THE FORGOTTEN GOTHIC:

Short Stories from the British Literary Annuals,

1823-1831

THE FORGOTTEN GOTHIC:

Short Stories from the British Literary Annuals, 1823-1831

Introduction and edited by

Dr. Katherine D. Harris

ZITTAW PRESS

2012

The Forgotten Gothic
Introduction © Katherine D. Harris

ISBN 978-0-9767212-4-6

CONTENTS

List of Plates	ix
Acknowledgements	xi
Texts, Formats, Editorial Principles, Abbreviations	xiii
Introduction	xvi

Forget Me Not

Anonymous, The Magic Mirror	38
Anonymous, The Ring; A True Narrative	48
Anonymous, The Grey Palmer	57
Anonymous, Pernicious Effects of Fortune-Telling	60
White, Joseph Blanco, The Alcazar of Seville and the Tale of the Green Taper	65
Jewsbury, Maria Jane [?], The Grave of the Suicide	76
Flora, Bolton Abbey	81
Stafford, William Cooke, Woman's Love	85
Hofland, Barbara, The Regretted Ghost	95
Harral, Thomas, Days of Old	107
T., A.D., The Fairies' Grot	111
A Traveller, The Lady of the Tower	119
Anonymous, The Phantom Voice	125
Thomson, Richard, Saint Agnes' Fountain	135
Dods, Mary Diana, The Three Damsels	148
Roby, John, The Haunted Manor-House	152
Roberts, Emma, Maximilian and his Daughter	166
Neele, Henry, The Comet	171
Shelley, Mary or Maria Jane Jewsbury [?], Lacy de Vere	186
Dods, Mary Diana, The Bridal Ornaments	197
Neele, Henry, The Magician's Visiter	209
Inglis, Henry, Kathed and Eurelia	213
Harral, Thomas, The House of Castelli	217
Roberts, Emma, The Halt on the Mountain	226
Bowdich, Sarah, Eliza Carthago	234
Shelley, Mary, The Euthanasia	239
Bird, John, The Cornet's Widow	252
Neele, Henry, The Houri. A Persian Tale	259

Rosa, Giuseppe Guercino	267
Inglis, Henry D., The Musician of Augsburg	275
Hofland, Barbara, The Maid of the Beryl	280
Anonymous, The Magician of Vicenza	288
MacNish, Robert, The Red Man	293
Galt, John, The Omen	302
Beevor, M.L., St. Feinah's Tree	306
Moir, D.L., Kemp, The Bandit	311
Richardson, David Lester, The Soldier's Dream	321
Barker, Matthew Henry, Greenwich Hospital	323
Thompson, W. G., Fanny Lee	331
Thomson, Richard, The Antiquary and His Fetch	337
Bird, John, The Convent of St. Ursula	349
Chorley, H. F., The Elves of Caer-Gwyn	358
Stone, William L., The Grave of the Indian King	370
Beevor, M.L., The Benshee of Shane	379
Thomson, Richard, The Haunted Hogshead	386
Hesketh, S. K., The Smuggler	391
McNaghten, Captain Sir William Hay, The Sacrifice	400
Bird, John, The Haunted Chamber	410
Moir, D.L., Bessy Bell and Mary Gray	421

Friendship's Offering

Anonymous, Lanucci	427
Anonymous, The Laughing Horseman	434
Anonymous, Forgiveness	447
Ainsworth, William Harrison, Rosicrucian	451
Gillies, Robert Pearch, The Warning	465
Inglis, Henry Rodolph, Rodolph, the Fratricide	472
Inglis, Henry Rodolph, The Unholy Promise	478
Kennedy, William, The Castle of St. Michael	484

The Keepsake

Shelley, Mary, Convent of Chaillot: or, Valliere and Louis XIV	495
Ainsworth, William Harrison, The Ghost Laid	506
Scott, Sir Walter, My Aunt Margaret's Mirror	515
Shelley, Mary, The Sisters of Albano	541
Scott, Sir Walter, The Tapestried Chamber	554

Shelley, Mary, Ferdinando Eboli	566
Shelley, Mary, The Mourner	582
Shelley, Mary, The Evil Eye	598
Shelley, Mary, The False Rhyme	615
Shelley, Mary, Transformation	618

The Literary Souvenir

Anonymous, The Golden Snuff-Box	633
D., L., New Year's Eve. The Omens	644
Maturin, Charles, Leixlip Castle	653
Ainsworth, William Harrison, The Fortress of Saguntum	662
Ainsworth, William Harrison, A Tradition of the Fortress of Saguntum	665
Anonymous, The Diamond Watch	674
Moir, D.L., The Old Manor-House	686
Hogg, James, The Border Chronicler	696
Roberts, Emma, Rosamunda	707
Wilson, John, The Two Fathers	711
Galt, John, The Witch	716
Roberts, Emma, The Bridal of St. Omer	719
Croker, Thomas Crofton, Clough Na Cuddy	728
Moir, D.L., Auld Robin Gray	734
Griffin, Gerald, The Dilemma of Phadrig	745
Maginn, William, The City of the Demons	754
Moir, D.L., The Pneumatologist	760
Anonymous, The Sisters	766
Bulwer, Edward Lytton, A Manuscript found in a Madhouse	782
Griffin, Gerald, The Rock of the Candle	788
Maginn, William, A Vision of Purgatory	808
Loundon, J.C., The Grotto of Akteleg	818
Grattan, Thomas Colley, The Love-Draught	825
Inglis, Henry, The City of the Desert	834
Galt, John, The Confession	838
Howitt, William, Ithran the Demoniac	841
Anonymous, Lady Olivia's Decamerone	851
Howitt, William, The Last of the Titans	858

Appendix A: Comparison of Gothic Content in the Annuals   867

Appendix B: Chronological Index of British Literary
Annual Titles   868
Appendix C: Other Literary Annual Contributions by Select Authors of
Gothic Short Stories   871
Appendix D: Chronological Index of British Literary
Annual Titles   884
References & Works Cited   891

LIST OF PLATES

Forget Me Not; A Christmas and New Year's Present for 1826
    Woman's Love   86
    The Regretted Ghost   94
    Days of Old   106

Forget Me Not; A Christmas and New Year's Present for 1829
    Fathime and Euphrosyne   238
    Vicenza   287

Forget Me Not; A Christmas, New Year's, and Birth-Day Present for 1830
    Greenwich Hospital   323

Forget Me Not; A Christmas, New Year's, and Birth-Day Present for 1831
    Bessy Bell and Mary May   421

Friendship's Offering. A Literary Album for 1826
    The Laughing Horseman   433

Friendship's Offering: A Literary Album, and Christmas and New Year's Present for 1829
    The Warning   464

Friendship's Offering: A Literary Album, and Christmas and New Year's Present for 1831
    The Mountain Torrent   491

The Keepsake for 1828
    The Convent of Chaillot, or La Valliere & Louis the XIV   502
    The Ghost Laid   512

The Keepsake for 1829
    The Magic Mirror   533
    Lake Albano   542
    The Tapestried Chamber   562
    Adelinda   578

The Keepsake for 1830
    Virginia Water [1]   581
    Virginia Water [2]   584
    Zella   607
    Francis the First & His Sister   614
    Juliet   630

The Literary Souvenir; or, Cabinet of Poetry and Romance for 1825
    Spain-Fortress of Saguntum   662

The Literary Souvenir; or, Cabinet of Poetry and Romance for 1827
    Auld Robin Gray   734

The Literary Souvenir for 1829
    The Sisters   765
    Minny O'Donnell's Toilet   790

The Literary Souvenir for 1831
    The Narrative   850

ACKNOWLEDGEMENTS

This project was initiated at the urging of Franz Potter, editor of Zittaw Press, after a rousing panel on Gothic literature at the South Central Society for Eighteenth-Century Studies annual conference in 2007. After fellow panelists offered cogent suggestions for expanding the relationship between literary annuals and Gothic literature, another version of the paper was presented, this time on a panel about literary annuals, periodicals, and nineteenth-century women at the Society for the History of Authorship, Reading and Publishing in 2008. Students of ENGL 113 in 2006 inspired the much fuller collection, and those in 2008 provided enthusiastic feedback and thoughtful comments.

Five intrepid research assistants formed the workforce, reading all 28 volumes cover-to-cover, suggesting stories, and transcribing many of the 100 short stories. In addition, they handled my nineteenth-century volumes with great care and offered wicked and sage commentary on nineteenth-century print culture, literary annuals, and Gothic short stories: Amy Leonard, Jennifer Cairns, Hai Nguyen, Maria Judnick, and Robyn McCreight. I would particularly like to thank colleagues, Revathi Krishnaswamy for thought-provoking comments on a draft of the introduction, Charles Robinson and Nora Crook for their insight on Mary Shelley, Erick Keleman for his technical expertise about editions and print culture. A few tough years in the California economy (and the California State University budget) stymied the progress of this project. Stephen Behrendt and the entire NEH Romanticism Summer Seminar crew of 2010 re-invigorated my interest in this project, restored my faith in the value of literary studies, and continue to be some of the most generous teachers and scholars around. I am grateful for the generosity of expert scholarly editors, Paula Feldman, Maura Ives, Martha Nell Smith, and Ann Hawkins. Since the idea of digitizing and re-printing my collection of annuals all started because Laura Mandell asked for my metadata, I thank her for the stalwart, unwavering support and excellent scholarship that she continues to contribute to women's nineteenth-century poetry and Digital Humanities. To the small, but passionate, cohort of literary annual scholars, I put this collection together as enticement. Finally, thank you, Franz Potter, for your scholarship, interest, anticipation, and patience.

San José State University supported this project with: a CSU Research Grant in 2005 and 2006 to purchase equipment and hire the first student assistant (who typed the entire 1831 Forget Me Not for my digital archive project); a Small Faculty

Grant for a student assistant in 2006; a Jr. Faculty Career Development Grant to fund a student assistant in Fall 2007; a College of Arts & Humanities Release Time grant to write and present at the 2007 conference.

TEXTS, FORMATS, EDITORIAL PRINCIPLES, ABBREVIATIONS

This type of collection would have been represented better as a facsimile collection in order to facilitate study of the short stories in concert with print culture, authorship, and history of the book in early nineteenth-century London. But because a facsimile edition would be too voluminous and too expensive to produce, we resolved to produce an accurate transcript of these printed texts, in essence a typographic facsimile. Because of the difficulty in optical character recognition (OCR) of nineteenth-century fonts and the tight bindings on many of these literary annuals, scanning was kept to a minimum and performed only on the images. Each transcription, saved as a plain text file, was proofread three times: for typographical errors; for page format; in comparison to the original's typography and word choice.

Printer's errors were retained. British spellings were not normalized. Some words were divided at a line break in the original; those hyphens were retained only if the word was truly meant to be two words without a hyphen. Otherwise, line-break hyphens were removed. Hyphenated words use the smaller hyphen symbol rather than an en dash to replicate the visual difference between an em dash (which visually signals a break in the narrative) and a hyphenated word (which would have been simply following the language protocols). Page-ending hyphens were retained.

All special characters and symbols were retained with the exception of Œ and Æ, each transcribed as OE and AE, respectively. Italicized words were also retained. Extra spaces before punctuation was deleted. All footnotes are from the original text. Em dashes are replicated without any spaces on either side in order to replicate the imposition of this typographical element. The font was normalized for publication purposes with the exception of those story titles that used a gothic font for the subtitle. Tabs and single spacing is preserved for paragraph division. Original page numbers were either flush left or flush margin right; in this volume, they have been embedded in the stories and encased in brackets. Inserted page numbers not in the original are encased in brackets. Running headers were used in some annuals 1825 and beyond; however, for ease of publication, they are not retained in the transcripts. Printer's registers appear in the originals but are not reproduced here. In the originals, right justification was used for most printings with apparent kerning to make each line fit to the page. That kerning has been removed to normalize spacing. Engravings are placed in the same position as the original. I realize that retaining spacing before punctuation or transcribing line length and kerning would have been optimal to facilitate study of a printer's idiosyncrasies and a printer's influence on the reader's response to the visual aspects of the printed text. As with any rare book, before studying the printer's errors or printing techniques as an influence on authorship or reading, consult the original printed text and the manuscript.

Anonymous authors are identified using Boyle's index where possible. Nora Crook, Betty Bennett, and Charles Robinson have made some discoveries about Mary Diana Dods' and Mary Shelley's contributions to the annuals. Though Boyle's index has become the standard for identifying anonymous authors in British literary annuals, some caution must be exercised; recent scholarship has uncovered editors' misattributions of writings, most likely because the writing had been provided from a secondary source or the editor was in need of a well-known author's name to help sell the annual. Most engravers', painters', publishers', and editors' biographies can be found in the *Oxford Dictionary of National Biography*.[1]

The volume is organized by literary annual title, year, and page number instead of offering the contents organized by author. Each of these annuals maintained consistent editors, with the exception of the early *Keepsake* volumes. Each editor subscribed to an aesthetic in the ordering of contents. Reading from the first to the concluding story in each annual will afford the reader a view of these stories' relationships and the distinctive tone of each annual. For author contributions, see Appendix B. To see these authors' contributions to other annuals, see Appendix C. To see a list of all contents in each of these annuals, check Harry Hootman's database, the *Poetess Archive* or the *Forget Me Not Archive*. The *Poetess Archive* contains some full text as does the *Forget Me Not*; but no full text of these stories is available other than a few annuals in Google Books and on microfiche. See the References section for a list of significant collections of literary annuals.

With the exception of *Friendship's Offering* for 1829, all literary annuals are held in the Katherine D. Harris private collection.

When this project began in 2007, the Google Books project had not yet progressed to scanning special collections and rare books. By July 2010, Google Books offered pdf page images and plain text OCR of many *Literary Souvenir*

---
1 See my forthcoming entry for Rudolph Ackermann in The Encyclopedia of Romantic Literature. Eds. Frederick Burwick, Nancy M. Goslee and Diane Long Hoeveler. Blackwell Publishers.

and some *Friendship's Offering* volumes. The rate of errors in Google Books' OCR has diminished significantly in the last year – to the point where it was more economical to use some of the plain text OCR from Google Books than to transcribe stories manually. If Google Books OCR plain text was used for the print text, it is indicated in a footnote and full bibliographical details are provided in the References section. Plain text from other online sources was used for some stories; those too are indicated in a footnote and in the References section. Each plain text file was proofread against the original nineteenth-century volume for typographical and OCR errors. With the 1829 *Friendship's Offering*, the transcribed text relies on the Google Books pdf of page images and photocopies from the Chadwyck-Healey microfiche collection, *English Gift Books and Literary Annuals 1823-1857*. The 1831 *Keepsake* does not exist in Google Books; instead, transcription is based on an online plain text source and proofread against the Chadwyck-Healey microfiche; the image is taken from Katherine D. Harris' 1831 Keepsake.

A fully searchable digital scholarly edition that incorporates textual analysis tools, exhibit builders, such as Collex, Omeka, TaPor, Monk, and visualization tools would be best suited for this type of project. With this in mind and with the permission of Zittaw Press, the plain text of each story and the engravings included here will be incorporated into the *Poetess Archive* database in the future.

The following abbreviations are used throughout:

FMN	*Forget Me Not*
FO	*Friendship's Offering*
KS	*The Keepsake*
LS	*The Literary Souvenir*

INTRODUCTION

Inspired by intercontinental literary forms and created by a successful art publisher, Rudoloph Ackermann, the literary annual first appeared in London in 1822 and was claimed by a myriad of publishers to represent the best of British ingenuity – even though the material form, the printing process, and the editorial methods were borrowed from French and German pocket-books, albums and emblems.[2]

The genre nevertheless served a larger purpose of exposing a burgeoning audience of women and girls to "very many of the best lyrical poems of nearly all our most popular contemporary writers appeared in the first instance in their pages," as is noted in the 1858 *Bookseller* article, "The Annuals of Former Days" (494). John Clare, James Hogg and even Wordsworth and Tennyson established a new audience through the annuals, an audience of those who had not previously purchased their single-author volumes of poetry.[3]

As I argue elsewhere, the British nineteenth-century literary annual in its textual production is best seen as a female body, its male producers struggling to make it both proper and sexually alluring, its female authors and readers attempting to render it their own feminine ideal.[4] At first, reviewers enjoyed the annuals, offering long excerpts and recommending particular annuals to their readers. Within five years, though reviewers began to write with disgust about the genre – primarily with objections to the *poetess* aesthetic.

Laura Mandell points out that "two myths pervade the study of this immensely important and influential body of writing. One is that canonical writers shunned this work, refusing to publish in well-paying annuals and choosing instead to create great, high art; the other is that poetess poetry is 'bad' writing."[5] Both myths rely on the production of aesthetics, and it was the reviewers who produced this demarcation about

---

[2] For a discussion about the literary annual's precursor forms and its evolution, see my article, "Borrowing, Altering and Perfecting the Literary Annual Form – or What It is Not: Emblems, Almanacs, Pocket-books, Albums, Scrapbooks and Gifts Books" *The Poetess Archive Journal* 1.1 (2007) <unixgen.muohio.edu/~poetess/PAJournal/index.html>.
[3] Though Thackeray is often noted for his acerbic review of the later annuals, but this did not keep him from contributing. Vanessa Warne discusses Thackeray's role in and critique of literary annuals in "Thackeray Among the Annuals: Morality, Cultural Authority and the Literary Annual Genre."
[4] See Katherine D. Harris, "Feminizing the Textual Body: Women and their Literary Annuals in Nineteenth-Century Britain," *Publications of the Bibliographical Society of America* 99:4 (Dec. 2005): 573-622.
[5] A 2007 NEH Scholarly Editions grant application is the source of this quote.

literary annuals – at first praising as possessing "a tone of romance, which, set off as it has been by poetry of a very high order, can have no other possible tendency than to purify the imagination and the heart" (Nov. 1826 *Monthly Review* 274). Lest we become mired wholly in the aesthetic reception of the annuals' contents, it's important to note the materiality and the genesis of this particular genre in order to understand its eventual "trashing."

Published in the German magazine *The Free Speaker* in 1815, the short story "Mimili" sold an unprecedented 9000 copies in 3 years (*Cambridge History of German Literature* 265) and inspired a genre of sentimental prose that capped the German Enlightenment. Based on the success of "Mimili," the author H. Clauren began publishing an annual publication, *Vergissmeinnicht* translated as forget me not, and named after the flower given to the young man by Mimili.[6] (See above.)

---

[6] The young shepherdess, Mimili, represents the story of ultimate propriety and chastity. A foreign traveler (a young man) approaches her home and is welcomed by her father. The young man falls in love with Mimili and offers descriptions of her voluptuousness for the reader. He makes several advances and is rebuffed. By the time he must leave, he begs Mimili's father for permission to marry her. Her father, not wanting to be hasty and acknowledging that this young man is the first

In November 1822, Rudolph Ackermann, a German immigrant and very successful lithography and periodical publisher, borrowed and translated this German form and title for the first literary annual, the *Forget Me Not*. The criteria for defining a literary annual are scattered throughout advertisements for and the Preface to the first *Forget Me Not* volume, published November 1822 and edited by either William Combe or Frederic Shoberl:

- *Purpose*: Annuals are "expressly designed to serve as annual tokens of friendship or affection" (Advertisement at conclusion of 1823 *Forget Me Not*). Ackermann establishes not only the purpose of the volume but also its sentiment and gift-giving status.

- *Publication Time Frame*: "It is intended that the Forget-Me-Not shall be ready for delivery every year, early in November" (Advertisement/Preface to 1823 *Forget Me Not* vii). Critics adhere to this criteria and blast any publication that appears outside the holiday time frame (November through January) yet still claiming to one of the literary annual family.

- *Continual Evolution*: "[T]he Publisher has no doubt that, in the prosecution of his plan, he shall be enabled, by experience, to introduce improvements into the succeeding volumes" (vii). Each editor hereafter uses the preface to proclaim improvements to his/her title for each succeeding year. This promise suggests a continued longevity to the title and asks readers to anticipate a better product the following year.

- *Authorship*: "[H]e shall neglect no means to secure the contributions of the most eminent writers, both at home and abroad" (vii). Ackermann establishes the literary annual as more than an anthology with this promise. The authors are generally contemporary figures of the period instead of classical authors, such as Shakespeare. The primarily British contributors will eventually be

---

that Mimili has encountered, asks him to return in a year to see if the passion still burns between them. During this year, the young man joins the military and disappears after a long battle. When Mimili receives a friend's letter informing her of her young man's fate, she mourns endlessly until the moment when the young man miraculously appears, having been wounded and survived the battle. They are married as evidence of their fortitude and genuine love. Ackermann's translation follows the same didactic path as the German original, including the more lascivious tests of Mimili's chastity. For a discussion of "Mimili" as it relates to German nationalism, authorial control and German parodies, see Todd Kontje's "Male Fantasies, Female Readers: Fictions of the Nation in the Early Restoration."

touted as representations of English superiority.[7]

- *Originality*: "To convey an idea of the nature of the pieces which compose the bulk of this volume, it will be sufficient to state that they will consist chiefly of original and interesting Tales and Poetry" (Advertisement at conclusion of 1823 *Forget Me Not*). This claim of originality plagues the editors of the annuals through the 1830s, but most will continue to declare the literature's originality regardless if pieces had been published prior to the annual's appearance.

- *Engravings*: "[W]hile his long and extensive connexion with the Arts, and the credit with which he has acquitted himself in his various undertakings in that line, will, he trusts, be a satisfactory pledge that his best exertions shall not be wanting to give to this Work in a decided superiority in regard to its embellishments, over every other existing publication of the kind" (Advertisement/Preface to 1823 *Forget Me Not* vii-viii). With a reminder about his expertise in and success with lithography publications, Ackermann assures readers that engravings and artwork will always accompany the literature within annuals. This marriage of the literary and the visual is an integral aspect of literary annuals: An annual must carry both in order to be considered within the family.

- *Useful Information*: "The third portion comprises a Chronicle of Remarkable Events during the past year: a Genealogy of the Reigning Sovereigns of Europe and their Families; a List of Ambassadors resident at the different Courts; and a variety of other particulars extremely useful for reference to persons of all classes" (Advertisement at conclusion of 1823 *Forget Me Not*). Ackermann attempts to establish the literary annual as referential and useful across class boundaries. However, one can assume that Ackermann is not offering this information to the working or lower classes because of the cost (twelve shillings). This element was eventually discarded by all annuals around 1825 in favor of additional creative contributions. (See Image 6 for an example of useful information.)

---

[7] In some instances, editors will include a note either within the preface or at the conclusion of the story, poem, song stating that a particular work had recently mistakenly been printed in a periodical and newspaper and was beyond the author's control or knowledge. Alaric A. Watts, editor of the *Literary Souvenir* for its entire run, used this strategy most often.

- *Exterior Format*: "The Forget Me Not is done up in a case for the pocket, and its external decorations display corresponding elegance and taste with the general execution of the interior" (Advertisement at conclusion of 1823 *Forget Me Not*). The diminutive size (3.5" x 5.5") represents a particular form of femininity that is portable in the pocket or the hand – specifically of a lady. Though the size eventually grew, the annual's embellished boards mark the elegance of the entire genre and were continued through its lifetime even in the rebindings.

The volume of reading material was immense at the introduction of literary annuals and competition for consumers was fierce. Periodicals, journals and cheap twopenny newspapers,[8] ranging from one to seven pence, captured the attention of readers who were interested in the mundane topics of daily life. For two to four shillings, ladies' magazines supplied readers with beautiful images and some useful information on a monthly or even quarterly production schedule. Critical and review periodicals published more intellectual copy for two to six shillings. Poetry volumes suffered a steady decline in sales, though, much the same as conduct manuals (Erickson 28).[9] But, almanacs, albums and commonplace books continued to attract consumers because of their raw information and invitation to create content. Even the three-volume novel enjoyed a healthy audience of consumers despite its fifteen to twenty-one shilling price. Sir Walter Scott's best-selling novels topped the list by selling at an enormous thirty-one-shillings each. By 1822, a middle class audience was primed for a literary object that was both beautiful and entertaining but not overtly didactic like conduct manuals.

---

[8] For a discussion of the twopenny newspaper's cultural capital, see Brian E. Maidment's article, "☒Penny' Wise, ☒Penny' Foolish?: Popular Periodicals and the ☒March of Intellect' in the 1820s and 1830s," in *Nineteenth-Century Media and the Construction of Identities*, ed. Laurel Brake, Bill Bell, and David Finkelstein (New York: Palgrave, 2000).

[9] Because of these declining sales, publishers (including Smith Elder, John Taylor, Longman and John Murray) refused to publish new poetry as well as second editions of major poets, including P.B. Shelley, Keats and Byron, regardless of their respective posthumous fame (Erickson 33). In the event of the few volumes that were published during the late 1820s and early 1830s, publishers often asked a poet to underwrite her or his volume's publication in order to guarantee against unprofitable sales. Erickson further argues that "despite lower printing costs, publishers found that most poetry appealed to an increasingly smaller portion of the reading public and so kept its price high," selling for approximately five shillings for over one hundred years (35). However, the single-author volume's demise does not account for the literary annual's success. Quite possibly, at twelve shillings and more, the annual's variety of authors, genres and engravings appeased a broader audience than a single-author volume of poetry.

Introduction

Retail Prices of Reading Materials, 1814-1835[10]

Cheap Weekly Magazines	1.5*d*.-6*d*. (*Mirror of Literature*, 1822)
Political tracts	2*d*.
Cheap Non-Fiction	6*d*. per part
	4*s*.6*d*. per complete volume (1827)
Weekly Magazine	6*d*.-1*s*.
Daily Newspapers	7*d*.
Recycled	1*d*.-3*d*. Illegally hired/lent to multiple readers
Re-prints (Literature)	1*s*-12*s*.(Shakespeare's plays)
Critical Periodicals	2*s*. (*Fraser's*)
Monthly Magazines	2*s*.6*d*.-4*s*.
Numbered Series (Fiction)	2*s*.-5*s*. per weekly installment
Poetry Volume	5*s*.
Review Periodicals	6*s*. (*Quarterly Review, Edinburgh*)
Literary Annual	12*s*.-£3
3 Volume Novel	15-21*s*. (1814-1823)
Serialized Novel	20*s*. total for parts
	21*s*. complete vol. (*Pickwick Papers*, 1836)
Scott Novel	31*s*.6*d*. (1820)
Circulating Library	35*s*. (per year for unlimited access)

By wrapping beauty, literature, landscape art, and portraits into an alluring package, for 12 shillings editors and publishers filled the 1820s with this popular and best-selling genre.[11] Originally published as duo-

---

10 Figures amassed from Richard Altick's *The English Common Reader: A Social History of the Mass Reading Public 1800-1900* (Chicago: University of Chicago Press, 1957), 260-293; 318-347.
11 For a detailed discussion about the editorial practices and authorial production of literary annu-

decimo or octavo[12] in paper boards, the annuals were usually whisked away to be re-bound in beautiful leather covers. (See below.)

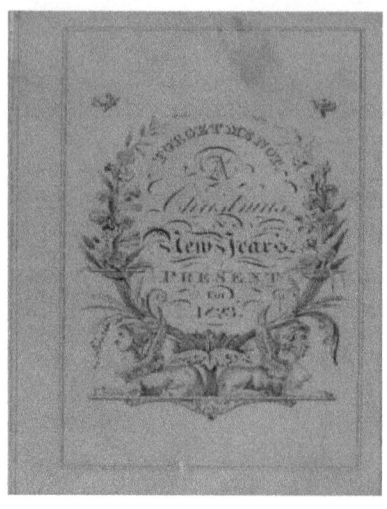

By 1828, publishers employed the latest innovations in binding and switched to silk to amplify the value of the material object. (See next page for *The Keepsake for 1841* silk boards)

---

als, see Paula Feldman's Introduction to facsimile edition of *The Keepsake for 1829*.
12 This term refers to the codex format and "is used to indicate the size of a volume in terms of the number of times the original printed sheet has been folded to form its constituent leaves. Thus in a folio each sheet has been folded once, in a quarto twice, in an octavo three times; the size being thus respectively a half, a quarter and an eighth that of the original sheet" (Carter 106). In response to public demand, in 1828 some literary annuals were published in the larger quarto form.

Introduction

Each annual typically offered a confined space for dedication. (See below: Dedication page from 1826 *Forget Me Not*)

Early annuals offered practical information similar to the Stationer's Company's almanac, but that would soon disappear in favor of more literary and visual content. (See next page: *Friendship's Offering* 1824 weather guide and hackney coach fares)

The Forgotten Gothic

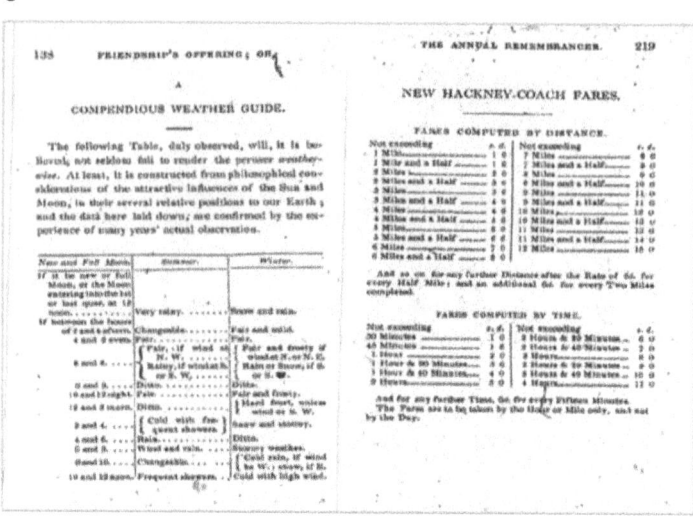

Engravings were cast from popular paintings but rarely garnered fame for the engraver who was deemed a mere copyist and denied entrance into the Royal Academy. (See below, John Martin's "Seventh Plague of Egypt" (1823) painting; see next page, Henry Le Keux's engraving in the 1828 *Forget Me Not*)

Introduction

Often engravings were commissioned like that in the image below for the 1825 *Literary Souvenir*, and then well-known poets were asked to render an accompanying poem, work for hire – eventually much to the poet's dismay.

But let me stress this: *everyone* contributed to the annuals, even if they despised the genre.[13]

With a large audience almost immediately clamoring for more literary annuals, Ackermann and his editor, Frederic Shoberl, created a second *Forget Me Not* for 1824 and found themselves competing with *Friendship's Offering* and *The Graces*. By 1828, with an aggregate retail

---

13 See Index of Prominent Contributors, *Forget Me Not Hypertextual Archive* <http://www.orgs.muohio.edu/anthologies/FMN/Authors_Prominent.htm>

value of over £70,000 for 100,000 copies, 15 English literary annual titles had joined the market only to vie for an audience against 30 more titles by 1830. (See Appendix D)

The trade in annuals had become so popular that various titles emerged with hopes and promises of continuing a yearly publication. But with titles like *Olive Branch* and *Zoölogical Keepsake* appearing and vanishing in a single year, more often than not, that promise was broken. Many factors led to the success or demise of a particular title – external appearance, engraving quality, literary contents, popular authors, editorial arrangement, marketing and reviews. This last element provided an introduction and public face to each annual by recommending, denouncing or simply excerpting its contents.

Even with all of this popular success, the critical condescension surrounding the literary annual would haunt the genre well into the nineteenth century:

> The Annuals created a *craze*, the craze denoted some *insanity* in the public mind of the period; and much of this insanity is apparent within the curious circle of prolific writers, from which the general contributions were obtained. ... This Annual was ephemeral not because it was effeminate; but because it was *unequal*, with a bias towards the trivial. It was one of the "*cakes*" of literature, not the bread. And even cakes become distasteful, when they provide only two or three currants each, notwithstanding that the surface is liberally endowed with *sugar*. (Tallent-Bateman 1902; 90, 97; emphasis added)

After finally sputtering out in England in 1857, the literary annual re-appeared as an homage to Rudolph Ackermann during the 1930s – even after Charles Tallent-Batement condescendingly recommends annuals and poetess poetry as the cakes of literature.

Gothic Short Stories in the Annuals

This collection of gothic short stories takes us further than perhaps eighteenth or nineteenth-century scholars are comfortable with – to extend our discussions about the Gothic in such a way that the tradition does not die at 1820, as is purported by Robert Mayo. We will, however, move past the deaths of Shelley, Keats and Byron – the spokespersons for the second wave of traditional Romanticism. Queen Victoria won't ascend to the throne for another six years, and Tennyson has not yet become the powerhouse poet who will eventually rise to Poet Laureate of England.

Introduction

Scholars touted 1820-1830 as a "dead zone" – without any literary guiding light. However, many studies have shown that the magazines were filled with literary fodder, more specifically, the Gothic short story. Another phenomenon occurs during this decade as well – the overwhelming popularity of the literary annual, begun in 1823 by Rudolf Ackermann and surviving right through the 1850s.

In 1831 not only did Mary Shelley publish the second edition of her popular novel, *Frankenstein* with its famous introduction, but the literary annual craze reached its peak, with titles such as *The Keepsake, Literary Souvenir, Friendship's Offering* and, finally, the *Forget Me Not*. Because parody is usually the marker of solidifying (and then moving beyond) a literary tradition, 1830 marked the year that the literary annual genre was solidified with Thomas Hood's parody, *The Comic Annual*.

Christine Alexander and Franz Potter have both urged the scholarly community to investigate the convergence of these two literary movements – the Gothic short story inside the literary annual's pages. Both suggest the return of an Old Gothicism and the creation of a New Gothicism because of this venue of publication. Before we get to an actual Gothic short story within a literary annual, we need to investigate the relationship between the Gothic short story and this literary form – for it is definitely not the magazines and periodicals that traditionally published Gothic short stories.

Jane Austen's parody, *Northanger Abbey*, published in 1818 but written two decades earlier in reaction to the overblown sentiments of Mrs. Radcliffe and Matthew Lewis' novels, solidifies the High Gothicism of the 1790s. Mary Shelley's *Frankenstein* (1818), John Polidori's *The Vampyre* (1819) and Charles Robert Maturin's *Melmouth, the Wanderer* (1820) follow closely on the heels of Austen's satirical fun along with several successful melodramas on the London stage. By 1818, though, the Gothic tradition had already transformed itself because of Sir Walter Scott's re-working of Gothicisim in his historical romances, including *Waverley* (1814). Even William Wordsworth participated in this evolution with his poem "The Ruined Cottage" (1814 in *The Excursion*). Marilyn Gaull notes that by 1820 Austen's satire had lost its popular appeal (xi) but not without solidifying the Gothic tradition's basic premise – to horrify and terrify its innocent readers.

Critiqued as leading to false notions of reality, the Gothic novel was thought to over-excite young women and mislead them to think that life was as romantic and suspenseful as any Gothic novel. Samuel Taylor Coleridge reviews Lewis' *The Monk* without enthusiasm:

> THE horrible and the preternatural have usually seized on the popular taste, at the rise and decline of literature. Most powerful stimulants, they can never be required except by the torpor of an unawakened, or the languor of an exhausted, appetite. The same phaenomenon, therefore, which we hail as a favourable omen in the belles lettres of Germany, impresses a degree of gloom in the compositions of our countrymen. We trust, however, that satiety will banish what good sense should have prevented; and that, wearied with fiends, incomprehensible characters, with shrieks, murders, and subterraneous dungeons, the public will learn, by the multitude of the manufacturers, with how little expense of thought or imagination this species of composition is manufactured. (194)

With this rebuke against sensational texts, reviewers attempted to save an entire generation of young women. Obviously, the critical disdain and the warnings don't work. In 1831, Mary Shelley revised her successful novel about the re-creation of life – downplaying the slightly incestuous relationship between Victor and Elizabeth – and added an Introduction which accounts for creative imagination in much the same way that Victor Frankenstein justifies his scientific experiments. With these publications beginning in 1818, the "New Gothic" tradition cements itself as the latest type of Gothicism, as is suggested by Robert B. Heilman: "novels that turned from old forms of external terror to 'an intensification of feeling'" (quoted in Alexander 409).

According to Robert Mayo, by 1810, the Gothic *short story* was well-established as fiction ("Gothic Short Story" 448) and came in the form of Gothic Romance, Historical Romance, Sensational Fiction and Sentimental Horror. They were published in *Blackwood's* and *London Magazine*, as well as the *Lady's Magazine* and *Lady's Monthly Museum* even prior to 1800. Between 1790 and 1820, Mayo describes the Gothic short story – usually only 2500 words or less to fit magazine page limitations, differing in its "machinery of terror" (454) and fragmentary at best. However, the Gothic short story was well-adapted to the magazine because "their moral tone accorded well with the didactic claims of the miscellanies ... and no matter how desperate the pressure of events, found room for a moral" ("Gothic Romance in the Magazines" 765). Mayo claims that the Gothic short story then fell out of favor by the 1820s. But, both Christine Alexander and Franz Potter question this assertion and ask that another literary form be considered the new venue for Gothic short stories. This form is the literary annual, the form that becomes "infected" with Gothicism from its very inception.

Introduction

Christine Alexander notices the appearance of this new type of Gothicism in the Brontës' novels and attributes it to their juvenile explorations of Scott's novels, *The Lady's Magazine* and a popular, but much maligned literary genre, the literary annuals, specifically *Friendship's Offering* for 1829, *The Literary Souvenir* for 1830 and the *Forget Me Not* for 1831.

As stated by early editors and publishers, the literary annual was intended to beautify and edify its readers, typically young women who poured over each volume's contents. The poetry, prose and engravings presented an opportunity for young poets to establish an audience (Tennyson and Hogg), novelists to perfect short story techniques (Mary Shelley and W. Harrison Ainsworth) and artists to disseminate scenes of country life and exotic locales (J.M.W. Turner). From 1823 to 1830, readers, authors and critics were in awe of the literary annual's inventive contents and beatific packaging, as described above. But, with everything within popular culture, the literary annual evolved to include the latest literary trends, much to the disdain of those same authors, readers and critics.

By 1820, Sir Walter Scott's historical realism had been re-appropriated in a manner that resurrected the Old or High Gothic tradition, according to Potter (95) – a move that Christine Alexander re-names as the New Gothic.

Alexander finds that this New Gothic tradition governs many of the short stories published in the annuals and links the specific plots of several of these stories to much of Charlotte Brontë's juvenilia as well as *Jane Eyre:*

> The Gothic frees her to achieve two apparently contradictory ends: on the one hand to imitate the Annuals and indulge in her love of the exotic, the licentious, and the mysterious, and increasingly to indulge in her fascination with the darker recesses of the mind and its relationship to natural phenomena; and on the other hand to assume the anti-Gothic stance that Heilman noted was so characteristic in the novels. (427)

Though Alexander finds much of the Brontës' New Gothic influence in the annuals, what she does not discuss is the parallel disdain that both the early Gothic Novel and the annuals suffered at the hands of reviewers. Critics writing these review articles considered themselves, like editors of the annuals, protectors of public literary tastes. One reviewer describes the duty of critic as knight-errant protecting the public against bad literature: "If the legitimate object of periodical criticism is to recommend to the public such works as deserve its patronage, and expose folly and false taste, we may, in the discharge of the first of these offices, be allowed to criticise the [1825] *Literary Souvenir*" (*British Critic* quoted in 1826 *Literary Souvenir*).[14] In their public duty, the critics initially applauded literary annuals, especially the *Forget Me Not* and *Literary Souvenir*, because they possessed "a tone of romance, which, set off as it has been by poetry of a very high order, can have no other possible tendency, than to purify the imagination and the heart" (Nov. 1826 *Monthly Review* 274).[15] The poetry was intended to stimulate the reader's sentiments, educate their intellect and christen their creativity. According to the critic's edict, reviewers were required to protect the public from bad literary choices or corrupting printed materials – treating readers and consumers like children: "We feel justified in pronouncing the [1828] Souvenir for the new year a failure, as compared with its predecessors" (Dec. 1827 *Monthly Review* 525). One reviewer declares a poem in the 1832 *Literary Souvenir* a disappointment and with that firmly defines the literary annual as a didactic tool for family consumption and hence reliance on morality as its guiding post:

> As a poem [Alaric Watts' "The Conversazione"] it is a most miserable affair. As a satire it betrays more of bad temper and malignant feeling . . . [W]e ask whether a work like the Literary Souvenir, intended for the drawing-room, very frequently within our own experience presented as a Christmas gift to youth of both sexes, and hitherto looked upon as a collection of amusing, light, and inoffensive articles, should be made the channel for such a scurrilous composition as this "Conversazione?" . . . [¶] *Poetry* like this is certainly not of the description, which we should wish to see in the hands of any young person, and we hope that the specimen, which we have given, will induce many persons to deliberate, whether they ought to admit the volume that contains it within their family circle. (Dec. 1831 *The Monthly Review* 524, 525)

---

14 This review was appended to the 1826 *Literary Souvenir* as a testimonial to the annual's superiority in a growing field of titles. After attesting to the annual's legitimacy, the review continues in glowing praise of the *Literary Souvenir*: "The leading character of the articles is superior, the design is excellent, and, if rightly prosecuted, the *Literary Souvenir* may take the highest rank among periodical publications. The most eminent literary characters of the day are among its contributors. With such writers, and published annually, the work has every chance of attaining to steady excellence and enduring reputation. The limitations of our work will not allow us to quote a sixth part of what we could, otherwise, dwell on with great pleasure: there is much that is beautiful in the longer tales. The engravings which accompany the *Literary Souvenir* are extremely beautiful."
15 *The Monthly Review*, a London monthly magazine published 1826-1845, was publicized as a gentler review periodical compared with the *Edinburgh Review* and *Quarterly Review*. Published by Charles Knight during 1826, the periodical was more dedicated to summary and quotation (Waterloo 716; *Waterloo Directory* online). However, this gentler nature does not seem the case with many of the reviews cited herein.

Because the annuals contained these short stories that were particularly Gothic, the genre was doubly indemnified. However, reviewers focused on critiquing the poetry rather than the short stories for their Gothic qualities. Indeed, this occurs because the gothicisim inherent to these prose pieces was not Matthew Lewis' sensationalism or even Mary Shelley's pseudo-science. Instead, the pieces contain the supernatural excitement of early Gothic novels. However, the conclusions to these short stories were often more appropriate for the literary annual and the young minds' of the readers – they were disappointingly didactic or explained away through circumstance, which makes them more Mrs. Radcliffe than Monk Lewis – a penchant for "natural terror" rather than the supernatural.

These stories, then, signal this shift in the Gothic tradition, from an old to a new intensity of feeling that was localized in a familiar setting, much the same as later novels such as *Dracula*, *The Woman in White* and *Wuthering Heights*. With this, the literary annuals act as catalysts (along with many other periodicals) for this evolution in literary tradition – even despite the disdain from critics and literati.

Christine Alexander discusses the impact of a few stories from the 1831 *Forget Me Not* on the Brontës' later novels, but what other Gothicism appears throughout the 1831 *Forget Me Not* – and even earlier in the annuals? This 1831 volume includes five Gothic stories and one engraving not discussed by Alexander. Each story presents elements of the Gothic and then just as quickly critiques or squashes those Gothic tendencies to fit the malleable minds of the literary annual audience.

Take for instance "The Elves of Caer-gwyn," a brief twelve-page story among the 371 pages of engravings, poetry, and prose in the 1831 *Forget Me Not*. It is not a fragment as with many other Gothic tales, but it does adhere to some of the conceits generally employed by authors of Gothic Romance. Robert Mayo defines this genre for us:

> [R]omance was the hallmark for barbarous superstition, unreason, moral depravity, and bad taste. And Gothic romance, above all, outrageously violated the canons of "truth to real life," and offended a morality in which the appeal to reason, common sense, and decorum was a conspicuous feature. The pious pretenses of the literature of terror–the unwavering chastity of the heroines, the inflexible devotion of the heroes, the strict avoidance of the real supernatural, and the wholesale operation of poetic justice in the final chapters. (Mayo, "Gothic Romance" 787)

Mayo continues by describing the particularities of the Gothic short story as lacking "plot framework ... [with] little or no exposition, no resolution of events, and no accounting, usually, for the mysteries and horrors which have been devised" (451).

"The Elves of Caergwyn" is not filled with overt examples of supernatural, nor does it violate those "truth to real life" requirements of novels. Instead, this piece resorts to a traditional Gothic framework of an undefined castle in an isolated land. The hero, Launcelot – reminiscent of medieval romance – validates the Gothic elements by arriving on a "very stormy evening in the autumn of 17–" (75). He returns to the land of his father, who ran off after he was jilted by a neighboring lady. No one knows him – at least until he presents letters of introduction to the now-old husband of the lady. One would expect that a battle or a revenge would ensue, but that is not so. Instead, Launcelot falls in love with the daughter, Anne, and privately sues for her hand in marriage. The twist is that a much-disliked and old landowner, Sir Purvill, is the intended betrothed by way of a long-standing family agreement. Launcelot, instead of battling for Anne's attention and favor, takes longing glances as Purvill disreputably manhandles Anne in front of her parents. But, a deal is a deal. Our hero wanders off to a glen to sing his desires away and is interrupted by giggling. He follows the sounds and happens upon a cave where he spies these tiny men and is then shot at by an unknown figure!

The rest of the story wraps up the opening scenes where Launcelot has stumbled into a witch's house for shelter from a storm. He overhears the witch taking money from a local peasant who has requested that a curse be placed upon Purvill. The denoument comes in the form of discovering that it was Purvill who shot at Launcelot, but not in the spirit of jealousy. Instead, the witch's curse plagues Purvill with voices and causes all of the house guests to restlessly lay awake every night. Purvill, suffering from a bit of dementia, flees the haunted, isolated land and thereby forfeits his right to marry Anne. Launcelot wins the girl!

The supernatural element of the elves is never explained away, but accepted by Launcelot. When he overhears the witch's curse, he thinks nothing more of it. Our narrator doesn't even connect those elements by the story's conclusion. Instead, Launcelot and Anne produce a prodigious line of great people – as the narrator returns to the facade of a legend. Neither Launcelot or Anne is a strongly motivated character. Instead, they seem to conform to the niceties of social interaction, declaring love only through their eyes.

This story is far from the incest, rape and demons of Lewis' *The Monk*. However, its setting smacks of Radcliffe's isolation. The story begins with:

> THERE remains to this day, or, at all events, there did remain till within the last few years, the spacious ivy-covered manor-house of Caer-gwyn, one of the finest specimens of domestic architecture in that part of the principality. It is situated far from any town, in the midst of its broad lands, and sheltered by hills, in the lone recesses of which is hidden many secluded valley with its tiny rivulet, and sparingly scattered among the extensive sheep pastures are small antique farm-houses, looking as though they were a part of the primitive rock on which they stand. (73)

And, it continues with a pastoral setting that is also part of the natural terror that Radcliffe presents. However, by 1831, the audience would have been acutely aware of the revolution in poetics, namely Wordsworth and Coleridge's *Lyrical Ballad,s* as well as the movement towards social responsibility by Shelley and Byron. Fancy and imagination had received a significantly different definition than Edmund Burke and Anna Letitia Barbauld presented on the sublime. In this 1831 story, fancy has been imprisoned. The narrator purports that a private viewing of this legend will free the reader's fancy.

> Many are the stories extant among the aged peasants of their tricksy gambols; and those who love a tale of their days and deeds for some stormy winter evening, when the fancy is set free, and there are none stern or unimaginative enough to chide or check her flights, may perhaps read, with some interest, my legend of the Elves of Caer-gwyn.

The implication is that there are still restrictions on a young woman's freedom of imagination. The literary annuals were intended to replace the conduct manuals and supplement the ladies magazines, but they are also intended as a permanent keepsake, marking friendship and love as well as material wealth. Richard Polwhele continuously published poems that defined women as players in the game of marriage, but only until they were married. After marriage, they were no longer participants – much the same way that Anne is portrayed in this story here. Conversely, women poets (specifically Felicia Hemans) presented empowered and intellectual female characters who displayed this "intensity of feeling" rather than suffering through supernatural terrors. The entire movement of the literary annuals was to highlight intensity of feeling – we get this from Launcelot throughout this short story in the 1831 *Forget Me Not* not only in the cave scene where he encounters both the elves and his rival, but also through the narrator's omniscient access to Launcelot's woeful plight. Everyone lives happily ever after in a socially defined relationship at the conclusion of the tale, but the narrator, inserting himself as an "I" at the conclusion of the tale, really conveys the intensity of a place or a space that is often the subject of that High Gothicism.

Here we have a melding of that old and new Gothicism that Alexander and Potter have pointed toward. The proximity to the often schizophrenic goals of the literary annuals causes just such a mixture. By 1831, the goal of the literary annual was not so much to educate or to model propriety. Instead, it was the middle class's beautifully packaged version of entertainment that shielded readers not from the impropriety of the Gothic tradition, but invited readers to secretly enjoy it. They could hide behind the beauty of the literary annual form and point to its ornamented hard covers – indeed, fancy and imagination were freed.

Interpreting Gothic Short Stories in the British Annuals 1823-1831

According to Franz Potter in *The History of Gothic Publishing*, 300 Gothic short stories were published in periodicals 1800-1834. He includes literary annuals in this list, though it is not technically a periodical. Potter notes that the first literary annual, the 1823 *Forget Me Not*, carries a Gothic short story, "The Magic Mirror." Apparently Ackermann also published a story or two in his very successful *Repository of Arts* in 1815 and would not, therefore, have been a stranger to the genre.

Potter's initial figures include 60 Gothic short stories in literary annuals through 1831. *Gothic Short Stories in British Literary Annuals* builds on Potter's initial assessment of 60 Gothic short stories in the annuals, uses the above criteria for selecting Gothic stories, and focuses on the most popular British literary annuals: *Forget Me Not* (1823-1847), *Friendship's Offering* (1824-1844), *The Keepsake* (1828-1857), *The Literary Souvenir* (1825-1835).[16]

Both *Friendship's Offering* and the *Forget Me Not* were originally published with paper boards and were perhaps perceived as more ephemeral than the *Keepsake*, published with silk-covered boards, or *The Literary Souvenir*, published in leather or cloth boards. Maintaining a resonance of eighteenth-century literary forms, the *Forget Me Not* and *Friendship's Offering* were published in duodecimo and octavo through 1831 and did

---

16 Popularity, for the purposes of this study, is marked by the longevity and economic success of each of these annuals.

not indulge in larger paper until later years, if at all. *The Literary Souvenir* offered octavo and quarto versions. And, *The Keepsake* was published only in quarto. Though the paper size evolves through the life of most literary annuals, the printed space, the printing plate, remains octavo and the page begins to incorporate large margins around the text blocks in 1825 with *The Literary Souvenir*. This was done to facilitate printing, and for some, printing on India paper and tipping-in engravings that were larger than the text blocks, all of which signals the eventual shift away from the annual's literary contents towards its visual contents.

The *Forget Me Not* maintained an editorial with Frederic Shoberl managing the annual until its demise in 1847. Alaric A. Watts founded and controlled *The Literary Souvenir*, previously *The Graces* in 1824, until it became the *Cabinet of Modern Poetry* in 1836. Charles Heath, an engraver and founder of the most popular and successful literary annual, *The Keepsake*, selected first, accomplished Gothic novel writer, William Harrison Ainsworth, then Frederic Mansel Reynolds as his editors. Letitia Elizabeth Landon and the Countess of Blessington briefly edited this annual and *Heath's Book of Beauty* after 1831. *Friendship's Offering* has, perhaps, the most mysterious beginnings and editorship: Thomas K. Hervey, Charles Knight, and Thomas Pringle each edited volumes through 1831. With the exception of William Harrison Ainsworth, none of the editors contributed Gothic short stories to the annuals represented in this collection, though they did contribute poems to various volumes. (See Appendix B for an alphabetical list of authors represented in this re-print collection.) Ainsworth contributed to all but the *Forget Me Not*. (See Appendix C for a list of his and other authors' contributions to other annuals.)

Though the *Forget Me Not* was not the most popular literary annual by 1831, after nine volumes in as many years, and led by Frederic Shoberl and Rudolph Ackerman's business acumen, the *Forget Me Not* publishes by far the most Gothic short stories of these four literary annuals. (See Appendix A for a comparison of Gothic content across annuals.) Beginning with a single, 21-page Gothic short story in the 1823 volume, the *Forget Me Not* incorporates eight stories, totaling 135 pages and representing 35% of the 1826 content. In 1830, the *Forget Me Not* again approaches 30% of their content dedicated to Gothic short stories, totaling 10 in number and 125 pages. The *Forget Me Not* 1828-1830 published over 400 pages of content, equaled only by *The Literary Souvenir*'s overall pages for 1826-1828. The more popular *Keepsake* maintained under 300 pages of content 1828-1831 but included four Gothic short stories over 109 pages in 1829, which is represented as 30% of the content. *Friendship's Offering*'s contents range anywhere from 222 to 418 pages but consistently contains the lowest number of Gothic short stories. Alaric Watts' *Literary Souvenir* was the *Forget Me Not*'s greatest competitor for number of Gothic short stories and number of pages dedicated to these stories. By 1829, the popularity of the Gothic short story is apparent: the *Keepsake, Forget Me Not*, and *Literary Souvenir* each dedicated 30% of their content to Gothic short stories.

In total, the *Forget Me Not* includes 50 Gothic short stories and 768 pages over nine years; *The Literary Souvenir* includes 28 Gothic short stories and 441 pages over seven years; and *The Keepsake* includes 10 Gothic short stories and 215 pages over 4 years. In comparison to the total number of pages produced overall by each literary annual title, the *Forget Me Not* reserves 21% of its pages for Gothic short stories against *The Literary Souvenir*'s 16.4% and *The Keepsake*'s 15.9%. In total, the *Gothic Short Stories in British Literary Annuals* contains 96 stories and 25 engravings from 28 volumes of literary annuals.

From 12 to 19 engravings were included in each of these literary annuals. Charles Heath, a well-known engraver, was adamant that *The Keepsake* would offer a higher number of engravings than any other annual. Because engravings were typically produced and then authors solicited for a poem, not many engravings accompany these Gothic short stories. *The Keepsake*, however, leads with eight engravings accompanying all of its Gothic short stories 1828-1831, something that the other annuals did not do. In fact, *The Keepsake* for 1830 includes two engravings with Mary Shelley's story, "The Mourner." The *Forget Me Not*, over nine years, includes only seven engravings to accompany its stories.

The quality of writing in these short stories varies; however, Mary Shelley, William Harrison Ainsworth, and William Howitt exhibit the most control over their prose and, for the most, avoid some of the tropes of Gothic short fiction: compacted beginnings; liberal typographical interventions; under-developed characters and action; abrupt conclusions; didactic overtones. Sir Walter Scott's story, "My Aunt Margaret's Mirror" in *The Keepsake* for 1829 is the longest story at 44 pages. Mary Shelley's story, "False Rhyme," in *The Keepsake* for 1830 is the shortest at only three pages. The stories in *The Literary Souvenir* are significantly shorter than those in the *Forget Me Not*. Often, *The Literary Souvenir*'s stories are didactic in nature. Gothic short stories do not appear with any frequency in *Friendship's Offering*, and annual which seems to focus more on poetry than any other literary form; in fact, Gothic short stories are completely absent from the 1824 and 1828 volumes of *Friendship's Offering*.

"The Ghost Laid," by William Harrison Ainsworth in *The Keepsake* for 1828, concludes abruptly but is decidedly ironic about the short

Introduction

story form and forced labor of writing to an engraving. The narrator mentions the image in a moment that breaks free from the narrative. The story concludes abruptly by admonishing the reader for wanting more details about the after-life of the characters – whether they lived happily and contentedly or were subjected to further horrors. In a parody of the short story format and Gothic fiction, Ainsworth, as was typical of his writing, lends levity to both the annual and his tale.

Potential Research Questions

Instead of offering a scholarly edition, fully annotated with editorial complexity, *Gothic Short Stories in British Literary Annuals* was produced to encourage research on the development of the Gothic short story in literary annuals. The production, dissemination, and reception of literary annuals definitely influenced the development of the short story form and the evolution of Gothic in its relationship to Victorian novels. It is not clear, however, how much editorial intervention facilitated, even forced, the abrupt format of this type of fiction. Since professional authors would have been accustomed to writing towards a word count, the brevity of conclusions and beginnings of short stories might have been through their own doing or the editor's control.[17]

The longest story in this collection, Sir Walter Scott's "My Aunt Margaret's Mirror," is a massive 11,660 words.[18] The story and characters are allowed to develop outside the constraints of a typical Gothic short story, though. But, Sir Walter Scott was an overwhelmingly popular and much-sought-after author. In fact, he was once offered £500 to edit *The Keepsake* but declined and offered an exorbitantly-priced story instead.

And, obviously, the amount of scholarship that can be produced based on the literary elements apparent in these short stories is immense. It is my hope that future studies based on this collection will also reflect the mode of dissemination, literary annuals.

---

17 Charles Robinson, editor of *Mary Shelley: Collected Tales and Stories with Original Engravings*, notes that Mary Shelley was asked to revise some short stories for *The Keepsake* to "fit" the page length.
18 The number of words per page in these literary annuals is approximately 265.

FORGET ME NOT

Literary Annual
Forget Me Not, A Christmas and New Year's Present for 1823. Ed. [Frederic Shoberl]. London: R. Ackermann, 1823. Printer: C.E Knight, Butcher Row, East Smithfield.

Title
Anonymous. "The Magic Mirror. A Polish Tale." FMN 1823. 133-153. [133]

THE
MAGIC MIRROR.
A POLISH TALE.

In the castle of Lapotka, in Poland, there was an ancient tower, concerning which many extraordinary reports were circulated: but as the door, composed of thick oaken planks, strengthened with iron, had not been opened, to any one's knowledge, from time immemorial. The most general notion was, that a former proprietor of the castle had practiced the black art in a dark apartment in this tower, that it was still haunted by his spirit, and that at the hour of midnight, the door of the tower flew open with a tremendous noise. [134]

Francis, a sprightly boy, the only son of the gentleman who owned the castle at the commencement of the eighteenth century, could therefore never approach the tower in question without a peculiar feeling of horror. He was growing up to manhood, when he once expressed a wish to his father that this unsightly tower, which disfigured the whole castle, were demolished; but the old man, with an air of mystery, replied, that he would probably some day think differently of the matter. Francis had been educated, agreeably to the wish of his mother, by a pious priest, who, having been frequently the dupe of the artful and designing, had conceived a disgust of the world, and embraced a monastic life. By him his pupil was instructed in the sciences; he instilled into him a spirit of piety and a love of virtue; but a suspicion and distrust of mankind were gradually infused, by the daily expressions of the preceptor, into the mind of his pupil. He had been from home some years to finish his education, when a letter from his father summoned him to return with all possible expedition, as he felt his health rapidly declining, and was desirous of speaking to him before his dissolution; especially as Charles the Twelfth of Sweden, after his victories at Narva and on the Dwina, was just then menacing the Polish frontiers. Francis obeyed his father's injunction, and hurried home, hoping to find him still alive. With an anxiously [135] throbbing heart he entered the castle-gate, and sought to read in every face the fulfillment of his most ardent wish, that his father might be yet living.

Old Ignatius came to meet him. "God be praised," cried he, "our master is yet alive, but extremely weak."

"Hasten, then," said Francis, "to prepare my dear father for my coming."

"Oh! he knew you would be here to-day," replied Ignatius, "so you had better go to him at once."

Francis could not conceive by what means his father had received such precise intelligence respecting the period of his return, but hurried to the bed of his parent, who was greatly rejoiced at his arrival, and immediately desired to be left alone with his son.

"My affairs," he began, "are exceedingly deranged; but my old and valued friend, the Starost Drebinski, has promised me the hand of his beautiful daughter for you. She possesses a large fortune in her own right. She is still young; her heart is disengaged; seek her love and the friendship of her brother; you will obtain both, and thereby raise our race, now nearly extinct, to new splendor. Perhaps, too, your mother's brother, though he and I have not been on good timers, may not transfer this hostility to you." [136]

The old man seemed nearly exhausted; his utterance became difficult; but he mustered his strength for another effort.

"I have still," said he, in a voice scarcely audible, "to communicate to you an important secret, which, if properly employed, may conduct you to the highest degree of prosperity. In yon tower—Ignatius—"

At these words he swooned. He again came to himself, indeed, and attempted to speak, but in vain; and in a few hours he was no more.

Francis was most affectionately attached to his father, and for a considerable time the thoughts of his deceased parent occupied his whole soul. He found his father's affairs in the utmost confusion. There were many points, indeed, on which Ignatius, the steward of the estate and the confidential agent of his father, was able to furnish information; but this was not the case with others, and particularly with a law-suit of the utmost importance; and Ignatius, to whom he addressed his enquiries on this subject in vain, at length said: "Probably nothing but the mirror can throw any light on this subject." Francis looked at him with astonishment, and on his requiring an explanation, it appeared that Ignatius had supposed that his dying master had made his son fully acquainted with the family secret. Finding that he was yet ignorant of it, he promised to give him all the necessary information at midnight. [137]

The air of mystery assumed by the steward who would not, and who indeed declared that he could not, then explain himself more fully, strongly excited the curiosity of his young master. He recollected the last words of his expiring father, and awaited the appointed hour with impatience. Midnight came, and with it Ignatius. He entered the room muffled up in a cloak, with a lantern in one hand, and a bunch of large keys in the other. At his desire, Francis wrapped himself in another cloak, "for," said his conductor, "I should wish, that if we happen to be seen, we may be taken for spirits." They proceeded to the tower, which Francis, owing to the recollection of his early years, could not approach without a secret awe; and this feeling was greatly increased by the harsh grating of the door, on being opened, and the sepulchral smell that issued from the tower.

"What," he asked, "am I to do here?"

"Only follow me," answered Ignatius; "you will see."

He unlocked a second door, that led into a ruinous chapel, and then lifting up a trap-door he descended. Francis hesitated a moment; but his curiosity was roused, and he followed. It was a funeral vault. Between two rows of moulding coffins and scattered bones, they advanced to an iron door, and passing it, entered a [138] small vaulted chamber, the walls of which were hung with black. The floor was covered with a black carpet; on it stood a small altar, upon which, between two black tapers, lay a skull, and before that a book in black binding.

"What means all this?" asked Francis.

"I am fulfilling the instructions of your deceased father," answered Ignatius, "which he gave me, in case he should not live till your arrival."

"But for what purpose is this mummery?"

"All I know about from the communications of my late master, is this:— One of your ancestors, a pious old gentleman, went on a pilgrimage with his son to Jerusalem. On their return, they fell into the hands of pirates, and were sold for slaves at Alexandria. As long as they continued together, the father's piety preserved the son from despair; but the old man, unused to hardships soon sunk under them. The son, without guide or friend, accustomed to live well and enjoy himself, not in his prime doomed to the most oppressive servitude, without any prospect of being ever redeemed, became accidentally acquainted with a Cophtic monk, who purchased his liberty, and with whom he passed several years. How they were both employed during that time is best known to God and his saints; but so much is certain, that your ancestor came back safe, and was rich [139] and respected. He constructed this little chamber by his family vault, and bequeathed to his descendants the magic mirror for the disclosure of future events, the use of which is explained in this book."

"Where is, then, this mirror?" asked Francis.

"Beware of drawing back the veil that conceals it: this must not be done except in the manner prescribed by the book. All that I can shew you, without danger, I will."

He drew up a curtain. Francis started back. In a niche in the wall stood a mummy, holding in both hands the mirror, covered with a black veil, on which unknown characters were embroidered in gold.

"None but a descendant of him who built this chamber may presume to look in the glass. You now know all that has been communicated to me; the book will inform you of the rest."

"Oh!" said Francis sorrowfully; "now I know why my dear good mother was so often weeping by herself: her friends called it melancholy, for she would not inform any one of the cause of her tears. No doubt she was acquainted with this horrid family-secret."

"You are right," replied Ignatius; "and your noble uncle, who was informed of the whole affair, when he came some years before you were born, to take leave your mother, previously to his departure from Poland with king [140] John Casimir, made your father promise to destroy this enchanted mirror. He believed that your father had done so, but was apprized, I know not by what means, of the contrary, and hence the coldness which ensued between them."

"Well then, out of respect for my beloved mother. I will destroy this abominable instrument of sorcery."

"Have patience, I beseech you! for even this cannot be done without the observance of certain circumstances, as directed in the book."

"Then take up the book, and let us begone out of this horrid place."

Francis threw the book for a moment into a book-case; but the troubles occasioned by the advance of the Swedes into Poland, numerous law-suits, and the importunity of creditors, immediately afterwards engaged his whole attention. He was soon convinced that there was no other way to avert impending ruin than the advantageous match proposed by this father. He hastened to Drebenski, by whom he was cordially welcomed, as the son of an old friend.

"I am heartily glad," said he "that you are come to see me just now, as I shall have an opportunity to introducing you to my daughter before she sets out for Warsaw. In the present troubles, the country is not a fit abode for a young lady; and therefore my sister, who lives [141] at Warsaw, is come provided with a Swedish passport to take her to that city.

This address strengthened the hopes of his young visitor. Rosalia presently entered the apartment; her extraordinary beauty captivated him at the first glance; but her childlike innocence, the noble simplicity of her manners, and the affection which she every moment expressed for her father, completely enchanted him. The possession of such a female seemed to him the highest felicity to which he could aspire in this world. Drebinski observed with peculiar satisfaction the impression made by his daughter's charms on the son of his friend. Francis found means also to ingratiate himself with Drebinski's sister, the Castellana Mozarski; and the young man, praised by all whom she loved and esteemed, soon began to be by no means indifferent to the fair Rosalia. Perceiving her growing partiality, he forgot all his troubles; his imagination pictured the most delicious prospects, and thus passed some of the happiest moments of his life. But the evening before the day fixed for the departure of the young lady, the conversation, which had previously been so lively, was at a stand. Francis eyed Rosalia with a look of dejection: he had acquainted her father with his wishes, but received no decisive answer, as the old man declared, that every thing depended on the choice of his [142] daughter. With downcast look sat Rosalia, only now and then venturing to raise her eyes to the handsome stranger, while many a gentle sigh heaved her fair bosom. The Castellana observed them both with a smile, and cast many a significant look at her brother.

Drebinski at length rose form his chair. "My dear Rosalia," said he, in a tender tone, "I should like to see you, before I die, united to a man deserving of your love."

Rosalia, sweetly blushing, kissed the hand of her father who thus proceeded:—"This young gentleman is the son of the friend and companion of my youth. I promised his father, on his death-bed, that he should have your hand, unless your heart were averse to the match. I will not forestall your choice; but, could I behold you united and happy together, this sight would cheer my declining days."

A tear trembled in the eye of the susceptible Rosalia: she extended her hand, in silence, to Francis, who pressed her to his heart, and imprinted the first kiss on her lips. The father raised his grateful eyes to heaven; and the Castellana shed tears of joy. The journey was postponed for a few days, and the lovers were inexpressibly happy. It was agreed, that the marriages should take place as soon as the storms of war had blown over. Francis now thought of nothing but his Rosalia, and made [143] every possible effort to retrieve his embarrassed affairs.

Thus had some months passed away, when Drebinski died. Will Rosalia, thought Francis, who gave me her hand only to gratify her father—will she, who is doubtless universally adored at Warsaw for her beauty, and perhaps surrounded by men, to whom I am in every respect inferior, still continue to bless me with her love? This thought haunted him incessantly. He wrote to Rosalia; he fancied that in her answer there was not the same tenderness as before; and at the same time he was informed by her, that her brother, who had resided some years in France, was on his return to his own country.

"O, ye saints!" exclaimed Francis, while the big tears trickled down his cheeks, "is it not likely that this brother, to whom I am an utter stranger, will make every effort to deprive one whose ruined circumstances are well known, of the hand of his sister?" This idea tormented him exceedingly. With a view to divert his mind by study, he sat down to the writing-table left him by his father. In examining the papers it contained, he discovered a secret drawer, in which were deposited letters from his uncle; who, on quitting Poland, had entered into the French military service, and held an important command. In every one of these letters the writer urged his brother-in-law to destroy the chamber described above and the magic mirror; [144] but the last contained the assurance, that unless, in the course of three months, he received a certificate form Father Dominic, that his wish was complied with, he would leave his large fortune to widows and orphans; but, in the contrary event, he should bequeath the whole of it to the son of his deceased sister. This letter had been written ten years, yet there was still a hope that he might be enriched by the kindness of his uncle, and thus rendered more worthy of Rosalia.

    He pulled the bell, and sent for Ignatius.
    "Do you know Father Dominic?"
    "Yes, he was confessor to your mother."
    "Is he still living?"
    He is prior of the neighboring convent."
    Francis posted away to the priory, and was most kindly received. Dominic knew nothing more than that his father occupied himself with magic, and that his pious mother and her brother had endeavored, by all the means in their power, to divert him from this abominable pursuit; the more particular circumstances of the case he was unacquainted with. So much, however, he could tell Francis, when he enquired concerning his uncle, that the latter was alive, and a general in the French army at the commencement of the late war; and he promised to forward any letter which his nephew might think fit to write to him. [145]

    Francis lost no time in writing to his uncle; he promised to destroy the unhallowed chamber, and took up the book to inform himself of the manner in which this intention might be executed without danger. At the beginning he found a description of the ceremonies with which the veil should be removed from the mirror, and the magic words which it was necessary to pronounce before looking into the glass. It required also, that any questions proposed to the mirror should be entered upon the blank leaves of this book, and also the answers returned to them by the mirror. Curiosity induced him to turn the last question proposed to the mirror by his father. It was as follows: "Has my son to expect wealth?"—The mirror presented a heap of bags full of money. Francis felt a momentary joy, which soon gave place to mistrust.—"To expect?" said he, "what a vague question! It should have been—Will he possess wealth?"

    At this moment a party of Swedes came to be quartered upon him.

Francis shut up his book, and went to receive them. The officers of a whole regiment had been sent to his castle. Francis, with a heart full of anxiety, sat pensive and silent; while the hilarity of the Swedes was heightened by the bottles of Tokay which they emptied at dinner. The elder officers forgot [146]their years, and joked the younger on their amours at Warsaw.

"Lilienström," said one of them, "is still in the dismals; he cannot forget the beautiful Rosalia."

Why should I deny it?" rejoined Lilienström, a young and very handsome man. "She is the most woman I ever beheld: and does not every body admire her?"

"In these sentiments the other officers coincided. The name of Rosalia had a painful effect on Francis; but he mustered courage, and asked, with apparent indifference, "Who is, then, the fair object of your commendations?"

"Rosalia Drebinski," replied one of the Swedes.

"If I am not mistaken," continued Francis, "the hand of that lady is engaged."

Her father," answered one of the half-intoxicated officers, "is said to have forced a match upon her; but it would be a miracle if the present suitors were not to supplant the absent one." A general laugh succeeded.

Francis, tormented by the most painful uncertainty, passed the following night without sleep. The thought of consulting the magic mirror frequently darted across his brain, but his guardian angel prevented him from carrying it into effect. In a few days the Swedes departed, and Francis was left alone with his [147] anxiety and his apprehensions. He projected a variety of plans; he thought of proceeding to Warsaw to watch Rosalia, and to remind her of him; but he had no money to defray the expense of such a journey, and to make a suitable appearance in the capital. Ignatius was consulted, and was of opinion that the mirror would be the best adviser. The idea of applying to the mirror frequently occurred, but it was not yet matured into a resolution.

Meanwhile Francis received a visit from the reverend Father Dominic. He loved and respected the aged prior. He was on the point of pouring forth his whole heart before him; but Dominic seemed himself to be deeply dejected, and observed, that man ought to put his trust in God, to look to him alone for happiness, and not to grieve or despair on account of any disappointment of his hopes.

"For heaven's sake, reverend father," cried Francis, turning pale as death, and trembling like an aspen leaf, "have compassion on me; conceal not from me the dreadful intelligence: my heart already tells me that Rosalia is false!"

"No, my son," replied Dominic; "I know nothing of Rosalia. The letter which you gave me for your uncle I sent to France; I hoped to be the messenger of good tidings, but yesterday I received accounts from Paris, informing me [148] that your uncle has fallen in battle. Not a word is said concerning his property, but the writer merely states, that I shall be apprized of farther particulars by the general's aid-de-camp, a Pole, who has returned to his own country." Painful as this intelligence was, yet Francis felt somewhat relieved for the moment. He had anticipated a more severe misfortunate. The idea of being persecuted by fate, and the probability of soon hearing that his last hope was blasted, preyed upon his heart. A feverish heat drove him to and fro; he knew not what to do, or where to find rest. In this state of mind he met Ignatius, and to him he complained of his distress. "How," cried he, "shall I put an end to this uncertainty, this infernal torment?"

"If you only wish to arrive at certainty, you may do that immediately."

"I understand you; well, be the result what it will—Fate summons. Come on, then!"

He hastened with the steward to the tower. Distant lightnings played about the horizon: the owl screeched, but Francis heeded it not. According to the directions in the book, he uncovered the glass, and demanded an answer to the question—whether Rosalia felt attachment to any other man than himself? He looked in the glass—Rosalia, in dishabille, attended by a maid carrying a light, hurried into a room by [149] one door, while a young officer entered it at another, and they clasped each other most tenderly in a mutual embrace. Francis was furious at this sight: he wished for further information, but the mirror could not be consulted oftener than every third night.

The next morning Francis looked extremely pale, and perturbed: Dominic attributing this to his communication, deferred his departure for some days, that he might console and cheer him. He advised Ignatius to send for a physician, which the steward, however, declined doing: and thus arrived the third night, when the mirror was to resolve the question—whether Rosalia would keep up the same connection with the officer which subsisted between them at that time? Both of them appeared in a carriage, attended by two outriders. "The faithless, perjured woman!" exclaimed Francis; "she is eloping with him!" He was in a state bordering on distraction. In vain did Dominic, who was ignorant of the real cause of his despair, offer all the consolations of religion. At times they seemed to have some effect; but fury and despair soon regained possession of his heart. Dominic then turned to a crucifix which hung in the room. "Father of mercies," cried he, "send him consolation and save his poor soul." Francis wildly paced the floor, resolving to consult the mirror once more, to take [150] revenge on his rival, and then to terminate his life and his misery at once.

At this moment a carriage drove up to the door, and a servant entered the room.

"Send them away," cried he; "I will not see any one. I am ill—I am not at home."

The servant returned, saying, that the strangers insisted on speaking with the master of the house. "Reverend Father," said Francis, "rid me of them, I entreat you."

Dominic went. He found a young officer, and a young lady, whom he recognized at the first glance. It was Rosalia and her brother. He told them that Francis was ill, and that it would be necessary to prepare him for their visit. Drebinski, therefore, related what follows:—

"On leaving Poland, I entered into the French service, and soon found a kind friend in General Strikowski who appointed me his aid-de-camp. In a few years, my father desired me, on account of his increasing infirmities, to demand my dismission, and return home to manage his estates. A sense of honor prevented me from complying with this injunction before the end of the campaign, when I received a letter from my sister acquainting me with her betrothal to the nephew of my good general. This intelligence gave us both infinite pleasure. I could not answer her, for the enemy and we were then face to face; a few days afterwards [151] an engagement ensued, and the noble Strikowski was mortally wounded. He declared his nephew heir to his considerable property, of which he ordered me to take charge. As soon as the campaign was over, I resigned my commission and hastened home. It was midnight when I arrived at Warsaw, and drove up to the house of my aunt. The family had retired to rest. Rosalia's maid heard me knock; I mentioned my name; and our joy at meeting again was not to be described. I begged my sister to make the nephew of him, to whom I was under such obligations, happy as speedily as possible by the gift of her hand. She acceded to my request, and has accompanied me hither for the purpose, on the way to my estates."

The eyes of the venerable prior overflowed with tears of joy. All's well, thought he, that ends well. He hastened to Francis to communicate to him the auspicious intelligence; but was astonished at his expression more horror than gratification. Francis wrung his hands, raised his eyes to heaven, and prostrated himself before the crucifix, while tears streamed down his pallid cheeks. Minutes seemed hours to Rosalia; she could wait no longer, and hastened to Francis, whom, on opening the door, she found on his knees. "Dear, good soul!" cried she, "my thanksgiving shall rise with thine to the throne of God." She fell on her [152] knees beside him—his face became more and more pale, and he sunk senseless on the floor. On coming to himself, he kissed Rosalia's hand and bedewed it with his tears. "O, thou angel of love!" cried he, "I am unworthy of thee!" With profound contrition he then related all that had passed with the magic mirror, and the cruel deception it had practiced upon him.

"Where is this accursed instrument?" cried Debrinski: "your uncle enjoined me to see to it, that it should be destroyed."

"Months," replied Francis, "would be required, according to the directions in the book, to accomplish this without danger."

"Whoever," said Dominic, "believes in him who deprived hell of its power, need not fear its threats."

Ignatius and some others of the household, were summoned. They proceeded to the subterranean chamber. Dominic laid hold of the mirror, but was seized by the mummy, whose eyes seemed to roll as they looked at him, while hideous howling resounded on all sides. The prior, however, wrested the mirror from its grasp, and dashed it in pieces. He caused every thing in the apartment to be burned, and threw the book also into the flames. Alternate horror and rage, joy and shame, had operated with such force on Francis, that he was like one intoxicated. Next morning he was seized [153] with a violent fever; the physician, summoned to his aid, declared him in great danger, and in three days he expired with profound contrition, amidst the prayers of the pious prior.

This event made the deepest impression on the susceptible heart of the fair Rosalia, who had been tenderly attached to the deceased. The world had lost all charms for her; she took the veil; and, as abbess of the convent, she lived to an advanced age, an example of virtue and piety to all the sisterhood.

Drebinski married happily, and often related this history to his children and grandchildren, warning them at the same time against superstition. "Be thankful," he would say upon such occasions, "to the all-wise Being, who has limited the sphere of mortal vision, and no doubt from the kindest motives concealed the future from our view. Strive not, with presumptuous hand, to draw the veil aside form it, but, resigned to the will of Providence, seek your highest felicity in piety and virtue alone."

Literary Annual

Forget Me Not; A Christmas and New Year's Present for 1824. Ed. Frederic Shoberl. London: R. Ackermann, 1824. Printer: Thomas Davison, Whitefriars.

Title

Anonymous . "The Ring; A True Narrative. From the Russian." FMN 1824. 107-126. [107]

THE RING;
A TRUE NARRATIVE.
FROM THE RUSSIAN.

"Look, who comes yonder, towards our house, in an open sledge with three horses?" cried the major's lady, as she happened to look through the window.

Her husband, Major Sundukow, to whom this question was addressed, rose slowly from the oaken sofa supported by eagles' claws with a ball in each, and stepped to the window.

"There are two persons in the sledge," continued his wife. "One of them has a white feather in his hat. Dear me! who can it be?"

"Why, who else but our neighbor, Chabarow, and his son," replied the major. "I quite forgot to tell you that while I was out a-hunting yesterday, I met the steward, who told me that his young master was come home on leave of absence. Go and see about some breakfast—tell Glafira to make herself a little [108] smart, and do you be sure to put on your best."

The lady retired to comply with these directions, while the major called a servant, and ordered him to fetch his uniform surtout, the carefully preserved memorial of his military career. Sundukow had served under the Empress Elizabeth, and had retired from the army about fifteen years before the time of which I am speaking.

While they are dressing, and the servants are opening the door, which at that period was always kept locked night and day even in the towns, I gain time to inform my readers, that Sundukow was a gentleman residing in the government of Wladimir, and that he had a beautiful daughter. The lily and the rose were blended in her lovely face; her figure was majestic as a queen's, and her parents, be it observed, were wealthy. Many suitors solicited the hand of Glafira; but would it have been prudent to give her to a man who perhaps possessed no more than about fifty peasants? Her parents had unfortunately the weakness to seek an opulent bridegroom for their daughter. We shall only observe, by the way, that the young Chabarow, after his father's death, would become the master of five hundred peasants, and then the reader may easily guess the reason why the major wished his wife and daughter to appear [109] to the best advantage on this occasion. It is true indeed that the lady, as a tender mother, had no need of this advice.

The visitors were introduced. After the first salutations, old Sundukow complimented the officer, called him a gallant youth, praised his dragoon uniform, inquired the particulars of the action on the Kagul, asked after field-marshal Rumjanzow, and was overjoyed to hear that hopes were entertained of peace, as he had been exceedingly apprehensive of a new recruiting. The young man never ceased boasting of his exploits, and answered all the questions put to him with the greatest accuracy; but when the lady entered with her daughter, he became manifestly confused—his stories were no longer intelligible—he confounded the names of the generals. Baur he called Bruce, and Plemjannikow, Potemkin; and all this was owing to nothing more or less than the appearance of Glafira.

During dinner he conversed with her on the subject of their rural occupations, and in so doing betrayed his levity. The modest damsel blushed, though not at every word; for she had been several times at parties at Wladimir, and had passed a whole month of the preceding winter in Moskwa.

On taking leave, Chabarow invited Sundukow and his family to dine with him the following day. [110]

"That would be a capital match for our Glafira," said the major to his wife, after he had attended his visitors to the door: "though he is rather an unlicked cub, according to the vulgar saying, still he is young and rich."

"I perfectly agree with you, my dear," replied Mrs. Sundukow; "but still I feel much for poor Kudrin. He is attached with his whole soul to our girl; and if he is not rich, he is so affectionate, so modest, and so pious."

"Well, but have we not flatly rejected his suit, and forbidden him the house? How silly you are to harbour such ideas!"

"One can't speak, but you fly into a passion immediately. I merely said what I thought; but it rests with you to act as you please. I shall be heartily glad myself for Glafira to cut a figure as the wife of an opulent man."

Kudrin—likewise a neighbor of Sundukow's—who had early been left an orphan, was now, at the age of twenty-five years, master of the like number of peasants, and was just what Mrs. Sundukow described him. He had acquired a little polish in the house of a Russian grandee, and was a particular favourite with the major's lady, because he could give a tolerably connected account of the lives of the saints from the legends of the church, and never missed the morning service on holidays.

Kudrin had cherished for above a year an [111] ardent passion for Miss Sundukow, and when he ventured to offer her his hand, it was without any reference to her fortune. It was her beauty and amiable disposition that captivated him. As to Glafira, she seemed to have no aversion to the young man; nay, she was pleased with his company and conversation and she loved to hear him play old tunes on the recumbent harp; but she felt no particular inclination for him, and therefore took the rejection of his overtures by her father very quietly.

This mortification, however, had not wholly broken off Kudrin's intercourse with the Sundukow's family. The nurse of the fair Glafira was wholly devoted to him, partly out of pity, and partly because he was as liberal in his presents to her as his circumstances permitted. She frequently gave him accounts of her mistress, and sometimes too contrived to remind the latter of her discarded lover.

A fortnight after the arrival of young Chabarow, Kudrin was informed by the nurse that Glafira was betrothed. Though the hapless lover had long been deprived of all hopes, still this intelligence afflicted him exceedingly. He wept, pined, and became quite melancholy.

Thus began and terminated the successful suit of Chabarow. At the very first interview he took a fancy to Glafira; after he had seen her a few times, he fell in love with her, and [112] communicated his sentiments to his father, who immediately drove off to Sundukow's. The old folks, after some conversation on the subject, gave each other their hands, and the affair was settled. They concerned themselves but little about the consent of Glafira; for in those happy days the will of the parents alone decided the fate of their daughters.

Glafira felt, as a bride, some kindness for Chabarow, but it was not that tender and yet mighty passion which is denominated love.

The two months' leave of absence obtained by Chabarow had expired, and he was obligated to return to the army. He seemed heartily sorry for it, and Glafira herself often sighed, to the great dissatisfaction of her nurse. The betrothal was celebrated before his departure; but the nuptials were deferred till the return of the bridegroom the following spring.

It was the middle of December when Sundukow's family, in their joy, resolved to take a jaunt to Moskwa, for the purpose of spending the Christmas holidays and the Carnival in that city, and likewise to show the bride to their friends, and to make the necessary purchases against the wedding. They accordingly set out, and agreeably to the custom of those times took a number of their serfs along with them; and the nurse, from whom the young lady had never yet been separated, was not forgotten. [113]

Kudrin also repaired to Moskwa, as he himself declared, merely to amuse himself; but on the very first Sunday he attended mass, and that at the church of St. Wassilij, which the major's lady preferred to all the rest. There he had the happiness to see Glafira, accompanied by her nurse, without being observed by either of them.

The good creature still continued to be faithfully devoted to him. Kudrin received many a useful hint from her, and occasionally found opportunities of speaking to her. Though Glafira was already affianced, and the last spark of hope was extinguished in Kudrin's Heart, still she urged many reasons why he ought not to despair. The young man cheerfully placed himself under the guidance of the nurse, and listened with pleasure to her consolations—consolations which seldom fail to soothe the unhappy. The Christmas holidays commenced: they were formerly the most delightful season of the year, awaited with equal impatience by the young of both sexes—a season which, by the variety of its amusements, occupied children, as well as diverted the parents, and which (thanks to the present illumination!) now pass off with as little ado as any other holidays. I shall not say a word about the capitals of governments, where every thing Russian has long been banished from social life; there are the ancient Christmas sports are happily compensated [114] by masquerades and balls, and in the circular towns, where too people are now ashamed of these innocent amusements, what has superseded them?—cards and the incessant rattle of glasses; the one as commendable as the other. But I have involved myself here in an unseasonable digression, and resume the thread of my narrative.

The Christmas holidays begin in this manner:—Whole families of acquaintances assembled in the evenings, to bury gold, to sing riddle-songs,[1*] to play at forfeits, and to disguise themselves. Glafira shared, as usual, in these amusements, but seemed to take less interest in them than formerly; she cared not about selecting any one whom she wished to please, or in whose hand she desired to put the gold ring more frequently than into that of any other.

"New-year's day will soon be here, and Miss has not yet had her fortune told," observed this sly nurse one evening. "Why should I?" replied Glafira. "Am I not already betrothed?"

"Well, and is not this the very time to learn whether your bridegroom is well, what he is [115] doing, and if he frequently thinks about you? I tell you, a great deal of water will yet flow before your wedding. Till the hour appointed by God arrives, who knows what may happen? Slip on your pelisse, and let us go into the street, and ask the first person we meet what is his name?"

Glafira, not accustomed to contradict her nurse, put on her pelisse, and went down with her into the street. They had not gone above ten paces before they met a man. "What is your name?" asked Glafira.

"Alexander," was the reply.

There, young lady!" whispered the old woman: "that is not your bridegroom's Christian name, but Kudrin's. Here, hard by, the streets cross: let us go and hear on which side the first dog will begin to bark."

They stopped at the crossing—a dog barked. "Aha! hark you, my dear!

---

1 The nature of this amusement is as follows:—While the whole company sing an appropriate song, any one who chooses puts some article or other belonging to him into a covered dish, and thinks of something. Another verse is then sung, the dish is shaken, one of the covered articles is taken out, and the fortune of the owner is predicted amid laughter and merriment from the subject of the song.

The dog does not bark from toward Kiew, to which Chabarow is gone, but from our own quarter, Wladimir, where Kudrin now is."

They listened at two or three houses to the Christmas songs which were singing within; but, owing to the double windows, they could not catch a single word, so that no omen was to be drawn from them.

Glafira hurried back to the house. Agitated by doubts, and impelled by curiosity, she told [116] her nurse, that next night she would consult the mirror—a kind of prognostication which she preferred to any other, on account of the many instances in which its accuracy had been demonstrated.

The old woman commended her design, and next night, at twelve o'clock, when all the family were in bed, went with her into a wing of the house that was uninhabited. Here all the necessary preparations were made. In the middle of the room were placed two tables with a mirror on each. The nurse made Glafira sit down between them; and with a piece of charcoal she drew a circle round the spot. "Be not afraid, my dear," said she: "I shall be at hand; sit still, but be sure don't look round; for no enemy dares pass this circle."

Hereupon she took post at the door of the room. All was still. The timid girl did not stir, but looked stedfastly at the mirror before her, and saw nothing but an endless row of lights. Half an hour elapsed—her eyes began to be dazzled—the brilliance of the lights was obscured, as it were, by smoke; but nothing appeared in the glass. All at once a slight noise was heard. Glafira's blood curdled, and in a moment she gave a loud scream, at the same time covering her face with both her hands.

The old nurse and a glass of water soon brought her again to herself.
[117]
"What is the matter with you, my dear child?"
"Ah, nurse! let us be gone from this frightful place! I saw—I saw—"
"But what did you see, love?"
"I saw—a—a—man."
"And did you know him?"
"I thought so—and would you believe it?—he had no resemblance to my bridegroom, but was exactly like Kudrin."
"There you see, my dear! who knows but he may be destined for you at last?"

The reader will easily guess how this apparition was conjured up. The sly nurse had made previous arrangements. Kudrin, at her invitation, was in waiting at the appointed hour, softly entered the room, advanced to the back of Glafira's chair, and hastily retired again, unobserved by the agitated girl.

Poor Glafira could not sleep a wink all night. Kudrin's image was continually present to her imagination. A slight fever, the consequence of her fright, left her in a few days; but the impression made by this circumstance on her mind was not to be erased. Her sharp-sighted attendant presently perceived the state of her mind, and began to operate upon it with so much the more effect.

Glafira, educated in superstitious notions heard from her nurse nothing but remarks to the [118] prejudice of Chabarow, and commendations of Kudrin. As the latter was really more polished, more affectionate, and more handsome in person than his rival, Glafira, conceiving that he was destined by a superior power to be her husband, began to love him.

Every thing went on according to the wishes of the nurse; but a melancholy and unexpected event frustrated her plans in a moment and blasted the hopes of old Sundukow; so little can we answer for the success of our most promising enterprises! Delighted with our progress, we imagine that we are already in sight of the goal which we are so strenuously striving to reach; but the hand of Omnipotence suddenly conceals it from our view, and often only that it may conduct us to the very same point, but by another way well-pleasing to itself.

After the Sundukows had spent nearly a month at Moskwa, they began to make preparations for returning home. One morning visitors called to see them. Glafira was just then engaged in some domestic occupation, which she immediately relinquished, and slipped into her mouth the ring with which she was affianced to Chabarow, while she washed her hands.

"My mistress begs you to step into the parlour, and to make haste if you please," said a servant to her. Glafira opened her lips to answer and swallowed the ring. Unluckily it met [119] with some obstruction, and stuck in her throat. In vain did she strive to rid herself of it—her strength failed—her respiration was suspended—the unfortunate girl sunk into the arms of the women who surrounded her, and expired in dreadful convulsions.

The whole house was in the utmost consternation. The wretched parents, the terrified visitors, and the inquisitive servants, all hurried to the spot. Tears and lamentations, which filled the room and the whole house, acquainted the neighbors with the fatal accident, but did not reach the ear of Glafira, who lay inanimate in the arms of her mother and her nurse.

In those days there were still but few physicians at Moskwa, and very little confidence was placed in these. One of the visitors set off in search of one of those gentlemen, and returned with him in about two hours. This disciple of Aesculapius, a German, in a powdered wig of monstrous size, looked at Glafira, felt her pulse, applied his hand to her temples, and shook his head, declaring the case hopeless, but adding, that had he been fetched half an hour earlier, he could have answered for her life.

The robe of white satin destined for Glafira's wedding-dress was now transformed into her shroud. Thus attired, the corpse, lovely even in death, was laid upon a table, her beautiful chestnut hair falling in large ringlets over her [120] shoulders. The parents, deeply shocked by the catastrophe, were conducted into a distant apartment. Two aged ladies, nearly related to the family, undertook the arrangements for the funeral—a melancholy and a painful duty to a susceptible heart, and which deserves the sincere gratitude of those for whom the sad office is performed.

The tidings of the sudden death of Sundukow's fair daughter soon spread through the city, and reached Kudrin's ears the same day. The heart of the unhappy lover, whose extinguished hopes had just begun to revive through the efforts of the nurse, was overwhelmed with anguish. At that moment he would rather that Glafira had been in Chabarow's arms: it seemed to him more desirable to die of the torments of hapless love, than to deplore the premature end of the charming girl to whom his whole soul was so strongly attached.

After the first vehement emotions of grief, he resolved, let it cost what it might, to see the deceased once more, to take a last farewell of her, and then to immure himself for the rest of his life in a distant convent. But how was he to gain access to the Sundukow's house? He could not reckon on this occasion upon the nurse; for she, afflicted by the death of her young mistress, could think of nothing but her loss. Kudrin [121] racked his brains for some time, and at length he adopted the following plan for want of a better.

He repaired to the church of the parish in which the Sundukows lived, sought the clerk, and inquired at what time he should have to recite the psalms by the deceased daughter of the gentleman of Wladimir. "At eleven o'clock," was his reply. Kudrin then informed him, under the seal of profound secrecy, that he had made a vow to read the psalms by twelve corpses; he therefore offered to perform the duty for him, and begged that he would lend him his gown.

The clerk, astonished at the proposal of the stranger, surveyed him with a scrutinizing look, and hesitated to comply; but when Kudrin threw down upon the table ten shining rubles—a handsome sum in those days—he bowed assent, delivered to him his blue gown, and afterwards talked a long time with his wife about the singular vow of this young gentleman.

In the simple modest garb of a servant of the church, with oppressed heart and pallid cheek, the unhappy Kudrin was ushered into the apartment of the lifeless Glafira. At the sight this beloved and lamented object he could scarcely support himself. At the farther end of the room, on a table surrounded by six tall candlesticks, beneath an awning of rich stuff, [122] her face covered with white muslin, lay the remains of her who was dearer to him than any thing in the world. But he was obliged to collect himself, for there were persons in the room. He went up trembling to the desk, opened up the Psalms, made the sign of the cross, and with a faltering voice began to read. In order not to betray himself, he strove to fix his eyes on the book before him, but they would wander in spite of him to the veiled face of the lovely slumberer.

About one o'clock all of the attendants retired from the apartment, excepting an old maid-servant, who, being fatigued, soon fell asleep. The nurse had taken the death of her young mistress so deeply to heart, that she was confined by illness to her bed. When all around was quiet, Kudrin quitted his place, went up to the table, and fell upon his knees, while tears streamed down his cheeks. "I loved thee," said he softly, "even when I was deprived of all hope of ever possessing thee. I could at least enjoy the consolation of praying for thy happiness, and of rejoicing if my prayers were granted. But now—"Here he rose, and threw back the veil from Glafira's face. What angelic beauty! no appearance of death! the lips wore the hue of health—a delicate red tinged her cheeks—she looked like one in a profound and tranquil slumber. Immoveable [123] and without uttering a word he contemplated her lovely features for some moments. His tears then began again to flow; with a deep drawn sigh he pronounced a last farewell, and resting his hands on the edge of the table, he bent over the corpse to kiss her. His lips almost touched the lips of the deceased—burning tears fell fast upon her cold face—when, all at once, the crazy legs of the table gave way, and down it fell under its load. In his first alarm Kudrin caught the corpse, raised it up, and held it in his arms. The crash roused the snoring maid-servant, and awoke the persons who slept in the contiguous apartments. The whole family hastened to the spot, and all stood motionless at beholding the scene which there presented itself.

But the universal astonishment was infinitely increased when they heard deep sighs issue from the bosom of Glafira, when, opening her eyes, she looked round on all sides, and in faint accents asked, "Where am I?—who holds me so fast and why?—where are my mother—my father—my nurse?" By this time the latter had come in, and they were not less amazed than the rest.—"But nobody answers me!—Ah! now I recollect!—you thought I was dead. But look—only look—I am alive, and there is the fatal ring!" She pointed with her finger—all eyes were turned to the floor, and there they beheld [124] the ring, from which the unfortunate girl had been relieved by the effect of the fall. They unanimously exclaimed, "She lives!" and ran up to Glafira, who, already able to stand without support, extended her arms to her overjoyed mother.

In a moment the candlesticks and all the other decorations of the former melancholy scene were removed. Joy beamed from every face. Each embraced her in turn, and not one with dry eyes. At length the general curiosity was directed to the supposed clerk, who, with enraptured heart, but modest look, stood motionless. At the first question from Sundukow respecting what had happened, he threw himself at his feet, and having frankly narrated all of the circumstances, he concluded with these words: "My love has restored your daughter to you: In my arms she returned to life. Can you still object to acknowledge me you son?"

"Father! mother!" exclaimed Glafira, casting a look of inexpressible tenderness at Kudrin: "this is my saviour! Never will I belong to any other, nor will I again put on my bridegroom's ring with which I was wedded to death!"

What course could the deeply affected father and the sobbing mother pursue after so solemn an assurance? After a mutual silent, but eloquent look, they embraced Kudrin as their beloved son. [125]

When the report of this extraordinary event was circulated through the city, many of the old inhabitants of which may still recollect it, Sundukow's consent was universally approved. The major, however, was uneasy on account of the violation of his promise; but Chabarow himself relieved him from this anxiety. News soon arrived from Tula, that the fickle youth, in passing through that town, had fallen in love with a handsome widow, to whom he had been privately married.

Is it necessary to finish this story? Does the reader need the assurance that Kudrin and Glafira were a happy couple? They, like every body else, acknowledge in the enviable lot a kind dispensation of Divine Providence.

Title
Anonymous. "The Grey Palmer: A Legend of Yorkshire." FMN 1824. 232-237.
[232]

THE
GREY PALMER:
A LEGEND OF YORKSHIRE.

Eight miles from the city of York, amidst picturesque scenery on the banks of the river Wharfe, stands the residence of Sir Thomas Milner, which was anciently the site of a convent, inhabited by nuns of the Cistercian order. There was a contemporary monastery of monks at Acaster Malbis; and tradition relates that a subterranean passage afforded the inmates of these institutions access to each other. In the year 1281, the lady abbess of Nun Appleton called upon the archbishop from Caywode, and the nuns of St. Mary's abbey, to chant high mass on the blessed of St. Mark, to lay at rest the wandering wailing spirit of sister Hylda, which had haunted the convent, the monastery, and adjacent country, during seven long years. The peasants fled from that district, for the spirit appeared to them in their houses, glared on them in the fields, or floated over their heads in passing the Wharfe; and if [233] they attempted to fell a tree in the woods, a hideous form in a Cistercian habit presented itself, showing a wound in its breast; and the morning-wind, raising its black veil, uncovered a ghastly countenance, and sunken eyes raining incessant tears.

A tempest, with loud, dismal, and portentous howlings, shook the high craggy cliffs above Otley:—fierce and more fierce it whirled along the river, and sent levin bolts and red meteors over the cloisters of Nun Appleton; showers descended as if the firmament of heaven were dissolved into rolling tides; and the Wharfe, swelling over all its banks, washed rocks from their base and lofty trees from their far-spreading roots. The holy archbishop, in sacred stole, is before the altar—the veiled sisters of St. Mary's stand by the choir—and the monks of Acaster Malbis are ranged beyond the fretted pillars of the chapel; they wait the solemn call of the bell to raise their voices in hymns of supplication—the walls resound with knocking at the convent-gate—The portress told her beads and crossed her breast, as she said to herself, while wending to the portal, "Here comes the pilgrim of Palestine, foretold by the dreary ghost of sister Hylda!"

She turned the lock with difficulty; it seemed to deny admission to the stranger, and the hinges resisted and creaked horribly against his ingress; [234] but the arm of the portress forced them to expand, and a Palmer, clad in grey weeds of penitence, strode within the threshold. The roaring thunder burst over his head, blue lightnings flashed around his gigantic figure, and in a hoarse sepulchral voice he thanked the portress for her gentle courtesy.

"By land and by sea," said he, "I have proved all that is terrible in danger or awful in the strife of war. My arm wielded the truncheon with gallant Richard, the chiefest knight of the Holy Rood; and the Paynims of Acre, with their mighty Soldan, have quaked in the tumult of our crusaders. The storm of the Red Sea and the rage of open ocean have rattled in mine ear. I have crossed burning sands, and met the wild lords of the desert in shocks of steel; but never was my soul so appalled as by the rage of elements this horrible night. To the sinner nought is so fearful as the workings of Almighty wrath in our lower world. I have visited every shrine of penitence and prayer to purge the stains of crime from this labouring bosom; I have trodden each weary step to the holy sepulchre in Palestine; I have knelt to the saints of Spain, of Italy, and of France; I have mourned before the shrine of St. Patrick and every saint of Ireland; in Scotland I have drunk of every miraculous fount and holy well; and but for the swollen waters of Wharfe, [235] I had sought the grey towers of Caywode, or the fair abbey of Selby, to crave prayers from the pure in heart for the worst of transgressors. At holy St. Thomas's tomb my pilgrimage ends. But for the wicked there can be no rest. The pelting hail-blast, the dark-red flashes of lightning, and the flooded Wharfe, oppose my course. I wandered through the dark wood—dire peals of thunder roared among the groaning oaks, and the ravening he-wolf rushed from his den across my path, while the flame of his eyes showed his gore-dripping jaws wide asunder to devour me. A spectre, more fell than the rage of a savage beast, drove him away—the croaking raven and ominous owlet sung a death-warning—and the spectre shrieked into my ear—'Grey Palmer, thy bed of dank, chill, deep earth, and they pillow of worms, are prepared! Thy fleshless bride waits to embrace thee!'"

Deep sounded the bell. "Haste thee, haste thee, holy Palmer!" said the portress; "the spectre of sister Hylda bade the lady abbess expect thee. Haste thee to join the choral swell. Why quakes thy stately form? Haste thee—the bell hath ceased its solemn invocation!"

Scarcely had the Palmer entered the sanctified dome of the chapel, when the seven hallowed tapers which burned in perpetual blaze [236] before the altar expired in blue hissing flashes—the full-swelling choir sunk to awful silence—a gloomy light circled along the vaulted roof—and sister Hylda, with her veil thrown back by her skeleton hand, revealed her well-known features; but pale, grim, and ghastly with the hue of the tomb, as she stood by the Palmer, who was recognised as friar John.

The archbishop raised his meek eyes and blanched countenance to Him that liveth and reigneth for ever. The cold dew of horror dropped from his cheeks; but in aspirations of prayer his courage returned, and in adjurations by the name of the Most High he commanded the spectre to tell why she broke the peace of the faithful. Unearthly groans issued from her colourless lips: the dry bones of her wasted carcase rattled with a fearful agitation as she thus spoke:—"In me behold sister Hylda, dishonoured, ruined, murdered by friar John in the deep penance-vault. He stands by my side, and bends his head lower and lower in confession of his guilt. I died unconfessed, and seven years has my troubled, my suffering spirit walked the earth, when all were hushed in peaceful sleep but such as the lost Hylda. Your masses have earned grace for me—I go to my long rest. Seek the middle pavement-stone of the vault for the mortal relics of a soul purified [237] and pardoned by the blood of the Redeemer. Laud and blessing to his gracious name for ever!"

Soft strains of melody swelled in the air, and a bright flame rekindled the holy tapers; but sister Hylda and the Palmer vanished, and were never seen more!

Title

Anonymous. "Pernicious Effects of Fortune-Telling." FMN 1824. 319-329.[319]

PERNICIOUS EFFECTS OF FORTUNE-TELLING.

The late Dr. Adam Nietzky, who, towards the conclusion of the last century, was professor at the University of Halle, had the vanity to wish to be thought not only an able physician and naturalist, but also an infallible fortune-teller. He, therefore, seized every opportunity of displaying this faulty, and foretelling future events; and also studiously propagated among his acquaintance the reputation of that power. Every prediction that was fulfilled, the admiration of his friends, and his own mysterious behaviour caused it to be whispered that Nietzky certainly possessed the key to futurity.

By these means, but more especially by his high character as a physician, and by his universal reputation for piety and integrity, he not only acquired the confidence of many venerable matrons, but became the oracle of his pupils to as great a degree as it is possible for any academical teacher to be. Hence, at the [320] conclusion of his lectures, his regular auditors seldom failed to assemble in groups before his house to discuss the dark enigmas which he had pronounced, and on which they made comments still darker and more absurd.

The impression produced by these effusions of his prophetic talent, however, was not equally strong on all his disciples. Some laughed at and ridiculed his silly vanity; others, from a spirit of orthodoxy, doomed him, as a necromancer, to the flames; while the majority were disposed and resolved to follow implicitly the supernatural light of their instructor.

Among the former was a student, whom we shall designate by his initial T., a native of Hanover, who was accidentally brought into company with some of the enthusiastic party. At first he launched forth sarcastic observations against his weak opponents, or pitied them on account of the derangement of their intellects; but though he could neither comprehend nor confute their senseless assertions, still the contagion of fanaticism began gradually to operate on his mind also. He was now frequently absorbed in serious meditation. The infatuation of his acquaintance appeared to him most insensate and ridiculous; but still there seemed to be some truth in the thing itself. At length he even contrived to compose from all these absurdities a serious whole. [321] There is, even in persons of sound understanding, a curiosity which is generated by a propensity to satire, and kept up by a love of the marvellous, and which is ultimately identified with the interest of truth itself. Impelled by this curiosity, and with a view either to discover and ascertain the truth of chiromancy, or to expose its uncertainty and absurdity, young T. resolved to have his own fortune predicted by Nietzky. Accordingly, he once followed him the lecture-room to his study, and acquainted him with his wish. Nietzky was accustomed to inquire minutely into the character and circumstances of each of his auditors, and a retentive memory treasured up these particulars, to be employed as occasion might serve. On the other hand, our inquisitive student had attended the lectures of several other professors as well as Nietzky's, but he had never had a private interview with any of them. The novelty of this tête-a-tête, the solemn look of the professor, and still more, the feeling that he was so near the accomplishment of his object, threw him into a sort of partly painful, partly pleasing anxiety, from which he could not immediately recover himself.

Nietzky had already asked and obtained correct answers to several obscure questions, and thus drawn from the youth many a circumstance [322] connected with his family before his confusion subsided, and he regained his self-possession.

The professor at length took his hand; and after the first glance at it, he thus addressed him:—"Young man, you will, in a twelvemonth, be recalled by your father from the university; six weeks afterwards you will lose your aunt; you will have the expectancy of an office, but an unforeseen circumstance will frustrate your hopes. Now, prepare to hear the worst—you will survive the disappointment only six months."

The prophet ceased; a servant summoned him away, and the thunder-struck student was dismissed for the present.

Our hero, as it may easily be conceived, was not a little confounded at what he had heard. At first, he could not help thinking of it for hours and days together, nay, it occupied his mind in many a sleepless night. But he was of a rather volatile disposition. Professor Nietzky's lectures were finished; he had himself attained the object of his wishes; his longing was satisfied; other occupations and amusements had by degrees weakened, or entirely erased, the impression made by the prediction; and it was not long before he felt convinced of his own folly, and of the fallacy of fortune-telling. He, therefore, amused every circle of his acquaintance and every party of his fellow-[323]students with the prediction levelled against him by Nietzky, and thought to make amends for his weakness by giving full scope to his satirical humour. In short, he regarded the affair with perfect indifference; and if he still sometimes called it to mind, it was only for the purpose of bestowing a smile of compassion on it and Nietzky.

He had now been three years at the university, when he received orders from his father to leave Halle. He aunt, who was not young, had lingered sixteen years in a consumption. It was evident, from the rapid decline of her strength, that her dissolution was fast approaching; and scarcely could joy for the return of her beloved nephew prolong her life for a few days. She died shortly after T.'s return home. When he strove to get rid of the thoughts and conclusions which naturally resulted from these events, the efforts which he made only served to increase his anxiety.

Nietzky's prediction began to be fulfilled, and the mind of the young man became more and more convinced of its probability, though he always deduced these occurrences from natural causes. The inactive life which he led at home began to be irksome to him. Several of his townsmen and fellow-students successively obtained appointments; and the ambition natural to his age stirred more and more powerfully [324] within his bosom. He applied first for one, and then for another vacant place; but his plans, being formed without due regard to the natural course of things, invariably proved abortive.

At length the post of town-clerk of his native city became vacant. He was not in want of patrons. His father was one of the oldest senators, and many of the other members of the magistracy were related to him by blood: these exerted all their influence to secure the office for him. He was actually elected, and nothing more was requisite but his confirmation by the court. One of the ministers, however, to whose department this district belonged, and who had, of course, paramount influence in the town, proposed his secretary for the office, and the magistrates durst not oppose this nomination.

Thus was T. once more disappointed. So far, therefore, almost all that Nietzky had predicted was most precisely fulfilled; and hence he inferred the danger that threatened his very life. He was, therefore, in continual apprehension of a near and inevitable death.

His understanding had abundance of arguments to oppose this silly anxiety; but they were only individual and distinct representations, which had to combat obscure feelings and ideas. Every victory gained by the former was at the same time a triumph for the latter; because they became more and more deeply impressed [325] upon his soul, and more familiar to his imagination. The once cheerful countenance of the pitiable young man became by degrees overspread with gloom. The colour forsook his cheeks; and his perturbation and unhappiness were manifest, in spite of the air of unconcern which he strove to assume. The thought of death, which haunted him incessantly, daily aggravated his melancholy and misery; and his free opinions in regard to religion were transformed into the excess of piety and devotion.

The nearer he approached to the last period of his life, the greater became his uneasiness. His ever busy imagination acted most prejudicially upon his body; every feeling of indigestion, or obstruction of the blood; every change in his pulse, to which he paid incessant attention; every cold arising from checked perspiration, was thereby rendered much worse; and these more pernicious effects of the fancy soon converted what had previously been imaginary into real disease. Just about this time, a sudden change of weather laid up a great number of the inhabitants of T.'s native town with catarrh and rheumatism. He, too, was attacked by this complaint—a circumstance not at all surprising: nor will the reader, on considering all the facts that have been related, be at all astonished to learn that out of hundreds of patients, he was the only one who, in [326] spite of all the care and attention of experienced physicians, was carried off by this slight complaint.

It may not be amiss to subjoin to this melancholy story one of a different character, in honour of the professors of astrology.

Louis XI of France, conformably with the spirit of his age, kept several astrologers at his court. It was probably in his excessive fear of death that this part of his establishment originated. This fear went so far, that no person durst pronounce the word death in his presence. If, nevertheless, any thing occurred to remind him of it, he would bury himself, out of anxiety and alarm, over head and ears in the bedclothes.

One day, intending to take the diversion of the chase, he asked an astrologer if the weather would continue fine? The astrologer confidently assured him that the day would be fair and serene. The king had not proceeded far towards the forest, when he met a charcoal-burner, driving his ass laden with coal before him. This man was bold enough to tell the king that he would do well to turn back, because in a few hours there would be a storm, accompanied with torrents of rain. The event justified his prediction.

Next day Louis sent for his humble monitor, and inquired where he had learned astrology, [327] and how he was able to foretell the weather with such accuracy. "Sire," replied the man, "I never went to school in my life, and can neither write nor read; but I keep in my service an excellent astrologer, who never deceives me."

"Who is he? what is his name?" asked the monarch, in astonishment.

"Please your majesty," answered the peasant, "it is my ass. Whenever a storm is at hand, he droops his ears forward and hangs down his head, goes more slowly than usual, and rubs himself against the walls. He did so yesterday, and from these signs I was enabled to warn your majesty of the approaching storm."

This adventure tended somewhat to enlighten the understanding of the king in regard to astrologers. He saw that even an ass knew more than they, and began to be ashamed of them. He bestowed a royal largess on the ass-driver for his unsolicited prediction, and dismissed from his service those whose duty it was to forewarn him of accidents.

One of these persons only contrived to preserve the good graces of the sovereign. He prophesied that a favourite mistress of the king's would die within a week. She did actually expire within the specified time. From a love of the marvellous, the narrators have not deemed [328] it worth while to acquaint posterity with any of the circumstances attending her decease. It is possible, that a week before her dissolution she might have been dangerously ill; or even have carried within her, in the form of poison, the seeds of approaching death; or perhaps some accident, or the same course of things which caused the fulfillment of Nietzky's prediction, might in this case have favoured the prophet of misfortune.

That this astrologer at least was not deficient in the sagacity to profit by time and circumstances, is partly evident from the presence of mind with which he contrived to avoid his own impending destiny. The king, deeply chagrined at the loss of his mistress, summoned the same astrologer into his presence, after he had given strict orders to his attendants to seize the poor fellow when he should give a certain sign, and to throw him out of a window on the second floor.

When he appeared, the king thus addressed him:—"As thou pretendest to be so clever, and to foresee the fate of other persons, tell me what thine own will be, and how long thou hast yet to live."

The sly astrologer, well knowing the weak side of the king, replied, without the least embarrassment: "I shall die just three days before your majesty." Louis was too superstitious to [329] persevere in his design, and to cause him to be actually thrown out of the window. On the contrary, he did all that lay in his power to defer to as late a period as possible a death which was to be so speedily followed by his own.

Literary Annual
Forget Me Not; A Christmas and New Year's Present for 1825. Ed. Frederic Shoberl. London: R. Ackermann, 1825. Printer: J. Moyes, Bouverie Street, Fleet Street.

Title
By the Author of "Doblado's Letters." [White, Joseph Blanco.] "The Alcazar of Seville and the Tale of the Green Taper." FMN 1825. 31-54. [31]

THE ALCAZAR OF SEVILLE,
AND THE
TALE OF THE GREEN TAPER
By the Author of Doblado's Letters

MY favorite haunt, while a student at Seville, was the Alcázar, the ancient abode of her kinds, both Moors and Christians. It is a place originally erected by the Arabs, at a short distance from the principal mosque, now the cathedral; and rebuilt upon a more extensive plan by Peter the Cruel, in 1360. The Spanish tyrant made it answer the double purpose of a mansion and a fortress, adding a wall, on the side of the town, which, though now concealed in many places by houses, shews, in its strength, how much he has to fear whom every body fears.

The gates in this inclosure marked to me the boundary between ancient and modern Seville,—I do not use the words ancient and modern in the precise sense of the antiquarian: with dates I neither had nor wished to have [32] any thing to do,—they have plagued me through life, so readily do they glide off my memory. Of the books which contain the history of native town, not one had then been in my hands; yet the Alcázar with its neighborhood was more than history to me; for the traditional tales which I had heard from the dear lips that taught me Castillian, made it an enchanted spot, where, scarcely noticing the present inhabitants, I mixed with the shades of both Moors and Spaniards who had dwelt there in the ages of love and romance.

I should indeed pity that Andalusian youth who, on a summer's day, could enter at the Huntsmen's Gate;[2] cast a look at the arabesque fretwork of the palace; pass in front of the grand saloons, which stretch on one side of the gardens; proceed to the King's Mews; and lastly, take shelter from the burning but enlivening heat of the sun in the labyrinth of Moorish streets at the back of the Alcázar, and be deaf the while to those sweet tales which language is too gross to translate from the whispers of fancy:—such as I heard from that ethereal babbler had a charm which time cannot destroy. When, descending fast into the vale of years, I strongly fix my mind's eye on those narrow, shady, silent streets, where I breathed

2 Puerta de los Monteros

the scented air which came rustling through [33] the surrounding groves; where the footsteps re-echoed from the clean, watered porches of the houses, and every object spoke of quiet and contentment,—of bare sufficiency of fortune enlarged by cheerfulness and moderation of wishes,—of modest gentility, supporting its claims to respect, not by riches and power, but by inherited nobleness and delicacy of feeling; the objects around me begin to fade into a mere delusion, and not only the thoughts but the external sensations which I then experienced revive with a reality that makes me shudder;—it has so much the character of a trance of vision! Alas! what is there left of the objects themselves but these mental traces, these deep and painful impressions, which, like unhealed wounds, must in the heart of many an exile bleed anew whenever they are examined!

The approach to the gardens of Alcázar is through a long, low, narrow passage, whose darkness and confined dimensions add to the effect of light and space on passing the iron gate of the first parterre. An Englishman would find here little but the novelty of the scene to gratify him. Every thing, even the plants and flowers, bears an artificial look. The high myrtle hedges, inclosing the square plots into which the ground is divided, are kept in the most precise shape by the smoothing [34] shares of the gardener. The thyme, lavender, and boxwood, are seen in rows, forming grotesque designs of animals, mottoes, and herald figures. The walks are paved with bricks; and iron railings separate the different portions, which go by the names of the Queen's, the Prince's, the Alcove, the Labyrinth, and the Ladies' Gardens. The centre of the last is occupied by two lines of dancers, cut out of the myrtle hedge on which they stand, all with heads and hands carved in wood; the rest of the body and dress formed of the living plant. A band of musicians, of the same vegetable growth, with harps, pipes, and tabors, is seen at one end; and two colossal savages, with maces of enormous dimensions, all connected by the same roots, and living on the same earth, stand sentinels at the entrance.

Such are the objects which might disgust the fastidious and unaccommodating taste of some travelers. But, Oh! how different are the felines of a native, taught by the climate and nature of his soil, not expect rural pleasure within the walls of a town, forest scenery on thirsty plains, or soft turfs under a fierce sun, which would leave no traces of vegetable green, were it not for the hardiness of some plants, and the artificial streams that water them! The inhabitant of the south looks in a garden for cool shade, and balmy breezes, and [35]the refreshing murmurs of fountains; the intoxicating breath of the organ flowers in their season; the thick, though invisible, clouds of odours which rise from millions of roses; the sights of the south wind; and, sweeter than they, the warbling of the nightingale. Such pleasures cannot be enjoyed in the cold open solitude of a park: but how wonderfully are they enhanced by the privacy of a Moorish garden!

Lost in the sensations just described, I used to sit, hour after hour, in a favorite corner where I could hear the sound of a copious stream, which, from the mouth of a marble lion, gushed into a large reservoir; and would not have exchanged the tall grey wall, incrusted with rustic work above, and clothed below with trained orange and lemon trees, for the finest park scenery which I have learnt to admire in England. There, with scarcely any one in view (for this place is frequented only three or four days in the year), and listening to the shears of the gardeners, which forced out the sweet cool scent of the box and myrtle, and awaked feelings not unlike the whetting of the scythe, where it announcers the long-expected summer; my fancy fluttered like a bird hatched in an aviary, beyond whose wire-work there is not a wish to tempt him. Had I not room enough for every dream of youthful happiness? [36]

Did not those very limits seem to secure me from intrusion, that bane and blight of the hearts which early learn to shrink from the gaze of the petty tyrants who subdivide the oppressive power of church and state in those countries? Oh no! liberty never smiles there but within walls and gates. The monarchs themselves, who contrived these bowers, felt the necessity of guards and enclosures. As to myself, who derived my best pleasures from fancy, I never passed between the threatening maces of the gee savages who stood at the entrance, without imagining that the blow which they suspended, as I chose to believe, out of pure good-will towards me, would fall upon the first intruder who should dare to break in upon my privacy.

The vegetable guards seemed, however, to be in collusion with many occasional visitors. Parties of strangers from the country used, now and then, to visit the gardens; but though their presence could not but disturb the enjoyment of my oriental reveries, they never staid long within view; while, on the other hand, the play of the water-spouts which, upon such occasions, is invariably the consequence of a small fee given to the chief gardener, made me full amends by adding freshness and brilliancy to the scene.

The reader should be informed, that [37] the brick walks, and the rustic incrustation of the walls, with all the artificial coral and shell rocks of which the decorations of the foundations consist, are perforated with innumerable small apertures, communicating with leaden pipes, which convey a large body of water form a much higher level. Upon turning a cock, walls, walks, and rocks are bristled over with a crop of streamiest, rising to the height of eight or ten feet, and preserving in their directions the outline of the figures from which they issue. Those in the walks are so contrived, that, rising on both sides with a certain obliquity, arches of shining drops are formed, under which any one might walk without being exposed to more than a light spray. Hydraulic organs were formerly connected with these waterworks, of which nothing remains but a figure blowing a trumpet. The sound it utters has a peculiar softness, and appears to proceed not from the figure itself, but from a wind instrument behind the wall, or rather under ground. The quaintness of these contrivances, and the coolness produced by the rapid evaporation which follows the play of the diminutive fountains, are in perfect harmony with the character of the whole place: they certainly never failed to freshen my thoughts and invigorate my fancy.

It was on one of these occasions that I made [38] the acquaintance of an excellent man—one of the best specimens of the Sevillian gentry, at a period when Spanish manners were making progress towards refinement, and just before the introduction of the affected ease and rude frankness, which now contrast so offensively with the remains of their ceremonious politeness. Don Antonio Montesdeoca was seldom seen in the modern French coat: his dress, except on a few church festivals, was the long Spanish cloak, of light-brown stuff, in summer, and of cloth of the same colour in winter. The hat was about ten inches broad in the brim, with a crown from three to four in height. His unshorn grey hairs were gathered into an oblong black silk net, with a string of tassels not unlike the tail of a paper kite, which hung over his back. He was tall, lean, and walked remarkably erect, bearing the left arm bent upon the breast, as if it still supported the long sword which, sixty years ago, all gentlemen carried about in the evening. I knew Don Antonio by name, and he knew me; yet, with the natural modesty of a boy, I used only to touch my hat to him, according to the good old style of Spanish civility, and pass on to my favourite seat. Both of us, however, being thus thrown together daily on the same spot, it was not long before the old gentleman, telling me that he had known my family many years, [39] asked what brought me so often to the gardens. He was highly delighted with the similarity of our tastes at such distant periods of life. From that day we often met to converse under the shade of the same tree. He knew a great deal about the palace, and all the antiquities of the town. I listened with much interest to his accounts of days long past; and will try to repeat such parts of them as I believe to be worthy of attention, by their having left the deepest impression on my memory.

There is an object in the gardens which, from my earliest childhood, I had looked upon with a mixture of awe and curiosity: it is a dark, dismal, subterraneous hall, supported by rows of double columns, and very scantily lighted from a few square apertures in the ceiling, secured by strong iron grates, as if they had been contrived for a keep or dungeon. In the middle of this hall is seen a large oblong tank of marble. The tank, at the time I am speaking of, was perfectly dry; though two large spouts, at the upper end, still showed the purpose for which it was constructed. The recollection of its original use is preserved in the name which the place bears to this day, of the Baths of Donna Maria Padilla. This lady, who is generally believed to have been, from her earliest youth to her death, the mistress of Peter the Cruel, was the butt of the party who [40] set on the throne the bastard Henry of Transtamare, the same that murdered the king, his brother, with his own hand, after the battle of Montiel. Such, however, were Maria's beauty, goodness of heart, and natural talents, that even the chronicles written during the ring of the successful usurper are forced to speak of her with respect; while, on the other hand, malice and calumny were employed in spreading the most shocking reports, which, in the shape of popular traditions, are still preserved among the Sevillians. I had once obtained admission to the baths, through the influence of my friend Don Antonio, when he asked me how many old gossips' stories of Donna Maria Padilla I had heard. I acknowledged that, like every other child in Seville, I had, in fact, heard the whole series: that I had often been frightened to bed by the nursery maid's story of the coach of fire in which Donna Maria was said, on certain nights to parade the town; and had even heard, as a proof of her shameless profligacy, that she took no pains to avoid the public gaze in these very baths. "Absurd," interrupted my old friend, "very absurd and wicked! I cannot endure calumny even against those who have been many centuries among the dead. Maria Padilla, to tell you the truth, is one of my historical favourites: she, from pure disinterested love of Peter, bore the reproach of [41] being his mistress, though she was the true and lawful queen of Castille. The most indubitable proofs of the marriage were given to the Cortes at Seville soon after her death: and no man would now pretend to doubt the fact, had not such a doubt been necessary to justify the usurpation of Henry. Heaven, in mercy to her virtues and sufferings, spared her seeing the last years of Peter's reign, and saved her (whatever the Spanish ballads say to the contrary) the humiliation of falling at the feet of her husband's murderer. Peter himself scarcely deserves compassion; yet few tyrants could say more in extenuation of their crimes. Placed on the throne a mere boy, two powerful and violent parties strove to make him the tool of their ambition. His wicked and lewd mother harassed a naturally violent character into downright ferocity; and the crowd of Peter's bastard brothers almost deserved the death which the enraged despot inflicted upon them: yet the amiable Padilla, whose enemies they were, exerted herself to the last to save them. The power of her charms must have been surprising, since they could bind through life a man of the most unbridled passions. But Peter, who, in the wantonness of youth, pampered by the unprincipled rives of the Padilla family, tried often to break the spell which bound his heart to Maria's, returned to her as [42] often, declaring that she was the loveliest of all women. Do you see the beautiful gallery of arches supported on groups of small columns, which runs over the city wall that terminates these gardens?" "Yes," said I; "it joins the Alcázar with the ancient tower called del Oro, which rises on the brink of the river."

"In that tower," continued my friend, "did Peter keep for some time one of the rivals whom the enemies of Maria Padilla contrived to set up against her. The lady's name was Aldonza Coronél, a sister of Maria Coronél, the celebrated foundress of the convent of Santa Clara, in this town; who, to avoid the dangers which threatened her virtue, destroyed her charms in a manner too shocking to relate. You have, no doubt, seen her body, in a glazed coffin, occupying the seat of honour in the choir of that nunnery. Well; Aldonza, a frailer beauty, came to implore the king's forgiveness for her husband, Alvar Perez de Guzman, who had been declared a traitor. The king was struck with her beauty; and the enemies of Maria Padilla procured interviews which proved the ruin of Aldonza. Maria was deserted in the Alcázar, while the faithless wife of Alvar Perez drew the whole court to the tower del Oro. The triumph of Aldonza was, however, of short duration. Maria's meek endurance of neglect soon rekindled affection in the heart of [43] the king; and Aldonza had to bury her shame in the cloister which her sister had just erected, as a retreat for herself and such females as wished to secure their virtue from the violence and profligacy of the times. The ill treatment and death of Blanch of Bourbon, generally supposed the legitimate queen of Castille, have in modern times been attributed to the direct influence of Maria Padilla. That the ever returning affection of Peter for the woman of his first love was the occasion of that barbarous treatment cannot be doubted; but the real cause of Blanche's misfortunes was the intrigues of the queen dowager, who made her defence a pretext for her own ambitious purposes. Maria Padilla appears to have loved Peter with the purest attachment. The tone and temper of her mind may be inferred from the fact that, during a temporary coolness in the king, she obtained a bull for the foundation of a convent, of which she was appointed abbess by the Pope. Yet she possessed towns and estates whither she might have retired, and maintained a splendid independence. But to return to the baths: they are to me in their present state an object of regret and vexation. I recollect them, when in my youth they preserved the original form which they received from the Moorish architect; for this place was the only unaltered remnant of the Mahometan palace. What you [44] now behold a dismal dungeon, was an orange grove of the same dimensions as the square yard which now stands over it. The upper branches of the trees rose to the level of the palace. These rows of columns supported two corridors which, crossing at right angles, gave access to the grand saloon, and afforded a delightful walk on the sides of the four squares into which they divided the garden below. I cannot conceive any thing more delicious in our hot climate, than a large bath, shaded by luxuriant trees, perfumed by numerous flower-plots; open to light and air, and yet scooped like a grot in the centre of a palace."

I once asked Don Antonio's opinion of the real character of Peter. "Some have of late represented him," said my friend, "as a man of great severity of character, but not cruel by nature. That he was goaded into ferocity, I have already told you. But it cannot be denied that in the latter part of his reign he grew faithless and treacherous to his friends, and a blood-thirsty monster to his enemies. Even in his best years, he at times gave way to fierce anger; though there still appeared a mixture of candour and justice in his character. Every body in this town knows the bust of Peter the Cruel, which still marks the spot where he killed a man in a chance affray, while walking in the night alone and in disguise. [45]

To believe the traditional story, the murderer would never have been suspected but for an old woman who, hearing the clash of swords, looked out with a lamp from her window. She soon withdrew the lamp in great fright, without seeing the man who had slain his adversary. When questioned by the magistrates the next day, she declared her persuasion that the murderer was no other than the kinghimself, whom she had discovered by the well-known rattling of his knees. Peter heard the accusation with composure, and neither contradicted nor injured the poor woman. Unable, however, to remove the suspicion which lay at his door, he ordered his own bust to be fixed in a niche upon the spot, as the heads of malefactors are set up to mark the scene of their crimes. The name of the narrow street which opens in front of the bust bears still, as we all know, the name of Candilejo, from the lamp said to have been brought out by the old woman.

"The state of public morals at that period, and the weakness of the law against the privileged orders, may be conceived from another traditional story which the annalists of Seville have preserved. A prebendary of the cathedral was, in the early part of Peter's reign, trying to seduce a beautiful woman, the wife of a mechanic. The frequency of the lover's visits roused the jealousy of the husband, and he [46] desired the clergyman to desist from troubling the peace of his household. The prebendary, incensed at what he conceived to be an insult, waylaid and killed the man. He then took sanctuary in the cathedral, and was soon after set free by the archbishop under a very slight punishment. A son of the murdered man, who though young and poor possessed a high spirit, appeared before the king, in an open space with seats, built of stone, near one of the gates of the palace, where he used daily to hear the complaints and petitions of his subjects. The structure I allude to was pulled down so lately as the middle of the seventeenth century. The orphan youth complained bitterly of the archbishop, who had allowed the murderer of his father to go unpunished. Peter heard the lad with great attention, and, taking him aside, asked him if he felt courage enough to avenge his father? The lad declared, he wished for nothing so ardently. 'Go, then,' said the king, 'and come to me for protection.' The heartblood of the murderer dripped soon after from the orphan's dagger. He was hotly pursued to the palace, where, being given in charge to the crossbowmen, a day was appointed for the trial. Peter, in open court, heard the archbishop's counsel against the prisoner; and asked the sentence of the ecclesiastical judge against the prebendary. 'He was, please your highness,' [47] answered the prosecutor, 'suspended a whole year from his office.' 'What is your trade or occupation, young man?' said the king. 'I am a shoemaker,' was the answer. 'Then, let it be recorded as the sentence of this court, that, for the space of a whole year, the prisoner shall not be allowed to make shoes.'

On another occasion I questioned Don Antonio concerning a report of a larger serpent having once attacked Peter the Cruel. "You mistake the story, my young friend," said he. "The allusion you have heard is to a very grave charge of sorcery, preferred by some writers of the fourteenth century against Maria Padilla. They assert that Blanch of Bourbon gave Peter, at their wedding, a beautiful belt, with which he was highly pleased. Maria, if we believe these writers, fearing to lose the king's affection, put this belt into the hands of a Jew, a great magician; and replaced it in her lover's wardrobe, after having had it exposed to the influence of a powerful spell. In full court the next day, the king, wearing the belt, was receiving the homage of the grandees, who came to congratulate him upon his marriage: suddenly a hideous serpent appeared coiled round the middle of his body. During the first alarm the monster glided rapidly out of sight: with it the king's belt, the gift of his bride, had disappeared. It is added, that from [48] that moment Peter could not endure the sight of Blanche."

"It would be desirable," said I, "to have a collection of tales of enchantment, from the traditionary legends of this part of the country."—"It would, indeed," answered Don Antonio, "and this quarter of the town would, I am sure, furnish a considerable contribution. All the streets to the south-east of the Alcázar were, from the conquest of Seville, allotted to the Moors who wished to remain under the dominion of the Christians. There is another portion of the town, on the same side, which, as you know, is still called the Jewry. The superior knowledge possessed by these two classes of people, when the Spaniards were almost exclusively employed in the arts of war, exposed them to the suspicion of their ignorant neighbours. Medicine, I believe, was at one time practised in Spain by none of Jews and Moors; and, as this science is intimately connected with chemistry, the vials, alembics, and furnaces of a laboratory, could not fail to confirm the prejudices of the Christians on the score of magic. These prejudices were, besides, industriously kept alive and strengthened by impostors, who, finding themselves already suspected, were glad to derive some profit from popular fear and credulity. I recollect that in one of the plays of Lope de Rueda, (the first [49] who introduced acting in Spain), a Moriscoe is consulted as the regular magician of the place. In later times, when all the descendants of Spanish Moors were, with as much cruelty as impolicy, expelled from the country, the notion that they had left their money concealed and secured by supernatural means became general. Stories of enchanted treasures are as common among us as in some parts of Germany. We are just in view of a house which, in my youth, I saw for a long time uninhabited, because it was said to be haunted by an unfortunate Moorish woman, whose ghost was bound in suffering to a concealed treasure."—"I know the house very well," said I, "but having heard it called Casa del Duende,[3] was led to believe that the supernatural story connected with it, belonged to the ludicrous part of the world of spectres."—"By no means," replied my friend, "the story, whether of itself, or from my having heard it when a child, has something melancholy and impressive

---

3 The Goblin-house.

to mind. I will tell it you as we walk home."

TALE OF THE GREEN TAPER.

"Among the unfortunate families of Spanish Moriscoes who were forced to quit Spain in 1610, there was one of a very rich farmer who [50] owned the house we speak of. As the object of the government was to hurry the Moriscoes out of the country without allowing them time to remove their property, many buried their money and jewels, in hopes of returning from Africa at a future period. Muley Hassem, according to our popular tradition, had contrived a vault under the large Zaguán, or close porch of his house. Distrusting his Christian neighbours, he had there accumulated great quantities of gold and pearls, which, upon his quitting the country, were laid under a spell by another Moriscoe, deeply versed in the secret arts.

"The jealousy of the Spaniards, and the severe penalties enacted against such of the exiles as should return, precluded Muley Hassem from all opportunities of recovering his treasure. He died, entrusting the secret to an only daughter who, having grown up at Seville, was perfectly acquainted with the spot under the charm. Fatima married, and was soon left a widow, with a daughter whom she taught Spanish, hoping to make her pass for a native of our country. Urged by the approach of poverty, which sharpened the desire to make use of the secret trusted to her, Fatima, with her daughter Zuleima, embarked on board a corsair, and were landed secretly in a cove near Huelva. Dressed in the costume of the peasantry, and having assumed Christian names, [51] both mother and daughter made their way to Seville on foot, or by any occasional conveyance which offered on the road. To avoid suspicion, they gave out that they were returning from the performance of a vow to a celebrated image of the Virgin, near Moguer. I will not tire you with details as to the means by which Fatima obtained a place for herself and daughter in the family then occupying her own paternal house. Fatima's constant endeavours to please her master and mistress succeeded to the utmost of her wishes: the beauty of innocence of Zuleima, then only fourteen, needed no studied efforts to obtain the affection of the whole family.

"When Fatima thought that the time was come, she prepared her daughter for the important and awful task of recovering the concealed treasure, of which she had constantly talked to her since the child could understand her meaning. The winter came on; the family moved to the first floor as usual, and Fatima asked to be allowed one of the ground-floor rooms for herself and Zuleima. About the middle of December, when the periodical rains threatened to make the Guadalquivir overflow its banks, and scarcely a soul stirred out after sunset, Fatima, provided with a rope and a basket, anxiously awaited the hour of midnight to com-[52]mence her incantation. Her daughter stood trembling by her side in the porch, to which they had groped their way in the dark. The large bell of the cathedral clock, whose sound, you are well aware, has a most startling effect in the dead silence of the night, tolled the hour; and the melancholy peal of supplication (Plegária) followed for about two minutes. All now was still, except the wind and rain. Fatima, unlocking with some difficulty, the cold hands of her daughter out of hers, struck a flint, and lighted a green taper not more than an inch long, which she carefully sheltered from the wind in a pocket-lantern. The light had scarcely glimmered on the ground, when the pavement yawned close by the feet of the two females. 'Now, Zuleima, my child, the only care of my life,' said Fatima, 'were you strong enough to draw me out of the vault where our treasure lies, I would not intreat you to hasten down by these small perpendicular steps, which you here see. Fear not, my love, there is nothing below but the gold and jewels deposited by my father.'—'Mother,' answered the tremulous girl, 'I will not break the promise I have made you, though I feel as if my breathing would stop, the moment I enter that horrible vault. Dear mother, tie the rope round my waist—my hands want strength—[53] you must support the whole weight of my body. Merciful Allah! my foot slips! Oh, mother, leave me not in the dark!'

"The vault was not much deeper than the girl's length; and upon her slipping from one of the projecting stones, the chink of coins, scattered by her feet, restored the failing courage of the mother. 'There, take the basket, child—quick! fill it up with gold,—feel for the jewels,—I must not move the lantern.—Well done, my love! Another basket full, and no more. I would not expose you, my only child, for . . . yet, the candle is long enough: fear not, it will burn five minutes . . . Heavens! the wick begins to float in the melted wax: out, out, Zuleima! . . the rope, the rope! . . . the steps are on this side!'

A faint groan was heard. Zuleima had dropped in a swoon over the remaining gold. At this moment all was dark again: the distracted mother searched for the chasm, but it was closed. She beat the ground with her feet; and her agony became downright madness on hearing the hollow sound returned from below. She now struck the flints of the pavement, till her hands were shapeless with wounds. Lying on the ground a short time, and having for a moment recovered the power of conscious suffering, she heard her daughter repeat the words, 'Mother, dear mother, leave [54] me not in the dark!' The thick vault, through which the words were heard, gave the voice a heart-freezing, thin, distant, yet silvery tone. Fatima lay one instant motionless on the flints; then raising herself upon her knees, dashed her head, with something like supernatural strength, against the stones. There she was found lifeless in the morning.

"On a certain night in the month of December, the few who, ignorant that the house is haunted, have incautiously been upon the spot at midnight, report that Fatima is seen between two black figures, who, in spite of her violent struggles to avoid the place where her daughter is buried alive, force her to sit over the vault, with a basket full of gold at her feet. The efforts by which she now and then attempts to stop her ears, are supposed to indicate that, for an hour, she is compelled to hear the unfortunate Zuleima crying, 'Mother, dear mother, leave me not in the dark!'"

Title

J. [Maria Jane Jewsbury]. "The Grave of the Suicide." FMN 1825. 219-230. [219]

THE GRAVE OF THE SUICIDE.

> Thou didst not sink by slow decay
> Like some who live the longest;
> But every tie was wrench'd away,
> Just when those ties were strongest.
>
> *Bernard Barton.*

WHOSE is that nameless grave, unmarked even by a rude stone or simple flower? And why is it lying solitary in the loneliest corner of the churchyard, beneath the frown of those dark trees, that in the storm swing their branches so heavily above it, and cast over it a desolate gloom even in the brightest hour of summer sunshine? Why is it apart from those other hillocks, that lie smilingly together, as though it alone were excluded from the peaceful communion of the dead?

That grave does not cover one who withered on the stalk of human life, and then quietly dropped from it in the sere and yellow leaf; nor one that was plucked by the spoiler in the bud [220] of infant promise; nor yet one who shed the leaves of life in the full beauty of maturity;—

it is not the grave of an old person who sustained life as a burden, and at last welcomed death as a refuge; or of the child who, snatched from the cherishing arms of its parents, was followed by them with deep but sinless sorrow; nor is it a matron's grave, "whose lovely and pleasant" life is embalmed in the memory of many friends. No—it is the memorial of a "sleepless soul that perished in its pride;" of one who made her grave with her own hand, and lay down in it without the Christian hope of awaking in heaven; and but for the terrible recollections of her last hours, which the grey-haired villager sometimes whispers in the ears of thoughtless youth, of one once so fitted to inspire affection and contribute to happiness, we might say in sorrow and in truth, "her memorial is perished with her."

There is an old man, feeble and nearly blind, often wandering about the churchyard, but not as he was wont in former and happier days. Then he leaned upon the arm of a fair and affectionate child, who cheered him by her smile, and soothed him by her tenderness. Life a hoary and tottering column wreathed with luxuriant ivy, her youthful influence preserved him desolation, and partially concealed even from his decay. Throughout the summer evenings [221] the churchyard was their favourite resort, for the old man loved to rest upon a grave and survey the wide and lovely valley lying at his feet, made glorious by the setting sun; while his spirit would melt within him, as, turning from that magnificent display of this world's beauty to the surrounding memorials of its perishable nature, he felt himself "a stranger and a pilgrim upon earth, as all his fathers were." And then would his young companion press near him with the deep affection of a young and untroubled heart, lay his head on her bosom, and bend over it till her long golden tresses mixed with his hoary locks, like sunbeams upon mountain snows. Then would she whisper to him sweet assurances of her filial love, or sing to him a stanza of some old quiet melody; till, with the eloquence of a faded and now tearful eye, he blessed her as the comfort and the glory of his age.

But he is now a neglected, desolate old man; he has no companion in his evening walks,—" none to watch near him,"—to smile upon him, or to speak kindly. Day after day, or stormy or fair, or summer or winter, he haunts that churchyard, and resting against the dark trees which shade that lonely corner, sighs bitterly over the neglected hillock at their feet:—and bitterly may he sigh, for his Ellen sleeps in that nameless solitary grave! [222]

Alas! how few comprehend the workings of a woman's soul! how few know the altitude of virtue which it can attain, or the depths of sorrow and degradation into which it can descend! The days of a woman's life glide along in sameness and serenity, like the tiny waves of a summer brook; her manners wear the same unperturbed aspect; her habitual thoughts and feelings seem to preserve a like "noiseless tenour;" and therefore few suppose that the anxieties of ambition, the strivings of passion, or the fierce tumults of pride, disappointment, and despair, can possibly exist beneath so quiet a surface. We forget that women are essentially capable of feeling every passion, good or bad, even more powerfully than men. We associate them too much in our thoughts with the petty details by which they are surrounded, and deem them constitutionally trifling, because from education, necessity, and habit, they are continually placed in contact with trifles. God forbid that the majority of females should manifest, or even know the passionate depths of the soul! Comparatively few acquire a knowledge which involves the surrender of their happiness, and too frequently also the sacrifice of their worth; but those few afford us warnings—salutary though terrible instruction to the rest of their sex. Ellen was one. [223]

Reflective, passionate, and proud, "emotions were her events." Not merely the mistress, but the companion of her own thoughts, the being of solitude and reverie, the child of impulse, and the slave of sensibility—while she existed in the real world, she could be said to live only in the ideal one of her own creation. Ambitious, yet unable to appreciate the true distinction which should be sought by women;—cherishing that morbid refinement of feeling, which destroys usefulness and peace by magnifying the evils of life, while diminishing their many alleviations;—dazzled by the gaudy fictions of imagination, and deluded by the vain flatteries of her own heart—she turned with disgust from the simplicities of nature and the sobrieties of truth,—from the regular routine of common duties, and the calm enjoyments of every-day life. Restless, weary, and discontented, she longed for something that should satisfy the grasp of her imagination—something that should fill the aching void within her heart. Alas! she forgot that this "infinite gulf can only be filled by an infinite and unchanging object."

Thus, by degrees, a complete change came over her spirit;—a change which those who surrounded her could not understand, and with which therefore they could not sympathize. The rose faded from her cheek, the smile played less frequently and less sweetly round her lips, [224] sadness too often shaded her young fair brow; and her manners, once so warm and courteous to all, became cold, abrupt, and reserved. These changes were not the work of a day; though the necessity of concentrating their history in a few short sentences makes that appear sudden and rapid, which was in reality gradual and slow.

Perhaps had Ellen at this critical period of her life been taken into the world by some judicious friend, and gently introduced to things as they really are, her mind might yet have recovered its energy and her spirits their tone; but limited to the seclusion of a village, she was debarred those little pleasurable excitements, whether of scene or society, which were necessary to prevent a mind like hers from preying on itself; and she yielded with proportionable enthusiasm to the first influence which broke the monotony of her life. That influence was love;—love as it ever will be felt and cherished by one of Ellen's disposition, in all the delirium and danger of intense passion. But alas! if she proved in her own experience the full truth of the observation, that "love is the whole history of a woman's life," she equally proved the justice of its conclusion, "that it is only an episode in the life of a man." A complete novice in the study of character, and accustomed to view every object alternately through the glare of imagination or the [225] gloom of morbid sensibility, it required little exertion to make her the dupe of a being, who added to seniority of years a consummate knowledge, not merely of books, but of men and manners, and the world; one, skilled to wear all aspects, suit all characters, and speak every language—excepting that of simple reality and truth—one of that class of men, who treat the young hearts they have won like baubles, which they admire, grow weary of, and fling aside.

But Ellen knew not this;—beguiled by the thousand dreams of romantic love, the present and the future shone to her ardent eye alike glorious with happiness and promise. "Her soul was paradised by passion;" every duty was neglected; every other affection superseded by this new and overwhelming interest. Even her old kind father felt, and sometimes sighed over the change; for he remembered the days when his comfort was the first and last of Ellen's anxieties, and his love her great and sufficient joy. But how could he chide his darling—the single ewe-lamb left of his little flock—the beautiful being that, like a star, irradiated the gloom of his evening pilgrimage!—he could not do it; and he made those excuses for her inattentions, which Ellen's better feelings would not have dared to offer for herself. [226]

At length, however, she discovered the fatal truth—that the passion which had formed the glory, the happiness, and indeed the whole business of her life, had been but one of many pastimes to her lover. Circumstances separated them, and after lingering through all the sickening changes of cherished—deferred—and annihilated hope,—she knew, in all the fulness of its misery, that she was forsaken and forgotten. It is well known that a strong mind can endure a greater portion of mental suffering without its producing bodily illness, than a weak one can. Many other girls in Ellen's situation would have had a violent fit of illness, been given over by their doctors, have recovered to the surprise of their friends; and after looking pale and interesting for a few weeks, would have married some one else, and lived very comfortably for the remainder of their days. Ellen was not such a character.

When she knew that the visions of fancy and the blossoms of hope were for ever scattered and destroyed, the stranger would have supposed her insensible to the blow. But the "the iron had entered into her soul." Throughout the whole of the night on which she received the "confirmation strong," she sat in her chamber motionless and solitary; she neither spoke, nor wept, nor sighed; and though every passion warred wildly in her bosom, she sat [227] and "made no sign:" and in the morning she resumed her station in her family, and went through her usual occupations and domestic pursuits with more minuteness and attention than she had manifested for a considerable time. Many knew the trial which had befallen her, but none durst offer sympathy; for the pride that sparkled in her eye, and the deep calm scorn which curled her pale lip, alike defied intrusion and forbade inquiry. She conversed, but appeared unconscious of the meaning of the words she mechanically uttered; she smiled, but the sweet expression of her smile had vanished; she laughed, but the melody of her laugh was gone: her whole bearing was high and mysterious. Now, her whole frame would shudder as at the suggestions of her own thoughts; then again, she would resume the quiet stern determination of her former manner:—one moment, her lip would quiver, and her eye fill with tears of mingled grief and tenderness; but the next, her burning cheek, compressed lip, and firm proud step, bespoke only deep and unmitigated scorn.

But who can portray the mysterious workings of pride, passion, doubt, horror, and despair, that crowd upon one who meditates self destruction? Oh! there is not the being in the existence who may imagine to himself, in the [228] wildest and most horrible of his dreams, all that must pass through the soul before it can violently close its earthly career! Could we summon from his scorned and unholy grave one who has lain down in it with his blood upon his own head, he only might adequately paint the emotions of that little hour between the action and its consequence! he only describe his state of mind, when the flimsy arguments which had cajoled his reason had vanished like evening shadows—when the sophistries which had lulled his conscience rose up like horrible deceits—when the home, friends, duties, comforts, even the life itself a moment before so despicable, appeared of an overwhelming importance;—and when, more terrible than all, he was left to grapple alone and altogether with the anguish of his body and the dying darkness of his soul—with the near and unveiled view of eternity, and the dread of future and unmitigated vengeance!

The sun was retiring behind the dark hills, like a warrior in the pride of victory, and field, and stream, and forest, lay glowing beneath them, in all the "melancholy magnificence of the hour," when the old man sought his beloved child, to take their accustomed walk to the churchyard. In vain he sought her in her flower-garden, in the arbour of her own planting, and in his quiet study. At length, he [229] tapped playfully at her chamber-door, and receiving no answer, he entered. There indeed was Ellen! There she stood—every limb shivering in that warm summer evening, while the cold perspiration gathered on her brow, and neck, and arms! There she stood—her fair hair dishevelled, her eye wild and glazed, and her whole countenance changed with mental and bodily torture: she might less be said to breathe than gasp; and the very motion of her dress shewed how wildly her heart throbbed beneath it. "Are you ill, my child?" said her father, terrified by her appearance. "Speak to me, my love," continued he, with increasing agitation, as he perceived the agony depicted on her countenance. Twice she strove to speak, but each effort was unavailing; no words escaped her parched and quivering lips;—at last, grasping his hands with convulsive energy in her cold and clammy fingers, she pointed towards the fatal phial, yet upon her table. The hideous tale was told!—The old man gave one long miserable groan, and the next moment fell senseless at his daughter's feet. There she stood, now turning her intense gaze upon her father, as he lay extended on the ground; and now, upon that setting sun, that bright sky, and brighter earth beneath it, which she must never, never view again!

But oh! the depth of that darkness within [230] her mind - that sickening desire of life, and that overwhelming certainty of death—the stinging conviction of her sin and folly—and the dread of impending judgment! All these, in a moment, passed over her soul like the ocean-billows in a raging storm, sweeping away in their fury every refuge of hope, every trace of consolation!

But it is time to draw the curtain over a scene "too loathly horrible" for thought or description. Succour was ineffectual—comfort unavailing! She existed for a few hours in agony and despair; and when the morning sun arose to gladden and refresh the earth, all that remained of the once fair and gentle Ellen was a livid and distorted corpse!

J.

Literary Annual
Forget Me Not; A Christmas and New Year's Present for 1826. Ed. Frederic Shoberl. London: R. Ackermann, 1826. Printer: J. Moyes, Bouverie Street, Fleet Street.

Title
Flora. "Bolton Abbey." FMN 1826. 19-26. [19]

BOLTON ABBEY.

> If thou wouldst view fair Melrose aright,
> Go visit it by the pale moon-light:
> For the gay beams of lightsome day
> Gild but to flout the ruins gray.
> Lay of the Last Minstrel.

THE sun had just risen, when Emma, De la Roche, and myself, mounted our horses, and set forward on our expedition to the abbey. It was one of those sultry days common towards the end of summer, and which contribute to render the cooling breezes of autumn, so soon to refresh the air, doubly welcome. Every thing seemed to foretell that the day would be intensely hot: as we rode along through a rich and highly cultivated country, we could observe the cattle collecting themselves to the sides of the pools or river, endeavouring to catch the slight breezes which played upon the face of the waters; while some, venturing into the stream, sought to cool their burning limbs in its waves, but even here they could find no repose: the warmth of the day had brought out all the insect tribes, which, buzzing around, stung them almost to madness. In vain they fled; the watchful foe pursued; nor could any stratagem elude his insatiable thirst for blood, until, worn out with the [20] race, the poor animals returned, wearied and dispirited, to the place from which they had commenced their career. Every now and then, we could discern small companies of reapers busy with the early harvest; even their work seemed to go listlessly on. In general the wheat remained uncut: while its rich golden waves, spreading in every direction over the face of the country, gave a pleasing variety to the landscape. "It is wonderful," I observed to De la Roche, "that you, who have been accustomed to all the magnificence and luxuriance of a southern climate, can still contemplate with pleasure the comparatively homely scene before us: I should always fear one of the effects of traveling would be, to render me dissatisfied with my own barren country." "Far otherwise," he replied: "the lofty mountain and the foaming cataract strike us at first with pleasure, with admiration, and with awe; the mind soars, as it were, above itself: but the higher its flight the sooner it becomes fatigued, and we gladly turn from scenes of lofty grandeur to the more smiling beauties of the plain. Besides all this, there is a magic in the name of home and country, which he only who has quitted them for a time can fully know. In a foreign land, we wander amidst the charms of nature, lonely, unconnected beings: separated from our kindred and our friends, we have none to sympathize in our feelings; we are, as it were, alone in [21]the world. But here we are identified in a manner with the scene around us; every peasant that we meet is a countryman and a kind of brother."

In conversation such as this we reached the abbey. It is now enclosed with a high park-wall, on opening a door in which the ruins in all their grandeur burst upon our view. Although the remaining vestiges but faintly shew what it was in the days of its former magnificence, in point of situation it can hardly be equalled. Close to the venerable pile, the Wharfe rolls peacefully along, overhung by rocks of a thousand various tints, from the deep rich purpose to the more sober saffron; the tops of these cliffs are crowned with overhanging brushwood; from several of their apertures fall cascades, sending their white foal high into the air, and swelling the stream below with their tributary waters. Crossing the river, by means of large stones placed at equal distances from each other, we sauntered along the foot of the rocks, which served as a protection from the powerful rays of the sun, until the river, narrowing at every step, rushes with impetuous fury (forming a kind of whirlpool) between two rocks, known by the name of "The stride." It was the fatal spot where "the Boy of Egremond," the last of his race, was dashed to pieces, as he attempted to leap the pass. The place is still shunned by the peasantry: oft in the silence of the night as the wind moans heavily by it, they [22] fancy they distinguish the screams of the childless mother mingling with the blast; fulfilling, as it were, her own reply to the herdsman, which has been handed down by tradition, and is still used as kind of a proverb by the men of Wharfedale.[4]

The heat at last obliged us to return to the ruin, in the hole that it might afford us a temporary retreat, until sufficiently refreshed to pursue our ramble. We soon reached the spot, where it stood screened by large venerable trees, and entered what had formerly been the nave of the church by one of the numerous

---

[4] "In the twelfth century, William Fitz-Duncan laid waste the valleys of Craven with fire and sword, and was afterwards established there by his uncle David, king of Scotland. He was the last of his race; his son, commonly called the Boy of Egremond, being dashed to pieces as he attempted to leap a narrow pass, owing to the hound which he held in his hand holding back. A priory was removed from Embsay to Bolton, that it might be as near as possible to the place where the accident happened: that place is still known by the name of the Strid; and the mother's answer to the serf, who informed her of the melancholy even, is to this day often repeated in Wharfe-dale."—WHITAKERS'S *History of Craven.*

The exclamation of the mother is thus introduced into a beautiful little poem, by S. Rogers, Esq.—

"'Say, what remains when hope is fled?'
She answered, ' Endless weeping!'
For in the herdsman's eye she read
Who in his shroud lay sleeping."

breaches which time, or the still more destroying hand of man, had made in the wall. There was a kind of silent awe in the scene, which suited well with [23] the tone of my feelings. Can any thing remind us forcibly of the brevity of human existence, than the sight of a vast edifice, raised with a care and a skill which seemed to promise that it should remain coeval with time itself, now mouldering in the dust; weeds and grass usurping the site of the fair pavement! Where once the window, stained with armorial bearings, "shed a dim religious light," is seen the creeping ivy; and instead of "the loud pealing organ," and swelling voices, hymning the praises of the Deity, are heard at times the screaming of the bittern, and the low complaining of the owl. And where are they, the proud founders of the building? where are the lordly abbots, with their long train of attendant monks?—all, all, are vanished! not one trace remains, to point out the spot which contains their ashes! The dust of the chivalrous baron and the mitred churchman is mingled in one indiscriminate mass, or scattered by the winds to the four corners of heaven. A few more revolving years, and they who now move so lightly and so gaily over the green turf, will, like those who sleep below, be swallowed up in the vast ocean of eternity, and be forgotten, as though they had never been!

Thus musing, or at times sauntering listlessly among the ruins, I heeded not the passing time, nor perceived that my companions had wandered far from me. In the morning no cloud had ob-[24]scured the serene azure of the sky, but for sometime one black spot had been visible in the distance; it had for the last half hour been rapidly increasing in size, and every now and then I could distinguish the low mutterings of the distant thunder, accompanied by a few faint flashes of lightning. Aware that the storm would not now pass away, I was on the point of leaving the building, when a peal of thunder shook it to its very foundation; at that moment my companions joined me. We wished to have reached the inn; but the storm was now raging with a violence which drowned the sound of our voices: the peals of thunder, bursting with sudden crashes over our heads, were reverberated by a thousand echoes amongst the rocks and dilapidated buildings; and long ere one sound died away, it was renewed by claps, each of which seemed longer and louder than the last, while the forked and vivid lightning flashed from every window and crevice, rendering the horrors of the scene without distinctly visible. We had entered that part of the abbey where divine service is still performed, and arranged ourselves in silence round the altar. Thus we remained for more than an hour, when the fury of the storm began to abate, but the thunder had been succeeded by floods of rain; and being at some distance from the inn, we were detained prisoners some time longer. We reached it at last; but the shower had been followed by [25] a kind of drizzling rain, which threatened to be of longer duration, and we were reluctantly obliged to give up all thoughts of returning home that night. Seated round a cheerful fire, talking over the pleasures and dangers of the day, our little party soon recovered its gaiety, nor separated until a late hour.

The window of the apartment which I occupied looked towards the abbey; and as I gazed from it, I could not but feel surprised at the change which a few hours had made in the scene. Nothing could be more profound than the calm which had succeeded the storm. The moon was risen, shedding her silver light all around, and the outline of the abbey was beautifully defined by her soft rays. I could not sleep, nor resist the wish, at this still and beautiful hour, when all around me were asleep, to revisit the scene of past pleasures. I proceeded about two hundred yards from the house, and then a feeling of the most perfect loneliness made me pause; I could proceed no further. Earth below seemed so peaceful, and the heavens above presented such an image of calm majesty; I alone seemed the only living being in the vast expanse. Evening certainly is the time for holy devotion; but Night, even when most beautiful, brings with her feelings of solemnity and awe. She speaks so forcibly of the end of all things, of our last long sleep! I had, however, seen Bolton by the pale moonlight. Beautiful [26] Bolton! four long years have passed away since the events I have been relating; and how have the little party, which on that day visited those ruins, been dispersed; how much of earth and ocean now separates hearts still as fondly united! But the only one of the three who still remains shall never see thy mouldering walls without a thought to the memory of her lost friends, and a tear to the recollection of their love.

Flora.

Title
Stafford, William Cooke. "Woman's Love." FMN 1826. 62-77. [62]

WOMAN'S LOVE.

IT was a fine day in the month of October 181-, when Alfred Montgomery, then on a visit to his uncle, an eminent merchant residing in the city of York, set out to stroll as far as Bishopthorpe, the seat of the venerable and respected archbishop of the province. His route lay through fields which had been lately covered with standing corn, and had now assumed the hue of autumn. On his left waved the majestic elms that decorate the magnificent walk which runs by the river Ouse for nearly two miles, and is the finest terrace-walk in the kingdom; their leaves shone in the rays of the autumnal sun like burnished gold; behind him rose the towers of that majestic temple, York Minster, perhaps the most elaborate Gothic structure in England; whilst in front, the palace of Bishopthorpe, rearing its head above the plantations in which it appeared to be enveloped, closed the scene. Alfred had a heart not insensible to the beauties of nature, and he seemed to gaze on the surrounding objects with feelings of admiration and delight. He had just taken out his pencil to make a sketch of the venerable cathedral as it appeared in the distance, rising like a giant above the pigmy

PLATE: Woman's Love.
Steel plate engraving; designed/drawn by Henry Corbould;
engraved by George Corbould.

[63] edifices by which it is surrounded, when a wild shriek burst upon his ear. It came from the high road which skirted the fields; and in an instant he leaped the hedge, and looked round to discover what it was that had alarmed him. A little way down the road, he saw two ruffians employed in rifling a female, who was extended on the ground; and, though armed only with a stick, he rushed to her rescue. The villains fled at his approach; for the guilty are generally cowards. Alfred

then turned his attention to the fainting form of the female whom they quitted. She was seemingly not more than eighteen; and though terror had blanched her cheek, yet it was evident that she possessed considerable personal attractions. Alfred raised her in his arms, and fortunately the terrified girl soon gave signs of returning animation; for my hero would have been at a loss how to proceed, if her insensibility had continued. Opening her eyes, she cast them on the ingenuous countenance of her young deliverer:—"Am I safe?" she murmured, in soft accents. "You have now nothing to fear; yet, as soon as you are able, we had better leave this spot, lest the villains who have escaped should return." "Oh, let us go now." "You will allow me to attend you; I cannot think of trusting you alone," said Alfred; a proposition which [64] was readily assented to by his fair companion; and they proceeded towards the cottage of her aunt, which she informed him was situated at only a short distance.

Arrived at the cottage of Mrs. Mildmay, Alfred was overwhelmed with the thanks of that lady for the service which he had rendered her niece; and he received them with a manly ingenuousness which strongly recommended him to the notice of both. His connexions were not unknown to Mrs. Mildmay, and during his stay in York he frequently repeated his visits; and when he departed for the metropolis, he carried with him the assurance that the heart of the lovely Amelia Mildmay was wholly his.

Alfred had some difficulty in tearing himself from the spot in which all his hopes and wishes centered; but the commands of his father were imperative. Sir James Montgomery was the head of an ancient house, and he looked to his son as one who was destined to perpetuate its honours. Alfred well knew that his father would never consent to his union with the orphan and portionless daughter of a country surgeon—for such Amelia Mildmay was—however amiable or however accomplished; and he obeyed his summons with a foreboding dread of much evil that was to come, but with a firm determination to withstand all efforts to induce him to break the vows he had pledged to Amelia. But Alfred [65] knew not his own heart; he depended too much on the strength and stability of his affections, and they deceived him.

Sir James had heard from his brother-in-law, Mr. Lawrence, with whom Alfred had been staying at York, that his son had formed an attachment to a young lady who had nothing to recommend her but beauty, amiable dispositions, and extensive accomplishments; which latter were bestowed upon her by a doating father, who, when in prosperity, with a lucrative profession, and the fair prospect of leaving the image of his regretted wife an ample if not an affluent provision, spared no expense in procuring her the most eminent masters; and Amelia did honour to their care. Adversity, however, soon blighted all the hopes of Mr. Mildmay, and he died a martyr to despair, leaving his child to the protection of the wife of his deceased brother, who had for six years supplied the place of her parents with an affection which Amelia dutifully repaid. Thus, though Miss Mildmay would have graced a ducal coronet, yet the want of high birth—that of fortune would have been no object—prevented Sir James Montgomery, who looked upon the enchant of the young people as a mere childish passion, from receiving her as his daughter.

Arrived at his father's splendid mansion in Grosvenor-square, Alfred found a large party as-[66] sembled to enjoy the festive gaieties of a "winter in London." At first he entered into the scenes of splendid dissipation in which he was immersed with reluctance, and his heart reverted to the banks of the Ouse and the lovely Amelia; but soon—such as the influence of bright eyes and fine forms—he joined in them with a degree of pleasure which was unaccountable to himself, but which a judge of poor human nature would have found no difficulty in tracing to the right cause. The fact was, Alfred, though gifted with many excellent qualities, inherited no small share of his father's family price. The seeds of vanity also were thickly sown in his composition, and strangely marred his otherwise amiable disposition. The heir of Sir James Montgomery's title and fortune, he was of course an object of desire to all the disengaged young ladies, whose mammas or other relatives were on terms of intimacy with the family; and many were the snares laid to entrap his affections. Some of these were so palpable, that they failed through their own grossness; but others were more delicately managed: and whilst the vanity of the young man was flattered on the one hand, his interest was excited on the other. For the honour of that sex, which Heaven, in pity to man, sent

"——— to cheer
The fitful struggles of our passage here,"

I must add, that these females, who were so [67] anxiously striving to win the youthful heir, were few in number; and that even of those, not one, I verily believe, would have endeavoured to captivate his affections, if they had known that a lovely fair one, to whom he had plighted his vows, was pining in secret for him.

In a few months Alfred almost ceased to remember that such a being as Amelia Mildmay existed. His days were devoted to the society of a number of dashing young fellows, who contrived to kill time at the clubs and other places of fashionable resort; his nights to the opera, the theatres, or Almack's, to splendid routs, fascinating balls, or scientific conversazioni. At every turn he was awaited by the blandishments of flattery; on all sides he was the object of the most assiduous attentions from the rich, and the young, and the beautiful. Is it wonderful, then, that his heart became entangled? Is it wonderful that the quiet, unobtrusive qualities of Amelia were forgotten amidst the glare, and pretensions, and fascinations of a London fashionable life? I offer no apology for his infidelity; I state facts, and lament that truth compels me to record the defection of Alfred Montgomery from his vows.

But how passed this time with Amelia? At first, with hope for her companion, she looked forward to future happiness as certain, and dwelt with delight upon the prospect of wedded bliss. But conscience interfered to damp these pleasing anticipations. She had concealed from her aunt, [68] at Alfred's request, the fact of a mutual engagement having taken place between them, and her heart bitterly smote her with having practised duplicity in regard to this revered relative. She soon, however, set her conscience at rest, by telling Mrs. Mildmay the whole little history of her guileless bosom; and a gentle chiding was the only reprimand which that kind and affectionate woman could bring herself to bestow on the lovely girl, who looked up to her for forgiveness and protection. Her self-approbation thus restored, Amelia anticipated with eager anxiety the receipt of a letter from town. It came, and was worded in a language as ardent as her own feelings—as pure as her own imaginings. Under the sanction of her aunt, she replied to this first love-epistle she had ever received; and such an effect had the few artless lines she penned upon Montgomery, that he absented himself from a gay party, made on purpose for him, in order to answer it. The next letter he received he thought less interesting; but replied immediately. After the third, he suffered a longer period to elapse; a still longer after the fourth: and to her fifth epistle it was such an interval before any answer was received, that Amelia's heart was filled with foreboding fears: and when it arrived, it was so cold, so distant, so reserved; it breathed so much of the language of prudence, and so little of that of love, that all those fears were confirmed. Still, not even to her aunt would she whisper a sus- [69] picion of Alfred's truth, though the conviction that he no longer loved—at least not as she did, with a pure, devoted, undivided attachment—preyed upon her spirits, robbed her cheeks of their bloom and her eyes of their lustre; and the once gay and animated Amelia was not only the shadow of her former self.

Whilst this amiable girl was thus lamenting the faithlessness of her absent lover, that lover was entangled in the snares which ambition and inclination entwined to captivate him. The Honourable Louisa Montague was the daughter of the gallant admiral of that name, and the two families of Montgomery and Montague were upon the most intimate terms with each other. Louisa loved; and she was besides ambitious of gaining one for whom so many females were contending. She assiduously paid court to Alfred, but in so delicate a manner that she never betrayed her doing so. She appealed to him on every disputed point; she chose her books by his direction; sang those songs and played those pieces of music which he approved: occasionally a beautiful bouquet, arranged by her hand, was presented to the youth; a purse was netted for him, and a thousand other bewitching little agrémens displayed, which women know so well how to call into action, and which are so seductive in their effects upon those whom they are intended to charm. Alfred by degrees found [70] Miss Montague's society almost necessary to his existence; he was her escort in the park, her attendant at the opera, her partner at the ball: and one morning, having called upon her to inquire after her health, as she had not been at Montgomery-house at all the preceding day—honour and Amelia being both forgotten—he made her an offer of his hand and fortune, and was accepted.

No sooner, however, had that magic word, which crowns the hopes of a true lover, passed the lips of the fair Louisa, than the thoughts of Amelia recurred to Alfred's breast. "He started like a guilty thing," his colour changed, and he sunk into a chair that happened to be close beside him. To the anxious inquiries of Louisa he returned the most incoherent answers, and at length rushed from her presence, in a state of mind which would have demanded pity, had it not been brought on by his own forgetfulness of what was due to the confiding girl who had bestowed her heart on him. He flew to solitude, but reflection maddened him; and he then resorted to society—but nothing could quiet the agitation of his mind. Had he confessed to Louisa the exact state of his heart, all might have still been well; for she was a noble-minded girl, though her amiable qualities were partially obscured by her ambition. But his pride would not allow him to acknowledge that he had acted [71] with duplicity, that he had professed to love her, when his heart was devoted to another; and he finally resolved to abide by the event of the morning, and to forget, if possible, Bishopthorpe and Amelia Mildmay.

Both the families received the intelligence of Alfred's offer to Louisa Montague with joy; and immediate preparations were made for the marriage. Alfred wrote one hurried note to Amelia, to intimate that she must prepare her mind to hear of a change; and then he gave himself up to the fascinations of his betrothed. Eager to get rid of the agonising thoughts which would intrude, and hoping he should feel more easy when it had become his duty to love and honour Louisa as his wife, he was anxious for the day which should unite them. Before that day arrived, he had totally forgotten Amelia; and when he led Louisa to the altar, not one thought of her disturbed his bosom. Such is man! and such, too frequently, is man's love! It rages with violence for a time; but absence cools the flame, and too often totally extinguishes it, even when the object possesses every qualification which can reflect honour on his choice.

The newspapers informed Amelia of the marriage of Alfred, and the next day she disappeared from the cottage of her aunt, whose most anxious inquiries could obtain no tidings of her. It would be vain to describe her anguish;—she loved [72] Amelia as her child; and when two days had elapsed, and no intelligence was received of the fugitive, she was laid on the bed of sickness, caused by anxiety for the fate, and exertion to discover the retreat, of her beloved niece.

Alfred and his wife departed, as soon as the marriage ceremony was performed, for a seat belonging to Sir James Montgomery, situated in the most beautiful part of Devonshire. There, blest in each other's society, the days flew swiftly away, and time seemed to have added new pinions to his wings; so short seemed the hours as they passed. But this was happiness too exquisite to be of long duration. On the tenth day of their residence at Chilton-house, Louisa was walking on the lawn in front of the building, equipped for riding, and waiting for Alfred, which was to accompany her to take a view of some picturesque objects in the neighbourhood. Suddenly her attention was excited by a female, who, with agitated step and a wild and distracted mien, approached, and surveyed her with a piercing eye, in which the fire of insanity was clearly to be distinguished. She spoke not, but gazed anxiously and steadfastly on Louisa, who shrunk from the close inspection, and yet seemed rooted to the spot, as if deprived of the power to move. Suddenly the figure approached nearer, and passing her hand across the fair brow of Mrs. Montgomery, she put aside the ringlets which over-[73] shadowed it, and exclaimed, after the pause of perhaps a minute, "Are you his wife?—but no!" the fair maniac (for such she was) continued, "for he is mine; his faith was plighted to me—you can have nothing to do with my Alfred!"

What an agonising moment was this for Louisa! She saw before her one who had been deceived by the man to whom she had plighted her vows, and whose reason had fallen a sacrifice to his base and unnatural desertion. What a thought for a doting wife—for a proud one too, who would never have accepted a divided heart, or been contented with a share only of her husband's affection!—But perhaps there might be some mistake; she would try.

"What Alfred do you mean, my poor woman?" she asked, in a tone of sympathy.

"Why, my own Alfred—Alfred Montgomery—him for whom I twined this wreath;—but the flowers are faded now—so methinks, is his love, for it is a long while since I have heard from him!" She took a wreath of flowers from her bosom as she spoke, and, pressing it to her lips, presented it to Mrs. Montgomery. "See," she cried, "these are the flowers he used to love! I plucked them from my own bower—that bower which Alfred decorated.—But I cannot give it to you: no, I must keep it for Alfred.—Alfred!" she exclaimed in a loud and piercing voice, "where art thou, Alfred?"—then adding [74] in a lower and plaintive tone, "They told me he was married, but I would not believe it. I wandered through wind and through rain, through brake and through brier, till I reached his home: there they told me too that he was married. Still I would not believe it: I followed him here, for is he not mine? what right then have you here?"

Amelia—for it was indeed that lost, unhappy girl—now seized Louisa wildly by the hand: she uttered a piercing shriek; and the well known voice reaching the ear of her husband, he was instantly by her side, eager to see what had occurred to alarm her. But what a sight met his eyes! He beheld his newly-married wife supported by her maid, who had hear her shriek, pale and inanimate, the picture of death; whilst at her feet lay the lovely being whom he had made wretched. How she came there he was at a loss to conjecture, and, not knowing what had passed between her and his wife, he was equally at a loss how to act. Before he could recall his scattered ideas, and resolve on what was to be done, Amelia raised herself from the ground, and catching his eye she sprang up, clinging to him exclaimed, "He is here! he is mine!—Oh, Alfred! they told me you were married; that you had ceased to love me: but would not believe that you could slight the heart which beats only for you!—Feel!" and [75] she took his hand, and placed it on her bosom, "how it flutters, poor thing!—it will soon be still. Alfred. I am dying!"—and her voice suddenly assumed a rational and composed tone—" I know not what I have said, what I have done; I have wandered I know not where or how: but—but———." She struggled to articulate something more, but nature was exhausted; she heaved one sigh—dropped her head upon his bosom—and expired.

Whilst this scene was passing, the servant had conveyed Louisa into the house, whither Alfred followed with his lifeless burden, almost as unconscious as the form he bore. He laid the corpse on a sofa in the parlour—he threw himself by the side of it, and called upon his Amelia once more to live for love and him. Then the recollection of his wife flashing across his mind, he rose, and throwing himself into a chair, covered his face with his handkerchief, and sobbed convulsively. This paroxysm over, he became rather calmer, and sought Louisa, who had retired to her chamber. To her he gave a full explanation of his acquaintance with Amelia, and pleaded so effectually for forgiveness, that it was soon granted. But a sting was planted in his heart, which time could never remove. In the midst of all that fortune could bestow, and blessed with happiness seemingly beyond the lot of humanity, the remembrance of Amelia [76] always intruded in the hour of retirement; it was the canker-worm which robbed his nights of repose, his days of happiness; and he lived a memorable instance of splendid misery. His wife's lot was more happy, for to her he was an attentive and affectionate husband; and at his death, which took place about a year after his marriage, her grief was sincere and heartfelt. She had numerous offers of marriage, but rejected them all, faithful to the memory of him who, as her first, she was determined should be her only love.

It remains, however, to be explained how Amelia reached Devonshire. She knew Alfred's residence in town from the address of his letters; and from the servants at Montgomery-house it was ascertained that a female, who answered her description, had been inquiring after him in a few days after the bridal party left town. On being told that he was gone to Chilton with his bride, she made no reply, but rushed out of the hall. It appeared that a stage-coach had set her down at an inn near the seat of Montgomery; but whether she had travelled in that manner all the way from London, or whether part of the journey had been performed on foot, was never known—most probably, from the state of her dress, the latter was the case. At the expense of Alfred, her corpse was removed to Bishopthorpe, and interred in the church-yard of that village. [77] Her aunt did not survive long survive her, and they lie in one grave.

This is a melancholy tale, but the incidents are facts which came within my own knowledge. I have seen the grave of this hapless girl, and dropped the tear of pity for her fate.

WILLIAM COOKE STAFFORD.
    YORK, Jan. 1825

Title
Hofland, Barbara Mrs. "The Regretted Ghost." FMN 1826. 79-101.

PLATE: The Regretted Ghost
Steel plate engraving; designed/drawn by Richard Westall, R.A.; engraved by Charles Heath; printed by McQueen [79]

THE REGRETTED GHOST
BY MRS. HOFLAND.

IN the winter of 1568-9, Blanche Devereux was unexpectedly called from her grandfather's seat in Brecknockshire, to enliven and console her elder sister, who was then suffering from illness, and who resided in the tower of London with their aunt, the Baroness Ferrars de Chartley.

Until this period, and for a few years afterwards, this fortress was also a palace; but Elizabeth, the reigning sovereign, never used it as such; and at the period in question it was inhabited only by a few persons of quality, to whom it afforded a convenient home on account of their confined circumstances, or to whom it was an agreeable resident, the pleasantness of which effaced their sense of its gloomy associations. But by many others its frowning portals and massy towers could not be entered without emotions of awe almost amounting to horror; for, during the last twenty years, so numerous had been the prisoners of distinction confined there, so often had noble and even royal blood been shed by the executioner, that every thing [80] bore a portentous aspect, likely to affect the spirits of the higher class of its inhabitants, and to awaken the superstitious fears of the lower.

The young Blanche, scarcely sixteen, wild and gay as the kids on her native mountains, (which she now left for the first time) thought little of the frowning battlements, for she had been accustomed to the cloud-capped beetling rocks of her own country; but she was terribly annoyed by the sense of being inclosed by impassable barriers. She had hitherto roved in the domains of her aged relative as freely as the birds and the butterflies; and her elastic form, sparkling eye, and buoyant heart, all demanded a wider range than was now offered by long, dark rooms, narrow passages, and sentineled entrances. Happily, however, Blanche had not only gaiety and curiosity, but tenderness and affection. In her love for her sister, and her power of solacing the tedium of confinement, she soon lost every feeling of personal annoyance; her sensibility was exercised, and her imagination awakened to the best purposes of existence.

These sisters, Adelaide and Blanche, were orphans, and co-heiresses to their mother's extensive property; and their relations on both sides were their guardians. They had been brought up together in infancy by their grandfather, Sir John Devereux; but when the elder [81]attained her eighteenth year, it was judged a proper duty to send her to London, for the advantage of being introduced to the queen and her court by her aunt, the dowager Lady Ferrars. It was a grievous thing to part the sisters, for none ever loved more fondly. Adelaide was four years the elder, and had therefore felt the trial longer, if not more acutely; though before this time the loss of Blanche had been supplied, in one sense, to her heart. Their meeting, however, restored and strengthened every early chord of affection; and she grew better so quickly, that her nurse predicted "she would soon leave her chamber, and probably be able to walk to the end of the gallery and see the Duke of Norfolk go to execution, if her majesty would be so good as to fix the day."

"To execution!" said Blanche, as the roses left her cheeks—"surely he will not be killed? why should he, poor gentleman?"

"Because," returned old Barbara, "he is condemned. In my time things were very different—people were not used to be kept wait, wait, wait, not knowing when their heads were to be chopped off—no, no, many a good time I have been up early to see persons executed in the morning, who were sentenced over night."

"But what has this poor duke done?"

"Why fallen in love, to be sure—(there are few things that do more mischief than love, I take it)—with the beautiful queen of Scots, (Who, by the bye, many people say, is the lawful queen, because this queen's mother was beheaded, as I saw with my own eyes, which I suppose was a sign she was no better than she should be,) and so somehow that has made him a rebel, and die he must."

"Poor man! I am extremely sorry for him."

"Most young ladies are so, I dare say; for a more proper persona of a man, or a sweeter, or a braver, did I never behold; and find heart-breaking scene it will be to see him lay down his head on the block, for certain. Not that I should cry for him as I did for my lady Jane Grey, and her handsome young husband: but still"—

The garrulous attendant, being called to prepare some medicine, left the sisters, and Blanche was diverted from her sympathies for the noble prisoner, by observing that Adelaide was exceedingly agitated—that her lovely face, so recently pale, was covered with blushes—and that she evidently sought to say something which is was difficult to reveal even to her.

At this time Lady Ferrars entered to bid them adieu for the day, as it was her duty to attend on the queen at Crosby Hall. Blanche, whose curiosity and sensibility were excited, made various inquiries respecting the duke of her aunt, who answered them all with an air of great mystery and an earnest assurance, "that it was her duty, as one too young to understand such subjects, never to enter upon them;" even forbidding her to take her usual walk in the courts, lest she should inadvertently look towards the apartments of the prisoner. She added—"We, alas! can do him no good, by expressing that compassion we feel, but we may do ourselves harm. I would not have your cousin Robert[5] here at this time for the world; for, boy as he is, some warm expression, dictated by his impulse, might injure him and the duke also, whose fate (she added in a subdued tone) will now be soon decided."

The lady departed, for her servant, mounted on a fine Flanders horse, with a huge pillion covered with crimson velvet fringed with gold, had been long

---

5 Robert Devereux, Earl of Essex, the favourite of queen Elizabeth, in the latter part of her reign.

waiting for her. Blanche would have attended her to the outer chamber, but the anxiety now more strongly expressed in the countenance of Adelaide prevented her; the moment the door was closed she ran to the couch, and flinging her arms round the neck of the invalid, inquired "if she could do any thing that could contribute to her ease and comfort?"

"Yes, my beloved Blanche, you certainly can.—Young as you are, I dare confide in you; [84] but the service to which I allude is one that requires not only prudence but courage."

"If you will afford occasion for the exercise of the former, I can answer for the latter, Adelaide.—I have the heart of a lion; I have climbed up to the very highest point of the Van, where the little people[6] live, and drunk water at their own spring without hearing any of them groan. I can do any thing, dear Adelaide, or you—even corfe candles†[7] will not alarm me."

"You will not meet any evils of this nature, my love. The objects of terror to myself, when I undertook the task I must now trust to you, were sentinels and spies; the danger, a severe cold, which, to tell you the truth, was the cause of my illness."

"I will wrap myself carefully up in my black cloak."

"But you must do that consistently with the dress of a royal page, which you will find in the bottom of that press. Take it out before Barbara's return, and between now and midnight, at which time precisely you must set out to carry my letter, I shall be able to give you exact directions."

Blanche conveyed the dress to her chamber, and in the course of the following evening [85] learned in what manner she was to proceed with secrecy, through open courts or subterraneous passages, to a small door in the postern, where some person, whose presence would be announced by three low taps, would be waiting to receive the letter through a certain chink. It was the great business of Adelaide, whose mental agitation almost conquered her indisposition, to keep up cheerful conversation; but this was unwittingly thwarted by Barbara, who told of deep groans heard at the foot of the stairs, where the royal infants*[8] had been buried; and even drew their attention to certain sounds near the chamber they inhabited, which, she maintained, were the death-sobs of the duke of Clarence, who, as they knew, met his death in the adjoining closet in a butt of malmsey. The very whistling of the wind brought to her ears the hysteric laugh of the unfortunate Anne Boleyn, and she deemed every distant step that of some unquiet spirit repenting past guilt, or seeking vengeance for past injuries.

At length even Barbara slept—the mighty fabric and its numerous inhabitants were all apparently locked in repose; and Blanche, eager yet tremulous, <u>excited by warm affection</u>, and somewhat, probably, by the novelty of the enterprise,

6 In South Wales the fairies are called the little people.
7 Lights which announce death, and universally believed in
8 Edward V. and his brother Richard, duke of York.

yet alive to all that might alarm her age [86] and her sex, prepared herself for the expedition. She felt almost angry that she should be obliged to make so much preparation for so short a journey, yet she said repeatedly to herself, "Within half an hour I shall be again in my own chamber," as if she wished that the deed were done.

Mystery has frequently a charm for young minds, but silence is appalling.—As Blanche descended with noiseless step and nearly hidden light, she would have been most thankful if she could have carolled away her own sense of the gloom which surrounded her, and the fearful thoughts which obtruded themselves. As she passed the armoury, the gloomy lights reflected from the single beam emitted by her own dark lantern, and the ghastly forms of untenanted suits of armour, affected her considerably; and when, after that, she walked over the burying-ground, and knew that she was approaching the spot where the innocent blood of lady Jane Grey had been shed, her emotion increased. Yet she was now to enter a low door, descend into a long passage, and shut out all aid from the external world—she had to enter a place to which she was an utter stranger, and from which it would perhaps be found impracticable to return—what should she do?

"Poor Adelaide depends upon me; besides she has done this herself, and is undoubtedly [87] rendering some person a service by this letter.—Why should I hesitate? the eye of God is upon me wherever I go; I will trust in him."

Blanche turned the key of the padlock which obtained her admittance, and found an exceedingly narrow staircase, down which she descended with the more celerity, from believing herself to be at least safe from the eye of man, which was the only cause of alarm in the mind of her sister, whose faith she now endeavoured to embrace. When the steps terminated, the air blew cold and fresh, and a distant door creaked upon its hinges, but so slightly, that the sound might arise from accident.—After a short pause she proceeded.

The passage, after a time, branched off, and, agreeably to her directions, she took the one which led circuitously to the entrance denominated the Traitors' Gate. Blanche continued her route, losing, as she proceeded, all fears save discovery, and listening only for creaking hinges and acing sentinels. Happily all remained silent; the current of air ceased, and on taking a turn to the left, which opened on a wider passage, which, though long, she expected would bring her to the steps she must ascend for the completion of her mission, she felt a degree of re-assurance and comfort.

How great, then, was her surprise and horror, when, on venturing to give herself a little more [88] light, and stopping for that purpose, she distinctly saw a bright beam advancing from a great distance towards her! At first she hoped that some reflection from her own light might occasion an appearance so alarming; and she took the cap from her head to cover the aperture by which the ray thus reflected had escaped; but alas! she now saw distinctly not only that there was a light, but that it was borne by a figure, tall though indistinct, advancing rapidly. To fly was impossible, nor was it less so to gaze on the terrific apparition, which approached with a kind of sweeping motion but noiseless tread, as if it were rather borne forward by the wind than supported by the earth. The form was majestic, and conveyed the idea of a man in its character of grace and strength; but it was completely swathed in white floating habiliments, which not only wrapped the lower part, but enveloped the head also. In the left hand it carried a lamp; the right grasped an unsheathed dagger, which glistened in the ray, and assisted in revealing the awful figure to the fascinated eyes of Blanche.

Unable to move from the universal trembling of her limbs, the only thought of the poor girl in this moment of horror arose from the hope, that this supernatural being would pass by her in this destined course, without adding to the infliction under which she suffered by his [89] presence; but at the moment when he arrived within a few paces, such was her increased agitation and the audible bearing of her heart, that the apparition heard her breathing suddenly stopped, and held his lamp in such a direction, that the light fell full upon her pale but lovely face, from which her cap was already removed.

Instantly throwing back the drapery that enveloped his head, the ghost at once discovered that face of a young and handsome man, and putting out his armed hand, he with two fingers grasped the arm of poor Blanche as well as he was able, in the most kind and re-assuring manner, saying, in a low but sweet voice, "My poor boy, do not be frightened; who can have been so cruel as to have sent thee hither?"

Instantly relieved from the belief of supernatural agency, Blanche was now covered with blushes, and forgetful of her disguise, felt only the impropriety of her situation; gasping for breath, she was incapable of articulating a single word, and, overcome by recent fears and present agitation, she burst into tears.

"Nay, cheer thee, my pretty child, and do thy lady's bidding. I meant not to distress thee by my question—be silent as to what thou hast seen, and if I live to behold these tresses again, thou shalt not want a friend."

As these words were spoken, the apparition playfully touched the clustering ringlets of Blanche, and then, as if considering that his [90] absence would be the best restorative to the terrified page, passed forward. So great was the transition which had taken place in the mind of the maiden, though still silent, that she now felt as if he were rather a guardian angel than an object of terror; and she determined not to lose a moment in executing her mission, that she might have the benefit of his lamp, and the power of appealing to him for aid, should she be again terrified.

Under this idea she passed swiftly forward, but her shoes, like those of the supposed ghost, being covered with felt, she was also noiseless. She had gone only a few yards, with her lantern still covered, when she was sensible of an aperture in the wall she was passing, and a voice said whisperingly, as if speaking to some one very near, "Do not fire till he ascends the steps; his lamp will then guide you."

Blanche instantly recollected that she had seen a flight of narrow stairs resembling the more distant ones by which she had descended, and the conviction flashed on her mind, that these hidden assassins were lying in wait for the cavalier who personated the ghost. She flew back to him, seized his arm just as he had reached the foot of the stairs, and saying only, "Be silent," took his lamp out of his hand.

In another moment she had placed it upon the fifth step, and descended; but before she had time to speak, a ball from a pistol aimed by a [91] sure hand had whizzed over head, and shattered the lamp. "Noble boy, thou hast saved my life!" cried the ghost, as for a moment he caught her in his arms and pressed her to his heart.

"What shall I do?" cried Blanche in new distress. "Only allow me they lantern to ascend, and I shall then be safe; thy own dark cloak will preserve thee, or I would not leave thee—no! not for the world."

So saying, the cavalier dropped his outer wrappings in the passage, took the lantern from her unresisting hand, and darted up the narrow and precipitous stairs, and probably secured his egress by some outlet unknown to her: in another moment the lantern was lowered to her feet by his scarf; she caught it, and ran eagerly forward in the direction which unavoidably led her once more close past the concealed assassins.

All was silent, and she reached the outer door just as three hurried taps were given, as if by a hand alarmed or weary of repeating them: she lost not a moment in projecting her letter through the chink, and saw another instantly returned, which she caught eagerly and placed in her bosom. As she retreated, the splashing of water and the sound of an oar met her ear; and alarmed by every thing which in the slightest degree disturbed the death-like silence [91] of this murderous passage, she fled back with even more celerity than she had advanced, yet could not forbear to pause a single moment at the foot of that staircase by which the noble-looking apparition had vanished, and listen for sounds indicative of his proximity or safety. All was perfectly quiet, but to her surprise and alarm the white drapery and the shattered lamp were removed; it was plain that the murderers had already been to seek their prey through some door or passage unseen by her, and from the celerity of her own movements, she could not doubt that they were close at hand.

Winged by new and justifiable fears, Blanch now fled with the speed of an arrow, venturing to increase her light for that purpose; nor did she stay her steps till she had ascended the stairs, and placed the heavy door betwixt herself and the bullet which she every instant expected to pursue her. She had the satisfaction to find the entrance in the precise state she had left it; when it was locked, she collected her faculties and pursued her former track, perfectly cured of all fear of the illustrious dead, and regained her room without injury, just before the first hour of morning had struck.

How much had passed in that single hour of absence! how impatient was she to reveal her adventure to Adelaide, who not only received her letter with the warmest gratitude, but [93] listened to her story with the deepest interest! After various questions as to the person and manners of the ghost, she pronounced it her decided opinion, "that it could be no other than the duke of Norfolk himself, who had under this disguise made an unsuccessful attempt to escape;" for she was aware that the narrow stairs described by Blanche led to the apartments occupied by his Grace as a prisoner.

"Poor man! would that he had gone," cried Blanche, "or that I could have aided him!—but, sister, to whom did I carry the letter?"

"To one," said Adelaide, blushing, "who is dear to me as a betrothed lover, the young Sir Henry Brudenell."

"Is he a friend of the duke's?" said Blanche with eagerness, pressing the hand of her sister, as if to spare her the confusion arising from this tender confession, but at the same time proving intense interest in the noble captive.

"No, his personal acquaintance with the duke is slight, for he is several years younger; but he is, I may assert safely, a brave, high-spirited youth, too likely to enter in this cause with enthusiasm; therefore his uncle, the Lord Montague, who, like our good aunt, is very cautious, from having like her lived in perilous times, thought it right to lay a positive interdict on his visits here during the time the noble prisoner continues captive. I have endeavoured to make Henry submissive to this mandate, to [94] which is love and his temper alike rendered him refractory, and trust he will now be prevailed upon to refrain from again exposing himself to private injury and public peril."

The sisters were interrupted by the arrival of the baroness, but their thoughts were soon turned from descriptions "of the queen's attire, Lord Leicester's appointments, the grand entertainments of the ambassador from France, and the action of Shakspeare at the Globe in a play of his own writing," by the news of Barbara, who insisted "that it was whispered all over the Tower, that a warrant for the execution for the duke of Norfolk had actually arrived."

Blanche passed another sleepless night, and rose only to find her fears confirmed; and such was the effect which the event produced upon her, that her aunt supposed that she had caught the disorder of her sister, and the hysterical floods of tears, which bespoke terror, compassion, and an interest beyond a name for one whom she had never seen, must be connected with latent fever. Since it was in vain to argue with one so evidently disordered in mind, the good lady adopted the wisest course the case admitted. Imputing the agitation of her young niece to her country education, her consequent superstition, and terror at the execution, she procured leave to quit her apartments immediately, and placing the sisters together in a litter, she pro-[95]bceeded to the house of a friend in Barbican, and soon after to retired lodgings in St. Martin's in the Fields.

In this situation Adelaide speedily recovered her health, for here her young lover and his noble family visited her, and contributed not less to her recovery than the pure air and the pleasant groves which surrounded her. But the blow was struck which appeared to sever the young heart of Blanche from society; and the more happiness she beheld, even in the possession of those with whom she fondly sympathised, the more did she shrink from partaking their emotions. So lately the gayest of the gay—a wild fluttering bird, singing from every spray—and filling every scene with her own sweetness and hilarity—she now became grave almost to melancholy; and, in her pensive countenance and measured step, exhibited a decorum of manners which astonished even the most stately dames who surrounded the virgin queen.

Time passed—Adelaide was married—the sisters were presented at court, and the beauty and gentle demeanour of the lovely Blanche admired by many. Various suitors became candidates for her hand. All were refused. For three years the young Blanche dwelt in the very zenith of gaiety, and inhaled the air of flattery unmoved; when, on the removal of her brother-in-law to his country seat, in order to [96] celebrate the christening of his heir, she accompanied her family thither.

The dowager viscountess Cobham, who always resided in the country since the death of her lord, and was the near neighbour of the Brudenells, had promised to become a sponsor on this occasion. She was a woman of high character, great power and wealth, and even yet said to possess much personal beauty. The family of Sir Henry were assembled for the purpose of celebrating the sacrament in question, when her attendants drew up before the house, and expectation was generally awakened on the subject of her appearance. She entered most splendidly apparelled, but covered with a long veil, which the gentlemen, who were united with her in the awful ceremony, hastened with all deference to remove.

At this moment Blanche started, and an involuntary exclamation passed her lips.

"Fair lady, you start as if you saw a ghost," said one of the visitants to her jestingly.

At these words lady Cobham fixed her eyes with a look of wild but steady scrutiny on the poor girl, who, though the colour had actually forsaken not only her cheeks but her lips, now blushed deeply. In the tall, stately form of lady Cobham, her brilliant eye, and more especially the contour of her face, she saw so strong a resemblance to the ghost of the vaulted [97] passage, that she immediately thought it possible that, aided by art, she might have been the very person whom her heart, in despite of her reason, had so long mourned as dead—the man whom she had heard spoken of as one endued with every virtue, and who had left on her mind the impression of every grace.

Whatever might be the confusion and varied expression of poor Blanche's countenance, it was equalled in that of the viscountess, who in a few words complained "that she was unwell, and overdone by her ride," and seizing the arm of Blanche, she retired with her.

"Young Lady," said she, the moment they were alone, "you must pardon my question—did you ever see an apparition resembling me?"

"Undoubtedly I did, in the vaults of the Tower."

"And you!—what did you do?"

"It spoke, and I became relieved from my terror, and was afterwards so happy as to save the life of the person in question."

"Ay! the lamp received the shot intended for his head—I know, I know it all—O God! I thank thee."

The lady stopped, overpowered with her recollections, and although a thousand questions rose to the lips of Blanche, she was unable to utter one. "Could this be the sister of the duke, and had she so conquered her sorrow [98] for his hard fate, as to rejoice in any thing connected with the memory of it?"

"I trust," said the lady at length, "you will have no objection to behold him whom you so befriended again?"

"How is that possible, madam?"

"Because he is now returned from the continent, and means to sup with us here this evening, little indeed hoping for the pleasure which awaits him. I need not say that you must meet as strangers, nor can he explain at this moment why he hazarded to so little purpose his valuable life on that eventful night. He is my only son, and has to my ear alone confided the history of that remarkable night, and the miraculous escape which he owed to your courage and presence of mind."

"How strange! I believed that I had seen the duke of Norfolk—therefore his death affected me deeply."

As Blanche spoke, "the pure and eloquent blood" again rushed to her face, and she felt as if she had said too much; the remembrance of that romantic devotion, that determined celibacy, which, although unavowed, had so long influenced her conduct, and thrown an air of pensive melancholy over her countenance and her actions, added to her confusion. The viscountess read her thoughts, abut had too much delicacy to shew her power, and immediately replied, [99] "No! it was my amiable son, his young and ardent friend, the lord Cobham, who has since then so far distinguished himself in the Netherlands, (whither he immediately went after the failure of his plan for the duke's release,) that if it were discovered we have little doubt of obtaining a pardon—But my son's secret was not penetrated, and from you we have, I am sure, not much to fear, my sweet girl—you will not betray the ghost?"

"Oh no, nor must I be myself betrayed. I entreat you, madam, do not inform your son that —"

"Listen to me," said the viscountess. "A little reflection convinced my son, that the apparent page of twelve years old must be a girl of sixteen or seventeen, since no child so young could have exhibited the talents and quick sightedness you displayed. The more he recollected of the beauty, the terrors, and the voice of the page, the more did his heart dwell with admiration and tenderness on the unknown object; and although sorrow for the death of his friend and the necessity of absence alike called on him to join his regiment without an hour's delay, such was his curiosity, and, I might add, his passion, that, but for my suggestion he would at all risks have endeavoured to discover you amongst the ladies of the court." [100]

"Your suggestion?" said Blanche, raising her blue eyes reproachfully.

"Yes! I shewed, that no motive could possibly have induced so young and timid a creature to venture upon such an expedition, save love!"

"Undoubtedly not!—I went most reluctantly, but it was to console my dear sister, who was then sick, and sent me to exchange letters with her present worthy husband."

"Thank you, my dear, candid girl, you have in these words restored me to health; we will now return to the company, for I am equal to my duty."

Happy was it for Blanche that this denouement had taken place, for the first person who approached lady Cobham was her anxious son, who had arrived during her absence, and whose astonishment and delight, on beholding his mother's arm fondly resting on the neck of the well-remembered page, may be better imagined than described. Surrounded by so many witnesses, scarcely could the eyes of either reply to inquiries; but a time came for explanation, and it will not surprise any of my readers to learn, that the ghost soon proved himself anxious to fulfil his promise, and become "a friend for life" to the page who had preserved him so singularly, and who was remembered so fondly.

That the coy and retired Blanch should [101] yield to the handsome and distinguished lord Cobham, excited little surprise in the court, and no displeasure from the queen, who was desirous of drawing the dowager from her solitude; but many persons were astonished at the change soon apparent in the manner of the bride. The innocent gaiety of heart so natural to youth now returned to the fair Blanche, and rendered her as charming in manner as she was lovely in person; yet was it always so far tempered by the shock which her spirits had received, and the habit of reflection which it had induced, as to render her wise, pious, gentle in temper, and steady in every virtuous pursuit, becoming her station as a woman of rank, and her situation as a wife and mother.

The incident which originally introduced this happy pair to each other remained a secret during the right of the maiden queen, but it gave a zest to the recollections of early life in many an hour of retirement; and when the curling tresses of the beauteous Blanche reposed in silvery white beneath her cap and pinners, her fond husband, with all the chivalric constancy which belonged to his times and his character, would still call them "the silver bands that bound his heart," and inquire if he were still "so blest as to be her beloved, her Regretted Ghost?"

The Forgotten Gothic

Title
Harral, Thomas. "Days of Old." FMN 1826. 107-115.

PLATE: Days of Old
Steel plate engraving; designed/drawn by Henry Corbould;
engraved by George Corbould [107]

DAYS OF OLD.
BY T. HARRAL, ESQ.*[9]

———— Whilst slow the curfew tolls,
Years and dim centuries seem to unfold
Their shroud, as at the summons.
BOWLES.

IT was on the morning of the 2nd of August, A.D. 1100, now seven hundred and twenty-five years ago, that an aged man was seen to walk slowly and feebly from a cottage on the western verge of the newly-formed forest in Hampshire. The sun's first rays were glittering on the Avon; his warmth had not yet exhaled the night-dew from the grass; the surrounding foliage retained the deep verdure of summer; and the birds, "sweet nature's happy choristers," enjoying the glory of their element, were warbling forth their hymns of joy and praise as blithely as in spring. The air was fresh and mild; and it seemed to play around the temples and amongst the few and thinly scattered white hairs of the time-bowed patriarch with reviving influence. His tottering steps were supported by a staff in his right hand, and by a [108] fair blooming boy, on whose shoulder his left hand rested. Many a wistful look did he cast around in sad and mournful silence. It was evident that some long-cherished painful feeling laboured in his breast. Inadvertently he raised his face towards the north, where, in the far-off distance, rose the massive towers of an ancient castle, frowning severe and gloomy defiance on the subjugated country. A slight convulsion shook his frame; seemingly in anger he averted his head, and endeavoured to pass more quickly on.

Why did the old man start, why did his cheek redden, on beholding the proud dwelling of the great? His blue eye, his florid complexion, the general countour of his features, unequivocally indicated a Saxon descent. Ask not, then, why the indignant blood rushed to his heart, as the towers of Hunlavintone, now inhabited by Pauncevolt the Norman, burst upon his view.

"Seat of my fathers!" exclaimed the aged Bertfred, as he once more turned his face in anguish towards the castle, "why hast thou not fallen—why hast thou not crushed the destroyer, whose unhallowed revels have so often polluted thy halls? There was a time when those halls were the abode of valour; when they were blessed by the prayers of the poor and the affection of the rich; when every guest was a hero, and truth, justice, and honour presided at the hospitable [109]

9 Author of an "Essay on the Life and Literary Character of Miss Seward," prefixed to the Supplementary Volume of the lady's Works: "Claremont, a Poem;" "Picturesque Views on the Severn," &c.

board. Yet, mark my words, boy," continued he, addressing his youthful page in the fervour of inspiration, "the Almighty Creator hath said—He who cannot lie hath said—' I will visit the sins of the fathers upon the children, unto the third and fourth generation!'"

Bertfred and the youth had not proceeded far when they met Godric, a feudatory resident on one of the neighbouring estates.

"A fine morning for a walk," said Godric, courteously saluting his aged friend. "Yes, or for a ride; but my enjoyments are, alas! nearly over in this world. It is not with me now as it was fifty or even forty years ago, when I could leap a dike or hunt a board"—" Ay," rejoined Godric, cutting short his speech, "or wield a sword with the best of them. I have heard many a tale of your prowess on the fatal field of Hastings, though you have generally been disposed to pass over the melancholy subject in silence."

"Ah! that was a day of blood, the wrongs of which have not yet been avenged by Heaven. Buy vengeance, though it may slumber awhile, will not sleep for ever.—Oh, had you seen our noble king, the brave, the gallant Harold!—But that was before your time; you were then only a child."

"True: but my father fought for him—bled for him—died for him." [110]

"Yes: bravely did he fight; fiercely did he repel the dark invader, who had dared to pollute the sacred soil of his dear native land. Ah, Godric! had we all fought as your worthy father fought that day, Harold, the rightful heir of England's throne, would have triumphed; the proud Norman would have been driven back into the ocean, and his bloody sceptre would never have been swayed over a free-born Saxon race."

At this moment the distant sound of bugles, the full cry of dogs, and the obstreperous shouts of huntsmen, were heard upon the gale. "There, there go some of the oppressors of the earth!" said Godric; "some of the base minions of the crown, for whose sport and pastimes our fair cities have been laid waste, our fields and our vineyards converted into a vast wilderness—the lair of beasts less brutal than their pursuers!"

"Well, let them pass," replied Bertfred; "their triumph is only for a season. The lives of men are held but lightly now: kill your brother, and you may atone for the crime by a paltry fine; but if you take the life of a deer, of a boar, or even a hare, (creatures which God gave for the common support of man,) the ferocious foreign tyrant will remorselessly deprive you of your sight. It was not thus that Alfred framed or administered his laws. Was it for this that Harold—the good, the pious Harold—offered up [111] his vows before he gave battle to the Norman invader? Surely, surely, there must be a day of retribution!"

"It will be six-and-thirty years ago next October," resumed Bertfred, after a brief pause; "yes, it was on a Saturday, the 14th day of October, that Harold perished—I have good cause to remember it, Godric."

"Yes: your son"—

"On his march he stopped at that stately temple, which he had founded for the worship of his God, in the wooded plains of Waltham; and there, attended by his nobles and his chiefs—I was honoured as one of the first of his train—he heard a solemn mass performed for the success of his arms.—Voices of the dead! methinks I hear you now.—Censers smoked with incense; the sacred anthem swelled in many a deep and awful strain upon the ear; the white-robed men of God, in prayers of fervent energy, implored the Father of all mercies to protect their King, and to crown his enterprise with glory. Alas! their pious orisons availed not."

The sound of the bugles, the cry of the dogs, and the shouts of the huntsmen in the chase, again assailed the ears of Bertfred and of Godric. The sound was nearer; but they allowed it not to interrupt their conversation.

"I need not dwell upon the battle," continued Bertfred: "your father and I fought by the side [112] of our king: it was his lot to fall—to die a soldier's death; and mine—detested boon!—to be disposed of by the spoiler of the land. We were in the thickest of the fight; we had twice repelled the furious and almost despairing duke. All that was great and sublime seemed to animate every bosom, and to invigorate every arm in the English host; the cry of victory was already raised—when, like the returning waves of the ocean, a countless multitude poured in upon us; the royal standard disappeared; your good father was no more; and Harold—I see his last looks, I hear his last words—'Tell my brothers,' said he, ' to fight to the death; 'tis England's crown, 'tis England's glory that they fight for!' Alas! those brothers, the royal-hearted Gurth and Leofwin, had already sealed their valour with their blood. Another moment—the deadly iron had entered his brain—I saw his half-glazed eye—he clutched my hand in convulsive agony of death—in an instant his spirit had fled! All was then"—

"But, your son?"

"Alas, poor Aelfric! he too perished; and the only hope, the last branch that now remains of the once noble and flourishing house of Bertfred is this hapless child, the offspring of his widowed sister. He fell in all the pride of youth and beauty—in all the rich lustre of rising manhood. But it was the will of the Almighty; to his will [113] we must all submit; and even to this day it cheers my old heart to know that he fell for his king."

Bertfred wiped away the tear that stole down his cheek, and then affectionately kissed the fair forehead of the youth, who bore the name of his long-lamented son.

"Aelfric," he resumed, "had the distinguishing honour of bearing the king's banner; a magnificent ensign, upon which was richly emblazoned the effigies of a warrior in combat; the border beset with gold and jewels and precious stones. The staff of that banner the dear boy had grasped firmly in death. After the battle, the invader sent it, in impious mockery, to the holy father of the church, at Rome, as a token of his victory over the last king of the Saxons. Oh, had the fortune of the day been reversed; had Harold, the beloved of his people, triumphed; the nation would not have been condemned to the bitter slavery of a foreign yoke, the poor man would not have been robbed or murdered with impunity, the rich demesne of Hunlavintone would not have been conferred upon an alien, the ruthless follower of an ambitious chief, nor would its lordly owners, the descendant of an ancient and noble race, have been doomed, in savage mercy, to wear out the worthless remainder of his days, bowed down by misery, in yon wretched hovel!"

Again the bugles sounded; again the joyous cry of the dogs was heard in their approach; [114] again the applauding shouts of the huntsmen made the wide forest ring. A stag emerged from the depths of an embowering wood—the pack was in full pursuit—a hundred voices exclaimed, in notes of adulatory rapture. "The king's! the king's!" as an arrow was seen to pierce his flank. The wounded stag rushed on—the royal train as swiftly followed—

> Many a lord with his lady bright,
> Forming a gay and gallant sight—

and, in another moment, turning an angle of the chase, the dazzling groups had vanished.

"Heartless, thoughtless wretch!" indignantly cried Godric; "has he so soon forgotten that his brother Richard was slain by a deer in this very forest?"

Suddenly the approach of horses was heard—confused sounds mingled in the fair—low murmurs, sobs, and cries of grief, and female lamentations, by turns prevailed. The first distinct articulate sounds that could be collected were, "He's dead! he's dead!—the king, the king is dead!" Hurriedly, and in rude disorder, the company—lords, ladies, huntsmen, knights, esquires—rode past the spot where Bertfred, Godric, and the young Aelfric were standing, mute with surprise, astonishment, and expectation. An arrow, shot by Sir Walter Tyrrel, and accidentally turned in its course, had pierced the breast of the king. [115] His followers were hastily bearing him towards some near cottage for relief: but, alas! no human aid could avail—the spirit of William Rufus had left its earthly tenement for ever!

The flush—not of joy, but of a more deep and anxious feeling—passed over the face of Bertfred as he heard the evil tidings of the throng. His voice assumed unwonted firmness, when he exclaimed, "Did I not tell thee, boy, that vengeance would not sleep for ever—that the ghost of the slaughtered Harold should be appeased?—William—Richard—Rufus! Thrice art thou avenged! The will of Heaven be done! I shall not depart in peace."

Title
T., A.D. "The Fairies' Grot." FMN 1826. 119-135. [119]

THE FAIRIES' GROT.

Nature has her expression, like individuals. The aspect of a wile and gloomy scene seems fitted to awaken remorse from its slumber, while a smiling region, and the pure air of the mountains, tend to produce tranquil and happy impressions. Such mysterious relations, subsisting between the creation and the creature, form a unison and harmony which reveal and proclaim the divine Author.

Switzerland, unquestionably is richer than any other portion of Europe in sublime scenery; and the brisk and lively air breathed from its skies adds to the enjoyment of the wanderer over this picturesque country: for in a warm climate, like that of Italy, the mind becomes enervated, and the feelings partake of the softening temperature of the atmosphere.

Near the little town of Orbe, in the canton de Vaud, is the Fairies' Grot, so named from some remote and obscure popular tradition. The real magic of this grotto is its situation:—the Orbe, a furious torrent, runs at the bottom of the valley, above which the grot seems suspended. No habitation is visible, although a fresh and luxuriant vegetation blooms all around; but the valley is of difficult access, nor is it an easy task [120] to arrive at the grotto: its ancient trees are thus protected from the destructive hand of man, and remain from age to age like the genealogy of the valley, nor is it without respect that they can be contemplated. There is no describing a spot so wildly romantic as to baffle imagination, but the thoughts which the sight of it awakens leave behind them an indelible remembrance. Few travellers visit the Fairies' Grot, and I probably should have never seen it, had not a duty and a sacred promise led me thither. This grotto was the scene of a very tragic event; and though years have since rolled by, my sensations, on finding myself there once more, were of the most poignant and lively nature. On the rocks which formed the grotto was every where graven the date, the 18th of August. I was accompanied by a youth whom I had educated. Adolphus, struck as though by instinct, was considerably affected. The day of our visit to this spot happened also to be the 18th of August, and my young friend on this same day completed his twenty-first year: he could hardly think that the sight alone of this wild place, and this strange concurrence of circumstances, could sufficiently explain my excessive agitation. The appointed hour drew night. "Adolphus," said I, "a mystery which has cost you many a sigh has enveloped your youth. It is time that it should cease the last wish of your father must [121] now be accomplished. Listen to the tale of his misfortunes." I pointed out a spot where I desired he should seat himself. "There," said I, "did I see your father fall, mortally wounded by the hand of the murderer of your mother;—that same had which engraved on these rocks the so often repeated date." Adolphus shuddered; his countenance assumed an expression of revenge: he was eagerly interrupting me, but I, replying to his thought, cried, "Peace be to the tomb! the victims and the murderer have disappeared!—my son, let us pray for them all." These words soothed the young man, and after the silent abstraction of a few moments I thus commenced my recital.

Count Leczinski, your father, had been in the Russian service; he possessed considerable estates in the environs of Cracow, and having suffered from the consequences of a dangerous wound, he retired to his domains at a period when he was no longer young. Being the last remaining branch of an illustrious house, his friends pressed him to marry, but a misanthropic turn of mind inclined him to shun society. In his earlier days, I suspect, he had loved; he never spoke to me of that, and I have only been led to this conjecture by vague circumstances. My father had been the constant attendant of count; he was his surgeon—a profession which I likewise followed; and to your father, my [122] generous benefactor, I owe every thing. I accompanied him in his retirement, and although the great disproportion of our ages seemed an obstacle to confidential friendship, yet his unvarying goodness, and the interest he took in me, awakened on my part the most sincere and tender attachment. Business called the count to Munich; thither we went, and there he became acquainted with a young and very interesting person, the daughter of his lawyer. She was but sixteen years of age; the expression of melancholy which softened her features touched the count even more than her beauty. The lawyer was not slow to perceive the impression his daughter had made, and, without once consulting her, employed his whole address to accomplish a union so flattering to his ambition. The count, withheld by a habitual timidity and self-distrust, dared not to explain himself further than with the lawyer; thus, then, was the marriage decided, and it speedily took place. Your mother made no resistance; the count understood her obedience as consent, and was satisfied. He carried his wife into Poland, and on his return to his own estate resumed his wonted occupations and his solitary habits—the young countess being left wholly to herself. A year afterwards you were born: the 18th of August, 1791, was a festival for all the numerous vassals of the count; and even he seemed to parti-[123]cipate in the public joy. I have often thought that he married merely as a duty, and that, continually a victim to the remembrance of a first passion, he had never been able to bestow on his countess, in spite of her attractions, more than the tribute of esteem and friendship; besides, he had become a husband at sixty years of age, and felt out of his place by the side of his young wife. Under these circumstances, we lived quite secluded from the world. Meanwhile the health of your mother became alarmingly precarious, and change of air was prescribed for her. You were too young to encounter the journey; the count left you to my care, and departed with the countess for Paris. They went immediately to the house of the baroness de

P., a very distant relation of the count's,—a woman who lived much in society. For the young countess, born in an humble sphere, and accustomed from the time of her marriage to great retirement, the contrast was striking. The count, who found this change of habits insupportable, confided his wife to the care of the baroness. Amongst those who frequented the house of this lady, a young Swiss, named Henry de C., was particularly distinguished; he was presented to the count, whom he found means to please, and to whom he was always a welcome visitor. The young man appeared inattentive to the countess, whom he [124] met continually either with her husband or with the baroness. Henry was endowed with all that enables man to please; nevertheless, the expression of his countenance seemed occasionally to betray sentiments such as one would scarcely venture to suspect:— accustomed to surrender himself to his passions, he spared no means for their gratification. He saw your mother, and loved, or at least fancied he loved her; and the more difficulty he anticipated in the pursuit, the greater was the stimulus to his purpose. The baroness became his confidante; the unprincipled woman saw merely in Henri's passion one of those casual and common circumstances, which only derived some interest in her eyes, from its being likely to awaken her dull cousin (as she called the count) from his apathy, and she lent herself without scruple to the projects of her ally. The seduction of the countess, however, was not to be easily effected: strict in her duties, to tempt her to a failure in them was impossible; and though her sentiments for the count were limited to esteem, she could never be induced to forget that she belonged to him by a sacred tie, and that he was the father of her child. Henri would not be repulsed; he gradually accustomed her to a language quite new to her ear; her very innocence weakened her distrust; she felt disturbed without knowing why;—the cunning seducer gave her the habit, [125] the necessity of being beloved, without alarming her suspicions by an abrupt declaration. He created, as it were, around her an atmosphere of love. Alas! how could she escape? Henry de C. was born with happy dispositions, but, abandoned from infancy to immoral influences, he became vicious, and the energy of his character, instead of being employed in noble designs, was perverted to the furtherance of evil ones.

 The countess, so different from the women whom he saw habitually, made a deep impression on him;—perhaps had he met her some years earlier, while she was yet free, she might have reclaimed him to virtue. Situated as he now found her, she was destined to add to the number of his crimes and of his victims.

 Count Leczinski was obliged to return to Cracow, to maintain a lawsuit which threatened to cost him a portion of his property. Compelled to travel rapidly, he left his wife, whose health was not yet re-established, in Paris, expecting to return to her at the end of a few weeks. the absence of the husband in no degree weakened the virtue of this wife. Henry redoubled his attentions, he dared even to speak, but he was repulsed—nevertheless he was beloved. He perceived that he never should succeed in his purpose; but his love was become madness. The count seldom wrote, for, over-[126] whelmed with business, he had but little leisure to dedicate to correspondence with his countess. Anxiety at length brought on him a tedious illness, of which it was my office to apprise your mother; at the same time the count ordered me positively to prohibit her coming to him, so fearful was he of her encountering the fatigue of a long journey. The illness furthered Henri's plans:—all letters addressed to the countess were first submitted to him, by a domestic whom he had corrupted. A second letter very soon arrived, as if from me, the hand-writing, the postmark, all so perfectly counterfeited, that it was impossible the countess should conceive any suspicion of their authenticity. Thus did she learn the supposed death of your father;—her letters were intercepted and suppressed, and others fabricated, and sent in their place. Six months passed away, during which the count continued ill, and Henri conducted himself with such apparent delicacy as at length to triumph over the scruples of the countess; and before the year of her mourning had expired, she consented to a secret marriage. A heavy melancholy oppressed her spirits on the eve of the day fixed for the ceremony. Henri urged her to explain the cause of her sadness; he was adored by her, and he could not solicit in vain. She had seen him smile at things which in her eyes were sacred, and she had scarcely courage to [127] confess to him a superstition in which she believed as implicitly as in her love.

"Thou wilt have it so," said she, "and I must speak. I have always haboured a notion that I should die young, and that sorrow would conduct me to the tomb. Until I loved thee I never knew happiness, and yet, now that I am so near becoming thine for ever, this gloomy presage returns upon me. I feel as though I were destined to die at a distance from thee. Oh, Henri! thou cants, it thou wilt, tranquillise my heart, and restore its confidence. We hold in Germany a belief, which softens the idea of death:—if two beings who love each other engage solemnly not to quit the world without appearing for the last time to one another, however wide may be the distance that separates them, then the survivor can never become inconstant. Henry, receive my vow! let me enjoy the certainty of being always beloved by thee! my promise, if not ratified by thy consent, would be vain and of no effect." Henri, shocked, and agitated by conscience, might perhaps at that moment have been surprised into an avowal of the whole plot, but she did not leave him time for explanation. Seeing his emotion, she seized a bible, and putting it into his hand—"Swear," said she, "that thou acceptest the vow I make, not to quit this life without communicating to thee the event: I will [128] not appear to thee, but my last sigh shall be thine, and thou shalt hear it. Then all will be over as to this world, and I shall be gone to love thee in another." Henri, not knowing what he did, but subdued and hurried along by her irresistible enthusiasm, pronounced the vow required; then, incapable of contending farther with his tumultuous feelings, he retired, leaving his victim on her knees praying for him, nor did he see her again till the following day, at the hour appointed for the ceremony of their marriage. A false priest officiated—the crime was consummated. The baroness continued in total ignorance of the means which Henry had employed. He exacted of her, who believed herself his wife, the strictest secrecy,—he neglected the correspondence which hitherto, under the name of the countess, he had maintained with me; consequently the count's inquietude became extreme; and, no longer able to suffer the uneasiness of suspense, he resolved on departing for Paris. His valet-de-chambre only accompanied him, as I continued to take charge of you. On arriving at the hotel of the baroness, he quitted his carriage, and, wrapt in his travelling cloak, entered the hotel without being recognised. He went straight to the apartment of his wife, who was alone. On perceiving him she uttered a piercing shriek, and fell senseless on the floor: for twenty-four hours every [129] assiduity was uselessly lavished upon her. The sudden apparition of the count, whom all believed dead, caused a powerful sensation in the household of the baroness: as for himself, occupied solely with his wife, whom he never quitted, he paid but little attention to what was passing around him. At length the countess exhibited symptoms of revival: she shuddered on beholding the count near her; he would have retired, but she withheld him. "Do not," she entreated, "refuse to hear me; my remaining moments are numbered, let us not lose them!" She faithfully related to him all that had passed. Without any attempt to dissemble her love, she attributed her misfortune to some cruel fatality; the idea of suspecting, of accusing Henri, never once presented itself to her; and until the count had fully unveiled the machinations of her seducer, she persevered in acknowledging her love.

This last stroke she was unable to resist—the horrible truth destroyed at once all her illusions—the name of Henri never again passed her lips; but her love and her life were one—to pluck the former from her heart was death. The count, at her earnest supplication, never quitted her, but neither of them could speak; nevertheless, a few moments before she breathed her last sigh, she entreated his blessing, and recommended you to his paternal care. The [130] count pronounced his blessing; she listened to his words of peace; a light smile passed over her lips; she expired. The count gazed on her remains for a moment, then rushing from the door—"Vengeance!" cried he, and disappeared. It was on the 18th of August, at six o'clock in the evening, that your mother died.

Henri, on learning the return of the count, fled. Goaded by remorse, tormented by jealousy, he never paused until he reached the frontiers of Switzerland. At Jougne, he was attacked by a violent fever, and during some days was entirely abandoned by his reason: he scarcely awaited his recovery to continue his route to Orbe, where he had passed some years of his infancy. One thought, one only sentiment possessed him; and yet, notwithstanding the boiling impetuosity of his disposition, he dared not to inquire what had become of the countess. He did not refresh the recollection of any of his old acquaintance, and was not recognised by them, since he had quitted Orbe at the age of fourteen, and was not twenty-eight. He passed his days and greater part of his nights in this grotto, and the superstitious neighbours, intimidated by his ferocious air, ventured not to approach it; thus his solitude remained undisturbed. Six weeks elapsed unmarked by any change, when one day—it was the 18th of August—he felt himself more than ever a prey to his [131] torments, and his agitation became insupportable. On the evening of that same day, a few minutes before six o'clock, he felt as if chained to the spot where you now sit. He trembled, scarcely dared to look round him, and held his breath, as though fearful to disturb the awful silence. Perhaps a presentiment, a mysterious revelation, compelled him to listen—at length he heard a sigh—a sigh which made him shudder. He started from his fixed position, and rushed forward a few steps as if in pursuit of some object, but sudden recollection returned, and he cried aloud, "Death! death!" Rendered furious by his remorse, he wandered through the cavern, repeating incessantly the word "Death! death!" During the two days that this state of frensy continued, he was in possession of his consciousness, for it was from himself that I had these details. At length the people with whom he lodged, uneasy at his continued absence, and aware that this was his habitual haunt, followed him hither, and found him stretched on the earth exhausted by his emotions. He spoke not, and allowed himself to be led away unresistingly; but the next day he returned, and assisted by some peasants, built himself a cottage near the grotto, which he furnished with a bed, table, and chair; and each morning they brought him his daily supply of provisions. At first he was the subject of a thousand conjectures, but was soon forgotten. Forgotten! no:—divine retribution, the [132] torments of conscience, were not sufficient expiation—human vengeance impended over him.

The count was not exempt from self-reproach. He was conscious that he neglected his wife, and had married her without consulting her inclinations; but that projects over which he now brooded drew him, as it were, out of himself, and diverted him from his deep sorrow. The search he caused to be made after Henri was long fruitless, but at length one of his emissaries believed he had discovered traces of its unhappy object, and communicated the tidings of his success. Not a moment did the count delay his departure for Switzerland. He arrived at Orbe, where he pursued his inquiries; and though the replies he received were vague and indefinite, yet the period of the arrival of the man who inhabited the grotto so far agreed with the date of the tragic event in which he was so deeply implicated, that he resolved at least to see him. Led by a guide, therefore, he reached the rock on which Henry had erected his cottage: he saw him, and, in spite of the change of his features, recognised him immediately. Concealing what he felt, he quitted the spot, having fixed on the following day for the execution of his project. That next day was the 18th of August, the fatal anniversary. Furnished with pistols, the count set out for the grotto—his valet was ordered to [133] remain at a certain distance from it, and forbidden to approach nearer, unless he should not appear again in the space of a short time, which he specified. It was then striking six. Henri, immovable, in that same place where he had received the mysterious intelligence of the death of his victim, (for he was convinced she was no more) plunged in a gloomy reverie, heard not the steps of the count, who, on approaching him, cried, "Villain, defend thyself!" offering him at the same time a pistol. Henri shuddered—for the first time, for so long a period, another voice other than his own echoed amid those rocks. He beheld the count, and at the same instant the phantom of the countess seemed to rise from the earth, and place herself between them. "Pardon!" cried he; "pardon!" while in the posture of a suppliant he implored the vision of his delirious imagination. The count felt compelled to regard him for a moment with something like pity; but soon recollecting himself—"Coward," said he, "defend thyself!" Henry did not seem to understand him; and the count, wrought into a fury, insulted and excited him by the most injurious epithets. Henri's passions were at last roused; he seized the pistol and fired it; the ball entered the right arm of the count—Henri remained unhurt. He approached your father, who staggered, and with difficulty supported himself, but who in a terrible voice [134] bade him "begone." At that moment the valet arrived; he supported his master, who, before he departed, said, "If I live, next year, in this same place, on this same day, at this same hour, expect me!" and having uttered those words he disappeared.

The count's wound was dangerous. He staid at Geneva, where every care was taken of him; still he did not recover: at length he wrote to me, requiring my attendance immediately. I left you in the charge of his bailiff, and departed. Ignorant of all that had passed since the count quitted Poland, I was now first informed by himself of his misfortunes, and of the resolution he had taken to perish by the hand of Henri or to deprive him of life. Vainly did I endeavour to calm him, and dissuade him from the horrible design—I found him implacable. At the time fixed, we departed for Orbe. The count had a presentiment that he should fall, and therefore made all necessary arrangements. He appointed me your tutor, and enjoined, that on my return to Poland I should cause you to travel under a fictitious name, and forbear to reveal to you the story of your parents until you should have attained your twenty-first year; he ordered me also to lead you to this grotto, and at six o'clock, in the spot where we now are, to recite to you these facts: but I have not yet completed my melancholy task. We went to [135] the grotto; Henri was there, and very long did he refuse to fight, until the outrages of the count compelled him to it. I saw him fire; he took no aim at your father, and, but for a movement of the latter, the ball never could have hit him:—but the decree of fate must be accomplished—the ball passed through his heart—he fell dead. Henri looked on him for a moment, then, with a burst of horrid laughter, more frightful than death itself, he fled. I saw him climb from rock to rock; he disappeared from my sight. Some days after, the neighbours found his body, which the torrents had swept down into the Orbe. The count had left a declaration, on my presenting which to the magistrates, they granted me permission to remove his body. I had it embalmed, and, on my return to Poland, buried it in the tomb of your ancestors, as well as that of the countess, according to the orders he had given me. Adolphus, may so many misfortunes warn you to resist the tyranny of the passions! You are free—may the remembrance of this day be useful to you!

    A long silence followed these words; my young friend seemed absorbed in his reflections—I durst not interrupt them. At length he rose, and casting a last look around him—"Peace to the tomb!" said he. He turned from the grotto, and I followed him.

    A.D.T.

Title
A Traveller. "The Lady of the Tower." FMN 1826. 166-177. [166]

THE LADY OF THE TOWER.

IN a remote part of the southern extremity of Ireland, not far from the sea-shore, lately resided a lady, who bore the name which we have prefixed to this narrative, and whose habits, manners, and history, so far as they have been developed, throw over real life all the colours of romance. She was of tall stature, and appeared to be about forty-five years of age. Her countenance, originally soft and impressive, had assumed, from the constant exposure to the weather, a hue of deep brown; and the agitation of alternate emotions, relapsing from gaiety into melancholy, had wrinkled her brow into deep furrows, and given to her features an occasional severity of expression, which, while it diminished the effect of lingering traces of early beauty, enabled her to unite with self-protection that feeling of dread which attached to her actions the character of supernatural agency, and gained her a striking though not singular ascendancy over the superstitious inhabitants who dwelt round her abode.

It is now seven years since this lady suddenly appeared in that neighbourhood. She arrived on foot, in the plain garb of the female peasantry [167] of the country, but wearing pendant upon her neck an embossed foreign gold chain of antique workmanship, to which was attached a cross of the same metal, exactly resembling those worn by superior persons in the convents of Catholic countries on the continent. Concealed upon her person she also carried a quantity of Spanish, and some letters, which, from subsequent circumstances, were conjectured to contain a power of commercial credit: for after she had at intervals forwarded them, whither it was not ascertained,—as she availed herself of some mode of transmission unknown to the rude people among whom she had fixed her abode,—she was always furnished with adequate means for subsistence and charity.

It is impossible to describe a more secluded and romantic spot than that selected by this lady for her sojourn—it has all the solitude which a poet's imagination could paint, without the abstract gloominess of an utter separation from the world; and it furnishes pastoral employment, which always gives a relish for the simpler beauties of nature: whilst the surrounding scenery, in moments of excitement, administers to the sublimity of enthusiasm, and also furnishes, from the splendid fragments of its scattered and diversified ruins, abundant objects for the devotional and historical reflections of a cultivated mind. Her abode was a [168] shepherd's hut, formed of the rude materials which compose the cabins of the Irish peasantry, the walls of dried mud, the roof a thatch of sticks, straw, and bushes, yielding in summer a wild luxuriance of neglected blossoms, which it would perplex the botanist to classify and describe. The face of the surrounding country is rude, though partially relieved by patches of pasturage, and the extended horizon bounded by a long chain of lofty and abrupt mountains, the iron base of which repels the waves of the Atlantic Ocean, and which give a sublime termination to the distant view. The immediate vicinity of the shepherd's cottage has also its attractions for the contemplative mind: a few scattered huts contain the population, living upon the dwellings of the poor are formed against the large sepulchral flag-stones which, according to the vulgar tradition, were once the tomb of a giantess famed for surprising exploits, but which are conjectured to be in reality the remains of heathen temples of the Druids, though they are better known in this particular spot, in later years, as the protecting barriers of the deep and winding caverns, which were placed of refuge and concealment from outlaws in the convulsed periods of Irish history; and subsequently the abodes and depositories of the smugglers, who were wont to infest this part of the coast in pursuing their [169] illicit traffic. As if to typify the progress of civilisation and the accompanying advancement of the arts, which are its handmaids, there was reared close to these druidical monuments a Franciscan friary or abbey, now in ruins, but still bearing some rich remains of its former magnificence. The walls of the steeple, the choir, with some of the cloisters, and a small chapel, supposed for morning prayer, still remain. The Gothic pillars, spacious windows, and noble arches, give a solemn air to this venerable pile, while the long, sounding aisles, intermingled with broken tombs, twilight vaults, and caverns piled with human bones, aided by the gloom of high and detached walls, held together by the overgrown verdure of centuries, which has interwoven itself into the very material, sadden all the scene, and illustrate Pope's beautiful lines:—

"In these deep solitudes and awful cells,
Where heav'nly pensive Contemplation dwells,
And ever-musing Melancholy reigns."

As if a spot not comprising more than twenty acres of land was destined to possess the successive fragments of man's labour and mental improvement, for nearly as many centuries,—close to this ruined abbey stands one of the ancient round towers, nearly one hundred feet high, of such dubious construction as to baffle [170] even the fertility of antiquarian conjecture: four of these structures only are known in Ireland, two in Scotland, in England none. The perfect appearance of this tower is beautiful; it is built of freestone, and the smallness of its symmetry, being no more than about twenty feet in circumference at the base, narrowing in its dimensions to the top, gives it the air of a look-out pillar, or watch-tower, to the majestic Gothic ruin which it adjoins. Some, however, consider these edifices to have been bell-towers, there being towards the top four opposite windows, calculated to let out the sound; and there are said to have been formerly found in them crosspieces of oak, from which to suspend a bell. Whatever may be their origin, their present slender and tapering form and fine state of preservation render them beautiful objects of curiosity, and more particularly when coupled with the more elaborate though ruinous architecture of the neighbouring edifice.

Wrapped in the seclusion and contemplation of such a scene, the Lady of the Tower passed her recent years, and her employment illustrated the wayward delusion of her mind, whilst her gentleness, except in moments of excitement which occurred at distant intervals, displayed the natural placidity of her temper.

Her manners were those of a well-bred woman, fashioned upon rather a foreign model: [171] she had the cheerfulness without the ease peculiar to the higher classes of our own country, though it is not impossible that her constrained and formal air sprang as much from mental aberration as from the education of her earlier life. Her employment consisted in wandering within that range of the adjacent country, and constantly amusing herself in the rural employments of the females and children, who have here the general care of the small flocks reared by the peasantry of the neighbourhood. She was kind and liberal to the crowded families in the wretched hovels around her, having always a supply of medicines for the sick, which she administered when required with anxiety and care. To the children she assiduously imparted the elements of education, stimulating them by occasional presents of schoolbooks, and mixing with them in their juvenile pastimes. It was upon one of these occasions, that the writer first saw this lady:—she was seated upon one of the druidical fragments described, surrounded by about forty children, many of them of tender years, to whom she was giving instruction from one of the common catechisms of this country. The tender and innocent expression of infantine piety, however the result of discipline and the habitual observance of form, is always interesting; but the sentiment which it must ordinarily inspire was [172] here heightened by an appearance of health and cleanliness, which seems indigenous to the spot, and presents a strong contrast to the squalid and uncleanly aspect of the naked juvenile part of the population, whom the traveller sees basking in the sun on the road-side, before he approaches this more favoured hamlet.

In contemplating this cheerful and contented little group, the eye naturally fell on the only adult who appeared in the circle. She adhered to the dress of the peasantry, but with a greater attention to particularity and neatness. Her voice had a peculiar solemnity of inflection, though entirely divested of severity; and the affectionate attention with which her admonitions appeared to be received, proved the maternal care which she had bestowed upon the little objects of her humane solicitude, and their reciprocal attachment. Who could have witnessed this edifying spectacle, presenting, as it did, such a contrast with the condition of humble society elsewhere in the same county, without inquiring into its cause? The answer to the interrogatory was simple—to the Lady of the Tower it was ascribed;

and she was invested with all the superhuman attributes, which the superstitious imaginations of the ignorant could invent, to account for acts of disinterested benevolence, and explain the eccentric wanderings of an amiable but distempered mind. [173]

This lady's mode of living partook of the simplicity and economy of the peasantry of the place. She rose early, and ascended the tower (a custom which gave her its name), from the summit of which, with her face towards the sun, she addressed an humble but fervent prayer. She then slowly descended, absorbed in silent meditation, and entered the nave of the ruined abbey, from one of the dilapidated chapels of which she invoked the Divine mercy and protection, with impassioned feeling. During the performance of these duties, she was quite regardless of the surrounding objects, and if addressed, turned away from the importunity with evident dissatisfaction. The knowledge of this feeling mostly spared her any interruption; and such was the reverence in which she was held, that even the children suspended their playful gambols, at her approach, while she was absorbed in her devotions. At times she ascended the precipitous cliffs, which command a view of the ocean, and in seasons of storm she partook of the troubled action of the elements, and appeared at such moments of excitement under the influence of a wild and irregular enthusiasm, often heightened into a frensy, which illustrated the distemper of her mind. On these occasions, she bore, hanging from her neck, a rude imitation of the Spanish guitar, constructed by herself from materials obtained at the place of her [174] residence, and from its strings she struck a plaintive sound to accompany the wild vocal strains, in which, in a foreign tongue, she seemed to address the ocean, at the moment when it most furiously buffeted the base of the rock on which she stood. Though her voice was usually lost amid the roaring of the tempest, yet she never ceased to exert it in this manner, with painful and ineffectual violence. The belief of the peasantry was, that she had been shipwrecked in a Spanish vessel, when a child, and had for years supported herself, before her appearance among them, in the caverns which the sea indents along the line of this bold coast; and they were full of as idle traditions about her food, in this amphibious sojourn, having been supplied by supernatural means. They also collected omens from her acts, which were interpreted as portentous not only of the weather but of the success of their domestic pursuits.

Invested, as she became, with all these ominous attributes, it was unlikely that the poor people would or indeed could, collect any authentic particulars of her real history, whilst the fertility of their invention (a characteristic property of the Irish peasantry) enabled them at all times to furnish a solution of her feelings and actions, from the traditions of which they had an inexhaustible stock. About two years ago, she suddenly disappeared, and, whether [175] her wayward fancy had led her to seek another abode, or, in her wanderings among the rocks, which became more frequent during a severe winter, she had perished by slipping from an overhanging precipice, and found a grave in the bosom of that ocean upon whose heavings she had poured the most plaintive and impassioned strains, remains uncertain—for all that can be gathered on the spot is, that she never returned from an evening walk towards the sea, but that at midnight her form was seen alighting upon the summit of the tower, where she was accustomed to pray, and thence to ascend upwards with an angelic buoyancy, which pointed to the bliss reserved for the penitent and the virtuous.

The information which the writer failed to acquire from the inhabitants of the hamlet, respecting this interesting object of so much just respect and superstitious veneration, he afterwards partially obtained, from a reference to which he was led by a perusal of the few manuscripts left by this lady in the cottage where she resided.

Upon inquiry in Dublin of the commercial gentlemen through whom she received her supplies, and afterwards in London, through a reference which he afforded—all that could be learned was this:—that an annuity of £160 a year was regularly remitted from the firm of [176] Messrs. Lynch, of Bourdeaux, to be placed in the use of a lady, who had, during the early part of the French campaign in Portugal, been induced to quit the asylum of a convent, whither she had been sent from some part of Ireland for the purpose of education, by a young officer of Massena's army, then occupying a considerable part of the peninsula—that in the retreat of the French, she had accompanied the object of her attachment, exposed to all the vicissitudes and perils of a rapid campaign, and refused to be separated from his society in the field, until the young soldier fell by almost the last cannon-shot fired at Marshal Soult's army, in the battle of Thoulouse.

His friends, who were of some rank, pitied her helpless and widowed condition, now aggravated—some might think relieved—by mental aberration, arising from excess of grief. In a moment of convalescence she left the neighbourhood of Bordeaux for Ireland, to see her mother, from whom for years she had not heard; and on her arrival she learned, for the first time, the death of her parent, the last member of her family. Stung with grief and disappointment, she had firmness and recollection enough to make the necessary arrangements for her future subsistence, or rather, for her means of serving others, out of the income assigned to her in France by the family upon whom her protection [177] had devolved, and then to ramble into the wild and romantic place we have described as being her last abode; where the acts of her closing life shed a new and virtuous interest over her history, and drew a veil of pity across that epoch of her earlier career, which had broken off all connexion with her own family, and exposed her to the sufferings and vicissitudes of premature declining years.

Among the imperishable curiosities of the hamlet where she last resided, the peasantry, with grateful affection, mark the granite seat on which she reposed: and the children, at stated periods, assemble round it, to pay an humble but not less sincere homage to the spot from which they were accustomed to receive instruction, and to deck with wild flowers the rude and broken tablets, both in the abbey and the tower, which seemed to possess such interest for their mysterious instructress, the remembrance of whom will long survive among the simple objects of her benefits.

A TRAVELLER.

Title
Anonymous. "The Phantom Voice." FMN 1826. 317-337. [317]

THE PHANTOM VOICE.

IT was at the close of a bright and memorable evening in October, that I had carelessly flung the reins upon the neck of my horse, as I traversed the bar and almost interminable sands skirting the north-west coast of our island.

On my right, a succession of low sand-hills, drifted by the partial and unsteady blasts from the ocean, skirted the horizon—their summits strongly marked upon the red and lower sky in an undulating and scarcely broken outline. Behind them, I heard the vast and busy waters, rolling on, like the voice of the coming tempest. Here and there some rude and solitary hut rose above the red hillocks, bare and unprotected; no object of known dimensions being near, by which its true magnitude might be estimated, the eye often seemed to exaggerate its form upon the mind in almost gigantic proportions. As twilight drew on, the deception increased; and starting occasionally from the impression of some keen and lacerating thought, I beheld, perchance, some huge and turreted fortress, or a pile of mis-shapen battlements, rising beyond the hills like the grim castles of romance, or the air-built shadows of fairy-land. . . . Night was fast closing; I was alone, out of the beaten track [318] amidst a desert and thinly inhabited region; a perfect stranger, I had only the superior sagacity of my steed to look to for safety and eventual extrication from this perilous labyrinth.

The way, if such it might be called, threading the mazes through a chain of low hills, and consisting only of a loose and ever-shifting bed of dry sand, grew every moment more and more perplexed. Had it been daylight, there appeared no object by which to direct my course, no mark that might distinguish whether or not my path was in a right line or a circle; I seemed to be rambling through a succession of amphitheatres formed by the sand-hills, every one so closely resembling its neighbour that I could not recognise any decided features on which to found that distinction of ideas which philosophers term individuality. In almost any other mood of the mind, this would have been a puzzling and disagreeable dilemma; but at that moment it appeared of the least possible consequence to me where the dark labyrinth might terminate.

Striving to escape from thought, from recollection, the wild and cheerless monotony of my path seemed to convey a desperate stillness to the mind, to quench in some measure the fiery outburst of my spirit. It was but a deceitful calm—the deadening lull of spent anguish; I awoke to a keener sense of misery, from which there was no escape. [319]

How am I wandering! It was not to lament over my own griefs that

I commenced my story. Let the dust of oblivion cover them; I would not pain another by the recital. There are sorrows—short ages of agony—into the dark origin of which none would dare to pry; one heart alone feels, hides, and nourishes them for ever!

Night now came on, heavy and dark; not a star twinkled above me; I seemed to have left the habitations of men. In whatever direction I turned, not a light was visible; all fellowship with my kind had vanished. No sound broke the unvarying stillness, but the heavy plunge of my horses' feet and the hollow moan of the sea. Gradually I began to rouse from my stupor; awaking as from a dream, my senses grew rapidly conscious of the perils by which I was surrounded. I knew not but some hideous gulf awaited me, or the yawning sea, towards which I fancied my course tended, was destined to terminate this adventure. It was chiefly, however, a feeling of loneliness, a dread, unaccountable in its nature, that seemed to haunt me. There was nothing so very uncommon or marvellous in my situation; yet the horror I endured is unutterable. The demon of fear seemed to possess my frame, and benumbed every faculty. I saw, or thought I saw, shapes hideous and indistinct, rising before me, but so [320] rapidly that I could not trace their form ere they vanished. I felt convinced it was the mind that was perturbed, acting outwardly upon the sense, rendered more than usually irritable by the alarm and excitation they had undergone—yet I could not shake off the spell that was upon me. I heard a sharp rustling pass my ear; I involuntarily raised my hand; but nothing met my touch save the damp and chilly hair about my temples. I tried to rally myself out of these apprehensions—but in vain: reason has little chance of succeeding when fear has gained the ascendancy. I durst not quicken my pace, lest I should meet with some obstruction; judging it most prudent to allow my steed to grope out his path in the way best suited to his own sagacity. Suddenly he made a dead halt. No effort or persuasion could induce him to stir. I was the more surprised, from knowing his generally docile and manageable temper. He seemed immovable, and moreover, as I thought, in the attitude of listening. I too listened eagerly—intensely; my senses sharpened to the keenest perception of sound.

The moan of the sea came on incessantly as before; no sound else could be distinguished. Again I tried to urge him forward; but the attempt was fruitless. I now fancied that there might be some dangerous gulf or precipice just at his feet, and that the faithful animal was un-[321] willing to plunge himself and his rider into immediate destruction. I dismounted, and with the bridle at arm's length, carefully stepped forward a few paces, but I could find no intimation of danger; the same deep and level bed of sand seemed to continue onwards, without any shelving or declivity whatever. Was the animal possessed?—He still refused to proceed, but the cause remained inscrutable. A sharp and hasty snort, with a snuffing of the win in the direction of the sea, now pointed out the quarter towards which his attention was excited. His terror seemed to increase, and with it my own.

I knew not what to anticipate. He evidently began to tremble, and again I listened. Fancy plays strange freaks, or I could have imagined there was something audible through the heavy booming of the sea—a more distinct, and as it were, articulated sound—though manifestly at a considerable distance. There was nothing unusual in this—perhaps the voice of the fisherman hauling out his boat, or of the mariner heaving at the anchor. But why such terror betrayed by the irrational brute, and apparently proceeding from this source?—being confident I could perceive some connexion between the impulses of the sound now undulating on the wind, and the alarm of my steed. The cause of all this apprehension soon grew more unequivocal—it was evidently ap-[322] proaching. From the sea there appeared to come at short intervals, a low and lengthened shout, like the voice of one crying out for help or succour. Presently the sounds assumed a more distinct and definite articulation. "Murder! Murder!" were the only words that were uttered, but in a tone, and with an expression of agony I shall never forget. It was not like any thing akin to humanity, but an unearthly, and, if I may so express it, a sepulchral shriek—like a voice from the grave.

 I crept closer to my steed; nature, recoiling from the contact of the approaching phantom, prompted me thus intuitively to cling to any thing that had life. I felt a temporary relief, even from the presence of the terrified beast, though I could distinctly perceive him shuddering, yet fixed to the spot. The cry had ceased; but still I continued to listen with intense anxiety, till a sudden rushing cleft the air, and a crash followed, as of some heavy body falling at a little distance from my feet. The horse burst from his bonds, galloping from me at full speed, and I stood alone! In this appalling extremity, I approached the object of my fears. I bent to the ground; stretching out my hand, my fingers rested on the cold and clammy features of a corpse. I well remember the deep groan that burst from my lips—nature had reached the extremity of en-[323] durance—I felt a sudden rush of blood to the heart, and fell beside my ghastly companion, equally helpless and insensible.

 I have no means of ascertaining the duration of this swoon; but with returning recollection I again put out my hand, which rested on the cold and almost naked carcass beside me. I felt roused by the touch, and started on my feet—the moon, at this instant emerging from a mass of dark clouds, streamed full on the dead body, pale and blood-stained, the features distorted, as if by some terrible death. Fear now prompted me to fly; I ran as if the wind had lent me wings—not daring to look back, lest my eyes should again rest on the grisly form I had just left. I fled onwards for some time; the moon now enabling me to follow the beaten track which, to my great joy, brought me suddenly, at the turn of a high bank, within sight of a cheerful fire gleaming through a narrow door, seemingly the entrance to some wayside tavern. Bursts of hilarity broke from the interior; the voice of revelry and mirth came upon my ear, as if just awakening from a dream. It was as if I had heard the dead laugh in their cold cerements. As I stept across the threshold, the boisterous roar of mirth made me shudder; and it seemed, by the alarm visible in the countenances of the guests, that my appearance presented something as terrible to their apprehensions. Every eye [324] became fixed intently on me, as I seated myself by a vacant table; and I heard whisperings, with suspicious glances occasionally directed to where I sat. The company, however, soon began to get the better of their consternation, and were evidently not pleased at so unseasonable an interruption to their mirth. I found that some explanation was necessary as to the cause of my intrusion, and with difficulty made them comprehend the nature of my alarm. I craved their assistance for the removal of the body, promising if possible to conduct them to the spot where the miserable victim was thrown. They stared at each other during this terrible announcement, and at the conclusion I found every one giving his neighbour credit for the requisite portion of courage, though himself, at the same time, declined participation in the hazards of the undertaking.

"Gilbert, ye towd me'at ye stood i' th' churchyard, wi' shoon bottoms upper most, looking for the wench ye wur to wed through the windows: Ise sure 'at ye'll make noa bauk at a bogle."

"Luk thee, Jim, I conna face the dead; but I wunna shew my back to a live fist, the best and the biggest o' the countryside—Wilt' smell, my laddy?"

Gilbert, mortified at the proposed test of his prowess, raised his clenched hand in a half-threatening attitude. A serious quarrel might [325]nhave ensued, had not a sudden stop been put to the proceedings of the belligerents by an interesting girl stepping before me, modestly inquiring where I had left the corpse; and offering herself as a companion, if these mighty cowards could not muster sufficient courage.

"Shame on ye, Will!" she cried, directing her speech to a young man who sat concealed by the shadow of the projecting chimney; "shame on ye! to be o'erfaced by two or three hard words. Ise gangin, follow 'at dare."

Saying this, she took down a huge horn lantern, somewhat dilapidated in the outworks, and burnt in various devices, causing a most unprofitable privation of light. A bonnet and cloak were thrown on hastily; when, surrendering the creaking lantern to my care, she stood for a moment contemplating the dingy atmosphere ere she stept forth to depart. During these ominous preparation, a smart sailor-looking man, whose fear of his mistress' displeasure had probably overcome his fear of the supernatural, placed himself between me and the maiden, and taking her by the arm, crustily told me that if I could point out the way, he was prepared to follow. Rather a puzzling matter for a stranger, who scarcely knew whether his way lay right or left from the very threshold. Thus admirably qualified for a guide, I agreed to make the attempt, being determined to spare no pains[326] in the hope of discovering the object of our search.

Company breeds courage. Several of the guests, finding how matters stood, and that the encounter was not likely to be made singlehanded, volunteered their attendance; so that our retinue shortly consisted of some half dozen stout fellows. The vanguard was composed of myself and the lovers; the rest creeping close in our rear, forming their rank as broad as the nature of the ground would admit.

Luckily I soon found the jutting bank, round which I had turned on my first view of the house we had just left. We proceeded in silence—except that a whisper occasionally arose from one of the rearmost individuals talking to his bolder neighbour in front when finding his courage on the wane. Following for some time what appeared to be the traces of recent footsteps, I hoped, yet almost feared, that every moment I might stumble on the bleeding corpse. An attendant in the rear now gave the alarm at something which he saw moving on our left, and at the same time making a desperate struggle to get into the front of his companions. This produced a universal uproar—each fighting for precedency, and thoroughly determined not to be the last. I soon beheld a dark object moving near and the next minute I was overjoyed to find my recreant steed, quietly searching amongst [327] the tufted moss and rushes for a scanty supper. My associated knew not what to make of this fresh discovery. Some of them, I believe, eyed him with deep suspicion; and more than one glance was given at his hoofs, to see if they were not cloven.

Order, however, being re-established, we again set forward with what proved a useful auxiliary to our train. We had not travelled far, when I was again aware of the peculiar snort by which he manifested his alarm, and it was with difficulty I got him onwards a few paces, when he stood still, his head drawn back, as if from some object that lay in his path. I knew the cause of his terror, and giving the bridle to one of my attendants, cautiously proceeded, followed by the maiden and her lover; who, to do him justice, shewed a tolerable share of courage—at any rate, in the presence of his mistress. Soon I recognised the spot, where yet unmoved lay the bleeding carcass. The girl started when she beheld the grim features, horribly drawn together and convulsed, as if in the last agony. I was obliged to muster the requisite courage to attempt its removal; and raising it from the sand, I procured assistance in placing it across the horse, though not without a most determined opposition on the part of the animal. Throwing a cloak over the body, we made the best of our way back; and on arriving at the house, I found [328] the only vacant apartment where I could deposit my charge was a narrow loft over the outhouse, the entrance to which was both steep and dangerous. With the assistance of my two friends, though with considerable difficulty, it was in the end deposited there, upon a miserable pallet of straw, over which we threw a tattered blanket. On returning, I found the guest-room deserted; the old woman to whom the tavern belonged—the mother, as I afterwards found, of my female companion—was hastily removing the drinking utensils, and preparing for an immediate removal to the only apartment above stairs which bore the honours of the bed-chamber. She kindly offered me the use of it for the night; but this piece of self-deprivation I could not allow; and throwing my coat over a narrow bench, I drew it near the fire, determining to snatch a little repose without robbing the good woman and her daughter of her night's comfort.

It was now past midnight; sleep was out of the question, as I lay ruminating on the mysterious events of the few past hours. The extraordinary manner in which the murdered wretch had been committed to my car, seemed an imperative called upon me to attempt the discovery of a foul and horrible crime. With the returning day I resolved to begin my inquiries, and I vowed to compass sea and land ere I gave up the pursuit. So absorbed was I in the project, [329] that I scarcely noticed the storm, now bursting forth in a continuous roll from the sea, until one wild gust, that seemed to rush by as if it would have swept the dwelling from its seat, put an end to these anticipations I watched the rattling casement, expecting every moment that it would give way, and the groaning thatch be rent from its hold. Involuntarily I arose, and approached the window. It was pitchy dark, and the roar of the sea, under the terrific sweep of the tempest, was truly awful. Never had I heard so terrible a conflict. I knew not how soon I might be compelled to quit this unstable shelter; the very earth shook; and every moment I expected the frail tenement would be levelled to its foundations. The eddying and unequal pressure of the wind heaped a huge sand-drift against the walls, which probably screened them from the full force of the blast, acting at the same time as a support to their feeble consistency; sand and earthy matter were driven about and tossed against the casement, insomuch that I almost anticipated a living inhumation. The next blast, however, generally swept off the greater portion of the deposit, making way for a fresh torrent, that poured upon the quaking roof like the rush of a heavy sea over a ship's bulwarks.

I was not destined to be left companionless in the midst of my alarms. The old woman and her daughter, too much terrified to remain quiet, [330] came down from their resting-place, which, being close within the thatch, was more exposed to the fierce beat of the tempest. A light was struck, and the dying embers once more kindled into a blaze. The old woman, whom I could not but observe with emotions of awe and curiosity, sat cowering over the flame, her withered hands half covering her furrowed and haggard cheeks; a starting gleam occasionally lighted up her grey and wasted locks, which, matted in wild elf-knots, hung about her temples. Occasionally she would turn her head, as the wind came hurrying on, and the loud rush of the blast went past the dwelling. She seemed to gaze upon it as though 'twere peopled, and she beheld the "sightless coursers of the air" careering on the storm; then, with a mutter and a groan, she again covered her face, rocking to an fro to the chant of some wild and unintelligible ditty. Her daughter sat nearly motionless, hearkening eagerly during the short intervals between the gusts; and as the wind came bellowing on, she huddled closer into the chimney corner, whither she had crept for protection.

"Such nights are not often known in these parts," said I, taking advantage as I spoke of a pause in the warfare without. The old woman made no answer; but the daughter, bending forwards replied slowly and with great solemnity: " Mother has seen the death-lights dancing upo' [331] the black sand; some ha' seen the sun gang down upon the waters that winna' see him rise again fro' the hill top."

"Is your mother a seer, then, my pretty maiden?"

"Ye're but a stranger, I guess, 'at disna ken Bridge o' the Sandy Holm— Save us! she's hearkening again for the"—

"There!—Once!" The old woman raised her hands as she spoke, and bent her head in an attitude of listening and eager expectation. I listened too, but could discover no sound, save the heavy swing of the blast and its receding growl.

"Again!" As she said this, Bridget rose from the low stool she had occupied, and hobbled towards the window. I thought a signal-gun was just then audible, as from some vessel in distress. Ere I could communicate this intelligence, another and a nearer roll silenced all conjecture. It was indeed but too evident that a vessel was in the offing, and rapidly driving towards the shore, from the increasing distinctness of the signals.

Old Bridget stood by the window; her dim and anxious eyes peering through the casement, as if she could discern the fearful and appalling spectacle upon the dark billows.

"Your last! your last, poor wretches!" she cried, as a heavy roll of wind brought another [332] report with amazing distinctness to the ear. "And now the death-shriek!—another, and another!—ye drop into the deep waters, and the gulf is not gorged with its prey. Bridget Robson, girl and woman, has ne'er watched the blue dancers but she has heard the sea-gun follow, and seen the red sand decked with the spoil—Wench, take not of the prey; 'tis accursed!"

The beldame drew back after uttering this anathema, and again resumed her station near the hearth.

The storm now seemed to abate, and, as if satisfied with the mischief at this moment consummating, the wind grew comparatively calm. The gusts came by fitfully, like the closing sobs of some fretful and peevish babe, not altogether ceasing with the indulgence of its wishes. As I stood absorbed in a reverie, the nature of which I cannot now accurately determine, the maiden gently touched my arm.

"Sir, will ye gang to the shore? Ise warrant the neighbours are helping, and we may save a life though we cannot gie it."

She was wrapped in a thick cloak, the hood thrown forward, and the horn lantern again put in requisition, fitted up for immediate service. We opened the door with considerable difficulty, and waded slowly through the heavy sand-drifts towards the beach. The clouds, shattered and driven together in mountainous heaps, were [333] rolling over the sky, a dark scud sweeping over their huge tops, here and there partially illuminated by the moonbeams; the moon was still obscured, but a wild and faint light, usually seen after the breaking up of a storm, just served to shew the outline of objects not too remote from our sphere of vision.

My companion acted as guide, and soon brought me to an opening in the hills, which led directly down to the beach. Immediately I saw lights before us, moving to an fro, and the busy hum of voices came upon the wind; forms were indistinctly seen hurrying backward and forward upon the very verge of the white foam boiling from the huge billows. Hastening to the spot, we found a number of fishermen—their wives assisting in the scrutiny—carefully examining the fragments of the wreck which the waves were from time to time casting up, and throwing with a heavy lunge upon the shore. Either for purposes of plunder, or for the more ostensible design of contributing to their preservation, sundry packages were occasionally conveyed away, subsequently to an eager examination of their contents. My associate ran into the thickest of the group, anxiously inquiring as to the fate of the crew, and if any lives had been preserved.

"I guess," cried an old hard-featured sinner, "they be where they'll need no lookin' after. Last brast' o' wind, six weeks agone next St. Barnaby, [334] I gied my cabin to the lady and her bairns—and' the pains I waur like to ha' for my labour—I didn't touch a groat till the parson gied me a guinea out o' th' 'scription—but I may gang gaily hoam to-night. There's no live lumber to stow i' my loft; the fishes ha' the pick o' the whole cargo this bout."

"Canna we get the boats? I can pull an oar, thou knows Darby, wi' the best on 'em," inquired the female.

"Boats!" exclaimed Darby, "ne'er a boat would live but wi' keel uppermost—Ise not the chap to go to Davy Jones to-night picked i' brine broth, my bonny Kate."

"Thou'rt a greedy glead; Ise go ask Simon Stockfish; but I'll warrant thou'lt be hankering after the reward, an' the biggest share to thine own clutches."

She turned away from the incensed fisherman; and proceeding to a short distance, we found a knot of persons gathered around a half-drowned wretch, who owed his appearance again upon land to having been lashed on a boom, which the sea had just cast ashore. Almost fainting from cold and exhaustion, he was undergoing a severe questioning from the by-standers—each wishing to know the name of the ship, whether bound, and the whole particulars of the disaster. We just came in time for his release; and I soon had the satisfaction to find the poor fellow in my [335] quarters, before a comfortable fire, his clothes drying, and his benumbed limbs chafed until the circulation was again pretty nigh restored. After drinking a tumbler of grog, he appeared to recover rapidly; and we found, on inquiry, that he was the master of the vessel just wrecked on the coast. He shook his head on a further inquiry as to the fate of her crew. "A score as good hands," said he, "are gone to the bottom as ever unreefed a clean topsail or hung out a ship's canvass to the win—I saw them all go down as I lashed myself to the jib-boom." He groaned deeply; but speedily assuming a gayer tone, requested a quid and a quiet hammock. "My lights are nearly stove in, my head hangs as loose as a Dutchman's shrouds; a night's sleep will make all taut again."

Old Bridget was gone to bed; and unless the sailor chose to occupy the straw pallet at present in the possession of a guest, whose mysterious arrival seemed to be the forerunner of nothing but confusion and disaster, there did not seem any chance of obtaining a birth, save by remaining in his present situation. I told him of the dilemma, but Kate replied: "We can just take the body fro' the bed; it winna' tak' harm upo' the chest i' the fur' nook. The captain will not may be sleep the waur' for quiet company."

He did not seem to relish the idea of spending the night even with so quiet a companion; but as [336] it seemed the least disagreeable alternative, we agreed to plot him to the chamber, and help the miserable pallet to change occupants. The corpse we concluded to lay on some clean litter, used for the bedding of the cattle. We conducted the stranger to his dormitory, which was formerly a hay-loft, until converted into an occasional sleeping-room for the humble applicants who sometimes craved a night's lodging at the Sandy Holm.

The only entrance was by a crazy ladder, and so steep, that I was afraid our feeble companion would find considerable difficulty in climbing to his chamber. It was my intention to have prevented him from getting a sight of the ghastly object that occupied his couch; but, pressing foremost, he ran up the ladder with surprising agility, gaining the top ere I had made preparations for the ascent. I mounted cautiously, and giving him the light whilst I made good my landing, he went directly to the bed. I had set my foot on the floor, and was lending a hand to Kate, who had still to contend with the difficulties of the way, when I heard a dismal and most appalling shriek. Starting round, I beheld the stranger gazing on the couch; his eyeballs almost bursting from their sockets, and the most vivid expression of horror and amazement visible in his countenance. I ran to him, as the light dropped from his grasp—catching it ere it fell, I [337] perceived his eyes rivetted on the livid and terrific features of the corpse. My limbs grew stiff with horror; imaginings of strange import crowded on my mind; I knew not how to shape them into any definite form, but stood trembling and appalled before the dark chaos whence they sprung. Scarcely knowing what I said, still I remember the first inquiry that burst from my lips—"Knowest thou that murdered man?"

The words were scarcely uttered, when the conscience-stricken wretch exclaimed, in accents which I shall never forget, "Know him! yesterday he sat at my helm. I had long borne him an evil grudge, and I brooded on revenge. The devil prompted it—he stood at my elbow. It was dark, and the fiend's eyes flashed when I aimed the blow. It descended with a heavy crash, and the body rolled overboard. He spoke not, save once; it was when his hated carcass rose to the surface. I heard a faint moan; it run on my ear like the knell of death; the voice rushed past—a low sepulchral shout; in my ear it echoed with the cry of 'MURDER!"

Little remains to be told; he persisted to the last in this horrible confession. He had no wish to live; and the avenging arm of retributive justice closed the world and its interests for ever on a wretch who had forfeited all claims to its protection—cast out, and judged unworthy of a name and a place amongst his fellow-men.

Title

By the Editor of the "Chronicles of London Bridge." [Thomson, Richard.] "Saint Agnes' Fountain. The Romance of a Finsbury Archer." FMN 1826. 350-378. [350]

SAINT AGNES' FOUNTAIN:
THE ROMANCE OF A FINSBURY ARCHER.
By the Editor of the "Chronicles of London Bridge."

> —— I am advised to give her music o'mornings;
> they say it will penetrate.
> SHAKSPEARE.

> A little Fountain-cell,
> Where water, clear as diamond-spark,
> In a stone basin fell.
> SCOTT'S Marmion.

IT is very well known to every one who is at all acquainted with the ancient history or topography of London, that the northern part of Finsbury-Fields, that is to say, from the present Bunhill Row almost to Islington, was once divided into a number of large irregular pieces of ground, enclosed by banks and hedges, constituting the places of exercise for the famous City Archers. Along the boundaries of each of these fields were set the various marks for shooting, formerly known under the names of Targets, Butts, Prickes, and Rovers; all of which were to be shot at with different kinds of arrows. They were also distinguished by their own respective titles, which were derived either from their situation, their proprietors, the person by whom there were erected, the name of some famous archer, or [351] perhaps from some circumstance now altogether unknown. These names, however, were often sufficiently singular; for in an ancient map of Finsbury-Fields, yet extant, there occur the titles of "Martin's Monkie." the "Red Dragon," "Theefe in the Hedge," and the "Mercer's Maid." Indeed one of these names, not less remarkable, was given so late as the year 1746, in consequence of a person, named Pitfield, having destroyed an ancient shooting-butt, and being obliged to restore it by order of an Act passed in 1632; the Artillery Company, to which it belonged, engraved upon the new mark the significant title of "Pitfield's Repentance." The general form of the Finsbury shooting-butts, was that of a lofty pillar of wood, carved with various devices of human figures and animals, gaily painted and gilt; but there was also another kind, of which some specimens have remained until almost the present day. These consisted of a broad and high sloping bank of green turf, having tall wings of stout wooden paling, spreading out on each side. Such shooting-butts, however, were chiefly for the practice of the more inexpert archers, and not for those, who, like Master Shallow's "old Double, would have clapt in the clout at twelve score, and carried you a forehand shaft at fourteen, and fourteen and a half." Upon this bank of turf was hung the target, and sometimes the [352] side paling stretched out so as to form a long narrow lane for the archers to stand in; the principal intent of them being to protect spectators or passers-by from the danger of a random arrow, or an unskilful marksman: the latter, however, if in the Artillery Company, was not responsible for any person's life, if, previously to letting fly his arrow, he exclaimed "Fast!" The marks were erected at various distances from shooting-places, some being so near as seventy-three yards, and others as far distant as sixteen score and two; though the ancient English bow is said sometimes to have been effective at so immense a distance as four hundred yards, or nearly a quarter of a mile. The fields in which these butts were place, were, in the time of Elizabeth, a morass, subdivided by so many dikes and rivulets, that the ground was often new-made where the bowmen assembled, and bridges were thrown over the ditches to form a road from one field to another. Like the Slough of Despond, however, they swallowed so many cart-loads, yea, waggon-loads of materials for filling them up, that old Stow once declared his belief to be, that if Moor-Fields were made level with the battlements of the City Wall, they would be little the drier, such was the marshy nature of the ground.

Notwithstanding all these inconveniences, however, the Finsbury and Moor-Fields were not [353] even anciently left wholly uninhabited: in 1498 they were occupied by orchards and gardens, and near the site of Chiswell-street stood the modern manorial residence of the Fynes family, which first gave name to the estate. Even in the moor itself, too, were scattered some few houses, connected by the bridges and causeway already mentioned; and one of these was, in the latter part of the reign of Elizabeth, a famous place of entertainment for the Archers frequenting the spot. It stood a little to the north of Bunhill-Fields, near the shooting-butt known by the name of "Friar Tuck;" and it mounted for a sign the head of an Archer in the gayest caparison of the time, under which the artist had very gravely written, "Thys is the Bowmanne of Lockesley," not considering that Robin Hood lived nearly three hundred years before. However, as old Jasper Butts, the host, could draw good ale and wine, play passing well at the quarter-staff, kept a plentiful table for the London Archers, was a merry man over a flagon, a tall fellow in a wrestling match, had a pretty ward—Mistress Mildred Paget,—and, above all, could deliver his shaft fairly at thirteen score and odd yards,—why, his guests marked not the anachronism of his sign, but filled his house and his pockets upon all occasions.

It was early in the morning of the 16th of September, 1583, when the sun was beginning [354] to dissipate the exhalations which ever arose from the marshes of Moor-Fields, that a party of young men, habited like City Archers, but carrying with them various instruments of music, arrived before the door of the Bowman of Lockesley. The foremost two formed a peculiar contrast to each other: one of them was a short thin figure, dressed in a suit of the most fashionable cut which his tailor could devise, and wearing his amber-coloured beard trimmed down to a curved point. His face expressed, if expression can exist in vacuity, a vast deal of satisfaction with himself, blended with that silly good-humour which laughs at every thing; and it seemed, by the bright flush of his cheeks, that he had been looking into the Malmsey-flaggon, notwithstanding the day was yet so young. He wore on his head a small, pert-looking, black velvet hat, adorned with a chain and medal, and several long gaudy feathers; and, besides his bow and quiver, he had a Spanish rapier, which, from its own length and his mismanagement, was more frequently between his legs than at his side. He was evidently come out upon an expedition of great mirth and importance, and since he often turned to his companions, and especially to the one who was walking with him, laughing and chatting with an overflowing degree of happiness. The other young man was of a moderate height, rather inclining to talness, of a good [355] figure, and more plainly but handsomely clad: wearing his clothes as if an elegant habit were both familiar and proper to him. In his manner he was not less good-humoured than the other, but he was without that silly kind of laugh which preceded and ended all of his speeches: in a word, the inhabitants of the Bowman of Lockesley, so far as their sight could reach, might have guessed that the latter was a gentleman, while they might have sworn that the former was a fool.

"In truth, cousin George Mowbray," began the first of these personages, "an young Mistress Mildred like not our music, I shall take it in snuff; good sooth but I shall; for it hath cost me a matter of twenty groats to set it forth for her. But I think, coz, that the dulcimer will touch her, and the viol that Master Strum playeth so deftly, and they most excellent witty words,—she cannot but love it unfeignedly." "Depend on't she will, Master Simpcox Bridbolt," replied his friend; "thou knowst that Orpheus moved rocks with his music;—go to, thou shalt soften the heart of this Finsbury Niobe an it were as hard as London-stone, man." "Why lo you there now!" answered Simpcox, "there it is; you can deck out your speeches with such marvellous taking words, and the women like them, coz, the women like them. Now when I would speak to Mistress Mildred thus, why I've not a word for a dog, when she looketh upon me,—[356] but in the Bear-Garden, oh coz! in the Bear-Garden—there I'm at home to an ace." "But Master Simpcox," interrupted another of the party, "when you talk to Mistress Mildred, you should woo here with a lover's oaths, and swear to her of your constancy and her own beauty. Trust me, a proper man like you should never lack with for a woman." "You say sooth, Master Halberject, I am a proper man, and I can wear a rapier with any body for grace; but Mistress Mildred marks it not, or doth but laugh at me when I note it unto her. Yet I hope in Saint Michael that our music shall penetrate, for the words be most admirable rich, and well-conceited. Master Mowbray here made them for the nonce, for, having erewhile been page to my Lord of Leicester, he hath dwelt much at court, and"——"Hist," cried Master Strum, the viol-player, "here we are under Mistress Mildred's windows; so now my masters sing ye in good time, and strike off sharply, lute, cittern, and dulcimer."

"Eos lifts the veil of Night,
Phoebus' steeds ascend the skies;
Flowers, and birds, and joy, and light,
Maiden, wait thine opening eyes.

"Mounteth now the lark on high
To the clouds with tuneful glee;
Like his, to Heaven mine anthems fly,
And soars my morning song to thee." [357]

"Stand close my mates, stand close," cried Simpcox as the strain concluded, "I hear her coming to open me the casement, and then I only should be seen, ye know, and accost her in an excellent witty speech which hath also been penned for me." "To it, man, then," said Mowbray, "for I hear somewhat moving in the hanging-chamber, and thou shouldst ever strike ere the iron cools." Simpcox made no reply, but throwing off his hat, and putting himself into a most affected attitude, stretching out both his arms and one leg, he plunged at once into the most extravagant piece of euphuism which the prevailing taste of the day could furnish. "Paragon of peerless perfection!" began he, "can thy couch detain thee, O Flower of Finsbury Virginity! now that the golden-haired god hath yoked his team of light quintessent, and drives joyously up the tyrian-tinted clouds in his chariot of molten gold? Come forth, O thou Mirror of maidens! Come forth, my Radiance, and say to thine Ardency who awaits thee below"—"By the bones of Saint Becket, I think the knave's bestraught!" exclaimed the merry voice of the landlord, as he put his broad face out at the casement, which Birdbolt gazed upon with an open mouth and a foolish stare. "How now, Master Simpcox, is't you guisarding under my windows to turn my girl's brain? Hold you there, man, till I don my trunks and hosen, and [358] we'll have a morning's quart of canary together, that shall make thine eyes flash fire, like Royal Harry's, the Tower Tiger's." "You say well Master Butts!—sooth now, you say well; but I came on another guess-errand, I promise you, which was to give pretty Mistress Mildred a morning's melody. I pray you now, an you love me, get her to come unto the casement." "That shaft will scarce hit, Master Simpcox," replied the landlord; "she will not fancy any but a courtly youth, a proud piet, and thou art all too city-bred for her: what then?—why let her go and"—"Nay, that may never be, good mine host," said Simpcox, "am not I as transmewed in mine apparel as heart can desire; so that none could deem I was a mercer in the Royal Exchange? I speak the tongue of the court too, and I have set forth this music to woo her withal at my own costs and charges." "And yet thou wilt not hit the white this round, Master Simpcox; but what of that? there be other matters better worth pursuing than a woman. And I warrant me now, we shall have the field filled anon with jolly archers to practise for the great show tomorrow. The Duke of Shoreditch and his goodly troop will rest them here."

With these words, the landlord having finished his toilet, left the window, and in a few minutes came out of the house, bearing a large [359] tankard. As he encountered the friends of Simpcox, he saluted each familiarly; as—"Hah! what Master Halberject, mine ancient clothworker, how weaves thy life, man?— Master Strum, of the City Waits, I perceive; and excellent musician, trust me. What! is't thou, Master Mullet of Paul's Wharf? ay! and thy valiant cousin Oldfish of Leadenhall: good men and true, all of ye, excellent Archers every one. What, ho, knaves! within there! ale and canary for my guests! But here's a gentleman," continued he, turning to Mowbray, "whom I know not." "Good, mine host," said Simpcox, "this is my cousin, Master George Mowbray: I pray you to know Master Butts, coz. He writ for me, mine host, that excellent conceited song which we sang erewhile. In good sooth he came but to try his bolt in the shooting, but that I persuaded him to take his lute, and come with me to Mistress Mildred." "Y'are a wag, to shoot in another man's bow, and hit the mark yourself: but you're welcome all, gentles, we shall have a brave day for sport; and see now, yonder come trooping our gallant archers.

"Jolly Poebus look down in thy glory below,
And inspire us to shoot, or to sing;
For Archers still hail thee as God of the Bow,
And Poets as God of the String,—
My old Buck!
And Poets as God of the String! [360]

"Then a health to our brave British Bowmen be crown'd
In the Forest, the Field, and the Park,
May their strings be unfailing, their bows be all sound,
And their arrows fly true to the mark,—
Merry Boys!
And their arrows fly true to the mark!"

The various troops of Archers which formed the celebrated pageant of the 17th of September, now began to assemble in Finsbury-Fields, for a trial of skill previously to that famous spectacle, habited in those sumptuous dresses by which the Bowmen of Elizabeth's reign were so eminently distinguished. There came Barlow, Duke of Shoreditch; Covell, Marquess of Clerkenwell; Wood, the Marshal of the Archers; the Earl of Pancras, the Marquesses of St. John's Wood, Hoxton, Shacklewell, and many other excellent marksmen, dignified by similar popular titles, long since forgotten. There was such glittering of green velvet and satin, such flapping of the coloured damask ensigns of the leaders, such displaying of wooden shields covered with gay blazonry, such quaintly dressed masquers, such pageant-devices of the various London parishes which contributed to the show, such melodious shouts, songs, flights of whistling arrows, and winding of horns, that, as an author of the time truly says, "such a delight was taken by the witnesses thereof, as they wist not for a while where they were." But for those would enjoy this pageant to perfection, let them turn [361] over the leaves of Marshal Wood's very rare tract of "the Bowman's Glory," which really blaze with his minute description of the dresses and proceedings. Many a deed of archery, well-befiting the fame of Robin Hood himself, was the day recorded upon the Finsbury shooting-butts; and of these none were more applauded than Master Mowbray's, who many times hit the white, and twice split to pieces the arrows of a successful shooter. "Now, by my holidame!" said Butts, as he drank the health of the young Archer in the rural banquet which followed the sports, "Finsbury-Fields have been honoured this day beyond what they ever were since Britain began." "Not so, mine host," said Mowbray, "for in them lies interred the heart of one of the last and bravest knights who ever went to Palestine; and he was mourned by such an ardent and holy affection, that the world itself can shew no equal to it." "Marry now," said Pipeclay, the potter of Moorgate, "I've lived by these fields man and boy any time these forty year, and I've never heard of that yet." "But I doubt not," returned Mowbray, "that you very well know St. Agnes' Spring, which lies to the east of these moors." "Ay," interrupted the host, "who knows not that? I remember me that in Queen Mary's days, Father Mumblemass, the priest of Cripplegate, used to say that it wrought miracles; but I never try [362] water whilst canary or sack is to be had." "Now truly, cousin George Mowbray," cried Birdbolt, and he was loudly joined in his request by several others of the party,—"if it may stand with your liking, I beseech you tell us the tale you wot of, and we shall be much bounden to you therefore." "Nay, my masters," replied Mowbray, "an that be your will, it is not worth a denial; and so ye will take it as a Bowman's romaunt, plain and undecked as it is,—why, give me your patient hearing."

Our old English Chronicles tell us, that after the death of Richard the Lion-hearted, his next successors, although they took the cross, as if intending like him to fight bravely in the Holy Land, never had the valour or the good fortune to get thither; for John Lackland assumed it, that he might be free from the demands concerning the Great Charter; and Henry of Winchester had too many wars in his own country to allow him to go abroad to look for fighting. All the succeeding crusades, therefore, with the exception of one, were undertaken by the French kings; but in the year 1240, Richard, Earl of Cornwall, King of the Romans, and brother to our Henry the Third, headed an expedition from England in the seventh crusade. The issue of this enterprise was not only unsuccessful in itself, but also terrible fatal to numbers of the brave men who [363] had engaged in it. The intrigues of the ambassadors of Frederick the Second, Emperor of Germany, and the Mahometan court, ended in a truce between them, which cut off all hope of aid from that quarter; while the dissensions of the Templars and the Knights of St. John of Jerusalem, were, in great degree, the cause of a sanguinary defeat of the crusaders at Gaza. Hence it was, that Richard Fitz-Roy could effect no greater benefit for the Christian cause than the conclusion of a peace with the Sultan of Egypt, in 1241, after which he returned to England.

In this crusade, one of the bravest knights who took the cross was Sir John de Fynes, a soldier who had been attached to the royal party throughout the continued anarchy to the royal party throughout the continued anarchy of John's reign, and the numerous discontents which had already disturbed that of Henry the Third. He was a knight of such well-known valour, that the insurgent barons had often attempted to draw him to their party, though his small castle, standing in these marshy grounds of Moor-Fields, was a fortress of too little value for them to march against. In the reign of Henry the Third, the district of London which we now call Finsbury, was an immense morass, or rather a number of large fens, in many places under water; which, in the winter, were commonly frozen into one sheet of ice. As the ground rose toward Isling-[364] ton, the remains of the great forest with which Middlesex was once covered, stretched itself out like a broad black belt skirting the northern boundary of the county; and the only way of approaching that place was by certain artificial paths, visible enough in dry weather, though, after a storm, the road to foot-passengers and those unacquainted with the country was wholly impassable. As these paths were originally made for the convenience of reaching certain particular points, so one of them, partly constructed of large stones rudely placed, formed a kind of causeway, leading to a tall and gloomy square tower, seated on a rising ground, and defended from the inundations of the neighbouring country by such skill as the age afforded. The shape of the edifice appeared to be of a Roman character, as if it had been built during the reign of the Caesars in Britain, and had been abandoned on account of its unhappy situation; but some later possessor had enclosed it with a strong embattled wall of chequered brick and stone, having a high gateway between two turrets, of that form which we still call King John's gates. Above the entrance appeared a shield, bearing the rude figure of a lion rampant, carved in stone, having a label issuing from his mouth, bearing the family legend, "Fynd to the Feld," in large Saxon characters. Of this, the literal signification is "Foe to the Field," and it was [365] adopted by the house of Fynes as its motto and war-cry of defiance. In this fortress then resided Sir John de Fynes, a plain, blunt, English soldier, the faithful companion of Richard the First in his crusades; and his earnest desire was that he might yet fall upon the plains of Palestine. His lady, Isabella de Fynes, had been dead some years; but yet so far was he from the rude spirit of his time, that he could never transfer to another the vow of affection which he had made to her. The knight therefore remained a widower, with two daughters, Agnes and Maria, who were rapidly approaching that age when the heart feels other affections than those which arise from filial love; and their father felt himself detained in Britain only until he should have bestowed them worthily in marriage—but his next hopes and wishes were centred in Jerusalem. He had given them the best education and accomplishments that the time was capable of furnishing; and he had the satisfaction of seeing in them his own firmness, courage, and loftiness of feeling, blended with the milder virtues of his departed Isabella.

Such were the inhabitants of Fynes Castle, to which, one morning, a horseman was observed approaching rapidly along the causeway; and in a short time he was discerned to be Sir John's chief esquire, Oliver Vauntbras, around whom, as he rode into the outer bailey, all the do-[366]mestics flocked for news from the court, from which he had so speedily returned. "Well, friend Oliver," began several voices at once, "what tidings, man? what tidings? where sits the court now? how looks King Henry to the barons? heard'st aught from the holy pope? who do men say now shall be archbishop of Canterbury? and"—"The foul fiend himself, for my part!" returned Oliver, shaking himself free, and giving some of the nearest inquirers no very gentle rebuffs with his mailed hand—"Here's a coil! by the bones, I think Satan is in you! what have ye to do with either king or court? But hark ye, fellows, thus stands the world: kings want gold, lords want power, the pope wants both, and the devil wants all. And now cease your questioning, and let Sir John know that I have sped his errand and would speak with him thereon; for I have tidings for him, though not for you."

When the esquire was summoned into the presence of his lord, he found himself seated on a kind of oaken throne, or settle, under a canopy in his great hall, upon the dais, or elevated platform at the upper end. He was engaged in feeding a hawk, whilst his daughters, according to the custom of the time, were seated on embroidered cushions below him, and near them stood a rude kind of ivory hard, as if Maria, the elder, who was gifted with a very peculiar talent [367] for sacred melody, had been delighting her father with some of those metrical hymns of the Roman church, the tunes of which were so ancient, that they have been supposed to be the identical music adapted to the Odes of Horace. "How now, Oliver!" began the knight as his esquire entered the hall; "what says the king?" "He greets you well, Sir Knight," answered the soldier, "and will think of your motion anon; but farther answer he gave me not, seeing that he is now pressed by raising supplies, and the factions between our bishops and the Italian priests, who are come to get gold for the pope and livings for themselves." "Alas, my poor master!" sighed Sir John, "thou art ever doomed, I fear, to be involved in strife with thine own followers in thine own land, instead of carrying fire and sword in Palestine at the head of an English army of crusaders. And what farther, Oliver?" "Briefly this my lord, that the brave Richard, Earl of Cornwall, much in grief for his lady's late death, hath vowed to collect soldiers and depart for the Holy Land. He also greets you well, and prays you to gather what force you may, and meet him at Dover on the feast of Saint Michael next, to join the crusade." "And that I will do blithely," cried Sir John, a martial delight spreading itself over his whole countenance; "by the soul of my father!" continued he, tossing the hawk to his perch, "but it's the [368] most spirit-stirring news I've heard these ten years. And know'st thou who goes with him, knave?" "The best of the baronage, so please you," returned the esquire, "but in chief, William Marshal, Earl of Pembroke, and William Longsword, Earl of Salisbury." "Be it so," said the knight; "braver leaders, or more loyal peers, I seek not: and now where sits the royal Richard until he embark?" "At his castle of Berkhamstead, in Hertfordshire," answered Oliver, "where he bade me bring him your answer straight, but first to deliver this ring as a true token, and to call on you by your ancient war-cry, Fynd to the Feld!" "And when I reply not truly to that call," exclaimed the knight, "my hand must be powerless, and my heart as cold, as the tomb can make them! Hasten to the prince then, Oliver; say that I will not fail him; and, God seconding our swords, we will plant the cross upon the towers of Gaza, or lay our bones beneath it. The Black Lion of Fynes will come forth to the battle; there is my signet-ring; away, good Oliver, away."

It is easy to conceive the emotions with which this message, so gratifying to the knight, was received by his daughters. They gazed upon each other with tears gushing from their eyes, as they thus beheld themselves about to be deprived of the only protector who was yet remaining to them; and when the esquire quitted the hall, [369] they gave full vent to their feelings, by throwing themselves, weeping aloud, upon their father's neck. "Why, how now, girls!" exclaimed Sir John in a jesting tone, "is this the countenance of an old crusader's daughters, to blench thus when war is made against the infidels? St. Mary defend! but I'd rather be the first to scale the walls of Gaza, than the proudest baron that ever bore pennon. I would truly," continued he, in a softened tone, "if it had pleased Heaven, have been content to rest here at home, at least until I had seen you both worthily bestowed in marriage, and then no matter how soon I had laid mine old bones in the Holy Sepulchre, and sought mine Isabella in heaven: but when a crusade marches from England, why ye wot well it would be foul scorn for a Knight of St. John, and a soldier who fought with Richard the Lion-hearted at Acre, to sit here unarmed like a hawk in his mewing." "The will of God be done!" said Agnes, "and it is his cause in which you are arming, my father; but"—"But what, my fearful little Agnes—hast not seen in thy missal, girl, how the stripling David overthrew me the Paynim, for all his brigandine and lance? And hath not Father Boniface told us full oft to take unto us the armour of God, which he saith meaneth going on the crusade? Dry your tears, lambkins, dry your tears, I shall return to you, fear not, and with a brave rich husband for each of you [370] from the crusading army—not a fellow who takes up arms against his king, under a specious device of liberty; but a knight of worth, who hath taken a pagan by the beard, and who when he dies may have his effigy cross-legged lying on his tomb." "Be it so, my father," cried Maria, in a composed, solemn voice, to that which the knight had spoken half in jest; "be it so—for until I see you again, may that God whose cross you go to defend forsake me if I marry or hold communion with any man!" "Sayst thou so, my girl!" replied the knight; "and whither wilt thou go whilst I am away then? for England is all too wild a place for two fair maidens to live alone in." "I will betake me to the Hospital of Bethlehem, adjoining the Moor-Fields, and there I will remain until you shall return to release me from my vow." "And for me," said Agnes, "I will remain in the castle which gave me birth; and the room from which my mother's spirit took its flight to heaven shall be to me as a cell: for until I shall again behold thee, my father, I will not go forth into the world to be made lady-queen of England itself. And God so bless me as I shall keep my vow!" "Well, but know ye, minions," asked Sir John, "that a voyage to Palestine is all another matter from going across the sea to Normandy; ay, and a battle in the holy country tenfold fiercer than a tilt with a Christian soldier? [371] for those dogs of Mahomet fight like the very sons of Satan. So then, girls, I would have ye bethink you that it may be long ere I come back again, and your youth will fly in time, as mine hath done." "Be it years or be it days, my father," said Maria, in the same tone of exalted feeling, "till I again behold you, I will not once think of man or of marriage; and for that the expedition is full of danger, I will cause to be erected for your sake, and for the sakes of all the souls of the crusaders, a cross of stone at the gate of Bethlehem Priory which I enter; and there will I offer up my orisons at morning and at midnight that we may meet again."

"Bless thee, my child!" said the crusader, "through thy piety, and our own cause, I trust to see the blessed land free from the very name of an infidel." "And now, my father," said Agnes, "hear my vow, and mark what I will do for thee. A short distance eastward from this place is a fair spring of crystal water continually flowing; from which, and because that the Christmas rose groweth there without culture, the city maidens call it the spring of St. Agnes le Claire; and the blessed martyr herself had endued it with a miraculous power of healing. I will enclose this holy spring in a fair stone well, and erect above it a crucifix, that the sick may remember from whom all healing virtue floweth, and bless Him by whom they are made whole. [372] And this little fountain shall be unto me as an oratory; for there will I offer up my matins and vespers in perfect maidenhood, till thou shalt return again from Palestine." "And if it be Heaven's will," said the knight, "we shall meet, although I should return from the dead to thee, or though the infidel cimeters were tenfold keener. What would ye say now to see me return suddenly some night, when ye are praying at the cross and fountain? stranger things have been." "Come, my father, only come," replied Agnes, "and whether at morn or at midnight, that I reck not." So concluded a conversation which had excited a much greater depth of feeling than any of the party had anticipated: and the knight left his daughters with more emotion than he was wont to express, to give orders for his departure, which followed in a few days.

The habit assumed by Sir John de Fynes, on the morning of his setting forth for Palestine, was that peculiar to the famous Knights Hospitallers of St. John of Jerusalem. He was clothed then in a massive suit of chain-mail, which hung in large heavy folds upon his body and arms; looking, for the most part, of a dark iron-grey colour, shining only in some few places which were exposed to a constant friction. His legs were also enclosed in armour of the same species. But a principal feature of the crusader's habit, was the large crimson war-mantle of his order. [373] On the left breast of his robe was the eight-pointed cross of the order, formed of white cloth, and alluding to the eight beatitudes of Christianity. Such was the costume of Sir John de Fynes, as he passed his portal with a thoughtful step, and threw himself upon his horse, which, barded as he was from counter to flank, bearing the knight's additional weight, reared up in seeming pride at having so brave a soldier upon his back. Sir John dashed one tear from his fine manly countenance as he looked for the last time upon his two pallid daughters; and then turning to his retinue, cried, in a voice of thunder, "Fynes to the field! set on!" The troop was instantly in motion, and in a short time it had left the marshy grounds of the castle, and even the city of London itself, far behind.

It is reported by those who have endeavoured to collect the scattered fragments of this legend, that when Agnes and Maria de Fynes entered on their solitary course of life, the maidens of London would often visit them, endeavour to recall them to the world and its pleasures, and particularly entreat them to marry. For it must be observed, that when the Duke of Cornwall and his diminished army of crusaders returned to England, neither Sir John de Fynes nor his esquire was with them. It was asserted, however, that they could not have fallen at Gaza, because all the [374] Christian corses had been recognized and carefully interred into the holy ground; nor had they died of the plague, which afterwards thinned the fragments of the army, because they had been missing long before it brake out. All that could be imagined of them, therefore, was that they had been either made captive by the infidels, or else had joined the crusaders of France, who yet remained in Palestine.

Years, however, rolled away; no tidings came of the knight; and the once peerless beauty of his daughters began to be changed into a wan and premature old age, occasioned by their anxiety, their solitary life, and the severities of their vows, which they continued to keep in all their primitive force. At length, when all hope seemed at an end, as Agnes de Fynes was one clear midnight keeping the vigil of her patroness at her blessed fountain, her thoughts turned upon her father, and his promise to return to them perchance during their night-prayers at the cross and the well. Her meditations were suddenly interrupted by a faint, but long-drawn sigh; and upon looking up, she saw a stranger sitting on the well-side, wrapped in a red mantle, bearing a white eight-pointed cross on the shoulder, whilst the moon, glancing faintly upon his figure, shewed that he was habited beneath in chain-armour. "Holy Virgin!" exclaimed Agnes, starting up, "in the name of God, what art [375] thou?" "Am I then forgotten, Agnes de Fynes?" said the figure, turning towards her the countenance of her father, though, greatly changed by time and the climate of Palestine, as well as by the warfare in which he had been engaged; "am I then forgotten, Agnes de Fynes? Said I not that I might return suddenly, when thou wert praying by the fountain reared by thy piety?—and lo! I have come; God hath permitted it." "Welcome, my father, welcome at noon, or at midnight welcome," cried Agnes; and she was about to cast herself upon his breast, when he prevented her by a sign, saying, "Not now, my child; I trust we shall embrace hereafter, but now mine arms are all too cold to clasp thine in them." "Alas! my father," said Agnes, looking with sorrow at his pale thin visage and silvery hair, "thou art sadly changed from the bold warrior who departed from England." "Yes, Agnes de Fynes, the withering gloom of the Turkish prison, in which myself and my follower were so long confined, changes the proud glance of the soldier like the grave; but I am now at rest! I have come from far to behold thee, my child, and thou, too, art sadly altered—but my stay must be brief, yet doubt not but my heart shall remain with you for ever!" He bent forward as he spake, stretching forth his hands as if to bless her, whilst Agnes, overcome by a feeling of awe, which the time and circumstances were [376] well calculated to inspire, fell on one knee before him. A cold spell seemed to detain her for some moments in that position, and when she found courage to rise—she was alone!

The remainder of the night was passed in anxious conjectures; and early in the morning Agnes walked out from Fynes Castle towards Bethlehem Priory to relate the adventure to Maria, who had there succeeded to the dignity of abbess. When she arrived at the gate and cross, she was met by her sister, who had evidently something of great importance to communicate, as she addressed her, saying, "Sister Agnes, I was about to make you an early visit this morning, by command of our father, whom I saw last night seated by this cross." "You saw him, sister Maria! why, he was with me at St. Agnes' Well as the bell chimed for lauds." "Holy St. Anne!" exclaimed Maria, "at that very hour he stood before me at this cross, wrapped in his red mantle; and when I would have embraced him, he waved it, saying, that the cold of his arms would chill my blood, but that his heart should remain with us for ever."

They soon reached the castle; and upon entering it, Agnes was informed that a stranger from Palestine was waiting to have audience of her. When the sisters passed with palpitating hearts into the hall, an ancient man, dressed in the torn fragments of an esquire's habit, and [377] wrapped in a dark mantle, in which he seemed to conceal something that he was bearing, was introduced to their presence. "You are then from the Holy Land, friend?" began Agnes to the soldier; "all who come from thence must be welcome unto us: if you seek food or relief, such as our poor house can offer is yours, were it for that single petition only." "Noble ladies," replied the stranger, "I have, it is true, but newly escaped from Gaza, where I have been these thirty years imprisoned by the infidels. With me also was confined a brave crusade knight, who died in his fetters; but ere he died, he caused me to swear that I would take his heart from him, and if I should ever escape, bear it with me to England, to be interred in the lands of his own castle in the Moor-Fields, near to London." "And," said Maria with anxiety, "the knight's name was"— "Sir John de Fynes," replied the soldier: "behold the casket!" he continued, producing an urn from beneath his cloak, "'Let my heart,' said he in dying, 'remain with my children forever!'"

The mysterious visitor of the preceding night was thus made clear to have been the spirit of the brave crusader; and Agnes and Maria de Fynes wept loud and bitterly over the last relics of their father. Indeed, they appear to have lamented him with a sorrow to which history shews no parallel; for it is related that they held a [378] solemn mourning for him for three hundred days, and then buried his heart in these fields, first called from that circumstance Fynes-bury. They both retired for life into the Priory of Bethlehem, and at their death they gave Finsbury-Fields to the City for the London maidens to walk in. An old song, to the tune of "Where is my True Love?" printed in the "Crown Garland of Golden Roses," yet commemorates some of these events; and the winter rose yet adorns, and healing virtues are yet to be found, in the pure crystal waters of SAINT AGNES' FOUNTAIN.

Literary Annual

Forget Me Not; A Christmas and New Year's Present for MDCCCXXVII. Ed. Frederic Shoberl. London: R. Ackermann, 1827. Printer: Thomas Davison, Whitefriars.

Title

Lyndsay, David. [Dods, Mary Diana.] "The Three Damsels. A Tale of Halloween." FMN 1827. 79-86.[10] [79]

THE THREE DAMSELS.
A Tale of Halloween.
By David Lyndsay, Esq.

"COME hither, my beautiful Jean, and my fairy Lilias," said the venerable Countess of Moray to her laughing, happy grand-daughters—"come hither, my children, and spend your Halloween with me. It is true I have not prepared the charms of the night, nor am I ready to join you in the incantations of the season, but I have a tale may suit it well; and you will not like it the less because the gray head tells you with her own lips the story of her day, when her locks were as bright as the berry, and her eyes as beaming as your own."

"That, in truth, shall we not, noble grandam," said the sparkling Lilias; "but yet would I have the charm of Halloween. Ah, little canst thou dream how dear this night is to the expecting maiden!—Let us perform the rites of the even, and to-morrow, grandam, thy tale shall find us most attentive listeners."

"Ah, true Scots!" said the Countess, "thus clinging to the wonderful, and seeking to peep into futurity: but try not the charm, my children, if you love me. Alas! I think not of it without tears and a sorrow unspoken till now; for the fate of a friend, dear to my early youth, gushes to my bosom. Sit, my children, and my story shall repay you for this loss of your time; me it will also please to speak of the things gone by: and if it convince you, as I trust it will, of the folly of these superstitions, I [80] shall have more than gained my purpose. Will my children listen?" "What is there we can refuse you, noble grandam?" said the lovely Jean, burying her locks of amber amid the snowy curls of the venerable Countess. "Speak on, then; you have made us listeners already—and hark! wind, and rain, and snow—a goodly night for a tale. Tell on, dear grandam; the fire is bright, the lamp is clear, and we are seated gravely, our thoughts composed to attention—now for thy wondrous tale!"

"It was on these very eve, many years since, my children," began the noble lady to her auditors, "that there three lovely daughters of a noble house assembled <u>together in a dreary</u> wood to try the charm of the night, which if successful was to

10 Maria Diana Dods (a cross-dressing poet) used the male pseudonym "David Lyndsay" when publishing in the annuals. See Betty T. Bennett's work, *Mary Diana Dods: A Gentleman and a Scholar* (Johns Hopkins UP, 1994).

give to their earnest sight the phantom form of the lover who was afterwards to become the husband. Their powerful curiosity had stifled their fear (for they were as timid as beautiful) on their first setting out on this expedition; but, on finding themselves alone in the dark and melancholy wood, some touches of cowardice and compunction assailed them together, and they determined by a somewhat holy beginning to sanctify the purpose which had brought them thither. They were too young to laugh at this mock compact between God and the Devil, and therefore when Catherine, the eldest sister, began, in an audible voice, to recite the prayer against witchcraft, the others joined in it most devoutly. Now then, fortified against evil, their courage rose with every additional sentence; and when the soft voice of the young Agnes, the loveliest and youngest of the three, steadily responded the [81] 'amen,' they were as courageous as was necessary, and no longer fearful of the power of the evil one. I know not, my children, all the forms used upon this occasion; but Catherine, after repeating certain words in a solemn voice, advanced before her sisters, and quietly placed upon the ground her offering to the shade she had invoked, as by his conduct towards it she was to judge of her future prospects. It was a beautiful rose-tree which she had chosen, and the flowers were full and many; and the sisters were contemplating from a little distance the richness of their hue, when they were startled by the clashing of arms and the loud outcries of men in fierce contention, breaking upon the stillness of the night. For a moment they hesitated whether to fly or remain concealed, when their doubts were decided by the rapid approach of a stern and stately Highland chief, who, brandishing his broad sword, swept on to the rose-tree as if he would annihilate from the earth its fair and fragile beauty. Suddenly he paused—his arm was no longer raised to destroy—the weapon drooped gently down beside the tree—and they saw his blue eye look mildly and kindly on the flowers, as, bending down to gather them, he faded from their sight in the action. Catherine was by no means displeased with her fortune; and the appearance of her handsome bridegroom gave courage to the other two to hasten the coming of theirs. Marian, the second sister, removed the rose, placed a lily bough in its stead, and then, with a beating heart and wandering eye, repeated the charm. Again the silence was broken, as the quick but steady tramp of a warrior's [82] horse struck upon the ear, and the shade of a noble cavalier, dismounting from his phantom steed, advanced slowly, very slowly, towards the lily: his face was beautiful, but sad—beyond expression sad; and they saw a tear fall upon the flower as he pressed it to his lips and deposited it gently in his bosom. He too had faded like a dream, when the beautiful Agnes advanced to perform her part in the witcheries of the night. She trembled, but she would not recede, and faintly repeating the charm, hung her white handkerchief on the branch of a distant tree. This time there was no sound, but a dread and solemn silence slowly ushered in her unexpected fate. From the wood came a long and sable procession of horse and foot, following a coffin, that was steadily borne towards them: many were the ghastly attendants supporting the pall, and many were the shadowy mourners who followed. Agnes watched with breathless attention the march of the phantom dead: they advanced slowly and steadily till they came under the tree, where her white offering fluttered lightly in the air; it was seen suspended a moment above then, then dropped amidst the cavalcade, and Agnes beheld the pale fingers of the chief mourner clutch at the offering as it fell.

"Days, weeks, months, passed away, and still found Agnes drooping over her blighted hopes, and expecting the death of which the omen of the forest had assured her; but still she died not, and was every succeeding month astonished that she yet lived. She now began to doubt the truth of the omen, more especially as the Highlander had not yet wedded her sister, who was betrothed to, and [83] about to become the wife of, a favourite of the king, who had earnestly sought her hand. Agnes thought she too might now listen to a tale of love; and such a one as was soon told her by a noble lover, and of her sovereign's blood, she listened to with pleasure. Walter was now her all, and the omen of the forest was forgotten.

"The marriage of Catherine was appointed to take place at a country residence of her affianced husband, and Agnes, with her betrothed, was invited to be present. Marian too was there, and no happiness could have been more complete than that of the bridal party; but a dark night set upon this brilliant morning: ere they could reach the church which was to be the scene of their union, the Highlanders had descended in force from their mountains and assailed the unarmed guests. 'The Camerons come!' cried the shrieking maidens, and flew in all directions from their sight; the bridegroom fell in the conflict; and the bride, as she rushed to the side of her dying husband, was clasped in the arms of the insolent chief, and borne away to *his* bridal bed in the Highlands. Marian escaped the tumult, and Walter preserved his adored by the effects of his desperate valour, cutting with his sword a passage through his foes, and encouraging the armed men, who now came to their assistance, to drive the invaders from their hold. They were successful; and silence, though accompanied by sorrow, again reigned in the halls of the young and hapless bridegroom.

"But the greatest evil resulting from this cruel inroad was the sad effect it had upon the mind of Agnes. Her [84] belief in the omens of the forest again returned: her confidence in her prospects was shaken; and with the same feeling the bids the giddy wretch throw himself at once from the precipice over which he fears he shall fall, she determined to hasten the destiny which she now firmly believed to await her. Convinced by the fate of her sister of the certain fulfilment of her own, she resolved to spare her lover the anguish of beholding her expire; and, for this purpose, suddenly broke off all connexion with him, and refused to admit him to her presence. Walter's hope still struggled with his despair: he made some earnest appeals to her tenderness, her reason, and her gratitude. Agnes was deaf to all: she believe herself destined to fall an early victim to death, and that that bridegroom would snatch her from an earthly one, even at the altar's foot. Walter, heart-broken, retired from his home, and joining the cavalier armor of the king, sought in the tumult of a military life forgetfulness of the wound his calmer days had given. In the intervals of his visits to his family Marian became interested in his welfare: she saw him frequently, spoke to him of Agnes, soothed his sufferings by her compassion, and gratified his pride by her admiration. He had no thought for any other: and though he loved not Marian, yet she became his trusted friend, his companion, and finally his wife. It was her will, not his: and what woman ever failed in her determination over the mind of man! They wedded and were wretched. The heart of Walter had not been interested, and the temper of Marian was not such as to acquire its delicate preference. [85] She became jealous, irritable, perverse, and soon taught her hapless husband the difference between herself and the gentle Agnes. Such a course could have but one termination: stretched at length on that sick bed which was to be her last, she sent to desire the attendance of her younger sister. Agnes obeyed the mandate, but only arrived in time to meet the funeral procession which conducted the hapless Marian to her early grave. The widower instantly recognised, from a distance, his young heart's love, and rapidly flew to meet her; and as she shed tears of unfeigned sorrow for his loss, he took the white handkerchief she held and tenderly dried them away. O! at that moment, how deeply Agnes sighed! She beheld in this scene the fulfilment of the omen, and wept to think she had thus wasted some of the best years of her life, and trifled with her lover's happiness and her own. 'Ah, silly delusion!' she exclaimed in bitterness of heart, 'of what has thou not bereaved me!' After the period of mourning had expired, she gave her hand to Walter, and endeavoured, in making his days tranquil, to forget the felicity she had lost."

"But they were wedded, grandam dear," said the beautiful Lilias, laughing—"what more would the people have had?" "Youth, and its love, and its hope, and all its bright and gracious feeling," said the venerable Countess: "*they* had all fled with time, and nothing but their remembrance remained with Agnes and her Walter, which made their lot more bitter. He was at their wedlock past even manhood's prime; she was no longer young; [86] and though not wretched, yet they were not happy; and it was only in their descendants they looked for felicity. Agnes had found it truly, but for Walter—"

"Grandam, it is your own tale you tell and our grandsire's, I am certain, by the tears which roll down your face," replied Lilias. "Ah, I will wait Heaven's own good time for a husband, and try these charms no more. Kiss me, noble grandam: your Lilias will never forget the Tale of Halloween." The bright maiden threw herself into the arms of her venerable ancestress, and at that moment it was scarcely possible to decide which was the nobler object, the damsel in the glory of her brilliant youth, or the Countess in the calmness of her majestic age.

Title

By the Author of "The Duke of Mantua". [Roby, John.]"The Haunted Manor-House." FMN 1827. 133-159. [133]

THE HAUNTED MANOR-HOUSE.
BY THE AUTHOR OF "THE DUKE OF MANTUA."

———THE mail coach had just set me down at the entrance to a dreary and unweeded avenue. There was a double row of dark elms, interspersed with beech, neither very bowery nor very umbrageous, though, as I passed, they saluted me with a rich shower of wet leaves, and shook their bare arms, growling as the loud sough of the wind went through their decayed branches. The old house was before me. Its numerous and irregularly contrived compartments in front were streaked in black and white zig-zags—vandyked, I think, the fairest jewels of the creation call this chaste and elegant ornament. It was near the close of a dark autumnal day, and a mass of gable-ends stood sharp and erect against the wild and lowering sky. Each of these pinnacles could once boast of its admired and appropriate ornament—a little weather-cock; but they had cast off their gilded plumage for ever, and fallen from their high estate, like the once neatly trimmed mansion which I was now visiting. A magpie was perched upon a huge stack of chimneys: his black and white plumage seemed perfectly in character with the mottled edifice at his feet. Perhaps he was the wraith, the departing vision of the decaying fabric; an apparition, unsubstantial as the honours and dignities of the ancient and revered house of Etherington.

I looked eagerly at the long, low casements: a faint glimmer was visible. It proceeded only from the wan [134] reflection of a sickly sunbeam behind me, struggling through the cleft of a dark hail-cloud. It was the window where in my boyhood I had often peeped at the village clock through my little telescope. It was the nursery chamber, and no wonder that it was regarded with feelings of the deepest interest. Here the first dawnings of reason broke in upon my soul; the first faint gleams of intelligence awakened me from a state of infantine unconsciousness. It was here that I first drank eagerly of the fresh rills of knowledge; here my imagination, ardent and unrepressed, first plumed its wings for flight, and I stept forth over its threshold, into a world long since tried, and found as unsatisfying and unreal as the false glimmer that now mocked me from the hall of my fathers.

A truce to sentiment! I came hither, it may be, for a different purpose. A temporary gush will occasionally spring up from the first well-head of our affections. However homely and seemingly ill adapted, in outward show and character, for giving birth to those feelings generally designated by the epithet romantic, the place where we first breathed, where our ideas were the first moulded, formed and assimilated, as it were, to the condition of the surrounding atmosphere, (their very shape and colour determined by the medium in which they first sprung) the casual recurrence of a scene like this—forming part and parcel of our very existence, and incorporated with the very fabric of our thoughts—must, in spite of all subsequent impressions, revive those feelings, however long [135] they may have been dormant, with a force and vividness which the bare recollection can never excite.

The garden-gate stood open. The initials of my name, still legible, appeared rudely carved on the posts—a boyish propensity which most of us have indulged; and I well remember ministering to its gratification wherever I durst hazard the experiment, when first initiated into the mystery of hewing out these important letters with a rusty penknife.

Not a creature was stirring; and the nature of the present occupants, whether sylphs, gnomes, or genii, was a question not at all, as it yet appeared, in a train for solution. The front door was closed, but as I knew every turn and corner about the house, I made no doubt of soon finding out its inmates, if any of them were in the neighbourhood. I worked my way through the garden, knee-deep and rank with weed, for the purpose of reconnoitring the back-offices. I steered pretty cautiously past what memory, that great dealer in hyperbole, had hitherto pretty generally contrived to picture as a huge lake—now, to my astonishment, dwindled into a duck-pond—but not without danger from its slippery margin. It still reposed under the shadow of the old cherry-tree, once the harbinger of delight, as the returning season gave intimation of another bountiful supply of fruit. Its gnarled stump, now stunted and decaying, had scarcely one token of life upon its scattered branches. Following a narrow walk, nearly obliterated, I entered a paved court. The first tramp awoke a train of echoes, that seemed as [136] though they had slumbered since my departure, and now started from their sleep, to greet or to admonish the returning truant. Grass in luxuriant tufts, capriciously disposed, grew about in large patches. The breeze passed heavily by, rustling the dark swathe, and murmuring fitfully as it departed. Desolation seemed to have marked the spot for her own—the grim abode of solitude and despair. During twenty years' sojourn in a strange land, memory had still, with untiring delight, painted the old mansion in all its primeval primness and simplicity—fresh as I had left it, full of buoyancy and delight, to take possession of the paradise which imagination had created. I had indeed been informed, that at my father's death it became the habitation of a stranger; but no intelligence as to its present condition had ever reached me. Being at L—, and only some fifty miles distant, I could not resist the temptation of once more gazing on the old manor-house, and of comparing its present aspect with that but too faithfully engrafted on my recollections. To all appearance the house was tenantless. I tried the door of a side-kitchen, or scullery: it was fastened, but the rusty bolts yielded to no very forcible pressure; and I once more penetrated into the kitchen, that exhaustless magazine, which had furnished ham and eggs, greens and bacon, with other sundry and necessary condiments thereto appertaining, to the progenitors of our race for at least two centuries. A marvelous change!—to me it appeared as if wrought in a moment, so recently had memory reinstated the scenes of my youth in all their [137] pristine splendour. Now no smoke rolled lazily away from the heavy billet; no blaze greeted my sight; no savoury steam regaled the sense. Dark, cheerless, cold,—the long bars emitted no radiance; the hearth unswept, on which Growler once panted with heat and fatness.

Though night was fast approaching, I could not resist the temptation of once more exploring the deserted chambers, the scene of many a youthful frolic. I sprang with reckless facility up the vast staircase. The shallow steps were not sufficiently accommodating to my impatience, and I leaped rather than ran, with the intention of paying my fist visit to that cockaigne of childhood, that paradise of little fools—the nursery. How small, dwindled almost into a span, appeared that once mighty and almost boundless apartment, every nook of which was a separate territory, every drawer and cupboard the boundary of another kingdom! Three or four strides brought me to the window;—the village steeple still rose abruptly from the dark fir-trees, peacefully reposing in the dim and heavy twilight. The clock was chiming: what a host of recollections were awakened at the sound! Days and hours long forgotten seemed to rise up at its voice, like the spirits of the departed sweeping by, awful and indistinct. These impressions soon became more vivid; they rushed on with greater rapidity: I turned from the window, and was startled at the sudden moving of a shadow. It was a faint long drawn figure of myself on the floor and opposite wall. Ashamed of my fears, I was preparing to quit the apartment, when my attention [138] was arrested by a drawing which I had once scrawled, and stuck against the wall with all the ardour of a first achievement. It owed its preservation to an unlucky but effectual contrivance of mine for securing its perpetuity: a paste-brush, purloined form the kitchen, had made all fast; and the piece, impregnable to all attacks, withstood every effort for its removal. In fact, this could not be accomplished without at the same time tearing off a portion from the dingy papering of the room, and leaving a disagreeable void, instead of my sprawling performance. With the less evil it appeared each succeeding occupant had been contented; and the drawing stood its ground in spite of dust and dilapidation. I felt wishful for the possession of so valuable a memorial of past exploits. I examined it again and again, but not a single corner betrayed symptoms of lesion: it stuck bolt upright; and the dun squat figures portrayed on it appeared to leer at me most provokingly. Not a slip or tear presented itself as vantage-ground for the projected attack; and I had not other resource left of gaining possession than what may be denominated the Caesarean mode. I accordingly took out my knife, and commenced operations by cutting out at the same time a portion of the ornamental papering from the wall, commensurate with the picture. I looked upon it with a sort of superstitious reverence; and I have always thought, that the strong and eager impulse I felt for the possession of this hideous daub proceeded from a far different source than mere fondness for the memorials of childhood. Be that as it may, I am a firm believer in [139] a special Providence, and that too, as discovered in the most trivial as well as the most important concerns of life. It was whilst cutting down upon what seemed like wainscoting, over which the room had been papered, that my knife glanced on something much harder than the rest. Turning aside my spoils, I saw what through the dusk appeared very like the hinge of a concealed door. My curiosity was roused, and I made a hasty pull, which at once drew down a mighty fragment from the wall, consisting of plaster, paper, and rotten canvas; and some minutes elapsed ere the subsiding cloud of dust enabled me to discern the *terra incognita* I had just uncovered. Sure enough there was a door, and as surely did the spirit of enterprise prompt me to open it. With difficulty I accomplished my purpose; it yielded at length to my efforts; but the noise of the half-corroded hinges, grating and shrieking on their rusty pivots, may be conceived as sufficiently dismal and appalling. I know not if once at least I did not draw back, or let go my hold incontinently as the din "grew long and loud." I own, without hesitation, that I turned away my head from the opening, as it became wider and wider at every pull; and it required a considerable effort before I could summon the requisite courage to look into the gap. My head seemed as a difficult to move as the door. I cannot say that I was absolutely afraid of ghosts, but I *was* afraid of a peep from behind the door—afraid of being frightened! At length, with desperate boldness, I thrust my head plump into the chasm! [140]

Now, reader, what was it, thinkest thou, that I beheld? Thy speculations on this subject will, of course, depend entirely upon thy nerves and constitution, likewise upon thy course of education and habits of study. If, as in all probability thou art, of the gender feminine, and a little addicted to romance, poetry, and the like, then wilt thou tickle thine imagination with delightful guesses about a white lady, a lamp, and a dagger. If thy brain hath been steeped in the savoury brine of novel-reading and sentimentality, then will thy thoughts be of gloomy rooms, prisoners immured by unfeeling relatives, &c. Shouldst thou happen to be cast in a more matter-of-fact mould, strongly addicted to cry "Fudge!" at every display of trickery and folly, then mayest thou opine, what any man with three grains of sense would have guessed long since, that it was nothing but a cupboard! I might thus frame solutions proper to every character and temperament. "As the fool thinks," &c. is a trite proverb; but, suffice it to say, not one of these fancies and speculations, I take upon myself to affirm, is correct. As before mentioned, I thrust my head suddenly into the chasm, more startled at the noise produced by the celerity of my own motions than I could possibly be at any thing that was visible. As far as the darkness would permit I explored the interior, which, after all, was neither more nor less than a small closet. From what cause it had been shut out from the apartment to which it belonged, it were vain to conjecture. All that was really cognizant to the senses presented itself in the shape of a shallow closet, some four feet [141] by two, utterly unfurnished, save with some inches of accumulated dust and rubbish, that made it a work of great peril to grope out the fact of its otherwise absolute emptiness. This discovery, like many other notable enterprises, seemed to lead to nothing. I stept out of my den, reeking with spoils which I much rather had left undisturbed in their dark recesses.

Preparing for my departure and a visit to my relation in the village, who as yet had no other intimation of my arrival than a hasty note, to apprize him that I had once more set foot on English ground and intended to visit him before my return, I stepped again to the window. Darkness was fast gathering about me: a heavy scud was driven rapidly across the heavens, and the wind wailed in short and mournful gusts past the chamber. The avenue was just visible from the spot where I stood; and looking down, I thought I could discern more than one dark object moving apparently towards the house. It may be readily conceived that I gazed with more than ordinary interest as they approached; and it was not long ere two beings, in human habiliments, were distinctly seen at a short distance from the gate by which I had entered. Feeling myself an intruder, and not being very satisfactorily prepared to account for my forcible entry into the premises, and the injury I had committed on the property of a stranger, I drew hastily aside, determined to effect a retreat whenever and wherever it might be in my power. Door and window alternately presented themselves for the accomplishment of this unpleasant purpose, [142] but before I could satisfy myself as to which was the more eligible offer, as doubters generally do contrive it, I lost all chance of availing myself of either. "*Facilis descensus*"— "Easier in than out—" &c., occurred to me; and many other classical allusions, much more appropriate than agreeable. I heard voices and footsteps in the hall. The stairs creaked, and it was but too evident they were coming, and that with a most unerring and provoking perseverance. Surely, thought I, these gentry have noses like the sleuth-hound; and I made no doubt but they would undeviatingly follow them into the very scene of my labours: and what excuse could I make for the havoc I had committed? I stood stupefied, and unable to move. The thoughts of being hauled neck and heels before the next justice, on a charge of housebreaking, mayhap—committed to prison—tried, perhaps, and— the sequel was more than even imagination durst conceive. Recoiling in horror from the picture, it was with something like instinctive desperation that I flew to the little closet, and shut myself in, with all the speed and precision my fears would allow. Sure enough the brutes were making the best of their way into the chamber, and every moment I expected they would track their victim to his hiding-place. After a few moments of inconceivable agony, I was relieved at finding from their conversation that no notion was entertained, at present, of any witness to their proceedings.

"I tell thee, Gilbert, these rusty locks can keep nothing safe. It's but some few months since we were here, [143] and thou knowest the doors were all fast. The kitchen door-post is now as rotten as touchwood; no bolt will fasten it."

"Nail it up,—nail 'em all up," growled Gilbert; "nobody'll live here now; or else set fire to 't. It'll make a rare bonfire to burn that ugly old will in."

A boisterous laugh here broke from the remorseless Gilbert. It fell upon my ear as something with which I had once been disagreeably familiar. The voice of the first speaker, too, seemed to sound like the echoes of childhood. A friendly chink permitted me to gain the information I sought: there stood my uncle, and his trusty familiar. In my youth I had contracted a some-what unaccountable aversion to the latter personage. I well remembered his downcast gray eye, deprived of its fellow; and the malignant pleasure he took in thwarting and disturbing my childish amusements. This prepossessing Cyclop held a tinder-box, and was preparing to light a match. My uncle's figure I could not mistake: a score of winters had cast their shadows on his brow since we had separated; but he still stood as he was wont—tall, erect, and muscular, though age had slightly drooped his proud forehead; and I could discern his long-lapped waistcoat somewhat less conspicuous in front. He was my mother's brother, and the only surviving relation on whom I had any claim. My fears were set at rest, but curiosity stole into their place. I felt an irrepressible inclination to watch their proceedings, though [144] eaves-dropping was a procedure that I abhorred. I should, I am confident—at least I hope so—have immediately discovered myself, had not a single word which I had overheard prevented me. The "will" to which they alluded might to me, perhaps, be an object of no trivial importance.

"I wish with all my heart it were burnt!" said my uncle.

"The will or the house?" peevishly retorted Gilbert.

"Both!" cried the other, with an emphasis and expression that made me tremble.

"If we burn the house, the papers will not rise out of it, depend on 't, master," continued Gilbert; "and that box, in the next closet, will not be like Goody Blake's salamander that she talks about."

I began to feel particularly uncomfortable.

"I wish they had all been burnt long ago," said mine honest uncle.—After a pause he went on: "This scape-grace nephew of mine will be here shortly. For fear of accident—accidents, I say, Gilbert—it were better to have all safe. Who knows what may be lurking in the old house, to rise up some day as a witness against us! I intend either to pull it down or set fire to it. But we'll make sure of the will first."

"A rambling jackanapes of a nephew!" said Gilbert; "I hoped the fishes had been at supper on him before now. We never thought, master, he could be alive, as he sent no word about his being either alive or dead. But I guess, [145] continued this amiable servant, "he might ha' staid longer an' you wouldn't ha' fretted for his company."

Listeners hear no good of themselves, but I determined to reward the old villain very shortly for his good wishes.

"Gilbert, when there's work to do, thou art always readier with thy tongue than with thy fingers. Look! the match has gone out twice-leave off puffing, and fetch the box—I'll manage about the candle."

I began to feel a strange sensation rambling about me. Gilbert left the room, however, and I applied myself with redoubled diligence to the crevice. My dishonest relation proceeded to revive the expiring sparks: the light shone full upon his hard features. It might be fancy, but guilt, broad, legible, remorseless guilt, seemed to mark every inflection of his visage: his brow contracted—his eye turned cautiously and fearfully round the apartment, and more than once it rested upon the gap I had made. I saw him strike his hand upon his puckered brow, and a stifled groan escaped him; but, as if ashamed of his better feelings, he clenched it in an attitude of defiance, and listened eagerly for the return of his servant. The slow footsteps of Gilbert soon announced his approach, and apparently with some heavy burden. He threw it on the floor, and I heard a key applied and the rusty wards answering to the touch. The business in which they were now engaged was out of my limited sphere of vision.

"I think, master, the damps will soon ding down the old house: look at the wall; the paper hangs for all the [146] world like the clerk's wig—ha, ha!—If we should burn the whole biggin, we'd rid it o' the ghosts. Would they stand fire, think you, or be off to cooler quarters?"

"Hush, Gilbert; thou art wicked enough to bring a whole legion about us, if they be within hearing. I always seemed to treat these stories with contempt, Gilbert, but I never could very well account for the noises that old Dobbins and his wife heard. Thou knowest he was driven out of the house by them. People wondered that I did not come and live here, instead of letting it run to ruin. It's pretty generally thought that I fear neither man nor devil, but—oh! here it is; here is the will. I care nothing for the rest, provided this be cancelled."

"Ay, master, they said the ghost never left off scratching as long as any body was in the room. Which room was it, I wonder?—I never thought on't to inquire; but—I don't like this a bit. It runs in my head it is the very place, and behind that wall, too, where it took up its quarters; like as it might be just a-back of the paper there. Think you, master, the old tyke has pull'd it down wi' scratching?"

"Gilbert," said my uncle solemnly, "I don't like these jests of thine. Save them, I prithee, for fitter subjects. The will is what we came for. Let us dispose of that quietly, and I promise thee I'll never set foot here again."

As he spoke, he approached the candle—it was just within my view—and opened the will, that it might yield more readily to the blaze. I watched him evidently pre-[147] paring to consume a document with which I felt convinced my welfare and interests were intimately connected. There was not a moment to be lost; but how to get possession was no easy contrivance. If I sallied forth to its rescue, they might murder me, or at least prevent its falling into my hands. This plan could only prolong its existence a few moments, and would to a certainty ensure its eventual destruction. Gilbert's dissertation on the occupations and amusements of the ghost came very opportunely to my aid, and immediately I put into execution what now appeared my only hope of its safety. Just as a corner of the paper was entering the flame, I gave a pretty loud scratch, at the same time anxiously observing the effect it might produce. I was overjoyed to find the enemy intimidated at least by the first fire. Another volley, and another succeeded, until even the sceptical Gilbert was dismayed. My uncle seemed riveted to the spot, his hands widely disparted, so that the flame and its destined prey were now pretty far asunder. Neither of the culprits spoke, and I hoped that little more would be necessary to rout them fairly from the field. As yet they did not seem disposed to move; and I was afraid of a rally, should reason get the better of their fears.

"Rats! rats!" shouted Gilbert. "We'll singe their tails for them." The scratching ceased. Again the paper was approaching to its dreaded catastrophe.

"*Beware*! " I cried, in a deep and sepulchral tone, that startled even the utterer. What effect it had produced on my auditory I was left alone to conjecture. The [148] candle dropped from the incendiary's grasp, and the spoil was left a prey to the bugbear that possessed their imaginations. With feelings of unmixed delight, I heard them clear the stairs at a few leaps, run through the hall, and soon afterwards a terrific bellow from Gilbert announced their descent into the avenue.

Luckily the light was not extinct, and I lost no time in taking possession of the document which I considered of the most importance. A number of loose papers, the contents of a huge trunk, were scattered about; but my attention was more particularly directed to the paper which had been the object of my uncle's visit to Etherington-house. To my great joy, this was neither less nor more than my father's will, witnessed and sealed in due form, wherein the possession of my ancestors were conveyed, absolutely and unconditionally, without entail, unencumbered and unembarassed, to me and to my assigns. I thought it most likely that the papers in and about the trunk might be of use, either as corroborative evidence, in case my uncle should choose to litigate the point and brand the original document as a forgery, or as a direct testimony to the validity of my claim. I was rather puzzled in what manner to convey them from the place, so as not to excite suspicion, should the two worthies return. I was pretty certain they would not leave matters as they now stood when their fears were allayed, and daylight would probably impart sufficient courage to induce them to repeat their visit. On finding the papers removed, the nature of this night's ghostly admonition would im-[149] mediately be guessed, and measures taken to thwart any proceedings which it might be in my power to adopt. To prevent discovery, I hit upon the following expedient.—I sorted out the waste paper, a considerable quantity of which served as envelopes to the rest, setting fire to it in such manner that the contents of the trunk might appear to have been destroyed by the falling of the candle. I succeeded very much to my own satisfaction. Disturbed and agonized as my feelings had been during the discovery, the idea of having defeated the plan on my iniquitous relative gave a zest to my acquisitions almost as great as if I had already taken possession of my paternal inheritance.

Before I left the apartment, I poured out my heart in thanksgivings to that unseen power whose hand, I am firmly convinced, brought me thither at so critical a moment, to frustrate the schemes and machinations of the enemy.

Bundling up the papers, my knowledge of the vicinity enabled me to reach a small tavern in the neighbourhood, without the risk of being recognized. Here I continued two or three days, examining the documents, with the assistance of an honest limb of the law from W—. He entertained considerable doubts as to the issue of a trial, feeling convinced that a forged will would be prepared, if not already in existence, and that my relative would not relinquish his fraudulent claim, should the law be openly appealed to. Mr. Latitat strongly recommended that proceedings of a different nature should be first tried, in hopes of enclosing the villain in his own toils; and these, if suc-[150]cessful, would save the uncertain and expensive process of a suit. I felt unwilling to adopt any mode of attack but that of open warfare, and urged, that possession of the real will would be sufficient to reinstate me as the lawful heir. The man of law smiled. He inquired how I should be able to prove, that the forgery which my uncle would in all probability produce was not the genuine testament: and as the date would inevitably be subsequent to the one I held, it would annul any former bequest. As to my tale about burning the will, that might or might not be treated as a story trumped up for the occasion. I had no witnesses to prove the fact; and though appearances were certainly in my favour, yet the case could only be decided according to evidence. With great reluctance, I consented to take a part in the scheme he chalked out for my guidance, and on the third day from my arrival, I walked a few miles from the village, returning by the mail that it might appear as if I had only just arrived. On being set down at my uncle's, I had the satisfaction to find, as far as could be gathered from his manner, that he had no idea of my recent sojourn in the neighbourhood. Of course the conversation turned on the death of my revered parents and the way in which their property had been disposed of.

"I can only repeat," continued he, "what I, as the only executor under your father's will, was commissioned to inform you at his decease. The property was heavily mortgaged before your departure; and its continued depression in value, arising from causes that could not have been foreseen, left the executor no other alternative but [151] that of giving the creditors possession. The will is here," said he, taking out a paper, neatly folded and mounted with red tape, from a bureau. "It is necessarily brief, and merely enumerates the names of the mortgages and amounts owing. I was unfortunately the principal creditor, having been a considerable loser from my wish to preserve the property inviolate. For the credit of the family I paid off the remaining incumbrances, and the estate has lapsed to me as the lawful possessor."

He placed the document in my hands. I read in it a very technical tribute of testamentary gratitude to Matthew Somerville, Esq. styled therein "beloved brother;" and a slight mention of my name, but no bequest, save that of recommending me to the kindness of my relative, in case it should please Heaven to send me once more to my native shores. I was aware he would be on the watch; guarding therefore against any expression of my feelings, I eagerly perused the deed, and with a sigh, which he would naturally attribute to any cause but the real one, I returned it into his hands.

"I find," said he, "from your letter received on the 23d current, that you are not making a long stay in this neighbourhood. It is better, perhaps, that you should not. The old house is sadly out of repair. Three years ago next May, David Dobbins, the tenant under lease from me, left it, and I have not yet been able to meet with another occupant fully to my satisfaction; indeed I have some intention of pulling down the house and disposing of the materials." [152]

"Pulling it down!" I exclaimed, with indignation.

"Yes; that is, it is so untenantable—so—what shall I call it?—that nobody cares to live there."

"I hope it is not haunted?"

"Haunted!" exclaimed he, surveying me with a severe and scrutinizing glance. "What should have put that into your head?"

I was afraid I had said too much; and anxious to allay the suspicion I saw gathering in his countenance, "Nay, uncle," I quickly rejoined; "but you seemed so afraid of speaking out upon the matter, that I thought there must needs be a ghost at the bottom of it."

"As for that," said he, carelessly, "the foolish farmer and his wife did hint something of the sort; but it is well known that I pay no attention to such tales. The long and the short of it, I fancy, was that they were tired of their bargain and wanted me to take it off their hands."

Here honest Gilbert entered, to say that Mr. Latitat would be glad to have a word with his master.

"Tell Mr. Latitat to walk in. We have no secrets here. Excuse me, nephew; this man is one of our lawyers from W—. He has nothing to communicate but what you may hear, I dare say. If he should have any private business, you can step into the next room."

The attorney entering, I was introduced as nephew to Mr. Somerville, just arrived from the Indies, and so forth. Standing, Mr. Latitat performed due obeisance.

"Sit down; sit down, Mr. Latitat," cried my uncle. "You need not be bowing there for a job. Poor fellow, [153] he has not much left to grease the paws of a lawyer. Well, sir, your errand?"

"I came, Mr. Somerville, respecting the manor-house. Perhaps you would not have any objections to a tenant?"

"I cannot say just now. I have had some thoughts of pulling it down."

"Sir! you would not demolish a building, the growth of centuries—a family mansion—been in the descent since James's time. It would be barbarous. The antiques would be about your ears."

"I care nothing for the antiquities; and, moreover, I do not choose to let the house. Any further business with me this morning, sir?"

"Nothing of consequence: I only came about the house."

"Pray, Mr. Latitat," said I, "what sort of a tenant have you in view—one you could recommend? I think my uncle has more regard for the old mansion-house of the Etheringtons than comports with the outrage he threatens. The will says, if I read aright, that the house and property may be sold, should the executor see fit; but as to pulling it down, I am sure my father never meant any thing so deplorable. Allow me another glance at that paper."

"Please to observe, nephew, that the will makes it mine, and as such I have a right to dispose of the whole in such manner as I may deem best. If you have any doubts, I refer you to Mr. Latitat, who sits smiling at your unlawyer-like opinions." [154]

"Pray allow me one moment," said the curious Mr. Latitat. He looked at the signature, and that of the parties witnessing.

"Martha Somerville—your late sister, I presume?"

My uncle nodded assent.

"Gilbert Buntwisle—your servant?"

"The same. To what purpose, sir, are these questions?" angrily inquired my uncle.

"Merely matters of form—a habit we lawyers cannot easily throw aside whenever we get sight of musty parchments. I hope you will pardon my freedom?"

"Oh! as for that, you are welcome to ask as many questions as you think proper: they will be easily answered, I take it."

"Doubtless," said the persevering man of words. "Whenever I take up a deed, for instance—it is just the habit of the thing, Mr. Somerville—I always look at it as a banker looks at a note. He could not, for the life of him, gather one up without first ascertaining that it was genuine."

"Genuine!" exclaimed my uncle, thrown off his guard. "You do not suspect that I have forged it?"

"Forged it! why how could that enter your head, Mr. Somerville? I should as soon suspect you of forging a bank-note, or coining a guinea. Ringing a guinea, Mr. Somerville, does not at all imply that the payee suspects the payer to be an adept in that ingenious and much abused art. We should be prodigiously surprised, Mr. Somerville, if the payer was to start up in a tantrum, [155] and say, 'Do you suspect me, sir, of having coined it?'"

Mr. Latitat, if you came hither for the purpose of insulting me—"

I came here upon no such business, Mr. Somerville; but as you seem disposed to be captious, I *will* make free to say, and it would be the opinion of ninety-nine hundredths of the profession, that it might possibly have been a little more satisfactory to the heir-apparent, had the witnesses to this the most solemn and important act of a man's life been any other than, firstly, a defunct sister to the party claiming the whole residue, and, secondly, Mr. Gilbert Buntwisle, his servant. Nay, Mr. Somerville," said the pertinacious lawyer, rising, "I do not wish to use more circumlocution than is necessary; I have stated my suspicions, and if you are an honest man, you can have no objections, at least, to satisfy your nephew on the subject, who seems, to say the truth, much astonished at our accidental parley."

"And pray, who made you a ruler and a judge between us?"

"I have no business with it, I own; but as you seemed rather angry, I made bold to give an opinion on the little technicalities aforesaid. If Mr. Etherington chooses," addressing himself to me, "the matter is now at rest."

"Of course," I replied, "Mr. Somerville will be ready to give every satisfaction that may be required, as regards the validity of the witnesses. I request, uncle, that you will not lose one more moment in rebutting these in- [156] sinuations. For your own sake and mine, it is not proper that your conduct should go forth to the world in the shape of which this gentleman may think fit to represent it."

"If he dare speak one word—"

"Nay, uncle, that is not the way to stop folks' mouths now-a-days. Nothing but the actual gag, or a line of conduct that courts no favour and requires no concealment, will pass current with the world. I request, sir" addressing myself to Latitat, "that you will not leave this house until you have given Mr. Somerville the opportunity of clearing himself from any blame in this transaction."

"As matters have assumed this posture," said Mr. Latitat, "I should be deficient in respect to the profession of which I have the honour to be a member, did I not justify my conduct in the best manner I am able. Have I liberty to proceed?"

"Proceed as you like, you will not prove the testament to be a forgery. The signing and witnessing were done in my presence," said Mr. Somerville. He rose from his chair, instinctively locked up his bureau; and, if such stern features could assume an aspect of still greater asperity, it was when the interrogator thus continued:—"You were, as you observe, Mr. Somerville, a witness to the due subscription of this deed. If I am to clear myself from the imputation of unjustifiable curiosity, I must beg leave to examine yourself and the surviving witness apart, merely as to the minutiae of the circumstances under which it was finally completed: for instance, [157] was the late Mr. Etherington in bed, or was he sick, or well, when the deed was executed?"

A cadaverous hue stole over the dark features of the culprit; their aspect varying and distorted, in which fear and deadly anger painfully strove for pre-eminence.

"And wherefore apart?" said he, with a hideous grin. He stamped suddenly on the floor.

"If that summons be for your servant, you might have saved yourself the trouble, Mr. Somerville," said Latitat, with great coolness and intrepidity, "Gilbert is at my office, whither I sent him on an errand, thinking he would be best out of the way for a while. I find, however, that we shall have need of him. It is as well, nevertheless, that he is out of the reach of signals."

"A base conspiracy!" roared the infuriated villain. "Nephew, how is this? And in my own house—bullied—baited! But I will be revenged—I will—"

"Here he became exhausted with rage, and sat down. On Mr. Latitat attempting to speak, he cried out—"I will answer no questions, and I defy you. Gilbert may say what he likes; but he cannot contradict my words. I'll speak none."

"These would be strange words, indeed, Mr. Somerville, from an innocent man. Know you that WILL? said the lawyer, in a voice of thunder, and at the same time exhibiting the real instrument so miraculously preserved from destruction. I shall never forget his first look of horror and astonishment. Had a spectre risen up, arrayed in all the terrors of the prison-house, he could not [158] have exhibited more appalling symptoms of unmitigated despair. He shuddered audibly. It was the very crisis of his agony. A portentous silence ensued. Some minutes elapsed before it was interrupted. Mr. Latitat was the first to break so disagreeable a pause.

"Mr. Somerville, it is useless to carry on this scene of duplicity: neither party would be benefited by it. *You have forged that deed!* We have sufficient evidence of your attempt to destroy this document I now hold, in the very mansion which your unhallowed hands would, but for the direct interposition of Providence, have levelled with the dust. On one condition, and on one only, your conduct shall be concealed from the knowledge of your fellow-men. The eye of Providence alone has hitherto tracked the tortuous course of your villainy. On one condition, I say, the past is for ever concealed from the eye of the world." Another pause. My uncle groaned in the agony of his spirit. Had his heart's blood been at stake, he could not have evinced a greater reluctance than he now showed at the thoughts of relinquishing his ill-gotten wealth.

"What is it?"

"Destroy with your own hands that forged testimony of your guilt. Your nephew does not wish to bring an old man's gray hairs to an ignominious grave."

He took the deed and, turning aside his head, committed it to the flames. He appeared to breathe more freely when it was consumed; but the struggle had been too sever even for his unyielding frame, iron-bound [159] though it seemed. As he turned trembling from the hearth, he sunk into his chair, threw his hands over his face, and groaned deeply. The next moment he fixed his eyes steadily on me. A glassy brightness suddenly shot over them; a dimness followed like the shadows of death. He held out his hand; his head bowed; and he bade adieu to the world and its interests for ever!

Title

Roberts, Emma. "Maximilian and his Daughter." FMN 1827. 219-226. [219]

MAXIMILLIAN AND HIS DAUGHTER.
BY MISS EMMA ROBERTS.

——LUDOLPH had faced many dangers without shrinking, but the appalling circumstances which now surrounded him excited a painful thrill: the blood rushed through his veins with fearful rapidity, his pulses throbbed, his heart beat, and with strained eye he gazed wildly around. He was conducted in silence through a gloomy passage, which led from his dungeon; a door opened, and he found himself suddenly thrust into a square apartment, the massy walls of which, dark and frowning, were bare, save that at intervals a staple or a chain of rusty iron was appended from the rough stone. Several instruments of strange shape were heaped together in a corner, apparently removed for the purpose of making room for some other apparatus, which was raised in the centre of the floor, covered with a black cloth. A grated window afforded sufficient light to reveal the melancholy accompaniments of this dismal chamber, and drawing towards it, the knight looked out upon a dreary court-yard, where he beheld a scaffold and all the insignia of death—the block, the axe, the heap of saw-dust, and the grim headsman standing beside them. For whom were these sickening preparations made?—the manacles which bound his fettered limbs, his close imprisonment of three days, and, above all, the accusations of a conscious heart, returned a ready answer; and his approaching fate was embittered by the conviction that it [220] was just. On the field of battle, or even on the gibbet or the wheel, in a better cause, Ludolph would have yielded his last breath with heroic fortitude: but to descend dishonoured to the grave, and to leave behind him the frail partner of his guilt exposed to the world's contumely, perchance to a more dreadful punishment than that which now awaited the author of her shame, wrung the warrior's heartstrings, and subdued his ardent soul.

Ludolph von Wilmenstein, descended from a younger branch of a noble family, was a soldier of fortune: he had sought and obtained renown under the banners of the Hungarian monarch against the invading infidels; and after two glorious campaigns repaired to the court of Duke Maximilian of—to offer his sword in the impending war with Lombardy. Undistinguished amid a crowd of knights, anxiously pressing their claims to high appointments in the same service, he received very slight notice from the haughty prince, who ruled with little less than imperial splendour: but Ludolph, though ambitious, was also modest, and, content to remain in obscurity during the silken pastimes of a court, he awaited with unmurmuring patience the moment wherein his feats of arms should attract attention to his prowess. Ludolph's fine person, expressive features, and noble bearing, had not passed wholly unnoticed: the admiring whispers of the damsels in her train drew the regards of their proud and scornful mistress, Ismengarde, only child of Maximilian, and heiress of the duchy. Fascinated as if by a spell, the hitherto icy heart of the princess was touched: the hand- [221] some stranger became the constant subject of her meditations, and she determined, if it were possible, to bring him to her feet. This was an undertaking fraught with difficulty, in consequence of the immeasurable distance which fortune had placed between them, and of the unbending stateliness and formal etiquette which, even in those rude times, marked the court of Maximilian. Ismengarde, cold and repelling, in the consciousness of her high birth and beauty, disdained to mingle with the crowd who shared in its festal splendours, and either withdrew early, or, calling her ladies of honour around her, sate aloof in a distant circle, which none except nobles of exalted rank dared approach. Love, however, soon pointed out a method by which the princess might hope to converse with the object of her affections: the season of the carnival approached; and in the masquing and disguising which distinguished its revels she contrived, without exciting suspicion, to engage Ludolph in the dance. The knight hung enamoured over the dark-eyed beauty, who, reposing on his arm, suffered gentle words to escape her lips, in reply to his ardent protestations. One evening the delighted pair had wandered away from the crowded hall; the sound of music stole faintly upon their ears; the glare of the tapers threw a softened light from the wide gothic windows upon banks and beds of flowers, and the gems of the spangled sky were reflected in the crystal mirror of a fairy lake below. It was in this sweet hour that Ludolph besought his mysterious companion to reveal herself—the veil dropped from her rich tresses, and he [222] beheld the princess Ismengarde, on whom he had been wont to gaze as upon the stars above them.

  From this fatal evening the knight haunted the palace-gardens, making the air musical with the witching melody of his fond guitar: the melting serenade, breathed beneath the lattice of Ismengarde's chamber, was answered by signals which repaid the minstrel's song. Sometimes a shower of rose-buds, detached from the alabaster vase which graced his lady's balcony, were dropped at his feet; at others, the soft waking of a lute, whose chords were swept at intervals, assured him that there was one listener within—a gentle heart wrought by the soft persuasiveness of his lay to answer with responsive notes. Thus emboldened, the adventurous cavalier climbed the marble balustrade, and the lovers met—too often for Ludolph's honour and for the peace of Ismengarde.

  It was the painful recollections connected with this breach of duty to the sovereign he served, to the woman he adored, which bleached Ludolph's cheek, and shook his tortured frame—the impossibility of making atonement by the sacrifice of his forfeit life, which added a sting to the disgraceful punishment awaiting him. The knight's minutes seemed now to be counted; the executioner passed his finger over the axe, and looked somewhat impatiently towards the place where he stood: he cast his eyes upwards to catch a glimpse of the narrow patch of blue sky which canopied the dismal court-yard—all below was buried in deep shade, but the dancing sunbeams played upon the opposite wall, and he drank in the golden [223] light which perchance would never meet his eager gaze again. Ludolph was roused from his agitating reflections by the opening of one of the three doors which the apartment contained: the bolts dropped one by one—it grated harshly upon its ponderous hinges—and, preceded by two domestics, the Duke Maximilian entered. Stern determination sate upon the avenger's brow; he signed to his attendants, and they removed the black drapery which had formerly attracted Ludolph's attention, in the supposition that it covered some of those diabolic engines of inventive cruelty, constructed for the prolongation of human suffering; but, as the sable train rolled off, it disclosed, to his surprise, a temporary altar, magnificently decorated. The servants, having performed the allotted task, retired, and the same door revolving a second time, Ismengarde was led forward, pale, trembling, and leaning upon the arm of a dignified ecclesiastic—her dark hair hanging dishevelled over her shoulders—the diadem falling from her head, and the loose folds of her jewelled robe sweeping disordered upon the ground. Still in this utter desolation and misery she preserved an air of grandeur; and though every limb was convulsed, the strong efforts which she made to preserve composure were not wholly unsuccessful; and there were moments in which her resolution appeared to be as unconquerable as that of her father: but Ludolph alone observed her sorrow, and he hid his face in his fettered hands, turning away from the sight of her beauty and her distress. "Approach!" exclaimed the duke, addressing the unhappy pair: "the [224] offspring of your mutual crime must be born in wedlock, and, the nuptial rites concluded, a just doom awaits its guilty parents. The convent and the scaffold are both prepared—take ye leave therefore of this world for ever." Ludolph, rejoicing in his misery that the life and the reputation of Ismengarde would be spared, drew near the altar: he would have spoken of comfort, but utterance was denied, and the priest commenced his melancholy office before he could rally the flagging spirits which had sunk in the uncontrollable anguish of this dread hour. How many tears were shed, how many sighs breathed, in the short interval which ensued! The knight's burning fingers clasped the clay-cold hand of his bride as he stood in chains beside her: a last embrace, a last farewell, was forbidden by the vindictive parent, who tore the shrieking wife from the wretched husband's outstretched arms.

The monk withdrew; the third and last door now opened, and disclosed a flight of stairs, which led directly to the scaffold. The court-yard below was filled with armed men, and Ludolph felt that the advance of a few steps would bring him to his grave. Death would have been a welcome release from the agony which had been crowded into the last few minutes, but the thought of Ismengarde's despair unmanned him; and if prayers would have availed, he would have sunk in prostrate humility before his earthly judge. The withering smile on the duke's lips, the savage glance of his flashing eyes, forbade hope. Maximilian waved him to depart; the intrepid warrior, disdaining to beg his life, and unwilling [225] to expose the situation of Ismengarde to the rude soldiery below, prepared to obey in silence. The princess followed her lover's receding form with a wild gaze, and, darting forward, shut the door which closed and opened by a spring, and then drawing a dagger from her bosom, ere Ludolph could raise his manacled hand to save, buried it deep in the breast of her father, who fell a corpse at the foot of the altar. Paralysed by this unexpected catastrophe, the knight stood aghast with horror: his first impulse was to rush upon the scaffold, to meet the death which had been prevented by a murder so barbarous and so unnatural; but his feet seemed chained to the spot, and he stood motionless, watching with intense solicitude the movements of the parricide.

Ismengarde betrayed no touch of remorseful feeling; she covered the body with the black drapery which lay conveniently near it, and then hurried out of the chamber. Ludolph, left alone with the stiffening remains of his relentless enemy, started from his frozen attitude, almost trusting that he should awake from a fearful dream, but he could not escape the horrible reality. He turned to the window, and there beheld the preparations still going forward for his own death. A friar had ascended the scaffold to administer the last rites, and the deep toll of a funeral bell smote heavily upon his ear. The priest who had performed the bridal ceremony now entered, followed by a few attendant monks, who, by their superior's directions, took up the duke's body, without removing the black winding-sheet which enveloped it. Ludolph's [226] chains were unclasped, a rich robe was thrown around him, and, conducted into the hall of audience, he saw Ismengarde seated on her father's throne, and heard the shouts which united their names in ducal sovereignty. Maximilian was reported to have died suddenly by the bursting of a blood-vessel—and the tale, if suspected, remained unquestioned.

Riches, power, rank—all that the world could offer—were laid by Ismengarde at her husband's feet: he turned away in silent horror from the fruits of guilt, but still he could not abandon one who had plunged her soul in crime for his sake, and they lived together in gloomy wretchedness. Untouched by repentance for a deed which had secured the idols of her ambitious heart, Ismengarde resented Ludolph's shuddering anguish; her proud eyes quailed beneath his melancholy glance; and, after vainly seeking to recover his lost affection, she gave herself up to the world's delusive pleasures.

In the soft gush of the rippling waters, in the waving of the flowers, the beaming stars, and golden sun-light, the unhappy knight saw only the sad remembrancers of departed happiness; he loathed his life, and he loathed the murderess who had preserved him from the axe.

Beneath a palm-tree, in a garden attached to the monastery of Mount Carmel, lie the bones of a knight, slain in the holy wars; and under a magnificent tomb, in the cathedral church of her native city, those of Ismengarde repose. Happily unconscious of the guilt and misery of his parents, their only child succeeded to the ducal throne.

Title
Neele, Henry. "The Comet." FMN 1827. 239-267. [239]

THE COMET.
BY HENRY NEELE, ESQ.

A few years ago at the little fishing town, or rather village, of G., on the coast of Cornwall, resided a gentleman who, from his appearance, might be estimated to be nearly sixty years of age, but I have since learned that he was not more than forty. Whatever his age might be, he was more than suspected to be the old gentleman, that is to say, no other than the devil himself. Now I, who happened to be obliged, for the arrangement of some family affairs, to reside a month or two at G., had the misfortune to differ from my worthy neighbours as to the identity of the occupant of the old manor-house with the enemy of mankind. In the first place, his dress bore no sort of resemblance to that of Beelzebub. The last person who had the good fortune to get a glimpse of the real devil was the late professor Porson, and he has taken the pains to describe his apparel very minutely, so that I am enabled to speak with some degree of confidence upon this part of the subject. The professor's description runs thus:

> And pray how was the devil drest?
> Oh! he was in his Sunday's best:
> His coat was black, and his breeches were blue,
> With a hole behind that his tail went through.
>
> And over the hill, and over the dale,
> And he rambled over the plain;
> And backwards and forwards he switch'd his long tail
> As a gentleman switches his cane. [240]

The "complement externe" of the old gentleman at G. was quite the reverse of all these. In the first place he had no Sunday's best; the sabbath and the working day saw him in precisely the same habiliments—a circumstance which confirmed the towns-people in their opinion; whereas I have no less an authority than that of Porson for deducing an opposite conclusion from the same premises, because the devil is scrupulously particular about his Sunday's apparel. Then again he was never seen in a coat, but always wore a loose morning gown. This however was a circumstance which, in the opinion of all, told decidedly against him; for why should he always wear that gown, unless it was for the purpose of hiding his tail beneath its ample folds? The goodwives of the town were especially pertinacious upon this point, and used to eye the lower part of the old gentleman's garment very suspiciously as he took his morning's walk upon the beach. As to his rambling over hill and dale, in the manner mentioned by the learned professor, that was quite out of the question, for he was a great sufferer by the gout, and wore bandages as large as a blanket round his leg. Whenever this fact was mentioned, the gossips used to smile, shake their heads, and look particularly wise, observing that it was clearly a stratagem which he resorted to for the purpose of concealing his cloven foot.

Another circumstance ought not to be omitted: he never went to the parish church—the only place of worship within twenty miles; and after he left G. an ivory crucifix was found in his house, over which there was no [241] doubt (in the opinion of the neighbours) that he used to say the Lord's prayer backwards, and repeat a variety of diabolical incantations. I ventured humbly to suggest that his absence from church, and the discovery of the crucifix, were proofs, not that he was the devil, but a catholic: upon which I was interrupted with a sneer, and an exclamation of "Where is the mighty difference?"

He gave great offence at the house of a fisherman who lived near him, and strongly confirmed the prejudices existing against him, by tearing down a horse-shoe which was nailed at the door as a protection against witchcraft, and calling the inhabitants fools and idiots for their pains. Seeing, however, the consternation which he had created, he laughed heartily, and threw them a guinea to make amends. The good folks were determined not to derive any pecuniary advantages from the devil's gold, but they gave it to their last born, an infant in arms, as a plaything. The child was delighted with the glittering bauble, but one day having got it down its throat, there it stuck, and instant suffocation ensued. The weeping and wailing of the family on this occasion were mingled with execrations on the author of the calamity, for such they did not hesitate to term the old gentleman, who had evidently thrown to them this infernal coin for the purpose of depriving them of their chief earthly comfort. They were not long in proceeding to the nearest magistrate, and begging him to issue his warrant to apprehend the stranger for murder. To this, however, his worship demurred, and the good folks changed their battery, and [242] begged to ask, as the guinea was of course a counterfeit, whether they could not hang the devil for coining. To this his worship replied, that though coining is an offence amounting to high treason, yet the devil, not being a natural-born subject of his majesty, owed him no allegiance, and therefore could not be guilty of the crime in question. The poor people departed, thinking it all very odd, and that the devil and the squire must be in collusion, in which opinion they were confirmed by a tallow-chandler, who was the chief tradesman of the town, as well as a violent radical, and who advised them to petition the House of Commons without delay.

I will explain to my readers the secret of the tallow-chandler's enmity. The old gentleman had of a sudden ceased to buy candles, and illuminated his house, inside and out, in a strange and mysterious manner by some means, which, from the brimstone-like smell occasionally perceived, were plainly of infernal origin. For several weeks previously, he had been employing labourers from a distant town (for he did not engage the honest man, whose pick-axe was the only one ever used by the good people of G.) in digging trenches, and laying down pipes, round his house. The towns-folk gazed on in wonder and terror, but at a careful distance; and although they had a longing desire to understand the meaning of all this, they cautiously avoided any intercourse with the only persons who could give them the least information, viz., the labourers who performed the work. At length, one night, without any obvious cause, the lamp before [243] the old gentleman's door, that in his hall, and another in his sitting-room, were seen to spring into light as if by magic. They were also observed to go out in the same way, and thereupon a smell, which could not be of this world, proceeded from them. One day, too, a dreadful explosion took place at the house, and a part of the garden wall was thrown down; all which were plain proofs that it could be no one but the devil who inhabited there. The good folks of G. had never heard of gas or its properties, and I was thought to be no better than I should be for endeavouring to explain all these phenomena by natural causes.

There was one more fact which proved (if proof were wanting) the accusation of the towns-people. He was a great correspondent, and put more letters into the post-office than all the rest of the inhabitants of G. together. These were generally directed to Berlin, a town which, after much inquiry, was ascertained to lie in a remote part of Devonshire, and to be inhabited by a horridly dissolute and profane set of people. What was stranger still, no part of the superscription could ever be read but the world Berlin: the rest was such a piece of cramp penmanship, that the most expert scholar in G. could not decipher it. The postmaster (without having ever heard of Tony Lumpkin or his aphorisms) knew that "the inside of a letter is the cream of the correspondence," and ventured one day to open an epistle which the mysterious one had just dropped into his box. The contents, however, did not much edify him. Not a letter was there 244] which resembled any one in the English alphabet—it was, therefore, some devilish and cabalistic writing, invented for the purposes of evil. My opinion being asked, I positively refused to look at the inside; but having perused the superscription, I said that it was addressed to some one in Berlin, which was a city in Germany, and that, although I did not understand German, I had no doubt that the direction was written in the German character. Being asked, whether even I, with all my scholarship, could read it, I candidly confessed that I could not; upon which I was asked, with a sneer, whether I expected to persuade them that the Germans were such a nation of fools as to write in a hand which nobody could read. The good folks were also firmly persuaded that, whatever I might say, I was in my conscience of the same opinion with them, and my refusal to look at the inside of the letter was set down as a plain proof that I was afraid of receiving some mysterious injury if I did.

My own opinions were so much opposed to those of my neighbours, that I felt rather a desire to be acquainted with the stranger, whose manners appeared to be open and good-humoured, although testy and eccentric. My naturally shy disposition prevented me, however, from accomplishing my wish; and, besides this, I found that my own affairs were enough to occupy me during the short time that I remained at G. I learned that the person who had created so much consternation had arrived at that town about four months before, and that the house had been previously engaged for him. Who, or what he was, or [245] why he came thither, no one who tried could ascertain. Whether I could have attained this wonderful height in knowledge, I do not know; but having something else to do, I never made the attempt. At length the old gentleman and his two servants, an elderly female, and a stout active man who talked a gibberish (so they called it at G.) which no one could understand, were one day seen very busily employed in packing up. A queer-looking, broad-bottomed vessel, from which a boat was lowered, appeared off the town. The three strangers sallied out with their boxes, and after depositing a packet at the post-office addressed to the former proprietor of the house (which was supposed to contain the keys, and was ordered to be kept until the arrival of the person to whom it was addressed), they got into the boat, rowed to the ship, and were never seen or heard of more.

During the short time afterwards that I continued at G. I was subject to repeated lectures for my obstinate infidelity as to the old gentleman's diabolisms; and whatever argument I advanced in support of my own opinion, it was sure to be met by the unanswerable question, "If he was not the devil, who the devil was he?"

Many years rolled over my head, and the memory of the mysterious inhabitant of G. had entirely vanished from it, when circumstances which it is unnecessary to detail obliged me to pay a visit to the north of Germany. At the close of a fine autumnal day in 18—, I found myself entering the splendid city of Berlin. Both my good steed and I were so much fatigued that a speedy resting was [246] very desirable for us; but it was long before I could choose an hotel out of the immense numbers which presented themselves to my view. Some were far too magnificent for my humble means, and the mere sight of their splendour appeared to melt away the guilders in my pocket. Some, on the other hand, were such as no "man of wit and fashion about town" would think of putting his head into. At length I thought that I had discovered one which looked like the happy medium, and the whimsicality of its sign determined me to put up there. The sign was DER TEUFEL: and since my departure from G. I had acquired a sufficient mastery of the German language to know what those two words signified in English. I entered, and after taking all due precautions for the accommodation and sustenance of the respectable quadruped who had borne me upon his back for nearly half a day, I began to think of satisfying that appetite which disappointment, anxiety, and fatigue, had not been able entirely to destroy. My worthy host, who did not seem to bear any resemblance to his sign, unless I could have the ingratitude to ascribe his magical celerity and marvellous good fare to the auspices of his patron saint, quickly covered my table with a profusion of tempting viands, while a flask of sparkling Hochheim towered proudly, like a presiding deity, above the whole. My good humour, however, was a little clouded when I saw plates, knives, and forks, laid for two instead of one. "What means this?" said I to the landlord. "Mein Herr," he answered submissively, "a gentleman who has [247] just arrived will have the honour of dining with you."—"But I mean to dine alone," I replied angrily—not that I doubted the sufficiency of the meal, but I did not choose to be intruded upon by strangers. "Pardon me, mein Herr," said the landlord with unabashed impudence, "I have told Herr von Schwartzman that dinner is ready. I am sure you will like his company. He is a gentleman of good fortune and family. He is moreover —"—"I care not who he is," I exclaimed, "but in order to cut thy prating short, and to get my dinner, if I must needs submit, let him come in at once, even if he be the devil himself!"

I had scarcely uttered these words when I started, as if I had really seen the person whom I mentioned, for the room-door opened, and in walked the old gentleman who had caused so much wonder and terror at G. The superstitions of the people of the town—the sign of the inn where I now was—the old fellow's name, Schwartzman, (which being interpreted in English meaneth black man)—my own petulant exclamation—and the sudden apparition of this unaccountable person, were circumstances that crowded my brain at once, and for an instant I almost fancied myself in the presence of the foul fiend. "You seem surprised," at length said Herr von Schwartzman, "at our unexpected meeting; and, indeed, you cannot be more so than I am. I believe it was in England that we met before."

"Even so, mein Herr," I answered, encouraged by the [248] earthly tone of his voice, and fancying that the good-humoured smile which mantled over his face must be of this world, and at any rate could be of no worse origins—"even so, mein Herr, and I have often regretted that, placed as we were among a horde of barbarous peasantry, an opportunity never occurred for our better acquaintance."

"It is at length arrived," he said, filling two glasses of Hochheim. "Let us drink to our better and our long acquaintance."

I pledged the old gentleman's toast with great alacrity, and it was not until the passage of the wine down my throat had sealed me to it irrevocably, that I reflected upon the sentiment to which I had drunk with so much cordiality, and I was again shaken with doubts as to the nature of the person with whom I had avowed my wish to be long and intimately acquainted.

I looked upon his feet—but that's a fable—and then I looked upon the viands on which he was feeding lustily while I (although he had the courtesy to load my plate with the best of every thing) was wasting the golden moments in idle alarms and superstitious absurdity. The more reasonable man was roused within me, and I fell to the work of mastication with a zeal and fervour that would have done honour to Dr. Kitchener himself.

"Well, my friend," said my companion, after we had pretty well satisfied the cravings of our stomachs, "our landlord has this day treated us nobly, and methinks we have not been backward in doing honour to his excel-[249]lent cheer. He is an honest fellow, who well deserves to prosper, and we will therefore, if you please, drink Success to Der Teufel."

I had raised my glass to my lips when I found that the old gentleman meant to propose a toast, but I set it down hastily as soon as I heard the very equivocal sentiment to which he wanted me to pledge myself. The fiend, I thought, is weaving his web around me, and wishes me to drink to my own perdition. A cold sweat came over me, a film covered my eyes, and I thought that I perceived the old man looking askew at me while his lip was curled with a malignant smile.

"You are not well," he said, taking my hand. I shrunk from his grasp at first, but to my surprise it was as cool and healthy as the touch of humanity can possibly be. "Let us retire to our worthy host's garden—the heat of this room overpowers you—and we can finish our wine coolly and pleasantly in the arbour."

He did not wait for my consent, but led me out; and our bottle and glasses were very quickly arranged upon a table in a leafy arbour, where we were sheltered from the sun, and enjoyed the refreshing fragrance of the evening breeze as it gently stirred the leaves about us.

"They were odd people," said my friend, "those inhabitants of G.; they stared at me, and shrunk from me, as if I had been the devil himself."

"And in truth, mein Herr," I replied, "they took you to be no less a personage than he whom you have just named." [250]

The old gentleman laughed long and heartily at my information. "I thought as much," he said. "It is an honour which has been ascribed to me from the hour of my birth, and in more countries than one."

"Indeed," said I, "you speak as if there were something in your history to which a stranger might listen with interest. May I crave the favour of you to be a little more communicative?"

"With all my heart!" he replied: "but in truth you will not find much to interest you in my story. A little mirth and a good deal of sorrow make up the history of most men's lives, and mine is not an exception to the general rule. I was born some threescore years ago, and was the son and heir of the Baron von Schwartzman, whose castle is a few miles to the southward of this city—and I am now, by your leave, mein Herr, the baron himself. (I made a lower bow than I had ever yet greeted him with). My mother had brought into the world, about two years previously, a daughter of such extraordinary beauty, that it was confidently expected that the next child would be similarly endowed; but I was no sooner presented to my father than he was so startled at my surprising ugliness, that he retreated several paces, and involuntarily exclaimed, 'The devil!' This was a christian name which stuck to me ever afterwards, and which, as you can bear witness, followed me even into a foreign country.

"My godfather and godmother, however, treated me much more courteously than my own natural parent, and [251] bestowed upon me, at the baptismal font, the high-sounding appellation of Leopold. Nothing worth describing occurred during the years of my infancy. I cried, and laughed, and pouted, and sucked, and was kissed, and scolded, and treated, and whipped, as often, and with the same alternations as children in general, only I grew uglier, and justified the paternal benediction more and more every day. In due time I was sent to a grammar-school. As I had at home been accustomed to independence and the exercise of my self-will, I soon became the most troublesome fellow there; and yet (I may now say it without the imputation of vanity) I contrived, by some means or other, to gain the heart of all, whether tutors or pupils. For solving a theme, or robbing an orchard; writing nonsense verses, or frightening a whole neighbourhood; translating Homer into German verse, or beating a watchman until his flesh was one general bruise, who could compete with Leopold von Schwartzman? One day I was publicly reprimanded and punished for some monstrous outrage, and the next rewarded with all the honours of the school for my proficiency in the classics. In short, it was generally agreed that there was not such another clever, pleasant, good-tempered, good-for-nothing fellow in the school. 'Certainly,' the wise people would say, *'the devil is in him.'*

"And now," added the old man, smiling, but smiling, I thought, somewhat solemnly and sadly, "I must let you into the secret of one of my weaknesses. I have ever had the most implicit belief in the science of astrology. [252] You stare at me incredulously, and I can excuse your incredulity. You, born in England perhaps some forty years ago, can have but few superstitions in common with one whose birth-place is Germany, and whose natal star first shone upon him above threescore years before the time at which he is speaking. Observe that comet," he said, pointing towards the west; "it is a very brilliant one, and this is the last night that it will be visible."

"It is the beautiful comet," I said, "which has shone upon us for the last six months, and which first appeared, I think, in the belt of Orion."

"True, true," replied the baron: "it is the comet which, according to the calculations of astronomers, visits the eyes of the inhabitants of this world once in twenty years, and I can confirm the accuracy of their calculations as far as relates to three of its visits. You will smile, and think that the eccentricity of my conduct and character is sufficiently accounted for, when I tell you that that comet is my natal planet. On the very day and instant that it became visible, sixty years and six months ago, did I first open my eyes in my father's castle. There is, however, a tradition connected with this comet, which has sometimes made me uneasy. It runs thus:

The comet that's born in the belt of Orion,
Whose cradle it gilds, gilds the place they shall die on.

However this is its third return that I have seen, and being now as hale and hearty as ever I was, the tradition, if it means any thing to interest me, means that I shall [253] live on to the good old age of fourscore. But to return to my history. I was a fervent believer in astrology, and I thought that if I could meet with a person, either male or female, who was born under the same star, to that person I might safely attach myself, and our destinies must be indissolubly bound together. I had however never met with such a person, and as yet I had never seen my natal star, for on the day on which I entered the university of Halle I wanted three days of attaining my twentieth year. Those three days seemed the longest and most tedious that I had ever passed; but at length the fateful morning dawned, on the evening of which, a few minutes before the hour of eight (the hour of my birth), I hastened to a secluded place at a short distance from the town, and planting myself there, gazed earnestly and intently upon the belt of orion. I had not gazed long before a peculiar light seemed to issue from it, and at length I saw a beautiful comet, with a long and glittering train, rising in all its celestial pomp and majesty. How shall I describe my feelings at this moment? I felt, as it were, new-born: new ideas, new hopes, new joys, seemed to rush upon me, and I gave vent to my emotions in an exclamation of delight. This exclamation I was astonished to hear repeated as audibly and fervently as it was made, and turning round, I beheld a female within a few paces of me to my right.

"She was tall, and exquisitely formed; her dress denoted extreme poverty; and her eye, which for a moment had been lighted up with enthusiasm, was downcast, and [254] abashed with a sense of conscious inferiority, when it met mine. Still I thought that I had never beheld a face so perfectly beautiful. Her general complexion was exquisitely fair, without approaching to paleness, with a slight tinge of the rose on each cheek, which I could not help thinking that care and tenderness might be able to deepen to a much ruddier hue. Her eyes were black and sparkling, but the long dark lashes which fell over them seemed, I thought, acquainted with tears. Her hair was of the same colour with her eyes, and almost of the same brightness. I gazed first upon her and then upon the newly-risen comet, and my bosom seemed bursting with emotions which I could not express, or even understand.

"'Sweet girl!' I said, approaching her, and taking her hand, 'what can have induced you to wander abroad at this late hour?'

"'The comet,' she said—'the comet!'—pointing to it with enthusiasm.

"'It is indeed a beautiful star,' I replied—and as I gazed I felt as if I were the apostle of truth for so saying—'but here,' I added, pressing my lip to her white forehead, 'is one still more beautiful, but alas! more fragile, and which ought therefore not to be exposed to danger.'

"'Ay,' she said, 'but it is the star which I have been waiting to gaze upon for many a long year; it is the star that rules my destiny, my natal star! Twenty years ago, and at this hour, was I brought into the world.'

"Scarcely could I believe my ears. I thought that [255] the sounds which I had heard could not come from the beautiful lips which I saw moving, but that some lying fiend had whispered them in my ears; I made her repeat them over and over again. I thought of the desire which had so long haunted me, and which now seemed gratified; I thought, too, of the beautiful lines of Schiller:

It is a gentle and affectionate thought,
That in immeasurable heights above us,
At our first birth this wreath of love was woven,
With sparkling stars for flowers!

In short, I thought and felt so much that I fell at the fair girl's feet, told her the strange coincidence of our destinies, revealed to her my name and rank, and made her an offer of my hand and heart without any further ceremony.

"'Alas! sir,' she said, permitting, but not returning the caress which I gave her, 'I could indeed fancy that fate has intended us to be indissolubly united, but I am poor, friendless, wretched; my mother is old and bed-ridden; and my father, I fear, follows desperate courses to procure even the slender means on which we subsist.'

"'But I have wealth, sweet girl!' I exclaimed, 'sufficient to remove all these evils, and here is an earnest of it'—endeavouring to force my purse into her hands.

"'Nay, nay,' she said, thrusting it back, 'keep your gold, lest slander should blacken the fair fame which is all Adeline's dowry!'

"'Sweet Adeline! beautiful Adeline!' I said, 'do not let us part thus. Can you doubt my sincerity? Would [256] you vainly endeavour to interpose a barrier against the decrees of fate? Believe that I love you, and say that you love me in return.'

"'It is the will of fate,' she said, sinking in my arms. 'Why should I belie what it has written in my heart? Leopold, I love thee.'

"Thus did we, who but half an hour previously were ignorant of each other's existence, plight our mutual vows; but each recognized a being long sought and looked for, and each yielded to the overruling influence of the planet which was the common governor of our destiny. I was anxious to celebrate our nuptials immediately, but Adeline put a decided negative upon it.

"'What,' she said, 'were you born under yon star, and know not the dark saying which is attached to it?—

The love that is born at the comet's birth,
Treat it not like a thing of earth;
Breathe it to none but the loved one's ear,
Lest fate should remove what hope deems so near;

Seal it not till the hour and the day
When that star from the heavens shall pass away.'

"I instantly recollected the saying, and acquiesced in the wisdom of not acting adversely to what I believed to be the will of destiny. 'It will then be six long months, sweet Adeline!' I said, 'ere our happiness can be sealed; but I must see thee daily—I cannot else exist.'

"'Call upon me at yon white cottage,' she answered, 'at about this hour. My father is then out; indeed he [257] has been out for some weeks now—but he is never at home at that hour; and my mother will have retired to rest. Farewell, Leopold von Schwartzman.'

"'Farewell, dearest Adeline—tell me no more of thy name. I seek not—I wish not—to know it: tell it not to me until the hour when thou art about to exchange it for Schwartzman.'

"Our parting was marked, as the partings of lovers usually are, with sighs, and tears, and embraces, protestations of eternal fidelity, and promises of speedily seeing each other again.

"The love thus suddenly lighted up within our bosoms I did not suffer to die away, or to be extinguished. Every evening, at the hour of nine, I was at the fair one's cottage door, and I ever found her ready to receive me; nay, at length I used to find the latchet left unfastened for me, and I stole up stairs to her chamber unquestioned. I soon discovered that her mind and manners were, at least, equal to her beauty; but the utmost penury and privation were but too visible around her. It was in vain that I offered her the assistance of my purse, and urged her to accept by anticipation that which must very shortly be hers by right. The high-minded girl positively refused to avail herself of this offer, and then I could not help, at all hazards, endeavouring to persuade her to consent to our immediate union, as that seemed to me to be the only means of rescuing her from the distressing state of poverty in which I found her.

"'Say no more, Leopold,' she said, one night, when I [258] had been urging this upon her more strenuously than ever—'say no more, lest I should be weak enough to consent, and so draw down upon our heads the bolts of destiny. And, Leopold, I find thy presence dangerous to me; let me, therefore, I pray thee, see thee no more until the hour which is to make us one. I dread thy entreating eyes—thy persuading tongue: one short month of separation, and then a whole life of constant union. Say that it shall be so, for my sake.'

"'It shall be so—it shall, for thy sake,' I said. For bitter as was the trial to which she put me, the tone and manner in which she implored my acquiescence were irresistible.

"'Then farewell,' she said; 'come not near me until that day. Should you attempt to see me earlier, I have a fearful foreboding that something evil will befall us.'

Forget Me Not

"This was the most sorrowful parting which I had yet experienced; but I bore it as manfully as I could. Three, four, five days, did I perform my promise, and never ventured near the residence of Adeline. I shut myself up in my own chamber, where I saw no one but the domestic who brought my meals. I could not support this life any longer, and at last I determined to pay a visit to Adeline.

"'Whither would you go, mein Herr?' said the centinel at the city gate, through which I had to pass.

"'I have business of importance to transact about a mile from the city,' I answered: 'pray do not detain me.'

"'Nay, mein Herr,' replied the centinel, 'I have no [259] authority to detain you; but if you will take the advice of a friend, you will not leave the city to night. Know you not that the noted bandit Brandt is suspected to be in the neighbourhood this evening; that the council have set a price upon his head; and that the city bands are now engaged in pursuit of him?'

"'Be it so,' I said: 'a man who is skulking about to avoid the city bands is not, methinks, an enemy whom I need greatly fear encountering.'

"The centinel shook his head, but allowed me to pass without further question. Love lent wings to my feet, and already was Adeline's white cottage in sight, when a violent blow on the back of my head with the butt-end of a pistol stretched me on the ground, and a man, whose knee was immediately on my chest, pointed the muzzle at my head.

"'Deliver your money,' he said, 'or you have not a moment to live.'

"'Ruffian,' I said, 'let me go. I am a student at Halle, son of the Baron von Schwartzman. Thou durst not for thy head attempt my life.'

"'That we shall soon see,' said the villain cooly; and my days had then been certainly numbered, had not three men, springing from a neighbouring thicket, suddenly seized the robber, disarmed him, and then proceeded very quietly to bind his hands behind him.

"'Have we caught you at last, mein Herr Brandt?' said one of my deliverers. 'We have been a long time looking out for you. Now we meet to part only once and for ever.' [260] "The robber eyed them sullenly, but did not deign a reply, as they marched him between them towards the town. We soon entered the gate, through which I had already passed, and were conducted before the commander of the garrison, who, as Brandt had been placed by proclamation under military law, was the judge appointed to decide upon his case.

"My evidence was given in a very few words, and, corroborated as it was by that of the policemen, was, I perceived, fatal to Brandt. I could not help, however, entreating for mercy to the wretched criminal.

"'Nay, sir,' said the officer, 'your entreaty is vain. Even without this last atrocious case to fix his doom, we needed only evidence to identify him as Brandt, to have cost him all his lives, were they numerous as the hairs upon his head. Away with him, and hang him instantly upon the ramparts.'

"'I thank thee, colonel,' sand the bandit, 'for my death. It is better to die than to witness such sights as have torn my heart daily. It was only to save a wretched wife and daughter from starvation that I resorted to this trade. But, fare thee well—Brandt knows how to die.'

"The unhappy man was instantly removed; and finding that there was no further occasion for my attendance, I rushed into the streets in a state that bordered upon frenzy. The idea that I had, however innocently, been the occasion of the death of a man shook every fiber in my frame; and while I was suffering under the influence of these feelings, the sullen roll of the death drums announced that Brandt had ceased to live. [261]

"I went home and hurried to bed, but not to rest. The violence of the blow which I had received from the bandit, as well as the mental agony which I had undergone, threw me into a dangerous fever. For ten days I was in a state of delirium, raving incoherently, and unconscious of every thing around me. At length I arrived at the crisis of my disorder, which proved favourable. The fever left my brain, and the glassy glaze of my eye was exchanged for its usual look of intelligence and meaning. I turned round my head in my bed, and looked towards the window of my chamber. It was evening; the arch of heaven was of one deep azure, and the comet was shining in all its brightness. Its situation in the heavens, which was materially different from that which it occupied when I was last conscious of seeing it, recalled and fixed my wandering recollections of all that was connected with it. I rang the bell violently, and was speedily attended by my valet, who had watched over me during my illness. I interrupted the expressions of delight which the sight of my convalescent state drew from him by inquiring eagerly what was the day of the month and the hour.

"'It is the eighth of August, sir; and the clock of the cathedral has just chimed the hour of seven.'

"'Heavens!' I exclaimed, starting from my bed, 'had this cursed fever detained me one hour longer, the destined moment would have passed away. Assist me to dress, good Ferdinand; I must away instantly.'

"'Sir,' said the man, alarmed, 'the doctor would chide.' [262]

"'Care not for his chiding,' I said. 'I will secure thee; but an affair of life and death is not more urgent than that on which I am about to go.'

"'The good curate, von Wilden, is below,' said Ferdinand, 'and told me that he must see you; but I dared not disturb you. He was just going away when you rang the bell, and is now waiting to know the result.'

"I remembered immediately that I had appointed the curate to meet me at that hour, for the purpose of proceeding to Adeline's cottage and tying the nuptial knot between us. I had told him the nature of the duty which I wished him to perform, without, however, disclosing so much as to break through the caution contained in the traditional verses. I lost no time in joining him in the hall, and proceeded to leave the house, accompanied by him, with as much celerity as possible, lest the intervention of my medical attendant or some other person should throw difficulty in the way.

"We soon reached the open fields. It was a beautiful star-light evening. The comet was nearly upon the verge of the horizon, and I was fearful of its disappearing before the ceremony of my nuptials could be accomplished. We therefore proceeded rapidly on our walk. An involuntary shudder came over me as I passed by the scene of my encounter with the bandit; but just then the white cottage peeped out from among the woods which had concealed it, and my heart felt reassured by the near prospect of unbounded happiness. We approached the door: it was on the latch, which I gently raised, and then pro-[263] ceeded, as usual, up the stairs, followed by the curate. I thought I heard a low moaning sound as we approached the chamber door; but it was ajar, and we entered. An old woman, who seemed scarcely able to crawl about, was at the bed-side with a phial in her hand; and stretched upon the couch, with a face on which the finger of death seemed visibly impressed, lay the wasted form of Adeline. 'Just heavens!' I exclaimed, 'what new misery have ye in store for me?'

"The sound of my voice roused Adeline from her death-like stupor. She raised her eyes, but closed them again suddenly, on seeing me, exclaiming, 'Tis he, 'tis he!—the fiend!—save me, save me!' The bitterness of death seemed to invade my heart when I heard this unaccountable exclamation. I gasped for breath, and cold drops of agony rolled from my temples. I ventured to approach the bed. I took her burning hand within my own, and pressed it to my heart. She again fixed her eyes upon me solemnly, and said, 'Know you whom you embrace? Miserable man, has not the universal rumour reached thy ears?'

"'Dearest Adeline,' I said, 'for the last ten days I have been stretched upon the bed of delirium and insensibility. Rumour, however trumpet-tongued to other ears, has been dumb to mine.'

"'You call me Adeline,' she said; 'is that all?'

"'The hour,' I answered, 'is at length arrived—I thought it would be a less melancholy one—when thou were to tell me that other name, ere thou exchangedst it for ever.' [264]

"'Know then,' she said, rising up in the bed with an unusual effort, in which all her remaining strength seemed to be concentrated, 'that my name is Adeline Brandt!'

"For an instant she fixed her dark eyes upon my face, which grew cold and pallid as her own; then the film of death came over them, and her head sank back upon her pillow, from which it never rose again.

"Weak and sickly, and stricken, as it were, with a thunderbolt, I know not how I preserved my recollection and reason at that moment. I remember, however, looking from the chamber window, and seeing the comet shining brightly, although just on the verge of the horizon—I turned to the dead face of Adeline, and thought of those ill-omened verses—

The comet that's born in the belt of Orion,
Whose credit it gilds, gilds the place they shall die on.

I looked again, and the comet was just departing from the heavens; its fiery train was no longer visible; and in an instant after the nucleus disappeared.

"I have but little to add in explanation. I learned that, on the evening of our meeting, the unfortunate Brandt, who had carried on his exploits at a distance, knowing that a price was set upon his head, had fled to the house where his wife and daughter lived, and between whom and him no suspicion of any connexion existed, resolving, if he escaped his present danger, to give up his perilous courses; but that he found those two females in such a state of wretchedness and starvation, that he rushed out and committed the act for which he forfeited his life. Had [265] I but asked Adeline her name, this fatal event would not have happened; for I should most assuredly have removed her to another dwelling, and provided in some way for her father's safety; or, had not the traditional verses restrained us from mentioning our attachment to any one until the hour of our nuptials, I should have revealed it to the bandit, and so taken away from him every inducement for following his lawless occupation. Ill news is not long in spreading. Adeline heard of her father's death, and that I was the occasion of it, a few hours after it took place. The same cause which sent her to her death-bed roused her mother from the couch of lethargy and inaction on which she had lain for many years; and I found that she was the wretched old woman whom I had seen attending the last moments of her daughter.

"The remainder of my history has little in it to interest you. I left the university, and retired to my father's castle, where I shut myself up and lived a very recluse life, until his death, which happened a few years afterwards, obliged me to exert myself in the arrangement of my family affairs. The lapse of years gradually alleviated, although it could not eradicate, my sorrow; but when I found myself approaching my fortieth year, and knew that the comet would very soon make its reappearance, I could not bear the idea of looking again upon the fatal planet which had caused me so much uneasiness. I therefore resolved to travel in some country where it would not be visible; and having received a pressing invitation from a friend in England to visit his [266] native land, accompanied by an intimation that his house at G. was entirely at my service, I did not hesitate to accept his offer. You know something of my adventures there, especially of the consternation which I occasioned by laying down gas-pipes round my friend's house, in consequence of a letter which I had received from him, requesting me to take the trouble to superintend the workmen. Twenty more years have now rolled over my head; the comet has re-appeared, and I can gaze on it with comparative indifference; and as it is just about taking its leave of us, suppose we walk out and enjoy the brightness of its departing glory."

I acceded to the old gentleman's proposal, and lent him the assistance of my arm during our walk. "Yonder fence," said he, "surrounds my friend Berger's garden, in which there is an eminence from which we shall get a better view. The gate is a long way round, but I think you, and even I, shall find but little difficulty in leaping this fence—I will indemnify you for the trespass"—and he had scarcely spoken before he was on the other side of it. I followed him, and we proceeded at a brisk pace towards a beautiful shrubbery, on an elevated spot in the centre of the garden. M. von Schwartzman led the way, but he had scarcely reached the summit before I heard an explosion, and saw him fall upon the ground. I hastened to his assistance, and found him weltering in his blood. I raised his head, saying, "no, no, my friend, it is all in vain—the influence of that malignant star has prevailed over me. [267] I forgot that my friend Berger had lately planted spring-guns in his grounds. But it is Destiny, and not they, which has destroyed me. Farewell—farewell!" On these words his last breath was spent: his eyes, while they remained open, were fixed upon the comet, and the instant they closed the ill-boding planet sunk beneath the horizon.

Title

Anonymous. [Shelley, Mary or Jewsbury, Maria Jane?] "Lacy de Vere." FMN 1827. 275-294.[11] [275]

LACY DE VERE

<blockquote>
Doom'd to be
The last leaf which, by Heaven's decree,
Must hang upon a blasted tree.
WORDSWORTH.
</blockquote>

The founder of the family of the de Veres came over with the first William but not as an adventurer allured by the prospect of gain and the hope of acquiring titular distinction, for the insignia of knighthood had already been bestowed upon him in his own land. When, however, the Conquest rendered it alike the duty and policy of William to attach his Norman followers to his person, Rupert de Vere was one of the first who received solid proofs of that monarch's favour. Generation followed generation; king after king succeeded to the throne; centuries of change, romance, and tragedy, fulfilled their chequered fate; and in the history of all, the de Veres were eminently conspicuous.

But Time, that lifts the low,
And level lays the lofty brow,

began, at length, to exercise an evil influence on the fortunes of the house; and towards the middle of the fifteenth century, Hugh, the then baron de Vere, had little to transmit to his children beyond the name and noble nature of his ancestors. Instead of the broad manors and princely dwellings once connected with the title, he found himself reduced to a single castle, situated on the sea-coast in the north of England; one, that in the proud days of the family, had been erected as a mere hold for the pro-[276]tection of the northern vassals from the incursions of the Scottish borderers. At the period in question, the WARS OF THE ROSES, those suicidal wars of the same people, were at their height. Every county became in turn a field of battle, till the whole kingdom was saturated with the blood of its inhabitants. The ties of neighbourhood, even of kindred, were dissolved. Inhabitants of the same village, members of one household, separated

---

11 According to Nora Crook and archival research, the author of this tale is either Mary Shelley or Maria Jane Jewsbury. In an April 18, 2008 email, Charles Robinson writes that "Maria Jane Jewsbury says that she has received £6 for a work of hers called 'Lucy de Vere' published in the *Amulet*. The particular researcher who turned that up has to be wrong about both Lucy and the *Amulet*, but could be referring to 'Lacy de Vere'— and Jewsbury is one person who could resemble MWS." See Nora Crook's note on the discrepancy in *Mary Shelley's Literary Lives and other Writings* (Vol. 4 xlv-xlvi). There is no Lucy/Lacy De Vere in the *Amulet* by anyone. Neither is there a Lucy/Lacy in the Anonymous entries identified by Boyle. In all of the popular titles, there's no other de Vere story at all. The most likely author of the story is Maria Jane Jewsbury.

only to meet again in hatred and blood-thirstiness—only to reunite in the fierce onset of battle—neighbours as strangers, friends as rivals, children of one mother as sworn foes!

Though it was in consequence of these wars that the family of the de Veres became extinct—from one sorrow, and one disgrace, they were free—they neither espoused the cause of rebellion, nor were they divided amongst themselves. At the first raising of king Henry's standard the old baron braced on his armour; and if, owing to the changed fortunes of his house, many went forth to the service of that monarch with a larger train of vassals, not one, whether prince or knight, could compete with Hugh de Vere in the value of his offering. He brought six brace sons, devoted to him and to each other, the pillars of his house, the guardians of his age. Even the youngest, the fair stripling Lacy, girt with the sword which his father, when himself a youth, had wielded at Agincourt—he too was there, stately in step and bold of heart as the mailed man of a hundred battles.

That was neither a time nor a court calculated to encourage tenderness of heart; and she, the guiding spirit [277] of both, was little subject to its influence; yet as the baron presented his sons, each after each according to his age, an expression of sorrow passed for an instant over the countenance of queen Margaret, when Lacy stepped from the circle and kneeled down. "Nay, nay, my lord," said she, hastily, "leave the boy behind; why expose a life that can benefit neither friend nor foe? Rise, rise, poor child; what canst thou do for us?"

"I can die," said the noble boy, with a passionate enthusiasm, that thrilled his father's heart with mingled pride and sorrow.

"Well said!" replied the queen, fixing her cold, proud eye on Lacy's countenance, yet glowing with emotion.

He understood its meaning, and returned the searching glance with something like an expression of indignant defiance.

"I perceive he is a de Vere," said the queen, turning to the old baron, for whom the compliment and its accompanying smile were intended. "But where is poor Blanche?" continued she, again addressing Lacy: "if thou hast left her in the north, she, too, may need a knight's protection: thou art a brave spirit; but dost thou well to leave her in charge of hirelings?—for her sake—for thine own, peril not thy youth in our cause. Lord Hugh, command him back to thy castle: if Warwick keep court in the north, he may chance to see fighting even there." This was no common strain with Margaret of Anjou; but her own princely boy, the magnanimous, ill-fated Edward, stood beside her, and the woman [278] and the mother triumphed for an instant over the imperious and dark-minded queen.

"Craving your grace's favour," said Lacy, in a determined tone, before his father had time to reply, "were Blanche my wife, instead of my sister, I would neither live nor die like a bird in a cage: when the arrow finds me"—and the boy pointed as he spoke to his device, a falcon in full flight—"it shall be thus, free and fearless."

No further explanation or entreaty was attempted. Lacy accompanied his father and brothers; and ere time had written manhood on his brow, he had borne his part in many a well-fought field. The various changes in the royal fortunes are, however, too well known to require enumeration here; indeed, except as connected with the fortunes of Lacy de Vere, they are irrelevant. On him and his they told so soon and so fatally, that, at the period to which this legend is supposed to refer, he was no longer the fair stripling who had vowed to die before he well knew the nature of death. The years that had elapsed since then were, it is true, few in number; but they had been years of strife and storm, crowded with fearful alternations of victory and defeat, flight and pursuit, alike grievous and unavailing. The great struggle was yet undecided—Lacy de Vere was still a youthful warrior: but, oh, how changed, how care-worn! The bloom had forsaken his cheek; buoyancy had left his spirit; prompt in fight, and cool in council, he played his part in the desperate game like one to whom life and death, success and failure, were alike uncertain and indifferent. And to [279] him all things else were changed. He no longer rode forth encouraged by the presence of his father and five brave brothers: one by one that little company was cut off; each after each, in the order of birth, fell by his side; and he, the youngest of his father's house, became its head—the sole heir of a race of heroes, the baron de Vere!

It was the battle of Towton which invested Lacy with these melancholy honours, and rendered him at the same time a fugitive; for that battle, so sanguinary in itself, was fatal to the queen and her adherents. Stung to madness by the death of his last surviving brother, and the utter ruin of that cause, in defence of which all that was dear to him had perished, the words of Margaret, the tears of Blanche, rushed upon his memory; that tie of kindred which he had once so lightly esteemed, now, that it was the only one remaining, assumed its rightful sway over his wounded spirit. He found that the relative love which God hath planted in the human heart, however it may be outraged for a time by stoicism, by worldly wisdom, or worldly glory, will return to the proudest bosom in the dark day of adversity. Lacy de Vere, who once, in the delirium of martial pride, scorned his home, and deserted her who, as the offspring of the *same* birth, was bound to him by a more than common sisterhood, now flung down the insignia of his rank and bearing, and fled from the field of battle. True to that instinct which governs all men in their misfortunes, he fled towards his long deserted home, and he found it, as his fears had well predicted, desolate and in ruins. One horrible peculiarity [280] in the present contest was the license assumed by both parties to devastate whatever part of the country they passed through, whether hostile or friendly to their interests. Even those engaged in the same cause were not always safe from each other; many an old feud was avenged; many a rival removed, or his property destroyed, apparently by some excess on the part of the troops, but frequently at the command of their more interested leaders. The devastation which had been wrought in the present instance seemed more than the result of destroyers animated by merely general motives; there appeared to have been a guiding spirit at word. There did not remain sufficient building to shelter a beggar from the storm; not a tree, not a shrub, but was either cut down or mutilated; the grass and corn had been consumed with fire as they stood; even the paltry hovels which had sheltered the domestic labourers were leveled with the earth: all was destroyed without distinction or remorse—destroyed in the spirit of *hatred*.

Lacy de Vere walked round the remains of this, the last hold of his race; and in the anguish of a noble spirit brought low by self-reproach, he rejoiced that his father and brothers were in the grave. But when he reached a spot which had once been a little herb-garden carefully walled round, now open on all sides, and choked with the drifted sea sand, rage and grief overcame him—he could no longer refrain from the expression of his inward emotions. "Yes," said he, with a bitter smile: "yes, an enemy hath done this; but no enemy of king Henry and [281] his cause: it was no Robin of Redsdale with his marauders; no vindictive Warwick; no savage borderers: it was *my* enemy, the enemy of my house, Lionel Wethamstede, *thou* didst this evil! Assassin serpent, *twice* I spared thee in battle, and twice didst thou ride off bidding me seek my flourishing home and fair sister!—blind, blind fool, to cherish a tiger till it longed for its keeper's blood! Lionel, Lionel Wethamstede," continued the speaker more vehemently, while his whole frame was tremulous with passion, "didst thou slaughter the lamb in the fold? was the bird crushed with the nest? Oh, Lionel, in thou *didst* spare Blanche in the day of destruction, all, all, were thy sins thousand-fold, shall be forgiven!—If Blanche lives—it thou has spared her—I, even I, thine enemy will bless thee!"

Lacy was too much engrossed by his own emotions to be aware that he was watched, or even observed, by a boy couched amongst the rubbish. At the first glance the intruder appeared nothing more than a young peasant, worn with fright and famine; but upon a second view, his attire, coarse as it was, could not disguise the natural grace of the wearer; nor even the dark cloth bonnet, though of the kind only worn by menials, give a sordid expression to the noble countenance which it shaded. Hitherto he had remained perfectly quiet, eyeing Lacy with mingled anxiety and interest; but when the last words of the young knight's passionate invocation died upon the air, he rose from his hiding-place with a slow and stately step, and addressed him in a tone that struck [282] like the east wind to the listener's heart—a tone of reproach, if aught so sweet could be said to convey reproach, of affection and deep sorrow. "And where wert *thou*, Lacy de Vere, when the spoiler stole upon thy heritage? Where was *thy* care when she for whom thou mournest prayed thee by that mystery of love which unites those born in the same hour, to stay and shield her from treachery and violence? And didst thou spare Lionel Wethamstede?—Look to it; for, of a truth, in the day of his power not so will he spare thee:—look to it, for he hath vowed vengeance against all who bear thy name and all who call thee master; but few, few are those. He hath begun his work well; think ye not he will finish? When thou wert young thou hatedst him; for the lying lip and craven spirit are hateful to the brave and true. But he saw it—he withered in the scornful glances of thy dark eye—and he swore to have vengeance—slow, secret, but sure vengeance, on thee and thine!"

"He hath it, he hath it!" groaned Lacy; "he hath it, to the last drop of bitterness."

"He hath it *not*," resumed the boy, solemnly. "Dost not thou, the offender, live? and she who spurned him as a reptile when he proffered her safety—and his hand?—Look to it, last of a lordly race; spare him not the *third* time. He hath laid thy dwelling in the dust; those who were hirelings he corrupted; those who were faithful he slew; and she who was born to mate with princes fled for her life to the dark and noisome cavern of the rock. Yet is the work of vengeance incomplete.—Weep on, [283] Lacy de Vere," continued the mysterious speaker, after a pause, only interrupted by the baron's convulsive sobs; "though thou art a warrior, weep on—what knows thou of *Grief?*—It hath come to thee in its royal robes, amid sounding trumpets, and gorgeous banners, and the shout of victory, and the presence of mighty warriors:—but grief hath come to me in lowlier guise—in darkness, and cold, and neglect, and hunger, and sickness of heart, and loneliness as of the grave; and I shall weep no more, unless perchance for thee!"

"Curse, curse me, Blanche!" said Lacy, vehemently; for his heart told him that she herself was by his side. "I can bear all things now I have found thee;" and saying this he drew her to his bosom, and wept over her like a child.

Further details of the conversation which ensued on the reunion of those who had so long been lost to each other are needless.

Love is a child that speaks in broken words. It is easy to conceive of the self-reproaches uttered by Lacy, and the sweet forgiveness and consolation spoken by Blanche; of the anxious question and fond reply; their mutual mourning over the past, and mutual cares for the future; both softened by the reflection that, come weal come woe, the bond of affection would never more be divided. There needed neither vow nor witness; yet there, amid the ruins of that home which had sheltered them throughout a happy childhood, on the hearth-stone round which for centuries their ancestors had gathered, the twins, the last [284] of their race, knelt down, and vowed to separate no more, but to have, living or dying, one fate, one home, one grave; and they called upon the spirits of their father and brethren, whose bones lay bleaching on many a field of battle, to witness and sanctify the vow. They arose, homeless and friendless—nevertheless they arose comforted; for that love, which neither change nor sorrow can lastingly embitter or absorb, again triumphed in the soul of each.

The refuge which Blanche had found for herself, on the destruction of her home and the death or flight of those left to guard it, was too fearful a spot to have been selected by one less courageous, or under circumstances less appalling. A line of rock extended along the seashore for about the space of half a mile, gradually rising from one extremity, and as gradually declining to the other. It appeared one vast parapet, a continued range of stone battlements, erected by Nature—at once to overlook and brave the ocean beneath. The front was as completely perpendicular as if hewn by the hammer and the chisel, while lichens, mosses, ivy—every variety of graceful creeping shrub—overspread its surface, as though trained there by the hand of man. It was wonderful to view what seemed a gigantic wall of cold hard stone, thus magnificently embroidered with the foliage of earth, while here and there masses of the hoary and weather-stained rock showed like ruined castles amid the clinging "greenery." Nearly at the summit of the highest point, inaccessible as it would seem except to the sea-bird and the goat, was a [285] natural arch, scooped out of the rock, and opening into a cavern. The ivy spread around that arch with peculiar beauty; adjacent parts of the rock brightened in the beams of the morning, or in the moonlight; but that cavern always retained the same aspect—dark, noisome, unearthly. This was Blanche's refuge—the dwelling-place of her who had been delicately reared, as befitted the only daughter of a noble house. Lacy was mute with surprise and terror when he first saw her ascend, what appeared to him as inaccessible to the foot as any castle wall. There were, however, though he perceived them not, inequalities on the surface; and now clinging to a bush—now grasping a root of ivy, her nailed peasant's shoes tinkling at every step against the stony path—her slight figure alternately hidden and revealed amongst the shrubs—Blanche, to whom habit had familiarized the perilous ascent, reached the cavern: but as she stood in the dark entrance, the moonlight glimmering on her countenance, and her voice coming down from that vast height a mere "filament of sound," Lacy could have believed her a creature of another world and species.

    She was not, however, companionless in this her aerial home: the goats often repaired thither to rest; the seabird there deposited her eggs; and to them had she frequently been indebted for sustenance when the rock and the shore failed to afford their natural tribute of berries and shell-fish.

    Necessity, that teacher sterner and more efficient even than duty, soon accustomed Lacy to that difficult ascent [286] and rude hiding place. He had been too familiar with hardship and sorrow to mourn over outward privations; and, ere long, he loved that "dim retreat," hallowed as it was by repose and safety, and cheered by the presence of her who was not only his sister, but his best and only friend.

> His garb was humble: ne'er was seen
> Such garb with such a noble mien:
> Among the shepherd-grooms no mate

> Had he, a child of strength and state!
> Yet lack'd not friends for solemn glee,
> And a cheerful company,
> That learn'd of him submissive ways,
> And comforted his private days.
> To his side the fallow-deer
> Came, and rested without fear;
> The eagle, lord of land and sea,
> Stoop'd down to pay him fealty
>
> WORDSWORTH.

The desires which once consumed his spirit were extinguished; the vain strife and yet vainer joys and ambitions of the world no longer occupied his mind. "Revenge and all ferocious thoughts were dead:" he could remember his enemies, ay, even Lionel Wethamstede, in peace; and when he walked among the neighbouring herdsmen, lowlier in lot than themselves, or stood in the opening of his mountain-hold, and looked on the ocean roaring beneath, or the host of heaven shining quietly above, Lacy de Vere forgot the past, and, calling his sister to his side, pronounced himself a happy man. [287]

But this retreat, this respite from misfortune, was not destined to remain long unmolested. The battle of Towton had, it is true, placed Edward Duke of York on the throne, and wholly destroyed or scattered the adherents of Queen Margaret; but that remorseless prince, deeming his power only to be secured by continued bloodshed, still allowed his followers to ravage the north, as having been the strong-hold of the Lancastrian cause. Among the most active in this murderous employment was Lionel Wethamstede. He knew that Lacy de Vere yet lived, concealed, as he had reason to suspect, in the neighbourhood of his former dwelling. Except as affording means of gaining fortune and distinction, the cause of king Edward or queen Margaret were alike indifferent to him; it was personal hatred which induced him to hunt out the Lancastrians with such relentless seal—the desire to discover and exterminate the last of that family, whose protection he had so long enjoyed and cruelly requited. During childhood and youth, he had been a favourite with the old Baron de Vere, and as such allowed to be an inmate of the castle; before him he had masked, under the show of humility and devoted zeal, the designing, treacherous spirit, which crouches that it may the more securely spring upon its prey, and lays in servile submission the foundation of despotic power. The young Lacy, bold and open as became his birth, instinctively scorned the minion, even before he discovered how well that scorn was merited. Many a proud glance and bitter taunt were bestowed by the fearless youth, little dreaming, that of [288] all such, however unnoticed at the time, Lionel kept a too faithful record, and would one day claim for them a deadly recompense. And now that day was near at hand. Hatred, once formed in the heart, turns neither to the right hand nor to the left till its work is done. Love, even the love of a mother for her babe, may be diverted—grief, though of a father for his dead first-born, be forgotten—gratitude may pass like the morning dew, and pity as a noon-day cloud—HATRED alone can survive all change, all time, all circumstance, all other emotions, nay, it can survive the accomplishment of revenge, and, like the vampyre, prey on its dead victim!

"I know not," said Lacy, as he and Blanche stood together one evening in the archway of their cavern, "I know not why, when all around me is so fair, sadness and forebodings of coming evil should hang so heavily on my heart."

"Nay, nay, dear Lacy," replied Blanche; "look at our castle, which will resist both fire and violence; our faithful rock, with all its luxuriant garniture flashing in the light of that departing sun: what should we fear? Art thou weary of repose, Lacy, or dost thou mistrust thy warder?" continued she with affectionate playfulness, at the same instant placing her arm within his.

But the cloud passed not from her brother's brow, and he replied in the low broken voice men use when troubled in spirit: "I tell thee, Blanche—nay, count not my words idle, for an influence is on me which I can neither gainsay nor resist—I tell thee, evil hangs over us—my [289] end is near. *Twice* I spared Lionel Wethamstede; and twice, since the last going down of yonder sun, have I beheld myself in his power. Oh! it was a dark vision, a dream more fearful than a field of battle!"

"Dreams, Lacy, visions!—what of them? When I dwelt here alone, oh, how often did I see thee prisoner—wounded—dying—dead! I, too, had dreams and visions, and yet they came not true; why, then, should thine?"

Lacy made no reply to this inquiry, for he heard it not: and when he again spoke, his words were but the expression of the melancholy reverie into which he had fallen. "Yes—it was down there—stealing along the foot of the rock, half hidden by the trees and underwood, Lionel and his black band—six—black in spirit as in outward guise—not one ever known to strike twice or to spare—I knew them all—and why they came."

"Lacy!—Baron de Vere!" exclaimed Blanche, shaking his arm, which she held, with her utmost strength, "rouse from this unmanly mood; let the babe and the peasant start at shadows, but thou, I pray thee—let me not have to blush for him who I ought to honour!"

"And whom thou wilt ere long weep," replied Lacy, in an unaltered voice. "Blanche de Vere, misjudge me not! I spoke neither of flight, nor fear, nor supplication for life, nor of aught that may disgrace a warrior—I did but speak of DEATH—death that were welcome if it came only to myself; but my sister, dearer than all the kindred I have lost, were all now living—my last, last friend, death is on its way to *thee* too!" [290]

"It will not be death if shared with thee," replied Blanche fervently;

"death would be to live when thou wert gone. I did thee wrong, noble, generous brother! forgive it." And she sat down at his feet, and covered her face with her hands.

"Glorious orb!" said Lacy, after having for some minutes earnestly regarded the sun, which was now slowly descending into the ocean with more than meridian pomp, "unchanged, unchangeable—bright at thy setting as on thy first rising—most glorious orb, farewell! And thou too, earth, steeped in the tears and blood of thy children, polluted with crime, groaning with sorrow, yet withal so beauteously appareled, many graves has though afforded my father's house—spare it ye another—the last—and now," said he—the steady solemn tone in which he had hitherto spoken changing to one of indignant defiance, while a change as complete overspread his countenance—"now, even now, that grave is needed—the appointed hour is arrived—yonder the murderers come, black and silent as in the vision; but the last de Vere dies not like a reptile, driven into its hold and crushed in darkness: the doom that is decreed shall be met. Rise, Blanche! sister by birth, companion in sorrow, daughter of heroes, arise, and let us descend! let not Lionel have to glory in our shame!— haste!—haste! I see his black plume waving to and fro—his spear glitters through the trees—nearer—brighter every instant."

"I am ready, ready to endure all," said Blanche, firmly; "but oh, let not Lionel see our parting anguish: [291] bless me for the last time here!"—and she laid her head upon her brother's bosom. They stood regarding each other, speechless and in tears; to part was harder than to die.

Lacy's visions and forebodings were indeed on the point of being realized. The implacable Lionel had learned but too surely their place of retreat, and but too truly was he, with his ruffians, winding along the foot of the rock; even now they were within view of the cavern, in the opening of which stood that devoted pair, whose doom was sealed before they knew it. A shout of brutal triumph suddenly burst from Lionel and his band, as they halted when sufficiently near the spot: at the same instant, two picked archers obeyed their leader's command with murderous precision, and ere the defenceless victims could look round or utter a cry, the arrows pierced them, clasped as they were in each other's arms! One of the shafts had entered Lacy's heart, and in the twinkling of an eye, without word or groan, he was numbered with the dead. For an instant, a single instant, his dying eyes were turned upon his fellow-victim; and that glance, though transient as the flash of lightning, revealed love stronger than death, love that would exist beyond the grave. The wound received by Blanche, though mortal, was not calculated to occasion instant death, and nobly did she employ the precious respite.

"My brother shall not become a prey to the birds of the air," were her first words on perceiving that he was indeed dead; and, with an energy scarcely human, she prepared [292] for her labour of love. Habit had, it is true, rendered the ascent and descent of that rock so easy, that in the darkest night she would scarcely have missed her footing; but wounded as she was at present, her intention to descend, and convey with her Lacy's yet warm and bleeding body, appeared impracticable. Love, however, enabled her to execute what love had induced her to determine. Carefully wrapping the corse in every garment she could afford from herself, to defend it in some measure from the sharp points of the rock, she partly drew and partly bore the precious burden down a pathway, which to any but herself would, under such circumstances, have assuredly been fatal. She felt neither fatigue nor pain; she heeded not that every shrub and stone in the descent was sprinkled with her own blood; her sold care was to shield the senseless body in her arms from wounds and injury. Heaven, in pity, strengthened her for the task, and she reached the ground in safety—her labour accomplished, her reward obtained. Those who had come out against the noble pair gathered round them in silence; some, in truth, touched by this last exhibition of love, passing even the love of women.

She unfolded the coverings from the body, which was now becoming cold and stiff; then looking upon the armed circle, she fixed her eye on him, the evil spirit, whose ministers they were, and addressed him like one gifted with unearthly authority. "Lionel, they work is finished! thou wert the nursling of our house, and hast become its destroyer! Thou hast rendered bitter for sweet, and evil [293] for good, and injuries for benefits! thou has brought low the old, the honourable, the young, the brave, the virtuous, and hitherto none hath stayed thy hand: but come near, Lionel Wethamstede, and I will advise thee of things that shall befall thee yet. By day thou shalt dread treachery, and by night dream visions of horror; thou shalt flee when none pursue, and be afraid where no fear is: thou hast built thy fortunes in thy master's blood; some around thee shall build theirs in thing: as thou hast hated, so shall others hate thee: scorn, and sorrow, and affliction, and want—every evil thou has wrought on us shall cleave fourfold and for ever to thee and thine—yea, cleave as the flesh cleaveth to the bone. Ay, go thy way, man of blood! brace they helmet, and mount thy steed—thou mayest escape me *now*; but I shall see thee again, where neither horse nor armour will avail thee—before God, who will condemn the murderer in the face of heaven, in the day of judgment—Lionel Wethamstede, thou shalt meet me *there*!"

She ceased. The livid paleness and the damps of death had gradually gathered on her countenance; every sentence had been uttered in mortal anguish: nevertheless she had maintained throughout the cold, calm bearing of one already separated from the body. The wretch to whom her words had been addressed shivered under their influence, as though exposed to an ice-blast; superstitious horror mastered the ferocious spirit till then scarcely satisfied with its revenge; and setting spurs to his horse, he departed from the spot like one pursued by an evil spirit. [294]

"Let those who shot the arrows complete their work!" said the dying maiden to the men, who remained fixed to the spot, subdued as by some supernatural agency, and scarcely conscious of their leader's departure—"let them wrap us in one shroud, and bury us in the same grave!"

One of the archers stepped forward; he was rude, even savage, in his exterior, but nature was not utterly extinct: he kneeled down beside the dying and the dead, and swore to observe the request.

"Thy victim blesses thee," replied Blanche; "farewell!" She spoke no more, for death claimed his conquest. She stretched herself on the ground beside him whom in life she had loved so well, whom dying she could not forget; placing one arm beneath his head and the other across his bosom, so that her cheek rested against his, she meekly closed her eyes, like a wearied child that sleeps on its mother's lap.

Thus died Lacy and Blanche de Vere, twins in birth, and twins also in the manner of their death. They slept not as their fathers before them, in marble monuments adorned with the stately devices; they were laid in the peasant's grave, beneath the green and trodden turf, with no record more lasting than its bright but perishable flowers. There was none to mourn over them, none to have them in remembrance, none to perpetuate their name; when they died, they died altogether, and with them the memory of a noble race passed for ever from the earth.

> So fails, so languishes, grows dim, and dies,
> All that this world is proud of!

Title

Lyndsay, David. [Dods, Mary Diana.] "The Bridal Ornaments. A Legend of Thuringia." FMN 1827. 393-416.[12] [393]

THE BRIDAL ORNAMENTS.
A legend of Thuringia.
By David Lyndsay, Esq.

The traveller, who some centuries ago had occasion to pass through the country of Thuringia, took care to choose his route by the Castle of Aarburg, unless disappointed love, or some other miserable heart-ache, cause him to seek a more solitary road. The warder stood night and day upon the watch-tower, gazing about for knights, pilgrims, or other strangers; and when lucky enough to discover one approaching, upon sounding a flourish on his cheerful horn, by the way of welcome, the gates creaked, the drawbridges rattled, the horses stamped, and the men-at-arms rode out to meet the traveller, and courteously invite him to refreshment and a night's comfortable rest. The knight of the castle had a kind word for every new comer, and, according to his rank, he either conducted him into the fall, or left him to the care of his retainers until he should think proper to depart.

The last knight of the family, Sir Thimo von de Aarburg, did not derogate from the fame acquired by his ancestors for hospitality. He had succeeded to the inheritances of his brothers, uncles, and cousins, and knew no care unless when strangers and guests were wanting to partake of the good things of his castle: in such cases it even sometimes happened that he sallied forth himself to meet travellers, and invite them to share his hospitality.

The greatest treasure in the Castle of Aarburg was [394] the knight's only daughter, celebrated throughout all Germany by the name of "the Beautiful Bertha."—Princes, counts, and knights, came from the four quarters of the earth to admire her and humbly solicit her love—but she was not to be pleased so easily: this knight she found too dull, that too presuming, and a third was splenetic—Frenchman, Britons, and Italians, all shared the same fate. "He who shall gain this bride," quoth gossip Rumour, "will be fortune's greatest favourite; for besides the enchanting beauty with which nature has endowed her, and the immense wealth which fortune has loaded her father, there is an invaluable casket of jewels—an ancient property of the house of Aarburg—which she, as the last of her family, will receive at her nuptials for her bridal ornaments."

At the distance of a few arrow-flights from the Castle of Aarburg stood an <u>ancient ruin, which</u> the late owner, Sir Heerwart, had left as the sole inheritance of

[12] Maria Diana Dods (a cross-dressing poet) used the male pseudonym "David Lyndsay" when publishing in the annuals. See Betty T. Bennett's work, *Mary Diana Dods: A Gentleman and a Scholar* (Johns Hopkins UP, 1994).

his only son Baldwin. Before the period when the emperor Maxmilian introduced the spreading plant of Roman law into German soil, and whilst every knight could protect his property with spear and sword, the good Sir Heewart was not the poorest among those of his own rank; for he was brave in battle, and made great profit by booty and ransom: but now, when the knightly spear was obliged to bend before the goose-quill, and the emperor, during public peace, laid heavy fines upon all private feuds against the property of others, he could not get on quite so well as usual. Year after year he was obliged to cede [395] apartments and towers of his ruinous castle to the bats and the owls, whose profession abroad was not prohibited life that of its luckless lord.

The young knight, Sir Baldwin, beheld with great pain the natural decay of the home of his ancestors. Little space as the whole of his personal property required, it appeared very much as if his castle would only grant him that little for the few warm days of summer, by no means promising him protection against the frost and snow of the ensuing winter. He held a private council with himself, as to what was to be done under such circumstances; but his thoughts always swerved from the tasks which he had given to his understanding, and amused his imagination with dreams and wishes, which had no sort of connexion with the case in question.

Sir Baldwin's heart was unfortunately as near to ruin as his paternal castle, with this only difference, that the cause was not from the attacks of age and pitiless enemies, but rather from the repeated assaults of youth and beauty, and against which his means of defence were still more slender. He had seen the daughter of the knight of Aarburg at a tournament, where she had been proclaimed the Queen of Beauty, and presented the prize to the victor. Sir Baldwin's arm was strengthened tenfold by the sight of her loveliness: he lifted the knights out their saddles as if they had been men of straw; and his blows fell as it spirits of the air conducted his arm. The fair Bertha was not more shortsighted than the rest of her lovely sex in these particular cases; she saw plainly enough that her [396] eyes were the sunbeams, and her soft words the breath of that spring, which produced such vigorous plants of valour in the bosom of the young knight: she therefore rewarded the judges of the combat with her sweetest smiles, when they with one accord decreed the prize to her hero; and she delivered it to him with a blush, that to an experienced eye would have betrayed what was passing in her bosom.

After the tournament, Sir Baldwin did not fail to pay frequent visits to the knight of Aarburg in his own castle; and as he was a lively companion, and assisted the baron not only to project, but also to execute many an excellent practical joke, he soon became a daily guest at Aarburg, and always found a seat ready for him at the table, with a chamber and a bed besides, when he did not like to ride home through fog and darkness. The Lady Bertha sent many an inquiring glance towards the active, slender knight; even challenged him sometimes to the dance, when awkward guests threatened her with a round or a saraband; and solicited his advice when she purposed to add something new to her ornaments or her attire. These little condescensions gave courage and strength to the hopes of the young knight; and one lovely summer's evening, when the Lady Bertha was seated in a bower, accompanying her harp with her sweet voice, he suddenly found his heart become too warm and too large for his bosom: so he sprang up from the bank of turf, sank at Bertha's feet, and swore roundly, that, like the sound of her song, he only lived by her breath, and fondly and [397] earnestly wooed for her sweet love in return. The lady was surprised, but not so much at the knight's glowing passion, which she had for a long time observed with secret satisfaction, as at its hasty and violent effect. In her consternation the harp slipped from her fair hands, and, as she bent forward to recover the instrument, her lips encountered those of Sir Baldwin; while her arms, which were accidentally extended, intertwining themselves with his, the lovers were guilty of a kiss and an embrace, before they were aware how much the demon Chance had played into the hands of the divinity Cupid. After the first few moments, they were somewhat startled upon considering how Sir Thimo, the rich lord of Aarburg, would regard his daughter's love for the poor knight of the ruins. They conned the subject over and over again many nights after this; and sat many an hour together without coming to any conclusion, except that Baldwin was to fix himself more firmly in the favour of the knight of Aarburg, and to take an early opportunity of disclosing his hopes and plans respecting Bertha. This opportunity soon offered itself. Notwithstanding all the magnificence and expense of the Castle of Aarburg, father Thimo's money-chests became fuller and fuller every day, so that there was really no end to his riches and purchases. On one occasion (the acquisition of a rich lordship), when his friends and guests wished him joy in full bumpers, he placed his cup gloomily upon the table before him, and would not accept their congratulations. "Of what use is it all to me?" said he; "you know I have no heir, to whom [398] to leave my property and possessions." "No," replied one of the guests; "but have you not a lovely daughter, who can give you just such a son-in-law as your heart would desire?" "True," replied the knight of Aarburg, sighing; "but I would rather have had a son: a son-in-law carries off his wife to his own castle, and the old father sits deserted and solitary in his empty hall. If I had a son now—a son, for instance, like Baldwin there—I should look out for a proper wife, and place him over this new lordship, or let him dwell in the castle of my ancestors, where there is room enough for a whole generation."

Sir Baldwin's courage rose at these words—it had already been considerably elevated by the quantity of wine which he had drunk; he did not hesitate as to how he should begin his speech, but commenced the attack straightforward: "Father Thimo," said he, "what hinders you from making me your son?"— Give me your daughter, the beautiful Bertha, to wife, and let us dwell in one of your castles, or, if it please you better, here at Aarburg: you shall have children and grandchildren to your heart's content."

But instead of accepting this friendly offer in a friendly manner, the knight of Aarburg turned coolly round, and showed a very long face to the speaker; and "Do you think so, knight of Heerwart?" was the only answer he deigned to give the petitioner, who beheld him quietly resume, without further remark, an indifferent conversation with one of his guests. Baldwin's anger rose at the coolness with which the knight of Aarburg received his courtship. In [399] the zeal of his heart he rose from his seat, repeated his words, and declared his love for the beautiful Bertha in terms of the most impassioned eloquence. Thimo allowed him quietly to go through with his oratory, and when he had finished, "Knight," said he, "how am I to know whether you really love my daughter, or only woo her for your own temporal advantage? Hear me quietly—I listened patiently to you. You appeal to your knightly word; that is certainly sufficient for me in all affairs of honour: but my Bertha is not only the pride of my house, but also the darling of my heart. Besides, I have, like all rich people, my whims, which all your eloquence will not make me resign: he who wins the hand of my Bertha must be rich in castles and lands, in order that she may not live in less splendour as a wife than she did as a maiden. I can add nothing as a fortune, for all I possess will be spent in the purchase of bridal ornaments, magnificent as those which a spirit once bestowed upon our family, and which, since that period, have unfortunately been lost. For this reason my son-in-law must be a rich man. Those bridal ornaments I will have, and their purchase will swallow up my fortune; but they are, notwithstanding, and acquisition too important to be neglected."

To Sir Baldwin this speech appeared extremely ridiculous, though he took care not to declare this as his particular opinion; on the contrary, he affected to treat the thing in a very different manner. "Sir Thimo," he began gravely, throwing a most sentimental expression into his face, placing his right hand pathetically upon his [400] heart, "surely you cannot imagine that I have any wish for these vanities and superfluous treasures; keep them all, I beseech you, for ever: it is Bertha herself alone I covet; is not her beauty a richer jewel than—" "Pshaw!" thundered the old man, now become exceedingly impatient, "don't I know beforehand all that you are going to say? Have I not sworn the same thing myself a thousand times, and could you do otherwise, professing love for my Bertha, than swear by all the saints that you preferred one lock of her fair to all the chains of gold that emperors and princes could bestow? There, now, you look rather foolish; but no matter. Bertha must have the ornaments, and I will have my whim; for the rest we may still be good friends if you choose; but you must first pass your knightly word, that there shall be no private tampering with Bertha's duty, neither inside nor outside the castle: I'll have no love-making, Baldwin, or we part company at once."

Sir Baldwin made a wry face or two at this bitter pill, which nevertheless he was obliged to swallow; and therefore, much against his will, gave his knightly word to Sir Thimo, lest he should be altogether deprived of the sight of his lovely mistress. The knights and gentlemen, friends of Sir Thimo, who were present at this scene, forgot to sympathise with the unsuccessful wooer, in the ardour of their curiosity respecting those valuable bridal ornaments, on the possession of which the lord of Aarburg seemed to have placed all his happiness. They anxiously inquired whence they came, whither they had gone, and [401] what were the particular virtues they possessed; swearing most manfully (for Sir Thimo's wine had inflamed their valour) to get them back for their good host, even from under the Grand Turk's beard. "Whither they are gone," replied Sir Thimo, "is more than I can tell you, since the loss was before my father's time. The last person who wore them was the Lady Urilda, the sole child and heiress of the then Baron von der Aarburg, and hers is a fearful history. She loved a knight, who was as poor, though not so honest, as Baldwin there; and upon her father's refusal to permit the match, she, on the suggestion of her admirer, murdered the poor old man, and, dressing herself in the bridal ornaments, waited at midnight for her lover to carry her off. He came, as the legend goes—but what he said or did, or whither they went, has never been known to this day; only during that dreary night frightful shrieks and loud wailings were heard, as of one in mortal agony beseeching for mercy; and in the morning it was known that the Lady Urilda and the bridal ornaments had strangely disappeared together. It is an ugly history, and the less is said upon the subject the better; but as to the 'how they came into the family,' the story being of a more pleasing character, I shall not hesitate to repeat it as it has been often related to me by our old confessor.

"The Countess Ursula von der Aarburg, who lived many centuries ago, and was a perfect pattern both as a wife and a mother, was sleeping quietly one night among her seven children (it was the Eve of St. John), when she [402] suddenly awoke from hearing herself called by a shrill clear voice. Opening her heavy eyelids, she was surprised to observe a singularly-dressed female figure, of great beauty but diminutive stature, standing by the side of her couch, and who said, in a sweet small voice, 'Arise, noble lady, and lend a sufferer your assistance; the Queen of the Mountain will die without your aid.' The countess rose, though utterly unable to understand the speaker, who waited upon her toilette, and officiated as her waiting-maid, and with as much readiness and zeal as if it had been the habit of years; and the countess herself, who was no very keen observer, could not help remarking, that with the several articles of her dress seemed to be instinct with life, or to possess some very extraordinary deference to her attendant, the motion of whose little finger they instantaneously obeyed, placing themselves upon their owner's person at the first signal given by the stranger. The Countess Ursula had never been so well attended before, and in pure gratitude for the honour done her (howbeit not loving moonlight walks, having seven children), quietly followed wherever her singular visitor thought fit to lead her. Away the went (not flying, but soberly walking) from the castle, unseen of the guards, through whom, however, they passed, over ramparts and drawbridges, through doors and gates, over fields and water, without even wetting their feet, till they arrived at a high mountain, at the foot of which her guide knocked upon a square tablet for admission. The stony doors gave way, and immediately a magnificent glittering arch [403] was formed in the mountain, under which the travellers passed to the splendid hall of a subterranean regal palace. Here many beautiful forms of men and women, but all proportionably small, met the countess and her companion, and respectfully saluting them, conducted them through many royal saloons, glittering with gold and silver, to one more superb than any of the rest, in which were a pair of golden folding-doors communicating with another chamber. These suddenly flew open, and another female advancing, took the countess by the hand, and saying that the Mountain-Queen longed for her impatiently, conducted her into the apartment. The little men fell back respectfully, but the waiting-maids accompanied the countess into the chamber of the sovereign. Here walls of pure marble were surmounted by a cupola of soft green emerald, under which stood a bed of beaten gold, and upon that reclined a lovely female, mild and gracious as the Italian representations of the Madonna. 'Noble lady,' said she, in a gentle tone, to dame Ursula, 'be not alarmed; you are even safer here than in the home of your fathers: approach me without hesitation, and assist me in this hour of mortal terror, which has fallen upon me in the Eve of St. John, when the spirits of the earth are powerless until morning. I bear beneath my heart a pledge of our sovereign-husband's love, which, without your aid, cannot see the light; assist me, then, in this my hour of need, as you would hope for help in yours.'

"Ursula was moved by this gentle address and the high confidence reposed in her: she spoke some words [404] of comfort to the royal patient, and then blessed her with the sacred sign of the cross, in order to make quite sure the devil had no hand in the affair. In fact, every thing remained unchanged except the beautiful face of the queen, which smiled still more sweetly than before; and the soft mountain-air, which met the nerves of the stranger, was loaded with fragrance, and breathed harmony around her; for wonderful music floated above them, while Ursula presented to the queen a lovely infant boy. As the mother folded him to her heart, a loud shot was heard, and the deep majestic tones of many trumpets, pouring forth sounds of triumph, rang through this subterraneous paradise. The folding-doors again opened; the king himself entered, took the child in his arms, kissed it, and then showed it to a great number of little men, who had fallen upon their knees before the doors: they bowed their heads to the earth, and then shouted as loudly as before.

"The Countess Ursula was an astonished spectator of this strange yet happy scene, till the silver voice of the queen recalled her attention. 'Take, noble lady,' it said, 'with the grateful acknowledgements of Saffira, the Mountain-

Queen, this little casket, which will serve as a rich and perpetual monument of the gratitude she owes for your service. Be careful to preserve in your family the jewels which it contains. As long as they make part of your possessions, your house shall be the first in its country, and the branches of your genealogical tree shall even overshadow the empire itself; but if you lose it, [405] prosperity will vanish and your name be extinguished for ever. You may, nevertheless, bestow a few of these jewels upon a beloved daughter, for they have the power of communicating happiness to their possessor; but in that case be careful to replace them with gems of the same kind and value, that the whole set may be preserved entire, and each bride of the house of Aarburg may adorn herself with them on her bridal day.' She then signed to the lady who had brought Ursula thither, and placing in her hand the casket of exquisite workmanship, requested to her to conduct the countess home. This was performed immediately: the attendant waited to undress the lady with all duteous attention, placed the casket upon the table, and retired, making a most profoundly respectful courtesy.

"When my good ancestress awoke in the morning, she was very well disposed to consider the whole as a dream, till the sight of the casket staring her in the face convinced her there was no delusion. Her husband was delighted with the present, for the blessing promised by the Mountain-Queen was fulfilled to the letter; the family grew immensely rich and prosperous, and there was not a town in German where an Aarburg had not a castle. But since the jewels have been lost, we have gone rapidly to decay. One Aarburg has died childless after another, and I, the last, have no offspring save Bertha. She, however, shall retrieve the fortunes of our family: one jewel I have in my possession which came to me by inheritance, and if the Mountain-Queen is to be believed, [406] will communicate its virtues to all the other articles made to match it. This is my purpose; I will have the set made entire; and you now understand why I can give Bertha no other fortune, since mine will be all consumed by the purchase of the jewels with which I am resolved to adorn her on her wedding-day."

At the close of this wonderful story, the knight's hearers began to discuss the Countess Ursula and her midnight adventure with no little merriment and freedom. Some declared that the ancestress must have had a lively imagination— that she dreamed the thing, and then invented the jewels afterwards. Others asserted that her ladyship must have been fond of a frolic, more especially as the Mountain-King himself figured upon the scene: but these were the freethinking reprobates. The true believers where shocked by their impiety, and gravely produced many instances of similar facts in support of their opinion. Sir Baldwin took no part at all in the discussion; he sat, in very ill humour, looking extremely grim, in the corner, and wishing, from his inmost soul, the bridal ornaments, which had thus robbed him of a bride, at the devil.

The autumn days now began to shorten, and the period of the equinox approached. The wind whistled frostily over the stubbles, and the rain and hail beat (without much difficulty, it must be confessed) through the windows of Sir Baldwin's castle. The coldness of his home determined him to quit it; and having formed his resolution, he hastened to the knight of Aarburg, to entreat his [407] assistance and approbation of the measure. "Good Sir Thimo," said he, "I can no longer sit idly down in my dismantled castle; the storms are playing as cruel a game with that as love is doing with my heart. I intend to set out for the emperor's armor, and endeavour to gain fame and fortune by valour. Buy my castle of me: you may give me for it what you think proper." The Baron of Aarburg did so (for between honest men bargains are soon struck), though he was sincerely grieved at the prospect of Baldwin's departure. He gave, however, a noble feast in his honour; allowed him to sit, for the last time, next to the beautiful Bertha: furnished him with letters to all his castellans in the different parts of German, commanding them to treat the knight as himself during the time he should stay there; and then, bestowing upon him a few kind words and a hearty shake of the hand, seized him by the shoulder, and thrust him out of the castle.

Baldwin, as he mounted his horse, cast many a sigh towards the chamber of his beloved Bertha; yet, remembering his knightly word, he would allow himself the indulgence of a farewell, but darted gallantly forward on his travels. He found his introductory letters of no small use in procuring him good cheer and lodging. Those castellans nearest to their lord were exceedingly civil; while the more distant being, of course, in less fear of his authority, were insolent and refractory. He had almost made up his mind to trouble no more of them, when a violent storm, which overtook him hear Leipzic, drove him [408] for shelter to Sir Thimo's castle of Frankenberg. Sir Baldwin, who was at heart a cheerful fellow, perceived the windows all gaily lighted up, and heard sounds of music and dancing with infinite delight; for he hoped to join the revellers, and shortly to be as merry as themselves. Three times he blew stoutly upon the horn before any one noticed his application; and at last a gruff old warder stumped towards him, and shrilly demanded his business. The knight could read on the warder's brow that he had disturbed their merriment, and was by no means a welcome guest; yet nothing daunted, he sent in his letter to the castellan, and was instantly admitted. "Sir knight," said the castellan, trying to look, and, what as infinitely more difficult, to speak soberly, "you see how we are doing—a marriage in my family is the occasion of this little festivity. Partake of our cheer, noble sir; eat, drink, and be merry. I can, according to my lord's directions, entertain you to your heart's content; only tonight, the castle being so crowded with company, I cannot find you a bed."

"Make yourself easy, I beseech you, Mr. Castellan," replied Sir Baldwin, quite coolly, notwithstanding this difficulty—"I do not intend to quit this roof to-night; and if you will not spare me the trouble, I will undertake the search myself, and depend upon it I will find a bed, even if I am obliged to share the bride's." The castellan looked angry, but said little, conscious that it was not to his interest to offend his master's guest; he therefore suddenly recollected that two chambers in the castle [409] were vacant—one a wretched hole, through which the wind whistled so loudly as to remind Sir Baldwin of his own desolate castle at Aarburg—the other a magnificent apartment, called "the Baron's" but in a most dreary state of neglect, owing to its being entirely appropriated to the use of some fantastical goblins who kept their revels there, and had had the good taste to select this, the noblest apartment in the castle, for their exclusive accommodation.

The poor castellan strongly persuaded the knight to sleep in the storm-visited attic, in preference to that tenanted by the ghosts; but to this Sir Baldwin would be no means consent after he had viewed the apartment. He had not the fear of ghosts before his eyes, and, at any rate, esteemed them better company than hail, rain, and sleet. "Gramercy! Sir Seneschal," said he, "for your kind advice, which I do not intend to follow: I had rather sleep with the goblins, more especially as you say there are females among them, than under the chilling influence of all the winds of heaven; so, in spite of the knights adventurers, who, on their return from this chamber, have found their hands and feet had changed places, I will pass the night in it, and dare the worst that may befall me." The seneschal said nothing in reply, but sent food, wine, and lights, to the baron's chamber. In a few hours the ball broke up, and the party of revellers dispersed: the castellan's family retired to rest, and Sir Baldwin, after disposing of the contents of a small flagon of choice Rhenish, threw himself heavily upon his magnificent bed to dream of his beloved Bertha. But his [410] sleep this night was not destined to be blessed with so fair a vision; his thoughts incessantly ran upon the unpromising state of his affairs, and the little prospect there was of a union with his beloved. Tired of these vexatious and unprofitable reflections, he tried hard to lose himself in sleep, but found it impossible to succeed: he turned fidgetily from side to side—pulled his pillow, now up, now down—shut his eyes, opened them—said his prayers over and over again; and finding this last remedy inefficacious, made up his mind, though in extreme ill-humour, to lie awake all night. No sooner had he come to this conclusion, than he was startled by a noise which seemed to issue from the chimney of this deserted apartment in which he was so unsuccessfully courting repose.

He now banished as anxiously all thoughts of sleep as he had before endeavoured to encourage them, and, suddenly facing round towards the seat of the odd noise which had disturbed him, beheld, to his utter astonishment, a human hand fall down the chimney; to this succeeded a foot, then another hand, and then again another foot, and so quietly, by degrees, all the requisites for making up a human body, each attired according to its own proper mode of dressing: and these rolling together, and kindly uniting, there arose from the fragments a gigantic figure, who, with belt and partizan, huge mustaches and grim looks, mounted guard on one side of the fire-place.

This organizing process was suspended for a few seconds, and then began again, and a second halberdier deliberately stalked forward, and placed himself opposite to [411] his elder brother, on the other side of this wondrous laboratory; but things did not long go on so quietly. The gentle rain of limbs, which had hitherto descended so modestly, was changed into a loud and rattling shower; and the delicate feet of women, fists of men, heads of children, a whole assortment of human limbs, rolled pellmell down the chimney. Amongst these were materials for tables, chairs, and footstools—kettles, covers, dishes, and goblets, followed in grand confusion, with every thing necessary for a great entertainment, so that one half of the chamber was filled with this lumber. The two first-born of this ghastly creation then stepped gravely forward, laid aside their partizans, and began their operations by reducing to order this chaos of materials for the creation of the latest of worlds. From this mass of human fragments they stuck folks together so cleverly, and with so much dexterity, despatch, silence, and taste, that it was impossible to doubt the extent of their practice in this their most extraordinary vocation. From their Promethean fingers, which beat the maker of poor Frankenstein all to nothing, there arose a whole train of stately-looking domestics, who bestirred themselves to prepare a splendid banquet, which soon sparkled upon the table. Guests only were wanting. These, however, were soon produced from the alchymical chimney. It really hailed men and women, who, in the most magnificent festival dresses, took their seats upon the chairs, or walked gaily about the apartment. The last comer was a young and lovely lady, beautiful as moonlight, and as pale: her countenance was like the sigh of [412] an angel, full of grief, but of unspeakable sweetness. By her side walked a gigantic knight, black and terrible to look upon: there was a laughing fury curling round his lips, and his eyes were dark thunder-clouds, emitting flashes of lurid lightning. He rudely dragged the lovely lady to a mirror, which reflected back to her eyes, not her own fair image, but a hideous phantom, to which, when she shrank from it in horror and disgust, he again compelled her to return and contemplate the figure, while the attendants brought her magnificent ornaments and a bridal crown. In these the monster-knight obliged her to array her beautiful person before the deceptious mirror; and these articles, to the horror of Sir Baldwin, he discovered to be red-hot, as well by their glowing light, as by the hissing of the beautiful lady's flesh, when the contents of this infernal jewel-box were displayed upon her person.

Until this moment, Sir Baldwin had, from his bed, been only a silent spectator of this curious adventure; but an involuntary burst of indignation at the conduct of the black knight, which escaped him, directed the stony looks of the whole assembly of spectres towards his bed. One of them solemnly rose, took a golden goblet from the table, presented it to the human guest, and by signs invited him to rise and partake of their midnight festivity. Sir Baldwin trembled; for brave as were the ancient knights when they had a human enemy to encounter, they did not deem it at all disgraceful to be sensible of fear when opposed to the spiritual world; and Sir Baldwin, like all the rest of his brethren, would rather have seen the glitter of a hun- [413] dred Saracen sword-blades than that golden goblet which the strange drinking-companion pressed upon him so pertinaciously with his fleshless bony hand. Notwithstanding his confusion, however, he saw that there was no escaping. As his delay began to put in motion the other guests, who now commenced a slow and regular march towards his bed. To a strong mind, in such moments, the transition from terrified hesitation to the most dauntless heroism is as easy and as rapid as the change from idle boasting to pusillanimous despondency in the heart of a coward. Sir Baldwin instantly recollected himself, leaped up lightly from his bed, seized his sword in his right hand, and with his left deposited the goblet with the infernal punch upon the table. "Whoever you may be," he then exclaimed in a firm and powerful tone of voice, "how dare you challenge an honourable knight to partake of your cheer, whilst you thus oppress weak maidens, like midnight murderers and robbers? If you are human, then meet me fairly, and let us fight it out, firmly and gallantly; if you are not, then begone from this castle, and do not disturb with your presence the dwellings of human beings."

A dismal silence of some seconds which followed this speech was suddenly broken by a ghastly laugh from the black knight, which shook the very walls of the castle. "This maiden," cried he, "is mine; she gave herself to me; she won me by a crime—a midnight crime—for which each midnight she must suffer. She is my bride; and my bride she must remain, and nightly be decked in these burning ornaments, till the jewels shall return to [414] their rightful owner: meddle not then with the matter, Sir Knight, but deign to partake of our cheer."

Sir Baldwin evinced not the smallest inclination to follow this impertinent advice, but advanced in a hostile manner towards the ugly goblin who had uttered it. The latter also drew his enormous sword, and stood on his defence, but could not prevent the descent of Sir Baldwin's blow, which, falling with all its strength on the black knight's head, divided him completely in two from the crown to chine. The two halves of the cloven knight stood quietly apart for some few seconds, and then collapsing, the black knight again stood before him, whole, upright, and ugly as before.

The bridal guests, encouraged by the failure of Sir Baldwin, pressed upon him more eagerly than before, holding in their withered hands goblets filled with red, smoking froth. The men invited him to drink, the women to dance, but neither of these invitations would he deign to accept; and finding that his sword-blade no longer terrified them, he presented to their eyes the crosletted hilt, from which they shrank back in horror, and made way to the right and left for him to pass. Perceiving this, and knowing the hapless maiden to be that Urilda who had last worn the bridal ornaments, and of whose disappearance the ugly company present gave a tolerably sufficient explanation, he made up his mind in an instant, and advancing boldly towards the bride, took from her brow and slender person the burning jewels, which, however, contained no fire for him. Then facing [415] the black knight, "I will do you justice, arch-fiend," said he, "but only, such as you deserve. This maiden is Urilda, of the family of Aarburg, and you have henceforth no further part in her, since I claim the jewels for their rightful owner, and seize them, in Our Lady's name, for Sir Thimo von der Aarburg."

This bold proclamation by word of mouth had an effect which the speaker himself scarcely anticipated. It fairly dislodged the enemy, who, apparently too lucky in getting safely away and securing their prisoner, left behind them all the treasure which Sir Baldwin contended for, even to the utensils of gold and silver produced for the banquet. One loud, ghastly, simultaneous shriek was the signal for their discomfiture; after which they all rushed to the chimney, and darted up en masse, and in much quicker time than they had descended from it.

I need not detail Sir Baldwin's uncontrollable delight on beholding the treasure of which his firmness had made him possessor. He could not sleep for gazing, and hoping, and speculating. Break of day brought to his apartment the seneschal, who, if he was astonished at finding the knight alive, was still more so by the flitter with which he was surrounded. His greedy fingers longed to clutch some part of the booty, but Sir Baldwin scared him away, by declaring the legacy to be the devil's own, which he had destined for Sir Thimo, and which, if any other dared to touch, would bring instant death to the sacrilegious offender. Carriages were then procured, and he hastened to depart for Aarburg, for he remembered that Urilda [416] would still be the demon's captive till the treasure should be in the hands of its rightful owner: this was soon effected. The baron, who had a "heavy miss" of his friend, welcomed him back with all his heart and soul; and Bertha—but all the lovers who read my legend—and all my readers either are, have been, or will be so—will understand her feelings better than I can describe them. Sir Baldwin was instantly acknowledged the knight's accepted son; and Bertha, without the sacrifice of Sir Thimo's fortune, wore the bridal ornaments on her wedding day. But before that period, on the first night Sir Baldwin passed in her father's castle, a gentle voice stole on his ear as he was endeavouring to compose himself to sleep—"Thanks, noble knight," it breathed, "thanks for your dauntless courage! I am the spirit of the redeemed Urilda; seek my body in the cavern under the castle of Frankenburg, and give it a tomb in the vaults of my ancestors. Farewell, noble knight! all happiness henceforth be the portion of you and yours!" Sir Baldwin awoke, obeyed the spirit, married Bertha, and, of course, lived very happily ever after.

Literary Annual
Forget Me Not; A Christmas and New Year's Present for MDCCCXXVIII. Ed. Frederic Shoberl. London: R. Ackermann, 1828. Printer: Thomas Davison, Whitefriars.

Title
Neele, Henry. "The Magician's Visiter." FMN 1828. 91-98. [91]

THE MAGICIAN'S VISITER.
BY HENRY NEELE, ESQ.

IT was at the close of a fine autumnal day, and the shades of evening were beginning to gather over the city of Florence, when a low quick rap was heard at the door of Cornelius Agrippa, and shortly afterwards a stranger was introduced into the apartment in which the philosopher was sitting at his studies.

The stranger, although finely formed, and of courteous demeanour, had a certain indefinable air of mystery about him, which excited awe, if, indeed, it had not a repellent effect. His years it was difficult to guess, for the marks of youth and age were blended in his features in a most extraordinary manner. There was not a furrow in his cheek, or a wrinkle on his brow, and his large black eye beamed with all the brilliancy and vivacity of youth; but his stately figure was bent apparently beneath the weight of years; his hair, although thick and clustering, was gray; and his voice was feeble and tremulous, yet its tones were of the most ravishing and soul-searching melody. His costume was that of a Florentine gentleman; but he held a staff like that of a palmer in his hand, and a silken sash, inscribed with oriental characters, was bound around his waist. His face was deadly pale, but every feature of it was singularly beautiful, and its expression was that of profound wisdom, mingled with poignant sorrow. [92]

"Pardon me, learned sir," said he, addressing the philosopher, "but your fame has travelled into all lands, and has reached all ears, and I could not leave the fair city of Florence without seeking an interview with one who is its greatest boast and ornament."

"You are right welcome, sir," returned Agrippa; "but I fear that your trouble and curiosity will be but ill repaid. I am simply one, who, instead of devoting my days, as do the wise, to the acquirement of wealth and honour, have passed long years in painful and unprofitable study, in endeavouring to unravel the secrets of nature, and initiating myself in the mysteries of the occult sciences."

"Talkest thou of *long* years!" echoed the stranger, and a melancholy smile played over his features:—"thou, who has scarcely seen fourscore since thou left'st thy cradle, and for whom the quiet grave is now waiting, eager to clasp thee in her sheltering arms! I was among the tombs to-day—the still and solemn tombs: I saw them smiling in the last beams of the setting sun. When I was a boy, I used to wish to be like that sun; his career was so long, so bright, so glorious. But tonight I thought 'it is better to slumber among those tombs than to be like him.' To-night he sank behind the hills apparently to repose, but to-morrow he must renew his course, and run the same dull and unvaried but toilsome and unquiet race. There is no grave for him, and the night and morning dews are the tears that he sheds over his tyrannous destiny." [93]

Agrippa was a deep observer and admirer of external nature and of all her phenomena, and had often gazed upon the scene which the stranger described, but the feelings and ideas which it awakened in the mind of the latter were so different from any thing which he had himself experienced, that he could not help, for a season, gazing upon him in speechless wonder. His guest, however, speedily resumed the discourse.

"But I trouble you, I trouble you;—to my purpose in making you this visit. I have heard strange tales of a wondrous mirror, which your potent art has enabled you to construct, in which whosoever looks may see the distant or the dead, on whom he is desirous again to fix his gaze. My eyes see nothing in this outward visible world which can be pleasing to their sight. The grave has closed over all I loved. Time has carried down its stream every thing that once contributed to my enjoyment. The world is a vale of tears, but among all the tears which water that sad valley, not one is shed for me—the fountain in my own heart, too, is dried up. I would once again look upon the face which I loved. I would see that eye more bright and that step more stately than the antelope's; that brow, the broad smooth page on which God had inscribed his fairest characters. I would gaze on all I loved and all I lost. Such a gaze would be dearer to my heart than all that the world has to offer me—except the grave, except the grave." [94]

The passionate pleading of the stranger had such an effect upon Agrippa (who was not used to exhibit his miracle of art to the eyes of all who desired to look in it, although he was often tempted by exorbitant presents and high honours to do so), that he readily consented to grant the request of his extraordinary visitor.

"Whom wouldst thou see?" he inquired.

"My child, my own sweet Miriam," answered the stranger.

Cornelius immediately caused every ray of the light of heaven to be excluded from the chamber, placed the stranger on his right hand, and commenced chanting, in a low soft tone, and in a strange language, some lyrical verses, to which the stranger thought he heard occasionally a response, but it was a sound so faint and indistinct that he hardly knew whether it existed any where but in his own fancy. As Cornelius continued his chant, the room gradually became illuminated, but whence the light proceeded it was impossible to discover. At length the stranger plainly perceived a large mirror which covered the whole of the extreme end of the apartment, and over the surface of which a dense haze or cloud seemed to be rapidly passing.

"Died she in wedlock's holy bands?" inquired Cornelius.

"She was a virgin spotless as the snow."

"How many years have passed away since the grave closed over her?" [95]

A cloud gathered on the stranger's brow, and he answered somewhat impatiently, "Many, many; more than I now have time to number."

"Nay," said Agrippa, "but I must know. For every ten years that have elapsed since her death once must I wave this wand; and when I have waved it for the last time, you will see her figure in yon mirror."

"Wave on, then," said the stranger, and groaned bitterly: "wave on, and take heed that thou be not weary."

Cornelius Agrippa gazed on his strange guest with something of anger, but he excused his want of courtesy on the ground of the probable extent of his calamities. He then waved his magic wand many times, but to his consternation it seemed to have lost its virtue. Turning again to the stranger he exclaimed:

"Who and what art thou, man? Thy presence troubles me. According to all the rules of my art this wand has already described twice two hundred years—still has the surface of the mirror experienced no alternation. Say, dost thou mock me, and did no such person ever exist as thou hast described to me?"

"Wave on, wave on!" was the stern and only reply which this interrogatory extracted from the stranger.

The curiosity of Agrippa, although he was himself a dealer in wonders, began now to be excited, and a mysterious feeling of awe forbade him to desist from waving his wand, much as he doubted the sincerity of his visitor. [96]

As his arm grew slack, he heard the deep solemn tones of the stranger, exclaiming, "Wave on, wave on!" and at length, after his wand, according to the calculations of his art, had described a period of above twelve hundred years, the cloud cleared away from the surface of the mirror, and the stranger, with an exclamation of delight, arose, and gazed rapturously upon the scene which was there represented.

An exquisitely rich and romantic prospect was before him. In the distance rose lofty mountains crowned with cedars; a rapid stream rolled in the middle, and in the fore-ground were seen camels grazing; a rill trickling by, in which some sheep were quenching their thirst, and a lofty palm-tree, beneath whose shade a young female of exquisite beauty, and richly habited in the costume of the East, was sheltering herself from the rays of the noon-tide sun.

"'Tis she! 'tis she!" shouted the stranger; and he was rushing towards the mirror, but was prevented by Cornelius, who said,

"Forbear, rash man, to quit this spot! with each step that thou advancest towards the mirror, the image will become fainter, and shouldst thou approach too near, it will vanish away entirely."

Thus warned, he resumed his station, but his agitation was so excessive, that he was obliged to lean on the arm of the philosopher for support, while, from time to time, he uttered incoherent expressions of wonder, delight, and lamentation. "'Tis she! 'tis [97] she! even as she looked while living! How beautiful she is! Miriam, my child, canst thou not speak to me? By Heaven, she moves! she smiles! oh speak to me a single word! or only breath, or sigh! Alas! all's silent—dull and desolate as this heart! Again that smile!—that smile, the remembrance of which a thousand winters have not been able to freeze up in my heart! Old man, it is in vain to hold me! I must, will clasp her!"

As he uttered the last words, he rushed franticly towards the mirror—the scene represented within it faded away—the cloud gathered again over its surface,—and the stranger sunk senseless to the earth.

When he recovered his consciousness, he found himself in the arms of Agrippa, who was chafing his temples and gazing on him with looks of wonder and fear. He immediately rose on his feet, with restored strength, and, pressing the hand of his host, he said, "Thanks, thanks, for thy courtesy and thy kindness, and for the sweet but painful sight which thou hast presented to my eyes." As he spake these words, he put a purse into the hand of Cornelius, but the latter returned it, saying, "Nay, nay, keep thy gold friend. I know not indeed, that a Christian man dare take it; but be that as it may, I shall esteem myself sufficiently repaid if thou will tell me who thou art."

"Behold!" said the stranger, pointing to a large historical picture which hung on the left hand of the room. [98]

"I see," said the philosopher, "an exquisite work of art, the production of one of our best and earliest artists, representing our Saviour carrying his cross."

"But look again!" said the stranger, fixing his keen dark eyes intently on him, and pointing to a figure on the left hand of the picture.

Cornelius gazed and saw with wonder what he had not observed before—the extraordinary resemblance which this figure bore to the stranger of whom, indeed, it might be said to be a portrait.

"That," said Cornelius, with an emotion of horror, "is intended to represent the unhappy infidel who smote the divine Sufferer for not walking faster, and was therefore condemned to walk the earth himself, until the period of that Sufferer's second coming."

"'Tis I! 'tis I!" exclaimed the stranger; and, rushing out of the house, rapidly disappeared.

Then did Cornelius Agrippa know that he had been conversing with THE WANDERING JEW.

Title
Conway, Derwent. [Inglis, Henry D.] "Kathed and Eurelia. A Bohemian Legend."
FMN 1828. 237-243. [237]

KATHED AND EURELIA.
A Bohemian Legend.
By Derwent Conway.

"The last time," said Reginald to his wife, "that there was a tempest such as this, was the night our Eurelia was born."

"I remember it well," said Therese. "Eurelia, my child, stir up the red embers, and lay some dry branches on the fire: let us be as cheerful as we can."

Eurelia rose at her mother's bidding, and did as she was desired. The dry wood made such a blaze, that the vivid flashes of lightning were scarcely seen; but their crackling could not prevent the thunder, and the wind, and the rain, from being heard.

"Hush!" said Reginald, at a sudden pause in the storm; "surely some one knocked at the door."

"God pity the traveller in this night!" exclaimed Therese: "go, see, husband."

Reginald went to the door, and inquired who was there. No one answered. He thought his voice might not have been heard for the storm, and he withdrew the bolts, and opened a small chink. "Strange!" said he, as he returned to his wife and Eurelia.

"Is nobody there?" asked Therese.

"No human being," replied Reginald; "there are only two large, shaggy, black hounds: where they have come from, and whither they are going, God knows!" [238]

"Let them come in, and crouch at the fire. Poor animals! mayhap they've lost their way."

"I was a-thinking of that; for dumb animals need warmth and shelter as well as we, who, God be thanked! have it: but just as I was about setting wide the door, a flash of lightning showed me their faces, and I thought I saw a sort of devilish laugh upon them, and so I shut it again."

"Nay, husband, this is foolery; you're wont to be a stout-hearted man."

"Stout-hearted or faint-hearted, the hounds shall stand there all night for me, open the door who may."

"May I let them in?" asked Eurelia.

"You may take shame to yourself, husband," said Therese, "when you see the tender child nowise alarmed."

"Her boldness," replied Reginald, "has all come of late; she used to fear a mouse stirring, but within a month or two she has feared nothing: she will walk out into the forest at all hours of the night, and sometimes not to gather wood, but only, as she says, to see the wild things that are roaming about. I wish good may come of it."

"Hush, hush!" said Therese: "if ever I heard fingers knocking, I hear them now."

"I'll go none to the door," said Reginald; "tis only the hounds' paws."

Just at this instant a terrific blast seemed to tear up the forest: a tree, wrenched from the ground, was [239] borne against the window, and shattered the shutters into a thousand shivers; and instantly, through the open window, in leaped the two hounds, and lay down before the fire.

"Heaven save us!" said Reginald.

"Poor animals! they're dripping wet," Said Therese. "Husband, put in the spare shutters."

"Let me first put out the hounds."

"Not so; let them lie still till the storm be over."

"It's well nigh nine o'clock, and time to go to bed: we cannot leave the hounds here; the half of that buck and the two boars' heads would be eaten up before morning."

"I will sit up," said Eurelia, "until the storm be over, and then I will let out the dogs; so you and my mother may go to bed."

The dogs lifted their heads and looked at one another, and then laid them down again.

"You are a good child," said Therese: "your father is weary, and has to be up betimes; we'll go to bed: the storm cannot last much longer; put out the dogs as soon as it has passed, and go to bed, and be sure to fasten the door." Therese kissed Eurelia, and went away with her husband.

The moment the door was shut, Eurelia put her finger upon her lips, and the two dogs rose and laid their heads upon her lap. "Down, good hounds!" said she; "wait a little." Frequently, she tripped [240] lightly to the door, and listened. At length she took down her bonnet, and gently pushed open the shutter.

The storm had ceased; the trees stood erect and stirless; for the wind was gone, and all was quiet, excepting the shiver of the forest, that comes seemingly when there is no wind. The sky was cloudless; and the moonshine fell, in its wane, white and slanting, among the deep foliage.

"Come," said Eurelia.

Do you see her tripping swiftly through the moonlight glades, and the two hounds running before her?

At last they have reached an open amphitheatre, all treeless but for one gigantic and aged sycamore, that lifted itself in the centre: and some one was waiting beneath.

"Eurelia," said a voice, "you have made me wait long."

"I could not come sooner," said she: "will you forgive me, Kathed?:

"Eurelia," cried he, gazing upon her, "never did the moonshine fall upon so much beauty."

"What is beauty?" replied she: "it is my love you value."

"But is beauty nothing?"

"Nothing," said Eurelia; but as she said this, she looked upon Kathed's countenance—a countenance more beautiful than mortal may possess; and she felt that she spoke not the truth. [241]

"Eurelia, I know your thoughts—you love me—you are my own. I could take you with me, and you could not resist me. Yes, Eurelia! I have told you that the penalty of loving me and being mine is to break asunder all ties with the race of men—to live among other beings, and—"

"No matter: I will go with thee."

"But there is yet another penalty."

"I care not: I will go with thee."

"Eurelia," continued Kathed, "look upon me: I seem young and beautiful; my hair is dark and abundant; my forehead white and unwrinkled; my eyes—are they not expressive of the spring-time of years?—See, my limbs are straight and firm: look at me; I am erect, and bear in my aspect the image of youth: but this will pass away."

"True, Kathed! You are not immortal."

"Eurelia, you think me young."

"You are young."

"No, Eurelia! before the oldest of the trees in this forest—before this aged sycamore sprung out of the soil— I was in being; and I shall live until their trunks be sapless—yet not for ever. I have but the seeming of youth, Eurelia."

"No matter: I will go with thee."

"Hear me yet farther, most loved among the daughters of men! It is our nature to possess the appearance and the qualities of youth, and such beauty as we may desire, for some centuries after our creation; but [242] when the appointed time has elapsed, there is no gradual change from youth to age: suddenly, in a moment, we are stricken with extreme age and take its likeness; and exactly in proportion to the beauty we possessed before do we become hideous. Look at me again, Eurelia: I chose this form, the most perfect, and this countenance, the most beautiful, that were permitted; and so this form and this face will become the most hideous that can be borne."

Eurelia looked at Kathed: "No matter," said she; "I will go with thee."

"But yet hear me, Eurelia!—this time fast approaches; I have but a short space to be as you now behold me!"

Eurelia trembled; but she felt the pressure of Kathed's arm around her, and she looked at him and said, "No matter: I will go with thee."

"Eurelia, I have said that my season of youth is short; but know you how short?"

"I know not," said Eurelia.

"To-morrow, at midnight, I shall be changed. It is midnight now; I have but twenty-four hours of youth and love to give to thee."

"I fear not the change; you will still be Kathed—you will still love me."

"No, Eurelia: I shall indeed by Kathed, but the season of love shall have passed away: I will be kind to thee, but I shall not love thee."

"Not love me!" said Eurelia. [243]

"Nay, but," continued Kathed, "neither, Eurelia, shalt thou love me; for neither in person nor voice shall I bear any resemblance to your Kathed."

"Not the voice of Kathed!" said Eurelia, mournfully.

"No, Eurelia; and even the character of Kathed shall be changed; for the characters of youth and age are different."

"No matter; I will go with thee. But how know you that there are but twenty-four hours between youth and age?"

"Eurelia, we know thus: precisely twenty-four hours previous to this change, the hand takes the appearance of age."

Kathed's hand was around Eurelia; she looked at it—it was shrivelled and yellow—and she shrunk from his embrace. "Why did you woo me?" said she.

"I knew not until this midnight that twenty-four hours was all that remained to me of youth. Ah, Eurelia! if you shrink thus from my hand, how will you shrink from me when no a trace of youth or beauty is left—when even the likeness of Kathed shall have passed away?"

Once more Eurelia looked in Kathed's face.—"I will go with thee," said she.

The hounds rose and bayed. The moon entered a thick cloud; and, when it emerged, its pale beams fell upon the green amphitheatre and the aged tree—but there was no one under its shade.

Title

Harral, Thomas. "The House of Castelli." FMN 1828. 339-356. [339]

THE HOUSE OF CASTELLI.
By Thomas Harral, Esq.

A brighter day never blessed the fertile plains of Italy—a softer, lovelier evening never smiled upon the bower of our first parents—a night of deeper glory never pictured to the rich and fervid imagination of Hafiz, the bard of Eastern song, than that which preceded the natal norm of Castelli's heir. Every zephyr was balm, was perfume. Who that has once witnessed the dark splendour of an Italian sky, when the early morn has disappeared can forget its awful grandeur—every radiant orb, perchance the abode of happier spirits, performing its destined evolution in the solemnity of silence!

It was in such an evening—such a night—that I beheld the marble ruins, magnificent even in their mouldering decay, of the Palazzo di Castelli. Yes, the noble structure was then in ruins; but, in the thirteenth century, the period to which this little sketch refers, it was seen towering in all its beauty, its greatness, and its glory. It was then the hereditary demesne of the ancient family of Castelli.

The hour of midnight was rapidly approaching, when its venerable possessor, the representative of a long race of heroic ancestors, walked forth into the gardens of his palace to enjoy the cooling breeze of night. Those gardens, had then been seen by the impostor Mohammed, or by the deluded votaries of the veiled [340] prophet of Khorassan, might have been sighed for as the promised paradise. And what was the fabled beauty of the houris, compared with that of the one lovely being, whose sylph-like form, seen dimly through the shades of night, was raised with mingled feelings of delight, and rapture, and adoration, towards the brighter world above?

Il principe di Castelli had been fatigued in planning and superintending the preparations for the approaching day, in honour of the birth—the anniversary of the birth—of his son. The air was redolent with sweets—the breeze played refreshingly amongst the old man's time-thinned silvery locks. All around was bright, was beautiful; never had he seen the stars performing their courses more gloriously in the heavens. He was happy; yet—and he knew not why—a shade of troubled feeling came across his mind. Again his eyes were raised: he beheld, or fancied that he beheld, over the great western turret of the palace, a particular planet, whose blood-red orb seemed to dart rays of lurid light upon the chamber of his son. What might the omen portend? The prince had, in his early youth, been addicted to the study of the occult science; and, although he had since neglected the pursuit, he had never ceased to entertain a firm belief in the truth of its indications. Fear came over him as though he had been a child; for his son, the last surviving hope of his hose, was far distant, fighting under the sacred banner of the cross in the Holy Land. It was during the time of the fifth [341] crusade, under Louis the Ninth, of France; and Giulio di Castelli, with a chosen band of knights and their retainers, had joined the army of that sovereign, in the pious hope of expelling the Saracens from Palestine—of again forcing the crescent to succumb to the cross.

The prince di Castelli, it has been said, had never withdrawn his faith from the science of the stars. It is not, therefore, to be wondered at, that, amongst the chief persons of his palace—one to whom he had for years assigned a handsome suite of apartments—was a celebrated astrologer, named Felice Il Dotto. To this sage, late as was the hour, the prince immediately determined to repair. He found him in his observatory, at the top of a lofty tower, which had been erected for the express purpose of enabling him more advantageously to prosecute his learned and mysterious art. Il Dotto was no tyro in astrological lore: he was deeply read in the works of Albumazar, the orientalist—he had studied under the far-famed Michael Scott—he was possessed of astronomical and magical talismans from Babylon—he had sympathetic stones, engraven with the heavenly signs, which were thought to have power over the spirits of the three regions—he cold divine by rods, by the crystal, and by the antimonial cup—he was profoundly skilled in the black and in the white magic, though he practised on the latter—and he had the angels Raphael, and Gabriel, and Uriel, and Zequiel, under his command.

"Il Dotto!" said the prince di Castelli, as he entered [342] the observatory:— "Il Dotto!" he repeated; but the mystical adept, absorbed in meditation over an astrological figure of the heavens that lay before him, heard him or heeded him not. "Il Dotto!" exclaimed the prince, in a louder and somewhat impatient tone; when at length the sage looked up, and the prince continued: "Seest thou yon baleful planet streaming its red and fiery glare over the western turret? Doth it bode evil to the house of Castelli? Speaks it of death? Tell me, what of my son?"

"Await the arrival of another day," answered Il Dotto: "twice to-night have I drawn this horoscope—twice have my calculations been broken; some sinister influence prevails—let us wait another day."

"Nay, but the morrow is the birth-day of my son: give me the response of the stars to-night, or I shall not sleep—I shall not be myself to-morrow."

Again Il Dotto cast a figure; but again he was unsuccessful. "It avails not," said he; "the stars will not be compelled; the time is not auspicious—I can tell thee nothing till to-morrow."

"But thou hast other arts," replied the prince: "exert thy deepest skill. Fear not my courage; I can face spirits of the upper, of the middle, of the lower sphere: command them, therefore, into my presence, and let them tell me of my son."

Il Dotto would willingly have refrained from the attempt, but the suit of his noble patron was urgent, was peremptory. On the central portion of the floor he [343] spread a rich, but much worn, ancient carpet, wrought in India by the sacred hands of a Brahmin in honour of the druids of the White Island, from whom the priests of Brahma are by some thought to have descended. It was embroidered with the signs of the zodiac, according to the astronomical system of the Egyptians. In the first of the four corners appeared the figure of a fierce warrior gloriously crowned, and riding upon a crocodile; in the second, mounted on a pale horse, a demoniacal king, with a leopard's face and griffin's wings; in the third, an archer, with a serpent's tail, a hawk perched on his right shoulder, and bestriding a dromedary; in the fourth, an armed chief, with the face of a lion, bearing a lance and a flag, and spurring forward a huge dragon breathing smoke and flame.—Il Dotto then cast the slippers from his feet, replaced them with a pair of perfumed sandals, arrayed himself in a costly linen robe, once the property of a famous Eastern magician, and covered his head with a coif of green and crimson velvet, from which depended three triangular lappets, terminated by tassels of pure gold. With his wand of ebony he drew a large circle on the eastern wall of his chamber. Within the circle he inscribed certain cabalistic characters of mysterious import. On a marble slab which stood near him he prepared to kind a fire of aromatic herbs, odoriferous woods, gums, and spices. The fire was lighted, the sage's lamp was extinguished, and the invocations were pronounced, and the fragrant suffumigation of the most potent spirits of the [344] earth—Zeminar, the monarch of the north; Gorson, the king of the south; Amaymon, the king of the east; and Goap, the prince of the west—proceeded.

The prince di Castelli sat in breathless expectation on the opposite side of the chamber. Ere the charmed fire had sent up its last, faint, quivering, blue flame, Il Dotto thrice again passed his ebony wand around the circle. At his request, the prince approached, and placed himself on a tripod in the centre of the embroidered carpet. The flame expired—the chamber was in utter darkness—a silence that might almost be felt prevailed. Faintly and slowly, a low, distant, rumbling sound was heard: a feeble, misty light, as of the earliest dawn, occupied the circle to its fullest extent. As the light gradually increased, remote strains of military music broke fitfully upon the ear. The sounds approached—the light increased—the sun arose, flashing a blaze of heat and splendour over a champaign country. White tents were seen in the distance—the din of arms came on—the battle-charge was heard—two hostile armies met in furious conflict. The shouts of Christians, the yells of infidels, arose to heaven. All was wild confusion. The clash of weapons, the cries of the wounded, pierced the ear. Suddenly the field was cleared. Then again the galloping of horse was heard—a countless host of Saracens fled across the fatal plain—the banners of the cross, with the brave cavaliero di Castelli at their head, were seen in quick and fierce pursuit—the trumpet- [345] sound of victory filled the welkin with its roar! Instantaneously a mighty crash was heard—and Castelli and Il Dotto were left in the solemn darkness of night.

* * * * * * * *

Visions of glory hovered around the pillow of Castelli's lord. Yet were not the slumbers of the aged prince unbroken: they were feverish and disturbed; and ever and anon the waking consciousness of impending evil darted across his brain. The morning arose, fresh, brilliant, and beautiful. It was the happy morn of Giulio de Castelli's birth. Gay flags, the proudly triumphant colours of the house of Castelli, were streaming and undulating with graceful splendour from every turret, and spire, and pinnacle, of the palace. The columns, the statues, the arches, the fountains, with which the wine-clustered plantations were profusely enriched, were garlanded with flowers of every hue—full strains of music, and the peasants' song of joy, arose upon the gale—and in every quarter, near and remote, the heart's revelry abounded.

The first repast was over, and the prince di Castelli was preparing to meet troops of assembled guests in the grand saloon of the palace. whence was that bugle sound? and whence that messenger covered with dust, and his foaming steed bearing him down the old avenue of limes? It was a courier with dispatches from the Holy Land; and his tidings were happy ones, for they announced a great and glorious victory achieved by the prowess of the young lord of Castelli over the hosts of [346] the infidel. Joy! joy to the old man his father! And he was joyful—and he blessed the starts of heaven in their beauty—and his soul was raised in grateful thanksgiving to the Supreme Lord!

There was high feasting that day within the walls of Castelli's palace; and the song and the dance prevailed—and the purple mist of evening descended in the vale, and floated around the hills—and the bright, young moon arose, and, for a time, gilded with her soft and silvery radiance every distant object. The moon sank; and, as the night came on, one dazzling blaze of artificial light illuminated the gardens of the Palazzo di Castelli. Abroad, thousands of many-coloured lamps glittered in every tree: every flower-decked arch and column was thickly gemmed with their resplendent fires. In the walks, too, and within the marble walls of the palace, rich festoons and chaplets, composed of roses and carnations, and hyacinths and anemones, and every beauteous flower that Italia's clime can boast, relieved with the tender, vivid, and brilliantly variegated greens of the jasmine, the laurel, the myrtle, and the geranium, ran from pillar to pillar, diffusing odours, and receiving lustre from transparent lights, displayed in never-ending variety of device.

Amidst the breathing sorcery of the scene, whose is that blithe and airy form, arrayed in virgin purity, that rests with fond solicitude upon the arm of the prince di Castelli, as he moves slowly through the admiring crowd? Her soft and graceful air—her com- [347] plexion, blending the fairest lily with the loveliest rose—her golden hair—her full blue eyes of light - seem to raise her above earth's brightest beauties. It is Rosaura, the young marchesa d'Obizzi, the orphan heiress of that great and honourable house. Around her waist is a zone thickly set with the finest pearls; over her snowy bosom is a necklace of corresponding beauty; within her hair appears one simple, modest rose of the faintest bella-donna tint; and over her shoulders is lightly thrown a pale blue scarf. It was the very dress which she wore, even to the rose and the scary, on the morning when Giulio de Castelli left his paternal home to make war upon the enemies of the christian faith.—Rosaura was the beloved ward of the prince di Castelli; she had nearly completed her sixteenth year; she have been affianced to Giulio from her birth; and, upon his return, she was to become the bride of him whom her young heart worshipped.

The hour was late—the guests had departed—Rosaura, with her maid, had retired to her chamber—and the prince di Castelli, glad to escape the fatigues of the day, went forth alone into the nearest orange grove of the palace. Wandering farther than he had intended, at every step in inhaled the breath of flowers, and the garden air rushed upon his cheek in all its refreshing coolness. He was absorbed in meditation—all his thoughts were thoughts of happiness. On his return, the sparkle of fountains from the yet unextinguished lights met his eye; presently afterwards, the [348] low and soothing murmur of a distant waterfall reached his ear; and, as he approached his palace, the soft and melancholy echo of a harp was borne upon the wind. The sounds were from Rosaura's chamber. She had taken her harp—for her heart, too, was filled with kind and gentle musings, and she had sung to it a sweet song of love.

Chance, or some secret impulse, again directed the eye of Castelli towards the western turret of the palace; and, blazing over it in portentous glare, the same blood-red planet that he saw the night before still shed its baleful rays. Notwithstanding the visionary forms that he had seen raised by Il Dotto's art—notwithstanding the confirmatory news of the morning—notwithstanding the joyous revelry of the day—a shivering sensation passed over the frame of the prince. Again he repaired to the magician's tower; and there again he found Il Dotto seated beneath a lamp of figured gold, that shed an almost dazzling refulgence upon his turbaned head. A celestial globe of large dimensions stood before him; themes, and positions, and horoscopes, were confusedly spread on the table. Il Dotto had not mingled in the festive throng: his air was grave, and sad, and abstracted. A spirit of anxious inquiry for the welfare, for the destiny, of his son, revived with all its force in the bosom of Castelli. Strange as it seemed, every sidereal calculation of Il Dotto throughout the day had failed. The ceremonies of the preceding night were therefore repeated in all [349] their solemnity. The carpet had been spread—the fire had been kindled—the circle had been traced—the cabalistic characters had been inscribed—the lamp had been extinguished—the prince was seated on his tripod—the chamber was in darkness and in silence. Soft music, as of the song of spirits, was heard: it was the selfsame air, but slower in time, more plaintive, more melancholy in its cadences, that Castelli had heard from Rosaura's harp not an hour before. Gradually the circle became illuminated: a stately edifice—Castelli started on beholding a pictured semblance of his own palace—appeared; and issuing from its portal was a warrior knight—it was Giulio—leading a richly caparisoned charger. By the warrior's side was a lovely maiden—Ah! it was Rosaura d'Obizzi! but, instead of a robe of virgin white, which she had worn at the departure of her betrothed lord, she was attired in a sable vest and veil: her look was pale, mournful, and dejected; and, instead of the cerulean scarf which she had bound upon her arm as the sacred talisman on love, the scarf which she now wore was black. In the far distance a shadowy and undefined form, of gaunt and terrific aspect, arose. The aged noble shuddered; perspiration, in large cold drops, bedewed his temples; he groaned audibly—the phantom palace sank in one vast sheet of flame—all was dark and silent as the grave!

Rosaura slept sweetly; but Castelli's night was a night of horrors.— Another morning dawned: alas! unlike its predecessors, it ushered in no day of bright-[350]ness! The lark sang not in heaven—the smaller specie of the feathered choir were mute—and the sun had passed his meridian before he shone forth in his wonted splendour. Castelli was sad, but he gave no tongue to the anguish of his heart. To-morrow—what was to-morrow? It was intended as another day of rejoicing; for it was the birthday of Rosaura. The prince, troubled as he was in spirit, caused every requisite preparation to be made; and in the gentle society of the young marchesa he sought for that consolation and repose of mind which he found not in himself.

The day passed—the shades of evening had come on—the crescent moon was riding brightly, yet serenely, in the firmament, her glories now and then momentarily obscured by a light flitting cloud. The sky had not yet attained its dark deep blue—the stars were yet but faintly seen—when Castelli, restless, impatient, and agitated, went forth, once more, to gaze upon the western turret. There—there—increased in magnitude and in power—still blazed that blood-red orb, whose rays had first created consternation in the breast of the widowed and now lonely prince. Once more—ah! for the last time, he said—once more would he visit Il Dotto in his tower!

Involuntarily—almost unconsciously—the prince di Castelli turned into a walk leading towards the chapel. He approached the sacred edifice with awe— he entered its walls with a sensation of dread: the close of the vesper-hymn died upon his ear, as the priest and the [351] choral train were about to retire into the cloister. Three waxen tapers burned in a recess before the altar; but the nave and aisles of the chapel were lighted by the mild splendour of the moon, whose rays fell streaming through the richly stained glass on many a costly monument and tomb. Contrasting with the variegated light thus produced, large and deep masses of shadow where formed by architectural projections, and by the military trophies

Forget Me Not

and monumental records of the departed great.

In passing towards the altar, Castelli saw, partly concealed by the mass sepulchre of one of his most renowned ancestors, a female form—it was Rosaura's—kneeling as in humble and devout supplication. A moon-beam fell on her cheek—her full eye was raised to heaven—her lips moved—she bent her head—she breathed another prayer, another blessing on her beads. Whiter than the veil she wore was that cheek of pale and placid loveliness. Rosaura, when she saw Castelli, would have retired; but the prince stepped forward, embraced her, kissed her cold forehead, pressed her affectionately, fervently to his bosom, and, without speaking, moved on. Scarcely had he left her, when a low, deep, hollow groan was heard. He started, looked around, and ere he could again reach Rosaura, the gigantic armed statue of a former prince di Castelli fell, untouched, from its pedestal, immediately before him. The sound produced by the fall of the huge mass, with its clashing armour of steel, upon the [352] stone pavement, was appalling. Rosaura shrieked: an ice-bolt seemed to pierce the heart of Castelli; for a mysterious, awful prophecy, darkly connected with the fate of that statue, had long threatened his princely race. For a moment the old man supported himself by grasping the carved figure of a cherub projecting from the angle of a tomb. He then turned to Rosaura, who had sunk motionless and senseless to the earth. The moon had suddenly become overcast; and the only light within the chapel was from the tapers before the altar. Rosaura, however, slowly but partially recovered; and, with much difficulty, the aged prince succeeded in bearing her to her apartments.

The midnight-hour had struck ere Castelli reached the tower of Il Dotto. The sage was seated, as on the two preceding nights; but his raiment was black—black from head to foot—and he changed it not during the awful solemnities which ensued. Few were the words that passed between Castelli and Il Dotto. This time the stars were not mentioned. Every ceremony that had been before performed was gone through now with, if possible, more deep attention. Il Dotto seemed as though he had been prepared, not only mentally but corporeally, for some great, some decisive event. When Castelli ascended the tripod, Il Dotto, placing a dried root of vervain in his hand, enjoined the strictest silence. "Whatever you may see," said he, "whatever you may hear, retain your seat firmly, and let not the slightest sound escape your lips. To violate this in-[353]junction may be fatal." Castelli bowed assent. The trumpet-sound of victory was heard: it was heavenly music to the ear of Castelli! and, oh! how beautiful was the landscape which appeared within the magic ring! The sun was setting, in all his gold and purple glories, behind the distant hills. It was sunset that only once beheld could never be forgotten—it was a sight to transport the fond imagination into the sphere of angels and beatified spirits. Yet was it not a scene for the painter's pencil, or even for the poet's pen: it was too radiant, too magnificent, too gorgeous, too sublime; but, raising the mortal to immortality, it softened and expanded, and gave to the rapt soul of Castelli the glowing, the dazzling, the awe-inspiring prospect of a future and a better world.

"Look again," said Il Dotto; "look, but speak not." The scene was changed. It was night—deep night—darkness that might be felt. Then came a strange unearthly light; and then the vault of heaven was filled with shooting stars, and flashing lights, and flaming meteors, and vast globes of fire exploding with terrific sound; and then the lightning's fierce and lurid glare, darting and hissing in arrowy and serpent forms, as it preceded the loud, rattling crashing thunder-burst which shook all nature to its adamantine base. Castelli trembled—shuddered—but spake not.

It was dawn—the mist was clearing from the hills—the sun rose in tranquil splendour. In the distance, on the left, lay the Saracen host encamped; the fore-[354] ground of the picture was occupied by the christian army, busily marshalling for the fight; and, elevated upon the right, stood the magnificent tent of the red-cross conquering chief. That chief was Giulio di Castelli. His attendant page had nearly completed the task of arming him for the field. The scarf—Rosaura's love-pledge—was upon his arm. To place the casque upon the warrior's head was all that remained. And by whom was that casque placed? Not by the youthful page—not by the trusty squire—whose love as well as duty had bound him to his master's service. In the grim features—the gaunt form—of the figure by whom that office was performed, the prince di Castelli recognised the dim shadow which, on a former night, had met his then undistinguishing gaze. The form was Death's! How cold was the thrill which ran through Castelli's heart!

Once more the scene was changed. The battle raged in all its fury. Conflicting squadrons, by turns, chased each other off the field; and still, with desperate energy, the fight was maintained. Again the red cross triumphed—again the infidel was routed with incalculable slaughter—again the air was filled with shouts of victory! Castelli's heart beat quickly, loudly, exultingly. Anon was seen the leader of the Saracen host, pursued at utmost speed by the triumphant chief—by Giulio di Castelli! The warriors wheeled round and round in many a swift and mazy circle. And now the infidel turns his steed and rallies—and now the chiefs [355] retreat a few paces—and now their meeting eyes flash fire—and now, with more than human strength, they hurl the lance—and now they rush, horse to horse, hand to hand, sword to sword, in mortal combat. What were the feelings of Castelli's lord? For a moment, by mutual consent, as it were, to recover breath, the hostile chiefs again retreat; and then, again, in rapid whirl, they seem to burst upon the very spot—the charmed spot—where sat the aged, breathless parent. Ah! now they meet more fiercely, more wildly, more recklessly than before. The sword of Giulio is raised—it falls to cleave the skull of the infidel! No, not so; by a dexterous movement he evades the blow—rallies—rushes upon his opponent. By their dreadful collision the chiefs are unhorsed: they recover—they fight—Giulio staggers—reels—is falling to the earth! "My son!" frantically exclaimed the prince, rushing forward to receive him in his arms, and striking with deadly force against the wall of the now dark chamber. A shock, as of an earthquake, was simultaneous with the interdicted exclamation of Castelli—with his involuntary rush towards the magic scene; and the tower of Il Dotto rocked, shook, and trembled to its foundation.

* * * * * * *

On the birthday of Rosaura there was mourning in the palace of Castelli. Its princely owner was no more; and Rosaura too—the loved, the lovely, and the gentle one—was in the kingdom of the blessed. She had met her lover in the dim visions of the night; [356] in the depth of sleep her pure spirit had passed away. Giulio and Rosaura were united in heaven.

* * * * * * *

Giulio had been slain in single combat by the leader of the Saracens, on the morning of Rosaura's birthday, as prefigured by the magic art of Il Dotto; and thus was fulfilled the prophecy— *"When the statue of the renowned Antonio di Castelli shall fall, the son, the father, and the bride, shall perish, and the succession of an ancient race be extinguished for ever."*

Title

Roberts, Emma. "The Halt on the Mountain." FMN 1828. 362-378. [362]

THE HALT ON THE MOUNTAIN.
A TALE OF THE SPANISH WAR.
BY MISS EMMA ROBERTS

The day's march had been long and wearisome, and still the exhausted party looked in vain through the lonely sierras in search of a human habitation. Roland de St. Pierre, the commander of a small detachment of French voltigeurs, became aware that he had missed the direct track, and that it was useless to expect to reach the outposts of the army on that night: he therefore made up his mind to spend the hours of darkness under the shade of one of those spreading cork-trees which made his present route a path of exceeding beauty. He halted his followers, and offered them the immediate repose of which they stood so much in need: unwilling, however, to relinquish the hope of obtaining refreshment after their harassing fatigues, the soldiers rallied their flagging spirits, and desired to proceed onward, upon the chance of finding the hut of some goatherd, which might afford a slight repast to assuage the cravings of their appetites.

It was a calm, lovely, autumnal evening; all was so hushed and tranquil, that not the slightest breeze agitated the leaves of the forest-trees: the dull tramp of the soldiers alone broke the deep silence; for, toil-worn and faint from long abstinence, they had ceased from the light catches and merry roundels which had [363] heretofore beguiled their march; and melancholy feelings, in unison with the sombre gloom around, began to steal over the mind of the youthful commander, destined to make his first campaign against the unoffending allies of his ambitious master. Roland troubled himself little with political questions; he sought to win rank and honour by the aid of his good sword, and had received his first summons to march into Spain with the enthusiastic delight of a heart panting to distinguish itself in some well-contested field, and reckless what sphere was selected for the theatre of his achievements; but he had that morning encountered scenes revolting to a mind unaccustomed to the horrors of war:—whole villages stretched in black ruins upon the desolated plains, farms, once smiling and prosperous, still smouldering in the flames which had reduced them to heaps of ashes, human bones strewed upon the greensward, and half-decaying corses tainting the sweet air of heaven, the frightful relics of those devoted peasants who had dared defend their hearts and their homes from the spoiler's hand.

Roland's unpractised heart grieved over the horrible devastation which greeted his shuddering glance, and he was surprised to find how deep an impression the ghastly spectacle of the morning had left upon his mind. No trace of war or carnage defiled the purity of the landscape which he now trod. The gurgling runnel

Forget Me Not

leaped clear and limpid over the rocks, its sparkling current unstained with blood, and nought [364] save the perfume of the orange-blossom came mingled with the aromatic fragrance of the thymy pastures; yet was the solitude so profound, the stillness of the coming nigh so awful, that, in his present state of languor, all the characteristic gaiety of his temper and nation was insufficient to remove the oppression which weighed heavily upon his soul.

The dim twilight faded away, and darkness, made more gloomy by the thick foliage above, succeeded; wearily the voltigeurs dragged their jaded limbs along, and, just as they despaired of advancing further, the sudden illumination of a moon upon the wane showed them at a considerable distance a roof, whence issued a thin column of smoke. Animated by this exhilarating prospect, the tired party pressed eagerly forward to the spot. Upon a closer inspection, they discovered the promised haven to be an outhouse, lofty and extensive, which had evidently been attached to a superior mansion, now levelled with the ground. A broken trellis, from which the untrained vine wandered along the damp earth, fountains choked with grass and fragments of sculptured marble, showed that the sword and the firebrand had performed their deadliest operations; but the work had not been sufficiently recent to display the most frightful ravages of war: time had thrown a slight veil over the wreck, and the moon glanced upon flowers springing up uncultured in a garden which had been defaced by hostile feet, and upon a rank vegetation of weeds, waving like banners from the prostrate walls. [365]

The high dark front of the barn-like building, which promised shelter for the night, frowned grimly in the moonlight: the unglazed windows were secured by strong wooden shutters, and the most dreary silence reigned throughout the interior; but a faint light, issuing from some of the numerous crevices in this dilapidated structure, gave tokens of habitation, although the inmates, whoever they might be, preserved a sullen silence for a considerable period, neither deigning to answer, nor seeming to hear, the supplications and threats with which the French soldiers alternately solicited and demanded attendance. Before, however, these rough guests had exhausted all their patience, a door opened, and the flame of a pine-wood torch threw a strong light upon the face and figure of the portress, as she stood upon her own threshold. Her tall spare form towered above the middle height; but if Nature had moulded it with a careful hand, its beauty was totally obscured by a cumbrous garment of sackcloth, girt about the waist with a cord. Her long gray hair, which streamed wildly from beneath a scanty covering of coarse black stuff, and the rigid lines in her gaunt countenance, gave her the appearance of age: but Roland, as he gazed upon her with an undefinable sensation of awe and wonder, saw that she had scarcely passed, if she had reached, the summer of her life; that there was also an air of dignity in her demeanour, which ill accorded with the meanness of her habiliments and the squalid poverty with which she was surrounded. A [366] ghastly smile passed across her pale and haggard face as she bade the weary party welcome; and though want, and wretchedness, and disease, had preyed with ravaging effect upon her features; though her eyes were sunk in her head, her lips parched and wan, and her skin wrinkled and jaundiced, Roland perceived that she still retained lineaments of severe and almost superhuman beauty: and a vague feeling of the existence of some mysterious danger came across his mind, as he observed the silent workings of that extraordinary countenance, while she bestirred herself with fearless alacrity to provide for the accommodation of men, whose intrusion upon her solitude must have been any thing but pleasing.

Ashamed of the dread which involuntarily crept over him—since he knew the impossibility, from the depopulated state of the country, and the strong cordon of troops with which the province now occupied by the French army was surrounded, of there being any concealed ambush even in this secluded spot— he strove to banish the apprehension of impending evil, and to make himself as comfortable as circumstances would admit: still he could not withdraw his looks from his hostess; and though not expecting to make any discovery from her answer, inquired whether she did not feel some alarm while living alone in so dreary a solitude.

"What should I fear?" she calmly replied: "I have lost everything but life, and that is now of so little [367] value, that its preservation is not worth a thought. And why," she continued, "should I wish for the protection of my countrymen?— they are more gloriously engaged in the great and holy cause which has armed all Spain in defence of its liberties."

Somewhat reassured by the undisguised frankness of this speech, Roland contented himself with a scrupulous examination of the place, which he still could not help fancying had been inauspiciously chosen for the night-halt of his party. Nothing alarming met his eye: the furniture was rude and scanty, the building ill calculated to conceal arms or snares of any kind; and what could a band of nine stout soldiers apprehend from the utmost malice of one woman? Struggling, therefore, with the forebodings of his spirit, he ate his portion of the frugal meal which was set before him with a keen relish, but declined the cup of wine offered at its completion, from a natural antipathy to the fermented juice of the grape, and a particular aversion to the vintage of Spain. The voltigeurs, delighted to obtain food and rest, unattracted by the person of the lone female who administered to their necessities, and more diverted than angry at her avowed enmity to their country, saw nothing to excite their suspicions; and their commander, perceiving that no one participated in the uneasy doubts which pertinaciously clung to him, was unwilling to betray his dread of lurking danger to his inconsiderate companions, lest they might attribute the communication to some ignoble feeling. [368]

The repast ended, the young officer was conducted by his singular and painfully-interesting hostess up a ladder to sort of a loft, occupying the upper part of the building. At first he disliked the idea of separation from his party, but perceiving that he could keep a watchful eye over them through several large apertures in the floor, he became more reconciled to an arrangement which would enable him to observe all that passed, without attracting attention by his vigilance. A coarse bed was spread in one corner of the room; but, too much agitated to think of repose, he took up a position which gave him an uninterrupted view of the premises below. A wood fire burned brightly; and within the influence of its genial warmth the toil-worn soldiers had stretched themselves at length upon the floor, and, wrapped in their cloaks, resigned their weary spirits to a death-like sleep. The lone inhabitant of the dwelling had withdrawn to a distant corner, and, in the fitful blaze, the dark drapery which enveloped her spare form could scarcely be distinguished from the inequalities of the floor which formed her couch. So profound was the slumber of the wayworn voltigeurs, that their breathing was not audible in the chamber above: a dead silence prevailed, disturbed only at intervals by a rustling sound, so slight, that Roland deemed it to proceed from the wing of some night-bird sweeping along the eaves. The fire, unreplenished, began to moulder away, the figures of the sleepers became indistinct, and drowsiness crept unconsciously over Roland's frame; [369] how long he remained in utter forgetfulness of his situation he knew not, but he was roused by a clear sweet voice, singing in low yet distinct tones the following ballad:

> The moors have rear'd the crescent high, the cross is lowly laid,
> And vainly to their patron saints the Spaniards shriek for aid:
> Sorrow and desolation reign throughout the bleeding land—
> But raise exulting shouts to Heaven, for vengeance is at hand!
>
> Our warriors lie in mangled heaps upon the gory plain;
> Our fathers, and our husbands, and our brothers, all are slain:
> But we will nerve our woman's arms to wield the flaming brand,
> and teach our proud and ruthless foes that vengeance is at hand!

This lay was evidently a fragment of the countless relics of the eventual struggle between the Spaniards and the Moors, which, in days of old, had so gloriously terminated in favour of the christian cause; but the coincidence of the words with the peculiar circumstances in which he was placed alarmed the French officer: he groped his way, by the imperfect light, to the spot whence the sound proceeded. "Who and what art thou," he exclaimed, "whose warning song has so effectually chased slumber from my eyelids?"

"An enemy!" replied the same clear soft voice; "but one who is sated, sick of shedding blood!—Force a passage for me through the decaying panels of the wainscot, and I will set you free!"

"Stand aside then!" cried Roland; and at one effort the worm-eaten barrier gave way: a flood of moonlight [370] passed in, and revealed a slight fair girl, whose countenance, bearing a striking resemblance to that of the female who had inspired him with such a strong feeling of awe, though pale and thin, was still so exceedingly beautiful, that the admiring gazer could not fancy that it had lost a single attraction from the calamity, whatever it might be, which had made such fearful havoc in the frame of her companion.

"Follow me," she cried, "and quickly: the delay of an instant may cost your life."

"I will but stay to rouse my party," returned Roland, struck with sudden surprise to find that they had not already gathered round him, disturbed by the crash of the falling wainscot.

"They will wake no more in this world," said the stranger: "look not to them, but save yourself. The poison has performed its work, and they are as the dust beneath them."

Rushing to the ladder, Roland, reckless of personal danger from the lapse of time, threw himself into the room below, stirred the fading embers, and the blaze that spring up, as it caught a fresh pine faggot, confirmed the dreadful truth. The pulses of the soldiers had ceased to beat; they breathed not—moved not; and their convulsed and distorted features told the horrid story of their fate. Roland stood shuddering and aghast amid the senseless clay around him; bolts of ice shot, in rapid succession, through his heart. Were these inanimate bodies the late companions of his toil, [371] men vigorous with life and health, who but and hour before had shared his march, stiffening in the cold grasp of death, murdered, and murdered before his eyes?—Drops of agony burst from his brows; and, drawing his sword in gloomy desperation, he exclaimed—"I will stay and avenge you!" The fair vision whose voice had broken his repose had followed him to the spot; and, preserving amid the appalling scene the same calm melancholy expression of countenance which seemed habitual to her, again addressed him.

"Justice," she cried, "claims this sanguinary deed, and vengeance is beyond your reach, unless the blow should fall on me. Strike if you will, and spare not; for dearer lives have fallen beneath the murderous weapons of your countrymen."

The French officer slowly dropped the point of his sword; he saw, indeed, that it would be worse than vain to abandon himself to the indignation which filled his heart; but, continuing to gaze upon the ghastly faces of his comrades, as they lay, bereft of sense and motion, on the earth which was so soon to close over them, a sickening sensation crept through his frame: he could bear no more; and clasping his hand across his eyes, moved from the spot.

His companion, taking advantage of this change of mood, seized his cloak, and drew him to the ladder. They ascended it in silence, crossed the two upper apartments, and gained the ground through a wooden balcony, furnished, according to the custom of the [372] country, with a flight of steps. Roland, in a few minutes, found himself in a wild and tangled path, with his preserver still at his side.

"I have saved you from death," she cried; "but my task is not yet ended. A secret avenue, which cannot be trodden without a guide, leads to the road at the mountain's base: I will conduct you thither in safety; and, strange, employ your rescued like in generous efforts to meliorate the sufferings of the hapless Spaniards: interpose your authority in aid of the weak and defenceless, and snatch them from the wanton butchery which spares neither sex nor age. Look on yonder shapeless ruin: once it smiled joyously in the moonlight—once a happy peasantry crowded to its now broken walls, to pay the tribute of glad and grateful hearts to their beloved lord: a family, blessing and blessed, made the air around them melodious with the hymn of praise and thanksgiving—a gush of song forever flowing, like the mountain stream. On the last day that tones of cheerfulness issued from human lips upon that desecrated spot, we celebrated a festival—the betrothing of my elder sister—and merrily were struck the cords of the gay guitar, and lightly, to the spirit-stirring sounds of the castanet, our flying footsteps touched the ground. Suddenly an armed band burst in upon our harmless revelry. There was a grotto carefully concealed, wherein our anxious friends placed Estella and myself for safety: through a fissure in the rock we saw the barbarians enter. I lost vision, [373] sense, and recollection, when, vainly struggling with overpowering numbers, my father fell; but Estella, incapable of moving, or withdrawing her eyes from the scene of slaughter, and acutely, miserably alive to all its horrors, turned a stony gaze upon the unequal contest, and saw, one by one, our parents, our three brave brothers, her lover, our friends and servants, perish by the unpitying hands of their assailants. The streams of blood, flowing down the pathway, penetrated the grotto, and, as I lay upon the damp ground, my festal garments were drenched with the vital current of all I loved on earth. The work of murder accomplished, the Frenchmen indulged themselves in pillage; and having seized every thing of value, our home, our once happy home, was devoted to the flames. Vainly did we hope that the smoke would suffocate us in our retreat; but the wind blew it away, and we were saved to execute a dreadful deed of vengeance. Three days passed, and at length, sated with plunder and with blood, our merciless enemies retreated: the sound of their bugles died upon her ear, and Estella, the fair, the gracious, the idolized Estella, emerged from the cave, with her golden tresses changed to dull gray—the beaming radiance in her eyes quenched—her flesh withered away—the gaunt spectre of her former self. She swore a fearful oath upon the mangled pile of our murdered relatives, and fearfully has she performed it. For every precious life taken on that fatal day, by her frail and feeble hands have ten been sacrificed. My spirit grows weary of [374] this constant slaughter; and when you refused the wine, and Estella, perceiving your suspicions, fled to procure the assistance of a trust friend, the Holy Virgin, to whom I pray incessantly, urged me to effect your deliverance, and I obeyed the mandate."

The narrator of this horrible tale paused, and Roland, bursting into a passionate exclamation, turned round to offer his fervent thanks to the fair and luckless creature to whom he owed his life, but she had vanished: the broad road lay before him, and no trace of his conductress appearing, he lingered for a moment and then pursued his way. The morning began to break as he trod the solitary path, and, but that he was alone, the agile voltigeur could have fancied the whole night's adventure a feverish dream: the rustling of the leaves, the twittering of the birds, were the only sounds that broke the stillness; he missed the light songs and lighter laughter of his late companions, and strode along, unheeding the distance, almost choked by the tumultuous emotions which crowded to his heart. As he approached the outposts, a dropping fire from the lines announced to the young soldier that preparations for action had commenced, and he only arrived in time to join his division, which was immediately engaged in a fierce contest with the enemy. Roland, wound up to the highest pitch of excitement, fought with desperate energy, striving, in the impetuosity of the onslaught, to banish the frightful scene which was ever before his eyes. The day, however, [375] notwithstanding the bravery of the troops, was not auspicious to France; evening saw the whole of the army in full retreat; and Roland, when bivouacking in a secure position, found himself in a distant province from the mountain scene which had proved so fatal to eight of the most gallant fellows in the service.

The beauty of Estella and Magdalena, the daughters of the count de los Tormes, was celebrated throughout Spain, and the tragic tale of their supposed murder formed a theme for the minstrels, who, while dwelling upon their virtues and their loveliness, incited every generous heart to avenge their wrongs. Some of these popular lays found their way to the French camp. Roland needed no auxiliary to perpetuate the recollection of these unhappy females; his thoughts dwelt continually on the fair form of Magdalena: insensibly he associated this gentle creature with all his future schemes and prospects, and many romantic visions were disturbed by the gaunt spectre of her stern sister, starting up, like a destroying angel, between him and his fairy hopes. Roland, a man, and a Frenchman, could not understand the possibility of owing his life to any cause save an impulse of tenderness in his favour. Unaccustomed to reflect deeply upon religious influence, he smiled at the alleged interposition of the Virgin, and admired the womanly contrivance which had so artfully veiled her own wishes under the pretence of obeying the commands of Heaven. Without too closely scanning his intentions, [376] he felt an irresistible desire to snatch the ill-starred Magdalena from the horrible situation in which she was placed; and already well acquainted with the Spanish language, he spared no pains to render himself so completely master of it as o enable him to pass for a native.

The fortune of war gave Roland the opportunity which he had so long desired: he was stationed in the neighbourhood of the humble residence of the sisters, and, in the disguise of a muleteer, he ventured to approach the fatal spot. Taking the same road which he had formerly trod, the bold mountain peaks frowned above him; the thick forest of cork-trees spread its umbrageous shade around; the ruined mansion, with its grass-grown gardens, brought sickening recollections to his heart. Accustomed to death in every shape—by the sword, by the bullet, and by the axe; by lingering tortures, and by wasting plagues—often fighting ankle-deep in blood, and treading on the corses of the slain; through lightly regarding these horrors, he never could banish from his memory the scene of that dreadful night, when, by the funeral light of the pinewood fire, he gazed upon the blackening faces of his comrades, as they lay in death's ghastly embrace on the floor. Often in his gayest revel did the lights, and the music, and the wine-cup, vanish from his eyes, and the dark hut and the dead were before him.

Now he was roused from his gloomy reverie by the same sweet, clear voice which had once broken upon [377] a dangerous slumber: he looked into a green dell below, and saw Magdalena, kneeling at a wooden cross, surmounted by an image of the Virgin, and singing her early matin hymn. Roland was by her side in an instant; and, with the confident vivacity of his country, poured out with passionate vehemence a thousand protestations of love. Magdalena, at first amazed, distrusting sight and sense, and listening with apparent patience, merely to be certain that she heard aright, no sooner caught the truth, than, starting from the ground, her fair melancholy countenance dilating with scorn and rage, she cast a look of ineffable contempt upon the handsome suppliant, and clinging to the rude altar before her, said—

"But that I loathe the sight of blood, presumptuous miscreant! thy heart's best vein should drain upon his outraged shrine! Begone!—judge not of me by the craven spirit that brought thee hither!—And before he could make a single attempt to appease her just indignation, she had fled.

The contemned lover lingered long and fruitlessly on the spot which had witnessed his disappointment: reluctantly obeying at last the dictates of prudence, which urged the folly of remaining to be discovered and sacrificed to the vengeance which he had provoked, he slowly and sullenly retreated. Though no longer daring to entertain a hope of inducing the fair Spaniard to exchange her dreary solitude for a life of luxury and ease, still the image of Magdalena haunted his ima- [378] gination; her dazzling beauty, her noble sentiments, her touching history, could not, would not, be forgotten. A third time the means of visiting her dwelling-place presented themselves; and, almost without a purpose, Roland again approached the ruined hovel:—he found her grave! A mound of green turf, a rude cross, inscribed with her name and age, marked the last resting-place of one of Spain's fairest flowers. Her sister had assumed a soldier's habit, and had joined the Guerillas.

The Forgotten Gothic

Literary Annual
Forget Me Not; A Christmas and New Year's Present for MDCCCXXIX. Ed. Frederic Shoberl. London: R. Ackermann, 1829. Printer: Thomas Davison, Whitefriars.

Title
Bowdich, Sarah. "Eliza Carthago." FMN 1829." 57-64. [57]

ELIZA CARTHAGO.
BY MRS. BOWDICH.

AT four o'clock one morning I stepped into a canoe, to go to Elmina, the Dutch head-quarters. The land-wind was blowing strongly, and, although only five degrees north of the equator, I was glad of all the shawls and great-coats I could find to protect me from the chilling blast. Notwithstanding these coverings, I was quite benumbed, and landed at seven with the feelings which I should have had during a hard frost in England.

My visit was to the king of Elmina, a Dutch mulatto, of the name of Neazer. He had, during the slave-trade, been possessed of considerable property, which, added to his maternal connexions, gave him great power among the people of that place. He had also resisted every thing like oppression on the part of the Dutch, and, although ruined in fortune, he was invested with the royal dignity, in gratitude for his signal endeavours to prevent the exactions of General Daendels. I had to pass through the town to reach his house; and the narrow streets were thronged with people going to and from the market, close to his door. It was like other African markets, except that there was a circle of dogs for sale; a circumstance which I had not witnessed at Cape Coast. They were long-eared, wretched-looking, little beasts, valued at half [58] an ackie, or half-a-crown, each, and were to be made into soup.

I found his majesty surrounded by a few remnants of his former splendour, such as dim looking-glasses and tawdry sofas, and in an immense house, composed of dark passages and staircases, large halls, and a dirty black kitchen at the top. His attendants were royal in number, for most of his subjects were willing to wait on him for the sake of his good feeding. He received me very hospitably, and immediately set before me a splendid breakfast, presenting not only African but European delicacies. His garden supplied him with the former, and his wide acquaintance with the masters of trading vessels, who gladly purchased his influence with the natives, procured him the latter.

During our meal Mr. Neazer begged to introduce to me his sons, two of whom were just returned from an English school. "To be sure," he said, "they were terrible rascals, but then they were well educated, and polite enough to talk to an English lady." These "young boys," as he called them, were accordingly summoned, and after a long interval, spent in decoration I believe, they appeared; but, instead of the infants I expected to see, they were tall, stout men. In lieu of the promised polish, each strove to make the other laugh at every word uttered by their papa; yet to me they were most respectful; for they heard my remarks with deference, assented to every observation, and bowed at the conclusion of every sentence as grace- [59] fully as they were permitted to do by the many yards of muslin which enveloped their throats, and by the scantiness of their best coats, which they had long outgrown. My risibility was so strongly excited that I feared I might not always command my gravity, and rejoiced at the proposal for a walk to see the garden and the garden-house.

The decays of his fortune had caused the decay of his country residence. Still Mr. Neazer loved to show it, and finding that I could not oblige him more, I sat down on a chair nearly demolished by white ants, but felt exceedingly nervous at the reptiles which I saw lurking in every crevice. Lizards chased each other with rapidity up and down the walls; centipedes and scorpions were not far off; and it only required a serpent to peep out to complete my apprehensions. I had passed two in my way, or rather they had rushed across my path; and I never could contemplate the possibility of their approach without a shudder. I tucked my gown close round me, and making ready with my parasol, I sat like a statue, till my attention was arrested by Mr. Neazer's account of the destruction of a Dutch fortress up the river Ancobra. I now repeat it as a curious exemplification of customs and manners, which will, I hope, through the endeavours of civilized Europe, ere long cease to exist.

The fortress named Eliza Carthago was built about the year 1700, in a lonely situation, fifty miles from the mouth of Ancobra, a river of Ahanta, and far [60] from the reach of European assistance. This loneliness was not remedied by internal strength; for the utmost force placed there consisted of a handful of soldiers, a drummer, and a serjeant. The governor had resided in it for many years, and had apparently conciliated the natives. It was in the neighbourhood of the gold-pits; and during his trade he had amassed a quantity of rock-gold, and was altogether so rich, from possessing the exclusive commerce of this part of the interior, that he at length excited the cupidity of his neighbours. They met in council, and vowed to abet each other till the white man was ruined, never taking into consideration that his wealth had been won by fair dealing with themselves that they had been the willing instruments of his success; and that they had also been enriched by their mutual barter. "No; it was not right that a white man should come and take away their gold, and they never would rest satisfied till they had it all back again." It was necessary for them, however, to act cautiously, for they had no desire that the fort should be for ever abandoned, as it kept the trade open, and supplied them with European articles at a much easier rate than by going to Elmina for them.

Their first plan was to invent some pretext for quarrelling with the governor; and, accordingly, the next bargain that took place between them was accompanied by so much extortion on their part, that the Dutchman could not comply with their demands. [61] His continued resistance at length produced the wished-for dispute, or palaver; and open hostility manifested itself on the side of the natives. His cattle disappeared, his plantations were destroyed, his trade was stopped, and he was not allowed to purchase food in the market. His slaves contrived for a while to procure provisions, as if for themselves; but, their trick being discovered, they were forbidden to come into the town again for that purpose under pain of death, and their master was reduced to live entirely on the salted stores of the fortress.

The governor now began to think more seriously of the quarrel than he had hitherto done, and dispatched a trusty messenger to head-quarters for assistance. He then summoned the chiefs of the town to the fortress to talk over the palaver. This only produced still greater irritation; and the next morning he found himself surrounded by the natives, who were well armed with muskets, bows, and arrows. He shut up the fort, loaded the few guns which he possessed, and, parleying with them from the ramparts, threatened to fire on them if they did not retire. They only answered him with shouts of defiance. Still the poor governor hesitated, because, this step once taken, the difficulty of ever coming to an amicable arrangement was increased. He lingered in the hope of assistance from Elmina; but, exasperated at the death of one of his soldiers, who was shot as he walked along the walls, he at length fired. Great destruction was occasioned; but [62] his enemies were like hydras, the more he killed, the more their numbers seemed to increase; and day after day was spent in regular warfare. His soldiers were cut off by the skillful aim of these excellent marksmen; and, what was worse than all, his ammunition was fast decreasing. His cannon became useless; for in a short time he had not a man left who could manage them, or a ball to load them with. As long as he possessed iron and leaden bars, and brass rods, all of which are articles of trade, he was enabled to fire on the people with muskets; but at length even these failed him, and he was reduced to a few barrels of gunpowder. Every day he hoped for relief; every day he resorted to the bastion which overlooked the path to Elmina; but every day he was disappointed. Still every hour held out a hope; and he melted his rock-gold into bullets, and fired with these till he had no more. He was now entirely destitute of the means of defence; his stores were daily lessening, and want had already occasioned the desertion of his followers, who secretly stole from the fort and took refuge with the enemy. When the unhappy man mounted the walls with his telescope to look towards Elmina, his adversaries insulted him, and asked him when he expected news from the coast, and how many bullets he had left; and they showed him the pieces of gold which they had either picked up, or taken out of the bodies of those who had been killed by them. Finding that he still watched and hoped, they brought in sight his [63] messenger, who had been intercepted and put in irons by the wretches, before he had proceeded many miles on his way to Elmina.

This was the stroke of despair to the ill-fated European: every resource was gone; his only companions were a man, who had lived with him many years, and an orphan boy, who had each refused to quit him. With these he consulted, and seeing his destruction inevitable, he determined at least to be revenged on the villains who had bayed him to death. Assisted by the two servants, he placed all his gunpowder, which still amounted to a considerable quantity, in a small room underneath the hall of audience. He then passed the night in arranging his papers, making up the government accounts, wiling away the property he had realised and sent home, and writing to a few friends. These dispatches he carefully secured on the person of the man, who had orders to try to make his escape with them the next morning, and to convey them to head-quarters.

At daybreak the governor appeared on the walls of his fortress, and made signs to the people without that he wished to speak with them. He gained a hearing, and then told them that he was now willing to give them whatever they asked, and to settle the palaver exactly as they wished; that, if the chiefs would come into the fort in about two hours to drink rum together, they would find him ready to deliver up his property to any amount they pleased. This proposal [64] was agreed to, the governor received his guests in the hall, and the people poured into the fortress. During the bustle which this occasioned, the faithful servant contrived to escape, and, creeping through the bushes, made the best of his way to Elmina. He had not proceeded far, however, when he heard a tremendous explosion; he turned round, and smoke, stones, and mangled human bodies were seen mingled together in the atmosphere. However prepared, the man involuntarily stopped to contemplate this awful catastrophe, and was only roused by the boy whom he had left with his master. It appeared that the governor affected to treat with the chiefs till he thought they were all assembled; he then reproached them with their perfidy and ingratitude, and exclaimed— "Now then, rascals, I will give you all I possess—all—all!" and stamped his foot with violence. This was the signal to the boy below, who instantly set fire to a covered train, sufficiently long to allow him to rush from the approaching mischief; and scarcely had he cleared the gates of the fortress, when all the chiefs perished with their victim, and many were killed who had assembled in the court.

The man and boy reached Elmina with the dreadful tale, and the ruin of the fortress, now and overgrown heap of stones, attests the truth of the story.

Title

Εως. [Shelley, Mary.] "The Euthanasia. A Story of Modern Greece." FMN 1829. 95-120.[13]

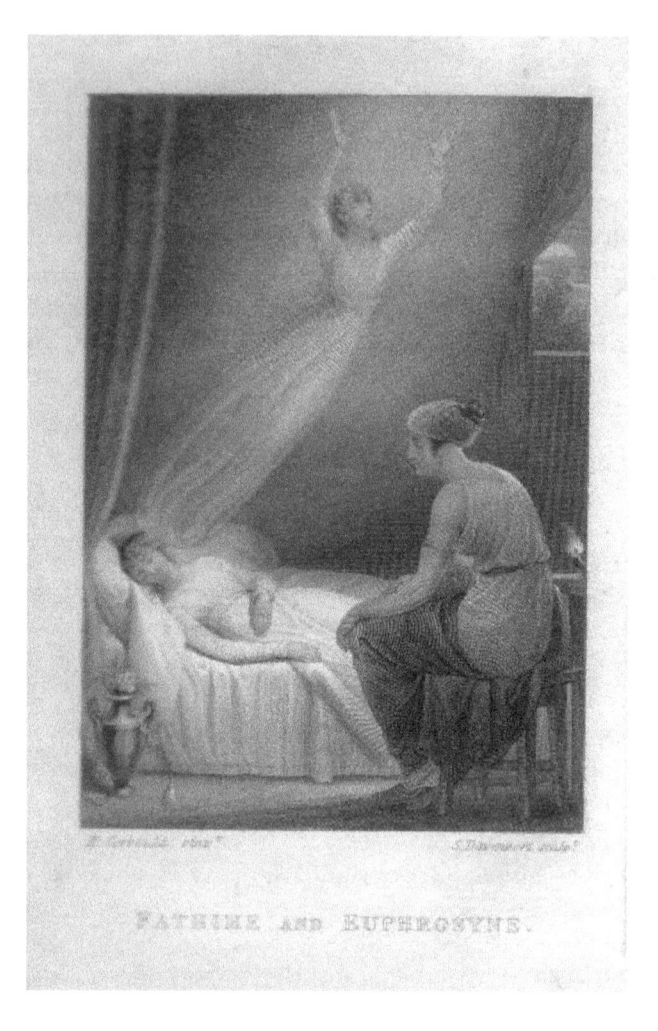

Plate: Fathime and Euphrosyne
Steel plate engraving; painted by Henry Corbould;
engraved by Samuel Davenport [95]

---

13 Mary Shelley identified as the author by Nora Crook; see "Sleuthing towards a Mary Shelley Canon," Women's Writing 6:3 (Oct 1999): 413-424.

THE EUTHANASIA.
A STORY OF MODERN GREECE.

— "THE sun is setting, and the doors must be shut before nightfall; it was Kalsandoni's last order. Girl, what can keep your lingering so long below?" was cried out from the top of the long steep stair that led to the summer chamber of the wife of Kalsandoni.

"I am coming, mother—I shall be with you in a moment; the sun is not going down yet," was the answer, in the silver voice of Euphrosyne, from the garden-door. But the voice was more silvery still in which she whispered— "Now be obedient, Carlo, and leave me. It will be dark immediately, and you will never be able to get into the town." The advice was received, as advice generally is, with a total disregard of its value, and the pretty giver of so much wisdom was obliged to give it over again. The listener was still sceptical in the extreme as to the necessity of so rapid a retreat. New arguments were of course necessary, and the dialogue was prolonged, until the wife of Kalsandoni was hear exerting her maternal tones yet more loudly from the summit of her tower: the sun gave a sudden dip into the sea, which he seemed to set on fire; and the noise of an authoritative foot coming down stairs made a separation inevitable.

"Farewell, then, my sweet! farewell, light of my soul, my own Euphrosyne!" was responded in the dusk, followed by a sound which proved the lips of the speaker could do more than talk, and which sent Eu-[96] phrosyne back half a dozen steps totally confounded, trembling from head to foot, and redder than the very roses that clustered over her.

"I shall never forgive you for this, Carlo," said she, when her breath came again. "You have never dared to presume on my patience before."

"Never!" said Carlo; "never, my sweet! it is my first offence, and should be forgiven; it may be my last, and must be forgiven."

"You last, Carlo!—Heavens, I hope not! What do you mean?"

Carlo laughed. "Well, Euphrosyne, that little speech of yours luckily falls into an ear that can remember nothing but that you are the loveliest child of nature. But what would you say, my beauty, my bride so soon to be, if I were going to take leave of you for a while?"

"Go, if you will, sir; I acquit you of all promise. But," and the laugh died away, "perhaps you are going to be married to Argyrophili's daughter? I ask the question through mere curiosity. You Italians are in love with every body for a week, and then, on the Sunday, marry some old woman or stranger for her money."

"I may be going to wed one whom I have often seen," said the Italian.

Euphrosyne's flashing eyes were fastened on his countenance, as if she heard with them.

"My bride is to some eyes the loveliest of all that are to be seen upon the earth." said Carlo. [97] Euphrosyne started from the hand that clasped her.

"Yet I think her, at this moment, the most hideous of all possible beings" continued Carlo.

Euphrosyne relentingly suffered her little taper fingers to twine with those of the hand still held towards her.

"Yet she is the most faithful creature that man ever trusted with his heart," said Carlo.

"Torture me no more with this raillery, but let me begone," sighed his agitated hearer.

"She ought to excite no emulation of yours,' replied the Italian; "for she is the wife of every husband that she can seize."

"Is she rich?"

"Immeasurably!"

"And young, fond, delicate, wise?" wept Euphrosyne. "Then go, Carlo, and be happy."

"She is all those: young, for she is the creature of a moment; fond, for where she has once attached herself no time can dissolve the tie; delicate, for the slightest flowers that bloom and breathe on her bosom are not more an emblem of fragility; and wise, for all that mankind knows becomes perpetually hers."

Euphrosyne clasped her hands on her forehead, that felt like a furnace, and blindly walked up the stairs.

"One word more," whispered the Italian, detaining her by the robe. "This possible bride is old, heartless, and rude."

"What am I to understand by all this? It is cruel [98] of you to perplex me, Carlo. But you will marry her, after all?" said the young Greek, pausing on the stair.

"In two days I will marry either you or her. Tomorrow night I must see this being whom I thoroughly hate," said Carlo with a languid smile. "But, come, my love, if we must part, let us part as friends. Never, while I retain my senses—never, while I have an eye that can feel the charms of matchless beauty, or a heart that can beat with passion for virtue, tenderness, and truth, can I willingly lead any other bride to the altar than my own Euphrosyne."

The words sank into her soul. She tottered forward, and fell upon his neck. The lover silently raised up that exquisite countenance, and sadly gazed upon it in the last gleam of the sunshine, as if in its fainting colours was going out the sunshine of his life. No words were spoken. Euphrosyne's tears fell large and quick from her eyelashes. Her red lips quivered.

"Farewell, my beloved, my bride!" at length sighed the Italian. He pressed a kiss on her white forehead, and, with one wild and long embrace, turned away. Both felt as if the spirit had departed from them at the moment.

Let me go back two months. Kalsandoni's dwelling had once been a wing of the palace of Beker Ali, pasha of Acarnania. The Turks, voluptuaries like the monks, knew like them how to choose a situation as well as any men in the world, and Beker Ali had built this summer pavilion on the brow of the richest hill that [99] was to be seen for leagues round Missolonghi. But Ali Pasha first shook the lazy Turk out of its pillows; then came the Greek patriots, and made a bonfire of a wing and the centre; and then came Kalsandoni, a chieftain of the klephts, who seized the remainder, in right of having cut off the ears of the commandant of Ali, and being the first to take possession.

The view from its upper chambers was boundless; and many an hour had Euphrosyne, the gentle daughter of so rough a sire, sat in the viranda, watching the glorious colours of the clouds, as they rose up in the sky, like successive fleets, to cast anchor on the mountain frontier of Acarnania; or following with her gaze the long flights of the sea-fowl, that, coming by thousands and tens of thousands from the rough precipices and furious snow-storms of the Pindus, made her wish for wings to fly with them in chase of summer to the groves and rills of Asia. The sea, brilliant as a sheet of lapis-lazuli, and made picturesque by green islands and mountains clothed with purple heaths and brown forests, was a perpetual mirror of the loveliest and the nobles aspects of nature; and, with the simply lyre of the Dalmatian and Albanian gypsies, she gave voice to the delight that filled her eye and heart.

On one of these evenings, when she had sat longer than usual making pictures in the clouds she was roused from her employment by the trampling of horses, and the sound of her father's voice, pitched in a remarkably high key. The gallant Albanian had returned un-[100] expectedly to supper, was as hungry as a wolf, and as little disposed to conceal any of his inclinations. The day's occurrences had ruffled his temper; for the little Ipsariote brig, in which he had a venture to the amount of three-fourths of his wealth, had gone the way of war. This swiftest of all sailers, commanded by the reis[14] who swore by the Panagia[15] that it cost him no trouble whatever to have fifty times hoodwinked, or out-sailed, or outfought, the keenest, the fleetest, and the boldest caravella[16], from the Dardanelles to the Gulf of Venice; this queen of smugglers, which he protested had made more trips from Zante and Corfu than ever plank and canvas had done before; which was scattered more brandy and broad cloth through the dominions of the sultan than the honest Turks thought could have been made by the united labours of man; and which had made the fortunes of half a dozen successive pashas by a mere toll out of her profits; on the very first voyage, when Kalsandoni committed to her the fruits of his valour, in the shape of sequins, with St. Mark's holy visage shining on them, was doomed to taste of the ill luck that at one time or other comes to all things, whether ships or men. The little brig had even now weathered a storm,

14 A captain.
15 The Virgin.
16 A Turkish frigate.

escaped a pirate, and was already in the full assurance of discharging her cargo of contraband, within the next half hour into the cellars of the richest and most conscientious seraff[17] of Pa- [101] tras, when the report of a gun shook the nerves of her crew; and, before they could recover from their astonishment, out swam from behind one of the rocks that bulge into the gulf of Lepanto a caravella, with her decks covered with musketeers, and the crescent flying in her tops. Battle, as the reis swore again by the Panagia, was hopeless; for the pursuing monster showed a row of teeth that would have made a meal of the little culprit at once. At all events, the reis, whatever might have been his affection for a metallic currency, felt none for the coin that the brazen messengers of the caravella were likely to send on board. The matter was by no means mended in Kalsandoni's opinion by his own person making a part of the cargo; and he heartily cursed the hour when his credit of the worthy reis beguiled him into sailing to receive his profits of his venture into his own pocket. A thousand times in the course of a quarter of an hour, while they were trying to trick the Turk by the masquerade of hoisting the colours of every nation under heaven, and were not ashamed to be Algerines, nor even Dutchmen for the time, Kalsandoni devoted to speedy ruin the fat old papas who had sold him a charm against accidents of all kinds for a week to come; the boasting captain who had offered to insure every hair on his head, and a voyage like the wind besides, for half a sequin; and every man of the community who had in any possible way been abiding or abetting, by advice or otherwise, to bring him into this scrape. [102]

    The council on board the brig was a model for councils of war: it was unanimous; it did not take up a minute; and it was followed by instant decision. The reis made a show of preparing for fight. A gun was fired ahead of the caravella, to let her know that there was powder and ball among his valuables; a piece of intelligence which the pursuers did not expect, and which caused the holding of a council of war upon her deck likewise. The Osmanlee were never famous for the rapidity of their deliberations; and before they had brought their perfumed bears to bear upon the subject, and had lighted their pipes in established form, the little Ipsariote had tacked, taken advantage of a gust, and shot like an arrow out of the gulf of Lepanto.

    The caravella followed, firing from her bowchasers, to the infinite disturbance of the wild geese and cormorants along the range of precipice that guards the shores of Acarnania; and which might have been additionally astonished at finding the great machine which they had so frequently contemplated as a roosting-place turned into such a flying fiend. By the Ipsariote, though the twelve-pound shot might as well have been fired against the moon, was under an unlucky planet. It was in vain that she showed all the knowledge of the coast that a long smuggling education could have taught her; that, on rounding the northern

---

17 An Armenian banker.

headland of the gulf, she ran direct for Zante, and steered within a boat's length of the tail of the southern shoal, in the hope of bringing the huge adversary on its middle: it [103] was in vain that she ran around Ithaca, and rubbed her planks against the rock, that every antiquary and old woman in the island pledge their souls and bodies to be the individual ship which brought Ulysses home from Troy; Santa Maura itself was tried in vain. For the first time since the creation of the world, the Turks knew their right hand from their left, steered within sight of rocks without running upon them, and fired for half an hour together without blowing up their ship.

The chase was drawing to a close, for the tall and heavy sails of the caravella were too much fro the little fluttering rags that wafted the Ipsariote. Within the last five minutes the fugitive must be on the rocks that save the town of Dragomestre from putting to sea in the first storm, or from the Osmanlee hands. The reis and his crew had made up their minds already. The picture of the Panagia was taken from the cabin, carried three times round the deck, and then deposited on the capstan, with a lantern burning in front. The gallant captain led the way for his crew; and, while the Turkish balls were dashing up the water about their ears, they began a hymn upon their bended knees.

Kalsandoni looked on this martial manoeuvre with a momentary surprise; for, as this was his first voyage, he was unacquainted with the received Mediterranean mode of meeting an enemy. But he recollected that he had to the amount of a thousand sequins under the [104] boards that served these men of piety for their prayers. He advanced to the reis, who was lying with his face rubbing the very deck before the great protectress, and applied a furious kick to the most prominent portion of the worshipper. The reis started up from his devotions, and attempted to prove to the angry klepht that singing a hymn to the Virgin was the true and only way to escape the Osmanlee. The klepht, inaccessible to virtue and reason, simply demanded whether he would fight the enemy or not. The reis, seconded by his chief mate and his crew, declared that such a thing was never heard of in the face of a superior force; that he would pray as much as any other captain in the trade, but that fight he would not. The demand was reiterated in a voice of thunder: it received the same answer; and Kalsandoni, taking the man of piety by the neck, lifted him in his giant grasp, and tossed him over the gunwale. The crew all screamed out with horror, and again took to their knees, from which, however, they were speedily disturbed by the klepht walking from stem to stern of the vessel, and distributing the same stimulant which had been so effectual with the reis. In the midst of the screams and execrations from this produced, one voice was heard in loud laughter. The klepht turned round to smite the scorner; but found before him a handsome tall Italian, who had just come upon deck, and was standing half convulsed at the sight of this unhallowed expedient.

The klepht saw at once that he was not of the [105] Mediterranean metal, and cried out to him, "Do you like to be hanged at the Turkish yard-arm, as these rascals are sure to be?"

"Not while I can help it," was the easy answer.

"Then take this lamp; go down into the magazine; and, when I call to you, blow us up, brig and all together."

The Italian took the lamp, and put his foot on the top-stair; but the crew had heard enough. To be blown up was worse than even the yard-arm. They gathered up their pikes and muskets from the deck; and the Turks, to their amazement, saw signs of a desperate resistance. Kalsandoni took the command, fired the first gun, and was knocked twenty feet from its breech by the shock. But the Italian had been an old artillerist, and he taught his mongrel crew to throw half a dozen of their discharges into the enemy's portholes. Nothing could be more surprising to the men of opium. The last shot had fallen into the depot of pipes for the voyage; their coffee-cups were falling fast; and the single hen-coop, on which they rested their hopes of pilau, was already sprinkled with the blood and feathers of its victims. The idea of fighting under such losses never yet entered the mind of any of the lords of Stamboul. Their captain gave orders to strike, and the flag was coming down, when, at the unlucky moment, the accursed reis, just dragging his limbs up the rocks, began to shout out in revenge, and point to the brig. [106]

The Turks, who did not understand a single syllable of what he was absolutely rending his lungs to tell them, but who deliberate upon everything, left the flag half-mast high, to save the trouble of repeating the operation; and quietly lighted their pipes, to discover the will of fortune. They had not long to wait. A heavy shot had struck the Ipsariote mast: shroud and sail were seen dropping from it one after the other; and at last came their naked prop over the side of the vessel. The crew sent up a general shriek; the reis roared with double revenge; the Turks said nothing, but shook out their pipes, fired a general broadside into the sinking brig, and ran on board. Kalsandoni and the Italian brandished their scimiters boldly. The klepht sheared off the head and turban of the renegade captain of the caravella, to whom he found at the moment of boarding that he had an old grudge. His companion was forced to content himself with the brawny wrist and well-ringed hand that the Turkish lieutenant laid upon the gunwale. But if they had both been tigers they could not be everywhere. On looking round, they perceived the crew at their devotions again. The vessel was tilting against the rocks; the water was running in and washing the knees of the worshippers. Kalsandoni gave his comrade a look, which he partly understood; and both, trampling backward over necks and shins without ceremony, sprang into the sea together. The exploit was not great, for the distance from shore was not a hundred yards. But the loss [107] was of another description; and the epithets with which Kalsandoni adorned his parting apostrophe to the crazy ship, the cowardly crew, the knavish reis, and the plundering Turks, would have done honour to an act of excommunication from the Vatican itself.

Standing on the shore, the klepht saw his sequins torn from his soul; but, if there was any comfort in their having escaped the pollution of the fingers of Islamism, he enjoyed it; for the brig had no sooner felt her deck incumbered with the unhallowed feet, than, as if indignant, down she went head-foremost. The feast of his wrath was to be fuller yet: for the caravella, lightened of half her crew, who were now swimming about to the advantage of the sharks and kites, which made no difference between Christian and nonbeliever, ran upon the rocks, and opened out, plank by plank the secrets of her prison-house to the buffeting of the waves. The turbans soon began to float independently of the heads of their owners; and, a single boat being the only thing belonging to the Turks that was in a condition to keep out the water, exactly ten of their two hundred escaped to carry the news of their victory to the feet of the great earthly disposer of the affairs of nations by sea and land, brother to the sun and moon, and cousin-german to the Georgium Sidus—the most magnificent sultan.

"Brother Palikar," said the klepht at last, with a groan to his companion, "is there any good in looking [108] at the wrecks of those dogs of Mahoun, or any comfort in standing here starving and shivering?"

"None whatever, that I can find," was the reply; "and rather than stay here, with nothing to eat but the sea-weed, and nothing to warm me but the sea-water, such is my habit of taking matters as they come, that I should not at all object to a good roof over my head, a cheerful fire at my feet, a well-dressed supper under my fingers, and a pretty woman, or even a brace of them, under my eyes."

"Then follow me," said the klepht, and darted down a ravine. The Italian followed; and as evening was just tinging the tops of the hills with that bright and living glory, which is like no other lustre in the world, but the light that steals on us from the half-sapphire, half-diamond, of a true Greek eye: "There," said the klepht, pointing to a white building peeping from a wilderness of vines and olives high up on the hill side, "there you shall sup with Kalsandoni."

On reaching the foot of the hill they found a rabble of palikars running out of their huts to welcome their sovereign lord, who returned their salutations with a few expressions suggested more by his recent wrath for the sequins, than his sense of their loyalty. The palikars are proverbially the most independent men on earth; they never swallow an insult, even to the extent of an oblique glance, and there are few among them who have not to be proud of shooting somebody for something or other. Many a man now [109] regretted that he had left his musket at home in the hurry of rejoicing; and, by singular fortune, there was not a loaded pistol among them, though they had been sitting in the midst of their friends. But no man can be prepared on all occasions, and Kalsandoni, before they have time to load, bethought himself of asking the heads of families to supper. Their resentment was buried at the sound, their honour was spunged clean, and with one accord they escorted their chieftain home, and made the trampling that broke up the vision of his daughter Euphrosyne.

From the rocky edge of Acarnania to the gentle shores of the Hellespont there was not a lovelier being than that daughter. Her mother, a Georgian, stolen or strayed from the establishment of the Mourad Ali, once pasha of the Morea, and famous for the most delicate taste in horses and women of any pasha that was ever decapitated, gave her all the beauty that could be added by loveliness of colour and brilliancy of eye to the classic features of the Greek. Delicately fair, yet with a hue over her countenance that looked like a meeting between the white and red rose; a pair of eyes that no one living could decide to be either hazel, or the deepest blue, or the most dazzling black, but which seemed alternately all; a form such as Nature loves to make when she is left to herself; and a heart as innocent and playful as the birds that fluttered and sang all morning, noon, and eve, under her window, Euphrosyne came down from the bower to fling herself into her father's [110] arms, and looked like a creature of Fairy Land, or Paradise, among the rough faces and mountaineer shapes of the palikars.

The Italian was smitten at once, and Euphrosyne, even in the simplicity of seventeen, found out, before supper was done, that she had a lover. The sensation was new, and its novelty kept her awake. Like another Juliet, she wooed the moon that night, and, like her, in the rustling of the vine branches heard more than the breathings of the wind. A sigh, a fragment of a song, a verse from Ariosto, and a few words of wonder, were all that she could collect of her audience of the young Italian. But, slight as it was, it was enough to keep her pillow unvisited by sleep, until Aurora came dropping dew and carnations over earth and heaven.

The klepht and his guest were breakfasting in the garden over the remnant of the sheep dressed the night before, and which the loyalty of the palikari had put into a state to do no harm to the appetite of an anchoret. The Italian fell into a reverie. He was roused by the cocking of a gun, looked up, and saw his entertainer with an eye piercing as a beam of fire fixed upon him.

"Young fellow," was the unceremonious address, "you are in love with my daughter—make no attempt to deny it—I suffer no liars to live. But, as I know no more of you that of the emperor of the yellow beards[18], let me have your story.— However, ob- [111] serve, that every word must be true, on penalty of two ounce balls in your brains.—I suffer no liars to live."

The Italian, laughing, gave up his brief biography. He was of a noble Piedmontese family. He had travelled in France, where all the old women and young men were boasting of a charter;—in Germany, where the schoolmasters whipped their boys to the sound of a charter;—in England, where every man talked of a charter, as their epicures talked of turtles—a luxury belonging to the

---

18 The Russians.

Forget Me Not

English appetite alone, and which all were proud of, though not one in a thousand was ever able to get a taste. He had then returned to Italy, and found not even a syllable about a charter, except in the whisperings of half-pay soldiers, disbanded douaniers, and discarded placemen. In his indignation at the public want of this essential comfort of life, he had joined the virtuous disgraced and proclaimed a charter. But the people were not ripe for so glorious a possession. They loved eating and sleeping, singing and cigars, after the manner of their fathers, better than being starved as banditti, or shot as rebels. The project died. The principals betrayed their subordinates, the subordinates betrayed their principals; generals ran away from their armies, and armies from their generals; until it was found that the true Italian genius of the nineteenth century was for organ-grinding and opera-singing, for flirting with other men's wives, and saving money on sixpence a day. He had fled, partly through love of liberty, and, he must ac- [112] knowledge, partly through fear of being handed At Ancona he had stepped into the Ipsariote brig, whose captain took his money on promise of conveying him straight to Tripolizza, starved him into a sick-bed, cheated him by going everywhere but where he promised, and, as he verily believed, would have kept him at sea for eve, but for the brig's going down.

Kalsandoni uncocked his musket and gave him his hand. "You are an honest fellow," was his remark, "and behaved so well yesterday that I even scarcely object to your being Italian. Your being a noble is rather a stumbling-block, and I could have almost forgiven a man for keeping such a misfortune out of sight. But, as you cannot help it, here's my hand. If Euphrosyne is not too proud to like you, you shall be an Albanian from this day, and my son-in-law."

Carlo Visconti would have been an Ethiopian under such a condition. The lovely young Greek had already made up her mind, but her words took a month more to put into that delicious shape, which, to a lover's ear, is worth all the music in the Nine. Carlo flew with the glad tidings to the klepht. The warrior's countenance took a shade of doubt. "What does her mother say? Ha!- I see you have not consulted her. I now know why your policies failed. Always consult the women first. Consult them from the weave of a riband to the choice of a wife. In war and wine, in trade, in travel, on all points, from the time that you can first ask a question till you are dumb or at least deaf, take their [113] opinions—they may set your right, or set you wrong; but, believe a husband of eighteen years' experience— take them if you value peace."

This omission cost another month, for Fathme ,the mother of his love, angrily insisted on time to make up her mind too. But at the close of their dreary month Fathme was more undecided than ever, for a private reason. She had been a celebrated beauty; she was still handsome; and what beauty ever voluntarily abdicated the sceptre? She had seen Euphrosyne driving her from her throne, and growing up into exquisite womanhood in her very presence. Still her fondness for this bewitching creature softened the defeat, and she took shelter under the belief that, seen at the distance favourable to the antique, they might sometimes pass for sisters. But, if Euphrosyne married, what conceivable escape was there from the fact of her being a grandmother? The stamp of age would be on her at once even though ten times her lilies and roses. In spite of her mirror, her feelings, and her worshippers, she must be that most alarming of all things, an old woman!

At length even Fathme gave way, and the marriage was to be celebrated on the 19th of August, 1823. The bride was shut up the week before, while those preparations that mothers delight in were going on. Carlo was daily and nightly under the window of his lady love. But for some nights he had been gloomy, and disturbed to a degree that excited the alarm of [114] Euphrosyne. She became jealous as he became enigmatical, and on the riddle which he left for her contemplation on the night on which our story began, drew many a tear down her feverish cheek. She spent the night thinking of the mysterious bride.

There was terrible cause for the lover's gloom. Mustapha Pasha, a man of blood, was marching with fourteen thousand troops down on Acarnania. To meet the ravager the Greeks could muster but two thousand. His passage on the hills on the frontier must sweep the land with fire and sword. In this dreadful emergency, Marco Bozzaris, a hero worthy of the days of Leonidas, offered to lead a corps of kindred heroes to die for their country. Carlo had taken service with the Greeks, but as Bozzaris, himself an Albanian, selected none but Albanians for the enterprise, he might have remained behind. Within two days of marriage, his whole soul engrossed by the charms of his bride, the thought of delay was bitterness, and he had at length flung aside his musket. But, as he was ascending the hill, he saw Kalsandoni coming to join the Sacred Band, and his knowledge of the destitution into which his loss must throw his wife and child decided the lover at once. He retuned to Missolonghi under the cover of the dusk, went instantly to Bozzaris, and by an arrangement which that generous soldier easily comprehended, contrived to have Kalsandoni appointed to another duty, and his own name substituted into the Albanian roll. [115]

At midnight these brave men mustered on the ramparts of Missolonghi, since made so memorable by their gallant defence against the Egyptian army and their worse assailants, famine and disease. The troops marched all night with such extraordinary rapidity, that by daybreak thy reached Carpovisa, at the foot of the mountains. The pasha's army were seen pitching their tents after descending from the defiles; and now nothing but the most vigorous determination could save the whole of the lowlands from ruin. During the day, Bozzaris concealed his forced behind some of the rugged projections of the hills, and continued watching the movements of the enemy, whom his sagacity discovered to be making preparation to march by daybreak. Calling together his Albanians, he declared his intention of anticipating them with a night attack. The attempt was tremendous; and all were conscious that, whatever might be the result, none could hope to return with his life. They received the proposal in the silence of men who heard their sentence of death; but they received it with the still more solemn evidence of their resolution, by throwing away the scabbards of their scimitars; a national custom, when they are determined to conquer or return no more.

On the night of parting from her lover, Euphrosyne remained at her casement for some hours, revolving the enigma of the bride whom her betrothed was to meet; whom he hated, yet whom he must not seem to shun; who was at once rich and poor, young and [116] old, lovely and terrible. Once or twice her quick ear caught the sounds of marching and arms; but at dawn the scene before her lay as tranquil as ever. Rumours, however had arrived of the approach of the enemy, and long before noon they were confirmed by the sight of the peasantry hurrying with their families and cattle from the frontier, across the plain toward Missolonghi and Anatolico. She now could rest no longer in the house, and, throwing on her veil, walked down to a little projection on the side of the hill, where Carlo, in a moment of his native romance, had piled together some fragments of marble, as a monument of the meetings; and where her own fair hand had adorned the spot with flowers. On the little altar she found a billet of a few lines, telling here that "duty and honour compelled him to join their troops, that he loved her alone, and that, living or dead, she should be his only bride." An ominous feeling smote her; she placed the billet in her bosom, and returned instantly to her chamber, where she flung herself on the bed, and was found by her mother weeping bitterly. She at length fell into a feverish slumber, and on awakening desired to be dressed in her bridal robes. Remonstrance was useless. She said, that Carlo had come and assured her that he would return at exactly twelve that night, and marry her. To soothe her mind she was suffered to put them on; and, to this hour, all who saw her in them talk of her singular beauty on that evening. She sat till twilight at her casement, alternately singing and [117] speaking to herself; and they describe her voice and language as of more than mortal sweetness and eloquence.

At nightfall she was awakened by this dangerous indulgence of her heart by her father's return, and she flew down stairs to meet him; but he was in ill-humour with what he thought the insult of sending him with his party to watch some Turkish stragglers, who had appeared within a dozen miles of the town, but whom he could not overtake. Of Carlo he knew nothing; but declared that he believed him to be nothing better than an Italian romancer, who had run away to avoid the marriage. Euphrosyne made no answer but tears, which her father, angry as he was, could not resist; he kissed her, and bade her go to rest.

The night was lovely, and after long breathing the air that came sweet and cool from the garden, she lay down, with her eyes fixed on the casement, which looked towards the mountains. Her mother, alarmed at every symptom of illness in a kingdom where death is frequently so rapid, sat watching by the bed, and moistening her lips with water from time to time. Euphrosyne slept awhile, and then suddenly starting up and saying, "He comes, I have seen him!" threw her arms around her mother's neck, kissed her repeatedly, and then turned to rest again. The bell was just tolling midnight from the church towers in Missolonghi; when a broad flash shot up suddenly in the direction of the mountains, illuminating the chamber, and covering Euphrosyne was light. She was asleep, [118] but evidently in a dream so happy, that her mother would not venture to awake her. She pronounced her lover's name, and by gestures seemed to welcome his arrival. The flash had disappeared; but even by the feeble light of the lamp, she looked so strikingly beautiful, that her mother declares all that she has ever seen of human loveliness before was but a shadow to the substance. The fever had totally left her, her cheek had the glow of health, and her slumbering lips continued to utter sounds of joy.

After a while her sleep seemed to be more profound, the house was hushed, and her mother's eyes grew heavy. She was startled by Kalsandoni's coming hastily into the room to inquire who was singing and playing at such a time of night; for the sound of voices and instruments was beginning to be heard round the house. No one could be seen. Her mother was in an agony lest so sweet a sleep should be disturbed; and Kalsandoni angrily took up his musket and rushed into the garden to drive away intruders. Still none were visible; but the sounds continued, swelling into a richer and more entrancing harmony every moment. At last alarm seized the household; they gathered from all quarters, and Kalsandoni, fearful that some attempt was about to be made on his dwelling; took his daughter's hand to awake her. It was cold; in surprise he held the lamp towards her face; nothing could be more glowing than its crimson; her features appeared full of animated beauty; her lips were [119] in a rosy smile—but the hand grew more icy. He held a mirror to her face, there were no signs of breath on it. He cried out that "Euphrosyne, his beloved, his angel was dead!" The priest came, the physician the paramana[19], but all was in vain. Beauty, genius and love, had there finished their mortal career. Euphrosyne had died at midnight; but her look, singularly lovely even on the bier, showed that she had died happy.

On that night, Marco Bozzaris had given Carlo the command of one of the divisions that were to break in upon the flanks of the Turkish camp, reserving for himself and his three hundred Souliotes the attack on the centre. The last words of this glorious Greek might be written in brass and marble, beside the noblest inscription of the Spartan soul. "If you lose sight of me during the battle, come and look for me in the pasha's tent." At midnight he stormed the lines, routed the Turks with immense slaughter, and set the whole encampment in a blaze Carlo had rushed in at the opposite quarter, and had reached the tent at the moment when Mustapha was mounting his horse to escape. He fired his musket,

---

19 Nurse.

and the horse fell; but a spahi galloping up, while he was in the act of grasping the pasha, fired his pistol into his bosom. Carlo fell mortally wounded. The fight was furious where he lay; and Bozzaris, stopping to lift him from the ground, received a ball in the loins. He revenged it by a blow of his scimitar, that swept off the Turk's head, and [120] he still persisted in carrying the young Italian from the field, where a second ball struck the hero in the forehead. They fell together.

A tress of Euphrosyne's hair was found in Carlo's bosom; Carlo's billet was found clasped in Euphrosyne's hand. He had indeed found the fatal bride whom he dreaded to meet, but whom none can shun. His life passed away with the last breath of Euphrosyne. Their last moment was the same; and in a little dell of wild olive and vine, on the side of the hill above Missolonghi, to the east, they sleep in the same grave.

Title
Bird, John. "The Cornet's Widow." FMN 1829. 131-144. [131]

THE CORNET'S WIDOW.
BY JOHN BIRD, ESQ.

IT was already known through the village that the arms of the Anglo-Spaniards were victorious, and the French in full retreat. Alarm at once gave place to joy. One deafening shout of acclamation arose to greet the returning victors; yet amid the impatient throng might be seen many a fair face looking with trembling eagerness for the moment that should kindle hope into ecstacy, or still the beating heart with the torpedo touch of despair. One there was, a pale yet lovely woman, who, screened behind the thin muslin curtain of a bay-window looking up the street, watched, with half-averted eyes, each scattered group that, waving their caps with exultation, or lamenting silently over some fallen comrade, passed in quick succession to the temporary guard-house. She was the wife of a cornet, beloved and respected through the regiment, and by that wife adored. Like one tottering on the verge of a precipice, she often closed her eyes, as if shrinking from the fate that awaited her; now awaking to breathless hope at a shout of triumph, and now dropping their swollen lids as the lifeless form of some remembered friend of her husband's was carried mournfully before her.—Alas! what pangs are like the pangs of suspense!—It was almost a relief when she perceived the bosom companion of her Arthur appear in the distance, although he came alone. Unable to re-[132] strain her impatience, she darted from her concealment and met him at the door.—He took her arm in silence and led her back into the apartment.—She grasped his hand convulsively.—Alas! she could not ask a tale which her own heart too well divined. The big tears that rolled down the manly cheek of captain Somers were a fatal confirmation of her worst fears. By a strong effort, however, she at once regained a calmness that astonished and awed the heart-stricken warrior.—"He is dead!"—A pressure of the hand was the emphatic reply.— "It is the will of Heaven—a hard lesson for a wife—my poor children!"—At a signal from Somers they were brought into the room, and a gush of tears, the first she had shed, seemed to relieve that intensity of grief, the calmness of which had alarmed her military friend, unused save to clamorous and murmuring lamentation.

"I must not yield to this!" she exclaimed, putting the wondering children from her: "go, go, poor orphans—fatherless—friendless!"

"Not so," cried the worthy Somers; my fortune,—my services (such at least as a soldier may offer) are at your command."

She smiled faintly—"Dear friend of my Lesley—mine!—oh, no—I must not dwell on this!—yet one thing I must ask!—the body, captain Somers?—

his precious remains?—you speak not!"

Somers, strongly agitated, would have evaded the inquiry, but her increasing emotion rendered this im- [133] possible. "I staid but to rescue all that is left of my departed friend from the hands of—we searched the plain, but were unable to recognise—"

She sunk back in her chair with a piercing shriek—"Trodden to death!"

"Not so," exclaimed Somers, with sparkling eyes: "he died the death of a soldier!—I saw him fall! A ball had entered his breast, and he expired on the instant.—At that moment the enemy gave way, and the rushing forward of a column—"

"It is enough!" she cried, closing her eyes, as if upon the painful truth—she remained silent a few moments—then, seeming to constrain herself into utterance—"leave me," she said, "kind, generous Somers:—I bow to the will of Heaven, but—I must be alone!"

The gallant officer, respecting the grief to which any effort at condolence had been but as mockery, bent in silence and withdrew.

The night that succeeded this eventful day was chill and gusty. The moon, obscured by swiftly coursing clouds, shed a dim, sepulchral light over that battlefield where the corses of the fallen brave lay festering into decay.—Sentinels had been stationed to guard the dying and dead that time had not yet permitted to remove or inter, but could not wholly prevent the ravages of those vultures in human form, who, brutalized by their thirst of plunder, had tracked the scent of blood. One of these sentries, a serjeant of Lesley's [134] regiment, was keeping watch near the spot where the unfortunate cornet had fallen, and silently meditating on the untimely fate of one whom he had loved and honoured, when a pale form, indistinct in the gloom, glided past him. At such a time a vague feeling of dread may be forgiven to the bravest. "Who goes?" he cried, somewhat tremulously.—No reply was given, but the white drapery of the being, who seemed pausing in utter inability to proceed, indicated her at once to be some unhappy mourner, in whose bosom love had stifled the throb of fear and the shrinkings of horror. Deeply affected at such a vision, the serjeant hastened eagerly to her aid, and at once recognised, with awe and amazement, the widow of the fallen cornet.

"Tell me," she cried, scarcely articulate from emotion—"tell me where—the spot—"

"Dear lady," he replied, unable to restrain his tears, "this is no place for you—it is in vain!—we have searched——"

"I know, I know," she exclaimed impatiently, "but I—hinder me not, Wilmot—it is the duty of a wife—a wife!—no, no, a widow—to seek out one who—" she leant on the serjeant's arm almost insensible, but soon recovering—"point but to the spot—"

He stretched his arm towards a heap of the unburied dead, a few paces from them, and with true delicacy relinquishing any further effort to restrain her purpose, retired. He retired, however, only behind the covert of a ruined wall, whence, unseen by the fair [135] mourner, he could observe her motions and watch over her safety.—With timid steps she glided to the gory mass that had baffled the scrutiny of friendship: but what can elude the piercing eye of love? An almost joyful shriek proclaimed that the precious form was found.—Alas, what a spectacle it presented to the gaze of a fond, doting wife!—The upper part of Lesley's face was wholly mangled and disfigured, the brow crushed, the eye extinguished—but a smile still played round the mouth, to which the cold lip of the scarcely breathing widow was eagerly prest in all the wild exuberance of woe. Having thus yielded to the first gush of passion, the voice of religion, the only true solace of the afflicted, seemed to regain dominion over the sweet mourner. Sinking on her knees by the corpse of her beloved husband, with clasped hands and eyes uplifted to Heaven, her pure and lowly spirit breathed itself forth in a blessing on the departed. At that moment the moon, emerging from her shadowy veil, shone full on the pale features of the widow, displaying to the admiring gaze of Wilmot a countenance beaming with love and resignation almost beatific.—And oh, what lovelier vision has life than that of a beautiful woman pouring forth her soul before her Creator!—Bowing her head, as if in submission to the divine will, and fondly stealing a farewell kiss from the cold lips of her Arthur, she rose and seemed intent to retire; but, ever turning to catch another glance, still lingered, as unequal to the effort of leaving [136] the spot. On a sudden a new feeling, incomprehensible to the observing serjeant, appeared to animate her.—Hastily stooping, he observed her remove carefully the cap of the departed, as though she feared to wake the slumber of the dead, and sever a lock of hair, which she hid with trembling eagerness in her bosom;—then looking wildly round for the friendly Wilmot, who hastened anxiously to her, she pointed to the spot—"That dear form—"

"Shall be cared for, my honoured lady!" exclaimed the serjeant, placing his hand solemnly on his breast.—She prest his hand.—He burst into tears.— "I would weep too," she said, looking tenderly on him, "but now I cannot—farewell!"

The serjeant, greatly affected, entreated her to remain a few minutes, till the relieving of the guard should enable him to quit his post, and protect her to her home.— "I need no protection but that of Heaven," she cried; "alas, Heaven only can protect me now!" She pointed once more to the spot she had quitted, and, the serjeant replying by an expressive gesture, again prest his hand and vanished.

The absence of Mrs. Lesley from her home, having been observed, had given rise to the most cruel suspicions. Somers, however, whose penetration had led him to divine the true cause, had eagerly followed her steps to the field, and, affected as he was by the recital of Wilmot, he was yet greatly relieved on hearing of her noble and unmurmuring resignation. The body [137] of Lesley was removed under his directions from the gory mass to await the rites of sepulture—rites which a recent order for the advance of the detachment on the following morning rendered it essential to carry into effect within a few hours. On this occasion it was his painful duty once more to seek the house of mourning.

He found the widow paler than before, but quiet, calm, and composed. "Somers," she said, "I have taken a last farewell of my Arthur"—her eyes began to fill— "I must not yield to this"—dashing the gathering drops away— "I have duties to perform towards the dead and the living, which forbid the indulgence of selfish feeling! You tell me that his remains will be interred with the honours of war:—it is well!—Yet, alas! have not those honours bereaved me of the best and dearest?—Oh! that he had never embraced this cruel profession!—then might his ashes have reposed in the lone tomb of his forefathers, beneath those broad beeches, where once we strayed—better for him that it had never been so!—You look surprised, dear friend of my Arthur!—Know you not that by marrying me he lost fortune—father—all—all!" The intensity of her feelings gradually overpowered that air of tender resignation to which she had tasked herself. Somers earnestly entreated her to spare herself the agonizing recital. "No!" she exclaimed, "it is fitting that you, the chosen of my husband's heart, should know the past story, the future purpose, of [138] his widow.—I was the daughter of the village rector in the parish where the father of my Arthur, General Lesley, resided. We were playmates in infancy, but the premature death of my parents transferring me to the care of an aunt, and the absence of Arthur at school and afterwards at college, separated us for several years. I need not tell you that my husband was one of the most perfect of beings. Noble in form, but oh, how much more noble in spirit! he seemed destined to realize the most ambitious hope of a doting father.—Why was it my fate to mar the dazzling prospect?—We met—the love of infancy expanded into a softer, dearer emotion; and yielding to the pleadings of my Arthur, the entreaties of an anxious because needy relative, and oh! more fatal than all, the whisperings of my own heart, I became a wife!—Anticipating the displeasure of the general, we wedded in secret.—Alas! is there not a curse on stolen nuptials?—Had it been my fate alone to expiate our fault!—but Heaven willed it otherwise—Nay, nay, no sympathy!—the sting is here; but I can endure it. Unmoved by our tears and supplications, the general cast us off, my poor Arthur's cornetcy being his last, his fatal benefaction:—the rest you know; our love, our sufferings, our privations—and oh! the dreadful issue!—But I am becoming weak again, and I have yet to inform you of my purpose. Somers, I carry within me the seeds of death: the malady that destroyed my parents is preying on my vitals, and will soon unite [139] me to my Arthur. Think not I grieve at this!—Oh! were it not for my poor babes, what bliss, what ecstasy were mine to close my eyes on this vale of woe, and awake to a blessed immortality!—But I distress you:—a few words more and I have done—We are near the coast—it is my intention to sail immediately for England, and to commit the dear pledges of my Arthur's love to the care and protection of their natural guardian, his father—Resentment cannot live after death—the good old general will not refuse to receive his grandchildren, or if he should—"

"I will protect them!" exclaimed Somers, with enthusiasm. The widow spoke not; but the warm pressure of her hand and the tear in her eye were all-eloquent. "I cannot resist your purpose," he replied; "it is the natural impulse of a noble heart: but remember," he continued, "that, while Somers lives, you and yours have a friend. I will take measures for your safe-conduct to the next port, and your embarkation from thence.—Nay, no thanks!" He pressed his lip silently and respectfully to her extended hand, while, with eyes beaming with gratitude, she took a long and last farewell of her kind and generous friend.

It was in the afternoon of a wintry day in November, that the widow and her orphans arrived at the little inn of the village where General Lesley resided. The sullen aspect of nature, the fallen leaves, the cold ungenial wind, all seemed in unison with the mournful and agitated feelings of the drooping wanderer. To [140] look on her birth-place—to retrace the spot where she first met her departed Arthur, the haunts where they had strayed, and the peaceful church in which they had together offered up their pure and humble prayers to Heaven—to gaze on these, and feel that the one pervading charm was no more—this was indeed a severe trial of that fortitude which religion had inspired and preserved. Even the artless and natural questions of the elder of her children, a boy of six years old, "Which is grandpapa's house?" and "Is he as kind and good-natured as papa?"—by recalling to her mind the uncertainty of her reception, awakened feelings that were but more acute from their exciting the childish wonder of her young charge. Without making herself known, she learned that the melancholy fate of his only child had already reached the general, whose grief was unbounded; that he was then at his mansion, but had hitherto obstinately refused to receive any visits, or to listen to the voice of consolation.

Short deliberation was requisite to direct her how to act. To pour forth her feelings on paper in a brief but affecting narrative, which she dispatched to the house of the general by a servant of the inn, was the work of a few minutes. Grief is eloquent: but, alas! the excitement of feeling arising from the performance of this duty soon gave way to a deepened depression, which she vainly attempted to subdue. To divert her thoughts from an issue she seemed never to have really dreaded till now, she occupied herself in consigning [141] her little daughter to rest, and was preparing to perform the same maternal office for the boy; but his innocent pleading to "sit another hour with poor mamma," was too affecting to be resisted. Never had his likeness to his unhappy father seemed so strong as at this moment, when, with childish earnestness, he pressed his artless supplication on his weeping mother.

"Do not cry, my own mamma," exclaimed the lovely prattler: "I shall soon be a man, and then you shall never weep again.—And, tell me, mamma, shall I not wear a red coat like my papa?"

"Heaven forbid, my child!" cried the agonised mother. The door opened, and the general stood before her. Scarcely knowing what she did, the agitated widow sunk on her knees before him, still holding the hand of her young son, who, with innocent wonder, gazing on his aged relative, silently and unconsciously kneeled beside her. His strong resemblance to his departed sire seemed the irresistible appeal of nature to the feelings of his progenitor. Snatching him to his heart, yet putting him away at intervals to observe the lineaments more attentively, tears, the first he had known, broke from the veteran's eyes, like springs from the burning desert, while the noble childe yielded to caresses, which he returned with eagerness and delight.

"Dear mamma, tell me, is this my own grandpapa?" [142]

"Yes, yes—bright image of my lost Arthur!" cried the white-haired grandsire— "of that Arthur who is wonderfully and mercifully restored to me in this dear boy.—Oh, shall I abandon thee also!—Ellen, my child!" he exclaimed, sinking on his knees by the side of the still kneeling widow, whom excess of feeling had kept silent and motionless: "Ellen, my own sweet daughter, can you ever forgive me?"

She could not speak, but, bathing his hand with her tears, attempted, with filial tenderness, to raise him.

"Not yet, not yet!" he cried, gently putting her child from him, while, with uplifted hands, he bent in mute gratitude to Heaven. In silent imitation, the wondering boy, kneeling between his grandsire and his mother, lifted, as he had been taught, his little hands in prayer, while his fond, his enraptured parent, flinging her arms round him, gave vent, in a torrent of tears, to the delighted feelings of an overcharged heart. It was a moment of bliss, cheaply purchased even by that strong emotion which threatened to accelerate the dissolution of her already wasted frame.

"Ellen, my child!" exclaimed the general some days after, when the widow and her orphans had been formally established in his mansion: "Ellen, these eyes, that cheek, are a continual reproach to my unnatural desertion of you!—You must have advice. I shall not think you forgive me while I see you thus pale and languid." [143]

"My friend—my father!" said the widow, taking his hand, "we must part!"

"Part!" repeated the old man, greatly affected—"Part, Ellen!—Would you then leave me?—Would you bereave me of your children—of my dear second Arthur?"

"No, no!" she cried: "in committing them to your fatherly care—in seeing them taken to your fostering bosom, my last duty, my last desire, is accomplished."

"And think you then, Ellen," resumed the general, "that I love you less than your children, or that I will ever resign you?" She held up her hand, so wasted that the light shone through, and the fatal truth at once struck on the affectionate old man. He burst into loud exclamations of grief. "It is I—it is I that have killed you!—that have murdered Arthur!—Oh, Ellen, why did you conceal this cruel malady from me!—But it may not yet be too late—we have skillful physicians—"

"Seek not to avert the will of Heaven," she exclaimed, faintly smiling; "it may not be controlled: and, oh, my father!" she continued, pressing her thin lip to his withered hand, "ought we to repine at a fate which will unite me for ever to my blessed Arthur? I do not ask you to protect his children—to rear them in the love of virtue—to teach them the way of pleasantness and the path of peace."

Overpowered by emotion, he vainly attempted to speak; but the children entering at the moment, he extended an arm round each, endeavouring by that [144] silent gesture to express the solemn purpose of his heart. The widow smiled as she drew from her bosom the lock of hair, severed on the night of her husband's death, and placed it in the general's hand.—"It is my only legacy—can I bequeath one more precious?"

He looked on it with glistening eyes, and turned, as if to express his sense of its value, when he perceived her lift her clasped hands to Heaven, and sink back fainting in her chair. The cries of the children brought servants into the room, who attempted to restore her, but in vain—the cornet's widow was no more!

Title
Neele, Henry. "The Houri. A Persian Tale." FMN 1829. 165-178. [165]

THE HOURI.
A PERSIAN TALE.
BY THE LATE HENRY NEELE, ESQ.

IN the 414th year of the Hegira, Shah Abbas Selim reigned in the kingdom of Iraun. He was a young and an accomplished prince, who had distinguished himself alike by his valour in the field and by his wisdom in the cabinet. Justice was fairly and equally administered throughout his dominions; the nation grew wealthy and prosperous under his sway; and the neighbouring potentates, all of whom either feared his power or admired his character, were ambitious of being numbered among the friends and allies of Abbas Selim. Amidst all these advantages, a tendency to pensiveness and melancholy, which had very early marked his disposition, began to assume an absolute dominion over him. He avoided the pleasures of the chase, the banquet, and the harem, and would shut himself up for days and weeks in his library (the most valuable and extensive collection of oriental literature extant), where he passed his time principally in the study of the occult sciences, and in the perusal of the works of the Magians and the astrologers. One of the most remarkable features of his character was the indifference with which he regarded the beautiful females, Circassians, Georgians, and Franks, who thronged his court, and who tasked their talents and charms to the utmost to find favour in the eye of the shah. Exclamations [166] of fondness for some unknown object would, nevertheless, often burst from his lips in the midst of his profoundest reveries; and, during his slumbers, he was frequently heard to murmur expressions of the most passionate love. Such of his subjects whose offices placed them near his person were deeply afflicted at the symptoms which they observed, and feared that they indicated an aberration of reason: but, when called upon to give any directions, or take any step for the management of the affairs of the nation, he still exhibited his wonted sagacity and wisdom, and excited the praise and wonder of all.

He had been lately observed to hold long and frequent consultations with the Magians. The kingdom had been scoured from east to west in search of the most skillful and learned men of this class; but whatever were the questions which Abbas Selim propounded, it seemed that none of them could give satisfactory answers. His melancholy deepened, and his fine manly form was daily wasting under the influence of some unknown malady. The only occupations which seemed at all to soothe him were singing and playing on his dulcimer. The tunes were described, by those who sometimes contrived to catch a few notes of them, to be singularly wild and original, and such as they had never heard before. A courtier, more daring than the rest, once ventured so near the royal privacy as to be able to distinguish the words of a song, which were to the following effect:— [167]

> Sweet spirit! ne'er did I behold
> Thy ivory neck, thy locks of gold;
> Or gaze into thy full dark eye;
> Or on thy snowy bosom lie;
> Or take in mine thy small white hand;
> Or bask beneath thy smilings bland;
> Or walk, enraptured, by the side
> Of thee, my own immortal bride!
>
> I see thee not; yet oft I hear
> Thy soft voice whispering in my ear;
> And, when the evening breeze I seek,
> I feel thy kiss upon my cheek;
> And when the moon-beams softly fall
> On hill, and tow'r and flow'r-crown'd wall,
> Methinks the patriarch's dream I see—
> The steps that lead to heaven and thee.
>
> I've heard thee wake, with touch refined,
> The viewless harp-strings of the wind,
> When on my ears their soft tones fell,
> Sweet as the voice of Israfel[20].
> I've seen thee, midst the lightning's sheen,
> Lift up for me heaven's cloudy screen,
> And give one glimpse, one transient glare,
> Of the full blaze of glory there.
>
> Oft midst my wanderings wild and wide,
> I know that thou art by my side;
> For flow'rs breathe sweeter 'neath thy tread,
> And suns burn brighter o'er thy head;
> And though thy steps so noiseless steal,
> And though thou ne'er thy form reveal,
> My throbbing heart and pulses high
> Tell me, sweet spirit, thou art nigh.
> [168]
> Oh, for the hour, the happy hour,

---

20 The angel of music.

> When Azrael's[21] wings shall to thy bow'r
> Bear my enfranchised soul away,
> Unfetter'd with these chains of clay!
> For what is he whom men so fear,
> Azrael, the solemn, and severe;
> What but the white-robed priest is he,
> Who weds my happy soul to thee?
>
> Then shall we rest in bow'rs that bloom
> With more than Araby's perfume,
> And gaze on scenes so fair and bright,
> Thought never soar'd so proud a height;
> And list to many a sweeter note
> Than swells th' enamour'd bulbul's throat;
> And one melodious Ziraleet[22]
> Through heaven's eternal year repeat.

One evening, when the shah was thus occupied, his prime minister and favourite, Prince Ismael, introduced into his apartment a venerable man, whose white hair, long flowing beard, and wan and melancholy but highly intellectual features, failed not to arrest the attention and command the respect of all who beheld him. His garments were plain and simple, even to coarseness, but he was profusely decorated with jewels, apparently of considerable value, and he bore a long white wand in his hand. "I have at length, oh king!" said the minister, "met with the famous Achmet Hassan, who professes, that if it be in the power of any mortal to procure the gratification of your highness's wishes, that power resides in him." [169]

"Let him enter," said the shah. The minister made an obeisance, introduced the sage, and retired.

"Old man, said Abbas Shah, "thou knowest wherefore I have sought thee, and what I have desired of thee?"

"Prince," said Achmet, "thou wouldst see the houri, the queen of thy bower of paradise; her who, in preference to all the other dark-eyed daughters of heaven, will greet thee there, and shall be thy chosen companion in those blissful regions."

"Thou sayest it," said the shah. "Can thy boasted art procure me a sight, be it even transitory as the lightning's flash, of that heavenly being?"

"King of Iraun," said the sage, "the heavenly houris are of two different natures. They are, for the most part, of a peculiar creation formed to inhabit those bowers; but a few are sinless and beautiful virgins, natives of this lower world, who,

---

21 The angel of death.

22 A song of rejoicing.

after death, are endowed with tenfold charms, which surpass even those of the native daughters of paradise. If thy immortal bride be of the former nature, she is beyond the reach of my art; but if she be of the latter, and have not yet quitted our world, I can call her spirit before thee, and thine eyes may be gratified by gazing upon her, although it will be only for a moment, transitory, as thou has said, as the lightning's flash."

"Try, then, thy potent art," said the prince. "Thou hast wound up my spirit to a pitch of intense desire. Let me gaze upon her, if it be but for an instant." [170]

"Prince," said the sage, fixing his dark, bright eye upon the shah, "hope not to possess her upon earth. Any attempt at discovering her abode, or making her thy own, will be disastrous to you both. Promise me that thou wilt not think of any such enterprise."

"I promise thee any thing—every thing. But haste thee, good Achmet, haste thee; for my heart is full, even to overflowing."

The sage then with his wand described a circle round the prince, within which he placed several boxes of frankincense and other precious spices, and afterwards kindled them. A light thin cloud of the most odorous fragrance began to diffuse itself over the apartment. Achmet bowed his head to the ground repeatedly during this ceremony, and waved his wand, uttering many sounds in a language with which the shah was unacquainted. At length, as the cloud began to grow rather dense, the old man drew himself up to his utmost height, leaned his right hand on his wand, which he rested on the floor, and, in a low, solemn tone, uttered an incantation, which seemed to be a metrical composition, but was in the same unknown language. It lasted several minutes; and while the old man was pronouncing it, the cloud, which was spread over the whole apartment, seemed gradually gathering together and forming a condensed body. An unnatural but very brilliant light pervaded the chamber, and the cloud was seen resolving itself into the resemblance of a human shape, until at length the [171] prince saw, or fancied that he saw, a beautiful female figure standing before him. His own surprise was not greater than that of the old man, who gazed upon the phantom he had raised, and trembled as he gazed. It appeared to be a young female, about fifteen years of age. She was tall, and her form exhibited the most wonderful symmetry. Her eyes were large, bright, and black. Her complexion was as though it had borrowed the combined hues of the ruby and the pearl, being of an exquisite white and red. Her lips and her teeth each exhibited one of these colours in perfection, and her long dark hair was crowned with flowers, and flowed in glossy ringlets down to her waist. She was dressed in a long flowing robe of dazzling whiteness: she neither moved nor spoke, only once the prince thought that she smiled upon him, and then the figure instantly vanished, the preternatural light left the apartment, and the mild moonbeams again streamed through the open lattices.

Before the exclamation of joy which was formed in the prince's bosom could reach his lips, it was changed into a yell of disappointment. "Old man," he said, "thou triflest with me—thou has presented this vision to my eyes only that thou mightst withdraw it immediately. Call back that lovely form, or, by Mahomet! thou shalt exchange thy head for the privilege which thou hast chosen to exercise of tormenting Abbas Selim."

"Is it thus, oh king!" said Achmet, "that thou [172] rewardest the efforts made by thy faithful subjects to fulfill thy wishes? I have tasked my art to its utmost extent: to call back that vision, or to present it again to thine eyes, is beyond my skill."

"But she lives—she breathes—she is an inhabitant of this world!" said the prince.

"Even so," returned the other.

"Then I'll scour all Iraun, I'll dispatch emissaries all over the world, that, wherever she be, she may be brought hither to fill up the vacuum in my heart, and to share the throne of Abbas Selim!"

"The instant," said Achmet, "that your highness's eyes meet hers, her fate is sealed. She will not long remain an inhabitant of this world. It is written in the Book of Fate that she shall not be the bride of mortal man."

"Death, traitor!" said the monarch; "am I not the shah? who shall gainsay my will?—what shall oppose it?"

"The will of Heaven!" replied the sage, calmly. "The irrevocable decrees of destiny."

"Away! avaunt! thou drivelling idiot!" said Selim, "let me not see thee more!"

The shah's maladies, both mental and bodily, increased alarmingly after this event. The lovely phantom haunted him sleeping and waking. He lost all appetite and strength, and appeared to be fast sinking into the grave. At length he bethought himself, that if he could, from memory, sketch the features which he [173] had beheld, he might possibly thence derive some consolation. He possessed some talent for drawing—his remembrance of the form and features was most vivid and distinct—and, guiding his pencil with his heart rather than his hand, he succeeded in producing a most extraordinary likeness. He then summoned into his presence a skilful and accomplished limner, in whose hands he deposited the sketch, and describing to him the colour of the hair, eyes, and complexion, of the original, he desired him to paint a portrait.

The limner gazed upon the sketch, and listened to the description with profound attention and evident surprise. "Surely," said he, "I have seen her whose features are here delineated. Indeed they are features which are not easily mistaken, for she is beautiful as one of the damsels of Paradise."

"Sayest thou so?" said the monarch, starting from his seat, while he tore from his turbans some jewels of inestimable value, which he thrust into the painter's hand. "Knowest thou where to find her?"

"She lives in the southern suburbs," answered the limner. "Her name is Selima, and her father is a poor but a learned man, who is constantly buried in his studies, and is unconscious of the value of the gem which is hidden under his humble roof."

"Haste thee, good Ali, haste thee! bring her hither—let no difficulties or dangers impede thee, and there is not a favour in the power of the monarch of Iraun to grant which thou shalt ask in vain." [174]

Ali flew rather than ran to the abode of his fair friend, in whose welfare he had always taken a lively interest. He knocked at the door, which was opened by the lovely Selima herself.

"Sweet Selima," he said, "I have strange news for thee."

"Speak it then," she answered smilingly; "be it bad or good, the sooner I hear it the better."

"I have a message for thee from the shah."

"The shah!" she said, and her eyes sparkled with a mysterious expression of intelligence and wonder; but she did not, extraordinary as was the information, appear to entertain the slightest doubt of its veracity. "'Tis wondrous strange!"

"'Tis true," said the limner. "He placed in my hands a sketch for a female portrait, in which I instantly recognised your features."

"It is but a few days ago," said she, "that I had an extraordinary dream. Methought I was in an apartment of surprising extent and magnificence. A cloud of fragrant odours filled the room; the cloud became gradually condensed, and then assumed the form of a young man of most majestic form and handsome features. Although I had never seen the shah, I soon knew by his pale, proud brow, so sad and yet so beautiful, his bright, sparkling blue eye, his tall, stately form, and his regal gait, that this could be none other than Abbas Selim. He smiled sweetly upon me—he took my hand in his, and his lips approached mine [175] I woke, and saw only the cold moonbeams gilding my chamber.

"Sweet Selima! why have I never heard of this before?"

"I told it all to my father," she said; "but he frowned upon me, and bade me think of it no more, and to tell my dream to no one. But thy strange message has made me violate his command. I have thought of nothing but Abbas Selim since. How happy ought the nation to be whom he governs; and, above all, how happy the maiden whom he loves!"

"Then art thou, my Selima, supremely happy," said the limner; "for of thee is he enamoured to desperation. Thou must accompany me immediately to the palace."

In the mean time the shah paced his apartment in an agony of impatience. "Curse on this lingering limner!" he exclaimed; "has he combined with the Magian to drive me to distraction? May every vile peasant press to his heart the being whom he adores, and am I, the lord of this vast empire, to sigh in vain, and to be continually tormented with faint and momentary glimpses of the heaven from which I am debarred?"

He had scarcely uttered these words, when the private entrance to his apartment, to which he had given the painter a passport, opened, and his messenger entered, leading his fair companion by the hand. No sooner did the monarch's eyes encounter those of Se- [176] lima, than he instantly knew that he was in the real, substantial presence of her whose phantom he had beheld. His wonder and delight knew no bounds, nor will the power of language suffice to describe them. He pressed to his heart the object for which it had so long panted. Health and strength appeared to be suddenly restored to him; new life seemed rushing through his veins; and his buoyant step and elastic tread seemed to belong to a world less gross and material than that in which he dwelt. When the first paroxysm of his rapture was over, he summoned the chief imaum into his presence, and gave him orders to follow him into the mosque attached to the palace, for the purpose of immediately celebrating his nuptials with Selima.

The priest gazed intently on his bride, and his features became strangely agitated. "The will of Abbas Selim," he said, "is the law of his faithful subjects; but if I have read the Koran aright, and if my studies have not been idly pursued, the finger of death is on yon fair maiden, and her nuptials with the shah will but accelerate the approach of Azrael."

"Dotard!" said the prince; and he gazed upon Selima, whose features glowed with all the hues of beauty and health. "Tell not to me thy idle dreams, but perform thine office, and be silent."

The chidden priest obeyed the last injunction of his prince, and, with head depressed and folded arms, followed him and his bride to the mosque, which was [177] hastily prepared for the celebration of these unexpected nuptials. Heavily and falteringly he pronounced the rites, which were just on the point of being concluded, when a man rushed into the mosque, and, with frantic and threatening gestures, placed himself between the bride and bridegroom. It was Achmet Hassan.

"Forbear, forbear!" he cried, "or Allah's curse light on you!"

"It is the traitorous Magian," said the shah. "Villain! wouldst thou beard thy sovereign at the nuptial hour?"

As he spoke, he unsheathed his scimitar, and rushed towards Achmet." "Save him! spare him!" shrieked the bride; "it is my father!" and rushing between them, the shah's weapon pierced her to the heart, and she sunk lifeless to the earth.

All were struck mute and motionless with horror at this fatal event. When they had somewhat recovered from their stupor, every eye was fixed upon the shah. Still and cold, and silent as a statue, he occupied the same place as at the moment of this fearful catastrophe. His eyes glared fixedly and unmeaningly. His lips and cheeks were of an ashy paleness. He returned no answer to the inquiries which were made of him, and the import of which it was evident that he did not comprehend. In fact, it was clear that reason had fled from the once highly endowed mind of Abbas Selim, and that the reign of [178] one of the greatest and most highly accomplished princes who had ever filled the throne of Persia was terminated.

In a state of listlessness and inanity he continued for above a twelvemonth. A few apartments of the palace were all that remained to him of his once mighty empire, and the sceptre passed into the hands of his brother. His most faithful and constant attendant was the unhappy Achmet Hassan, whom he had rendered childless, and on whose bosom he breathed his latest sigh. As the hour of death approached, his intellects seemed to return; but his malady had so entirely exhausted his strength, that he could not utter a syllable. Once, from the motion of his lips, it was supposed that he was endeavouring to pronounce the name of Selima; then a faint smile illumed his features, while he pointed to the casement and the deep blue sky which was seen through it, and his spirit fled to the bowers of Paradise.

Title
Rosa. "Giuseppe Guercino." FMN 1829. 193-208. [193]

GIUSEPPE GUERCINO.

THE sun was sinking in the west, the labours of the day were over, and the cheerful peasantry of the Neapolitan suburbs assembled to close the evening with the accustomed dance and song. Apart from the group stood, with abstracted air, a youth, whose slight form and graceful mien pointed him out as one well fitted to mingle in, and to adorn, the festivities of which he was but an inactive spectator. It was evident, however, that the scene of gaiety had lost its charm for him; and with a sigh, heaved from the inmost recesses of his heart, he turned aside, and walked dejectedly away; directing his steps, unconsciously as it seemed, not towards his home, but to a small village which lay exactly in an opposite direction.

"Giuseppe Guercino has actually gone away then without once asking me to dance," said the gay Theresa, a lovely dark-eyed girl, who had been watching him with an interest he little suspected. "Rosetta is not here to-night, and so I thought I might have been his partner: but no matter; here comes our neighbour Carlo, he will ask me, I am sure:" and no sooner was her anticipation fulfilled, than, forgetful of him who was gone, she took her part in the lively waltz, with all the animation of her age and of her country.

Meanwhile Giuseppe wandered on, totally uncon- [194] scious of the transient disappointment caused by his abrupt departure; and, as he drew nearer, and nearer still to the cottage of Rosetta's parents, the shadow deepened on his brow.

"Why should I seek her now," he exclaimed in accents of sorrow, "to hear that hope is denied to me? Ah! if it had not been so, she would have come to tell me of our brightened prospects; but, no! she did not come—there is no hope. I know, I feel that there is none. Too cruel destiny! we are condemned to part for ever!"

The story of Giuseppe's griefs was simple. His father, the aged Andrea, had inhabited the cottage where he now resided ever since his earliest youth; and although, from its immediate vicinity to the volcano, it had been not unfrequently threatened with destruction, and his property, consisting wholly of vineyards, had been often materially injured, he still persisted in the resolution of remaining there to the latest day of his existence.

Petrone, Rosetta's father, was not a native Neapolitan; he had taken up his abode in the neighbourhood entirely from necessity. He had become possessed of rich vineyards in the suburbs of Naples by the death of a distant relative, and, unused to the alarming aspect of the burning mountain, could only reconcile himself to the idea of living on his new property by building himself a cottage at the very farthest extremity of the village most remote from its influence. [195]

Under these circumstances, when Giuseppe solicited the hand of his beloved Rosetta, the anxious father stipulated, that the first proof of his affection for her should be his instantly quitting the dangerous spot where he now dwelt, and removing to that inhabited by his new relations.

Giuseppe heard the proposal with mingled surprise and sorrow; for Andrea, having been a helpless cripple for the last three years of his protracted existence, depended upon him for every comfort, and he had vowed that he would never leave him while he lived. With a countenance which plainly showed the conflict of his soul, Giuseppe looked up mournfully at Petrone, exclaiming—

"Can I have heard you right, my friend? and is it possible that you wish me to abandon him, whose life depends upon my care? Can I, ought I, to forsake him? to leave him to die in his misery alone? does *she* require me to do this?"

"Oh, no!" replied Petrone soothingly; "she has required nothing of the kind, nor indeed do I: but surely you can quit that cottage for another, and your afflicted father may still be your inmate.

"Impossible!—I have often implored him to remove from a dwelling so dangerously situated, but he would never listen to my prayers. 'I built it with my own hands,' will he reply, 'when I was young and happy, raised its rude walls, constructed its rustic roof. It was to this beloved home I brought my bloom- [196] ing bride; it was here I reared my smiling infants: I cannot, will not leave it, hallowed as it is by ever dear remembrance. Go, if you will, and seek a safer shelter; I will remain here while I live.' Say then, my friend, shall I again urge him on a point he holds so dear? I dare not touch the string that wakes so sad an echo in his heart!"

Petrone could not enter into the feelings of Giuseppe, or make allowance for the prejudices of his father. He answered him with a coldness of manner which both wounded his sensibility and offended his ride, and they parted mutually disconcerted. Ere he returned to his now melancholy home, Giuseppe contrived to say a few words to Rosetta: he told her of the conference he had had with her father: and, taking a sad farewell of her, he made her promise that she would try her powers of persuasion; and they agreed, that if she should succeed in making him reverse the stern decree that he had passed, she would join the dance upon the green, and give him the happy news.

And it was on this eventful evening that Rosetta's absence from the gay group of cottagers had told Giuseppe all he had to fear. He knew that his fate was fixed, but yet he could not rest till he had heard the cruel sentence confirmed by herself: and now he stood beneath the latticed window, from which she had been wont to look on him with her sweetest smile. Here he heard her speaking in low tones, and at broken [197] intervals, to her younger sister. He feared to let her knew that he was there; he feared that he must hear the dreaded words—"My father is inexorable."

Suspense, however, is the worst of all love's torments. Giuseppe found it so; and thought that he could better bear even the painful certainty. He drew still nearer, with slow and hesitating step.

"Rosetta! Cara mia Rosetta!" whispered he, in faint and trembling accents.

"Giuseppe! mio ben amato!" was the quick reply; and, springing to the window, Rosetta held out her hand, and bent forward to meet her lover. He clasped it silently in his, and raised his eyes to hers—they were bathed in tears.

"Ah, Rosetta! those tears tell me all I have to fear—your father's resolution is unalterable! Is it not so? tell me, my beloved! from your lips let me hear my sentence!"

"Alas! it is even so!" answered the weeping girl: "Giuseppe—we must part!"

"Rosetta! do not kill me by those cruel words! who is there that will dare to part us? Say that you will still be mine! Believe me—the dangers of that burning mountain, which seem so dreadful in your father's eyes, are little thought of, little cared for, by those who have seen more of it than you have done. You are not native here; your fears are natural, but indeed you do wrong to nurse them."

"I have but one fear only," replied Rosetta, more [198] calmly—"the fear of disobeying the commands laid on me by a father whom I love."

"Where then is the love you have so often vowed to me?—oh, faithless one! Alas! I fear it weighs but lightly in the balance."

"These are keen reproaches, Giuseppe, and I feel them bitterly—more bitterly," she added, with increased emotion; "because it was from your example that I learnt the sacredness of filial duties." She ceased; she bent her head upon her bosom, and sobbed convulsively.

"The saints forbid that I should grieve thee, my beloved! I did not mean to doubt thy truth; forgive the hasty words I uttered in the anguish of my soul! Rosetta, pardon me!"

She answered only by her tears; and they flowed fast, and faster. Her sister came to her, raised her drooping head, spoke tenderly, and begged her to be more composed. "I hear my mother's step," she said; "Oh! she will chide you, if she sees you thus." Then, turning to Giuseppe—"Leave her, I implore you! leave her, now! Come back to-morrow, early, before my parents are awake; she will then answer you, but now she cannot." She drew back Rosetta's hand, which hung languidly upon the window-sill, then closed the lattice hastily, and, placing her finger on her lips, retired.

Giuseppe lingered awhile in hopes that they would reappear, but they came not, and at length he tore himself away, and retraced his homeward route. On his [199] road he met in quick succession the laughing peasants who had been enjoying the dance from which he had absented himself. They passed him two by two, apparently fatigued by their exertions, but with spirits still unwearied, and all too gay and happy to bestow more than a passing word upon the sad Giuseppe, or to notice the lowering aspect of the coming night.

Among the rest, Theresa, with her handsome partner, came tripping by. She was fanning herself with her broad hat, which she had taken off, leaving her long ringlets to flow unconfined over cheeks, the natural brilliancy of which was heightened by exercise and animation. Her companion was carrying some luxuriant bunches of the rich purple grape, which he offered to her with an air of gallantry, and she accepted the grateful fruit with an answering smile. Yet she did not forget to speak to Giuseppe as she passed him.

"You have come too late for the dance," she said; "it is all over now, and we are going home. Well, you'll come to-morrow evening; then, perhaps you may find it pleasanter; it really is too warm to-night; there is not a breath of air; Carlo and I are tired to death—are we not, Carlo?"

The question having received the expected answer of "Who could ever be weary when dancing with Theresa?" they wished him good night, and proceeded on their way.

Theresa however looked back, after they had passed, and said, "What think you of the weather? Carlo [200] says that there will be a storm to-morrow, because there is such a red light right at the crest of the mountain. I am sure I hope he is wrong, for it would spoil our dance."

Left to the silence of his solitary walk, Giuseppe looked towards Vesuvius, and, for the first time, saw the ominous appearance which it presented. He became also sensible of an extreme oppression in the air, which he had not before observed. He loosened the handkerchief round his neck, threw open his vest, and parted the jet black locks that hung clustering on his forehead; but still he was overpowered by the sultry heat; it seemed increasing every moment; and, by the time he reached his home, he felt so thoroughly depressed in mind and body, that he threw himself upon his bed, and tried to forget himself in sleep.

But sleep withheld its gentle influence. Hour after hour rolled on, and he was still restless—wakeful—feverish. He rose—opened his window and looked out. The night was unusually dark—the atmosphere was thick and hazy—and, where an occasional glimpse of the blue sky was seen, it served but to make a stronger contrast with the mass of vapoury clouds that were rolling heavily together, gradually veiling the bright face of heaven. Here and there a single star shot with a bright but transitory ray athwart the gloom—then disappeared—and then shone out again with faint and fading lustre.

The breathless stillness of the night gave a yet more [201] awful character to the stormy portents overhead. The living world was sleeping—and Nature too might have seemed to be at rest, but for the groaning of the troubled mountain, the inward thunders of which murmured deeply and incessantly, but, as yet, not angrily.

Giuseppe, with an anxious eye, marked all these ominous bodings of a storm. He thought of his father's helpless age—he walked to his bedside, and gazed on his features with intense and melancholy interest—he was pleased to see him sleeping so calmly. "The storm may pass, perhaps, ere he awakes," said he; "for worlds I would not break his slumber—would that my own perturbed spirit could find so sweet a solace!"—and, as he spoke, he softly stole from the apartment—gently unlatched the cottage-door, and wandered forth, in the vain hope of finding in the open air some slight relief from the intolerable heat. He strayed to a considerable distance from his home—but no breeze fanned his burning cheek—panting and exhausted, he threw himself upon a bank, and at length fell into an uneasy sleep.

How long he remained there he scarcely knew—the gray dawn was just appearing when he was awakened from a horrid dream by the sound of a deep hollow voice, while at the same instant a powerful hand was laid on his. A female figure, dimly seen in the misty light of morning, stood bending over him. She was tall, hard-featured, dark-complexioned, and her eyes gleamed on him with a fierce expression that betokened a wandering intellect. Even in his calmer moments [202] such an apparition might have startled the young peasant; but now, abruptly roused from a broken slumber, his senses yet confused by the bewildering images of his disturbed fancy, while the rising tempest raged around him, she seemed to him the very spirit of the storm—

"Wither'd and wild in her attire
She look'd not like a habitant of earth,
And yet was on it."

While he still gazed on her, in wondering silence, she seized him by the wrist, and shook his nerveless arm. "Why are you sleeping here, young man?" she cried, in a shrill, discordant tone; "are there no natural ties that call you to your home when danger threatens it? I did not think there was another being on this breathing earth so desolate as I—but you must be an outcast like myself, or else why do I find you here at such an hour as this? Look to the burning mountain! look to the village at its foot! How long, think you, will those lowly tenements withstand the rushing torrent?"

Giuseppe turned—and saw, with speechless agony, the inevitable ruin that was impending over the humble dwelling of his father. He rose, and with instinctive speed rushed towards it with a cry of terror. But the maniac, far more swift of foot than he, soon left him in the distance, and, long ere he could reach the village, he lost sight of her entirely.

As he hurried on towards Andrea's cottage, he found [203] the narrow street in which it stood thronged with the frightened crowd of its inhabitants; who, roused from their morning slumbers by the thundering voice of the volcano, were hastily collecting their trifling stores of worldly wealth, and preparing for instant flight. Some were endeavouring to still the screams of their scared infants—others looked up with death-pale countenances to the frowning canopy of clouds above them, which threw a lurid light far on the swelling sea and blackened earth. Here was one, who, palsied by his fears, stood as if rooted to the ground—and there another, invoking to his aid his patron saint—while others shrieked loudly to their flying kindred, or exclaimed, in accents of despair, "*Oime! Oime! fuggiamo!— fuggiamo!*"

Giuseppe forced his way with difficulty through the desperate crowd, and rushed towards his father's house. The miserable man, awakened by the crashing of the storm, and the tumultuous voices of the alarmed villagers, had called to his son for help; and when he found his oft-repeated cries unanswered, he imagined that he had fled and left him to his fate, and, in a paroxysm of despair, he threw himself upon his bed, and burying his face in his pillow, vainly tried to close his eye against the flashing lightning, and his ear to the rolling thunder.

"My father! my beloved father!" cried Giuseppe, "behold me here! see, I am come to save you! Exert yourself for one short hour only, and I *will* save you—[204] rouse, rouse yourself—look up! look up and speak to me—one word, my father! only one word to say you recognise your son! hear me, father! hear, and answer me!

In vain, Giuseppe spoke—for, overcome at once by the quick transition from despair to hope, Andrea sunk into a state of stupor, from which no effort could recall him. His distracted son saw that no time was to be lost; and, trusting to the unassisted strength of his young arm, he raised the old man from his bed, and bore him rapidly to the cottage-door. Here he paused awhile, and cast a hurried glance around him: he saw that the threatened ruin could not now be long delayed; he knew too that it would be necessary to bear his helpless burthen to a considerable distance before he could ensure his safety—and how could this be done? Unnerved as he already was, and sinking under the baneful influence of the sulphureous atmosphere, he dared not trust his father's precious life to such a doubtful rescue. Was there no friend at hand to share with him the toils and perils of his hasty flight?

Alas! no—all the energies of every human being were engrossed by the necessity of providing for their own individual safety. He saw that the search was hopeless, and he was about to commence his painful pilgrimage alone, when suddenly the maniac stood again before him. "What has brought you," he cried, "to this devoted place?—You said there were no ties that linked you to this world." [205]

"And I said truly—for all those who were dearest to my heart have perished long, very long ago. I lost them by one fatal blow—for they were swept away by the last most terrible eruption of that destructive mountain. I fled from them—I left them in my panic: I returned afterwards to gaze upon the havoc—but they were gone from me for ever! Since that tremendous day, one hour's peace I have not known: I have wandered I know not where—but I saw the storm-cloud, and I followed it—it was by beacon-light!" She drew nearer to Giuseppe, lowered her voice, and said, with unnatural calmness—"I have come back now that I may be reunited to my husband and my children. Are you, too, waiting for your doom?"

"No!" replied Giuseppe; "I am preparing to flee this wretched place with my poor helpless parent.—Heaven protect me! how am I to save him?—There is no mortal hand but mine to succour him!"

"Do not say so," replied the woman, hastily, "for I am here to help you: you shall see the strength of this poor wasted form. Oh, if I could yet save one miserable creature from this fearful fate!" Then, with a frightful vehemence of action, she tore from its rude hinge the open door, and flung it on the ground with a force that shook the feeble fabric to its base. "See," she cried, in a loud exulting tone, "what supernatural strength my griefs have given me!" And, as she spoke, she threw her ragged mantle over it, and without the help of the amazed Giuseppe, who stood petrified with [206] surprise and fear, she laid the old man on the litter she had made, then turning to his son—"Quick! quick!" she cried, "let us take him from this scene of horrors!" And in obedience to the orders of this strange associate, Giuseppe lifted the rude couch from the floor, and assisted to convey it from the house, his feet scorched by the heated earth on which he trod, and his senses stunned by the reverberated thunder which echoed through the vault of heaven.

The fugitives had not proceeded far when a vivid flash of lightning darted across the haggard features of the maniac, with such terrific brilliancy that she started with a piercing shriek, and fell insensible. Giuseppe ran to her, chafed her throbbing temples, opened her clenched hands, and spoke to her in tones of kindness and encouragement. At length she slowly raised her head and looked at him. He saw in that wild and vacant look that the transient gleam of reason was eclipsed for ever.

All thoughts of the task to which she had so lately bound herself were now obliterated. She fixed her gaze upon the fiery mountain, and called on it to finish her career of misery. "Rage on!" she cried, "and do thy worst! I am prepared to perish—but let thy work of death be swift!—let me not hear my husband's dying groan—my infants' stifled cries!—I am coming! I am coming!—Farewell! fare—well!" And, as she spoke, she flew to meet the rushing stream of fire, and left Giuseppe once again, alone, and hopeless of escape. [207]

Despair however seemed to awaken all his powers; he raised Andrea's lifeless form, and, like the pious Trojan, bore him from the far-spread conflagration. But, ah! unlike Aeneas, he could not leave the destroying flame behind him: it still pursued him, like some savage beast, raging and roaring for his prey.

He looked back, and saw its speed increasing as his strength diminished. Spent with toil, overwhelmed with agitation, and suffocated by the poisonous vapours that wreathed in inky columns around him, Giuseppe felt further flight impossible, and gave up the useless struggle.

The liquid lava flowed like molten ore behind: before him was a rising ground, as yet untouched by the destructive torrent. A ray of hope again inspired him: he gained the summit of the slight ascent, and the red river, parting at its foot into two narrowed channels, left him, with his father, unscathed, uninjured, the only living object in a wide waste of desolation!

Words cannot paint the feeling of the moment, nor tell with what intense devotion he lifted up his voice to Heaven, offering his tributary thanks to that Almighty Power which had preserved him so miraculously: he then threw himself upon the neck of his reviving parent, and wept delicious tears.

It would be idle to relate with what sensations Giuseppe and his father were received by those whose earlier flight had saved them from the volcano's fury; or to say how they afterwards venerated the spot which had been their resting-place and refuge in their last [208] distress. They gave to it a name commemorating the event of which it had been the scene, and from that time it was called by all the neighbouring peasantry, "Il Monte di Carità."

Rosetta's parents offered Andrea the shelter of their roof until his son rebuilt for him a home; but he did not long survive his change of residence; he lived but to bless Rosetta as Giuseppe's bride, and then, without a sigh, expired in her arms.

ROSA.

The dénouement of this little tale is a fact which occurred at one of the last eruptions of Vesuvius.

Title
Conway, Derwent. [Inglis, Henry D.] "The Musician of Augsburg." FMN 1829. 235-244. [235]

THE MUSICIAN OF AUGSBURG.
BY DERWENT CONWAY.

THERE lived, at some former time, in the city of Augsburg, a musician whose name was Nieser. There was no kind of musical instrument that he could not fashion with his own hands, nor was there any upon which he could not perform indifferently well. He was also a composer; and although none of his compositions are now extant, tradition informs us that his reputation in that, as well as in the other departments of the art, not only filled the city, but extended throughout the whole circle of Suabia. Other causes contributed to swell his fame: he possessed great wealth—acquired, it was sometimes whispered, not in the most creditable way; and the only inheritor of it was a daughter, whose beauty and innocence might well have been deemed dowry sufficient, without the prospective charms of her father's possessions. Esther was indeed almost as celebrated for the softness of her blue eyes, and the sweetness of her smile, and her many kind actions, as old Nieser was for his wealth, and the excellence of his stringed instruments, and the paucity of his good deeds.

Now, in spite of the wealth of old Nieser, and the respect which it had obtained for him, and the musical celebrity which he enjoyed, one sore grievance pressed heavily upon him. Esther, his only child, the sole representative of a long line of musicians, could scarcely [236] distinguish one tune from another; and it was a source of melancholy anticipation to Nieser, that he should leave behind him no heir to that talent which he held in almost equal estimation with his riches. But, as Esther grew up, he began to take consolation in thinking that, if he could not be the father, he might live to be the grandsire, of a race of musicians. No sooner, therefore, was she of a marriageable age, than he formed the singular resolution of bestowing her, with a dowry of two hundred thousand florins, upon whomsoever should compose the best sonata, and perform the principal part in it. This determination he immediately published throughout the city, appointing a day for the competition; and he was heard to affirm, with a great oath, that he would keep his promise, though the sonata should be composed by the demon, and played by the fiend's own fingers. Some say this was spoken jocularly; but it would have been better for old Nieser had he never spoken it at all: it is certain, however, that he was a wicked old man, and no respecter of religion.

No sooner was the determination of Nieser the musician known in Augsburg, than the whole city was in a ferment. Many who had never dared to raise their thoughts so high now unexpectedly found themselves competitors for the hand of Esther; for, independently of Esther's charms and Nieser's florins, professional reputation was at stake; and where this was wanting, vanity supplied its place. In short, there [237] was not a musician in Augsburg who was not urged, from one motive or another, to enter the lists for the prize of beauty. Morning, noon, and night, the streets of Augsburg were filled with melodious discord. From every open window proceeded the sound of embryo sonatas; nor was any other subject spoken of throughout the city than the approaching competition, and its probable issue. A musical fever infected all ranks: the favourite airs were caught, and repeated, and played, and sung, in every house in Augsburg; the sentinels at the gates hummed sonatas as they paced to and fro; the shopkeepers sat among their wares singing favourite movements; and customers, as they entered, took up the air, forgetful of their business, and sung duets across the counter. It is even said, that the priests murmured allegrettos as they left the confessional; and that two bars of a presto movement were found upon the back of one of the bishop's homilies.

But, amidst all this commotion, there was one who shared not in the general excitation. This was Franz Gortlingen, who, with little more musical talent than Esther, possessed one of the best hearts and handsomest persons in Suabia. Franz loved the daughter of the musician; and she, on her part, would rather at any time have heard her own name, with some endearing word prefixed to it, whispered by Franz, than listened to the finest sonata that ever was composed between the Rhine and the Oder. Nieser's decree was therefore of sad import to both Esther and Franz. [238]

It was now the day next to that upon which the event was to be decided, and Franz had taken no step towards the accomplishment of his wishes: and how was it possible that he should? He never composed a bar of music in his life: to play a simple air on the harpsichord exhausted all the talent he was master of. Late in the evening Franz walked out of his lodgings, and descended into the street. The shops were all shut, and the streets entirely deserted; but lights were still visible in some of the open windows; and from these came sadly upon the ear of Gortlingen the sound of instruments in preparation for the event which was to deprive him of Esther. Sometimes he stopped and listened, and he could see the faces of the musicians lighted up with pleasure at the success of their endeavours, and in anticipation of their triumph.

Gortlingen walked on and on, until at length he found himself in a part of the city which, although he had lived in Augsburg all his life, he never recollected to have seen before. Behind him the sounds of music had all died away, before him was heard the low rush of the river, and mingled with it there came at times upon the ear faint tones of wondrous melody. One solitary and far distant glimmer showed that the reign of sleep was not yet universal; and Gortlingen conjectured, from the direction of the sound, that some anxious musician was still at his task, in preparation for the morrow. Gortlingen went onwards, and as he drew nearer to the light, such glorious bursts of har- [239] mony swelled upon the air, that, all unskilled as he was in music, the tones had a spell in them which more and more awakened his curiosity as to who might be their author. Quickly and noiselessly he went forward until he reached the open window, whence the sound proceeded. Within, an old man sat at a harpsichord, with a manuscript before him: his back was turned towards the window, but an antique and tarnished mirror showed to Gortlingen the face and gestures of the musician.

It was a face of infinite mildness and benevolence; not such a countenance as Gortlingen remembered to have ever seen the likeness of before, but such as one might desire to see often again. The old man played with the most wondrous power; now and then he stopped, and made alterations in his manuscript, and as he tried the effect of them he showed his satisfaction by audible expressions, as if of thanksgiving, in some unknown tongue.

Gortlingen could at first scarcely contain his indignation at the supposition that this little old man should dare to enter the lists as one of Esther's suitors; for he could not doubt that he, like the others he had seen, was preparing for the competition: but as he looked and listened, gradually his anger was quelled in contemplating the strangely mild countenance of the musician, and his attention fixed by the beauty and uncommon character of the music; and at length at the conclusion of a brilliant passage, the performer per- [240] ceived that he had a sharer in his demonstrations of pleasure, for Gortlingen, in his unrestrained applause; quite drowned the gentler exclamations of the mild old man. Immediately the musician rose, and throwing open the door, "Good evening, master Franz," said he; "sit down, and tell me how you like my sonata, and if you think it likely to win Nieser's daughter." There was something so benignant in the old man's expression, and so pleasing in his address, that Gortlingen felt no enmity, and he sat down and listened to the player. "You like the sonata, then?" said the old man, when he had concluded it.

"Alas!" replied Gortlingen, "would that I were able to compose such a one!"

"Hearken to me," said the old man: "Nieser swore a sinful oath, that he would bestow his daughter upon whomsoever might compose the best sonata, 'even although it were composed by the demon, and played by the fiend's own fingers.' These words were not spoken unheard: they were borne on the night-winds, and whispered through the forests, and struck on the ear of them who sat in the dim valley; and the demon laugh and shout broke loud upon the calm of midnight, and were answered from the lone depths of a hundred hills: but the good heard also; and though they pitied not Nieser, they pitied Esther and Gortlingen. Take this roll; go to the hall of Nieser: a stranger will compete for the prize, and two others will seem to accompany him: the sonata which I have given to you is the [241] same that he will play; but mine has a virtue of its own: watch an opportunity, and substitute mine for his!" When the old man had concluded this extraordinary address, he took Gortlingen by the hand, and led him by some unknown ways to one of the gates of the city, and there left him.

As Gortlingen walked homewards, grasping the roll of paper, his mind was alternately occupied in reflections upon the strange manner in which he had become possessed of it, and in anticipation of the morrow's event. There was something in the expression of the old man that he could not mistrust, though he was unable to comprehend in what way he could be benefited by the substitution of one sonata for another, since he was not himself to be a competitor. With these perplexing thoughts he reached home, and lay down and fell asleep, while all night long Esther's blue eyes were discoursing with him, and the tones of the old man's sonata were floating in the air.

At sunset next evening Nieser's hall was to be thrown open to the competitors. As the hour approached, all the musicians of Augsburg were seen hurrying towards the house, with rolls of paper in their hands, and accompanied by others, carrying different musical instruments, while crowds were collected at Nieser's gate to see the competitors pass in. Gortlingen, when the hour arrived, taking his roll, soon found himself at Nieser's gate, where many who were standing knew him, and pitied him, because of the love he [242] bore the musician's daughter; and they whispered one to another, "What does Franz Gortlingen with a roll in his hand: surely he means not to enter the lists with the musicians?" When Gortlingen entered the hall, he found it full of the competitors and amateurs, friends of Nieser's, who had been invited to be present, Nieser sat in his chair of judgment at the upper end of the room, and Esther by his side, like a victim arrayed for sacrifice. As Gortlingen made his way through the hall, with his roll of music in his hand, a smile passed over the faces of the musicians, who all knew each other, and who also knew that he could scarcely execute a march, much less a sonata, even if he could compose one. Nieser, when he saw him, smiled from the same cause; but when Esther's eye met his, if she smiled at all, it was a faint and sorrowful smile of recognition, and soon gave place to the tear that stole down her cheek.

It was announced that the competitors should advance and enrol their names, and that the trial should then proceed by lot. The last that advanced was a stranger, for whom every one instinctively made way. No one had ever seen him before, or knew whence he came; and so forbidding was his countenance, so strange a leer was in his eye, that even Nieser whispered to his daughter that he hoped *his* sonata might not prove the best.

"Let the trial begin," said Nieser: "I swear that I will bestow my daughter, who now sits by my side, [243] with a dowry of two hundred thousand florins, upon whomsoever shall have composed the best sonata, and shall perform the principal part." "And you will keep your oath?" said the stranger, advancing in front of Nieser. "I will keep my oath," said the musician of Augsburg, "though the sonata should be composed by the demon, and played by the fiend's own fingers." There was a dead silence; a distant shout and faint laughter fell on the ear like an echo. The stranger alone smiled: every one else shuddered.

The first lot fell upon the stranger, who immediately took his place, and unrolled his sonata. Two others, whom no one had observed before, took their instruments in their hands, and placed themselves beside him, all waiting the signal to begin. Every eye was fixed upon the performers. The sign was given; and as the three musicians raised their heads to glance at the music, it was perceived with horror that the three faces were alike. A universal shudder crept through the assembly; all was silent confusion; no one spoke or whispered to his neighbour; but each wrapt himself up in his cloak and stole away; and soon there was none left, excepting the *three* who still continued the sonata, and Gortlingen, who had not forgotten the injunction of the old man. Old Nieser still sat in his chair; but he, too, had seen, and as he remembered his wicked oath, he trembled.

Gortlingen stood by the performers, and as they approached what he remembered to be the conclusion [244] he boldly substituted his for the sonata that lay before them. A dark scowl passed over the face of the three, and a distant wail fell upon the ear like an echo.

Some hours after midnight the benign old man was seen to lead Esther and Gortlingen out of the hall; but the sonata still proceeded. Years rolled on. Esther and Gortlingen were wedded, and in due course of time died; but the strange musicians still labour at their task, and old Nieser still sits in his judgment-chair, beating time to the sonata. When it ends—if it ever shall end—Esther will be far beyond the reach of the wicked vow made by the musician of Augsburg.

Title

Hofland, Barbara. "The Maid of the Beryl." FMN 1829. 253-267. [253]

THE MAID OF BERYL.
BY MRS. HOFLAND.

ONE bright evening in September, 1587, the sun shone cheeringly on many a gay boat and fancy-formed vessel, sporting on the silver bosom of the Thames, between the regal palace of Greenwich and the city of London; but one boat shot forward before all the rest, as if impelled by bolder hands or more buoyant spirits. The owner attracted the admiration of all eyes as he glided along, and many a low obeisance, or friendly recognition, was returned by him with an air of lofty courtesy, or kindly frankness, which displayed his character and his feelings. He was a very young man, with a handsome ingenuous countenance, expressive of joyous confidence and conscious power. His eyes were dark and lustrous, his forehead high and polished, his mouth small, but symmetrically formed. His beard at this period was light and curling, contrasting with his hair, which was of a dark brown. His figure, tall end elegant in its proportions, was attired in the height of the reigning mode, which was alike splendid and becoming. He wore a white satin doublet embroidered in strips of the same colour, intermingled with costly pearls: the sleeves were made extremely large about the shoulders, and an answering appearance of fulness was given about the hips, in the lower part of his clothing, which was in texture and ornament the same as the upper, and, from the middle of the thigh to the ankle, fitted closely, and displayed his finely-proportioned limbs to [254] great advantage. White shoes, with large roses, and a small crimson velvet cap, with three drooping white feathers placed on one side of his head, completed his clothing. His hands were embellished by rings; the left was covered by an embroidered glove; the right was employed in caressing a greyhound, so beautiful as to divide attention with his master, who lay in a reclining position on a crimson cloak of Genoa velvet, under an awning of blue damask. Six rowers in gay liveries completed the spectacle presented by this gallant young nobleman to the floating world around him.

By degrees all were left behind him; but, as the shadows of evening deepened, his attention was drawn to one small bark which had lately followed in his wake. It was rowed by a young boy of foreign aspect, and contained only one other person, who was so entirely enveloped in a large garment of a dusky hue, that the sex of the wearer could not be known. It appeared to the man of rank that these persons were gipsies, a race much proscribed at that time; and he apprehended that they sought protection from the watermen, amongst whom they were threading their way with great skill, by keeping in his vicinity. His attendants had the same conception of the case, without the same will to befriend the despised foreigners; and when, on arriving near the Temple stairs, the poor boy tried to land, in the spirit of malicious sport they so manoeuvred their own vessel, that the principal occupant of the boat was [255] thrown by a violent jerk into the water, in the direction of the pleasure barge.

To seize the floating vestment with a strong and agile hand, and to rescue the slight form which it enfolded, was the work of a moment with our favourite of nature and fortune; and as his loud reproof showed the necessity of reparation to his followers, all were soon placed in safety on the steps. It now appeared that the person still trembling in the preserver's arms was a woman, and the approach of a flambeau, in the hand of a man who was lighting a party to their boat, showed that she was young and beautiful, and of singular and striking appearance.

Like the inhabitants of Africa in general, she had been covered with an haïek, or wrapper: but this being now dropped, she appeared dressed in a caftan or jacket, richly embroidered, drawers and petticoat of white camlet, and a head-dress of gauze handkerchiefs, becomingly intermingled with her own dark, braided hair. Her neck was encircled by links of gold. She had bracelets and armlets of the same precious metal, enriched with emeralds; but these articles of value, however unexpected, were forgotten the moment she began to speak; for her coral lips and pearly teeth, aiding the effect of her large, dark eyes, seemed to throw a lustre on her countenance, and to produce an impression of beauty new even to one wont to distinguish and to admire it. The melody of her low and trembling voice, her solicitude to regain the haïek that would shroud her beauties, and her desire [256] to be left alone with the boy, whom she called her brother, proved the retirement of her habits and the modesty of her nature, and added to the curiosity which her appearance was calculated to excite. As pity for her distressing situation superseded even his desire to see more of her, the young nobleman hastened to engage the bearer of the flambeau to see her safely home. Reassured by his unobtrusive affability, and the near prospect of being suffered to depart, she ventured to express her gratitude warmly and even eloquently, though in somewhat imperfect language, and had once half drawn a ring from her finger, and was on the point of beseeching him to wear it in memory of his own good deed, when she suddenly replaced it, saying, "No; if I read the heavens aright, rings are to you unfortunate, whether given or received."

"So, then," said he internally, "this girl is a gipsy fortuneteller after all!" and, half ashamed of his adventure, he jumped hastily into the boat, and, by ordering it to Essex-house, informed the few bystanders that they had enjoyed the good fortune of beholding the young earl of that title, who had lately been introduced at court by the all-powerful earl of Leicester, and on whom the queen had already bestowed marks of her distinguished approbation.

Eager as the African girl had hitherto been to depart, yet she now lingered, as if to catch the last sound of his oars, and ascertain the painful truth that he was indeed removed beyond observation. From this event- [257] ful night the lovely stranger received an impression dangerous to all her sex, but to her decidedly unhappy, since it communicated hopeless and intense interest in one so completely divided from her by superior station, country, and faith.

Yet was she not forgotten. Many a time did the bright eyes of the admired and flattered Essex dart anxious glance through the dense crowds that pressed near him, as he slowly rode towards the palace, or walked from his garden in the Strand to take the water, in the hope of beholding her again. Constantly disappointed, he at length questioned Sir Horatio Pallavicini on the subject, as being a person likely to be acquainted with all resident foreigners. He was an Italian merchant of great repute, in the queen's service, residing in Lollesworth, a part of the bishop of London's fields, towards which the stranger had directed her steps.

"Your lordship must inquire after Arsinöe el Abra, the Maid of the Beryl; yet surely one so favoured by fortune has no temptation to task her skill?"

"You do not mean to say, that one so young as this Arsinöe practises witchcraft, or pretends to the learning of an astrologer?"

"No; she is distinct from both, and equally so from the tribe of dissolute and idle vagabonds which have lately infested this country. Arsinöe is highly, and even royally, descended, and from her ancestors inherits a knowledge in occult science distinct from that [258] of the wizard, termed sorcery or magic, and which professes to receive aid from good spirits alone. Of these curious and forbidden matters I know nothing but that this young creature has rare talents and great virtues also I can testify: she was an excellent daughter to the parents she has lost, is of a noble nature, and endowed with equal modesty and dignity."

A sudden call to attend the earl of Leicester to Holland, where, at the battle of Zutphen, the favourite gave signal proof of his valour, and witnessed the death of the brave Sir Philip Sidney, suspended his inquiries after Arsinöe; but when he returned a knight banneret, and was received with more than usual honours by the queen, his desire to see the eastern maid, not only for herself but for her art, revived, and by the assistance of Sir Horatio the interview was effected.

The visit was made with that secrecy which belongs to mysterious and forbidden things. Under the sole guidance of Akra el Abra, the brother of Arsinöe, and wrapped in a large cloak, the earl set out at midnight, unknown to his household, and reached in due time a retired house, situate among dilapidated buildings, and exhibiting in its appearance much that might excite suspicion. After opening the outer door, his guide proceeded up so many stairs, that at length the earl recollected that he had been too successful not to have made enemies, and it was possible that he might be throwing himself into their power.

Just as he was instinctively grasping his sword, the [259] guide stopped, and desired him to place that weapon, together with his cloak, cap, and shoes, in his hands.

Essex hesitated; but being always more valiant than prudent, in another moment he complied with the request. The door of a room, evidently devoted to the pursuits of Arsinoë, was then unlocked, and he entered a place well calculated to make a stronger impression on the mind of a young and ardent inquirer into the secrets of futurity.

The room in question was an exact square, with a dome roof. The walls were hung with crimson cloth, on which numerous hieroglyphics were curiously wrought; and the floor was covered with that rare article of oriental luxury, a Persian carpet. In the centre of the dome was a skylight, from which was suspended a beryl of extraordinary size and brilliance, and of the form of a globe. The rays of the full moon fell directly on this precious stone, from which they were so reflected as to illumine the room, which was small, and completely surrounded by a divan or sofa, except at the east end, which was occupied by a white marble sarcophagus, filled with pure water, on each side of which stood beautiful statues of the Egyptian Isis.

Essex had scarcely had time to notice the objects in this singular boudoir, when Arsinoë entered, bearing in her hands a refulgent lamp. She was splendidly attired in the costume of her country, and exhibited in her carriage the majesty of a princess; while [260] her graceful form, regular features, and finely tinted complexion, confirmed the previous impression of her extraordinary beauty. Her countenance mingled with the lofty expression conferred by conscious power, anxiety, and solemnity; and since the earl did not advert to their former meeting, but merely announced himself as the friend of the Italian merchant, Arsinoë received him as such by a silent movement. When he proceeded to inquire if her prophetic powers were connected with the precious stone before him, she replied: "Yes; it is in the beryl that I must read so much of your future destiny as my instructors see it meet to reveal. He who has lifted his hand against his fellow-man cannot distinctly descry those images which will shortly people the clear expanse before us."

"Be it so," said the earl, seating himself on the divan, yet looking towards the beryl, beneath which Arsinoë placed the brilliant lamp, uttering at the same few time a kind of incantation in her own tongue. In a few moments the beryl, originally of the size of a small orange, appeared to expand considerably; dark lines divided it into four distinct parts, and numerous moving forms were delineated on the surface of each portion, in a manner equally beautiful, miraculous, and awful.

Arsinoë knelt down, and gazed on the eastern side. "I see," said she, "the queen of these realms riding through a camp, prepared for battle, and you, as the master of the horse, accompanying her.—The pageant [261] changes—you return home from foreign conquest, and your sovereign now receives you rather with the tenderness of woman than the condescension of majesty. You kneel at her feet, and rise earl marshal of England."

At these words Essex sprang from his seat, as if to convince himself of the fact; but the eastern maid waved her hand majestically, as one born to be obeyed, and placed herself at the southern side of the beryl as soon as he was re-seated and silent.

"I see you again kneeling, but it is by the side of a young and lovely woman. Her shape is fine, her eyes dark, her complexion of northern whiteness; but there is an expression of melancholy in her countenance. She is the widow of one whose name will go down to posterity with honours even brighter than yours.—Ah! she listens to your vows, she receives from you a ring—that ring I saw in the heavens—it is the harbinger of sorrow to the giver and receiver."

"Your spirits play false, fair damsel: Robert Devereux is as little likely to wed a young widow as an ancient maiden."

"It is written here—she is your wedded wife now, and will be another's in days to come."

A sigh of unutterable anguish followed this declaration, and the fair sorceress, changing her situation, gazed eagerly on the eastern side in silence, until her auditor inquired what she beheld.

"I see battle and victory, honour and anger; the [262] presumption of a favoured subject, the weakness of an aged queen. Again the guerdon of valour is bestowed on you, but enemies are around, and the whispers of calumny assail you. The sovereign gives a ring as the pledge of safety, but trust not to it. Now I behold you again at the head of armies, but your look is dispirited, and rather befitting an exile than a general."

"That is not the expression I should choose to wear, or can brook to consider.—Try the fourth part of your magic globe, my sibyl."

Arsinöe fulfilled the wishes of her impatient guest. She bent her dark eyes on the northern quarter of the beryl with penetrating gaze, but in a moment recoiled—then looked again and shrieked aloud. The earl rose in alarm, and approached close to the beryl; but when he reached it the forms became indistinct, the supernatural expansion was withdrawn, and the precious stone remained in its natural state. Casting his eyes around in disappointment not unmixed with terror, he perceived Arsinöe pale and senseless on the floor, her fine features bearing the impression of that agony which had given her temporary death.

"Alas! why did I come hither? why did I dare, like Saul, to seek the knowledge which God has hidden?" were the first exclamations of the earl, whose religious principles, deeply implanted by a pious father, now rushed upon his mind, and, while they condemned him for the sin of seeking forbidden knowledge, pro-[263] hibited further inquiry as to the object which had so severely affected Arsinöe. Pity for her state, indeed, soon obliterated every other impression; he bore her to the sarcophagus, sprinkled her temples and hands with the water, and, as life returned, soothed her by gentle words indicative of pity towards herself, unmixed with those inquiries which it would have embarrassed her to answer.

Casting upon him a look of animated gratitude, which was followed by one of the sincerest compassion, Arsinöe rose, and with great solemnity loosed the golden chain by which the beryl was suspended, and suffered it to drop on the floor, saying at the same time in a voice of deep emotion, "I resign thee for ever."

Sincerely did the earl, as a Christian, rejoice in a resolution which he considered to be for the "soul's health" of one in whose well-being he felt deeply interested; but, in congratulating so young and fair a woman, it is but too possible that the ardour and tenderness of his nature might express too strongly the feelings of the moment. It is at least certain that, fearful of the power of Arsinöe or of his own susceptibility, the earl hastily fled from her presence, and endeavoured in the career of ambition and the pleasures of literature to banish from his mind both the predictions of the beryl and the charms of its possessor.

The history of this nobleman, his rapid rise to almost sovereign power, his secret marriage with the widow [264] of Sir Philip Sidney, and his unfortunate end, are known to every one. It is probable that when he received from the queen that ring which the cruelty of his enemies eventually rendered useless to him, he thought of the adventure of this memorable night; but no part of his story induces us to conclude that it dwelt upon his mind. As a warrior or a statesman, he was too perpetually employed to look back on that action, which he probably considered as the frolic of a boy, or the sin of a legislator.

Far different were the feelings of Arsinöe; her occupation was gone, and with it that sense of power which, however blameably, had allied her to higher natures; while she had drunk more deeply of that unhappy passion which, though hopeless, was incurable. To wean her from that unknown sorrow which destroyed her faculties and threatened her life, her young brother, now advancing to manhood, prevailed upon her to travel, and, under the auspices of Sir Horatio Pallavicini, she wandered for years in Italy and Sicily. The mildness of the climate counteracted her apparent disease, but neither that nor the beauties of the country could restore her spirits. The only relief that her melancholy admitted arose from the enjoyment which music afforded her, and which she constantly sought at the hours of worship in the august ceremonies of the catholic churches. Every where her finished beauty, rendered more touching by the gentle melancholy that pervaded her classic features, awoke admiration, which [265] was confirmed by the melting softness of her voice; but the language of flattery fell on her ear as on that of the dead, and, save in gratitude towards her generous and devoted brother, no smile parted the coral lips of Arsinöe, and no word of hope or cheerfulness interrupted the pensive sadness of her meek dejection.

In the winter of 1600-1, circumstances occurred which rendered it desirable that Akra should visit England, and Arsinöe made no objection to accompany him, as the season was favourable. They landed below the Tower of

London, and observing many persons entering the principal gate of that fortress, as they believed, for the purpose of worship, for it was Ash-Wednesday, they entered with them; the brother being desirous of seeing a person resident there, whilst his sister should seek her wonted solace in the church. They had, however, proceeded only a short distance within the enclosed space, when they perceived, with extreme horror, that a scaffold was erected, on which was a block, and by its side two executioners were already stationed.

Arsinöe gazed wildly around.—The black object before her, the dark towers in the back-ground, the stern faces of the headsmen, and the appalled countenances of the spectators, were all recognised, and she looked as if bound by fascination to the objects she loathed and dreaded. In another moment, and the whole of that terrific vision was realised. A noble-looking man, in the very prime of life, stepped upon [266] the scaffold. He was arrayed in a dress of black satin, which showed to advantage the singular grace and dignity of his person. His beard was long and full, his face pale but composed, and his dark eyes, though somewhat robbed of their youthful lustre, told the trembling Arsinöe, in their first penetrating glances, that he the worshipped idol of her young heart, stood before her a sufferer and a victim.

It was believed by all around until the last moment, that the mercy of the queen would interpose to snatch from destruction one so dear and so distinguished. Whisperings to that effect mingled with the audible sighs of those present. Arsinöe heard them not; with one convulsive sob she sank fainting on the ground, unheeded at this awful period by all but her brother. When life returned—when in eagerness and terror she again looked towards the scaffold, the newly dissevered head, bleeding and ghastly, met her view, and again she sank senseless to the earth.

The sorrows of Arsinöe now drew rapidly to a close. She had loved, as woman only loves, in silent hopelessness and unabated admiration, that object which imagination, not less than memory, endured with its power to charm. Her brother knew not, till this terrific circumstance revealed the mystery, the cause of the deep-seated sorrow which had desolated the best years of her life, and subdued the energies of her capacious mind; but he found himself unable, as before, to alleviate the sorrow which he so sincerely pitied. [267]

Happily the extreme anxiety evinced by Arsinöe to learn every word uttered by the unfortunate Essex in his last moments, and which she besought her brother to repeat daily, led her to seek consolation from that religion which sustained him in that awful hour, and had influenced him during life. In Italy, she had attended christian worship to soothe and divert her mind, but she now sought its sacred truths as the consolation of her heart; and, under its divine influence, hopes of a glorious and exalted nature illuminated the deathbed of the Maid of the Beryl.

Title
Anonymous. "The Magician of Vicenza." FMN 1829. 273-283.

PLATE: Vicenza
Steel plate engraving; designed/drawn by Samuel Prout;
engraved by Alfred Robert Freebairn [273]

THE MAGICIAN OF VICENZA.

IN the year 1796, on one of the finest evenings of an Italian autumn, when the whole population of the handsome city of Vicenza were pouring into the streets to enjoy the fresh air, that comes so deliciously along the currents of its three rivers; when the Campo Marzo was crowded with the opulent citizens and Venetian nobles; and the whole ascent, from the gates to the Madonna who sits enthroned on the summit of Monte Berrico, was a line of the gayest pilgrims that ever wandered up the vine-covered side of an Alpine hill; the ears of all were caught by the sound of successive explosions from a boat running down the bright waters of the Bachiglione. Vicenza was at peace, under the wing of the lion of St. Mark, but the French were lying round the ramparts of Mantua. They had not yet moved on Venice; though her troops were known to be without arms, experience, or a general, and the sound of a cracker would have startled her whole dominions.

The boat itself was of a singular make; and the rapidity with which this little chaloupe, glittering with gilding and hung with streamers, made its way along the sparkling stream, struck the observers as something extraordinary. It flew by every thing on the river, yet no one was visible on board. It had no sail up, no steersman, no rower; yet it plunged and rushed along with the swiftness of a bird. The Vicentine populace are behind none of their brethren in superstition, and, [274] at the sight of the flying chaloupe, the groups came running from the Campo Marzo. The Monte Berrico was speedily left without a pilgrim, and the banks of the Bachiglione were, for the first time since the creation, honoured with the presence of the Venetian authorities, and even of the sublime podesta[23] himself.

But it was fortunate for them that the flying phenomenon had reached the open space formed by the conflux of the three rivers, before the crowd became excessive; for, just as it had darted out from the narrow channel, lined on both sides with the whole thirty thousand old, middle-aged, and young, men, maids, and matrons of the city, a thick smoke was seen rising from its poop, its frame quivered, and with a tremendous explosion, the chaloupe rose into the air in ten thousand fragments of fire.

The multitude were seized with consternation; and the whole fell on their knees, from the sublime podesta himself, to the humblest saffron-gatherer. Never was there such a mixture of devotion. The *douanier* drooped down beside the smuggler; the *cavaliere* servente beside the husband; the Vicentine patriot beside the Venetian *sbirro*; the father-confessor beside the blooming penitent, whom he had condemned but that morning to a week's confinement on dry bread and the breviary; the bandit beside the soldier; and even the husband beside his own wife. Never was there such a concert of exclamations, sighs, callings on the

---

23 The governor, a Venetian noble.

saints, and rattling of [275] beads. The whole concourse lay for some minutes with their very nose rubbing to the ground, until they were all roused at once by a loud burst of laughter. Thirty thousand pair of eyes were lifted up at the instant, and all fixed in astonishment on a human figure, seen calmly sitting on the water, in the very track of the explosion, and still half hidden in the heavy mass of smoke that curled in a huge globe over the remnants. The laugh had proceeded from him, and the nearer he approached the multitude, the louder he laughed. At length, stopping in front of the spot where the sublime podesta, a little ashamed of his prostration, was getting the dust shaken out of his gold-embroidered robe of office, and bathing his burning visage in orange-flower water, the stranger began a sort of complimentary song to the famous city of Vicenza. In Italy every man is a poet, which accounts for the Italian poetry being at this hour the very worst in the world; and panegyric is the only way to popularity, which accounts for the infinite mass of folly, laziness, beggary, and self-admiration that makes Italy pre-eminent in masquerades, monks, madonnas, and marquises.

  The stranger found a willing audience; for his first stanza was in honour of the "most magnificent city of Vicenza;" its "twenty palaces by the matchless Palladio;" much more "its sixty churches;" and much more than all "its breed of Dominicans, unrivalled throughout the earth for the fervour of their piety and the capacity of their stomachs." The last touch made [276] the grand-prior of the cathedral wince a little, but it was welcomed with a roar from the multitude. The song proceeded; but, if the prior had frowned at the first stanza, the podesta was doubly angry at the second, which sneered at Venetian pomposity in incomparable style. But the prior and podesta were equally outvoted, for the roar of the multitude was twice as loud as before. Then came other touches on the cavalieri serventi, the ladies, the nuns, and the husbands, till every class had its share: but the satire was so witty, that keen as it was, the shouts of the people silenced all disapprobation. He finished by a brilliant stanza, in which he said, that "having been sent by Neptune from the depths of the ocean to visit the earth, he had chosen for his landing-place its most renowned spot, the birth-place of the gayest men and the handsomest women—the exquisite Vicenza." With these words he ascended from the shore, and was received with thunders of applause.

  His figure was tall and elegant: he work a loose scarlet cloak thrown over his fine limbs, Greek sandals, and a cap like that of the Italian princes of three centuries before, a kind of low circle of green and vermilion striped silk, clasped by a large rose of topaz. The men universally said that there was an atrocious expression in his countenance; but the women, the true judges after all, said, without exception, that this was envy in the men, and that the stranger was the most "delightful looking *Diavolo*" they had ever set [277] eyes on. The *cavalieri serventi*, were never in less repute than within that half hour; and quarrels ensued in the most peaceable establishments, that dismissed from combing their dogs, carrying their pocket-handkerchiefs, and yawning six hours a day in their presence, full five hundred of the most faithful adorers of the most exalted matrons of Vicenza.

The stranger, on his landing, desired to be led to the principal hotel; but he had not gone a dozen steps from the water-side, when he exclaimed that he had lost his purse. Such an imputation was never heard before in an Italian city; at least so swore the multitude; and the stranger was on the point of falling several fathoms deep in his popularity. But he answered the murmur by a laugh; and, stopping in front of a beggar, who lay at the corner of an hospital roaring out for alms, demanded the instant loan of fifty sequins. The beggar lifted up his hands and eyes in speechless wonder, and then shook out his rags, which, whatever else they might show, certainly showed no sequins. "The sequins, or death!" was the demand, in a tremendous voice. The beggar fell on the ground convulsed, and from his withered hand, which every one had seen empty the moment before, out flew fifty sequins, bright as if they had come that moment from St. Mark's mint. The stranger took them from the ground, and with a smile flung them up in a golden shower through the crowd. The shouts were immense, and the mob insisted on carrying him to the door of his hotel. [278]

But the Venetian vigilance was by this time a little awakened, and a patrol of the troops was ordered to bring the singular stranger before the sublime podesta. The crowd instantly dropped him at the sight of the bayonets, and, knowing the value of life in the most delicious climate of the world, took to their heels. The guard took possession of their prisoner, and were leading him rather roughly to the governor's house, when he request them to stop for a moment beside a convent gate, that he might get a cup of wine. But the Dominicans would not give the satirist of their illustrious order a cup of water.

"If you will not give me refreshment," exclaimed he, in an angry tone, "give me wherewithal to buy it. I demand a hundred sequins."

The prior himself was at the window above his head; and the only answer was a sneer, which was loyally echoed through every cloister.

"Let me have your bayonet for a moment," said the stranger to one of his guard. He received it; and striking away a projecting stone in the wall, out rushed the hundred sequins. The prior clasped his hands in agony, that so much money should have been so near, and yet have escaped his pious purposes. The soldiers took off their caps for the discoverer, and bowed them still lower when he threw every sequin of it into the shakos of those polite warriors. The officer, to whom he had given a double share, showed his gratitude by a whisper, offering to assist his escape for [279] as much more. But the stranger declined the civility, and walked boldly into the presence-chamber of the sublime podesta.

The Signior Dominico Castello-Grande Tremamondo was a little Venetian noble, descended in a right line from Aeneas, with a palazzo on the

Canale Regio of Venice, which he let for a coffeehouse; and living in the pomp and pride of a *magnifico* on something more than the wages of an English groom. The intelligence of this extraordinary stranger's discoveries had flown like a spark through a magazine, and the *illustrissimo* longed to be a partaker in the secret. He interrogated the prisoner with official fierceness, but could obtain no other reply than the general declaration, that he was a traveler come to see the captivations of Italy. In the course of the inquiry the podesta dropped a significant hint about money.

"As to money," was the reply, "I seldom carry any about me; it is so likely to tempt *rascals* to dip deeper in roguery. I have it whenever I choose to call for it."

"I should like to see the experiment made, merely for its curiosity," said the governor.

"You shall be obeyed," was the answer; "but I never ask for more than a sum for present expenses. Here, you fellow!" said he, turning to one of the half-naked soldiery, "lend me five hundred sequins!"

The whole guard burst into laughter. The sum would have been a severe demand on the military chest of the army. The handsome stranger advanced to him, [280] and, seizing his musket, said loftily, "Fellow, if you won't give the money, this must." He struck the butt-end of the musket thrice upon the floor. At the third blow a burst of gold poured out, and sequins ran in every direction. The soldiery and the officers of the court were in utter astonishment. All wondered, many began to cross themselves, and several of the most celebrated swearers in the regiment dropped upon their knees. But their devotions were not long, for the sublime podesta ordered the hall to be cleared, and himself, the stranger, and the sequins, left alone.

For three days nothing more was heard of any of the three, and the Vicenzese scarcely ate, drank, or slept, through anxiety to know what was become of the man in the scarlet cloak, and cap striped green and vermilion. Jealousy, politics, and piety, at length put their heads together, and, by the evening of the third day, the *cavalieri* had agreed that he was some rambling actor or Alpine thief, the statesmen that he was a spy, and the Dominicans that he was Satan in person. The women, partly through the contradiction natural to the lovely sex, and partly through the novelty of not having the world in their own way, were silent; a phenomenon which the Italian philosophers still consider the true wonder of the whole affair.

On the evening of the third day a new Venetian governor, with a stately cortège, was seen entering at the Water Gate full gallop from Venice: he drove straight to the podesta's house, and after an audience, was pro- [281] vided with apartments in the town-house, one of the finest in Italy, and looking out upon the *Piazza Grande*, in which are the two famous columns, one then surmounted by the winged lion of St. Mark, as the other still is by a statue of the founder of our faith.

The night was furiously stormy, and the torrents of rain and perpetual roaring of the thunder drove the people out of the streets. But between the tempest and curiosity not an eye was closed that night in the city. Towards morning the tempest lulled, and in the intervals of the wind strange sounds were heard, like the rushing of horses and rattling of carriages. At length the sounds grew so loud that curiosity could be restrained no longer, and the crowd gathered towards the entrance of the *Piazza*. The night was dark beyond description, and the first knowledge of the hazard that they were incurring was communicated to the shivering mob by the kicks of several platoons of French soldiery, who let them pass within their lines, but prohibited escape. The square was filled with cavalry, escorting waggons loaded with the archives, plate, and pictures, of the government. The old podesta was seen entering a carriage, into which his very handsome daughter, the betrothed of the proudest of the proud Venetian senators, was handed by the stranger. The procession then moved, and last, and most surprising of all, the stranger, mounting a charger, put himself at the head of the cavalry, and, making a profound adieu to the new governor, who [282] stood shivering at the window in care of a file of grenadiers, dashed forward on the road to Milan.

Day rose, and the multitude rushed out to see what was become of the city. Every thing was as it had been, but the column of the lion: its famous emblem of the Venetian republic was gone, wings and all. They exclaimed that the world was come to an end. But the wheel of fortune is round, let politicians say what they will. In twelve months from that day the old podesta was again sitting in the government-house—yet a podesta no more, but a French prefect; the signora Maria, his lovely daughter was sitting beside him, with an infant, the image of her own beauty, and beside her the stranger, no longer the man of magic in the scarlet cloak and green and vermilion striped cap with a topaz clasp, but a French general of division in blue and silver, her husband, as handsome as ever, and, if not altogether a professed *Diavolo*, quite as successful in finding money whenever he wanted it. His first *entrée* into Vicenza had been a little theatrical, for such is the genius of his country. The blowing-up of his little steam-boat, which had nearly furnished his drama with a tragic catastrophe, added to its effect; and his discovery of the sequins was managed by three of his countrymen. As an inquirer into the nakedness of the land, he might have been shot as a spy. As half-charlatan and half-madman, he was sure of national sympathy. During the three days of his stay the old podesta had found himself accessible to reason, the [283] podesta's daughter to the tender passion, and the treasures of the state to the locomotive skill of the French detachment, that waited in the mountains the result of their officer's diplomacy. The lion of St. Mark, having nothing else to do, probably disdained to remain, and in the same night took wing from the column, to which he has never returned.

Literary Annual
Forget Me Not; A Christmas, New Year's, and Birth-Day Present for MDCCCXXX.
Ed. Frederic Shoberl. London: R. Ackermann & Co., 1830. Printer: Thomas Davison, Whitefriars.

Title
By a Modern Pythagorean. [MacNish, Robert.] "The Red Man." FMN 1830. 49-65. [49]

THE RED MAN.

IT was at the hour of nine, in an August evening, that a solitary horseman arrived at the Black Swan, a country inn about nine miles from the town of Leicester. He was mounted on a large fiery charger, as black as jet, and behind him a portmanteau attached to the croup of his saddle. A black travelling cloak, which not only covered his own person, but the greater part of his steed, was thrown around him. On his head he wore a broad-brimmed hat, with an uncommonly low crown. His legs were cased in top-boots, to which were attached spurs of an extraordinary length; and in his hands he carried a whip, with a thong three yards long, and a handle which might have levelled Goliath himself.

On arriving at the inn, he calmly dismounted, and called upon the ostler by name.

"Frank!" said he, "take my horse to the stable; rub him down thoroughly; and, when he is well cooled, step in and let me know." And, taking hold of his portmanteau, he entered the kitchen, followed by the obsequious landlord, who had come out a minute before, on hearing of his arrival. There were several persons present, engaged in nearly the same occupation. At one side of the fire sat the village schoolmaster—a thin, pale, peak-nosed little man, with a powdered periwig, terminating behind in a long queue, and an expression of self-conceit strongly depicted upon his countenance. He was amusing himself with a pipe, [50] from which he threw forth volumes of smoke with an air of great satisfaction. Opposite to him sat the parson of the parish—a fat, bald-headed personage, dressed in a rusty suit of black, and having his shoes adorned with immense silver buckles. Between these two characters sat the exciseman, with a pipe in one hand, and a tankard in the other. To complete the group, nothing is wanted but to mention the landlady, a plump, rosy dame of thirty-five, who was seated by the schoolmaster's side, apparently listening to some sage remarks which that little gentleman was throwing out for her edification.

But to return to the stranger. No sooner had he entered the kitchen, followed by the landlord, than the eyes of the company were directed upon him. His hat was so broad in the brim, his spurs were so long, his stature so great, and his face so totally hid by the collar of his immense black cloak, that he instantly attracted the attention of every person present. His voice, when he desired the master of the house to help him off with his mantle, was likewise so harsh that they all heard it with sudden curiosity. Nor did this abate when the cloak was removed, and his hat laid aside. A tall, athletic, red-haired man, of the middle age, was then made manifest. He had on a red frock coat, a red vest, and a red neckcloth; nay, his gloves were red! What was more extraordinary, when the overalls which covered his thighs were unbuttoned, it was discovered that his small-clothes were red likewise. [51]

"All red!" ejaculated the parson, almost involuntarily.

"As you say, the gentleman is all red!" added the schoolmaster, with his characteristic flippancy. He was checked by a look from the landlady. His remark, however, caught the stranger's ear, and he turned round upon him with a penetrating glance. The schoolmaster tried to smoke it off bravely. It would not do: he felt the power of that look, and was reduced to almost immediate silence.

"Now, bring me your boot-jack," said the horseman.

The boot-jack was brought, and the boots pulled off. To the astonishment of the company, a pair of red stocking were brought into view. The landlord shrugged his shoulders, the exciseman did the same, the landlady shook her head, the parson exclaimed, "All red!" as before, and the schoolmaster would have repeated it, but he had not yet recovered from his rebuke.

"Faith, this is odd!" observed the host.

"Rather odd," said the stranger, seating himself between the parson and the exciseman. The landlord was confounded, and did not know what to think of the matter.

After sitting for a few moments, the new-comer requested the host to hand him a nightcap, which he would find in his hat. He did so: it was a red worsted one; and he put it upon his head.

Here the exciseman broke silence, by ejaculating, [52] "Red again!" The landlady gave him an admonitory knock on the elbow: it was too late. The stranger heard his remark, and regarded him with one of those piercing glances for which his fiery eye seemed so remarkable.

"All red!" murmured the parson once more.

"Yes, Doctor Poundtext, the gentleman, as you say, is all red," re-echoed the schoolmaster, who by this time had recovered his self-possession. He would have gone on, but the landlady gave him a fresh admonition, by trampling upon his toes; and her husband winked in token of silence. As in the case of the exciseman, the warnings were too late.

"Now, landlord," said the stranger, after he had been seated a minute, "may I trouble you to get me a pipe and a can of your best Burton? But, first of all, open my portmanteau, and give me out my slippers."

The host did as he was desired, and produced a pair of red morocco slippers. Here an involuntary exclamation broke out from the company. It begun with the parson, and was taken up by the schoolmaster, the exciseman, the landlady, and the landlord, in succession. "More red!" proceeded from every lip, with different degrees of loudness. The landlord's was the least loud, the schoolmaster's the loudest of all.

"I supposed, gentleman," said the stranger, "you were remarking upon my slippers."

"Eh—yes! we were just saying that they were red," replied the schoolmaster. [53[

"And, pray," demanded the other, as he raised the pipe to his mouth, "did you never before see a pair of red slippers?"

This question staggered the respondent: he said nothing, but looked to the parson for assistance.

"But you are all red," observed the latter, taking a full draught from a foaming tankard which he held in his hand.

"And you are all black," said the other, as he withdrew the pipe from his mouth, and emitted a copious puff of tobacco smoke. "The hat that covers your numskull is black, your beard is black, your coat is black, your vest is black; your smallclothes, your stockings, your shoes, all are black. In a word, Doctor Poundtext, you are—"

"What am I, sir?" said the parson, bursting with rage.

"Ay, what is he, sir?" rejoined the schoolmaster.

"He is a black-coat," said the stranger, with a contemptuous sneer, "and you are a pedagogue." This sentence was followed by a profound calm. Not a word was spoken by any of the company, but each gazed upon his neighbour in silence. In the faces of the parson and the schoolmaster anger was principally depicted: the exciseman's mouth was turned down in disdain, the landlady's was curled into a sarcastic smile; and as for the landlord, it would be difficult to say whether astonishment, anger, or fear, most predominated in his mind. During this ominous tran- [54] quillity the stranger looked on unmoved, drinking and smoking alternately with total indifference. The schoolmaster would have said something had he dared, and so would the parson; but both were yet smarting too bitterly under their rebuff to hazard another observation.

In the midst of this mental tumult, the little bandy-legged ostler made his appearance, and announced to the rider that his horse had been rubbed down according to orders. On hearing this, the Red Man got up from his seat, and walked out to the stable. His departure seemed to act as a sudden relief to those who were left behind. Their tongues, which his presence had bound by a talismanic influence, were loosened, and a storm of words broke forth proportioned to the fearful calm which preceded it.

"Who is that man in red?" said the parson, first breaking silence.

"Ay, who is he?" re-echoed the schoolmaster.

"He is a bit of a conjurer, I warrant," quoth the exciseman.

"I should not wonder," said the landlord, "if he be a spy from France."

"Or a travelling packman," added the landlady.

"I am certain he is no better than he should be," spake the parson again.

"That is clear," exclaimed the whole of the company, beginning with the pedagogue, and terminating as usual with the host. Here was a pause: at least Doctor Poundtext resumed—"I shall question him [55] tightly when he returns; and if his answers are impertinent or unsatisfactory, something must be done."

"Ay, something must be done," said the schoolmaster.

"Whatever you do," said the landlady, "let it be done civilly. I should not like to anger him."

"A fig for his anger!" roared her husband, snapping his fingers; "I shall give him the back of the door in the twinkling of an eye, if he so much as chirps."

"Anger, indeed!" observed the exciseman; "leave that to me and my cudgel."

"To you and your cudgel!" said the stranger, who at this moment entered, and resumed his place at the fireside, after casting a look of ineffable contempt upon the exciseman. The latter did not dare to say a word; his countenance fell, and his stick, which he was brandishing a moment before, dropped between his legs.

There was another pause in the conversation. The appearance of the Red Man again acted like a spell on the voices of the company. The parson was silent, and by a natural consequence his echo, the schoolmaster, was silent also: none of the others felt disposed to say any thing. The meeting was like an assemblage of quakers. At one side of the fire sat the plump parson, with the tankard in one hand, and the other placed upon his forehead, as in deep meditation. At the opposite side sat the schoolmaster, puffing vehemently from a tobacco-pipe. In the centre was the [56] exciseman, having at his right hand the jolly form of the landlady, and at his left the Man in Red; the landlord stood at some distance behind. For a time the whole, with the exception of the stranger, were engaged in anxious thought. The one looked to the other with wondering glances, but, though all equally wished to speak, no one liked to be the first to open the conversation. "Who can this man be?" "What does he want here?" "Where is he from, and whither is he bound?" Such were the inquiries which occupied every mind. Had the object of their curiosity been a brown man, a black man, or even a green man, there would have been nothing extraordinary; and he might have entered the inn and departed from it as unquestioned as before he came. But to be a Red Man! There was in this something so startling that the lookers-on were beside themselves with amazement. The first to break this strange silence was the parson.

"Sir," said he, "we have been thinking that you are—"

"That I am a conjurer, a French spy, a travelling packman, or something of the sort," observed the stranger. Doctor Poundtext started back on his chair, and well he might; for these words, which the Man in Red had spoken, were the very ones he himself was about to utter.

"Who are you, sir?" resumed he, in manifest perturbation. "What is your name?" [57]

"My name," replied the other, "is Reid."

"And where, in heaven's name, were you born?" demanded the astonished parson.

"I was born on the borders of the Red Sea." Doctor Poundtext had not another word to say. The schoolmaster was equally astounded, and withdrew the pipe from his mouth: that of the exciseman dropped to the ground: the landlord groaned aloud, and his spouse held up her hands in mingled astonishment and awe.

After giving them this last piece of information, the strange man arose from his seat, broke his pipe in pieces, and pitched the fragments into the fire; then, throwing his long cloak carelessly over his shoulders, putting his hat upon his head, and loading himself with his boots, his whip, and his portmanteau, he desired the landlord to show him his bed, and left the kitchen, after smiling sarcastically to its inmates, and giving them a familiar and unceremonious nod.

His disappearance was the signal for fresh alarm in the minds of those left behind. Not a word was said till the return of the innkeeper, who in a short time descended from the bed-room over-head, to which he had conducted his guest. On re-entering the kitchen, he was encountered by a volley of interrogations. The parson, the schoolmaster, the exciseman, and his own wife, questioned him over and over again. "Who was the man in red?—he must have seen him before—he must have heard of hi,—in a word, he must know something about him." The host protested "that he [58] never beheld the stranger till that hour: it was the first time he had made his appearance at the Black Swan, and, so help him God, it should be the last!"

"Why don't you turn him out?" exclaimed the exciseman.

"If you think you are able to do it, you are heartily welcome," replied the landlord. "For my part, I have no notion of coming to close quarters with the shank of his whip, or his great, red, sledge-hammer fist." This was an irresistible argument, and the proposer of forcible ejectment said no more upon the subject.

At this time the party could hear the noise of heavy footsteps above them. They were those of the Red Man, and sounded with slow and measured tread. They listened for a quarter of an hour longer, in expectation that they would cease. There was no pause: the steps continued, and seemed to indicate that the person was amusing himself by walking up and down the room.

It would be impossible to describe the multiplicity of feelings which agitated the minds of the company. Fear, surprise, anger, and curiosity, ruled them by turns, and kept them incessantly upon the rack. There was something mysterious in the visitor who had just left them—something which they could not fathom—something unaccountable. "Who could he be?" This was the question that each put to the other, but no one would give any thing like a rational answer.

[59]   Meanwhile the evening wore on apace, and though the bell of the parish church hard by sounded the tenth hour, no one seemed to inclined to take the hint to depart. Even the parson heard it without regard, to such a pitch was his curiosity excited. About this time also the sky, which had hitherto been tolerably clear, began to be overclouded. Distant peals of thunder were heard; and thick sultry drops of rain pattered at intervals against the casement of the inn: every thing seemed to indicate a tempestuous evening. But the storm which threatened to rage without was unnoticed. Though the drops fell heavily; though gleams of lightning flashed by, followed by the report of distant thunder, and the winds began to hiss and whistle among the trees of the neighbouring cemetery, yet all these external signs of elementary tumult were as nothing to the deep, solemn footsteps of the Red Man. There seemed to be no end to his walking. An hour had he paced up and down the chamber without the least interval of repose, and he was still engaged in this occupation as at first. In this there was something incredibly mysterious; and the party below, notwithstanding their numbers, felt a vague and indescribably dread beginning to creep over them. The more they reflected upon the character of the stranger, the more unnatural did it appear. The redness of his hair and complexion, and, still more, the fiery hue of his garment, struck them with astonishment. But this was little to the freezing and benumbing [60] glance of his eye, the strange tones of his voice, and his miraculous birth on the borders of the Red Sea. There was now no longer any smoking in the kitchen. The subject which occupied their minds were of too engrossing a nature to be treated with levity; and they drew their chairs closer, with a sort of irresistible and instinctive attraction.

     While these things were going on, the bandy-legged ostler entered, in manifest alarm. He came to inform his master that the stranger's horse had gone mad, and was kicking and tearing at every thing around, as if he would break his manger in pieces. Here a loud neighing and rushing were heard in the stable. "Ay, there he goes," continued he. "I believe the devil is in the beast, if he is not the old enemy himself. Ods, master, if you saw his eyes: they are like—"

     "What are they like?" demanded the landlord.

     "Ay, what are they like?" exclaimed the rest with equal impatience.

     "Ods, if they a'n't like burning coals!" ejaculated the ostler, trembling from head to foot, and squeezing himself in among the others, on a chair which stood hard by. His information threw fresh alarm over the company, and they were more agitated and confused than ever.

During the whole of this time the sound of walking over-head never ceased for one moment. The heavy tread was unabated: there was not the least interval of repose, nor could a pendulum have been more re- [61] gular in its motions. Had there been any relaxation, any pause, any increase, or any diminution, of rapidity in the footsteps, they would have been endurable; but there was no such thing. The same deadening, monotonous, stupefying sound continued, like clockwork, to operate incessantly above their heads. Nor was there any abatement of the storm without; the wind blowing among the trees of the cemetery in a sepulchral moan; the rain beating against the panes of glass with the impetuous loudness of hail; and lightning and thunder flashing and pealing at brief intervals through the murky firmament. The noise of the elements was indeed frightful, and it was heightened by the voice of the sable steed like that of a spirit of darkness; but the whole, as we have just hinted, was as nothing to the deep, solemn, mysterious treading of the Red Man.

Innumerable were their conjectures concerning the character of this personage. It had been mentioned that the landlady conceived him at first to be a traveling packman, the landlord a French spy, and the exciseman a conjurer. Now their opinions were wholly changed, and they looked upon him as something a great deal worse. The parson, in the height of his learning, regarded him as an emanation of the tempter himself; and in this he was confirmed by the erudite opinion of the schoolmaster. As to the ostler, he could say nothing about the man, but he was willing to stake his professional knowledge that his horse was [62] kith and kin to the evil one. Such were the various doctrines promulgated in the kitchen of the Black Swan.

"If he be like other men, how could he anticipate me, as he did, in what I was going to say?" observed the parson.

"Born on the borders of the Red Sea!" ejaculated the landlord.

"Heard ye how he repeated to us what we were talking about during his absence in the stable?" remarked the exciseman.

"And how he knew that I was a pedagogue?" added the schoolmaster.

"And how he called on me by name, although he never saw nor heard of me before?" said the ostler in conclusion. Such a mass of evidence was irresistible. It was impossible to overlook the results to which it naturally led.

"If more proof is wanting," resumed the parson after a pause, "only look to his dress. What Christian would think of travelling about the country in red? It is a type of the hell-fire from which he is sprung."

"Did you observe his hair hanging down his back like a bunch of carrots?" asked the exciseman.

"Such a diabolical glance in his eye!" said the schoolmaster.

"Such a voice!" added the landlord. "It is like the sound of a cracked clarionet."

"His feet are not cloven," observed the landlady. [63]

"No matter," exclaimed the landlord; "the devil, when he chooses, can have as good legs as his neighbours."

"Better than some of them," quoth the lady, looking peevishly at the lower limbs of her husband.

Meanwhile, the incessant treading continued unabated, although two long hours had passed since its commencement. There was not the slightest cessation to the sound, while out of doors the storm raged with violence, and in the midst of it the hideous neighing and stamping of the black horse were heard with pre-eminent loudness. At this time the fire of the kitchen began to burn low. The sparkling blaze was gone, and in its stead nothing but a dead red lustre emanated from the grate. One candle had just expired, having burned down to the socket. Of the one which remained the unsnuffed wick was nearly three inches in length, black and crooked at the point, and standing like a ruined tower amid an envelopment of sickly yellow flame; while around the fire's equally decaying lustre sat the frightened coterie, narrowing their circle as its brilliancy faded away, and eyeing each other like apparitions amidst the increasing gloom.

At this time the clock of the steeple struck the hour of midnight, and the tread of the stranger suddenly ceased. There was a pause for some minutes—afterwards a rustling—then a noise as of something drawn [64] along the floor of his room. In a moment thereafter his door opened; then it shut with violence, and heavy footsteps were heard trampling down the stair. the inmates of the kitchen shook with alarm as the tread came nearer. They expected every moment to behold the Red Man enter, and stand before them in his native character. The landlady fainted outright: the exciseman followed her example: the landlord gasped in an agony of terror: and the schoolmaster uttered a pious ejaculation for the behoof of his soul. Doctor Poundtext was the only one who preserved any degree of composure. He managed, in a trembling voice, to call out "Avaunt, Satan! I exorcise thee from hence to the bottom of the Red Sea!"

"I am going as fast as I can," said the stranger, as he passed the kitchen-door on his way to the open air. His voice aroused the whole conclave from their stupor. They started up, and by a simultaneous effort rushed to the window. There they beheld the tall figure of a man, enveloped in a black cloak, walking across the yard on his way to the stable. He had on a broad-brimmed, low-crowned hat, top-boots, with enormous spurs, and carried a gigantic whip in one hand, and a portmanteau in the other. He entered the stable, remained there about three minutes, and came out leading forth his fiery steed thoroughly accoutered. In the twinkling of an eye he got upon his back, waved his hand to the company, who were surveying him through [65] the window, and, clapping spurs to his charger, galloped off furiously, with a hideous and unnatural laugh, through the midst of the storm.

    On going up the stairs to the room which the devil had honoured with his presence, the landlord found that his infernal majesty had helped himself to every thing he could lay his hands upon, having broken into his desk and carried off twenty-five guineas of king's money, a ten pound Bank of England note, and sundry articles, such as seals, snuff-boxes, &c. Since that time he has not been seen in these quarters, and if he should, he will do well to beware of Doctor Poundtext, who is a civil magistrate as well as a minister, and who, instead of exorcising him to the bottom of the Red Sea, may perhaps exorcise him to the interior of Leicester gaol, to await his trial before the judges of the midland circuit.

A MODERN PYTHAGOREAN.

Title

Galt, John. "The Omen." FMN 1830. 99-105. [99]

THE OMEN
BY JOHN GALT, ESQ.

* * * * * WE were thirteen, the ominous number, and all strangers to each other. It is true that Von Hesse and I had travelled from Prague together, but we had no previous acquaintance; indeed, we had been three days in company before either of us knew the other's name.

Our host, the banker, was a jolly facetious personage, with a dash of freethinking in his conversation, which, through regulated by some feeling allied to good taste, was yet sufficiently obtrusive. He appeared to be sensible that an open display of his religious opinions might give offence, and evidently repressed his inclination to sport irreverent jests; but habit, in despite of resolution, now and then broke out, and an occasional expression indicated that with more intimate friends his infidelity would have been probably less mitigated. As often as any of these expressions escaped him, the thoughtful countenance of Von Hesse was darkened; and twice or thrice, when the banker went a little too far, he gently contrived to check the mirth which the unchristened gibe was calculated to awaken.

The air and demeanour of Von Hesse were at all times mild and winning. His physiognomy was serene, almost solemn; his voice soft and pleasing; and a slight touch of sadness in his accent increased the interest which his calm and engaging manners universally [100] inspired. It bespoke something like pity; for it suggested an apprehension that his spirit was affected by forebodings, or laden with the remembrance of misfortunes. Once, and once only, in the course of our journey to Frankfort, I saw him agitated. It was but for a moment; something wilder than sadness gleamed as it were through the habitual seriousness of his features; an ashy and ghastly hue, the complexion of horror or of dread.

It happened in the twilight of an evening, as we approached a little village where we were to pass the night, that, at the turn of the road, we came suddenly on a small burying-ground, the most spectral and dismal place of the kind I had ever seen. It was indeed like no other. Tall, black, and fantastical wooden memorials served for tombstones; some of them bore a mysterious resemblance to hatchments and funeral banners, others reminded me of skeletons: they suggested frightful associations, and I could not help saying, "These are surely the sepulchres of men who have made dreadful confessions!"

It was at that moment his countenance became so strangely changed from its wonted pensiveness; but I then ascribed the change to his participating in the momentary superstition with which I was myself affected, nor did I afterwards think of what I had noticed till our host, in his jocular sallies, derided the communion of spirits and the visitation of ghosts.

His remarks were playful and ingenious, and, to [101] some of the guests, afforded amusement. To me they were disagreeable; not, however, I frankly confess, so much owing to their irreverence, as to their visible effect on Von Hesse.

It was at this turn of the conversation that the slow and meditative eye of Professor Khüll became fixed upon him so earnestly, that I could not but think he was actuated by a curiosity similar to my own. Strange, I had travelled four weeks with Von Hesse without discovering any symptom of his mysterious disease, and yet the professor, who had never seen him before, in less than an hour had discerned that he was one of those peculiar beings who have "that within which passeth show." But the extraordinary metaphysical discernment of Khüll has often been the wonder of his friends.

Falling in with the current of the conversation, Khüll remarked, in reply to our host, that whatever the generality of mankind might think of the communion of spirits, and of ghosts and dreams, it is impossible to dissipate by reason the faith of those who believe in them; "because," he added, looking at Von Hesse, "the faith is built up of experiences. The believers do not adopt their creed upon persuasion, but have had testimonials to its truth in themselves, influencing them to believe. The soundness of a man's judgement would not suffer much, in my opinion, by his assuring me that he had seen a ghost."

This singular observation drew from the banker one [102] of his sharpest jokes; for the professor was not esteemed very orthodox, but suspected of cherishing notions adverse, not only to every kind of superstition, but even to some of the popular dogmas of religion.

Von Hesse interfered, and said, with evident emotion, "But you must allow, professor, that the experience of such mysteries can only affect ourselves: we have no faculty by which we can adequately convey the horror of our experience to others."

"I should infer from that, sir," replied Khüll, "that you have tasted of 'that horror.' "

"I have," said Von Hesse, firmly, "but I have seen no ghosts, nor held communion with spirits, nor—but I will tell you of an instance of my experience."

The table was solemnly hushed as he spoke. all save our host were touched with awe; his attempt, however, to rally, by pushing round the wine, was interrupted by Khüll saying "A good metaphysical tale is worth a tun of Johannisberger—pray, do let him proceed."

"At the close of the war," said Von Hesse, "I was ordered, along with three other officers, to investigate some of the army accounts which remained at Basle unsettled. Being at the time slightly indisposed, I found it necessary to travel by easier stages than my companions, and accordingly allowed them to go on before.

"On the morning after they left me, I was sensible of the remarkable change in my disease; the slow fever [103] with which I had for weeks been affected went suddenly off—I should say, it passed from the body to the mind; for, although the corporeal hectic was extinguished, an acute moral excitement succeeded, and my reflections became so hurried and morbid that a dread of madness fell upon me. My sleep was unrefreshing, and filled with dismal and ominous dreams, the imagery of which was sometimes fearfully distinct, at others dark, indistinguishable, and prophetical. I was depressed without cause, and apprehensive without reason; and often, in the still of the evening, while solitary in the inns where I halted for the night, I felt as if I have been conscious of the presence of invisible spirits of departed friends compassionately regarding me.

"By the time I rejoined my companions at Basle, this comfortless state had produced a visible change in my appearance. They said that my complexion had become strangely wan, and that my eyes shone with something more like light than the natural lustre.

"One morning, after a restless night, I fell into a profound sleep—so profound that every trace and sentiment of existence might be said to have been obliterated for the time. From this syncope I was suddenly startled by an indescribable alarm. I heard no voice, nor any sound, and yet I received a supernatural intimation of a dreadful misfortune having befallen one of my dearest friends.

"When I joined my companions they were shocked [104] at my appearance, and one of them anxiously inquired what had happened. I told them, and they looked gravely at each other: they seemed to think it was a warning to myself.

"I then noted the hour and day of this alarm in my pocket-book; and, strange to tell, from that time I felt myself released from the singular enchantment of dismay which had so invested my spirit; my health revived, my complexion regained its wonted hue, and I laughed at superstition.

"When our inquiries were finished we returned to Vienna, and, soon after, I resolved to visit the friend on whose account I had been so disturbed. He resided at Prague; but just as I was on the eve of setting out on the journey, I received from him a letter, which at once froze me with awe and overwhelmed me with sorrow.

"He described himself as having been for a long time afflicted with an irresistible depression of spirits, a foreboding of calamity, while all things with him were prosperous. Then he proceeded to relate that one morning, quoting the date—I referred to my pocket-book, it was the same, the day and hour, on which I had received the intimation—he dreamt that he saw a hand with a knife a the throat of one of his children; he was at the same moment roused by a message from the nursery that the child was ill. The doctor was sent for, the disease was croup of the worst kind, and to relieve the sufferer the doctor made an incision [105] with an instrument precisely similar to the knife he had seen in his dream. The same hour one of the servants was found to be ill of a fatal fever, the infection of which spread so rapidly in the family, that the utter desolation of his house at one time seemed to be ordained.—Now, Professor Khüll, what explanation can you give, either by sympathies or associations, of the fact, the sublime fact, of this sense of an event which was taking place at a great distance, and of which there could have been no possible fore-knowledge?"

Title

B., M.L. [Beevor, Miss M.L.] "St. Feinah's Tree. A Legend of Loch Neagh." FMN 1830. 155-163. [155]

ST. FEINAH'S TREE.
A LEGEND OF LOCH NEAGH.

ONE evening Collogh (Goody) M'Gragh say by her peat fire, and her three sons sat around her; fine lads they were too—I do not mean in dress, but in person—possessing brave hearts and hangs for a row, and frisky legs enough for a dance; when such things were going, as oftentimes they be, in merry Ireland;—fine, spirited *craturs*, were Dan, Mike, and Pat M'Gragh, as young Irishmen ought to be; and their handsome faces and their large black eyes glowed and glistened, as the *ould* mother looked upon them, with pride in her heart, as well she might. The lads had just come in from a neighbouring wedding among the gentry, where prizes had been bestowed on the most agile in rustic spores; consequently, Dan, Mike, and Pat, had each carried off from it something *honestly*; a proceeding not without a precedent on their parts, although it must be confessed that such was rare.

"And the *what* will I do with my hat, mother?" said San, in answer to a query of Collogh's, twirling the ribbon-decked beaver round his hand; "why, sell it to be sure, is it that I shall still in such a jewel!—Faith no!"

"And I'll lay up my shirt for the burying," cried Mike.

"Then, Mick M'Gragh," said Collogh, "bad luck be wi' ye, my lad, and boderation: it is the ould mo- [156] ther ye're thinking to bury? O, Mike, Mike! 'tis yeeself, and no other, I tell ye."

Michael stared; for though he really meant to wear his new Irish surtout as a shroud, when he was dead, yet he intended, though he did not exactly mean so to express himself, to put it on, clean, white, well-made, and ornamented as it was, at his mother's funeral and his own wedding, events which in his ideas were neither of them far distant: he therefore stared; for the anticipation of an early death was furthest from his thoughts.

"And what's the lad looking at? ay, honey; do stare, an ye will, *now*;—night is the hour when your sightless eyes shall be turned on the desolate Collogh M'Gragh! But why would I spake to *you*, Mike? Isn't it all my brave lads? and meself am the ould des'late cratur to go down to the grave alone!"

The young men were astonished, and prayed her to explain herself; which, after a couple of hours' persuasion, and more that a couple of horns of whiskey, she did, by desiring them on no account whatever to go to their still.

Now in Church Island, one of the little isles of Loch Neagh, the M'Graghs had an illicit distillery, which was the subject of endless contention between the mother and sons; because, whilst the old lady did not in the least object to drink many a hearty draught of the beverage they prepared, she had many conscientious qualms respecting the legality of their proceedings; [157] and oft times, after vainly entreating them to pursue some *honest* calling, she prophesied a heavy curse upon their disobedience. But the lads knew very well that to an Irishman a still is both an idle and a profitable source of revenue, and therefore continued to work at their own, together or in turns, as occasion required. When, therefore, they heard her present prohibition, imagining it to be but the revival of the old subject, they ridiculed her fears, and one and all declared that the *would*, whatever were the consequences, continue the business upon Church Island. Collogh, heated with wrath and whiskey, flew into a hurricane of passion, cursed them in the bitterness of her heart; and when they turned out of the cabin, in order, as they said, "to leave her to cool a bit," she wished she might never see their undutiful faces again!

The Irish character is peculiarly ardent and fickle: suddenly its anger or its love burns like a devouring and unquenchable fire, and as suddenly is extinct. No sooner were her sons gone than the mother's heart began to soften, and she reflected, that young men could never endure to be governed by the fancies of a woman: and such young men too!—bold, handsome, and joyous lads as they were;—that she had been drinking the finest poteen in Ireland, the produce of their *still*, and had cursed them to their faces, and banned them from her door. She then remembered her prophecy of their deaths, and fearing it might come true, her heart was [158] wrung with an agony too sore for speech; so at first the poor dame sat down and cried for the *certain* death coming upon her dear boys; and then, her grief vanquished by hope, she bestirred herself to provide for them a good supper.

Hour after hour passed, and it seemed to her that they came not: but at midnight, uncovering her face (for over it long had she spread her apron, as she sat in her sorrow), she beheld, seated round the table, Dan, Mike, and Pat, as pale as death, and as silent. They fixed their large, mournful, and glazed eyes upon her, but spake not. She put before them the hot potatoes, milk, and bacon, urging them, in the kindest manner, to eat and to answer her; but they neither touched the food, nor moved, nor spoke: indeed, the young men looked more like corpses than living bodies; and horrible thoughts and apprehensions thronged thick and fast upon the soul of Collogh M'gragh. She conjured them in an agony to speak, to tell her what ailed them, and not to trick and fright a lone woman like her, by appearing as their own *fetches*;—she assured them of her pardon, of her unchanged affection, and many times retracted the curses she had called down upon her children in her grievous fury;—she addressed them generally and separately, but without avail: Dan, Mike, and Pat, answered not, neither did their bluish-white, chilly, ghastly faces, betray that they even heard her words; not a muscle moved; the large dead-look- [159] ing black eyes were fixed and vacant; and Collogh, remembering that she had not heard them enter, uttered a cry of horror, and fell senseless on the floor.

When consciousness returned, the pale, dewy light of morning was beaming in at the cabin, through the smoke-vent, for it had no window; and Collogh M'Gragh found herself alone, bating the pig that always slept in a corner of her house. Her first thought was for her sons, who, it as evident, had been out all night; but had not the memory of the horrible apparitions flashed at the same time athwart her brain, this circumstance would not have alarmed her, as they usually worked during the night at the still, and slept in the day-time: she hoped, therefore, that they might be home in an hour or two—but they came not; and it was no consolation to think, that one or all of them might have been overwhelmed by the holy stone, which she knew it was their favourite freak to endeavour to lift. She remembered that Pat, once choosing to hazard a shot at some of St. Feinah's Wild-fowl on Church Island, his gun burst; and though he remained uninjured, the thousand fragments of the weapon flew upwards, and never a splinter of it came down again! she also recollected, that sundry misfortunes, and even death, had attended such persons as, with sacrilegious temerity, had plucked a twig off St. Feinah's tree, that sacred and wondrous elder, the age of which is incalculable; and which, though overthrown and hacked by [160] sundry cuttings, still flourishes, covering a great portion of the interior ground of that ruined sanctuary which gives title to the island. A thousand vague suspicions and apprehensions presented themselves to the mind of Collogh M'Gragh, and at length, as the day wore away, she resolved to take a boat at the ferry, and cross over to Church Island in search of her sons.

Now this island is a kind of fairy place, both from the circumstances already mentioned concerning it, and because it is rich in antiquities, relics, and white-thorn trees, whose odorous, delicious blossoms, in their season, are as grateful to the wanderer, as those gales that greet the mariner from lands of spice and roses; consequently, all tourists of taste, when they visit Loch Neagh, which deserves consideration as well as its rival Killarney, never fail to land upon Church Island, as a something to a see of course. Accordingly, the day being bright and beautiful, Collogh M'Gragh, upon her arrival at the ferry, found a number of visitors taking their places in the holiday boat to cross to the island, upon which, she understood, a gay party was already landed. The strangers were good-natured, and insisted on the poor woman taking the opportunity to cross with them; and as the sun shone, the streamers floated in the sweet air, and the bagpipes struck up a merry tune, Collogh could not prevent her old heart dancing for pleasure. Notwithstanding her [161] heavy fears for Dan, Mike, and Pat, she felt as if her old limbs could have danced too, lightly, mirthfully, and buoyantly, as in the days of her buxom youth, on the very surface of the cool, calm, shining lake.

On reaching the island, many persons stood upon its shore, and, as

Collogh observed before they opened their lips to hail the fresh party, with very anxious and woebegone countenances: at length, several voices asked whether they had heard of the accident, or seen any of the bodies? "What accident? what bodies?" was the reply from the fresh company: but Collogh M'Gragh shrieked forth—"My sons! my sons!" and, alas! she spoke but too truly. After the clamour had ceased, which the desire of all to relate the circumstance occasioned, the wretched mother gleaned a succinct account of the dreadful catastrophe, from which it appeared that the three M'Graghs, who were well known to the boatmen who took the first party over to Church Island, had been seen by the strangers, on their visit to the old church, lopping and hewing St. Feinah's tree, because, as they said, they wanted the wood, and elder was, of all others, the wood for their purpose. What they cut they carried off in a boat, which, when about halfway between Church Island and the Ferry, suddenly, without a breeze, without a ripple, and beneath the broad unclouded sunshine—sunk. A rush and splash of water was heard—a deathful, piteous shriek—and to these succeeded a deep, [162] awful, grave-like silence! Boats were immediately dispatched, to render, if possible, assistance to the sufferers, but in vain; their bodies even had not risen—no, nor were they ever seen or heard of again. The English strangers attributed the accident to natural causes, but the Irish inhabitants of the shores and islands of Loch Neagh believe nothing less than that St. Feinah thus avenged the insult and sacrilege committed by the M'Graghs upon his, or her (for this saint's name is not in the calendar) favourite and sacred elder-tree.

    Little remains to be added, but that poor Collogh M'Gragh, the wretched mother, was inconsolable: she had cursed her children in the bitterness of her soul—and with that curse upon their heads had they quitted her presence—never to return—never to learn that they were forgiven: they were gone—the comforts of her age, the life of her heart—to their untimely graves, and in her misery and desolation she became deranged, and died soon afterwards. Her spirit, it is said, wanders yet upon the shores of Loch Neagh, chanting, in a low but awfully plaintive tone, the words of a keen, or song, which she improvised for her children, and died singing; and of which the following is a nearly literal translation:

        They say, my sons are sleeping
           Beneath the treach'rous wave,
        And I—their mother—keeping
           A wild watch o'er their grave;
        [163]
        But are they dead?—nay, seeming
           Deep in the lake to lie,
        They're whisp'ring love, or dreaming,
           And will not heed my cry.
                                  Ullah!

Flow on, flow on, glad waters—
    The loved, the young, the brave,
Are gone to court thy daughters,
    The blithe ones of the wave.
Shine on, thou lake of pleasure,
    When late thy breast was spread,
Each sunk, to seek his treasure,
    As on a rosy bed.
                  Ullah!

Bloom on, green isles of beauty,
    Ye'll sparkle not in vain;
For though to mortal duty
    The loved ne'er rise again;
Yet, since they did not adore ye,
    By the moon's melting ray
They'll rove with sea-maids o'er ye,
    Or elves, more bright than they.
                  Ullah!

Rise, dear ones, from the waters!
    And glad me with your smile;
The lage's enamour'd daughters
    May spare ye for a while:
Quit, quit their love, too tender,
    Their music, and their wine:
Leave, leave their homes of splendour
    On hour, to brighten mine!
                  Ullah!

M.L.B.

Title

Delta. [Moir, D.L.] "Kemp, The Bandit. A Legend of Castle Campbell." FMN 1830. 209-227. [209]

KEMP, THE BANDIT
A LEGEND OF CASTLE CAMPBELL.
BY DELTA.

SIR JOHN DE CAMPBELL, a young and gallant knight of Argyleshire, had long sued for the hand of the fair Lady Madeline, daughter of the Duke of Rothsay, at that time resident at the Scottish court, at Dunfermline; but, owing to family differences, his suit had been unavailing, although the affections of the gentle lady were known to be his. The power and influence of the Rothsay family, together with their allegiance to royalty, rendered a daughter of that line an object of political ambition among the young nobles; and, if the fair young creature remained single until twenty summers had shone in her blue eyes, it may be veritably set down to a determinate resolution of her own, and not to lack of suitors. In connexion with our little narrative, however, it need only be remarked, that among the rivals was Lord Duffus, a gallant of handsome person, but of loose manners and dissolute conduct. He was soon destined to find himself in the bad graces of both sire and child; his suit, amounting to importunity, received a flat negative; and the discarded wooer gave way to feelings of revenge and affronted pride.

At this remote and unsettled era of Scottish legislation, a freebooter, named Jasper Kemp, whose daring deeds and personal prowess rendered him the [210] terror of all the surrounding districts, occupied the Castle of Gloom a magnificent fortalice, situated in a gorge at the foot of the Ochills, in the parish of Dollar, Clackmannanshire. Although in the immediate precincts of the royal court, many attempts for ejecting him had failed; the natural and artificial strength of his situation rendered his castle almost impregnable, especially when defended by spirits so bold and daring; while success, hardihood, and immunity from punishment, had combined to render the outlaw so fearlessly resolute, that he is said once, for a wager, to have burst with his band, in open daylight, into the palace of Dunfermline itself, and succeeded in carrying off the dinner from the king's table.

This person had collected about him men of determined courage and desperate fortunes—ruffians who set death at defiance, and who were ready for hire to put all to the last stake; indeed, so extensive were their rapines and so unfeeling the cruelties they exercised, that they were never known to be abroad without the neighbouring country quaking in terror and alarm. Strong, as we have said, in its natural site—the Castle of Gloom being surrounded, except at one approachable point, by picturesque mountains, towering to the clouds,—Kemp felt, after the royal troops had ineffectually invested it twice or thrice, that his principal risk of being at any time obliged to capitulate must arise from being cut off from his supply of water; but the energetic mind of the outlaw determined on overcoming even [211] this mighty deficiency; and he accomplished the gigantic task of cutting downwards through the solid rock to the bed of a rivulet, a descent of more than a hundred feet; the frightful chasm, almost closed with weeds and brambles, remaining to this day a monument of enterprise and perseverance.

To this determined and resolute character Lord Duffus communicated his design of carrying away by force the fair Lady Madeline De Rothsay; and, by a large bribe, he succeeded in bringing him over to his designs. The plan was laid in secresy, and managed with Kemp's usual adroitness; for, soon afterwards, when the lady, escorted by two female attendants, was one summer evening riding in apparent security along the plain towards Inverkeithing, she was suddenly surrounded by an armed train, which burst from a neighbouring copse, bound her on her palfrey, separated her from her maidens, and hurried her furiously along the coast, in the direction first of Culross, then of Alloa. Kemp, immediately on getting her into safe possession, threw off his cloak of disguise, and rode by her side in splendid armour, mounted on a war-horse proportioned to his Herculean bulk; and, notwithstanding the ferocity of his exterior, he behaved towards his fair and fainting prisoner with a courtesy unwonted to his nature. On nearing the hamlet of Dollar, the part wound around a wooded path, picturesquely overhung with rocks, where, in an opening between the Ochills, the magnificent Castle of Gloom frowned before them [212] in the fairy dusk of twilight. At the accustomed signal the gates were thrown open; the train entered; the heavy portcullis fell behind them; and the heart of Madeline died within her, when she found that the Castle of Gloom was to be her prison, and that her captor was none other than Kemp, the dreaded freebooter.

The better to cloak his designs, and to obviate all suspicion of his partnership in this nefarious transaction, Lord Duffus remained at court—the boon companion of the dissolute and extravagant; while he appeared to enter with more than common feeling into the general sorrow that overhung it, on the news of Lady Madeline's forcible abstraction; and, such an adept was he in the arts of hypocrisy and cunning, and he played his part so well, by making protestations of service to the duke, that even the idea of his being the main spring of the enterprise seemed not for a moment to be entertained by his most vigilant enemies. So, when week after week of fruitless search had elapsed, when liberal rewards had been offered, and offered in vain, and, when the buzz of the alarm began to subside, even hope itself becoming extinct, Lord Duffus, found or fancied, that he might now venture to act with greater boldness, and risk his projected visit to the Castle of Gloom itself.

It were vain to attempt a description of what must have been the feelings of Lady Madeline in her awful, forlorn situation: but a few weeks ago the pride of her father's eye, the ornament of a royal court, "the observed of all observers;" and now, separated from her friends, shut up in a secluded castle, and the prisoner of a lawless ruffian, of whose ultimate designs against her nothing good could possibly be surmised, however present circumstances might concur to keep them concealed. She had no doubt of Kemp being her captor, and what was she to expect from such a man? Meanwhile, though he paid her only a short and respectful visit every day, inquiring into her comforts, and offering the fulfillment of every wish she might breathe consistent with her situation as a prisoner, her heart died within her when she thought of her forlorn and awful situation, and that the present calm could only be a prelude to the bursting of the terrible tempest-cloud. A dismal mystery overhung her, which was soon to be dispelled. Duffus she never suspected, and De Campbell how could she suspect?—"Ah!" thought she, "if De Campbell knew my situation, neither gates of brass, nor bolts of steel, would deter him from accomplishing, or at least attempting my rescue. But that is never to be, and I am destined to—no, I will not be dishonoured—to perish here!"

Stoicism is an article beyond the creed of human nature; the coldest bosom has embers which may be fortuitously kindled up, and there is no calculating on the power of female beauty over the heart of man. Kemp himself, the daring and desperate outlaw, whose cruelties and atrocities were proverbial, was touched with the divine loveliness of his victim, whose tears and whose tenderness began at length to melt his rugged spirit. But with passion ambitious designs also entered his bosom; and these were fostered by the impression, that either Duffus was too much suspected at court to be able to visit his unfortunate prisoners; or that he had that nobleman sufficiently in his power to compel him to hush up the matter, whatever might be the result. Kemp therefore determined to play a bold game; and, screwing up his resolution to the point, he at once made an offer of his services to Lady Madeline, on particular conditions. It is also unnecessary to add, that these conditions were instantly and indignantly refused; and finding that he had committed himself, by preceding too precipitately and too far, he had some difficult in managing with Lord Duffus, who arrived at the Castle of Gloom that very evening with the intention of visiting his victim, and communicating to her his plan of carrying her beyond seas—a vessel, hired for the express purpose, being at the time riding off the coast. The bandit was taken unawares, but, under some shrewd pretence or other, he prevailed upon him to deter his visit until the succeeding day, when, as he said, Lady Madeline had agreed voluntarily to afford him an opportunity of explanation.

Kemp now found that his fortune with regard to his beautiful captive must at once be put to the die. Through a sleepless night he revolved his dark schemes [215] in his mind, until he had fixed on one that seemed most likely to help him to their bloody issue.

A great quantity of game abounding at that time in the neighbourhood of the Castle of Gloom—there being much wood and thicket, as well as shelter and inequality of ground—Kemp summoned his guest, at daybreak, to the chase, and a gallant hunting train, with hound, and hawk, and bugle, issued from the gates into the morning sunlight. Kemp led the way up the defile, and they winded along the pathways from grove to glen, until a buck was started. The animating notes of pursuit were sounded; and, after a short but rapid run, the animal was taking to his accustomed ford, with the dogs close upon him, when Kemp, who was immediately behind Duffus spurred furiously upon him, and, without uttering a syllable, put forth his whole gigantic force in the thrust of his spear. His transfixed him, and bore him from his saddle to the ground. It was but one shriek of agony, and then the coldness, the stiffness, the repose, of death.

'Twas now the month of September; the foliage withering on the forest-trees was silently preaching to man of the vicissitudes of time, and, by a premature decline of the season, the evening rains had already degenerated into snow-showers, when two or three of Kemp's trustiest followers, coming to the place where the body of the unfortunate wretch had been hid at morning in the thicket, spread out a mantle on the ground, in which they enveloped the corpse, and bore [216] it away on their shoulders, through the duck of twilight, to the adjoining sequestered burial-ground. The sun had sunk behind the far western Grampians;—the night-hawk gave his faint aërial scream as he flitted over the forbidding orgies;—the evening became clear and starry;—and a north wind sweeping over the layer of snow hardened its surface into a polished iciness. They reached the lonely burial-ground, which they entered in silence. The grave had already been dug—the body was tumbled into it—the earth shovelled over;—and a quantity of leaves, collected for the purpose, were scattered around, to prevent any traces of recent digging being observable.

The ruffian, Kemp, seemingly untouched by a feeling of remorse, had in person beheld this last consummation of his atrocious deed; and now, exulting in the security of success, he returned through the copse by a direct path to the postern door of the Castle, which he entered, followed by his bravoes, who sate down to their prepared and promised carousal.

The fears of Lady Madeline, were, in the mean time, deepening into despair—the hopes that sustained her were gradually waning away, like the traces of sunset from the west—and, after brooding over the misery of the preceding evening, her heart sank within her, and she began to give up every thing for lost. Worn out by hope deferred, and by tears, and terror, and agitation of mind, she felt driven to utter desperation; and, rising from her knees, after imploring the pardon of [217] Heaven, she gazed forth on the stars, twinkling in the serenity of the blue sky, as it were for the last time, and hid in her bosom the dagger with which, should necessity urge, she had come to the terrible determination of putting a period to her sufferings.

The night was now far advanced—the wine-cup had circled freely—the sounds of wassail cheer waxed louder in the hall, while song and jest went round till the roofs rand, when a loud and hasty summons shook the gate, and a herald, with an armed band, demanded, in the king's name, the surrender of the person of Lord Duffus. Heated with wine, and exasperated with rage, Kemp appeared on the battlements, and told them that they had been sent on a false errand—that Lord Duffus was not in his keeping—and that if they would find him, they must seek him elsewhere. He then made some scoffing remarks on their embassy, wished them a pleasant ride back, and returned to his companions.

Some clue to the sudden disappearance of Lady Madeline de Rothsay having been given by one of the attendants of Lord Duffus, who had been privy to the secret meetings with the notorious Kemp, and had afterwards been dismissed from his service in a drunken frolic, the suspicions of her friends had been suddenly awakened; while the king, who had long in private favoured the suit of De Campbell, contrived to have that young knight sent on this mission to recover the lost fair one. [218]

De Campbell having traced the journey of Lord Duffus to the neighbourhood of Castle Gloom, his suspicions were more forcibly awakened. Aware, however of the daring and desperate character of the freebooter, and knowing that the tocsin of alarm had been now sounded in his ears, to put him upon his guard, he judged it best, the night having become dark and gloomy, to leave the rugged and dangerous by-paths, and proceed without delay in the direction of Clackmannan Tower, where he was assured of hospitable accommodation for the night. Here too, if requisite, he could readily augment his force, so that he might invest the place in the morning with better chance of success.

The party had not proceeded far over the rugged hill-paths among the trees, when, by the light of the torches, by which they were necessarily preceded, the track of recent footsteps in the snow attracted their attention, and a sudden thought struck De Campbell, that, by following the foot-prints, they might discover something of Duffus, who, he strongly suspected, must be lurking somewhere in the neighbourhood. They pursued the traces on and on, until they led first round the edge of an ancient quarry, then off by the skirts of a copse-wood, and then, leaving the common track, away to the left, down a dell, to the sequestered burial-ground. There, typing their horses to the yew-tress, they groped about with their lights, until, at the northeast corder, they came to the scattered leaves, and re- [219] marked the traces of recent digging. Suspicion, strong before, now became still stronger. Can it be, thought De Campbell, that the monsters have murdered beautiful Madeline de Rothsay, and buried her fair body here in this lone and dreary spot? A cold sweat burst over his limbs, his helmet pressed with a heavier weight on his forehead, and his heart shrunk within his breast. Words may not describe his emotions, as the grave was re-opened, and the body discovered and disinhumed. The torchlight, playing on the cheek of De Campbell, showed it to be pale as the snow at his feet; for, as they were unwrapping the war-cloak, he every moment dreaded to see, from the attire, some dreadful token that the lady of his love slept within in. His terrors however were removed, but his amazement certainly increased, when he recognised on the instant the blood-bedabble features of Duffus; and, in the bosom of it all, commiseration for his untimely and wretched fate almost stifled the memory of his failings and his crimes.

Having so far unriddled a most mysterious business, the next step was to track the foot-marks round the enclosures. These, after some little tediousness of search, were found to lead to an opening in the hedge of evergreens, evidently but very recently made, as was observable from some detached branches and berries, which lay on the ground unbesprinkled with the snow, and which must have been torn off subsequently to the shower. Through the thicket behind, the traces were [220] found to lead onwards to the postern gate of the castle, beside which De Campbell, having collected his men, held them in readiness for effecting a forcible entry.

With the greatest secrecy and silence, the party reached the postern gate of Castle Gloom, which, to their surprise, was unlocked and unguarded; either so careless of consequences were Kemp and his associates in the midst of their villainy, or so secure did they feel as to deem themselves beyond the reach of surprise. Accompanied by only one trusted yeoman, De Campbell explored his way in darkness, sword in hand, along the winding passages, while his band kept possession of the postern, in order to assure his retreat, if necessary. For some time he wandered aimlessly in shade and bewilderment, until struck by the sounds of revelry and riot beneath him in the hall. These he neared, and at length was attracted towards the eastern angle of the building, in one of the lattices of which he had, from without, discerned a light. While standing to listen, the tones of a human voice were distinctly heard, sometimes elevated, in loud altercation, and as others, as if melting into the tender pathos of persuasion. He trode along on a swan's down, and reached the doorway unmolested.

"Yield to thy fate!" said some one, in whose address assumed mildness could not entirely conquer native ferocity—"yield with a good grace, fair maiden; and it will be well for thee. Thou shalt be mistress of all around thee. As for rescue, foster not a hope of that. [221] It is needless to indulge in vain imaginations. Make the best of thy present situation, and know thyself inevitably in my power. Nay, weep not; thou must be aware, that what thou refusest I can take; that thou art my prisoner, the bondswoman of Jasper Kemp; that they fate must ever remain a mystery; that Lord Duffus is dead; and that of this castle and these demesnes

I am sole master. Think not that the force of man, or the fear of man, can ever compel me to deliver up them or thee; for against the king and the might of his kingdom I could hold them with bloodshed and battle to my opponents for a year and a day.—Consider them well, fair lady. Yet would I compel thee not; give me a ray of hope—say that thou wilt be mine, be it to-morrow, or next day, or the day after that; and all I ask of thee now is, the delight of pressing that fair soft hand to my rude lips."

A faint female shriek ascended as the ruffian approached. "Advance not another step! or behold, I plunge this dagger into my bosom!" cried a female voice, suffocating in the agony of indignation and terror. "Know that I am prepared for the worst; and if you do not desist from your purpose, and on the instant leave this chamber, into which you have brutally intruded on a defenceless woman, I hold unsheathed in my hand the instrument, which shall dye the rushes of its floor with my heart's blood!"

"He! he! Lady Madeline," sneered the bandit, "I [222] know thy pretty secret. Shall I send for De Campbell to comfort thee?"

The listener could no more: the door was impetuously burst open, and, armed cap-à-pie, De Campbell stood, spectre-like, before his panic-struck adversary. "Wretch!" he cried, "I needed not to be sent for; lo, Heaven hath wafted me hither to defend innocence and to punish guilt! Take, then, the reward due to your atrocities!"

Kemp quivered through all the fibres of his gigantic frame, and gnashed his teeth in rage, as, grasping round for his weapon, he felt himself unarmed; but, with the presence of mind for which he was ever remarkable, he touched a spring in the paneling, and instantly disappeared, the blow of De Campbell falling on the half-closed door, through which the freebooter had eluded him.

All was at once uproar and alarm. Bells rang, voices shouted, and the jangle of armour resounded above and below, while the party of De Campbell rushed pell-mell into the castle, and, barricading the entrances to the hall, effectually prevented the revellers from assisting their master in the defence of the place. Confused with terror-struck, Kemp soon found that matters had come to a desperate pass; and, ignorant of the extent of force brought against him, he judged it best to attempt escape with a few collected followers: a plan which he could not have effected, but from his intimate [223] knowledge of localities. De Campbell, on the other hand, equally ignorant as to the real state of the matters, and well aware of the intrepidity of the opponent whom he had so fortuitously and unexpectedly surprised, judged it best, for the safety of his lovely and beloved change, to make every preparation for departure by the earliest light of morning.

The surprise, the joy, the rapture, of the Lady Madeline, on being so providentially rescued from the jaws of destruction, at such a critical juncture, and by him in whom her whole happiness on earth was centred, cannot be expressed.

Her blood-forsaken cheek now glowed with a crimson beyond the most delicate tints of the carnation, and her faded eye kindled with an eloquent lustre, whose silence spoke the depth of her gratitude and affection. She would have thrown herself at his feet—but at her feet he knelt, and raising her hand to his lips, he declared that even his life-blood had been cheerfully poured in attempting her deliverance; and that, while his cuirass wore her badge, his arm should ever be ready to wield a sword in her service.

The revelling and riotous banditti having been secured, and the castle left in the keeping of Ramage, De Campbell's lieutenant; scarcely had the sun, rising from the great German Ocean, purpled the eastern heavens above the Bass and May islands, when the horses, saddled and caparisoned, were led out before the gate leading into the court, and Lady Madeline de [224] Rothsay, escorted by her deliverer and his gallant train, set out towards Dunfermline. All were armed and on the look-out; for, until gaining the champaign, they were not without the suspicion of an attack by Kemp and his infuriated gang. Well it was for them that they kept as much aloof as the paths admitted from the wooded overhanging rocks, and from the narrower defiles, where they were most liable to be stopped or overwhelmed: for, with a falcon eye, the bandit had tracked their route; and on approaching the ford of the Devon, his well-known and far-feared trumpet-call was heard. It sounded before, and was answered from behind; and, as the troop of De Campbell paused to listen, the trampling of approaching horses was heard amid the adjoining copse woods.

The time called for instant decision. "On!—on!—let us onwards!" cried the young knight, spurring his charger to the gallop, and seizing the rein of Lady Madeline's palfrey. "Our only safety is pushing onwards to Dunfermline, through the opposers in front. To halt is to be surrounded—delay is destruction; then onwards, onwards, my merry men! Balfour," said he, turning round to one of his trustiest followers, while bidding his fair ward be of good cheer, he handed to him the rein of Lady Madeline's palfrey—"Balfour, to thee I commend the safeguard of this lady; and see that thou act as becomes a Scottish soldier, to whom a precious charge is committed." Then, addressing his train, he added—"Let us keep around [225] her, my gallants, till we have wedged our way through yonder caitiffs; and while we face round and hold them at bay, do thou, Balfour, with an escort, hurry on thy journey, and Heaven grant that thou deliver up thy charge in safety!"

Just as he had finished these words, and the horses were put to a hand gallop, an armed troop appeared guarding the ford on the hither side of the Devon; and in the centre rode the redoubted Kemp himself, conspicuous by his gigantic size and the lofty plume of his helmet. Every thing was now at stake, and De Campbell shrank not from the encounter, as, putting his spear in rest, he bore full on in the teeth of his formidable antagonist. In the twinkling of an eyelash both parties had closed in deadly combat, men and horses were overthrown, blows rang on cuirass and casque, and the life-blood flowed from many a gallant heart. Balfour, with Lady Madeline, was at first necessitated to fall back into the rear, from the imminent danger of forcing a passage through the strait so completely blockaded; but, alive to the importance and honour of his trust, he watched his opportunity when the contest was hottest, and, seizing the reins of the alarmed palfrey, clove down the only bandit who endeavoured to bar his path, plunged into the water, and gained the opposite bank. He then threw aside his heavy armour, put spurs to his horse, and carried his fair and fainting charge triumphantly beyond the din of conflict and the reach of her pursuers. [226]

Having calculated on a deep and easy revenge, Kemp became completely infuriated at the resistance he had so unexpectedly encountered; but when he perceived the escape of his beautiful captive—the tender being towards whom his own rude feelings seemed to have been so unaccountably attracted—his self-possession entirely forsook him, and he rushed headlong on De Campbell, to sacrifice him to his frenzy. As is customary in cases of over-excitement, he overshot his mark; and De Campbell, though much his inferior in mere brute strength, had by far the vantage-ground of him in science and coolness. For a while he contented himself in parrying the savage thrusts of his assailant, and, when the exhausting vigour of the monster gave him some chance of success, he rushed at him full title, and with a tremendous blow of his battle-axe smote him from his horse into the river. With a gurgling groan the ponderous corse sank in the still deep water under the projecting hazel-bank, and the spot of the Devon, which was the scene of this sanguinary achievement, is called "Kemp's Pool" to this day.

It is almost unnecessary to add that, immediately on the death of their commander, the followers of the bandit were discomfited, and made but a feeble resistance. A considerable number were already wounded or slain, and the remainder, finding opposition unavailing and success without an aim, threw down their arms and betook themselves to flight. Meanwhile, faithful to his trust, Balfour had carried his lovely [227]

charge in safety to Dunfermline, where she was received with ecstasy by her despairing friends; and when De Campbell arrived—oh may true love be ever so rewarded!—he was waited upon by the Duke of Rothsay, who, grateful beyond the reach of unmeaning family pride, or the power of words, for the recovery of his lovely and beloved child, quenched the remembrance of former differences, and generously gave his sanction to her union with her deliverer.

The king was himself present at the ceremony, which in a brief space followed at the Chapel Royal; and, on giving away Lady Madeline de Rothsay, he said to the bridegroom—"The life of this fair lady you have gallantly preserved; and my friend the duke has acted but with justice in bidding you be blessed together. As her dowry, accept from me the Castle of Gloom, and it domains, the usurped property of the sanguinary monster from whom you have freed my kingdom. Lady, that castle was the scene of your miseries. Sir knight, that castle was the scene of your gallantry. To both, be it the scene of the felicities, which, I pray Heaven to shower down bounteously on your heads! Let guilt and gloom abide in its halls no more; but, in remembrance of the beauty that adorns and the valour that won it, be it hence-forth and for ever known by the appellation of Castle Campbell."

Title
Richardson, David Lester. "The Soldier's Dream." FMN 1830. 234-237. [234]

THE SOLDIER'S DREAM[24].
BY DAVID LESTER RICHARDSON, ESQ.

The victory was decisive, and the whole force had returned to Gwalioh, a distance of several miles from the scene of action. The night was cold and gloomy; but, being too feeble to move, and suffering intensely in mind and body, I remained upon the field, surrounded by the dead. My wounds were galled by the shard midnight air, and I groaned aloud. I soon, however, felt ashamed of my idle lamentations, and, by smothering the voice of pain, I endeavoured to fortify myself against its power. During this silent struggle with my fate, I was startled by the sound of a footstep, and, gazing stedfastly towards the spot whence it proceeded, I could just discover the dim shadow of a man. At this moment the red moon emerged from behind a cloud, and displayed the form of one whom I had hated from my earliest youth. He seemed not to recognise my features, though I had fought and received my wounds by his side.

"Who art thou?" cried he.

"A soldier!"

"And doubtless, fellow," he continued, "the trade of blood is suited to thy spirit!" This said, he drew his cloak around him, and glided past me like a phantom. [235]

The moon again disappeared; the winds became still more piercing; the heavy dew wetted me to the skin; and, notwithstanding the chillness of the atmosphere, I was almost overpowered with the effluvia of dead, some of whom had been long exposed beneath a burning sun. At last, worn out with toil and suffering, after collecting a quantity of clothing from the bodies of my silent comrades, the touch of whose cold clay thrilled me with horror, I wrapped myself up as warmly as I could, and soon fell insensibly into a bewildered dream.

I thought I was wandering about upon the field of battle, and congratulating myself that the pain of my wounds had considerably abated, when, at the skirt of a gloomy forest, I was surprised and shocked by the appearance of a being whose aspect was inexpressibly hideous and appalling. I soon found that it was the Spirit of Death! I paused awhile in speechless terror, and at length heard him exclaim, in a voice whose tones fell upon my ear like the echoes of a charnel vault, "Miserable mortal! thy career of murder is over—thou hast provided me with many a victim, but it is now thy turn to be sacrificed—follow me." After struggling long and painfully through the close and thorny forest, I sank down exhausted with fatigue

---

24 This was the ground-work of the blank verse poem with the same title which appears in Mr. Richardson's volume of "Sonnets, and other Poems."

and emotion. The spirit's eye then fixed fearfully upon me, and in a moment I was lost to every sensation. I know not how long I remained in this silent trance; but I was at last roused by the din of clashing swords, [236] shrieks, and horrid cries, that seemed to proceed from an immense inclosure, whose walls of adamant reached higher and farther than the eye could follow. Beneath the portal of a glorious temple, which rose opposite to these interminable walls, I beheld a form of surpassing beauty, but whose glance was searching and severe. I mingled in the crowd which stood before him, and discovered the faces of many of my fellow-soldiers. The angel, for such he appeared, at length addressed us. We listened with fear and trembling, for his words were spells upon our souls. After unveiling the secrets of our hearts with terrible precision, and scrutinizing our motives of action in the world we had left, he smiled with divine benignity upon a youth who had died defending his farther from a party of the enemy that had surrounded him, and upon another, who had wielded his sword in the cause of freedom. "These two alone," said he, "out of this vast assemblage, have righteously shed human blood, and been uninfluenced by selfish principles. The rest have made kingdoms ring with the cries of widows and of orphans, for no other purposes than gain and glory. I leave them to their fate." He then turned towards an immense golden gate, which opened as he approached, and discovered a flight of steps, at the summit of which we could just the lower part of a throne, but it dazzled our eyes like the sun at mid-day. He was accompanied by the champion of freedom and the defender of his father, and the gate instantly closed behind them. [237]

  The air then grew darker, and a thick cloud rose from the ground, and, as it gradually expanded, disclosed a shape of indescribable deformity, that regarded us for some time with a look of demoniacal exultation. He then commanded us to follow him, and led us through a variety of gloomy passages into the interior of the inclosure, whence proceeded the sounds of agony and strife, that aroused me from the trance of death. We here beheld an innumerable throng in dreadful warfare, and felt a strange, but irresistible impulse to join the combatants. "On," cried the field who had brought us hither, "on to the Hell of Battle!" At these words we were inspired with relentless rage, and rushed to the scene of action. I suddenly recognised the being who had case a shade across my path in life, and excited my deadly hatred. I now struck fiercely at his heart. My aim did not fail; but what was my surprise, disappointment, and dismay, when I found that death here relinquished his power; and that we were condemned to feel its pangs without a prospect of release! My antagonist now turned on me—defence was vain. He stabbed me in the most vital parts, and, in unutterable agony—I awoke.

  It was morning, and the sun's pale and level rays just gleamed upon the ghastly faces of my dead companions. I threw off their infected garments, and as I felt my wounds less painful, I was glad to hasten from a scene which had inspired such a dream of horror.

Title

By The Old Sailor. [Barker, Matthew Henry.] "Greenwich Hospital ." FMN 1830. 241-255.

PLATE: Greenwich Hospital
Steel plate engraving; painted by Samuel Owen;
engraved by Robert Wallis [241]

GREENWICH HOSPITAL.
BY THE OLD SAILOR.

"What do you say to get some of the worthy old blues, me messmate,"
—(Dick is a pensioner)—"to spin out a yarn or two about the shattered old hulks in Greenwich moorings?"
"Say no more, say no more!" exclaimed I; "it shall be done directly."
"And get 'em printed in one of your periodicals?" continued Dick.
"The very thing!—the very thing!"

Greenwich Hospital; a Series of Naval Sketches.

Ay, there it is!—the grand depository of human fragments—the snug harbour for docked remnants—Greenwich Hospital! Who is there that has stood on that fine terrace, when the calm of evening has shed its influence on the spirit, and Nature's pencil, intermingling light and shade, has graced the landscape with its various tints, without feeling delighted at the spectacle? No sound is heard to break the stillness of the hour, save where the sea-boy trills his plaintive ditty, studious to grace the turnings of his song; for it was his mother taught it him, and for he strives to imitate. To him the tide rolls on unheeded; he sees not the tall mast, the drooping sail; ah, no! his heart is in the cottage where he knew his first affection, when, with a smile of infantile delight, he drew his nourishment from that fond bosom lately bedewed with tears at parting. Who is there that has not exulted in the scene, when the proud ship has spread her canvas to the breeze, to carry forth the produce of our country to distant lands; or, when returning to her own homeshores, laden with the luxuries of foreign climes, the gallant tars have "hailed each well-known object with [242] delight?" Ay, there they stand! the veterans of the ocean, bidding defiance to the frowns of fate, although they are moored in *tiers*. They are critics too—*deep* critics; but they cannot fancy the steam-vessel, with a chimney for a mast, and a long line of smoke for a pendant. These are the men that Smollett pictures—the Jack Rattlins and the Tom Pipes of former years. Ay, those were *rattling* days, and *piping* times! There is no place upon earth except Greenwich in which we can now meet with them, or find the weather-roll or the lee-lurch to perfection. They are all thoroughbred; and a thorough-bred seaman is one of the drollest compounds in existence: a mixture of all that is ludicrous and grave—of undaunted courage and silly fear. I do not mean the every-day sailor, but the bold, daring, intrepid man-of-war's man; him who in the time of action primed his wit and his gun together, without a fear of either missing fire. He has a language peculiarly his own, and his figures of rhetoric are perfect reef-knots to the understanding of a landsman. If he speaks of his ship, his eloquence surpasses the orations of a Demosthenes, and he revels in the luxuriance of metaphor. The same powers of elocution, with precisely the same terms, are applied to his wife, and it is a matter of doubt which engrosses the greatest portion of his affection: to him they are both *lady-ships*. Hear him expatiate on his *little barky*, as he calls his wooden island, though she may be able to carry a hundred and fifty huns, and a crew of a thou- [243] sand men. "Oh! she is the fleetest of the fleet—sits on the water like a duck—stands under her canvas as stiff as a crutch—and turns to windward like a witch!" Of his wife he observes, "what a clean run from stem to stern! She carries her t-gallants through every breeze, and in turning hang for hang never misses stays." He will point to the bows of his ship, and swear she is as sharp as a wedge, never stops at a sea, but goes smack through all. He looks at his wife, admires her headgear and bow-lines, compares her eyes to dolphin-strikers, boasts of her fancy and fashion-pieces, and declares that she darts along with all the grace of a bonnetta. When he parts with his wife to go on a cruise, no tear moistens his cheek: there is the honest pressure of the hand, the fervent kiss, and then he claps on the topsail-halliards, or walks round at the capstan to the lively sounds of music. But when he quits his ship, the being he has rigged with his own fingers, that has stood under him in many a dark and trying hour, whilst the wild waves have dashed over them with relentless fury, then—then—the scuppers of his heart are unplugged, and overflow with the soft droppings of sensibility. How often has he stood upon that deck and eyed the swelling sails, lest the breezes of heaven should visit their "face too roughly!" How many hours has he stood at that helm, and watched her coming up and falling off! and when the roaring billows have threatened to ingulph her in the bubbling foam of the dark waters, he has eased her to the sea [244] with all the tender anxiety that a mother feels for her darling child. With what pride has he beheld her top the mountain wave, and climb the rolling swell, while every groan of labour that she gave carried a taught strain upon his own heart-strings!

Place confidence in what he says, and he will use no deception; doubt his word, and he will indulge you with some of the purest rhodomontade that ingenious fancy can invent. He will swear that he had a messmate who knew the man in the moon, and on one occasion went hand-over-hand up a rainbow to pay him a visit. He himself was once a powder-monkey in the Volcano bomb, and will tell you a story of his falling asleep in the mortar at the bombardment of Toulon, and his body being discharged from its mouth instead of a *carcass*. With all the precision of an engineer, he will describe his evolutions in the air when they fired him off, and the manner in which he was saved from being dashed to pieces in his fall.

All this he repeats without a smile upon his countenance—and he expects you to believe it: but you may soon balance the account; for, tell him what absurdity you will, he receives it with the utmost credulity, and is convinced of its truth. His courage is undoubted, for he will stand on the deck undismayed, amidst the blood and slaughter of battle; yet on shore he is seized with indescribable apprehensions at the sight of a coffin. The wailings of distress find a ready passport to his heart; but, to disguise the real motives [245] which prompt immediate aid, he swears that the object of his charity does not deserve a copper, yet gives a pound, with only this provision, that the individual relieves does not bother him about gratitude. You may know him from a thousand; for though in his dress conspicuously neat, and his standing and running rigging in exact order, yet they are arranged with a certain careless ease, as if he had but just come down from reefing topsails. The truck at the mast-head does not sit better than his tarpawling hat, neither does the show upon the pea of the anchor fit tighter than his long-quartered pumps. Grog is his ambrosia, his *neck-tar*, and he takes it cold, without sugar, that he may have the full smack of the rum.

And these are the characters at Greenwich Hospital, who, after fighting the battles of their country, are honoured with a palace. Oh, it was a proud display of national gratitude to such brave defenders! England has been compared to a huge marine animal, a sort of lobster, whose ports were its mouths, and whose navy formed its claws. What, then, is Greenwich but a receptacle for superannuated claws? I dearly love to get amongst them—nearly two thousand shattered emblems of Britain's triumphs. then, to see them strolling about the park, luxuriating on its green mossy banks, or holding strange converse with the deer, they always remind me, in their blue dresses, of bachelor's buttons springing from the sward.

"You were with Nelson then?" said I to a pen- [246] sioner with whom I had entered into conversation. He was a short, thickset man, apparently between sixty and seventy years of age; and, as he hobbled along on his wooden leg, he strongly reminded me of a heavy-laden Indiaman, with a heel to port, rolling down before the wind from the Cape of Good Hope to Saint Helena. His countenance was one of mild benevolence; and yet there was a daring in his look that told at once a tale of unsubdued and noble intrepidity; whilst the deep bronze upon his skin was finely contrasted with the silky white locks with hung straggling on his brow.

"You were with Nelson?" said I.

"I was, your honour," he replied; "and those were the proudest days of my life. I was with him when he bore up out of the line off Cape St. Vincent, and saved old Jarvis from disgrace. I was in his own ship too—the Victory—fighting on the same quarter-deck."

This was spoken with such an air of triumph that the old man's feature's were lighted up with animation; it called to his remembrance scenes in which he had shared the flory of the day and saved his country. His eye sparkled with delight, as if he again saw the British ensign floating in the breeze, as the proud signal for conquest, or was labouring at the oar, with his darling chief, like a tutelar deity of old, guiding the boat through the yielding element, and leading on to some daring and desperate enterprise. At this moment I felt somewhat of a mischievous inclination to try the [247] veteran's temper, and therefore remarked: "Nelson was a brave man, no doubt, but then he was tyrannical and cruel."

The hoary tar stopped, and looked me full in the face: a storm was gathering in his heart, or rather, like a vessel taken aback in a sudden squall, he stood perplexed which way to scud. But it was only for a moment; and, as his features relaxed their sternness, he replied: "No matter, your honour!—no matter! You have been kind to me and mine, and I'm no dog to bite the hand that helped me in adversity."

This seemed to be uttered with the mingling emotions of defiance and melancholy; and, to urge him further, I continued:—"But, my friend, what can you say of the treatment poor Caraccioli experienced? You remember that, I suppose?"

"I do, indeed!" he replied. "Poor old man! how earnestly he pleaded for the few short days which nature at the utmost could have allowed him! But, sir,"

Forget Me Not

add he, grasping my arm, "do you know what it is to have a fiend at the helm, who, when Humanity cries 'Port!' will clap it hard a-starboard in spite of you?—one who, in loveliness and fascination, is like an angel of light, but whose heart resembles an infernal machine, ready to explode whenever passion touches the secret spring of vengeance?"

I had merely put the question to him by way of joke, little expecting the result; but I had to listen to a tale of horror. [248]

"You give a pretty picture, truly, old friend," said I. "And, pray, who may this fiend be?"

"A woman, your honour; one full of smiles and sweetness, but she could gaze with indifference on a deed of blood, and exult over the victim her perfidy betrayed. It is a long story, but I must tell it you, that you may not think Nelson was cruel or unjust. His generous heart was deceived, and brought a stain upon the British flag, which he afterwards washed out with his blood. Obedience is the test of a seaman's duty—to reverence his king, and to fight for his country. This I have done, and therefore speak without fear, though I know nothing of parliaments and politics. Well, your honour, it was at the time when there was a mutiny among the people at Naples, and prince Caraccioli joined one of the parties against the court; but afterwards a sort of amnesty, or *damnification* I think they call it, was passed, by way of pardon to the rebels, many of whom surrendered, but they were all made prisoners, and numbers of them were executed.

"Well, one day I was standing at the gangway, getting the barge's sails ready, when a shore-boat came alongside, full of people who were making a terrible noise. At last they brought a venerable old man up the side; he was dressed as a peasant, and his arms were pinioned so tight behind that he seemed to be suffering from considerable pain. As soon as they had all reached the deck, the rabble gathered round him, some [249] cursing, others buffeting, and one wretch, unmindful of his gray hairs, spat upon hi,. This was too much to see and not speak about; the man was their prisoner, and they had him secure—the very nature of his situation should have been sufficient protection; so I gave the unmannerly fellow a tap with this little fist"—holding up a hand like a sledge-hammer—"and sent him flying into the boat again without the aid of a rope. 'Well done, Jack!' exclaimed a young midshipman, who is now a post-captain; 'Well done, my boy! I owe you a glass of grog for that; it was the best summerset I ever saw in my life.'—'Thank you for your glass o'grog, sir,' said I; 'you see I've made a *tumbler* already.' And indeed, your honour, he spun head over heels, head over heels, astonishingly clever. I was brought up to the quarter-deck for it, to be sure, because they said I had used the *why-hit-armis*; but I soon convinced them I had only used my fist, and the young officer who say the transaction stood my friend, and so I got off.

"Well, there stood the old man as firm as the rock of Giberaltar, not a single feature betraying the anguish he must have felt. His face was turned away from the quarter-deck, and his head was uncovered in the presence of his enemies. The Neapolitans still kept up an incessant din, which brought the first lieutenant to the gangway; he advanced behind the prisoner, and, pushing aside the abusive rabble, swore at them pretty fiercely for their inhumanity, although, at the same [250] time seizing the old man roughly, he brought him in his front. 'What traitor have we here?' exclaimed the lieutenant; but checking himself on viewing the mild countenance of the prisoner, he gazed more intently upon him. 'Eh, no—it surely cannot be—and yet it is'—his hat was instantly removed, with every token of respect, as he continued—'it is the prince!'

"The old man, with calm dignity, bowed his hoary head to the salute, and at this moment Nelson himself, who had been disturbed by the shouting of the captors, came from his cabin to the deck. He advanced quickly to the scene, and called out in his hasty when vexed, "Am I to be eternally annoyed by the confusion these fellows create! What is the matter here?' But when his eye had caught the time-and-toil-worn features of the prisoner, he sprang forward, and with his own hands commenced unbinding the cords. 'Monsters!' said he, 'is it this that age should be treated?—Cowards! do you fear a weak and unarmed old man?—Honoured prince, I grieve to see you degraded and injured by such baseness, and now,' he added, as the last turn released his arms 'dear Caraccioli, you are free!' I though a tear rolled down Nelson's cheek as he cast loose the lashing, which having finished, he took the prince's hand, and they both walked aft together.

"They say the devil knows precisely the nick of time when the most mischief is to be done, and so it [251] happened now, for a certain lady followed Nelson to the deck, and approached him with her usual bewitching smile. But oh! your honour, how was that smile changed to the black scowl of a demon when she pierced he disguise of the peasant and recognised the prince, who, on some particular occasion at court, had thwarted her views and treated her with indignity. It had never been forgiven, and now—he was in her power. Forcibly, she grasped Nelson by the arm, and led him to the cabin.

"'His doom is sealed,' said one of the lieutenants, conversing in an undertone with a brother officer; 'no power on earth can save him.' 'On earth!' rejoined the other, 'no, nor in the air, nor in the ocean, for I suspect he will meet his death in the one, and find his grave in the other.' 'Yet surely,' said the surgeon, who came up, 'Nelson will remember his former friendship for the prince, who once served under him. Every sympathetic feeling which is dear to a noble mind must operate to avert his death.' 'All the virtues in your medicine-chest, doctor,' rejoined the first, 'would not preserve him many hours from destruction, unless you could pour an opiate on the deadly malignity of'—here he put his finger upon his lip and walked away.

"Well, your honour, the old man was given up to his bitter foes, who went through the mockery of a court-martial, for them condemned him first and tried him afterwards. In vain he implored for mercy; in [252] vain he pleaded the proclamation, and pointed to his hoary head; in vain he solicited the mediation of Nelson, for a revengeful fury had possession of his better purposes, and dammed the rising tide of generosity on the hero's soul; in vain he implored the pardon and intercession of ——; but here I follow the example of my officer, and lay my finger on my lip.

"A few hours more, and the brave old man, the veteran prince, in his eightieth year, hung suspended for the fore-yard-arm of a ship he had once commanded. Never shall I forget the burst of indignation with which the signal-gun was heard by our crew, and a simultaneous execration was uttered fore and aft.

"Nelson walked the deck with unusual quickness, nay he almost ran, and every limb seemed violently agitated. He heard the half-suppressed murmurs of the men, and a conviction of dishonour seemed to be awakening in his mind. But, oh sir! where was pity, where was feminine delicacy and feeling? The lady approached him in the most seducing manner, and attracted his attention: he stopped short, looked at her for a moment with stern severity, and again walked on. 'What ails you, Bronté?' said she; 'you appear to be ill!' and the witchery of her commanding look subdued the sternness of his features—he gazed upon her and was tranquil. 'See!' said she, pointing out at the port to where the body of Caraccioli was still writhing in convulsive agony; 'see! his mortal struggles will [253] soon be over. Poor prince! I grieve we could not save him. But some, Bronté, man the barge, and let us go and take a parting look at our old friend.' I shuddered, your honour, and actually looked down at her feet to see if I could make out any thing like a cloven hoof. 'The devil!' exclaimed a voice in a half-whisper behind me that made me start, for I thought the speaker had certainly made the discovery, but it was only one of the officers giving vent to his pious indignation.

"Well, the barge was manned, and away we pulled, with Nelson and the lady, round the ship where the unfortunate prince was hanging. He had no cap upon his head, nor was his face covered, but his white hair streamed in the breeze above the livid contortions which the last death-pang had left upon his features. The Neapolitans were shouting, and insulting his memory; but they were rank cowards, for the truly brave will never wreak their vengeance on a dead enemy.

"Nelson and the lady conversed in whispers, but it was plain to be seen his spirit was agonized, and his fair but frail companion was employing every art to soothe him. She affected to weep, but there was a glistening pleasure in her eyes, as she looked at the corpse, which had well nigh made the boat's crew set all duty at defiance. Nelson—and no man was better acquainted with the characteristics of a sailor—saw this, and ordered to be rowed on board. She upbraided [254] him for what she called his weakness, but his soul was stirred beyond the power of her influence to control his actions.

"A few days afterwards, a pleasure party was made up amongst the nobility for an excursion on the water, and the barge, with Nelson and his mistress, took the lead. It was beautiful sight to see the gilded galleys, with their silken canopies and pennons flashing in the sun and reflecting their glittering beauties, on the smooth surface of the clear blue waters, whilst the measured sweep of the oars kept time with the sweet sounds of music. Not a cloud veiled the sky, not a breath curled the transparent crest of the gentle billow; all was gaiety and mirth.

"After pulling for some miles to the entrance of the bay, we were returning towards the shore, when a dark objet, resembling a bale of goods, appeared floating ahead of the barge. The bow men were directed to lay in their oars and see what it was. They obeyed, and stood ready with their boat hooks, which, the moment they were near enough, were used in grappling the supposed prize. But in an instant they were loosened again, and 'A dead body! a dead body!' was uttered in a suppressed tone by both. They boat held on her way, and, as the corpse passed astern, the face turned upwards, and showed the well-remembered countenance of poor Caraccioli. Yes! as the lieutenant had said, he met his death in the air, and the ocean had been his grave; but that grave had [255] given up its dead, and the lady seldom smiled afterwards.

"Nelson hailed one of the cutters that were in attendance, and directed that the body should be taken on board, and receive the funeral ceremonies suitable to the rank of the unfortunate prince had held whilst living. The music ceased its joyous sounds for notes of melancholy wailing, and the voice of mirth was changed to lamentation and sadness.

"Years passed away, and Nelson fell in the hour of victory; but the lady! ah! her end was terrible. The murdered prince was ever present to her mind; and as she lay upon her deathbed, like a stranded wreck that would never more spread canvas to the breeze, her groans, her shrieks, were still on Caraccioli. 'I see him!' she would cry, 'there, there!—look at his white locks, and his straining eyeballs! England—England is ungrateful, or this would have been prevented. But I follow—I follow'—and then she would shriek with dismay, and hide herself from sight. But she is gone, your honour, to give in her dead reckoning to the Judge of all. She died in a foreign land, without one real friend to close her eyes; and she was buried in a stranger's grave, without one mourner to weep upon the turf which covered her remains."

Title
Thompson, W. G. "Fanny Lee." FMN 1830. 261-271. [261]

FANNY LEE
BY W. G. THOMPSON, ESQ.

There is many a lovely vale in England, but perhaps none more lovely than the sweetly sequestered spot which bears the name of Heaton Dean; there is none, at least, so sacred or so dear to me. I well remember, even at this distant hour, the inexpressible joy with which I have trodden that fragrant scene, when the sweets of summer were strewn around with nature's amplest profusion, in the company of one who has long since ceased to be an inhabitant of this earth; one to whom I have listened till the delight of hearing had absorbed all inclination to reply, and every feeling was wrapt up in the music of a voice which is now mingling with the melody of the spheres, and which, to me, was only excelled by the warblings of that brilliant race which seemed ever the most animated and the most musical in her presence. even when the naked grove emitted no sound but the bleak and melancholy moanings of the dying year; when the rapid rivulet rushed impetuously to bury itself in the bosom of the upheaving ocean, or was indurated by the chilling breath of hoary winter; the severe grandeur of its ridgy outlines, of its steep and inaccessible banks of snow, had a charm which, when shared with her, neither the radiance of summer nor the sweet and cheering voice of spring has since imparted. When she—But why is this? I meant merely to relate her favourite [262] legend, and find myself entering into particulars which can never interest any heart but the baffled and disappointed one that beats in my bosom. I believe that there are spots hallowed to every memory; that there are walks, and trees, and stones, and jutting rocks, associated with the mind by tenderest affinity; the scenes of a thousand spirit-stirring things; where youthful hearts have poured the overflowings of affection; where the tears of kindred sorrow have dropped and mingled; where friendships have been formed, which it was the business of after life to cement; where wrongs have been perpetrated and reproaches interchanged, which ended in heart- breakings, misery, and despair. It is with feelings generated by such a belief, that I have glanced for one moment at Heaton Dean. ——But to the legend.

Little Fanny Lee was an orphan, and entered at an early age into the service of honest Mable, the miller of the Dean. The miller and his wife were kind creatures, and as they had n children of their own, the orphan Fanny became unto them as a daughter. The equable tenor of an humble occupation, like that of which I speak, affords but few facilities for description, being merely the reciprocal succession of labour and repost, never interrupting the quiet interchange of good nature, gentleness, and peace; in the language of the poet,

"Pursuing thus the ever running year
with profitable labour to the grave."
[263]

Years rolled on—the ripening buds of spring burst forth to flower and beauty; the brilliant summer deepened into the gorgeous hues of autumn; till the seared tints faded and twirling leaves fell, and winter came, like the shade of buried pleasures, and gemmed the trees with icicles, and strewed the fields with snow. Fanny Lee, no longer little Fanny, had also sprung from bud to beauty, and the charms of womanhood were dawning in as sweet a form as ever sought and received shelter in a rustic valley; her autumn was far in the distance, and the winter of gray age had no place in the aerial perspective. She knew the debt of gratitude which she owed to her honest protectors, and se was faithful in its assiduous discharge: perhaps there never was a happier family. Fanny had her moments of inquietude, and these consisted in wild and vague imaginings respecting the authors of her being; who and what they were, and whence they came, and how they had departed. On these themes she would sit and commune with her own heart through many an anxious hour, till her flushed cheek and glistening eye sufficiently declared the fruitlessness of her reveries. Her kind mistress would say at such times, "Why shouldst thou be unhappy, Fanny, in the absence of information which, if known, might not be productive of satisfaction to thee? Be content, my dear child, that thou art here, and good and kind, and in the paths of happiness. Whoever were thy parents here, thy heavenly Father, Fanny, has been kind to thee." And [264] Fanny would clasp her hands, and with upturned and streaming eyes acknowledge that it was so.

Of the various inherent energies of the human mind, none is stronger than love. It cannot be constrained by mastery. When once it is lighted up in the heart of a young and generous creature, its sway is as the sway of death—irresistible and destroying. Fanny Lee loved! It were tedious to detail the means which led to this very natural occurrence—to follow the lovers in their evenings walks,

"When but the silent stars stood witness of their joy" —

to relate the eloquent appeal, the murmuring fond reply, and all the ecstasies of young and extravagant passion. There was a little moss-grown seat, overarched by high and leafy trees, close to the margin of a naturally-formed reservoir, which, from the amplitude of the stream, usually wore the appearance of a sweetly sheltered lake. Here would the lovers sit for hours, and entertain the fondest anticipations of future bliss, and here, on this seat, and underneath these trees, in the presence of approving Heaven, was the small silver coin broken between them, the several parts of which were never to come in contact more, whilst love or life remained in either heart.

Henry Thornhill was the pride of Heaton Dean. Tall in stature, and beautiful in proportion, he was as manly in heart and feeling as he was in action and appearance. He was the approved lover of Fanny Lee—her affianced husband—the future father of her child- [265] dren—the guardian of her fortunes—and, above all, the one sole idol of her own pure, and gentle, and affectionate heart. Loud have been the exclamations against the evils of this world, the worthlessness of its pleasures, and the depravity and wickedness of its passions. In nine cases out of ten these are mere miserable affectations, the result of disappointed intrigue or satiated indulgence. This world has many a bright and beautiful scene, and there are hours in the life of a man which are well worth the living for. Say, ye who have stood in the situation of Henry Thornhill, with the panoply of hope on your hearts, and the flowery path of life before you, in which you go hand in hand and step by step with a young, intelligent, and confiding creature—in her beauty radiant as the morning—in her affection warm as the mid-day sun—what can be conceived of delight to equal the visions of such a time? But I must return to my story.

A rich and glorious harvest had just been swept, as it were, from the generous soil by the laborious hand of the husbandman; the air rang with mirth, and gaiety was in the faces and gratitude in the hearts of all. In this season of universal joy our lovers drank deeply of rural delight, and with the approbation of the kind miller they were immediately to ratify the hymeneal contract. Young Henry departed to the neighbouring town to purchase the wedding-ring, cheered by the cordial benedictions of amiable friends, and animated by the blushing smiles of his betrothed. [266]

The autumn nights of England are beautiful. The moon held soft and undivided sway throughout the clear and glorious expanse of her sweet and silent dominion. The air was filled with the balm of fragrant shrubs and odour-breathing flowers, and the stillness of night was broken only by the gentle murmur of the rivulet. Fanny Lee came forth to meet her lover on his return, to see his small but sacred purchase, to hear a few syllables of ardent affection, to return the pressure of a fond embrace, and seek the dreams of innocence and joy which still await the happy heart of contentment, even on the lowly pillow of a cottage-couch. The hallowed beauty of the evening communicated a balm to her feelings inexpressibly delicious. She had no power of expressing the sensations which thronged on her pure and grateful heart. Her situation was like that of one who wanders under the influence and amid the fairy scenery of a wild dream of enchantment. She had crossed the burn and passed the stile, but still the manly figure of Henry rose not on her sight. She went on, for there was nothing in that lovely scene to blanch the cheek of innocence: she reached the bridge, but still he was not there. She paused, she listened, but no step disturbed the stirless leaves; no snatch of rustic melody broke on the balmy air. She sat down with something like a feeling of disappointment—she would wait one moment, for she knew he would come. Perhaps there is nothing more trying than the breathless suspense of such a moment. [267] The air seems thick, and laden with low and dreamlike murmurs of every sound but that you wish to hear. The very beatings of your own anxious heart arise in tumult on the pained ear, and bury sounds remote. Still, still he came not. With the sense and the modesty which characterized all her actions, and possibly with a feeling of regret, she returned—returned to commune with her agitated heart, till "nature's sweet restorer" should wrap her in deep repose.

On the ensuing day it was known that Henry Thornhill had never reached his home. One, two, three long days elapsed, and yet no tidings of the fugitive. The feelings of the forlorn Fanny must be imagined—to attempt a description of them would be a presumption of which I shall not be guilty. It was now the serious duty of Mable to repair to the town, and ascertain, if possible, what had become of the lost lover. By a mere accident did Mable learn the fate of young Thornhill. At the time of which I am writing, England was in the triumphant prosecution of a devastating war—the service wanted men, and Thornhill had been impressed. The athletic form of the peasant had attracted the attention of the lieutenant; he entered into conversation with him; part of the gang appeared; the officer insulted his victim, who indignantly struck him to the earth; he was seized, and, after a desperate resistance, overpowered, manacled, and borne away. Complaint was fruitless, for redress was unknown. Henry Thornhill departed with a bleed- [268] ing heart for new scenes—to face his country's foes on a dangerous element, and without the hope of return.

The distressing tidings were communicated to Fanny Lee; and, oh! the havoc they made in the heart of that young, and sanguine, and confiding creature! When the first burst of her exquisite agony had subsided, a deep and solemn melancholy overpowered her for many days. She spoke to no one; she seemed not to recognise any object, however well known before.

The last leaves of autumn were dropping from the trees, and the bleak wintry winds began to howl through the woods of Heaton, when a poor, weak maniac was observed wandering over the scenes of former gladness—it was Fanny Lee! The light and bounding step of youth was changed to the cold and cheerless shuffle of idiot imbecility; the vivid hue of health was banished by the sepulchral colour of despair; the eye that beamed the lustre of love and gratitude was quenched in the dim and glassy glare of madness. The seat above the little lake was her favourite resort: there she would sit, and weep, and gaze for whole hours on the piece of broken silver suspended from her neck by a blue riband, singing at times, in melancholy tones, of seamen on the far and tempest troubled ocean—and many a broken ditty which has long since been forgotten. One has been preserved—a rude and simple strain. How she came by it was never known. The country people said she made it all herself, as she [269] wandered in the cold moonlight. She sang it, in her solemn and impressive moments, on the accustomed seat where the silver piece was broken. Of the air I have no record—I believe it was entirely her own. The words were nearly as follows:

> He comes from afar,
>   Where the billows are sounding
> He comes from afar,
>   Where the wild waves are bounding!
> He comes to his trysting
>   Beneath the green tree:—
> But, alas, for the maiden
>   He never shall see!
>   Never, oh, never!—
>   Blighted for ever!
> Alas, for the maid whom he never shall see!
>
> Deep, deep in the wild glen
>   A grave is preparing;
> And, hark! to her lone home
>   The maid they are bearing.
> Full sweet will her sleep be
>   From sorrow and pain;
> But ne'er shall she meet with
>   Her lover again!
>   Never, oh, never!—
>   Blighted for ever!
> Ne'er shall she meet with her lover again!
>
> O whisper, ye trees! when
>   His lost one he's seeking;
> Bear to him the words of
>   A heart that is breaking!
> Say how well she loved him
>   In sorrow and pain,
> [270]
> When madness came over
>   Her heart and her brain.
>   Buried for ever!
>   Never, oh, never
> Shall he maid of his bosom behold him again!

Winter was now raging with all his fury, and it was the peculiar care of old Mable to make Fanny Lee abide the warmth and the comforts of his fireside. One day the poor heart-broken creature, always gentle, had demeaned herself with unusual affection and resignation. She had moaned over many of her rude rhymes, when she suddenly lifted her head, and said—"Mistress, think you, will Harry come back again? I will —" she added, with a deep sigh—"It was my hope to be the mistress of this bonnie mill when kind old Mable's head was laid: but, oh, the changes!" said she, bursting into tears; "now will old Mable see me lying low, and he a strong old man still. But I will come again, mistress; and when the waters thunder down the Dean, and Mable works all night, I'll sing some of my bonniest verses, and he will wipe his eyes, as he does now, and say, 'Poor Fanny Lee!'" A flood of tears prevented her proceeding, and her auditors were too much affected to reply. Towards evening she became quite collected, and said she would walk to the seat among the trees before it grew darker. She went out accordingly—but in a few minutes she was lost—no one had seen her—no one could find her. A heavy fall of snow came on, accompanied by intense frost, which continued for several days. Deep was [271] the interest created by the disappearance of Fanny. Had she wandered to the town?—she would have been seen. Had she destroyed herself?—oh, no! she was too good for that. Had she perished in the snow?—some one surely would have found her. On the breaking up of the frost, she was discovered by two little girls lying in the lake below the mill, into which she had probably fallen in returning from her favourite seat. And so they laid her in her early grave, amid the tears and regret of the few who had known her in the short season of her joy, and the heavy hours of her adversity. A white stone, with her name and age, still marks the spot where her once beautiful form has mingled with the dust of congregated generations, on which the rustic chronicler has engraven the touching words—

"THERE IS REST IN THE GRAVE."

What became of Henry Thornhill I never could learn; but it was said that, when honest old Mable lay on his death-bed, the mournful voice of Fanny was heard every night, in low melodious chant, until the good old man was gathered to the house of his fathers.

The Dean is as romantic, and the mill as picturesque, as ever—the trees still wave in verdant grandeur above the little seat—but in summer the lake is almost dry. I sometimes think—a foolish fancy, perhaps—that the rivulet has wept itself away in the very sorrow for its instrumentality in the death of poor Fanny Lee.

Title

Thomson, Richard. "The Antiquary and His Fetch. A Legend of the Strand." FMN 1830. 279-302. [279]

THE ANTIQUARY AND HIS FETCH
A LEGEND OF THE STRAND
BY RICHARD THOMSON, ESQ.,
AUTHOR OF "TALES OF AN ANTIQUARY," &c. &c.

> "Speak to me what thou art.—
> Thy evil spirit, Brutus."
>   SHAKSPEARE.

Several years before that period when "Anne and piety" endeavoured to amend the morals of London, by erecting within it fifty new churches, that part of the Strand nearly opposite to Somerset-House was a broad piece of unoccupied ground, in the centre of which stood its famous and very capital May-pole. Towering to the height of a hundred and thirty feet over the low shops and antique dwellings in its vicinity, it looked like "the mast of some great ammiral;" or, to a romantic fancy, seemed to be the staff of Brutus Greenshield, or Gerard the Giant, or any other of the ancient and invincible heroes of Londinum, planted in barren magnificence before the gates of his beloved metropolis. For the greater part of the year it appeared little more than a plain shaft of cedar, blackened by exposure to the smoke and weather, which it had endured ever since 1661, when it was erected to commemorate the Restoration: but, "when the sweet spring-time did fall," its gilded vane and other ornaments were carefully cleaned; and on May-day eve it was decorated with flags and flower-garlands, silver [280] plate and green boughs, being one of the principal scenes of festivity in the ensuing holiday.

Without making the reader acquainted with all the residents in this part of London at the time when our story commences—namely, in the afternoon of Monday the eighth of September, in the year of grace 1701—we must introduce him to one rather strange character, Master Nicolaus Mouldwarp, who lodged opposite the May-pole, on the north side, with a noted druggist of the time, whose sign was a rhinoceros, in allusion to the medical properties of that animal's horn, though it was most generally referred to as "The Hog in Armour." Master Mouldwarp was a very famous collector of curiosities, or those wonderful stray fragments of antiquity which perpetually puzzle use to imagine how they could possibly have escaped the tooth of Time, since the old *Edax Rerum* is continually devouring morsels which are far less delicate and *recherché*. In person, our antiquary was a very tall, thin, melancholy, and yet fierce-looking, old gentleman, with a coarse sandy wig; sunken gray eyes, continually lowering with discontent;

a perpetual sneer curling between his hooked nose and upper lip; very hollow cheeks, and a visage of the colour and texture of old stained parchment. From this last feature, connected with his being a most zealous supporter of the Prince of Orange, whom he followed to England, and his boasted descent from several of the most ancient Dutch families, he was not unfrequently called Myn- [281] heer Illskin. Indeed his property had been amassed in Holland, for as *Dogberry* says, he was a "rich fellow enough;" though it was often suspected that he had acquired it with more good fortune than honesty, since the real heir to it, to whom Mouldwarp was left guardian, though he had never seen him, was said to have died in that receptacle for idiocy, the Dull-house of Amsterdam. At any rate, he was on morning missing, and, as his fits of lunacy were sometimes rather powerful, there was good hope for Master Mouldwarp that he would never return; and so, converting his property into dollars and guilders, under pretence of searching for him, he brought it away to England, and arrived her about the close of the seventeenth century. The predominating feature of our antiquary's mind was an unbounded selfishness; and he often rejoiced in being a bachelor, who could indulge his humours without having to provide for either "kith or kin;" so that it will be readily imagined his disposition was not much better than his looks. He was infected, past cure, with the endemic disease of antiquaries and all collectors—jealousy; and some of his contemporaries declared that he had fretted his skin yellow by repining over the increase of his fraternity, and the treasures which they were continually snatching from him, though he always contrived to hint that they were counterfeits. His vexation, thus awkwardly concealed, he also made yet more evident, by striving to mask it under a seemingly philanthropic inquiry [282] after his contemporaries, which usually contained some distant allusion to their decease, and the probable dispersion of their museums; though occasionally his temper would suddenly break out, when he was informed of any very extraordinary rarity passing into the possession of another.

Of all Master Mouldwarp's associated and rivals, he viewed none with more envy than the famous Sir Hans Sloane and his *protégé* and *ci-devant* valet, Don Saltero, whom, in reward of his services, had set up as a *curioso* and coffee-house keeper, with a small gratuity, and the odds and ends of his own collection. And truly he possessed some astonishing rarities, which caused Master Mouldwarp to look still more like discoloured parchment with vexation, and more melancholy with despair; though there were still some rather wonderful matters to be found in the cabinet at "The Hog in Armour:" so that it was s sort of neck-and-neck between the two virtuosi. For, if Don Saltero justly prided himself upon having a genuine piece of the skin of Queen Catherine of Arragon, Master Mouldwarp could show a tall glass of spirits enclosing a tail—of a monkey, as some said and swore—but in reality taken from the very last of those Kentishmen whom Thomas á Becket gifted with such an appendage, as a penance for their having wantonly

Forget Me Not

docked his horse. This was a noble acquisition; and so was our antiquary's genuine mooncalf, also preserved in an antique bottle. But then Don Saltero had [283] a whole child petrified! and the trunk of a large tree, shaped by nature so wonderfully like a swine, that many considered it to be actually "a lignified hog!" Then he had the body of a starved cat, supposed to be upwards of two centuries old, having belonged to the abbots of Westminster; being taken, during a repair, from between the two walls in the Abbey;—and he had Queen Elizabeth's work-basket, and her strawberry-dish, and Pontius Pilate's wife's sister's chambermaid's hat! and, in short, so many other rarities, that altogether Master Mouldwarp was little less than weary of his life, and quite disgusted with the disappointments and vanities of the world.

As the reader has seen that he had rather a peculiar taste for supernatural curiosities, he will not be surprised to learn that our antiquary was nor principally desirous of obtaining a jewel of that kind which would certainly go near to immortalise his museum, and make it famous through the civilised world. This was that mysterious book, belonging to the noted Dr. Simon Forman, wherein was the following remarkable memorandum: "This I made the devil write with his own hand in Lambeth Fields, 1596 in June or July, as I now remember." After the death of Forman, about 1624, Master Mouldwarp traced his manuscripts to Elias Ashmole, and from him the university of Oxford; though, after all his inquiries, he never could find if the wondrous volume were with them. He was nevertheless perfectly convinced of its existence, and [284] hope—flattering hope, which so often proved a will-o'-the-wisp to collectors—induced him to believe that it might one day be his own; but, until he should arrive at this consummation, he viewed his museum as fair, but imperfect; as we may conceive Allah ad Deen looked upon his genie-palace when he was told that it wanted a roc's egg suspended in the dome; or Perie-Zadeh saw her beautiful villa deficient in the golden water, singing-tree, and talking-bird.

It was with this feeling that he set out on the afternoon of that day when our story commences, to spend the remained of it at Don Saltero's coffee-house; which, as every one knows, originally stood, and still does stand, about the middle of Cheyne-walk, near Battersea-bridge, overlooking the broad stream of the silver Thomas. To visit this very celebrated museum was the general recreation and employment of the antiquaries and citizens of a former day; though, to such as Master Mouldwarp, it was at least equally a plague and a delight, since the whole building was literally crammed with curiosities which they could have no hope of rivalling. An alligator stuffed was stretched along the ceiling of the passage, and ancient armour and firelocks guarded the walls; as of old your fiery dragons and armed giants kept watched over the treasures of enchanted castles. The front apartment in the first story, was, however, the grand scene of attraction, it being covered in every part, excepting the floor, with that miscellaneous kind of varieties

[285] which gave unlearned visitors the greatest satisfaction: since they embrace all sorts of subjects, undisturbed by any scientific arrangement, and are more calculated to excite wonder than to convey instruction.

Having ascended the stairs, we must just point out to the reader that Master Salter, or Don Saltero, as he calls himself, the host, is that tall, sharp-faced, foreign-looking man, who is gliding about the room in a full-dress suit of dirty light blue, and tarnished silver lace; with a silk hat under one arm, a napkin beneath the other, a white apron before him, and a pair of snuffers suspended at his girdle, which was at this time the ordinary badge of waiters and men of his profession. The afternoon glided tranquilly away: Master Mouldwarp inspected the curiosities for perhaps the twentieth time, drank his coffee, deposited his fee, and then was about to set forward to London, as the evening appeared darker than usual, and in 1701 the road was not considered very safe after dusk. "Well, Don Saltero! well!" began Master Mouldwarp, in retiring from the coffee-room, and for the last time glancing discontentedly around him, "anything new with the virtuosi? any more antiquaries and collectors, eh, don? though, Heaven knows, there's enough of us, if the one half were to devour the other."

"Your worship hath said right wisely," answered Saltero in a grave tone, and bowing very profoundly; "there be already more mouths than food, as it hath been my fate to note in the western Indies, whither I [286] went with the most erudite Sir Hans Sloane. Touching news, I trow your honour knoweth how Master Cankerworm hath gotten a very curious word, dug up in the foundation of the new cathedral of St. Paul, and thought to have belonged to the British kind Lever Mawr, or Lucius."

"The plague take that fellow Cankerworm!" ejaculated Master Mouldwarp, "he's always snatching the bread out of my mouth; for, do you know, Don Saltero, that I gave a handsome fee to the clerk of the works at that same cathedral, only to have the first sight of any thing which might be dug up in my poor way? for I never wish to supplant other people. However, Don Saltero, I don't believe old Cankerworm's sword can be genuine. I think it's a flam, Don Saltero; and we're not sure that KING Lever Mawr ever existed, Don Saltero; Bishop Nicolson thinks he never did, and I think so too, Don Saltero."

"And your worship will indubitably have heard," replied the unmoveable host, not noticing his visitor's vexation; "your worship will have heard, that Master Polypus hath had a new stoke of apoplexy."

"Poor Polypus! poor Polypus!" rejoined Mouldwarp, with a kind of complacent melancholy; "he'll mend again, I trust; though, to be sure, I doubt it. And pray, Don Saltero, if any thing should happen to him—which God defend!—but there may, you know,—what do you think will become of his museum? will it come to the market, eh, Don Saltero?" [287]

"By no means improbable, your honour," answered the coffe-house keeper.

"Why, then if it should, don" replied Mouldwarp, "I'll have out of it that piece of Noah's ark, from the Mountains of the Moon, in Armenia, if I go to the workhouse for it; for I can do as I like; I've neither kith nor kin to provide for, you know. Old Polypus snatched it away from me at Dr. Frowzy's sale, and I take it to be one of the greatest curiosities in the world, except that piece of the devil's handwriting, which I could never yet find out."

"But which," said Don Saltero, "I am now to give your honour joy at having procured."

"How! what! you rascal!" exclaimed Master Mouldwarp passionately; then, adding, in his usual discontented tone, "But I see, don, it's a joke. Well, well! I can take a joke with any body; but we antiquaries are a thin-skinned generation touching our hobbies, you know."

"Heaven forbid that I should just with your honour!" returned Don Saltero; "but your worship assuredly said yesterday, in my poor house here, that you had the devil's handwriting."

"Why, thou villanous old travelling tonsor," rejoined Mouldwarp, "I've not seen the inside of your den of monsters for this month before; and will you persuade me that I was here yesterday?"

"In the society of several other honourable and in- [288] genious gentlemen," answered the don, in a calm unaltered voice, "curious to see so great a rarity."

"Then let them go where it is to be had," said Mouldwarp, turning away; "for, I believe in my conscience, that the writers has had back his manuscript. I tell you, once more, Don Saltero, that I've searched every where for the devil's handwriting, and never yet could find it."

"Then I'll show it to you," said a voice behind them, exactly resembling Mouldwarp's; "ay, and the pen with which it was written, and the ink dried upon its point! I had them from my father."

As they started round at this speech, there appeared on the other side of Don Saltero a figure, in every respect resembling Mouldwarp, with yellow hair, a sallow and sinister-looking visage, and clothed in that particular Dutch habit which it was the antiquary's pride and custom to retain."

"Worthy Master Mouldwarp," exclaimed the alarmed Don Saltero, "speak again, that I may know which is your honour in flesh and blood; for I deem that one of you is the other's ghostly fetch, come to give notice of his death."

"Why, here I am, you old fool!" returned he of the Hog in Armour, in something of a passion, to cover his fear; "it is all a fetch indeed, I well believe; but I'll be better acquainted with this person before I leave the house. And so pray, sir, what may you be?" [289]

"Half a man," was the brief reply.

"Indeed! and what brings you here?" continued Mouldwarp.

"To look for my other half, which ran away from me two years ago. But, to pass from this matter, which some of my good friends say has turned my brain, let's talk like virtuosi, who are madmen of another sort. I'll assure you, sir, that it's very true which I said touching the devil's handwriting; and as I'm most anxious that you should see it, as we walk through Chelsea together, you shall step into my house and look at it."

"I thank you, sir," replied the antiquary, hesitating and looking up at the sky; "but I must hasten home; the evening looks lowering, and part of the road to London is not very safe to travel late upon."

"Ay," returned his counterfeit, also looking upwards, "there will indeed be a storm to-night, and that of no common-sort: but you'll be in no greater danger than you are now; I'll see you safe myself, and I well believe you have no fear from me," added he sarcastically.

"Oh no!—by no means," said Mouldwarp, swallowing some odd doubts which were beginning to arise in his mind; "and if it stand with your liking we'll set out at once." To this the stranger agreed, and the antiquary and his fetch departed from Don Saltero's coffee-house.

The skies had grown dark, both with the approach- [290] ing storm and the shades of evening, when the strangers stopped at a dilapidated and seemingly empty house in the oldest part of Chelsea. The shutters of the windows had been originally closed, but they were now dropping piecemeal from this place, and discovered the discoloured and broken glass and the decaying frames beneath them; whilst within the building nothing was to be seen but an almost impenetrable darkness. However, Master Mouldwarp's companion pushed open the broken and creaking door, groped his way to a gloomy staircase, and calling upon the antiquary to follow him, seized his hand and led him on to an upper apartment, which he unlocked, and which seemed something to resemble the habitation of a human being. The furniture was old and stately; there were hung against the dark and broken windows some fragments of ancient stained glass; a few stuffed animals and other curiosities lay scattered about the apartment; and the walls were hung with several fine specimens of armour and swords, which were preserved in the most beautiful order, especially the latter. Having lighted a lamp, the owner of these treasures produced two tall Flemish glasses, and an ancient leathern bottle in a case of camel's hair, such as the Turks use in the journeys to Mecca, which had probably come originally from some Egyptian caravan. Out of this he poured a curious sort of thin sparkling wine, seemingly of great age; and, inviting his guest to sit down and taste it, assured him that it was probable no other person in [291] Europe could produce so wondrous a beverage. They partook of it together, and Master Mouldwarp found it to be a kind of cordial of most exquisite flavour, though of a fiery quality, and declined drinking any more of it; upon which his host said in an ironical tone, "Well, as you will; but the first cup's enough, and another would make you neither better now worse. However, this wine's all too rare to give to such as don't know its value. But I pray you, honest friend, what do you think you're been drinking of?"

"Why," replied Mouldwarp, feeling very dissatisfied upon the subject, "perhaps some Greek or Egyptian wine of the last century. You surely have not given me poison, villain?"

"What, I!" said the stranger, "and took a glass of it myself! no, no, worthy sir, I trust that you'll live long and grow better. But to see, now, how good things may be thrown away! The wine which we have drunk together is full fourteen hundred years old, being a bottle of that very elixir which St. Macarius saw the devil carrying through the desert to tempt the hermits withal, towards the end of the fourth century, you know."

"Why, you rascal!" exclaimed Mouldwarp, "I'll have you taken up and burned for a wizard! A proper story, truly, to decoy me into an old house, fit only for thieves or cut-throats, and to tell me a lying legend, after giving me poison for wine!" [292]

"If the legend lies," answered the stranger calmly, "'tis no sin of mine, for you may read it for yourself in the *Legenda Aurea* of the learned Jacobus de Voragine; and, as for poisoning, you've the very man of all the world to be mended by that elixir, having, as you say, neither kith nor kin; for if any two persons drink of the same bottle, their fates are untied for ever afterwards; all that happens to one falls upon the other, and they die at the same time, and in the same manner. I've been taken for you already, you know, and now you'll be taken for me. I told you I was looking for my other half. But it's a pity that we're not of the same way of thinking, for you're a Williamite and I'm a Jacobite. However, that will be all one now, for I shall be taken for a whig, and you will be suspected for a tory."

"You shall be clapped up for a rebel, or a madman, and that before I'm an hour older," said Mouldwarp, preparing to depart.

"What!" replied his host, "without seeing the devil's handwriting?"

"Pshaw!" exclaimed the antiquary, "I've seen enough of his works already; so let me go, fellow, and be quit of you."

"I will detain you but little longer," said the stranger. "But, tell me, did you ever hear of Andrew Greysteil, the sword-maker, who stabbed his son for discovering his secret of tempering his blades?" [293]

"Yes," answered Mouldwarp, impatiently, "I think I heard of one Andreas Stahl at Amsterdam, of whom such a story was told: and what of him?"

"Why," said his host, taking up a beautifully rapier encrusted with ancient stains of blood, "this is the weapon which he did it withal. Say, then, was not that murder a crime written with the very hand of the fiend? and was not this direful blade the pen which he traced it, dipped in his own fatal stream?"

"Man of evil and folly!" cried Mouldwarp, "let me begone; I'll listen to you no longer."

"Only a few moments more," rejoined the stranger, "whilst I come to your own matters, and then depart where you list, until fate brings us together again. Greysteil fled from his country, and became that Andreas Stahl whom you knew at Amsterdam, where he realised a fortune, and made you guardian to his remaining son, Walter, who—"

"Who was an idiot, a lunatic," interrupted Mouldwarp, "and died in the Dull-house there. He, too, was said to have done murder, or—"

"Say rather homicide," hastily returned his host, "and how deeply he repented it, his long confinement, unsettled reason, and miserable wanderings, might best prove. It was nevertheless accidental; for, shooting one day with a cross-bow at a mark, his arrow glanced from the target, struck one of his fellows, and left him a lunatic for life! There lies the shaft," continued he, [294] pointing to it, "the pend with which the fiend wrote a second time in the annals of our house; for I am Walter Greysteil, and you—are my treacherous guardian!"

When Mouldwarp recovered from the first shock of this announcement, he exclaimed with a hesitating voice, "If—if—it be as you say—I—I—really am rejoiced to find you, Master Greysteil,—that is to say, if you are he,—and—and—"

"And now begone in truth!" exclaimed his ward, interrupting him with a voice of strong contempt, "begone, thou grovelling worm, begone! Keep the miserable dollars which thou hast raked together from the mad orphan; I want them not, and thou wilt not long enjoy them. They will dishonour thee to return them, and damn thee to retain them, and thou wilt always possess in them the stamp and signature of the demon. But begone, begone! pollute my dwelling no longer! and remember, that for the future our fates are indissolubly united!" He then fell into the wild paroxysm of a maniac, and Mouldwarp hastened from the house, scarcely knowing where he went.

It was a dark and stormy night, when the antiquary, troubled in mind, fatigued in body, and drenched with rain arrived in London, and continued to walk hastily onward without observing the course which he took. At last his strength began to fail, and he looked round him for a coach or a shelter; but not a coach was to be seen, and moreover, he found that he had [295] mistaken his way, and now stood opposite to that famous old tavern in the Haymarket called the Blue Posts, from two painted and carved pillars which stood beside the door. It was at this period celebrated as a house for political meetings, and especially for the supposed *metallic* influence which Monsieur Poussine, the French ambassador to James II., was said to exert over its visitors, on behalf of the exiled king, together with his occasional entertainments, at which it was considered an indisputable sign of Jacobitism to be present. Without remembering these circumstances,—for if he had he would as soon as have entered the den of a dragon,—Master

Mouldwarp was attracted thither by the blazing fire and the cheerful sounds which used to distinguish the ancient taverns of London until the late hour of the night. Without listening to the waiter's address, he followed him into a large room, where a part of well-dressed persons were seated round a table smoking, drinking, and singing. The antiquary, supposing this to be no more that one of the ordinary clubs of the time, to which all strangers are indiscriminately admitted, seated himself without hesitation, and called for brandy; upon which one of the guests near him, pushing a bottle to him, said "There, sir, there are the goods, and so help yourself. That article, sir, is the right thing; real French, I'll promise you, and fit only for such *honest men*," a name generally assumed by the Jacobites, "as we are. There's good French wine, too, upon the table; but we're no [296] great friends to Hollands, oranges, or punch; eh, sire, d'ye take me?"

Whilst Mouldwarp was refreshing himself the host entered, and looking round said, "Gentlemen, if you're all honest men here, and love a good tune well played, perhaps you would like to hear a Scotch piper, who has brought some of the rarest music from France that you ever listened to: but he plays only to such as are very honest, I'll assure you."

"Send him up, landlord," answered the person who had spoken to Mouldwarp, glancing round the table with an intelligent look; "we're better than those who are worse, at any rate."

The suppressed sound of the pipes was now heard in the passage playing a lament, which caused the guests to look rather seriously upon each other, though the tune was shortly changed to that lively air entitled "Up and waur them a' Willie!" the inspiring sounds of which, joined to the good French wine and brandy, set hands and feet beating time to it. The performer then entered, playing a Highland march; and though habited in the ordinary dress of a person of his profession, his general air and manners seemed to hint that he was really of much higher rank than he appeared to assume. This might also be supposed from his speaking in French very rapidly to one of the party, of which the words, "Saturday, September the 6th," were whispered round the table with much consternation. He continued, however, to support his character, [297] and to play several other tunes with equal effect, such as "The welcome over the main;" "Lang awe', but welcome here;" "Auld Stuarts back again," &c. until at length he laid down his pipes, took up a rather capacious glass of brandy, and said, "Weel, gentles, here's to a' honest man, baith here and ower the water:

"'To one who abroad is, but should be at home,
Let the cups be all fill'd, and the tankards all foam;
Here's a sigh for all such as have no staunch defender,
Here' a health to the KING, and confound the Pretender!"

"Well, done, friend Piper," said the president; "I move that you give us another stave."

"I'm not sure that I can," returned the musician; "I could ne'er bide at a buik lang aneugh to learn a haill sang, for ye see I've aye been a wandered; but I'se gie ye a ballad of all sorts;" and he then began a kind of medley, commencing with that lament which he had already played upon his pipes.

> "'Oh hone a rie! oh hone a rie!
>   The Flower of Albyn lies fu'low'
> That banish'd rose, sae fair to see,
>   Hath closed for aye its leaves of snow!'"

Then, after a short melancholy pause, he added in a blither tone,

> "'But there's a bonnie white rose-bud
>   Yet left upon the bough, Willie,
> And clans and chiefs of noble blood
>   Will stand to guard it now, Willie.'

"Weel, gentles, ye'll no forget— [298]

> 'The sun it rises bright in France,
>   And fair sets he;
> And there's a lad in yonder land
>   Wha should in Britain be.'

"And sae I'll give ye guid nicht, with

> 'Another cup before we part;
> Another toast to warm the heart;
> Another shout sae loud and bra',
> To ane that's sad and fare awa.'
>
> 'Oh, the rose, the white, white rose!
> Oh, my bonnie, white, white rose!
> There;s not a flower on earth that blows
> That e'er I loved like my white, white rose.'"

The performer then took up his pipes and left the house, and our antiquary had the satisfaction of discovering that he had passed the evening with a part of the most notorious Jacobites in London, which made him hasten from the tavern as if he had been followed by fire, sword, or pestilence. As he passed silently and secretly from the door, however, he heard a voice say, "Good night to you Master Mouldwarp; I give you joy upon having become a tory so soon: you'll find your visit here has been no secret." He knew that these words could proceed from no other person than Walter Greysteil, and he turned round with the charitable intention of giving him to the watch, when he was nowhere to be seen, nor was any other person within sight: so that, vexed and weary, he once more set out for his own dwelling, where he arrived soon after midnight. [299]

Most of the May-pole decorations, mentioned in the beginning of this narrative, had been of course either faded or removed by the time to which we are referring; but, the morning after Master Mouldwarp's excursion, the inhabitants of the spot were extremely surprised by finding the gild iron crowns, which decked in the middle of it, had been wreathed about with white roses in the preceding night, by some unknown hand, and for some unspoken purpose. A very few hours, however, cleared up the latter mystery, since it was speedily whispered by the merchants and politicians, that, for certain, the exiled James II. had died of a lethargy at ST. Germain's, on Saturday the 6th; that Louis XIV had proclaimed the Prince of Wales, James the Third of England; that the French resident would doubtless be forthwith ordered out of this kingdom, and war be declared with all possible expedition. But the secret decoration of the Strand May-pole was not so easily explained, as it had been effected under all the disadvantages of night, parading watchmen, three great lanterns erected upon the shaft itself, and a height of sixty-seven feet, where the flowers were suspended.

Although suspicion and superstition furnished abundance of evidence upon this occasion, yet there was none sufficiently accurate and satisfactory for the Honourable James Vernon, then secretary of state, to proceed upon. Those of King James's party attributed the whole work to a miracle, and confidently swore that [300] seven angels were seen placing the garlands, amidst the inspiring strains of the most melodious music; whilst the supporters of William, resolving not to be outdone, affirmed that they were hung up in a storm by an equal number of devils. "Person of honours and credit," however, who never could be found, were the only other witnesses of either of these wonderful visions. The various insinuations and reports against such as were suspected of being Jacobites were but little less unreasonable; since one was condemned as a concealed papist, simply because he had not shown himself so zealous a protestant as to get heartily drunk on the fourth and fifth of November, the birthday and landing of the Prince of Orange, and the discovery of the "horrid popish Jacobite plot" as the old almanacs have it. Another was thought to be secretly truckling to the king of France, because an old French limner, who was justly considered as a most dangerous spy, since nobody understood him and he understood nobody, lodged in one of his attics. A third was to be sure no friend to England, being neither more nor less than a wily Scots tobacconist, called James Stuart; and a fourth was positively a wolf in sheep's clothing, who could have no hope, since he had actually been wigmaker to King James, who absolutely went away in an article of his manufacture; and it was even said that he had sent another to St. Germain's! Such, with almost a thousand variations of "a new tout on an old horn," were some of the reports concerning those who [301] lived in the immediate vicinity of the Stand May-pole; and similar tales were to be heard in nearly every part of London. It was certainly true that the exiled James Francis Edward Stuart had numbers of secret friends in England, and that the nation was in a very disturbed state; since a war with France was inevitably approaching, and William III, was lying dangerously ill in Holland, though the fact was studiously concealed, and scarcely known until after his recovery.

It was not long before a shrewd suspicion fell upon Master Mouldwarp, and he was rather earnestly invited to attend the secretary of state, to give some account of his proceedings that evening; when there were sundry exclamations of wonder from all his acquaintance, that a person whom they had always esteemed as a staunch supporter of William III. Should at last turn out to be a concealed Jacobite and Jesuit in disguise. The principal point against him was his having been seen at the Stuart Club at the Blue Posts, when a famous leader of James's party arrived there in disguised with the news of his death, and the proclamation of the prince by Louis. To this, Argus Blink, the watchman, who slept opposite the May-pole, added, that some time between midnight and morning he saw a figure like the antiquary walking near it, and at length retire towards the Hog in Armour. In his own defence, Master Mouldwarp related part of the narrative of his wonderful resemblance; but though the dilapidated house in Chelsea was searched, the [302] rooms were all deserted, and Walter Greysteil was never found again in London.

Nothing having been proved against him, the antiquary was at length set at liberty, though he was still closely watched, and generally regarded as a suspected person; in addition to which, the wild humours and zealous Jacobitism of his lunatic representative were frequently involving him in new difficulties, though he could never lay hold of the actual author. At length, his landlord, wearied with sheltering so suspicious a person, dismissed him from the Hog in Armour; on which he sold his museum, and again quitted England to search after Walter Greysteil, and endeavor, by restoring him his fortune, to regain his own quiet of mind. Some traditions say that they are still alive, and still looking for each other, without being able to meet, though nearly one hundred and thirty years have passed way since these events happened. But, whilst some may esteem that to be a fiction, invented only to excited wonder, and unworthy of being added to this sort, my own notion is, that it is true; and I think there is rather a wholesome lesson to be derived from the supposition; namely, that when men lost a good conscience they may wander over the world till doomsday, ere they recover their peace of mind. If to this it be added, that evil men are tormentors to each other, and that crime is the handwriting of the arch-fiend upon our lives, the reader will have all the morality which I can extract from this narrative.

Title
Bird, John. "The Convent of St. Ursula." FMN 1830. 361-379. [361]

THE CONVENT OF ST. URSULA
BY JOHN BIRD, ESQ.

IT was near the close of a brilliant autumn day, that a solitary horseman, descending a mountain road seldom visited by travellers, and rough in proportion to its disuse, stopped at the door of a wretched posada, that seemed to possess few attractions for a guest of his apparent quality. But though the tenement itself was mean almost to repulsion, the rich province of Granada could boast few more lovely or romantic valleys than that where he had chosen to make his halt. The deep masses of forest trees, just tinted with the golden glow of the waning year, threw their broad shadows around the margin of a lake, where ever-flowing rills, that leaped fantastically from rock to rock, glided gracefully into repose beneath the slanting rays of the sunset. The luxuriant hills scarcely yet denuded of the purple wealth that soared even to their summits; and the long line of shadowy mountains beyond, reflecting with diminished lustre rather than loveliness the bright radiance of evening; might well have atoned, to a less susceptible heart, for any lack of accommodation, in a country more celebrated for its scenery than its hospitality. Yet the pause of the traveller, though his eye wandered eagerly through the valley, seemed actuated by some deeper feeling than mere enthusiasm. It was the glance of one whose soul was in his gaze. In the absorbing interest of the moment he saw that object alone on which his eye was fixed, and he withdrew his attention only to pass into the house, whither the hostess, in some [362] amazement, and even consternation, at so unlooked-for an arrival, hastened to attend him. The trepidation of the poor woman was not diminished by a nearer view of her guest, whose dress, through travel-soiled, was rich in material, and whose form and manner were in a high degree commanding and dignified. He was tall and eminently handsome; but though his years could not have numbered thirty, care or toil had already left traces on his cheek and brow even more indelible than those of time. His first inquiries, in a voice of melancholy sweetness, where of a neighboring convent.

"You might have seen the spires above the forest, senor," replied the hostess: "it lies but a short way behind those old cork-trees, and few there are that visit it now-a-days, except on some grand ceremony, like that of tom-morrow."

"To-morrow!" repeated the stranger, in faltering accents—"What ceremony is this of which you speak?"

"One seldom witnessed at the convent of St. Ursula, senor," replied the good woman; "though in my mind it is a sad sacrifice of a beautiful young lady: for if all be true that I have heard, God's light never shone on a fairer creature than that novice who is to take the black veil to-morrow."

"To-morrow!—and the black veil!" said the stranger, shuddering.

"It is even so," cried the hostess. "Her great wealth, [363] no less than her loveliness, will bring the country from far and near to look on one who, in the flower of youth, can cast from her the golden gifts of fortune! But there is One who reads the heart, and hers, poor lady, may have been wrong."

"Know you her name?" demanded the stranger, hastily.

"Juana de Guidova."

He groaned, and struck his clenched hangs on his forehead with a violence that affrighted the poor hostess.

"Alas! I fear me these are bitter tidings for you, senor!"

"They are, indeed! but, brief as is the space, Juana, I will tear thee from thy bondage, ay, though it be even at the foot of the altar!"

"Saints and angels protect us, senor!—if you are come for aught but to witness the ceremony, you had better have been in your grave! The abbess is a stern, proud woman, who will rather die than loose her grasp of a prize like Lady Juana—one that can bring riches and fame to a poor, decayed convent; and, alas! were it not impious to wish—"

"I cannot reason it with you, hostess," returned the stranger, with a bitter smile; "I must see this abbess, and that quickly. Expect me back to sleep—if indeed it be my fate ever to sleep again—and let my good steed, I pray you, be cared for: he hath served me well at need, though something seems to whisper that I shall [364] never mount steed more!" He waved his hand impatiently, as if to forbid reply, and walked rapidly forth in the direction of the convent. The hostess looked anxiously after him: "Poor gentleman!" she exclaimed, "he will run himself into danger; and all in vain!—A true lover, I'll warrant him! but what can true love do against the power of the church?—The abbess has a heart of stone, and Father Miguel is watchful and wary.—Come what will, I must warn him of his peril, even though a heavy penance should be my only reward."

The stranger meanwhile pursued his way to the convent, now scarcely distinguishable, amid the closing shades of evening, from the dark foliage by which it was encompassed. On knocking at the gate, and inquiring for the abbess, he was conducted, after a pause, to the parlour of the superior, who with some difficulty consented to give audience to a guest that declined to announce his name.

"You will pardon me, senor," cried the abbess, coldly, "if I request you to be brief: there are yet arrangements to be completed for our holy rites of to-morrow, which at this time demand my undivided attention."

"I have a boon to ask," replied the stranger, faltering—"It is to speak—for one moment only—but alone—with the Lady Juana de Guidova."

"Holy St. Ursula!" exclaimed the abbess, raising her hands, "what impiety is this!—to break in on the [365] awful communing's of one devoutly praying to become weaned and purified from all earthly feelings, and longing for her acceptance as a bride of him—"

"It may not be!" interrupted the stranger: "Juana is bound by vows, which not even the church has power to unloose, to me, her betrothed husband!—Her own breath alone can dissolve our solemn contract."

"What profane mocker art thou," cried the indignant superior, with flashing eyes, "who darest to impugn the power of the church, and vainly seekest to withdraw from her saintly purpose one whose heart is irrevocably fixed on divine love?—But it recks not who or what thou art—thy boon is rejected; and as thou wouldst escape the vengeance due to a scoffer at holy rites, begone, ere the hour of mercy be past!"

"Of mercy!" repeated the stranger scornfully; "say rather of cruelty unexampled, of treachery unparalleled, but not, I trust in Heaven, of craft or force to consummate thy unholy will. Know me, proud abbess, for one fearless of thy power, and resolute to defeat thy purpose. Ere the command of our emperor claimed my devoted service on the distant plains of war, Juana was affianced to me in the presence of her deceased father, by the hand of a venerable priest, who yet lives to avouch our hallowed contract. My long absence and reported fall may have aided a belief that her vows were absolved by death; but when she knows that I live, live to demand the fulfillment of her promise—" [366]

"It is too late," cried the abbess with vehemence; "the church has power to bind and to loose! and potent as you may deem yourself, Alphonso de Mondemar—for I know you now—you have yet to learn, that the weak woman who stands before you is stronger in the delegated service of Heaven, than you, the favoured servant, it may be, of the mighty Charles! Be wise, therefore, in time, lest I denounce your impiety to the grand inquisitor, whose will not our righteous emperor himself dares dispute. Were he in presence—"

"Behold his signet!" cried Mondemar; "his mandate requiring you to deliver up Juana, on pain of forfeiture!"

"It is an imposture—he has been deceived," interrupted the superior, with increasing vehemence: "our gracious monarch is too fast a friend of holy church to dispute her decrees; but were he now before me, I would tell him, that, sovereign as he is, there is a power superior to that even of God's vicegerent upon earth— a power derived from Heaven alone, whose vengeance, Mondemar, you would do well to avoid."

"Say rather that I will brave; ay, at the foot even of that altar, whence Mondemar will rend thy devoted victim, or perish in the attempt."

The abbess involuntarily trembled as she listened to the denunciations of one inflexible as herself, and potent in the favour of a mighty monarch; yet her eye blanched not, her brow relaxed not; and Mondemar, perceiving the hopelessness of expostulation with a [367]being wholly devoted to the interests of her order, looked his defiance, and departed.

The indignation that had excited and sustained him during his interview with the abbess faded into doubt and dread as he slowly retraced his steps towards the posada. He knew too well the power of the church, more especially in a remote valley, to hold the threats of the superior lightly. Aid was distant and uncertain; the danger pressing and imminent. Foreign as it was to the high-souled impulses of his nature, he now regretted that he had not endeavoured to oppose art to art; to have gained by gold or daring some means of at least apprising Juana that he yet lived and loved. He trembled to meditate on the effect that the surprise even of joy might produce on so sensitive a frame; yet to hope that now, when the suspicions of the abbess were roused, and her vigilance alarmed, he could succeed in gaining access to Juana, was beyond even the sanguine expectation or enterprise of a lover. Yet still he lingered in faltering irresolution, lingered till a deep and heavy step warned him of the danger of discovery. Silently and steadily he then sought a neighbouring thicket, whence the thick enshrouding darkness only enabled him to perceive the dim outline of a shadowy figure that passed, hastily onward. "Some homeward-bound peasant probably," he exclaimed: "oh that I could change destinies with one who, if he hath not wealthy, power, or nobility, is far richer in contentment, lowliness, and love, that [368] precious balm and solace of existence! Oh, Juana! that with thee I might retire to some humble cottage, some peaceful vineyard, far from the reach of worldly cares or riches! Through the shelter of this night even might I have borne thee, but for my fatal rashness, swiftly and securely. Why not now? Yet no; 't were hopeless to expose myself, or that sweet deluded one, to the vindictive rage of the abbess. In the face of day only must I confront our foes, and trust in Heaven to uphold the right"

It was with difficulty that he retraced his route to the posada; the darkness of the hour, increased by an impending storm (the distant thunders of which were heard to tremble along the mountains) preventing all recognition of the path by means of external objects. Large heavy rain-drops began now also to patter among the leaves; and he had probably been overtaken by the tempest, but for the care of his good-natured hostess, who placed a lamp at her door, which served as a beacon to his uncertain steps. She met him on the threshold. "There is one awaiting you, senor," she cried in a low voice; "the confessor of the convent, Father Miguel. He pretends much good-will towards you; and prays Heaven he may be sincere! but trust him not too far."

Mondemar, murmuring his tanks, yet musing on so singular a warning, passed on to the inner apartment, where he was saluted by an aged ecclesiastic, with an air of humility too strongly contrasted with [369] the haughty demeanor of the abbess not to excite suspicion as to the sentiment which so unlooked-for a deportment might express. The monk was a thin spare man, whose deeply-lined features seemed rather to speak of the austerities of his religious practice than of the ravages of time, though he was evidently declining into the vale of years. His looks were meek and lowly, and his hand was placed on his breast, as if to denote the sincerity of his vocation.

"Your blessing, father!" exclaimed Mondemar, with a sullen inclination of the head: "how may I have deserved this late visit from so holy a man?"

"By your misfortunes, my son, your unmerited misfortunes," replied the monk, with an air of sympathy. "I grieve to know that I am weak in power, though strong in will to aid you."

"My misfortunes, father?" cried Mondemar.

"I have not to learn, my son," interrupted his companion; "in fact, I know the purport of your visit to our convent. I know also its unsuccessful termination. To me, as father confessor to the community, the abbess has divulged all that passed; and I lament that you have been seduced into the utterance of threats as vain as irreverent."

"Father," replied Mondemar, "on this head I am impenetrable as adamant: if you know my wrongs, if you are apprised of the arts which would tear from me one bound by vows which Heaven alone can absolve, you must feel that I have now no choice but in the [370] face of Heaven to claim from my deceived Juana a renunciation of oaths which it was impious even to administer."

"My son," interrupted the monk, "a cause may be just; but if rashly urged—"

"What other course remains?" said Mondemar, with vehemence. "Your abbess has defied me—has denounced, as the most flagrant profanation, my request to see or communicate with the Lady Juana, who will be lost to me unless redeemed by that one bold act which you stigmatize as rash and irreverent."

"I would," said the old man, mildly, "that I had the power to join your hands; but I can only pray that right may prevail, and counsel you to a reliance on above as your best stay: for what, alas! is all mortal wisdom but weakness and folly?"

"We must use the means vouchsafed to us, father," returned Mondemar. "We must act by that light which Heaven hath permitted; and those means—that light—impel me—"

"Yet, my son," interrupted the confessor, "the counsels of age not vainly temper the fervour of youth. I will own to you, our superior is firmly bent that the Lady Juana shall become a nun. The wealth, the distinction, I may confess, which our house will acquire by the intended rite, are too alluring to be easily abandoned; and the zeal of the Marquis D'Aranda—the guardian of our novice, and her near relation—in the same course, renders all opposition nearly hopeless. [371] Yet, my son, if I have not power, save by those gently admonitory breathings which, like the airs of heaven, steal softly and sweetly to the heart, these humble aids shall not be wanting to awaken a purer feeling."

"Father!" cried the drooping Mondemar, "my spirit sickens at such aids, which seem to me but unavailing fantasies."

"Fantasies you call them!" said the friar, reddening. "But you are wet and travel-worn, and the inward man requires to be sustained no less in strength than in spirit. Within there, hostess!—Wine, wine, and viands!—You are faint, my son from exhaustion: take freely—your fare, though rude, is salutary. Come, my son!" he continued, seizing a drinking-cup; "follow the example of an old man, who, for your sake, will this once indulge in the generous juice of the grape. You have need of its exhilarating influence. Why, how now, daughter?" he exclaimed, angrily:—"you have spilled, by your carelessness, a portion of the wine I had poured out for your guest."

"Your pardon, Father Miguel!" said the hostess, submissively; "I will bring in another flask."

"How! would you waste the remainder?" demanded the monk, angrily: "thus disregarding the sin of misusing the gifts of Heaven."

"I will not tempt her to rebel," said Mondemar, raising the cup, and hastily swallowing its contents. In the abstraction of the moment, he had not marked the changed and excited features of the monk—an ex- [372] citement altogether disproportioned to the occasion; but he now regarded with no less astonishment the inflamed countenance of the self-subduing friar than the mournful and disappointed looks of the hostess. The monk, perceiving this effect, so contrary to his desires, hastened to reassume his meek and humble port; but, finding that other feelings than those which had marked their latter conference now possessed the bosom of Mondemar, he murmured something of the lateness of the hour, and rose at once to depart. "I must to my sacred calling, and chiefly to labour, not, I would fain hope, without success, in your cause. But, be that issue as it may, depend on me as your true friend and advocate; one who can at least prepare the Lady Juana for your unexpected appearance, should you still persevere in that public appeal, which, as a servant of the convent, no less than as a minister of religion, I would yet deprecate, as tending to scandal and disgrace on our holy order. Yet I pray that Heaven may order it otherwise, and that those who have dared to outrage the sanctity of holy vows may be fearfully punished."

"Father, if I am to depend on your words—"

"Say rather on my deeds!" cried the retreating monk; "for it is only on these that I rely." He lifted his hands above the bending form of Mondemar, and slowly retired with the hostess, with whom he remained some time in deep conference.

Exhausted alike in mind and body, the hapless lover sought a restless couch, where, some time insensi- [373] ability, but scarcely in sleep, the hours of night passed slowly on. If slumber at any time sunk on his over-wrought frame, the fearful visions of an excited and distempered imagination destroyed in its balmy influence: wild creations of fancy, combining with real yet uncertain fears, awakened his sensitive spirit to transitory horrors, but too well aided by the convulsions of the elements. At one moment he beheld Juana in the power of an exasperated inquisitor, condemned to the tortures that await a relapsed man; while he, spell-bound and powerless, was denied the use of speech and motion. At another, he seemed to be flying with her from the pursuit of her prosecutors, whose steps he distinctly heard gaining rapidly on them. Again, he stood with her on the brink of a precipice, from which she was hurled by an unseen hand, shrieking for help, while he remained in impotent despair. Now they were abandoned to the fury of wild beasts; and now were hurried to the flames kindled to avenge their delinquency to the mandates of the church. It was from a dream of hopeless imprisonment within walls never again to unclose, with the cry of the fainting, dying Juana still ringing in his ear, that he suddenly awoke to a consciousness of life and liberty. It was morning, and a morning of great beauty. Hill and dale, flower and forest, glistened alike in tearful loveliness, as each slowly kindled into light and animation beneath the smiling sunbeam and the freshening breeze. Mondemar only arose pale, languid, and dispirited. He looked [374] from the lattice with an anxious eye on the crowds already assembling to witness the gorgeous spectacle which the profession of a noble and wealthy novice offered to their curiosity.

"Yes!" he exclaimed, with a bitter smile, "it is time that I also should nerve myself to that effort which must terminate in rapture or despair!—It is time that I should throw off this torpid feeling that presses on my heart, and gird up my limbs and my spirit, to abide the issue of my fate!— Why look you so strangely on me?" he cried, as the hostess clasped her hands in seeming terror on meeting his morning salutation.

"Holy mother!" she replied, "you are ill, senor, and, I fear—"

"What my good hostess?" said Mondemar, faintly smiling.

"That which it were vain even to speak," answered the trembling dame, "even if I dared. Yet go not to the convent, senor;—it will be in vain; it is but rushing into danger."

"Nay, but I have a friend there in the holy confessor."

"A friend!" repeated the hostess, crossing herself. "One moment only, senor: if you will go, trust not in aught but your own true heart; and may He who upholds the virtuous give you good deliverance."

Mondemar looked, as if to demand an explanation of her warning, but the hostess had already retired within her own dwelling, and he passed languidly on- [375] ward among the smiling groups, who gazed with wonder on one unmoved by the general festivity. It was not that his resolution was less firm, his hope less vivid;—his frame alone, that frame which ha defied the fatigues, the perils of war, now shrunk from the impending crisis on which his future destiny depended. Yet, feeling the necessity of exertion, he rallied his fainting strength, and, mingling with the throng, entered the chapel of the convent where the ceremony was to take place, seemingly unrecognised, and certainly unmolested. Seeking the shelter of a massive pillar, where unseen he could thence command a full view of the altar, he looked anxiously around for the father confessor; but, though he once thought that he perceived the monk looking warily on the assembled multitude, he was either deceived, or the monk eluded discovery by immediately retiring. In the mean time the throng gradually increased, till the chapel was entirely filled, excepting the space kept apart from the performance of the ceremony. At length the pealing organ woke on the listening ear, the voices of the nuns arose in one triumphant strain, and the novice, preceded by the archbishop, who was to receive her vows, and the superior, decorated with the insignia of her office, advanced towards the altar. Her guardian, the Marquis D'Aranda, and a train of attendant nobles, slowly followed.

With intense, with almost overpowering interest, did Mondemar gaze on the mistress of his affections, his [376] betrothed, his chosen bride;—on one who believed him to be no more, who was to listen to his voice as to a voice from the dead;—on one who was to seal his bliss, or confirm his despair. Now, now was the hour for effort; and now he felt his strength, his resolution, yield to a torpor unknown till this fatal moment. He gazed on her as in a bewildered dream, from which he vainly endeavoured to awake. Juana looked pale, yet calm; her eye was tranquil, but it was the tranquility of extinguished hope:—she smiled, but her smile was beamless. Her obedience seemed the yielding of an unresisting or uninterested victim, rather than the eagerness of an aspirant for divine love. The impassioned, the elevating principle, that, soaring from earth to heaven, rapturously embraces the self-interdiction that bars a return to an abjured world, Juana knew not. Hers was the meek submission of one who delegates to others the exercise of that will which seeks only to hide a blighted heart in silence and seclusion. Yet pale, passionless, as she looked, never had Juana appeared so lovely in the eyes of Mondemar as at the moment when he beheld her, as it were, snatched from his powerless grasp. His eyes grew dim;—he scarcely saw the severing of those lovely locks which at their parting he had ornamented with a chaplet of pearls, the last offering of his love;—he scarcely beheld her cast aside the rich jewels, those vain symbols of her former state, which she was about to resign for ever;—he heard not the inaugural discourse of the archbishop, [377] nor marked the glance of hatred and alarm which the haughty abbess threw around the chapel as the fatal ceremony commenced. But when the vow, the irrevocable vow, fell trembling on his ear, and the faint response of Juana faltered on her lip, life, power, and energy seemed rushing through his veins like the vivid blaze of an expiring flame.—"Juana! Juana!" he exclaimed in a voice that thrilled to every heart, "forbear!—thy vows are mind—mine, they betrothed husband's—the living, the faithful Mondemar's!"

"Mondemar!" repeated the shrieking Juana; "am I awake!—do I look on thee!—or is it but a fantasy of the deceiver to wean me from my holy purpose!"

"No, no! thy purpose is unholy—is impious! thou art mine—mine only!" continued the frantic Mondemar, rushing forward, regardless of the stern denunciations, or the impeding multitude that would have barred his progress. It was a nobel but an expiring effort. Even as he reached the sinking Juana he met the glance of the confessor, a glance of almost demoniacal rage, and, as he fell in the agonies of death, of horrid triumph. It revealed to his awakening sense the source of those pangs which were consuming his vitals. The crafty friar had mingled poison with his wine; poison so deadly, that, but for the well-intentioned but vain stratagem of the hostess, it had numbered him with the dead ere the morning rose. "Juana! we meet but to part," cried Mondemar faintly, as the last agony dimmed his sight and speech; "yet to hold [378] thee once more in these arms—to impress this last kiss on thy cold lips—to die in thy dim embrace!—Yes, there is bliss even in death!—Look on me, sweet! speak but one word to the expiring Mondemar—tell him that he was still loved, and that treachery alone—but I grow faint—"

"Mondemar!—my love,—my husband!" cried the heart-stricken Juana, "you must not die; these lips shall yet breathe life. Oh, had I but known!—Cruel, cruel that ye were," she exclaimed, turning to D'Aranda and the abbess, "to deceive me thus!—Has Heaven no thunderbolts—has earth no justice?"

"Yes," cried the emperor, suddenly entering the chapel, while the terrified superior and her guilty instrument quailed before his frown, "you shall have such justice, Mondemar, as no less befits my regal oath, than my gratitude to a brave and worthy servant."

"It is too late," murmured the dying Mondemar; "but for this sweet innocent, let her not be compelled to utter vows—"

"My vows are thine, Mondemar, thine only!" cried the frantic Juana, clasping her expiring lover to her bosom; "in life or death we will not part."

He pressed his lips to hers with a convulsive effort; looked one moment upward, and expired. They hastened to unclasp the living Juana from his grasp. She waved them off, and gazing wildly at those distorted features which had only beamed on her with love and tenderness, turned to the monarch, as if to demand [379] vengeance on his destroyers. The emperor seemed to understand her silent appeal, and at a glance the trembling abbess and the conscience-stricken confessor were led away guarded. A smile of exultation lightened for an instant on the brow of Juana; she clasped her hands, sunk on the silent corpse, and in one wild sob her spirit fled for ever.

Literary Annual
Forget Me Not; A Christmas, New Year's, and Birth-Day Present for MDCCCXXXI.
Ed. Frederic Shoberl. London: R. Ackermann, 1831. Printer: Thomas Davison, Whitefriars.

Title
Chorley, H. F. "The Elves of Caer-Gwyn." FMN 1831. 73-95. [73]

THE ELVES OF CAER-GWYN.
BY H. F. CHORLEY, ESQ.

"Heaven defend me from that Welch fairy."
MERRY WIVES OF WINDSOR.

"All courteous are by kind, and ever proud
With friendly offices to help the good."
THE FLOWER AND THE LEAF.

THERE remains to this day, or, at all events, there did remain till within the last few years, the spacious ivy-covered manor-house of Caer-gwyn, one of the finest specimens of domestic architecture in that part of the principality. It is situated far from any town, in the midst of its broad lands, and sheltered by hills, in the lone recesses of which is hidden many secluded valley with its tiny rivulet, and sparingly scattered among the extensive sheep pastures are small antique farm-houses, looking as though they were a part of the primitive rock on which they stand. There is, however, on the estate, one ravine in particular of great beauty, though little known to the tourist; it is terminated by a waterfall, where the brook, after having long been pent up in a narrow channel, shoots over a perpendicular rock of considerable height into the valley below: a rude path has been formed beneath the fall, so that you can return by the other side of the stream, after having passed under the cascade. Large trees have grown in the crevices of the stones, their branches in many places meeting above the water; ferns and other shade-loving plants spring up on every side in rich profusion, and, for may yards, the path [74] is overhung by a luxuriant drapery of ivy, the branches of which nearly sweep to the ground. In short, it is a haunt of such wild and lonely beauty, that it is not difficult to believe the popular tradition, that elves and fairies there loved to dwell and disport themselves; and a cave is yet shown said to be their chosen stronghold and retreat. Many are the stories extant among the aged peasants of their tricksy gambols; and those who love a tale of their days and deeds for some stormy winter evening, when the fancy is set free, and there are none stern or unimaginative enough to chide or check her flights, may perhaps read, with some interest, my legend of the Elves of Caer-gwyn.

Few families of note lived in the fairy-favoured days without their signs or omens attendant on good and evil fortune, and the house of Caer-gwyn was by no means an exception to this general rule. Its family sprites, too, were supposed to exercise an unwearied, and often an unwelcome interference in the destinies of the sons and daughters of its race—nay, rumour-loving gossips declared that, owing to their influence (how, it was never very accurately explained), the lady Jane Welles, then heiress to the property, broke her faith with a long-attached lover, and married Sir Cyril Vavasour. The rejected one went abroad upon her marriage, and never returned to England; his lands were left to the care of a steward, and, as little was heard of him for a long series of years, his name, at length, seemed gradually to pass from remembrance; [75] except when, twice a-year, old Barnabas opened a part of the desolate manor-house, when the tenants came to pay their rents; and then, as they went homewards, the honest farmers would spend themselves in conjectures (for Barnabas was impenetrable to questions), as to what had become of Mr. Tyrrell.

It was on a very stormy evening in the autumn of 17—, that a gentleman reined up his steed at the door of a miserable hut, and, knocking loudly, requested shelter and rest, at least till the thunder and rain, which fell in torrents, should have abated. He had travelled far, and ridden hard all day, through a wild and thinly peopled district; and though his good horse had long been tired, and his rider anxious to pause upon his journey, this dwelling, in a lone and craggy valley, was the first he had seen for many miles. It was situated at a little distance from the road (if road that might be called, which in many places was nothing more than the bed of a mountain torrent, where the stream had been diverted to some other channel), and a smoke rising among the trees had directed him, through a kind of rift in the rocks, to a small hollow, surrounded on every side by huge, fantastically-shaped fragments of stone. Among these there seemed hardly room for the cottage and its garden, and the wanderer wondered what singular being could inhabit such a strangely-situated dwelling. After some pause the door was opened by a tall, stern-looking woman, far advanced in years, as might be seen by the wrinkles [76] on her brow, and the whiteness of her hair, though her figure was still erect and unbending. Her dress was very clean and neat; she even wore ornaments of some cost—rings of gold upon her fingers—and a bunch of keys suspended at her side by a silver chain. Almost before she could open the door he heard her say, "Why have you come so much too early?" but when she perceived that her visiter was no inhabitant of that country, but young and handsome, and richly dressed in a foreign costume, she stepped back, and seemed to hesitate, when he said, "I am a stranger in these parts, and have lost my way; can you give me shelter?" "I do not know," she replied ungraciously, "this is no house of entertainment for wayfaring folk;" and then, looking out upon the stormy sky, she added, "but you may come in." "And my horse, good mother?" "I will show you where you may stable him," said she, pointing to the door of a small shed in another corner. Upon this the rider dismounted, and, having led the tired steed to the stable, and with some trouble found for him a small bundle of musty hay, he next began to think of his own comforts, and returned to the cottage, which promised warmth at least from the bright fire blazing within.

The inside of the small dwelling suited well the neat appearance of its owner. At first, Launcelot was too intent upon drying his wet garments, and doing justice to the good cheer of bread, eggs, new milk, *et cetera*, set before him, to notice much else; but when [77] his hunger was in some measure satisfied, and his hostess left him, he began to use as a keen a pair of black eyes as were ever set in human head, to make observations withal. The apartment was strangely set out with old furniture, which had once been handsome and costly; and by degrees he came to the conclusion that this must be the dwelling of some devotee who had withdrawn herself from the world to this retired spot. He was confirmed in his conjecture, by observing in one corner, above a slab of stone, the image of his hand was a huge black-letter Bible. There was no sign of any other inhabitant, and he was beginning to meditate a chain of subtle questions, which might throw some light on the history and calling of his stately hostess, when she entered, and after removing the food from the table, drew a chair to the fire, and commenced the conversation herself.

"The storm is over," said she, "and your garments (laying her hand on his cloak), are dry; are you ready to depart, or have you any further business here?"

"Why, my good lady," said the youth, "you would not surely turn out a stranger who has lost his way, and who cannot tell where else he is to find a night's lodging. How should I have any other business here who never was in the country before?"

"It matters not," she said; and then in an undertone began to think aloud. "No one will be coming to-night, and if he be a stranger, he will never be able [78] to find his way out of this place in the dark;" then raising her voice, "if you think you can sleep in this chair, I shall be glad to accommodate you for the night."

"Sleep! I could sleep anywhere after being tossed about for a week on shipboard," rejoined Launcelot good-humouredly, "and, upon my honour, this is the only clean cottage I have seen since I set foot in Wales—but do no you find it very solitary to live here all alone?"

She answered coldly in the negative, and there was again a dead pause, when suddenly she drew close to her guest, and said, in a low and earnest tone, while she fixed her cold gray eyes steadily upon his, "Young man, have you ever an enemy on whom you wish to be avenged?"

"Parbleu! mother, what a question!" replied Launcelot, a little startled: "I cannot guess what interest you can have in knowing my enemies."

"What if I could help you to a revenge upon them?"

"Upon my honour this is a strange country, where I cannot sit comfortably down by the first good fire I have seen, without having to answer such inquiries, No, mother!—once for all, I have no enemies that I remember just now; and, if I had, this good sword of mine is sufficient to chastise them all."

"I am satisfied," she said, and then again sunk into a moody silence. Her guest, after one or two more vain attempts at conversation, was silent too—with him an unusual circumstance. [79]

Thus passed on an hour, when suddenly she sprang from her seat, saying hastily, "I hear feat!—Young man, you must hide yourself."

"Nay—I will fly from no danger!—and let me still sit by this warm fire," replied the youth, who had curled himself up into an attitude of great comfort, and was fast approaching a happy state of forgetfulness.

"No, no—you must either be contented to hide for a time," replied his hostess, "or at once leave the house.—Here, this way—Coming!" she cried, in answer to a low tap on the door; and she thrust her guest, who was too sleepy to resist much, behind a clay partition, where was a chair, cautioning him to be silent.

People are rarely too drowsy for curiosity, and Launcelot (who had yielded because he know not whether his non-compliance with her request might not involve his hostess in some danger), having found a loophole of observation in the ruinous wall, soon awakened up to a brisk interest in what passed; and the scene was truly a singular one.

The door was opened, and another woman entered, obviously of a much lower rank than his hostess, who testified much surprise on beholding her.

"Why, Winifred, are you here again?" said she; "and such a distance as you have to come. What has brought you out to-night?—The old errand, I suppose—and you wish me to show you the way to the well?" [80]

The old woman, when she had recovered her breath, made some answer unintelligible to the listener.

"And who is it that you wish to doom now?" inquired the other eagerly.

"Take a piece of lead, and write the name I shall tell you."

"What! is old Purvill's turn to come at last?" exclaimed the sibyl of the spring, when she had traced the required name for her visiter, whose own palsied hand was unable to aid the scheme of vengeance. "It is no more than I have long expected; but what has he done to you?"

"He has sold my last cow for rent; and it was but the other day he bade his bailiff whip my poor little Morgan, for only gathering a few nuts in his wood, the Saxon! And you know"—here she lowered her voice, and the listener could only catch the words "my daughter."—"Well," added she, in her usual tone, "they say now that he is going to court Sir Cyril Vavasour's lady daughter.—Evil befall them both!"

"Hush, hush Winifred!" said the sibyl; "but where is your money?"

The old woman produced from her pocket a piece of silver, and then her hostess opened the Bible, and, pointing to a few verses, desired her to follow her, while she read them backwards. Then came a muttered imprecation on the head of her victim—"that his eyes might fail, that his body might grow thin, that his heart might be grieved, that his flocks might die, [81] that his corn might be blighted, that he might not sleep by night, and that the curses of the poor and houseless might attend his up-rising and down-lying." These, and other such wishes, were poured forth in profusion, with all the earnestness of concentrated malignity; and then Launcelot watched them leave the cottage, and, in an instant afterwards, heard distinctly the sound of a plash in water. Presently they returned, but the ceremony was over; an, as there was nothing more to be learned for they spoke fast and fluently, but in such a low voice that he could not comprehend or follow the subject of their discourse, he became gain overcome with sleep, which, in spite of his efforts, compelled him to yield to its influence.

He prepared, as soon as he awoke, which was very early in the morning, to continue his journey; and when he sought his hostess to recompense her hospitality, she returned his money to him, saying, "Keep your gold—I do not need it; but if you fancy that you owe me any thing, let me ask you a favour, which is, that you will promise me, on the word of a gentleman, never to mention what you saw or heard last night." Launcelot carelessly gave the required promise, and, after having received some necessary directions as to the road he was to follow, departed.

A week from that time found Launcelot Bellasis an inmate at Caer-gwyn. He had brought letters of introduction from the continent, and old Sir Cyril Vavasour, who had been somewhat of a courtier in [82] his youth, was so much pleased with the sprightliness and polish of his manner, that he requested him to prolong his stay. Lady Vavasour, too, who had for many years been a confirmed invalid, seemed to find enjoyment in their guest's society: but these would have weighed little with the young many as inducements to remain, had there not been another inmate in the old manor-house, sweet Anne Vavasour. Inexperienced and country-bred; only seventeen, and beautiful withal; of a rare and radiant loveliness; with the grace and symmetry of a fairy, and with all the frank confidence of a guileless and simple nature—neither concealing nor wishing to conceal the delight she took in Launcelot's merry tales and courtly songs—in having some more gentle companion on her riding excursions than old Gregory the huntsman, and a French master, who taught her twice as well and ten times as pleasantly as Father Edwards the priest—was not his beauty, this confidence, likely to enchain a heart as frank and as open as her own? Never had Caer-gwyn been so cheerful for many a long day: the house was full of the sounds of merriment and music, and at evening the hall rung with the hearty laugh of the old knight, who looked on and enjoyed their mirth. And, in fact, they were never grave, except for one half hour, when they differed on the colour of a set of ribbons Anne was to wear at the approaching harvest-home festival, which was to be kept with all the gaiety and profusion of former days in honour of their guest; [83] and, on another occasion, when Sir Cyril, at breakfast, announced, looking very significantly at Anne, the approaching arrival of Master Purvill, and bade her put on her best looks to welcome her bridegroom.

Launcelot bit his lip on hearing this intelligence, and after breakfast demanded a private interview with Sir Cyril. He told him at once that he was in love with his daughter; and, when he had finished his tale, waited breathlessly for an answer. The old man sighed and spoke kindly; but he replied, that, by an old family compact, Anne had long been engaged to marry Master Purvill—that, in fact, they were betrothed; and he felt that in honour he could not retract from the agreement: but he told Launcelot, that if he would promise not to attempt to engage the affections of his daughter, and remain with them patiently, the, should any circumstance occur to break a connexion, which must otherwise, he said, go on, he might renew his suit, nor fear rejection. It was in vain that Launcelot besought some further mark of grace: the old gentleman, who had passed his word, was inexorable, even when Launcelot urged that he was of Welsh origin, the son of the long-departed Mr. Tyrrell, who had married abroad, and taken his wife's name, whereas Purvill was an Englishman. To his pleading Sir Cyril answered, that he had given his word; and extorted from him a further promise, that he would not directly or indirectly make Anne acquainted with what had passed; and thus the interview ended. [84]

On the second evening from this day arrived Mr. Purvill, to the great discomfiture of Anne, and the great diversion of Launcelot, who saw at once that his chance was better than he had dared to hope. "Old Purvill" (as he was unanimously called by every one in the house, from the father-in-law to the bride-elect) was singularly ungainly and awkward in his appearance. He had to stoop in his shoulders; he was slightly lame; he was slow in speech; and he never looked any one in the face to whom he was speaking. His demeanour was as disagreeable as his appearance: he came into the house with the air of one who knows he is, or is to be, lord and master; and, excepting the moments in which he was left alone with Anne (who took care that such opportunities should be few and far between), his manner was insufferably overbearing, as he took little pains to conceal how regardless he was of pleasing any one. There was soon a very substantial enmity kindled between him and Launcelot. They were careful, however, that no one should perceive it; and each was to the other "civil as an orange, and somewhat of the same jealous complexion." On some pretext or other, the gay young cavalier would always contrive to join the riding party, or break off the interview by his intrusion; and a fortnight passed on, bringing the harvest-home revel very near, without the occurrence of any decisive event.

Nevertheless, the family of Caer-gwyn was, during that time, far from being a comfortable or settled [85] household. The servants at first, one by one, began to complain of nocturnal disturbances: they could not sleep as they used to do. Gradually these rumours increased; and then, they knew not how, it was discovered that no domestic work prospered: the milk would not make butter as it should do, the fires would not burn, the chimneys smoked, the cows overthrew three milkmaids in succession, the horses were restive and broke the fences, and every thing animate and inanimate, from the chamber of dais to the *basse cour*, two seemed out of order and out of joint. Presently Sir Cyril and Lady Vavasour complained that they lost their rest; or, if they did sleep, that their dreams were sprite-haunted: then Anne began to grow pale and vigilant like the rest, and to tell of whispering voices heard in the corridor at midnight. As to Master Purvill, the gay wooer, he was seized with a violent fit of the cramp; and all, except Launcelot, seemed to be the prey of some trifling but frequently repeated annoyance, whence Master Purvill charitably conjectured that *he* was the cause; and endeavoured, by frequent insinuations to that effect, and by dwelling upon the circumstance of his being the son of Sir Cyril's rival, to darken his sunshine at Caer-gwyn. So came on the harvest festival: and the hall, dressed out with huge branches of autumn flowers, and such green branches as could be procured, presented a cheerful and lively sight that evening, filled as it was with the sturdy yeomen, their wives and fresh inno- [86] cent-looking daughters, collected from far and near, and all in their gayest holiday clothes. The dancing commenced early, and was carried on with spirit; though the lights went out once or twice in a most unaccountable manner, and the harper declared that he had never known his strings break so often. But these were minor failures, and the entertainment was proceeding much to the enjoyment of the company, when Launcelot, rather than endure the unwelcome sight of Anne dancing with Master Purvill, walked out into the bright moonshine to digest his vexation as best he might.

It was a glorious night, mild, and fresh, and clear—a night on which the spirit of rancour might well feel its own petty jealousies rebuked by the silent loveliness of the sleeping earth and the solemn majesty of the sky; and Launcelot, though he had that day received much provocation from his rival, which had bred high words between them, felt his own chafed spirit imperceptibly soothed by the tranquillity of all around him. On he went, scarcely knowing wither he was wandering, till upon rousing himself from a reverie he perceived that he was at the entrance of the Fairies' Glen, which looked so bewitchingly lovely in that soft and bright light that he went in, though he remembered countless legends, told him during many a forest walk, of charms wrought there on the night of the full moon, and the sometimes beneficent, sometimes malicious, deeds of the small people who dwelt [87] therein. But he had a good conscience and a careless heart, so he feared not: indeed, as he walked along he could not forbear singing to his guitar, his constant companion, this romance, the remembrance of which that fairy-haunted valley seemed to awaken:

> I would I were a fay,
>   To dwell beneath a tree,
> And sleep the noon away,
>   Where none my rest might see:
> But when with stars the sky
>   By night was shining gay,
> Perchance the poet's eye
> Might mark me floating by.
>   I would I were a fay.
>
> Then lightly would I pass
>   To where tall night-flowers spring,
> And in the dewy grass
>   The fairies trace their ring:
> I'd feast beneath their oak,
>   And join their charmed lay,
> And hear the echo mock
> Their music from the rock.
>   I would I were a fay.
>
> When winter nights are cold,
>   And lords and ladies sleep
> In the castle parlour old,
>   To its warm fire I'd creep;
> Our weave a vision bright
>   Where Beauty slumb'ring lay,
> That she might bless the sprite
> Who brought her dreams by night.
>   I would I were a fay.
>   [88]

There was yet another verse unsung, when, on pausing for an instant to adjust the strings of his guitar, his attention was immediately arrested, and he stood fixed in an attitude of amazement; for some musician (and he thought by the sound some one almost close to him) took up the air, which was a very remarkable one, and sung, in a distinct voice, the words of the last verse. Launcelot crossed himself, for he believed that none in England knew that song but himself; and then, as silently as he could, advanced in the direction whence the sound seemed to proceed; but he saw nothing save the waterfall, which appeared as a stream of silver falling from heaven to earth—when again the verse was repeated. He was now close beneath the cascade; but the shrill clear strain of the music rose high above the steady and measured cadence of the water, and then ceased.— Still he saw nothing. In great perplexity Launcelot bethought him to try another air, pausing in the middle as before. After a moment's silence the viewless minstrel again answered it, completing the strain; and as often as he repeated the experiment, so often did he meet with the same result. The moon was then in her zenith, pouring a flood of light through the most shady places, when, on raising his eyes towards the sky, he imagined that about half way up the rock he descried a pair of very bright eyes like sparks of fire. A little observation confirmed this, and presently he became aware that they belonged to a very small creature clad [89] in green, who was gazing down upon him; while every now and then was heard the suppressing sound of laughter, as though others were behind him in that rocky recess.

"So you have found us out at last, Launcelot," said that tiny minstrel. "Come up, and you shall hear some good news."

Launcelot was bold enough to say—"And who are you that live in such a place? and why cannot you come down to me, if you have anything to say?"

Here there was a louder laugh from the rock.

"Oh! most doughty champion of the Lady Anne, you are afraid," answered the little man promptly; "nevertheless you must come up and hear the good news. We have taken a fancy to your music, and will do you no harm. Mount, I say!"—and the youth, who loved adventure and feared nothing, managed by dint of branches and projecting stones to raise himself, and, in a few minutes, to gain the platform whence the voice proceeded.

When he had fairly reached the small shelf of rock, he perceived that he was at the entrance of a vast cavern. The walls were formed of glittering spar of every colour of the rainbow, and the interior was brilliantly illuminated by countless pendent lamps. At the entrance were seated in great state about seven small beings, all richly clad in green: beside each was laid a musical instrument. They received their guest with another chorus of laughter. [90]

"What a mighty trouble the gentleman has taken!" said the spokesman of the party.

"Yes," cried another mischievous-looking little personage, who had just laid aside a trumpet as large as himself; "when there are only such a handful of us to receive him. Pity our master and mistress are not at home."

"Why, where are they gone?" asked the first.

"Oh! they are down at Caer-gwyn," was the answer.

"But, gentlemen," said Launcelot good-naturedly, though he felt rather strangely when he saw their wild looks and heard their shrill voices, "as I have come, I hope that you will not disappoint me of the good news you promised me."

At this there was another loud burst of laughter, and the elves cried, "Oh ho! so you cannot wait till our master comes home. Well, you are a good sort of fellow, and belong to our craft, so we will sing you a stave, and then you must be gone." Thus saying, they arose, and all standing on tip-toe, as though they wished to exert their voices to the utmost, they joined in a melody quaint and sweet, which filled every crevice of the vaulted chamber, and was answered by a distant and musical echo. The *refrain* ran thus:

"Peace shall come to never a one
Till the accursed home is gone."

These homely words were reiterated again and again, with every change of melody; and then the musicians, [91] with many a fantastic gesture, disappeared into the cavern. As suddenly, the light which had illuminated the interior faded away, and in an instant all was dark. It was like on of the changes of a dream. There was the waterfall roaring within a yard of him, and above were the dark ivy-branches waving in the air; but, in his excited state of mind, he almost fancied that a whispered sound, as of "Go! go!" mingled with the gentle night wind. He felt that he was to expect nothing more that night; and after having vainly sought the entrance to the fairy cavern, now no longer visible, he descended the rock, full of the oracular distich, the melody of which was yet ringing in his ears.

But his adventures were by no means at an end. He was hastily returning homewards, for the first time remembering how long he had been absent, when he heard footsteps near him, beneath the deep shadow of the trees. He stood entirely still to listen whence they proceeded; but the ceased as suddenly, and for an instant all was breathless silence, which was succeeded by another sound, the motive whereof he could not misunderstand:—it was the cocking of a pistol. In a second, ere his eyelid could drop, he had sprung to one side: that very instant the piece was discharged; and, guided now by the sound of retreating footsteps, he rushed through the brushwood, while the distinct and crashing tread of his unseen adversary was a certain guide. But the person whom Launcelot pursued knew the woods much the better of the two. Launcelot, in [92] deed, was every instant stumbling over huge stones, or coming to tangled places impossible to pass, while the fugitive was obviously escaping, as the sound of his steps gradually grew fainter; and, ere long, Launcelot saw, in the clear moonshine, a figure cross the path at a lower point, and again disappear in the darkness. Aware that the individual was now beyond his reach, he made the greatest haste homewards, resolving, if possible, to arrive at the house first; for he was sure that this must be some one who had marked his departure, and dogged him unseen; and he knew of only one person who could bear any grudge towards him.

His suspicion was speedily destined to become certainty. On approaching yet nearer to the house, he perceived that its inhabitants and guests were all gathered together upon the lawn. There were Sir Cyril Vavasour, and his servants, and the priest, all talking at once. What was the centre of the circle he could not at first discern; but, on coming nearer, he heard the knight say, in a tone that savoured of much contempt, "Nay, Lord help thee, Master Purvill! but try to bear it like a man.—Why, Lancie, thou art come back in good time: here has our Master Purvill been a night-walking tool and, missing you both from the hall, I stepped out, judging it best that you should not meet, if I could help it, when I heard something roaring like a bull; and on coming here, I found this poor fellow lying—a most pitiable figure as you see—crying for mercy in a voice loud enough to reach to Caermar- [93] then, and he cannot yet tell what has befallen him. Come, get up, and tell us what is the matter."

"I am fairy-struck! Release me! oh, release me!" cried the prostrate lover, who certainly looked anything but amiable; his clothes torn with briars, and his wig having fallen off, while he yet lay on the ground, kicking fiercely at every one who approached. "I will never fire pistol more! I will never be married! never! never! Why do you pinch me so?"

"Let me come near him," said Father Edwards, who bustled through the crowd; "I will drive out the evil one!—Anathema, Sathanas!"—as he spoke, making the sign of the cross in the air, and sprinkling his face with a few drops of holy water. "Come, sir, rise! your tormentors have left you." And assisting Master Purvill to rise, "See! my brethern," he said, taking a pistol from his unresisting hand, "how vain is the arm of flesh to prevail against the powers of darkness! Tell me, did you wrestle sorely with them ere you were overcome?" But Master Purvill, although restored to his senses, seemed confused, and in no wise willing to speak.

It was now Launcelot's turn to step forward. He took his rival's hand, and, pressing it emphatically, said, "My good sir, I am glad to see you restored; but I fear that the air of Caer-gwyn is not salutary to you, and these moonlight walks after fairies must be very prejudicial to you health. I have studied medicine abroad, and would recommend your returning [94] homeward as speedily as may be: you require rest and quiet, and cannot find it here."

"Any thing!—that is—to-night, if you please!" gasped out the much-humbled man. "I will not sleep another night within those walls, to suffer a repetition of what I have already undergone."

"I am sorry, Master Purvill," said Sir Cyril gravely, "that you should have been so much disturbed as to be obliged to carry fire-arms in my peaceful house; but we will say nothing more about it now, and talk these things coolly over to-morrow."

"Yes," cried a shrill voice from the crowd; "and
  "Peace shall come back anon,
  When the accursed is gone."

"Who spoke?" cried Purvill wildly; and then turning to his host in an agony of fear—"As you are a Christian man, I pray you let me depart to-night."

"Well, Master Purvill, as you please; but my daughter?"—And just then, as they reached the hall door, the blithe face of the Lady Anne was seen, who eyed her betrothed with a glance in which merriment and contempt were blended.

"Let me speak for the gentleman," said Launcelot. "I have good reason to know that circumstances have happened to-night which render him no longer desirous of the honour of the alliance; only he is diffident, and finds it not easy to speak upon the matter. Is it not so, sir?" [95]

"Yes, yes!" replied Purvill. "Since I have thought on it I have never had an hour's peace. Pray for me, and let me depart."

"Oh, sir," said Sir Cyril, with the air and tone of a much-injured and proud man, "you shall not be compelled to fulfil your engagement. And now, as the hour is late, let us all to bed. Come with me, Lancie, and tell me all about these strange passages." The guests then departed, busily talking over the late events; and, for the first time since the arrival of Master Purvill, all the inhabitants of Caer-gwyn enjoyed good rest.

The next morning found Anne and Launcelot at an unusually early hour standing in the porch to watch Master Purvill's departure. To her, and to her alone, did he ever tell the tale of his encounter with the fairies, whose malevolent influence, it was said, ceased from that hour for ever. There was now no obstacle to the happiness of the lovers. In a few weeks they were married; and, truly, the prospered as much as if the tales of fairy gifts were true. I must tell, ere I conclude, that Master Purvill did not long survive the breaking off the connexion. The cursing-well remains to this day, and is yet resorted to; though I am not aware that any of those sprung from Launcelot Tyrrel and Anne Vavasour have ever had recourse to its waters for the purpose of vengeance, as they have the reputation of being an unusually good-humoured and placable race.

Title

Stone, William L. "The Grave of the Indian King." FMN 1831. 101-118. [101]

THE GRAVE OF THE INDIAN KING.
BY WILLIAM L. STONE, ESQ.

"When the hunter shall sit by the mound, and produce his food at noon—'Some warrior rests here' he will say, and my fame shall live in his praise."
OSSIAN.

NATURE seems to have made the fair west in one of her sweetest and kindest moods. Beyond the Onondaga hills, for a long distance, there are no mountains lifting their bleak and rugged summits to the clouds to break the landscape; no beetling cliffs and shagged precipices frowning upon the startled beholder; no dark and gloomy ravines "horrid with fern, and intricate with thorn;" but the whole region, for hundreds of miles, presents a scene of placid and uninterrupted beauty, varied only by gentle hills and moderate declivities, broad plains and delightful valleys. The entire face of the country is, moreover, diversified by a succession of clear and beautiful lakes—fit residences for the Naiads—and traversed by rivers, which wend their way tranquilly to the north, until, by one mighty bound, they leap from the table-land into the embrace of the majestic Ontario, and are lost in the immensity of its waters. But, of all the lesser lakes with which this charming country has been rendered thus picturesque and delightful, Skaneatelas is deemed by all travellers the most beautiful. Its very name, in the language of the proud race who once ranged the forests, and bounded along its shores with the lofty tread of heaven's nobility, or darted across its bright surface in [102] the light canoe with the swiftness of an arrow, signifies the LAKE OF BEAUTY. It is true that, being thus divested of the wilderness and grandeur of mountain scenery, the stranger's attention is less powerfully awakened at the first view, than if it had been cast among the adamantine towers of a more rugged region; but there is in the country by which it is surrounded a quiet loveliness, and air of repose, eminently calculated to please and to captivate the heart. The lands descend on all sides in a gentle slope to the margin of the lake, forming as it were a spacious amphitheatre, having a fountain of liquid silver sparkling in its bosom. Its shores are alternately beautified by the hand of man with cultivated fields, adorned by the living verdure of the meadow, or fringed with banks of flowers; while, to augment the charm of variety, some of Nature's own stately picturings are left, consisting of groves of the primitive forest, here towering aloft in giant pride, and there overhanging the shore, and dipping their pendent branches in the clear cool element, in which every object is reflected with fresh and vivid distinctness. Combining so many of the elements of beauty, few spots in the broad map of the occidental world have equal pretensions to admiration. Still, however, in the eye of untutored man, how much more beautiful must the Skaneatelas have been before the dense forests in which it was embosomed fell, as though struck by the wand of a magician; when it lay amidst the awful stillness and venerable grandeur which pre- [103] vailed around—the dark foliage, the rich and solemn covering of the woods, giving it an air of indescribable magnificence and beauty, in perfect keeping with the moody and contemplative habits of the might chieftains of the wilderness.

The attractive sheet of water which we have thus briefly described is sixteen miles long, and from one to two miles in breadth. The village, which takes its name from the lake, is pleasantly situated upon a little plain at its western extremity, elevated but a few feet above the pebbly beach, upon which the little crisped billows break so gently as scarcely to give sound enough to hush an infant to repose. The view is charming at all times; but nothing can be more delightful, more exquisitely beautiful, than the prospect from this lovely village on a cool summer's evening, when the queen of night throws her silver mantle over the sparkling waters, lighting them up like a mirror of surpassing brightness. Behind the village the land rises, by an easy ascent, into a hill of moderate height, upon the summit of which an open grove of primitive forest trees, to the extent of some fifty acres, as been suffered to remain by the proprietor—an English gentleman, who has thus far followed the westward march of empire. From this elevated spot the prospect is enlarged, and if possible yet more attractive than below. It includes a wide sweep of fertile country, embracing sections both wild and cultivated, farm houses and country seats, fields diversified with gardens, and [104] meadows, orchards, copses, and groves. Near the centre of this forest rises a little mound, covered with wild and luxuriant herbage, like a Druid's grave; and which, time immemorial, has been respected by the pale-faces, who have succeeded the dusky lords to whom the Creator originally granted the fee-simple of the soil, as the lone and hallowed sepulchre of an Indian king. Indeed, tradition has invested it with more interest than often attaches to the last narrow habitation even of those who may have figured largely in story or in song. Be mine the humble task to gather up the history of the sacred spot, and rescue the fleeting tradition alike from the danger of exaggeration or the yawning repository of oblivion.

The district in which the incidents of our drama occurred is situated in the heart of what was formerly the territory of the Five Nations of Indians— the Iroquois of the French, and the Mingoes of the early English history. These nations consisted of the Mohawks, the Oneydoes, the Onondagoes, the Cayugas, and the Senekas. They were a noble race of the American aboriginals, and have been appropriately designated as the Romans of the western world. Their league resembled a confederated republic, although they had not advanced much beyond the first stage in the science of government. Their conquests, like those of the

Romans, were pushed to a vast extent, so that, by the right of inheritance, or of arms, their subject territory extended from the mouth of the Sorel, on [105] the St. Lawrence, up the great chain of lakes to the Mississippi, thence to the junction of the Ohio with this Father of Rivers, thence south to the country of the Creeks and Cherokees, and back on the whole extent, from the ocean to the lakes. Like the Romans, they added to their strength by incorporating their vanquished foes into their own tribes; and, if the prisoners thus adopted, those who behaved well were treated as though of their own blood. If wise at the council-fire and brave on the war-path, they were advanced to posts of honour. Like the Romans, moreover, they were ambitious to extend their conquests, even when their power and influence were on the decline. They cherished a high and chivalrous sense of good faith and honour, according to their own rude notions; and carried on a war of thirty years for a single infraction of the rights of the calumet. Their power was great, and their name a terror to other savage nations, long after the Whites had planted themselves over a wide space of the country. The grand councils of this powerful confederacy were held in the deep and romantic valley of the Onondaga, where, as they believed, "there was from the beginning a continual fire kept burning."

The Five Nations, moreover, being the friends and allies of the English, were consequently much of their time involved in hostilities with the French, then in possession of the Canadas, and also with the Indians, who had been induced to adhere to them by the Jesuits; [106] for "The Holy Order of Jesus" had even thus early insinuated its priestly emissaries into every tribe. Indeed, their fidelity to the English was sometimes put to the severest trials; and whoever traces their history will find their conduct to have been regulated by an elevated and punctilious regard to honour, and marked by disinterestedness "above all Greek and Roman fame." "When the Hatchet-makers," said the eloquent Sadekanaghtie to Governor Fletcher, at Albany, in 1694, "first arrived in this country, we received them kindly. When they were but a small people we entered into a league with them, to guard them from all enemies whatsoever. We were so found of their society that we tied the great canoe which brought them, not with a rope make of bark, to a tree, but with a strong iron chain, fastened to a great mountain. Then the great council at Onondaga planted a tree of peace at Albany, whose top will reach the sun, and its branches spread far abroad, so that it shall be seen a great way off; and we shall shelter ourselves under it, and live at peace without molestation. The fire of love burns at this place as well as at Onondaga; and this house of peace must be kept clean. Let the covenant-chain be kept bright like silver, and held fast on all sides; let not one pull his arm from it." Alas! noble, generous chief! how fleeting were thy glowing visions! and thy brightest anticipations of peace with the white man, how soon were they overcast! How soon, in the bitterness of grief and disappointment, was thou com- [107] pelled to exclaim—"Our arms are stiff and tired of holding fast the chain, whilst others sit still and smoke at their ease. The fat is melted from our flesh, and fallen on our neighbours, who grow plump while we become lean. They flourish, while we decay." Even the race of the tribe which numbered the illustrious Sadekanaghtie, Tachanoontia, Decanesora, and Garangula, whose simple and unstudied eloquence, clothed in the rich and beautiful imagery furnished from this store-house of Nature, shone more brightly than the blaze of their council-fires, has been swept from the face of the earth; and a few straggling remnants of the other tribes, who formed this celebrated confederacy, are all now left of the once mighty and terrible ONGUEHONWE.[25] But, in our desire to bestow a passing tribute of honourable and well-deserved praise upon an illustrious race, whose merits have never been properly appreciated, whose noble qualities have not been well understood, and whose proud character all history has united to calumniate, we may have digressed too far, and will now return to our subject—"The grave of the Indian King."

The frequent hostilities in which the Five Nations were involved with the Canadian French and Indians, in consequence of the alliance with the English, have already been mentioned. And cruel were the conflicts and retaliatory massacres on both sides, as might be [108]instanced in the battle between the Five Nations and the Hurons, near Quebec, the destruction of Schenectady, and the slaughter at Montreal. Too often, moreover, were they encouraged and pushed into hostilities by the English, and in time of need left without adequate succour or supplies. In the year 1690, Count Frontenac, one of the most cruel efficient and politic, as well, perhaps, as the most cruel of the French governors in Canada, attempted to detach the Five Nations from the friendship of the English colony, and the negotiate a separate peace. With this view, through the agency of the Jesuits, the Count succeeded in persuading the Indians to call a grand council of their chiefs at the old council-fore in Onondaga, to which he dispatched messengers with his proposals. There were present eighty sachems; and the council was opened by Sadekanaghtie. The French commissioners laboured assiduously to accomplish their purpose, and the conference continued several days. But a messenger from Albany informed the chiefs that a separate peach would displease the English, and the proposals were therefore promptly rejected. Shortly afterwards, the Count determined to avenge himself on the Five Nations, for having preferred maintaining inviolable their good faith and honour, to the peace which he had proffered. For this purpose he assembled all his disposable troops, amounting to four battalions, with the Indians in his service and under his control; and departed from Montreal on the 9th of July, with two[109] small pieces of cannon, two mortars, a supply of grenades, &c. After a wearisome march of twelve days, during which the utmost circumspection was necessary to avoid ambuscades, the Count reached the foot of the Cadarackui lake (now called Ontario), and crossed thence in canoes to

---

25 Signifying "Men surpassing all others;" a name which the Five Nations conferred upon themselves.

the estuary of the Ohswega river, which flows from the northern extremity of the Onondaga or Salt Lake; the Onondaga river flowing into the southern end, near the great salt licks. The expedition cautiously ascended the Ohswega, and crossed the salt lake, keeping strong scouts on the flanks, to prevent any surprise that might be attempted by a crafty enemy. This precautionary measure was the more necessary, inasmuch as the Indians against whom they were marching, with their wonted chivalry, had given the French notice that they were apprised of their hostile approach. A tree had been discovered by one of the scouts, on the trunk of which the savages had painted a representation of the French army on its march; and at the foot of the tree two bundles of rushes had been deposited, serving at once as a note of defiance, and giving the invaders to understand that they would be compelled to encounter as many warriors as there were rushes in the bundles. These being counted were found to number fourteen hundred and thirty-four.

The castle of the Onondagas was situated in the midst of the deep and beautiful valley to which we have already referred, and through which the Onondaga river [110] winds its way to the lake. Count Frontenac with his motley forces had made a halt near the licks, and thrown up some temporary defences. The site of the castle was but five or six miles distant from the French camp. It was a sacred spot in the eyes of the Indians, as the seat of the grand councils which had for ages regulated the affairs of the fierce and wild democracy of the Five Nations. They had, therefore, resolved to defend it to the last, and their women and children had been sent from the rude village deeper into the recesses of the forest. Circumstances, however, changed this determination on the morning of the day upon which Count Frontenac intended to advance. Two of the Hurons deserted from the forces of the Count, and gave the Onondagoes, to whose assistance neither of the associate tribes had yet arrived, such an appalling description of the French, that they dared not remain and give battle. Yonnondio's[26] army, they said, was like the leaves on the trees—more numerous than the pigeons that fly to the north after the season of snows. They were armed, they said, with great guns, that threw up huge balls high towards the sun; and when these balls fell into their castle they would explode, and scatter fire and death everywhere. Upon this intelligence, the sachems gathered into a group around the council-fire for consultation. There piercing eye-balls, which were at first burning with in-[111] dignation, soon dropped suddenly to the earth, as they reflected upon the impossibility of contending against such weapons, while their dusky countenances gathered darkness with the gloom. Some of the principal chiefs having interchanged a few words in an under-tone, there was a call to bring Thurensera[27] to the council-fire. A dozen young warriors instantly sprung upon their feet, and bounded towards the principal wigwam of the village with the swiftness of greyhounds. Ere many

[26] The name by which the Five Nations designated the French governor. *Cayenguirago* was the name they gave to the English governors.
[27] A name among the Five Nations signifying the "Dawning of the Light."

seconds had elapsed they returned, bearing upon a rudely-constructed litter an aged and venerable-looking chief, whose head was whitened by the snows of more than a hundred winters. He had been foremost on the war-path and first at the council-fire, before the great canoes of the pale-faces had touched the shores which the Great Spirit had given them. The young men treated their burden with the utmost care and deference, and the aged chieftain was seated at the foot of a tall, weeping elm, against the huge trunk of which he leaned upon for support. A brief but solemn pause ensued, during which all eyes were directed to the venerable father of the council. At length the veteran sachem raised his head, and, looking about upon the group of chiefs and warriors gathered anxiously around him, he broke silence as follows:

"Why have my children brought Thurensera to the council-fire? The Great Spirit will soon call him to [112] his hunting-grounds. Thurensera's eyes are dim, and his limbs, no longer like the bending sapling, are stiff, like the scathed trees of the burnt prairies. He can no more bend the strong bow. He cannot go forth on the war-path, or recount the deeds of his fathers to the young men at the council-fire. Thurensera is a woman, but his father was a great chief; and," elevating his voice, he added, "I can now see him sitting upon a cloud fringed with the red lightning, and beckoning me to come. Why have my children called Thurensera? and why do their eyes rest upon the ground, and their spirits droop like the hawk, when struck by the young eagle?"

After another pause, and a moment's consultation among the chiefs, one of the bravest warriors informed the sage of the intelligence received from Yonnondio's camp, and of the peril of their situation; they had, therefore, sent to their father for council in this emergency.

Once more there was silence—still as the forest shades, when not a leaf rustles in the breeze, not a stick breaks beneath the light tread of the fox. The venerable sage hid his furrowed countenance in his withered hands, as if deeply engaged in thought, while the dark group of chiefs and warriors gathered more closely around, all ready to obey his counsel, be it what it might; and all anxious, as it were, to drink in the wisdom that was for the last time, perhaps, to flow from his lips. At length the chieftain of more than [113] thirteen hundred moons slowly raised his head, and spake as follows:

"My children! a cloud has gathered over our council-fire, and you must fly! Yonnondio is come among us with his people, like a flock of birds. You must not wait till you see the big ball of thunder coming to your destruction, or the star of day and night, that breaks when it falls to burn your castle and your wigwams.

"My children! you have been like the lynx on the trail, and made the war-path red with the blood of your enemies. But you must fly, until joined by the Oneydoes, the Cayugas, and the Senekas, when you can come back upon your enemies, and spring upon them like the hungry panther. You will spring on them while they are asleep, and the fire-balls cannot burst upon you, to kill my warriors and burn up their wigwams.

"My children! Thurensera will stay to show Yonnondio's pale-faces how to die. Yonnondio shall see what a Mingo can bear without a cry of pain. He shall see what his children will have to fear, when my sons assemble their warriors, and come upon his settlements in their wrath.

"My children! when you pass this way, look for my bones. Bury them deep in the bosom of the earth, who is my mother, on the hill looking towards the rising sun, by the lake that is beautiful. Put into my grave my pipe, my hatchet, and my bow, that I may chase the moose and the buffalo in the hunting-grounds [114] of the Great Spirit. Put in my canoe, that is on the beautiful lake, that when the Great Spirit tells me I may come and look upon my children, I may paddle again on the bright waters of Skaneatelas. I will come when the moon in her fulness steals over the lake to let her light sleep on its calm bosom. As I glide onward, the lovers among our young men and women will dream of other days; and the spirits of the clouds will whisper—'The grave of the old warrior, who taught Yonnondio how to die.' They will tell the white man to cross it with a soft step.

"My children! you must fly! Keep the covenant chain of our tribes bright as silver, and let it bind you together like strong iron. Put the brand to your castle and you wigwams, that Yonnondio may get no booty but the scalp of Thurensera. Let the rain of heaven wash all the bad from your hearts, that we may again smoke together in friendship in the happy country of the Great Spirit. Thurensera has no more to say."

The aged chief was listened to throughout with the most profound attention. The subsequent deliberation was brief, for time was pressing, and the decision of the council was unanimous, to avoid engagement and retire into the forest. The chiefs and warriors, and the young men in particular, were exceedingly reluctant to leave the venerable sachem, by whose arm so often led to victory; but he was resolute in his purpose, and [115] inflexible in his determination. He gathered himself into an attitude of perfect composure, and, turning his face in the direction from which Frontenac was expected, prepared to meet his fate. Meantime the sachems and warriors, having hastily completed their arrangements, took their final leave of the old chieftain, applied the brand to their dwellings, and disappeared in the thick wilderness.

The Count Frontenac, astonished at the sight of the ascending columns of smoke, as they rose in dense and curling masses towards the sky, moved rapidly forward, but it was to an empty conquest. The huts and the rude words of the Indians were already in ashes. The old chief, Thurensera, was found by the trunk of the elm, with the same stoical composure with which he had been left; and Frontenac's Indians had, by his permission, the pleasure of tormenting him. He bore their tortures with unflinching firmness. Not a muscle moved, not a limb quivered: not a sight, not a groan escaped him. At length they stabbed him in several places.

"Go on, ye tormentors!" he exclaimed with an energy belonging to former days: "the old eagle has received the death-arrow in his breast. He will never soar again but in the bright skies of the Great Spirit. You cannot harm him. The Great Spirit," he continued, "has touched my eyes, and I see through the clouds of death the warriors who have raised the war-cry with me in other times. They are walking on the [116] winds, and playing on the clouds. I see the dark waters which all must pass. Those dark waters are the tears shed by the Great Spirit for the evil deeds of his children. Go on, ye tormentors! ye Indians who take the scalp for Yonnondio! ye dogs of dogs! but why stab me with the long knife? You had better burn me with fire, that the Frenchman my know how to die. Tear me to pieces: roast me at the war-feast: scatter my ashes to the winds: crumble my bones in the salt lake. Yonnondio's Indians! listen to the voice of the Manitto, while he bids Thurensera tell what is to come upon you. Your race is to be as the river dried up—as the dead trees of the forest, when the fire has gone over it. The white man who sent Yonnondio over the great salt lake, in the big canoe, will lose his power. A Wolf is to walk abroad, that will scatter the pale-faces at Quebec like a flock of sheep, and drive them out of the red man's land. The white man with Cayenguirago, who is our friend, will come over the land like the leaves. the panther is bounding to the setting sun; the bear moves slowly off the ground; the deer and the buffalo leap over the mountains and are seen no more. The forest bows before the white man. The great and little tree fall before his big hatchet. The white man's wigwams rise like the hill-tops, and are as white as the head of the bald eagle. The waters shall remain; and when the red man is no more, the names he gave them shall last. The Great Spirit has said it. A hundred warriors are [117] coming to lead me on the trail to the happy hunting-grounds. Think of me, ye tormentors, when my sons come upon you like the chafed panther in his swiftness and his strength. Great Spirit! I come!" Thus died Thurensera, with a greatness of soul worthy of a sachem of the Five Nations.

When the invader had retired, the Onondagoes conveyed the remains of the lofty Thurensera to the hill of the Skaneatelas, and buried him in the "Grave of the Indian King." And in this hallowed spot his ashes have reposed in peace, the little mound becoming more holy by the lapse of years, and the tradition more interesting as lights and shadows were imparted to it by those whose imaginations were kindled by the relation, until the autumn of the year of grace 1829, when it was visited by an English savant, who spent some months with the hospitable proprietor of the consecrated mound. This gentleman had travelled much, and been a great collector of curiosities. He had killed alligators in the Delta of the Mississippi, and chased buffaloes in California. He had hunted elephants in South Africa, and tigers in the jungles of Bengal. He had rescued an urn from the ruins of Herculaneum, and dug an Ibis, and a thigh-bone of on of the Pharaohs, from the pyramids of Grand Cairo. And he was resolved to penetrate the secrets of the Indian's grave, and if possible to obtain the pipe, the tomahawk, and the hunting apparatus, if not the canoe, of the venerable chief, to enrich the great [118] museum of the capital of his native land. Accordingly, with great secrecy, he repaired thither one moonlight night in October, armed with crowbar and shovel. But, alas, for the worthy collector of curiosities, and the veracity of traditional history! a bed of compact limestone rock, within a few inches of the surface of the earth, soon taught the Gothic invader of the Grave that no grave had ever been there!

Title

B., M.A. [Beevor, Miss M.L.] "The Benshee of Shane. A Tradition of the North of Ireland." FMN 1831. 123-136. [123]

THE BENSHEE OF SHANE.
A TRADITION OF THE NORTH OF IRELAND.

> "The night hath been unruly . .
> . . . . as they say,
> Lamentings heard i' the air; strange screams of death;
> And prophesying—with accents terrible
> Of dire combustion!"
>
> MACBETH.

THE shades of evening were veiling the romantic woods that encircled the ancient castle of Shane, when Moira O'Neill walked joyously and lovingly forth, leaning fondly on the arm of her idolized Meredith, to whom, on the evening of the third day from that period, she was to be united for ever.

How holy is the loveliness of nature! and how thrillingly is it felt by the young, by those whose hearts glow with almost ethereal fire, and who, deeply loving and as deeply loved, behold in its deliciousness an answer to, and a felicitation upon, their own immeasurable bliss! The lovers wandered on, silent from excess of happiness, but beautiful and light of step as the guardian angels of those delicious solitudes. The dreamy wind of holy evening, lavish of woodland odours, sighed around them. The brilliant glow of rich sunset, streaming at interval through breaks in the luxuriant bowery foliage, shed on their sweet countenances "celestial rosy red, love's proper hue;" and their minds, lulled to a blessed and indescribable repose, intensely participated in the sylvan voluptuousness around them. The gentle rush of waters down [124] mossy crags—the farewell song of some lone, silvery-voiced bird to dying day—the aromatic odour of dark sad pines, with that besides of a thousand greenwood and mountain plaints—the celestial tones of a bugle heard afar, and seeming in that dim, tender hour, the sad, sweet voice of the spirit of the wilds—and the luxurious affection of confiding and guileless hearts, formed in the apprehension of the devoted Moira and Melville a very heaven upon earth.

The sky deepened to a darker gray, the pale full moon edged the forest trees and turrets of Shane's Castle with silvery light, softened the rough contour and aspect of the mountains, seemed cradled in the clear placid waters of Loch Neagh, and glinted in the little joyous cataracts that dashed down many a rock, when a lugubrious wail, heard now as if from some aerial being hovering over the castle, and now as from one floating above the woods, startled the lovers, and broke the ethereal repose of their souls.

"It is Mavin Rho," sighed Moira; "this is her hour, and ill methinks does her superhuman lament bode to us, dear Melville!"

"Let us return," replied Meredith, passing his arm round the waist of his trembling betrothed, and urging her on towards the castle. "Who heeds the Benshee now? say rather the owl, for an owl indubitably it is. Come, dearest, we are out too late!"

"And owls," replied Moira, "do not they also screech to warn of approaching death? But sure [125] is the Benshee's cry, and long, long hath she flitted and shrieked about the ancestral patrimony of the O'Neills!"

"And yet, Moira, not one O'Neill hath died of late—why so superstitious?"

"Ah, Melville! and do you accuse me of *superstition*, who know so well the acts of Mavin Rho, the Benshee of Shane's Castle, and the mysterious influence she possesses over the destinies of its inhabitants?"

Meredith kissed the affrighted girl's pale cheek, and was silent; first, because he liked not to dispute with Moira; and secondly (although he wished to conceal the fact even from himself), because he was but too sensible that round his heart also crept a cold fear, as he heard floating in the breeze tones at once so dreary, melancholy, and wild. Silently and swiftly he walked on, catching, in mere absence of mind, at every protruding twig from every bush in his way.

"Oh Melville, Melville! what have you done?" cried Moira, as they stood in the moonlight on the steps of the castle. "Put it down, put it down immediately!"

"Ay," replied Meredith, smiling: "What indeed! I suppose our Benshee, like the rest of our race, will be for avenging the rape of the white thorn; but, Moira, as for putting it away, that, craving your pardon, I certainly shall not do: in an hour I return to Antrim, and this little branch will serve me as a me- [126] mento of the past and an anticipation of the future. When we are married, I may perhaps oblige you."

At this instant a fierce and dismal yell, as if from a fiend perched on the turrets of the old castle, harrowed the souls of the lovers, who immediately retreated some paces from the edifice and looked up, but in vain; they could discover nothing. A sound, however, resembling the tempestuous roaring of a conflagration, now struck their astonished senses, whilst the words "*Away! away! away!* were distinctly uttered by an unearthly voice, shrill as that of the curlew in the storm, and sad as that of the angle of death. Meredith hurried Moira into the castle; there the ominous voice had been heard, and the portentous sounds of destruction; and in the great hall its denizens had assembled in the utmost consternation. The father and brother of Moira advanced to meet her, but the terrified maiden, hiding her head in her mother's bosom, wept, and rejected all consolation and all endeavours to prove her presentiments groundless.

Now rushed in, with eyes fixed, and glaring wildly, as if opened to behold some being of the viewless world, and with his long silver locks streaming in disorder over his pale and haggard features, Ryan O'Neill, the bard of Neill O'Neill's household, and one of the poorer members of a branch of that family.

"And did I not see her?" exclaimed he; "and will I not know again Mavin Rho, the ould Benshee, that screeched when my angle-child lay dying?" [127]

"The what have you seen?" asked many voices, whilst all attention was quickly transferred from Moira to Ryan; around him every creature thronged in an agony of curiosity and superstitious terror.

"Didn't she, thrice ere my Vauria died, clench her cloudy hands, and shake her sad, sad face at me? and didn't she do it now?—Didn't she then stand at the entry of this castle, even as now she's just in the middle of this hall?—See ye not, hear ye not, the wild Benshee? Her dim form is like cloud in the moonshine, and vivid roaring fires about her!"

Ryan fell back, with eyes upturned, with mouth open, with a countenance distorted and ghastly pale, whilst every limb of his aged frame shook with convulsive tremors. His affrighted auditors cast a fearful glance around the hall, where nothing save themselves being visible, promptly afforded succour to the wretched bard. During this interval, Meredith contrived to slip the bridal ring into the hand of his affrighted Moira, and, in spite of tears, remonstrances, and tender entreaties, tore himself from her, and proceeded on his wild and solitary road to Antrim.

When Ryan O'Neill recovered from the species of ecstacy into which he had fallen, he rose and commenced chanting an irregular, melancholy song, conceived in numbers, to which his gigantic stature, his impressive gestures, the worn and pallid appearance of his venerable face, and the deep pathos of his hollow voice, gave dreadful import and interest, although, [128] from its oracular incoherence and the disturbed state of his auditors' minds, they gleaned from it little, save that some horrible catastrophe threatened the house of O'Neill; that "the brightness and the darkness of destruction would shortly envelope Shane's Castle," which Mavin Rho could not save; for, that she numerous and powerful enemies of the White Thorn were now to have their hour to prevail and to rejoice.

Now, to Benshees of every grade, and belonging to every ancient family, the white thorn, it is well known, is sacred, which accounts for the alarm of Moira on observing a spray of that plant in the hand of Melville Meredith; and the prophecy of Ryan seemed to every individual in Shane's Castle indicative of supernatural conflicts and the desertion of the family and castle by Mavin Rho, who, though she was accustomed to wail ominously to prepare the O'Neills for a family loss, was upon the whole regarded as a friendly and guardian being. The domestics, and some cottagers, whom strange aerial cries without the castle, and stranger reports of what was passing within, had drawn thither, eyed Neill O'Neill askance—for rumours of unhallowed confederacies into which he had entered, and arts, mysterious and forbidden, in which he was engaged, were current amongst the tenantry of Shane. But far more did all eyes turn suspiciously upon the lord of the castle, when, upon the proposition of the domestic chaplain, that, in this harrowing juncture, the aid of the Ruler of the Spirits should be sought, Neill O'Neill [129] exclaimed—"Pray ye that will; prayer suits not me!" and, ordering a plentiful supply of whiskey to be distributed amongst his drooping vassals, he quitted the hall. Moira, and the remainder of her near and dear relations, also left the apartment; and the dependents, commencing a hearty carousal, related deeds of the invisible world fully sufficient to make their flesh quiver and creep upon their bones. All that dreary night was a voice heard moaning and lamenting above the old castle; and though its tones were low and plaintive, yet, in the still murky hour, they seemed to penetrate the most secret recesses of the antique structure, and to search the finest fibres of the heart.—That voice was the voice of *Mavin Rho*!

Next day the preparations for Moira's bridal recommenced with abundant activity, and the arrival of a party of gay young people, who had been invited to attend the ceremony, would, it was hoped, revive the drooping spirits of the bride, especially, too, as some of them had that morning seen and spoken to Melville Meredith in the town of Antrim. Moira, however, brought up in the beautiful and sublime solitudes of the castle and vicinity of Loch Neagh, suffered to wander at will, and alone, through wood, wild, and the passes of the mountains, and to imbibe a taste for the mythology of the peasants, where every cottage afforded its hoard of tales of terror, became strangely timid and superstitious. In the night-hour, oft would her heart beat, almost to bursting, at the remembrance[130] of those supernatural stories; oft, in broad daylight, would she tremble, she knew not why, save that she seemed to feel the presence of some invisible being; and oft would she rush homewards from the lone romantic beauties that she loved, impelled and harrowed by a fancy that portrayed a thousand beings, viewless to human ken, peopling the deep sylvan solitudes, a thousand voices roaring in the winds and waters, and a thousand careering wings pursuing her in the fleet blasts, whose song was so unearthly, between the mountains. Moira, a prey to such appealing phantasms, secretly believed that her friends had seen and conversed with Meredith's *fetch* and that she should, in the course of the day, hear of his demise, or see his corpse brought in covered with gore, or sodden by the waters of the lake; therefore, though tranquil, she was sad, and under forced gaiety but ill concealed the disquietude of her soul.

That night mirth was within Shane's Castle, and the voice of Mavin Rho without. Loud and long, fierce and drear, was the Benshee's cry, and there were who heard, if the lord of the mansion did not, "*Up! Up! Neill O'Neill! why tarry here?*" But O'Neill when he retired to rest was informed of this circumstance, as also that some of the villagers had discerned the misty, indistinct figure of a woman, standing on one of the parapets, wringing her hands, and uttering grievous lamentations, whilst a dun, fiery halo seemed to surround the castle as if to consume it. [131]

"Pshaw!" cried O'Neill, "very pretty stories to scare the village brats; but I'm not so to be imposed on."

"*O'Neill! O'Neill!*" shrieked a voice, apparently at the casement of the chamber, "*why tarry here?*"

The fearless lord of Shane's Castle then said, after a while, to his terrified lady, in a low smothered tone, and with the countenance of ghastly affright, "Let your servants attend you; this is no imposition; I must see the chaplain." In half an hour the chapel-bell had rung, and the festive castle-party, together with most of the domestics, and a few villagers, whom the novelty of the sound had attracted from their quiet pillows, were at public prayers in the sacred fane; exhibiting on the part of Neill O'Neill, who had scoffed at the means of averting calamity until a warning had been particularly addressed to himself, a very striking instance of the perverseness and presumption of man. The remainder of the night passed tranquilly, and the blush of morning relieved the fears of Moira for the safety of her lover, since Meredith himself appeared with the break of day.

More lovely than the roseate tint of early morn is the blush that mantles on the cheek of the youthful bride upon the blessed day of her espousals; more radiant and joyous than the newly-wakened sun is the smile that lights her delicate features, and the bliss that gleams in her loving eyes. Such beauty arrayed the countenance of Moira, and, in a less degree, that [132] of the elegant Melville, when, meeting on this happy morning, the enamoured pair knew that in this world they should never, never part again.

The interesting ceremony was fixed to take place in the evening, according to a custom prevalent in many noble families; and, after "one long summer's day of holiday and mirth," which, but for a sultry and tempest-boding afternoon, would have been perfection, the hour arrived, and at about ten o'clock the happiest of bridal parties entered the chapel of Shane's Castle. Moira was arrayed in white, and a beautiful wreath of green clustering shamrock encircled her bright hair. She trembled as the awful ceremony commenced, but became like an aspen-leaf when the terrific shriek of Mavin Rho, mingled with the growling of distant thunder, rang through the chapel. The good priest paused, and thrice the shrill cry of "Away!" accompanied by the same awful and unaccountable sound of a devouring conflagration, which had caused so much alarm on the third previous evening, chilled the assembly, and the dismayed lovers gazed on each other in unutterable sorrow and despair.

"*Lost! Lost! Lost!*" shrieked the dreary and superhuman voice; a vivd flash of red and angry lightning preluded a thunderclap that rocked the castle from its foundations, and stunned its horrified inmates, whilst cries and shrieks of the most hideous kind were heard above and around it. Every soul rushed for protection to the alter; the sacred apartment became filled [133] with vapour, and in the centre of it was apparent, all misty, and in lineaments undefined, a female form. *"Tis she! 'Tis she!"* cried Ryan O'Neill, and hid his face in his hands, whilst most of the spectators of this unexpected apparition fled from the chapel as for their lives. Dim were the lineaments and features of the Benshee; her cloudy frame was like the mists of night when moonbeams faintly struggle through; her countenance was not unpleasing, but very, very sad, and resembling that of a female O'Neill who had years before been burnt to death in Castle Shane: her attire was strictly antique, and exactly similar to the old costume in which the unfortunate Hilda hung portrayed in the great gallery. The apparition shook mournfully her misty head, and fixed, in melancholy gaze, her vapoury, dim eyes upon the few trembling beings who yet remained at the alter. Her pale, thin lips emitted mournful screams, such even as proceed form the agonized hearts of the despairing dying. She wrung her airy hands, apparently in excessive sorrow, and floated slowly forward to the alter.

"Fire! fire!" now shouted that multitude, who, having quitted the castle, beheld it almost immediately enveloped in volumes of fierce flame and sooty smoke. "Fire! fire!" The terrible cry resounded far and wide, and the tenantry of Neill o'Neill quitted the bridal festivities to aid their lord in this dreadful extremity. Shouts, shrieks, lamentations, tremendous thunderings, terrific lightnings, red, streaky fires, that [134] seemed aspiring to the very heavens; black, heavy clouds of smoke, slowly rising from the conflagration, and adding, in their solemn spread, a lurid darkness to the night, combined to form a scene of horrors surpassing description.

But louder, far louder, than the voice of man and the roar of the elemental conflict, were the direful and exulting shouts of malignant powers, who, black and fearful in form, were, by the red light of the flames, beheld fluttering over this scene of devastation, and chasing each other on busy wing, with infernal laughter, through the terrific fires and curled volleys of dense suffocating smoke.

Morning presented a spectacle too dismal to be delineated, and to the last degree affecting and awful, when the desolated and incinerated relic of Shane's Castle was compared with that proud structure, in the brilliancy and joyousness of the preceding day! Let us be brief: our tale would record events that have formed for years a portion of the superhuman lore of the peasants who reside on or near the O'Neill estate, and the borders of Loch Neagh; but events that are now fast fading into oblivion. Neill O'Neill was found scorched to death; as it was apprehended, the flames had seized him during his flight from the chapel towards his laboratory. The eye-sight of Ryan O'Neill was extinguished for ever; but he survived the destruction of the castle for some years, and was supported by the only son of Neill O'Neill, who had [135] escaped without injury, and afterwards rebuilt the edifice, and inherited the domain. The mother of Moira, the domestic chaplain, and some of the servants, were found dead beside the alter, to which they had fondly clung for protection, destroyed either by fear or suffocation. Moira and Melville were never heard of more. Some pretend that Mavin Rho transported them uninjured to Fairy Land; some imagine that, in striving to escape through the fire and smoke, they perished—a circumstance at least probable; nevertheless, the chapel remained unscathed by the flames, whilst neither they nor any remnants of them were ever discovered. Some assert that they have met, when belated in the woods of Shane's Castle, rather floating forward than walking, a youth and a maiden of blessed and smiling aspect; sometimes they are silent, sometimes they seem to converse; and the virgin, clad in pure white, which glistens in the pale moon rays, wears round her golden hair a coronet of clustering shamrock, that sparkles with the clear and vivid light of green gem of other climes. And other affirm, that when the enamoured moon throws over the loch her pale, broad blaze, a bark, swifter and fairer than was ever mortal vessel, glides over the quiet, shining expanse of dreamy waters, whilst voices, sweet as the voices of the just, issue thence, uttering delicious songs! Oft, too, is that aerial music heard in melancholy wood and sequestered dell, or amid the lonely, gust passes of mountains, romantic and sublime, flinging afar, in [136] the deep silence of holy night, its tones of unutterable peace and blessedness! But for Mavin Rho, it is generally agreed, that on the night of the burning of Shane's Castle, the friendly Benshee resigned her trust; never since has she there been heard of or beheld. Some also, in these latter days of scepticism and refinement, pretend, notwithstanding the preceding authentic tradition of her actual apparition, to doubt that she ever existed. To such we might reply in the sacred words of Holy Writ, did we not fear to commit profanation, in mingling the Scriptures of Truth with the wild legend of Erin.

M. L. B.

Title

Author of "Tales of An Antiquary," etc. [Thomson, Richard.] "The Haunted Hogshead. A Yankee Legend." FMN 1831. 145-154. [145]

THE HAUNTED HOGSHEAD.
A YANKEE LEGEND.
BY RICHARD THOMSON, ESQ.
AUTHOR OF "TALES OF AN ANTIQUARY," ETC.

"Oh, wonderful! wonderful! and most wonderful, wonderful! and yet again wonderful! and after that, out of all whooping!"
SHAKSPEARE.

YOU don't live to Boston, then, do you? No; I calculate you are from the old country, though you speak English almost as well as I do. Now, I'm a Kentucky man, and my father was to Big-bone Creek, in old Kentucky, where he could lather every man in the state, but I could like my father. Well! when I first came to Boston, I guess, I was a spry, active young fellow, and cruel tall for my age; for it's a pretty considerable long time ago, I calculate. So first I goes to look out for Uncle Ben—you've heard of him and his brown mar, I reckon—and I finds Uncle Ben at Major Hickory's Universal Transatlantic Hotel, by Charles Bay, in East Boston, taking a grain of mighty fine elegant sangaree, with Judge Dodge and President Pinkney the Rowdey, that built the powerful large log mansion-house in Dog's Misery, in the salt-marshes out beyond Corlear's Hook, in New York. I was always a leetle bit of a favourite with Uncle Ben, and so he says to me—

"Jonathan W.," says he, for he calls me Jonathan W. for short; "I'll tell you what it is," says Uncle Ben, "you come out mighty bright this morning, I motion that you take a drop of whisky-toddy or so." [146]

"Oh yes, Uncle Ben," says I; "I should admire to have a grain, if it's hansome."

"Considerable superb," says he; "it's of the first grade, I guess, for Major Hickory keeps wonderfully lovely liquors; and I can tell you a genuine good story about them, such as, I guess, you never heard before, since you was raised."

And then he up and told such a tale, that the helps all crowded round him to hear it, and swore it was better than a sermon, so it was. And as you're a stranger from the old country, and seem a right slick-away sort of a chap, without a bit of the gentleman about you, and are so mighty inquisitive after odd stories, why I don't mind telling it to the 'Squire myself; and you may depend upon it that it's as true and genuine as if you had heard it from Uncle Ben himself, or July White, his old woolly-headed nigger.

You must know, then, that the Universal Transatlantic Hotel was built an awful long time before I was raised; though my Uncle Ben remembered a powerful grand wood house that stood there before it, which was called the Independent Star of Colombia, kept by Jacobus Van Soak, who came to Boston from the old, ancient, veteran Dutch settlers of New York. It was some time after fall in the year 77, that a mighty fierce squall of wind blew down some of the wall of the house where the cellar was, quite to the very foundation. I reckon that the old host was a leetle bit madded at this, he was; though he bit in his [147] breath, and thought to drive in some new stakes, put up fresh clap-boards, and soon have it all slick and grand again; but, in so doing, as he was taking out the piles underneath the house, what does he find but an awful great big barrel, and a cruel heavy on it was, and smelled like as if it was a hogshead of astonishingly mighty fine old ancient rum. I'll lay you'll never guess how they got it out of the cellar, where they found it, because they never moved it at all, I calculate; though some of the helps and neighbours pulled and tugged at it like natur! But the more they worked, the more the barrel wouldn't move; and my Uncle Ben said that might strannge sounds came out of it, just as if it didn't like to be disturbed and brought into the light; and that it swore at the helps and niggers in English and Spanish, Low German and High Dutch. At last, old Van Soak began to be a leetle bit afeard, and was for covering it up again where he found it, till my Uncle Ben vowed it shouldn't be buried without his having a drop out of it, for he was a bold active man, that cared for nothing, and loved a grain of rum, or sangaree, or whisky-toddy, or crank, or any other fogmatic, to his heart, he did. So down in the cellar he sets himself, drives a spigot into the barrel, and draws him a glass of such mighty fine elegant rum, as was never seen before in all Boston.

"Handsome! considerably handsome! mighty smart rum, I guess," says my Uncle Ben, as he turned it down; "mild as mother's milk, and bright as a flash [148] of lightning! By the pipe of St. Nicholas, I must have another grain!" So he filled him another glass, and then Jacobus plucked up heart, and he took a grain or two, and the helps and bystanders did the same, and they all swore it was superbly astonishing rum, and as old as the Kaatskill mountains, or the days of Wouter Van Twiller, the first Dutch Governor of New York, Well! I calculate that they might at least be a leetle bit staggered, for the rum ran down like water, and they drank about, thinking, you see, that all the strength was gone; and as they were in the dark cellar, they never knew that the day was progressing powerfully fast towards night; for now the barrel was quiet again, and they began to be mighty merry together. But the night came on cruel smart and dark, I reckon, with a pretty terrible loud storm; and so they all thought it best to keep under shelter, and especially where such good stuff was to be had free, gratis, for nothing, into the bargain.

  Nobody knows now what time it was, when they heard a mighty fierce knocking on the top of the barrel, and presently a hoarse voice from the inside cried out, "Yo ho, there brothers! open the hatchway and let me out!" which made them all start, I calculate, and sent Van Soak reeling into a dark corner of the cellar, considerably out of his wits with fright and stout old rum.

"Don't open the hogshead," cried the helps and neighbours, in mighty great fear; "it's the Devil!"

"Potstausend!" says my Uncle Ben;—for you must [149] know that he's a roistering High-German;—"You're a cowardly crew," says he, "that good liquor's thrown away upon."

"Thunder and storm!" called out the voice again from the barrel, "why the Henker don't you unship the hatches? Am I to stay here these hundred years?"

"Stille! mein Herr!" says my Uncle Ben, says he, without being in the least bit afeard, only a leetle madded and wondered he was; "behave yourself handsom, and don't be in such a pretty particular considerable hurry. I'll tell you what it is; before you come out I should like to make an enquerry of you:—Who are you? where were you raised? how have you got along in the world? and when did you come here? Tell me all this speedily, or I shall decline off letting you out, I calculate."

"Open the hogshead, brother!" said the man in the tub, says he, "and you shall know all, and a pretty considerable sight more; and I'll take mighty good care of you for ever, because you're an awful smart, right-slick-away sort of a fellow, and not like the cowardly land-lubbers that have been sucking away my rum with you."

"Hole mich der Teufel!" said my Uncle Ben, "but this is a real rig'lar Yankee spark, a tarnation stout blade, who knows what a bold man should be; and so, by the Henker's horns, I'll let him out at once."

So, do you see, Uncle Ben made no more ado but broke in the head of the barrel; and what with the [150] storm out of doors, and the laughing and swearing in the cask, a mighty elegant noise there was while he did it, I promise you: but at last there came up out of the hogshead a short, thick-set, truculent, sailor-looking fellow, dressed in the old ancient way, with dirty slops, tarnished gold-laced hat, and blue, stiff-skirted coat, fastened up to his throat with a mighty sight of brass buttons, Spanish steel pistols in a buffalo belt, and a swinging cutlass by his side. He looked one of the genuine privateer, bull-dog breed, and his broad swelled face, where it was not red with rage, or the good rum, was black or purple; marked, I reckon, with a pretty considerable many scars, and his eyes were almost starting out of his head.

If the helps and neighbours were afeard before, they were no astounded outright, I calculate; and 'specially so when the strannge Sailor got out of his hogshead, and began to lay about him with a fist as hard and as big as a twelve-pounder cannon-shot, crying like a bull-frog in a swamp,—"Now I shall clear out! A plague upon ye all for a crew of cowardly, canting, lubberly knaves! I might have been sucked dry, and staid in the barrel for ever, if your comrade had borne no stouter a heart than you did."

Well, I guess, that by knocking down the helps and the neighbours he soon made a clear ship; and then, striding up to my Uncle Ben, who warn't not at all afeard, but was laughing at the fun, he says to him, says he, "As for you, brother, you're a man after my [151] own kidney, so give us your fin, and we'll soon be sworn friends, I warrant me." But as soon as he held out his hand, Uncle Ben thought he saw in it the mark of a red horse-shoe, like a brand upon a nigger, which some do say was the very stamp of the Devil put upon Captain Kidd, when they shook hands after burying his treasure at Boston, before he was hanged.

"Hagel!" says my Uncle Ben, says he, "what's that in your right hand, my friend?"

"What's that to you?" said the old Sailor. "We mariners get many a broad and deep red scar, without talking about, or making them; but then we get the heavy red gold, and broad pieces along with them, and that's a tarnation smart plaster, I calculate."

"Then," says my Uncle Ben again, says he, "may I make an enquerry of you? Where were you raised? and who's your Boss?"

"Oh!" says the Sailor, "I was born at Nantucket, and Cape Cod, and all along shore there, as the nigger said; and for the Captain I belong to, why, he's the chief of all the fierce and daring hearts which have been in the world ever since time began."

"And, pray, where's your plunder?" says my Uncle Ben to the strannge Sailor; "and how long have you been in that hogshead?"

"Over long, I can tell you, brother; I thought I was never going to come out, I calculate. As for my plunder, I reckon I don't show every body my locker; but [152] you're a bold fellow enough, and only give me your paw to close the bargain, and I'll fill your pouch with dollars for life. I've a stout ship and comrades ready for sea, and there's plunder everywhere for lads of the knife and pistol, I reckon; though the squeamish Lord Bellamont does watch them so closely."

"Lord who?" says Uncle Ben, a leetle bit madded and wondered.

"Why, Lord Bellamont, to be sure," answered the strannge sailor, "the English Governor of New England, and Admiral of the seas about it, under King William the Third."

"Governor and Admiral in your teeth!" says my Uncle Ben again; for now his pluck was up, and there warn't no daunting him them; "what have we to do with the old country, your kings, or your governors? this is the Free City of Boston, in the Independent United States of America, and the second Year of Liberty, Seventy-seven, I reckon. And as for your William the Third, I guess he was dead long before I was raised, and I'm no cockerell. I'll tell you what it is, now, my smart fellow, you're got pretty considerably drunk in that rum cask, if you've been there ever since them old ancient days; and, to speak my mind plain, you're either the Devil or Captain Kidd. But I'd have you to know, I'm not to be scared by a face of clay, if you were both; for I'm an old Kentuck Rowdey, of Town-Fork by the Elkhorn; my breed's half a horse and [153] half an alligator, with a cross of the earthquake! You can't poke your fun at me, I calculate; and so, here goes upon you for a villain, any way!"

My Uncle Ben's pluck was now all up; for pretty considerably madded he was, and could bit in his breath no longer; so he flew upon the strannge Sailor, and walked into him like a flash of lightning into a gooseberry-bush, like a mighty, smart, active man as he was. Hold of his collar laid my Uncle Ben, and I reckon they did stoutly struggle together for a tarnation long time, till at last the mariner's coat gave way, and showed that about his neck there was a halter, as if he had been only fresh cut down from the gibbet!—Then my Uncle Ben did start back a pace or two, when the other let fly at him with a pretty considerable hard blow, and so laid him right slick sprawling along upon the ground.

Uncle Ben said he never could guess how long they all laid there; but when they came to, they found themselves all stretched out like dead men by the niggers of the house, with a staved rum cask standing beside them. But, now—mark you this well—on one of the head-boards of the barrel was wrote, "W. K. The Vulture. 1701," which was agreed by all to stand for William Kidd, the Pirate. And July White, Uncle Ben's woolly-headed old nigger, said that he was once a loblolly-boy on board that very ship, when she was a sort of pickarooning privateer. Her crew told [154] him that she sailed from the old country the very same year marked on the cask, when Kidd was hanged at Execution-Dock, and that they brought his body over to be near the treasure that he buried; and as every one knows that Kidd was tied up twice, why, perhaps, he never died at all, but was kept alive in that mighty elegant rum cask, till my Uncle Ben let him out again, to walk about New-York and Boston, round Charles Bay and Cape Cod, the Old Sow and Pigs, Hellegat, and the Hen and Chickens. There was a fat little Dutch Parson, who used to think that this story was only a mighty smart fable, because nobody could remember seeing the Pirate besides Uncle Ben; and he would sometimes say, too, that they were all knocked down by the rum, and not by the Captain, though he never told Uncle Ben so, I calculate; for he always stuck to it handsomely, and wouldn't 'bate a word of it for nobody.

When Uncle Ben had finished, he says, "Jonathan W." says he, "I'll tell you what it is: I'll take it as a genuine favour if you'll pay Major Hickory for the sangaree and the toddy, and we'll be quits another day." And so I paid for it every cent; but would you believe it? though I've asked him for it a matter of twenty times, and more than that, Uncle Ben never gave me back the trifle that he borrowed of me from that day to this!

Title

Hesketh, S. K. "The Smuggler." FMN 1831. 165-182. [165]

THE SMUGGLER.

"WHY, then, what in the wide world are ye standing there fore, and the lugger coming up into your very mouths?" exclaimed a young peasant, as he joined a group who were inactively gazing on the scene before them.

"And don't you know, Jem," said one of the crowd, "that Serjeant Jones—bad luck to his ugly soul!—took every one of the oars from us, before we could put them in hide; and the Peelers [anglicé, police] are all along the shore; the devil so much as a cockle-shell can stir unknownst to them."

"I would not doubt him, the English blackguard," said the first speaker. "Isn't this a cruel case? and we breaking our heart all the winter, making them caves; and now, between the Peelers and the revenee cruiser, 'tis empty they'll be always."

"Whisht! whisht! Jem, you fool," said a patriarchal-looking old man, coming forward; "do you think the captain will let them on board of him? He'd rather see the lugger and all down Poul-carca."

"And how can he help himself, why?" persisted Jem. "Won't them boats of the cruiser be at him, before he can say Jack Robinson? Oh! 'tis himself that's fairly bothered, whatever came over him, that he didn't keep out at sea till the night. What'll we do at all, and where's Tom Sullivan?"

"Oh, then, where is Tom, sure enough?" said several voices eagerly. [166]

"I'll tell you, boys," said the old man already mentioned, lowering his voice as the circle closed round him, "'tis on board of the lugger he is."

A general murmur of approbation broke from the crowd.

"And that same is a comfort, any way," said the loquacious Jem; "the never a one in the whole country is a match for Tom; he'll give 'em the slip surely." And all agreed that "there was no coming up to Tom."

Now, perhaps, the reader may wish to learn where and wherefore all this consultation was held. The group stood on the extreme point of one of the many little promontories, which with their corresponding inlets are included in a large bay, the most fatal to mariners of any on the iron-bound south-western coast of Ireland. Many are the wild and dismal tales told by the peasantry of the shipwrecks which have from time to time occurred there; and for many years, no merchant vessel has been known voluntarily to approach the "Mal-bay," save one unfortunate ship, whose master, mistaking it for Galway bay, to which it bears some resemblance, ran in before the wind. He did not discover his error until too late; for, a gale springing up, his vessel struck upon a sunken rock, and instantly went down. She was freighted with rich cargo; and elephants' teeth are still occasionally found by the fishermen amongst the rocks, perpetuating the recollection of her melancholy fate. [167]

The bad character of the bay was rather favourable than otherwise to the practice of smuggling. The masters of vessels engaged in this illegal traffic made themselves acquainted with every lonely spot where it was possible to run their cargoes, and had acquired so accurate a knowledge of the position of every rock and shoal in the bay, as to render its very dangers subservient to their purposes, by enabling them to sail in safety where no other vessel dared to follow. They avoided the peril of lingering on that coast by the zealous co-operation of the peasantry, who, on the appearance of the smuggler, surrounded her in their canoes, (little wicker boats covered with horse hides, or tarred canvas) and conveyed her cargo, in an incredibly short time, to different places of concealment. Their eagerness to become purchasers to tea, brandy, &c., was quite unchecked by any apprehension of the consequences; and many, who were supposed to be literally penniless, often produced considerable sums of money to procure the proscribed luxuries, of which they afterwards found means to dispose on very advantageous terms.

It is a singular fact that, of the many hundreds by whose means these illegal practices were carried on, scarcely one individual could be found who entertained the least conscientious scruple with regard to them. Smuggling was almost universally viewed in the same light in which the Spartans are said to have regarded theft, viz. as highly meritorious unless discovered. To baffle the revenue officers, in their frequent searches [168] for contraband goods, was their greatest care, and the seizures were consequently rare and inconsiderable.

One of the modes of concealment which their ingenuity had devised deserves to be recorded. In a small island at the mouth of the bay, they formed several deep pits, working perpendicularly downwards for some feet; and then, enlarging the lower part, they placed small beams across to prevent the earth from falling in, and lined the whole carefully with timber. The only access to these caves, as the peasantry called them, was from above, by an opening about the size and appearance of a grave. This opening was occupied by a large box, the bottom of which rested on a ledge at a distance from the surface equal to its own depth. The box was nearly filled with earth, which was accurately covered with green turf, so that when the box was let down into its birth, it was impossible to distinguish the turn which was placed over it from the rest of the field, tis verdure being preserved and its growth nourished by the earth beneath it.

It as early in the month of April, 18—, that the event occurred which forms the subject of this tale. The morning of the 13th was dark and lowering. The sea was unusually calm, though not perfectly still; for the strife of those great waters is unceasing. Even in the sultriness of the long midsummer days, when the air is motionless, and the burning sun has subdued all else into breathless stillness, the beating of the ocean surge against its rocky boundaries falls ever on the [169] ear, as if to tell that the pride of its mighty undulations may not be repressed save by the hand of the Eternal.

About noon, a light breeze sprang up, and a large schooner, rounding the headland of Moher, and emboldened by the impunity with which she had often before run her cargoes, stood in shore, without waiting, as was usual, for the obscurity of night. The tide of her prosperity had turned. The revenue officers at Kilrush had, the previous night, received intelligence of her intended visit to the coast, and hastily concerted a plan for her capture. Directions were accordingly sent to the powers at Miltown-Malbay, and measures were there taken, as we have seen, to prevent any communications between the lugger and the shore. A revenue cruiser, also, sailed from Scattery Roads, in the Shannon, with orders to lie concealed until the smuggling vessel had neared the land, when, appearing at the mouth of the bay, she was cut off her retreat. This manoeuvre was executed with the most complete success, and the new and beautiful schooner, with her valuable cargo, was left, apparently without a possibility of escape, to the tender mercies of the amiable guardians of his majesty's excise. But here a difficulty occurred in the eagerness of the aforesaid gentlemen to intercept their prey. The lugger kept so close in shore as to render it very dangerous, if not quite impossible, for the cruiser to approach her; and it would have been equally imprudent to attempt boarding an enemy so formidably [170] manned and armed with the small force which they could muster in their boats. It was impossible to procure any assistance from shore, as it was necessary that the few police there should be in readiness to oppose the landing of the smuggler's crew. The disconcerted cruiser was, therefore, obliged to be content with keeping a gloomy watch over her victim, until an additional force, which she had signaled for, should arrive. Her armed boats meantime rowed about the bay, to prevent any attempt of the smugglers to escape in their boats; but the commander of the cruiser, well knowing the danger of being left without sufficient number of hands on so dangerous a coast, and also to guard against any stratagem of the smuggler to separate him from his boats, had given strict orders that they should keep within a certain distance of their vessel.

It as at this juncture of affairs that the conversation which has been recorded took place. We left the group rejoicing in the circumstance of Tom Sullivan's being on board the schooner. Now as Tom is, in some sort, the hero of our tale, and also a very fair specimen of his genus, it is fit that he should be introduced to the reader. But, to account for his appearance in "such a questionable shape," we must speak a little of his "birth, parentage, and education." His father, Patrick Sullivan, was a fisherman, who had added to his principal occupation the care of a few acres of land, which had prospered under his ma- [171] nagement, so that he was more comfortably established that "the neighbours." His cottage was situated on the sea-shore, under shelter of a steep hill, and flanked by one or two offices for the reception principally of those favoured animals, the pigs, which are generally allowed, at proper seasons, amongst the class to which Patrick belonged, an unrestrained freedom of access to all parts of their owner' cabins. Opposite to the front of the house, the shore was covered with huge stones, completely rounded by the action of the sea, nearly down to low-water mark; beyond which extended a low range of rocks, covered with short sea-weed. At either side the rocks rose into bolder and more varied diversities of form; and still farther on, high and abrupt cliffs opposed the waves. Three or four canoes, placed high on the beach, bottom upward, denoted Patrick's occupation, and the precaution taken to secure even the roof of his cottage from the effects of storms, by fastening on the thatch with straw ropes, hinted at the danger of his vocation. The interior of the dwelling scarcely differed in the least particular from those of his brother fishermen around; for he would be there considered a daring innovator, who should presume to deviate from their usual style of architecture, or system of internal arrangement. The unplastered mud walls, the earthen floor with its thousand irregularities, the huge tapering chimney with its coronet of straw, and the wicker half-door to keep the childer in and the pigs out, [172] at those seasons when their absence was considered desirable, were all to be seen in every fishing hamlet on the coast. The nets, lines, poles, and other apparatus were, as usual, stretched across the rafters; and sometimes, when all collected, formed a sort of ceiling, which gave the cottage a warmer appearance than if the rafters had been unfurnished with these implements of industry. Tom was a fisherman almost from his cradle, and had scarcely arrived at manhood before he was famed as being one of the most skilful and daring between Loop-head and Moher. His life, however, was not one of unremitting employment. The tempestuous Atlantic cannot at all times be spoiled of its finny inhabitants; and even the canoes, which live in a higher sea than any other description of boat, are sometimes obliged to lie idle on the beach. At these times Tom was at liberty to pursue his favourite sport. Pulling a rusty, dangerous-looking, old fowling-piece from under his bed, he would sally forth, and, taking a range of the shore for two or three miles, he was pretty sure to meet some one of those young sportsmen, who, with a laudable contempt of every less rational pursuit, devote themselves with untiring assiduity to the destruction of sea-gulls and cormorants, and who, were their abilities but equal to their zeal, would doubtless ere now have exterminated those obnoxious portions of animated nature. To such Tom was always welcome. He was familiar with every rock and cave in the whole bay, and was [173]mgenerally able to procure for them better sport than they would have otherwise had. Indeed Tom was the most desirable guide that could possibly be procured. There was something infectious in his light-hearted gaiety, and his strokes of genuine Irish humour were quite irresistible. No one ever thought of keeping Tom at "a proper distance;" the thing was absolutely impossible. There was so much drollery and originality in his remarks, that you felt glad to have an opportunity of conversing with him on terms of equality.

His natural shrewdness and quick insight into character were continually showing themselves, and there was never any offensive vulgarity to check the pleasure you felt in listening to him. Amongst his own class he was absolutely idolized. A pattern was not "a pattern" if Tom was absent; and in graver matters his advice and assistance were sought before that of many older and more experienced men. His very prepossessing personal appearance was no small addition to his other good qualities, in the judgement, at least, of his female acquaintance. But Tom was provokingly indifferent to the admiration which he excited in the fairer portion of the creation, and his careless hilarity was for a time unrepressed by any symptoms of the tender passion. However, the assertion of his invulnerability, which was a favourite one amongst the rural coquettes of the neighbourhood, was at length completely disproved. In other words, poor Tom fell desperately in love. Al- [174] though his passion was returned with equal warmth, yet the relative situation of the parties rendered it very unlikely that he should ever be able to attain the object of his wishes, by making the tall, slender, and even elegant-looking Mary Cassidy his wife. Tom's father and hers were the leaders of two adverse factions, and neither would listen to any proposals of so closely connecting their families. Since the time of the Montagues and Capulets, perhaps, no more sincere and lasting hostility had ever existed between near neighbours; and yet Tom was not without hope, that, could he amass what he considered a tempting fortune, it might prove a sufficient inducement to her father to forego all further hostility, and consent to a reconciliation and its consequences.

  To this object he turned all his attention; and it was in the prosecution of this scheme that he had recourse to the rather exceptionable means which his being on board the smuggler implied. His conscience, however, our English readers may doubt the fact, did not at all reproach him; and when at last he found himself outgeneraled, and counselled the opposing of force to force, he did so on the simple principle of self-preservation.

  The bold and desperate crew of the smuggler, finding that all hope of saving their vessels must be relinquished, determined that she should be entirely destroyed rather than suffered to fall into the hands of the enemy. They therefore ran her on a rock, about a hundred yards from shore, and, having set fire to her in several [175] places, prepared to effect a landing in defiance of all opposition. In putting this hazardous purpose into execution, the presence of Tom Sullivan was particularly useful. As they had returned the fire of the cruiser, when chased in the morning, their lives depended upon their making their escape. Although the night had now set in, Tom was able to guide them to a spot apparently well calculated for their purpose. At the point which he selected, a ledge of rocks, which ran out into the sea from the base of the cliff, terminated almost perpendicularly. The face of this rock was not difficult of ascent, and at about five feet from the summit was a projection running along its whole length, from which, without exposing themselves, they might observe all that was passing to landward. They scarcely expected that they should be allowed to land without opposition; however, seeing that the police were disposed to remain on the cliff above, the boats were lowered, manned, shoved off, and almost at the same instant reached the rocks, so closely had they run the schooner to the shore. The first burst of flame from the burning vessel, while it announced to the police that the work of her destruction had commenced, gave also to view her two boats, as they at that instant left her side. The desired position was however gained before the police were able to offer any resistance; and as they at length began awkwardly to descend the cliff, the light from the blazing vessel became sufficiently strong to enable [176] the smugglers to wound two of the party severely, on which they quickly retreated to their former post.

In the mean time the flames increased rapidly on board the devoted schooner, and soon exhibited one immense sheet of flame, that cast a strong unearthly light on all around, while it was unsteadily reflected on the trembling waters. Vast numbers of the peasantry flocked together from all quarters, many attracted by the novelty of the sight, but by far the greater number influenced by a stronger feeling that mere curiosity. There was one group in particular which showed the deepest interest in what was going forward. In the midst stood Tom Sullivan's father. He saw his son's danger to an extent of which her could not himself have been aware when he led his party to the spot which they now occupied. He knew that, could they succeed in passing along under cover of the rocks for some yards, they would be able to approach the cliff at a point which, from its apparent inaccessibility, was left unguarded by the police; but he had not seen that, before they could gain this point, they must pass a spot where, from a cleft in the rock, they should be fully exposed to the fire of the enemy. To this spot the police had also turned their attention. They had thrown themselves on the ground at the edge of the cliff, and, pointing their carbines in that direction, remained motionless. One only of the party traversed a small space which separated them from the peasantry, as a precaution against surprise. [177]

Tom Sullivan's friends hoped that he would perceive the danger before it was too late, and not make an attempt which much almost inevitably prove fatal. The smugglers, however, who, as long as the police were visible, had kept up a brisk fire, were deceived by their disappearance, and, concluding that they had retired from the cliff, were proceeding to that part of the shore from which, as we have said, they would have been almost certain to escape, when suddenly they came upon the opening in the rock, which was only about fifty yards distant from the cliff. The mate of the schooner passed forward. The instant his dark figure became visible, a volley was fired from above, and he fell lifeless into the sea. A murmur of horror ran through the crowd, who were spectators of this catastrophe. Though the night was extremely dark, yet every object was so brilliantly illuminated by

Forget Me Not

the flames, that the sailor's dress of the unfortunate mate had been distinguished; and there was no apprehension that it was Tom Sullivan who had fallen. But his danger was now manifestly imminent. His distracted father was surrounded my numerous friends, all suggesting plans equally impracticable for his son's rescue.

"Oh! boys, boys!" whispered one of the party, "if't was the red-coats instead of them Peelers we had to dale wid—." But the police were regarded with a superstitious horror, and no one dared directly to propose an attempt to overpower them. Indeed, the [178] attempt, had such been made, would probably have proved fruitless, as the police, who were apprehensive of an attack, had, in addition to the sentinel we have mentioned, placed themselves so as to interpose a high hedge between them and the people, whose numbers were now become very formidable.

"Only 'tis entirely impossible, Patrick," said our friend Jem, "I know the way to get them off clear and clean: but 'it is no use in life, unless they knew it themselves—and who's to tell them? 'Tis myself would think but little of going down the cliff to them," continued he; "only 'tis a dead man I'd be, surely, before I got there. Look at them black divels watching the rock as a cat would watch a mouse's hole."

However, Jem's despair of the practicability of his expedient did not prevent him from communicating it to those around, and certainly, as he himself said, there was but one obstacle to its being put into execution. None could be found, even amongst those most solicitous for the escape of the little band, who would consent to face almost inevitable death. But there was one who had stood in silent agony during the whole scene, and who seemed unconscious that there was a thronging crowd around her, or that she was the subject of general remark and sympathy. She had remained with her eyes fixed on the fatal opening in the rock, and had witnessed the death of the sailor with less emotion than any other spectator. Her whole soul seemed engrossed by one feeling. It was Mary Cas- [179] sidy, Tom Sullivan's love. But when the possibility of his escape was suggested by some one near her, she started from her stupor, and, learning that his safety depended on communicating their plan to him, she burst wildly through the circle which surrounded his father, entreating to be sent on this errand, which the bravest shrank from. None could believe that she understood the full extent of the danger to which she would thus expose herself. They pointed to the police, whose eyes were fixed on the rock, by which it was death to pass; and they showed the precipice down and along which she must clamber. But she could only see that there was a possibility of saving her lover, and she was deaf to all remonstrances. In truth, these remonstrances were not urged as eagerly as in any other case they would have been, for there was a ray of hope which no one would intercept.

The hedge which we have said separated the people from the police, making at this point a sudden turn, was completely hid from the view of the latter.

This was a favourite haunt of poor Tom's, and he used often to conceal himself in one of the many clefts in the rocks half-way down, to shoot at the large sea-gulls in their heavy coasting flight along the shore.

To an eye unaccustomed to these scenes, it appeared quite impossible to descend, and certainly no woman had ever before attempted it. But the delicate and timid Mary did not for an instant shrink from the dizzy precipice. Her friends could not venture [180] sufficiently near the edge of the cliff to witness her descent, lest they should have been observed by the police; but there was a death-like silence through all the people, which told their intense anxiety, as she passed from among them on her almost hopeless way. She had not foreseen many of the dangers which crowded round her as she advanced. The rock, which at first afforded a few natural steps, soon became broken and irregular, and afforded a footing so precarious, that the small stones on which she stepped often passed from under her feet, and went rolling and bounding into the deep and heaving sea beneath. But in spite of all dangers she, at length, stood on the natural platform, which we have described as running under cover of the rocks, along almost their whole length, and reached the fatal point where they ceased for a few yards to interpose between the cliff and the sea. She expected to have seen the imprisoned band on the other side of the cleft, and her heart died within her when she found herself disappointed. A little further on the rock again projected, and prevented her from seeing beyond; and, concluding that they were screened by it from her view, she closely examined her farther way, and perceived that there rose from the ledge or platform a very small portion of the rock, under which she thought she could creep without being seen above. The poor girl trembled violently as she attempted this most dangerous experiment. Should the rock for a moment prove insuf- [181] ficient to conceal her, she would inevitably be fired on, as the police could not even suspect that any other than one of the smugglers could be there at such a moment. This, the greatest danger, was passed in safety; and almost overcome with excess of agitation, Mary, turning the projecting rock, stood before the astonished group. The superstitious sailors started back in horror from the pale phantom-like figure seen by the strong blaze of their own vessel; but Tom Sullivan knew that it was no apparition, and though his daring courage had not been shaken by all the past scene, he now burst into tears. But there was no time to be lost, and Mary rapidly pointed out the means of escape which their friends had devised, and which they instantly adopted with the joy of men already saved from death.

The whole party stood by the spot which Mary had just passed, and, every thing begin ready, a pistol-hot, the appointed signal, was fired. Instantly there rose from the multitude on the cliffs a shout so simultaneous, so sudden, and so deafening, that the terrified police, concluding that the apprehended attack was about to be made by the people, drew together, and prepared for resistance.

The shot died away, and unbroken silence again settled down on the assembled throng. The police again, though with more caution, returned to their watch; but the one moment gained was invaluable; the opening was passed, and the little band, ascending the cliff in safety, mingled with the [182] crowd. To this day, Tom Sullivan's share in the adventures of the night is not known by any but his own friends, comprehending, as has been shown, no very inconsiderable number; and it has often afforded matter of wonder to Serjeant Jones how it came to pass that Patrick Sullivan and Darby Cassidy, those inveterate foes, whose desperate battles he was often summoned to terminate with strong arm, should now be such loving neighbours; and, above all, how a wedding, which soon after took place, could ever be suffered to unite the families so long at deadly feud.

S.K. HESKETH

Title

M'Naghten [McNaghten], Captain Sir William Hay. "The Sacrifice. An Indian Tale." FMN 1831. 193-213. [193]

THE SACRIFICE.
AN INDIAN TALE.
BY CAPTAIN M'NAGHTEN.

THE earliest beams of the rich sun of an eastern morning changed the crystal waters of the Nerbuddah into living gold, as the broad bright river caught the gorgeous ray on its clear untroubled bosom. How lovely and how tranquil seemed the delightful valley, enriched by the every-flowing springs of that fertilizing stream, and how beautiful a contrast did its verdant surface present with the dark and wild chain of the Goand mountains which stretched almost around it! Not a trace was now visible of the desolating track of the fierce Pindarries, whose predatory incursions into that and the surrounding districts had till lately been made with the regularity of the harvests, which twice in the year the generous soil presented, almost spontaneously, to the inhabitants. Terror preceded and the most wanton devastation followed the march of these organized freebooters; for, not content with merely sweeping the flocks and herds of the defenceless people, they applied various species of torture to the young, the aged, and the feminine, in order to extort a discovery of the places where it was supposed they had, in anticipation on the inroad, concealed their more valuable and portable effects. The villages were destroyed by fire, after they had been ransacked even to nakedness, and the cool murder of children, with the violation of the females, were the usual concomi- [194] tants of the plunder and destruction. Such were the fruits of the wretched policy adopted by the Mahratta princes regarding the internal security of their dominions, and such the miserable situation of their deserted subjects, till the humane, wise, and energetic exertions of the late Marquis of Hastings put an end to that singular system of lawless depredation, which had for so long a period of years devastated the fairest and the fruitfullest tracts of India.

So complete had been the extirpation of the whole race, and so sudden the blessed effects of security, that in the beautiful valley connected with our tale, not a trace was now discernible of the desolation caused by those fierce intruders; whose steps, but two years before, might have been too easily traced by the smouldering ruins which marked heir ruthless progress from their own wild abodes, along the whole extent of the now fair and smiling valley. That dark and blood-stained host had for ever disappeared; and in the neighbouring topes[28] or

---

28 *Tope*.—The use of this term, which is not a perfectly legitimate one, even in an Indian tale, reminds me of an error into which the genius-filled author of Waverley has fallen, in his late tale of the Surgeon's Daughter. In attempting to localize a part of that story in India, Sir Walter uses the word tope as synonymous with a *knowl*, or hill; whereas it signifies merely a *grove*, without reference to

groves of thick-leaved mangoe trees, and [195] under the shade of the widely-spreading and magnificent banian, which erected its green and curious colonnades near to a peaceful dwelling, that lay half-sequestered amid groups of the plantain, and partly shadowed by the lofty tufts of the stately palmyra, nought was to be seen more wild or savage than that troops of various, but sacred monkeys, frolicking among the branches; and flocks of the beautiful parroquet, which delighted and dazzled the eye that marked their flight from one part of the grove to another, or plumed their variegated wings in the sunshine. The young Heena, advancing from the door of her father's lowly dwelling, surveyed the peaceful scene with a happy and a [196]grateful heart. She had known the grief of the late insecurity, and her father, an old soldier, in the service of the Rajah of Nagpore, had been severely wounded in the defence of his native village against the hands of the spoiler: but these sorrows had ceased, and young and sanguine, both hope and joy had resumed their natural places in her breast; and she fondly trusted hat thenceforward the path of life would be as brilliant, and strewed with as many flowers of pleasure, as the sunlit and highly luxurious vale around her. She contemplated with calm and thankful pleasure those flocks and hers, which, preserved from the Pindarrie raids, now promised to secure a future competency to the beloved family so lately on the brink of irremediable upon the security afforded by the vigorous measures of the Company's government, and the vicinity of her present residence to Nagpore, the capital of the kingdom, for the permanency of the tranquil state which had happily succeeded fearful periods of alarm, havoc, and bloodshed. Still the smile which occasionally played around the rich, soft life of the beautiful and modest girl, and which illuminated her full, dark, and tender eye, had in it a pensiveness which gave to it a character of needless melancholy, in the view of an ignorant and surprised beholder, who could not perceive the cause of uneasiness in a scene and a person of such sweet serenity. Her yet budding bosom, like the wave but newly lulled to rest, heaved at [197] intervals with greater emotion than could easily be concealed by the folds of the graceful saree, the light and negligent, but

---

whether the trees composing it happen to stand upon a hillock, or a mound, or on a plain; on which last the *tope* is, in nineteen cases out of twenty, to be found. But there is not, in truth, any such Indian word as *tope* applied in that manner, the proper phrase being a *bagheecha*; and I notice this as one, among several errors of Indian scenery and names, into which the above-named most accomplished author has fallen; the rather, as I apprehend, from more than one of his hints, that he "has a mind" to enter upon the magnificent field which the East presents to his stupendous powers of picturing and description. I hope he will enter upon it, (after the little reading and inquiry necessary to perfect him in the technicalities); for the history of India contains hundreds of authentic anecdotes of valour and enterprise, before which the fictions—even the fictions—of our chivalry must fade. But as Horace said of the "vixere fortes ante Agamemnona," they have had no chroniclers known to the western world, and the consequence is that they there remain unknown. The corrective remarks of this note I make with great diffidence, though I believe they will not offend Mr. Croftangry; but so large a portion of his readers are Indians, and to those such errors as I allude to are so apparent, that it deducts greatly from the interest a tale should excite, and which all of his do excite, to have the fancy disturbed by any thing which at once recalls them to the matter of fact.

not neglected drapery of which partially enveloped a figure, light and elastic in its movements, and exquisite in its elegantly rounded proportions. With gentle, yet convulsive swells, the remembrance of former misfortunes would intrude, if not absolutely to darken, at least to cloud, the felicity of the present prosperous hour. She thought, and a tear glittered the while in the long black lashes of her dropping eyelids, of the idolized brothers and sisters, who one by one, by some awful and sudden calamity, had been swept away in the pride of their youth, or the innocence of their childhood; any many and bitter were the floods of sorrow she had wept over the pale corses of those gentle relatives, too early hastened to a violent dissolution. The fierce assault of the treacherous hyena, the more awful gripe of the wary alligator, the quick-working poison of the cobra capella, and the base dagger of the remorseless assassin, had at different, but shortly distant periods, been fatal to her nearest relatives; and two brothers, with herself, who was the eldest offspring, alone survived out of a fair and numerous family, who had gladdened the warm hearts of the anxious parents, and promised to excel in manly bravery and feminine loveliness; and Heena's grief was renewed and perpetuated by the painful solicitude of her mother's watchful eye, which tearfully followed every movement of those beloved children [198] who still remained, and for whose safety she suffered incessant and agonizing, but unexplained apprehensions. Yet the brightly variegated sky, the dancing, pearly waters, the glowing landscape; and, above all, the thoughts of one the absent and the dear; whose dauntless and well-aimed javelin had saved her from a fate perhaps more terrible than the worst deaths that had visited her family, combined to chase away the memory of deeper griefs; and again Heena looked up, and smiled less pensively.

The peasants, happily relieved from the dangers that formerly attended their daily toils, speeded cheerfully to the labours of the field; and, with a view to a similar occupation, for which a healthy old age did not render him unfit, the mild and venerable Agundah blessed his daughter, as she passed forth from his cottage; and Jumba, the brother of Heena, and only one year her junior, embraced his young wife, and kissed his laughing infant, ere he sought the thriving plantation of sugar-cane, which, under his skilful management, promised to yield a crop of unusual abundance.

"Give me, Heena," cried Kyratee, a fine manly boy seven years of age, "give me the koorpa, that I may follow my father and brother to the field."

"Alas! no," exclaimed the too anxious mother, darting forward from the interior of the hut, and clasping her boy with an eagerness for which there was not apparent reason; "think, should some of the savage and lurking Goands still linger in the vicinity, they may [199] tear thee away even before my eyes, mocking at my vain defence, and regardless of my agonized supplications. Ah! no, my son; till thou art able to defend thyself against the rude and warlike man, thou must not wander from the precincts of the cottage."

"Speak for me, Heena!" cried the bold but wayward boy. "I can throw the javelin well, I can draw the bow, and poise the difficult lance; for Muttaree taught me all, and his arm thou knowest never yet has failed. I have a dagger, too, at my belt; and I fear not the worthless and womanly people of the hills. Nay, I shame to remain at home, sitting at ease, while I might be aiding my father to till the ground, or helping to plant the rice, or bringing down with my sling or my arrows the birds who might come to disturb the grain in the furrows. You will win my mother to let me go, kind Heena, I know you will; and the other boys of the village will not cry shame upon the indolent Kyratee."

Heena looked fondly on the the coaxing, ingenuous urchin, and was about to plead in his behalf; but she caught at the instant her mother's imploring eye, saw the colour fade from her cheek, and compassionating the terror which she could not share, undertook to pacify the too adventurous boy, who now began to display the juvenile frowardness which follows disappointment. Offering to feather his arrows from the eagle's wing, and to bind his quiver like that of Muttaree, if he would remain contentedly by her side, Kyratee, [200]

pleased with the idea of the martial occupation, relinquished his project; and Heena's filial respect to her mother's slightest wish was rewarded by one of those tender, approving, but pensive smiles, which alone illumined the wan countenance of the care-worn parent. It was those gentle tokens of deep affection which repaid Heena for the assiduity with which she studied the happiness of those around her, and which she considered to be lightly earned by the greatest efforts she could make to obtain them. Bending with patient and inexhaustible sweetness over her self-imposed employment, while amusing her young and highly-interested companion, she solaced her own heart with sweet thoughts of her approaching felicity. Hitherto, though she had been sought by many in marriage, she had chosen to remain in virgin solitude, anxious only to lighten the domestic cares of her mother, to gladden with her light step and melodious voice the home which she was the invaluable blessing, and to soothe the sorrows, which, with little cessation, had, from her earliest remembrance, oppressed the hearts of those she loved; but now that her parents had removed from the exposed village, wherein all the disasters they so deeply mourned had befallen them, to a more secure locality; and that a young family, the offspring of her brother, were springing up, to bind new ties around those she was at last about to leave, she had unreluctantly consented to shorten the probation of her lover, and, the betrothed bride of the enraptured Muttaree, a few days [201] only were to elapse ere she had promised to become his wife. Soon a well known step bounded over the verdant sod—soon a well known voice shed its music on her ear, and the shadow of a beloved form fell upon the spot where she sate—when Kyratee uttered a shout of joy. Heena flew to the embrace of the cherished guest, and the fond mother, as she surveyed the meeting, in silence clasped her hands and raised her eyes, in which might be read the invocation of a blessing, to the bright and joy-inspiring heaven above her. Eda, the young and lovely sister-in-law of Heena, sate toying with her prattling child, under the shade of a superb tamarind tree, which spread its light, green, delicate leaves in full luxuriance above her; and seldom, in sooth, could the monarch's palace present so sweet a scene of love and peace as that which blessed the straw-roofed hut of the venerable Soobrattee. At this moment, the calmness of the clear, blue air was destroyed by a wild and piercing shriek:—"It is the death-cry of my son!" screamed the frenzied and prophetic mother, as desperately she darted forward; and in another instant, an enormous tiger was observed bounding rapidly towards the neighbouring jungle, and bearing his victim in his enormous jaws with the same ease that Eda dandled her reposing infant. While the females stood stupefied by terror and grief, the young Kyratee seized, with impotent courage, his tiny javelin; but the collected Muttaree took up his bow, from which the well-directed arrow flew to the heart of the [202] savage, with more than the lightning's celerity and the lightning's fatal power. The tiger dropped his prey, but the mangled and bleeding body lay motionless—as utterly devoid of life as that of the monster who stretched his huge bulk beside it. The almost petrified Eda, uttering long, heart-piercing, and unearthly shrieks, flung her infant frantically into the arms of Kyratee, and rushing towards the corpse, gazed upon the dismal spectacle till, unable to bear longer the ghastly sight, feeling and sense forsook her, and she sank lifeless on the gory grass and partly on the corpse of her dilacerated husband. Paralyzed by the fatal event which so suddenly passed before her, Heena remained for a moment motionless and almost apathetic, but the distracted state of her mother soon roused her to exertion. Until that dreadful day, the unhappy woman had borne all the misfortunes which had unremittingly pursued her devoted offspring with a calm, enduring sorrow. That she felt them deeply was manifested by her fading, grief-worn form, her pallid cheek, and her ever-tearful eye. She wept abundantly, but it was in patient silence; and the keenness of the sufferings, which wrung the core of her heart, could only be discovered by the heavy sighs and the smothered groans, which all her efforts could not wholly suppress. But now she gave loose to a burst of grief, which threatened to end (and happy for her if it had ended) in madness; and vainly, as earnestly, did Heena endeavour, by soothing words and affectionate caresses, to [203] allay the storm of wildly bursting passion. It would not be controlled; and breaking, with unwonted strength, from the gentle bondage of her daughter's twining arms, she flew towards a distant thicket with a speed which distanced all pursuit, and Heena could only track her wretched parent's footsteps by the cries which burst from her overcharged heart, with all the shrillness of oriental grief, and beheld her at last, half-kneeling and half-lying on the ground, beneath a tall pepul-tree, where, exhausted by the violence of her emotion, she had sunk in utter helplessness. Fearful of approaching too closely, as it was evident her mother had sought to indulge her sorrows in solitude, the weeping and anguished girl stood a little distance off, concealed by the intervening shrubbery of the jungle, and watching, with the acutest solicitude, the actions of one who seemed to meditate some desperate purpose, and listening with the tenderest compassion, to her wild shrieks and passionate exclamations.

"My son, my son!" she cried; "brave as a lion in the field, mild and gentle as a dove beneath the palm-leaved roof of thy father's hut; beautiful as the young Camdeo, and wise as the favourite friend of Vishnoo; the parched and thirsty earth drinks thy heart's blood, the vulture's red eye already marks thee for its prey. No more shall thy fleet steps follow the deer, and thy sure matchlock carry death to the panther! No more shalt thou bring home the shaggy skin of the lion in triumph to those who rejoiced in thy valour! Oh! Too [204] revengeful goddess! will nothing avail, neither prayers nor offerings, to move thee to be merciful? Must all I prize beneath yon glorious orb be doomed to a miserable death to satisfy thy vengeance? Will not a mother's cries be heard?—Will not the red hand be stayed—the insatiable sword be arrested, by those just powers who see that the measure of my grief is full, and that this torn and burthened heart can endure its agony no longer? The penalty of my disobedience has been paid with the lives of six, for that one which my trembling hands refused to sacrifice; and will nought appease thee, thou too vindictive deity! nothing suffice to atone for the maternal weakness, the fond and strong affection, which could not immolate at thy tremendous altar the loved one, the first-born, the welcome guest, who gave the sweet assurance that the curse of a barren bed had been removed! Could my hand snap the tender thread of my smiling, my fist, my only babe's existence? Could my lip devote the innocent to instant and most awful destruction?—No! no!—and on me then let the punishment be inflicted. Let my life pay the forfeit of my crime—but spare the guiltless!—let me not behold the few remaining and fragile branches of a decaying tree lopped off successively by the ruthless fiat of an unmerciful judge!—and let not for my offence my husband suffer in the loss of his children!"

"Mother, mother!—dearest mother!" said Heena, coming forward, "thy words pierce my soul. Tell me, I beseech thee—I, who am thine eldest born—am I, [205] and in what manner, the miserable cause of the calamities which have pursued thee from my birth? Let not the dark and fatal secret prey longer on thy lacerated heart; and perchance some means may still, though late, be found to avert the dreadful evils which threaten annihilation to all our race."

"Alas, my child!" returned the sorrowing parent, "how wilt thou listen to the tale of thy mother's frailty? Bright was the morning of my life. No bird in the glad valley ever sang more gaily, no flower ever bloomed more freshly, than she who was the pride and delight of a tribe, all of whom were lavishly endowed with the choicest of Nature's gifts. I loved, and was loved by, a youth of my own high caste, worthy of my virgin heart; and joyously sounded the guitar, the timbrel, and the conch-shell at our nuptial, and golden were the flowers that decked the festal ceremony. I was the cherished treasure of one whose heart was tender and faithful as the turtle-dove's; and I—but vain are words to paint the excess of my idolatry. Months fled away—brief and blissful months—but the flower-treading time brought no sweet hope that a mother's joys would be added to the bliss of a most happy wife. Years at length went over; and although no reproach escaped from lips which could not utter a chiding expression, there was a silent sorrow in the eye which had been wont to beam with unalloyed gladness; the listless languor of hopelessness stole over a frame so lately lithe and active as that of the antelope, I looked [206] round my childless home; I saw the scorning glances of my more fortunate companions—I heard their deriding words, and strove—long and sorely strove—to bear my shame and my grief in silence: but when a fourth year had winged its flight—and my miserable expectation made it fly rapidly as felicity would have urged it—and still no gentle voice greeted me with the fond and glorious name of mother; when the involuntary cloud deepened of the brow of my ever affectionate husband; and when his relatives crowded round him with cruelly commiserating sorrow, I became miserable and desperate. Often in the silence and the darkness of the night I had pondered on the means of procuring the blessing I so earnestly desired, till at length, goaded to distraction by the failure of every plan, every drug, and every prayer, I flew to the temple of the stern goddess Bhowanee, and there registered a solemn vow, that if she blessed me with the wished-for fruit, which a frowning destiny had so long denied, I would devote the first-born—the pledge that the curse of barrenness had been removed—to the bestower of the coveted boon. Alas, my Heena! when thy infant eyes opened to the light, sparkling and lustrous as the gem from which we named thee; when thy coral lips parted in a cherub smile, such as I had never till them beheld, for I could not endure to look upon another's offspring; and thy tiny and helpless fingers clasped mine in a soft and innocent embrace—could I part with a gift so precious?—Could I see those dark beaming eyes quenched [207] in a death of my own infliction—thy tender limbs stained with blood—thy fair and clinging form mangled and distorted? I could not, would not, fulfill my rash, inhuman vow; and, striving, by frequent sacrifices of less precious things, to propitiate the deity I dreaded to offend, I lived for some times in the fond expectation that I should escape the punishment to which I had rendered myself obnoxious. Every year that now glided away brought with it a new and welcome claimant upon my affection; but still to thee, the loved, the treasured object of my heart's warmest feelings, I clung with fond and prophetic tenacity. Every new grace, every fresh virtue, that developed itself in thy expanding mind and person, rendered thee still more dear, more cherished, and more prized; and though I saw my other darlings torn away, I nursed a hope, in spite of my utter conviction of its fallacy, that each victim seized by the wrathful goddess would be the last, and that yet I might descend to the grave, having my eyes closed, and my pile lighted up, but the offspring I had purchased at so terrible a price. But now that weak prop is removed, and now I see too plainly that I shall be doomed to live a bleeding witness of the cruel destruction of the only remaining blessings of my existence."

Heena listened with a sinking heart to this fearful narrative. She had long felt assured that a mysterious fate hung over her devoted family, and, though not most distantly imagining how deeply she was involved [208] in the direful cause of the calamity which she mourned, she too had wreathed garlands upon the altars of the gods, and poured out honey, and milk, and oil, and grain, before each hallowed shrine, in the hope of suspending or averting the infliction. Now, shuddering with cold horror, she felt the conviction that a higher, a more dreadful oblation was required from her; and she saw the fearful path she was destined to tread plainly revealed before her. Though she trembled, and wept tears even of blood, as she contemplated the terrible duty she was called upon to perform, her feminine hear did not for a moment waver, but, locking within it the awful secret of her resolution, prepared to execute the purpose which she fondly and piously believed to be holy. Her tender voice and her unremitting endearments succeeded at length in partially tranquillizing the violent emotions of her parent's breast, and they returned to their forlorn and dismal home together, bearing the meek patience the evils of their destiny; but the mother's tears streamed forth anew, as she surveyed the melancholy arrangements which were already in preparation for the obsequies of her gallant son; and had Heena's purpose been less stedfast that it was, she could not have withstood the imperious necessity which demanded the sacrifice she secretly meditated. Eda, the lovely and gentle Eda, but too happy in being permitted to share her husband's repose, was calmly and (as she believed) virtuously preparing to ascend his funeral pile. Decked in her [209] bridal ornaments, and wreathed in the fairest flowers, she wept only when she turned her eyes upon her unconscious infant, who uttered at intervals low, wailing cries, strangely according with the awfulness of the proceedings. This babe, thought Heena, and thou, too, my only remaining brother, must all perish as miserably as he did, who lies before me, if I fail to perform the appalling conditions of my mother's vow. Oh Muttaree! beloved and lost for ever! should I be spared the agony of witnessing thy grief, I feel that I could unshrinkingly perform the sacrifice.

The sequestered spot of the valley was now a scene of lamentable activity; for the heart-stricken parents of the deceased saw their sympathizing neighbours preparing to perform the ceremonies of the Suttee to the widow of him who had so long been the solace of their lives; and though tenderly anxious to prevent her pious purpose, they feared to oppose the selfish wish to a choice which was uncompulsorily made. Heena busied herself amongst the mourners. The lofty project which engrossed her whole soul gave to her eye a majesty almost divine; her pale, interesting countenance assumed a sublime expression, which did not, however, derogate from its natural softness; and her movements, always graceful, were marked with a dignity, hitherto not in accordance with her characteristic meekness and modesty. Every pulse throbbed wildly as she beheld Eda, with a smiling countenance, ascend the funeral pyre, and, amidst the choral hymns [210] of the attendant brahmins, the deafening sound of the numerous instruments, and the cordial prayers of the admiring spectators, take the head of her beloved husband on her lap, and consign herself to the destructive element. Turning her eyes from the appalling spectacle, they encountered the fond and commiserating glance of Muttaree; and it was then that the contrast between her fate and that of the fast consuming Suttee smote her inmost soul with an almost overpowering agony. Eda was going to be reunited, and for ever, to the object of her fondest affection; while she must leave the worshipped idol of her heart to despair and misery. Was there no spot beneath the face of heaven to which they might fly—no refuge from the fury of that inextinguishable enmity, which had already achieved such deep and deadly revenge? Or if there were, could she selfishly consult her own solitary happiness, and leave her parents to suffer the continuing wrath of the unappeased Bhowanee? It was impossible! And, as fresh vision arose in her mind, she saw her young brother and her orphan nephew springing up into the blooming manhood only to be cut down in the prime of their strength and beauty, by the same relentless hand which had nearly exterminated her unoffending family. Again were her nerves restrung, and again she firmly resolved to execute her original design, which, however horrible, presented the only certain means of preserving the lives of those who were far dearer to her than her own. [211]

Aware that the hapless family who were plunged into mourning by the late tragical event attributed their misfortunes to the pursuit of an evil destiny, Muttaree was not surprised when Heena, taking him aside, besought him to journey as far as the temple of Boodha, near the town of Azimgurh, and there perform certain religious ceremonies before the high altar. But too happy to obey the slightest wish of her whom he loved to distraction, he lost no time in departing on his mission; but, on his arrival there, he found the hold edifice shut, and the place deserted, in consequence of a dreadful contagion which had spread death and desolation throughout the adjacent country; and, depressed by so ill an omen, he bent his way homewards again, but determined to visit a far-famed temple of Mahadeo, which was wildly situated in the midst of the Goand hills, and at a small distance from Puchmurree, the principal hold of the savage inhabitants. As he drew near to the spot he heard the loud sounds of sacrificial instruments, and observed a numerous company winding up the adjacent defile towards the summit of a rock which was sacred to Bhowanee, the wife of Mahadeo. The scenery was wild and gloomy. Deep ravines, which might have been deemed bottomless, but for the hoarse roar of the invisible waters which rushed beneath; rugged steeps, and masses of jungle-covered hills, the abode of unmolested beasts of prey of every hideous kind, formed the character of that dreadful locality. At the foot of the stupendous [212] rock, adverted to before, was a cavern, hollowed by nature's hand out of a huge, but lower, rock; and within this dark recess, and beyond a fountain which the every-dripping roof supplied, was the altar of the goddess; and it was to the foot of this cave, from the fearful summit of the rock of sacrifice, that infatuated mothers were wont to hurl their first-born children, in return for the curse of barrenness being taken off their beds by the power of Bhowanee. A strange sensation, a fearful presentiment, agitated the bosom of Muttaree as he approached the frightful precipice, which, rising perpendicularly and ruggedly to the height of one hundred and seventy feet, was associated with awful tales of the inexorable goddess, to whose horrid and revolting rites it had been dedicated for ages. A light female form, whose white garments fluttered in the breeze, was seen gliding to the summit. Muttaree darted forward; but ere he reached the spot, the officiating brahmin had humanely drawn the intended victim back, and, by his actions, seemed to expostulate with anxious earnestness against the desperate enterprise. Muttaree rushed forward, and beheld the soul-harrowing sight of which his prescient heart had warned him.

"Strike, strike the gong and the cymbal!" exclaimed Heena, "to drown the voices of those who would dissuade me: but for this delay I had been spared the agonizing looks of one who may not melt my resolution, though his presence calls my soul too strongly [213] back to earth from the heaven it was approaching. In pity, Muttaree, tear away those sad, those beseeching eyes—I must complete the sacrifice!—Ha! wouldst thou grasp me?" she exclaimed, as, dashing away his outstretched arms, and crying, "Thou art saved, oh, my mother!" she, with one wild and desperate bound, leaped from the topmost point of the rock, and sank, whirling like a stricken eagle, into the awful gulfs beneath it.

Title

Bird, John. "The Haunted Chamber." FMN 1831. 279-300. [279]

THE HAUNTED CHAMBER.
BY JOHN BIRD, ESQ.

"JOCK, JOCK!" cried the horseman impatiently, "let me not curse the chance that threw a knave in my way instead of an honest fellow! There is scant time to argue this matter."

"Scant enough!" muttered Jock, "seeking that the horses are to sort, the pigs to feed, and Cicely—"

"To be kissed," interrupted the traveller, laughing: "yet if thou lovest that Cicely half so well as thou hast sworn—"

"Ay, ay, Master Frank," exclaimed Jock, "you are one of those roundheads that swear none, but lie plaguily, if all tales by true. And what if Cicely like a little swearing, by way of security, as she calls it? where is the mighty harm? Lying is far worse, I trow: yet I have deceived neither Cicely nor you."

"And I have broke no head," rejoined the traveller; "though I feel strongly inclined to try the hardness of this cudgel on thy numskull. Fie, fie, Jock, to palter thus with an old friend, when all he asks is but to be helped to the speech of thy pretty mistress Mabel."

"That all," returned the serving-man, "being as much, perhaps, as my place is worth."

"And how much is that?" said his companion, laughing louder than before: "with thy old crab of a master, who keeps thee on bare blade-bones and swipes (Jock writhed a little at this), why, thou art not half the man thou wast."

"He would brain me," cried Jock, arguing the matter with himself.

"He knows better than to look for ought but maggots in thy brain-pan, Jock," retorted his antagonist. "But, in one word, wilt thou pleasure me?—ay or no?"

"One word!" repeated Jock; "nay, there go two to that matter—mine and my master's."

"And here is a single argument," returned the traveller, holding up a gold Carolus as he spoke, "which, sufficiently urged, shall go far to secure both."

"Marry, and you speak sense now, mun," cried Jock, looking on the coin with eager eyes as it glistened in the bright moonlight; "for, truly, broad pieces come not to tempt a poor fellow like me every day: and seeing that my young lady was betrothed to thee, as it were, by her old sour guardian ere thou wert ill-conditioned enough to write thyself roundhead, and that a few more of such weighty arguments might tempt guardy himself to turn round—"

"Thou knave! thou rascal! thou villain!" exclaimed a voice from behind, which Jock, conscious of being caught in the manner, knew to belong to his master; "what treachery is this? How, Master Colyton? is it well done, sir, to tamper with my servant? to entice an ignorant booby like this (ignorant, quotha! muttered Jock) to betray the small trust which necessity obliges me to confide to him?"

"Master Gisborne," returned Colyton, somewhat [281] abashed, "I have broke no faith with you, for I owe you none. You, sir, can hardly avouch so much to me, after refusing me the hand of your ward, which, if a promise availed aught—"

"Promise," interrupted Gisborne, "are always made, or ought to be (which is the same thing), with a reservation, mental or otherwise. Times are changed, Master Colyton; and in deserting the good cause"—

"This is but cheatry, miserable cheatry!" returned the indignant Colyton. "Thou knewest my sentiments, Master Gisborne, when thy promise was made; and other motives—"

"You will do well to spare your insinuations, sir," interrupted Gisborne; "seeing that my power over Miss Darrell is absolute till she attains the age of twenty-one. But come, Frank; since chance or design has brought you to my gate, and you are desirous to see Mabel, on one condition I consent."

"Name it," cried the lover in sudden and delighted surprise.

"It is," said Gisborne, "that you converse with her only in my presence, which, of course, implies that love-stories are to be postponed *sine dic*. I will have no whispering in corners, no back-stair meetings. Give me your word of honour as to this, and you shall go with me to the house—deny me, and your way lies before you."

"I have no option for this evening," answered Colyton, "which will terminate our compact: I must [282] depart ere daybreak on my mission to the lord general."

"To Cromwell!" returned Gisborne, starting, "pah! the very name stinks in my nostrils! But no matter: we must bend or break, it seems. Jock, take Master Colyton's mare, and see that she be well sorted. I will set you forth at daybreak myself, and thus be assured (with a smile) that you depart alone. The guardian of a young skittish damsel cannot be too wary."

The mansion to which young Colyton was conducted by his ancient acquaintance was one of those rambling yet picturesque dwellings that trace their erection to the age of Elizabeth. Gisborne himself was a royalist, and suspected of having aided the recent attempt to place the second Charles on the throne of his ancestors; yet the fact, if such it were, had been so well concealed as to give no handle on which the opposite party could lay hold to molest his person or property. Colyton, we have already seen, had attached himself to the side of Cromwell as on whom he believed able and willing to build up anew the tottering fabric of government on a broad and liberal basis. He was, moreover, of good family and fortune; and Gisborne's motives, in refusing the young and blooming Mabel where she had been affianced, were variously attributed to his expectations that the triumph of his party might enable him to grasp the forfeited lands of the delinquent Colyton, or that in any case the possession of his ward's person and wealth might be rendered sub- [283] servient to his safety of even advancement. Be this as it may, the fair Mabel herself blushed rosy red when her quondam lover was introduced so suddenly to her presence by him whom she believed most anxious to separate them for ever.

"I have brought an old friend to partake our cheer, Mabel," cried Gisborne, spitefully enjoying her embarrassment. "But hey-day! you do not look overpleased, methinks, to see Master Colyton."

"Pleased, sir!" repeated Miss Darrell, looking anxiously at Colyton; "I am surprised, as well I may be; and a little more ceremony"—

"My dearest Mabel," began Colyton.

"Hoity-toity!" interrupted Gisborne; "have you so soon forgotten that this is a mere visit of ceremony, or friendship if you will, and that love is an interdicted topic?"

"You may chain my tongue, sir," cried the lover indignantly, "but you cannot change my heart."

"I shall change nothing, sir," returned the host drily; "not even my own will, which you know already. But come, no to be inhospitable to my guest, I trust your passion will not spoil your appetite, as a savoury odour which issues even now from the kitchen assures me that supper is not far distant. A friendly meal and a cheering glass, Master Colyton, and then to bed, will, methinks, be no bad arrangement for one who is to rise before the lark. Mabel, will you charge [284] yourself with the office of seeing the tapestried chamber made ready for your old acquaintance?"

"The tapestried room, sir!" replied Mabel, looking the image of astonishment; "and why not the damask chamber?"

"Simply because I have determined otherwise, Miss Darrell," returned the master of the mansion.

"But, sir, the tapestried room is—is—-"

"Is what, foolish girl?"

"Very damp, sir," replied Mabel.

"What, with the dry-rot in the walls!" returned the host with a grim smile. "But no matter; a good fire shall banish all fear of catching cold."

"There may be other fears, sir," rejoined Mabel, hesitating.

"What, for a lad of Frank's mettle?—No,no! I suppose you are thinking of the walking lady. Colyton, to encounter a fair lady were of course pleasant enough—but a ghostly fair—"

"Would be an adventure worth boasting of, sir," returned Frank, laughing.

"I remember now to have heard of this haunted chamber, and, to say truth, have often desired the opportunity of putting the ghost or the story to rest; but other thoughts," looking tenderly at Mabel, "were wont to banish this."

"Bravo!" cried Gisborne; "the lad is the hero I always took him for: but soft—break we off; for here comes—no ghost, but a substantial supper." [285]

Colyton, all enamoured as he was, had ridden too far that day not to address himself in good earnest to the excellent cheer before him; and not even the anxious glances of Mabel, which he encountered in the intervals of mastication or deglutition, could, for a while, detach him from grosser thoughts. Gisborne gazed and sniggered at what he deemed an unerring proof that his guest was no longer "all for love;" and his favourable estimation rose as that of his ward declined. Mabel pouted, frowned, and at last looked so cross that Frank was half frightened; when his host, having despatched one cheerer, begged his excuse for a few minutes, departing with a hint as to that promise, the observance of which he maliciously hoped would ruin Colyton now and for ever with his attached but high-spirited mistress.

"And now, Frank," said the young lady as the door closed, "that this odd guardian of mine has so oddly left us to ourselves, let us make the most of the very few minutes he will give us to concert—why, what ails the man?—he looks as dismal as midnight—to concert—poh! are you mad or silly?—Have you lost your wits or your heart? No answer!—Are you dumb?"—Frank shook his head, and looked the picture of despair.—"What, only sulky!—Very pretty, sir! If this be your mode of entertaining me—if all your protestations of love—Frank, Frank, it must be so!—you have fallen in love with somebody else—you are going to be married, to be married (with a gulp) [286] to one of that filthy Cromwell's daughters, I dare swear."

"N—o!"—The word as intercepted in its passage from poor Colyton's lips, to the infinite danger of his respiration; when, recollecting his promise, he, as a last resource, shoo, his head more violently than before.

"This is playing the fool with a witness, Frank: Will you be pleased to tell me what ails you?"

Frank sighed deeply as he put his finger on his lip.

"You are forbidden to speak, then:—the more fool you, Frank, to make any such promise. In the name of patience, why came you here at all?—but that you can't tell me."—Frank blew a kiss towards her.—"Psha, nonsense! a true lover would have found a thousand expedients rather than have sewn up his own lips!—Provoking! when guardy will be upon us in a few moments, and I am at my wits' end with vexation at having all the talk to myself."—Frank laughed outright.—"Don't laugh, sir. I may have another lover, and in this house, for aught you know."—He became instantly grave, and seemed strongly disposed to forget his engagement.—"Tell me, sir; did you come in with guardy this afternoon, muffled up in a horseman's cloak?"

"No, no!" exclaimed Colyton, in a sudden transport of passion.

"You have broke your promise, Master Frank!" cried Gisborne, opening the door. [287]

"He should have done so to better purpose, then, sir," retorted Mabel, almost crying with vexation; "since No is the only word that has passed his lips. But I can say No too; ay, and you may both repent of trifling with the feelings of one who is like enough to circumvent you both." She looked daggers at her astonished auditors, and, dropping a profound curtsy, vanished from the room.

"Nay, nay, Master Colyton, you shall not follow her," exclaimed Gisborne, as his guest rose in great perturbation: "our engagement—"

"You have acted ungenerously, unjustly by me, Master Gisborne!" returned Colyton warmly; "you have betrayed me."

"No such thing, Frank; it was your own choice," replied his host: "you might have gone forward, and welcome. But come, take not this rebuff to heart—it is a froward little pet, whom you would do well to forget: but of this we can talk another time; at present I have other and more weighty matters for your ear. You have heard of the disastrous issue of Worcester fight—disastrous at least to our party, though a real triumph to yours."—Colyton shook his head.—"Frank, it is useless to contend; I must swim with the stream: will you bear this packet for me to Cromwell, and assure him that he has not a firmer, a more devoted adherent, than old Ralph Gisborne:—nay, never stare, man, when we are of the same side.—Mabel—" [288]

"May be mine!" cried Colyton in an ecstasy.—"You have, then, been only playing with our impatience."

"It may be so, or not," returned Gisborne drily: "private happiness must, at all events, give place to public weal. Will you do my bidding?"

"Gladly and willingly," answered Colyton; "for, much as I pity the unhappy prince, I feel with you that our only reliance now is on Cromwell, though his ambition, I fear, may incited him—"

"Walls have ears sometimes, Frank," whispered Gisborne, looking mysteriously and timidly round him. "The night wanes, and you will need rest ere you recommence your journey. With the first light of day I will arouse and let you out by the postern that leads to the stables. You must e'en manage to saddle your own steed, since neither Jock nor any one shall know our movements, lest it brew mischief. And now, Master Frank," he continued, as he ushered his guest into the tapestried chamber, "Commend yourself to sleep, and be careful that no ghost steals away this packet, on which both our fortunes depend.—Good night!"

Left alone in the chamber, Colyton felt little inclination for slumber. The events of the last few hours had been too various and perplexing not to excite other feelings than those of repose; yet the idea that Gisborne, though from worldly motives perhaps, might again favour his suit to Mabel, was too delightful not to overmaster every other thought. Meanwhile, after securing the door, he seated himself before the ample chimney, up which roared a cheerful wood fire, and surveyed the important packet of which he was to be the bearer. It was carefully sealed, and addressed to Cromwell by his usual titles. A smile of disdain passed over the countenance of the youth as he surveyed this instrument of his host's defection from a falling cause. "Patriotism, or loyalty at least, should be made of sterner stuff!" he exclaimed, "or what has poor Charles Stuart to hope from his adherents?" A low sigh seemed to echo his sentiments. He started from his seat, and looked anxiously round the chamber, but perceived nothing that could in any degree strengthen the opinion that his ear had not deceived him. The story of the haunted room returned to his memory; and, free as he was from all superstition, the hour, the seeming evidence of his senses, produced a feeling of awe which he could not wholly overcome. Smiling at his own credulity, he cast himself, drest as he was, on the bed; and though sleep came not, and indeed was scarcely sought, fatigue, cooperating with agitation of mind, gave birth to that species of waking delusion which combines objects present to the sense with wild and visionary ideas. The faded nymphs and shepherds depictured on the tapestried walls seemed gradually to become animated, and, by strange, uncouth gestures, to invite him to the dance they were represented as pursuing. The reeds sounded, hands were clasped, the damsels pranced and pirouetted, and their gallants pirouetted yet more fiercely, till the very velocity with which they swept round dispelled the illusion. He raised himself on the bed and rubbed his eyes. They resumed their old grim forms on the tapestry, and the only motion was from the flickering of the wood fire and the tapers that flared in the breeze admitted through a casement, which, from a long disrepair, was only imperfectly closed. The legend of the chamber arose on his memory: it bore that an ancestress of the family had buried a sum of money in that room, which the suddenness of her last summons not permitting her to indicate, no after-occupant (not even the griping Gisborne himself) had ever been able to discover it, and that the spirit still wandered where her dearest treasure reposed. Smiling at the tradition, Colyton once more assumed his recumbent postured, and his indistinct perceptions again returned, in the midst of which he seemed to perceive the very form his fancy and portrayed, that of an old woman, dancing before his eyes, yet looking in the midst of her gambols the very personation of anxiety. Uncertain as to whether he was dreaming, awake, or asleep, he lay motionless; but the rotatory vagaries of the figure still continued; and by degrees he saw, or thought he saw, other shadowy figures in the darkened part of the chamber. Brave as he was by nature, terror gradually assumed her usual empire over his dormant faculties. He lay helpless and unable to articulate, or to withdraw his gaze from the visionary female, who, at every flitting, approached nearer his couch, till at length a withered hand drew back the bed-curtain, and a ghastly face glared in on him. So palpable an impression of the actual presence of some incorporeal being called forth a strong effort, by dint of which he started upright on the bed, a motion which put the ghost fairly to flight; while the rustling of the stiff damask draperies seemed to indicated the possession of greater substantiality in his visitant than is attributed to the airy race of spirits, if indeed the suddenness of his own movement had not been the only exciting cause. Doubtful of all but the unwonted disorder perturbation which such an occurrence might produce on the firmest mind. The embers in the grate waxed low, the candle-wicks had reached a most portentous length, and the figures on the walls looked more grim and ghastly than before. He even fancied that he heard a low murmuring of voices, and a creaking of shoes from a closet at the farther end of the chamber. He attempted to call out, but his tongue cleaved to the roof of his mouth, and in sudden desperation he was in the act of springing from the bed to catch at the bell, when the closet door slowly opened, and the ancient dame whom he had before seen once more advanced towards him. No longer doubting that the chamber was haunted by that unquiet spirit of whose vagaries he had been so incredulous, he threw himself [292] back in despair of resisting the will of an incorporeal being, and awaited the event in silence, if not composure. Again, as before, she stole forward with a slow and noiseless step, and withdrawing the curtain once more looked in upon him; but in that moment the spell dissolved, for the features were seen and known. "Bridget!" he cried, recognising in his nightly visitant the good old housekeeper.

"Hush, hush!" she replied, in a half-breathed whisper; "as you valued life, be still. Why, la! Master Francis, you are not afraid of me, sure?"

"Afraid, my dear old woman? and of thee? No, no; but—"

"Well, well, no buts—you may be sure I come on no idle errand at such a time as this: yet how to speak it I know not."

"You come to me," cried Colyton, quaking inwardly, "from Mabel?"

"Ay, from her, and another whom you wot not of."

"It is so then, and she has forgotten her faith!"

"Hush, hush, Master Frank, for mercy's sake!"

"How can I hush when you speak of another, who is doubtless a new lover of Mabel's?"

"Yes—no—I can't tell—Lord help my poor brain that wanders till I know no more what I am saying—but good lack! how lucky that you have your clothes on, Master Frank, for now Mistress Mabel may e'en come and tell you herself." [293]

"It is well my stipulation with Master Gisborne is out," thought Colyton, "or I must have broken my word at all hazards."

The closet door again opened, and Bridget returned with Miss Darrell, while another figure hovered in the shade, whom, however, Frank plainly discovered to be a man, and his jealous feelings seemed at once to be confirmed.

"It is well, Mistress Mabel," he began—

"That is as it may turn out, Frank," replied the young lady sharply; "meanwhile I am glad you have recovered your speech, though hand as well as tongue may be needful in the service I am about to require of you. I come to bespeak your good offices for one—"

"Whom you have promoted to the vacant post of your lover," cried Colyton with an inflamed visage and bitter smile.

"Don't be a fool, Frank! If the post be vacant, it is more than I know, though I might have guessed as much when you were tongue-tied after so long an absence. But no matter. Frank, can you be faithful?"

"I ought rather to ask that question of you, Mabel," returned he reproachfully.

"Do, for Heaven's sake, put our love-affairs out of your foolish head for one hour at least," answered his mistress, "and listen to matters more important."

"To you, Mabel?"

"To me, to you, to every one," she replied with kindling eye, "who values faith, honour, and loyalty above base and selfish considerations. Frank, you [294] know the issue of Worcester fight—you are the adherent of Cromwell:—is it a part of your creed, of your duty, to hunt down and destroy the survivors of that fatal combat?"

"I see how it is, Mabel," interrupted he; "you have given your heart to some cavalier, whom, at the risk even of your reputation, you are endeavouring to rescue from the penalty of his rash devotion to an unfortunate prince. Resign this attempt to me, and on my life I will save your lover, or—"

"Not my lover!" cried Mabel, leading forward the silent cavalier; "not my lover, Frank, but my King!"

"Yet, Master Colyton," exclaimed the stranger, throwing aside his cloak, "I am that unhappy Charles Stuart, the second of the name, who, in the failure of my attempt to regain my crown and kingdom, am compelled to trust my life to the uncertain loyalty of those who may build their fortunes, and yet more save their own necks, by the certain sacrifice of mine. Such was the chance that brought me into this house. In my flight from Worcester with two trusty friends, we encountered Gisborne, known to both, so at least they said, for long and persevering attachment to the royal cause. He knew me at once, and offered for the night that rest and shelter which exhaustion of body and mind rendered so needful. I had no choice but to accept the offer, while my friends sought that vessel which, I trust, is on the coast hard by to bear me from the block. Gisborne brought me in, as he and I [295] thought, unseen; but what fugitive," continued he, smiling archly at Mabel, "ever escaped the sharp eye of a woman? There was a mystery to be fathomed— it yielded to female penetration. Accompanied by her trusty duenna, this young lady discovered it only to fill me with alarms, possibly unfounded, yet bearing too much of probability to be disregarded by one whose safety is so precarious as mine. Colyton, I distrust Gisborne, though pledged to me by his own voluntary oath. You are my foe, but an honourable one; so at least your kind mistress affirms. Say, then, are you aid the descendant of a line of kings to escape the fate of an erring, perhaps, but right-minded father? or will you take the surer, the more profitable, path of betraying a fugitive?"

"No, no, my liege," interrupted Colyton, sinking at the feet of Charles; "my adherence to Cromwell extends not here. Would I might restore you to that throne which is your inheritance! yet all I can—"

"Time presses," exclaimed Charles smiling; "and we must come to the point. I have already said that I distrust Gisborne: he has, my sweet spy here informs me, given you a pacquet to convey to Cromwell."

"It is even thus," returned Colyton; "and its contents, so far as I am informed—"

"The exigency of my affairs," interrupted Charles, coolly breaking the seal, "must wave all ceremony. [296]

Nay, nay, Master Colyton, no scruples; they were mistimed when life is at stake."

"Yet consider, my liege," cried Colyton, "my faith, my plighted word to Master Gisborne, who would not surely have deceived me!"

"You may thank the courage, sir," returned the prince, "that cut the knot at which you would have boggled till your neck had paid the forfeit of your delicacy; and for faith—look here, at Master Gisborne's own hand! This scroll, sir—this infamous scroll—is to make his peace with Cromwell by betraying into the clutches of the usurper him whom he had sworn to protect at the hazard of his life, while you are flatly accused to your general of disobedience to the trust reposed in you! Yes, Master Colyton, your ruin was to be his rise, and my head to pay the forfeit of my rash confidence! From this, sir, the sagacity, the vigilance, the courage, of your angelic mistress has redeemed us both, I trust; yet are we still in the meshes! What is to be done? Cannot we escape from the window?—the darkness will befriend us? and yet, if my eyes deceive me not, light is already dawning in the east."

"And at daybreak," cried Colyton, "Gisborne himself has promised to arouse and let me out: he may even now be listening."

"No, no," interrupted the housekeeper, whose awe at the presence of royalty had hitherto kept her mute and motionless, "no; master could not suspect aught, [297] seeing that none but myself ever knew of the secret passage between the king's chamber and this; and I heard him lock the door at the end of our gallery before he went to rest, so that he could reckon on our being safe for the night."

"I see but one chance," cried Mabel, arousing from a trance of anxious thought: "your majesty must personate Frank, and be let out by the very betrayer who is most anxious to keep you in. You are about the same height, and, once fairly muffled in Master Colyton's cloak, on my life poor guardy in his tremor will never discover you."

"Yet if I pass the door unseen," said the king, "how even then am I to escape?"

"You will find my mare in the stable," returned Colyton, "who will carry your Majesty with the speed of lightning: but can you contrive to saddle her? for Gisborne fairly told me to look to be my own groom."

"I must risk every thing," answered Charles, laughing, "even the breaking of my neck from slackened girths, rather than be taken like a mouse in a trap: and hark! the clock strikes five; we must be speedy!"

A low tap at the door gave added celerity to their speed. "Are you stirring, Master Colyton?" murmured the voice of Gisborne from the passage.

"Ay, ay," returned Frank in a drowsy tone, as if arousing from sleep; "I will but slip on my cloak and be with you."

It was the work of a moment to muffle the fugitive [298] in the cloak of Colyton, the conspirators afterwards withdrawing silently to the closet, from which they anxiously watched the intrepid monarch, as he unbarred the chamber-door, and gave admittance to his self-purposed betrayer.

"So, so, you have not rested much I see," cried Gisborne, looking at the disordered bed-clothes—"disturbed by ghosts, eh?" with a low chuckle.

The king gave a sign of impatience, murmured a faint "Hush!" and attempted to pass forward.

"You are right, quite right," said Gisborne; "we cannot be too wary; Mabel has ears like a cat, and might pounce upon us, only that like a cat she is locked up—he, he! So you have the pacquet safe, I see. Now, then, to despatch you."

The disappeared. In a few moments the door was heard to open, and after a short pause—a pause of agony to the listeners—they had the unspeakable satisfaction to hear the bolts once more cautiously secured; a signal that the wanderer had eluded the vigilance of his host, and fairly given him the slip. Daylight now appeared; and Gisborne, curious, perhaps, rather than suspicious, returned to the haunted chamber, from the window of which he could observe the departure of the traveller.

"What a pize! Frank is plaguy slow or confoundedly clumsy this morning; he could never else be all this time saddling his own mare! He little thinks how neatly I have done his business and my own at the [299] same time! So, so he comes at last!—Ha! whom do I see?—the king! Treason! treason!—He will escape!—Yet how shall I get out? I dare not jump. Treason!—I must ring the alarm-bell; I must raise the country!—That confounded Colyton—"

"Must take the liberty to putting a little gentle restraint on you even in your own house, Master Gisborne," said Frank, pouncing from the closet on the ill-starred master of the mansion, whose struggles quickly brought Mabel and old Bridget to aid in his caption. This, however, was complete. Snared in his own toils, threats or entreaties were alike unavailing to procure his release for the obdurate Frank. A pretext of sudden illness, promulgated by Miss Darrell and her female coadjutor, easily accounted to the servants for the non-appearance of the master, whose involuntary durance continued till the safety of Charles could no longer be compromised by his self-destined betrayer.

The intelligence of the monarch's embarkation was the signal for Gisborne's liberation, who, having wisely considered that times might again change, and that his story, if truly told, would sound but ill even in the ears of Cromwell, saw fit to make common cause with Colyton, and even to consent to his union with Mabel. Whether the grand motive for this compliance was the discovery of Bridget, that Miss Darrell had, by passing her minority, become her own mistress, has not been certainly authenticated. It is however known, that yet [300] farther discoveries, assigned by rumour to the visitant of the haunted chamber, transferred the mansion and demesne of Gisborne to Frank, as the rightful inheritance of Mabel; and that the discomfited guardian, albeit his knaveries were glossed over and his person protected by those whom he had most injured, pined over the loss of his wealth and influence, till he at last fretted himself to death in pure despair of regaining either. Whether the share of Colyton in the escape of the fugitive ever reached the ear of Cromwell may well be doubted, as it was not till the king's restoration that the circumstances of his flight were accurately known, when, fortunately for Frank, he needed not those substantial acknowledgements for which other adherents of royalty were anxiously but vainly seeking. The merry monarchs, however—remembering, perhaps, that he owed his life and crown to the intrepidity of Mabel and her adoring husband—eagerly invited them to his court, holding out at the same time the promise of a baronetcy as a lure to Colyton; but the latter, gaining wisdom from happiness, shrunk from so equivocal an honour, content, on a forced journey to town, to laugh over, in his own person only, with a good-humoured but misguided king, their night of memorable adventure in the Haunted Chamber.

Title
Delta. [Moir, D.L.] "Bessy Bell and Mary Gray. A Scottish Legend of 1666."
FMN 1831. 361-370.

PLATE: Bessy Bell and Mary Gray.
Steel plate engraving; painted by J.R. West painter;
engraved by William Finden. [361]

BESSY BELL AND MARY GRAY.
A SCOTTISH LEGEND OF 1666.
BY DELTA.

IT was in the yet Doric says of Scotland (comparing the present with the past) that Kenneth Bell, on of the lairds of the green holms of Kinvaid, having lost his lady by a sudden dispensation of Providence, remained for a long time wrapt up in the reveries of grief, and utterly inconsolable. The tide of affliction was at length fortuitously stemmed by the nourice bringing before him his helpless infant daughter—the very miniature of her departed mother, after whom she had been named.

The looks of the innocent babe recalled the father's heart to a sense of the duties which life yet required of him; and little Bessy grew up in health and beauty, the apple of her father's eye. Nor was his fondness for her diminished, as year after year more fully developed those lineaments which at length ripened into a more mature likeness of her who was gone. She became, as it were, a part of the old man's being; she attended him in his garden walks; rode out with him on her palfrey on sunny mornings; and was as his shadow by the evening hearth. She doted on him with more than a daughter's fondness; and he, at length, seemed bound to earth by no tie save her existence.

It was thus that Bessy Bell grew up to woman's stature; and, in the quiet of her father's hall, she was now, in her eighteenth year, a picture of feminine loveliness. [362] All around had heard of the beauty of the heiress of Kinvaid. The cottager who experienced her bounty drank to her health in his lonely jug of nut-brown ale; and the squire, at wassail, toasted her in the golden wine-cup.

The dreadful plague of 1666 now fell out, and rapidly spread its devastations over Scotland. Man stood aghast; the fountains of society were broken up; and day after day brought into rural seclusion some additional proofs of its fearful ravages. Nought was heard around but the wailings of deprivation; and omens in the heavens and on the earth heralded miseries yet to come.

Having been carried from Edinburgh (in whose ill-ventilated closes and wyndes it had made terrible havoc) across the Frith of Forth, the northern counties were now thrown into alarm, and families broke up, forsaking the towns and villages to disperse themselves under the freer atmosphere of the country. Among others, the laird of Kinvaid trembled for the safety of his beloved child, and the arrival of young Bruce, of Powfoulis Priory, afforded him an excellent opportunity of having his daughter escorted to Lynedoch, the residence of a warmly attached friend and relative.

Under the protection of this gallant young squire, Bessy rode off on the following morning, and, the day being delightful, the young pair, happy in themselves, forgot, in the beauty of nature, the miseries that encompassed them. [363]

Besides being a youth of handsome appearance and engaging manners, young Bruce had seen a good deal of the world, having for several years served as a member of the body guard of the French king. He had returned from Paris only a few months before, and yet wore the cap and plume peculiar to the distinguished corps to which he still belonged. The heart of poor Bessy Bell was as sensitive as it was innocent and unsophisticated; and, as her protector made his proud steed fret and curvet by her side, she thought to herself, as they rode along, that he was like one of the knights concerning whom she had read in romance, and, unknown to herself, there awoke in her bosom a feeling to which it had hitherto been a stranger.

Her reception at Lynedoch was most cordial; nor the less so, perhaps, on the part of the young lady of that mansion, because her attendant was Bruce, the secret but accepted suitor for the hand of Mary Gray. Ah! had this mystery been at once revealed to Bessy Bell, what a world of misery it would have saved her!

From the plague had our travellers been flying; but the demon of desolation was here before them, and the smoke was ceasing to ascend from many a cottage-hearth. It became necessary that the household of Lynedoch should be immediately dispersed. Bruce and Lynedoch remained in the vicinity of the dwelling-house, and a bower of turf and moss was reared for the young ladies on the pastoral banks of the Brauchie-burn, a tributary of the Almond. [364]

It was there that Bessy Bell and Mary Gray lived for a while in rural seclusion, far from the bustle and parade of gay life, verifying in some measure what ancient poetry hath feigned of the golden age. Bruce was a daily visitant at the bower by the Brauchie-burn: he wandered with them through the green solitudes; and, under the summer sun and a blue sky, they threaded oft times together the mazes of "many a bosky bourne and bushy dell." They chased the fantastic squirrel from bough to bough, and scared the thieving little weasel from the linnet's nest. Under a great tree they would seat themselves, as Bruce read aloud some story of chivalry, romance, or superstition, or soothed the listless hours of the afternoon with the delightful tones of the shepherd's pipe. More happy were they than the story-telling group, each in turn a queen, who, in like manner, flying from the pestilence which afflicted Florence, shut themselves up in its delightful gardens, relating those hundred tales of love which have continued to delight posterity in the glowing pages of Boccaccio.

Under whatever circumstances it is placed, human nature will be human nature still. When the young and the beautiful meet together freely and unreservedly, the cold restraints of custom and formality must be thrown aside; friendship kindles into a warmer feeling, and love is generated. Could it be otherwise with our ramblers in their green solitude?

Between Mary Gray and young Bruce a mutual and [365] understood attachment had long subsisted; indeed they only waited his coming of age to be united in the bonds of wedlock; but the circumstance, for particular reasons, was cautiously concealed within their own bosoms. Even to Bessy Bell, her dearest and most intimate companion, Mary had not revealed it. To disguise his real feelings, Bruce was outwardly less marked in his attention to his betrothed than to her fried; and, in her susceptibility and innocent confidence, Bessy Bell too readily mistook his kind assiduities for marks of affection and proofs of love. A new spirit began to pervade her whole being, almost unknown to herself; she looked on the scenes around her with other eyes; and life changed in the hues it had previously borne to the gaze of her imagination. In the absence of Bruce she became melancholy and abstracted. He seemed to her the being who had been born to render her blessed; and futurity appeared, without his presence, like the melancholy gloom of a November morning.

The physiological doctrine of temperaments we leave to its difficulties;

although we confess, that in Bessy Bell and Mary Gray something spoke in the way of illustration.

The countenance of Bessy was one of light and sunshine. Her eyes were blue, her hair flaxen, her complexion florid. She might have sate for a picture of Aurora. Every thing about her spoke of "the innocent brightness of the new-born day." Mary Gray [366] was in many things the reverse of this, although perhaps equally beautiful. Her features were more regular; she was taller, even more elegant in figure; and had in her almost colourless cheeks, lofty pale brow, and raven ringlets, a majesty which nature had denied to her unconscious rival. The one was all buoyancy and smiles; the other subdued passion, deep feeling, and quiet reflection.

Bruce was a person of the finest sense of honour; and, finding that he had unconsciously and unintentionally made an impression on the bosom-friend of his betrothed, became instantly aware that it behoved him to take some step to dispel the unfortunate illusion. Fortunately the time was speedily approaching, which called him to return, for a season, to his military post in France; but the idea of parting for Mary Gray had become doubly painful to his feelings, from the consideration of the circumstances under which he was obliged to leave her. The ravages of death were extending instead of abating; and the general elements themselves seemed to have become tainted with the unwholesomeness. There was an unrefreshing langour in the air; the sky wore a coppery appearance, and over the face of the sun was drawn as it were a veil of blood. Imagination might no doubt magnify these things; but victims were falling around on every side; and no Aaron, as in the days of hoary antiquity, now stood between the living and the dead, to bid the plague be stayed. [367]

With the noble resolution Bruce took his departure, and sorrow, like a cloud, brooded over the bower by the Brauchie-burn. Mary sate in a quiet, melancholy abstraction; but ever and anon the tears dropped down the cheeks of Bessy Bell, as her "softer soul in woe dissolved aloud." Love is lynx-eyed, and Mary saw to well what was passing in the mind of her friend; but, with a kind consideration, she allowed the lapse of a few days to moderated to turbulence of her feelings ere she ventured to impart cruel truth. So unlooked for, so unexpected was the disclosure, that for a while she harboured a spirit of unbelief; but conviction at once flashed over her, extinguishing every hope, when she was shown a beautiful necklace of precious stones, which Bruce had presented to his betrothed on the morning of his bidding adieu to the bower of the Brauchie-burn. As it were by magic, a change came over the spirit of Bessy Bell. She dried her tears, hung on the neck of her friend, endeavoured to console her in her separation from him who loved her, and bore up with a heroism seemingly almost incompatible with the gentle softness of her nature. She clasped the chain round the neck of Mary, and, kneeling, implored Heaven speedily to restore the giver to her arms.

Fatal had been that gift! It had been purchased by Bruce from a certain Adonijah Baber, a well-known Jewish merchant of Perth, who had amassed consider- [368] able riches by traffic. Taking advantage of the distracted state of the times, this man had allowed his thirst after lucre to overcome his better principles, and lead him into lawless dealings with the wretches who went about abstracting valuables from infected or deserted mansions. As a punishment for his rapacity, death was thus in a short time brought to his own household, and he himself perished amid the unavailing wealth which sin had accumulated.

Fatal had been that gift!—In a very little while Mary sickened; and her symptoms were those of the fearful malady afflicting the nation. Bessy Bell was fully aware of the danger; but, with an heroic self-devotion, she became the nurse of her friend; and, when all others kept aloof, administered, though vainly, to her wants. Her noble and generous mind was impressed with the conviction that she owed some reparation for the unintentional wound which she might have inflicted on the feelings of Mary, in having appeared to become her rival in the affections of her betrothed.

As an almost necessary consequence, she was herself seized with the malady of death. The evening heard them singing hymns together—midnight listened to the ravings of delirium—the morning sun shone into the bower of death, where all was still!

The tragedy was consummated ere yet Bruce had set sail for France; but the news did not reach him [369] for a considerable time, the communication between the two countries being interrupted. His immediate impulse was to volunteer into the service of the German emperor, by whom he was attached to a squadron sent to assist Sobieski of Poland against the Turks. He never returned; and was supposed to have fallen shortly afterwards, in one of the many sanguinary encounters that ensued.

The old Laird of Kinvaid awoke from the paroxysm of his grief to a state of almost dotage, yet occasionally a glimpse of the past would shoot across his mind; for, in wandering vacantly about his dwelling, he would sometimes exclaim, in the spirit so beautifully expressed in the Arabian manuscript, "Where is my child?" and Echo answered, "Where?"

The burial vaults of both the Kinvaid and Lynedoch families, who were related, were in the church of Methven; but, according to a wish said to have been expressed by the two young friends, "who were lovely in their lives, and in death were not divided," they were buried near a beautiful bank of the Almond. Several of the poets of Scotland have sung their hapless fate: Lednoch bank has become classic in story; and, during the last century and a half, many thousands of enthusiastic pilgrims have visited the spot, which the late proprietor of Lynedoch has enclosed with pious care.

Of the original ballad only a few lines remain: they are full of nature and simple pathos. [370]

> Bessy Bell and Mary Gray
>   They were twa bonny lasses;
> They biggit a bower on yon burn brae,
>   And theekit it owre wi' rashes.
>
> They wouldna lie in Methven kirk,
>   Beside their gentle kin;
> But they would lie on Lednoch braes,
>   To beek them in the sun.

FRIENDSHIP'S OFFERING

Literary Annual

Friendship's Offering; or, The Annual Remembrancer: A Christmas Present, or New Year's Gift, for 1825. Ed. Thomas K. Hervey. London: Lupton Relfe, 1825. Printer: D.S. Maurice, Fenchurch-street.

Title

Anonymous. "Lanucci. A Tale of the Thirteenth Century." FO 1825. 247-260. [247]

LANUCCI.
A Tale of the Thirteenth Century.

———

Whence it comes that the most inveterate hatred frequently disunites the hearts of those whom heaven appears to have destined most truly to love each other? Nothing is more dreadful than fraternal enmity. Yet, how often did brothers shed each others blood at the period of the feuds between the Guelphs and Ghibelines, in Italy.

At the time when these two parties were contending, with equal boldness and insatiable hatred, Pisa and Florence, the two most considerable republics of Tuscany, desolated by the horrors of civil war, were frequently the theatre of the most fatal family feuds, of which the following story is a melancholy instance.

Two sisters, equally distinguished by beauty and high birth, had married a Bandinelli of Florence, of the party of the Guelphs, and a Lanucci of Pisa, of the party of the Ghibelines. These sisters, who had been united from their earliest infancy, by the tenderest friendship and sisterly [248] affection, became the mothers of two sons, Antonio Bandinelli and Frederick Lanucci.

The morose disposition of the young Florentine had conceived from his childhood, even during their boyish sports, the most violent animosity towards his cousin, which increased with his years. He was scarcely eighteen, and had acquired sufficient skill in the management of his horse and arms, when, with a heart full of hatred and lust of combat, he one day determined to ride to Pisa. He was already in sight of the walls of the city; when, riding along the solitary banks of the Arno, he perceived his enemy, who was exercising his horse, unsuspicious of any evil. Without any provocation on his part he loaded him with the bitterest reproaches, drew his sword, and dismounted to attack him. The other, compelled to defend himself, did the same. Lanucci was, however, more expert in the management of his arms, and had the additional advantage of an unruffled temper. He avoided wounding his antagonist, only wearying him, by forcing him to retreat step by step. At length, he had him entirely in his power, and might have taken his life; but his generous heart hoped to subdue him by love. He placed his sword on his breast, saying, "You see that your life is in my hands, but I joyfully spare it. Think, too, of our mo- [249] thers, I conjure you; and for their sake let all enmity between us from this moment cease." Bandinelli, in this situation, promised all that his brave adversary required; but scarcely had he restored him to liberty, when he rose, with re-doubled fury, and aimed a blow at him from behind, which would infallibly have brought him to the ground, had he not avoided it by a sudden and instinctive motion.

Lanucci, indignant at this inconceivable treachery, was unable to check his just anger: "Wretch!" cried he, "you will not have peace; receive the reward of your baseness." Thus saying, he, with one blow, brought him to the ground, and left him weltering in his blood. Returning to Pisa, Lanucci, stained with the blood of his cousin, would not go to his mother's house, but concealed himself with a friend, whence he sent a written account of the event to Florence, to justify himself by a simple and faithful narrative. The death of Bandinelli filled his heart with despair, though he had been obliged to wound him by the necessity of self-defence.

But the monster, Bandinelli, was still alive, and was to live long, to embitter the life of Lanucci. Some peasants had found him weltering in his blood, and conveyed him to Florence; where his wound being dressed, was pronounced [250] dangerous indeed, but not mortal. The traitor, who, as he recovered his health, felt his hatred revive, and, if possible, increased through shame and rage at being conquered, or rather from vexation at having made in vain his cowardly attempt at assassination: the traitor, I say, meditated the foulest calumny to gratify his revenge. He, therefore, declared that he had been suddenly and perfidiously attacked. As he was one of the Guelphs, they took his part against Lanucci, whom, as a Ghibeline, they already considered as a traitor; and their faction being at that time predominant, he was sentenced, in spite of his most solemn protestations, to banishment from Pisa, and the confiscation of his property.

Lanucci possessed the rarest treasure to be found on earth, the most valuable blessing in adversity, which, in prosperity, we can seldom acquire or retain; Lanucci had a friend—Belfiore was his only support; especially as his inconsolable mother, plunged in sorrow, began at times to entertain doubts of the virtue of her son. Belfiore having in vain exerted himself to the utmost in Lanucci's defence, offered to give him an asylum at one of his country seats. There, at a distance from the tumult of the world, they hoped to lead a tranquil life in the enjoyment of mutual regard and friendship. But the measure of [251]the sufferings, which inexorable fate had destined for Lanucci, was not yet full.

In this retreat, the prohibition to return to his native city was doubly painful, when he received news of the illness of his mother, which, to complete his misery, was soon succeeded by that of her death. From that time he was plunged in silent melancholy, while some pleasing recollections of his childhood but rarely cheered the gloom that enveloped his mind. The room which he inhabited, and in which he usually slept, was separated from that of his friend and host, only by a saloon, into which both their doors opened.

One night, when he had hardly fallen asleep, he was waked by a noise, which seemed to proceed from the salon. He raised himself up and listened, but was unable to hear any more. Fancying that it was only one of those melancholy dreams, which haunt the unfortunate in their sleep, he tried to compose himself to rest, but in vain. Soon after, he thought he heard a groan, and it seemed to him to come from his friend's chamber. He listened with double attention, and heard the groan repeated; he immediately rose, and hastened to Belfiore's bed-side. He calls to him, but receives no answer. In the darkness of the night, he has no means of ascertaining his situation, but by feeling him; he [252] raises and presses him to his breast, but cannot awake him. With his heart filled with anxious foreboding and terror, he runs back to his own apartment, and returns with a lamp to the bedside of his friend. But, oh dreadful sight! he finds him bathed in his blood! the deadly steel plunged into his generous bosom, and himself stained with blood, from having taken his friend in arms, who just then heaved his last sigh. At this heart-rending scene, overcome by his feelings, he utters a piercing cry, and throws himself on the corpse of his friend. He, unconsciously, lets fall the lamp—it is extinguished—and night again envelopes in a gloomy veil this scene of horror!

Meantime, the domestics being awakened by the noise, hasten to the assistance of their master. They find him murdered; Lanucci stretched upon his corpse: he regards them with a fixed eye, and a pale and terrified countenance, and the just extinguished lamp is still smoking at his feet. A cry of horror proceeds from all present. Lanucci awakes to the most fearful recollection: with convulsive fury he leaps up, exclaiming, "Where is he? Where is the perfidious assassin? Why cannot I plunge this dagger into his breast? O, Belfiore! O, my beloved Belfiore!" A flood of tears rushed from his eyes, and he [253] again sunk senseless on the corpse. Amazement, grief, and horror deprived all present of the power of utterance. At day break the news of this dreadful event was spread on all sides. With the rapidity of lightning, it extended to Pisa. The human dispensers of divine justice sent their officers, who arrested all the inmates of the house, and carried Lanucci himself before the chief judge, who was of the party of the Guelphs. He was here confronted with all those who appeared, as being suspected of this heinous crime; all the evidence united to point him out as the criminal. The place where he was found by the servant, the blood which stained his hands and breast, his terror, the newly extinguished lamp, which was found at this feet, his previous condemnation, and its cause, and still more, his cypher on the dagger, which was taken from Belfiore's breast, and which every body recognised to be his, all conspired to mark him as the murderer. Even his despair seemed to accuse him. "I," said he, "I murder the only friend whom I have met with in the world! him, to whom I am indebted for the preservation of that life which I now feel to be a curse! him, whom I loved more than myself! for whom I would have joyfully have shed the last drop of my blood! I deprive him of life, sully my hand with so foul a [254] deed! and, at what hour, in what place? Am I accused of murdering him in the silence of the night,—in his peaceful slumber? I, his friend, to whom he afforded protection and hospitality? can I be thought capable of such cowardice? Oh heaven! to what an excess of sorrow hast though doomed me! Oh great and merciful God! are the trials which thou hast appointed me not yet sufficiently severe? Oh, spirit of my mother, pray for thy son, for they unhappy child, to the Almighty who knows his innocence!"

When he had uttered these words, the unfortunate Lanucci was completely exhausted; but nothing transpired to weaken the evidence against him, or even to lessen the suspicion. But among his judges there was one of those rare men, who, particularly in times of civil dissentions, are hardly ever met with; his name was Cardegha. Though of the Guelph faction, he did not think that a Ghibeline, accused before the tribunal, ought to be found guilty merely because he was a Ghibiline; and by his just and equitable sentiments he gave his contemporaries an example of a conscientious and upright judge. Moved by Lanucci's anguish, by the honest frankness which appeared in his looks and his words, he openly defended him. The rest of the judges, on the other hand, considered the despair of the accused as the effect [255] of remorse, or as one of the artifices usual with criminals. They said, that the proofs of his guilt were too clear and manifest; his murderous hand, accustomed to assassination, had already attempted the life of his cousin, the young Florentine; that it was necessary to suffer the useful rigor of the law to take its course; the enormity of the crime required exemplary punishment; besides this, that the populace cried aloud for vengeance, they demanded his condemnation, and they durst no longer delay it. Lanucci was almost unanimously sentenced to death. Cardegha in vain attempted to defend him; in vain he reminded them of the curse of heaven, which overtakes the unjust judge; he could obtain nothing save only the melancholy consolation of imparting to the unfortunate Lanucci the dreadful sentence which had been passed.

At the sound of the massy bolts and hinges of the prison, the heart of this worthy man was oppressed, and an involuntary tear started into his eye, but he wiped it away, for he wished to appear calm and composed, and in every case to administer comfort. The gates of the subterraneous vault now opened, and by the faint glimmering of a lamp, he beheld the miserable Lanucci stretched upon the earth, absorbed in grief, and oppressed by the weight of his chains. His [256] compassion was again awakened, and his eyes filled with tears, which he was no longer able to repress.

"You accuse me of murder," said the prisoner, "you consider me as a traitor!"—"My son," rejoined the humane judge, "the being we call man, is but a tissue of error and illusion; I believe you innocent, and therefore pity you, less than I do the judges who pronounced your sentence of death."—"My sentence of death! Then it is decided! Loaded with infamy, I shall descend into my grave!" At the melancholy train of images which this terrific word excited, Lanucci was seized with a kind of suppressed rage, which ended in a perfect stupor. A long and horrible gloom hung over his soul. Those who approached him melted into tears, and tried in vain to tranquillize him. The Thought of death was not terrible to him; since the death of his mother and the loss of his friend, he considered it as the only termination to his sufferings. But to survive in the memory of his fellow citizens as a murderer, to be executed in the square of his native city, where every object recalled to his mind the sports of a happy childhood, it was this that overpowered his lofty soul.

Cardegha returned, and taking advantage of an interval of apparent composure, he kindly took [257] the hand of the unhappy sufferer, and pointing at the same time to the crucifix, which hung on the opposite wall, "Do you think," said he, "that He was guilty? Behold His wounds, admire his resignation to the Divine Will, and think of the sufferings of Him who died on the cross for your sake." Lanucci gazed in silence on the cross: then, as if suddenly inspired, he exclaimed,—"O my God, my God all power is thing! Pardon the wavering of my soul; I do not dread death, and I will even submit to infamy; my death is just and equitable, if thou in thy wisdom hast determined it. What is it to me the opinion of the world, O my divine Redeemer? Thrice wast thou denied by the most faithful of thy apostles, and to me the most unworthy of thy creatures, thou dost send an angel of comfort into my gloomy prison. O Cardegha, I owe thee more than life; I die full of faith in God and his blessed Son; soon I shall again hear the welcome voice of my mother, and embrace my friend whom I could not save from the murderer's blow!"

All who were witnesses of this painful struggle of the guiltless youth were now perfectly convinced of his innocence, and they all sincerely wished that he might be saved. The news of his pious resignation had already spread itself in the city, which was followed by a general belief in [258] his innocence, and murmurs arose on all sides. The people wished the execution of the sentence to be delayed. Time, they said, would discover the criminal, for it was impossible that Lanucci should be guilty.

A considerable party of moderate persons had resolved to make a solemn application to the judges, and public opinion had already decided in his favour. But the noble Cardegha had not lost a moment. Immediately after the first depositions were taken, he had sent an express to Florence; this messenger had returned, and everything assumed a different aspect.

The murderer of Belfiore was a Banditto, hired by Bandinello, Not content with having caused his cousin to be deprived of his property and banished from his native city, he aimed at the life of the Lanucci, which he considered as a disgraceful monument of his own treachery. On the day of their first encounter, Lanucci's dagger had fallen from his girdle, and was picked up by the peasants who conveyed Bandinelli home, and who delivered this weapon to him, supposing it to be his. He put it into the hands of a Banditto, and promised him a large reward if he executed his nefarious design.

Cardegha's friends at Florence had caused all persons to be strictly watched, who went [259] in and out of the Bandinelli palace: by this means they had discovered the murderer. It appeared form his confession, that he had secretly entered Belfiore's house, where he concealed himself till midnight; but that, mistaking the apartments of the two friends, he had murdered Belfiore instead of Lanucci. In order to make it believed that Lanucci had killed himself, he had been ordered to leave in the wound, the dagger given him by Bandinell. Hastening, as soon as the deed was accomplished, to fly the Pisan territories, he was attacked at the gates of Florence, by one of his comrades, whom Bandinelli had commanded to lie in wait and murder him on his return. His comrade, whom he had overcome, made this confession to save his life. He was arrested by the Florentine police in the vestibule of the Bandinelli palace, where he wanted to conceal himself, in order to punish Bandinelli, for his treachery. The chief magistrate, of the same party as Cardegha, had voluntarily given up the banditto, and the more readily, as the two republics were at that time at peace, and Belfiore was of a great family at Pisa; and, on the other hand, there was nothing to be feared for Bandinelli, who, according to the barbarous custom of those times, had to dread no punishment for his crime, but the pangs of his own conscience. [260]

As soon as this news was known in Pisa, the citizens, who felt the deepest interest in Lanucci, gave themselves up to the greatest rejoicings. But the sudden and unexpected transition, from grief to joy, nearly proved fatal to him. When he saw his innocence thus solemnly recognised, he was so overcome that he sunk on the grown, without consciousness, and almost without life. Cardegha, who did not quit him, afforded him all possible assistance; and when Lanucci recovered, they both prostrated themselves before the image of our Saviour.

"O, religion," cried Lanucci, "the strength which thou givest, taught me to endure the idea of an ignominious death; this day thou dost still more; thou teachest me the duty of living. O, my mother! O, Belfiore! your son, your friend, has constantly remained worthy of your love and your esteem. Merciful Father! deign to turn Bandinelli's heart; pardon him, and may judges, in all ages, learn, through my unhappy story, how often deceitful appearances can mislead! And you, noble Cardegha, to whom I am indebted for my life, my honour, tell me what return I can make you?" He replied:—"By doing that for others, which Heaven has permitted me to do for you."

Literary Annual

Friendship's Offering. A Literary Album. Ed. Thomas K. Hervey. London: Lupton Relfe, 1826. Printer: D.S. Maurice, Fenchurch-street.

Title

Anonymous. "The Laughing Horseman. A Tale." FO 1826. 109-134.[1]

PLATE: The Laughing Horseman.
Steel plate engraving; drawn by Richard Westall, R.A.; engraved by Edward Finden; printed by McQueen. [109]

---

[1] Plain text for this transcription was obtained from Google Books <http://books.google.com/books?id=8jofAAAAMAAJ&lpg=PR13&ots=KaxUOMikST&dq=friendship's%20offering%201826&pg=PR1#v=onepage&q&f=false> and then compared against the original volume. For full citation, see References.

THE LAUGHING HORSEMAN.

> What a strange creature is a laughing fool!
> As if man were created to no use,
> But only to shew his teeth.
>
> WEBSTER.

"WHERE was the body found?" said the parish clerk.

"In the Deadman's Clough," replied the landlord," close under the roots of the big black elm."

"It is the strangest thing of the kind,"—said the clerk,

"That has happened in England, in my time," added the landlord.

There was a dead pause. No one else thought fit to join in the conversation of the two worthies, who were, in a manner, the secondary oracles of the parish. But the bystanders filled the yard of the Crow and Teapot, and peeped over each other's shoulders, and under their arms, with a shuddering curiosity, to catch a glimpse of the corse. At times, a half-suppressed whisper would rise among the crowd; and, occasionally, a scuffle took place, as those behind pushed forward those in the front ranks [110] who, as vehemently, resisted the suggestion. For, anxious as all were to see the mangled and hideous spectacle, none were willing to approach beyond a certain degree of appropinquity, seemingly marked out, by common consent, as the extremity of their advances.

"Lost for three weeks!" ejaculated the landlord, "and found in such a state!"

"Most unfit," said the clerk, "for a Christian body, under an old tree; and might have lain time unknown, without bell or book;—what of his immortal soul!"

"True, true! and such a life as he led, drinking at home—never spent a penny at a public; and gambling abroad, and getting money, the Lord knows how, and, yet, never a farthing to a starving body."

"Nor a penny in the poor's box; but, as to that, he never came within ten graves' length of a church door," said the clerk.

"Never, since the day that we first heard of his winning three hundred guineas from Will Codicil, the rich lawyer's son; and that was the first winning Gripe Gibbons ever made, one way or other," added the host.

"Aye, but he made many a one after; never rattled a dice-box, or chucked a guinea, or dealt a card, but sure it was, great or small, the sweepings always came to one pocket," said the landlord's plump wife,—who began to feel impatient at the long silence under which she had remained. [111]

"Even so," replied the clerk: "it is to be prayed for, that he may not have lost more than he gained. It ever seemed strange to me, the run of luck he had. I never knew of a gambler that always won,—not one; saving, always, when it might be with the help, with the abetting of—of him—of one that's not to be named."

The insinuation, conveyed by these words, was not lost on the audience. Those who had been most eager in pressing forward towards the centre, now shrunk back a rank. The whole assembly presented a galaxy of faces, most unduly exaggerated in length; and looked at the speaker, as if eager to devour the words of strange import that fell from a man, who, according to his station, spake with authority.

"And I would fain know," continued the speaker, lowering his voice, and assuming a more mysterious tone, "I would fain know the meaning of that bauble that never left him when living, and hangs to his neck, now that he lies there, a mangled corse."

When the rising horror, which the sayings of the clerk had given birth to, had a little subsided, a woman, one of the bystanders, ventured to offer an answer to the implied query.

"I have heard Sukey Barnes, his old housekeeper, when she was well and hearty,—as blythesome an old woman as one would see on a summer's day,—say her belief, that it was a charm against him that we know of, and that he prized it more than all his ill-gotten winnings; and often, after his rioting, [112] when those fearful fits came on him, he would grasp it with his clasped hands, and cry to it to save him. Morning and night, sleeping and waking, he had it on him; but why, or for what, a Christian soul should put such a faith in a senseless thing o' metal, *He* only knows."

An oracular "humph!" accompanied with a look from under the bent eyebrows of the clerk, betokened his deep consideration of Meg Symonds' account; which increased so much the terror of the crowd, (and crowds were not by far so enlightened in those times, as in our own,) that, although it was yet day-light, many a one looked, fearfully, over the left shoulder, and seemed only to wait an example to depart, with all possible speed, from the vicinity of the fearful thing. At length, the landlord revolved his circumference, and, leading the way with the clerk into the house, was followed by the whole assembly, man, woman, and child, emulously disputing the priority of entrance, and alike desirous of being the last to quit the yard in which lay the unfortunate object of their anxiety.

The approaching gloom of the evening was dispelled by the fire of larch faggots, that roared, and fumed, and flustered, in the huge chimney of the inn-kitchen, a cheering defiance to the chills of February. A capacious semicircle, widely expanding around this welcome point of attraction, was speedily formed within which, divers round and square tables were laden with earthen jugs, brown as the [113] English barleycorn juice wherewith they were replete. As the contents of the measures diminished, the courage of the inmates waxed higher; and stories, dark and mysterious, were dealt out in lavish profusion. The atmosphere seemed infected with the contagion of the strange and the supernatural; no subject was broached but savoured of more than earthly interest: none listened to but what spake of the grave, and its fearful scenery, or the still more exciting theme of the delusions and machinations of the enemy of man. The old ran through the memory of their days, and the days of their fathers, to cull from the traditions of the murdered and the slayer. The swollen corpse of the water-fiend's victim—the black damning marks of the strangled—the rattling of the gibbet chains—and the noiseless step of the things that mortal eye may hardly look upon and live, were, by turns, presented to the thirsting and fevered imagination; whilst the young drank in, with greedy ears, the sleep-destroying histories, till not a soul in the room but was saturated with the dreadful topic that thrilled their blood, with the nervous excitement of an irresistible stimulant.

One of the company, in particular, was chained in attention to these narratives. The subject seemed, by a sort of enchantment or fascination, to enwrap his soul, and chain down every faculty; yet, to look at him, no one would have selected him as an object likely to be affected, in any peculiar degree, by [114] supernatural terrors. He was a young man, apparently not more than five and twenty; his hale frame, and ruddy cheeks, indicated bodily health, as well as freedom from any burthensome excess of care; and he seemed well able to defend himself from such foes as might be overcome by dint of strength: but, under the influence of the fears which at present assailed, he became like Samson, weak, not indeed, 'as another man,' but chicken-hearted as a child. Never was man so translated by terror.

He of the timorous mind sat on a pedlar's box, which, at once, denoted his profession, and inclosed the chief of his worldly substance. Though not immoderate in its dimensions, it, on this occasion, carried double; for, squatted upon it, close by the owner, sat a favoured she, the faultless Phyllis of the perambulant Corydon, whose left arm half surrounded her reluctant waste, while the right in part supported its owner, as he leaned against the huge chimney-piece into whose comfortable vicinity he had drawn. It was a moot point, whether the occasional squeezes which the pedlar bestowed on the object of his affections, were, in fact, the designations of love or of fear; whether produced by an ebullition of tender feeling, or by a desire of being certified that he was in the immediate companionship of tangible creatures of flesh and blood—things of his own nature. And so he sat and listened, and listened and sat, till his blood curdled cold in his veins, and [115] his naturally curled locks began to assume an inclination to perpendicularity. Briefly, he was frightened to death, as near as a man might be.

Time passed on. It had grown quite dark—without a light you could not have seen your hand. Moon and stars were as effectually be-clouded, as if they had ceased to exist. The broad blaze flickered in the chimney, jollily, and gleamed on the little snug diamond window-panes, with infinite gaiety. The ghosts and goblins became familiar; and this, added to the cheery look of the apartment, with, here and there, glimpses anticipatory of the wherewith preparing for supper,—taking into consideration, too, the ennobling powers of the stout ale,—raised up the hearts of the wondering company. We must except, however, the pedlar; he, nerveless to shake away his fear, still clung to Cicely Simkins;—and peeping, now over his right, now over his left shoulder, quivered inwardly at his own shadow, as it rose and fell, with the waving of the flame.

The conversation was suddenly interrupted. A loud calling at the outer door of the inn betokened the traveller impatient to deliver his horse to the care of the ostler, and himself to the shelter of the house. The landlord was, extempore, on his legs; and, in a few moments, ushered in, with the customary phrases of hospitiary welcome, the new-comer.

The traveller, though a good-looking man in the main, had something odd about him,—so much so that his appearance, for a time, put an end to the [116] converse, and a dead blank ensued. He gazed about him, carelessly; marched, with great slinging steps, to the hearth; and, rubbing his hands briskly over the flame, took the seat by the pedlar's Dulcinea, which the landlord had recently deserted, and called for a pint of usquebaugh.

Now, there was nothing strange in all this:—you or I, or any other traveller, on a cold night, and after a ride, it may be of thirty miles, would have done the same. Yet so it was, that the guests stared, first at each other, and then at the stranger, as if at a loss what to make of it. They looked at the traveller, and scrutinized, as if they would have seen through him,—which they certainly would, had he been transparent, or only *semi*-opaque. But his frame was too dense to admit of such researches; and he lolled as he sat, and stretched his legs to the fire, and sipped his liquor, like a man of middle earth.

Stay!—We have given no account of his personal appearance; which, as before hinted, was a little queer. He was a tall man, not corpulent, his legs degenerating to spindle; but what they wanted in natural coatings, was made up by a prodigy of jackboots, with huge spurs, that jingled and jaunted like a whole company of the tenth hussars. His coat and light pantaloons of a parson's grey, were worse for wear, and began to rustify. A prim small ruff betokened him of the old school, and accorded well with a steeple-crowned beaver, with superlative rims; when laid aside, this disclosed a head of un- [117] combed grizzly hair, black as soot. His countenance was of a dark dingy hue, penetrating in expression; he had great beetle brows, and his eyes pierced into you, as if they shot needles. His age might be some fifty—fifty-five, perhaps. There was nothing more in his person worthy of note, except that his features, from time to time, were distorted with an intolerable inclination to laugh.

The landlord interrupted the gathering silence. "Master Thummins!" said he, "that was a good story you told us awhile ago: can nobody match it? Adzooks! that a can of good ale should pass away, without a song or a tale to bear company. Rob Saunders, man! tell us the tale of Old Bess Baudlin and the Evil One. There's many a one, here, has never heard it; and it's a good tale, well worth the listening."

"Aye, what was that?" said the stranger, joining in the conversation, "what was that tale, landlord?"

"A tale, sir!—and, as I said, a good tale—of an old woman that cheated the—the—"

"The Devil, you mean to say," said the traveller.

"The very same," said the landlord.

"Do you know any thing of this tale?" said the traveller, suddenly turning round, and addressing himself to the pedlar, who was almost struck dumb at this unexpected address; but he recovered himself, and made answer,—

"An' please you, sir! I know nothing at all about it—a thing wholly out of my line of business; but [118] think, may it please you, that he must be a longheaded lad that cheats the Devil."

"Or a pedlar," answered the other, drily; "both of them hard to deal with, as I am informed."

There was something irresistibly comical in the stranger's manner, though not in his words. He looked around the apartment, and no one could withstand it. Even the gravity of the parish-clerk gave way. An universal laughter pervaded; and yet there were many who, though unable to resist the impulse, felt the laughter was strange and fearful. Amid the hubbub, the stranger himself, rising from his seat, and sticking his hands in his pockets, burst into a peal of merriment that immediately silenced the rest. So loud, so long, so prodigious a laugh was never before heard in a mortal change-house. The very rafters trembled, and the soot fell down the chimney, out of sheer amazement.

When the paroxysm was past, the stranger walked out into the yard. Clink—clink—clink—his huge spurs sounded as he went, and every jingle went to the hearts of the hearers, and, at each, their visages grew paler. The stout-hearted landlord quavered, the parish-clerk was dumb-foundered with consternation. What was strange, the faint pedlar seemed the least affected by the stranger's appearance and demeanour. When the traveller shut the door upon the company, they respired more easily; but they recovered courage only to disperse, and, in two minutes, every guest but the clerk and the pedlar [119] were gone. They stood their ground, with the landlord, in the spacious kitchen. The cook, barmaid, waiter, and scullion had all disappeared, in the person of a stout lass, Nancy Swindells by name; and, with her, had vanished the host's niece and pedlar's mistress, Cicely Simkins.

"This will never do," said the landlord;— "to have my customers laughed away, in such a style, is no joke; and who ever heard such a roaring hyena!"

"The bells often parish-churches could not, I opine, have clanged out such a rattling," said the clerk.

"And such a strange looking man, too! One must take all customers, and be thankful, Mr. Passover! but, to my thinking, I never saw such an outlandish man in my days. I should not be very extremely astonished if he be a Papist, for no good Protestant ever indulged, as I may say, in such a merriment; and then his raiment, Mr. Passover! was hardly the comely dress of a Christian man. For myself, on a holiday,—when one can rest, in a manner, from the cares and labors of the world, and appear in a decent attire, something better than ordinary,—I, mainly, wear a coat of good blue, of a respectable cut, with bright buttons, that corresponds gaily with my best red flush waistcoat, and other things conformable, which—"

Longer had he spoken, had not Giles Passover gently laid his hand upon the open mouth.

"With submission, Master Simkins! I doubt whether a dress similar to the one you describe, and [120] which, as my eyes can testify, becomes you well, would sit gaily upon the merry gentleman, your guest. I doubt, too, whether this— you are a man of discretion, Mr. Simkins!—I doubt whether he be a Papist."

He assumed, as he spoke, the attitude of doubt, his fore-finger dubiously keeping time to his words; then, drawing the landlord still closer to him, he hemmed, looked round suspiciously, and gasping thrice, as if to take his breath, ejaculated to the host's ear, in a hurried and fearful whisper, "I doubt, sir!—I doubt he's something worse." He had no sooner spoken, than he fell extended upon the floor, senseless and motionless, to the astonishment of his companions; who, ignorant of the cause of this sudden prostration, were like to follow, involuntarily, the example thus set them,—so great were the fears to which it gave birth; for none, save the clerk, had seen the cold shining eyes which, through the window that adjoined the yard, had glared upon him as he spoke, with a concentration of malice and sneering triumph, too fearful for the endurance of mortality.

On recovering from his fit, the clerk staid no longer question, but ran for his life, leaving, behind him, his hat and mull; he even forgot his ivory-headed cane,—a companion whose society he was never before known to quit, no, not since he was elected clerk to the parish-church of Crowdundle.

"What can be the matter with Mr. Passover?" [121] said the pedlar, when, after sundry fruitless efforts, he, at length, regained the faculty of speech.

"The Lord of Heaven only knows," replied the bewildered man of liquors; "I think the house is bewitched, and all that's in it. Another such a stir, and my wits are clean gone. Jack!" continued he, addressing himself to the ostler, who, at that moment, entered from the yard, "have ye seen ought of the gentleman?"

"What he in the queer hat and boots? Sure I have."

"Where—where is he?" inquired the host and the pedlar, in one breath.

"I left him in the yard, staring at old Gibbons, yonder, by the light of the stable lamp. Every man to his taste! say I; or else, it's a queer amusement to be gaping at a dead body, at this time o' night, by the light o' a stable lamp. Indeed, you mun know, master! that when he first came in,—for I was cleaning his worship's horse"—

"What!—oh, aye, I remember now, he came o' horseback; but what sort of cattle may it be? more bones than beauty, I'll warrant."

"Never saw, never will see again, such a piece of flesh: the bravest black ever wore a tail, and a swinging one he has. Stands eighteen hands if an inch; such flanks—such joints—such eyes! but, as I was saying, in comes my gentleman, as I was combing his horse. Now, d'ye see, my mind misgave me; for, seeing such a codger come in, and a [122] dead man lying, may be, some ten yards off, and a dark night too, and no light but a farthing rush in a horn lanthorn, my heart jumped into my mouth, in a moment; but, howsomever, I put a bold face on the thing;—I were woundily frightened though ; and so, says I, ' Good night to you, friend.'— 'Good night,' says he. My God! such a voice; it was like—it was like—let me see: splice me if I know what it were like! but it made me drop my comb, and turn round with a flisker. 'Take care of my horse, my lad!' quoth he. '*Your* horse,' says I to myself; 'you're a rum customer, too:—carry that tale a step farther, my dear!' By the holy! he might have heard every word I had thought; for he cocks up his glim at me,—such a blinker!—I shook, like a leaf in a March wind, and kept my tongue safe from that time. So, he takes no more notice, but marches up to the corpse, as it was lying there, on Tim Shunter's old barn door, that they pulled down to carry it on. And I looked slily, with half an eye,—for I didn't care that he should spy me noting him,—and, as I live, he was grinning and laughing to himself, like, and snuffing up the air; though one would think he might have found somewhat more pleasing to his eyes and his nose."

Further communication was prevented, by the entry of the object of the discourse; who requested to be shewn to his lodging for the night. With great internal reluctance, the landlord complied. The stranger courteously bade the pedlar a good night, [123] and departed, without removing his boots, the clank of which rang in the ears of every inmate of the dwelling. The landlord returned, looked at his doors, and retired to rest. The pedlar crept, with hesitation and doubt, to his chamber, and the ostler withdrew to his den.

It was long ere the pedlar slept; and then, his dreams were troublous and strange. He awoke again, and lay tossing on his hard couch,—his thoughts full of the stranger horseman and his marvellous laugh. Though the stranger had shewn himself more complaisant to him than to the rest, and this had, in some degree, emboldened him, yet, to divest himself of fear was impossible. He lay long, panting and wishing for the morning light, to deliver him from the horrors that assailed him, till at length, a doubtful lethargy stole over his senses.

He had lain thus—to his conception the time appeared infinite—when a sudden sound seemed to drop upon his ear, and he shivered, as he recognized in it the creak of the stranger's boot, and the clank of his spur, suppressed, as if by the cautious and stealthy step of the owner: he shrunk under the bedclothes—he listened—the step approached—his nightcap, perforce, abandoned his head—he felt, he *knew* that the stranger was in his room! Every nerve was unhinged; a cold sweat burst from him; the bed shook audibly under his tremblings; all was silent, till a voice, which the pedlar's fears instantly [124] acknowledged, called him by his name, "Peter Tapeyard, shew thy face, man!"

The miserable pedlar, thus invoked, raised his countenance above the bed-linen, and beheld, gazing upon him, the traveller, attired as before. There was the same complacence in his looks that had before been manifested in his demeanour towards the man of goods; but, when the latter essaying to speak, ejaculated, "For the love of God!"—his exordium was cut short, by the stranger's altered look; the hue of his face deepened almost to blackness, and his brows contracted hideously, over eyes that suddenly gleamed like plates of fire, with a cold and shining light. The pedlar's faculties were suspended, until the voice of his visitor, jarring on his ear, recalled him from his trance of horror.

"Peter Tapeyard! listen to me,—to thy friend: thou art poor as the poorest of thy trade. Is it not so?"

A deep groan, from the pedlar, announced a woful affirmative.

"Yes, thou art poor: I know thee well, though thou knowest not me, Peter! and—but look up, man! and fear not."

The pedlar obeyed. The fearfulness of the traveller's aspect had passed away.

"Thou would'st wed Mistress Simkins, the landlord's niece. Thou necd'st not say aye; thy looks speak for thee, and the girl would have thee." [125]

"Surely she would," replied the pedlar," if—"

"If, thou would'st say, thou wert richer. The landlord is a prudent man, and will not trust his chicken to a cold nest. Now, what would'st thou do to get thee wherewith to obtain the damsel?"

"I would,–" exclaimed the pedlar, then stopped abruptly; for all the stories he had recently heard of the Evil One and his dealings, rushed upon his mind, and he shuddered at the thought of consigning his soul to perdition, even for Cicely Simkins. The stranger laughed his intolerable laugh. "Fear not, man! thy soul is safe; what have I to do with thy soul? or who would barter the cast of a bent sixpence for a pedlar's soul,—worn threadbare, too, like thine? But time is short. Listen then; there is hung round the neck of yonder dead fool, a box of gold."

"Of gold!" exclaimed the pedlar: "it seemed but as mouldy brass."

"Peace, man!" said the other. "I tell thee it is gold; though, to the clowns that thronged hither, it seemed the base thing thou speakest,—else, their reverence for the dead had not held out so long. I wish the gold had been coined into red guineas, such as thou mayest turn them to, if wise. Hesitate not:—they call it a charm, to keep away him they call the Evil One. Asses! to think a metal box can guard against his power! Remove the box—take it to the goldsmith of the next town—sell it him—marry [126] Cicely Simkins—thrive, and be happy!—What sayest thou?"

The temptations hung out dazzled the pedlar's mind. He might acquire his Cicely—he need no longer tramp about, with the huge box hanging on his back—he might settle in a snug cottage—he might even, in due season, succeed to Cicely's uncle, in the lucrative supremacy of the Crow and Teapot. And then, where was the harm of taking from the dead what could so well avail the living! besides, here was no contract, supposing his unknown adviser the being he was suspected; there was no agreement to give that gentleman the least controul over the natural or spiritual man of Peter Tapeyard. Why, then, should he delay in taking the benefit of the mode pointed out to him of so easily making his fortune?

"Worthy sir!" said he, "I will gladly, and with many thanks, accept your kind offer; as soon as daylight"—

"I know what thou would'st say," interrupted the other, "but it may not be. Daylight will bring hither the coroner, and the quacks of the law, and where then will be thy opportunity? The cock must not crow before thy prize is won: hasten, then, for the morning is coming;—report to me at the breakfast board thy success. Up, then, and be active!—the dead tell no tales."

He seized, as he concluded, the arm of the pedlar, [127] as if with the purpose of enforcing his recommendation of a speedy completion of the undertaking. A cry of horror burst from the tortured and terrified man of wares, as he sprung from his trance, awakened by the burning grasp of the stranger. He opened his eyes, and, looking around, found himself alone. The pain that had so acutely pierced him was vanished. He arose from his bed, and looked from the narrow casement:—the moon was up, and shining broadly and brilliantly. He looked into the yard—he gazed at the door of the stable, in an outer part of which lay the corpse. Should he descend or not?—Was his dream a mere phantom of a disturbed imagination, or an actual indication of a speedy way to the acquisition of wealth? He wavered—turned towards his bed,—when, in so doing, his eye fell upon the sleeve of his shirt. It was burnt, as if a band of glowing iron had surrounded it; and, on his arm, was scorched the visible impress of a man's hand. Here was a sufficing proof of the reality of the visit with which he had been favoured.

He descended the stairs softly and fearfully, casting about him many a wistful look. Often did he stop to tremble and to doubt, as the wind whistling through some crevice, or the cough of a sleeper, arrested his attention. Once, he thought some one passed him;—a cold sweat testified his terrors. More than once, his flesh quivered like a jelly; for he thought he saw glaring on him, through the darkness, the cold blood-chilling light of eyes not mortal. [128]

He gained the yard—he approached the stable-door; he would have lingered, but could not—suspense was worse than all his fears could fashion. He rushed in—he stood by the dead—seized the box that hung suspended to the neck of the deceased. Ere he could remove it, the cock sounded his triumphing note—The traveller's steed, at the moment, neighed loud and shrill! The pedlar snatched away his prize, and darted, in an agony of terror, from the spot. He thought the stranger passed him, as he went, dark and frowning;—and his eyes!—at last, he regained his chamber.

Early in the morning, as the stranger had predicted, came the officers of the law, to hold an inquest over the body of Gripe Gibbons, Esq. Nothing satisfactory was elicited, as to the manner of his death; the verdict of 'accidental death' was returned, and preparations had been made for interring the deceased in the afternoon.

The stranger appeared not at breakfast; nor had any one seen him since the preceding evening,—the pedlar excepted, who had reasons for not being communicative on the subject. Many were the debates occasioned by the traveller's absence; nor was the disappearance of the amulet overlooked, which all connected with the strange guest. All who had been terrified on the preceding evening, resorted to the inn to satisfy their curiosity, bringing with them multitudes of others, who knew, by hearsay only, what had happened; so that, if the landlord had pro- [129] fited little by Gripe Gibbons, Esq. in his life-time, that gentleman proved a source of considerable emolument to him, when dead.

The parish-clerk, too, called in, on his way to church,—a double degree of mysterious importance in his demeanour, from the events of the preceding night. He spoke little—doubted not the Evil One was looking after the soul of the dead—and intimated the propriety of a watch being kept, that night, in the church-yard. As usual on such occasions, his advice was much approved, but not followed; for no one cared to put himself in peril, for the sake of Mr. Gibbons' soul.

The only known relative of the deceased, the successor to all his wealth, attended as mourner, in the ceremony of interment, which was performed without parade. The church was not more than a stone's throw from the house; but, from some reason, the bearers thought proper to take a circuitous route, running by the Deadman's Clough, the place where the body had been discovered. They paused a moment, as they arrived there. It was a dismal spot—a dark dreary hollow, whose rugged sides were thick with brambles and wild shrubs. It was filled with vapours, and the rank vegetation that grew there was wet with pestilent dews. A solitary elm, whose black and leafless arms were flung around with a spectrous wildness, grew near the bottom of the abyss. It was under the half-covered roots of this tree, that a truant lad had been frightened, nigh out [130] of his senses, by discovering the body of the defunct; which, preserved by an intense frost, was, at the end of three weeks' exposure, yet recognizable. All gazed, with fearful interest,—but most the pedlar, who sprung back with horror; for, through the gloom which filled the place, it seemed to him that he discerned, fixed upon him, the glaring eyes whose cold light he too well remembered. They proceeded, and the funeral was duly solemnized.

The pedlar seized the first opportunity, as they returned, of escaping from the company; he was impatient to realize his golden dreams, and obtain a remuneration for the sore squeeze the stranger had given him. The money arising from the sale of the golden box, he conceived, would furnish a pleasing salve for the scorched arm; so, he trudged off with more than usual celerity.

The company, meanwhile, adjourned to the Crow and Teapot; and the spacious kitchen was, again, crowded with the guests who, the preceding night, had been scattered away in dismay. Again, the ale flowed—again, the subject of the unknown visitor was resumed, and sundry ingenious conjectures published, as to his identity with the arch foe of man. The black horse came in for a share of the conversation; and the visitors thronged to behold the stud of the very Satan. They marvelled at his prodigious size, and seeming strength; and found, in his appearance, numberless circumstances denoting his infernal origin. Their curiosity satisfied, they slunk [131] back to their ale; and, as a huge fire blazed in the grate, grew snug, and determined to make a night of it.

The pedlar's absence was not unnoticed; but the more immediate and momentous subject of their disquisitions was of a nature too exclusively engrossing to admit of participation with another topic; and Peter Tapeyard's absence was speedily forgotten by all,—save only the fair Miss Simkins, who, as she busied about, cast many a glance around, to ascertain if the truant swain had not yet appeared.

There is an easy, comfortable coziness in an inn–especially if a country one—and prevailing mostly in the kitchen, towards evening, that mellows the temperament of a guest into a pleasing and indifferent indolence. There is a freedom from all controul—a lolling leg-stretching liberty, that comes sweetly, as the dimness of the latter winter grows into darkness, and the chill descending frost gives zest to the ruddy blaze of a roasting fire. There, between cup and lip, there is no slip—no balk—no hindrance of the passive luxury. There time ambles withal; and the measured tick of the family clock comes, with a friendly and home-breathing voice, to the ear. Should the cold wind whistle without, with what added delight does the guest cherish his palms, and edge still more encroachingly on the hearth! Or, if one of a circle, how rejoices he in the kindly fellowship and participation in the good things within his power! How gaily rises the song—how freely the [132] laugh! How briskly the mantling cup pours forth its contents, lending light to the eye, and smiles to the lip! The guests of the Crow and Teapot were of a class peculiarly fitted to enjoy the pleasing delirium of the spot,—men whose enjoyments were all social, and qualified, neither by nature or education, for refined pleasures. So, they ate, and drank, and rejoiced, jollily; and were, indeed, in the very riot of their felicity, when the door opened, and the pedlar, with starting eyes, pale cheeks, perpendicular hair, and quivering frame, fell flat on the ground, exclaiming, with a voice that was almost a shriek of terror, "Brass, and not gold!"

When raised and interrogated, no answer could be obtained from him but an iteration of those words; nor, from that hour to his dying day, could any explanation be got from him of the cause which had so bereaved him of his faculties. It is probable, from the short sentence he uttered, that the box purloined from the dead was, in truth, of base material; and the representations held out by the stranger designed only to answer some private end of his own, in the removal of the amulet. The further cause of the pedlar's violent agitation we presume not to guess at; nor does history afford any, the remotest, light on the subject. However this may be, a strong impression remained on the minds of the spectators that all was not right with Peter Tapeyard;—one consequence of which was, that, in the course of the following month, Miss Simkins re- [133] signed her hand and name to a substantial and Godfearing dealer in small wares, in the neighbouring town of Crowdundle.

That night, the landlord and parish-clerk determined to watch in the chamber of the former, which commanded a prospect of the church-yard. The stranger had not, yet, made his appearance; the black steed, much to the host's annoyance, remained in his stable, unclaimed. They sat patiently: at last, they started, for both heard a noise, seemingly proceeding from the stable. They were, yet, undetermined whether to descend the stairs or not, when the hollow tramp of the horse was heard, under the window; and, looking forth, they beheld the stranger, leading his steed in the direction of the church-yard! It was a bright, beamy, moonlight night; and the figures of the horse and his leader seemed doubly dark and black, as they intercepted the beams. Arrived at the church-yard, the stranger abandoned his horse, and entered the place where the grave-stones were shining in the light.

The gazers were cold with terror.

"There, there!" said the landlord, "he's at the grave! listen, hear him calling the dead!" And they listened, and fancied they heard the summons that was to break the bonds of death.

"See, see!" said the clerk," the ground is moving, like the burrow of a mouldy warp! He's there!—he's there! Gripe Gibbons himself! Fire, man!—fire the blunderbuss!" [134]

Absurd as this suggestion was, the landlord instantly complied. The echo was followed by the deep, high, unnatural laughter of the stranger; but the recoil of the weapon prostrated both the host and his companion, with a violence that left them, for a moment, senseless. The thunder-beat of the strong black horse aroused them—they rushed to the casement:—far away, the horse sprung over hill and hollow, under a double burthen!

"Gripe Gibbons has paid his reckoning this night!" said the clerk, at length.

"I wish," said the landlord, after a pause, "the other had done so, too."—For, the horseman had forgotten to discharge his shot.

Title
Anonymous. "Forgiveness. A Tale." FO 1826. 240-247. [240]

FORGIVENESS.[2]
A TALE.

The night was dark and tempestuous:—heavy gusts of wind shook the abbey walls, and resounded, in deep murmurs, along the cloisters;—while the moon, occasionally breaking through the thick clouds which enveloped her, cast an uncertain and awful light over the surrounding scenery.

The monk, Pierre, had lain down to rest,—but sleep fled from his eyes; and a broken slumber, which neither absorbed sense nor yielded repose, alone answered his solicitations. The groans of the distressed seemed to mingle with the sighing of the blast; and he frequently started from his couch, under the impression that he heard the well-known signal of his trusty dog, Fidele. In this manner he spent the hours, till the heavy bell of St. Gothard announced that midnight had passed. The storm was, in some degree, abated; and the beams of the moon were less interrupted. Pierre, however, no longer endeavoured to sleep. He fixed his eyes upon the bright luminary, which now shone full through the [241] casement of his little apartment, —and a train of thought, involuntarily, stole over his mind.

"Behold," said he, mentally, "a picture of myself! Delivered up to the dominion of my own wayward desires, every image was distorted in my imagination; and the common evils of life became burthens too great for endurance. The still small voice of reason was unheard in the whirlwind of passion; and–like the leaf, severed from its parent stem, and hurried down the torrent—I was alone on the sea of life, the sport of every breeze, and at the direction of every current. Oh, Father of Mercies!" he cried, energetically, "I thank Thee for the correction Thou hast given me, and for the light Thou hast communicated to me! A wanderer no more—though poor and feeble, friendless, and forgotten by the crowds that once hung on my smiles, —I pursue my path with joy, because it leads to Thee; and lose the sense of individual suffering in the humble, but active, endeavour to mark my gratitude,—and imitate Thee, by bringing my fellow wanderers to a place of earthly rest, and preparing them for a heavenly one!"

He was silent. A gentle calm diffused itself over his mind, and sleep began to steal over his eyelids; when, suddenly, he was roused by the reiterated barking of Fidele. He instantly obeyed the summons; and, wrapping his cloak around him, hurried into the air. Fidele fawned upon him with delight—then sprang forward—again barked loudly—and [242] then, as if dissatisfied at the

---

2 Plain text for this transcription was obtained from Google Books <http://books.google.com/books?id=8jofAAAAMAAJ&lpg=PR13&ots=KaxUOMikST&dq=friendship's%20offering%201826&pg=PR1#v=onepage&q&f=false> and then compared against the original volume. For full citation, see References.

slow pace that his master was obliged to observe, (for the path was rugged, and impeded with snow,) he returned—jumped upon him—licked his hand—and, with redoubled speed, pursued his own way, through the windings of the mountain. At length, he stopped. Exerting all his strength, Pierre pressed forward; and beheld the apparently lifeless remains of a man, stretched upon the snow. He knelt down, and perceived,—by the rays of his torch, aided by the beams of the moon,—that the ground was covered with blood. He laid his hand upon the breast of the stranger, and, to his joy, some slight pulsation evinced that life was not quite departed. He now dispatched Fidele for further assistance; and, in a short time, the wounded man was conveyed to the Abbey.

Pierre laid him upon his own bed; and, anxious to ascertain the extent of the injury he had received, he proceeded to examine the head, from whence the blood still flowed copiously. With this view he removed his cap, and parted the thick curls that covered his forehead. The light now shone full on his livid countenance. Pierre started back,—his eyes remained fixed upon the stranger,—his whole frame shook with violent and increasing emotion,—and the placid expression of his features was entirely lost. Recovering himself, he hid his face with his hands; and,—after an apparent struggle with his feelings,—he knelt down, and in a short, but earnest prayer, deplored his present weakness, and suppli- [243] cated the Divine assistance for the future. He then arose;—the smile of benevolence again illumined his pale, but venerable face; and, approaching the sufferer, he applied every remedy in his power, and watched, with trembling anxiety, the result of his cares. With feelings of pure delight, he observed, at length, the heaving of his breast, and heard a deep sigh issue from his lips. In a short time, the stranger opened his eyes, and fixed them upon his benefactor; but seemed to have no recollection of the past, or apprehensions for the present. Pierre took his station by his bedside, and, for many days, assiduously attended him.

At the end of a week, Abdallah—as he called himself—was able to converse; and Pierre now asked the particulars of his disaster, and the meaning of the incoherent expressions of wrath which had, frequently, escaped from his lips, during his late delirium. "You behold," said Abdallah, "a man who has seen the reverses of fortune, in their greatest extent. I have basked in the smiles of monarchs; I have held the highest posts of office; and wealth unbounded has swelled my coffers. My rank, however, was unable to shield me from malevolence; and the envy of one who had long hated me wrought my ruin. I was disgraced, to make room for my rival; and I became an outcast from that country which had owed its prosperity to my cares, and a vagabond in lands that had lately trembled at the sound of my name." [244]

Overpowered with the acuteness of his feelings, he paused;—nor was Pierre less affected. He wrapped his face in his garments, and groaned aloud. "You feel for me," said Abdallah, "but what are your sensations compared with mine!

Listen, however, good Pierre! and rejoice with me. My injuries have not slept in the dust!—no, no!"—added he, his countenance assuming an expression which made his auditor shudder, as he regarded him; —"I swore to be revenged, and I have performed my oath! Night and day has the desire of vengeance pursued me. It has been my food—my occupation—the height of my wishes, and the very end of an existence of which I had, long ago, rid myself, but for the hope of living to witness the destruction of my enemy."

"But, surely," interrupted Pierre, "you destroyed, by this means, your own happiness, (for, doubtless, sources of happiness were still open to you,) without injuring his." "Happiness!" scornfully replied Abdallah, "I desired no happiness but to be revenged; though, perhaps, I could not have wished my rival to endure a more bitter punishment than the state into which he had reduced me. The hope of vengeance haunted me every where. I had sufficient wealth,—but I despised it. I had a wife and children,—but their caresses were poisoned by the image of my foe. I forgot to take my food; and even sleep brought no repose. Frequently, in my slumbers, I thought I felt him in my grasp, and [245] raised my arm to stab him to the heart,–when, awakened by the action, I found he had yet escaped, and I wept for disappointment. My wife and children were all swept off by a fever," added he, in a low voice; "my wealth was dissipated. I renounced every connexion, and hired myself with bravoes. At length, I heard that my rival had received a commission which would compel him to cross these mountains. I instantly bent my course hither; and, having encountered his train, I managed to separate him from his attendants. And now, hear me, old man!—hear the completion of my long-protracted hopes. I met him in the pass. I struck him to the earth; and while he lay bleeding on the ground, I proclaimed myself my avenger, and upbraided him with his perfidy! I witnessed the convulsions of his frame! I heard his dying groans—they were music to my ears! and, in a delirium of joy, I still hung over him, when a blow, from an unknown hand, precipitated me down the precipice. Tell me, am I not to be envied! Can happiness, now, be greater than mine, or revenge more complete!"

He seized the arm of Pierre, as he spoke. The countenance of the latter was pale as marble, and it was some moments before he could make any reply. "Abdallah," at length, he cried, "I also was once rich, powerful, and renowned;—and I also had an enemy. He was once my friend–my brother–the beloved of my heart. I raised him to power, and gratified all his desires. But, he betrayed my love,—he brought dis- [246] grace and ruin upon my name, and drove me an exile from my country and mankind. Like you, I carried revenge into my retreat; and, like you, I suffered it to prey upon my heart. I planned various schemes of vengeance, but none answered the extent of my wishes. At length, I, fortunately, became acquainted with one who was well skilled to assist my research, and guide me in the right way to obtain satisfaction for my past wrongs. It was long, however, before I could obey his suggestions, or listen to his entreaties;—but, in the end, he prevailed, and opportunity alone was wanting to complete my projected plan."

"And has that opportunity been granted?"—eagerly enquired Abdallah." "I thank heaven," replied Pierre, fervently, "it has! Years had passed away, when, in an unlooked-for hour, my treacherous friend was thrown into my power. His life was in my hands;—no one was near to witness the deed;—he was alone, undefended, and—" "And," cried Abdallah, in a voice which shook with emotion, "you slew him!" *My* revenge," returned Pierre, "was not to be so gratified." He raised his eyes to heaven; and then, extending his arms towards Abdallah, he exclaimed,—"*I forgave him!* Look at me, Abdallah!—Poor and mean as I am, do you not recognize, under these weeds, your once loved, once Honoured, Hamet? Nay, hide not your face, but lose, again, on the bosom of friendship. I have learned a better lesson than to take vengeance. I [247] have exchanged the slavery of passion for the freedom of the Christian; and entreat you to partake of that peace which has long filled my bosom,–and which now swells it with joy unutterable! —Your enemy still lives, and is sheltered, with yourself, in these walls."

Abdallah paused for a few minutes,–and his varying countenance shewed the perturbation of his mind. Then, throwing his arms round the neck of Pierre, he sobbed—"Hamet! teach me this lesson, and bring me to your God; and let the restoration of your friendship be the promise of his pardon and acceptance!"

Literary Annual
Friendship's Offering. A Literary Album. Ed. Thomas K. Hervey. London: Lupton Relfe, 1827. Printer: D.S. Maurice, Fenchurch-street.

Title
By the Author of "Sir John Chivertons." [Ainsworth, William Harrison.] "Rosicrucian. A Tale." FO 1827. 38-63. [38]

THE ROSICRUCIAN.
A TALE.
BY THE AUTHOR OF "SIR JOHN CHIVERTON."

―――――

"Who is that singular-looking man?" said Carl Merler, to one who stood near him, in a Coffee-house, in Manheim.

"Who?—the tall man in brown?"

"The same;—do you know him?"

"I can hardly tell;—every one who comes here knows him,—and, yet, he is known to nobody. He is said to be an Immortal!—how?—Invisible! The man is six feet, or more;—you jest."

"More plainly, he is a worshipper of the Rosy Cross,—a visionary; half chemist,—half mystic; whose character you may hear from every body in the room, all of whom will speak confidently of him, and all differently. From one, you will hear that he is a man of genius and a philosopher,—from another, a fool; from a third, a madman."

"An illuminate, perhaps?"

"No—not exactly so. There is nothing, as it seems, political in his reveries,—nothing relative [39] to the ordinary concerns of humanity. He mixes with no one. It is not known that he keeps up any correspondence by letters. His manners are mild and urbane, and his demeanor, as you may observe, serious and contemplative. You, now, know all that any one appears to know of his habits or character."

"What is his name?"

"I know not,—nor have I ever heard him addressed by name."

"Does he inhabit this city?"

An old château, two miles hence, close by the Rhine, is his residence. He has no visitors, and of his domestic life, of course, nothing is known.⊠What is the hour?"

"Half after eight."

"So late?—I must be gone. Farewell!"

The individual, who had given rise to the young man's inquiries, was a man whose appearance was, at once, striking and prepossessing:—the latter phrase is, perhaps, too weak. His large frame, it is true, gave him, at the first glance, a somewhat ungainly appearance, which, however, vanished, when his countenance was observed. It was pale and clear. The features of the face were deeply traced; the forehead broad and capacious, the temples full and bare. Merler gazed and gazed, and became more and more anxious for a more intimate knowledge of this visionary,—if such he was.

The room began to assume the mellow, deep tinge of an autumn evening. The stranger laid down [40] the paper he had been reading, and left the house.

Day after day, Carl Merler resorted to the same place; and it generally happened that he saw the individual of whom he was, in fact, though almost unconsciously to himself, in quest. Still he was not better acquainted with him than before. If he made inquiries, he learnt nothing from the answers which added to his previous stock of information. It happened too, (remarkably as he thought,) that no opportunity ever occurred for the interchange, between them, of those little civilities that, continually, take place between persons whom habit or accident brings together. His curiosity increased.

One evening, it chanced that all the company had left the room, except Carl Merler and the object in whom he felt so unaccountable an interest. The latter, was reading a pamphlet; the former as usual, alternately studying the appearance of his companion, and creating theories of his real character and station.

It was while involved in one of these reveries, that his attention was awakened by some one's drawing a chair to the table where he sat. He looked up, and saw, opposite to him, the subject of his thoughts. He was confused,—rose up, resumed his seat, and looked hesitatingly at his companion, who calmly returned his glance.

The stranger smiled. "Do you want any thing with me?" he said, turning his full bright eyes, not unpleasantly, on Carl Merler. [44]

"Sir!"

The stranger repeated his question.

"No!—I am not aware that—that is—"

"Pardon me—you *are* aware. You have sought me here, not once, nor twice, nor thrice, but day after day, and for weeks. I know that you sought *me*. And, yet, you say, that you have no business with me.

"At least, I know of none."

"Well, then, I will tell you. You would know who and what is the solitary individual, of whom you have heard that he is alchemist, dreamer, Rosicrucian,—what not. Is it not so?"

"I confess that my curiosity has been strongly—I fear impertinently—at work, since my first visit to this place."

"Impertinently? Why so? Every man is, and ought to be, subject to the inquisition of his fellows. He, only, who has cause to fear, will object to the jurisdiction;—I have none. Once, again,—you wish to know who I am, and what are my pursuits?"

"Since you ask me,—I do."

"Very well—come and see!"

The stranger arose, took his hat, and departed, accompanied by Merler. They passed through several streets, and, proceeding beyond the confines of the town, found themselves on the pleasant borders of the abundant river. They wound their course among the vineyards that clothed the banks.

"See, what an evening!" said the stranger, as they [42] lingered, for a moment, under the shade of a lime trees.—And it *was* an evening fit to be spent and enjoyed on the banks of the Rhine.

The sun, just sinking over the green levels of the vine plantations,—the rapid waters, rejoicing in his purple glow—the little neat cottages of the peasants,—and the gay song and happy step of the peasants themselves, as they rejoiced in the work of the harvest,—fell, at once, on the eye and ear, with such a lively accordancy, that the spirit was charmed, and forgot that the days of purity and bliss—the reign of paradise—were no longer of the earth.

They walked on, still admiring the scene, that changed every instant;—looking, now, at some lazy vessel, that came floating down the stream, with its great sails flapping idly about, in quest of the breeze; and, now, at some half-ruined tower or dismantled dwelling, that stood gloomy and discontented, where every thing around was jocund, fresh, and delightful. It was at once of these habitations, in somewhat better repair than the others which they had seen, that the stranger stopped, and announced to his companion that their journey was at an end.

Taking its external aspect, it was a sombre and comfortless building,—half French and half Gothic; surrounded by a garden, dark cheerless, and neglected. The gate in the garden wall creaked, dolefully, as it opened; and again, as the owner of the pile closed and locked it, as they entered.

The path, along which they proceeded, was over- [43] grown with thick weeds; and, here, and there, a fallen garden-statue interrupted their progress. They arrived at the door of the mansion, a wicket in which was opened by an old and feeble woman.

"Let me now introduction you to my mansion," and Merler's host:—"no very splendid one, perhaps, for one whose fame has passed through the converse of all the good people of Manheim. It suffices, however, for my wants, and more is not needed. This is my library!"

It was a capacious room, three sides of which were covered with shelves, well stocked with books. The third was occupied, partly by the window which admitted light to the apartment,—partly by a cabinet, the doors of which were open,—and partly by one or two full length portraits, suspended in huge, heavy, painted frames. A large table occupied the centre of the floor; upon which, as well as around the room, were arranged numerous mathematical and philosophical instruments, books, maps and papers. The shelves of the cabinet were loaded with phials.

The stranger took a place in the window-seat, and motioned to Merler to follow his example.

"Are you not convinced," said he, "that you have to do with a wizard? Does this apparatus capture your imagination?"

"I see nothing here," replied Merler, "unsuited to the library of any man of scientific habits."

"What! yet incredulous!" returned the other, with a smile,—"follow me, then!" [44]

Merler complied; as his host, taking a key from the cabinet, unlocked a small door, near the window, and descended a flight of stone stairs. Arrived at their termination, Merler found himself in a low vaulted chamber. It was full of the instruments with which the alchemists were said to torture the elements of things, in their endeavours to attain boundless wealth and unceasing health. Several furnaces were burning with a light-green flame.

"Now," said his conductor to Merler, "you see what are my occupations."

"You are an alchemist, then,—a seeker for that which so many have failed to find?"

"Hardly so. I have wealth to satisfy my wants, without resorting to the transmutation of metals; and he who has passed half a century on the earth will scarce wish for the *elixir vitae*.

"Perhaps, you disbelieve in their existence?"

"No!—The powers of the human mind, when free from the clogs of sensual desires, are nighly illimitable. I could discover those secrets,—I have accomplished more. But I wish not for them."

"What, then, has been the object of your inquiries?"

"Neither, as I have told you, to acquire golden dross, (which many have prostituted the paths of philosophy to obtain, as a means of gaining luxuries and indulgences, and which the motive of their search has, alone, withheld them form discovering;) nor to increase the number of my days, here. My [45] object has been, during the time allotted to me, to partake of a double existence,—a spiritual one, peculiar to those who have had firmness and courage to attain to it,—as well as the fleshly one, which I enjoy, in common with the rest of my species."

"I do not, perfectly, comprehend."

"I know it. When we have left this place, I will explain myself."

There was a short pause, during which Merler examined, more minutely, the appearance and furniture of the apartment. The walls, ceiling, and floor were of stone; the various utensils, which were placed on all sides, were partly of glass, and partly of metal.

"How is it," said Merler, "that, though your furnaces are apparently at work, I perceive none of the deleterious vapours with which their operations are, usually, accompanied?"

"Because," replied his companion, "every thing, here, has reached that state in which matter is sublimed, and loses its grosser particles. My labours, now, are not to find, or to invent, but to continue and perfect that of which I have long been possessed. Look at this!"

"I see nothing more than an empty phial—off crystal I think—and very transparent," said Merler, as he held the vessel between his eye and the lamp.

"So it seems to you," said his companion. "Yet it is full—full to the stopper."

"What, then, is this invisible substance?" [46]

"Dew—the purest, most refined, dew of heaven,—the most powerful dissolvent of matter."

"I remember to have heard of it, as one of the agents employed by the alchemical philosophers. Light is, I think, another."

"It is. Look, once again!"

He unstopped one of his retorts, and poured in the contents of the phial. A light, brilliant beyond imagination, but, withal, so soft that it dazzled not Merler's eyes, issued from the aperture. At the same moment, the lamp became extinguished.

"See," said Merler's conductor, "how the grosser light is unable to sustain the pressure of the pure element! If you please, we will withdraw."

They ascended the stairs, and again entered the library.

"I have displayed to you," said the philosopher, "the agents with which I work; and this, because I can read the characters of men at a glance, and yours pleased me. I know, that I can confide in you:—nay, no protestations! I know it. The end to which I have applied these agents you shall know, before we part. Meanwhile, partake of my humble meal;—the body has its wants, as well as the mind."

The host eat only of a sallad; though, in regard to his visitor, more substantial food had been prepared. When the meal was ended, the former rose.

"I will now," said he, "perform my promise:—but, first, examine this picture!" He pointed to one of the portraits that hung from the wall. [47]

It was of a man, apparently about thirty, clothed in the dress of a monk, and whose square cowl betokened him of the order of Capuchins. Merler examined the features, again and again; and, as often, turned from the contemplation of the picture, to look upon his host.

"Enough!" said the latter; "you discern the resemblance?"

"Perfectly!" said Merler.

"Look there, then!"

It was the picture of a female, to which Merler's attention was thus directed. The countenance was sad, but full of intelligence, and beautiful as the depth of a summer's evening. Under each of the pictures, the letters F.R.C., and the symbol of the cross, denoted that the originals were followers of what has been, generally, called the Rosicrucian philosophy.

"Be seated!—and you shall know what I have to relate.

"My name is Freybourg. I am, by birth, a German, though of French parentage. I was, by nature, studious; and my attention was soon directed to the marvels of natural philosophy. An eager, and even painful, thirst after novel information kept me, constantly, on the alert; and, as my family was good, and their resources liberal, the opportunities and facilities of acquiring were not withheld,— the less, as, being a younger son, it was, of course, expected that I should turn my learning to account. [48]

"There was little, however, in the objects towards which my curiosity was directed, to which the instruction of tutors was not rather an obstacle than otherwise. I learnt what they had to teach, and felt that, in so doing, I had made not one step towards that which, even without knowing what it was, I inwardly panted after. Something I wanted, to satisfy the ravenous appetite I felt;—something to which the cumbersome frippery of learning, which I met around me, was wholly foreign. Yet, where to seek for any satisfaction I knew not.

"I grew lonely and melancholy in my habits; I sought the deepest recesses of the woods, and spent whole days sitting idly, in dark and solitary brakes, or under the shade of trees, by the side of dull and unmoved waters. I did this, till the inanimate things, among which I wandered, became my sole companions and friends.

"In a chance conversation, I heard mention of the Rosicrucian doctrines, of the sixteenth century. To my mind, in its excited state, a spark was sufficient. I hailed the suggestion with rapture; rejoicing that a path was, thus, opened, by which to direct and steady the wandering, feverish wishes with which I was haunted.

"I acquired, without much difficulty, the writings of Fludd, Kuhlman, Rosenberg, and others who had treated of the divine science. I studied them, incessantly. Their phraseology was, purposely, obscure, and their meaning enveloped in terms, to the [49] right understanding of which I had no clue. But my aim was a noble one, and my perseverance unconquerable. By degrees, I became master of the secrets which, hitherto, I had possessed in those volumes,—as a man who has a rich jewel secured in a casket which he cannot open.

"Still, here was one step, only, advanced. The philosophers, who had discovered the means of acquiring the hidden and mysterious knowledge that I desired, had either never attained the end of their inquiries, or had forborne to promulgate the detail of their process. I had, thus, my tools given me; but I was, still, to learn whether I could use them successfully, where so many, before me, had failed. I bent all my energies to the task, and gained my object. In doing this, I did no more than any one may do, whose will is decided and exertions undeviating.

Before I proceed, it is necessary that I state to you something of the additional faculties which I had now acquired. The soul, of which our fleshly body is but the habitation, is not, like the latter, bounded by the fetters of place, but, when freed from its tenement, possesses ubiquity. To liberate the spirit,—so fully as to enable it to enjoy, completely, this omnipresence—is, indeed, beyond the power of divine science; and can be accomplished only by that mysterious process which, terminating our progress here, returns to their proper sources as well our material as spiritual constituents. But this power may, still, be [50] exerted in an inferior degree,—greater or less, as the aspirant has qualified himself for the possession of the faculties he covets.

"To me, it was a source of infinite and glorious delight to disentangle myself from the narrow limits to which the observation of fallen man is confined, and dismiss, as it were, a twin spirit from myself, to pererrate the extremest parts of the earth, and, taking the wings of the morning, to gather, from every clime, all that might be culled of fair, and beautiful, and good. Thus, I enjoyed a double existence; and, whilst I pursued my ordinary avocations at Strasbourg, was, at the same time, roaming in thickets and jungles, by the banks of the Ganges, or contemplating, at the Balbec, the prostrate temples of the Sun, and the ravages of time on the mighty cities of the earth.

"It was, one day, when rambling, in my other self, through one of the delightful vallies that sink at the foot of the Apennines, that I became, I may well say the *victim* of a sensation as novel as enrapturing. I was seated in my study, chasing away the hours by the perusal of those enduring riches which the intellect and genius of antiquity have delivered down to us, and which shew, strikingly, the weakness and the superiority of their authors,—when a perception, which I well knew was conveyed through the medium of my distant spirit, burst upon me:—such a dream of purity, and excellence, and loveliness, as my wildest moods of enthusiasm (and I was, ever, a [51] trafficker in the ideal and contemplative) had never fashioned! To you, who are yet in ignorance and thraldom, I should, in vain, endeavour to explain the manner in which this ray,—for such it seemed, and a most bright one,—burst upon me. It came, not as a picture conveyed by the sense,—not as a remembered idea, nor as a vivid creation of the fancy;—it came as an inward impulse, newly born, springing up in the mind, indefinite, uncreated, but existing and fervent.

"The object, which had thus been made present to me, continued not so for more than an instant; but the effect was complete. I was as one entranced;—one thought alone possessed me, until I became almost unconscious of even *that*.

A sort of lethargy of the imagination succeeded; and I hailed the hour which, bringing on the gloom of night, enabled me to seek for rest, in sleep.

"Sleep came; but not, with it, extinction of the thoughts that, for the last few hours, had filled my waking existence. In dreams, the same vision still haunted my mind,⌧the same idea of inexpressible beauty was still present. Associated images, too, arose, in all the wild phantasms of dreaming. Bright eyes,⌧burning kisses,⌧all the array of passion, danced before me. Sometimes, I half started from these incoherent slumbers; and, at such a time, light and aërial forms seemed to float around me. At length, I became exhausted with the excitation of these [52] restless fancies, and sank into a profound and refreshing sleep.

"In awaking, the first idea that presented itself was the one by which I had been haunted, the preceding day. Wherever I went, whatever I did, it followed me, still. It became the unceasing companion of my thoughts, by day and by night.

"The anxiety which I underwent affected by constitution; and, by the advice of my family, I left home, to travel in search of health. The first place I visited was the valley of the Apennines, which was so strangely connected with me. Here I wandered, for some days; but could learn nothing to direct me in my quest after the unknown object of my thoughts.

"Why need I detain you, with a long and useless detail of the pains I suffered, the countries I traversed, and the disappointments I endured! Two years elapsed;—and, weary of myself, of the knowledge I had laboured so hard to acquire, and in short, of the world and every thing it could offer,—I determined to take the vows and habits of a capuchin, and, rooting from my breast every remembrance of the past, to devote my future life to the meditation of nobler and more enduring subjects.

"Vain were the expectations that prompted me to take this step. Had I, resolutely devoting myself to the discharge of active duties, applied my leisure hours to the cultivation of religious feelings, all would have been well. The enemy within me, then, [53] would have lost his sharpest sting; and I might, in time, have abandoned studies which, I fear, it is but too presumptuous in mortals to pursue.

"I soon found that, if there be any place peculiarly consecrated to peace and content, it is not within the walls of a monastery. There is, there, no exclusion of the evil passions of the world; and, as poison acts more vigorously within a narrow compass, so it is in these societies. Besides, the uniformity of our life,—the uninterrupted stream of existence in which we flowed along, threw me, more forcibly than ever, back upon myself,—the very evil most to have been avoided. Amid the exercises of devotion, I found my thoughts, still chained to another subject. I strove against them,—and the irritation induced by the conflict, increased my calamity.

"My brethren were, with few exceptions, men of coarse and vulgar minds,—indolent, proud and malicious, (the natural infections of the monastic atmosphere.) Every thing conspired to induce me to avoid their society;—my present feelings, and the habits of my past life. They perceived it, and were not long in manifesting their sense of it.

"I was, however, too much involved in those things which continually oppressed me, to regard, very greatly, the petty annoyances to which I was exposed. I endeavoured to submit to these evils, contentedly; and, in this manner, five years passed on, without seeing any material change in my situation, my thoughts, or my sufferings. [54]

"About this time, our physician died; and as, when at home, I had disguised my philosophical pursuits, under the pretext of studying medicine, I had acquired a slight knowledge of the science, and was not, now, unwilling to improve it. I offered by services to our superior, and, after a few trials in trifling cases, they were accepted.

"The occupation in which I thus engaged was, necessarily, beneficial, as it occupied a portion of my thoughts, and diverted them, in some degree, from the recollections to which they incessantly veered. There was another advantage. I had occasion to make short excursions beyond the bounds of the monastery, for the sake of gathering plants and roots, for my simple pharmacy. There was something of liberty in this, and the exercise was a luxury to me.

"The monastery of ——— was situation upon a high and almost perpendicular rock. It was rarely visited by any one, although a carriage-path had been hewn out by it, and was tolerably passable. This road divided into two branches,—one of which led to some neglected stone quarries, as an approach to which the road had originally been constructed,—and the other had been extended for the purposes of traveling. From this station, there was a magnificent view. Elevated far above the level of the earth, I have seen the storm raging, and the lightning flashing below, while the unchecked sun-beams fell around me, above. Beyond the thick and tem- [55] pestuous cloud that filled the valise, and hung on the surrounding declivities, a smiling champagne country extended, bounded by hills distinguishable, only by a faint outline, from the sky, with which they seemed to blend.

"It happened that the storm-clouds had, one day, gathered in such prodigious masses, that, though the autumn had but just commenced, the monastery and every thing around, for miles, were enveloped in a thick haze, through which the rain fell slightly but incessantly. The contemplation of natural phenomena was the only thing I could call a recreation, and I came forth to enjoy the threatening of the elements.

"I was well acquainted with every foot of ground in the neighborhood; otherwise, it had been madness to have ventured beyond the walls,—so easily might an incautious step have precipitated one down a precipice whose height left no possibility of escape from destruction.—Even versed as I was, I found it needful to move with great care.

"Whilst I was endeavoring to distinguish the forms of rocks and trees, through the gloom, and watching the dim blue fires that flossed idly, at intervals,—a sudden dull sound met my ear, which I was, at first, unable to account for. It was not, however, many moments before I felt convinced that a carriage was passing, at no great distance. It could not be on the direct road, for I was standing on that; and the sound had passed me. At once, it [56] struck me that the travelers, if such they were, had taken he wrong branch of the road; for, though a direction-post was placed at the point where the path divided, it would be useless, in such a gloom. The thought was terrible; for, in three minutes, unless some aid offered, they would be dashed down the precipice, which the darkness, momentarily increasing, would conceal, until discovery was too late. Already, the noise had ceased,—so imperfectly is sound conducted, as you are aware, in those altitudes. I had nothing to guide me; but sprung forward, and, dropping a bank of about fifteen feet, found myself on the road that led to the quarries.

"Along this I speeded, almost in desperation. Again, I caught the rumbling of the wheels against the uneven surface of the rock. The vehicle was going, apparently, very leisurely; and this consideration seemed to add to the horrors of the situation,—there was something so sickening and appalling in the idea of human creatures going thus slowly and unconsciously, step by step, to destruction. This, however, was not of long continuance. A flash of lightning, blazing across the path, frightened the horses, and they set off at a rate that almost extinguished my hopes.

"One circumstances was in my favour. The road took a sweep round the base of a broad, but not very high, rock of granite; and, directly over this, was a footpath. I crossed it, and saved so much [57] ground as to meet the carriage, within ten yards of the edge of the precipice. I endeavoured to seize the reins; the horses plunged and reared almost upright; the motion of the carriage was stayed for a moment, and, in that moment, I sprang to the door, tore it open, and received, in my arms, a female, who fell senseless in the moment of her rescue. I heard the fearful cry of the expiring horses, as they were dashed under the carriage, on the rocks beneath. Two human creatures,—the father and fellow-traveller of the lady, and the driver,—shared the same destruction.

"I lingered not, but bore her whom I had saved, as speedily as I might, to the monastery. The brethren whom I met stared, with malicious surprise, as I entered. I loudly demanded our superior: he came, and consented, on hearing my account, that the lady should have refuge, until her friends could be found, within the walls of our retirement—prison, I might better say.

"I was preparing, in the presence of some of the senior brethren, to administer such slight medicines as I deemed necessary, tot he object of my anxiety, when, for the first time, I saw her face. The phial which I held dropped from my hand! I lost all sense and recollection!

"When I recovered, I found myself in my cell reclined on my pallet. By my side, sat an old brother, whom I had lately attended during a severe illness, and whose gratitude, for the services I had [58] rendered him, had been proof against all the ill-nature of the many, who looked upon me with an evil eye. He had undertaken the office of my nurse, and from him I made my inquiries.

"'Where is the lady, Hilarius?'

"'In the dormitory. They have sent for old Margaret, from the village, to attend her.'

"'It is well!—is she sensible?'

"'Quite;—she has inquired for you.—But what caused your illness?'

"'I know not;—a sudden pang!—Have you learnt who she is?'

"'No;—her dress and ornaments bespeak her, probably, of wealthy connexions.'

"'I should like, much, to see her. Does our Abbot know that she has inquired for me?'

"'I believe not.'

I would he knew;—I wish to visit their patient, but not without his knowledge.'

"'I will see that he knows,' said brother Hilary; and he rose from his seat and left me. He returned presently.

"'I have seen the father,' said he; 'moreover, I have seen your patient, and she insists, whatever Margaret says, on not retiring to rest until she has seen her preserver. You are at liberty to visit her.'

"'Let me then, brother, request your company.' And he conducted me to the chamber where *she* was whom I panted to behold.

"We arrived at the door. It was with difficulty [59] that I could conceal from my companion the violent agitation that possessed me, and which shook every nerve, to trembling,—as the autumn wind shakes the quivering autumn leaves.

"We entered the apartment. She sat at one end. I approached her;—she lifted up her eyes;—'Holy Virgin!' she exclaimed, 'it is—it is he!' She sprang from her seat, as she spoke,—gazed earnestly at me for a moment,—sand down again,—and, covering her face with her hands, burst into tears.

"I was astonished and confounded. 'Does she know her father's fate?' I whispered to Hilary.

"'No,' he replied; 'she believes he is in the house, but unwell, and we have been scarcely able to avoid her requests to see him.'

"'What, then, could cause her present grief?' I drew nearer to her, and spoke. I told her that I was, for the present, her physician;—she interrupted me.

"'I know you well,' said she,—'too well!'

"'Nay, daughter,'—the word stuck in my throat,—'nay, how can that be?'

"'Ask me not,' she replied; 'it were a strange and incredible tale.'

"'Surely,' said I, half addressing myself, 'the dream cannot have been mutual.'

"'How—what is it you say?' said she, eagerly.

"I looked around. Brother Hilary had left the apartment; the nurse sat at the farther end of the room. I sat down by my patient, and detailed to her what I have already made known to you. [60] Yes!—dead to the world,—vowed to solitude and religion,—I told her of the passion I had felt,—and the pangs I had suffered; knowing, the while, that there was now a gulf between us which no means could pass.—It was like the dead recounting, to the living object, the history of his buried love!

"I concluded. She was still in tears, but checked them.

"'It is most wonderful!' said she;—'I, too,'—she stopped, blushed and trembled,—'Yet why,' she resumed, 'this foolish weakness! why should I not, now, confess that I, too, have loved and suffered for a hitherto unknown object! At the moment when your spirit caught the fatal infection, in the valley of the Appennines, mine, too, was on the wing, and hovered round you. I need not say more;—your history will suggest the main features of mine. And, now, answer me a question sincerely;—where is my father? They told me I should see him, in an hour;—the time is past. Is he here? Is he ill? Heaven! your colour changes!—tell me—tell me, by all we have suffered, is he dead?'

"'Oh no—no—no!' I answered, hastily; but the confusion of my manner gave the lie to my words. She perceived it;—and, with a shriek, fell senseless to the ground.'

Freybourg pause din his narrative. "Excuse me," said he to Merler, "if even the *remembrance* of what I tell you stifles my voice and calls forth my tears."

"Be assured," answered Merler, "I respect your [61] grief. It is, perhaps, unpleasant for you now to continue your narrative;—if so"—

"No;—it is over," said his companion; "I will proceed.'

"I raised her from the ground, and directed the nurse to place her, whilst thus unconscious, in her bed. I retired, to prepare a draught for her. That done, I threw myself on my pallet,—myself half distracted with what had passed. The vesper bell aroused me from the lethargy of misery, and summoned me—heaven knows how unprepared!—to join in the evening devotions. These past,—in coming away from them, we had to pass the dormitory. I listened, for a moment, at the door. One of the friars, who, more than the rest, had shown a marked dislike, whispered an observation to another upon this circumstance. I turned around;—a malicious smile was on his countenance. Forgetful of all, save the indignation which I felt, I struck him to the earth.

"The consequence of this was, that I was confined, strictly, to my cell. I was not even allowed to see my patient; word was brought me, by Hilary, of her state, from time to time, and, on this information, I was expected to proceed.

"She became delirious. In vain I represented that, in order properly to treat her malady, I must be admitted to visit her.—Ignorance and malice were blind to everything.

"Day after day, this continued. Hilary was as- [62] siduous in bringing me intelligence,—for he alone pitied me. This was observed: he was forbidden my cell, and another deputed to act in his stead.

"You may, probably, think it was in my power easily, to baffle this rigour, by using my faculty of spiritual visitation. But this faculty I had neglected, for a long period, to exert; and, when I essayed it, I found the perturbing passions which had taken possession of me deprived me of my power. I had no longer the calm self-possession necessary for the enjoyment of the divine science. Like all uncommon powers, it failed me when most needed.

"Why should I linger in my tale! One morning, on awaking, I found Hilary by my side. I was about to inquire how he had obtained admittance, but he motioned me, cautiously, to silence; and, placing a folded paper in my hand, withdrew on tiptoe.

"I opened it. Its contents ran thus:

"'You will receive this from brother Hilary; but, before he gives it you, the writer will be no more! Its only purport is to wish you farewell! The reason of your absence I have been informed. *Here* we have both suffered deeply;—that we shall meet again, in happiness, I doubt not. Do not—but I know you will not—forget me. Once more, farewell!—my last breath will bless you.'

"I pass over my feelings on the receipt of this.—I determined to escape from the monastery. I did [63] so, and returned, in disguise, to Strasbourg. My parents and my elder brother were dead.—A distant relative had succeeded to the family estates.

"I had known him in youth. I sought him, and he offered me an asylum, which I accepted. I continued with him for two years, in concealment,—for the Capuchins were hot in pursuit of their victim. At length, I was liberated. The revolution commenced, and the friars were no longer powerful.

"My relation addressed me, one day, thus: 'Freybourg, I am about to join the royal party. In this bag is a sum which, with your habits, will supply your wants;—however the struggle ends, I shall not need it.'

"I retired hither. With some occasional interruptions during the troubles, I have lived here since. Now we are, again, at peace; and I abide solitary and unknown,—having resumed, as you have seen, my ancient studies."

"He ceased;—the clock, striking, announced midnight. Merler made due acknowledgments for the confidence reposed in him, and rose to depart.

The Forgotten Gothic

Literary Annual

Friendship's Offering: A Literary Album, and Christmas and New Year's Present for MDCCCXXIX. Ed. Thomas Pringle. London: Smith, Elder, and Co., 1829. Printer: Littlewood & Co., Old Bailey.

Title

Gillies, Robert Pearch. "The Warning. A German Legend." FO 1829. 93-105.

PLATE: The Warning.
Steel plate engraving; painted by Abraham Cooper, R.A.;
engraved by Ambrose William Warren [93]

THE WARNING.[3]
A GERMAN LEGEND.
BY R. P. GILLIES, ESQ.

It was on a very beautiful day in the end of October, when on my way back from Hildsburghausen to Weimar, I happened to pass through a wild and seldom explored valley of the Thuringian mountains. On this excursion, I had the good fortune to fall into company with an intelligent *Jäger*, one of the Prince of Meinungen's under-foresters, of whom it might well be said, that he "knew every haunted dell and bosky bourne of that wild wood," and if we came in sight of any old ruin, or trod any remarkable spot of ground, he was generally prepared with his traditionary legend. Thus my time was agreeably beguiled, till towards the close of the second day, we found ourselves in the lonely glen already mentioned. Naturally, the scene was both beautiful and romantic. A clear and rapid stream enlivened the valley, which towards the south, extended for some distance into a level plain, while on the north-west, the hills rose abruptly. The ground was diversified here and there with such patches of [94] dwarf oak, hazel, and birch wood, as generally mark the site of an old forest. One might almost have concluded, from their appearance, that the district had long ago been scathed by fire, and that the woods had never rightly grown again. But principally my attention was attracted by a ruin on the eastern slope of the mountain, the remains of what might once have been a formidable stronghold. There is a *je ne scai quoi* about such edifices, that reminds one, by a rather far-fetched association, of the science of physiognomy. One draws conclusions from the aspect of the mouldering walls, regarding the character and fortunes of the people who heretofore resided there, and seldom have I been mistaken in the conjectures which I hazarded in this way. Some deserted dwellings and fortresses have, even in their decay, an attractive if not cheerful appearance,—"*en freundliches aus-sehen*" (kindly looks) as my friend the *Jäger* would have expressed it. Others, on the contrary, exhibit far more of gloom than mere antiquity confers—a solemnity of aspect which the dazzling splendour of noon-day mocks indeed, but cannot overcome nor enliven—mysterious indications that within those walls inhabitants may have lived, powerful indeed, but neither good nor prosperous. Especially I am apt to cherish a prejudice against mansions that are built on the eastern side of a steep mountain, for their inmates are never blessed with the farewell rays of the long-lingering summer sun. At silent eventide, when "lovers love the western star," they [95] alone see it not; at those hours when one most wishes to be cheered, they alone are debarred that placid amber-coloured refulgence, which remains in the north-west, till opposed in the south by the rising splendour of the moon. But not only

[3] Plain text for this transcription was obtained from Google Books http://books.google.com/books?id=1vcdAAAAMAAJ&pg=PA92-IA2#v=onepage&q&f=false> and then compared against the Google Books PDF. For full citation, see References.

did the castle, which now came under our survey, stand according to my system on the wrong side of the valley, but there was in its exterior a specific attribute of ghostliness or diablerie, for its walls were absolutely black. It reared itself like the swarth figure of some colossal demon in that wilderness, and as we passed under it, I could hear the autumnal breeze sweep through its open windows and forlorn pathless corridors, in cadences almost like the moans and shrieks of a female captive in despair!—I stood still and gazed at it, expecting that the *Jäger* would as usual commence his illustrations, but on this occasion he did not say a word. "How comes it that you are silent here?" said I; "that is a frightful old fortress, and I feel confident you must have something interesting to tell."

"Nay, little or nothing," said the *Jäger*; "and we have at all events no time to explore the ruin, for we shall be late enough at our next resting-place. The legend here," (he continued) "is meagre, and in its details very uncertain. Some people insist that the castle is as old as the twelfth century, for its walls are of enormous thickness, and, formerly, there were vaulted passages and dungeons extending a great way under ground. Of its last resident owner, we are told that he had been dis- [96] tinguished by several princes as a brave soldier, but was to boot dissolute in manners, hideous in aspect, and a ferocious marauder. His name was Conrad von Zechenthurm. The proper hero of the story, however, was Gottfried von Schwarzenfels, lord of another castle, several miles distant from hence, and no less gloomy in appearance than that which we have just left. About the year 1221, Gottfried having at an early age gained high military renown in Palestine, returned to his native country, and became deeply enamoured of the beautiful Lady Bertha von Wittenrode, who had been rendered a prey to grief and despondency, by the loss of a former lover, whose fate was extraordinary, for he had disappeared from the world, no one could tell where nor how. He also had intended to join the Hungarian army on their way to Palestine;—the troop which he was to command had advanced a few hours march before him, and after bidding his beautiful bride farewell, he proceeded with the attendance only of a single squire. From that expedition he never returned, nor did he ever make his appearance at the appointed rendezvous. The lady was inconsolable, but it was long ere she would be convinced that he had in reality perished. At last, a woodman brought to her a finely wrought iron cross and chain, which he had found in a wild thicket of the forest, and for which he was in search of a purchaser. With horror she recognized in this cross a valuable relic, which she had obtained from the Abbess of St. Mary's convent, at Fulda; it had been [97] her gift, at parting, to her unfortunate admirer, and she well knew that it never could have been wrested from his possession, except with the loss of life. She hung the chain around her own neck, wearing the cross concealed on her bosom, and vowed that so long as she survived, this relic should be her constant companion, so that the remembrance of her departed lover might never be effaced from her heart. It was understood, moreover, that the Lady Bertha had determined on secluding herself in the convent at Fulda, whence she would never more return into the world; yet affliction did not triumph over her personal charms, for in all Saxony, no one could contest with her the palm of beauty. Numberless, therefore, were her admiring but almost despairing suitors, among whom, Gottfried alone, not without long perseverance, succeeded in gaining her affections. In features and person we are told that he bore a considerable resemblance to her first accepted lover, but that on at last becoming Gottfried's affianced bride, the lady suffered direfully from reproaches of conscience, inasmuch as she was already the betrothed of the dead. After their union, nevertheless, they lived together apparently in great happiness, or if any alloy were mixed in their cup of felicity, it proceeded but from the warlike temper of Gottfried, who could not desist from engaging in petty feuds with neighbouring barons, and was over-addicted to violent pleasures of the chace.

"In the year 1228, it happened, that by the Pope's command, the heroic Frederic II prepared [98] to set out on a new crusade, and on this occasion, Gottfried for many reasons determined that he would not remain an idle spectator. When the disclosure of his intentions could not any longer be delayed, he explained to Bertha, that in consistency with his duty as a Christian and a soldier, it was impossible for him to avoid following under the banners of Frederic. Thereupon it is said, that the lady for the first time in her life, addressed him in the tone of reproach. She insisted that it was not the sense of duty, far less the spirit of religion by which he was then actuated, but rather his own self-will, vain-glory, and impetuosity of temper. At last, desisting from such painful admonitions, she suddenly threw herself at his feet, and besought him, for heaven's sake, to abandon his design, for she could not overcome the mysterious and deep-felt conviction, that no good fortune would attend him on that expedition;—but like the far-famed knight of Rodenstein, Gottfried was inexorable. To the last moment, her entreaties were repeated, and with no better success;—still the knight pleaded that his enterprize was a sacred duty; and finally he departed rather in an angry mood, leaving with Bertha, a moderate train of squires and other retainers, to protect the castle during his intended long absence.

"So he rode on his way, with a numerous troop, and was accompanied at the commencement of his journey by the hard-favoured and ferocious, though valiant Conrad von Zechenthurm, who was bound [99] on the same warlike expedition. Towards the evening of the second day's march, the latter turned from the high road, attended by a single squire, to visit an ancient knight, one of his relations, while Gottfried remained at a neighbouring village, whither in the morning news was brought to him that the Baron von Zechenthurm had been so severely injured by a violent fall from his horse, that his proceeding any farther would then be impracticable. Moved with compassion, Gottfried immediately took a retrograde course, in order to enquire after his friend, with whom he condoled on this extraordinary accident; expressing some surprize, however, when the baron seemed to regard this adventure as an evil omen, and declared his intention of being carried back immediately to his own castle. It is said that even then, though Gottfried's resolution remained unshaken, he yet felt a mood of distrust and apprehension stealing over his mind, and under such impressions, he wrote a brief but affectionate letter to Bertha, requesting her forgiveness, if she had been offended by his obstinacy, and enclosing in it one of his rings as a love token: finally he gave this billet in charge to the knight of Zechenthurm, who promised that he would, in person, present it to the lady. This conduct of Gottfried seems rather strange and improbable;—but so says the legend.

"Thereafter he pursued his way towards Palestine, and there are many inconsistent stories of his adventures in the holy land. Most accounts, however, agree on this point,—that in an early engage- [100] ment with the Saracens, he was dangerously wounded; and although as if by miracle he recovered, yet he was unable to render any effectual service at the siege of Jerusalem, his mind being so much harassed by the visitation of an extraordinary and frightful dream, that involuntarily his whole thoughts centred on his far distant home. In the dead of the night, it had seemed to him as if he awoke from perturbed slumber, and he once more heard, as if actually present, the last despairing accents of Bertha at his departure. Moreover, it appeared as if a large and dimly illuminated mirror were placed before him, and he beheld her in a vaulted dungeon, pale, trembling, with features convulsed by terror, while, approaching her, was visible a figure with a drawn sword,—and in this assassin he recognized the hideous aspect of his friend, Conrad von Zechenthurm. Gottfried now started up in affright, but even when actually awake, he heard the same mournful accents that wailed around him, amid the flapping of his tent in that foreign wilderness,—and he could at last distinguish the words, 'Farewell—farewell for ever!'

"Our hero, it is almost needless to say, was a brave soldier, little disposed to cherish apprehension founded on such visionary warnings, but to his own astonishment the impressions of that dream haunted him night and day, and were indelible. Fortunately it chanced that Frederic wished to send home a confidential ambassador, with important dispatches, and was easily led to make choice of Gottfried [101] for that purpose. Thereupon the knight set out with the greatest eagerness; and it is said that one day on his homeward route, when resting his horses during the noonday heat, he was accosted by a gipsey-woman, who predicted that if he arrived at his own castle before the fifteenth day of a certain month, all would be well. His utmost endeavours, however, could not bring him into Thuringia till a later period, and on his arrival in the district which we have just now traversed, he and his attendants were overtaken at nightfall by a tremendous thunderstorm. For some time the darkness was so profound that but for the lightning no object could be discerned. Gottfried, however, believing that he was not far distant from the castle of his friend Conrad von Zechenthurm, continued to spur his horse right onward, and amid the tumult of the storm had unconsciously left his attendants behind him, so that he was now quite alone. Throughout his long and rapid journey, the knight had not suffered his attention to dwell on that frightful dream which haunted him in Palestine, but now its impressions returned suddenly and irresistibly. Again he beheld the phantom of his beautiful lady with hair dishevelled, her countenance pale with horror, and the hideous Zechenthurm about to plunge a dagger into her heart, while amid the rushing noise of the forest, during the pauses of the thunder, he could distinctly hear the long-drawn moans and sobs of a female voice."

The mountain side had now become almost com- [102] pletely dark,—and—was it the effect of fancy or some natural phenomenon? We both heard a long protracted wailing sound that rose from a spot on which, as my guide informed me, still were extant the ruins of a small oratory or chapel.

"Yes," said the *Jäger* observing that the tones had attracted my attention—"we are told that the subterraneous passages from the castle extended even to this distance, and that many awful crimes had been perpetrated and concealed in the dungeons beneath that very chapel. But to return:—Gottfried's favourite charger, who had hitherto never failed to obey his rider's commands, all of a sudden became restive, while in every limb and sinew he felt the animal trembling as if convulsed. This was the more unaccountable, because at that moment he had emerged from the forest into an open glade, whence the towers of his friend Zechenthurm's castle were at intervals distinctly visible. The storm, too, seemed to have passed away; only harmless gleams of sheet-lightning coursed over the firmament, while the stars and crescent moon began to emerge from the clouds. Gottfried spurred his steed, but to no purpose; the animal reared, plunged, retreated, and continued to tremble as if struck with supernatural terror; the knight dismounted and wished to lead him onward, but still in vain. No stratagem nor effort could make him proceed; but the cause of this affright soon became apparent. A form was seen floating along the heath,—at first like a wreath of white vapour, through which were almost distin- [103] guishable the moon and stars of the southern sky. The figure advanced nearer and became clearly defined; silently it came up almost close to Gottfried, and the reflection from a broad gleam of lightning disclosed to him the now ghastly countenance of his beloved and once beautiful Bertha! With one hand she pointed to a wound in her bosom; the other was upraised to warn him that on that path he must not advance farther. The appearance was but momentary. At first a chill shivering of horror passed over Gottfried's frame, but this also was but of short duration, for the whole truth seemed as if by supernatural inspiration revealed, and the duties of an avenger were yet to be fulfilled. *Alone* he must not approach the castle of Zechenthurm, of which the owner must be called to a last and fearful reckoning, if indeed he had been accessory to the fate of Bertha. With his bugle horn he made a signal, which after a space was acknowledged by his followers, but their answer seemed to come from afar distance, and he believed that they had sought shelter under some cliff of the mountains, which intercepted the sounds. Their signal was repeated, and at that moment the phantom was again visible; it had now passed him, and pointed in the direction from whence the sounds proceeded. He followed, for his horse now suffered himself to be led quietly; and watched the figure, till it became stationary near the spot where, as I have told you, there are the ruins of a small chapel. The storm renewed its violence; a cloud collected; the lightning descended like a ball of fire accompa- [104] nied simultaneously by a deafening thunder-clap. The bolt seemed to strike the spectre, for both vanished together, while for a space Gottfried felt himself stunned and dazzled; but he had marked the spot, and on coming up, perceived a deep chasm, for the earth and the vaulted roof of a subterraneous building had been rent asunder. Some say that he recognized there the garments and mangled remains of the beautiful Bertha; but this much is certain,—a sudden gleam fell on the consecrated relique,—the iron cross and chain which by their electric attraction had effected the discovery, and which he directly lifted up and hung round his own neck. At the same instant his attendants made their appearance, for he had with him a band of thirty horsemen, and without drawing bridle, or encountering any opposition, they all rode onwards to the castle of Zechenthurm. There it happened that the warder, overpowered by wine and wassail, was asleep on his post; the porter and guards in the outer court were soon made prisoners, and confessed that the baron was alone in his banquet hall. "*Alone*, then shall I now reckon with him!" exclaimed Gottfried, and rushed up the staircase. No one indeed was present at their first meeting, nor is it known what awful words were interchanged between them; only a furious clashing of swords became audible, and some of Gottfried's party entered, anxious for the safety of their leader; but the hour of retributive justice had come; the ferocious knight of Zechenthurm soon received a mortal wound, [105] and fell uttering fiend-like imprecations. By the confession of his confidential squire, it was afterwards proved that this detestable baron was in truth the assassin of Bertha's first accepted lover, to which crime he had been incited by rage at the disdain and abhorrence with which she received his addresses; though his resentment was concealed, nor did he betray to any other the repulse he had met with. During our hero's absence, Zechenthurm had also found means to force Bertha into his power, though in what precise manner her death was perpetrated, no one has ever explained. In their fury Gottfried's troop set the baron's castle on fire, and massacred most of his adherents; the pine tree woods had also been kindled by lightning, and for ten days thereafter the whole district was in a conflagration—"

"Good heavens!" he exclaimed, turning to the *Jäger*, "and it burns now!"

A fierce flash of lightning at this moment seemed to scorch my forehead; I saw nothing around me but fire, and heard only the roaring of the flames.

Nor was all this to be wondered at; for (to descend from romance to sober fact), after I had read myself to sleep, over a volume of German legends, the bed curtain, by a not uncommon accident, had come in contact with my candle. Luckily *Filou* (the most sagacious of poodles,) awoke me by vehement barking—and I had never been in Thuringia, nor spoken with the prince of Meinungen's forester, except in a dream.

Literary Annual

Friendship's Offering: A Literary Album, and Christmas and New Year's Present for MDCCCXXX. Ed. Thomas Pringle. London: Smith, Elder, and Co., 1830. Printer: Littlewood & Co., Old Bailey.

Title

Conway, Derwent. [Inglis, Henry Rodolph.] "Rodolph, the Fratricide." FO 1830. 200-211. [200]

RODOLPH, THE FRATRICIDE
BY DERWENT CONWAY

"Would to God it were otherwise," said Rodolph, as, from the window at which he stood, musingly, he saw the baronial equipage pass along the bridge that led into Erfurt. "'Twas a sinful wish," said Margaret, "forgive," said her husband; "I recall the wish:" and he trend to her, and kissed her forehead, and lifted the little boy from the stool where he sat at Margaret's feet, and held him to his neck.

Rodolph was the first-born of the Baron of Erfurt, whose barony is the richest in the province of Thuringia, and is indeed accounted one of the most considerable in Upper Saxony. Shortly before the death of the Baron, Margaret became the wife of Rodolph: she was of respectable, but not of noble origin; and this alliance was contracted, not only in opposition to the express commands of the Baron, but also without the consent of the Duke of Saxony, who, in those days assumed the prerogative of regulating the alliances of the most considerable among his nobles. The consequences of Rodolph's disobedience may be easily imagined: the [201] destination of the Barony was altered; and upon the death of the Baron, Frederick, the brother of Rodolph, was Lord of Erfurt. Since that event, the disinherited had lived, though not in indigence, yet in a sphere that, to the first-born, seemed scarcely removed from it.

Margaret had been Rodolph's choice: he had chosen her because he loved her; but love, that formed Margaret's existence, was but an episode in his. Ambition had been, in Rodolph, an earlier passion than love; all that he had seen from childhood upwards had contributed to foster it; the pageantry of rank, the homage paid to wealth, and the power it conferred: even in boyhood he had revelled in the vision of his coming greatness; and when, for a season, love claimed an undivided rule, it was but the rule of an usurper: the master-passion was quenched, but not extinguished.

Long, very long, did Margaret cling to hope. She saw a change in Rodolph; but oh! it could not be that he loved *her* less: had he not chosen her? had he not wedded her, in despite of the world and its threatenings? and was she not as worthy of his love as when he led her from the altar?—as fond—almost as fair?

Alas! Margaret knew little of the human heart,—less of the world.

Harshness was not the sin of Rodolph; his sin was neglect, the most withering blight that falls upon the human heart: the prostrate flower will raise its head when the tempest has passed by, but it cannot survive the withdrawing of those sweet influences by which it lives and is nourished. Margaret could not conceal [202] from herself the coldness of her husband: yet so confiding was she, so full of affection was her heart, that it was long ere district could gain entrance there; but it entered in at last, and grew into the sad reality, that Rodolph loved her less than the things she had deprived him of. Yet hope would not quite forsake her; one kind word—a look—a tone, such as she remembered, would send joy into her heart, and call to her cheek the smiles of other days; and when Rodolph said, "I recall my wish—Margaret, forgive me!" and turned to her and kissed her brow, and embraced their boy, she might have said truly, if she had spoken from the heart, "Have we not happiness enough?" But gleams of returning kindness from Rodolph were "few and far between;" they were like the sun-beams that flash for a moment through November mists; and after the incident with which this little history begins, a whole year elapsed, during which no kind word, no fond look, no remembered tone, dispelled for a moment, from the heart of Margaret, the darkness that dwelt there.

Rodolph grew more silent and morose; the images of grandeur that had once been familiar to him began to assume, in his mind, a more palpable form; the contrast between the present, and that which might have been, became every day more apparent, till at length he hated the brother who inherited his rights, and scarcely less than hated the woman for whom he had sacrificed them. Margaret could but weep in secret; for kindness and endearments—all she had to bestow, except her tears,—could only renew the recollection of [203] his folly, in having exchanged, for baubles such as these the splendid inheritance of his fathers.

Rodolph dreamt one night a dream. He thought he was the possessor of his father's inheritance; and although he retained in his dream a conviction in his own identity, he fancied that *he* was the younger brother, and that Frederick, the first-born, was placed in his circumstances—the disinherited—and living in obscurity. He lay, as he thought, in bed, and awake, revolving in his mind the events that had elevated him to the Barony; and glancing now and then at a huge chest in one corner of the chamber, in which he imagined was deposited the deed that excluded his brother, and secured to him his possessions. The room in which he lay was familiar to him; it had been the sleeping apartment of his father; and the portraits of many generations, lords of Erfurt, hung upon the walls. One door opened upon the corridor; and another, opposite to the foot of the bed, and visible between the somewhat parted curtains, led to a stair case, which terminated in another door opening into the vaults below the castle. As he thus lay ruminating upon the past, the present, and the future, the Castle clock struck twelve; and as the last chime died away, he saw the door into the chamber slowly open, and his brother Frederick enter; he saw his brother to the huge chest, lift the lid, and take out the deed; he sprung from his bed to save it—and, in the act of struggling with his brother, he awoke.

This dream made a powerful impression upon the [204] mind of Rodolph: the deed, the evidence of his disinheritance, was doubtless deposited somewhere; and if, by any means, he could obtain possession of it, what should then hinder him from claiming the rights of which he was dispossessed by that deed alone. Might not the chamber his dream had pictured to him be in reality that in which the deed was deposited; for there, he well knew, stood the chest in which the family archives were inclosed. The more he revolved upon the dream, the strong became the conviction that it had revealed the truth; and the more intense was his desire to recover the evidence of his disinheritance, and the more eager his longing after the power and honours enjoyed by his brother.

It was late on the evening of a day in the latter end of October, that Rodolph, after having been absent on a pretended journey of business to a neighbouring town, arrived within the precincts of his paternal house. The young crescent moon yet hung in the sky, and threw a pale and sombre light upon the well-known towers, and upon the open space between the walls and the family tomb, within whose shadow stood Rodolph. He waited till the moon sunk; and then, by paths long familiar to him, he passed lightly towards a low archway that led into the vaults. Once he fancied he heard the rustling of fallen leaves behind him, and paused for a moment; but concluding it to have been the sighing of the night wind, or some startled bird, he went onwards, and, creeping through the archway, dropt into the vaults. He speedily gained the small door that [205] opened upon the stair, and with a slight push it gave way. At the door of the chamber Rodolph stopped and listened. Within, all was still; but again, he fancied, a sound, as of a light tread, came from below: again he listened, but heard it no more. The possibility of his dream proving literally true, flashed across his mind—his brother springing from his bed to save the deed—and how then should he act? He felt the hilt of his poniard in his hand; but he said mentally—"No, no; I have not come hither to kill my brother—I come to seek my right; but I am no murderer."

Rodolph laid his hand upon the door, as the Castle clock struck twelve; and, as the last chime died away, he gently pushed it open, and stood within the well-known chamber. Through the parted curtain he saw his brother: a lamp which burned upon the table threw a steady light upon his face, and Rodolph saw that he slept. He approached the bed. "He is my brother," said he; "I have not come to take his life: is he not my brother? But how! my brother?—has he not robbed me of my rights? does he not possess my inheritance?"—and the visions of years, and the hopes of youth, and the disappointments of manhood, rushed in a collected torrent upon the mind of Rodolph. At that moment the countenance of the sleeper seemed agitated; a smile passed over his lips, and he whispered in an eager noiseless whisper—"It is mine, it is mine; I will keep it." As Rodolph gazed, his hand insensibly clutched the poniard with a firmer grasp: he raised his arm; and at the moment he would have struck, his hand [206] was arrested: he turned, and beheld—Margaret. But the demons of envy and hatred had taken possession of Rodolph; he flung Margaret from him, and, as the sleeper started from his disturbed vision, Rodolph buried the poniard in the bosom of his brother. One loud and long shriek recalled the fratricide to a sense of his danger; he threw down the red reeking proof of his guilt, and fled towards the vaults, calling upon Margaret to follow. But Margaret followed not; Margaret understood not; the blow that told her husband was a murderer, had struck reason from its throne: Margaret was a maniac; and when the household of the Baron, roused by that appalling shriek, the herald of madness, entered the chamber, she was sitting calmly beside the murdered Baron, with the poniard in her hand.

One word of retrospect is necessary. Indistinct words, muttered in sleep, had revealed to Margaret the design of her husband, and from night-fall she had watched for him. The purpose revealed by Rodolph in sleep, regarded on the proofs of his disinheritance; but undefined suspicions of greater evil had crept upon the mind of Margaret, and it was these that led her to follow the steps of her husband.

It was speedily known throughout the province that the Baron was murdered; and the maniac found in his chamber was deemed the murderer. The wife of Rodolph was well known to many, even among the Baron's household; and although it was surmised that ambition, oftentimes a powerful passion in the female breast, had [207] crazed the mind of Margaret, Rodolph stood free from suspicion; he could not be responsible for the actions of one bereft of reason. No sooner had sufficient time elapsed for the Duke of Saxony, who was then at the Imperial Court, to have received authentic information of the death of the Baron of Erfurt, than Rodolph repaired to Vienna, and preferred his claim to the succession. His brother had left not child; and as the insanity of Margaret afforded sufficient ground for an application for divorcement, there was no longer any objection on the part of the Duke to the recognition of his title.

Rodolph had now reached the object of his ambition; but at what price? the murder of his brother! the madness of his wife! And although the Lord of Erfurt was caressed and smiled upon; though, amid the gaieties of the imperial Court, he affected to be that which the world believed him to be—careless and happy; visions of more innocent days, past for ever, and fears of coming evil, dashed at times the untasted cup of pleasure from his lips, or lent bitterness to the draught. His brother, in boyish days, mirthful and kind; or sleeping, unconscious that a fratricide stood by his bed; Margaret, smiling and happy, as he led her from the altar; or tender, gentle, uncomplaining, as she had ever been; the one murdered—the other a maniac; these were the images that poisoned the streams of pleasure, and withered every blossom that springs on the pathway of wealth and honours.

Rodolph dreaded a return to the castle of his fathers. [208] The din of festivity that filled the capital, if it could not altogether drown the voice of conscience, yet dulled the sound; and if, amid the flourish of trumpets, or the chorus of syren ones, the maniac shriek of Margaret was sometimes heard, louder, and more thrilling than them all,—yet it seemed as if in the baronial hall, it would be more frequent and more appalling. But Rodolph must conform to the usage of his ancestors, and the practice of other nobles; and it was announced to this vassals and retainers, that the castle should be prepared for his reception.

Merrily did the silver-tongued bells of Erfurt proclaim the approach of the Lord Rodolph. The elevation of the younger brother had been deemed by the people an act of tyranny; and Rodolph was welcomed to his ancestral domains, as one who ought to have inherited them long ago. It was a universal holiday in Erfurt; crowds thronged the streets waiting the arrival of the Baron; and when towards evening he rode through the barrier, the air was rent with the welcoming acclamation of thousands. A deafening shout announced the entrance of the Baron within the hall of the castle,—but in Rodolph's fancy another cry came mingled with it. Anon the sounds of welcome died away,—fainter, and less frequent, became the tokens of rejoicing,—at length all was still,—night gathered round; and with it came the visions that oppress the guilty.

Rodolph tried to dispel them; the board was spread, the cup was filled and drained, and filled and drained [209] again. The hall blazed with artificial light, and the musicians exhausted their skill to do honour to their patron. But in vain: the portraits of his ancestors seemed the living witnesses of his guilt, and every eye was fixed upon him. Music was a mockery, in painful contrast with the troubled mind; and light itself, that to the guilt is sometimes felt to be protection, Rodolph would have exchanged for darkness, for it served but to aid the delusions of imagination, by magnifying and distorting every object that surrounded him.

Eleven chimed on the castle clock, and Rodolph desired his attendants to lead the way to his chamber: orders had been given to prepare for the Baron another apartment than that which had been the scene of blood; but the order had been misunderstood or neglected; and it was with feelings which none but the guilty can understand, that Rodolph glanced around the chamber, when the departing footsteps of his attendants could no longer be heard.

* * * *

Rodolph lay on the bed of his murdered brother; not, as in his dream, revolving on the events that had raised him to the inheritance, but striving to keep afar off the reminiscences that would yet force themselves in fearful distinctness upon his wakeful fancy. It was agony to be awake, and yet he feared to sleep, dreading the visions that might pursue him; and shrinking instinctively from that state of helplessness which, to [210] the guilty, is felt to be a state of danger. At times drowsiness nearly obtained the mastery over fear; but the embryo visions of troubled sleep—his brother entering the door, or Margaret's maniac shriek, recalled him to consciousness. But sleep at length overcame him; his eye-lids closed; and he lay as his brother had lain ere the poniard reached the heart of the sleeper.

Who is it that stands by the bed of Rodolph? Margaret—the maniac Margaret; she has burst her bonds, and has sought, by the remembered path, the chamber where last she saw her husband. She gazes earnestly on the face of Rodolph; and though she knows him not, yet that countenance wakes a gleam of recollection, a faint wandering ray of reason, an indistinct dream of some once connecting link,—and softly she creeps and lays her down by his side, and throws her arm over him.

Rodolph dreams a fearful dream: he dreams that his murdered brother is stretched on the same bed, and locks him in the cold arms of death; and in striving to shake form him his dreadful visitor, he awakes; but the gripe of a maniac is strong. Rodolph believes himself in the grasp of the dead—and terror does the work of justice!

Hush! it is Margaret's shriek that rends the castle! She knew not her husband living, but she knows him in death: reason for a moment illumined the mind; but life fled from the revelation of misery.

Literary Annual

Friendship's Offering: A Literary Album, and Christmas and New Year's Present for MDCCCXXXI. Ed. Thomas Pringle. London: Smith, Elder, and Co., 1831. Printer: Littlewood & Co., Old Bailey.

Title

Conway, Derwent. [Inglis, Henry Rodolph.] "The Unholy Promise. A Norwegian Legend." FO 1831. 115-125. [115]

THE UNHOLY PROMISE.[4]
A Norwegian Legend.
BY DERWENT CONWAY.

It was impossible to go farther than Rinesager. A journey of forty miles on mountainous roads, and scanty fare by the way, had made the sight of the village extremely acceptable; but my expectations of comfortable accommodation were considerably damped by the constant beating of a drum,—the music of a pandean pipe,—repeated shouts,—and occasional reports of fire-arms—all pretty clearly indicating that Rinesager was that evening the scene of festivity, and consequently no resting-place for a weary traveller. I resolved therefore to quarter with the Minister,—and having found an old man whose infirmities kept him seated at the door of his hut, to point out the way, I proceeded to the lowly habitation of the reverend pastor. He had gone to the church to perform the marriage ceremony; so that the occasion of the rejoicings was sufficiently explained; and, guided by the sound of the rustic music, I soon reached the church yard, where I found [116] all the village assembled—some, as "wedding guests," and others hoping to come in for a share of the libations which upon such occasions are liberally dealt out. It was not without the necessity of partaking in this hospitality that I was able to reach the porch; and a louder roll of the drum, more piercing notes from the pipe, and a more deafening shout from the villagers, announced the general satisfaction at this proof of good-will from a stranger. The interior of the building was almost as crowded as the area outside; but I contrived to make my way to the altar, where stood the bride and bridegroom and their respective relatives,—and before them, the minister whose good offices I intended to claim. The ceremony had already begun,—and I was more occupied in endeavouring to obtain a glimpse of the bride's countenance, than in listening to the questions and responses, when my attention was arrested by hearing the minister say, "Has any unholy promise been the means of bringing you and this maiden together?"—a question quite unintelligible to me,

---

4 Plain text for this transcription was obtained from Google Books < http://books.google.com/books?id=0PcdAAAAMAAJ&ots=vzYElBobmQ&dq=friendship's%20offering%201831&pg=PR7#v=onepage&q=friendship's%20offering%201831&f=false> and then compared against the original volume. For full citation, see References.

and of which I resolved to ask an explanation.

Soon after, the ceremony ended; the bride, wearing her gilded crown,[5] passed through the avenue that was made for her, followed by the sturdy Hedemarke to whom she belonged; and the church being cleared of its visitors, I turned to the Minister and introduced myself as a stranger and a traveller,—two characters, [117] that in Norway claim the instant exercise of hospitality. We left the church together, each carrying a basket containing provisions—the marriage fees in this country being paid in kind; and were soon seated in the good man's parlour, with a table before us spread with the simple fare of the country.

"The religious part of the marriage ceremony with you is of course the same as with us," said I; "but there was one question put by you that sounded oddly in my ears,—I mean, when you asked whether any UNHOLY PROMISE had brought the bride and the bridegroom together."—"It might well seem strange to you," replied the Minister, smiling; "it is a remnant of an old superstition, which, however, yet retains so much power over the minds of these simple mountaineers, that no maiden in this part of Hedemarkens would consider herself safe in entering into a matrimonial engagement, unless the Minister put the question which you heard. Upon my naturally expressing some curiosity to know the origin of so singular an addition to the marriage ceremony, "I have it in my power," said the Minister, "to satisfy your curiosity. I regret I cannot present you with the original copy of the legend,—but I will willingly transcribe it for you; and you will then carry back to your country a Scandinavian relic which I believe is altogether unknown beyond the boundaries of this narrow district." So saying, my hospitable entertainer left the room for a few moments, and returned with the object of his search. "You perceive" said he, "that care is re- [118] quired in handling this paper: it is already almost in tatters, nor indeed is this wonderful, since, judging by the antiquity of the hand-writing, I should guess it to have been the work of some one who has been in his grave these two hundred years." "I am afraid," said I, "even to touch so venerable and so frail a relic, and will therefore postpone the gratification of my curiosity until you have fulfilled your kind promise." And while I admired the prospects from the window, and looked over a copy of the Edda, my kind host transcribed the manuscript,—of which the following is a literal translation.

"Who, in the valley of *Hammer*,—who, on the *Louver* mountains, so fair as Una!—Her hair was like the golden light that bathes the *Reen Field* ere the sun sinks behind it: her eyes were soft as the gentle stars that sleep in the waters of the *Miosen Soe*,—Una the beloved—Una the good. The lake rests tranquil in the bosom of the hills,—they shelter its infancy, and look down upon its repose,—and so rested Una in the valley of *Hammer*. She was the daughter of Eldred, but she

---

5 Throughout Scandinavia it is the custom of every bride to stand at the altar with a gilded crown—meant as a symbol of chastity.

was the child of all; and she was long fenced round by the prayers of the good. The young men of the valley and the young men of the mountains strove for a smile from Una, for her smile was like the tender light of the blessed moon when it peers above the hilltops: but Una smiled upon none,—and least of all upon Uric.

It is the still hour when innocence rests,—and when [119] the guilty are abroad. Why is it, oh night, that on thy calm and fair dominion wickedness intrudes? Why is thy peacefulness disturbed by the tread of the unholy? Una sleeps in peace: but Uric is abroad. Night is around him; but the moon mounts up the sky and will soon look down upon his path.

Uric walks in silence. Beneath sleeps the Miosen See;—beyond, the mountains stand in their dim and solemn greatness:—the woods are dim and solemn too, and silent as the hills.

"Now," said Uric in his heart,—for he was afraid to break the stillness of night, "Una shall be mine: I see the ruin's dim outline before me;"—and he hastened on his way,—and reached the rugged mound, and saw the dark walls above him,—and the moonbeams falling through the rents, and upon the shapeless rocks and the old and dwarfish trees that were scattered here and there.

Uric toils up the mound,—and now he stands within the ruin. The broad shadow of the wall falls darkly across the silent court, but beyond the shadow the moonshine lies white upon the tall weeds, and the matted grass, and the hoary dandelion—and Uric stands within the shadow of the wall.

Why is the stillness of the ruin broken by the beating of Uric's heart? Behold! a tall shade crosses the moonlight; and Uric remembers his dream and wherefore he standeth there.

Like the whisper of the night-wind, the name of Uric fell upon the expecting ear. [120]

"I am here" said Uric.

And again, like the shiver of the forest, came these words to the ear of Uric,—"Una may be thine—but the price must be paid."

Now when Uric heard these words, his heart beat no more with fear, but for joy,—and he said—"what price?—be it the body, or be it the soul, it shall he paid;" and again he listened for the voiceless words of the unseen—and when they came, they fell chill upon the heart of Uric—for the price of Una was her first-born.

"Tis an unholy compact," said Uric—"but be it a compact."

No sooner had Uric spoken these words, than a tall shadow crossed the moon's light,—and he knew that he was alone. And he passed from the shade where he stood, into the fair moonshine, where it lay white upon the matted grass: and soon the dark walls rose behind him, and the dwarfish and branchless trees stood around like crooked old men; and he hastened on his way, while the night-wind, as it crept over the surface of the lake, or gently stirred the leaves of the forest, whispered in the ear of Uric, "Thy first-born!"

Who can tell the dreams of Uric? Were they of the dark ruin, and the white moonshine,—and the tall shadow that swept across it? Were they of the fair Una,—of her golden hair, and her star-like eyes, and her blessed smile? Were they of an innocent babe, and its infant caress? Who can tell!

Fair broke the morning upon the couch of Uric. [121] Who on such a morning would remember the visions of the night!

Ere yet the sun had drank the dew, Una had arisen, and with her braided hair and morning smile, she looked out upon the calm lake and the misty mountains:—and "wherefore," said she, "cometh Uric this way?"

Uric sitteth in Una's bower: her spindle is in her hand,—but she plies it not; nor listens she to the distant waterfall or the tinkling bells of the straying herds,—her ear drinks softer tones than the sound of falling waters—and sweeter words than the silver-tongued music of the hills.

Una sitteth in her summer bower,—but she sitteth alone,—the birds alone are her companions,—and the sweet Sowers that turn to her their scented coronals; her cheek is tinged with the rosy hue of eve, and the star that loveth the sun twinkles through the foliage; and now she hears the distant waterfall and the tinkling bells,—but her heart tells her that there are sweeter and more welcome sounds than these. The rosy tint has left her cheek,—the star has set, and the moon climbs up the sky,—but Una yet sitteth in her bower.

It is the bridal morning of Una. Eldred, the father of the beloved, the lovely and the good, lays his hand upon her and blesses her; and, clothed in her white garment of innocence, he leads her forth to the altar. "Una," says he, "needs no gilded crown; is she not the child of all the valley?—and all the valley knows that she [122] is chaste," and he lifted the crown from the head of his child,—and her golden hair was her crown; and thus did Una become the spouse of Uric.

Nine times hath the young moon pillowed her head upon the calm waters of the Miosen—and Uric heareth the cry of his first-born. Una smiles,—and the joy of a mother is in her heart and sparkles in her eyes; but Uric's heart remembers his unholy promise.

"Why art thou silent?" said Una;—"chosen of my heart, why art thou silent?—and why look ye not upon your first-born? Take him to thy bosom and bless him; his mother hath blessed him already, and he waiteth for the blessing of a father."

Uric took to his bosom the babe of his Una,—his "first-born," and as the babe opened his eyes upon him, a father's love gushed into his heart, but no blessing came from his lips; how could Uric bless his "first-born!"

Dark are the pines that stretch over the head of Uric,—but darker is his soul: he wanders into the depths of the forest,—and his companions are his tears: he sees the happy living things that sport on the green amphitheatres,—and the nimble creatures that play among the lofty pines—and faster fall his tears.

Now four times have the sunbeams lingered through the midnight hours upon the summit of the Sogne Field. Four times have the herds been led out to feed on the green and yellow-tinted mountains;[6] and the glow of [123] four summers rests on the cheek of the infant Uric: his hair is golden as his mother's; and, as the child of Una, he is the adopted child of the valley.

Una sitteth not now in her summer bower, listening to the distant waterfall or the tinkling bells. She sitteth among her maidens,—listening to the prattle of her boy, while he plays with the tender and sweet-scented shoots of the fir-trees that are strown around: and still is she Una the beloved. And the darkness has departed from the heart of Uric. Why should he remember the dim ruin,—and the white moonshine,—and the tall shadow,—and the voiceless words,—and his unholy promise? Four years have passed away,—and it is as but a dream; and six years yet must pass ere the price be due. For Uric had heard these words, "Ten years may the price be unpaid,—but then, and at this hour, I will expect thee and it."

It is the season when the moon and the stars rule over the midnight hour,—and when twilight fades away upon the mountains of Gulbrandsdalen.[7] The time of flowers is past,—and the sloping hills are crimson and yellow with the changing cloudberry;[8] and Una wanders through the fields with the youthful Uric, gathering the mellow fruit; but Uric wanders alone,—for his first-born hath numbered nine summers—and the summer is past.

And Una saw the shade that rested upon the brow of Uric—and she said, "Why, Uric, doth a shadow [124] cross thy brow like an unwelcome guest? Hast thou not Una, thy beloved;—dwellest thou not where thy fathers have ever dwelt;—knowest thou not thine own mountains;—is not thy home a home of peace, and the smile of Una the same that used to gladden thee;—and oh! hast thou not a treasure greater than these, even our first-born?—"

Darker and yet darker grew the shade upon the brow of Uric;—for as Una spoke, she kissed her blue-eyed boy, and "Go, my child," she said, "to thy father,—and caress him,—and tell him to smile upon thee, for if God spareth thee this night, ten years thou shalt have blessed us."

Long hath the moon risen,—and who are they that walk in her light?

"Come, my boy," said Uric, "it is thy father's hand that holdeth thine; 'tis sweet to walk in the moonshine, and to see how white and calm it lies between the shadows of the pines."

"Father," said the blue-eyed boy, "I love not the moonshine,—and I am weary; take me from these tall shadows—lead me to my mother."

"Yet a little farther," said Uric: and now they toil up the rugged mound,—

6 The mountains of Norway are thickly covered with a yellow flower during the summer months.
7 Alluding to summer being past.
8 The cloudberry is crimson until quite ripe,—it then takes a yellow tint.

and the dark walls rise above them; and, here and there around them, stand in the moonlight the dwarfish and crooked trees. "Father," said the child, "these stunted trees look like decrepid old men: take me from this place—lead me to my mother!" And Uric sat down upon the rugged mound,—and there, in the bright moonshine, sat the father and child. [125]

Fast fall the tears of Uric,—and sad is his punishment,—for he loveth his child; yet well he knoweth, that if that midnight moon be not the witness of the offering the compact is broken—and he doth himself become the forfeit.

Midnight waits within the silent court of the ruin: white are the matted grass and the tall weeds,—but no one standeth within the shadow of the wall. Midnight is come and passed—and the unholy promise is broken.

Long were the evening hours in the home of Una; the sun sunk in the forest,—and the mountains grew dim,—and the moon arose and bathed them in light; but Uric came not,—neither came her blue-eyed boy. And Una fell upon her knees and prayed; and even as the accents of prayer murmured upon her lips, her uplifted eyes closed,—and her head gently dropped upon her clasped hands. And Una knew in a vision the charm that for ten years had bound her to Uric, and the unholy promise. And Una awoke—and midnight was passed; and a mother's love was deep in her heart,—but the love she had borne to Uric was no more.

Fly, Una!—speed to thy blue-eyed boy: yonder is the rugged mound—see! beneath the fair moonbeams lieth thy child unhurt; take him to thy bosom, for he is chill,—and the chill of fear is at his heart.

"Mother," said the blue-eyed boy,—"whose was the tall shadow that glided by my father's side as he left me?—"

And Una shuddered; and closer she clasped her child to her bosom.

Title

Kennedy, William. "The Castle of St. Michael. A Tale." FO 1831. 159-178. [159]

THE CASTLE OF ST. MICHAEL,[9]
A Tale.
BY WILLIAM KENNEDY.

I.

My family, by the paternal side, was originally of Berne, in Switzerland, whence a branch of it removed to the Milanese, to improve its fortunes. The name of Reding—well known in the Cantons—was sustained with credit by my father. He inherited a thriving mill and farm, about a quarter of a league from the straggling village and venerable castle of St. Michael, within sight of the Tyrolese Alps. Travelling to Zurich, where he had distant connexions, he returned with a companion who weaned him from the desire of wandering any more. She was the daughter of a pious pastor on the borders of the lake. From him she derived a dower of upright principles and solid acquirements, which it was her dearest wish to transmit with interest to her children, all of whom died early, except my sister and myself.

The Castle of St. Michael, with the estate on which our little property was situated, belonged to an Austrian noble, who managed it by deputy, and lived in courtly [160] splendour at Vienna. Count Mansfeldt was equitably represented by his steward, Engel; and under him, our house enjoyed prosperity from the days of my grandsire.

We were the only persons in the place who professed the Protestant faith. My father's temperate conduct gained him the unrestrained indulgence of his opinions. The dread of proselytism did not preclude my entrance into a Catholic school. The teacher, a liberal Piedmontoise, was a lover of learning, and separated austerity from instruction. He observed, and gratified, my partiality for history and the classics, and thus unconsciously assisted in the formation of my future character.

My mother was the sole superintendent of my sister's education; she thought the feminine mind, so susceptible of impressions, should never be spontaneously consigned to foreign culture. Katherine was worthy of her preceptress. It is not for me to dilate upon her excellence—a portrait by my hand might be deemed the glowing creation of a brother's fondness. It is enough to mention the strength of our attachment. I was two years her senior; and when her age qualified her for sharing in childish pastimes, she was the welcome partner of all my amusements. I showered into her lap the first flowers of spring, and brought her

---

9 Plain text for this transcription was obtained from Google Books < http://books.google.com/books?id=0PcdAAAAMAAJ&ots=vzYElBobmQ&dq=friendship's%20offering%201831&pg=PR7#v=onepage&q=friendship's%20offering%201831&f=false> and then compared against the original volume. For full citation, see References.

the wild strawberry from heights where few would venture. In her friendship I reposed the confidence of ripening boyhood—frequently were the overflowings of a sanguine temperament repressed by her mildness. [161] With innocent wiles she endeavoured to veil my errors from parental eyes: when I did incur displeasure, her accustomed gaiety was gone, and the voice that recalled her truant smile was ever that which pardoned the offender.

A cheerful home is the paradise of the young: our's was illuminated by mutual love. The lightsome moments spent by the domestic hearth, form the only period of my life that I would willingly live over again. The music of the camp and of the theatre, heard in after years, failed to awaken the emotions I experienced long ago, when my mother sang the plaintive melodies of her mountain land. I have seen the most renowned generals of an age memorable for strife——among them, one to whom an astonished world did reverence—but no warrior have I beheld to rival my conceptions of William Tell. The peasant of Uri was the hero of our fireside. When the casement shivered to the gusts of winter, and the headlong flood thundered down the ravine, we called to mind the intrepid hand that steered the bark of Gesler over the stormy waters. Altorf and the Austrians were to us exhaustless themes; and I prayed that I might yet have the opportunity of imitating the courage of my namesake, Albert, the Patriot's unshrinking son.

II.

I was entering my twentieth year, when our situation underwent an important change. Our landlord was gathered to his ancestors, having bequeathed his Lom-[162] bardy estate to his second son, Count Rainer. Engel, the good old steward, was soon after dismissed from office, and retired, with the fruits of faithful service, to his native town in Carniola.

Count Rainer was a captain in the imperial army. He was with his regiment at Pavia when informed of his father's death. Devolving his authority on an emancipated sergeant of hussars, the purveyor of his libertine pleasures, he dispatched him to St. Michael to wring money from the tenantry, and prepare for his reception.

Ludolf was a swaggering bravo, emulous, at middle age, of the vices of profligate youth. On his arrival, he circulated a pompous intimation that he came vested with full powers to treat with the vassals of the Count, and renew their engagements.

My sister had gone to the village to make purchases, and I left the mill at vesper chime with the intention of meeting her. The path was abrupt, and little frequented. I was cherishing discontent at the husbandman's unvaried existence, when I was roused by the distant accents of a female in distress. They were clearly distinguishable, and I rushed to the quarter whence they proceeded. In a corner of an open spot, backed by a deep ditch, fenced with luxuriant underwood, Katherine was keeping a man, unknown to me, at bay: he was above the middle size, and in his beard and costume affected the fashion of the military. He faced me as I approached, and my sister, with disordered dress and agitated frame, flew to my side. [163] Defenceless as I was, my first impulse was to chastise the ruffian, though he wore a sabre; but consideration for the terrified girl, who clung to me imploringly, induced me to forego my purpose. We had not receded many paces, when Katherine relinquished her hold, and uttered a warning cry:—the hand of violence was already at my throat; and a harsh voice, unsteady from rage or intemperance, demanded why a contemptible slave dared to interfere with the representative of Count Rainer.

Unequal to my opponent in bulk and inert force, I was far above him in activity and the resources of a vigorous constitution. A sudden jerk freed me from his hold, and a well-applied push sent him reeling to the verge of the ditch. He drew his weapon with a rapidity on which I had not calculated: Katherine's coolness saved my life: she arrested his arm in its sweep. Ere he could disengage himself, I collected all my energy for one buffet, and laid him supine in the reservoir of mud.

III.

Count Rainer was greeted at St. Michael with the show of rustic rejoicing usual on the appearance of a new master. He was accompanied by a train of riotous associates. The roar of bacchanalian merriment shook the dusky halls of his patrimonial fabric, which, in the blaze of unwonted festivity, seemed to have renewed its youth. Nought, from the evening of the rencounter, had we heard or seen of Ludolf. His rude- [164] ness might have originated in the coarse jocularity of a soldier, stimulated by too fervid an application to the bottle. Prudence required that I should abstain from needlessly irritating a man whose enmity might mar my father's arrangements with his lord: I therefore avoided the chance of collision.

I was strolling about the fields with my gun on my shoulder, when a pet pigeon of Katherine's whirred past me, pursued by a hawk. I fired at the bird of prey, which dropped in an adjoining meadow. Springing across the intervening hedge, I found myself in the presence of a group of mounted sportsmen and their attendants. One of the horsemen was examining the dead hawk; his attention was directed towards me by a retainer, in whose brawny proportions, husky voice, and ferocious moustachios, I recognised my adversary, Ludolf.

My gun was demanded, in the name of Count Rainer: I refused to surrender it. The party formed a circle around, pinioned me, and wrested it from me, ere I could attempt resistance. "Mr. Steward," said the Count, "you may now acquaint your friend with the consequences of destroying a nobleman's falcon."

The ready villain and his servile followers dragged me to the earth; they profaned my person by stripes. When they left me in my abasement, the air felt pestilent with their brutal laughter.

I lay with my face to the greensward long after their departure. My brain was eddying in a hell-whirl. I could have welcomed the return of chaos, that the cir- [165] cumstance of my shame might be obliterated in the clash of contending elements. Had the sun been blotted from the heavens, and the summer earth turned to blackness and desolation, I should have thought them fit and natural occurrences. I raised my burning brow; but the orb of day was riding high in his glory, and the meadow grass and wild flowers were fresh and fragrant as if they had not witnessed the act of degradation. I discovered that a stranger had been regarding me with a vigilant eye. I confronted him, and darted at him a devouring glance; his firm, contemplative look remained unaltered. Placing a hand on my shoulder, he said, "Albert Reding, consider me your friend."

"I know you not," I answered, "nor care to know you." He smiled benevolently: "Young man, I am no Austrian. I shall be with you to-morrow."

IV.

The stranger kept his word—on the ensuing day he came to our dwelling. Making, he said, a tour through the North of Italy, the picturesque scenery tempted him to prolong his sojourn at St. Michael. In his excursions, he had chanced to hold random converse with my father, whom he professed to value as the worthy descendant of an independent and intelligent people.

I had forborne to grieve my family by the story of my disgrace, nor had it yet been detailed to them by the officious communicativeness of pretended friends. Our visitor made no allusion to it, but expatiated very agreeably on topics of general interest. He described [166] the passes of the Alps with the accuracy of a mountaineer, and displayed an intimacy with the localities of the Cantons that filled my parents with pleasure and surprise. In pursuit of knowledge, he had traversed the most remarkable sections of the globe; and his observations, affluent in instruction, proved that his wanderings had been of a different order from the capricious migrations of sight-seeking wealth.

The warmth with which I seconded some of his sentiments appeared to please him. He complimented my father on my education; adding, that the judgment with which I developed its resources designated me for a wider sphere of action than belonged to a tiller of the soil of Lombardy. I had been vain enough to entertain the same opinion; and its confirmation, by a competent authority, was balm to my spirit. Gladly I acceded to his request, of guiding him to the Baron's Font, a romantic cascade, where, to use his own language, he sighed to offer allegiance to Nature.

The Baron's Font was distant about three leagues, among the hills. Rustic tradition ascribed the origin of its name to the cruelty and profanity of a feudal noble, who, in mockery of the Christian's initiatory rite, precipitated the objects of his ferocity from an impending cliff into the basin of the waterfall. My companion noted the peculiarities of the route, and committed to writing the information I furnished respecting the district. We rested on the summit of a steep, skirted by the foaming stream of the cascade, beyond which rose wooded grounds in bold acclivity, [167] mellowing, with their dusky greenness, the gloomy grandeur of a mouldering tower.

The stranger abruptly adverted to the hateful humiliation of the preceding day. He descanted on the contumely I had suffered, with a vehement bitterness that chafed my young blood to flame. I denounced endless hostility against the Count and his minions. He calmly commented on the futility of the threat. In the frenzy of exasperation, I insinuated the possibility of resorting to the darkest means of accomplishing revenge. He replied, that in cooler moments I would spurn the idea of Italian vengeance. Requiring a pledge of secresy, he proceeded to point out an honourable mode of lowering the crest of the oppressor.

"My name," he said, "is Philippon—my profession, a military engineer, in the service of the French Republic. The armies of Liberty only await the capture of Toulon to sever the chains of Italy. I am terminating a secret journey of observation through Piedmont and the Milanese. Come with me to Paris, and join the standard of Freedom. In France, no parchment barrier excludes untitled youth from fame and fortune; draw a blade in her cause, and relieve the place of your nativity from the thraldom of its petty tyrant. These brutal and stolid Austrians must be driven to their land of hereditary bondage—justice demands it. The time has gone by for insulted and injured Humanity to shed tears in secret. Five dreary years I pined in the dismal solitudes of the Bastille—I saw it fall, amidst the curses of my countrymen; and never shall the spirit of a [168] liberated nation taste repose, until every stronghold of remorseless power is patent to the winds of heaven as yon grim old fortress, where the Count Rainers of the past outraged with impunity the natural equality of man!"

The majesty of generous indignation irradiated his brow: the eloquent thunders of the Roman forum seemed to roll around me.—I agreed to attend him to the capital of the young Republic.

V.

Bent on entering the field of martial adventure, I anticipated much difficulty in obtaining the concurrence of my father. A lover of tranquillity, he had sickened at the sanguinary measures that crimsoned the cradle of the French Revolution. Yielding also to age and infirmity, he had been accustomed to the prospect of resigning to me the chief management of our affairs. The narrative of my shame, however, which led him to tremble for the consequences, determined him against opposing my departure. Of my military project, and the pursuits of my patron, I made no disclosure—I barely stated the fact, that he had promised to provide for me at Paris, and proposed, in the mean time, giving me employment as an amanuensis.

Sorrow and Joy are twin daughters of Affection. Notwithstanding the excitement of curiosity and ambition, reluctantly and despondingly I crossed our humble threshold. I went away at night, and this added to the melancholy character of the separation. [169] My mother was unwell, and at her bedside I received her blessing. The features of my gentle-natured sister gave dim and pallid testimony to the fullness of her affliction. When I had parted with my parents, she escorted me to the extremity of the orchard. "Oh, Albert!" were the only words she had power to utter; and her face looked so mournful—so heart-appealing, in the moonlight—that to desert her smote me as a sin. One embrace, and I bounded off like a chamois—then paused, till weeping relieved my soul—Katherine! Katherine!

Through provinces where every man appeared fearful of his fellow, we journeyed to the metropolis of France. That city, the great political heart of the empire, more than participated in the feverishness of its members. Armed artizans patrolled the streets; the shrine of St. Guillotine had left the Romish Kalendar destitute of homage, and ecclesiastical processions were rendered obsolete by the morning march to the scaffold. Terror stalked gigantic in the citadel of Freedom: the dead were thrown into unhonoured graves, and the living cowered timorously in corners to lament them. I entered the Assembly, whose decrees had struck down the proud and elevated the lowly. Here, thought I, are sages congregated worthy of creation's golden sera! The Chiefs of the Convention pronounced their orations: — Proscription! Proscription! — was the cry; and, as the elements of discord raged, the scene resembled a hideous melée of savage beasts in an ancient amphi- [170] theatre.

I could not conceal from Philippon the extent of my disappointment: "You talk of regenerating the world," I exclaimed, "and you have revived the horrors of the Triumvirate!"

"Your's," he replied, "is the decision of inexperience, that condemns the fruit ere it has had time to ripen. The healthful wind, which ministers to the drooping frame of Nature, at the same moment dissipates contagion and whelms the mariner in the deep. Neither political nor physical good is gratuitously granted; rather let our fields be irrigated with blood than that their harvests should be gathered by the hands of bondmen! What is the doubtful lease of life—this brief and irksome tenure—to the happiness of posterity? Were I to linger here for centuries, would not my native land still survive me with its millions of kindred beings, to whom social law must prove the mighty instrument of evil or of good?"

VI.

I remained about a year at Paris in the house of my patron. Toulon had fallen, and the army of Italy had commenced operations by a successful movement on the Sardinian frontier. Profiting by the opportunity I possessed of studying the theory of the military art, I was rewarded with a commission in a regiment of the line—one of those destined for the invasion of the Milanese. I received, with alacrity, the order to proceed to Nice. I was shocked and disgusted by the dreary spectacle of civil broil, and I thirsted for distinction. [171] The memory of wrong also rankled in my bosom, and in my dreams I planted the revolutionary banner on the battlements of St. Michael, and heard myself hailed in the halls of the insolent Austrian with the acclamations due to a hero.

I joined my regiment and learned, not many months after, that my protector, Philippon, had fled to England, to escape the fate which, as a philosophic patriot, he affected to disregard. His exile grieved me. I had shared largely in his favours; and he had never neutralized their influence by the slightest alloy of unkindness.

A government weakened by vacillations in its form, and dissensions in the capital, permitted the army, with which my hopes were associated, to languish ill-appointed and inactive. Instead of running a career of glory, it was forced to contend with the most depressing privations. In my despondency, a long-delayed letter arrived from my father. Its contents were almost limited to the earnest request, that I would immediately hasten home.

Its emphatic urgency, unaccompanied by explanation assured me that all went not well. I would fain have obeyed the summons, but it was impracticable. The Directory, established in authority, ordered the army of Italy to the field. General Bonaparte, an officer in his twenty-sixth year, marshalled the way to the Alps.

VII.

Napoleon's campaigns in 1796 are familiar to all Europe. It was my fortune to be present in the most [172] remarkable engagements, and to escape without a wound. When Wurmser, after repeated defeats, succeeded in recruiting his forces in the Tyrol, a strong body of our troops, headed by the Commander-in-chief, advanced against a division of 20,000 Austrians stationed at Roveredo. Our line of march lay through the district of my birth. A few hours before we were in motion I was summoned to the quarters of the General. It was the well-known characteristic of this extraordinary man scrupulously to ascertain the extent of his resources, even to the qualifications of an individual soldier.

Aware of my knowledge of the country he was about to penetrate, he wished to make it subservient to his purpose. He questioned me as to the correctness of some local information, which I perceived had been derived from the documents of Philippon. Satisfied on these points, he sportively enquired, if I had any dislike to act as his herald to my old neighbours. I related my obligations to our German superior, and he promised me ample powers for discharging them in full.

    We were evidently unexpected. No artificial obstacle opposed our progress, and we proceeded with unexampled celerity. Our advanced posts were only separated from St. Michael by a few miles of broken ground, when I was despatched with a detachment to surprize it. The troops halted in a chesnut grove, about half a league from the mill, while I, grappling a fowling-piece, assuming a light hunting-cap, and covering my uniform with an ordinary cloak, went forth to reconnoitre the place, and to provide for the safety of my relatives.

Plate: The Mountain Torrent
Steel plate engraving; drawn by W. Purser;
engraved by Edward Goodall [173]

    I skirted round the village and castle, which I found were occupied by a company of Hungarian infantry under Count Rainer. Not anticipating the irruption of an enemy into their secluded fastness, camp indulgences had relaxed order. My informer, a poor peasant, seemed afraid of confiding to a stranger his opinion of the Count and his followers. I asked concerning my family, but with the name of Reding he was unacquainted.

    It was the beginning of September. There had been a continuance of unusually sultry weather, and the melting of the mountain snows had swelled the stream at St. Michael, to an impetuous torrent. Twilight was approaching when I reached a sheltered position on the bank opposite the castle. The waters dashed furiously against the base of the building, and the crazy supports the antiquated bridge quivered like a harpstring.

I resolved on a nocturnal attack, and was about to seek a passing interview with the dear domestic circle, when, looking towards the castle, I saw what stayed my step. A female ran wildly to the stream, pursued by some menials, in the rear of whom, on horseback, came the Count their master. The fugitive cleared the bridge just as her pursuers gained it. At that moment the centre of the infirm structure gave way to the torrent. Concealed among the trees, I perceived the female on bended knees, distractedly blessing God for her deliverance; and I knew that it was Katherine, my only—my beloved sister!

I fired a shot at him who had been foremost in the [174] chace—the infamous Ludolf—as he clambered up a remnant of the shattered bridge. He stood unhurt amidst the group that surveyed me, while I sheltered the dove of my boyhood in my bosom. In the confusion I exposed my uniform; the alarm was given, and every instant became precious. I supported Katherine until out of sight of the foe. "Fly!" I cried, "fly to our parents, dear sister! tell them I shall bring glad tidings in the morning!"

I counselled in vain. The sense of injury had unsettled her mind—she hung helplessly upon me—her lips moved but I could distinguish nothing of what she spoke, save the repetition of the words "Home! I have no home!"—Oh God! she was sadly altered!

A bugle echoed among the cliffs. I bore her to a cavern, the discovery of my youth, and wrapt her in my cloak. Hurrying, by familiar paths, with a speed I had never before exerted, I rejoined my associates.

VIII.

An intricate and circuitous track brought us at midnight to the isolated church of St. Michael, commanding the village and the narrow road to the castle. We crouched in the churchyard, until every sound ceased, and the lights that had blazed in different directions were no longer visible. Leaving part of my force to intercept the communication with the village, I led the remainder to a point of the fortress which I had scaled in my youthful rambles.

The pacing of the sentinels, and the noisy vigils of [175] the Count and his guests, were clearly audible as I descended the ivied wall. My party followed, one by one, and our success would have been signally complete, but for the accidental discharge of a musket. This was answered by a volley from the guard, the din of arms, and the hasty gathering of a tumultuous body of defenders. Ordering my men to keep close and follow me, we pressed forward to a private door that opened into the body of the pile.

This barrier was quickly shattered by a shower of balls, and in a second the great hall resounded with the groans of the dying and the shouts of the triumphant. In that arena of slaughter I was collected as I am now. Once had Rainer's bloated visage confronted me in the fray, but the baleful meteor vanished, and bootless to me was the issue of the conflict, until blade or bullet did its work on him and his subordinate.

The hall gave indications of a carousal. The red wine streaming from flaggons overturned in the struggle, mingled with the life-drops of the wassailers. Death derived a more appalling aspect from the relics of recent revelry. Some intoxicated wretches had been bayonetted with the goblets in their hands. One had fallen backwards on the hearth above the burning embers; he was mortally wounded, and the blood gushed freely in the flames. I stooped to raise him from his bed of torture. The streaks of gore did not disguise the lineaments of Ludolf. The reprobate had closed his reckoning with mortality.

Victory was ours, but discipline was at an end; I [176] could with difficulty muster sentinels for the night; the cellars were ransacked, and weariness and intemperance soon produced their effects. Sending confidential messengers to attend to my sister's safety and convey intelligence to my father, I prepared to await the dawn of morning.

Feverish from anxiety, I felt no inclination to grant my wearied limbs repose. My brain was racked with the thought of Katherine, and apprehension for my parents. I had seen enough to convince me that Rainer had done his worst.—What confederate demon had enabled him to escape me?

I paced from post to post, execrating the sluggish march of time. Leaning over an eminence near the broken bridge, I listened to the turbulent music of the waters. A subterraneous opening cut in the rocky soil below communicated with the vaults of the castle. Hearing the echo of a foot-fall, I bent cautiously over the outlet. A lamp glimmered beneath. A muffled figure raised it aloft to guide its egress, then extinguished it hastily. The light fell on the face of the Count.

I grasped his cloak as he emerged, but, slipping it from his shoulders, he retreated towards a shelving wood-walk on the margin of the stream. Had he gained it, the darkness must have saved him. Both my pistols missed fire. I outstripped him in the race, and bore him back to the very edge of the ravine. He made a thrust at me with his sword. I neither paused for a trial of skill, nor attempted to ward off the weapon; the butt end of a pistol found its way to his [177] forehead; not a sound passed his lips; down he went—down—down—passively bounding over the jagged declivity, till a heavy plash told that he was whirling with the torrent.

Vengeance was satisfied: I recoiled involuntarily from the scene of the encounter. Suddenly arose an explosion, as if a volcano had torn up the foundation of the castle: I was felled to the earth ere I could speculate upon the cause.

IX.

My campaigns were over. Rainer had laid a train, and fired the powder magazine of his captured hold. The bravest of my men perished; and I, crushed beneath a fragment of the toppling towers, lived to curse the art that returned me, mutilated and miserable, to a world in which I was henceforth to have no portion.

I left the hospital a phantom, and set forth on a pilgrimage, the performance of which was the only business that remained to me in life. The tide of battle had ebbed from St. Michael, when I crawled up its steep—the church and castle were blackened ruins—the habitations of the villagers roofless and deserted—the mill a shapeless mass of timber and stones. Our orchard was unfolding the buds of spring—I fancied that the hoary apple-trees wore the aspect of friends—the voice of singing floated on my ear, as I neared the dwelling of my infancy, and the fountain of my heart re-opened.

Close to the spot where our pretty porch once [178] stood, a matron, in the garb of extreme penury, was bending over the trampled remains of a plot of flowers. Her features were only partially revealed, but the mountain melody she sang could not be mistaken—I fell at my mother's feet! Shading back the hair from my scarred temples, she asked me if I had come from her children!

Mercy was vouchsafed to her and to me. She soon slumbered with the clods of the valley. My father had died, ere my departure from France; and the story of our injuries from the Austrian lightened the burden of remorse for the shedding of blood. I have discovered no trace of Katherine since I quitted her at the cave.

X.

My day has been without a meridian—divided between eventide and morn: heavy were the clouds that eclipsed its sunshine, but they are fleeting away; and, now that night is waxing apace, my up-turned soul beholds its moon rising resplendent with hope.

If I have not experienced felicity in the friendly shades of the Lake of Zurich, I have at least cast off the poisoned garment of reflection. Ever be they blessed, the kind ones who smoothed the pillow of the spirit-broken!

War has been over the globe. The arch-destroyer and a myriad of the unnoted slain are wrapt alike in the undiscerning dust, yet man is still unredeemed from bondage. When shall Peace go forth as a conqueror, arrayed in the panoply of Wisdom?

THE KEEPSAKE

Literary Annual
The Keepsake for 1828. Ed. William Harrison Ainsworth. London: Hurst, Chance, and Co., 1828. Printer: Thomas Davison, Whitefriars.

Title
Anonymous. [Shelley, Mary.] "Convent of Chaillot: or, Valliere and Louis XIV." KS 1828. 267-283.[1] [267]

THE CONVENT OF CHAILLOT: OR, VALLIÈRE AND LOUIS XIV.

L'amour me conduisait, je faisais tout pour lui.
Adélaide du Guesclin.

HISTORIANS have recorded the amours of princes, and perpetuated the names of the sharers of their affections, not because love is the province of history, but because, where power has centred in individuals, the stream of history has often been directed by love. In despotic governments this is ever the case; and the name of Maintenon is little less closely interwoven than those Richelieu and Mazarin with the events of their country. The royal mistresses of France have swelled the annals of their times: their arts, their policy, their ambition, are the history of their nation. Their charms and their blandishments won the hearts of their sovereigns; and, while freedom remained a yet unsolved problem, the caprices of kings were the fluctuations of states.

Of this notoriety, which is not fame, little is attached to the memory of the amiable but not happy woman, the only stain on whose name arises from her connexion with Louis the Fourteenth. He has been designated the Great: a bitter irony, in which impartiality sees only the flimsy cloud thrown by the breath of flattery over the ineffaceable epithets of selfish, unfeeling, and tyrannical. Louise de la Vallière loved without prudence, but also without ambition; she has therefore been

---

[1] Mary Shelley identified as author by Nora Crook; see "Sleuthing towards a Mary Shelley Canon," Women's Writing 6:3 (Oct 1999): 413-424.

almost forgotten, though genius has twined the charms of fiction round the realities [268] of her life, like the setting, with which the hand of the lapidary displays and enhances the pure product of the diamond mine.

The father of Louise filled a conspicuous office in the court of Gaston of Orleans, brother of Louis XIII. His death, which happened in the early youth of his daughter, was a source of deep grief to her, and contributed to augment the pensive and melancholy temperament natural to her disposition. Her secluded and almost solitary habits deepened these traits. She mingled as little as possible, and always with reluctance, in the gayeties of the court, where she was brought up. Wrapt in sweet but vague imaginings, she sought acquaintance with the loveliness of nature; and, beneath the shady woods of Orleans, or on the banks of the sparkling Loire, encouraged that dangerous susceptibility, with which her heart was by nature but too deeply fraught.

The society with which she had hitherto come in contact was not of a kind, to win her from these seductive abstractions. Gay, unthinking, and devoted to pleasure and coquetry, her companions of the court, their occupations and their objects, awakened no corresponding echo in her own breast. They existed only for levity and admiration; but Louise lived for feeling and for love.

Accident, however, introduced her to a friend in the following slight adventure. Meditating, as usual, on the banks of the river—sighing for that unexperienced sympathy, of which imagination had alone suggested to her the existence—she perceived a young man, who rushed by her in apparent anxiety, bearing water from the stream in his hat. An intervening cluster of thick shrubs almost instantly hid him from her sight; but, after advancing [269] a few yards, she perceived him again. He was kneeling on the ground by the side of a female, endeavouring in vain to awaken her from a state of insensibility. The powerful aromatic which Louise hastened to apply proved efficient. The revising figure opened her eyes, fixing them first on the youth, and then on Louise, when they returned with alarmed quickness to those of her companion. Louise divined the cause of this look, and was departing hastily, when the voices of those she left, uniting in thanks, retarded her steps.

The result of this adventure was an intimacy between Louise and Clemence Beaumelle—that was the lady's name—which afterwards ripened into a closer connexion, and gave to La Vallière a friend, in whom she could repose confidence.

Mademoiselle Beaumelle resided in a neighboring chateau with her aunt, Madame Savonne. Their whole establishment consisted of themselves and two domestics: they were not wealthy, and their dwelling, though sufficiently comfortable, was enriched with few luxuries. Louise found her new companion tender, sensible, and engaging. She was, perhaps, not beautiful, but interesting; and, at least, was possessed of mental and personal qualities, which had evidently enthralled the heart of Theodore Blanzac. This young man, attached to Clemence Beaumelle, and equally beloved in return, felt the deep pain of being prevented by a scanty fortune from completing a union, to which fortune was the only obstacle. Too much in love to relinquish the affection he had formed, but too generous to gratify it by exposing its object to the privations of wedded poverty, he contented himself in joining his Clemence in hopes, which, [270] as being such, were more than pleasant; but of the accomplishment of which there was little immediate prospect.

The sensitive heart of Louise de la Vallière felt deeply for the situation of her friends, though themselves bore the pressure of delay without repining, and even with cheerfulness. To Louise a new existence seemed opening in the enjoyments of friendship. Her mother, her only surviving parent, she honoured and loved as her kindness deserved; but there are confidences, which the very love, and still more the respect, of a child prevent a mother's sharing. The airy fabrics, the day dreams, the romance of a young and sanguine heart, it shrinks from disclosing, except to one, that, like itself, may be throbbing with the same feelings, and vibrating on the same chords. To find such a one was a prize to Louise; the dearer, because so long panted for in vain.

If Mademoiselle de la Vallière loved Clemence with the affection of a sister, it was with the esteem, at least, of a friend, that she regarded M. Blanzac: the blended ardour and sweetness of his disposition, his frankness, his interesting conversation, so different from the vapid frivolities and stale conceits of the courtiers of Gaston d'Orleans, pleased her as much by their novelty as their worth. Her walks were no longer solitary; accompanied by the inhabitants of the Chateau Savonne, she retraced with increased satisfaction her familiar rambles.

Still, however, she found something to wish for; for the vacancies of the heart, like the gulf of the Roman forum, never close but with the sacrifice of what it holds most dear and precious; never till it has no longer fears or wishes. In her lonely moments her busy fancy would [271] pain the happiness she could feel, were she, too, beloved like Clemence; were she the object of an affection so pure, so disinterested, the chosen and worshipped one of another Theodore Blanzac. Of *another*!—the word was fraught with a fund of self-inquiry: Louise did not enter into it, for she was unconscious of her danger. A circumstance, however, occurred, which revealed to her the terrors of the precipice on which she stood.

The chevalier St. Remi was now engaged in those assiduities towards Madame de la Vallière, which shortly afterwards terminated in their marriage. His station in the household of Monsieur gave him some influence, and his kindness towards Louise encouraged her to solicit his interest towards procuring an appointment, then vacant, for Theodore Blanzac. St. Remi exerted himself, the place was gained, and the great obstacle to the union of the lovers removed.

It was not until her grateful and rejoicing friends overwhelmed her with the thanks due to her efforts in their behalf, that the almost terrified Louise discovered, mingling with her joy in their happiness, a feeling of bitterness, which, even to herself, she trembled to acknowledge, but durst not deny. Perhaps the emotions from which this feeling arose were not yet those of love, but they are those from which it is born; and the step which Louise took for their extinguishment was decisive and prompt.

She had once more recourse to St. Remi, but this time the request was for herself. The situation of maid of honour to Madame was asked and obtained for her. Taught by her feelings, that not a moment should be [272] lost, she made immediate preparation for her departure to St. Germain.

These were soon completed. She took leave with little regret of her acquaintance at Orleans; they on their part felt no concern at the loss of one, with whom they had nothing in common; some wondered at her sudden departure, and others envied her the scenes of gayety and splendour, for which she was about to exchange the *ennui* of Orleans. It was not thus, however, that she parted with Clemence Beaumelle.

She had purposely chosen a time for paying this farewell visit to her friend, when she knew that Blanzac would be absent. Clemence lamented his being away. "It would have been such a pleasure to him," she said, "to have seen you; he loves you almost as well as I do." These words sent a thrilling chill through the heart of Louise. "Alas!" she thought, "he may confess his love for me; it is the love of a friend, but mine——" She made a violent effort to master her rebellious feelings, and succeeded.

The friends at length separated, after having been long together. They made no protestations of eternal friendship, but they wept, for neither could restrain her tears.

We shall surely see each other again," said Louise, as she lingered at the outer gate, to which her friend conducted her: "I feel, that our fortunes are linked together, and I rejoice in the thought. Farewell! do not forget me, Clemence, in your happiness."

"Forget you, dear Louise! oh no! we shall always think of you." [273]

Louise heard not her friend's concluding words; her heart echoed the sounds, "*We* shall always think of you." She pressed her friend in her arms, and left her in haste.

She was alone: how much alone, those know, who have parted for a long absence from one, whose place in the affections there is none to fill up. The heart, while yet possessed of what it loves, supports itself against the knowledge of its approaching loss: it is not until after the moment of separating, that it wonders at its former acquiescence, and feels the bitterness of its privation.

It was thus with Louise; she revisited all her favourite haunts, and wept to think, she should no more return to them in the company of the friends, who had so much endeared them to her.

The excitement, which the energy of her resolve had afforded, her conscious triumph over her own weakness, and the hurry of thought and action in which she had been involved, had hitherto sustained her. They failed her now; and by one of those revulsions, that naturally succeed powerful emotions, she felt languid, despondent, and irresolute.

In this state of weakness the thoughts of Blanzac recurred to her, as if still more to overwhelm her. Bursting into tears, she exclaimed, "If it be my lot hereafter to love, I may surely hope to taste the pleasures of the passion, for I feel all its pain." She was deeply, though naturally mistaken. In the first disappointment of our affections, we fondly imagine, that our affliction, as it is the heaviest we have known, is also the greatest we can experience, and that time can have nothing in store for us more painful than the wounds of the present. [274] Orleans was no longer her home. She was at St. Germain, and the novelty of her situation for a while distracted, but did not soothe her mind. This effect soon wore off, and her habitual depression resumed a dominion, from which it was speedily to be expelled by feelings, on the operation of which was suspended the destiny of Louise.

Whatever differences of opinion may exist as to the character of Louis le Grand in its more important traits, the accounts are uniform of his personal address and powers of pleasing. To women, his unfailing and almost submissive courtesy united with his handsome person and impressive manners, to render him an object of more than admiration. The eminence of a throne, while to the eyes of a court it diminishes, if it do not conceal blemishes, only magnifies the graces or virtues of its possessor. But the deportment of Louis had a majestic suavity, which flattery itself could scarcely do more than faithfully describe.

To the eyes, and still more to the heart of Louise, these qualities shone in unclouded lustre. The former feelings of her mind were weakened; and such is the delusion which the heart practises on itself, that Louise applauded her own resolution, in being able to withdraw her remembrances from the forsaken Orleans. The new feeling, to which she gave the name of loyalty, seemed to her sanctioned by prudence and duty; nor did she trouble herself to inquire into the lurking sophistry of her reasonings.

A universal admirer of beauty, and devoted to gallantry, the king, who was a regular attendant at the soirées of Madame, failed not to observe and be struck [275] with the timid loveliness of the new maid of honour. The deep expression of her features, her graceful form and exquisite complexion, repeatedly attracted him; the more so, that she sought to avoid observation, and shrunk from the glances that were bent upon her. Long ere Louise suspected, that she was even noticed by the monarch, his admiration was fixed; and with Louis to admire and to covet were one and the same. To win the affections of this beautiful and interesting girl became an object not less eagerly desired by him who formed the design, because her honour and her peace must be sacrificed in its accomplishment.

Whilst, however, Louise, though assailed by all that ambition, and all that female tenderness could urge, yet remained innocent, a fresh disappointment fell upon the friends she had left at Orleans. Theodore, on the event of marriage with his Clemence, was summoned by the duties of his station to a distant province. In the midst of the grief which this event caused to the lovers they were united; they parted at the altar that witnessed their vows, and Theodore left his weeping bride at the moment she received the name. Desirous of leaving a place where they had now no ties, and where to Clemence every object was imbued with mournful remembrances, Madame Savonne and her niece retired from the Chateau, and took up their temporary residence, as boarders, in the convent of St. Mary, on the heights of Chaillot.

Situate not more than half a league from Paris, Chaillot overlooks the waters of the Seine, on the opposite side of which lies the Champ de Mars. It was with pleasure that Clemence looked forward to being able to meet again the friend, from whom she had been now severed [276] for many months: she conjectured the surprise with which Louise would welcome her, and not to diminish it, she resolved to conceal her change of residence from her friend, until she could personally communicate the intelligence. Her aunt was distantly allied to the Duchess of Noailles, the governess of the maids of honour, and the intercourse between the friends might, on this account, be more easy and frequent than it would otherwise have been.

On arriving at Chaillot, late in the day, and wearied with their journey, the travellers hastened to seek the repose, of which they stood so much in need.

The next day Clemence surveyed the building, in which so many had been immured from the world and its vanities. The dim light that fell in irregular masses on the brown walls, the clam silence, interrupted only by the quiet footsteps of the nuns as they passed and repassed, conveyed to her imagination a soothing idea of peaceful abstraction from care. Clemence thought of the absent Theodore and his busy toils: she thought of Louise and her gay sojourn. "She would like these quiet recesses better," thought Clemence, "than the splendour of the court; her inclinations are wedded to solitude and privacy: at St. Germain she may seem happy, but here, with me, she would be so."

At this moment her eye fell on an object, that arrested all her attention. It was a female figure kneeling at the foot of a lofty cross, which stood in the cloister where Clemence was walking. The kneeler did not wear the monastic habit; she seemed in deep agitation; her face was concealed, but the form was familiar to Clemence. The deepening shadows of evening however prevented [277] her from discerning more, and a natural feeling of delicacy prompted her to withdraw, unnoticed, from the scene of the mourner's solitude. As she retreated in stealthy silence, she heard a footstep approaching in an opposite direction. It was one of the novices. Clemence stayed her, to inquire who the kneeling figure was.

"I do not know," replied the novice; "she is from the court of St. Germain; she arrived here last night shortly after you came. You must endeavour to see her;

she is very beautiful, but pale, and she seems very amiable."

Beautiful! amiable! and from St. Germain! was it possible that it might be——" Clemence was prevented from pursuing her conjectures by a sudden noise, that sent a thousand unaccustomed echoes through the cloister and aisles of the convent. It was the rapid approach of a carriage, which entered the court yard, succeeded by the sudden sound of many voices. Through a dim succession of arches Clemence beheld the superior of the Convent, passing in haste, attended by several of the sisters, all of whom wore their veils down. The confusion increased; on a sudden the gates at the extremity of the cloister jarred from the force with which they were thrown open. The kneeling figure sprung up from the foot of the cross; she looked wildly around her: as her eye fell on the man who advanced towards her, she uttered a faint shriek, and would have fallen to the ground, had not the king sprung forward, and caught her in his arms.

Louise was pressed to his heart; she heard the passionate breathings of affection from the lips of France's best and noblest, so at least she thought him. She loved him too; she could no longer conceal from herself, that she did so. [278] Loyalty, duty, admiration were no more, for they were extinguished in love. Love boundless, irrepressible—that love for which fond and passionate woman will sometimes sacrifice what the heart sighs to think, that lovely and spotless woman should ever sacrifice.

But it was not thus yet with Louise. Loving, adoring, even to despair, she remained not a second moment in the encircling arms that supported her. She sprung from the embrace of Louis, and flinging herself once more at the foot of the cross, "Holy mother of God!" she exclaimed, "help me or I perish!" She twined her arms round the pedestal of the cross, and, pressing it to her breast with almost phrensied violence, she wept bitterly and intensely.

Kneeling by her side, the agitated Louis entreated her to rise: with the tenderest words, and the most winning protestations, he besought her confidence. Trembling with emotion, confused, distracted, Louise one moment vowed internally to close her heart against the blandishments, that fell *too* sweetly on her ear. The next, her unresisting hand was clasped in that of the king. He raised her from the ground. The moment of energy, of resolution, was gone by: Louise burst again from the fatal embrace; her bosom leaned upon his, her head sunk on his shoulders, and her tears streamed on his neck.

"Can you not love me then, Louise?" The words were simple; but the look, the tone, spoke every thing to the heart of the overcome girl.

"*Love* you! oh God!" She hid her face; her bosom rose and fell yet more vehemently. The conquest of love over virtue was accomplished.

The Forgotten Gothic

PLATE: The Convent of Chaillot
Steel plate engraving; drawn by Alfred Edward Chalon, R.A.;
engraved by Charles Heath; printed by McQueen;
published by Hurst, Chance & Co. & Robert Jennings

Availing himself of her emotion, Louis hastened to bear her to the voiture in which he had come, and which was to bear them back to Paris. This movement aroused Clemence, who had remained an almost petrified spectator of this interview. Heedless of consequences, she rushed forward, and throwing herself before the king, cried in a voice of almost agony, "Spare her, sire! crush me—kill me, but spare her!"

The voice was as a spell on the spirit of her for whom she interceded. "Clemence! Clemence! Louise sprung convulsively into the arms of her friend, and was again insensible.

The imperious temper of Louis kindled at this interruption of his will. He looked at the trembling and abashed Clemence with indignation, with fury: he added words; he condescended to threaten.

Nothing else could have given to Clemence the self possession needed in that hour. A soothing word might have overwhelmed her, the display of unjust severity made her calm.

"Sire," said she, "the being whom I hold in my arms is my benefactress; the friend, almost the only one, of my youth. Should your majesty remove her hence, I may perhaps never behold her again; this friend, this benefactress, will be lost to me forever. Spare her to me then for an hour, for a few minutes. In the name," she continued, her voice growing more firm, and her countenance flush with the earnestness of her entreaty, "in the name of the God, who has made you the father of your country, I entreat you not to refuse the prayer of one of the lowliest of your children!" [280]

The meek courage of Clemence, and her attachment to Louie thus displayed, awakened those better feelings of which Louis was not devoid.

"I forgive you," said he, "nay, more, I admire your friendship. Take the hour you have so well asked for; and let this," he added, "be the pledge of your sovereign's esteem."

He unfastened, as he spoke, a jewelled chain which he wore around his neck, and would have placed it on that of Clemence. She retired a step with respect, but with firmness put back the offered gift.

"Pardon me, sire; your majesty's approbation is enough. You take from me my friend, and I cannot accept this splendid jewel. That you have granted what I asked, I will acknowledge with my prayers for your majesty."

With a profound reference she hastily withdrew, bearing with her the half reviving Louise.

The hour was passed in bitterness, mingled with happier feelings. Clemence at first endeavoured to detach her friend from the court and its master; but she soon desisted from her attempts. "I cannot act now," said the weeping La Vallière: "had I earlier asked and received your support, all might have been well. But yesterday I thought myself firm; I fled from danger, and it has pursued me hither;

now my strength is gone, my course is no longer my own; impelled by a feeling I cannot resist, I return to meet the fate which I dread, but cannot struggle with.

"Do not think harshly of me, Clemence, my friend, my sister. If I fall, it is not as a willing victim; my [281] struggles, my sufferings, have been great; do not condemn me if they have been in vain. Farewell, we *may* meet again."

They parted. La Vallière returned to the splendour and misery of a court. The rest as regards her is matter of history, which has less faintly, it at all, touched on the more obscure passages of her life on which I have dwelt; perhaps, because the rapid glance of the historian, like that of the heedless admirer of nature, regards only the hues of the flower which lie nearest to the eye, while it passes over the lovelier and more delicate streaks, that tinge the base of the petals.

Clemence ere long rejoined her husband. The remote district to which his duties confined him combined with other obstacles, to prevent any but a very rare correspondence between Clemence and her friend, now Duchess de la Vallière, the avowed mistress of the king's affections, and the mother of his children. Madame Blanzac rejoiced to hear of the tenderness of the monarch for her friend; her hope was for its continuance; but the hope was blended with fears, unhappily too well grounded.

The passion of the king, though long unchanged, at length, like all other passions rooted in selfishness, veered to a new object. The charms, the talent, and still more the artifice of Madame de Montespan, destroyed the influence of the more estimable but now familiar La Vallière. The heart of the latter sunk beneath the blow. It was long ere she could persuade herself of the truth. It seemed impossible that her fidelity, her devotion, her sacrifices, could be thus rewarded.

The favourites of royalty have in general found a [281] compensation for the fluctuating regards of those on whom they depend, in the facilities afforded them of gratifying their avarice, their ambition, or their vanity. La Vallière was without these resources; she had devoted herself to love alone, and when love proved treacherous she found the world a wilderness.

It was then that the pure feelings, which, though like all new feelings, had been insufficient to give strength to her resolves, began to ripen into principles. She left the world, which had no charms for her; a world, that could not fail to admire the spectacle of a woman, who at thirty years of age, and possessed of yet unfaded beauty, preferred religion and the rigours of a Carmelite monastery to a court and temptations of pleasures.

She entered the monastery, and, after the usual year of noviciate, received the veil before a concourse of the noble, and the proud, who thronged, along with those whom better motives inspired, to view the adieu to the world of one, who had long been dead to its enjoyments.

Shortly after her profession, she was informed, that a young female boarder, who had just entered the convent, was desirous of conversing with her.

Sister Louise desired that the stranger might be introduced to her cell. She was so—it was Clemence.

It was Clemence, a widow and a mourner. Blanzac was no more; and Clemence, husbandless and childless, had entered Paris the day before the profession of Louise; an event, the expectation of which then engrossed that loquacious city. Her long watchings on her husband, whom she attended, as she might be expected to attend the husband of her love, had prevented her from hearing the rumours, which were wafted from the distant capital. [283]
It was therefore with astonishment that she met the intelligence; it was also with sudden but fixed determination, to share with her friend the seclusion and austerities of the life she had chosen.

"You said, that there was a tie that linked us," said Clemence to Louise; "you prophesied truly, it will last to the uttermost!" And it did. The death of Madame Blanzac, which happened some years before that of Sister Louise, was the first, as it was the last interruption of their friendship.

It was to the Duchess de la Vallière that Madame de Sévigné applied the epithet of the "humble violet." It was well applied to her gentle spirit while she lived, and a fragrance, like that of the violet, has embalmed her memory in death.

"*I am not happy, but content*," was her touching reply to the insulting inquiries of her rival, who visited her after her profession. It united the meekness of a Christian with the philosophy of a sage. And if the feelings, in which these words originated, were the only fruit of a long life, of which the gay and happy scenes had not been the most prevailing, her life and her sufferings were not in vain.

Title

Anonymous. [Ainsworth, William Harrison.] "The Ghost Laid." KS 1828. 286-300. [286]

THE GHOST LAID.

SWEET village of ROSTHERNE! Gem of my youth's localities! How powerless has been the lapse of years to erase from among the chronicled regrets of memory they soothing and sequestered beauties. Thy fertile undulating plains, thy clustered trees, thy time-tinted church (where lie the remains of one most honoured and most beloved); across the bushy banks of, dearest of all, thy Mere, with its placid waters, I see them all, the idly waving branches, the light rippling waves. In fancy I see them all; perhaps my eye may again dwell on them, but with what feelings? with such as when last I saw thee? Can I bear with me to the scene of my [287] youth and, its pleasantness the buoyant spirit, the hope, yet dear, though blighted, the faith, the confident, the energy, that were then mine? Never—I think of these things and ask, where are they? The echo is from my heart, that answers, *where?*

ROSTHERNE is one of the loveliest spots in Cheshire, placed on the banks of a small lake, which, taking its name from the village, is called Rostherne Mere. The few dwellings it contains are rustic habitations, occupied by the cultivators of its rich meadows and pastures; they were so, though still fewer in number, fifty years back.

It was one fine autumn evening, about this time, that two lovers parted on a spot, equally distant from the brink of the river and a snug white-washed cottage that stood some one or two hundred yards eastwardly.

The year was sinking towards its end, the leaves covered the ground, and the reddish brown hue had usurped the place of the livelier green on the trees. It was a lovely night, deep pensive moonlight, the very night for love and love's votaries.

The two individuals, who on this occasion fell under this designation, were a pretty, neat, or rather more than neat, rather romantic-looking girl, of eighteen, perhaps, or a summer's shad more, it might be; and a person of the other sex, some years older, but yet young, tall, well made, with a countenance, which, amongst a good deal of better expression, indicated a spice of the scape grace in his composition. Their conversation, though wonderfully interesting to the parties, might possibly be otherwise to my readers, and is therefore kept in reserve. In fact, love conversations, like Cinderella's slipper, are essenti- [288] ally exclusive, and fit for nobody, except those for whom they are made.

"God be with you, my dear Walter," said the maiden, as, parting from the last embrace, she looked wistfully at her lover.

"And with you, my own Mary, till I return."

"Ah! till you return: but when?"

"Once more, I assure you, my love, I will return and bring success with me. Our scheme cannot fail. Farewell then, and fear nothing."

"Farewell," echoed the maiden, but in a tone, that showed how vainly she endeavoured to comply with the lover's last behest. One other *last* embrace, and they parted.

Mary Spenser was the daughter of the farmer who occupied the little snug cottage already mentioned. He was, though not a niggardly, a saving man; and, to use his own phrase, rarely spent twopence where a penny would do.

He was not however without sense in the application of his worldly treasures. While the mass was laid out to profit, a portion of it was devoted to the fitting his only daughter to fill hereafter some superior station to that, which she now held, of her mother's assistant in the government of their small household. He had, after much cogitation, determined to afford the advantages of a "ladies' seminary," some twenty miles distant. It was from this hotbed of improvement, that Mary had now lately returned.

She brought with her, as usual from such places, some sentimentality, cultivated by the perusal, in secret, of [289] divers of those "half-bound volumes in marble covers," which Sir Anthony Absolute pronounces so detrimental to all rule and authority.

I do not pretend to decide whether her acquirements—Good Heavens! that word reminds me, that I have given no account of my heroine's personal charms:—never mind now, but look at the engraving prefixed to this history. She is there leaning against a door.

Is she not beautiful?

Whether her own endowments, then, as I was about to say, or her father's wealth, formed her principal charm in the eyes of the neighbouring bachelors, I do not know. Certain it is, however, that many felt or feigned a flame; men of substance, having cattle, and herds, and the good things of the earth. Their cattle, and their herds, and their good things signified not a stiver. Mary would none of them.

In truth, Mary had made her choice and lost her heart before she came home: nothing very new, I am informed. It is true, that she had gained another heart in lieu of the one she had lost; at least, so Walter Markham told her, and she had great faith in his sayings. Now Walter Markham was the very man, and therefore ought to know best.

However it did so happen, that Mr. Benjamin Spencer, father of Miss Mary Spencer, by no means looked on Walter Markham with his daughter's eyes, preferring to assist his own sight with a pair of silver-rimmed spectacles. Somehow or other Walter Markham never got into the exact focus of these spectacles, so as to be seen to advantage through them. He might be very. [290] clever, and very pleasant, and very full of all manner of talk to please foolish girls; but Benjamin insisted he was not a pain's-taking, hard-working, calculating lad; and as he had not the needful, which there was no denying, neither had he, in Benjamin's estimation, the wherewith to scrape the same together. So after several conferences between the old man and the young man, their intercourse ended by a very decided intimation to Walter Markham not to make his appearance there again. At the same time Mary was forbidden to see him again; in consequence of which she met him by appointment the same night, when they talked and wept, and squeezed hands and lips, and parted as before-mentioned, which brings me back to the present tense of my story.

It was about a week after the time of this party, that Dame Spenser, *la mère*, paid a visit to a relation at some two or three miles distance. A most comfortable it was; the tea excellent, the cherry brandy supreme, and to crown all, Mistress Spencer won from her relative three silver threepences at all-fours. Such a concatenation of sleek and soothing things naturally produced a corresponding smoothness, and a more extensive philanthropy in their object: so that when, on returning homewards, the dame beheld, at a short distance before her, an object which appeared to her a wayfaring female mendicant seated at the foot of a hedge, she instinctively instituted an inquiry after a penny in her huge pocket. Her charity however in this instance proved superfluous.

"Keep your money for them that ask it," said the supposed pauper, rejecting the offered bounty.

"Well, well," replied the dame, "king George's head [291] has no need to go a begging in these times. If you kept a civiler tongue in your head it might be none the worse though," and the dame walked on.

"Stay!" said the other. It was with such a stern commanding tone, that the dame halted involuntarily. She looked more narrowly at the speaker, whose figure was more striking than prepossessing. A discoloured complexion, strongly marked and shaded by tangled masses of long black hair, repelled rather than invited observation. Her dress was coarse and much worn; the predominating colours were, or had been, blue and red. Two or three tin utensils, that lay by her, seemed to form a small portable stock in trade.

"Stay!" said the gipsy: "would you have your fortune told?"

"Not I, troth," answered the consort of Benjamin; "I want no better fortune than I have."

"Yet I could tell you want you would fain know: once more, shall I speak what I can tell?"

"Just as pleases yourself, good woman, only it is growing late, so the quicker you are, the better."

"I hinder you not," returned the prophetess; "begone then, since the fate of your own blood troubles you less than the occupation of your trumpery household. Follow your way, as I will mine."

The curiosity, which, implanted in the first of her progenitrixes, had descended to the good woman, and was just beginning to show itself, was extinguished in indignation at the slight case on her housekeeping, on which, and with justice, she greatly prided herself. Her wrath was indeed about to express itself in words, but the gipsy, paying no further attention to the farmer's wife, [292] slung her bundle over her shoulder, and set off in the contrary direction at great speed.

Dame Spencer too resumed her route, though in a less tranquil mood than had hitherto possessed her. Sometimes she wished she had heard the gipsy's tale; then her cheek would glow at the remembrance of the audacious disrespect, with which her household had been mentioned.

By the time, however, that she had arrived within half a mile of the cottage her displeasure had almost subsided, when, on a sudden, she started. She rubbed her eyes, she pinched her arms, she was convinced she was well awake. She saw sitting on the grown before her the identical woman, who had already occasioned her so much uneasiness. There she was, with her red and blue cloak and her tin kettles.

"Will you have your fortune told?" said the gipsy, as the farmer's wife drew night, in the same deep harsh tone as before.

"No,—I thank you; but I have no need."

"Your daughter's——"

"What have you to say of her?" exclaimed the now anxious mother, delaying her steps.

"I have little to say of her. She is a bright and a bonny flower."

"I could tell you that, and so could the whole village; so——"

"Ay," interrupted the sybil, "but I can tell you what neither you, nor all the wise heads of your village together, can tell me. Mary Spencer will be married."

"Like enough: my lass may have a husband without the asking." [293]

"True; few would ask for the husband she is doomed to have. Here, take this; open it when you are home; it will tell you who——" And she snatched up her burden, and was out of sight in the twinkling of an eye.

When Spencer's wife opened the case the gipsy had given her, she beheld the miniature resemblance of a young many named Tylson, well known in the neighbourhood, and at the time in question the subject of general conversation: a distinction he had earned by drowning himself in the Mere a few days before.

The appalled and astonished parent gazed with a fearful anxiety on this ominous picture. She was bewildered, and knew not what to do. Her husband was from home on some of his more distant business, nor was his return expected for at least a day or two. From her daughter she felt naturally desirous to conceal her fears and their cause. Thus in want of a confidant, her only resource was to seek the counsel of a neighbour, who had long been her nearest and closest gossip.

To this neighbour's house, a bright summery spot on the opposite side of the Mere, she accordingly went, though the day was closing, and herself fatigued with her excursion. Committing her own dwelling to the care of her daughter, and the one female servant, a somewhat aged crone, then confined to her bed by rheumatism, the good lady of the house wended to her friend's habitation. She was a widow woman with an only son, a good-humoured, sturdy, hard-headed lad, the favourite of the village, and, from having once enlisted in the Blues, known by the name of Corporal Crucifix. To [294] Mrs. Crucifix therefore did her neighbour recount her woes and fears.

The recital was barely finished, when the expected observations of Mrs. Crucifix were prevented by a sudden shriek; and a red-haired serving lass, rushing into the room, fell head foremost on the ground, apparently in a paroxysm of terror. The barking of the dog, and the exclamation of the Corporal without, concurred in announcing something extraordinary, and probably alarming.

Rising hastily from their seats, the two confabulators threw their cloaks over their heads, and ventured to undo the front door, which commanded the Mere.

The moon was up, but the evening mist on the lake was so thick, and the night gloom so far advanced, that it was with an indistinctness, more fear-exciting than any defined object, however, terrifying its nature, that the gazers beheld a tall upright figure gliding, as it seemed, along the surface of the lake with great rapidity. As well as it could be discerned, the figure, on arriving at the extreme end of the Mere, took to the land, and disappeared in the direction of farmer Spencer's cottage.

"My child! my child!" exclaimed the terrified mother: all her fears rising into certainties on seeing, as she doubted not she did, the spirit of the drowned Tylson, the predicted spouse of her daughter. "Good god! what will become of her!"

"Never fear, never fear," cried her almost equally alarmed friend, "the Corporal shall run down and take Jem Thatcher; I'll warrant them a match for ten Tylsons, dead or alive."

"That we are any day," shouted the Corporal, and [295] bracing his regimental sword on, and handing down the blunderbuss for Thatcher, the distressed mother, who could not be prevailed on to remain behind, sallied forth attended by her two squires.

In a few minutes, but which to the anxious mind of the mother seemed a long duration, the party stood at the door of farmer Spencer's cottage. The door was fastened; they knocked, but no answer was given; there was not light emitted from the windows.

"Stay," said the Corporal, "let us peep in upon them." And he looked in at the window, in which his companions joined him.

There was no candle in the kitchen; the only light was that of the pale moon-beam peering in through the opposite window. In the dimmest corner of the apartment stood a white and shadowy figure. Its ill defined outline seemed to sink into the gloom of the place, of which it was the sole inhabitant.

"Heaven by merciful!" said the farmer's wife, as she shrunk back in terror from the sight: "my poor Mary, my child, what has befallen her?" And she wrung her hands in distress and perplexity.

"Better go to the back door," said Corporal Crucifix, "and take them in the rear." And he led the way, going round by the stables, where the Corporal, under the direction of Mistress Spencer, struck a light and possessed himself of the horn lantern. He whistled after him two misanthropical curs, who swore heartily at the interruption of their slumbers.

Nothing obstructed their progress. As they passed the door of the chamber in which old Made, the invalid, lay, the mistress went in, with a faint hope of finding her daughter there. But the only voice that responded to her queries was that of Madge. When her mistress, however, who put much faith in Madge's sagacity, had in a few hurried words hinted at the cause of alarm, Madge's rheumatism could not hinder her from joining the hue and cry. "She had once seen a ghost," she said, "and was a better Christian than to fear a hundred." In two minutes she had huddled on her clothes, and with uneven steps followed the party in their descent on the enemy's land.

Beneath the kitchen door gleamed some rays of light. The Corporal, with a hand and heart a shade less steady than usual, laid hold on the latch. It sprung up, and the door yielded. They entered cautiously by the light of the half-clouded moon, and the penurious gleam of the Corporal's lantern. In the spot where the unearthly figure had stood nothing was seen. But against the door of the pantry, which opened on the far side of the room, leaned, apparently in a state of insensibility, Mary Spender. "One would not sure be frightful when one's dead," said the poet's Narcissa. Mary carried the principle farther, and would not be frightful in a swoon. She had fainted with a half suppressed smile on her sweet lips, and all the blood had not run to her heart, but blushed in roses, though lighter than usual, on her cheeks.

On the conviction, that the figure before her was her daughter, the farmer's wife sprung forward and caught her in her arms. She was easily brought to herself, and able to respond to her mother's eager inquiries.

She said, that, expecting her mother would be late, she had prepared her own supper, from which, only a few

PLATE: The Ghost Laid
Steel plate engraving; drawn by Philip Francis Stephanoff; engraved by Edward Portbury; printed by McQueen

[297] minutes before, she had been disturbed by a knocking at the back of the house. On going to discover its cause, she saw no one, and returned; when, on entering the kitchen, she found the light extinguished; and, looking around her, perceived a white and dim figure—tall, with its face covered, creeping across the floor. She rushed towards the front door, but, palsied by fear, had sunk against the pantry, senseless.

Every thing coincided with this account. The table was spread; the quenched candle still emitted a curling stream of smoke; and a plate or two broken on the floor was natural enough.

Meanwhile one of the curs aforesaid had been attracted by something of a light hue appearing under the pantry door, and was barking and snapping at it most doggedly. One the cessation of Mary's story, the attention of the whole party was attracted to this quarter. The Corporal opened his mouth to encourage the dog; it remained to with horror, when from the pantry issued a tall figure in the sheeted habiliments of the grave.

The appearance of the vision was instantaneously effective. The mother, snatching her daughter in her arms, fell into a chair; the Corporal, falling over another, extinguished the lantern. The Thatcher was overthrown by the Corporal, and in his prostration discharged the blunderbuss, the contents of which lodged in a beautiful pickled ham, which was then partially smoked. As for old Madge, she stood rooted at the top of the steps, like a Dutch image.

When the alarm had somewhat subsided, the cause of it had disappeared. As the front door was found un- [298] barred, it might have been thought, that the ghost had chosen this mortal mode of exit, had not old Madge protested, that, as she lived, she saw it vanish through the fireplace, which, she said, showed a slovenly, dirty disposition, as it was dressed in white garments.

But the most awful thing of all was, that, in the moment of confusion, the ghost had approached Mary and placed a ring on her finger, the fatal marriage finger. The mother had nearly gone distraught.

When the farmer returned home next day, he could make nothing of it; but, like his wife, was frightened, though he endeavoured to conceal it. The only one who seemed indifferent to it was Mary.

The story spread like wildfire. All Mary's suitor's gave up their pretensions *en masse*, being unwilling to rival the devil, and the poor girl seemed in a fair way for leading apes in the other world.

Time passed on, when, one evening, as dame Spencer was standing at the open door of the cottage, she saw advancing towards her the identical gipsy, who had prophesied such evil. Whatever she might be as a soothsayer, it seemed she was an indifferent merchant, for the farmer's wife would have sworn, that she carried the very same tin pans and kettles, that she travelled with six weeks before. She brought her in, and spread the table with mighty food.

"Be quiet," said the gipsy, as the farmer's wife was about to speak. "I know all you would say—all that has happened."

"But, good mother, can the ill be cured?"

"It can: give me your daughter's ring and a night's [299] lodging; the being you have seen shall give up your daughter to a mortal husband, ay, and a young and a gentle."

The dame joyfully acquiesced, but waited for her husband's sanction. He came in presently, and at once concurred: being, as he said, "weary and *fashed* with this senseless ghost."

The gipsy took Mary aside, examined the marks of her palms, and studied her countenance. She made many inquiries in a low tone and eager manner, and concluded by drawing from her finger the fatal ring.

As night advanced she was ushered into a small spare room, destined for her accommodation. When the door was closed upon her, a great talk took place between Spencer and his wife, as to the probable result of the gipsy's labours. Their daughter joined little in the conversation; she was melancholy and low-spirited. At length the whole household retired to rest, in earnest anticipation of the morning.

When the morning came, neither the gipsy nor Mary Spencer was to be found. The house was searched; the village was searched; all work and occupation was suspended; the wise and the foolish alike gathering together into those small knots, into which light particles naturally gather. Not a few stood on the banks of the Mere, poring into the waters with some expectation of seeing Mr. and Mrs. Tylson in the shape of the ghost and the late Mary Spencer.

The day passed, but neither ghost, gipsy, nor daughter came. The small knots broke up, formed fresh knots, and finally dispersed; some to the sign of the "Gray [300] Barb," and some to their respective dwellings, where the case was again and again argued over.

Twelve o'clock.——The disconsolate parents were still sitting in their kitchen, for they had no heart to go to bed. A knock at the door; another, and another.

"Open the door, Benjamin," said his wife.

"What can any one want here at this time?" muttered he, rising as he spoke. A faint glimpse of hope came over him. He opened the door, and caught his daughter in his arms. "But who the devil is this?" said he, as he gave up his daughter to her mother.

"A witch, a ghost, or a son-in-law, at your service," replied a voice.

"Watt!" Watt Markham!" The father's brown darkened, then cleared up. "Come in; thou art a bit of a devil, but better than a ghost, after all!"

There are several things unexplained in this story for want of room; as who the witch was, the ghost, and so forth: how the ghost came to sup with Mary Spencer, and so on. If any one is so dull as to require all this telling,

I am very sorry for it, but cannot help it.——

Literary Annual
The Keepsake for MDCCCXXIX. Ed. Frederic Mansel Reynolds. London: Hurst, Chance, and Co., and R. Jennings, 1829. Printer: Thomas Davison, Whitefriars.

Title
By the Author of Waverley. [Scott, Sir Walter.] "My Aunt Margaret's Mirror." KS 1829. 1-44. [1]

MY AUNT MARGARET'S MIRROR.[2]
BY THE AUTHOR OF WAVERLEY.
"There are times
When Fancy plays her gambols, in despite
Even of our watchful senses—when in sooth
Substance seems shadow, shadow substance seems—
When the broad, palpable, and mark'd partition
'Twixt that which is and is not seems dissolved,
As if the mental eye gain'd power to gaze
Beyond the limits of the existing world.
Such hours of shadowy dreams I better love
Than all the gross realities of life."

ANONYMOUS.

My Aunt Margaret was one of that respected sisterhood upon whom devolve all the trouble and solicitude incidental to the possession of children, excepting only that which attends their entrance into the world. We were a large family, of very different dispositions and constitutions. Some were dull and peevish—they were sent to Aunt Margaret to be amused; some were rude, romping, and boisterous—they were sent to Aunt Margaret to be kept quiet, or rather that their noise might be removed out of hearing; those who were indisposed were sent with the prospect of being nursed; those who were stubborn, with the hope of their being subdued by the kindness of Aunt Margaret's discipline;—in short, she had all the various duties of a mother, without the credit and dignity of the maternal [2] character. The busy scene of her various cares is now over. Of the invalids and the robust, the kind and the rough, the peevish and pleased children, who thronged her little parlour from morning to night, not one now remains alive but myself, who, afflicted by early infirmity, was one of the most delicate of her nurslings, yet, nevertheless, have outlived them all.

It is still my custom, and shall be so while I have the use of my limbs, to visit my respected relation at least three times a week. Her abode is about half a

---

2 Plain text for this transcription was obtained from Project Gutenberg <http://www.gutenberg.org/ebooks/1667> and then compared against the original volume. For full citation, see References.

mile from the suburbs of the town in which I reside, and is accessible, not only by the highroad, from which it stands at some distance, but by means of a greensward footpath leading through some pretty meadows. I have so little left to torment me in life, that it is one of my greatest vexations to know that several of these sequestered fields have been devoted as sites for building. In that which is nearest the town, wheelbarrows have been at work for several weeks in such numbers, that, I verily believe, its whole surface, to the depth of at least eighteen inches, was mounted in these monotrochs at the same moment, and in the act of being transported from one place to another. Huge triangular piles of planks are also reared in different parts of the devoted messuage; and a little group of trees that still grace the eastern end, which rises in a gentle ascent, have just received warning to quit, expressed by a daub of white paint, and are to give place to a curious grove of chimneys.

It would, perhaps, hurt others in my situation to reflect that this little range of pasturage once belonged to my father (whose family was of some consideration in the world), and was sold by patches to remedy distresses in [3] which he involved himself in an attempt by commercial adventure to redeem his diminished fortune. While the building scheme was in full operation, this circumstance was often pointed out to me by the class of friends who are anxious that no part of your misfortunes should escape your observation. "Such pasture-ground! — lying at the very town's end — in turnips and potatoes, the parks would bring £20 per acre; and if leased for building — oh, it was a gold mine! And all sold for an old song out of the ancient possessor's hands!" My comforters cannot bring me to repine much on this subject. If I could be allowed to look back on the past without interruption, I could willingly give up the enjoyment of present income and the hope of future profit to those who have purchased what my father sold. I regret the alteration of the ground only because it destroys associations, and I would more willingly (I think) see the Earl's Closes in the hands of strangers, retaining their sylvan appearance, than know them for my own, if torn up by agriculture, or covered with buildings. Mine are the sensations of poor Logan: —
"The horrid plough has razed the green
          Where yet a child I strayed;
     The axe has fell'd the hawthorn screen,
         The schoolboy's summer shade."

I hope, however, the threatened devastation will not be consummated in my day. Although the adventurous spirit of times short while since passed gave rise to the undertaking, I have been encouraged to think that the subsequent changes have so far damped the spirit of speculation that the rest of the woodland footpath leading to Aunt Margaret's retreat will be left undisturbed for her time and mine. I am interested in this, for every step of [4] the way, after I have passed through the green already mentioned, has for me something of early remembrance:—There is the stile at which I can recollect a cross child's-maid upbraiding me with my infirmity as she lifted me coarsely and carelessly over the flinty steps, which my brothers traversed with shout and bound. I remember the suppressed bitterness of the moment, and, conscious of my own inferiority, the feeling of envy with which I regarded the easy movements and elastic steps of my more happily formed brethren. Alas! these goodly barks have all perished on life's wide ocean, and only that which seemed so little seaworthy, as the naval phrase goes, has reached the port when the tempest is over. Then there is the pool, where, manoeuvring our little navy, constructed out of the broad water-flags, my elder brother fell in, and was scarce saved from the watery element to die under Nelson's banner. There is the hazel copse also, in which my brother Henry used to gather nuts, thinking little that he was to die in an Indian jungle in quest of rupees.

There is so much more of remembrance about the little walk, that—as I stop, rest on my crutch-headed cane, and look round with that species of comparison between the thing I was and that which I now am—it almost induces me to doubt my own identity; until I find myself in face of the honeysuckle porch of Aunt Margaret's dwelling, with its irregularity of front, and its odd, projecting latticed windows, where the workmen seem to have made it a study that no one of them should resemble another in form, size, or in the old-fashioned stone entablature and labels which adorn them. This tenement, once the manor house of the Earl's Closes, we still retain a slight hold upon; for, in some family arrangements, it had been [5] settled upon Aunt Margaret during the term of her life. Upon this frail tenure depends, in a great measure, the last shadow of the family of Bothwell of Earl's Closes, and their last slight connection with their paternal inheritance. The only representative will then be an infirm old man, moving not unwillingly to the grave, which has devoured all that were dear to his affections.

When I have indulged such thoughts for a minute or two, I enter the mansion, which is said to have been the gate-house only of the original building, and find one being on whom time seems to have made little impression; for the Aunt Margaret of to-day bears the same proportional age to the Aunt Margaret of my early youth that the boy of ten years old does to the man of (by'r Lady!) some fifty-six years. The old lady's invariable costume has doubtless some share in confirming one in the opinion that time has stood still with Aunt Margaret.

The brown or chocolate-coloured silk gown, with ruffles of the same stuff at the elbow, within which are others of Mechlin lace; the black silk gloves, or mitts; the white hair combed back upon a roll; and the cap of spotless cambric, which closes around the venerable countenance—as they were not the costume of 1780, so neither were they that of 1826; they are altogether a style peculiar to the individual Aunt Margaret. There she still sits, as she sat thirty years since, with her wheel or the stocking, which she works by the fire in winter and by the window in summer; or, perhaps, venturing as far as the porch in an unusually fine summer evening. Her frame, like some well-constructed piece of mechanics, still performs the operations for which it had seemed destined—going its round with an activity [6] which is gradually diminished, yet indicating no probability that it will soon come to a period.

The solicitude and affection which had made Aunt Margaret the willing slave to the inflictions of a whole nursery, have now for their object the health and comfort of one old and infirm man—the last remaining relative of her family, and the only one who can still find interest in the traditional stores which she hoards, as some miser hides the gold which he desires that no one should enjoy after his death.

My conversation with Aunt Margaret generally relates little either to the present or to the future. For the passing day we possess as much as we require, and we neither of us wish for more; and for that which is to follow, we have, on this side of the grave, neither hopes, nor fears, nor anxiety. We therefore naturally look back to the past, and forget the present fallen fortunes and declined importance of our family in recalling the hours when it was wealthy and prosperous.

With this slight introduction, the reader will know as much of Aunt Margaret and her nephew as is necessary to comprehend the following conversation and narrative.

Last week, when, late in a summer evening, I went to call on the old lady to whom my reader is now introduced, I was received by her with all her usual affection and benignity, while, at the same time, she seemed abstracted and disposed to silence. I asked her the reason. "They have been clearing out the old chapel," she said; "John Clayhudgeons having, it seems, discovered that the stuff within—being, I suppose, the remains of our ancestors—was excellent for top-dressing the meadows." [7]

Here I started up with more alacrity than I have displayed for some years; but sat down while my aunt added, laying her hand upon my sleeve, "The chapel has been long considered as common ground, my dear, and used for a pinfold, and what objection can we have to the man for employing what is his own to his own profit? Besides, I did speak to him, and he very readily and civilly promised that if he found bones or monuments, they should be carefully respected and reinstated; and what more could I ask? So, the first stone they found bore the name of Margaret Bothwell, 1585, and I have caused it to be laid carefully aside, as I think it betokens death, and having served my namesake two hundred years, it has just been cast up in time to do me the same good turn. My house has been long put in order, as far as the small earthly concerns require it; but who shall say that their account with, Heaven is sufficiently revised?"

"After what you have said, aunt," I replied, "perhaps I ought to take my hat and go away; and so I should, but that there is on this occasion a little alloy mingled with your devotion. To think of death at all times is a duty—to suppose it nearer from the finding an old gravestone is superstition; and you, with your strong, useful common sense, which was so long the prop of a fallen family, are the last person whom I should have suspected of such weakness."

"Neither would I deserve your suspicions, kinsman," answered Aunt Margaret, "if we were speaking of any incident occurring in the actual business of human life. But for all this, I have a sense of superstition about me, which I do not wish to part with. It is a feeling which [8] separates me from this age, and links me with that to which I am hastening; and even when it seems, as now, to lead me to the brink of the grave, and bid me gaze on it, I do not love that it should be dispelled. It soothes my imagination, without influencing my reason or conduct."

"I profess, my good lady," replied I, "that had any one but you made such a declaration, I should have thought it as capricious as that of the clergyman, who, without vindicating his false reading, preferred, from habit's sake, his old Mumpsimus to the modern Sumpsimus."

"Well," answered my aunt, "I must explain my inconsistency in this particular by comparing it to another. I am, as you know, a piece of that old-fashioned thing called a Jacobite; but I am so in sentiment and feeling only, for a more loyal subject never joined in prayers for the health and wealth of George the Fourth, whom God long preserve! But I dare say that kind-hearted sovereign would not deem that an old woman did him much injury if she leaned back in her arm-chair, just in such a twilight as this, and thought of the high-mettled men whose sense of duty called them to arms against his grandfather; and how, in a cause which they deemed that of their rightful prince and country,

'They fought till their hand to the broadsword was glued,
They fought against fortune with hearts unsubdued.'

Do not come at such a moment, when my head is full of plaids, pibrochs, and claymores, and ask my reason to admit what, I am afraid, it cannot deny—I mean, that the public advantage peremptorily demanded that these things should cease to exist. I cannot, indeed, refuse to allow the justice of your reasoning; but yet, being con- [9] vinced against my will, you will gain little by your motion. You might as well read to an infatuated lover the catalogue of his mistress's imperfections; for when he has been compelled to listen to the summary, you will only get for answer that 'he lo'es her a' the better.'"

I was not sorry to have changed the gloomy train of Aunt Margaret's thoughts, and replied in the same tone, "Well, I can't help being persuaded that our good King is the more sure of Mrs. Bothwell's loyal affection, that he has the Stewart right of birth as well as the Act of Succession in his favour."

"Perhaps my attachment, were its source of consequence, might be found warmer for the union of the rights you mention," said Aunt Margaret; "but, upon my word, it would be as sincere if the King's right were founded only on the will of the nation, as declared at the Revolution. I am none of your *jure divino* folks."

"And a Jacobite notwithstanding."

"And a Jacobite notwithstanding—or rather, I will give you leave to call me one of the party which, in Queen Anne's time, were called, *Whimsicals*; because they were sometimes operated upon by feelings, sometimes by principle. After all, it is very hard that you will not allow an old woman to be as inconsistent in her political sentiments as mankind in general show themselves in all the various courses of life; since you cannot point out one of them in which the passions and prejudices of those who pursue it are not perpetually carrying us away from the path which our reason points out."

"True, aunt; but you are a wilful wanderer, who should be forced back into the right path."

"Spare me, I entreat you," replied Aunt Margaret. [10] "You remember the Gaelic song, though I dare say I mispronounce the words—

'Hatil mohatil, na dowski mi.'

'I am asleep, do not waken me.'

I tell you, kinsman, that the sort of waking dreams which my imagination spins out, in what your favourite Wordsworth calls 'moods of my own mind,' are worth all the rest of my more active days. Then, instead of looking forwards, as I did in youth, and forming for myself fairy palaces, upon the verge of the grave I turn my eyes backward upon the days and manners of my better time; and the sad, yet soothing recollections come so close and interesting, that I almost think it sacrilege to be wiser or more rational or less prejudiced than those to whom I looked up in my younger years."

"I think I now understand what you mean," I answered, "and can comprehend why you should occasionally prefer the twilight of illusion to the steady light of reason."

"Where there is no task," she rejoined, "to be performed, we may sit in the dark if we like it; if we go to work, we must ring for candles."

"And amidst such shadowy and doubtful light," continued I, "imagination frames her enchanted and enchanting visions, and sometimes passes them upon the senses for reality."

"Yes," said Aunt Margaret, who is a well-read woman, "to those who resemble the translator of Tasso,—

'Prevailing poet, whose undoubting mind
Believed the magic wonders which he sung.'

It is not required for this purpose that you should be [11] sensible of the painful horrors which an actual belief in such prodigies inflicts. Such a belief nowadays belongs only to fools and children. It is not necessary that your ears should tingle and your complexion change, like that of Theodore at the approach of the spectral huntsman. All that is indispensable for the enjoyment of the milder feeling of supernatural awe is, that you should be susceptible of the slight shuddering which creeps over you when you hear a tale of terror—that well-vouched tale which the narrator, having first expressed his general disbelief of all such legendary lore, selects and produces, as having something in it which he has been always obliged to give up as inexplicable. Another symptom is a momentary hesitation to look round you, when the interest of the narrative is at the highest; and the third, a desire to avoid looking into a mirror when you are alone in your chamber for the evening. I mean such are signs which indicate the crisis, when a female imagination is in due temperature to enjoy a ghost story. I do not pretend to describe those which express the same disposition in a gentleman."

"That last symptom, dear aunt, of shunning the mirror seems likely to be a rare occurrence amongst the fair sex."

"You are a novice in toilet fashions, my dear cousin. All women consult the looking-glass with anxiety before they go into company; but when they return home, the mirror has not the same charm. The die has been cast—the party has been successful or unsuccessful in the impression which she desired to make. But, without going deeper into the mysteries of the dressing-table, I will tell [12] you that I myself, like many other honest folks, do not like to see the blank, black front of a large mirror in a room dimly lighted, and where the reflection of the candle seems rather to lose itself in the deep obscurity of the glass than to be reflected back again into the apartment, That space of inky darkness seems to be a field for Fancy to play her revels in. She may call up other features to meet us, instead of the reflection of our own; or, as in the spells of Hallowe'en, which we learned in childhood, some unknown form may be seen peeping over our shoulder. In short, when I am in a ghost-seeing humour, I make my handmaiden draw the green curtains over the mirror before I go into the room, so that she may have the first shock of the apparition, if there be any to be seen, But, to tell you the truth, this dislike to look into a mirror in particular times and places has, I believe, its original foundation in a story which came to me by tradition from my grandmother, who was a party concerned in the scene of which I will now tell you."

THE MIRROR.

CHAPTER I.

You are fond (said my aunt) of sketches of the society which has passed away. I wish I could describe to you Sir Philip Forester, the "chartered libertine" of Scottish good company, about the end of the last century. I never saw him indeed; but my mother's traditions were full of his wit, gallantry, and dissipation. This gay knight flourished about the end of the seventeenth and beginning of [13] the eighteenth century. He was the Sir Charles Easy and the Lovelace of his day and country—renowned for the number of duels he had fought, and the successful intrigues which he had carried on. The supremacy which he had attained in the fashionable world was absolute; and when we combine it with one or two anecdotes, for which, "if laws were made for every degree," he ought certainly to have been hanged, the popularity of such a person really serves to show, either that the present times are much more decent, if not more virtuous, than they formerly were, or that high-breeding then was of more difficult attainment than that which is now so called, and consequently entitled the successful professor to a proportional degree of plenary indulgences and privileges. No beau of this day could have borne out so ugly a story as that of Pretty Peggy Grindstone, the miller's daughter at Sillermills—it had well-nigh made work for the Lord Advocate. But it hurt Sir Philip Forester no more than the hail hurts the hearthstone. He was as well received in society as ever, and dined with the Duke of A—— the day the poor girl was buried. She died of heartbreak. But that has nothing to do with my story.

Now, you must listen to a single word upon kith, kin, and ally; I promise you I will not be prolix. But it is necessary to the authenticity of my legend that you should know that Sir Philip Forester, with his handsome person, elegant accomplishments, and fashionable manners, married the younger Miss Falconer of King's Copland. The elder sister of this lady had previously become the wife of my grandfather, Sir Geoffrey Bothwell, and brought into our family a good fortune. Miss Jemima, or Miss Jemmie [14] Falconer, as she was usually called, had also about ten thousand pounds sterling—then thought a very handsome portion indeed.

The two sisters were extremely different, though each had their admirers while they remained single. Lady Bothwell had some touch of the old King's Copland blood about her. She was bold, though not to the degree of audacity, ambitious, and desirous to raise her house and family; and was, as has been said, a considerable spur to my grandfather, who was otherwise an indolent man, but whom, unless he has been slandered, his lady's influence involved in some political matters which had been more wisely let alone. She was a woman of high principle, however, and masculine good sense, as some of her letters testify, which are still in my wainscot cabinet.

Jemmie Falconer was the reverse of her sister in every respect. Her understanding did not reach above the ordinary pitch, if, indeed, she could be said to have attained it. Her beauty, while it lasted, consisted, in a great measure, of delicacy of complexion and regularity of features, without any peculiar force of expression. Even these charms faded under the sufferings attendant on an ill-assorted match. She was passionately attached to her husband, by whom she was treated with a callous yet polite indifference, which, to one whose heart was as tender as her judgment was weak, was more painful perhaps than absolute ill-usage. Sir Philip was a voluptuary—that is, a completely selfish egotist—whose disposition and character resembled the rapier he wore, polished, keen, and brilliant, but inflexible and unpitying. As he observed carefully all the usual forms towards his lady, he had the art to deprive her [15] even of the compassion of the world; and useless and unavailing as that may be while actually possessed by the sufferer, it is, to a mind like Lady Forester's, most painful to know she has it not.

The tattle of society did its best to place the peccant husband above the suffering wife. Some called her a poor, spiritless thing, and declared that, with a little of her sister's spirit, she might have brought to reason any Sir Philip whatsoever, were it the termagant Falconbridge himself. But the greater part of their acquaintance affected candour, and saw faults on both sides—though, in fact, there only existed the oppressor and the oppressed. The tone of such critics was, "To be sure, no one will justify Sir Philip Forester, but then we all know Sir Philip, and Jemmie Falconer might have known what she had to expect from the beginning. What made her set her cap at Sir Philip? He would never have looked at her if she had not thrown herself at his head, with her poor ten thousand pounds. I am sure, if it is money he wanted, she spoiled his market. I know where Sir Philip could have done much better. And then, if she *would* have the man, could not she try to make him more comfortable at home, and have his friends oftener, and not plague him with the squalling children, and take care all was handsome and in good style about the house? I declare I think Sir Philip would have made a very domestic man, with a woman who knew how to manage him."

Now these fair critics, in raising their profound edifice of domestic felicity, did not recollect that the corner-stone was wanting, and that to receive good company with good cheer, the means of the banquet ought to have been furnished by Sir Philip, whose income (dilapidated as it was)[16] was not equal to the display of the hospitality required, and at the same time to the supply of the good knight's *menus plaisirs*. So, in spite of all that was so sagely suggested by female friends, Sir Philip carried his good-humour everywhere abroad, and left at home a solitary mansion and a pining spouse.

At length, inconvenienced in his money affairs, and tired even of the short time which he spent in his own dull house, Sir Philip Forester determined to take a trip to the Continent, in the capacity of a volunteer. It was then common for men of fashion to do so; and our knight perhaps was of opinion that a touch of the military character, just enough to exalt, but not render pedantic, his qualities as a *beau garçon*, was necessary to maintain possession of the elevated situation which he held in the ranks of fashion.

Sir Philip's resolution threw his wife into agonies of terror; by which the worthy baronet was so much annoyed, that, contrary to his wont, he took some trouble to soothe her apprehensions, and once more brought her to shed tears, in which sorrow was not altogether unmingled with pleasure. Lady Bothwell asked, as a favour, Sir Philip's permission to receive her sister and her family into her own house during his absence on the Continent. Sir Philip readily assented to a proposition which saved expense, silenced the foolish people who might have talked of a deserted wife and family, and gratified Lady Bothwell, for whom he felt some respect, as for one who often spoke to him, always with freedom and sometimes with severity, without being deterred either by his raillery or the *prestige* of his reputation.

A day or two before Sir Philip's departure, Lady Both- [17] well took the liberty of asking him, in her sister's presence, the direct question, which his timid wife had often desired, but never ventured, to put to him:—

"Pray, Sir Philip, what route do you take when you reach the Continent?"

"I go from Leith to Helvoet by a packet with advices."

"That I comprehend perfectly," said Lady Bothwell dryly; "but you do not mean to remain long at Helvoet, I presume, and I should like to know what is your next object."

"You ask me, my dear lady," answered Sir Philip, "a question which I have not dared to ask myself. The answer depends on the fate of war. I shall, of course, go to headquarters, wherever they may happen to be for the time; deliver my letters of introduction; learn as much of the noble art of war as may suffice a poor interloping amateur; and then take a glance at the sort of thing of which we read so much in the Gazette."

"And I trust, Sir Philip," said Lady Bothwell, "that you will remember that you are a husband and a father; and that, though you think fit to indulge this military fancy, you will not let it hurry you into dangers which it is certainly unnecessary for any save professional persons to encounter."

"Lady Bothwell does me too much honour," replied the adventurous knight, "in regarding such a circumstance with the slightest interest. But to soothe your flattering anxiety, I trust your ladyship will recollect that I cannot expose to hazard the venerable and paternal character which you so obligingly recommend to my protection, without putting in some peril an honest fellow, called Philip Forester, with whom I have kept company for [18] thirty years, and with whom, though some folks consider him a coxcomb, I have not the least desire to part."

"Well, Sir Philip, you are the best judge of your own affairs. I have little right to interfere—you are not my husband."

"God forbid!" said Sir Philip hastily; instantly adding, however, "God forbid that I should deprive my friend Sir Geoffrey of so inestimable a treasure."

"But you are my sister's husband," replied the lady; "and I suppose you are aware of her present distress of mind—"

"If hearing of nothing else from morning to night can make me aware of it," said Sir Philip, "I should know something of the matter."

"I do not pretend to reply to your wit, Sir Philip," answered Lady Bothwell; "but you must be sensible that all this distress is on account of apprehensions for your personal safety."

"In that case, I am surprised that Lady Bothwell, at least, should give herself so much trouble upon so insignificant a subject."

"My sister's interest may account for my being anxious to learn something of Sir Philip Forester's motions; about which, otherwise, I know he would not wish me to concern myself. I have a brother's safety too to be anxious for."

"You mean Major Falconer, your brother by the mother's side? What can he possibly have to do with our present agreeable conversation?"

"You have had words together, Sir Philip," said Lady Bothwell.

"Naturally; we are connections," replied Sir Philip, "and as such have always had the usual intercourse." [19]

"That is an evasion of the subject," answered the lady. "By words, I mean angry words, on the subject of your usage of your wife."

"If," replied Sir Philip Forester, "you suppose Major Falconer simple enough to intrude his advice upon me, Lady Bothwell, in my domestic matters, you are indeed warranted in believing that I might possibly be so far displeased with the interference as to request him to reserve his advice till it was asked."

"And being on these terms, you are going to join the very army in which my brother Falconer is now serving?"

"No man knows the path of honour better than Major Falconer," said Sir Philip. "An aspirant after fame, like me, cannot choose a better guide than his footsteps."

Lady Bothwell rose and went to the window, the tears gushing from her eyes.

"And this heartless raillery," she said, "is all the consideration that is to be given to our apprehensions of a quarrel which may bring on the most terrible consequences? Good God! of what can men's hearts be made, who can thus dally with the agony of others?"

Sir Philip Forester was moved; he laid aside the mocking tone in which he had hitherto spoken.

"Dear Lady Bothwell," he said, taking her reluctant hand, "we are both wrong. You are too deeply serious; I, perhaps, too little so. The dispute I had with Major Falconer was of no earthly consequence. Had anything occurred betwixt us that ought to have been settled *par voie du fait* , as we say in France, neither of us are persons that are likely to postpone such a meeting. Permit me to say, that were it generally known that you or my Lady Fo- [20] rester are apprehensive of such a catastrophe, it might be the very means of bringing about what would not otherwise be likely to happen. I know your good sense, Lady Bothwell, and that you will understand me when I say that really my affairs require my absence for some months. This Jemima cannot understand. It is a perpetual recurrence of questions, why can you not do this, or that, or the third thing? and, when you have proved to her that her expedients are totally ineffectual, you have just to begin the whole round again. Now, do you tell her, dear Lady Bothwell, that *you* are satisfied. She is, you must confess, one of those persons with whom authority goes farther than reasoning. Do but repose a little confidence in me, and you shall see how amply I will repay it."

Lady Bothwell shook her head, as one but half satisfied. "How difficult it is to extend confidence, when the basis on which it ought to rest has been so much shaken! But I will do my best to make Jemima easy; and further, I can only say that for keeping your present purpose I hold you responsible both to God and man."

"Do not fear that I will deceive you," said Sir Philip. "The safest conveyance to me will be through the general post-office, Helvoetsluys, where I will take care to leave orders for forwarding my letters. As for Falconer, our only encounter will be over a bottle of Burgundy; so make yourself perfectly easy on his score."

Lady Bothwell could *not* make herself easy; yet she was sensible that her sister hurt her own cause by *taking on*, as the maidservants call it, too vehemently, and by showing before every stranger, by manner, and sometimes by words also, a dissatisfaction with her husband's journey, that was [21] sure to come to his ears, and equally certain to displease him. But there was no help for this domestic dissension, which ended only with the day of separation.

I am sorry I cannot tell, with precision, the year in which Sir Philip Forester went over to Flanders; but it was one of those in which the campaign opened with extraordinary fury, and many bloody, though indecisive, skirmishes were fought between the French on the one side and the Allies on the other. In all our modern improvements, there are none, perhaps, greater than in the accuracy and speed with which intelligence is transmitted from any scene of action to those in this country whom it may concern. During Marlborough's campaigns, the sufferings of the many who had relations in, or along with, the army were greatly augmented by the suspense in which they were detained for weeks after they had heard of bloody battles, in which, in all probability, those for whom their bosoms throbbed with anxiety had been personally engaged. Amongst those who were most agonized by this state of uncertainty was the—I had almost said deserted—wife of the gay Sir Philip Forester. A single letter had informed her of his arrival on the Continent; no others were received. One notice occurred in the newspapers, in which Volunteer Sir Philip Forester was mentioned as having been entrusted with a dangerous reconnaissance, which he had executed with the greatest courage, dexterity, and intelligence, and received the thanks of the commanding officer. The sense of his having acquired distinction brought a momentary glow into the lady's pale cheek; but it was instantly lost in ashen whiteness at the recollection of his danger. After this, they had no news whatever, neither from Sir Philip, nor even from their [22] brother Falconer. The case of Lady Forester was not indeed different from that of hundreds in the same situation; but a feeble mind is necessarily an irritable one, and the suspense which some bear with constitutional indifference or philosophical resignation, and some with a disposition to believe and hope the best, was intolerable to Lady Forester, at once solitary and sensitive, low-spirited, and devoid of strength of mind, whether natural or acquired.

CHAPTER II.

As she received no further news of Sir Philip, whether directly or indirectly, his unfortunate lady began now to feel a sort of consolation even in those careless habits which had so often given her pain. "He is so thoughtless," she repeated a hundred times a day to her sister, "he never writes when things are going on smoothly. It is his way. Had anything happened, he would have informed us."

Lady Bothwell listened to her sister without attempting to console her. Probably she might be of opinion that even the worst intelligence which could be received from Flanders might not be without some touch of consolation; and that the Dowager Lady Forester, if so she was doomed to be called, might have a source of happiness unknown to the wife of the gayest and finest gentleman in Scotland. This conviction became stronger as they learned from inquiries made at headquarters that Sir Philip was no longer with the army—though whether he had been taken or slain in some of those skirmishes which were perpetually occurring, and in which he loved to distinguish himself, or whether he had, for some unknown reason or capricious [23] change of mind, voluntarily left the service, none of his countrymen in the camp of the Allies could form even a conjecture. Meantime his creditors at home became clamorous, entered into possession of his property, and threatened his person, should he be rash enough to return to Scotland. These additional disadvantages aggravated Lady Bothwell's displeasure against the fugitive husband; while her sister saw nothing in any of them, save what tended to increase her grief for the absence of him whom her imagination now represented—as it had before marriage—gallant, gay, and affectionate.

About this period there appeared in Edinburgh a man of singular appearance and pretensions. He was commonly called the Paduan Doctor, from having received his education at that famous university. He was supposed to possess some rare receipts in medicine, with which, it was affirmed, he had wrought remarkable cures. But though, on the one hand, the physicians of Edinburgh termed him an empiric, there were many persons, and among them some of the clergy, who, while they admitted the truth of the cures and the force of his remedies, alleged that Doctor Baptista Damiotti made use of charms and unlawful arts in order to obtain success in his practice. The resorting to him was even solemnly preached against, as a seeking of health from idols, and a trusting to the help which was to come from Egypt. But the protection which the Paduan Doctor received from some friends of interest and consequence enabled him to set these imputations at defiance, and to assume, even in the city of Edinburgh, famed as it was for abhorrence of witches and necromancers, the dangerous character of an expounder of futurity. It was at length rumoured that, for a certain [24] gratification, which of course was not an inconsiderable one, Doctor Baptista Damiotti could tell the fate of the absent, and even show his visitors the personal form of their absent friends, and the action in which they were engaged at the moment. This rumour came to the ears of Lady Forester, who had reached that pitch of mental agony in which the sufferer will do anything, or endure anything, that suspense may be converted into certainty.

Gentle and timid in most cases, her state of mind made her equally obstinate and reckless, and it was with no small surprise and alarm that her sister, Lady Bothwell, heard her express a resolution to visit this man of art, and learn from him the fate of her husband. Lady Bothwell remonstrated on the improbability that such pretensions as those of this foreigner could be founded in anything but imposture.

"I care not," said the deserted wife, "what degree of ridicule I may incur; if there be any one chance out of a hundred that I may obtain some certainty of my husband's fate, I would not miss that chance for whatever else the world can offer me."

Lady Bothwell next urged the unlawfulness of resorting to such sources of forbidden knowledge.

"Sister," replied the sufferer, "he who is dying of thirst cannot refrain from drinking even poisoned water. She who suffers under suspense must seek information, even were the powers which offer it unhallowed and infernal. I go to learn my fate alone, and this very evening will I know it; the sun that rises to-morrow shall find me, if not more happy, at least more resigned."

"Sister," said Lady Bothwell, "if you are determined upon this wild step, you shall not go alone. If this man [25] be an impostor, you may be too much agitated by your feelings to detect his villainy. If, which I cannot believe, there be any truth in what he pretends, you shall not be exposed alone to a communication of so extraordinary a nature. I will go with you, if indeed you determine to go. But yet reconsider your project, and renounce inquiries which cannot be prosecuted without guilt, and perhaps without danger."

Lady Forester threw herself into her sister's arms, and, clasping her to her bosom, thanked her a hundred times for the offer of her company, while she declined with a melancholy gesture the friendly advice with which it was accompanied.

When the hour of twilight arrived—which was the period when the Paduan Doctor was understood to receive the visits of those who came to consult with him—the two ladies left their apartments in the Canongate of Edinburgh, having their dress arranged like that of women of an inferior description, and their plaids disposed around their faces as they were worn by the same class; for in those days of aristocracy the quality of the wearer was generally indicated by the manner in which her plaid was disposed, as well as by the fineness of its texture. It was Lady Bothwell who had suggested this species of disguise, partly to avoid observation as they should go to the conjurer's house, and partly in order to make trial of his penetration, by appearing before him in a feigned character. Lady Forester's servant, of tried fidelity, had been employed by her to propitiate the Doctor by a suitable fee, and a story intimating that a soldier's wife desired to know the fate of her husband—a subject upon which, in all probability, the sage was very frequently consulted. [26]

To the last moment, when the palace clock struck eight, Lady Bothwell earnestly watched her sister, in hopes that she might retreat from her rash undertaking; but as mildness, and even timidity, is capable at times of vehement and fixed purposes, she found Lady Forester resolutely unmoved and determined when the moment of departure arrived. Ill satisfied with the expedition, but determined not to leave her sister at such a crisis, Lady Bothwell accompanied Lady Forester through more than one obscure street and lane, the servant walking before, and acting as their guide. At length he suddenly turned into a narrow court, and knocked at an arched door which seemed to belong to a building of some antiquity. It opened, though no one appeared to act as porter; and the servant, stepping aside from the entrance, motioned the ladies to enter. They had no sooner done so than it shut, and excluded their guide. The two ladies found themselves in a small vestibule, illuminated [27] by a dim lamp, and having, when the door was closed, no communication with the external light or air. The door of an inner apartment, partly open, was at the farther side of the vestibule.

"We must not hesitate now, Jemima," said Lady Bothwell, and walked forwards into the inner room, where, surrounded by books, maps, philosophical utensils, and other implements of peculiar shape and appearance, they found the man of art.

There was nothing very peculiar in the Italian's appearance. He had the dark complexion and marked features of his country, seemed about fifty years old, and was handsomely but plainly dressed in a full suit of black clothes, which was then the universal costume of the medical profession. Large wax-lights, in silver sconces, illuminated the apartment, which was reasonably furnished. He rose as the ladies entered, and, notwithstanding the inferiority of their dress, received them with the marked respect due to their quality, and which foreigners are usually punctilious in rendering to those to whom such honours are due.

Lady Bothwell endeavoured to maintain her proposed incognito, and, as the Doctor ushered them to the upper end of the room, made a motion declining his courtesy, as unfitted for their condition. "We are poor people, sir," she said; "only my sister's distress has brought us to consult your worship whether—"

He smiled as he interrupted her—"I am aware, madam, of your sister's distress, and its cause; I am aware, also, that I am honoured with a visit from two ladies of the highest consideration—Lady Bothwell and Lady Forester. If I could not distinguish them from the class of society which their present dress would indicate, there would be small possibility of my being able to gratify them by giving the information which they come to seek."

"I can easily understand—" said Lady Bothwell.

"Pardon my boldness to interrupt you, milady," cried the Italian; "your ladyship was about to say that you could easily understand that I had got possession of your names by means of your domestic. But in thinking so, you do injustice to the fidelity of your servant, and, I may add, to the skill of one who is also not less your humble servant—Baptista Damiotti."

"I have no intention to do either, sir," said Lady Bothwell, maintaining a tone of composure, though somewhat surprised; "but the situation is something new to me. If [28] you know who we are, you also know, sir, what brought us here."

"Curiosity to know the fate of a Scottish gentleman of rank, now, or lately, upon the Continent," answered the seer. "His name is Il Cavaliero Philippo Forester, a gentleman who has the honour to be husband to this lady, and, with your ladyship's permission for using plain language, the misfortune not to value as it deserves that inestimable advantage."

Lady Forester sighed deeply, and Lady Bothwell replied,—

"Since you know our object without our telling it, the only question that remains is, whether you have the power to relieve my sister's anxiety?"

"I have, madam," answered the Paduan scholar; "but there is still a previous inquiry. Have you the courage to behold with your own eyes what the Cavaliero Philippo Forester is now doing? or will you take it on my report?"

"That question my sister must answer for herself," said Lady Bothwell.

"With my own eyes will I endure to see whatever you have power to show me," said Lady Forester, with the same determined spirit which had stimulated her since her resolution was taken upon this subject.

"There may be danger in it."

"If gold can compensate the risk," said Lady Forester, taking out her purse.

"I do not such things for the purpose of gain," answered the foreigner; "I dare not turn my art to such a purpose. If I take the gold of the wealthy, it is but to bestow it on the poor; nor do I ever accept more than the sum I have [29] already received from your servant. Put up your purse, madam; an adept needs not your gold."

Lady Bothwell, considering this rejection of her sister's offer as a mere trick of an empiric, to induce her to press a larger sum upon him, and willing that the scene should be commenced and ended, offered some gold in turn, observing that it was only to enlarge the sphere of his charity.

"Let Lady Bothwell enlarge the sphere of her own charity," said the

Paduan, "not merely in giving of alms, in which I know she is not deficient, but in judging the character of others; and let her oblige Baptista Damiotti by believing him honest, till she shall discover him to be a knave. Do not be surprised, madam, if I speak in answer to your thoughts rather than your expressions; and tell me once more whether you have courage to look on what I am prepared to show?"

"I own, sir," said Lady Bothwell, "that your words strike me with some sense of fear; but whatever my sister desires to witness, I will not shrink from witnessing along with her."

"Nay, the danger only consists in the risk of your resolution failing you. The sight can only last for the space of seven minutes; and should you interrupt the vision by speaking a single word, not only would the charm be broken, but some danger might result to the spectators. But if you can remain steadily silent for the seven minutes, your curiosity will be gratified without the slightest risk; and for this I will engage my honour."

Internally Lady Bothwell thought the security was but an indifferent one; but she suppressed the suspicion, as if she had believed that the adept, whose dark features wore a half-formed smile, could in reality read even her most [30] secret reflections. A solemn pause then ensued, until Lady Forester gathered courage enough to reply to the physician, as he termed himself, that she would abide with firmness and silence the sight which he had promised to exhibit to them. Upon this, he made them a low obeisance, and saying he went to prepare matters to meet their wish, left the apartment. The two sisters, hand in hand, as if seeking by that close union to divert any danger which might threaten them, sat down on two seats in immediate contact with each other—Jemima seeking support in the manly and habitual courage of Lady Bothwell; and she, on the other hand, more agitated than she had expected, endeavouring to fortify herself by the desperate resolution which circumstances had forced her sister to assume. The one perhaps said to herself that her sister never feared anything; and the other might reflect that what so feeble-minded a woman as Jemima did not fear, could not properly be a subject of apprehension to a person of firmness and resolution like her own.

In a few moments the thoughts of both were diverted from their own situation by a strain of music so singularly sweet and solemn that, while it seemed calculated to avert or dispel any feeling unconnected with its harmony, increased, at the same time, the solemn excitation which the preceding interview was calculated to produce. The music was that of some instrument with which they were unacquainted; but circumstances afterwards led my ancestress to believe that it was that of the harmonica, which she heard at a much later period in life.

When these heaven-born sounds had ceased, a door opened in the upper end of the apartment, and they saw Damiotti, standing at the head of two or three steps, sign [31] to them to advance. His dress was so different from that which he had worn a few minutes before, that they could hardly recognize him; and the deadly paleness of his countenance, and a certain stern rigidity of muscles, like that of one whose mind is made up to some strange and daring action, had totally changed the somewhat sarcastic expression with which he had previously regarded them both, and particularly Lady Bothwell. He was barefooted, excepting a species of sandals in the antique fashion; his legs were naked beneath the knees; above them he wore hose, and a doublet of dark crimson silk close to his body; and over that a flowing loose robe, something resembling a surplice, of snow-white linen. His throat and neck were uncovered, and his long, straight, black hair was carefully combed down at full length.

 As the ladies approached at his bidding, he showed no gesture of that ceremonious courtesy of which he had been formerly lavish. On the contrary, he made the signal of advance with an air of command; and when, arm in arm, and with insecure steps, the sisters approached the spot where he stood, it was with a warning frown that he pressed his finger to his lips, as if reiterating his condition of absolute silence, while, stalking before them, he led the way into the next apartment.

 This was a large room, hung with black, as if for a funeral. At the upper end was a table, or rather a species of altar, covered with the same lugubrious colour, on which lay divers objects resembling the usual implements of sorcery. These objects were not indeed visible as they advanced into the apartment; for the light which displayed them, being only that of two expiring lamps, was extremely faint. The master—to use the Italian phrase for persons of this description—approached the upper end of the room, with a genuflection like that of a Catholic to the crucifix, and at the same time crossed himself. The ladies followed in silence, and arm in arm. Two or three low broad steps led to a platform in front of the altar, or what resembled such. Here the sage took his stand, and placed the ladies beside him, once more earnestly repeating by signs his injunctions of silence. The Italian then, extending his bare arm from under his linen vestment, pointed with his forefinger to five large flambeaux, or torches, placed on each side of the altar. They took fire successively at the approach of his hand, or rather of his finger, and spread a strong light through the room. By this the visitors could discern that, on the seeming altar, were disposed two naked swords laid crosswise; a large open book, which they conceived to be a copy of the Holy Scriptures, but in a language to them unknown; and beside this mysterious volume was placed a human skull. But what struck the sisters most was a very tall and broad mirror, which occupied all the space behind the altar, and, illumined by the lighted torches, reflected the mysterious articles which were laid upon it.

 The master then placed himself between the two ladies, and, pointing to the mirror, took each by the hand, but without speaking a syllable. They gazed intently on the polished and sable space to which he had directed their attention. Suddenly the surface assumed a new and singular appearance. It no longer simply reflected the objects placed before it, but, as if it had self-contained scenery of its own, objects began to appear within it, at first in a disorderly, indistinct, and miscellaneous manner, like form arranging itself out of chaos; at length, in distinct and

PLATE: The Magic Mirror
Steel plate engraving; drawn by John Massey Wright; engraved by E. Portbury; printed by McQueen

[33] defined shape and symmetry. It was thus that, after some shifting of light and darkness over the face of the wonderful glass, a long perspective of arches and columns began to arrange itself on its sides, and a vaulted roof on the upper part of it, till, after many oscillations, the whole vision gained a fixed and stationary appearance, representing the interior of a foreign church. The pillars were stately, and hung with scutcheons; the arches were lofty and magnificent; the floor was lettered with funeral inscriptions. But there were no separate shrines, no images, no display of chalice or crucifix on the altar. It was, therefore, a Protestant church upon the Continent. A clergyman dressed in the Geneva gown and band stood by the communion table, and, with the Bible opened before him, and his clerk awaiting in the background, seemed prepared to perform some service of the church to which he belonged.

At length, there entered the middle aisle of the building a numerous party, which appeared to be a bridal one, as a lady and gentleman walked first, hand in hand, followed by a large concourse of persons of both sexes, gaily, nay richly, attired. The bride, whose features they could distinctly see, seemed not more than sixteen years old, and extremely beautiful. The bridegroom, for some seconds, moved rather with his shoulder towards them, and his face averted; but his elegance of form and step struck the sisters at once with the same apprehension. As he turned his face suddenly, it was frightfully realized, and they saw, in the gay bridegroom before them, Sir Philip Forester. His wife uttered an imperfect exclamation, at the sound of which the whole scene stirred and seemed to separate.

"I could compare it to nothing," said Lady Bothwell [34] while recounting the wonderful tale, "but to the dispersion of the reflection offered by a deep and calm pool, when a stone is suddenly cast into it, and the shadows become dissipated and broken." The master pressed both the ladies' hands severely, as if to remind them of their promise, and of the danger which they incurred. The exclamation died away on Lady Forester's tongue, without attaining perfect utterance, and the scene in the glass, after the fluctuation of a minute, again resumed to the eye its former appearance of a real scene, existing within the mirror, as if represented in a picture, save that the figures were movable instead of being stationary.

The representation of Sir Philip Forester, now distinctly visible in form and feature, was seen to lead on towards the clergyman that beautiful girl, who advanced at once with diffidence and with a species of affectionate pride. In the meantime, and just as the clergyman had arranged the bridal company before him, and seemed about to commence the service, another group of persons, of whom two or three were officers, entered the church. They moved, at first, forward, as though they came to witness the bridal ceremony; but suddenly one of the officers, whose back was towards the spectators, detached himself from his companions, and rushed hastily towards the marriage party, when the whole of them turned towards him, as if attracted by some exclamation which had accompanied his advance. Suddenly the intruder drew his sword; the bridegroom unsheathed his own, and made towards him; swords were also drawn by other individuals, both of the marriage party and of those who had last entered. They fell into a sort of confusion, the clergyman, and some elder and graver persons, labouring apparently to keep the peace, while the [35] hotter spirits on both sides brandished their weapons. But now, the period of the brief space during which the soothsayer, as he pretended, was permitted to exhibit his art, was arrived. The fumes again mixed together, and dissolved gradually from observation; the vaults and columns of the church rolled asunder, and disappeared; and the front of the mirror reflected nothing save the blazing torches and the melancholy apparatus placed on the altar or table before it.

The doctor led the ladies, who greatly required his support, into the apartment from whence they came, where wine, essences, and other means of restoring suspended animation, had been provided during his absence. He motioned them to chairs, which they occupied in silence—Lady Forester, in particular, wringing her hands, and casting her eyes up to heaven, but without speaking a word, as if the spell had been still before her eyes.

"And what we have seen is even now acting?" said Lady Bothwell, collecting herself with difficulty.

"That," answered Baptista Damiotti, "I cannot justly, or with certainty, say. But it is either now acting, or has been acted during a short space before this. It is the last remarkable transaction in which the Cavalier Forester has been engaged."

Lady Bothwell then expressed anxiety concerning her sister, whose altered countenance and apparent unconsciousness of what passed around her excited her apprehensions how it might be possible to convey her home.

"I have prepared for that," answered the adept. "I have directed the servant to bring your equipage as near to this place as the narrowness of the street will permit. Fear not for your sister, but give her, when you return [36] home, this composing draught, and she will be better to-morrow morning. Few," he added in a melancholy tone, "leave this house as well in health as they entered it. Such being the consequence of seeking knowledge by mysterious means, I leave you to judge the condition of those who have the power of gratifying such irregular curiosity. Farewell, and forget not the potion."

"I will give her nothing that comes from you," said Lady Bothwell; "I have seen enough of your art already. Perhaps you would poison us both to conceal your own necromancy. But we are persons who want neither the means of making our wrongs known, nor the assistance of friends to right them."

"You have had no wrongs from me, madam," said the adept. "You sought one who is little grateful for such honour. He seeks no one, and only gives responses to those who invite and call upon him. After all, you have but learned a little sooner the evil which you must still be doomed to endure. I hear your servant's step at the door, and will detain your ladyship and Lady Forester no longer. The next packet from the Continent will explain what you have already partly witnessed. Let it not, if I may advise, pass too suddenly into your sister's hands."

So saying, he bid Lady Bothwell good-night. She went, lighted by the adept, to the vestibule, where he hastily threw a black cloak over his singular dress, and opening the door, entrusted his visitors to the care of the servant. It was with difficulty that Lady Bothwell sustained her sister to the carriage, though it was only twenty steps distant. When they arrived at home, Lady Forester required medical assistance. The physician of the family attended, and shook his head on feeling her pulse. [37]

"Here has been," he said, "a violent and sudden shock on the nerves. I must know how it has happened."

Lady Bothwell admitted they had visited the conjurer, and that Lady Forester had received some bad news respecting her husband, Sir Philip.

"That rascally quack would make my fortune, were he to stay in Edinburgh," said the graduate; "this is the seventh nervous case I have heard of his making for me, and all by effect of terror." He next examined the composing draught which Lady Bothwell had unconsciously brought in her hand, tasted it, and pronounced it very germain to the matter, and what would save an application to the apothecary. He then paused, and looking at Lady Bothwell very significantly, at length added, "I suppose I must not ask your ladyship anything about this Italian warlock's proceedings?"

"Indeed, doctor," answered Lady Bothwell, "I consider what passed as confidential; and though the man may be a rogue, yet, as we were fools enough to consult him, we should, I think, be honest enough to keep his counsel."

"*May* be a knave! Come," said the doctor, "I am glad to hear your ladyship allows such a possibility in anything that comes from Italy."

"What comes from Italy may be as good as what comes from Hanover, doctor. But you and I will remain good friends; and that it may be so, we will say nothing of Whig and Tory."

"Not I," said the doctor, receiving his fee, and taking his hat; "a Carolus serves my purpose as well as a Willielmus. But I should like to know why old Lady Saint Ringan, and all that set, go about wasting their decayed lungs in puffing this foreign fellow." [38]

"Ay—you had best set him down a Jesuit, as Scrub says." On these terms they parted.

The poor patient—whose nerves, from an extraordinary state of tension, had at length become relaxed in as extraordinary a degree—continued to struggle with a sort of imbecility, the growth of superstitious terror, when the shocking tidings were brought from Holland which fulfilled even her worst expectations.

They were sent by the celebrated Earl of Stair, and contained the melancholy event of a duel betwixt Sir Philip Forester and his wife's half-brother, Captain Falconer, of the Scotch-Dutch, as they were then called, in which the latter had been killed. The cause of quarrel rendered the incident still more shocking. It seemed that Sir Philip had left the army suddenly, in consequence of being unable to pay a very considerable sum which he had lost to another volunteer at play. He had changed his name, and taken up his residence at Rotterdam, where he had insinuated himself into the good graces of an ancient and rich burgomaster, and, by his handsome person and graceful manners, captivated the affections of his only child, a very young person, of great beauty, and the heiress of much wealth. Delighted with the specious attractions of his proposed son-in-law, the wealthy merchant—whose idea of the British character was too high to admit of his taking any precaution to acquire evidence of his condition and circumstances—gave his consent to the marriage. It was about to be celebrated in the principal church of the city, when it was interrupted by a singular occurrence.

Captain Falconer having been detached to Rotterdam to bring up a part of the brigade of Scottish auxiliaries, who were in quarters there, a person of consideration in the [39] town, to whom he had been formerly known, proposed to him for amusement to go to the high church to see a countryman of his own married to the daughter of a wealthy burgomaster. Captain Falconer went accordingly, accompanied by his Dutch acquaintance, with a party of his friends, and two or three officers of the Scotch brigade. His astonishment may be conceived when he saw his own brother-in-law, a married man, on the point of leading to the altar the innocent and beautiful creature upon whom he was about to practise a base and unmanly deceit. He proclaimed his villainy on the spot, and the marriage was interrupted, of course. But against the opinion of more thinking men, who considered Sir Philip Forester as having thrown himself out of the rank of men of honour, Captain Falconer admitted him to the privilege of such, accepted a challenge from him, and in the rencounter received a mortal wound. Such are the ways of Heaven, mysterious in our eyes. Lady Forester never recovered the shock of this dismal intelligence.

"And did this tragedy," said I, "take place exactly at the time when the scene in the mirror was exhibited?"

"It is hard to be obliged to maim one's story," answered my aunt, "but to speak the truth, it happened some days sooner than the apparition was exhibited."

"And so there remained a possibility," said I, "that by some secret and speedy communication the artist might have received early intelligence of that incident."

"The incredulous pretended so," replied my aunt.

"What became of the adept?" demanded I.

"Why, a warrant came down shortly afterwards to arrest him for high treason, as an agent of the Chevalier [40] St. George; and Lady Bothwell, recollecting the hints which had escaped the doctor, an ardent friend of the Protestant succession, did then call to remembrance that this man was chiefly *proné* among the ancient matrons of her own political persuasion. It certainly seemed probable that intelligence from the Continent, which could easily have been transmitted by an active and powerful agent, might have enabled him to prepare such a scene of phantasmagoria as she had herself witnessed. Yet there were so many difficulties in assigning a natural explanation, that, to the day of her death, she remained in great doubt on the subject, and much disposed to cut the Gordian knot by admitting the existence of supernatural agency."

"But, my dear aunt," said I, "what became of the man of skill?"

"Oh, he was too good a fortune-teller not to be able to foresee that his own destiny would be tragical if he waited the arrival of the man with the silver greyhound upon his sleeve. He made, as we say, a moonlight flitting, and was nowhere to be seen or heard of. Some noise there was about papers or letters found in the house; but it died away, and Doctor Baptista Damiotti was soon as little talked of as Galen or Hippocrates."

"And Sir Philip Forester," said I, "did he too vanish for ever from the public scene?"

"No," replied my kind informer. "He was heard of once more, and it was upon a remarkable occasion. It is said that we Scots, when there was such a nation in existence, have, among our full peck of virtues, one or two little barley-corns of vice. In particular, it is alleged that we rarely forgive, and never forget, any injuries received—that we make an idol of our resentment, as poor Lady [41] Constance did of her grief, and are addicted, as Burns says, to 'nursing our wrath to keep it warm.' Lady Bothwell was not without this feeling; and, I believe, nothing whatever, scarce the restoration of the Stewart line, could have happened so delicious to her feelings as an opportunity of being revenged on Sir Philip Forester for the deep and double injury which had deprived her of a sister and of a brother. But nothing of him was heard or known till many a year had passed away.

"At length—it was on a Fastern's E'en (Shrovetide) assembly, at which the whole fashion of Edinburgh attended, full and frequent, and when Lady Bothwell had a seat amongst the lady patronesses, that one of the attendants on the company whispered into her ear that a gentleman wished to speak with her in private.

"In private? and in an assembly room?—he must be mad. Tell him to call upon me to-morrow morning."

"I said so, my lady," answered the man, "but he desired me to give you this paper."

"She undid the billet, which was curiously folded and sealed. It only bore the words, "*On business of life and death*," written in a hand which she had never seen before. Suddenly it occurred to her that it might concern the safety of some of her political friends. She therefore followed the messenger to a small apartment where the refreshments were prepared, and from which the general company was excluded. She found an old man, who, at her approach, rose up and bowed profoundly. His appearance indicated a broken constitution, and his dress, though sedulously rendered conforming to the etiquette of a ballroom, was worn and tarnished, and hung in folds about his emaciated person. Lady Bothwell was about to feel for her purse, ex- [42] pecting to get rid of the supplicant at the expense of a little money, but some fear of a mistake arrested her purpose. She therefore gave the man leisure to explain himself.

"I have the honour to speak with the Lady Bothwell?"

"I am Lady Bothwell; allow me to say that this is no time or place for long explanations. What are your commands with me?"

"Your ladyship," said the old man, "had once a sister."

"True; whom I loved as my own soul."

"And a brother."

"The bravest, the kindest, the most affectionate!" said Lady Bothwell.

"Both these beloved relatives you lost by the fault of an unfortunate man," continued the stranger.

"By the crime of an unnatural, bloody-minded murderer," said the lady.

"I am answered," replied the old man, bowing, as if to withdraw.

"Stop, sir, I command you," said Lady Bothwell. "Who are you that, at such a place and time, come to recall these horrible recollections? I insist upon knowing."

"I am one who intends Lady Bothwell no injury, but, on the contrary, to offer her the means of doing a deed of Christian charity, which the world would wonder at, and which Heaven would reward; but I find her in no temper for such a sacrifice as I was prepared to ask."

"Speak out, sir; what is your meaning?" said Lady Bothwell.

"The wretch that has wronged you so deeply," rejoined the stranger, "is now on his death-bed. His days have been days of misery, his nights have been sleepless hours [43] of anguish—yet he cannot die without your forgiveness. His life has been an unremitting penance—yet he dares not part from his burden while your curses load his soul."

"Tell him," said Lady Bothwell sternly, "to ask pardon of that Being whom he has so greatly offended, not of an erring mortal like himself. What could my forgiveness avail him?"

"Much," answered the old man. "It will be an earnest of that which he may then venture to ask from his Creator, lady, and from yours. Remember, Lady

Bothwell, you too have a death-bed to look forward to; Your soul may—all human souls must—feel the awe of facing the judgment-seat, with the wounds of an untented conscience, raw, and rankling—what thought would it be then that should whisper, "I have given no mercy, how then shall I ask it?"

"Man, whosoever thou mayest be," replied Lady Bothwell, "urge me not so cruelly. It would be but blasphemous hypocrisy to utter with my lips the words which every throb of my heart protests against. They would open the earth and give to light the wasted form of my sister, the bloody form of my murdered brother. Forgive him?—never, never!"

"Great God!" cried the old man, holding up his hands, "is it thus the worms which Thou hast called out of dust obey the commands of their Maker? Farewell, proud and unforgiving woman. Exult that thou hast added to a death in want and pain the agonies of religious despair; but never again mock Heaven by petitioning for the pardon which thou hast refused to grant."

"He was turning from her.

"Stop, she exclaimed; "I will try—yes, I will try to pardon him." [44]

"Gracious lady," said the old man, "you will relieve the over-burdened soul which dare not sever itself from its sinful companion of earth without being at peace with you. What do I know—your forgiveness may perhaps preserve for penitence the dregs of a wretched life."

"Ha!" said the lady, as a sudden light broke on her, "it is the villain himself!" And grasping Sir Philip Forester—for it was he, and no other—by the collar, she raised a cry of "Murder, murder! seize the murderer!"

"At an exclamation so singular, in such a place, the company thronged into the apartment; but Sir Philip Forester was no longer there. He had forcibly extricated himself from Lady Bothwell's hold, and had run out of the apartment, which opened on the landing-place of the stair. There seemed no escape in that direction, for there were several persons coming up the steps, and others descending. But the unfortunate man was desperate. He threw himself over the balustrade, and alighted safely in the lobby, though a leap of fifteen feet at least, then dashed into the street, and was lost in darkness. Some of the Bothwell family made pursuit, and had they come up with the fugitive they might perhaps have slain him; for in those days men's blood ran warm in their veins. But the police did not interfere, the matter most criminal having happened long since, and in a foreign land. Indeed it was always thought that this extraordinary scene originated in a hypocritical experiment, by which Sir Philip desired to ascertain whether he might return to his native country in safety from the resentment of a family which he had injured so deeply. As the result fell out so contrary to his wishes, he is believed to have returned to the Continent, and there died in exile."

So closed the tale of the MYSTERIOUS MIRROR.

Title
By the Author of *Frankenstein*. [Shelley, Mary.] "The Sisters of Albano." KS 1829. 80-100. [80]

>THE SISTERS OF ALBANO.
>BY THE AUTHOR OF *FRANKENSTEIN*.

>And near Albano's scarce divided waves
>Shine from a sister valley;—and afar
>The Tiber winds, and the broad ocean laves
>The Latian coast where sprang the Epic war,
>"Arms and the Man," whose re-ascending star
>Rose o'er an empire; but beneath thy right
>Tully reposed from Rome; and where yon bar
>Of girdling mountains intercepts the sight
>The Sabine farm was till'd, the weary bard's delight.

It was to see this beautiful lake that I made my last excursion before quitting Rome. The spring had nearly grown into summer, the trees were all in full but fresh green foliage, the vine-dresser was singing, perched among them, training his vines: the cicala had not yet begun her song, the heats therefore had not commenced; but at evening the fireflies gleamed among the hills, and the cooing aziolo assured us of what in that country needs no assurance, fine weather for the morrow. We set out early in the morning to avoid the heats, breakfasted at Albano, and till ten o'clock passed our time in visiting the Mosaic, the villa of Cicero, and other curiosities of the place. We reposed during the middle of the day in a tent elevated for us at the hill top, whence we looked on the hill-embosomed lake, and the distant eminent crowned by a town with its church. Other villages and cottages

PLATE: Lake Albano
Steel plate engraving; drawn by J.M.W. Turner, R.A.;
engraved by Robert Wallis; printed by McQueen

[81] were scattered among the foldings of mountains, and beyond we saw the deep blue sea of the southern poets, which received the swift and immortal Tiber, rocking it to repose among its devouring waves. The Coliseum falls and the Pantheon decays—the very hills of Rome are perishing, but the Tiber lives for ever, flows for ever—and for ever feeds the land-encircling Mediterranean with fresh waters.

Our summer and pleasure-seeking party consisted of many: to me the most interesting person was the Countess Atanasia D——, who was as beautiful as an imagination of Raphael, and good as the ideal of a poet. Two of her children accompanied her, with animated looks and gentle manners, quiet, yet enjoying. I sat near her, watching the changing shadows of the landscape before us. As the sun descended, it poured a tide of light into the valley of the lake, deluging the deep bank formed by the mountain with liquid gold. The domes and turrets of the far town flashed and gleamed, the trees were dyed in splendour; two or three slight clouds, which had drunk the radiance till it became their essence, floated golden islets in the lustrous empyrean. The waters, reflecting the brilliancy of the sky and the fire-tinted banks, beamed a second heaven, a second irradiated earth, at our feet. The Mediterranean gazing on the sun—as the eyes of a mortal bride fail and are dimmed when reflecting her lover's glance—was lost, mixed in his light, till it had become one with him. —Long (our souls, like the sea, the hills, and lake, drinking in the supreme loveliness) we gazed, till the tool full cup overflowed, and we turned away with a sigh.

At our feet there was a knoll of ground, that formed [82] the foreground of our picture; two trees lay basking against the sky, glittering with the golden light, which like dew seemed to hang amid their branches—a rock closed the prospect on the other side, twined round by creepers, and redolent with blooming myrtle—a brook crossed by huge stones gushed through the turf, and on the fragments of rock that lay about, sat two or three persons, peasants, who attracted our attention. One was a hunter, as his gun, lying on a bank not far off, demonstrated, yet he was a tiller of the soil; his rough straw hat, and his picturesque but coarse dress, belonged to that class. The other was some contadina, in the costume of her country, returning, her basket on her arm, from the village to her cottage home. They were regarding the stores of a pedlar, who with doffed hat stood near: some of these consisted of pictures and prints—views of the country, and portraits of the Madonna. Our peasants regarded these with pleased attention.

"One might easily make out a story for that pair," I said: "his gun is a help to the imagination, and we may fancy him a bandit with his contadina love, the terror of all the neighborhood, except of her, the most defenceless being in it."

"You speak lightly of such combination," said the lovely countess at my side, "as if it must not in its nature be the cause of dreadful tragedies. The mingling of love with crime is a dread conjunction, and lawless pursuits are never followed without bringing on the criminal, and all allied to him, ineffable misery. I speak with emotion, for your observation reminds me of an unfortunate girl, now one of the Sisters of Charity in the convent in Santa Chiara at Rome, whose unhappy passion for a man [83] such as you mention, spread destruction and sorrow widely around her."

I entreated my lovely friend to relate the history of the nun: for a long time she resisted my entreaties, as not willing to depress the spirit of a party of pleasure by a tale of sorrow. But I urged her, and she yielded. Her sweet Italian phraseology now rings in my ears, and her beautiful countenance is before me. As she spoke, the sun set, and the moon bent her silver horn in the ebbing tide of glory he had left. The lake changed from purpose to silver, and the trees, before so splendid, now in dark masses, just reflected from their tops the mild moonlight. The fire-flies flashed among the rocks; the bats circled round us: meanwhile thus commenced the Countess Atanasia:

The nun of whom I speak had a sister older than herself; I can remember them when as children they brought eggs and fruit to my father's villa. Maria and Anina were constantly together. With their large straw hats to shield them from the scorching sun, they were at work in their father's *podere* all day, and in the evening, when Maria, who was the elder by four years, went to the fountain for water, Anina ran at her side. Their cot—the folding of the hill conceals it—is at the lake side opposite; and about a quarter of a mile up the hill is the rustic fountain of which I speak. Maria was serious, gentle, and considerate; Anina was a laughing, merry little creature, with the face of a cherub. When Maria was fifteen, their mother fell ill, and was nursed at the convent of Santa Chiara at Rome. Maria attended her, never leaving her bedside day or night. The nuns thought her an angel, she deemed them saints: her mother died, and they persuaded her to make one of them; her father could not but acquiesce in her holy in- [84] tention, and she became one of the Sisters of Charity, the nun-nurses of Santa Chiara. Once or twice a year she visited her home, gave sage and kind advice to Anina, and sometimes wept to part from her; but her piety and her active employments for the sick reconciled her to her fate. Anina was more sorry to lose her sister's society. The other girls of the village did not please her: she was a good child, and worked hard for her father, and her sweetest recompense was the report he made of her to Maria, and the fond praises and caresses the latter bestowed on her when they met.

It was not until she was fifteen that Anina showed any diminution of affection for her sister. Yet I cannot call it diminution, for she loved her perhaps more than ever, though her holy calling and sage lectures prevented her from reposing confidence, and made her tremble lest the nun, devoted to heaven and good works, should read in her eyes, and disapprove of the earthly passion that occupied her. Perhaps a part of her reluctance arose from the reports that were current against her lover's character, and certainly from the disapprobation and even hatred of him that her father frequently expressed. Ill-fated Anina! I know not if in the north your peasants love as ours; but the passion of Anina was entwined with the roots of her being, it was herself: she could die, but not cease to love. The dislike of her father for Domenico made their intercourse clandestine. He was always at the fountain to fill her pitcher, and lift it on her head. He attended the same mass; and when her father went to Albano, Velletri, or Rome, he seemed to learn by instinct the exact moment of his departure, and joined her in the *podere*, labouring with her and for her, till the old man was seen descending [85] the mountain-path on his return. He said he worked for a contadino near Nemi. Anina sometimes wondered that he could spare so much time for her; but his excuses were plausible, and the result too delightful not to blind the innocent girl to its obvious cause.

Poor Domenico! the reports spread against him were too well founded: his sole excuse was that his father had been a robber before him, and he had spent his early years among these lawless men. He had better things in his nature, and yearned for the peace of the guiltless. Yet he could hardly be called guilty, for no dread crime stained him; nevertheless, he was an outlaw and a bandit, and now that he loved Anina these names were the stings of an adder to pierce his soul. He would have fled from his comrades to a far country, but Anina dwelt amid their very haunts. At this period also, the police established by the French government, which then possessed Rome, made these bands more alive to the conduct of their members, and rumours of active measures to be taken against those who occupied the hills near Albano, Nemi, and Velletri, caused them to draw together in tighter bonds. Domenico would not, if he could, desert his friends in the hour of danger.

On a *festa* at this time—it was towards the end of October—Anina strolled with her father among the villagers, who all over Italy make holiday, by congregating and walking in one place. Their talk was entirely of the *laddri* and the French, and many terrible stories were related of the extirpation of banditti in the kingdom of Naples, and the mode by which the French succeeded in their undertaking was minutely described. The troops scoured the country, visiting one haunt of the robbers after the [86] other, and dislodging them, tracked them, as in those countries they hunt the wild beasts of the forest, till drawing the circle narrower, they enclosed them in one spot. They then drew a cordon round the place, which they guarded with the utmost vigilance, forbidding any to enter it with provisions, on pain of instant death. And as this menace was rigorously executed, in a short time the besieged bandits were starved into a surrender. The French troops were now daily expected, for they had been seen at Velletri and Nemi; at the same time it was affirmed that several outlaws had taken up their abode at Rocca Giovane, a deserted village on the summit of one of these hills, and it was supposed that they would make that place the scene of their final retreat.

The next day, as Anina worked in the *podere*, a party of French horse passed by along the road that separated her garden from the lake. Curiosity made her look at them; and her beauty was too great not to attract: their observations and address soon drove her away—or a woman in love consecrates herself to her lover, and deems the admiration of others to be profanation. She spoke to her father of the impertinence of these men, and he answered by rejoicing at their arrival, and the destruction of the lawless bands that would ensue. When, in the evening, Anina went to the fountain, she looked timidly around, and hoped that Domenico would be at his accustomed post, for the arrival of the French destroyed her feeling of security. She went rather later than usual, and a cloudy evening made it seem already dark; the wind roared among the trees, bending hither and thither even the stately cypresses; the waters of the lake were agitated into high waves, and dark masses of thunder-cloud lowered over the [87] hills tops, giving a lurid tinge to the landscape. Anina passed quickly up the mountain-path: when she came in sight of the fountain, which was rudely hewn in the living rock, she saw Domenico leaning against a projection of the hill, his hat drawn over his eyes, his *tabaro* fallen from his shoulders, his arms folded in an attitude of dejection. He started when he saw her; his voice and phrases were broken and unconnected; yet he never gazed on her with such ardent love, nor solicited her to delay her departure with such impassioned tenderness.

"How glad I am to find you here!" she said: "I was fearful of meeting one of the French soldiers: I dread them even more than the banditti."

Domenico cast a look of eager inquiry on her, and then turned away, saying, "Sorry am I that I shall not be here to protect you. I am obliged to go to Rome for a week or two. You will be faithful, Anina mia; you will love me, though I never see you more?"

The interview, under these circumstances, was longer than usual: he led her down the path till they nearly came in sight of her cottage; still they lingered: a low whistle as heard among the myrtle underwood at the lake side; he started; it was repeated, and he answered it by a similar note: Anina, terrified, was about to ask what this meant, when, for the first time, he pressed her to his heart, kissed her roseate lips, and, with a muttered "Carissima addio," left her, springing down the bank; and as she gazed in wonder, she thought she saw a boat cross a line of light made by the opening of a cloud. She stood long absorbed in reverie, wondering and remembering with thrilling pleasure the quick embrace and impassioned farewell of [88] her lover. She delayed so long that her father came to seek her.

Each evening after this, Anina visited the fountain at the Ave Maria; he was not there; each day seemed an age; and incomprehensible fears occupied her heart. About a fortnight after, letters arrived from Maria. They came to say that she had been ill of the mal'aria fever, that she was now convalescent, but that change of air was necessary for her recovery, and that she had obtained leave to spend a month at home at Albano. She asked her father to come the next day to fetch her. These were pleasant tidings for Anina; she resolved to disclose every thing to her sister, and during her long visit she doubted not but that she would contrive her happiness. Old Andrea departed the following morning, and the whole day was spent by the sweet girl in dreams of future bliss. In the evening Maria arrived, weak and wan, with all the makers of that dread illness about her; yet, as she assured her sister, feeling quite well.

As they sat at their frugal supper, several villagers came in to inquire for Maria; but all their talk was of the French soldiers and the robbers, of whom a band of at least twenty was collected in Rocca Giovane, strictly watched by the military.

"We may be grateful to the French," said Andrea, "for this good deed: the country will be rid of these ruffians."

"True, friend," said another; "but it is horrible to think what these men suffer: they have, it appears, exhausted all the food they brought with them to the village, and are literally starving. They have not an ounce of maccaroni among them; and a poor fellow, who was taken [89] and executed yesterday, was a mere anatomy; you could tell every bone in his skin."

"There was a sad story the other day," said another, "of an old man from Nemi, whose son, they say, is among them at Rocca Giovane: he was found within the lines with some *baccalà* under his *pastrano*, and shot on the spot."

"There is not a more desperate gang," observed the first speaker, "in the states and the regno put together. They have sworn never to yield but upon good terms: to secure these, their plan is to way-lay passengers and make prisoners, whom they keep as hostages for mild treatment from the government. But the French are merciless; they are better pleased that the bandits wreak their vengeance on these poor creatures than spare one of their lives."

"They have captured two persons already," said another; "and there is old Betta Tossi half frantic, for she is sure her son is taken: he has not been at home these ten days."

"I should rather guess," said an old man, "that he went there with good will: the young scape-grace kept company with Domenico Baldi of Nemi."

"No worse company could he have kept in the whole country," said Andrea: "Domenico is the bad son of a bad race. Is he in the village with the rest?"

"My own eyes assured me of that," replied the other. "When I was up the hill with eggs and fowls to the piquette there, I saw the branches of an ilex move; the poor fellow was weak perhaps, and could not keep his hold; presently he dropt to the ground; every musket was levelled at him, but he started up and was away like a hare among the rocks. Once he turned, and then I saw Domenico as [90] plainly, though thinner, poor lad, by much than he was, as plainly as I now see—Santa Virgine! what is the matter with Nina?"

She had fainted; the company broke up, and she was left to her sister's care. When the poor child came to herself she was fully aware of her situation, and said nothing, except expressing a wish to retire to rest. Maria was in high spirits at the prospect of her long holiday at home, but the illness of her sister made her refrain from talking that night, and blessing her, as she said good night, she soon slept. Domenico starving!—Domenico trying to escape and dying through hunger, was the vision of horror that wholly possessed poor Anina. At another time, the discovery that her lover was a robber might have inflicted pangs as keen as those which she now felt; but this, at present, made a faint impression, obscured by worse wretchedness. Maria was in a deep tranquil sleep. Anina rose, dressed herself silently, and crept down stairs. She stored her market basket with what food there was in the house, and, unlatching the cottage-door, issued forth, resolved to reach Rocca Giovane, and to administer to her lover's dreadful wants. The night was dark, but this was favourable, for she knew every path and turn of the hills; every bush and knoll of ground between her home and the deserted village which occupies the summit of that hill: you may see the dark outline of some of its houses about two hours' walk from her cottage. The night was dark, but still; the libeccio brought the clouds below the mountain-tops, and veiled the horizon in mist; not a leaf stirred; her footsteps sounded loud in her ears, but resolution overcame fear. She had entered yon ilex grove, her spirits rose with her success, when suddenly she was challenged by a sentinel; [91] no time for escape; fear chilled her blood; her basket dropped from her arm; its contents rolled out on the ground; the soldier fired his gun and brought several others round him; she was made prisoner.

In the morning, when Maria awoke, she missed her sister from her side. I have overslept myself, she thought, and Nina would not disturb me. But when she came down stairs and met her father, and Anina did not appear, they began to wonder. She was not in the *podere*; two hours passed, and then Andrea went to seek her. Entering the near village, he saw the contadini crowding together, and a stifled exclamation of "Ecco il padre!" told him that some evil had betided. His first impression was that his daughter was drowned; but the truth, that she had been taken by the French carrying provisions within the forbidden line, was still more terrible. He returned in frantic desperation to his cottage, first to acquaint Maria with what had happened, and then ascend the hill to save his child from her impending fate. Maria heard his tale with horror; but an hospital is a school in which to learn self-possession and presence of mind. "Do you remain, my father," she said: "I will go. My holy character will awe these men, my tears move them: trust me; I swear that I will save my sister." Andrea yielded to her superior courage and energy.

The nuns of Santa Chiara when out of their convent do not usually wear their monastic habit, but dress simply in a black gown. Maria, however, had brought her nun's habiliments with her, and thinking thus to impress the soldiers with respect, she now put it on. She received her father's benediction, and asking that of the Virgin and the saints, she departed on her expedition. Ascending the [92] hill, she was soon stopped by the sentinels. She asked to see their commanding officer, and being conducted to him, she announced herself as the sister of the unfortunate girl who had been captured the night before. The officer, who had received her with carelessness, now changed countenance: her serious look frightened Maria, who clasped her hands, exclaiming, "You have not injured the child! she is safe!"

"She is safe—now," he replied with hesitation; "but there is no hope of pardon."

"Holy Virgin, have mercy on her! what will be done to her?"

"I have received strict orders; in two hours she dies."

"No! no!" exclaimed Maria impetuously, "that cannot be! you cannot be so wicked as to murder a child like her."

"She is old enough, madame," said the officer, "to know that she ought not to disobey orders; mine are so strict, that were she but nine years old, she dies."

These terrible words stung Maria to fresh resolution: she entreated for mercy; she knelt; she vowed that she would not depart without her sister; she appealed to Heaven and the saints. The officer, though cold-hearted, was good-natured and courteous, and he assured her with the utmost gentleness that her supplications were of no avail; that were the criminal his own daughter he must enforce his orders. As a sole concession, he permitted her to see her sister. Despair inspired the nun with energy; she almost ran up the hill, out-speeding her guide: they crossed a folding of the hills to a little sheep-cot, where sentinels paraded before the door. There was no glass to the windows, so the shutters were shut, and when Maria first went in from the bright daylight she hardly saw the slight figure of her sister leaning against the wall, her dark hair fallen [93] below her waist, her head sunk on her bosom, over which her arms were folded. She started wildly as the door opened, saw her sister, and sprung with a piercing shriek into her arms.

They were left alone together. Anina uttered a thousand frantic exclamations, beseeching her sister to save her, and shuddering at the near approach of her fate. Maria had felt herself, since their mother's death, the natural protectress and support of her sister, and she never deemed herself so called on to fulfil this character as now that the trembling girl clasped her neck; her tears falling on her cheeks, and her choked voice entreating her to save her. The though—O could I suffer instead of you! was in her heart, and she was about to express it, when it suggested another idea, on which she was resolved to act. First she soothed Anina by her promises, then glanced round the cot; they were quite alone: she went to the window, and through a crevice saw the soldiers conversing at some distance. "Yes, dearest sister," she cried, "I will—I can save you—quick—we must change dresses—there is no time to be lost! —you must escape in my habit."

"And you remain to die?"

"They dare not murder the innocent, a nun! Fear not for me—I am safe."

Anina easily yielded to her sister, but her fingers trembled; every string she touched she entangled. Maria was perfectly self-possessed, pale, but calm. She tied up her sister's long hair, and adjusted her veil over it so as to conceal it; she unlaced her bodice, and arranged the folds of her own habit on her with the greatest care—then more hastily she assumed the dress of her sister, putting on, after a lapse of many years, her native contadina costume. [94] Anina stood by, weeping and helpless, hardly hearing her sister's injunctions to return speedily to their father, and under his guidance to seek sanctuary. The guard now opened the door. Anina clung to her sister in terror, while she, in soothing tones, entreated her to calm herself.

The soldier said, they must delay no longer, for the priest had arrived to confess the prisoner.

To Anina the idea of confession associated with death was terrible; to Maria it brought hope, She whispered, in a smothered voice, "The priest will protect me—fear not—hasten to our father!"

Anina almost mechanically obeyed: weeping, with her handkerchief placed unaffectedly before her face, she passed the soldiers; they closed the door on the prisoner, who hastened to the window, and saw her sister descend the hill with tottering steps, till she was lost behind some rising ground. The nun fell on her knees—cold dew bathed her brow, instinctively she feared: the French had shown small respect for the monastic character; they destroyed the convents and desecrated the churches Would they be merciful to her, and spare the innocent! Alas! was not Anina innocent also? Her sole crime had been disobeying an arbitrary command, and she had done the same.

"Courage!" cried Maria; "perhaps I am fitter to die than my sister is. Gesu, pardon me my sins, but I do not believe that I shall out-live this day!"

In the meantime, Anina descended the hill slowly and tremblingly. She fears discovery—she feared for her sister—and above all at the present moment, she feared the reproaches and anger of her father. By dwelling on this last idea, it became exaggerated into excessive terror, and she determined instead of returning to her home, to make a circuit among [95] the hills, to find her way by herself to Albano, where she trusted to find protection from her pastor and confessor. She avoided the open paths, and following rather the direction she wished to pursue than any beaten road, she passed along nearer to Rocca Giovane than she anticipated. She looked up at its ruined houses and bell-less steeple, straining her eyes to catch a glimpse of him, the author of all her ills. A low but distinct whistle reached her ear, not far off; she started—she remembered that on the night when she last saw Domenico a note like that had called him from her side; the sound was echoed and re-echoed from other quarters; she stood aghast, her bosom heaving, her hands clasped. First she saw a dark and ragged head of hair, shadowing two fiercely gleaming eyes, rise from beneath a bush. She screamed, but before she could repeat her scream three men leapt from behind a rock, secured her arms, threw a cloth over her face, and informed her of the horror and danger of her situation.

Pity, they said, that the holy father and some of his red stockings did not command the troops: with a nun in their hands, they might obtain any terms. Coarse jests passed as they dragged their victim towards their ruined village. The paving of the street told her when they arrived at Rocca Giovane, and the change of atmosphere that they entered a house. They unbandaged her eyes: the scene was squalid and miserable, the walls ragged and black with smoke, the floor strewn with offals and dirt; a rude table and broken bench was all the furniture; and the leaves of Indian corn, heaped high in one corner, served, it seemed, for a bed, for a many lay on it, his head buried in his folded arms. Anina looked round on her savage [96] hosts: their countenances expressed every variety of brutal ferocity, now rendered more dreadful from gaunt famine and suffering.

"O there is none who will save me!" she cried. The voice startled the man who was lying on the floor; he leapt up—it was Domenico: Domenico, so changed, with sunk cheeks and eyes, matted hair, and looks whose wildness and desperation differed little from the dark countenances around him. Could this be her lover?

His recognition and surprise at her dress led to an explanation. When the robbers first heard that their prey was no prize, they were mortified and angry; but when she related the danger she had incurred by endeavouring to bring them food, they swore with horrid oaths that no harm should befall her, but that if she liked she might make one of them in all honour and equality. The innocent girl shuddered. "Let me go," she cried; "let me only escape and hide myself in a convent for ever!"

Domenico looked at her in agony. "Yes, poor child," he said; "go, save yourself: God grant no evil befal you; the ruin is too wide already." Then turning eagerly to his comrades, he continued—"You hear her story. She was to have been shot for bringing food to us: her sister has substituted herself in her place. WE know the French; one victim is to them as good as another: Maria dies in their hands. Let us save her. Our time is up; we must fall like men, or starve like dogs: we have still ammunition, still some strength left. To arms! let us rush on the poltroons, free their prisoner, and escape or die!"

There needed but an impulse like this to urge the outlaws to desperate resolves. They prepared their arms with looks of ferocious determination. Domenico, meanwhile, [97] led Anina out of the house, to the verge of the hill, inquiring whither she intended to go. One her saying, to Albano, he observed, "That were hardly safe; be guided by me, I entreat you: take those piastres, hire the first conveyance you find, hasten to Rome, to the convent of Santa Chiara: for pity's sake, do not linger in this neighbourhood."

"I will obey your injunctions, Domenico," she replied, "but I cannot take your money; it has cost you too dear: fear not, I shall arrive safely at Rome without that ill-fated silver."

Domenico's comrades now called loudly to him: he had no time to urge his request; he threw the despised dollars at her feet.

"Nina, adieu for ever," he said: "may you love again more happily!"

"Never!" she replied. "God has saved me in this dress; it were sacrilege to change it: I shall never quit Santa Chiara."

Domenico had led her a part of the way down the rock; his comrades appeared at the top, calling to him.

"Gesu save you!" cried he: "reach the convent—Maria shall join you there before night. Farewell!" He hastily kissed her hand, and sprang up the acclivity to rejoin his impatient friends.

The unfortunate Andrea had waited long for the return of his children. The leafless trees and bright clear atmosphere permitted every object to be visible, but he saw no trace of them on the hill side; the shadows of the dial showed noon to be passed, when, with uncontrollable impatience, he began to climb the hill, towards the spot where Anina had been taken. The path he pursued was in part the [98] same that this unhappy girl had taken on her way to Rome. The father and daughter met: the old man saw the nun's dress, and saw her unaccompanied: she covered her face with her hands in a transport of fear and shame; but when, mistaking her for Maria, he asked in a tone of anguish for hi youngest darling, her arms fell; she dared not raise her eyes, which streamed with tears.

"Unhappy girl!" exclaimed Andrea, "where is your sister?"

She pointed to the cottage prison, now discernible near the summit of a steep acclivity. "She is safe," she replied: "she saved me; but they dare not murder her."

"Heaven bless her for this good deed!" exclaimed the old man, fervently; "but you hasten on your way, and I will go in search of her."

Each proceeded on an opposite path. The old man wound up the hill, now in view, and now losing sight of the hut where his child was captive: he was aged, and the way was steep. Once, when the closing of the hill hid the point towards which he for ever strained his eyes, a single shot was fired in that direction: his staff fell from his hands, his knees trembled and failed him; several minutes of dead silence lapsed before he recovered himself sufficiently to proceed: full of fears he went on, and at the next turn saw the cot again. A party of soldiers were on the open space before it, drawn up in a line as if expecting an attack. In a few moments from above them shots were fired, which they returned, and the whole was enveloped and veiled in smoke. Still Andrea climbed the hill, eager to discover what had become of his child: the firing continued quick and hot. Now and then, in the pauses of musquetry and the answering echoes of the [99] mountains, he heard a funeral chant; present, before he was aware, at a turning of the hill, he met a company of priests and contadini, carrying a large cross and a bier. The miserable father rushed forward with frantic impatience; the awe-struck peasants set down their load—the face was uncovered, and the wretched man fell lifeless on the corpse of his murdered child.

The countess Atanasia paused, overcome by the emotions inspired by the history she related. A long pause ensued: at length one of the party observed, "Maria, then, was the sacrifice to her goodness."

"The French," said the countess, "did not venerate her holy vocation; one peasant girl to them was the same as another. The immolation of any victim suited their purpose of awe-striking the peasantry. Scarcely, however, had the shot entered her heart, and her blameless spirit been received by the saints in Paradise, when Domenico and his followers rushed down the hill to avenge her and themselves. The contest was furious and bloody; twenty French soldiers fell, and not one of the banditti escaped; Domenico, the foremost of the assailants, being the first to fall."

I asked, "And where are now Anina and her father?"

"You may see them, if you will," said the countess, "on your return to Rome. She is a nun of Santa Chiara. Constant acts of benevolence and piety have inspired her with calm and resignation. Her prayers are daily put up for Domenico's soul, and she hopes, through the intercession of the Virgin, to rejoin him in the other world.

"Andrea is very old; he has outlived the memory of his sufferings; but he derives comfort from the filial attentions of his surviving daughter. But when I look at [100] his cottage on this lake, and remember the happy laughing face of Anina among the vines, I shudder at the recollection of the passion that has made her cheeks pale, her thoughts for ever conversant with death, her only wish to find repose in the grave."

Title

By the Author of Waverley. [Scott, Sir Walter.] "The Tapestried Chamber, or The Lady in the Sacque." KS 1829. 123-142. [123]

THE TAPESTRIED CHAMBER,[3]
OR
THE LADY IN THE SACQUE.
BY THE AUTHOR OF WAVERLEY.

The following narrative is given from the pen, so far as memory permits, in the same character in which it was presented to the author's ear; nor has he claim to further praise, or to be more deeply censured, than in proportion to the good or bad judgment which he has employed in selecting his materials, as he has studiously avoided any attempt at ornament which might interfere with the simplicity of the tale.

At the same time, it must be admitted that the particular class of stories which turns on the marvellous possesses a stronger influence when told than when committed to print. The volume taken up at noonday, though rehearsing the same incidents, conveys a much more feeble impression than is achieved by the voice of the speaker on a circle of fireside auditors, who hang upon the narrative as the narrator details the minute incidents which serve to give it authenticity, and lowers his voice with an affectation of mystery while he approaches the fearful and wonderful part. It was with such advantages that the present writer heard the following events related, more than twenty years since, by the celebrated Miss Seward [124] of Litchfield, who, to her numerous accomplishments, added, in a remarkable degree, the power of narrative in private conversation. In its present form the tale must necessarily lose all the interest which was attached to it by the flexible voice and intelligent features of the gifted narrator. Yet still, read aloud to an undoubting audience by the doubtful light of the closing evening, or in silence by a decaying taper, and amidst the solitude of a half- lighted apartment, it may redeem its character as a good ghost story. Miss Seward always affirmed that she had derived her information from an authentic source, although she suppressed the names of the two persons chiefly concerned. I will not avail myself of any particulars I may have since received concerning the localities of the detail, but suffer them to rest under the same general description in which they were first related to me; and for the same reason I will not add to or diminish the narrative by any circumstance, whether more or less material, but simply rehearse, as I heard it, a story of supernatural terror.

About the end of the American war, when the officers of Lord Cornwal-

---

[3] Plain text for this transcription was obtained from Literature Online <http://www.online-literature.com/walter_scott/2568/> and then compared against the original volume. For full citation, see References.

The Keepsake

lis's army, which surrendered at Yorktown, and others, who had been made prisoners during the impolitic and ill-fated controversy, were returning to their own country, to relate their adventures, and repose themselves after their fatigues, there was amongst them a general officer, to whom Miss S. gave the name of Browne, but merely, as I understood, to save the inconvenience of introducing a nameless agent in the narrative. He was an officer of merit, as well as a gentleman of high consideration for family and attainments.

Some business had carried General Browne upon a tour [125] through the western counties, when, in the conclusion of a morning stage, he found himself in the vicinity of a small country town, which presented a scene of uncommon beauty, and of a character peculiarly English.

The little town, with its stately old church, whose tower bore testimony to the devotion of ages long past, lay amidst pastures and cornfields of small extent, but bounded and divided with hedgerow timber of great age and size. There were few marks of modern improvement. The environs of the place intimated neither the solitude of decay nor the bustle of novelty; the houses were old, but in good repair; and the beautiful little river murmured freely on its way to the left of the town, neither restrained by a dam nor bordered by a towing-path.

Upon a gentle eminence, nearly a mile to the southward of the town, were seen, amongst many venerable oaks and tangled thickets, the turrets of a castle as old as the walls of York and Lancaster, but which seemed to have received important alterations during the age of Elizabeth and her successor, It had not been a place of great size; but whatever accommodation it formerly afforded was, it must be supposed, still to be obtained within its walls. At least, such was the inference which General Browne drew from observing the smoke arise merrily from several of the ancient wreathed and carved chimney-stalks. The wall of the park ran alongside of the highway for two or three hundred yards; and through the different points by which the eye found glimpses into the woodland scenery, it seemed to be well stocked. Other points of view opened in succession—now a full one of the front of the old castle, and now a side glimpse at its particular towers, the former rich in all the bizarrerie of the Elizabethan school, while the simple [126] and solid strength of other parts of the building seemed to show that they had been raised more for defence than ostentation.

Delighted with the partial glimpses which he obtained of the castle through the woods and glades by which this ancient feudal fortress was surrounded, our military traveller was determined to inquire whether it might not deserve a nearer view, and whether it contained family pictures or other objects of curiosity worthy of a stranger's visit, when, leaving the vicinity of the park, he rolled through a clean and well-paved street, and stopped at the door of a well-frequented inn.

Before ordering horses, to proceed on his journey, General Browne made inquiries concerning the proprietor of the chateau which had so attracted his admiration, and was equally surprised and pleased at hearing in reply a nobleman named, whom we shall call Lord Woodville. How fortunate! Much of Browne's early recollections, both at school and at college, had been connected with young Woodville, whom, by a few questions, he now ascertained to be the same with the owner of this fair domain. He had been raised to the peerage by the decease of his father a few months before, and, as the General learned from the landlord, the term of mourning being ended, was now taking possession of his paternal estate in the jovial season of merry, autumn, accompanied by a select party of friends, to enjoy the sports of a country famous for game.

This was delightful news to our traveller. Frank Woodville had been Richard Browne's fag at Eton, and his chosen intimate at Christ Church; their pleasures and their tasks had been the same; and the honest soldier's [127] heart warmed to find his early friend in possession of so delightful a residence, and of an estate, as the landlord assured him with a nod and a wink, fully adequate to maintain and add to his dignity. Nothing was more natural than that the traveller should suspend a journey, which there was nothing to render hurried, to pay a visit to an old friend under such agreeable circumstances.

The fresh horses, therefore, had only the brief task of conveying the General's travelling carriage to Woodville Castle. A porter admitted them at a modern Gothic lodge, built in that style to correspond with the castle itself, and at the same time rang a bell to give warning of the approach of visitors. Apparently the sound of the bell had suspended the separation of the company, bent on the various amusements of the morning; for, on entering the court of the chateau, several young men were lounging about in their sporting dresses, looking at and criticizing the dogs which the keepers held in readiness to attend their pastime. As General Browne alighted, the young lord came to the gate of the hall, and for an instant gazed, as at a stranger, upon the countenance of his friend, on which war, with its fatigues and its wounds, had made a great alteration. But the uncertainty lasted no longer than till the visitor had spoken, and the hearty greeting which followed was such as can only be exchanged betwixt those who have passed together the merry days of careless boyhood or early youth.

"If I could have formed a wish, my dear Browne," said Lord Woodville, "it would have been to have you here, of all men, upon this occasion, which my friends are good enough to hold as a sort of holiday. Do not think you have been unwatched during the years you have been ab- [127] sent from us. I have traced you through your dangers, your triumphs, your misfortunes, and was delighted to see that, whether in victory or defeat, the name of my old friend was always distinguished with applause."

The General made a suitable reply, and congratulated his friend on his new dignities, and the possession of a place and domain so beautiful.

"Nay, you have seen nothing of it as yet," said Lord Woodville, "and I trust you do not mean to leave us till you are better acquainted with it. It is true, I confess, that my present party is pretty large, and the old house, like other places of the kind, does not possess so much accommodation as the extent of the outward walls appears to promise. But we can give you a comfortable old-fashioned room, and I venture to suppose that your campaigns have taught you to be glad of worse quarters."

The General shrugged his shoulders, and laughed. "I presume," he said, "the worst apartment in your chateau is considerably superior to the old tobacco-cask in which I was fain to take up my night's lodging when I was in the Bush, as the Virginians call it, with the light corps. There I lay, like Diogenes himself, so delighted with my covering from the elements, that I made a vain attempt to have it rolled on to my next quarters; but my commander for the time would give way to no such luxurious provision, and I took farewell of my beloved cask with tears in my eyes."

"Well, then, since you do not fear your quarters," said Lord Woodville, "you will stay with me a week at least. Of guns, dogs, fishing-rods, flies, and means of sport by sea and land, we have enough and to spare—you cannot pitch on an amusement but we will find the means of pursuing [129] it. But if you prefer the gun and pointers, I will go with you myself, and see whether you have mended your shooting since you have been amongst the Indians of the back settlements."

The General gladly accepted his friendly host's proposal in all its points. After a morning of manly exercise, the company met at dinner, where it was the delight of Lord Woodville to conduce to the display of the high properties of his recovered friend, so as to recommend him to his guests, most of whom were persons of distinction. He led General Browne to speak of the scenes he had witnessed; and as every word marked alike the brave officer and the sensible man, who retained possession of his cool judgment under the most imminent dangers, the company looked upon the soldier with general respect, as on one who had proved himself possessed of an uncommon portion of personal courage—that attribute of all others of which everybody desires to be thought possessed.

The day at Woodville Castle ended as usual in such mansions. The hospitality stopped within the limits of good order. Music, in which the young lord was a proficient, succeeded to the circulation of the bottle; cards and billiards, for those who preferred such amusements, were in readiness; but the exercise of the morning required early hours, and not long after eleven o'clock the guests began to retire to their several apartments.

The young lord himself conducted his friend, General Browne, to the chamber destined for him, which answered the description he had given of it, being comfortable, but old-fashioned. The bed was of the massive form used in the end of the seventeenth century, and the curtains of faded silk, heavily trimmed with tarnished [130] gold. But then the sheets, pillows, and blankets looked delightful to the campaigner, when he thought of his "mansion, the cask." There was an air of gloom in the tapestry hangings, which, with their worn-out graces, curtained the walls of the little chamber, and gently undulated as the autumnal breeze found its way through the ancient lattice window, which pattered and whistled as the air gained entrance. The toilet, too, with its mirror, turbaned after the manner of the beginning of the century, with a coiffure of murrey-coloured silk, and its hundred strange-shaped boxes, providing for arrangements which had been obsolete for more than fifty years, had an antique, and in so far a melancholy, aspect. But nothing could blaze more brightly and cheerfully than the two large wax candles; or if aught could rival them, it was the flaming, bickering fagots in the chimney, that sent at once their gleam and their warmth through the snug apartment, which, notwithstanding the general antiquity of its appearance, was not wanting in the least convenience that modern habits rendered either necessary or desirable.

"This is an old-fashioned sleeping apartment, General," said the young lord; "but I hope you find nothing that makes you envy your old tobacco-cask."

"I am not particular respecting my lodgings," replied the General; "yet were I to make any choice, I would prefer this chamber by many degrees to the gayer and more modern rooms of your family mansion. Believe me that, when I unite its modern air of comfort with its venerable antiquity, and recollect that it is your lordship's property, I shall feel in better quarters here than if I were in the best hotel London could afford." [131]

"I trust—I have no doubt—that you will find yourself as comfortable as I wish you, my dear General," said the young nobleman; and once more bidding his guest good-night, he shook him by the hand, and withdrew.

The General once more looked round him, and internally congratulating himself on his return to peaceful life, the comforts of which were endeared by the recollection of the hardships and dangers he had lately sustained, undressed himself, and prepared for a luxurious night's rest.

Here, contrary to the custom of this species of tale, we leave the General in possession of his apartment until the next morning.

The company assembled for breakfast at an early hour, but without the appearance of General Browne, who seemed the guest that Lord Woodville was desirous of honouring above all whom his hospitality had assembled around him. He more than once expressed surprise at the General's absence, and at length sent a servant to make inquiry after him. The man brought back information that General Browne had been walking abroad since an early hour of the morning, in defiance of the weather, which was misty and ungenial.

"The custom of a soldier," said the young nobleman to his friends. "Many of them acquire habitual vigilance, and cannot sleep after the early hour at which their duty usually commands them to be alert."

Yet the explanation which Lord Woodville thus offered to the company seemed hardly satisfactory to his own mind, and it was in a fit of silence and abstraction that he waited the return of the General. It took place near an hour after the breakfast bell had rung. He looked fatigued [132] and feverish. His hair, the powdering and arrangement of which was at this time one of the most important occupations of a man's whole day, and marked his fashion as much as in the present time the tying of a cravat, or the want of one, was dishevelled, uncurled, void of powder, and dank with dew. His clothes were huddled on with a careless negligence, remarkable in a military man, whose real or supposed duties are usually held to include some attention to the toilet; and his looks were haggard and ghastly in a peculiar degree.

"So you have stolen a march upon us this morning, my dear General," said Lord Woodville; "or you have not found your bed so much to your mind as I had hoped and you seemed to expect. How did you rest last night?"

"Oh, excellently well! remarkably well! never better in my life," said General Browne rapidly, and yet with an air of embarrassment which was obvious to his friend. He then hastily swallowed a cup of tea, and neglecting or refusing whatever else was offered, seemed to fall into a fit of abstraction.

"You will take the gun to-day, General?" said his friend and host, but had to repeat the question twice ere he received the abrupt answer, "No, my lord; I am sorry I cannot have the opportunity of spending another day with your lordship; my post horses are ordered, and will be here directly."

All who were present showed surprise, and Lord Woodville immediately replied "Post horses, my good friend! What can you possibly want with them when you promised to stay with me quietly for at least a week?"

"I believe," said the General, obviously much embarrassed, [133] "that I might, in the pleasure of my first meeting with your lordship, have said something about stopping here a few days; but I have since found it altogether impossible."

"That is very extraordinary," answered the young nobleman. "You seemed quite disengaged yesterday, and you cannot have had a summons to-day, for our post has not come up from the town, and therefore you cannot have received any letters."

General Browne, without giving any further explanation, muttered something about indispensable business, and insisted on the absolute necessity of his departure in a manner which silenced all opposition on the part of his host, who saw that his resolution was taken, and forbore all further importunity.

"At least, however," he said, "permit me, my dear Browne, since go you will or must, to show you the view from the terrace, which the mist, that is now rising, will soon display."

He threw open a sash-window, and stepped down upon the terrace as he spoke. The General followed him mechanically, but seemed little to attend to what his host was saying, as, looking across an extended and rich prospect, he pointed out the different objects worthy of observation. Thus they moved on till Lord Woodville had attained his purpose of drawing his guest entirely apart from the rest of the company, when, turning round upon him with an air of great solemnity, he addressed him thus:—

"Richard Browne, my old and very dear friend, we are now alone. Let me conjure you to answer me upon the word of a friend, and the honour of a soldier. How did you in reality rest during last night?"

"Most wretchedly indeed, my lord," answered the [134] General, in the same tone of solemnity—"so miserably, that I would not run the risk of such a second night, not only for all the lands belonging to this castle, but for all the country which I see from this elevated point of view."

"This is most extraordinary," said the young lord, as if speaking to himself; "then there must be something in the reports concerning that apartment." Again turning to the General, he said, "For God's sake, my dear friend, be candid with me, and let me know the disagreeable particulars which have befallen you under a roof, where, with consent of the owner, you should have met nothing save comfort."

The General seemed distressed by this appeal, and paused a moment before he replied. "My dear lord," he at length said, "what happened to me last night is of a nature so peculiar and so unpleasant, that I could hardly bring myself to detail it even to your lordship, were it not that, independent of my wish to gratify any request of yours, I think that sincerity on my part may lead to some explanation about a circumstance equally painful and mysterious. To others, the communication I am about to make, might place me in the light of a weak-minded, superstitious fool, who suffered his own imagination to delude and bewilder him; but you have known me in childhood and youth, and will not suspect me of having adopted in manhood the feelings and frailties from which my early years were free." Here he paused, and his friend replied,—

"Do not doubt my perfect confidence in the truth of your communication, however strange it may be," replied Lord Woodville. "I know your firmness of disposition too well, to suspect you could be made the object of im- [135] position, and am aware that your honour and your friendship will equally deter you from exaggerating whatever you may have witnessed."

"Well, then," said the General, "I will proceed with my story as well as I can, relying upon your candour, and yet distinctly feeling that I would rather face a battery than recall to my mind the odious recollections of last night."

He paused a second time, and then perceiving that Lord Woodville remained silent and in an attitude of attention, he commenced, though not without obvious reluctance, the history of his night's adventures in the Tapestried Chamber.

The Keepsake

"I undressed and went to bed so soon as your lordship left me yesterday evening; but the wood in the chimney, which nearly fronted my bed, blazed brightly and cheerfully, and, aided by a hundred exciting recollections of my childhood and youth, which had been recalled by the unexpected pleasure of meeting your lordship, prevented me from falling immediately asleep. I ought, however, to say that these reflections were all of a pleasant and agreeable kind, grounded on a sense of having for a time exchanged the labour, fatigues, and dangers of my profession for the enjoyments of a peaceful life, and the reunion of those friendly and affectionate ties which I had torn asunder at the rude summons of war.

"While such pleasing reflections were stealing over my mind, and gradually lulling me to slumber, I was suddenly aroused by a sound like that of the rustling of a silken gown, and the tapping of a pair of high-heeled shoes, as if a woman were walking in the apartment. Ere I could draw the curtain to see what the matter was, the figure of a little woman passed between the bed and the fire. The back of this form was turned to me, and I could [136] observe, from the shoulders and neck, it was that of an old woman, whose dress was an old-fashioned gown, which I think ladies call a sacque—that is, a sort of robe completely loose in the body, but gathered into broad plaits upon the neck and shoulders, which fall down to the ground, and terminate in a species of train.

"I thought the intrusion singular enough, but never harboured for a moment the idea that what I saw was anything more than the mortal form of some old woman about the establishment, who had a fancy to dress like her grandmother, and who, having perhaps (as your lordship mentioned that you were rather straitened for room) been dislodged from her chamber for my accommodation, had forgotten the circumstance, and returned by twelve to her old haunt. Under this persuasion I moved myself in bed and coughed a little, to make the intruder sensible of my being in possession of the premises. She turned slowly round, but, gracious Heaven! my lord, what a countenance did she display to me! There was no longer any question what she was, or any thought of her being a living being. Upon a face which wore the fixed features of a corpse were imprinted the traces of the vilest and most hideous passions which had animated her while she lived. The body of some atrocious criminal seemed to have been given up from the grave, and the soul restored from the penal fire, in order to form for a space a union with the ancient accomplice of its guilt. I started up in bed, and sat upright, supporting myself on my palms, as I gazed on this horrible spectre. The hag made, as it seemed, a single and swift stride to the bed where I lay, and squatted herself down upon it, in precisely the same attitude which I had assumed in the extremity of horror, advancing her diabolical countenance within half a yard of mine,

PLATE: The Tapestried Chamber.
Steel plate engraving; drawn by Philip Francis Stephanoff;
engraved by Joseph Goodyear; printed by McQueen

[137]with a grin which seemed to intimate the malice and the derision of an incarnate fiend."

Here General Browne stopped, and wiped from his brow the cold perspiration with which the recollection of his horrible vision had covered it.

"My lord," he said, "I am no coward, I have been in all the mortal dangers incidental to my profession, and I may truly boast that no man ever knew Richard Browne dishonour the sword he wears; but in these horrible circumstances, under the eyes, and, as it seemed, almost in the grasp of an incarnation of an evil spirit, all firmness forsook me, all manhood melted from me like wax in the furnace, and I felt my hair individually bristle. The current of my life-blood ceased to flow, and I sank back in a swoon, as very a victim to panic terror as ever was a village girl, or a child of ten years old. How long I lay in this condition I cannot pretend to guess.

"But I was roused by the castle clock striking one, so loud that it seemed as if it were in the very room. It was some time before I dared open my eyes, lest they should again encounter the horrible spectacle. When, however, I summoned courage to look up, she was no longer visible. My first idea was to pull my bell, wake the servants, and remove to a garret or a hay-loft, to be ensured against a second visitation. Nay, I will confess the truth that my resolution was altered, not by the shame of exposing myself, but by the fear that, as the bell-cord hung by the chimney, I might, in making my way to it, be again crossed by the fiendish hag, who, I figured to myself, might be still lurking about some corner of the apartment.

"I will not pretend to describe what hot and cold fever-fits tormented me for the rest of the night, through broken sleep, [138] weary vigils, and that dubious state which forms the neutral ground between them. A hundred terrible objects appeared to haunt me; but there was the great difference betwixt the vision which I have described, and those which followed, that I knew the last to be deceptions of my own fancy and over-excited nerves.

"Day at last appeared, and I rose from my bed ill in health and humiliated in mind. I was ashamed of myself as a man and a soldier, and still more so at feeling my own extreme desire to escape from the haunted apartment, which, however, conquered all other considerations; so that, huddling on my clothes with the most careless haste, I made my escape from your lordship's mansion, to seek in the open air some relief to my nervous system, shaken as it was by this horrible rencounter with a visitant, for such I must believe her, from the other world. Your lordship has now heard the cause of my discomposure, and of my sudden desire to leave your hospitable castle. In other places I trust we may often meet, but God protect me from ever spending a second night under that roof!"

Strange as the General's tale was, he spoke with such a deep air of conviction that it cut short all the usual commentaries which are made on such stories. Lord Woodville never once asked him if he was sure he did not dream of the apparition, or suggested any of the possibilities by which it is fashionable to explain supernatural appearances as wild vagaries of the fancy, or deceptions of the optic nerves, On the contrary, he seemed deeply impressed with the truth and reality of what he had heard; and, after a considerable pause regretted, with much appearance of sincerity, that his early friend should in his house have suffered so severely. [139]

"I am the more sorry for your pain, my dear Browne," he continued, "that it is the unhappy, though most unexpected, result of an experiment of my own. You must know that, for my father and grandfather's time, at least, the apartment which was assigned to you last night had been shut on account of reports that it was disturbed by supernatural sights and noises. When I came, a few weeks since, into possession of the estate, I thought the accommodation which the castle afforded for my friends was not extensive enough to permit the inhabitants of the invisible world to retain possession of a comfortable sleeping apartment. I therefore caused the Tapestried Chamber, as we call it, to be opened, and, without destroying its air of antiquity, I had such new articles of furniture placed in it as became the modern times. Yet, as the opinion that the room was haunted very strongly prevailed among the domestics, and was also known in the neighbourhood and to many of my friends, I feared some prejudice might be entertained by the first occupant of the Tapestried Chamber, which might tend to revive the evil report which it had laboured under, and so disappoint my purpose of rendering it a useful part or the house. I must confess, my dear Browne, that your arrival yesterday, agreeable to me for a thousand reasons besides, seemed the most favourable opportunity of removing the unpleasant rumours which attached to the room, since your courage was indubitable, and your mind free of any preoccupation on the subject. I could not, therefore, have chosen a more fitting subject for my experiment."

"Upon my life," said General Browne, somewhat hastily, "I am infinitely obliged to your lordship—very particularly indebted indeed. I am likely to remember for [140] some time the consequences of the experiment, as your lordship is pleased to call it."

"Nay, now you are unjust, my dear friend," said Lord Woodville. "You have only to reflect for a single moment, in order to be convinced that I could not augur the possibility of the pain to which you have been so unhappily exposed. I was yesterday morning a complete sceptic on the subject of supernatural appearances. Nay, I am sure that, had I told you what was said about that room, those very reports would have induced you, by your own choice, to select it for your accommodation. It was my misfortune, perhaps my error, but really cannot be termed my fault, that you have been afflicted so strangely."

"Strangely indeed!" said the General, resuming his good temper; "and I acknowledge that I have no right to be offended with your lordship for treating me like what I used to think myself—a man of some firmness and courage. But I see my post horses are arrived, and I must not detain your lordship from your amusement."

"Nay, my old friend," said Lord Woodville, "since you cannot stay with us another day—which, indeed, I can no longer urge—give me at least half an hour more. You used to love pictures, and I have a gallery of portraits, some of them by Vandyke, representing ancestry to whom this property and castle formerly belonged. I think that several of them will strike you as possessing merit."

General Browne accepted the invitation, though somewhat unwillingly. It was evident he was not to breathe freely or at ease till he left Woodville Castle far behind him. He could not refuse his friend's invitation, however; and the less so, that he was a little ashamed of the peevish- [141] ness which he had displayed towards his well-meaning entertainer.

The general, therefore, followed Lord Woodville through several rooms into a long gallery hung with pictures, which the latter pointed out to his guest, telling the names, and giving some account of the personages whose portraits presented themselves in progression. General Browne was but little interested in the details which these accounts conveyed to him. They were, indeed, of the kind which are usually found in an old family gallery. Here was a Cavalier who had ruined the estate in the royal cause; there a fine lady who had reinstated it by contracting a match with a wealthy Roundhead. There hung a gallant who had been in danger for corresponding with the exiled Court at Saint Germain's; here one who had taken arms for William at the Revolution; and there a third that had thrown his weight alternately into the scale of Whig and Tory.

While Lord Woodville was cramming these words into his guest's ear, "against the stomach of his sense," they gained the middle of the gallery, when he beheld General Browne suddenly start, and assume an attitude of the utmost surprise, not unmixed with fear, as his eyes were suddenly caught and riveted by a portrait of an old lady in a sacque, the fashionable dress of the end of the seventeenth century.

"There she is!" he exclaimed—"there she is, in form and features, though Inferior in demoniac expression to the accursed hag who visited me last night!"

"If that be the case," said the young nobleman, "there can remain no longer any doubt of the horrible reality of your apparition. That is the picture of a wretched ancestress of mine, of whose crimes a black and fearful catalogue [142] is recorded in a family history in my charter-chest. The recital of them would be too horrible; it is enough to say, that in yon fatal apartment incest and unnatural murder were committed. I will restore it to the solitude to which the better judgment of those who preceded me had consigned it; and never shall any one, so long as I can prevent it, be exposed to a repetition of the supernatural horrors which could shake such courage as yours."

Thus the friends, who had met with such glee, parted in a very different mood—Lord Woodville to command the Tapestried Chamber to be unmantled, and the door built up; and General Browne to seek in some less beautiful country, and with some less dignified friend, forgetfulness of the painful night which he had passed in Woodville Castle.

Title

By the Author of Frankenstein. [Shelley, Mary.] "Ferdinando Eboli. A Tale." KS 1829. 195-218. [195]

FERDINANDO EBOLI.[4]
A TALE.
BY THE AUTHOR OF *FRANKENSTEIN*.

DURING this quiet time of peace, we are fast forgetting the excitements and astonishing events of the last war; and the very names of Europe's conquerors are becoming antiquated to the ears of our children. Those were more romantic days than these; for the revulsions occasioned by revolution or invasion were full of romance; and travellers in those countries in which these scenes had place hear strange and wonderful stories, whose truth so much resembles fiction, that, while interested in the narration, we never give implicit credence to the narrator. Of this kind is a tale I heard at Naples. The fortunes of war perhaps did not influence its actors; yet it appears improbable that any circumstances so out of the usual routine could have had place under the garish daylight that peace sheds upon the world.

When Murat, then called Gioacchino, king of Naples, raised his Italian regiments, several young nobles, who had before been scarcely more than vine-dressers on the soil, were inspired with a love of arms, and presented themselves as candidates for military honours. Among these was the young Count Eboli. The father of this youthful; noble had followed Ferdinand to Sicily; but his estates, lay principally near Salerno and he was naturally desirous of [196] preserving them; while the hopes that the French government held out of glory and prosperity to his country made him often regret that he had followed his legitimate but imbecile king to exile. When he died, therefore, he recommended his son to return to Naples, to present himself to his old and tried friend, the Marchese Spina, who held a high office in Murat's government, and through his means to reconcile himself to the new king. All this was easily achieved. The young and gallant Count was permitted to possess his patrimony; and, as a further pledge of good fortune, he was betrothed to the only child of the Marchese Spina. The nuptials were deferred till the end of the ensuing campaign.

Meanwhile the army was put in motion, and Count Eboli only obtained such short leave of absence as permitted him to visit for a few hours the villa of his future father-in-law, there to take leave of him and his affianced bride. The villa was situated on one of the Apennines to the north of Salerno, and looked down, over the plain of Calabria, in which Paestum is situated, on to the blue Mediterranean. A precipice on one side, a brawling mountain torrent, and a thick grove of

---
4 Plain text for this story was obtained from *The Last Man: A Romantic Circles Edition* <http://www.rc.umd.edu/editions/mws/lastman/eboli.htm> and then compared against the original volume. For full citation, see References.

ilex, added beauty to the sublimity of its site. Count Eboli ascended the mountain path in all the joy of youth and hope. His stay was brief. An exhortation and a blessing from the Marchese, a tender farewell, graced by gentle tears, from the fair Adalinda, were the recollections he was to bear with him, to inspire him with courage and hope in danger and absence. The sun had just sunk behind the distant isle of Istria, when, kissing his lady's hand, he said a last "Addio," and with slower steps, and more melancholy mien, rode down the mountain on his road to Naples. [197]

That same night Adalinda retired early to her apartment, dismissing her attendants; and then, restless from mingled fear and hope, she threw open the glass door that led to a balcony looking over the edge of the hill upon the torrent, whose loud rushing often lulled her to sleep; but whose waters were concealed from sight by the ilex trees, which lifted their topmost branches above the guarding parapet of the balcony.

Leaning her cheek upon her hand, she thought of the dangers her lover would encounter, of her loneliness the while, of his letters, and of his return. A rustling sound now caught her ear: was it the breeze among the ilex trees? her own veil was unwaved by every wind, her tresses even, heavy in their own rich beauty only, were not lifted from her cheek. Again those sounds. Her blood retreated to her heart, and her limbs trembled. What could it mean? Suddenly the upper branches of the nearest tree were disturbed; they opened, and the faint starlight showed a man's figure among them. He prepared to spring from his hold, on to the wall. It was a feat of peril. First the soft voice of her lover bade her "Fear not," and on the next instant he was at her side, calming her terrors, and recalling her spirits, that almost left her gentle frame, from mingled surprise, dread, and joy. He encircled her waist with his arm, and pouring forth a thousand passionate expressions of love, she leant on his shoulder, and wept from agitation; while he covered her hands with kisses, and gazed on her ardent adoration.

Then in calmer mood they sat together; triumph and joy lighted up his eyes, and a modest blush glowed on her cheek; for never before had she sat alone with him, nor heard unrestrained his impassioned assurances of affection. [198] It was indeed Love's own hour. The stars trembled on the roof of his eternal temple; the dashing of the torrent, the mild summer atmosphere, and the mysterious aspect of the darkened scenery, were all in unison, to inspire security and voluptuous hope. They talked of how their hearts, through the medium of divine nature, might hold commune during absence of the joys of re-union, and of their prospect of perfect happiness.

The moment at last arrived when he must depart. "One tress of this silken hair," said he, raising one of the many curls that clustered on her neck. "I will place it on my heart, a shield to protect me against the swords and halls of the enemy." He drew his keen-edged dagger from its sheath. "Ill weapon for so gentle a deed," he said, severing the lock, and at the same moment many drops of blood fell fast on the fair arm of the lady. He answered her fearful inquiries by showing a gash he had awkwardly inflicted on his left hand. First he insisted on securing his prize, and then he permitted her to bind his wound, which she did half laughing, half in sorrow, winding round his hand a riband loosened from her own arm. "Now farewell," he cried; "I must ride twenty miles ere dawn, and the descending Bear shows that midnight is past." His descent was difficult, but he achieved it happily, and the stave of a song, whose soft sounds rose like the smoke of incense from an altar, from the dell below, to her impatient ear, assured her of his safety.

As is always the case when an account is gathered from eye-witnesses, I never could ascertain the exact date of these events. They occurred however while Murat was king of Naples, and when he raised his Italian regiments, Count Eboli, as aforesaid, became a junior officer in them, [199] and served with much distinction; though I cannot name either the country, or the battle in which he acted so conspicuous a part, that he was on the spot promoted to a troop.

Not long after this event, and while he was stationed in the north of Italy, Gioacchino, sending for him to head-quarters late one evening, intrusted him with a confidential mission, across a country occupied by the enemy's troops, to a town possessed by the French. It was necessary to undertake the expedition during the night, and he was expected to return on that, succeeding the following, day. The king himself gave him his despatches and the word; and the noble youth, with modest firmness, protested that he would succeed, or die, in the fulfillment of his trust.

It was already night, and the crescent moon was low in the west, when Count Ferdinando Eboli mounting his favourite horse, at a quick gallop, cleared the streets of the town; and then, following the directions given him, crossed the country among the fields planted with vines, carefully avoiding the main road. It was a beauteous and still night; calm, and sleep, occupied the earth; war, the bloodhound, slumbered; the spirit of love alone had life at that silent hour. Exulting in the hope of glory, our young hero commenced his journey, and visions of aggrandizement and love formed his reveries. A distant shout roused him; he checked his horse and listened; voices approached; when recognising the speech of a German, he turned from the path he was following, to a still straighter way. But again the tone of an enemy was heard, and the trampling of horses. Eboli did not hesitate; he dismounted, tied his steed to a tree, and, skirting along the enclosure of the field, trusted to escape thus unobserved. He succeeded after an hour's painful progress, and arrived on the borders of a [200] stream, which, as the boundary between two states, was the mark of his having finally escaped danger. Descending the steep bank of the river, which, with his horse, he might perhaps have forded, he now prepared to swim. He held his despatch in one hand, threw away his cloak, and was about to plunge into the water, when from under the dark shade of the argine, which had concealed them, he was suddenly arrested by unseen hands, cast on the ground, bound, gagged and blinded, and then placed in a little boat, which was sculled with infinite rapidity down the stream.

There seemed so much of premeditation in the act that it baffled conjecture, yet he must believe himself a prisoner to the Austrian. While, however, he still vainly reflected, the boat was moored, he was lifted out, and the change of atmosphere made him aware that they entered some house. With extreme care and celerity, yet in the utmost silence, he was stripped of his clothes, and two rings he wore, drawn from his fingers; other habiliments were thrown over him; and then no departing footstep was audible: but soon he heard the splash of a single oar, and he felt himself alone. He lay perfectly unable to move; the only relief his captor or captors had afforded him being the exchange of the gag for a tightly bound handkerchief. For hours he thus remained, with a tortured mind, bursting with rage, impatience, and disappointment; now writhing, as well as he could, in his endeavours to free himself; now still, in despair. His despatches were taken away, and the period was swiftly passing when he could by his presence have remedied in some degree of this evil. The morning dawned; and though the full glare of the sun could not visit his eyes, he felt it play upon his limbs. As the day advanced, hunger preyed on him, and though amidst the visitation of mightier, he [201] at first disdained this minor, evil; towards evening, it became, in spite of himself, the predominant sensation. Night approached, and the fear that he should remain, and even starve, in this unvisited solitude had more than once thrilled through his frame, when feminine voices and a child's gay laugh met his ear. He heard persons enter the apartment, and he was asked in his native language, while the ligature was taken from his mouth, the cause of his present situation. He attributed it to banditti: his bonds were quickly cut, and his banded eyes restored to sight. It was long before he recovered himself. Water brought from the stream, however, was some refreshment, and by degrees he resumed the use of his senses, and saw that he was in a dilapidated shepherd's cot; with no one near him save the peasant girl and a child who had liberated him. They rubbed his ankles and wrists, and the little fellow offered him some bread, and eggs; after which refreshment, and an hour's repose, Ferdinando felt himself sufficiently restored to revolve his adventure in his mind, and to determine on the conduct he was to pursue.

He looked at the dress which had been given him in exchange for that which he had worn. It was of the plainest and meanest description. Still no time was to be lost; and he felt assured that the only step he could take was to return with all speed to the head-quarters of the Neapolitan army, and inform the king of his disasters and his loss.

It were long to follow his backward steps, and to tell all of indignation and disappointment that swelled his heart. He walked painfully but resolutely all night, and by three in the morning entered the town where Gioacchino then was.

He was challenged by the sentinels; [202] he gave the word confided to him by Murat, and was instantly made prisoner by the soldiers. He declared to them his name and rank, and the necessity he was under of immediately seeing the king. He was taken to the guard-house, and the officer on duty there listened with contempt to his representations, telling him that Count Ferdinando Eboli had returned three hours before, ordering him to be confined for further examination as a spy. Eboli loudly insisted that some impostor had taken his name; and while he related the story of his capture, another officer came in, who recognised his person; other individuals acquainted with him joined the party; and as the impostor had been seen by none but the officer of the night, his tale gained ground.

A young Frenchman of superior rank, who had orders to attend the king early in the morning, carried a report of what was going forward to Murat himself. The tale was so strange that the king sent for the young Count; and then, in spite of having seen and believed in his counterfeit a few hours before, and having received from him an account of his mission, which had been faithfully executed, the appearance of the youth staggered him, and he commanded the presence of him who, as Count Eboli, had appeared before him a few hours previously. As Ferdinand stood beside the king, his eye glanced at a large and splendid mirror. His matted hair, his blood-shot eyes, his haggard looks, and torn and mean dress, derogated from the nobility of his appearance; and still less did he appear like the magnificent Count Eboli, when, to his utter confusion and astonishment, his counterfeit stood beside him.

He was perfect in all the outward signs that denoted [203] high birth; and so like him whom he represented, that it would have been impossible to discern one from the other apart. The same chestnut hair clustered on his brow; the sweet and animated hazel eyes were the same; the one voice was the echo of the other. The composure and dignity of the pretender gained the suffrages of those around. When he was told of the strange appearance of another Count Eboli, he laughed in a frank good humored manner, and turning to Ferdinand, said, "You honour me much, in selecting me for your personation; but there are two or three things I like about myself so well, that you must excuse my unwillingness to exchange myself for you." Ferdinand would have answered, but the false Count, with greater haughtiness, turning to the king said, "Will your majesty decide between us? I cannot bandy words with a fellow of this sort." Irritated by scorn, Ferdinand demanded leave to challenge the pretender; who said, that if the king and his brother officers did not think that he should degrade himself and disgrace the army by going out with a common vagabond, he was willing to chastise him, even at the peril of his own life. But the king, after a few more questions, feeling assured that the unhappy noble was an impostor, in severe and menacing terms reprehended him for his insolence, telling him that he owed it to his mercy alone that he was not executed as a spy, ordering him instantly to be conducted without the walls of the town, with threats of weighty punishment if he ever dared to subject his impostures to further trial.

It requires a strong imagination, and the experience of much misery, fully to enter into Ferdinand's feelings. From high rank, glory, hope, and love, he was hurled to utter beggary and disgrace. The insulting words of his [204] triumphant rival, and the degrading menaces of his so lately gracious sovereign, rang in his ears; every nerve in his frame writhed with agony. But, fortunately for the endurance of human life, the worst misery in early youth is often but a painted dream, which we cast off when slumber quits our eyes. After a struggle with intolerable anguish, hope and courage revived in his heart. His resolution was quickly made. He would return to Naples, relate his story to the Marchese Spina, and through his influence obtain at least an impartial hearing from the king. It was not, however, in his peculiar situation, an easy task to put his determination into effect. He was pennyless; his dress bespoke poverty; he had neither friend nor kinsman near, but such as would behold in him the most impudent of swindlers. Still his courage did not fail him. The kind Italian soil, in the autumnal season now advanced, furnished him with chestnuts, arbutus berries, and grapes. He took the most direct road over the hills, avoiding towns, and indeed every habitation; travelling principally in the night, when, except in cities, the officers of government had retired from their stations. How he succeeded in getting from one end of Italy to the other it is difficult to say; but certain it is, that, after the interval of a few weeks, he presented himself at the Villa Spina.

With considerable difficulty he obtained admission to the presence of the Marchese, who received him standing, with an inquiring look, not at all recognising the noble youth. Ferdinand requested a private interview, for there were several visitors present. His voice startled the Marchese, who complied, taking him into another apartment. Here Ferdinand disclosed himself, and, with rapid and agitated utterance, was relating the history of [205] his misfortunes, when the tramp of horses was heard, the great bell rang, and a domestic announced "Count Ferdinando Eboli." "It is himself," cried the youth, turning pale. The words were strange, and they appeared still more so, when the person announced entered; the perfect semblance of the young noble, whose name he assumed, as he had appeared, when last, at his departure, he trod the pavement of the hall. He inclined his head gracefully to the baron, turning with a glance of some surprise, but more disdain, towards Ferdinand, exclaiming, "Thou here!"

Ferdinand drew himself up to his full height. In spite of fatigue, ill fare and coarse garments, his manner was full of dignity. The Marchese looked at him fixedly and started as he marked his proud mien, and saw in his expressive features the very face of Eboli. But again he was perplexed when he turned and discerned, as in a mirror, the same countenance reflected by the new comer, who underwent this scrutiny somewhat impatiently. In brief and scornful words, he told the Marchese that this was a second attempt in the intruder to impose himself as Count Eboli; that the trick had failed before, and would again; adding, laughing, that it was hard to be brought to prove himself to be himself, against the assertion of a briccone, whose likeness to him, and matchless impudence, were his whole stock in trade.

"Why, my good fellow," continued he, sneeringly, "you put me out of conceit with myself, to think that one, apparently so like me, should get on no better in the world."

The blood mounted into Ferdinand's cheeks on his enemy's bitter taunts; with difficulty he restrained himself from closing with his foe, while the words "traitorous im-[206] postor!" burst from his lips. The baron commanded the fierce youth to be silent, and, moved by a look that he remembered to be Ferdinand's, he said, gently, "By your respect for me, I adjure you to be patient; fear not but that I will deal impartially." Then turning to the pretended Eboli, he added that he could not doubt but that he was the true Count, and asked excuse for his previous indecision. At first the latter appeared angry, but at length he burst into a laugh, and then, apologizing for his ill breeding, continued laughing heartily at the perplexity of the Marchese. It is certain, his gayety gained more credit with his auditor than the indignant glances of poor Ferdinand. The false Count then said that, after the king's menaces, he had entertained no expectation that the farce was to be played over again. He had obtained leave of absence, of which he profited to visit his future father-in-law, after having spent a few days in his own palazzo at Naples. Until now, Ferdinand had listened silently with a feeling of curiosity, anxious to learn all he could of the actions and motives of his rival; but at these last words he could no longer contain himself. "What!" cried he, "hast thou usurped my place in my own father's house, and dared assume my power in my ancestral halls?" A gush of tears overpowered the youth; he hid his face in his hands. Fierceness and pride lit up the countenance of the pretender. "By the eternal God and the sacred cross, I swear," he exclaimed, "that palace is my father's palace; those halls the halls of my ancestors!" Ferdinand looked up with surprise. "And the earth opens not," he said, "to swallow the perjured man." He then, at the call of the Marchese, related his adventures, while scorn mantled on the features of his rival. The Marchese, looking at [207] both, could not free himself from doubt. He turned from one to the other: in spite of the wild and disordered appearance of poor Ferdinand, there was something in him that forbade his friend to condemn him as the impostor; but then it was utterly impossible to pronounce such the gallant and noble-looking youth, who could only be acknowledged as the real Count by the disbelief of the other's tale. The Marchese, calling an attendant, sent for his fair daughter. "This decision," said he, "shall be made over to the subtle judgment of a woman, and the keen penetration of one who loves." Both the youths now smiled—the same smile; the same expression—that, of anticipated triumph. The baron was more perplexed than ever.

Adalinda had heard of the arrival of Count Eboli, and entered, resplendent in youth and happiness. She turned quickly towards him who resembled most the person she expected to see; when a well-known voice pronounced her name, and she gazed at last on the double appearance of the lover. Her father, taking her hand, briefly explained the mystery, and bade her assure herself which was her affianced husband.

"Signorina," said Ferdinand, "disdain me not because I appear before you thus in disgrace and misery. Your love, your goodness will restore me to prosperity and happiness."

"I know not by what means," said the wondering girl, "but surely you are Count Eboli." [208]

"Adalinda," said the rival youth, "waste not your words on a villain. Lovely and deceived one, I trust, trembling I say it, that I can with one word assure you that I am Eboli."

"Adalinda," said Ferdinand, "I placed the nuptial ring on your finger; before God your vows were given to me."

The false Count approached the lady, and bending one knee, took from his heart a locket, enclosing hair tied with a green riband, which she recognised to have worn, and pointed to a slight scar on his left hand.

Adalinda blushed deeply, and turning to her father, said, motioning towards the kneeling youth,

"He is Ferdinand."

All protestations now from the unhappy Eboli were vain. The Marchese would have cast him into a dungeon; but, at the earnest request of his rival, he was not detained, but thrust ignominiously from the villa. The rage of a wild beast newly chained was less than the tempest of indignation that now filled the heart of Ferdinand. Physical suffering, from fatigue and fasting, was added to his internal anguish; for some hours madness, if that were madness which never forgets its ill, possessed him. In a tumult of feelings there was one predominant idea: it was, to take possession of his father's house, and to try, by ameliorating the fortuitous circumstances of his lot, to gain the upper hand of his adversary. He expended his remaining strength in reaching Naples, entered his family palace, and was received and acknowledged by his astonished domestics.

One of his first acts was to take from a cabinet a miniature of his father encircled with jewels, and to invoke the aid of the paternal spirit. Refreshment and a bath restored him to some of his usual strength; and he looked forward with almost childish delight to one night to be spent in peace under the roof of his father's house. This was not permitted. Ere midnight the great bell sounded; his rival entered as master, with the Marchese Spina. [209] The result may be divined. The Marchese appeared more indignant than the false Eboli. He insisted that the unfortunate youth should be imprisoned. The portrait, whose setting was costly, found on him, proved him guilty of robbery. He was given into the hands of the police, and thrown into a dungeon. I will not dwell on the subsequent scenes. He was tried by the tribunal, condemned as guilty, and sentenced to the galleys for life.

On the eve of the day when he was to be removed from the Neapolitan prison to work on the roads in Calabria, his rival visited him in his dungeon. For some moments both looked at the other in silence. The impostor gazed on the prisoner with mingled pride and compassion: there was certainly a struggle in his heart. The answering glance of Ferdinand was calm, free, and dignified. He was not resigned to his hard fate, but he disdained to make any exhibition of despair to his cruel and successful foe. A spasm of pain seemed to wrench the bosom of the false one; and he turned aside, striving to recover the hardness of heart which had hitherto supported him in the prosecution of his guilty enterprise. Ferdinand spoke first.

"What would the triumphant criminal with his innocent victim?"

His visitant replied haughtily, "Do not address such epithets to me, or I leave you to your fate: I am that which I say I am."

"To me this boast," cried Ferdinand, scornfully; "but perhaps these walls have ears."

"Heaven, at least, is not deaf," said the deceiver; "favouring Heaven, which knows and admits my claim. But a truce to this idle discussion. Compassion—a distaste [210] to see one so very like myself in such ill condition—a foolish whim, perhaps, on which you may congratulate yourself—has led me hither. The bolts of your dungeon are drawn; here is a purse of gold; fulfil one easy condition, and you are free."

"And that condition?"

"Sign this paper."

He gave to Ferdinand a writing, containing a confession of his imputed crimes. The hand of the guilty youth trembled as he gave it; there was confusion in his mien, and a restless uneasy rolling of his eye. Ferdinand wished in one mighty word, potent as lightning, loud as thunder, to convey his burning disdain of this proposal: but expression is weak, and calm is more full of power than storm. Without a word, he tore the paper in two pieces, and threw them at the feet of his enemy.

With a sudden change of manner, his visitant conjured him, in voluble and impetuous terms, to comply. Ferdinand answered only by requesting to be left alone. Now and then a half word broke uncontrollably from his lips; but he curbed himself. Yet he could not hide his agitation when, as an argument to make him yield, the false Count assured him that he was already married to Adalinda. Bitter agony thrilled poor Ferdinand's frame; but he preserved a calm mien, and an unaltered resolution. Having exhausted every menace and every persuasion, his rival left him, the purpose for which he came unaccomplished. On the morrow, with many others, the refuse of mankind, Count Ferdinando Eboli was led in chains to the unwholesome plains of Calabria, to work there at the roads.

I must hurry over some of the subsequent events; for a detailed account of them would fill volumes. The assertion [211] of the usurper of Ferdinand's right, that he was already married to Adalinda, was, like all else he said, false. The day was, however, fixed for their union, when the illness and the subsequent death of the Marchese Spina delayed its celebration. Adalinda retired, during the first months of mourning, to a castle belonging to her father not far from Arpino, a town of the kingdom of Naples, in the midst of the Apennines, about fifty miles from the capital. Before she went, the deceiver tried to persuade her to consent to a private marriage. He was probably afraid that, in the long interval that was about to ensue before he could secure her, she would discover his imposture. Besides, a rumor had gone abroad that one of the fellow-prisoners of Ferdinand, a noted bandit, had escaped, and that the young Count was his companion in flight. Adalinda, however, refused to comply with her lover's entreaties, and retired to her seclusion with an old aunt, who was blind and deaf, but an excellent duenna.

The false Eboli seldom visited his mistress; but he was a master in his art, and subsequent events showed that he must have spent all his time disguised in the vicinity of the castle. He contrived by various means, unsuspected at the moment, to have all Adalinda's servants changed for creatures of his own; so that, without her being aware of the restraint, she was, in fact, a prisoner in her own house. It is impossible to say what first awakened her suspicions concerning the deception put upon her. She was an Italian, with all the habitual quiescence and lassitude of her countrywomen in the ordinary routine of life, and with all their energy and passion when roused. The moment the doubt darted into her mind, she resolved to be assured; a few questions relative to scenes that had passed between [212] poor Ferdinand and herself sufficed for this. They were asked so suddenly and pointedly that the pretender was thrown oft his guard; he looked confused, and stammered in his replies. Their eyes met, he felt that he was detected, and she saw that he perceived her now confirmed suspicions. A look such as is peculiar to an impostor, a glance that deformed his beauty and filled his usually noble countenance with the hideous lines of cunning and cruel triumph, completed her faith in her own discernment. "How," she thought, "could I have mistaken this man for my own gentle Eboli?" Again their eyes met: the peculiar expression of his terrified her, and she hastily quitted the apartment.

Her resolution was quickly formed. It was of no use to attempt to explain her situation to her old aunt. She determined to depart immediately for Naples, throw herself at the feet of Gioacchino, and to relate and obtain credit for her strange history. But the time was already lost when she could have executed this design. The contrivances of the deceiver were complete—she found herself a prisoner. Excesses of fear gave her boldness, if not courage. She sought her jailor. A few minutes before, she had been a young and thoughtless girl, docile as a child, and as unsuspecting. Now she felt as if she had suddenly grown old in wisdom, and that the experience of years had been gained in that of a few seconds.

During their interview, she was wary and firm; while the instinctive power of innocence over guilt gave majesty to her demeanour. The contriver of her ills for a moment cowered beneath her eye. At first he would by no means allow that he was not the person he pretended to be: but the energy and eloquence of truth bore down his [213] artifice, so that, at length driven into a corner, he turned—a stag at bay. Then it was her turn to quail; for the superior energy of a man gave him the mastery. He declared the truth. He was the elder brother of Ferdinand, a natural son of the old Count Eboli. His mother, who had been wronged, never forgave her injurer, and bred her son in deadly hate for his parent, and a belief that the advantages enjoyed by his more fortunate brother were rightfully his own. His education was rude; but he had an Italian's subtle talents, swiftness of perception, and guileful arts.

"It would blanch your check," he said to his trembling auditress, "could I describe all that I have suffered to achieve my purpose. I would trust to none—I executed all myself. It was a glorious triumph, but due to my perseverance and my fortitude, when I and my usurping brother stood, I, the noble, he, the degraded outcast, before our sovereign."

Having rapidly detailed his history, he now sought to win the favorable ear of Adalinda, who stood with averted and angry looks. He tried by the varied shows of passion and tenderness to move her heart. Was he not, in truth, the object of her love? Was it not he who scaled her balcony at Villa Spina? He recalled scenes of mutual overflow of feeling to her mind, thus urging arguments the most potent with a delicate woman: pure blushes tinged her cheek, but horror of the deceiver predominated over every other sentiment. He swore that as soon as they should be united he would free Ferdinand and bestow competency, nay, if so she willed it, half his possessions, on him. She coldly replied, that she would rather share the chains of the innocent and misery, than link herself [214] with imposture and crime. She demanded her liberty, but the untamed and even ferocious nature that had borne the deceiver through his career of crime now broke forth, and he invoked fearful imprecations on his head, if she ever quitted the castle except as his wife. His look of conscious power and unbridled wickedness terrified her; her flashing eyes spoke abhorrence: it would have been far easier for her to have died than have yielded the smallest point to a man who made her feel for one moment his irresistible power, arising from her being an unprotected woman, wholly in his hands. She left him, feeling as if she had just escaped from the impending sword of an assassin.

One hour's deliberation suggested to her a method of escape from her terrible situation. In a wardrobe at the castle lay in their pristine gloss the habiliments of a page of her mother, who had died suddenly, leaving these unworn relics of his station. Dressing herself in these, she tied up her dark shining hair, and even, with a somewhat bitter feeling, girded on the slight sword that appertained to the costume. Then, through a private passage leading from her own apartment to the chapel of the castle, she glided with noiseless steps, long after the Ave Maria sounded at twenty-four o' clock, had, on a November night, given token that half an hour had passed since the setting of the sun. She possessed the key of the chapel door—it opened at her touch; she closed it behind her, and she was free. The pathless hills were around her, the starry heavens above, and a cold wintry breeze murmured around the castle walls; but fear of her enemy conquered every other fear, and she tripped lightly on, in a kind of ecstasy, for many a long hour over the stony mountain-

PLATE: ADELINDA
Steel plate engraving; drawn by Alfred Edward Chalon, R.A.;
engraved by Charles Heath; printed by McQueen

[215] path—she, who had never before walked more than a mile or two at any time in her life,—till her feet were blistered, her slight shoes cut through, her way utterly lost. At morning's dawn she found herself in the midst of the wild ilex-

The Keepsake

covered Apennines, and neither habitation nor human being apparent.

She was hungry and weary. She had brought gold and jewels with her; but here were no means of exchanging these for food. She remembered stories of banditti; but none could be so ruffian-like and cruel as him from whom she fled. This thought, a little rest, and a draught of water from a pure mountain-spring, restored her to some portion of courage, and she continued her journey. Noonday approached; and, in the south of Italy, the noonday sun, when unclouded, even in November, is oppressively warm, especially to an Italian woman, who never exposes herself to its beams. Faintness came over her. There appeared recesses in the mountain-side along which she was travelling, grown over with bay and arbutus: she entered one of these, there to repose. It was deep, and led to another that opened into a spacious cavern lighted from above: there were cates, grapes, and a flagon of wine, on a rough hewn table. She looked fearfully around, but no inhabitant appeared. She placed herself at the table, and, half in dread, ate of the food presented to her, and then sat, her elbow on the table, her head resting on her little snow-white hand; her dark hair shading her brow and clustering round her throat. An appearance of languor and fatigue diffused through her attitude, while her soft black eyes filled at intervals with large tears, as pitying herself, she recurred to the cruel circumstances of her lot. Her fanciful but elegant dress, her feminine form, her beauty and her [216] grace, as she sat pensive and alone in the rough unhewn cavern, formed a picture a poet would describe with delight, an artist love to paint.

"She seemed a being of another world, a seraph, all light and beauty; a Ganymede, escaped from his thrall above to his natal Ida. It was long before I recognised, looking down on her from the opening hill, my lost Adalinda." Thus spoke the young Count Eboli, when he related this story; for its end was as romantic as its commencement.

When Ferdinando had arrived a galley-slave in Calabria, he found himself coupled with a bandit, a brave fellow, who abhorred his chains, from all the combination of disgrace and misery they brought upon him. Together they devised a plan of escape, and succeeded in effecting it. On their road, Ferdinand related his story to the outlaw, who encouraged him to hope a favourable turn of fate; and meanwhile invited and persuaded the desperate man to share his fortunes as a robber among the wild hills of Calabria.

The cavern where Adalinda had taken refuge was one of their fastnesses, whither they betook themselves at periods of imminent danger for safety only, as no booty could be collected in that unpeopled solitude; and there, one afternoon, returning from the chase, they found the wandering, fearful, solitary, fugitive girl; and never was lighthouse more welcome to tempest-tost sailor than was her own Ferdinand to his lady-love.

Fortune, now tired of persecuting the young noble, favoured him still further. The story of the lovers interested the bandit chief, and promise of reward secured [217] him. Ferdinand persuaded Adalinda to remain one night in the cave, and on the following morning they prepared to proceed to Naples; but at the moment of their departure they were surprised by an unexpected visitant: the robbers brought in a prisoner—it was the impostor. Missing on the morrow her who was the pledge of his safety and success, but assured that she could not have wandered far, he despatched emissaries in all directions to seek her; and himself, joining in the pursuit, followed the road she had taken, and was captured by these lawless men, who expected rich ransom from one whose appearance denoted rank and wealth. When they discovered who their prisoner was, they generously delivered him up into his brother's hands.

Ferdinand and Adalinda proceeded to Naples. On their arrival, she presented herself to Queen Caroline; and, through her, Murat heard with astonishment the device that had been practised on him. The young count was restored to his honours and possessions, and within a few months afterwards was united to his betrothed bride.

The compassionate nature of the Count and Countess led them to interest themselves warmly in the fate of Ludovico, whose subsequent career was more honourable but less fortunate. At the intercession of his relative, Gioacchino permitted him to enter the army, where he distinguished himself, and obtained promotion. The brothers were at Moscow together, and mutually assisted each other during the horrors of the retreat. At one time overcome by drowsiness, the mortal symptom resulting from excessive cold, Ferdinand lingered behind his comrades; but Ludovico refusing to leave him, dragged him on in spite of himself, till, entering a village, food and fire restored him, [218] and his life was saved. On another evening, when wind and sleet added to the horror of their situation, Ludovico, after many ineffective struggles, slid from his horse lifeless; Ferdinand was at his side, and, dismounting, endeavoured by every means in his power to bring back pulsation to his stagnant blood. His comrades went forward, and the young Count was left alone with his dying brother in the white boundless waste. Once Ludovico opened his eyes and recognised him; he pressed his hand, and his lips moved to utter a blessing as he died. At that moment the welcome sounds of the enemy's approach roused Ferdinand from the despair into which his dreadful situation plunged him. He was taken prisoner, and his life was thus saved. When Napoleon went to Elba, he, with many others of his countrymen, was liberated, and returned to Naples.

Literary Annual

The Keepsake for MDCCCXXX. Ed. Frederic Mansel Reynolds. London: Hurst, Chance, and Co., and R. Jennings, 1830. Printer: Thomas Davison, Whitefriars.

Title

By the Author of Frankenstein. [Shelley, Mary.] "The Mourner." KS 1830. 71-97.

PLATE: Virginia Water
Steel plate engraving; drawn by J.M.W. Turner, R.A.;
drawn by Robert Wallis; printed by E. Brain [71]

THE MOURNER.[5]
BY THE AUTHOR OF "FRANKENSTEIN."

> One fatal remembrance, one sorrow that throws
> Its bleak shade alike o'er our joys and our woes,
> To which life nothing darker or brighter can bring,
> For which joy has no balm, and affliction no sting!
> Moore

A GORGEOUS scene of kingly pride is the prospect now before us!—the offspring of art, the nursling of nature—where can the eye rest on a landscape more deliciously lovely than the fair expanse of Virginia Water, now an open mirror to the sky, now shaded by umbrageous banks, which wind into dark recesses, or are rounded into soft promontories? Looking down on it, now that the sun is low in the west, the eye is dazzled, the soul oppressed, by excess of beauty. Earth, water, air, drink to overflowing, the radiance that streams from yonder well of light: the foliage of the trees seems dripping with the golden flood; while the lake, filled with no earthly dew, appears but an imbasining of the sun-tinctured atmosphere; and trees and gay pavilion float in its depth, more clear, more distinct, than their twins in the upper air. Nor is the scene silent: strains more sweet than those that lull Venus to her balmy rest, more inspiring than the song of Tiresias which awoke Alexander to the deed of ruin, more solemn than the chantings of St. Cecilia, float along the waves and mingle with the lagging breeze, which ruffles not the lake. Strange, that a few dark scores should be the key to this fountain of sound; the unconscious link between unregarded noise, [72] and harmonies which unclose paradise to our entranced senses!

The sun touches the extreme boundary, and a softer, milder light mingles a roseate tinge with the fiery glow. Our boat has floated long on the broad expanse; now let it approach the umbrageous bank. The green tresses of the graceful willow dip into the waters, which are checked by them into a ripple. The startled teal dart from their recess, skimming the waves with splashing wing. The stately swans float onward; while innumerable water fowl cluster together out of the way of the oars. The twilight is blotted by no dark shades; it is one subdued, equal receding of the great tide of day, which leaves the shingles bare, but not deformed. We may disembark and wander yet amid the glades, long before the thickening shadows speak of night. The plantations are formed of every English tree, with an old oak or two standing out in the walks. There the glancing foliage obscures heaven, as the silken texture of a veil a woman's lovely features: beneath such fretwork we may indulge in light-hearted thoughts; or, if sadder meditations lead us to seek darker shades,

---

5 Plain text for this story was obtained from *The Last Man: A Romantic Circles Edition* <http://www.rc.umd.edu/editions/mws/lastman/mournr.htm> and then compared against the original volume. For full citation, see References.

we may pass the cascade towards the large groves of pine, with their vast undergrowth of laurel, reaching up to the Belvidere; or, on the opposite side of the water, sit under the shadow of the silver-stemmed birch, or beneath the leafy pavilions of those fine old beeches, whose high fantastic roots seem formed in nature's sport; and the near jungle of sweet-smelling myrica leaves no sense unvisited by pleasant ministration.

Now this splendid scene is reserved for the royal possessor; but in past years, while the lodge was called the Regent's Cottage, or before, when the under ranger in- [73] habited it, the mazy paths of Chapel Wood were open, and the iron gates enclosing the plantations and Virginia Water were guarded by no Cerberus untamable by sops. It was here, on a summer's evening that Horace Neville and his two fair cousins floated idly on the placid lake,

"In that sweet mood when pleasant thoughts
Bring sad thoughts to the mind."

Neville had been eloquent in praise of English scenery. "In distant climes," he said, "we may find landscapes grand in barbaric wildness, or rich in the luxuriant vegetation of the south, or sublime in Alpine magnificence. We may lament, though it is ungrateful to say so on such a night as this, the want of a more genial sky; but where find scenery to be compared to the verdant, well wooded, well watered groves of our native land; the clustering cottages, shadowed by fine old elms; each garden blooming with early flowers, each lattice gay with geraniums and roses; the blue-eyed child devouring his white bread, while he drives a cow to graze; the hedge redolent with summer blooms; the enclosed cornfields, seas of golden grain, weltering in the breeze; the stile, the track across the meadow, leading through the copse, under which the path winds, and the meeting branches overhead, which give, by their dimming tracery, a cathedral-like solemnity to the scene; the river, winding 'with sweet inland murmur;' and, as additional graces, spots like these—Oases of taste—gardens of Eden—the works of wealth, which evince at once the greatest power and the greatest will to create beauty?

"And yet," continued Neville, "it was with difficulty that I persuaded myself to reap the best fruits of my [74] uncle's will, and to inhabit this spot, familiar to my boyhood, associated with unavailing regrets and recollected pain."

Horace Neville was a man of birth—of wealth; but he could hardly be termed a man of the world. There was in his nature a gentleness, a sweetness, a winning sensibility, allied to talent and personal distinction, that gave weight to his simplest expressions, and excited sympathy for all his emotions. His younger cousin, his junior by several years, was attached to him by the tenderest sentiments—secret long—but they were now betrothed to each other—a lovely, happy pair. She looked inquiringly; but he turned away. "No more of this," he said; and giving a swifter impulse to their boat, they speedily reached the shore, landed, and walked through the long extent of Chapel Wood. It was dark night before they

The Forgotten Gothic

met their carriage at Bishopsgate.

A week or two after, Horace received letters to call him to a distant part of the country: it even seemed possible that he might be obliged to visit an estate in the north of Ireland. A few days before his departure, he requested his cousin to walk with him. They bent their steps across several meadows to Old Windsor churchyard. At first he did not deviate from the usual path; and as they went they talked cheerfully—gaily: the beauteous sunny day might well exhilarate them; the dancing waves sped onwards at their feet, the country church lifted its rustic spire into the bright pure sky. There was nothing in their conversation that could induce his cousin to think that Neville had led her hither for any saddening purpose; but when they were about to quit the churchyard, Horace, as if he had suddenly recollected himself, turned from the

PLATE: Virginia Water
Steel plate engraving; drawn by J.M.W. Turner, R.A.; drawn by Robert Wallis; printed by E. Brain

path, crossed the greensward, and paused beside a grave near the river. No stone was there to commemorate the being who reposed beneath—it was thickly grown with rich grass, starred by a luxuriant growth of humble daisies: a few dead leaves, a broken bramble twig, defaced its neatness; Neville removed these, and then said, "Juliet, I commit this sacred spot to your keeping while I am away."—-

"There is no monument," he continued; "for her commands were implicitly obeyed by the two beings to whom she addressed them. One day another may lie near, and his name will be her epitaph.—I do not mean myself," he said, half smiling at the terror his cousin's countenance expressed; "but promise me, Juliet, to preserve this grave from every violation. I do not wish to sadden you by the story; yet, if I have excited your curiosity—your interest, I should say—I will satisfy it; but not now—not here."

Leaving the churchyard, they found their horses in attendance, and they prolonged their ride across Bishopsgate Heath. Neville's mind was full of the events to which he had alluded: he began the tale, and then abruptly broke off. It was not till the following day, when, in company with her sister, they again visited Virginia Water, that, seated under the shadow of its pines, whose melodious swinging in the wind breathed unearthly harmony, and looking down upon the water, association of place, and its extreme beauty, reviving, yet soothing, the recollections of the past, unasked by his companions, Neville at once commenced his story.

"I was sent to Eton at eleven years of age. I will not dwell upon my sufferings there; I would hardly refer to them, did they not make a part of my present narration. I was a fag to a hard taskmaster; every labour he could invent—and the youthful tyrant was ingenious—he devised for my annoyance; early and late, I was forced to be in attendance, to the neglect of my school duties, so incurring punishment. There were worse things to bear than these: it was his delight to put me to shame, and,—finding that I had too much of my mother in my blood,—to endeavour to compel me to acts of cruelty from which my nature revolted—I refused to obey. Speak of West Indian slavery! I hope things may be better now; in my days, the tender years of aristocratic childhood were yielded up to a capricious, unrelenting, cruel bondage, far beyond the measured despotism of Jamaica.

"One day—I had been two years at school, and was nearly thirteen—my tyrant, I will give him no other name, issued a command, in the wantonness of power, for me to destroy a poor little bullfinch I had tamed and caged. In a hapless hour he found it in my room, and was indignant that I should dare to appropriate a single pleasure. I refused, stubbornly, dauntlessly, though the consequence of my disobedience was immediate and terrible. At this moment a message came from my tormentor's tutor—his father had arrived. 'Well, old lad,' he cried, 'I shall pay you off some day!' Seizing my pet at the same time, he wrung its neck, threw it at my feet, and, with a laugh of derision, quitted the room.

"Never before—never may I again feel the same swelling, boiling fury in my bursting heart;—the sight of my nursling expiring at my feet—my desire of vengeance—my impotence, created a Vesuvius within me, that no tears flowed to quench. Could I have uttered—acted—my passion, it would have been less torturous: it was so when I burst into a torrent of abuse and imprecation. My [77] vocabulary—it must have been a choice collection—was supplied by him against whom it was levelled. But words were air—I desired to give more substantial proof of my resentment—I destroyed every thing in the room belonging to him; I tore them to pieces, I stamped on them, crushed them with more than childish strength. My last act was to seize a timepiece, on which my tyrant infinitely prided himself, and to dash it to the ground. The sight of this, as it lay shattered at my feet, recalled me to my senses, and something like an emotion of fear allayed the tumult in my heart. I began to meditate an escape: I got out of the house, ran down a lane, and across some meadows, far out of bounds, above Eton. I was seen by an elder boy, a friend of my tormentor. He called to me, thinking at first that I was performing some errand for him; but seeing that I *shirked*, he repeated his 'Come up!' in an authoritative voice. It put wings to my heels; he did not deem it necessary to pursue.—But I grow tedious, my dear Juliet; enough that fears the most intense, of punishment both from my masters and the upper boys, made me resolve to run away. I reached the banks of the Thames, tied my clothes over my head, swam across, and, traversing several fields, entered Windsor Forest, with a vague childish feeling of being able to hide myself for ever in the unexplored obscurity of its immeasurable wilds. It was early autumn; the weather was mild, even warm; the forest oaks yet showed no sign of winter change, though the fern beneath wore a yellowy tinge. I got within Chapel Wood; I fed upon chestnuts and beechnuts; I continued to hide myself from the gamekeepers and woodmen. I lived thus two days.

"But chestnuts and beechnuts were sorry fare to a [78] growing lad of thirteen years old. A day's rain occurred, and I began to think myself the most unfortunate boy on record. I had a distant, obscure idea of starvation: I thought of the Children in the Wood, of their leafy shroud, gift of the pious robin; this brought my poor bullfinch to my mind, and tears streamed in torrents down my cheeks. I thought of my father and mother; of you, then my little baby cousin and playmate; and I cried with renewed fervour, till, quite exhausted, I curled myself up under a huge oak among some dry leaves, the relics of a hundred summers, and fell asleep.

"I ramble on in my narration as if I had a story to tell; yet I have little except a portrait—a sketch—to present, for your amusement or interest. When I awoke, the first object that met my opening eyes was a little foot, delicately clad in silk and soft kid. I looked up in dismay, expecting to behold some gaily dressed appendage to this indication of high-bred elegance; but I saw a girl, perhaps seventeen, simply clad in a dark cotton dress, her face shaded by a large very coarse straw hat; she was pale even to marmoreal whiteness; her chestnut-coloured hair was parted in plain tresses across a brow which wore traces of extreme suffering; her eyes were blue, full, large, melancholy, often even suffused with tears; but her mouth had an infantine sweetness and innocence in its expression, that softened the otherwise sad expression of her countenance.

"She spoke to me. I was too hungry, too exhausted, too unhappy, to resist her kindness, and gladly permitted her to lead me to her home. We passed out of the wood by some broken palings on to Bishopsgate Heath, and after no long walk arrived at her habitation. It was a solitary, dreary-looking cottage; the palings were in disrepair, the [79] garden waste, the lattices unadorned by flowers or creepers; within, all was neat, but sombre, and even mean. The diminutiveness of a cottage requires an appearance of cheerfulness and elegance to make it pleasing; the bare floor—clean, it is true—the rush chairs, deal table, checked curtains of this cot, were beneath even a peasant's rusticity; yet it was the dwelling of my lovely guide, whose little white hand, delicately gloved, contrasted with her unadorned attire, as did her gentle self with the clumsy appurtenances of her too humble dwelling.

"Poor child! she had meant entirely to hide her origin, to degrade herself to a peasant's state, and little thought that she for ever betrayed herself by the strangest incongruities. Thus, the arrangements of her table were mean, her fare meagre for a hermit; but the linen was matchlessly fine, and wax lights stood in candlesticks which a beggar would almost have disdained to own. But I talk of circumstances I observed afterwards; then I was chiefly aware of the plentiful breakfast she caused her single attendant, a young girl, to place before me, and of the sweet soothing voice of my hostess, which spoke a kindness with which lately I had been little conversant. When my hunger was appeased, she drew my story from me, encouraged me to write to my father, and kept me at her abode till, after a few days, I returned to school pardoned. No long time elapsed before I got into the upper forms, and my woful slavery ended.

"Whenever I was able, I visited my disguised nymph. I no longer associated with my schoolfellows; their diversions, their pursuits, appeared vulgar and stupid to me; I had but one object in view—to accomplish my lessons, and to steal to the cottage of Ellen Burnet. [80]

"Do not look grave, love! true, others as young as I then was have loved, and I might also; but not Ellen. Her profound, her intense melancholy, sister to despair—her serious, sad discourse—her mind, estranged from all worldly concerns, forbade that; but there was an enchantment in her sorrow, a fascination in her converse, that lifted me above common-place existence; she created a magic circle, which I entered as holy ground: it was not akin to heaven, for grief was the presiding spirit; but there was an exaltation of sentiment, an enthusiasm, a view beyond the grave, which made it unearthly, singular, wild, enthralling. You have often observed that I strangely differ from all other men; I mingle with them, make one in their occupations and diversions, but I have a portion of my being sacred from them:—a living well, sealed up from their contamination, lies deep in my heart—it is of little use, but there it is; Ellen opened the spring, and it has flowered ever since.

"Of what did she talk? She recited no past adventures, alluded to no past intercourse with friend or relative; she spoke of the various woes that wait on humanity, on the intricate mazes of life, on the miseries of passion, of love, remorse, and death, and that which we may hope or fear beyond the tomb; she spoke of the sensation of wretchedness alive in her own broken heart, and then she grew fearfully eloquent, till, suddenly pausing, she reproached herself for making me familiar with such wordless misery. 'I do you harm,' she often said; 'I unfit you for society; I have tried, seeing you thrown upon yonder distorted miniature of a bad world, to estrange you from its evil contagion; I fear that I shall be the cause of greater harm to you than could spring from association with your fellow- [81] creatures in the ordinary course of things. This is not well—avoid the stricken deer'

"There were darker shades in the picture than those which I have already developed. Ellen was more miserable than the imagination of one like you, dear girl, unacquainted with wo, can portray. Sometimes she gave words to her despair—it was so great as to confuse the boundary between physical and mental sensation—and every pulsation of her heart was a throb of pain. She has suddenly broken off in talking of her sorrows, with a cry of agony—bidding me leave her—hiding her face on her arms, shivering with the anguish some thought awoke. The idea that chiefly haunted her, though she earnestly endeavoured to put it aside, was self-destruction—to snap the silver cord that bound together so much grace, wisdom, and sweetness to rob the world of a creation made to be its ornament Sometimes her piety checked her; oftener a sense of unendurable suffering made her brood with pleasure over the dread resolve. She spoke of it to me as being wicked; yet I often fancied this was done rather to prevent her example from being of ill effect to me, than from any conviction that the Father of all, would regard angrily the last act of his miserable child. Once she had prepared the mortal beverage; it was on the table before her when I entered; she did not deny its nature, she did not attempt to justify herself; she only besought me not to hate her and to sooth by my kindness her last moments.—'I cannot live!' was all her explanation, all her excuse; and it was spoken with such fervent wretchedness that it seemed wrong to attempt to persuade her to prolong the sense of pain. I did not act like a boy; I wonder I did not; I made one simple request, to which she instantly ac- [82] ceded, that she should walk with me to this Belvidere. It was a glorious sunset; beauty and the spirit of love breathed in the wind, and hovered over the softened hues of the landscape. 'Look, Ellen,' I cried, 'if only such loveliness of nature existed, it were worth living for!'

"True, if a latent feeling did not blot this glorious scene with murky shadows. Beauty is as we see it—my eyes view all things deformed and evil.' She closed them as she said this; but, young and sensitive, the visitings of the soft breeze already began to minister consolation 'Dearest Ellen,' I continued, 'what do I not owe to you? I am your boy, your pupil; I might have gone on blindly as others do, but you opened my eyes; you have given me a sense of the just, the good, the beautiful—and have you done this merely for my misfortune? If you leave me, what can become of me?' The last words came from my heart, and tears gushed from my eyes. 'Do not leave me, Ellen' I said; 'I cannot live without you—and I cannot die, for I have a mother—a father.' She turned quickly round, saying, 'You are blessed sufficiently.' Her voice struck me as unnatural; she grew deadly pale as she spoke, and was obliged to sit down. Still I clung to her, Prayed, cried; till she—I had never seen her shed a tear before—burst into passionate weeping. After this she seemed to forget her resolve. We returned by moonlight, and our talk was even more calm and cheerful than usual. When in her cottage, I poured away the fatal draught. Her 'good night' bore with it no traces of her late agitation; and the next day she said, 'I have thoughtlessly, even wickedly, created a new duty to myself, even at a time when I had forsworn all; but I will be true to it. Pardon me for making you familiar with emotions and [83] scenes so dire; I will behave better—I will preserve myself, if I can, till the link between us is loosened, or broken, and I am free again.'

"One little incident alone occurred during our intercourse that appeared at all to connect her with the world. Sometimes I brought her a newspaper, for those were stirring times; and though, before I knew her, she had forgotten all except the world her own heart enclosed, yet, to please me, she would talk of Napoleon—Russia, from whence the emperor now returned overthrown—and the prospect of his final defeat. The paper lay one day on her table; some words caught her eye; she bent eagerly down to read them, and her bosom heaved with violent palpitation; but she subdued herself, and after a few moments told me to take the paper away. Then, indeed, I did feel an emotion of even impertinent inquisitiveness; I found nothing to satisfy it—though afterwards I became aware that it contained a singular advertisement, saying, 'If these lines meet the eye of any one of the passengers who were on board the St. Mary, bound for Liverpool from Barbadoes, which sailed on the third of May last, and was destroyed by fire in the high seas, a part of the crew only having been saved by his majesty's frigate the Bellerophon, they are entreated to communicate with the advertiser: and if any one be acquainted with the particulars of the Hon. Miss Eversham's fate and present abode, they are earnestly requested to disclose them, directing to L. E., Stratton-street, Park-lane.'

"It was after this event, as winter came on, that symptoms of decided ill health declared themselves in the delicate frame of my poor Ellen. I have often suspected that, without positively attempting her life, she did many [84] things that tended to abridge it and to produce mortal disease. Now, when really ill, she refused all medical attendance; but she got better again, and I thought her nearly well when I saw her for the last time, before going home for the Christmas holidays. Her manner was full of affection: she relied, she said, on the continuation of my friendship; she made me promise never to forget her, though she refused to write to me, and forbade any letters from me.

"Even now I see her standing at her humble door-way. If an appearance of illness and suffering can ever be termed lovely, it was in her. Still she was to be viewed as the wreck of beauty. What must she not have been in happier days, with her angel expression of face, her nymph-like figure, her voice, whose tones were music? 'So young—so lost!' was the sentiment that burst even from me, a young lad, as I waved my hand to her as a last adieu. She hardly looked more than fifteen, but none could doubt that her very soul was impressed by the sad lines of sorrow that rested so unceasingly on her fair brow. Away from her, her figure for ever floated before my eyes;—I put my hands before them, still she was there: my day, my night, dreams were filled by my recollections of her.

"During the winter holidays, on a fine soft day, I went out to hunt: you, dear Juliet, will remember the sad catastrophe; I fell and broke my leg. The only person who saw me fall was a young man who rode one of the most beautiful horses I ever saw, and I believe it was by watching him as he took a leap, that I incurred my disaster: he dismounted, and was at my side in a minute. My own animal had fled; he called his; it obeyed his voice; with ease he lifted my light figure on to the saddle, contriving [85] to support my leg, and so conducted me a short distance to a lodge situated in the woody recesses of Elmore-park, the seat of the Earl of D——, whose second son my preserver was. He was my sole nurse for a day or two, and during the whole of my illness passed many hours of each day by my bedside. As I lay gazing on him, while he read to me, or talked, narrating a thousand strange adventures which had occurred during his service in the Peninsula, I thought—is it for ever to be my fate to fall in with the highly gifted and excessively unhappy?

"The immediate neighbour of Lewis' family was Lord Eversham. He had married in very early youth, and became a widower young. After this misfortune, which passed like a deadly blight over his prospects and possessions, leaving the gay view utterly sterile and bare, he left his surviving infant daughter under the care of Lewis' mother, and travelled for many years in far distant lands. He returned when Clarice was about ten, a lovely sweet child, the pride and delight of all connected with her. Lord Eversham, on his return—he was then hardly more than thirty—devoted himself to her education. They were never separate: he was a good musician, and she became a proficient under his tutoring. They rode—walked—read together. When a father is all that a father may be, the sentiments of filial piety, entire dependence, and perfect confidence being united, the love of a daughter is one of the deepest and strongest, as it is the purest passion of which our natures are capable. Clarice worshipped her parent, who came, during the transition from mere childhood to the period when reflection and observation awaken, to adorn a common-place existence with all the brilliant adjuncts which enlightened and devoted affection can be- [86] stow. He appeared to her like an especial gift of Providence, a guardian angel—but far dearer, as being akin to her own nature. She grew, under his eye, in loveliness and refinement both of intellect and heart. These feelings were not divided—almost strengthened, by the engagement that had place between her and Lewis:—Lewis was destined for the army, and, after a few years' service, they were to be united.

"It is hard, when all is fair and tranquil, when the world, opening before the ardent gaze of youth, looks like a well-kept demesne, unincumbered by let or hinderance for the annoyance of the young traveller, that we should voluntarily stray into desert wilds and tempest-visited districts. Lewis Elmore was ordered to Spain; and, at the same time, Lord Eversham found it necessary to visit some estates he possesses in Barbadoes. He was not sorry to revisit a scene, which had dwelt in his memory as an earthly paradise, nor to show to his daughter a new and strange world, so to form her understanding and enlarge her mind. They were to return in three months, and departed as on a summer tour. Clarice was glad that, while her lover gathered experience and knowledge in a distant land, she should not remain in idleness—she was glad that there would be some diversion for her anxiety during his perilous absence; and in every way she enjoyed the idea of travelling with her beloved father, who would fill every hour, and adorn every new scene, with pleasure and delight. They sailed.—Clarice wrote home, with enthusiastic expressions of rapture and delight, from Madeira:—yet, without her father, she said, the fair scene had been blank to her. More than half her letter was filled by the expressions of her gratitude and affection for her adored and [87] revered parent. While he, in his, with fewer words, perhaps, but with no less energy, spoke of his satisfaction in her improvement, his pride in her beauty, and his grateful sense of her love and kindness.

"Such were they, a matchless example of happiness in the dearest connexion in life, as resulting from the exercise of their reciprocal duties and affections. A father and daughter; the one all care, gentleness, and sympathy, consecrating his life for her happiness; the other, fond, duteous, grateful:—such had they been,—and where were they now—the noble, kind, respected parent, and the beloved and loving child? They had departed from England as on a pleasure voyage down an inland stream, but the ruthless car of destiny had overtaken them on their unsuspecting way, crushing them under its heavy wheels—scattering love, hope, and joy, as the bellowing avalanche overwhelms and grinds to mere spray the streamlet of the valley. They were gone: but whither? Mystery hung over the fate of the most helpless victim; and my friend's anxiety was, to penetrate the clouds that hid poor Clarice from his sight.

"After an absence of a few months, they had written, fixing their departure in the St. Mary, to sail from Barbadoes in a few days. Lewis, at the same time, returned from Spain: he was invalided, in his very first action, by a bad wound in his side. He arrived, and each day expected to hear of the landing of his friends; when that common messenger, the newspaper, brought him tidings to fill him with more than anxiety—with fear and agonizing doubt. The St. Mary had caught fire and had burned in the open sea. A frigate, the Bellerophon, had saved a part of the crew. In spite of illness and a physician's com- [88] mands, Lewis set out the same day for London, to ascertain as speedily as possible the fate of her he loved. There he heard that the frigate was expected in the Downs. Without alighting from his travelling chaise, he posted thither, arriving in a burning fever. He went on board, saw the commander and spoke with the crew. They could give him few particulars as to whom they had saved: they had touched at Liverpool, and left there most of the persons, including all the passengers rescued from the St. Mary. Physical suffering for awhile disabled Mr. Elmore; he was confined by his wound and consequent fever, and only recovered to give himself up to his exertions to discover the fate of his friends;—they did not appear nor write; and all Lewis' inquiries only tended to confirm his worst fears; yet still he hoped, and still continued indefatigable in his perquisitions. He visited Liverpool, and Ireland, whither some of the passengers had gone, and learnt only scattered, incongruous details of the fearful tragedy, that told nothing of Miss Eversham's present abode; though much, that confirmed his suspicion that she still lived.

"The fire on board the St. Mary had raged long and fearfully before the Bellerophon hove in sight, and boats came off for the rescue of the crew. The women were to be first embarked; but Clarice clung to her father, and refused to go till he should accompany her. Some fearful presentiment that, if she were saved, he would remain and die, gave such energy to her resolve, that not the entreaties of her father, nor the angry expostulations of the captain, could shake it. Lewis saw this man, after the lapse of two or three months, and he threw most light on the dark scene. He well remembered that, transported with anger by her woman's obstinacy, he had said to her, 'You will [89] cause your father's death—and be as much a parricide as if you put poison into his cup—you are not the first girl who has murdered her father in her wilful mood.' Still Clarice passionately refused to go—there was no time for long parley—the point was yielded and she remained pale, but firm, near her parent, whose arm was around her, supporting her during the awful interval. It was no period for regular action and calm order: a tempest was rising, the scorching flames blew this way and that, making a fearful day of the night which veiled all except the burning ship. 'The boats returned with difficulty,

The Keepsake

and one only could contrive to approach; it was nearly full: Lord Eversham and his daughter advanced to the deck's edge, to get in. 'We can only take one of you,' vociferated the sailors: 'keep back on your life! throw the girl to us—we will come back; for you if we can. Lord Eversham cast with a strong arm his daughter, who had now entirely lost her self possession, into the boat; she was alive again in a minute, she called to her father, held out her arms to him, and would have thrown herself into the sea, but was held back by the sailors. Meanwhile Lord Eversham feeling that no boat could again approach the lost vessel, contrived to heave a spar overboard, and threw himself into the sea, clinging, to it. The boat, tossed by the huge waves, with difficulty made its way to the frigate; and as it rose from the trough of the sea, Clarice saw her father struggling; with his fate—battling with the death that at last became the victor—the spar floated by, his arms had fallen from it—were those his pallid features? She neither wept nor fainted, but her limbs grew rigid, her face colourless, and she was lifted as a log on to the deck of the frigate.

"The captain allowed that on her homeward voyage, the [90] people had rather a horror of her, as having caused her father's death; her own servants had perished, few people remembered who she was; but they talked together with no careful voices as they passed her, and a hundred times she must have heard herself accused of having destroyed her parent. She spoke to no one, or only in brief reply when addressed; to avoid the rough remonstrances of those around, she appeared at table, ate as well as she could; but there was a settled wretchedness in her face that never changed. When they landed at Liverpool, the captain conducted her to an hotel; he left her, meaning to return, but an opportunity of sailing that night for the Downs occurred, of which he availed himself, without again visiting her. He knew, he said, and truly, that she was in her native country, where she had but to write a letter to gather crowds of friends about her; and where can greater civility be found than at an English hotel, if it is known that you are perfectly able to pay your bill?

"This was all that Mr. Elmore could learn, and it took many months to gather together these few particulars. He went to the hotel at Liverpool. It seemed that as soon as there appeared some hope of rescue from the frigate, Lord Eversham had given his pocket-book to his daughter's care, containing bills on a banking-house at Liverpool to the amount of a few hundred pounds. On the second day after Clarice's arrival there, she had sent for the master of the hotel, and showed him these. He got the cash for her; and the next day, she quitted Liverpool in a little coasting vessel. In vain Lewis endeavoured to trace her. Apparently she had crossed to Ireland; but whatever she had done, wherever she had gone, she had taken infinite pains to conceal, and all clue was speedily lost. [91]

"Lewis had not yet despaired; he was even now perpetually making journeys, sending emissaries, employing every possible means for her discovery. From the moment he told me this story, we talked of nothing else. I became deeply interested, and we ceaselessly discussed the probabilities of the case, and where she might be concealed: that she did not meditate suicide was evident from her having possessed herself of money; yet, unused to the world, young, lovely, and inexperienced; what could be her plan? What might not have been her fate?

"Meanwhile I continued for nearly three months confined by the fracture of my limb; before the lapse of that time, I had begun to crawl about the ground, and now I considered myself as nearly recovered. It had been settled that I should not return to Eton, but be entered at Oxford; and this leap from boyhood to man's estate elated me considerably. Yet still I thought of my poor Ellen, and was angry at her obstinate silence. Once or twice I had, disobeying her command, written to her, mentioning my accident, and the kind attentions of Mr. Elmore: still she wrote not; and I began to fear that her illness might have had a fatal termination. She had made me vow so solemnly never to mention her name, never to inquire about her during my absence, that, considering obedience the first duty of a young inexperienced boy to one older than himself, I resisted each suggestion of my affection or my fears, to transgress her orders.

"And now spring came; with its gift of opening buds, odoriferous flowers, and sunny genial days. I returned home, and found my family on the eve of their departure for London; my long confinement had weakened me—it was deemed inadvisable for me to encounter the bad air and fatigues of the metropolis, and I remained to rusticate. [92] I rode and hunted, and thought of Ellen; missing the excitement of her conversation, and feeling a vacancy in my heart which she had filled. I began to think of riding across the country from Shropshire to Berks for the purpose of seeing her. The whole landscape haunted my imagination—the fields round Eton—the silver Thames—the majestic forest—this lovely scene of Virginia Water—the health and her desolate cottage—she herself pale, slightly bending from weakness of health, awakening from dark abstraction to bestow on me a kind smile of welcome. It grew into a passionate desire of my heart to behold her, to cheer her as I might by my affectionate attentions, to hear her, and to hang upon her accents of inconsolable despair, as if it had been celestial harmony. As I meditated on these things, a voice seemed for ever to repeat, Now go, or it will be too late; while another yet more mournful tone responded, "You can never see her more!

"I was occupied by these thoughts, as, on a summer moonlight night, I loitered in the shrubbery, unable to quit a scene of entrancing beauty, when I was startled at hearing myself called by Mr. Elmore. He came on his way to the coast; he had received a letter from Ireland, which made him think that Miss Eversham was residing near Enniscorthy; a strange place for her to select, but as concealment was evidently her object, not an improbable one. Yet his hopes were not high; on the contrary, he performed this journey more from the resolve to leave nothing undone, than in expectation of a happy result. He asked me if I would accompany him; I was delighted with the offer, and we departed together on the following morning.

"We arrived at Milford Haven, where we were to take our passage. The packet was to sail early in the morning [93] —we walked on the beach, and beguiled the time by talk. I had never mentioned Ellen to Lewis; I felt now strongly inclined to break my vow, and to relate my whole adventure with her; but restrained myself, and we spoke only of the unhappy Clarice—of the despair that must have been hers, of her remorse and unavailing regret.

"We retired to rest, and early in the morning I was called to prepare for going on board. I got ready, and then knocked at Lewis' door; he admitted me, for he was dressed, though a few of his things were still unpacked, and scattered about the room. The morocco ease of a miniature was on his table; I took it up—' Did I never show you that? said Elmore; poor dear Clarice! she was very happy when that was painted!

"I opened it;—rich luxuriant curls clustered on her brow and the snow-white throat; there was a light zephyr appearance in the figure; an expression of unalloyed exuberant happiness in the countenance but those large dove's eyes, the innocence that dwelt on her mouth, could not be mistaken, and the name of Ellen Burnet burst from my lips.

"There was no doubt: why had I ever doubted? the thing was so plain! who but the survivor of such a parent, and she the apparent cause of his death, could be so miserable as Ellen? A torrent of explanation followed, and a thousand minute circumstances, forgotten before, now assured us that my sad hermitess was the beloved of Elmore. No more sea voyage—not a second of delay—our chaise, the horses' heads turned to the east, rolled on with lightning rapidity, yet far too slowly to satisfy our impatience. It was not until we arrived at Worcester that the tide of expectation, flowing all one way, ebbed. Suddenly, even while I was telling Elmore some anecdote to prove that, in [94] spite of all, she would be accessible to consolation, I remembered her ill health and my fears. Lewis saw the change my countenance underwent; for some time I could not command my voice; and when at last I spoke, my gloomy anticipations passed like an electric shock into my friend's soul.

"When we arrived at Oxford, we halted for an hour or two, unable to proceed; yet we did not converse on the subject so near our hearts, nor until we arrived in sight of Windsor did a word pass between us; then Elmore said, 'To-morrow morning, dear Neville, you shall visit Clarice; we must not be too precipitate.'

"The morrow came. I arose with that intolerable weight at my breast, which it is grief's worst heritage to feel. A sunny day it was; yet the atmosphere looked black to me; my heart was dead within me. We sat at the breakfast table, but neither ate, and after some restless indecision, we left our inn, and (to protract the interval) walked to Bishopsgate. Our conversation belied our feelings; we spoke as if we expected all to be well, we felt that there was no hope. We crossed the heath along the accustomed path. On one side was the luxuriant foliage of the forest; on the other, the wide-spread moor: her cottage was situated at one extremity, and could hardly be distinguished, until we should arrive close to it. When we drew near, Lewis bade me go on alone, he would wait my return; I obeyed, and reluctantly approached the confirmation of my fears. At length it stood before me, the lonely cot and desolate garden; the unfastened wicket swung in the breeze; every shutter was closed.

"To stand motionless and gaze on these symbols of my worst forebodings, was all that I could do. My heart seemed to me to call aloud for Ellen—for such was she [95] to me—her other name might be a fiction—but silent as her own life-deserted lips were mine. Lewis grew impatient, and advanced—my stay had occasioned a transient ray of hope to enter his mind—it vanished when he saw me, and her deserted dwelling. Slowly we turned away, and were directing our steps back again, when my name was called by a child. A little girl came running across some fields towards us, whom at last I recognised as having seen before with Ellen. 'Mr. Neville, there is a letter for you!' cried the child. 'A letter—where?—who?' 'The lady left a letter for you. You must go to Old Windsor, to Mr. Cooke's; he has got it for you.'

"She had left a letter:—was she then departed on an earthly journey? 'I will go for it immediately. Mr. Cooke! Old Windsor! where shall I find him? who is he?

"'Oh, Sir, every body knows him,' said the child; 'he lives close to the churchyard, he is the sexton. After the burial, Nancy gave him the letter to take care of.'

"Had we hoped? had we for a moment indulged the expectation of ever again seeing our miserable friend? Never! O never! Our hearts had told us that the sufferer was at peace—the unhappy orphan with her father in the abode of spirits! Why then were we here? Why had a smile dwelt on our lips, now wreathed into the expression of anguish? Our full hearts demanded one consolation—to weep upon her grave; her sole link now with us, her mourners. There at lust my boy's grief found vent in tears, in lamentation. You saw the spot; the grassy mound rests lightly on the bosom of fair Clarice, of my own poor Ellen. Stretched upon this, kissing the scarcely springing turf; for many hours no thought visited me, but the wretched one—that she had lived—and was lost to me for ever!

"If Lewis had ever doubted the identity of my friend with her he loved, the letter put into our hands undeceived him; the handwriting was Miss Evershamʼs, it was directed to me, and contained words like these:—

"April 11.

"I have vowed never to mention certain beloved names, never to communicate with beings who cherished me once, to whom my deepest gratitude is due; and, as well as poor bankrupt can, is paid. Perhaps it is a mere prevarication to write to you, dear Horace, concerning them; but, Heaven pardon me! my disrobed spirit would not repose, I fear, if I did not thus imperfectly bid them a last farewell.

"You know him, Neville; and know that he for ever laments her whom he has lost. Describe your poor Ellen to him, and he will speedily see that she died on the waves of the murderous Atlantic. Ellen had nothing in common with her, save love for, and interest in him. Tell him, it had been well for him, perhaps, to have united himself to the child of prosperity! the nursling of deep love; but it had been destruction, even could he have meditated such an act, to wed the parrici—-.

"'I will not write that word. Sickness and near death have taken the sting from my despair. The agony of woe which you witnessed, is melted into tender affliction and pious hope. I am not miserable now. Now! When you read these words, the hand that writes, the eye that sees, will be a little dust, becoming one with the earth around it. You, perhaps he, I will visit my quiet retreat, bestow a few tears on my fate, but let them be secret; they may make green my grave, but do not let a misplaced feeling adorn it with any other tribute. It is my last request; let no stone, no name, mark that spot. [97]

"'Farewell, dear Horace! Farewell, to one other whom I may not name. May the God to whom I am about to resign my spirit in confidence and hope, bless your earthly career! Blindly, perhaps, you will regret me for your own sakes; but for mine, you will be grateful to the Providence which has snapt the heavy chain binding me to unutterable sorrow, and which permits me from my lowly grass-grown tomb to say to you, I am at peace.

"Ellen."

Title

By the Author of Frankenstein. [Shelley, Mary.] "The Evil Eye." KS 1830. 150-175. [150]

THE EVIL EYE.[6]
BY THE AUTHOR OF FRANKENSTEIN.

> "The wild Albanian kirtled to his knee,
> With shawl-girt head, and ornamented gun,
> And gold-embroider'd garments, fair to see;
> The crimson-scarfed man of Macedon."
> LORD BYRON.

The Moreot, Katusthius Ziani, travelled wearily, and in fear of its robber-inhabitants, through the pashalik of Yannina; yet he had no cause for dread. Did he arrive, tired and hungry, in a solitary village—did he find himself in the uninhabited wilds suddenly surrounded by a band of Klephts—or in the larger towns did he shrink at finding himself sole of his race among the savage mountaineers and despotic Turk—as soon as he announced himself the Pobratimo[7] of Dmitri of the Evil Eye, every hand was held out, every voice spoke welcome.

The Albanian, Dmitri, was a native of the village of Korvo. Among the savage mountains of the district between Yannina and Tepellen, the deep broad stream of Argyro-Castro flows; bastioned to the west by abrupt wood-covered precipices, shadowed to the east by elevated mountains. The highest among these is Mount Trebucci; and in a romantic folding of that hill, distinct with minarets, crowned by a dome rising from out a group of [151] pyramidal cypresses, is the picturesque village of Korvo. Sheep and goats form the apparent treasure of its inhabitants; their guns and yataghans, their warlike habits, and, with them, the noble profession of robbery, are sources of still greater wealth. Among a race renowned for dauntless courage and sanguinary enterprise, Dmitri was distinguished.

It was said that in his youth, this Klepht was remarkable for a gentler disposition and more refined taste than is usual with his countrymen. He had been a wanderer, and had learned European arts, of which he was not a little proud. He could read and write Greek, and a book was often stowed beside his pistols in his girdle. He had spent several years in Scio, the most civilized of the Greek islands, and had married a Scote girl. The Albanians are characterized as despisers

---

6 Plain text for this story was obtained from *Arthur' Classic Novels* <http://arthursclassicnovels.com/shelley/eviley10.html> and then compared against the original volume. For full citation, see References.

7 In Greece, especially in Illyria and Epirus, it is no uncommon thing for persons of the same sex to swear friendship; the church contains a ritual to consecrate this vow. Two men thus united are called *pobratimi*, the women *posestrime*.

of women; but Dmitri, in becoming the husband of Helena, inlisted under a more chivalrous rule, and became the proselyte of a better creed. Often he returned to his native hills, and fought under the banner of the renowned Ali, and then came back to his island home. The love of the tamed barbarian was concentrated, burning, and something beyond this—it was a portion of his living, beating heart—the nobler part of himself—the diviner mould in which his rugged nature had been recast.

On his return from one of his Albanian expeditions, he found his home ravaged by the Mainotes. Helena—they pointed to her tomb, nor dared tell him how she died; his only child, his lovely infant daughter, was stolen; his treasure-house of love and happiness was rifled; its gold-excelling wealth changed to blank desolation. Dmitri spent three years in endeavours to recover [152] his lost offspring. He was exposed to a thousand dangers—underwent incredible hardships: he dared the wild beast in his lair, the Mainote in his port of refuge; he attacked, and was attacked by them. He wore the badge of his daring in a deep gash across his eyebrow and cheek. On this occasion he had died, but that Katusthius, seeing a scuffle on shore and a man left for dead, disembarked from a Moreot sacoleva, carried him away, tended and cured him. They exchanged vows of friendship, and for some time the Albanian shared his brother's toils; but they were too pacific to suit his taste, and he returned to Korvo.

Who in the mutilated savage could recognise the handsomest amongst the Arnaoots? His habits kept pace with his change of physiognomy—he grew ferocious and hard-hearted—he only smiled when engaged in dangerous enterprise; he had arrived at that worst state of ruffian feeling, the taking delight in blood. He grew old in these occupations; his mind became reckless, his countenance more dark; men trembled before his glance, women and children exclaimed in terror, "The Evil Eye!" The opinion became prevalent—he shared it himself—he gloried in the dread privilege; and when his victim shivered and withered beneath the mortal influence, the fiendish laugh with which he hailed this demonstration of his power, struck with worse dismay the failing heart of the fascinated person. But Dmitri could command the arrows of his sight; and his comrades respected him the more for his supernatural attribute, since they did not fear the exercise of it on themselves.

Dmitri had just returned from an expedition beyond Prevesa. He and his comrades were laden with spoil. They killed and roasted a goat whole for their repast; [153] they drank dry several wine skins; then, round the fire in the court, they abandoned themselves to the delights of the kerchief dance, roaring out the chorus, as they dropped upon and then rebounded from their knees, and whirled round and round with an activity all their own. The heart of Dmitri was heavy; he refused to dance, and sat apart, at first joining in the song with his voice and lute, till the air changed to one that reminded him of better days; his voice died away—

his instrument dropped from his hands—and his head sank upon his breast.

At the sound of stranger footsteps he started up; in the form before him he surely recognised a friend—he was not mistaken. 'With a joyful exclamation he welcomed Katusthius Ziani, clasping his hand, and kissing him on his cheek. The traveller was weary, so they retired to Dmitri's own home a neatly plastered, white-washed cottage, whose earthen floor was perfectly dry and clean, and the walls hung with arms, some richly ornamented, and other trophies of his Klephtic triumphs. A fire was kindled by his aged female attendant; the friends reposed on mats of white rushes, while she prepared the pilaf and seethed flesh of kid. She placed a bright tin tray on a block of wood before them, and heaped upon it cakes of Indian corn, goat's milk cheese, eggs, and olives: a jar of water from their purest spring, and skin of wine, served to refresh and cheer the thirsty traveller.

After supper, the guest spoke of the object of his visit. "I come to my Pobratimo," he said, "to claim the performance of his vow. When I rescued you from the savage Kakovougnis of Boularias, you pledged to me your gratitude and faith; do you disclaim the debt?"

Dmitri's brow darkened. "My brother," he cried, "need [154] not remind me of what I owe.

Command my life—in what can the mountain Klepht aid the son of the wealthy Ziani?"

"The son of Ziani is a beggar," rejoined Katusthius, "and must perish, if his brother deny his assistance."

The Moreot then told his tale. He had been brought up as the only son of a rich merchant of Corinth. He had often sailed as caravokeiri[8] of his father's vessels to Stamboul, and even to Master of a merchant ship Calabria. Some years before, he had been boarded and taken by a Barbary corsair. His life since then had been adventurous, he said; in truth, it had been a guilty one—he had become a renegade—and won regard from his new allies, not by his superior courage, for he was cowardly, but by the frauds that make men wealthy. In the midst of this career some superstition had influenced him, and he had returned to his ancient religion. He escaped from Africa, wandered through Syria, crossed to Europe, found occupation in Constantinople; and thus years passed. At last, as he was on the point of marriage with a Fanariote beauty, he fell again into poverty, and he returned to Corinth to see if his father's fortunes had prospered during his long wanderings. He found that while these had improved to a wonder, they were lost to him for ever. His father, during his protracted absence, acknowledged another son as his; and dying a year before, had left all to him. Katusthius found this unknown kinsman, with his wife and child, in possession of his expected inheritance. Cyril divided with him, it is true, their parent's property; but Katusthius grasped at all, and resolved to obtain it. He brooded over [155] a thousand schemes of murder

---
8 Master of a merchant ship.

and revenge; yet the blood of a brother was sacred to him; and Cyril, beloved and respected at Corinth, could only be attacked with considerable risk. Then his child was a fresh obstacle. As the best plan that presented itself, he hastily embarked for Butrinto, and came to claim the advice and assistance of the Arnaoot whose life he had saved, whose Pobratimo he was. Not thus barely, did he tell his tale, but glossed it over; so that had Dmitri needed the incitement of justice, which was not at all a desideratum with him, he would have been satisfied that Cyril was a base interloper, and that the whole transaction was one of imposture and villany.

All night these men discussed a variety of projects, whose aim was, that the deceased Ziani's wealth should pass undivided into his elder son's hands. At morning's dawn Katusthius departed, and two days afterwards Dmitri quitted his mountain-home. His first care had been to purchase a horse, long coveted by him on account of its beauty and fleetness; he provided cartridges, and replenished his powder-horn. His accoutrements were rich, his dress gay; his arms glittered in the sun. His long hair fell straight from under the shawl twisted round his cap, even to his waist; a shaggy white capote hung from his shoulder; his face wrinkled and puckered by exposure to the seasons; his brow furrowed with care; his mustachios long and jet black; his scarred face; his wild, savage eyes; his whole appearance, not deficient in barbaric grace, but stamped chiefly with ferocity and bandit pride, inspired, and we need not wonder, the superstitious Greek with a belief that a supernatural spirit of evil dwelt in his aspect, blasting and destroying. Now prepared for his journey, [156] he departed from Korvo, crossing the woods of Acarnania, on his way to the Morea.

"Wherefore does Zella tremble, and press her boy to her bosom, as if fearful of evil?" Thus asked Cyril Ziani, returning from the city of Corinth to his own rural abode. It was a home of beauty. The abruptly broken hills covered with olives, or brighter plantations of orange-trees, overlooked the blue waves of the Gulf of Aegina. A myrtle underwood spread sweet scent around, and dipped its dark shining leaves into the sea itself. The low-roofed house was shaded by two enormous fig-trees: while vineyards and corn-land stretched along the gentle upland to the north. When Zella saw her husband, she smiled, though her cheek was still pale and her lips quivering—"Now you are near to guard us," she said, "I dismiss fear; but danger threatens our Constans, and I shudder to remember that an Evil Eye has been upon him."

Cyril caught up his child—By my head!" he cried, "thou speakest of an ill thing. The Franks call this superstition; but let us beware. His cheek is still rosy; his tresses flowing gold—Speak, Constans, hail thy father, my brave fellow'" It was but a short-lived fear; no ill ensued, and they soon forgot an incident which had causelessly made their hearts to quail. A week afterwards Cyril returned, as he was wont, from shipping a cargo of currants, to his retreat on the coast. It was a beautiful summer evening; the creaking water-wheel, which produced the irrigation of the land, chimed in with the last song of the noisy cicala; the rippling waves spent themselves almost silently among the shingles. This was his home; but where its lovely [157] flower? Zella did not come forth to welcome him. A domestic pointed to a chapel on a neighbouring acclivity, and there he found her; his child (nearly three years of age) was in his nurse's arms; his wife was praying fervently, while the tears streamed down her cheeks. Cyril demanded anxiously the meaning of this scene; but the nurse sobbed; Zella continued to pray and weep; and the boy, from sympathy, began to cry. This was too much for man to endure. Cyril left the chapel; he leant against a walnut-tree: his first exclamation was a customary Greek one—Welcome this misfortune, so that it come single!" But what was the ill that had occurred? Unapparent was it yet; but the spirit of evil is most fatal when unseen. He was happy—a lovely wife, a blooming child, a peaceful home, competence, and the prospect of wealth; these blessings were his: yet how often does Fortune use such as her decoys? He was a slave in an enslaved land, a mortal subject to the high destinies, and ten thousand were the envenomed darts which might be hurled at his devoted head. Now timid and trembling, Zella came from the chapel: her explanation did not calm his fears. Again the Evil Eye had been on his child, and deep malignity lurked surely under this second visitation. The same man, an Arnaoot, with glittering arms, gay attire, mounted on a black steed, came from the neighbouring ilex grove, and, riding furiously up to the door, suddenly checked and reined in his horse at the very threshold. The child ran towards him: the Arnaoot bent his sinister eyes upon him:—"Lovely art thou, bright infant," he cried; "thy blue eyes arc beaming, thy golden tresses fair to see; but thou art a vision fleeting as beautiful;—look at me!" The innocent looked up, uttered a shriek, and fell gasping on [158] the ground. The women rushed forward to seize him; the Albanian put spurs to his horse, and galloping swiftly across the little plain, up the wooded hill-side, he was soon lost to sight. Zella and the nurse bore the child to the chapel, they sprinkled him with holy water, and, as he revived, besought the Panagia with earnest prayers to save him from the menaced ill.

Several weeks elapsed; little Constans grew in intelligence and beauty; no blight had visited the flower of love, and its parents dismissed fear. Sometimes Cyril indulged in a joke at the expense of the Evil Eye; but Zella thought it unlucky to laugh, and crossed herself whenever the event was alluded to. At this time Katusthius visited their abode. 'He was on his way," he said, "to Stamboul, and he came to know whether he could serve his brother in any of his transactions in the capital." Cyril and Zella received him with cordial affection: they rejoiced to perceive that fraternal love was beginning to warm his heart. He seemed full of ambition and hope: the brothers discussed his prospects, the politics of Europe, and the intrigues of the Fanar: the petty affairs of Corinth even were made subjects of discourse; and the probability that in a short time, young as he was, Cyril would

The Keepsake

be named Codja-Bashee of the province. On the morrow, Katusthius prepared to depart—"One favour does the voluntary exile ask; will my brother and sister accompany me some hours on my way to Napoli, whence I embark?"

Zella was unwilling to quit her home, even for a short interval; but she suffered herself to be persuaded, and they proceeded altogether for several miles towards the capital of the Morea. At noontide they made a repast under the shadow of a grove of oaks, and then separated. [159] Returning homeward, the wedded pair congratulated themselves on their tranquil life and peaceful, happiness, contrasted with the wanderer's lonely and homeless pleasures. These feelings increased in intensity as they drew nearer their dwelling, and anticipated the lisped welcome of their idolized child. From an eminence they looked upon the fertile vale which was their home: it was situated on the southern side of the isthmus, and looked upon the Gulf of Aegina: all was verdant, tranquil, and beautiful. They descended into the plain; there a singular appearance attracted their attention. A plough with its yoke of oxen had been deserted midway in the furrow; the animals had dragged it to the side of the field, and endeavoured to repose as well as their conjunction permitted. The sun already touched its Western bourne, and the summits of the trees were gilded by its parting beams. All was silent; even the eternal water-wheel was still; no menials appeared at their usual rustic labours. From the house the voice of wailing was too plainly heard.—"My child!" Zella exclaimed. Cyril began to reassure her; but another lament arose, and he hurried on. She dismounted, and would have followed him, but sank on the road's side. Her husband returned—"Courage, my beloved," he cried; "I will not repose night or day until Constans is restored to us—trust to me—farewell!" With these words he rode swiftly on.

Her worst fears were thus confirmed; her maternal heart, late so joyous, became the abode of despair, while the nurse's narration of the sad occurrence tended but to add worse fear to fear.

Thus it was: the same stranger of the Evil Eye had appeared, not as before, bearing down on them with eagle speed, but as if from a long journey; his horse lame and with drooping head; [160] the Arnaoot himself covered with dust, apparently scarcely able to keep his seat. "By the life of your child," he said, "give a cup of water to one who faints with thirst." The nurse, with Constans in her arms, got a bowl of the desired liquid, and presented it. Ere the parched lips of the stranger touched the wave, the vessel fell from his hands. The women started back, while he, at the same moment darting forward, tore with strong arm the child from her embrace. Already both were gone—with arrowy speed they traversed the plain, while her shrieks, and cries for assistance, called together all the domestics. They followed on the track of the ravisher, and none had yet returned. Now, as night closed in, one by one they came back; they had nothing to relate; they had scoured the woods, crossed the hills—they could not even discover the route which the Albanian had taken.

On the following day Cyril returned, jaded, haggard, miserable; he had obtained no tidings of his son. On the morrow he again departed on his quest, nor came back for several days. Zella passed her time wearily—now sitting in hopeless despondency, now climbing the near hill to see whether she could perceive the approach of her husband. She was not allowed to remain long thus tranquil; the trembling domestics, left in guard, warned her that the savage forms of several Arnaoots had been seen prowling about: she herself saw a tall figure, clad in a shaggy white capote, steal round the promontory, and on seeing her, shrink back: once at night the snorting and trampling of a horse roused her, not from slumber, but from her sense of security. Wretched as the bereft mother was, she felt personally almost reckless of danger; but she was not her own, she belonged to one beyond expression [161] dear; and duty, as well as affection for him, enjoined self-preservation. He, Cyril, again returned: he was gloomier, sadder than before; but there was more resolution on his brow, more energy in his motions; he had obtained a clue, yet it might only lead him to the depths of despair.

He discovered that Katusthius had not embarked at Napoli. He had joined a band of Arnaoots lurking about Vasilico, and had proceeded to Patras with the Protoklepht; thence they put off together in a monoxylon for the northern shores of the gulf of Lepanto: nor were they alone; they bore a child with them wrapt in a heavy torpid sleep. Poor Cyril's blood ran cold when he thought of the spells and witchcraft which had probably been put in practice on his boy. He would have followed close upon the robbers, but for the report that reached him, that the remainder of the Albanians had proceeded southward towards Corinth. He could not enter upon a long wandering search among the pathless wilds of Epirus, leaving Zella exposed to the attacks of these bandits. He returned to consult with her, to devise some plan of action which at once ensured her safety, and promised success to his endeavours.

After some hesitation and discussion, it was decided that he should first conduct her to her native home, consult with her father as to his present enterprise, and be guided by his warlike experience before he rushed into the very focus of danger. The seizure of his child might only be a lure, and it were not well for him, sole protector of that child and its mother, to rush unadvisedly into the toils.

Zella, strange to say, for her blue eyes and brilliant complexion belied her birth, was the daughter of a Mainote: [162] yet dreaded and abhorred by the rest of the world as are the inhabitants of Cape TÃ¦narus, they are celebrated for their domestic virtues and the strength of their private attachments. Zella loved her father, and the memory of her rugged rocky home, from which she had been torn in an adverse hour. Near neighbours of the Mainotes, dwelling in the ruder and most incult portion of Mama, are the Kakovougnis, a dark suspicious race, of squat and stunted form, strongly contrasted with the tranquil cast of countenance characteristic of the Mainote. The two tribes are embroiled in perpetual quarrels; the narrow sea-girt abode which they share affords at once a secure place of refuge from the foreign enemy, and all the facilities of internal mountain warfare. Cyril had once, during a coasting voyage, been driven by stress of weather into the little bay on whose shores is placed the small town of Kardamyla. The crew at first dreaded to be captured by the pirates; but they were reassured on finding them fully occupied by their domestic dissensions. A band of Kakovougnis were besieging the castellated rock overlooking Kardamyla, blockading the fortress in which the Mainote Capitano and his family had taken refuge. Two days passed thus, while furious contrary winds detained Cyril in the bay.

On the third evening the western gale subsided, and a land breeze promised to emancipate them from their perilous condition; when in the night, as they were about to put off in a boat from shore, they were hailed a party of Mainotes, and one, an old man of commanding figure, demanded a parley. He was the Capitano of Kardamyla, the chief of the fortress, now attacked by his implacable enemies: he saw no escape—he must fall—and his chief desire was to save his treasure and [163] his family from the hands of his enemies. Cyril consented to receive them on board: the latter consisted of an old mother, a paramana, and a young and beautiful girl, his daughter.

Cyril conducted them in safety to Napoli. Soon after, the Capitano's mother and paramana returned to their native town, while, with her father's consent, fair Zella became the wife of her preserver. The fortunes of the Mainote had prospered since then, and he stood first in rank, the chief of a large tribe, the Capitano of Kardamyla.

Thither then the hapless parents repaired; they embarked on board a small sacoleva, which dropt down the Gulf of Aegina, weathered the islands of Skvllo and Cerigo, and the extreme point of Tarus: favoured by prosperous gales, they made the desired port, and arrived at the hospitable mansion of old Camaraz. He heard their tale with indignation; swore by his beard to dip his poniard in the best blood of Katusthius, and insisted upon accompanying his son-in-law on his expedition to Albania. No time was lost—the gray-headed mariner, still full of energy, hastened every preparation. Cyril and Zella parted; a thousand fears, a thousand hours of misery rose between the pair, late sharers in perfect happiness. The boisterous sea and distant lands were the smallest of the obstacles that divided them; they would not fear the worst; yet hope, a sickly plant, faded in their hearts as they tore themselves asunder after a last embrace.

Zella returned from the fertile district of Corinth to her barren native rocks. She felt all joy expire as she viewed from the rugged shore the lessening sails of the sacoleva. Days and weeks passed, and still she remained in solitary and sad expectation: she never joined in the [164] dance, nor made one in the assemblies of her country-women, who met together at evening-tide to sing, tell stories, and wile away the time in dance and gaiety. She secluded herself in the most lonely part of her father's house, and gazed unceasingly from the lattice upon the sea beneath, or wandered on the rocky beach; and when tempest darkened the sky, and each precipitous promontory grew purple under the shadows of the wide-winged clouds, when the roar of the surges was on the shore, and the white crests of the waves, seen afar upon the ocean-plain, showed like flocks of new-shorn sheep scattered along wide-extended downs, she felt neither gale nor inclement cold, nor returned home till recalled by her attendants. In obedience to them she sought the shelter of her abode, not to remain long; for the wild winds spoke to her, and the stormy ocean reproached her tranquillity. Unable to control the impulse, she would rush from her habitation on the cliff, nor remember, till she reached the shore, that her papooshes were left midway on the mountain path, and that her forgotten veil and disordered dress were unmeet for such a scene. Often the unnumbered hours sped on, while this orphaned child of happiness leant on a cold dark rock; the low-browed crags beetled over her, the surges broke at her feet, her fair limbs were stained by spray, her tresses dishevelled by the gale. Hopelessly she wept until a sail appeared on the horizon; and then she dried her fast flowing tears, fixing her large eyes upon the nearing hull or fading topsail. Meanwhile the storm tossed the clouds into a thousand gigantic shapes, and the tumultuous sea grew blacker and more wild; her natural gloom was heightened by superstitious horror; the Moirae, the old Fates of her native

PLATE: Zella
Steel plate engraving; drawn by H. Corbould;
engraved by Charles Heath; printed by McQueen

[165] Grecian soil, howled in the breezes; apparitions, which told of her child pining under the influence of the Evil Eye, and of her husband, the prey of some Thracian witchcraft, such as still is practised in the dread neighbourhood of Larissa, haunted her broken slumbers, and stalked like dire shadows across her waking thoughts. Her bloom was gone, her eyes lost their lustre, her limbs their round full beauty; her strength failed her, as she tottered to the accustomed spot to watch—vainly, yet for ever to watch.

What is there so fearful as the expectation of evil tidings delayed? Sometimes in the midst of tears, or worse, amidst the convulsive gaspings of despair, we reproach ourselves for influencing the eternal fates by our gloomy anticipations: then, if a smile wreathe the mourner's quivering lip, it is arrested by a throb of agony. Alas! are not the dark tresses of the young, painted gray; the full cheek of beauty, delved with sad lines by the spirits of such hours? Misery is a more welcome visitant, when she comes in her darkest guise, and wraps us in perpetual black, for then the heart no longer sickens with disappointed hope.

Cyril and old Camaraz had found great difficulty in doubling the many capes of the Morea as they made a coasting expedition from Kardamyla to the gulf of Arta, north of Cefalonia and St.

Mauro. During their voyage they had time to arrange their plans. As a number of Moreots travelling together might attract too much attention, they resolved to land their comrades at different points, and travel separately into the interior of Albania: Yannina was their first place of rendezvous. Cyril and his father-in-law disembarked in one of the most se- [166] cluded of the many creeks which diversify the winding and precipitous shores of the gulf. Six others, chosen from the crew, would, by other routes, join them at the capital. They did not fear for themselves; alone, but well armed, and secure in the courage of despair, they penetrated the fastnesses of Epirus. No success cheered them: they arrived at Yannina without having made the slightest discovery. There they were joined by their comrades, whom they directed to remain three days in the town, and then separately to proceed to Tepellene, whither they immediately directed their steps. At the first village on their way thither, at "monastic Zitza," they obtained some information, not to direct, but to encourage their endeavours. They sought refreshment and hospitality in the monastery which is situated on a green eminence, crowned by a grove of oak-trees, immediately behind the village. Perhaps there is not in the world a more beautiful or more romantic spot, sheltered itself by clustering trees, looking out on one wide-spread landscape of hill and dale, enriched by vineyards, dotted with frequent flocks; while the Calamas in the depth of the vale gives life to the scene, and the far blue mountains of Zoumerkas, Sagori, Sulli, and Acroceraunia, to the east, wrest, north, and south, close in the various prospects. Cyril half envied the Calovers their inert tranquillity. They received the travellers gladly, and were cordial though simple in their manners. When questioned concerning the object of their journey, they warmly sympathised with the father's anxiety, and eagerly told all they knew. Two wrecks before, an Arnaoot, well known to them as Dmitri of the Evil Eye, a famous Klepht of Korvo, and a Moreot, arrived, bringing with them a child, a bold, spirited, beau- [167] tiful boy, who, with firmness beyond his years, claimed the protection of the Caloyers, and accused his companions of having carried him off by force from his parents.—"By my head!" cried the Albanian, "a brave Palikar: he keeps his word, brother; he swore by the Panagia, in spite of our threats of throwing him down a precipice, food for the vulture, to accuse us to the first good men he saw: he neither pines under the Evil Eye, nor quails beneath our menaces." Katusthius frowned at these praises, and it became evident during their stay at the monastery, that the Albanian and the Moreot quarrelled as to the disposal of the child. The rugged mountaineer threw off all his sternness as he gazed upon the boy. When little Constans slept, he hung over him, fanning away, with woman's care, the flies and gnats. When he spoke, he answered with expressions of fondness, winning him with gifts, teaching him, all baby as he was, a mimicry of warlike exercises. When the boy knelt and besought the Panagia to restore him to his parents, his infant voice quivering, and tears running down his cheeks, the eyes of Dmitri overflowed; he cast his cloak over his face; his heart whispered to him—"Thus, perhaps, my child prayed. Heaven was deaf—alas! where is she now?"—Encouraged by such signs of compassion, which children are quick to perceive, Constans twined his arms round his neck, telling him that he loved him, and that he would fight for him when a man, if he would take him back to Corinth. At such words Dmitri would rush forth, seek Katusthius, remonstrate with him, till the unrelenting man checked him by reminding him of his vow. Still he swore that no hair of the child's head should be injured; while the uncle, unvisited by compunction, meditated his [168] destruction. The quarrels which thence arose were frequent and violent, till Katusthius, weary of opposition, had recourse to craft to obtain his purpose. One night he secretly left the monastery, bearing the child with him. When Dmitri heard of his evasion, it was a fearful thing to the good Caloyers only to look upon him; they instinctively clutched hold of every bit of iron on which they could lay their hands, so to avert the Evil Eye which glared with native and untamed fierceness. In their panic a whole score of them had rushed to the iron-plated door which led out of their abode: with the strength of a lion, Dmitri tore them away, threw back the portal, and, with the swiftness of a torrent fed by the thawing of the snows in spring, he dashed down the steep hill: the flight of an eagle not more rapid; the course of a wild beast not more resolved.

  Such was the clue afforded to Cyril. It were too long to follow him in his subsequent search; he, with old Camaraz, wandered through the vale of Argyro-Castro, and climbed Mount Trebucci to Korvo. Dmitri had returned; he had gathered together a score of faithful comrades, and sallied forth again; various were the reports of his destination, and the enterprise which he meditated. One of these led our adventurers to Tepellenè, and hence back towards Yannina: and now chance again favoured them. They rested one night in the habitation of a priest at the little village of Mosme, about three leagues to the north of Zitza; and here they found an Arnaoot who had been disabled by a fall from his horse; this man was to have made one of Dmitri's band: they learned from him that the Arnaoot had tracked Katusthius, following him close, and forcing him to take refuge in the monastery of the Prophet [169] Elias, which stands on an elevated peak of the mountains of Sagori, eight leagues from Yannina. Dmitri had followed him, and demanded the child. The Caloyers refused to give it up, and the Klepht, roused to mad indignation, was now besieging and battering the monastery, to obtain by force this object of his newly-awakened affections.

At Yannina, Camaraz and Cyril collected their comrades, and departed to join their unconscious ally. He, more impetuous than a mountain-stream or ocean's fiercest waves, struck terror into the hearts of the recluses by his ceaseless and dauntless attacks. To encourage them to further resistance, Katusthius, leaving the child behind in the monastery, departed for the nearest town of Sagori, to entreat its Belouk-Bashee to come to their aid. The Sagorians are a mild, amiable, social people; they are gay, frank, clever; their bravery is universally acknowledged, even by the more uncivilized mountaineers of Zoumerkas; yet robbery, murder, and other acts of violence, are unknown among them. These good people were not a little indignant when they heard that a band of Arnaoots was besieging and battering the sacred retreat of their favourite Caloyers. They assembled in a gallant troop, and taking Katusthius with them, hastened to drive the insolent Klephts back to their ruder fastnesses. They came too late. At midnight, while the monks prayed fervently to be delivered from their enemies, Dmitri and his followers tore down their iron-plated door, and entered the holy precincts. The Protoklepht strode up to the gates of the sanctuary, and placing his hands upon it, swore that he came to save, not to destroy. Constans saw him. With a cry of delight he disengaged himself from the Caloyer who held [170] him, and rushed into his arms: this was sufficient triumph. With assurances of sincere regret for having disturbed them, the Klepht quitted the chapel with his followers, taking his prize with him.

Katusthius returned some hours after, and so well did the traitor plead his cause with the kind Sagorians, bewailing the fate of his little nephew among these evil men, that they offered to follow, and, superior as their numbers were, to rescue the boy from their destructive hands.

Katusthius, delighted with the proposition, urged their immediate departure. At dawn they began to climb the mountain summits, already trodden by the Zoumerkians.

Delighted with repossessing his little favourite, Dmitri placed him before him on his horse, and, followed by his comrades, made his way over the elevated mountains, clothed with old Dodona's oaks, or, in higher summits, by dark gigantic pines. They proceeded for some hours, and at length dismounted to repose. The spot they chose was the depth of a dark ravine, whose gloom was increased by the broad shadows of dark ilexes; an entangled underwood, and a sprinkling of craggy isolated rocks, made it difficult for the horses to keep their footing. They dismounted, and sat by the little stream. Their simple fare was spread, and Dmitri enticed the boy to eat by a thousand caresses. Suddenly one of his men, set as a guard, brought intelligence that a troop of Sagorians, with Katusthius as their guide, was advancing from the monastery of St.

Elias; while another man gave the alarm of the approach of six or eight well-armed Moreots, who were advancing on the road from Yannina; in a moment every sign of encampment had disappeared. The Arnaoots began to climb the hills, getting under cover of the rocks, [171] and behind the large trunks of the forest-trees, keeping concealed till their invaders should be in the very midst of them. Soon the Moreots appeared, turning round the defile, in a path that only allowed them to proceed two by two; they were unaware of danger, and walked carelessly, until a shot that whizzed over the head of one, striking the bough of a tree, recalled them from their security. The Greeks, accustomed to the same mode of warfare, betook themselves also to the safeguards of the rocks, firing from behind them, striving with their adversaries which should get to the most elevated station; jumping from crag to crag, and dropping down and firing as quickly as they could load: one old man alone remained on the pathway. The mariner, Camaraz, had often encountered the enemy on the deck of his caick, and would still have rushed foremost at a boarding, but this warfare required too much activity. Cyril called on him to shelter himself beneath a low, broad stone: the Mainote waved his hand. "Fear not for me," he cried; "I know how to die!"—The brave love the brave. Dmitri saw the old man stand, unflinching, a mark for all the balls, and he started from behind his rocky screen, calling on his men to cease. Then addressing his enemy, he cried, "Who art thou? wherefore art thou here? If ye come in peace, proceed on your way. Answer, and fear not!"

The old man drew himself up, saying, "I am a Mainote, and cannot fear. All Hellas trembles before the pirates of Cape Matapan, and I am one of these! I do not come in peace! Behold! you have in your arms the cause of our dissension! I am the grandsire of that child—give him to me!"

Dmitri, had he held a snake, which he felt awakening in [172] his bosom, could not so suddenly have changed his cheer:—"the offspring of a Mainote!"—he relaxed his grasp;—Constans would have fallen had he not clung to his neck. Meanwhile each party had descended from their rocky station, and were grouped together in the pathway below. Dmitri tore the child from his neck; he felt as if he could, with savage delight, dash him down the precipice—when, as he paused and trembled from excess of passion, Katusthius, and the foremost Sagorians, came down upon them.

"Stand!" cried the infuriated Arnaoot. "Behold Katusthius! behold, friend, whom I, driven by the resistless fates, madly and wickedly forswore! I now perform thy wish—the Mainote child dies! the son of the accursed race shall be the victim of my just revenge!"

Cyril, in a transport of fear, rushed up the rock; he levelled his musket, but he feared to sacrifice his child. The old Mainote, less timid and more desperate, took a steady aim; Dmitri saw the act, and hurled the dagger, already raised against the child, at him—it entered his side—while Constans, feeling his late protector's grasp relax, sprung from it into his father's arms.

Camaraz had fallen, yet his wound was slight. He saw the Arnaoots and Sagorians close round him; he saw his own followers made prisoners. Dmitri and Katusthius had both thrown themselves upon Cyril, struggling to repossess themselves of the screaming boy. The Mainote raised himself—he was feeble of limb, but his heart was strong; he threw himself before the father and child; he caught the upraised arm of Dmitri. "On me," he cried, "fall all thy vengeance! I of the evil race! for the child, he is innocent of such parentage! Maina cannot boast him for a son!" [173]

"Man of lies!" commenced the infuriated Arnaoot, "this falsehood shall not stead thee!"

"Nay, by the souls of those you have loved, listen!" continued Camaraz. "and if I make not good my words, may I and my children die! The boy's father is a Corinthian, his mother, a Sciote girl!"

"Scio!" the very word made the blood recede to Dmitri's heart. "Villain!" he cried, dashing aside Katusthius's arm, which was raised against poor Constans, 'I guard this child—dare not to injure him! Speak, old man, and fear not, so that thou speakest the truth."

"Fifteen years ago," said Camaraz, "I hovered with my caick, in search of prey, on the coast of Scio. A cottage stood on the borders of a chestnut wood, it was the habitation of the widow of a wealthy islander—she dwelt in it with her only daughter, married to an Albanian, then absent;—the good woman was reported to have a concealed treasure in her house—the girl herself would.be rich spoil—it was an adventure worth the risk. We ran our vessel up a shady creek, and, on the going down of the moon, landed; stealing under the covert of night towards the lonely abode of these women."—Dmitri grasped at his dagger's hilt—it was no longer there; he half drew a pistol from his girdle—little Constans, again confiding in his former friend, stretched out his infant hands and clung to his arm; the Klepht looked on him, half yielded to his desire to embrace him, half feared to be deceived; so he turned away, throwing his capote over his face, veiling his anguish, controlling his emotions, till all should be told. Camaraz continued:

"It became a worse tragedy than I had contemplated. The girl had a child—she feared for its life, and struggled [174] with the men like a tigress defending her young. I was in another room seeking for the hidden store, when a piercing shriek rent the air—I never knew what compassion was before—this cry went to my heart—but it was too late, the poor girl had sunk to the ground, the life-tide oozing from her bosom. I know not why, but I turned woman in my regret for the slain beauty. I meant to have carried her and her child on board, to see if aught could be done to save her, but she died ere we left the shore. I thought she would like her island rave best, and truly feared that she might turn vampire to haunt me, did I carry her away; so we left her corse for the priests to bury, and carried off the child, then about two years old. She could say few words except her own name, that was Zella, and she is the mother of this boy!"

A succession of arrivals in the bay of Kardamyla had kept poor Zella watching for many nights. Her attendant had, in despair of ever seeing her sleep again, drugged with opium the few eates she persuaded her to eat, but the poor woman did not calculate on the power of mind over body, of love over every enemy, physical or moral, arrayed against it. Zella lay on her couch, her spirit somewhat subdued, but her heart alive, her eves unclosed. In the night, led by some unexplained impulse, she crawled to her lattice, and saw a little sacoleva enter the bay; it ran in swiftly, under favour of the wind, and was lost to her sight under a jutting crag. Lightly she trod the marble floor of her chamber; she drew a large shawl close round her; she descended the rocky pathway, and reached, with swift steps, the beach—still the vessel was invisible, and [175] she was half inclined to think that it was the offspring of her excited imagination—yet she lingered.

She felt a sickness at her very heart whenever she attempted to move, and her eyelids weighed down in spite of herself. The desire of sleep at last became irresistible; she lay down on the shingles, reposed her head on the cold, hard pillow, folded her shawl still closer, and gave herself up to forgetfulness.

So profoundly did she slumber under the influence of the opiate, that for many hours she was insensible of any change in her situation. By degrees only she awoke, by degrees only became aware of the objects around her; the breeze felt fresh and free—so was it ever on the wave-beaten coast; the waters rippled near, their dash had been in her ears as she yielded to repose; but this was not her stony couch, that canopy, not the dark overhanging cliff. Suddenly she lifted up her head—she was on the deck of a small vessel, which was skimming swiftly over the ocean-waves—a cloak of sables pillowed her head; the shores of Cape Matapan were to her left, and they steered right towards the noonday sun. Wonder rather than fear possessed her: with a quick hand she drew aside the sail that veiled her from the crew—the dreaded Albanian was sitting close at her side, her Constans cradled in his arms—she uttered a cry—Cyril turned at the sound, and in a moment she was folded in his embrace.

Title

By the Author of Frankenstein. [Shelley, Mary.] "The False Rhyme." KS 1830. 265-268.[9]

Plate: Francis the First & His Sister
Steel plate engraving; painted by Richard Parkes Bonington;
engraved by Charles Heath; printed by McQueen [265]

---

9 Mary Shelley's authorship identified by Nora Crook; see "Sleuthing towards a Mary Shelley Canon," Women's Writing 6:3 (Oct 1999): 413-424.

THE FALSE RHYME[10]
BY THE AUTHOR OF "FRANKENSTEIN"

> "Come, tell me where the maid is found
> Whose heart can love without deceit,
> And I will range the world around
> To sigh one moment at her feet."— Thomas Moore.

On a fine July day, the fair Margaret, Queen of Navarre, then on a visit to her royal brother, had arranged a rural feast for the morning following, which Francis declined attending. He was melancholy; and the cause was said to be some lover`s quarrel with a favourite dame. The morrow came, and dark rain and murky clouds destroyed at once the schemes of the courtly throng. Margaret was angry, and she grew weary: her only hope for amusement was in Francis, and he had shut himself up—an excellent reason why she should the more desire to see him. She entered his apartment: he was standing at the casement, against which the noisy shower beat, writing with a diamond on the glass. Two beautiful dogs were his sole companions. As Queen Margaret entered, he hastily let down the silken curtain before the window, and looked a little confused.

"What treason is this, my liege," said the queen, "which crimsons your cheek? I must see the same."

"It is treason," replied the king, "and therefore, sweet sister, thou mayest not see it."

This the more excited Margaret`s curiosity, and a playful contest ensued: Francis at last yielded: he threw himself on a huge high-backed settee; and as the lady drew back the curtain with an arch smile, he grew grave and sentimental, as he reflected on the cause which had inspired his libel against all womankind. [266]

"What have we here?" cried Margaret: "nay, this is lêse majesté—
> 'Souvent femme varie,
> Bien fou qui s`y fie!'

Very little change would greatly amend your couplet:—would it not run better thus—
> 'Souvent homme varie,
> Bien folle qui s`y fie?'

I could tell you twenty stories of man's inconstancy."

"I will be content with one true tale of woman's fidelity," said Francis, drily; "but do not provoke me. I would fain be at peace with the soft Mutabilities, for thy dear sake."

"I defy your grace," replied Margaret, rashly, "to instance the falsehood of

---

10 Plain text for this story was obtained from *Great Literature Online* <http://shelley.classicauthors.net/falserhyme/> and then compared against the original volume. For full citation, see References.

one noble and well reputed dame."

"Not even Emilie de Lagny?" asked the king.

This was a sore subject for the queen. Emilie had been brought up in her own household, the most beautiful and the most virtuous of her maids of honour. She had long loved the Sire de Lagny, and their nuptials were celebrated with rejoicings but little ominous of the result. De Lagny was accused but a year after of traitorously yielding to the emperor a fortress under his command, and he was condemned to perpetual imprisonment. For some time Emilie seemed inconsolable, often visiting the miserable dungeon of her husband, and suffering on her return, from witnessing his wretchedness, such paroxysms of grief as threatened her life. Suddenly, in the midst of her sorrow, she disappeared; and inquiry only divulged the disgraceful fact, that she had escaped from France, bearing her jewels with her, and accompanied by her page, Robinet Leroux. It was whispered that, during their journey, the lady and the stripling often occupied one chamber; and [267] Margaret, enraged at these discoveries, commanded that no further quest should be made for her lost favourite.

Taunted now by her brother, she defended Emilie, declaring that she believed her to be guiltless, even going so far as to boast that within a month she would bring proof of her innocence.

"Robinet was a pretty boy," said Francis, laughing.

"Let us make a bet," cried Margaret: "if I lose, I will bear this vile rhyme of thine as a motto to my shame to my grave; if I win—-"

"I will break my window, and grant thee whatever boon thou askest."

The result of this bet was long sung by troubadour and minstrel. The Queen employed a hundred emissaries—published rewards for any intelligence of Emilie—all in vain. The month was expiring, and Margaret would have given many bright jewels to redeem her word. On the eve of the fatal day, the jailor of the prison in which the Sire de Lagny was confined sought an audience of the Queen; he brought her a message from the knight to say, that if the Lady Margaret would ask his pardon as her boon, and obtain from her royal brother that he might be brought before him, her bet was won. Fair Margaret was very joyful, and readily made the desired promise. Francis was unwilling to see his false servant, but he was in high good humour, for a cavalier had that morning brought intelligence of a victory over the Imperialists. The messenger himself was lauded in the despatches as the most fearless and bravest knight in France. The king loaded him with presents, only regretting that a vow prevented the soldier from raising his visor or declaring his name.

That same evening as the setting sun shone on the [268] lattice on which the ungallant rhyme was traced, Francis reposed on the same settee, and the beautiful Queen of Navarre, with triumph in her bright eyes, sat beside him. Attended by guards, the prisoner was brought in: his frame was attenuated by privation, and he walked with tottering steps. He knelt at the feet of Francis, and uncovered his head; a quantity of rich golden hair then escaping, fell over the sunken cheeks and pallid brow of the suppliant. "We have treason here!" cried the king: "sir jailor, where is your prisoner?"

"Sire, blame him not," said the soft faltering voice of Emilie; "wiser men than he have been deceived by woman. My dear lord was guiltless of the crime for which he suffered. There was but one mode to save him:—I assumed his chains—he escaped with poor Robinet Leroux in my attire—he joined your army: the young and gallant cavalier who delivered the despatches to your grace, whom you overwhelmed with honours and reward, is my own Enguerrard de Lagny. I waited but for his arrival with testimonials of his innocence, to declare myself to my lady, the Queen. Has she not won her bet? And the boon she asks——"

"Is de Lagny's pardon," said Margaret, as she also knelt to the king: "spare your faithful vassal, sire, and reward this lady's truth."

Francis first broke the false speaking-window, then he raised the ladies from their supplicatory posture.

In the tournament given to celebrate this "Triumph of Ladies," the Sire de Lagny bore off every prize; and surely there was more loveliness in Emilie's faded cheek—more grace in her emaciated form, type as they were of truest affection—than in the prouder bearing and fresher complexion of the most brilliant beauty in attendance on the courtly festival.

Literary Annual

The Keepsake for MDCCCXXXI. Ed. Frederic Mansel Reynolds. London: Hurst, Chance, and Co., and Jennings and Chaplin, 1831. Printer: Thomas Davison, Whitefriars.

Title

By the Author of *Frankenstein.* [Shelley, Mary.] "Transformation." KS 1831. 18-39. [18]

TRANSFORMATION[11]

> Forthwith this frame of mine was wrench'd
>   With a woful agony,
> Which forced me to begin my tale,
>   And then it set me free.
>
> Since then, at an uncertain hour,
>   That agony returns;
> And till my ghastly tale is told
>   This heart within me burns.
>   *Coleridge's Ancient Mariner.*

I HAVE heard it said, that, when any strange, supernatural, and necromantic adventure has occurred to a human being, that being, however desirous he may be to conceal the same, feels at certain periods torn up as it were by an intellectual earthquake, and is forced to bare the inner depths of his spirit to another. I am a witness of the truth of this. I have dearly sworn to myself never to reveal to human ears the horrors to which I once, in excess of fiendly pride, delivered myself over. The holy man who heard my confession, and reconciled me to the church, is dead. None knows that once—

Why should it not be thus? Why tell a tale of impious tempting of Providence, and soul-subduing humiliation? Why? answer me, ye who are wise in the secrets of human nature! I only know that so it is; in spite of strong resolve— of a pride that too much masters me—of shame, and even of fear, so to render myself odious to my species—I must speak.

Genoa! my birth-place-proud city! looking upon the blue waves of the

---

11 Plain text for this story was obtained from <http://www.columbia.edu/itc/english/f1102-005x01/readings/transformation.htm>, which was, in turn, transcribed from *The Mary Shelley Reader*, eds. Betty T. Bennett and Charles E. Robinson (Oxford University Press, 1990), pp. 121-35.; reprinted from Mary Shelley's *Tales and Stories*, pp. 286-300. This 1990 reprint is based on an 1891 edition published by W. Patterson, London, in the series, *The Treasure house of tales by great authors.* Comparison was made against microfiche created by Chadwyck-Healey, *English Gift Books and Literary Annuals* and was compared again to the 1831 physical volume.

Mediterranean sea—dost thou remember me in my boyhood, when thy cliffs and promontories, thy [19] bright sky and gay vineyards, were my world? Happy time! when to the young heart the narrow-bounded universe, which leaves, by its very limitation, free scope to the imagination, enchains our physical energies, and, sole period in our lives, innocence and enjoyment are united. Yet, who can look back to childhood, and not remember its sorrows and its harrowing fears? I was born with the most imperious, haughty, tameless spirit, with which ever mortal was gifted. I quailed before my father only; and he, generous and noble, but capricious and tyrannical, at once fostered and checked the wild impetuosity of my character, making obedience necessary, but inspiring no respect for the motives which guided his commands. To be a man, free, independent; or, in better words, insolent and domineering, was the hope and prayer of my rebel heart.

My father had one friend, a wealthy Genoese noble, who in a political tumult was suddenly sentenced to banishment, and his property confiscated. The Marchese Torella went into exile alone. Like my father, he was a widower: he bad one child, the almost infant Juliet, who was left under my father's guardianship. I should certainly have been an unkind master to the lovely girl, but that I was forced by my position to become her protector. A variety of childish incidents all tended to one point,—to make Juliet see in me a rock of refuge; I in her, one, who must perish through the soft sensibility of her nature too rudely visited, but for my guardian care. We grew up together. The opening rose in May was not more sweet than this dear girl. An irradiation of beauty was spread over her face. Her form, her step, her voice—my heart weeps even now, to think of all of relying, gentle, loving, and pure, that was enshrined in that celestial tenement. When I was eleven and Juliet eight years of age, a cousin of mine, much older than [20] either—he seemed to us a man—took great notice of my playmate; he called her his bride, and asked her to marry him. She refused, and he insisted, drawing her unwillingly towards him. With the countenance and emotions of a maniac I threw myself on him—I strove to draw his sword—I clung to his neck with the ferocious resolve to strangle him: he was obliged to call for assistance to disengage himself from me. On that night I led Juliet to the chapel of our house: I made her touch the sacred relics—I harrowed her child's heart, and profaned her child's lips with an oath, that she would be mine, and mine only.

Well, those days passed away. Torella returned in a few years, and became wealthier and more prosperous than ever. When I was seventeen my father died; he had been magnificent to prodigality; Torella rejoiced that my minority would afford an opportunity for repairing my fortunes. Juliet and I had been affianced beside my father's deathbed—Torella was to be a second parent to me.

I desired to see the world, and I was indulged. I went to Florence, to Rome, to Naples; thence I passed to Toulon, and at length reached what had long been the bourne of my wishes, Paris. There was wild work in Paris then. The poor king, Charles the Sixth, now sane, now mad, now a monarch, now an abject slave, was the very mockery of humanity. The queen, the dauphin, the Duke of Burgundy, alternately friends and foes now meeting in prodigal feasts, now shedding blood in rivalry-were blind to the miserable state of their country, and the dangers that impended over it, and gave themselves wholly up to dissolute enjoyment or savage strife. My character still followed me. I was arrogant and selfwilled; I loved display, and above all, I threw all control far from me. Who could control me in Paris? My young friends were eager to foster passions which furnished them with pleasures. I [21] was deemed handsome—I was master of every knightly accomplishment. I was disconnected with any political party. I grew a favourite with all: my presumption and arrogance were pardoned in one so young: I became a spoiled child. Who could control me? not the letters and advice of Torella—only strong necessity visiting me in the abhorred shape of an empty purse. But there were means to refill this void. Acre after acre, estate after estate, I sold. My dress, my jewels, my horses and their caparisons, were almost unrivalled in gorgeous Paris, while the lands of my inheritance passed into possession of others.

The Duke of Orleans was waylaid and murdered by the Duke of Burgundy. Fear and terror possessed all Paris. The dauphin and the queen shut themselves up; every pleasure was suspended. I grew weary of this state of things, and my heart yearned for my boyhood's haunts. I was nearly a beggar, yet still I would go there, claim my bride, and rebuild my fortunes. A few happy ventures as a merchant would make me rich again. Nevertheless, I would not return in humble guise. My last act was to dispose of my remaining estate near Albaro for half its worth, for ready money. Then I despatched all kinds of artificers, arras, furniture of regal splendour, to fit up the last relic of my inheritance, my palace in Genoa. I lingered a little longer yet, ashamed at the part of the prodigal returned, which I feared I should play. I sent my horses. One matchless Spanish jennet I despatched to my promised bride; its caparisons flamed with jewels and cloth of gold. In every part I caused to be entwined the initials of Juliet and her Guido. My present found favour in hers and in her father's eyes.

Still to return a proclaimed spendthrift, the mark of impertinent wonder, perhaps of scorn, and to encounter singly the reproaches or taunts of my fellow-citizens, was no [22] alluring prospect. As a shield between me and censure, I invited some few of the most reckless of my comrades to accompany me: thus I went armed against the world, hiding a rankling feeling, half fear and half penitence, by bravado and an insolent display of satisfied vanity.

I arrived in Genoa. I trod the pavement of my ancestral palace. My proud step was no interpreter of my heart, for I deeply felt that, though surrounded by every luxury, I was a beggar. The first step I took in claiming Juliet must widely declare me such. I read contempt or pity in the looks of all. I fancied, so apt is conscience to imagine what it deserves, that rich and poor, young and old, all regarded me with derision. Torella came not near me. No wonder that my second father should expect a son's deference from me in waiting first on him. But, galled and stung by a sense of my follies and demerit, I strove to throw the blame on others. We kept nightly orgies in Palazzo Carega. To sleepless, riotous nights, followed listless, supine mornings. At the Ave Maria we showed our dainty persons in the streets, scoffing at the sober citizens, casting insolent glances on the shrinking women. Juliet was not among them—no, no; if she had been there, shame would have driven me away, if love had not brought me to her feet.

I grew tired of this. Suddenly I paid the Marchese a visit. He was at his villa, one among the many which deck the suburb of San Pietro d'Arena. It was the month of May—a month of May in that garden of the world the blossoms of the fruit trees were fading among thick, green foliage; the vines were shooting forth; the ground strewed with the fallen olive blooms; the fire-fly was in the myrtle hedge; heaven and earth wore a mantle of surpassing beauty. Torella welcomed me kindly, though seriously; and even his shade of displeasure soon wore away. Some resem- [23] blance to my father-some look and tone of youthful ingenuousness, lurking still in spite of my misdeeds, softened the good old man's heart. He sent *for his daughter-he presented me to her as her betrothed. The chamber became hallowed by a holy light as she entered. Hers was that cherub look, those large, soft eyes, full dimpled cheeks, and mouth of infantine sweetness, that expresses the rare union of happiness and love. Admiration first possessed me; she is mine! was the second proud emotion, and my lips curled with haughty triumph. I had not been the *enfant gâté* of the beauties of France not to have learnt the art of pleasing the soft heart of woman. If towards men I was overbearing, the deference I paid to them was the more in contrast. I commenced my courtship by the display of a thousand gallantries to Juliet, who, vowed to me from infancy, had never admitted the devotion of others; and who, though accustomed to expressions of admiration, was uninitiated in the language of lovers.

For a few days all went well. Torella never alluded to my extravagance; he treated me as a favourite son. But the time came, as we discussed the preliminaries to my union with his daughter, when this fair face of things should be overcast. A contract had been drawn up in my father's lifetime. I had rendered this, in fact, void, by having squandered the whole of the wealth which was to have been shared by Juliet and myself. Torella, in consequence, chose to consider this bond as cancelled, and proposed another, in which, though the wealth he bestowed was immeasurably increased, there were so many restrictions as to the mode of spending it, that I, who saw independence only in free career being given to my own imperious will, taunted him as taking advantage of my situation, and refused utterly to subscribe to his conditions. The old man mildly strove to recall me to reason. Roused [24] pride became the tyrant of my thought: I listened with indignation—I repelled him with disdain.

"Juliet, thou art mine! Did we not interchange vows in our innocent childhood? are we not one in the sight of God? and shall thy cold-hearted, cold-blooded father divide us? Be generous, my love, be just; take not away a gift, last treasure of thy Guido—retract not thy vows—let us defy the world, and setting at nought the calculations of age, find in our mutual affection a refuge from every ill."

Fiend I must have been, with such sophistry to endeavour to poison that sanctuary of holy thought and tender love. Juliet shrank from me affrighted. Her father was the best and kindest of men, and she strove to show me how, in obeying him, every good would follow. He would receive my tardy submission with warm affection; and generous pardon would follow my repentance. Profitless words for a young and gentle daughter to use to a man accustomed to make his will, law; and to feel in his own heart a despot so terrible and stern, that he could yield obedience to nought save his own imperious desires! My resentment grew with resistance; my wild companions were ready to add fuel to the flame. We laid a plan to carry off Juliet. At first it appeared to be crowned with success. Midway, on our return, we were overtaken by the agonized father and his attendants. A conflict ensued. Before the city guard came to decide the victory in favour of our antagonists, two of Torella's servitors were dangerously wounded.

This portion of my history weighs most heavily with me. Changed man as I am, I abhor myself in the recollection. May none who hear this tale ever have felt as I. A horse driven to fury by a rider armed with barbed spurs, was not more a slave than I, to the violent tyranny of my temper. A fiend possessed my soul, irritating it to mad- [25] ness. I felt the voice of conscience within me; but if I yielded to it for a brief interval, it was only to be a moment after torn, as by a whirlwind, away—borne along on the stream of desperate rage—the plaything of the storms engendered by pride. I was imprisoned, and, at the instance of Torella, set free. Again I returned to carry off both him and his child to France; which hapless country, then preyed on by freebooters and gangs of lawless soldiery, offered a grateful refuge to a criminal like me. Our plots were discovered. I was sentenced to banishment; and, as my debts were already enormous, my remaining property was put in the hands of commissioners for their payment. Torella again offered his mediation, requiring only my promise not to renew my abortive attempts on himself and his daughter. I spurned his offers, and fancied that I triumphed when I was thrust out from Genoa, a solitary and penniless exile. My companions were gone: they had been dismissed the city some weeks before, and were already in France. I was alone—friendless; with nor sword at my side, nor ducat in my purse.

I wandered along the sea-shore, a whirlwind of passion possessing and tearing my soul. It was as if a live coal had been set burning in my breast. At first I meditated on what *I should do*. I would join a band of freebooters. Revenge!—the word seemed balm to me:—I hugged it—caressed it—till, like a serpent, it stung me. Then again I would abjure and despise Genoa, that little corner of the world.

I would return to Paris, where so many of my friends swarmed; where my services would be eagerly accepted; where I would carve out fortune with my sword, and might, through success, make my paltry birth-place, and the false Torella, rue the day when they drove me, a new Coriolanus, from her walls. I would return to Paris-thus, on foot—a beggar—and present myself in my poverty [26] to those I had formerly entertained sumptuously? There was gall in the mere thought of it.

The reality of things began to dawn upon my mind, bringing despair in its train. For several months I had been a prisoner: the evils of my dungeon had whipped my soul to madness, but they had subdued my corporeal frame. I was weak and wan. Torella. had used a thousand artifices to administer to my comfort; I had detected and scorned them all-and I reaped the harvest of my obduracy. What was to be done? Should I crouch before my foe, and sue for forgiveness?—Die rather ten thousand deaths!—Never should they obtain that victory! Hate—I swore eternal hate! Hate from whom?—to whom?—From a wandering outcast to a mighty noble. I and my feelings were nothing to them: already had they forgotten one so unworthy. And Juliet!—her angel-face and sylphlike form gleamed among the clouds of my despair with vain beauty; for I had lost her—the glory and flower of the world! Another will call her his!—that smile of paradise will bless another!

Even now my heart fails within me when I recur to this rout of grim-visaged ideas. Now subdued almost to tears, now raving in my agony, still I wandered along the rocky shore, which grew at each step wilder and more desolate. Hanging rocks and hoar precipices overlooked the tideless ocean; black caverns yawned; and for ever, among the seaworn recesses, murmured and dashed the unfruitful waters. Now my way was almost barred by an abrupt promontory, now rendered nearly impracticable by fragments fallen from the cliff. Evening was at hand, when, seaward, arose, as if on the waving of a wizard's wand, a murky web of clouds, blotting the late azure sky, and darkening and disturbing the till now placid deep. The clouds had strange fantastic shapes; and they changed, [27] and mingled, and seemed to be driven about by a mighty spell. The waves raised their white crests; the thunder first muttered, then roared from across the waste of waters, which took a deep purple dye, flecked with foam. The spot where I stood, looked, on one side, to the wide-spread ocean; on the other, it was barred by a rugged promontory. Round this cape suddenly came, driven by the wind, a vessel. In vain the mariners tried to force a path for her to the open sea—the gale drove her on the rocks. It will perish!—all on board will perish!—Would I were among them! And to my young heart the idea of death came for the first time blended with that of joy. It was an awful sight to behold that vessel struggling with her fate. Hardly could I discern the sailors, but I heard them. It was soon all over!—A rock, just covered by the tossing waves, and so unperceived, lay in wait for its prey. A crash of thunder broke over my head at the moment that, with a frightful shock, the skiff dashed upon her unseen enemy. In a brief space of time she went to pieces. There I stood in safety; and there were my fellow-creatures, battling, how hopelessly, with annihilation. Methought I saw them struggling—too truly did I hear their shrieks, conquering the barking surges in their shrill agony. The dark breakers threw hither and thither the fragments of the wreck: soon it disappeared. I had been fascinated to gaze till the end: at last I sank on my knees—I covered my face with my hands: I again looked up; something was floating on the billows towards the shore. It neared and neared. Was that a human form?—It grew more distinct; and at last a mighty wave, lifting the whole freight, lodged it upon a rock. A human being bestriding a sea-chest!—A human being!—Yet was it one? Surely never such had existed before-a misshapen dwarf, with squinting eyes, distorted features, and body deformed, till [28] it became a horror to behold. My blood, lately warming towards a fellow-being so snatched from a watery tomb, froze in my heart. The dwarf got off his chest; he tossed his straight, straggling hair from his odious visage:

"By St. Beelzebub!" he exclaimed, "I have been well bested." He looked round and saw me. "Oh, by the fiend! here is another ally of the mighty one. To what saint did you offer prayers, friend—if not to mine? Yet I remember you not on board."

I shrank from the monster and his blasphemy. Again he questioned me, and I muttered some inaudible reply. He continued:—

"Your voice is drowned by this dissonant roar. What a noise the big ocean makes! Schoolboys bursting from their prison are not louder than these waves set free to play. They disturb me. I will no more of their ill-timed brawling.—Silence, hoary One!—Winds, avaunt!—to your homes!—Clouds, fly to the antipodes, and leave our heaven clear!"

As he spoke, he stretched out his two long lank arms, that looked like spider's claws, and seemed to embrace with them the expanse before him. Was it a miracle? The clouds became broken, and fled; the azure sky first peeped out, and then was spread a calm field of blue above us; the stormy gale was exchanged to the softly breathing west; the sea grew calm; the waves dwindled to riplets.

"I like obedience even in these stupid elements," said the dwarf. "How much more in the tameless mind of man! It was a well got up storm, you must allow—and all of my own making."

It was tempting Providence to interchange talk with this magician. But *Power*, in all its shapes, is venerable to man. Awe, curiosity, a clinging fascination, drew me towards him. [29]

"Come, don't be frightened, friend," said the wretch: "I am good humoured when pleased; and something does please me in your well proportioned body and handsome face, though you look a little woebegone. You have suffered a land—I, a sea wreck. Perhaps I can allay the tempest of your fortunes as I did my own. Shall we be friends?"—And he held out his hand; I could not touch it. "Well, then, companions—that will do as well. And now, while I rest after the buffeting I underwent just now, tell me why, young and gallant as you seem, you wander thus alone and downcast on this wild sea-shore."

The voice of the wretch was screeching and horrid, and his contortions as he spoke were frightful to behold. Yet he did gain a kind of influence over me, which I could not master, and I told him my tale. When it was ended, he laughed long and loud: the rocks echoed back the sound: hell seemed yelling around me.

"Oh, thou cousin of Lucifer!" said he; "so thou too hast fallen through thy pride; and, though bright as the son of Morning, thou art ready to give up thy good looks, thy bride, and thy well-being, rather than submit thee to the tyranny of good. I honour thy choice, by my soul!—So thou hast fled, and yield the day; and mean to starve on these rocks, and to let the birds peck out thy dead eyes, while thy enemy and thy betrothed rejoice in thy ruin. Thy pride is strangely akin to humility, methinks."

As he spoke, a thousand fanged thoughts stung me to the heart. "What would you that I should do?" I cried.

"I!—Oh, nothing, but lie down and say your prayers before you die. But, were I you, I know the deed that should be done."

I drew near him. His supernatural powers made him an oracle in my eyes; yet a strange unearthly thrill [30] quivered through my frame as I said, "Speak!—teach me—what act do you advise?"

"Revenge thyself, man!—humble thy enemies!—set thy foot on the old man's neck, and possess thyself of his daughter!"

"To the east and west I turn," cried I, "and see no means! Had I gold, much could I achieve; but, poor and single, I am powerless."

The dwarf had been seated on his chest as he listened to my story. Now he got off; he touched a spring; it flew open!—What a mine of wealth—of blazing jewels, beaming gold, and pale silver-was displayed therein. A mad desire to possess this treasure was born within me.

"Doubtless," I said, "one so powerful as you could do all things."

"Nay," said the monster, humbly, "I am less omnipotent than I seem. Some things I possess which you may covet; but I would give them all for a small share, or even for a loan of what is yours."

"My possessions are at your service," I replied, bitterly—"my poverty, my exile, my disgrace—I make a free gift of them all."

"Good! I thank you. Add one other thing to your gift, and my treasure is yours."

"As nothing is my sole inheritance, what besides nothing would you have?"

"Your comely face and well-made limbs."

I shivered. Would this all-powerful monster murder me? I had no dagger. I forgot to pray—but I grew pale.

"I ask for a loan, not a gift," said the frightful thing: "lend me your body for three days—you shall have mine to cage your soul the while, and, in payment, my chest. What say you to the bargain?—Three short days." [31]

We are told that it is dangerous to hold unlawful talk; and well do I prove the same. Tamely written down, it may seem incredible that I should lend any ear to this proposition; but, in spite of his unnatural ugliness, there was something fascinating in a being whose voice could govern earth, air, and sea. I felt a keen desire to comply; for with that chest I could command the world. My only hesitation resulted from a fear that he would not be true to his bargain. Then, I thought, I shall soon die here on these lonely sands, and the limbs he covets will be mine no more:—it is worth the chance. And, besides, I knew that, by all the rules of art-magic, there were formula and oaths which none of its practisers dared break. I hesitated to reply; and he went on, now displaying his wealth, now speaking of the petty price he demanded, till it seemed madness to refuse. Thus is it: place our bark in the current of the stream, and down, over fall and cataract it is hurried; give up our conduct to the wild torrent of passion, and we are away, we know not whither.

He swore many an oath, and I adjured him by many a sacred name; till I saw this wonder of power, this ruler of the elements, shiver like an autumn leaf before my words; and as if the spirit spake unwillingly and per force within him, at last, lie, with broken voice, revealed the spell whereby he might be obliged, did he wish to play me false, to render up the unlawful spoil. Our warm life-blood must mingle to make and to mar the charm.

Enough of this unholy theme. I was persuaded—the thing was done. The morrow dawned upon me as I lay upon the shingles, and I knew not my own shadow as it fell from me. I felt myself changed to a shape of horror, and cursed my easy faith and blind credulity. The chest was there—there the gold and precious stones for which I [32] had sold the frame of flesh which nature had given me. The sight a little stilled my emotions: three days would soon be gone.

They did pass. The dwarf had supplied me with a plenteous store of food. At first I could hardly walk, so strange and out of joint were all my limbs; and my voice—it was that of the fiend. But I kept silent, and turned my face to the sun, that I might not see my shadow, and counted the hours, and ruminated on my future conduct. To bring Torella to my feet—to possess my Juliet in spite of him—all this my wealth could easily achieve. During dark night I slept, and dreamt of the accomplishment of my desires. Two suns had set-the third dawned. I was agitated, fearful. Oh expectation, what a frightful thing art thou, when kindled more by fear than hope! How dost thou twist thyself round the heart, torturing its pulsations! How dost thou dart unknown pangs all through our feeble mechanism, now seeming to shiver us like broken glass, to nothingness now giving us a fresh strength, which can do nothing, and so torments us by a sensation, such as the strong man must feel who cannot break his fetters, though they bend in his grasp. Slowly paced the bright, bright orb up the eastern sky; long it lingered in the zenith, and still more slowly wandered down the west: it touched the horizon's verge—it was lost! Its glories were on the summits of the cliff—they grew dun and gray. The evening star shone bright. He will soon be here.

He came not!—By the living heavens, he came not!—and night dragged out its weary length, and, in its decaying age, "day began to grizzle its dark hair;" and the sun rose again on the most miserable wretch that ever upbraided its light. Three days thus I passed. The jewels and the gold—oh, how I abhorred them! [33]

Well, well—I will not blacken these pages with demoniac ravings. All too terrible were the thoughts, the raging tumult of ideas that filled my soul. At the end of that time I slept; I had not before since the third sunset; and I dreamt that I was at Juliet's feet, and she smiled, and then she shrieked—for she saw my transformation—and again she smiled, for still her beautiful lover knelt before her. But it was not I—it was he, the fiend, arrayed in my limbs, speaking with my voice, winning her with my looks of love. I strove to warn her, but my tongue refused its office; I strove to tear him from her, but I was rooted to the ground—I awoke with the agony. There were the solitary hoar precipices—there the plashing sea, the quiet strand, and the blue sky over all. What did it mean? was my dream but a mirror of the truth? was he wooing and winning my betrothed? I would on the instant back to Genoa—but I was banished. I laughed—the dwarf's yell burst from my lips—I banished! 0, no! they had not exiled the foul limbs I wore; I might with these enter, without fear of incurring the threatened penalty of death, my own, my native city.

I began to walk towards Genoa. I was somewhat accustomed to my distorted limbs; none were ever so ill adapted for a straight-forward movement; it was with infinite difficulty that I proceeded. Then, too, I desired to avoid all the hamlets strewed here and there on the sea-beach, for I was unwilling to make a display of my hideousness. I was not quite sure that, if seen, the mere boys would not stone me to death as I passed, for a monster: some ungentle salutations I did receive from the few peasants or fishermen I chanced to meet. But it was dark night before I approached Genoa. The weather was so balmy and sweet that it struck me that the Marchese and [34] his daughter would very probably have quitted the city for their country retreat. It was from Villa Torella that I had attempted to carry off Juliet; I had spent many an hour reconnoitering the spot, and knew each inch of ground in its vicinity. It was beautifully situated, embosomed in trees, on the margin of a stream. As I drew near, it became evident that my conjecture was right; nay, moreover, that the hours were being then devoted to feasting and merriment. For the house was lighted up; strains of soft and gay music were wafted towards me by the breeze. My heart sank within me. Such was the generous kindness of Torella's heart that I felt sure that he would not have indulged in public manifestations of rejoicing just after my unfortunate banishment, but for a cause I dared not dwell upon.

The country people were all alive and flocking about; it became necessary that I should study to conceal myself; and yet I longed to address some one, or to hear others discourse, or in any way to gain intelligence of what was really going on. At length, entering the walks that were in immediate vicinity to the mansion, I found one dark enough to veil my excessive frightfulness; and yet others as well as I were loitering in its shade. I soon gathered all I wanted to know—all that first made my very heart die with horror, and then boil with indignation. To-morrow Juliet was to be given to the penitent, reformed, beloved Guido—to-morrow my bride was to pledge her vows to a fiend from hell! And I did this!—my accursed pride—my demoniac violence and wicked self-idolatry had caused this act. For if I had acted as the wretch who had stolen my form had acted-if, with a mien at once yielding and dignified, I had presented myself to Torella, saying, I have done wrong, forgive me; I am unworthy of your angel- [35] child, but permit me to claim her hereafter, when my altered conduct shall manifest that I abjure my vices, and endeavour to become in some sort worthy of her. I go to serve against the infidels; and when my zeal for religion and my true penitence for the past shall appear to you to cancel my crimes, permit me again to call myself your son. Thus had he spoken; and the penitent was welcomed even as the prodigal son of scripture: the fatted calf was killed for him; and he, still pursuing the same path, displayed such open-hearted regret for his follies, so humble a concession of all his rights, and so ardent a resolve to reacquire them by a life of contrition and virtue, that he quickly conquered the kind, old man; and full pardon, and the gift of his lovely child, followed in swift succession.

0! had an angel from Paradise whispered to me to act thus! But now, what would be the innocent Juliet's fate? Would God permit the foul union—or, some prodigy destroying it, link the dishonoured name of Carega with the worst of crimes? To-morrow at dawn they were to be married: there was but one way to prevent this—to meet mine enemy, and to enforce the ratification of our agreement. I felt that this could only be done by a mortal struggle. I had no sword—if indeed my distorted arms could wield a soldier's weapon—but I had a dagger, and in that lay my every hope. There was no time for pondering or balancing nicely the question: I might die in the attempt; but besides the burning jealousy and despair of my own heart, honour, mere humanity, demanded that I should fall rather than not destroy the machinations of the fiend.

The guests departed-the lights began to disappear; it was evident that the inhabitants of the villa were seeking repose. I hid myself among the trees—the garden grew [36] desert—the gates were closed—I wandered round and came under a window-ah! well did I know the same!—a soft twilight glimmered in the room—the curtains were half withdrawn. It was the temple of innocence and beauty. Its magnificence was tempered, as it were, by the slight disarrangements occasioned by its being dwelt in, and all the objects scattered around displayed the taste of her who hallowed it by her presence. I saw her enter with a quick light step-I saw her approach the window-she drew back the curtain yet further, and looked out into the night. Its breezy freshness played among her ringlets, and wafted them from the transparent marble of her brow. She clasped her hands, she raised her eyes to Heaven. I heard her voice. Guido! she softly murmured, Mine own Guido! and then, as if overcome by the fullness of her own heart, she sank on her knees:—her upraised eyes—her negligent but graceful attitude—the beaming thankfulness that lighted up her face—oh, these are tame words! Heart of mine, thou imagest ever, though thou canst not pourtray, the celestial beauty of that child of light and love.

  I heard a step-a quick firm step along the shady avenue. Soon I saw a cavalier, richly dressed, young and, methought, graceful to look on, advance.—I hid myself yet closer.-The youth approached; he paused beneath the window. She arose, and again looking out she saw him, and said—I cannot, no, at this distant time I cannot record her terms of soft silver tenderness; to me they were spoken, but they were replied to by him.

  "I will not go," he cried: "here where you have been, where your memory glides like some Heaven-visiting ghost, I will pass the long hours till we meet, never, my Juliet, again, day or night, to part. But do thou, my love, retire; the cold morn and fitful breeze will make thy cheek

PLATE: Juliet
Steel plate engraving; drawn by Miss Sharpe;
engraved by J.C. Edwards [37]

pale, and fill with languor thy love-lighted eyes. Ah, sweetest! could I press one kiss upon them, I could, methinks, repose."

And then he approached still nearer, and methought lie was about to clamber into her chamber. I had hesitated, not to terrify her; now I was no longer master of myself. I rushed forward—I threw myself on him—I tore him away—I cried, "0 loathsome and foul-shaped wretch!"

I need not repeat epithets, all tending, as it appeared, to rail at a person I at present feel some partiality for. A shriek rose from Juliet's lips. I neither heard nor saw—I *felt* only mine enemy, whose throat I grasped, and my dagger's hilt; he struggled, but could not escape: at length hoarsely he breathed these words: "Do!—strike home! destroy this body—you will still live: may your life be long and merry!"

The descending dagger was arrested at the word, and he, feeling my hold relax, extricated himself and drew his sword, while the uproar in the house, and flying of torches from one room to the other, showed that soon we should be separated—and I—oh! far better die: so that he did not survive, I cared not. In the midst of my frenzy there was much calculation:—fall I might, and so that he did not survive, I cared not for the death-blow I might deal against myself. While still, therefore, he thought I paused, and while I saw the villanous resolve to take advantage of my hesitation, in the sudden thrust he made at me, I threw myself on his sword, and at the same moment plunged my dagger, with a true desperate aim, in his side. We fell together, rolling over each other, and the tide of blood that flowed from the gaping wound of each mingled on the grass. More I know not—I fainted.

Again I returned to life: weak almost to death, I found [38] myself stretched upon a bed—Juliet was kneeling beside it. Strange! my first broken request was for a mirror. I was so wan and ghastly, that my poor girl hesitated, as she told me afterwards; but, by the mass! I thought myself a right proper youth when I saw the dear reflection of my own well-known features. I confess it is a weakness, but I avow it, I do entertain a considerable affection for the countenance and limbs I behold, whenever I look at a glass; and have more mirrors in my house, and consult them oftener than any beauty in Venice. Before you too much condemn me, permit me to say that no one better knows than I the value of his own body; no one, probably, except myself, ever having had it stolen from him.

Incoherently I at first talked of the dwarf and his crimes, and reproached Juliet for her too easy admission of his love. She thought me raving, as well she might, and yet it was some time before I could prevail on myself to admit that the Guido whose penitence had won her back for me was myself; and while I cursed bitterly the monstrous dwarf, and blest the well-directed blow that had deprived him of life, I suddenly checked myself when I heard her say-Amen! knowing that him whom she reviled was my very self. A little reflection taught me silence-a little practice enabled me to speak of that frightful night without any very excessive blunder. The wound I had given myself was no mockery of one—it was long before I recovered—and as the benevolent and generous Torella sat beside me, talking such wisdom as might win friends to repentance, and mine own dear Juliet hovered near me, administering to my wants, and cheering me by her smiles, the work of my bodily cure and mental reform went on together. I have never, indeed, wholly recovered my strength my cheek is paler since—my person a little bent. Juliet sometimes ventures [39] to allude bitterly to the malice that caused this change, but I kiss her on the moment, and tell her all is for the best. I am a fonder and more faithful husband—and true is this—but for that wound, never had I called her mine.

I did not revisit the sea-shore, nor seek for the fiend's treasure; yet, while I ponder on the past, I often think, and my confessor was not backward in favouring the idea, that it might be a good rather than an evil spirit, sent by my guardian angel, to show me the folly and misery of pride. So well at least did I learn this lesson, roughly taught as I was, that I am known now by all my friends and fellow-citizens by the name of Guido il Cortese.

THE LITERARY SOUVENIR

Literary Annual
The Literary Souvenir; or, Cabinet of Poetry and Romance. Ed. Alaric A. Watts. London: Hurst, Robinson and Co. and A. Constable and Co. Edinburgh, 1825. Printer: B. Bensley, Bolt Court, Fleet Street.

Title
Anonymous. "The Golden Snuff-Box." LS 1825. 127-148. [127]

THE GOLDEN SNUFF-BOX

When fortune frowns and hope grows dark,
Or warms my bosom but to mock it,
I think of thee, my golden ark,
And, smiling, take thee from my pocket.

Pandora's was a box of sadness,
And sure mankind but little owes it;
Thy lid's the door to mines of gladness,
And such it proves when I unclose it.
Old Song.

Oh! what a thrilling joy the snuff-box gives.
Southey.

The wild and feverish dominion of the marvellous, circumscribed and invaded as it has been by the increasing lights of civilization, and attacked by moralists and philosophers, still retains—in one of its regions at least—its ancient influence over the hearts and feelings of men. The appearance on earth of departed spirits continues even now to be a subject of fearful and anxious interest. In vain do many declare their scepticism; we all more or less, as circumstances affect us, evince some degree of practical belief; and no one listens to a narrative of this description without deep and concentrated attention. [128] What is the cause of this real faith breaking forth amid assumed incredulity? Whence this fear, we know not wherefore nor of what, that lays such firm hold upon our feelings? Does not an answer suggest itself—a reply, of which those who acknowledge the truth would fain stifle the expression? "The belief in preternatural appearances," says Dr. Johnson, "could have become universal only by its truth." Let infidelity then listen to the following adventure, of which the narrator is at the same time the hero.—

It was the first night after my departure from Frankfort that I arrived at Gottingen, weary with my journey, and low spirited at leaving a home (how much it costs to know the true force of that one word!) which was hallowed to me as the scene not only of past joy, but of past sorrow; for even grief lends a charm to its localities. My depression was augmented by the desolate appearance of my new habitation. The spaciousness of the rooms only served to render their bareness of furniture and the chilling nakedness of the walls the more obvious. How different from the snug neatness of the abode I had quitted! There, every thing was pleasant and delightful,—the inmates afforded me agreeable society when so inclined, and at other times never thought of interrupting the occupations of their lodger. But here every thing was different. The man of the house[129] and his wife were two of the common-places of creation, and on the strength of some alleged relationship to me—heaven knows whence derived—on the side of the latter, conceived that I must feel interested in whatever interested them. Their expectations, their disappointments, their squabbles, were therefore all so many inflictions on myself. Nor did I see any prospect of relief from the many vexations I was constrained to endure. I had changed my abode at the suggestion of an individual, to whom my friends, though not myself personally, were under some obligations, and I foresaw the reproaches I should provoke, if, in consulting my own comfort, I neglected to comply with their wishes. Thus circumstanced, I felt as a prisoner deprived of my free power of locomotion; and every thought in which I indulged upon the subject increased my inquietude. I escaped as soon as possible from the persecution of my host and hostess, and betaking myself to my miserable chamber, gave a free vent to my feelings;—I sat down "and wept when I thought of Babylon."

I threw open my window, and the free air rushed upon me in all its freshness. The moon was up, but the west was yet dyed with the lingering beams of the departed sun. Masses of silver-ridged clouds floated along, and caught a deeper tinge of beauty as some of the dying rays fell upon them. I thought how delightful it would have been, on such an evening, to [130] have sat in my little garden at Frankfort, with my book, refreshed with as pure a breeze, and haunted by no internal disquiet to subdue the glow of my delight. But now the luxuries of eternal nature seemed but a mockery of my regret. I should have hailed with satisfaction the tempest, whose clouded and lowering sky would have better accorded with my own dark and melancholy temperament.

My nearest kindred I had lost early in life, and, that outlet of the affections closed, I contracted a stronger attachment to places and inanimate objects. The soul ever seeks something to love, and, disappointed in its hopes, clings fondly to the places where they grew and perished. Of these even, I was now bereft; and unfriended and companionless, my cup seemed full of bitterness, and wild and dreary the waste that lay before me. At length I threw myself on my bed, and strove to seek in the forgetfulness of sleep, a temporary relief from the conflicting thoughts by which I was distracted. The attempt was fruitless: the same uneasiness pursued me—the same figures rose before me;—the cheerful fire-side of my residence at Frankfort, the smiling eyes and happy faces of its inmates, again presented themselves to my imagination, and were as suddenly and inexplicably changed into the dismal and soul-appalling desolation of my new abode, with its repulsive nakedness, its scant accommodations,—the one or two broken and [131] tattered daubs that were gibbeted upon its walls, and the sour and meagre visages of my host and hostess.

After a feverish dozing of two or three hours—an eternity of torment—I awoke, if I could be said to awake from what was not sleep, more weary and exhausted than ever. The moonbeams, intercepted by the mere remnant of a curtain, spread their broad white light on the floor: and every object in the chamber was distinctly visible: I arose, and descended into the sitting-room; from the dying embers that cast their flickering glimmer on the hearth, I contrived to light a lamp, and, rejecting any further ideas of sleep, sat down to look over the few torn volumes which lay in the room, my own books not having arrived from Frankfort. But had I expected much amusement from my researches, I should speedily have been undeceived. A work on Cookery, Jacob Behmen's book on Regeneration, and a fragment of the Life of Martin Luther, formed the most considerable part of the collection. I had no courage to inquire further, so, pushing the books from me, I stretched out my legs, and lolled on the table in a spirit of determined endurance.

Suddenly, it became dark: it seemed that the moon was totally eclipsed, though from this room it was not previously visible. The wind rose, and whistled, and now and then puffed down the chimney, raising a momentary gleam from the expiring [132] ashes. At last, it sank into a low moaning that lulled me with its melancholy wildness. I fancied, at times, that the distant, sullen roll of the thunder mingled with the blast, and heavy drops of rain dashed faintly against the windows.

My mediations were too confused to admit of my calculating the progress of time, and I know not how long they had lasted, when I was interrupted in my reverie by a loud knock apparently at the outer door of the house. I started; the knock was repeated, and before it was possible for any one to have given admission to the applicant, the door of the room in which I sat, opened, and a stranger, to my perfect astonishment, walked deliberately in. If he took no notice of me, I was more inquisitive concerning him, and watched his motions with intense curiosity; though, as I have since recollected with surprise, without feeling the slightest inclination to address him, or to move away from my seat.

The intruder was a man seemingly advanced in years, but remarkably tall and erect. An enormous great coat dripping with wet covered him, and the water poured also from a hat with a low crown and most exaggerated brims. A leathern belt was buckled around his waist, and a kind of gaiter of rough hide secured his legs. Such was his dress. He carried moreover in his hand a stout staff tipped with buckshorn. [133]

After having advanced to the hearth, he unbuckled his belt, and, drawing a chair to the fire, which had suddenly blazed up and threw a wild glare over the apartment, he removed his upper coat. He then placed it on the chair as if to dry, took off his portentously brimmed hat, and dashing from it a shower of water, hung it upon a peg on the wall. All this was done in silence, and with a coolness that might have been natural in the master of the house, but seemed exceedingly odd in a stranger entering the Lord knows how in the middle of the night,—and one too who appeared to conceive it altogether superfluous to explain the cause of so extraordinary a visit.

The removal of the great coat and hat exhibited the wearer as apparently very old, but still firm, and, as I have said, of unusual stature. His countenance must once have been handsome, and wore even then a mild, dignified, and benevolent aspect, which was not diminished by the few venerable hairs that were strewed upon his forehead. There was a good deal of acuteness in his look, especially in his eyes, which were bright and dark. He did not sit down, but, standing before the fire with folded arms, gazed on the flames as they rose and fell, and was seemingly buried in deep meditation.

I had no power to remove my eyes from the object which was thus unexpectedly presented to my view. I continued to gaze, and my 'great unknown' [134] remained in his original attitude, until the flames once more drooped into their former waning and expiring state. He stood there, immoveable as a statue. I began to regard him with some degree of awe—perhaps of terror. My lamp emitted a faint and fitful glimmer around the apartment, and the light from the hearth was unsteady and precarious in the extreme. I could no longer trace the features of my companion; a sort of fearful and mysterious gloom pervaded the room—the house stood along—I was the only inhabitant out of bed—the wind had ceased its low booming,—and the night was silent as death!

Suddenly the stranger turned towards me, and looking in my face with a wistful and melancholy gaze, expressive as I fancied, of a feeling of compassion. My consternation redoubled. His bright eyes were fixed steadily upon me with a fascination as unavoidable as that of the serpent—it might be as fatal. My blood crept and curdled n my veins, and an icy chill thrilled through my frame. I wished and endeavoured in vain to address the old man. It was not so much that I seemed to myself to have lost the power, as that I wanted the courage, to speak. Matters remained in this state some time; at last, by a violent effort, like that by which one casts off an incipient nightmare, I sprang up—"In God's name!" I exclaimed, "who and what are you?" [135]

I was astounded. Instead of answering me, he took out an antique gold box, highly chased, and taking form it a pinch of snuff, held it to me. I durst not refuse his civility, and therefore took a portion of the dust, though without an intention of applying it to my nostrils. He replaced the box in the pocket from which he had taken it; was silent a few minutes, and then addressed me:

"You have heard of Von Steivenhauss, your great grandfather?" His voice was firm, but hollow and deep.

I replied, "I have."

"You have heard perhaps, of Carl Heiderflitcher, his friend?"

"Frequently."

"You know that they twice saved each other's lives?"

"I do;"—and as my courage was now on the increase, or, as I became more used to the presence of my companion, I ventured to continue:—"I know also, that they died together in battle, each striving as much for his fellow as himself."

"They did so. Your grandfather died first, and Carl fell, oppressed with numbers, upon his body.—I am he."

Notwithstanding my boasted courage, I confess, this direct acknowledgement of personal identity with a man who had been slain upwards of seventy years, [136] startled me a not a little. However, he allowed me small time for meditation.

"Well," pursued he, "thus much do you know. But you do not know that before their death they entered into a compact, that each should, if permitted, watch over the descendents of the other, and assist them to the utmost when in danger or distress."

I professed my entire ignorance of such an arrangement.

"So it was," he continued; "we judged it better thus to decide, than that either should be the protector of his own race. Our reasons are immaterial."

There was no denying the likelihood of a ghost's reasons being immaterial; so I asked no questions, but suffered my informant to proceed with his narration.

"I was the last of my race. Your ancestor's covenant is therefore expired. He, however, yet survives in you. You will ere long be in danger. It is my business to protect you,"

He again took out his snuff-box—"Let this," he said, "be your constant companion. In trifling difficulties open this box, and you will receive assistance. Should any serious evil overtake you, open it thrice and close it; but beware you part not with it—beware also that no criminality of your own brings upon your head the evil from which you seek to relieve yourself:—and now take your snuff." [137]

From a personage to whom I laboured under such serious obligations, I could not refuse a proffered courtesy; I took one pinch, sneezed violently, and recovering with a start, found myself alone. The fire and the lamp were totally extinguished, and the gray light of the morning streamed through the windows. In vain did I look around; the old man was gone; the great coat and huge brimmed hat had likewise vanished. I began to think, despite of the strength of my impressions, that all that had passed was the progeny of a dream,—when resting my arm on the table, it encountered some hard substance. On turning my head, I found the golden snuff-box. There needed no further evidence of the correctness of my recollections.

Some months passed away without an appearance or intimation of the threatened evil. Meanwhile I diligently pursued my studies, and regularly attended old Bluffershwinkle, the cabbage-wigged lecturer on humanities. I lived frugally, read constantly, and had no occasion to resort to my box to deliver me from difficulties.

Returning, however, one day from the Professor's, deeply busied in meditation on a metaphysical query which he had just propounded for my consideration, my eye accidentally encountered those of a young female who was passing accompanied by an elderly domestic. Either from the con-[138] fused haste with which she averted her looks, or from some inequality in the path, she half slipped, and in recovering herself dropped the delicately fashioned basket which she carried in her hand. My utmost alertness was in requisition to seize the basket sufficiently soon to prevent its contents from being scattered on the pavement; I succeeded, and on restoring it to the owner was rewarded with such a blushing smile and so sweet a murmur of thanks, that unused as I was to the society of any females,—except my hostess at Frankfort, who was much older, and her daughters who were much younger than myself,—I doubt whether I was not more confused by the loveliness and grace of this fair creature than by the appearance of my midnight visitor. So greatly was I disconcerted, that I suffered her to pass without making any reply to her acknowledgements, and stood stupidly gazing after her, until remembering that I was in the public street, I cursed my own folly, and half determined to follow her, but perceived on looking back that she had already disappeared. I continued my walk homeward; and went to the Professor in the morning, indifferently prepared to solve the problem he had desired me to study.

Time passed; yet at intervals the idea of the fair incognita would introduce itself, with a mingled sensation of pleasure and disappointment, and [139] I frequently detected myself casting inquisitive glances at females in whom I had traced, or imagined I had traced, a resemblance to the goddess of my idolatry. But on a nearer approach the delusion always vanished, and I sought in vain for the lovely features and inimitable smile I remembered so well.

It was my usual custom at the latter end of the day to walk a mile or two into the environs of the town, and when one path grew familiar to me, to ramble in some different direction. In this manner I one evening explored a new track, which after various windings led me by the spacious garden of a handsome habitation, and was terminated by a small lake, the banks of which were clothed with various species of pines, and with willows whose pendulous branches kissed fondly and constantly the surface of the waters. The beauty of the spot detained me awhile in admiration, and I continued to gaze upon it and on the sky whose gorgeous and melting sunset radiance was unequalled save by the reflection of their splendour in the liquid mirror beneath.

Whilst thus occupied, the sound of two female voices saluted my ear, and speedily approached so near that I could distinctly hear the conversation of the speakers, one of whom, and as it seemed to me a very young girl, was soliciting her companion, [140] whom I guessed to be somewhat older than herself, to sing.

"Now, do, dear Lisette, do pray sing for me," said the younger.

"You know I have a cold, and cannot sing, Margaret."

"Now that I wont believe, and so sing for me; do sing."

Apparently the entreaties of the little girl produced the desired effect, for presently I heard a very sweet voice singing: the words, as nearly as I can render them, were—

From flower to floweret winging
The lightsome busy bee—

I was unable to catch more, as the fair vocalist had proceeded to too great a distance. However, she returned with her companion, and I heard the conclusion of her song.

Would I were gaily ranging
With heart as free from cares.

"Thank you, dear Lisette," said the child, "thank you;—but can't you—wont you sing it again?"

"Why, you little unconscionable creature, do you think I can sing all night for you?"

"No, not all night,—only just sing that song again." [141]

I listened, and the sweet voice against charmed my ear.

From flower to floweret winging,
    The lightsome busy bee,
His hum of gladness singing,
    Sweet riches gathereth he;
Delights for ever changing,
    Whose breast no poison bears;—

Would I were gaily ranging
> With heart as free from cares.

In less than two minutes after the songstress had ceased, I heard a loud cry of distress, and clearing the enclosures of the garden, rushed forward, and had no occasion to inquire the cause. The little girl had, in her gambols, wandered too far from her companion, and, her foot slipping, had fallen into the lake, close by the margin of which stood the other female (in whom I instantly recognized the lady of my meditations) in the utmost agony, but unable, from the alarm of the moment, to speak,—scarcely to sustain herself. I was no swimmer, but I sprang into the water, and caught the child as she rose to the surface;—we both sank,—and again rising, I snatched at the branch of a huge willow which hung over the lake, and, thus supported, contrived to keep partially above the water. But a fresh cause of terror speedily arose. The bough by which I held, not strong enough to sustain the double weight thus suspended from it, stained and cracked, and seemed [142] every moment on the point of breaking. Lisette had fainted—my cries for assistance were in vain;—I was beginning to despair, when my talisman, which I carried constantly about me, occurred to me. Seizing the child's clothes by my teeth, and clinging with one hand to our failing support, I grasped with the other the box, and opened and closed it as it lay within my pocket. Immediately the willow branch was lifted up, and a boat was rowed beneath us. We were not three yards from shore, and were instantly landed. I turned around to return my thanks to the rower, but the vessel had disappeared.

I ran with the child into the house, and committing her to the care of the domestics, hastened back to assist Lisette. I met her, however, recovered from her swoon, and flying with distracted looks towards the place I had just left. I loudly proclaimed the safety of her change; the joy over came her, and had I not caught her, she would have fallen to the ground. It was a moment worth an existence. As she lay panting and trembling in my arms, she raised her beautiful and gentle eyes, and gave me a look—such a look of joy and of thankfulnes, so deep, so rapturous, that in the many happy years I have since enjoyed, I have scarcely known one moment of bliss equally intense. The wind played among her light tresses, and one drifted to my cheek. If every there was magic in a [143] touch it surely thrilled in that. I pass over the subsequent meetings, the warm vows and the gentle confessions which followed: we both loved, and our stolen interviews were as delightful as they were pure and holy. It is unnecessary to be more minute: love narratives, the readers of my own sex would not thank me for, and the ladies have imaginations to picture for themselves.

The next occasion on which I found it necessary to resort to my snuff-box, was of a very different complexion. In a public room a few weeks afterwards, I had the misfortune to be involved in a quarrel with a man of dashing appearance, who thought proper to make some observations, which, I conceived, reflected upon my character. In the course of the dispute, I said something implying a want of gentlemanlike conduct in my opponent. He asked, with an appearance of great indignation, whether I doubted his being a gentleman.

"Sir," replied I, in as marked a tone as I could assume, "I have no doubt."

The issue was an arrangement to settle the dispute next morning, in an unfrequented spot, about a mile from the town.

Without incurring reputation for cowardice, I may confess that I returned home with a heavy heart. Whatever might be the event of the conflict, it could not fail of being productive of much injury, and [144] probably of much misery to me. The rank and reputation I had hitherto maintained n the university, my expectations in life, and that dearest one which twined around my heart with the strength of something more than mere worldly interest, the hope that my fond Lisette would be indeed mine, would, even if I escaped, be, if not wholly blighted, yet deeply affected by my share in the unfortunate affair in which I had become engaged. These and other reflections sufficiently painful, forced themselves upon my mind, until, defeated by their own vividness, they were succeeded by that stupor and heartless torpidity, which follows over-excited animation. In this state I rushed headlong into the street, and ignorant of what I was doing, entered a tavern and called for wine, which I drank till my brain whirled round with frenzy under its influence.

How I got home, I know not. But in the morning I found myself in my bed, suddenly awakened by the rude grasp of men whom I had no recollection of having before seen,—hard, cold, villainous looking wretches, in whose countenances no trace of human feeling was visible. For a moment I gazed round unconsciously; the next, the horrid remembrance of my engagement flashed upon me like a death-stroke. But the occasion or meaning of the interruption I had experienced, I neither knew nor could learn from my unwelcome guests, who compelled me has- [145] tily to dress myself, and then hurried me away in silence. We arrived at the public gaol. Here I was incarcerated alone in a damp and miserable cell.

It would be useless to detail the examinations I underwent or the hardships I endured. I stood charged, I was informed, with murder,—with the murder of the very man with whom I had quarreled the night previous. His body was found early in the morning in a retired street. I had been seen passing that way a short time before its discovery, with a violent and agitated demeanour, and my dispute with the deceased was so public, that suspicion immediately attached to me. What was worse, I had no means of rebutting the presumption of my guilt arising from those unhappy coincidences.

Remanded to my loathsome cell, my first impulse was to open and shut three times, according to the old man's directions, the box which was to preserve me in extremity. Once-twice-my heart palpitated violently as I closed it the third time. I looked around—some minutes elapsed, and I despaired. There was no appearance of assistance; I remained alone, and the iron door of the prison continued inexorably closed.

Hours, days, and weeks passed, without any aid or comfort for the wretched captive. My mental torments increased every moment. I thought of my home on the pleasant banks of the Maine. I thought of the [146] bright eyes and fond heart of Lisette. Then darker dreams took possession of my bewildered soul. Was it possible that I was actually guilty of the crime alleged? That in my mad insensibility, and infuriated by wine, I had met and destroyed my victim? Of all my pangs, this supposition struck the deepest. The horrid phantom thus conjured up, hovered continually around me, and the thought of my ignominious and public death increased the misery of my situation.

My trial came on. I had no witnesses whose testimony might exculpate me. Presumption was against me. I stated my case; was heard was respect and attention, but with evident incredulity.

Nothing remained but for sentence to be pronounced. The judge had prepared himself—had opened his lips to fulfill this last part of his awful duty, when he was interrupted by a sudden disturbance; and a confused murmur arose in the court of "witnesses for the criminal." Deserted as I had been by the expectation of relief, the hope now given birth to was too strong for me. A mist darkened my vision—I heard nothing—I saw nothing, till aroused from my insensibility by the information that I was free.

A witness had appeared—had exculpated me by his testimony, from the suspicion of the alleged crime, and had pointed out the real murdered, who, ,on his apprehension, had confessed his guilt. I reeled away, [147] scarcely conscious of what had happened, to my lodgings, where I was received with congratulations which I wanted not, mingled with admonitions as to my future conduct, which I despised.

I sought the privacy of my own apartment. The first object that met my sight was the figure of Carl Heiderflitcher, with his broad rimmed beaver. I was about to speak, but he motioned me to be silent.

"The threatened danger is past," said he, "I have saved your life, it yet remains to make your life worth enjoying. You love Lisette, the merchant's daughter, and are beloved by her; go to her father and make your proposals. I shall await your return."

I went, though with little hope of making any impression upon the purse-proud citizen. I saw him, and spoke of my love for his daughter; when he asked if I had 30,000 rix dollars.

A pretty question to a man who had never in his life been possessed at one time of fifty!

"I am not able to command that sum, but—"

"Then you may go about your business."

"Supposing," I said, "I should be able to raise that sum?"

"Why, then, and supposing also that my daughter liked you, I might, perhaps, on inquiry respecting you, have no great objection to the match. [148] But in the mean time I wish you a good morning."

I returned, cursing the avarice of the man, and the wantonness which had occasioned me to be sent upon this fool's errand. Carl Heiderflitcher were waiting for me. I recounted to him all that had passed.

"Humph—give me the box I lent you; you will have now no further occasion for it."

I took out the box.

"Empty it before you give it to me."

I opened it to shake out the snuff, and there followed a shower of gold pieces, which lasted some seconds. I turned in amazement to the stranger; he was gone, having taken with him his box, which had dropped from my hand in my excessive and delighted surprise.

I gathered up the money and counted it. There was gold to the amount of 40,000 rix dollars.

I was married a fortnight afterwards.

Title

D., L. "New Year's Eve. The Omens." LS 1825. 159-175. [159]

NEW YEAR'S EVE
THE OMENS.

And coming events cast their shadows before.
Campbell.

"Hark! the clock strikes eleven," said the Baron Rosenthäl to his assembled smiling guests; "let us each drink a glass to the parting year, and the memory of all the happy hours which it has brought us."

His wish was immediately complied with; the glasses were cheerfully brought into contact with each other, and the kindly recollection of past happiness glistened in every eye.

"It is, however, a strange though serenely serious thing, to watch the death of the old and the birth of the new year," said Hermann: "properly speaking, each instant is the commencement or end of a year; or if you please, of a century, or a millennium; and it is custom merely which gives solemnity to the mid-night hour betwixt the last of December and the first [160] of January."—"Just so," replied the Flak, "the consent of whole nations, founded perhaps upon religious uses, has given solemnity to the festival, and what do we require more? I am delighted that we are all seated together again, in pursuit of the same object in the same manner as last year, and that the old year smiles upon us in its dying hour, as if it had to accuse itself of nothing evil against us. But the circumstance that gives solemnity to its departure, is not our gaiety, but rather something more exalted,—the consciousness of a universal sympathy,—for, on these occasions, each individual celebrates his neighbour's festival no less than his own. The old year exhibits itself to our imaginations as a placid, smiling, dying mother, and the new one as a gay laughing babe; and between the coffin of the one, and the cradle of the other, prophetic feelings overshadow our souls, which in the mouths of human beings become either wishes or apprehensions."

"Let wishes rest till midnight," said the Baron, interrupting the speaker, "though no doubt we shall be glad to be convinced that new year's wishes are prophetic feelings—for as we all intend to wish for good things, it will be worth while to believe that those wishes will be realized, and our anticipations fulfilled: but alas! dear Falk, experience overturns your delightful theory, as it does too many others equally attractive." [161]

"We ladies at least," said the Baroness, "shall be happy to agree with you in the magic of new year's anticipations—explain therefore, to us, why so many of our wishes remain ungratified."

"It is because we are apt to form them too frequently and too idly," replied Falk, "and thus the new year's wishes become an empty ceremony, of which even you yourselves do not expect the fulfillment. I must observe, too, that I have only endowed with magical power those wishes which are pronounced from some overmastering feeling or irresistible impulse at the moment of the new year's birth; and I have thus lessened by a considerable number the amount of unfulfilled anticipations."

"In some countries, especially in Germany, great stress is laid upon words involuntarily spoken at certain seasons, and under certain circumstances. People shun words of evil purport with the great circumspection; but more particularly those which are ambiguous, and which, though pronounced with a good intention, are applied by the demons of Fate in an opposite sense, and may, perhaps be accomplished in a destructive manner."

"Falk," cried Hermann laughing, "I believe there is not a miraculous tradition nor a popular superstition, but you are able to produce examples in illustration of it; do, therefore, let us have a receipt for the magical power of words." [162]

"To invent an interesting little tale of this kind," replied Falk, "would perhaps not be a very difficult task, but I will only request your attention to a simple fact which I am going to relate, and of which I was myself a witness."

"Many years ago, I was acquainted at Karlsbad with the widow of a privy counsellor, Madame Amelia de Kulm; she had visited the baths with her little daughter for the sole purpose of accompanying thither a sick uncle, who did not however experience the benefit which he had anticipated from them. In consequence of his disappointment he was advised by his physicians to return home; and as the period fixed for my residence at Karlsbad had also expired, I acceded to the proposal of Madame de Kulm to depart at the same time with her, and to take the more distant route over the estate of her uncle. She had a singular motive for making this proposal; she entertained a positive conviction that her uncle would die on the road; for the mistress of the house where she lodged, who passed for a kind of visionary, had several times hinted her suspicion that one of the family would never arrive at the place of his destination alive.

"The weakness of the old gentleman did not admit of our continuing our journey without interruption; we therefore determined to have a day of rest in a pleasant village, the appearance of which had attracted our [163] notice. The landlady of the inn at which we put up, undertook the care of the invalid; and as he received the greatest attention from her, and was amused with her lively chat, his niece and myself indulged ourselves with a walk round the gardens of the village. The tranquil night which her uncle had enjoyed, had enlivened the spirits of Madame de Kulm, and she related to me with much humour several scenes of her past life, and anecdotes of her acquaintances. Suddenly we heard the tolling of a bell from the village. 'It is a funeral,' said she, 'let us meet it; it is long since I have beheld any interment in the country: during my childhood I would not have missed a funeral upon any account.' The little Minna wept at this observation, and prayed her momma not to go to the churchyard among the cold dead; but we laughed at her childish fear, and walked quietly into the cemetery. As is usual in villages, the coffin was placed by the side of the grave, and opened once more to afford the relatives a farewell glance. When the lid was removed we beheld a beautiful and youthful corpse reposing within its narrow home. Soon afterwards an aged peasant approached with a little girl, both dressed in mourning; they gazed long and sorrowfully upon the beautiful deceased, and then placed flowers of the dead in her folded hands. 'Sleep tranquilly,' said the old man; 'I hoped that thou wouldst have rendered me this service; but it has [164] been ordained otherwise.' The clergy man then approached, and delivered a sublime and consoling oration, to which Madame de Kulm prayed the deepest and most delighted attention. Shortly before its conclusion, her uncle appeared; who had allowed himself to be supported by the hostess to the church-yard. 'Oh, how I wish that you had heard this delightful oration from the commencement,' said she, springing towards him: and when the clergyman approached them, after the solemnity, in order to pay his respects to the strangers, she said 'I should wish for no other than you, Sir, to pronounce the funeral oration for me; accept of my thanks for the delight your eloquent discourse has afforded me.' The little Minna was terrified. 'Mamma,' said she, half weeping, 'do not speak thus, I beseech you.' 'No, it is for me rather to indulge in such a wish, my dear niece,' said the uncle; but the child again cried out more vehemently than before. The clergyman and I looked at each other with surprise; but Madame de Kulm said, smiling, 'I am unable just at this moment to furnish you with an explanation of my precipitate speech; but I request that you will favour us with your company to dinner at the inn.' The clergyman consented, and the explanation was then given; namely, that she intended to offer him a very valuable benefice upon her estate. The old man requested time for consideration; for [165] although his present income was small, he loved his congregation, and could not easily resolve to part from it; it was therefore determined that the affair should be settled by letter.

"But the proposed correspondence never took place. The following morning Madame de Kulm complained of indisposition, and requested that our departure should be delayed. Her sufferings increased in a short time to a dangerous illness, which baffled the science of the physicians: the result was death; and eight days after the former funeral, the clergyman delivered a funeral oration over the corse of the hapless Amelia de Kulm. It agonized us deeply, to stand by the side of the open coffin, and to behold thus the former ceremony (which we now felt had been but a prophecy of this,) so sadly repeated before us. Her uncle lived some years after this occurrence, and we often recalled to our minds the singular fulfilment of his niece's wish."

"It would have been still more singular," said Hermann, "if her death had happened accidentally,—sickness always allows of a natural explanation; perhaps Madame de Kulm was herself alarmed at her precipitate words, and still more so at the observation of her uncle; in that case her own fears were probably the sole cause of her illness and death."

"I beg you will pardon me," said Falk, gravely; "but I am always vexed when I hear people talk of [166] natural explanation; as if any thing in nature could happen unnaturally—all that occurs is natural of course, otherwise it could not occur."

"But we are not speaking of what is natural or unnatural," said the Baroness, "your story, Falk, has nothing to do with the question, because you leave it doubtful whether the sickness was not occasioned less through the words themselves, than through the observation occasioned by the words."

"Certainly though neither," replied Falk; "I observed, I believe, that Amelia was in an excited state of mind before the words were spoken. The unlimited praise which she bestowed upon the funeral oration, which, although clever, was by no means so uncommonly excellent, proved that this excitement existed in a most unusual degree; her words, therefore, which might have been caused by her approaching sickness, received a prophetic appearance from this singular coincidence of circumstances."

"Then you acknowledge," rejoined the Baroness, "that there was nothing wonderful or supernatural in the case?"

"Supernatural, certainly not," returned Anselm; "I am of Falk's opinion, that throughout nature, which occasions every thing we see, nothing can happen unnaturally."

"I am going to request of you," said Gertrude, "to [167] tell me the meaning of that which is called the supernatural:—may there not be appearances which you are obliged to call supernatural, which, if I may be allowed the expression, only pervert nature, and are unwillingly made use of by her, like authoritative sentences of a foreign power?"

"Undoubtedly there are," replied Falk; "but, in the mean time, tell us of some such appearances, as we can then argue upon them with more certainty."

"Thus we shall at length fall upon stories of ghosts," said Gertrude, smiling.

"I am glad of it, with all my heart," said Hermann, "every body likes to hear them—only observe in what a proper attitude for listening Anselm is already seating himself."

But Gertrude declined the narration of the story to which she had referred; she declared, that, fond as she was of listening to ghost stories, she yet felt a kind of dread at relating them. Her affianced lover smiled, and said, that as he could guess the occurrence alluded to, he would undertake its narration for her. To this she consented, and he thus proceeded:—

"A very near relation of my Gertrude, but a little visionary like herself—we will, if you please, call her Caroline—had formed with her young neighbour, Angelica, the closest and most affectionate intimacy. The father of the latter had, in [168] in his early years, exchanged some intercourse with the well-known Cagliostro, and still retained a great fondness for the mystical and wonderful, notwithstanding the exposure of that worker of miracles. His collection of books therefore contained, besides the best literary works, a great number of tales of wonder, legends, and ancient chronicles, which Angelica had, from her childhood, perused with the greatest avidity. The friends often sat until late in the night, inflaming their imaginations with stories of spectres and apparitions. During one of the paroxysms of mental excitement, they made each other a solemn promise, that she who departed first from this life should appear to her who remained. They had just been reading some instances of these kind of promises; and, in order to bind each other the more firmly, they mutually agreed that even a remission of their pledge should not release them from their engagement. Whilst they still held their hands solemnly clasped in each other the clock struck midnight. 'The sound of the hour of my death!' exclaimed Angelica suddenly, as if inspired—'in this hour the promise will be fulfilled.' Caroline sprang up, alarmed at this ill-boding observation. 'Be not so terrified at my mistake,' said Angelica, smiling; 'I meant to say it is the hour of my birth that strikes—sixteen years since at midnight I was born—doubly dear to me therefore is the promise given, and I am[169] probably destined to fulfill it.' The girls continued plunged in their romantic reveries till the lights burned down to the sockets warned them to retire to rest.

"Some time after this precipitate vow, Caroline was attacked by a malignant and infectious fever, and Angelica, contrary to her inclination, was compelled by her parents to avoid going to the house of her friend. As long as there was no danger to the life of Caroline, Angelina obeyed; but when the messages in reply to her inquiries seemed more desponding, no prohibition could prevent her from hastening to the couch of her sick friend. Her promise had begun to make a painful impression on her mind, and she hastened to Caroline, determined rather to hazard her life from the infection than any longer to suffer under the influence of so much terror. She implored her to retract her vow; and Caroline, who felt herself the less bound by it, as it had occasioned so much uneasiness in Angelica, willingly complied, when she observed the painful and distressing effect it had produced upon her friend. This interview, from which the relations of both parties had anticipated the greatest danger to the invalid, was attended the most favourable results. The exertion had a beneficial effect, and Caroline recovered rapidly, to the astonishment of the physicians. From that moment she regarded Angelica as her preserver, and both the friends declared that they would never [170] again hazard a wish or a question respecting the mysteries of the unknown world. Sickness and the vow were forgotten by degrees, and they from this time became more attached to each other than ever. Angelica had one day accompanied her parents to a ball in a neighbouring town. Caroline had excused herself on some trivial pretence, but in reality because she wanted to surprise Angelica, with a festival which she had arranged against the anniversary of her friend's birth-day, which was to happen on the following day. She sat until late at night at work with her attendant, and was just on the point of retiring when she heard the clock strike the hour of midnight. At that moment a singular current of air wafted around her, so that her working materials which lay upon the table were thrown down and strewed upon the ground. Starting at the circumstance, Caroline looked up, and beheld the shadow of Angelica standing before her; she saw it turn itself slowly round, then sink down upon the floor, and suddenly disappear. Her shriek of terror summoned her attendant, but Caroline had become insensible before she could enter. The servant had observed nothing but the singular current of air; but a few hours brought the melancholy intelligence that Angelica had actually been overtaken by sudden death that night as the clock struck twelve."

"This is horrible," exclaimed the Baroness. [171]

"What appears the most horrible to me," added Falk, "is the mysterious power of the words which Angelica had pronounced—'the sound of the hour of my death,'—thus, against her will, uttering her own death prophecy."

"How can you explain this to be natural?" demanded Gertrude.

"I beseech you do not give me the character of a general interpreter of mysteries," replied Falk; "I cannot explain these singular occurrences—but if they have really happened, they are certainly according to the order and law of nature, although this law is unknown to us. I know of nothing more presumptuous than to say, 'this I cannot understand, therefore it cannot be true;'—nevertheless, such a conclusion is the basis of all the criticisms on these kind of occurrences. The popular belief in which is called superstition, is, in reality, a fun of inquiry for the naturalist:—the truth, indeed, is not immediately to be discovered; but does a man of experience assert that in a mine nothing but rock is to be found, because the ore must be first worked out by art?"

"Have you not observed," interrupted the Baron, "that the will has much influence upon the success of the thing?—at least, this objection is made to the inferences."

"No doubt the will has influence upon the suc- [172] cess, or failure, of experiments," replied Anselm, "and must have it; for the experiment itself is to prove nothing else but that physical phenomenon—the direction of the will in physical phenomena; only you must distinguish that kind of will which imparts itself intentionally to the body, and directs its motions to the expected result, from the will which acts, not voluntarily, but according to an inward law of nature upon the body.

"Well, well," observed the Baron, "let us adjust our differences of opinion thus—touch glasses friends."

They all obeyed—the clear glasses rung, and the large drinking cups, in which the host had presented his oldest and most fragrant wine, sent out a tone like the solemn sound of bells. "Hark! the sound of a clock!" said Hermann softly,—"Hush!" exclaimed the Baron, opening the window. From the steeple of the tower resounded the stroke of the last quarter. Deeper and louder the knell of the midnight hour immediately followed. The assembled company sat in silence, and listened with solemn earnestness to the last tones of the departing year.

Still louder, deeper, and more solemnly, the clock from the high church-steeple repeated the melancholy sounds. Gertrude looked towards her affianced husband. Her eyes spoke a thousand happy hopes and wishes. The Baroness tenderly kissed her white forehead, surrounded with clustering curls, but no one [173] uttered a single word, in order not to interrupt the deep and awful solemnity of the moment. Still more powerfully, then, the colossal bell of the second church-steeple sounded also the midnight hour, and they looked towards Falk, who slowly unfolded a paper, and began in a solemn tone of voice to read some verses which he had recently composed.

INVOCATION.

"Oh mother year! into thy viewless tomb
Now art thou sinking, and thy friends forsaking.
We weep, oh mother! o'er thy coming doom,
As slow we mark it thy loved steps o'ertaking.
The faintest! o'er thy brow we see it linger—
The shadow of Decay's pale wasting finger;
Yet o'er they viewless grave fair angels sit—
The joys thy fondess gave, like guardians watching it.
                    Mother, farewell!

"And if, oh mother! all thou couldst not bless,
If still some downcast eye is stained by weeping—
Dying thou leav'st unto our fond caress
Thy babe alive, each cherished hope still keeping
Soon shall the music of the solemn bell
Thy infant's birth and thy departure tell;
And in thy dying hour thy brow is bright,
For thy consoling child comes smiling into light.
                    Mother, farewell!"

[174] Scarcely had he concluded, when a piercing shriek resounded through the apartment;—Gertrude looked up, and, in the next instant uttered a cry of horror, and sank upon the floor insensible.

"What was that?" was the general exclamation;—they had all heard the scream, but some insisted that it was Gertrude's own voice, whose shuddering had been just before remarked; others, that it had come from a distance, and that her cry of horror had been the result of it. Whilst they were still recovering, Gertrude, relived by the restoratives which had been administered to her, recovered her senses;—she declared that on looking up in the direction of the scream which had so terrified her, she had beheld a wild and ghastly apparition—the face of the beautiful Madonna which hung opposite to her, was changed into the distorted visage of a corpse, and gazed downward upon her, with a fixed and threatening look; and this sight it was, which had occasioned her subsequent fit of fainting.

"Respecting the phantom," said the Baron, "I can tranquilize your mind immediately—the Madonna seen from various parts of the room has a totally different appearance, and when the lights are placed in a particular direction, she acquires so ghastly an expression, that I have more than one determined to conceal her by night with a curtain: but you shall convince yourself." He conducted Gertrude to her for- [175] mer seat, and she really observed the change in the appearance of the painting. The holy mother was entirely without colour, and, contrasted with the child, appeared like a shadow;—the threatening expression in the face, Gertrude now acknowledged to have sprung from her own excited imagination.

"We must next inquire into the cause of the scream," said the Baroness, and summoned the domestics.

"It was nothing of consequence, "said the nurse, "the night light went out, and little Emilius shrieked because he was afraid of being in the dark,—but he is once more quietly asleep."

The usual new year's wishes, which were not introduced, enlivened the spirits of the party, and banished the remembrance of this unpleasant occurrence from their minds. They sung, laughed, and told stories for some time longer; and, when on the point of separating, the Baron invited the whole company to pass the next New Year's Eve together with him at the Castle of Hartenstein in the country. They all promised to attend, and gaily filled their goblets to the next happy meeting. "Keep your promise," exclaimed Gertrude, at parting,—"none of us can be absent next New Year's Eve—remember all, that the first promise of the year will not admit of an excuse—it must be absolutely kept."

Title

Maturin, Charles. "Leixlip Castle. An Irish Family Legend." LS 1825. 211-232.
[211]

LEIXLIP CASTLE
An Irish Family Legend.
BY THE REV. C. R. MATURIN

The incidents of the following tale are not merely *founded* on fact, they are facts themselves, which occurred at no very distant period in my own family. The marriage of the parties, their sudden and mysterious separation, and their total alienation from each other until the last period of their mortal existence are all *facts*. I cannot vouch for the truth of the supernatural solution given to all these mysteries; but I must still consider the story as a fine specimen of Gothic horrors, and can never forget the impression it made on me when I heard it related for the first time among many other thrilling traditions of the same description.

The tranquility of the Catholics of Ireland during the disturbed periods of 1715 and 1745, was most commendable, and somewhat extraordinary; to enter [212] into an analysis of their probably motives, is not at all the object of the writer of this tale, as it is pleasanter to state the fact to their honour, than at this distance of time to assign dubious and unsatisfactory reasons for it. Many of them, however, showed a kind of secret disgust at the existing state of affairs, by quitting their family residences and wandering about like persons who were uncertain of their homes, or possibly expecting better from some near and fortunate contingency.

Among the rest was a Jacobite Baronet, who, sick of his uncongenial situation in a Whig neighbourhood, in the north—where he had heard of nothing but the heroic defence of Londonderry; the barbarities of the French generals; and the resistless exhortations of the godly Mr. Walker, a Presbyterian clergyman, to whom the citizens gave the title of "Evangelist;"—quitted his paternal residence, and about the year 1720 hired the Castle of Leixlip for three years, (it was then the property of the Connollys, who let it to triennial tenants); and removed thither with his family, which constituted of three daughters—their mother having long been dead.

The Castle of Leixlip, at that period, possessed a character of romantic beauty and feudal grandeur, such as few buildings in Ireland can claim, and which is now, alas, totally effaced by the destruction of its noble woods; on the destroyers of which the writer [213] would wish a "minstrel's malison were said."—Leixlip, though about seven miles only from Dublin, has all the sequestered and picturesque character that imagination could ascribe to a landscape a hundred miles from, not only the metropolis but an inhabited town. After driving a dull mile (an *Irish* mile) in passing from Lucan to Leixlip, the road,—hedged up on one side by the high wall that bounds he demesne of the Veseys, and on the other by low enclosures, over whose rugged tops you have no view at all,—at once opens on Leixlip Bridge, at almost a right angle, and displays a luxury of landscape on which the eye that has seen it even in childhood dwells with delighted recollection.—Leixlip Bridge, a rude but solid structure, projects from a high bank of the Liffey, and slopes rapidly to the opposite side,, which there lies remarkably low. To the right plantations of the Veseys' demesne—no longer obscured by walls—almost mingle their dark woods in its stream, with the opposite ones of Marshfield and St. Catherine's. The river is scarcely visible, overshadowed as it is by the deep, rich and bending foliage of the trees. To the left it bursts out in all the brilliancy of light, washes the garden steps of the houses at Leixlip, wanders round the low walls of its churchyard, plays with the pleasure-boat moored under the arches on which the summer-house of the Castle is raised, and then loses itself among the rich [214] woods that once skirted those grounds to its very brink. The contrast on the other side, with the luxuriant vegetation, the lighter and more diversified arrangement of terraced walks scattered shrubberies, temples seated on pinnacles, and thickets that conceal from you the sight of the river until you are on the its banks, that mark the character of the grounds which are now the property of Colonel Marly, is peculiarly striking.

Visible above the highest roofs of the town, though a quarter of a mile distant from them, are the ruins of Confy Castle, a right good old predatory tower of the stirring times when blood was shed like water; and as you pass the bridge you catch a glimpse of the waterfall, (or salmon-leap, as its called,) on whose noon-day lustre, or moon-light beauty, probably the rough livers of that age when Confy Castle was "a tower of strength," never glanced an eye or cast a thought, as they clattered in their harness over Leixlip Bridge, or waded through the stream before that convenience was in existence.

Whether the solitude in which he lived contributed to tranquilize Sir Redmond Blaney's feelings, or whether they had begun to rust from want of collision with those of others, it is impossible to say, but certain it is, that the good Baronet began gradually to lose his tenacity in political matters; and except when a Jacobite friend came to dine with [215] him, and drink with many a significant "nod and beck and smile," the King over the water;—or the parish-priest (good man) spoke of the hopes of better times, and the final success of the *right* cause, and the old religion;—or a Jacobite servant was heard in the solitude of the large mansion whistling "Charlie is my darling," to which Sir Redmond involuntarily responded in a deep base voice, somewhat the worse for wear, and marked with more emphasis than good discretion;—except, as I have said, on such occasions, the Baronet's politics, like his life, seemed passing away without notice or effort. Domestic calamities, too, pressed sorely on the old gentleman: of his three daughters, the youngest Jane, had disappeared in so extraordinary a manner in her childhood, that thought it is but a wild, remote family tradition, I cannot help relating it:—

The girl was of uncommon beauty and intelligence, and was suffered to wander about the neighbourhood of the castle with the daughter of a servant, who was also called Jane, as a *nom de caresse*. One evening Jane Blaney and her young companion went far and deep into the woods; their absence created no uneasiness at the time, as these excursions were by no means unusual, till her playfellow returned home alone and weeping, at a very late hour. Her account was, that, in passing through a lane at some distance from the castle, an old woman, in the *Fingallian* dress, [216] (a red petticoat and a long green jacket,) suddenly started out of a thicket, and took Jane Blaney by the arm: she had in her hand two rushes, one of which she threw over her shoulder, and giving the other one to the child, motioned to her to do the same. Her young companion, terrified at what she saw, was running away, when Jane Blaney called after her—"Good bye, good bye, it is along time before you will see me again." The girl said they then disappeared, and she found her way home as she could. An indefatigable search was immediately commenced—woods were traversed, thickets were explored, ponds were drained,—all in vain. The pursuit and the hope were at length given up. Ten years afterwards, the housekeeper of Sir Redmond, having remembered that she left the key of a closet where sweetmeats were kept, on the kitchen-table, returned to fetch it. As she approached the door, she heard a childish voice murmuring—"cold—cold—cold—how long it is since I have felt a fire!"—She advanced, and saw, to her amazement, Jane Blaney, shrunk to half her usual size, and covered with rage, crouching over the embers of the fire. The housekeeper fled in terror from the spot, and roused the servants, but the vision had fled. The child was reported to have been seen several times afterwards, as diminutive in form, as thought she had not grown an inch since she was ten years of age, and always crouch- [217] ing over a fire, whether in the turret-room or kitchen, complaining of cold and hunger and apparently covered with rags. Her existence is still said to be protracted under these dismal circumstances, so un-like those of Lucy Gray in Wordsworth's beautiful ballad:
Yet some will say, that to this day
   She is a living child—
  That they have met sweet Lucy Gray
   Upon the lonely wild;
  O'er rough and smooth she trips along,
   And never looks behind;
  And hums a solitary song
   That whistles in the wind.

The fate of the eldest daughter was more melancholy, though less extraordinary; she was addressed by a gentleman of competent fortune and unexceptional character: he was a Catholic, moreover; and Sir Redmond Blaney signed the marriage articles, in full satisfaction of the security of his daughter's soul, as well as of her jointure. The marriage was celebrated at the Castle of Leixlip; and, after the bride and bridegroom had retired, the guests still remained drinking to their future happiness when suddenly, to the great alarm of Sir Redmond and his friends, loud and piercing cries were heard to issue from the part of the castle in which the bridal chamber was situated. [218]

Some of the moral courageous hurried up stairs; it was too late—the wretched bridegroom ha burst, on that fatal night, into a sudden and most horrible paroxysm of insanity. The mangled form of the unfortunate and expiring lady bore attestation to the mortal virulence with which the disease had operated on the wretched husband, who died a victim to it himself after the involuntary murder of his bride. The bodies were interred, as soon as decency would permit, and the story hushed up.

Sir Redmond's hope of Jane's recovery were diminishing every day, though he still continued to listen to every wild tale told by the domestics; and all his care was supposed to be now directed towards his only surviving daughter Anne living in solitude, and partaking only of the very limited education of Irish females of that period, was left very much to the servants, among whom she increased her taste for the superstitious and supernatural horrors, to a degree that had a most disastrous effect on her future life.

Among the numerous menials of the Castle, there was one "withered crone," who had been nurse to the late Lady Blaney's mother, and whose memory was a complete *Thesaurus terrorum*. The mysterious fate of Jane first encouraged her sister to listen to the wild tales of this hag, who avouched, that at one time she saw the fugitive standing before [219] the portrait of her late mother in one of the apartments of the Castle, and muttering to herself—"Woe's me, woe's me! how little my mother thought her wee Jane would ever come to be what she is!" But as Anne grew older she began more "seriously to incline" to the hag's promises that she could show her future bridegroom, on the performance of a few ceremonies, which she at first revolted from as horrible and impious; but, finally, at the repeated instigation of the old woman, consented to act a part in. The period fixed upon fro the permanence of these unhallowed rites was now approaching;—it was near the 31st of October,—the eventful night, when such ceremonies were, and still are supposed, in the North of Ireland, to be most potent in their effects. All day long the Crone took care to lower the mind of the young lady to the proper key of submissive and trembling credulity, by every horrible story she could relate; and she told them with frightful and supernatural energy. This woman was called *Collogue* by the family, a name equivalent to Gossip in England, or Cummer in Scotland, (though her real name was Bridget Dease;) and she verified the name, by the exercise of an unwearied loquacity, an indefatigable memory, and a rage for communicating and inflicting terror, that spare no victim in the household, from the groom, whom she sent shivering to his rug, to the [220] Lady of the Castle, over whom she felt she held unbounded sway.

The 31st of October arrived,—the Castle was perfectly quiet before eleven o'clock; half an hour afterwards, the Collogue and Anne Blaney were seen gliding along a passage that led to what is called King John's Tower, where it said the monarch received the homage of the Irish princes as Lord of Ireland, and which, at all events, is the most ancient part of the structure. The Collogue opened a small door with a key which she had secreted about her, and urged the young lady to hurry on. Anne advanced to the postern, and stood there irresolute and trembling like a timid swimmer on the bank of an unknown stream. It was a dark, autumnal evening; a heavy wind sighed among the woods of the Castle, and bowed the branches of the lower trees almost to the waves of the Liffey, which, swelled by recent rains, struggled and roared amid the stones that obstructed its channel. The steep descent from the Castle lay before her, with its dark avenue of elms; a few lights still burned in the little village of Leixlip—but from the lateness of the hour it was probably they would soon be extinguished.

The lady lingered—"And must I go alone?" said she, foreseeing that the terrors of her fearful journey could be aggravated by her more fearful purpose.

"Ye must, or all will be spoiled," said the hag, [221] shading the miserable light, that did not extend its influence above six inches on the path of the victim.

"Ye must go alone—and I will watch for you here, dear, till you come back, and then see what will come to you at twelve o'clock."

The unfortunate girl paused. "Oh! Collogue, Collogue, if you would but come with me. Oh! Collogue, come with me, if it be but to the bottom of the castle-hill."

"If I went with you, dear, we should never reach the top of it alive again, for there are them near that would tear us both in pieces."

"Oh! Collogue, Collogue—let me turn back then, and go to my own room,—I have advanced too far, and I have done too much."

"And that's what you hae, dear, and so you must go further, and do more still, unless,, when you return to your own room, you would see the likeness of *some one* instead of a handsome young bridegroom."

The young lady looked about her for a moment, terror and wild hope trembling at her heart;—then, with a sudden impulse of supernatural courage, she darted like a bird from the terrace of the Castle, the fluttering of her white garments was seen for a few moments, and then the hag who had been shading the flickering light with her hand, bolted the postern, and, placing the candle before a glazed loophole, [222] sat down on a stone seta in the recess of the tower, to watch the event of the spell. It was an hour before the young lady returned; when her face was as pale, and her eyes as fixed, as those of a dead body, but she held in her grasp *a dripping garment*, a proof that her errand had been performed. She flung it into her companion's hands, and then stood panting and gazing wildly about her, as if she knew not where she was. The hag herself grew terrified at the insane and breathless state of her victim, and hurried her to her chamber; but here the preparations for the terrible ceremonies of the night were the first objects that struck her, and, shivering at the sight, she covered her eyes with her hands, and stood immoveably fixed in the middle of the room.

It needed all the hag's persuasions (aided even by the mysterious menaces), combined with the returning faculties and reviving curiosity of the poor girl, to prevail on her to go through the remaining business of the night. At length she said, as if in desperation, "I *will* go through with it: but be in the next room; and if what I dread should happen, I will ring my father's little silver bell which I have secured for the night,—and as you have a soul to be saved, Collogue, come to me at its very first sound."

The hag promised, gave her last instructions with eager and jealous minuteness, and then retired to her own room, which was adjacent to that of the young [223] lady. Her candle had burned out, but she stirred up the embers of her turf fire, and sat nodding over them, and smoothing her pallet from time to time, but resolved not to lie down while there was a chance of a sound from the lady's room, for which she herself, withered as her feelings were, waited with a mingled feeling of anxiety and terror.

It was now long past midnight, and all was silent as the grave throughout the Castle. The hag dozed over the embers till her head touched her knees, then started up as the sound of the bell seemed to tinkle in her ears, then dozed again, and again started as the bell appeared to tinkle more distinctly;—suddenly she was roused, not by the bell, but by the most piercing and horrible cries from the neighbouring chamber. The Crone, aghast for the first time, at the possible consequences of the mischief she might have occasioned hastened to the room. Anne was in convulsions, and the hag was compelled reluctantly to call up the housekeeper (removing meanwhile the implements of the ceremony), and assist in applying all the specifics known at that day, burnt feathers, &c. to restore her. When they had at length succeeded, the housekeeper was dismissed, the door was bolted, and the Collogue was left alone with Anne; the subject of their conference might have been guessed at, but was not known until many years afterwards; but Anne that night held in her hand, in the shape of a weapon with the use of [224] which neither of them was acquainted, an evidence that her chamber had been visited by a being of no earthly form.

This evidence the hag importuned her to destroy, or to remove, but she persisted with fatal tenacity in keeping it. She locked it up, however, immediately, and seemed to think she had acquired a right, since she had grappled so fearfully with the mysteries of futurity, to know all the secrets of which that weapon might yet lead to the disclosure. But from that night it was observed that her character, her manner, and ever her countenance, became altered. She grew stern and solitary, shrunk at the sight of her former associates, and imperatively forbade the slightest allusion to the circumstances which had occasioned this mysterious change.

It was a few days subsequent to this event that Anne, who after dinner had left the Chaplain reading the life of St. Francis Xavier to Sir Redmond, and retired to her own room to work, and, perhaps, to muse, was surprised to hear the bell at the outer gate ring loudly and repeatedly—a sound she had never heard since her first residence in the Castle; for the few guests who resorted there came and departed as noiselessly as humble visitors at the house of a great man generally do. Straightaway there rode up the avenue of elms, which we have already mentioned, a stately gentleman, followed by four servants, all mounted, [225] the former two having pistols in their holsters, and the two latter carrying saddle-bags before them: though it was the first week in November, the dinner hour being one o'clock, Anne had light enough to notice all these circumstances. The arrival of the stranger seemed to cause much, though not unwelcome tumult in the Castle; orders were loudly and hastily given for the accommodation of the servants and horses;—steps were heard traversing the numerous passages for a full hour—then all was still; and it was said that Sir Redmond had locked with his own hand the door of the room where he and the stranger sat, and desired that no one should dare to approach it. About two hours afterwards, a female servant came with orders from her master, to have a plentiful supper ready by eight o'clock, at which he desired the presence of his daughter. The family establishment was on a handsome scale for an Irish house, and Anne had only to descend to the kitchen to order the roasted chickens to be well strewed with brown sugar according to the unrefined fashion of the day, to inspect the mixing of the bowl of sago with its allowance of a bottle of port wine and a large handful of the richest spices, and to order particularly that the pease pudding should have a huge lump of cold salt butter stuck in its centre; and then, her household cares being over, to retire to her room and array herself in a robe of white damask for [226] the occasion. At eight o'clock she was summoned to the supper-room. She came in, according to the fashion of the times, with the first dish; but as she passed through the ante-room, where the servants were holding lights and bearing the dishes, her sleeves was twitched, and the ghastly face of the Collogue was pushed close to hers; while she muttered, "Did not I say *he would come for you* dear?" Anne's blood ran cold, but she advanced, saluted her father and the stranger with two low and distinct reverences, and then took her place at the table. Her feelings of awe and perhaps terror at the whisper of her associate, were not diminished by the appearance of the stranger; there was a singular and mute solemnity in his manner during the meal. He eat nothing. Sir Redmond appeared constrained, gloomy and thoughtful. At length, starting, he said (without naming the stranger's name,) "You will drink my daughter's health?" The stranger intimated his willingness to have that honour, but absently filled his glass with water; Anne put a few drops of wine into hers, and bowed towards him. At that moment, for the first time since they had met, she beheld his face—it was pale as that of a corpse. The deadly whiteness of his cheeks and lips, the hollow and distant sound of his voice, and the strange lustre of his large dark moveless eyes, strongly fixed on her, made her pause and even tremble as she raised the glass to her lips; [227] she set it down, and then with another silent reverence retired to her chamber.

There she found Bridget Dease, busy in collecting the turf that burned on the hearth, for there was no grate in the apartment. "Why are you here?" she said, impatiently.

The hag turned on her, with a ghastly grin of congratulation, "Did not I tell you that *he* would come for you?"

"I believe he has," said the unfortunate girl, sinking into the huge wicked chair by her bedside; "for never did I see a mortal with such a look."

"But is he not a fine stately gentleman?" pursued the hag.

"He looks as if he were not of this world," said Anne.

"Of this world, or of the next," said the hag, raising her bony fore-finger, "mark my words—so sure as the—(here she repeated some of the horrible formularies of the 31st of October)—so sure he will be your bridegroom."

"Then I shall be the bride of a corse," said Anne; "for he I saw tonight is no living man."

A fortnight elapsed, and whether Anne became reconciled to the features she had thought so ghastly, by the discovery that they were the handsomest she had ever behalf—and that the voice, whose sound at first was so strange and unearthly, was subdued into a [228] tone of plaintive softness when addressing her;—or whether it is impossible for two young persons with unoccupied hearts to meet in the country, and meet often, to gaze silently on the same stream, wander under the same trees, and listen together to the wind that waves the branches, without experiencing an assimilation of feeling rapidly succeeding an assimilation of taste;—or whether it was from all these causes combined, but in less than a month Anne heard the declaration of the stranger's passion with many a blush, though without a sigh. He now avowed his name and rank. He seated himself to be a Scottish Baronet, of the name of Sir Richard Maxwell; family misfortunes had driven him from his country, and for ever precluded the possibility of his return: he had transferred his property to Ireland, and purposed to fix his residence there for life. Such was his statement. The courtship of those days was brief and simple. Anne became the wife of Sir Richard, and, I believe, they resided with her father till his death, when they removed to their estate in the North. There they remained for several years, in tranquility and happiness, and had a numerous family.

Sir Richard's conduct was marked by but two peculiarities: he not only shunned the intercourse, but the sight of any of his countrymen, and, if he happened to hear that a Scotsman had arrived in the neighbouring town, he shut himself up till assured of the stranger's depar- [229] ture. The other was his custom of retiring to his own chamber, and remaining invisible to his family on the anniversary of the 30th of October. The lady, who had her own associations connected with that period, only questioned him once on the subject of this seclusion, and was then solemnly and even sternly enjoined never to repeat her inquiry. Matters stood thus, somewhat mysteriously, but not unhappily, when on a sudden, without any case assigned or assignable, Sir Richard and Lady Maxwell parted, and never more met in this world, nor was she ever permitted to see one of her children to her dying hour. He continued to live at the family mansion, and she fixed her residence with a distant relative in a remote part of the country. So total was the disunion, that the name of either was never heard to pass the other's lips, from the moment of separation until that of dissolution.

Lady Maxwell survived Sir Richard forty years, living to the great age of 96; and, according to a promise, previously given, disclosed to a descendant with whom she had lived, the following extraordinary circumstances.

She said that on the night of the 30th of October, about seventy-five years before, at the instigation of her ill-advising attendant, she had washed one of her garments in a place where four streams met, and performed other unhallowed ceremonies under [230] the direction of the Collogue, in the expectation that her future husband would appear to her in her chamber at twelve o'clock that night. The critical moment arrived, but with it no lover-like form. A vision of indescribable horror approached her bed, and flinging at her an iron weapon of a shape and construction unknown to her, bade her "recognize her future husband by *that*." The terrors of this visit soon deprived her of her senses; but on her recovery, she persisted, as has been said, in keeping the fearful pledge of the reality of the vision, which on examination, appeared to be encrusted with blood. It remained concealed in the inmost drawer of her cabinet until the morning of her separation. On that morning, Sir Richard Maxwell rose before day-light to join a hunting party;—he wanted a knife for some accidental purpose, and, missing his own, called to Lady Maxwell, who was still in bed, to lend him one. The lady, who was half asleep, answered, that in such a drawer of her cabinet he would find one. He went, however, to another, and the next moment she was fully awakened by seeing her husband present the terrible weapon to her throat, and threaten her with instant death unless she disclosed how she came by it. She supplicated for her life, and then, in an agony of horror and contrition, told the tale of that eventful night. He gazed at her for a moment with a countenance which rage, hatred, and despair con- [231] verted, as she avowed, into a living likeness of the demon-visage she had once beheld (so singularly was the fated resemblance fulfilled), and then exclaiming, "You won me by the devil's aid, but you shall not keep me long," left her—to meet no more in this world. Her husband's secret was not unknown to the lady, though the means by which she became possessed of it were wholly unwarrantable. Her curiosity had been strongly excited by her husband's aversion to his countrymen, and it was so stimulated by the arrival of a Scottish gentleman in the neighbourhood some time before, who professed himself formerly acquainted with Sir Richard, and spoke mysteriously of the causes that drove him from his country—that she contrived to procure an interview with him under a feigned name, and obtained from him the knowledge of circumstances which embittered her after-life to its latest hour. His story was this:—

Sir Richard Maxwell was at deadly feud with a younger brother; a family feast was proposed to reconcile them, and as the use of knives and forks was then unknown in the Highlands, the company met armed with dirks for the purpose of carving. They drank deeply; the feast, instead of harmonizing, began to inflame their spirits; the topics of old strife were renewed; hands, that at first touched their weapons in defiance, drew them at last in fury, [232] and, in the fray, Sir Richard mortally wounded his brother. His life was with difficulty saved from the vengeance of the clan, and he was hurried towards the sea-coast, near which the house stood, and concealed there till a vessel could be procured to convey him to Ireland. He embarked *on the night of the 30th of October*, and while he was traversing the deck in unutterable agony of spirit, his hand accidentally touched the dirk which he had unconsciously worn ever since the fatal night. He drew it, and praying "that the guilt of his brother's blood might be as far from his soul, as he could fling that weapon from his body,"—sent it with all his strength into the air. This instrument he found secreted in the lady's cabinet, and whether her really believed her to have become possessed of it by supernatural means, or whether he feared his wife a secret witness of his crime, has not been ascertained, but the result was what I have stated.

The separation took place on this discovery:—for the rest,
I know not how the truth may be,
I tell the Tale as 'twas told to me.

Title

By the Author of "December Tales." [Ainsworth, William Harrison.] "The Fortress of Saguntum." LS 1825. 259-263.

PLATE: Spain-Fortress of Saguntum
Steel plate engraving; drawn by William Brockedon;
engraved by Edward Francis Finden [259]

THE
FORTRESS OF SAGUNTUM.

Journeying, many years ago, through the Eastern provinces of Spain, I lingered in Valencia to survey the ruins at Morviedro, the ancient Saguntum. Early one bright morning, I ascended the mountainous range, on the summit of which the remains of the ancient town are situated, and which, stretching out to the waves of the Mediterranean, separates the valleys of Valencia and Almenara.

I gazed with enthusiastic admiration on the beauties by which I am surrounded,—on the perfect picture whose loveliness met my view on every side. Wide to the east expanded the dark waters of the sea, foaming and glistening in the beams of the rising day-God; north and south the valleys glowed in the same life-giving splendour. The newly risen spring was gushing forth in very wantonness; and the fertile olives and the golden foliage of the mulberry trees, clothed the sides of the hills and the beau- [260] tiful plain of Valencia; beyond which, with its light steeples and sun-gilt spires, lay the city itself gleaming in the all-pervading radiance. Herbage, abundant and luxuriant, rioted in fulness; wild flowers sprang up at every step; and the breezes redolent with perfumes, and freshened by the waves over which they were wafted, bore with them a coolness more than delicious; nothing was wanting to the perfect unity of loveliness—the rich natural enchantment of the scene. The songs of innumerable birds saluted the ear, and as the muleteer followed his quadruped companions along the paths that wound around the hills, their jingling bells rang with many a merry peal.

And then with what seeds of reflection, what food for fancy did the spot on which I stood furnish me. The remains of empires, each powerful and splendid in its day of triumph, but now alike faded and vanished, lay crumbling around me. The ancient Fortress mingled in its remains the architectures of nations and times far distant and unlike. The walls that long withstood the power and skill of the Carthaginian, were varied with the barbaric masonry of the Saracen. The strange inscription, the horse-shoe arches, and fantastic ornature of the East, were employed to deck the unadorned strength of its former defences. The works of two dynasties had faded away, leaving in their decay one common [261] monument to the might of Time, their common destroyer.

The glorious recollections of chivalry, too, haunted, and hovered over the spot. The wild dreams of poetry—of knights and ladies-rich banquets and gorgeous festivals—the joust and the tournament; schools of romantic honour which lent a polish to the stern and warlike character of the age,—the submission of power to beauty, and strength to weakness;—these, and similar reflections, thronged upon my mind, until fancy almost upreared the perished halls and shattered towers, and people the scene with plumed dames and crested warriors,, with enthusiastic minstrels and liveried retainers,—all the enchanting pomp and circumstance with which we love to array times and localities, whose distance softens their harsher lineaments, as the veil that hides the features of loveliness, whilst it weakens our perception of their imperfections, enhances in imagination the influence of their charms.

"Alas!" the dreamer would say, in his moments of creative musing, "that these things should be no more! That the noble thoughts and lofty aspirations of the children of chivalry should be lost in the cold policy of statesmen and the mechanic organization of modern warfare. Their love and deep loyalty, courage, and fond devotion; a watchfulness of honour, that knew no stain and brooked no insult,— [262] that hung a living halo, an impelling spirit around the hearts and feelings of men. Then love was purchased with long service, and service was no burthen when love lightened its chains:—devoted to two ends only, the candidate for love and fame pursued hi way, regardless of consequences, either to win by success, the rewards of his endeavours, or to perish in the pursuit, attended to the grave by the tears of beauty and the approval of valour."

I determined not to leave this part of the country without paying some further visits to a spot which had laid so forcible a hold upon my feelings. Accordingly I went once, and again. I traced ruins, examined inscriptions, studied arches, and busied myself as much and to as little purpose as a zealous antiquarian who has just added to his name the importance of F.A.S. would have done.

In my researches, I met with an old man who was a more curious, I had almost said, a more antique relic than any I had encountered at Saguntum. Besides his extraordinary physiognomy, the keenness and tenuity of which seemed the most positive and captious old gentleman I had ever met with. In the course of his investigations he had formed divers theories, some of them, it must be admitted, almost as plausible as many which the kindness and generosity of my own countrymen, have, at various times, [263] benevolently patronized. Jerome Casos, for so my ancient friend was entitled, lamented exceedingly his not having lived at the time of the Saracens—from his appearance one would have sworn he had—in order that he might have done the state some service by putting in practice a recipe of his own for conversion of the unbelievers to christianity.

What, however, constituted the principal attraction which induced me to seek an acquaintance with this eccentric person, was the fun of traditionary stories he had accumulated relative to the Fortress and its former possessors. To all other relations, historical or topographical, he turned a deaf ear; they were to him foolishness: but when I indulged in any conjecture or observation at all connected with this, his local hobby-horse, his instantaneous attention, the gleaming of his little eyes, and the pricking up of his chin and nose, expressed the interest he took in the subject. One of these stories, in some measure pruned of the redundancies with which he had encumbered it, I have translated from my journal for the amusement of the reader:

Title

Anonymous. [Ainsworth, William Harrison.] "A Tradition of the Fortress of Saguntum." LS 1825. 264-282. [264]

A TRADITION OF THE FORTRESS OF SAGUNTUM.

And many a lady there was set,
   In purple and in pall;
But fair Christabelle, so woe-begone,
   Was the fairest of them all.

Then many a knight was mickle of might
   Before his lady gay:
But a stranger wight, whom no man knew,
   He won the prize that day.

His action, it was all of black,
   His hawberk and his shield:
No, no man wist whence he did come:
No, no man knew where he had gone,
   When he came off the field.

Sir Eauline.

DURING the early contentions between the native Spaniards and their Moorish invaders, (the exact period my informant's chronology was inadequate to supply) the fortress of Saguntum was in the possession of a Spanish Grandee the representative of [265] an ancient and distinguished family. The patrimony which had descended to him, unwasted by the excesses of the succeeding owners, had rather increased than otherwise, and Sebastian de Alzavar found himself consequently, on the death of his father, a man of considerable opulence and importance; that is to say, he was owner of the castle of Saguntum, with its domains, and of divers quantities of armour, offensive and defensive, the use of which to define, would infallibly turn the brains of a society of antiquaries of the present day. His sway extended over a tolerable range of territory, the cultivation of a small part of which supplied the Hidalgo and his retainers with the means of pasture for their cattle, and some few vegetable productions; and the much larger portion which constituted the remainder of his petty kingdom, (for, in those days, every noble in his own domain was a monarch) lay waste and barren, except where a few wild olives and straggling shrubs benevolently sprang up of their own accord to enliven the scene. A host of raggamuffins, who protected themselves from the weather by steel caps and quilted doublets, strong enough to withstand a smart stroke from a sword, occupied one spacious department of the buildings, and, on condition of killing and being killed whenever their lord thought proper to demand their services, and of amusing themselves in the interim with duck stones and [266] other rational recreations, were allowed to eat, drink, and sleep, at the expense of him under whose banner they had enlisted themselves.

But the treasure upon which Sebastian chiefly prided himself, and which had, at all times, attracted much attention to his habitation from wandering knights, good swords and men of worship all, was a daughter whose fame extended beyond the limits of the province, and whose accomplishments were as great as her beauty,—a theme lauded by bards and celebrated by roving minstrels. Besides working tapestry equally to that of Flanders,—being expert at all the domestic exercises in which women were then accustomed to occupy themselves,—expert, I say, beyond any female on record,—it was positively affirmed by those rhodomontading vagabonds the poets, that she was able not merely to spell, but actually to read; whilst some of the boldest of her panegyrists added the useful though difficult and mysterious art of writing, to the list oft he lady's acquirements. Then her skill on the guitar was exquisite, and she sang the romantic ballads which once formed the national poetry of Spain (a poetry worthy of a proud nation), with a spirit and feeling sufficient to inspire with heroism a hundred coats of mail. In accomplishments, therefore, Donna Estafina was without a peer.

But brilliant as might justly be the expectations of [267] one possessed of such unheard-of perfections, there were traits in the lady's character, more touching, though less splendid than those which were sung of in halls at banquets. It was true her admirers praised her beauty; but whilst they lauded the brightness and blackness of her eyes, with all the hyperboles which poets claim to use, the mild expression in which virtue and benevolence beamed from them was little spoken of; and the loveliness of her form was praised and worshipped, when the pure spirit which it served to enshrine was unheeded and unvalued.

I by no means intend to assert, that the lady though blessed with all these excellent qualities was wholly exempt from the failings of her sex: Good and gentle as she was, she was descended from the same original stock as the rest of her species, and, like them retaining a spice of the perverseness of our first mother, was apt to be obstinate when requested to do any thing which warred with her own notions of propriety. Under the influence of this disposition she had refused to take her place in the common hall, when a neighbouring Grandee of great power, wealth, and ancestry, dined at her father's table; and this merely because he was reputed to be addicted to drunkenness and passionate in his cups, as an instance of which it was alleged that he had killed his first wife by his violence, at a time when women claim more [268] than common kindness from those with whom they are associated.

It happened by the chance of war, that, in an excursion against the Saracens, Alzavar was taken prisoner. In the hope of gaining his freedom, he offered for his ransom enormous sums to the leader who had made him captive. Unfortunately the Saracen being among his own people a man of rank and affluence, was not to be tempted by the Hidalgo's proposals, and they were consequently rejected; not that he was maintained on jail allowance, far from it. On the contrary, he was provided for with due consideration to his station and character; for there was a spirit of wild and romantic generosity in those wards, which prevented men from oppressing or treating with indignity those whom fortune had placed within their power.

But whilst Mirza Abu'l Anwar resisted without effort the temptation of treasure, he was less invulnerable to that of beauty; and the report of the charms of La Bella Estafina, had reached his ear with all the garnishings of fame. In the spirit of the times, he immediately fell in love with this lady although he had never seen her, and at once determined to make the daughter's hand the condition of the liberation of the father; imagining that he should thus without difficulty obtain her for his tribe. The difference of religion he considered as a trifling [269] obstacle, for he was determined to convert his intended to the truths of Moslemism; and as to a thousand other difficulties which presented themselves, they only added fuel to the fire, and lent fresh allurements to the enterprise in which he was determined to engage.

With all these thoughts and these resolutions, Mirza betook himself to the apartments of his captive. But here he soon found that he had reckoned without his host; the proud Spaniard refused indignantly his consent to the compact, and the Moslem retired in a fit of disappointment and offended haughtiness.

But in the process of time, and as his captivity by being prolonged grew more irksome, Alzavar began to think that there might be no very great harm in coming to some terms with the infidel. He proposed therefore to give him his daughter on the condition of his own immediate liberation, and on the further stipulation that he should vanquish, in single combat, any three Spanish warriors who should successively present themselves to the trial. Spurred on by his passion, and not doubting but that he could overcome the choicest of the knights of Spain, the Saracen consented to his captive's proposal, and fixed that day month for the fulfilment of the contract. Other arrangements were then entered into for the regulation of the combat, and their mutual words having been pledged for performance of the [270] stipulations, the only security required, the Spaniard was conducted to the boundary of his own territory and dismissed in safety.

The dismay of Estafina when informed of the peril in which she stood was overwhelming. She had not known love, and thus in her breast the Saracen had no rival; but she was imbued with a strong attachment to her religion, and internally vowed that if she must indeed be yielded to her purchaser, it should not be as a living bride. With no one of her own sex and rank in whom she could confide or with whom she might converse, she had been compelled to seek companionship in her own internal resources, and had resorted to her religion, the only study in which her situation allowed her to engage, with a warmth and ardour of devotion which burned, uninterrupted by meaner considerations, purely and steadily in her breast.

The report was soon spread that the beautiful Estafina was to be the price of her father's liberty, unless ransomed by the disinterested valour of some knightly champion of beauty. But though her father had not doubted, from the celebrity of his daughter's charms, that a warrior would speedily be found able and willing to encounter with success the lance of Mirza Abu'l Anwar, yet he had reckoned too precipitately and without due regard to circumstances; for, surrounded as his domains were on almost every side by the [271] enemy; occupied as were the Spanish chivalry, and every individual engaged in a warfare of more than common interest to bosoms in which a spark existed of that flame which binds us to our country and our home; and formidable as was the well tried skill and prowess of the Saracen, the intelligence of the proposed combat neither spread so widely, nor was followed by so ready a disposition to engage in it, as Alzavar had looked for. Two knights only had appeared, and the moon was fast waning whose decline was to bring the challenger to the plain of Valencia.

Time galloped withal, yet no succor came; nothing from which even misery could extract the shadow of consolation; and (for hope delayed maketh the heart sick) the fortitude of the victim sank as the time approached which was to give her up to the arms of an infidel, or leave her the dreadful alternative of closing by self-violence her own existence; a course which she had persuaded herself would, under the circumstances be, if not laudable, at least justifiable. Suns rose and set, and the hours hurried onwards, until the day arrived whose morrow was to determine her fate. Determined, indeed, it already seemed; for it was evident that the two champions who had offered themselves would prove no match for the renowned leader of the Saracens. The day declined, and no other knight had appeared to engage in the next morning's trial. [272]

It was a deep, rich autumnal evening—the winds moaned softly, and the branches quivered in their passing embraces. The small light wave, that curled up its foaming crest to meet the kiss of the breeze, indented the sand with its uniform ripple, whose monotonous beat fell on the ear with a languid and measured iteration of sound. The few birds that yet lingered from their rest, poured forth sad and melancholy strains; the sun blazed over the broad bosom of the tideless Mediterrauean, expanded to receive his sinking splendour; and directly opposite, his yellow rival began to throw her watery beams over the dusky mountains. One or two stars dimly twinkled; a dewy mist rose from the herbage, and hung like a mantle over the earth. The sun sank deeper into the waves; the moon rose brighter and higher above the horizon, whilst the blue sky deepened in beauty with the commingling hues of splendour that were interwoven in its glorious canopy.

At this hour of deep and solemn stillness sat the unhappy Estafina, in a tapestried chamber of Saguntum, her mind's tumult a decided contrast to the peace which pervaded the scene before her. The stirring superstitions of the Roman faith, aided as their influence was by the solitary situation, and too great mental susceptibility of the daughter of Alzavar, and cherished and kept alive within her by the legends of saints and the raptures, real or feigned, of the writers whose [273] works alone she studied, had raised, to a state of feverish and irritable excitement, a mind already enfeebled by anxiety, and tormented by the anticipation of her destiny; until she determined, at length, rather to devote herself to martyrdom than become a victim of the enemy of her faith and her country. To those who know the power of religious fanaticism in straining the mind to an undue and supernatural tension, this will not appear stranger, and still less so that it was followed by its constant attendant, a more than proportionable degree of depression and relaxation. Extremes generate each other; and the paroxysm of enthusiasm past, its place in the soul is often usurped by a deep and settled despair. In an agonized state of mind she seated herself in the recess of a window, whose tressilled stone-work and stained panes admitted scantily the red and doubtful light reflected from the yet glowing clouds.

The apartment was one of sombre magnificence. The painted roof was intersected with richly carved groins of cypress, black with antiquity, springing from a cornice of the same material, and adorned with the grotesque representations of a thousand monsters. The walls were covered with tapestry from the looms of Flanders, on which were delineated the wild legends of an age yet more rude and more romantic. But the most remarkable of the ornaments of the chamber, was a picture placed at the [274] end of the room, near where Estafina sat, presenting a full length portrait of an ancestor of her family—a warrior clad in complete armour. On his shield, and on the mantle in which he was partly enveloped, the red cross denoted him as one of the champions of the faith: a golden chain hung around his neck, and his helmet was decorated with a lofty and sable plume. His countenance, to the extent of the painter's skill, was marked with the lineaments of sternness approaching to ferocity. A black steed stood beside him, decked in the now obsolete trappings of ancient warfare.

Upon this specimen of art Estafina gazed with half unconscious awe. The warrior whom it represented had been handed down to his posterity as famou for his destroying among the infidels. In a fierce encounter he once bestrode the body of a wounded comrade, and brought him away amid the adverse clashing of a hundred blades, having with his own hand killed five of the enemy. Her familiarity with this tradition caused the wretched maid to gaze with anxious feelings upon the portrait. Had she such an arm (she thought) to smite the Moslem in her behalf, she might be safe; but the warrior had gone to his home long years ago, and there was no one like him at hand to succour her. The sun's last glow had now faded, and the moon and stars held undisputed dominion over the night, yet no help was nigh, [275] and hope had long since expired. It was then that almost distracted with boundless and irrepressible grief, and deserted by all expectation of human aid, she called on the holy ones of heaven to assist her; it was then that in the weakness and agony of her broken spirit, she cast herself before the picture, and wildly implored her ancestor to deliver her from the perdition that threatened her; and then it was—doubt it who may—that the warrior bowed his head, and his features melted into a look of promise and protection; the air, fanned by his waving plume, wafted over her cheek as she sank to the ground in a state of insensibility, overcome by the mingled hope and terror that throbbed with resistless violence in her breast.

It was long ere she recovered; and when, at last, reviving nature awoke her from the trance into which she had fallen, she found herself in almost total darkness. The moon was no longer abroad casting her rich flood of light around her; the stars were shrouded in thick, full vapours, and it was with difficulty she explored the way to her sleeping apartment, where she found her attendants wondering at her prolonged absence, and on the point of setting forth in search of her.

She threw herself on the bed, but her slumbers were restless and perturbed. Dismal dreams arose in succession with all their hideous concomitants [276] of confused and indefinite shapes—dim, loathsome, and terrible. Exhausted more than refreshed, she awoke in the morning to exchange the fears and fever of the imagination, for the yet more dreadful realities which seemed to await her. The attendant maidens busily engaged themselves in the duties of ministering at her toilet—services which she submitted to with sickly and unresisting apathy.

Meanwhile the hammers of the distant workmen, who were laboriously engaged in staking out the place of combat on the level plain of Valencia, fell upon her ear, mingled with the clashing of armour and the clanging tools of the armourers. Every stroke went to her heart, and seemed to ring a death-knell to her peace. At last they died way; but were almost immediately succeeded by a new and, to her, more dreadful note.

It was a faint far-away measure of barbaric music—the wild romantic melody of the East, that, floating on the air, and vibrating in a prolonged and fantastic strain, jarred with horrible discord on her ear. Her maidens gazed on her, and on each other, with looks that required not the aid of language to convey their meaning; and despair beamed in every eye as it was strained in the direction from whence the music appeared to proceed, to catch the first glimpse of the feared and hated Saracen.

One by one, their armour gleaming in the splen- [277] dour of the morning, the Saracen and his retinue bounded down the steeps that border the plain of Valencia. Spurring their fiery steeds, that needed no such appliances to impel them along, they speedily arrived at the lists. A solemn courtesy was exchanged between the chieftains. Mirza passed to the place assigned for him on the field, and cast down, as he rode along, his glittering gauntlet in token of challenge to his opponents.

Had Estafina been less deeply interested in the scene before her, as she gazed from the lattice of her apartment upon the preparation fro the combat, she could not have beheld without pleasure, scarcely without admiration, the noble appearance and bearing of the Saracen. He was clad in a superb suit of scale armour richly embossed, which, fitting close to his person, displayed the symmetry of his well-knit athletic frame; the plume, with which his casque was adorned, adding in appearance to the advantages of a form uncommonly tall and well proportioned. The fleet Arabian on which he rode, was caparisoned in a manner worthy of his rider and himself. It was a beautiful chestnut, and in its mould were admirably blended the requisites of strength and fleetness. His flowing man sported wildly around the serpent sweep of his proudly arched neck, while bounding on is elastic haunches, he seemed with his sonorous neigh to sound a [278] haughty triumph over the inferior, though beautiful and valuable steeds of the two knights; and it was difficult which to admire most, the beauty of the animal or the skill with which his rider governed his every motion.

Meanwhile one of the champions of Estafina slowly advancing, raised on the point of his spear the gage of the Saracen, and in a moment the combatants were at their stations urging and checking their fiery steeds, and waiting but for the signal to try on each other the strength and skill of lance and arm.

It was a moment of fearful and intensely agonizing suspense to the devoted daughter, who in her tower, incapable of speech, sank on her knees uttering silent petitions to heaven, accompanied by the frequent and irrepressible sobs and tears of her weeping maidens. The father's heart, stung with remorse, bled within him,—for no one could doubt the issue of the conflict. At last the marshals of the field gave the expected signal, the thunder of the horses' hoofs beat heavily on the ear—it was followed by a momentary crash, and the Saracen's opponent rolled horse and man on the yellow dust. No one wondered at this termination, yet the certainty that one chance, weak as it was, was lost, chilled the hearts of the father and his daughter.

No sooner was the first conflict terminated than [279] the other knight presented himself, and the Saracen again returned to his station. Again a period of dread suspense occurred, and again at the sound of the trumpet, the combatants gave the spur to their steeds. They met half-way, and now, for a moment, hope rallied in the breasts of the partisans of Alzavar for so well directed was the lance of the Christian knight, that his opponent seemed to reel in the saddle. It was but for an instant, however, for speedily recovering himself, he bore on his adversary with such force, that the knight's horse slightly rearing, fell upon his haunches, whilst his rider, discomfited by the animal's movements, was unable to withstand the lance of the Saracen, and sinking on the ground, left to his opponent the field and honour of victory.

It was then that Estafina, still retaining, from the mysterious event of the preceding evening the glimmer of a hope that some assistance would yet be rendered her, despatched a messenger to her father, requesting that the lists might be kept open till sunset, to await the possibility of the arrival of some third champion. To this arrangement the Saracen had no power to object; and retiring to a tent which was pitched close by the lists, he partook of the refreshments which had been prepared, and awaited the arrival of a new opponent.

The hours were passing swiftly, and Estafina looked [280] in vain from her tower; no knight was visible. Overcome with agony, she lay fainting in the arms of one of her attendants, when a sudden cry of exultation arose from the plain, and awoke her to life and hope. She looked forth and saw, interposed between her and the melting radiance of the setting sun, the dim dark figure of a warrior on horseback. He seemed at a great distance, but advanced with such celerity that he was soon distinctly visible to every eye. A few moments more and he was at the lists, and snatching a horn from one of the pursuivants, sounding a long and loud note of defiance.

That trembling, fluttering thing, a woman's heart, vibrates between the opposite extremes of joy and sorrow, and hopes and fears, with such enthusiasm, that it was not strange that Estafina, casting off every shadow of a doubt, considered herself as already rescued, and half rebuked the damsel who expressed a hope that the new comer might be successful.

It was evident, to those on the field, that the Saracen did not prepare for the contest with so much indifference as he had previously manifested. His antagonist was, indeed, in appearance, a man not rashly to be encountered. His height and bulk were remarkable, and seemed to require all the strength of the large-made sinewy black steed that bore him. His armour was sable, a broad gold chain hung around his neck, and the mantle which flowed around his form [281] was marked with a blood-red cross. A large plume of black feathers streamed above his helmet.

All was in readiness. The followers of the Saracen seemed dismayed, whilst those of Alzavar gazed on the scene with confident anticipations. The warriors started on their course, and the earth absolutely quaked beneath the rapid beat of their chargers' feet. The red-cross knight descended like a thunderbolt on his adversary; the violence of his attack was irresistible, and the Saracen, hurled headlong from his seat, lay senseless and motionless on the earth.

To talk of the joy which inspired Alzavar and his daughter would be idle. To the acknowledgements which were heaped upon their deliverer, he answered only by his gestures. He spoke not, and when pressed to remove his helmet, declined by a wave of his hand, compliance with the request. To Estafina, his appearance and demeanor were a subject of fearful interest, for in him she well recognized her warrior ancestor of the picture. To her expressions of gratitude he replied with a courteous inclination of his head, but not even to her could he be prevailed upon to speak. All were astonished, but too deeply indebted to the stranger to question him on the peculiarities of his demeanor.

When pressed to partake of their evening meal, he assented, and sat down with the rest of the company to the banquet. It was richly and variously heaped [282] and luscious spiced wines mantled in golden goblets upon the table. Alzavar pledged his guest, who lifted in return the cup, and seemed about to raise his vizor to drink, when at that moment the priest arose and pronounced the customary blessing. The stranger knight replaced the cup, and folding his arms on the board, reclined his head upon them. After he had continued a short time in that posture, his host intimated his apprehensions that his guest was wounded, and desired someone near him to removed his helmet. This request was no sooner complied with than the guests sprang up from the board with a start of horror; beneath the helmet all was void. Dismay and confusion filled every breast, whilst, amid the perturbation that ensued, the empty armour fell rattling to the ground.

The Forgotten Gothic

Literary Annual
The Literary Souvenir; or, Cabinet of Poetry and Romance. Ed. Alaric A. Watts. London: Hurst, Robinson and Co. and A. Constable and Co. Edinburgh, 1826. Printer: T. and J.B. Flindel, 67, St. Martin's-Lane.

Title
Anonymous. "The Diamond Watch." LS 1826. 53-74.[1] [53]

THE DIAMOND WATCH.

He holds him with his glittery eye.
Coleridge.

It was a glorious evening in the summer of 1793—sky and cloud blending in one uniform flood of splendour. The brightness of the heavens was reflected on the broad bosom of the Saale, a river which, passing Jena, falls lower down into the Elbe, whence the commingled waters roll onward till lost in the Noordt Zee.

On the banks of this stream, not more than a mile from Jena, rose a mound of some extent, its sloping banks clothed in the beautiful uniformity of a vine plantation. Its summit was open and spacious; intersected, at intervals, by narrow dells redolent of flowery perfume, and eloquent with the voice of babbling rivulets. The hour of sunset was past, and the evening mist was already rising from the green bosom of the earth.

In one of these dells, so shaded by shrubs and the branches of a clump of dwarf oaks as to be almost impervious to the light, sat two persons, enjoying the delicious [54] coolness of the hour, after one of the most oppressive days of an unusually sultry summer. Their dress was remarkable, and sufficiently indicative of their pursuits. Their sable garments and caps of black velvet, their long streaming hair, combed down the shoulders and back, and the straight swords suspended from their right breasts, denoted them to be two of the, burschen, or students of the University of Jena.

"Such an evening as this," said the elder youth, addressing his companion, " and thou here? Thyrza is much indebted to thee for thy attention! Thou a lover!"

" Thyrza is gone with her mother to Carlsbad," rejoined his companion, " so thou mayst cease thy wonderment."

"So far from it that I wonder the more. A true lover knows not the rela-

---

[1] Plain text for this transcription was obtained from Google Books <http://books.google.com/books?id=OF8EAAAAQAAJ&pg=PA414&dq=1826+The+Literary+Souvenir;+or,+Cabinet+of+Poetry+and+Romance&hl=en&ei=WbRHTd39PISBlAfJ94ykBA&sa=X&oi=book_result&ct=result&resnum=3&ved=0CDMQ6AEwAg#v=onepage&q&f=false> and then compared against the original volume. For full citation, see References.

tions of space. To Carlsbad! why 'tis no more than—but *seht*! who have we here?"

As he spoke, they were approached by a little old man, whose garments of brown serge appeared to have seen considerable service. He wore a conical hat, and carried in his hand an antique gold-headed cane. His features betokened great age; but his frame, though exceedingly spare, was apparently healthy and active. His eyes were singularly large and bright; and his hair, inconsistent in some respects with the rest of his. appearance, crowded from under his high-crowned hat in black and grizzly masses. ,

"A good evening to you, Meine Herren," said the little [55] old man, with a most polite bow, as he approached the students.

They returned his salutation with the doubtful courtesy usual in intercourse with a stranger, whose appearance induces an anxiety to avoid a more intimate acquaintance with him. The old man did not seem to notice the coolness of his reception, but continued: "What think you of this?" taking from his pocket a golden watch richly chased, and studded all over with diamonds.

The students were delighted with the splendid jewel, and admired by turns the beauty of the manufacture and the costliness of the materials. The elder youth, however, found it impossible to refrain from bestowing one or two suspicious glances on the individual whose outward man but little accorded with the possession of so valuable a treasure.

He must be a thief and have stolen this watch, thought the sceptical student. "I will observe him closely."

But as he bent his eyes again upon the stranger he met the old man's look, and felt, he knew not why, somewhat daunted by it. He turned aside, and walked from his companion a few paces.

"I would," thought he, "give my folio Plato, with all old Blunderdrunck's marginal comments, to know who this old man is, whose look has startled me thus, with his two great hyaena-looking eyes, that shoot through one like a flash of lightning. He looks for all the world like a travelling quack-doctor, with his threadbare cloak and his [56] sugar-loaf hat, and yet he possesses a watch fit for an emperor, and talks to two burschen as if they were his boon companions.

On returning to the spot where he had left his friend, he found him still absorbed in admiration of the watch. The old man stood by, his great grey eyes still riveted upon the student, and a something, not a smile, playing over his sallow and furrowed countenance.

"You seem pleased with my watch," said the old man to Theophan Guscht, the younger student, who continued his fixed and longing gaze on the beautiful bauble:—"Perhaps you would like to become its owner?"

"Its owner!" said Theophan, "ah, you jest;"—and he thought, "What a pretty present it would be for Thyrza on our wedding-day."

"Yes," replied the old man, its owner, "I am myself .willing to part with it.

What offer do you make me for it?"

"What offer, indeed; as if I could afford to purchase it. There is not a bursche in our university who would venture to bid a price for so precious a jewel."

"Well then, you will not purchase my watch?"

Theophan shook his head, half mournfully.

"Nor you, Mein Herr?" turning to the other student.

"Nein," was the brief negative.

"But," said the old man, again addressing Theophan, "were I to offer you this watch,—a free present,—you would not refuse it perhaps?"

"Perhaps I should not:—*perhaps*,—which is yet more [57] likely,—you will not put it in my power. But we love not jesting with strangers."

"It is rarely that *I* jest," returned the old man; "those with whom I do, seldom retort. But say the word, and the watch is yours."

"Do you really"—exclaimed Theophan, his voice trembling with joyful surprize,—"do you really say so!—Ach Gott!—Himmell! what shall I—how can I sufficiently thank you?"

"It matters not," said the old man, "you are welcome to it. There is, however, one condition annexed to the gift."

"A condition,—what is it?"

The elder student pulled Theophan by the sleeve: "accept not his gifts," he whispered; "come away,—I doubt him much." And he walked on.

"Stay a moment, Jans," said Theophan; but his companion continued his steps. Theophan was undecided whether or not he should follow him; but he looked at the watch, thought of Thyrza, and remained.

"The condition on which you accept this bauble,—the condition on which others have possessed it,—is that you wind it up every night, for a year, before sunset."

The student laughed. "A mighty condition, truly;—give me the watch."

"Or," continued the old man, without heeding the interruption, "if you fail in fulfilling the condition, you die within six hours after the stopping of the watch. It will stop at sunset if not wound up before." [58]

"I like not that condition," said Theophan. "Be patient,—I must consider your offer."

He did so;—he thought of the easiness of avoiding the possible calamity;—he thought of the beauty of the watch,—above all, he thought of Thyrza, and his wedding-day.

"Pshaw! why do I hesitate," said he to himself: then turning to the old man, "Give me the watch,—I agree to your condition."

"You are to wind it up before sunset for a year, or die within six hours."

"So thou hast said, and I am content: and thanks for thy gift."

"Thank me at the year's end if thou wilt," replied the old man, "meanwhile, farewell."

"Farewell,—I doubt not to be able to render my thanks at the end of the term."

Theophan was surprised, as he pronounced these words, to perceive that the old man was gone. "Be he who he may, I fear him not," said he, "I know the terms on which I have accepted his gift. What a fool was Jans. Herwest to refuse his offer so rudely."

He quitted the spot on which he stood, and moved homewards. He entered Jena, sought his lodging, put by his watch, and, lighting his lamp, opened his friend's folio Plato, (with Blunderdrunck's marginal comments), and endeavoured to apply to the Symposion. But in ten minutes he closed the book with impatience, for his excited [59] friend rejected the philosophic feast; and he strolled into the little garden which his chamber-window commanded, to think of the events of the evening, and, with a lover's passion, to repeat and bless the name of his Thyrza.

There is perhaps no nature upon which the character of your true lover can be better engrafted than on that of a retired and contemplative student,—the child of imagination,—the denizen of a fancy-created world. Such was Theophan Guscht. In him a passion once awakened burned strongly and steadily; and his introduction to Thyrza Angerstell came like a fairy charm to conjure up an hitherto unknown world, peopled with new passions, new desires, new hopes, and new fears.

Time waned, and the watch was regularly wound up. Love smiled, for Thyrza was not cruel. Our bursche had resumed his studies, and was in due time considered as one of the most promising students of the whole university of Jena. All loved, and all admired Theophan Guscht; and even professor Von Steffhenback relaxed the gravity of his visage when he spoke of him; and was even heard to say, that he himself was, in his youth, much similar to Theophan; an assertion which those who compared the blear-eyed, flint-faced doctissimus with the free and open gaze and Grecian physiognomy of the student, could by no means understand in its literal sense.

But, as we have already observed, time flew apace; and the day but one before the happy day that was to give to Theophan his blooming bride, had arrived. In [60] truth, though not to be won without wooing, Thyrza had been from the first by no means insensible to Theophan's many advantages, personal and mental, over those whom chance had brought within the sphere of her observation. Although, therefore, when his attentions first began to be such as to attract notice, the maiden considered herself bound in duty to affect all that ignorance of his meaning, and prudence of demeanour, which we understand to be essentially requisite on such occasions; yet it was without any idea of utterly extinguishing, when the proper time should arrive for their disclosure, those feelings which Thyrza, with a woman's tact, speedily perceived were entertained for her by the handsome and amiable student. And as the lover's family and worldly expectations were, to say the least of them, respectable, and his character as an individual held in high estimation among the oracles of Jena, her parents were not likely to be so perversely opposed, as papas and mamas are sometimes said to be, to their children's inclinations, should she think proper to encourage her lover's suit. His visits were, therefore, allowed: Thyrza unbent by little and little from her reserve; and that portion of their neighbours, at least one in a hundred, who disinterestedly loved to give every body's business a preference over their own, nodded, and winked, and looked wise, whenever an allusion was made to a certain matrimonial connexion, which might possibly,—they would not say when,—take place between a certain young couple,—they mentioned no names,—one of [61] whom resided,—though they would not mention where,—at a certain house not a hundred miles distant, &c. &c.

But to proceed: it was, as we have affirmed, the day but one before *the* day which had been long looked forward to with such joyful anticipations, and Theophan had bidden adieu to most of his fellow-students, and taken leave of the learned professors whose lectures he had attended with so much benefit. It was a fine morning, and, being at leisure, he bethought him in what manner he should pass the day. Any novice can guess how the problem was solved. He would go and visit Thyrza. He set out accordingly, and was presently before the gate of David Angerstell's garden. A narrow, pebbled walk intersected it, at the top of which stood the house, an old quaint black and white building, with clumsy projecting upper stories, that spread to almost twice the extent of the foundation. A quantity of round, dropsical-looking flower-pots were ranged on either side of the door. The casement of a projecting window was open to receive the light breezes that blew across the flower beds, at which a young female was seated,—a beautiful, taper-waisted girl, with a demure, intelligent countenance, light twining hair, and a blue, furtively laughing eye. True as fate, that blue eye had caught a glimpse of her approaching lover. In a moment he was by her side, and had kissed with eager lips the soft little white hand that seemed almost to melt in his pressure. [62]

It is of little use describing love scenes at this time of day. Those who are born to be lovers have either felt or can well enough imagine such things, and those dull creatures who are not, are by far too dull to glean any tolerable idea, of them from what we could say. The lovers met in all the confiding tenderness of mutual affection,—happy mortals! the moments flew fast,—fast,—so fast that But let us take time.

They had strolled out into the garden; for the considerate parents of Thyrza had shown no disposition to interrupt their discourse further than by a mere welcome to their intended son-in-law. The evening was one of deep, full stillness,—that rich, tranquil glow, that heightens and purifies happiness, and deprives sorrow of half its bitterness. Thought was all alive within their breasts, and the eloquence of words seemed faint to the tide of feeling that flashed from their eyes.

Theophan and Thyrza rambled, and looked, and whispered,—and rambled, looked, and whispered again and again,—and time ambled too gently for his motion to be perceived. The maiden looked on the sky: "How beautifully the sun has set," said she.

"The sun set!" echoed Theophan, with a violence that terrified his companion,—"the sun set! then I am lost. We have met for the last time, Thyrza."

"Dearest Theophan," replied the trembling girl, "why do you terrify me thus? Met for the last time! Oh! no, it cannot be. What! what calls thee hence?"
[63]
"He calls who must be obeyed,—but six short hours,—and then Thyrza wilt thou bestow one thought on my memory?"

She spoke not,—moved not:—senseless and inanimate she lay in his arms, pale and cold as a marble statue, and beautiful as a sculptor's brightest dream. Theophan bore her swiftly to the house, placed her on a couch, and called for assistance. He listened, and heard approaching footsteps obeying the summons,—pressed his lips to her cold forehead, and, springing from the casement, crossed the garden, and in ten minutes was buried in the obscurity of a gloomy wood, or rather thicket, some mile or thereabouts from Jena.

Overcome by the passionate affliction that fevered his blood and throbbed in every pulse, Theophan threw himself down on a grassy eminence, and lay for some time in that torpid state of feeling in which the mind, blunted by sudden and overwhelming calamity, ceases to be aware of the horrors of its situation, and, stunned into a mockery of repose, awaits almost unconsciously the consummation of evil that impends it.

He was attracted from this lethargy by the plashing rain, which fell upon him in large thunder-drops. He looked around, and found himself in almost total darkness. The clouded sky, the low, deep voice of the wind, booming through the trees and swaying their high tops, bespoke the approaching storm. It burst upon him at length in all its fury! Theophan hailed the distraction, for the heart loves
[64] what assimilates to itself, and his was wrung almost to breaking with agony. He stood up and shouted to the raging elements! He paused, and listened, for he thought some one replied. He shouted again, but it was not, this time, in mere recklessness. Amid the howling of the tempest he once more heard an answering shout: there was something strange in the voice that could thus render itself audible above the din of the storm. Again and again it was the same: once it seemed to die away into a fiend-like laugh. Theophan's blood curdled as it ran; and his mood of desperation was exchanged for one of deep, fearful, and overstrained attention.

The tempest suddenly ceased: the thunder died away in faint and distant moanings, and the lightning flashes became less frequent and vivid. The last of these showed Theophan that he was not alone. Within his arm's reach stood a little, old man: he wore a conical hat,—leaned on a gold-headed cane,—above all, he had a pair of large glaring eyes that Theophan had no difficulty in instantly recognizing.

When the momentary flash had subsided, the student and his companion were left in darkness, and Theophan could with difficulty discern the form of his companion.

There was a long silence.

"Do you remember me?" at length interrogated the mysterious stranger.

"Perfectly," replied the student.

"That is well,—I thought you might have forgotten [65] me; wits have short memories. But perhaps you do not aspire to the character."

"You, at least, must be aware I have little claim to it, otherwise I had not been the dupe I am."

"That is to say, you have made a compact, broken your part of it, and are now angry that you are likely to be called upon for the penalty. What is the hour?"

"I know not,—I shall shortly."

"Does *she* know of this;—you know whom I mean."

"Old man!" exclaimed Theophan fiercely, "begone. I have broken the agreement,—that I know. I must pay the penalty,—of that too I am aware, and am ready so to do; but my hour is not yet come:—torment me not, but leave me. I would await my doom alone."

"Ah, well,—I can make allowances. You are somewhat testy with your friends; but that we will overlook. Suppose now, the penalty you have incurred could be pretermitted."

The student replied with a look of incredulous scorn.

"Well, I see you are sceptical," continued the old man; "but consider. You are young, active, well gifted in body and in mind."

"What is that to thee?—still more, what is it to me—now?"

"Much: but do not interrupt me. You love, and are beloved."

"I tell thee again, cease and begone to—hell"— [66]

"Presently:—You are all these now,—what will you be, what will Thyrza Angerstell be, to-morrow?"

The student's patience was exhausted: he sprang on the old man, intending to dash him to the earth. He might as well have tried his strength on one of the stunted oaks that grew beside him. The old man moved not,—not the fraction of an inch.

"Thou hast wearied thyself to little purpose, friend," said he: "we will now, if it pleases you, proceed to business. You would doubtless be willing to be released from the penalty of your neglect?"

"Probably I might."

"You would even be willing that the lot should fall upon another in preference to yourself?"

The student paused. "No,—I am content to bear the punishment of my own folly. And still—oh, Thyrza!" he groaned in the agony of his spirit.

"What! with the advantages you possess!—the prospect before you,—the life of happiness you might propose to yourself,—and more, the happiness you might confer on Thyrza,—with all these in your reach, you prefer death to life? How many an old and useless being, upon whom the lot might fall, would hail joyfully the doom which you shudder even to contemplate."

"Stay: were I to embrace your offer, how must the lot be decided,—to whom must I transfer my punishment?"

"Do this,—your term shall be prolonged twenty-four hours. Send the watch to Adrian Wenzel, the goldsmith, [67] to sell; if, within that time, he dispose of it, the purchaser takes your place, and you will be free. But decide quickly,—my time is brief, yours also must be so, unless you accede to my terms."

"But who are you to whom is given this power of life and death,—of sentencing and reprieving?"

"Seek not to know of what concerns you not. Once more, do you agree?"

"First, tell me what is your motive in offering me this chance?"

"Motive?—none. I am naturally compassionate. But decide;—there is a leaf trembling on yonder bough, it will fall in a moment. If it reach the ground before you determine—Farewell!"

The leaf dropped from the tree. "I consent!" exclaimed the student. He looked for the old man, but found that he was alone. At the same time the toll of the midnight clock sounded on his ear: it ceased,—the hour was passed, and he lived!

It was about the noon of the following day that the goldsmith, Adrian Wenzel, sold to a customer the most beautiful watch in Jena. Having completed the bargain, he repaired immediately to Theophan Guscht's lodgings.

"Well, have you sold my watch? "

"I have; here is the money, Mein Herr."

"Very well; there is your share of the proceeds."

The goldsmith departed, and Theophan shortly afterwards directed his steps towards Angerstell's house [68] meditating as he went on his probable reception, and what he could offer in extenuation of his behaviour the day before. Ere he had settled this knotty point to his satisfaction, he arrived at the garden-gate. He hesitated,—grew cold and hot by turns: his heart throbbed violently. At last, making a strong effort at self-command, he entered.

At the same window, in the same posture in which he had seen her the day before, sat Thyrza Angerstell. But the Thyrza of yesterday was blooming, smiling, and cheerful,—to-day she was pale and wan, the image of hopeless sorrow; even as a rose which some rude hand has severed from its stem. Theophan's blood grew chill; he proceeded, and had almost reached the porch of the house when Thyrza perceived him. With a loud cry, she fell from her seat. He rushed into the room, and raised her in his arms!

She recovered,—she spoke to him. She reproached him for the agony he had needlessly caused her by his cruel conduct the evening before. He obtained a hearing, and explained just so much of the history of the watch as related to its purchase, and the condition annexed to it. This he asserted was a mere trick of the donor, he having broken the condition and being yet alive. They wondered, he with affected and she with real surprize, that any one should have been tempted to part with so valuable a watch for the idle satisfaction of terrifying the recipient. However, love is proverbially credulous;— [69] Theophan's explanation was believed, and the, reconciliation was complete.

The lovers had conversed about a quarter of an hour, when Thyrza suddenly reverted again to the subject of the watch.

"It is strange," said she, "that I too am connected with a watch similar to yours."

"How,—by what means?"

"Last night I lay sleepless—'twas your unkindness, Theophan—"

Theophan hastened to renew his vows and supplications.

"Ah, well!—you know I have forgiven you. But as I lay, the thought of a watch, such as you describe, presented itself to my mind; how, or why, I cannot guess. It haunted me the whole night, and when I rose this morning it was before me still."

"What followed, dear Thyrza?" enquired the anxious student.

"Listen, and you shall hear. Thinking to drive away this troublesome guest, I walked out. I had scarcely left my home two minutes when I saw a watch, the exact counterpart of my ideal one."

"Where,—where did you see it?"

"At our neighbour's, Adrian Wenzel's. "And,—you,—you!" His words almost choked him.

"I was impelled by some inexplicable motive,—not [70] that I wanted or wished for so expensive a jewel,—to purchase this watch."

"No,—no!" exclaimed the agonized student, "you could not do so!" He restrained himself by an exertion more violent than he had believed himself capable of. He rose from his seat, and turned away his face.

Not now, as before, did his anguish vent itself in passion and violence. It seemed that the infliction was too heavy, too superhuman a calamity to be accompanied by the expression of ordinary emotions. He was deadly pale; but his eye was firm, and his lip trembled not.

"Theophan," said his mistress, "what ails you? and why should what I have said produce so fearful an effect upon you? I shall—"

"It is nothing,—nothing, dearest Thyrza!—I will return instantly, and tell you why I have appeared so discomposed. I am not quite myself,—I shall return almost immediately. I will but walk into the lane, and catch a breath of the fresh breeze as it comes wafted from the water."

He left her, and passed out of the garden. "I could not," said he inwardly, "tell her that she was murdered,—and by me too!"

He hastened on without an object, and scarcely knowing whither he was directing his steps, passed down the path which led by Angerstell's house, in that depth of despair which is sometimes wont to deceive us with the appearance of calmness. He had no distinct idea of the calamity he [71] had brought upon Thyrza,—even she was almost forgotten; and nothing but a vague apprehension of death, connected in some unintelligible manner with himself, was present to his mind. So deep was the stupefaction in which he was involved, that it was not until some one on the road had twice spoken to him that he heard the question.

"What is the time of day?"

Theophan looked round, and encountered the large, horribly-laughing eyes of the giver of the fatal watch. He was about to speak, but the old man interrupted him.

"I have no time to listen to reproaches: you know what you have incurred. If you would avoid the evil, and save Thyrza, I will tell you how."

He whispered in the student's ear. The latter grew pale for a moment, but recovered himself.

"She shall be safe," said he, "if I accept your terms? No equivocation now,—I have learnt with whom I deal."

"Agree to what I have said, and fetch hither the watch within half an hour, and she is delivered from her doom. She shall be yours, and "

"Promise not more, or give thy promises to those who value them. Swear that she shall be safe! I request no more,—wish for no more on earth."

"Swear!" repeated the old man; "by what shall *I* swear, I pr'ythee? But I promise,—begone and fetch the watch,—remember, half an hour; and, hark! thou accedest to my terms?"

"I do!" [72]

So saying, Theophan sped back to the house, unchecked even by the loud laugh that seemed to echo after him. He had walked farther than he had any idea of, and swiftly as he sprang over every impediment to his course, one-third of the allotted time had elapsed before he reached the room in which he had left his beloved.

It was empty!

"Thyrza! Thyrza!" shouted the student,—"the watch! the watch!—for Heaven's sake, the watch!"

The reverberation of his voice from the walls alone replied.

He rushed from chamber to chamber in a state of mind little short of desperation! He descended into the garden; the dull ticking of the family clock struck on his ear as he passed it, and he shuddered. At the extremity of the principal walk he beheld Thyrza.

"The watch! the watch! as you value your life and my—but haste, haste,—not a word,—a moment's delay is death!"

Without speaking, Thyrza flew to the house, accompanied by Theophan.

"It is gone," said she; "I left it here, and—"

"Then we are lost! forgive thy—"

"Oh! no, no, it is here," exclaimed she, "dearest Theophan! but why—"

He listened not even to the voice of Thyrza;—one kiss on her forehead, one look of anguish, and he was gone!

He sped! he flew!—he arrived at the spot where he [73] had left the old man. The place was solitary; but on the sand were traced the words—*The time is past!*

The student fell senseless on the earth.

When he recovered he found himself on a couch,—affectionate but mournful glances were bent upon him.

"Thyrza, Thyrza!" exclaimed the wretched youth, "away to thy prayers! but a soul like thine hath nought to repent. Oh! leave me,—that look!—go, go!"

She turned away, and wept bitterly. Her mother entered the room.

"Thyrza, my love, come with me. The physician is here."

"What physician, mother?—is it—"

"No, he was from home, this is a stranger; but there is no time to lose." She led her daughter from the apartment. "Your patient is in that room," she added, to the physician. He entered, and closed the door.

The mother and daughter had scarcely reached the stair-head, when a cry, which was almost a yell of agony, proceeding from the chamber they had left, interrupted their progress. It was followed by a loud and strange laugh, that seemed to shake the building to its foundation The mother called, or rather screamed, for her husband! the daughter sprang to the door of the patient's chamber! It was fastened, and defied her feeble efforts to open it. From within arose the noise of a fearful struggle,—the brief exclamations of triumph, or of rage,—the groan of pain,—the strong stamp of heavy feet,—all betokening a [74] death-grapple between the inmates. Suddenly, something was dashed upon the ground with violence, which, from the sound, appeared to have been broken into a thousand pieces.

There was a dead silence, more appalling than the brunt of the contest.

The door resisted no longer.

Thyrza, with her father and mother, entered the room: it was perfectly desolate. On the floor were scattered innumerable fragments of the fatal watch. Theophan was heard of no more.

On the fifth day from this terrible catastrophe, a plain flag of white marble in the church at——, recorded the name, age, and death of Thyrza Angerstell. The inscription is now partly obliterated; so much so as, in all probability, to baffle the curiosity of any gentle stranger who may wish to seek it out, and drop a tear on the grave of her who sleeps beneath.

Title

Delta. [Moir, D.L.] "The Old Manor-House." LS 1826. 181-200. [181]

THE OLD MANOR-HOUSE

> It is impossible for man to tell
> What things in nature are impossible,
> Or out of nature; or to prove to whom,
> Or for what purposes, a ghost may come.
> *Crabble.*

"Now, nurse, I won't go to bed, unless you promise to tell us a story; something about old castles, or about witches, or about ghosts,—or about any thing you like nurse, so that it be a frightful story," said little George, in an earnest tone, untying his shoe, and addressing himself to Mrs. Margery.

"I never heard the like of you, George," whined out his brother Philip; "you are always for that sort of thing. No, no, nurse, never mind him;—let us have something funny,—something to make us laugh. Mind, I won't go to bed any more than he, if you don't: he shan't always have his will. Do you hear that now:" and the spoiled urchin gave his head a most significant shake.

"Nursey, nursey!" bawled out Jack, the youngest and last, but by no means least importunate personage of the triumvirate, "I will neither take off a stitch of my clothes, nor let you undress me, mind that; unless you do as [182] George bids you, and tell us a nice, horrible little story about ghosts or robbers."

"Well, be good boys," answered the beseiged Mrs. Margery, who was allowed to exercise a very limited degree of authority over the indulged and forward imps; "be good boys, and get into bed, and I will tell you one of my best stories."

"Now it must be a frightful one," ejaculated George and Jacky in one breath.

"Very well, it shall be so; and we shall have a droll one to-morrow evening, Philip,—will that do?"

"Yes, it will do; but see that you don't forget your promise, Mrs. Margery."

"Believe me, I shan't forget. Now you are all in bed. But, George, that is not your night-cap," added Margery, taking one of her own caps from his head, and handing him the right one. "Lie down, like good little boys."

"We are all ready now, cried Jacky; why don't you begin, nursey? Let it be a terrible one."

"Give me a moment,—give me a moment; let me snuff the candle, mend the fire, get my needle threaded, and my seam on my lap—"

"And then we shall be all asleep,—ha, ha, ha!—a very clever one!"

"A moment patience then. Do you hear how the wind is whistling?—It would be an awful thing to be out travelling alone in this dark night!"

"Now, now, nurse! do give us our story; we don't mind the wind;" was the immediate rejoinder of the impatient trio.

"Hear how the rain is rattling against the panes!—Dear me! what was that came flap, flap, against the window!—I dare say it was one of the young ravens, falling down from the old tower:—I don't like these birds.—Witches always keep ravens about them, and talk to them, and the birds in due time learn their ways, and are alive to all their doings, which are wicked, and for no good. I recollect, when I was a young girl,—that is long, long, ago,—"

"That cannot be so very long, long ago. You know you told us, only the other night, that you was not forty yet;" said George, interrupting her, with considerable archness.

Mrs. Margery coughed, and proceeded: "—not a very great while, to be sure; but not yesterday either. Well, I mind about a raven, with a little bell tired to its foot, which went in among the ruins of an old—"

"Never mind the ravens," bawled George angrily; "do you think, you old witch, we will lie here to listen to you and your ravens. I shall get out of bed immediately, if you do not tell us our story, and begin at the beginning. See! here goes," added he, throwing down the bed-clothes.

"Stop!—stop!" cried nurse, rising hastily, "lie down, like a sweet fellow, and I will begin in a moment."

"Do, so, then" mumbled Jack, who had started to her elbow, "or, mind you now, we shall all get up:—do you hear that, nursey?"

"Very well, then; I shall begin at the beginning."

"There was an old woman who lived in a small cottage at the edge of a forest. She was infirm, and bent down with age; and, though she had no other help in the world, poverty compelled her to part with her only daughter, who was taken into a great old manor-house,—just like this of our own,—to be the companion and attendent of her master's eldest daughter.

"Her mother had been attentive to her during her tender years, and had brought her up in the dread of sin, giving her much good advice, and instructing her in the knowledge of the bible: so the poor girl knew that it was the will of Providence she should separate from her mother; and, though she did so with a heavy heart, she restrained her tears, in the hope that time would accommodate her to her situation, and that her earnings might add to the comfort of her parent's declining age. In a short time, by the sweetness of her temper,—for she was a kind, affectionate creature,—and by many amiable and friendly offices, she became a great favourite with every one in the house."

"Now, you see what you would be at," cried George, "can't you say at once she was a very good girl, and get one. We see that plain enough, so if you please—"

"You are always in a hurry, George; but just as you like,—Well, then; there was another young woman in the house, who was, like the rest, most kindly disposed towards Mary, until she found out that Mary's beauty had decoyed away her lover's heart from her; and then, though Mary did not know what had happened, nor could have prevented it if she had known, she hated her with a bitter hatred. Her sweetheart was the son of a small farmer, who lived about a mile from the manor, on the eastern side of the policy; and he came frequently of an evening to spend a cheerful hour by the great hall fire, as he said he was fond of music. Ah! those were the hospitable days;—those were the days of toasted cakes and foaming ale!—but one may like music for all that. So Jacob, the old coachman,—I remember Jacob, he had grown grey in the service, and very fat; for, poor old soul, he had nothing to do but ride behind my lady, through the grounds, on sunny forenoons, and make of himself what he liked for the rest of the day. The last time he ever mounted the coach-box was on his master's return from London; and, the night being dark, Jacob had remained too long by the inn fire-side to see clear; so it fell out that the carriage was upset, and Jacob was found on the other side of the hedge against which he had driven them. His son afterwards drove for him; but Jacob was often heard to say, after telling all the wonderful feats, that the days of driving were now over. But he had still an amusement wherewith to console him. Oh, how he would sit with his knees crossed, and his head awry, [186] scraping, for hours and hours, on the old violin, till every heart was glad, and the very roof rung! Poor Jacob! he was a good-natured fellow.

"But to return to my tale. The young farmer loved music, may be, well enough, and that was a good errand; but he loved Ellen the house-maid better, with her black bright eye and blue rose-knots; and, as she was fond of music too, she used always to come, as if by chance, and stand with her hand shading her face, by the side of the great roaring fire, right opposite to where young Hodges the farmer was sitting; so she couldn't help sometimes looking in his face, nor he in hers, till both feel deeply in love. Ah! boys, if you knew what it was like to be in love!"—and here Mrs. Margery fetched a deep sigh.

"What are you groaning at nurse?—pray get on."

"It was now towards the end of harvest; and, on fine moonlight nights, Farmer Hodges had more than once persuaded Ellen to take a stroll with him down the old chestnut-tree avenue; and, as they sauntered kindly together, he whispered many sweet things into her ear, which she would afterwards lie down and dream about. But the fine moonlight nights came and passed away, while Ellen was hoping and hoping,—and, alas! in vain. Hodges seemed even to shun her,—at least she thought so,—nor ever opened his lips to her but when he could not help it. No doubt she must have felt it severely, for it is a sore thing, boys, to be slighted,—mind that you never slight your sweethearts when you get them! So Ellen [187] would sometimes contrive to throw herself in his way, amid the clustering trees, but he never spake to her more than a civil word in passing. She grew very dull, and delighted to sit by herself, moping and cheerless; and when she heard Mary, at her work, singing away like a linnet on a sunny morning, she would almost fret herself into a fever. Her very heart was changed, and she became an altered creature. Her temper, which was pleasant, and rather kind, grew sullen and sour; so that, observing in the course of time that the same things were goin on, and that matters did not mend, she was rendered desperate. Her good looks forsook her, her cheek was sunk, and the wildness in her eyes, oh! it was terrible to look upon.—Mary, poor soul, listened to the warm speeches of Hodges, for he was madly in love with her, and would have given every thing in the world to have made her his wife; but she never know, had never heard, of his courting Ellen, before she came to be a servant; so she told all her secrets to her rival, with the hope of amusing her in ill health, and even asked for her advice in the matter.

"One evening, however, strange to say, Mary was a-seeking, and no one knew where to find her. She had been home, on the day before, to tell her mother of the change which was shortly to take place in her situation; and how a kind Providence had put into her power to be of use to her, as Hodges had agreed to take her home to live with them, after their marriage. The preliminaries had been settled: Sir William agreed to dispense with [188] Mary's services, and the young ladies, in testimony of their regard for her, had made her sundry little presents, which they considered might prove useful to her. The banns were to have been proclaimed in the neighbouring church on the Sunday following; and every thing was in a fair train for making poor Mary the wife of a loving husband. But, as I told you before, on the Friday evening she was a-seeking, and none knew aught about her. The night was comfortless and gloomy, something like this, but without rain; and the winds, blowing hard from the east, made a dreary noise among the trees; for there was a great deal of wood around the house.

"Hodges came in the evening, as he was accustomed to do, to inquire for his young and blooming bride; but how was he shocked to be told that she was off, like a leaf torn from the tree whereon in grew, and whirled away none knew whither. He was like one distracted. He went to and fro, in an agony of perturbation, and almost gasping for breath, while only the pride of his being a man kept the tears from bursting from his eyes, as his friends vainly endeavoured to console him. Every inquiry was made after Mary, but without effect; and, when almost midnight, he set out alone through the woods, towards the cottage of her mother. Heedless of the darkness, the loneliness, or the wind, he hurried away until he had got clear of the trees; but when he knocked up the old woman from her sleep, and asked her concerning her child, her knees tottered, and she fell back into her [189] wicker-arm chair, weeping, and crying out in anguish—'It is as my heart dread,—but the will of Heaven be done! It has come, not without warning, this awful dispensation! All night I have heard the ticking of the death-watch!—it is even as my heart foreboded. Ay! the four magpies too,—what caused them to fly across my window? It is death-death-death!—Well do I know that. I shall never see Mary,—I shall never shake the hand of my child again! What will become of me!'—and with that she pressed her hands to her eyes, and wept as if her old heart would break.

"Hodges was too much shocked to think of comforting her, and out again he rushed, and back through the forest. The stream came roaring down, but he waded recklessly through it, through, by so doing, he ran the greatest risk of being swept away along with it. He saw the lights over the trees, and made direct for the manor, through ditch and over hedge, till he stood near the orchard gate."

"Then he was not drowned?" asked Philip, pulling the curtain aside, and popping his head from beneath the bed-clothes. "I shouldn't like to see a drowned man—his face would be all sucked and wrinkled like old Nancy the washerwoman's hands."

"No:—he climbed the rocks on the opposite side, and forcing his way through the brambles and underwood, gained the postern—door, by which you pass through the orchard into the house. His hand was upon the lock, when a sudden terror came over his heart,—his knees [190] trembled,—and a cold sweat broke out over his face. He turned round,—and saw a figure, in white, under a tree: something told him it was Mary's ghost, but so great was his fear that he had no power to speak to it. At length he tried to step forward,—but nothing was to be seen, or heard, save the dreary sough of the wind among the trees.—On going to the room where Mary used to sleep, all her clothes were found, save a few articles of apparel. The things she had thrown off in the morning were still lying on a chair, and her Sunday-bonnet was hanging on a peg in the corner. No one knew what to think.

"Next day some labourers, returning from their work in the fields, discovered some traces of her. By the side of the road, at the place where the water runs out from the policy, there was a long wooden bridge, at one end of which was a shawl, belonging to Mary, was found lying on the grass. But this was all. The river was dragged, and the woods were searched, but no other token of Mary, dead or alive, was discovered. Weeks and months passed on; and at length every one thought that she had been drowned, and her body hurried out to sea.

"All in the manor-house were grieved, for they all loved Mary, excepting Ellen to be sure, as I have said; and poor Hodges grew an altered man. He did not seem to care any longer about his farm. Every thing he saw around him only rendered him more miserable. If he had been sure that Mary was dead, her loss would scarcely have afflicted him so keenly; but the mystery [191] which hung over her fate sank him in deeper and deeper dejection. At length he determined to leave his country, and enlisted into a regiment that was going over the sea. Poor fellow! he was never heard of more. Many were the battles that were fought abroad, and many, and many were killed, but his name was never known to be among them. I dare say he died long ago, whether he was killed or not; for no one lives on to see grey hairs who has a breaking heart."

"Poor Hodges!" said Philip, somewhat affected, "I am sorry for poor Hodges. No doubt he would have married Mary, and taken care of her old mother. But was it really a ghost he saw?"

"Have patience a moment, child, and you shall hear all I know about it. But let us speak a little lower, for I am afraid we may waken Jacky,—and that would be a pity."

"Never fear, nursey," cried George impatiently; "let the brat sleep or wake as he chooses; but pr'ythee go on with your story. What more about the ghost?"

"A good deal more. But first let me tell you that, when all agreed that Mary was dead, Sir William gave a sweet little cottage to her mother, that she might live comfortably in her old age: and I dare say she was as happy as the unaccountable loss of her daughter would allow her to be, for all her neighbours were very kind to her.

"In a short time after the disappearance of Mary, every thing at the old manor seemed to be going to wrack. [192] The servants whispered to each other strange things; and gave up their places. Scarcely any one would venture out after dark. The chambers, which before looked full of comforts, with their rich old paintings, and carved frames,—with their gilded high-back chairs, and their squares of Arras tapestry, now seemed lonely, dismal, and gloomy. The very trees around appeared to have grown darker and drearier, while the noises, which the winds made at night among their boughs, were likened to what was unearthly. The yelling of a hound from the neighbouring kennel made the bravest start, and hold his breath;—ah, children you needn't laugh, no person at the old manor thought it was a laughing matter.

"I have already told you that the hall was formerly a cheery place, where they used all to meet at night, and amuse themselves, fiddling, dancing, singing, and telling old stories; but now, scare any one went near it; and when they did they crowded round the fire, not caring for one another, and seeming to wish themselves any where, rather than where they were.

"Miss Lucy—ah! boys she was a pretty girl when I first knew her,—what a neck! and what fingers!—Well, she had always been a good friend of Mary's, and very very kind to her. So, to be sure, was also Miss Caroline; but to Miss Lucy the thing happened.

"It was on a winter evening, and the moon had a wild and watery look. The wind came driving against the old gable with a loud noise, and whistled through every [193] chink and open seam. The tall chimnies bellowed like thunder; the leaves whirled round in eddies, below every angle of the building; and the clouds drifted from east to west, like mighty armies flying from a field of battle. Miss Lucy had been sitting alone reading, when the turret clock, striking twelve, warned her to retire, and think of sleep. Suddenly a great slap came against the wainscot, which made her start. She turned round, but saw nothing. I should not like to have been in her place at such an hour, for it was a high apartment, almost separated from the body of the building, which she could not reach without wandering through a long, dark passage, and down a flight of steps. It never occurred to her, that she might bring the servants to her assistance by ringing her bell; or, if she did, she was unwilling to disturb any one, the whole family having retired to rest. Besides, it might have looked foolish for her to have called up people from their beds, merely to tell them she had heard a noise; so she proceeded to undress herself, for she would not keep her maid up,—ah! she was a considerate, as well as a lovely creature,—when, casting her eyes up to the great mirror, she saw something like a white handkerchief waving over her head. What could she now do?—her heart was failing within her, and her knees tottered; strength being scarcely left her to throw herself down into a chair. The candle burned dimly, and the apartment looked dreary and desolate; so she still thought that she was only troubled with a nervous terror. She rallied her [194] spirits, snuffed the candle, which diffused around a more cheerful light; and, endeavouring to sing to herself a snatch of some old tune, she prepared for bed.

"She had lain in the dark for some time, before any thing extraordinary happened. All was quiet,, save the wind rumbling in the large chimneys, and the roaring noise of the trees around the house."

"You frighten me, nurse," said Philip. "Pray George don't be pulling the clothes off from me.—And what did she see?"

"She saw something that almost froze the blood in her veins. Without the door being opened, a white figured glided in, and sate down in a chair opposite the bed. The pale moonlight found a passage between the chinks of the shutters; and lay in scattered lines of light upon the floor. Miss Lucy gasped, and gazed— and her hair stood on end with terror;—her tongue became parched;—she tried to speak, but could not, whilst the figure mournfully moving its head from side to side, kept its eyes fixed upon her. At length it rose up, and beckoned her to follow, for it seemed as it wished Miss Lucy to speak to it; but she could neither rise nor speak, for she was weaker than a new-born babe; so it put its fingers as it were to its lips, as if to enjoin silence; and, while she looked, and looked at it, she saw at length only the moonlight streaming through the shutters; and, at the same moment, the turret clock struck one.

"It was a long, long time before Miss Lucy closed an [195] eyelid; and the breakfast bell had run before she awoke, pale, feverish, and unrefreshed. She told no one of what she had seen and heard; but her looks indicated that something extraordinary had happened to her. She never slept alone afterwards.

"On another occasion, when the groom was going to get his pails filled at the well, he saw a figure standing by the pump; and his terror being greater than his curiosity, he threw away the empty buckets, took to his heels, and did not halt until he had bolted the stable door behind him. Joe was never again caught out after dark without a lantern."

"Nurse," cried George, "I wish you would snuff the candle, the place is looking dark; and give the fire a poke. Oh dear! what noise was that?"

"Oh! it was only I knocked over the tongs. Shall I go on still?" rejoined Dame Margery.

"Oh, I don't know," said George hesitatingly. "Perhaps—"

"No perhaps, nurse," cried the undaunted Philip; "let us have the whole of your story. We know now that they saw ghosts every night—and were terribly frightened—and never spoke to them. What came next, nurse?"

"The thing that came next, and now we are drawing near to a close, was the falling ill of Ellen the house-maid. She had left her place, and gone home to her friends: she was in great danger, and at time grew delirious, saying wild and frightful things, which made all who heard her [196] shudder. Even from the first, the doctors had small hopes of her, but she became weaker and weaker; and it was plain that she was not long for this world.

"According to her desire, the minster of the village was sent for, as she wished to speak with him alone; and, when he came, he sate down by her bedside.

"The man of God held up his hand in horror, at the confession which she made to him. He then called in her friends; and they all knelt down in prayer at her bedside. When they arose, they looked at Ellen, but she was dead, with her hands clasped upon her bosom, and her fingers pointing upwards.

"The minister alighted, on the next day, at the gate of the manor; and, having found Sir William, made the whole story known to him."

"And pray what was it, nurse? Come, be quick now, you are always so tedious," said George. "It is better, I am sure, to come to the point at once."

"To be sure, nurse," echoed Philip, "you like to keep us from sleeping. You wish to finish that large seam, we know well enough, mind that; and you are just afraid to sit by yourself, lest something bad should come, and whisk you away."

"Very well, children, I have just done. Ellen had confessed on her death-bed, that she was the murderer of Mary. Having seen that Mary's face had stolen away the heart of her lover from him, she hated her bitterly, and sought her destruction. [197]

"The manor-house had, long-ago, in the troublesome times of England, been a kind of castle, having places for cannon, a moat, and drawbridge. There were also some old vaults below ground, which had been used as dungeons in former days but which had been locked up for a great many years, and were full of damp and mould. A soldier had much rather have been shot at once, than have been buried alive in such a place.

"One day as the maids were about to go to the bleaching green with their baskets of wet linen, Ellen attracted the curiosity of Mary, by telling her stories about the vaults; and asking her, if she would just like to see them. They lighted a lamp, and went down the dark steps together; for the cruel Ellen had the large rusty keys in readiness. No sooner had she got her to the door, than she pushed her in, and shut the massive bolts upon her. She listened for a moment, astonished at her own wickedness, and heard a wild scream from below; but her hatred, stifling every feeling of humanity in her breast, she blew out her lamp, and hurried upwards to the light of day. Oh! was it not an awful situation for poor Mary!—What horror, and what misery must have endured, when she cried for help hour after hour, and no one could hear her!—When she knocked and knocked at the door of her coffin—for she was only in a larger grave—and knew that earthly help was not to be expected!

"The body was found lying upon the steps; and after it had received christian burial, no more strange sights were [198] seen at the manor. Almost every one within the walls had, at one time or other, been haunted by the figure; but no one had possessed sufficient presence of mind either to speak to it, or follow where it led. Though all the neighbourhood was now quiet, the place never looked so pleasant as before; and, since the family forsook it for another residence, the country people will not pass it after sunset, but in pairs; and the bravest of the two is fond to whistle, that he may keep up the courage of his comrade.

"Now children, my tale is ended, and you must go to sleep."

"Jacky and Philip are sleeping already," said George, "but is there no more of it? Mind you now, I wish to hear it all."

"Upon my word there is no more of it, George. Go to sleep now, like a dear boy."

"Is your seam not finished yet, nurse. The tailor can make new clothes for Jacky, and Philip, and myself, all in a week; but you women are sewing, sewing from one year's end to the other. Pray who wears them all?"

"Now, George, you just want to teaze me. Lie still, and sleep like your brothers."

"Sing me a song, then; some old thing or other. Not the Babes in the Wood—nor Barbara Allen—nor the Bloody Garland—nor any of that sort; in case I never sleep a wink to-night."

"Well then, any thing you please. What wouldn't one do for a quiet life! any thing to please you, child; I will sing you one that you never heard before." [199]

> A pretty young maiden sat on the grass,
> Sing heigh-ho, sing heigh-ho;
> And by a young shepherd lad did pass,
> In the summer morning so early;
> Said he, "my lass will you go with me,

My cot to keep, and my bride to be,
Sorrow and want shall never touch thee,
    And I will love you rarely?"

"Oh! no, no, no," the maiden said,
    Sing heigh-ho, sing heigh-ho;
And bashfully turned aside her head,
    On the summer morning so early;
"My mother is old, my mother is frail,
Our cottage it lies in yon green vale,
I dare not list to any such tale,
    For I love my kind mother rarely."

The shepherd took her lily-white hand,
    Sing heigh-ho, sing heigh-ho;
And on her beauty did gazing stand,
    On that summer morning so early.
"Thy mother I ask thee not to leave
Alone in her frail old age to grieve,
But my home can hold us all, believe,
    Will that not please thee fairly?"

[200]
    "Oh! no, no, no I am too young,
    Sing heigh-ho, sing heigh-ho;
I dare not list to a young man's tongue,
    On a summer morning so early."—
But the shepherd to gain her heart was bent;
Oft she strove to go—but she never went,
And at length she fondly blushed consent;
    Heaven blesses true lovers so fairly.

So every maiden learn by this,
    Sing heigh-ho, sing heigh-ho,—

"George, are you sleeping? Softly! no answer! that's well. Good night to you all, teasing brats, you would have plagued Job out of his wits;—and now for my bumper of Cognac!

Title

Hogg, James. "The Border Chronicler." LS 1826. 257-279.[2] [257]

THE BORDER CHRONICLER.
BY JAMES HOGG.
CHARLIE DINMONT.

As I was sauntering about Prince's-street a few months ago, I espied, at a distance, some one walking along, at whom all the passers-by turned round and gazed; indeed, the person or persons seemed to be moving on in the midst of a considerable crowd of people, all of whom expressed, by their looks, no small degree of interest. I hastened forward, and soon discovered the object of their curiosity. He was a tall, herculean countryman, rather coarsely and singularly dressed. He had huge topped boots, all of one colour; steel spurs; a rough coat of Galashiel's grey; a good oak staff under his arm; and immense whiskers that curled over his cheek. "How silly these people are," said I to myself, "thus to interest themselves in everything of country extraction. Certainly, if I may judge from appearances, yon farmer is a very clownish and ignorant fellow." I have heard it remarked, that "the multitude are never wrong." Of this [258] I shall not pretend to judge; but I had not overtaken this man, and walked by his side half a minute, before I discovered that there was something original about him; his very manner of walking the streets had somewhat of novelty in it. When any well-dressed or beautiful woman met him, he looked her full in the face, with a sort of good-natured familiarity, as if he had wished to address her with—"How's a' w'yethe day, my bonnie lassie?"—while she in return could scarcely maintain the gravity of her deportment till fairly past him. At length, a little spruce old man, with a powdered wig, was pushed against him by the crowd,—"Tak care, callant!" said he, "ye'll ding wee fock owre if ye stite that way;" and then, turning his face up to the sun, and laughing at his own jest, he strode on.

It struck me that I had somewhere seen such a figure before, though I could not remember in what place, and I therefore kept close by him, in hopes of finding an opportunity of introducing myself. Soon afterwards he stepped into an auction room, and sauntered some time in the front shop. He took some papers and prospectuses from the counter, and pretended to be reading their contents , but was all the while looking out at the corner of his eye at the clerk, as if he were a fellow of whom he had some jealousy, or with whom he wanted to pick a quar-

---

[2] Plain text for this transcription was obtained from Google Books <http://books.google.com/books?id=OF8EAAAAQAAJ&pg=PA414&dq=1826+The+Literary+Souvenir;+or,+Cabinet+of+Poetry+and+Romance&hl=en&ei=WbRHTd39PISBlAfJ94ykBA&sa=X&oi=book_result&ct=result&resnum=3&ved=0CDMQ6AEwAg#v=onepage&q&f=false> and then compared against the original volume. For full citation, see References.

rel; but perhaps he only suspected that the man was angry with him, or might not quite understand what was his business there. At length, seeing some gentlemen pass [259] up the staircase, he ventured up likewise, but with a considerable degree of caution. The sale was over, at which he appeared disappointed, looking always around as if he wished to see the auctioneer. A tall, spare gentleman now made up to him, and accosted him instantly with some common-place observations about the weather, and the books at which they were looking. I drew near, and, affecting to read, listened to the following curious conversation between them:

"What news from the country? How are matters going on there?"

"How do ye ken that I come frae the country, lad?"

"Oh! quite well; we know a countryman at first sight, from his very appearance."

"Appearance!—what do you mean by his appearance?" Here the farmer looked at his clothes on both sides, and all around, to see if there was anything particularly wrong in them.

"Though not easily to be defined, yet there is always something materially different in the manner, air, and make."

"Make! yes, thank God, there is some little odds there. I doubt aye that you town bodies get nae feck o' meat!"

"Rather doubt that the greater part of us get far too much, friend."

"It disna kythe on ye, man! for deil hae me, if there is na a hantle o' ye just like reested kippers, but ye war [260] speering about the news? Indeed, honest man, they were never so ill i' my day, nor my father's afore me. I hae heard him say that things gat a sair slump at the end o' the 'Merican war; but nothing ava like this. The hauf o' the farmers are maistly ruined already; but the weather's turned unco guid,—the braxy has na been ill this year,—Candlemas-day turned out foul, an' we would fain hope that things are gaun to turn a wee better wi' us."

"Do not you hope any such thing. The vain and foolish hopes of the farmers have ruined them! Young man, you must look farther than a change of the weather, before you begin again to cherish such ridiculous and extravagant expectations. We are a ruined nation,—a nation on the very verge of bankruptcy, and its attendants, anarchy and confusion; and, instead of things growing better, to every reflecting person it is as plain as that two and two make four, that they will yet be many degrees worse.

"I am unco vexed to hear that, man; for I cam just nto Edinbroch to tak twa or three farms, trowing that things could na be waur wi' us. The sheep stocks are comed to hauf naething, an' there's plenty o' land out. There's my Lord Hickathrift, Sir Duncan M'Grip o' the Hungrey-hall, an' Mr. Screwhimup the laird o' Bareboddam, have a' sequestered their tenants, an' warned them away, an' now they canna get a single bode for their land; they daurna stock it theirsels, an' by this time, I trow, they 'll gie ane a' farm for a sma matter. Now, [261] sir, if ye binna gayan sure o' what ye're saying, I like unco ill to gang hame. wanting a farm or twa; for to tell the truth, there's a bit bonny lassie that I hae an ee to,—I downa bide to want her muckle langer;—I canna bring her in ower the head o' my auld mither an' my titties,—an' unless we get a mailen o' our ain we'll be obligated to pit off. I hae a gay pickle siller, she has mair, an' my uncle Dan, he's to be cation for the lave; Ye'll, may be, ken him?—a hantle o' fock ken him."

"I do not, at this moment, recollect. Pray, sir, may I ask your name?"

"I'm Charlie Dinmont o' the Waker-cleuch; I leeve just a wee bit off the hee-road, as ye gang to the Cauldstaine kirk, where Dr. Christoff, the original-sin man, preaches, ye ken; an' if ever ye gang by that way, ye 'll find a prime road to the right, through Drown-cow, along the Pikestane-brae, an' out owre the mids o' Hobblequamoss, till ye come in sight o' a lang theeket-house wi' three chimleys,—that's ours; an' my mither an' titties will be happy to see you; an' I'll tak in hand to make ye fatter than ye're just now in eight days, though I sude pit ye i' the kirm!"

"You are very kind,—very kind indeed, sir; but—"

"Come, nane o' your buts; ye had better do't, ye hae muckle need on't: we hae aye plenty o' meat, sic as it is, about the Waker-cleuch, an' we hae whiles something to drink too;—for, d'ye ken, our, herd keeps a bit 'ewie wi' the crooket horn,' in his ben-end, that gies mair milk, an' [262] straunger milk, an' heartsomer milk, than a' the ewes o.' Dead-for-cauld. I count mysel muckle behadden t'ye for your advice about the farms; an' if I war sure that ye warna for some of them yoursel, I wad mak na ill use o' it, for I hae great hopes that ye 'll may be prove wrang in your calculations."

"I wish that there were but a bare possibility of it; no one would rejoice more heartily than I. But whoever considers the state of our finances, and the enormous load of debt under which the nation is groaning, must soon perceive that neither private nor public credit can longer be maintained. We are duped, cheated, and ruined!"

"Hout, man! I dinna like these sweeping halesale remarks; we hae studden some dowrer striffles than ony that are facing us just now. D'ye ken I hae thought a great deal about that national debt; an' there was ae year I had very near comprehendit it. I countit,—an' I reckoned,—an' I addit,—an' I multiplied, till I had a grit lang raw o' nothings, that gaed amaist across the slate; but when I cam to subtract, it didna answer ava;—it was aye nothing fra nothing, an' we's no mention the remainder. Weel, sir, I thought it was a' owre wi' us, as ye say; but instead o' that, things gaed aye just on as weel as ever, an' rather better, an' I saw that I had never fathomed it in the least; sae I am now resolved never to puzzle my harns more about the cause o' ony thing, but just stand by the effects. If ony body war to speer at ye, how the cauld moon could gar the sea rise an' fa?—how a wee [263] bit clippit thing, that gangs harling athwart the lift, sud heeze up the great ocean fra its very marl-pits?—Lord! ye wad think the thing impossible! Aha! look at the effect, lad! I can lippen til her that she 'll keep her time wi' the tide to a second. But the thing that has convinced me maist ava is the staine stairs in this new town o' Edinbroch; od! ye wad think they're hanging i' the air. An' tak me beuk-sworn, I canna comprehend how they stand, an' yet I can trust to them, an' gang up an' down them as freely as I war on the solid yird. I was aince a wee concerned about the national debt, till I saw the staine stairs o' Edinbroch; but they hae satisfied me that a man should nae count a' things absurd that he canna comprehend. Now, sir, I rede you do the same. Wad ye but just look upon the nation as a great staircase, an' the *debt* neither more nor less than the stair that bears a man up or down, precisely as he behaves an' manages himsel, I'll lay thee a guinea thou turns a third fatter. Look at me; I think, for a' the warld, you an' I standing thegither, are exactly like cause an' effect!"

About this time I went forward and shook honest Charlie by the hand, reminding him of our having once met before. I soon drew him into a conversation about Border tales and Border manners, and at length he took me by the hand, and without asking my leave, trailed me down stairs into the street, and there, instead of placing his arm within mine, put it round my shoulder, impelling me on at no ordinary pace. "Aha, man, but I is glad I ha' [264] met wi' thee!" said he, "for hadna thou sae many poetical flights in thy head, thou's the man could give ane a sound advice anent the times. Whatten a lang, doure, grumbling chap is he yon?"

"He is a radical Whig," said I, "and the most discontented, ill-boding person in this city; you need not regard his surmises; but I think you have hit him down for once about the national debt and the stone stairs of Edinbro'." He laughed at this remark till he made the street echo, and every person turn round and gaze who was in the division. By this time we had reached the door of a tavern, at the east end of Rose-street, and into that Charlie hurried me as fast as possible, without waiting to ask my consent, or to hear any remonstrances.

"I hae waggled up an' down on them hard free-stains," said he, "till I'se like to swairf wi' baith hunger an' drouth, but we shall vanquish them baith or we twa part." I began to expostulate, and declare off, talking of engagements elsewhere; Charlie regarded all that I said the same as if I had not been speaking, and, in the very midst of my excuses, was ordering a cold round of beef, with which he had had some former acquaintance, cold mutton-pies, and cockamers, as he called them; I said I was engaged to dinner and could *not* eat.

"Never mind! never mind!" said he, "tak the less, man,—tak the less; I'll, may be, mak up for your deficiencies. Deil a hair the waur you 'll be o' a snack; for me, I tak my dinners as weel again when I get something [265] to eat an' drink on a forenoon. Whenever get a hard booze my auld mither gars me aye eat a saut herring next day, some strang ewe milk cheese, an' twa or three brandered legs o' a fowl, made as hot as fire wi' pepper, to sharpen my appetite a wee; an' then she'll say (for she has maistly aye ae address to me on sic occasions);" here he mimicked the voice of an old woman, "now Charlie, my man, how is thy sharping-stane gaun to fit?—is the stomach o' thee getting ony bit edge yet?"

"Troth, no, mither, it is as blunt as a bittle!"

"Dear Charlie, man, does thou no ken thysel a bit hungrier for a' thou hast eaten?"

"I really canna say that I do, mither; I am no' ae straw hungrier than when I began."

"Ha, ha, ha! that is, indeed, very hard, Charlie, poor man!—I'm unco wae for thee—ha, ha, ha!"

I had before this time agreed to join Charlie in his meal, and confess that it did my heart good to see with what lest he enjoyed it; neither did he spare the liquor in washing it down;—he mimicked everybody with great effect, and appeared in reality the Mathews of the Border. We talked about farms, and various other subjects; but ever and anon his conversation manifested a prejudice against all town people. Whenever he touched upon their character it was apparently with a degree of prejudices for which I could not account; and these sentiments, from a man so shrewd, convinced me that there is something radically wrong in the ideas of the country people, [266] relating to their town neighbours, which must have been handed down, by father to son, from the ages of chivalry. I rallied Charlie, as bitterly as I could, on his false and exaggerated calculations; but he hemmed, shook his head, and remained apparently incredulous.

TOWN AND COUNTRY APPARITIONS.

"After a', man," said Charlie Dinmont, in a tone which seemed only half in earnest, "after a', man, how can it be that they 're as upright an' conscientious men i' the city as thou hauds them up to be?—how can there be ony conscience, or fear o' God, wi' focks that hae neither deils, ghosts, nor bogles amang them? Ay, thou may'st laugh the fill o' thee; but, in truth an' verity, I think the want o' deils, ghosts, an' bogles, are the greatest want that a community can be subjected to. They are the greatest of a' checks on human crimes; an' I marvel that there are none o' them at Edinbroch, where heinous wickedness is so abundant."

"I believe that there are very many of them in Edinbro', Charlie," said I, striking in with his whimsical humour, "but here it is impossible to distinguish them. I am well assured that ghosts of hapless females, who have fallen a prey to the selfish voluptuousness of the other sex, roam these streets every night, and to a certain hour in the morning." [267]

"Lord preserve us!—do you think sae?" said Charlie.

"I am quite certain of it," returned I, "having frequently seen them myself moving about, after midnight, with a melancholy and desponding air: but their forms throw no shadows on the pavement; their footsteps make no noise, not so much as the falling of a leaf; and, whenever they chance to look one in the face, their eyes have that dead stillness in them, that white moveless opacity, that denotes them, at first sight, to be only the ghosts of what they were."

"That's perfectly awsome, an' dreadful, an' terrible'." said he, "thou gars a' my flesh creep to hear thee! but I hae no doubt o' the circumstance, not ae grain;—poor undone, misfortunate beings! kicked out of a' rational happiness here, an' out o' heaven hereafter! 0! man, I had aye some hopes that creatures like these might be made without answerable souls; but it seems my hopes have been ill-foundit. Is it not a terrible thing to think that they should come back to linger and lament round the altars on which they sacrificed heaven an' earth at the same instant! I canna think of ony state sae dreadfu' an' hopeless as a spirit o' that kind."

"There are sights to be seen here every night, Charlie," said I, "that cannot fail of impressing every serious heart with the deepest awe, and would be enough to drive the inhabitants of a whole glen out of their senses."

"Thou never said a truer word, man, a' the days o! thy pilgrimage here on earth," said he; "for I hae seen [268] sights in it mysel, that, wi' a little change o' scene; wad hae freezed the blood. Consider for ane instant, a countryman setting hame his sweetheart on a Sunday evening; after saying o' questions, reading lang skreeds o' sermons, an' hearing prayers. Weel; the twa chop on;—the rood grows aye eirier an' darker, an' they cling aye closer thegither; hardly daring to talk above their breath, till, just at the corner o' a dark pine wood, they perceive a glimmering light shining from behind the trees across their path;—they stand still—hesitate, but dare not speak, an' their hearts beat as they would burst their tenements.; at length the maid ventures to whisper, "what can yon be?" "God only kens!" says the other; when, at that instant, there issues from behind the corner, a hideous figure wrapped up in sack-cloth; his head swathed in a white napkin with a cowl over it. This demon carries a dark lantern in its horrid paw, that only tends to make darkness visible, an' hideousness ten times more hideous; an' just as the couple are ready to sink into the earth, the horrid apparition cries out aloud—"*past twill o'clock!!!*"

Here I could not help bursting into a fit of laughter, at the humourous manner in which he had exaggerated the picture; but he went on, adding, "eh! what think ye o' the effect there, sir?—as I am an honest man, I saw sic a sight the last night, an' could na help thinking that if I had been at the Gird-wood corner, it was as muckle as my seven senses were worth."

"I am a believer in apparitions myself," said I, "and [269] in the existence of fairies and witches; at least I believe that these last did exist, and am never quite sure that the greater part of the women are not still witches to this day; and I am even so antiquated in my notions, as to believe in the existence of the devil likewise, and also in that of innumerable spirits, both good and evil;—what say you to all these, Charlie?"

"I believe in them a' as sternly as I believe the gospel," said he; "I canna but say that we wad be muckle the better of a new deil now, for the auld ane is rather beginning to lose his effect. I notice that the bits o' prime weel-bred minister lads think it shame now to bring him forward, an' seem rather inclined to mak a laughingstock o' him. But I wadna wonder should he play them a smirl by-and-by, though he is rather in the back ground just now. But wha wadna believe in spirits?—what a cauldrife, insignificant, matter-o'-fact world, this wad be without hoards o' spirits bustling amang us?—it makes a man of nae importance at a' when neither good nor ill spirits are looking after him, an' counteracting ane another on his account. But weel may I believe in such interferences! for I hae mysel seen some o' the grandest instances o' them that ever fell to the lot o' man to recount; an' there was ane o' them na farther gane than the last Hempton market, at Carlisle, whilk I 'll tell thee." [270]

GILLANBYE'S GHOST.

"I was gaun across to Annandale at that time, to see Willie Byrrell an' John Church, an twa or three friends; an' so I leaves Carlisle with a dozen o' Scotsmen, an' three ministers amang them, an' we takes the near road across the Solway sands at the mouth of the Esk. Several o' them pretended to ken the fords; but there was a whisper o' high tides rase amang them, an' we resolved to hae a guide on horseback. When we called at the guide's house he was gane across wi' a party, and the wife doubted whether he would get back that night, before the advance of the tide. We asked if there was danger; and she answered, that unless we were very expeditious there certainly would be danger: so with that we spurred into the level sand, and kept always shouting out, hoping we should meet the guide on his return. The water soon began to deepen; and we were fairly at a stand, for it was very near pitch dark. I 'll never forget that night! So as we were standing deliberating, ane o' the ministers o' the gospel says, "Na, na, sirs, we'll no venture in wanting a guide, for there is just the deil's dozen o' us, an' something will befal one or more of us before we get o'er."

"Count again, honest man!" said a stranger gentleman, whom never ane o' us had seen till that moment. Now I [271] was as sure that that man, an' his black, horse, rase out of the earth, as that I am flesh and blood; for there were thirteen o' us a' the way, an' no man could approach us, on that light-coloured plain o' sand, without having been seen. "Count again, honest man!" said he. I counted, an' sundry of us counted, an' in verity there were fourteen. From that time forth, my tongue an' the roof o' my mouth grew as dry as a whistle, an' I keepit near the hinder end o' the troop." "Wha 's this?" said one. "Where came he from?" whispered another; an' ilka body was muttering something. But there was a Mr. Little, who was hauf drunk, he rides up to him, an' he says, "whae the deil are you, sir?—an' where did ye cam fra?—for, as I'm a sinner, I never saw you till this moment."

"I came from the market, sir," says the stranger, "where I have had a busy,

busy day, and am hastening across to Scotland:—do you ford the river?"

"We proposed as much," said Little, "but are rather grown eiry about finding the track."

"I have crossed it at all seasons, and at all weathers," said the stranger; "but I have not time to trifle,—if you want to cross follow me; if not, good night."

"Have wi' ye!" says Little; "I like a chap that cries *follow me*, better than ane that cries *lead on*, at sic a time as this. Have with thee, I say;—at any rate thou's have to drown first,—that's ay some comfort."

"I should have brought my hogs to a bad market then," said the stranger.

"An' thysel to nae good ane," said Little.

"But pray now, hast thou done muckle business at the Hempton to-day?"

"A little, a little," said he; "but I intend doing more before the turn of the night. I have a grand scheme in view to-night, and hope to effect it."

"Ay; but dinna thou count afore the point, guid man," says Little, "for may be thou may'st be mista'en. I's wager thou's a dealer in bacon; I sees by thy face an' thy way o' riding."

"Yes, I sometimes deal a little in the flesh," said the stranger, "but rather more in the spirit,—the former is a vile drudgery, but in the latter I take delight."

"Ay, ay! an' so thou's a smuggler then?" says Little. "Confound thee! an' I did'na find a strang reekit saur about thee a' this time, an' coudna ken what it was. But, lad, where art thou leading us, for dost thou ken my beast is up to the thrapple, an' snorting like a whale."

"Only a deep step or two," cried the stranger, who was riding on with all the ease imaginable; "only a deep step or two;—come on, fine footing here." Some time before this, we had all stopped, except Little, owing to the depth of the tide; but more on account of a figure which approached us, on a white horse, with the swiftness of the wind, calling on us to turn back. We thought it ane going to cross in our company, an' paid little attention to him for a space. Which made him ride still faster, an' call the louder. At length we did pause, all in a body, as we were like to be swamped, an' then we heard him calling these words—

"Stop! stop!—for the sake of heaven and your own souls, stop! Do you know where you are going?—or whom you are following?"

Some of our party hearing this vehement interrogatory were stunned, an' involuntarily answered—"No, we do not."

"I wot that is true!" said he, "for you are going direct into the middle of the crooked swamp,—into which man never went and escaped; and, in the second place, you are following old Gillanbye, or rather the devil in hit likeness."

"I was almost petrified, for I had heard of the ghost of that old wretch leading people into jeopardies and death: and the moment our preserver uttered these words, I looked after our hellish guide, who at the same instant left us with a loud guffaw of a laugh, an' scoured, at a light gallop, across the tide, till he vanished in the dark. In the meantime, Little and his horse were swamped: for he was so busy talking to the devil, whom he took for a bacon-dealer and smuggler, that he never heard our preserver calling after us.

"There is only a deep step or two," says the deil; "come on, fine footing here!" Those were the last words that I heard him say; and poor Little, who saw him riding with such ease, spurred on after him, but in half a second he was over the head. He was riding a [274] good black mare; an' loth, loth was she to take the tide after the deil's horse; for she baith snorted an' reared on end; but her rider clapped the spurs in her side, an' plunge she went ower the head!—she gave two or three flounders, as if struggling in a bog, then down both of them went, an' the billows came up with the bursts o' their parting breath. "Ha! ha! ha!" quo' the deil; an' away he flew across the Solway, as if he had been riding for a broose."

"Little's down!" cried ane; "come on! come on! an' let us save Little," cried every body at ance; an' we were a' rushing in after him, but the figure on the white horse stopped us again, held up his hand, an' charged us, in God's name, to keep back. "All Cumberland cannot save him," said he, "for by this time he is five fathoms deep in quicksands. That swamp will suck a thing of half the weight of that poor fellow and his horse down in three seconds, never more to be seen. Turn, and follow me; there is only one possible path to Scotland to-night, by which I will lead you."

"We did as he commanded us, without a murmur, or without one gainsaying. It was manifest that he had saved all our lives, and the scenes which we had witnessed made so deep an impression on our minds, that we rode after him scarcely uttering a word. He kept galloping considerably a-head of us; but his white horse appeared so conspicuous through the gloom, that we followed him [275] with whip and spur, and always kept him in view. Whether it was an inlet of the firth, or the mouth of the river Eden, that we crossed, I do not know, but we rode on in deep water for a considerable while, and all of us believed that we had crossed the beds of the Esk to the Scottish side.

"However, none asked any questions. In a short time we came upon the high road, on which he said,—"you are safe now on the high road for Annandale; keep together in a body, and see that you fall not out by the way,"—saying which, he rode gently on before us; but on reaching the top of the first declivity, we lost him, and never saw or heard of him any more.

"We rode on, and rode on, expecting to come upon Graitney; till at length we thought we must have passed it, and should arrive at Annan; but, ere ever we kend, we found ourselves in the middle of Langtown, on the Border. There we heard that there had been a terrible tide in the firth, that came running up breast high, like the dam of a river broken open; that several persons had been lost, and others in great jeopardy; an' that it was suspected that either the deil, or the ghost of old Gillanbye, had been acting as a guide that night.

"I am perfectly assured that it was the devil, who would have led us into the crookit swamp; how else could he have galloped across that, an' the broad firth? And I am as well convinced that the man on the white horse was [276] an angel of mercy sent to save us; and who, indeed, took us by the only path by which any of us could have reached our homes that night.

"'Od! sir, I wadna hae exchanged my feelings o' gratitude to heaven that night, for a' the cauldrife dogmas of a' the heartless philosophers that ever drew the breath o' life.

"Now, sir, this is but one o' many, many instances that I could relate to you of the interference of Providence, by means out o' the common course o' nature to preserve life; an' that gars me believe baith in good an' ill spirits. I dinna believe in a' the hallanshaker spirits that are supposed to haunt every eiry spot through the hale country; I dinna believe that a ghost wad arise frae the dead, an' stand up in its winding-sheet, like a bog-stalker, merely to fright a body out o' his judgment that was half crazed afore. But if there is human life or innocence to preserve, or guilt and murder to bring to light, an' no earthly hand to help, I'll trust to an over-ruling Providence yet, be the means as incomprehensible as they may.

"Didst thou ever hear the story of the White Lady of Glen-Tress?"

"I think I have printed an edition of that story myself, Charlie."

"Deil ma care! thou 'it be none the waur o' hearing my way o' it. It is an excellent story, soon told, and very pat to the purpose." [277]

THE WHITE LADY OF GLEN-TRESS.

"In my grandfather's days, the house of Glen-tress was a farm-house, which had long been in the possession of a family of the name of Tait; a douss, decent, pious family they were, an' suffered muckle for religion's sake. At length they fell back in the warld; and then their farm was taken frae them, an' laid into that of Colquhar: but the family was sae respectable an' weel likit, that the new tenant wadna turn them out, but keepit them as his shepherds. John Tait, the elder brother, had a wife an' seven children, an' his brother lived with him; an' they remained in the old farm-house, in which their fathers had lived for generations, an' in which they had always been devout worshippers o' the Almighty.

"Weel, it sae happened that one fine summer's evening, after the sun had gone down, a' the family were assembled, save one little maid. They had taken their supper, an' the goodman had reached down the bible to begin family worship. He had taken it down, an' laid aside his bonnet; he had not begun the psalm, but sat waiting till little Mary should come in. She soon came in, breathless with haste, and said:—

"Come a' out, sirs!—haste ye!—come a' out, an' see wha's coming!" [278]

"Wha 's coming here at this time o' night, bairn?" said her mother.

"The grandest lady that ever was seen in this warld!" said the child; "she's as bonny as an angel, an' a' clad in white!—she was close on me ere ever I ken'd, an' she bade me tell you to come all to her directly. Haste ye, an' come away!—I tell you she's coming!—she's coming!"

"We had better defer the worship till we see what she wants," said John; an' with that he went out, wi' the big bible under his arm. The moment he had passed the threshold, he saw a figure, as white as a meteor, coming towards him, an' beckoning him, with an air of impatience, to meet her. He answered this singular summons, an' this brought the whole family out to the green. They every one saw her coming to meet John Tait, an', at that time, they two did not appear to be mere than ten or twelve yards asunder; they viewed her for a moment, in silence, when the attention of all was taken off by a tremendous crash, which was followed by a scream from the family group. John started, an' looked round; and behold the house was fallen in, an' the dust from the rubbish was rising, like a cloud, to heaven! With a palpitating heart, an' a head 'mazed with astonishment, he perceived that he an' his numerous family had been miraculously saved from instantaneous death. He turned to address his splendid guest, but she was gone, once an' for ever! By no one but themselves had this benevolent apparition been observed. [279]

"Now wha will venture to deny the interference of a kind Providence there, in saving an amiable an' devout family from momentary destruction?—an' who wadna rather hae heard poor Johnny Tait express his gratitude to his Maker an' Preserver that night, than a moral harangue fra ane that attributes ilka thing, baith in salvation an' providence, to our ain doings? Ay! poor Johnny Tait didna miss the prayers that night, though he had e'en to sing his psalm, an' kneel to his God, in the shieling ahind the kie."

I have a great many more of Charlie's instances noted down, which shall be forthcoming in the next volume of the *Literary Souvenir*, although it is probable they may not prove as interesting and congenial to the enlightened and polished part of the community as they did to me.

Altrive Lake, April 17, 1825.

Title
Roberts, Emma. "Rosamunda. A Venetian Fragment." LS 1826. 305-312. [305]

ROSAMUNDA.
A VENETIAN FRAGMENT.
BY MISS E. ROBERTS.

Rose of the world, Flower of Italy, Bright star of Venice, were the titles applied by the whole population of the city to the lovely Rosamunda di Guarini. When the last sound of the vesper-bell died upon the ear, masqued musicians stole from the ambush of the clustering pillars, or paused in their gondolas opposite her palace windows, and poured out strains of melody in her praise; prolonging the soft serenade until the dawn of morning, each note more wincing than the last. Nobles sighed at her feet,—minstrels and poets made her the theme of song,—and the most gifted artists of the age transferred to their glowing canvas charms which are still the wonder and delight of admiring worlds. How light was her footstep in the dance,—how joyously she warbled wild notes of thrilling sweetness,—and how brightly her blue eyes flashed through the living tapestry of leaves and flowers which she had twined across the fretted stone-work of her balcony. [306]

There, coyly shrinking from the gaze of men, she would sometimes venture, trusting to the clustering roses and mantling jessamine, to screen her fairer form and brighter blushes. Gay and gallant suitors crowded to the Di Guarini Palace, and princes were candidates for the hand of Rosamunda. She was neither ambitious of wealth or of power, but perhaps a little dazzled by the fame which proudly emblazoned the youthful career of Manfred Camaldano, she gave her heart to the bravest warrior, the most enchanting minstrel, and the most esteemed gentleman of the Venetian states. Manfred was a younger branch of a noble family: nature had been lavish in her gifts, yet fortune was unkind; his sword had purchased for him everlasting renown; but the policy of the Republic, in keeping her defenders poor, had denied him a more substantial recompense. He was, however, regarded as the probably heir of his rich uncle, the Count Andreas; and Rosamunda, young, sanguine in hope, and buoyant in spirit, looked forward to the period when the possession or the promise of this inheritance would enable him to demand her from her parents in marriage.

The sparkling waves of the Adriatic, when rippled by the gales of June, and kissed by the summer sun, danced not more gaily than Rosamunda's heart, when the lips of Manfred whispered in her ear his vows of everlasting love, and his dark eyes beamed upon her with the glance of true affection. Secure in his constancy, and exulting in the deep, the boundless attachment which absorbed her [307] own pure heart, fear and distrust were to her equally unknown; and she rejoiced, with as little foreboding of the future, as a bird in the spring, a flower in the sunshine, or an infant at play in the lap of its mother. It was in these days of felicity that all Venice hung enraptured on the charms of its loveliest daughter; that the church which Rosamunda frequented was thronged by the multitudes of every class; and the gondolieri abandoned the flowing verse of Tasso, the immortal chronicle of Armida's fascinations, Clorinda's valour, and Erminia's love, to chant the strain which celebrated the beauty and the virtue of the fair pearl of Italy, the sweet rose of the Di Guarini Palace.

At this period the Count Andreas died, somewhat unexpectedly to be sure, although the suddenness of his death excited no suspicion at the time that he had been unfairly dealt by. Manfred Camaldano succeed to his uncle's wealth; and now possessed of rank as well as riches, as soon as the first days of mourning were over, flew to the habitation of his beloved, and claimed her as his promised bride; but Rosamunda was changed,—she would not listen to him, she would not even see him. She gave no reason for this alteration in her sentiments: tears, entreaties, persuasions, and commands were alike unavailing; she continued inexorable. Although her disposition had hitherto been gentle even to timidity, she suddenly assumed an unyielding steadfastness, and even solicited to be allowed to retire to a convent; but with this request her parents were unwilling to comply. They had opposed her union with [308] Manfred so long as he remained poor; but no sooner had he attained to riches and distinction that they warmly espoused his cause, and led their trembling daughter into the gay world, where she was continually brought into contact with her lover. Manfred strove, by every art which love could dictate, to win from his cold auditor a single smile, a single sigh, a single tear; but she turned a deaf ear to all his blandishments. It was not sternness, it was not obstinacy, it was not caprice,—but a fixed, immoveable determination, which swayed her mind and restrained her tongue. "I can never be your wife,"—"I never will reveal the cause,"—were the only replies which hours of entreaty could wring from her averted lips. At one time Manfred would turn indignantly away, and join the dance with some bright beauty, proud of the attentions of one so handsome and distinguished amid the youths of Venice; at another, he would suffer the angry feelings of his soul to rise, and vent them in the bitterest reproaches; or he would pass his hand across his burning brow, and dash himself upon the earth in utter despair. Meanwhile the carnation faded from the cheek of Rosamunda, and growing paler still every day, she looked more like the marble production of some gifted sculptor, than a breathing personification of female beauty: once only did a momentary tint of crimson suffuse her pallid brow. Manfred, unable to restrain the rage and disappointment which burned within him, scornfully told her that she had lost her self-esteem, and dared not consent to sully the name of 309] Camaldano. The blood rushed to her cheek,—fire flashed from her eyes,—and she darted a withering glance of offended innocence upon him. It pierced him to the soul, and he knelt before her in an agony of contrition, and implored her

forgiveness for the frenzied words which had escaped him. She resumed the usual melancholy yet calm expression of her countenance, and turned away from him in silence. He came no more to the Guarini palace, yet his persecutions did not altogether cease; though Rosamunda was seen
>Less oft at masque and festival,
>More frequent at confessional,

she could not emerge from the solitude of her chamber without being aware of his immediate proximity. If she stole out upon the balcony to breathe the evening gale, as cooled by the waters of the Adriatic, as it came freshly through the flower-wreathed trellice, it brought with it the deep mellow tones of one to whose gentle serenade in happier hours she was wont to listen with delight. If languidly reclining in the curtained gondola she floated over the surface of those unruffled streams which intersected her native city, still those well-known sounds thrilled upon her ear, Manfred's gliding vessel would shoot beside hers, and she felt that a plank, a silken drapery, alone divided her from that once loved object to whom she had clung with such fond tenacity; whose breath was as incense to her, whose smile brightened her existence, and from whom she would at one time have thought it worse [310] than death to part; though now she would willingly have planted oceans and mountains between her heart and that of the discarded Manfred.

Kneeling before the shrine of her patron saint, though her spirit ascended on high and held communion with the blissful beings of a brighter sphere, the sigh and the groan of a prostrate form at her side would sometimes recall her to earth. Manfred shared in her orisons; and when, in obedience to the command of her parents, she sought the illuminated saloon, amid the glitter of innumerable lamps, the splendour of countless jewels, the flash of flowers, and the waving of plumes, her conscious eyes rested alone upon Manfred Camaldano. He was near her, he had touched her flowering veil, she inhaled the same air, stood upon the same spot with one who gazed upon her still with undiminished affection; but whatever were her secret feelings, those features which had formerly revealed with silent eloquence every thought, every sensation of her guileless heart, were now fixed in the expression of pensive sadness: the blue eye, beaming or tearful as joy or grief prevailed, had lost its lustre and its sparkling glance: the deep dye of the rose, which was wont to mantle and crimson on her cheek at every words and every look, was gone; and the unvarying alabaster hue betrayed not aught that was passing, perchance, an agitated breast. All Venice gazed upon her with wondering eyes, and almost deemed that the incantations of some evil spirit had unsettled the mind of the fair Rosamunda;— [311] for what could be alleged against Manfred? he who, his country's boast and pride, was handsome and generous, gallant and gay, gifted with genius, blessed with prosperity, and the truest, the fondest, and most ardent lover that ever poet feigned or historian recorded.

The brave sons of the republic rushed out upon the waters at the call of danger! The banner of St. Mark floated on high in the bright blue air,—the guardians of the golden-winged lion exalted their victorious standard! and the hearts of the Genoese quailed beneath it. The then unspotted bride of Venice, the curling Adriatic, proved a grave to those whose adventurous prows invaded the acknowledged rights of the Island City; and Manfred Camaldano, pre-eminent in the glorious strife, bound fresh laurels round his triumphant brows, and, leaping from his stout bark upon the shore, was hailed by applauding multitudes as the preserver of his country's honour. Garlands of flowers were strewed in the dust in the wide square of St. Mark—the fronts of the houses were draped with rich tapestry, or wreathed with blushing roses,—and silken flags waved from the summit of every tower. The shout of the populace came upon the ear mingled with the bray of the trumpet, the roar of artillery, the loud clash of the cymbals, and the deep boom of the double drum, whilst every bell in Venice rang out a peal of joy. At the gates of the ducal palace stood the Doge, surrounded by a crowd of senators, and a broad platform raised for the occasion was occupied by the noblest and fairest ladies of the city. [312] Amid her bright and blooming companions, like a drooping lily of Sharon, sat Rosamunda. The proudest moment of Manfred's existence had arrived,—the most distinguished gift which Venice could bestow was offered to him by the hand of its chief magistrate.

Suddenly, a squalid wretch, worn to a skeleton by disease or famine, pierced through the dense multitude; and, flinging up his arms to Heaven, exclaimed, "I accuse Manfred Camaldano of murder!—of the murder of the Count Andreas!" The whole assembly for a moment remained paralyzed with astonishment, and the intruder profited by the opportunity to narrate his mysterious tale. "Dark was the deed!" he cried, "and dark the scene wherein the crime was perpetrated: the vaults beneath the ruined church of St. Ildefonso, where few are wont to pray; but on that fatal night there were two suppliants at the subterranean shrine of the saint beside the Count Andreas, though both were hidden from the assassin's views. I was one witness,—and I call upon the Lady Rosamunda di Guarini to substantiate the charge, for she was the other!" The eyes of the spectators were immediately turned upon the trembling being thus fearfully adjured. She was pale,—so pale, that the gazers marvelled at the increasing paleness of one who already seemed to have whitened into stone; her blue orbs were veiled by their dropping lids,—her lips were closed,—her limbs had stiffened,—she was dead!

Literary Annual
The Literary Souvenir; or, Cabinet of Poetry and Romance. Ed. Alaric A. Watts. London: Longman, Rees, Orme, Brown, & Green; and John Andrews, 1827. Printer: T. and J.B. Flindel, 67, St. Martin's-Lane.[3]

Title
Wilson, John. "The Two Fathers." LS 1827. 19-27. [19]

THE TWO FATHERS
BY THE AUTHOR OF "LIGHTS AND SHADOWS OF SCOTTISH LIFE."

THERE was the sound of stifled sobbing throughout the whole house, the fires were extinct on all the hearths, and by the glimmer of neglected lights small groups of weeping friends were sitting in remote rooms, silent, or now and then uttering a few words from which all the tones of hope had faded away, and that struck their hearts, at intervals, like the very toll of the passing bell. In one apartment there was a perfect hush, and no more motion than on a frozen sea. Therein lay on her deathbed, but still breathing, as sweet a child as ever folded hands before God,—over her countenance, white as the shroudlike sheet, her parents had long been hanging, and dropping their last kisses on the closed unconscious eyes,—he whose skill had been in vain bestowed on the sufferer night and day, stood at the foot of the couch with a solemn face overspread with that profound pity which melteth not in tears,—and the holy man who had continued to read to her the words of Him who died to save sinners, even after [20] her speech was gone and her resignation was seen only in a few fast vanishing smiles, now bowed down his silver hairs in the gloom, and at the very moment of her soul's departure to heaven remained in the posture of reverential prayer.

 The change from life to death, gradual as it may have been in its progress, smites the loving heart that beholds it with a pang as sudden as if there had been no previous despair. There had been a faint irregular breath for the parents to listen to,—there had been a motion of the bosom for them to gaze on,—a quivering of the eyelids that, miserable though it was to see, showed that their child was yet among the living. But now breath or motion there was none,—her name was the name of a shadow—for her life had ceased to be,—she had left the world in which they dwelt and would continue to dwell;—the separation was infinite, the loss beyond the power of their smitten hearts to conceive, and religion itself, that had

---

3 Plain text for all short stories included here for the 1827 *Literary Souvenir* obtained from Google Books and then compared against the original volume. For full citation, see References. <http://books.google.com/books?id=aFUJAAAAQAAJ&ots=BUhL22ZoX1&dq=The%20Literary%20Souvenir%3B%20or%2C%20Cabinet%20of%20Poetry%20and%20Romance&pg=PR1#v=onepage&q&f=false

hitherto borne them up, deserted them in that extremity, and they both sank down together on the floor. No foot approached them—no hand was stretched out to succour them in their swoon,—for the friends who beheld the agony stood aloof in their awe, and left them to the care of him who in his most dreadful judgments is still the God of mercy.

For an hour the parents were left alone in that chamber—for scenes of suffering there are, which to witness is almost to profane. None went near them; and the few [21] dear friends that were in the house dropped away one by one to their own homes. The servants watched every louder groan that echoed through the stillness of the dark, and in whispers spoke of the saintly character of the beloved dead. "Too good was she," they said; "too beautiful to live long;" and she who had tended her from her birth showed a ringlet of her hair cut off during her last mortal sleep, while many a tear fell on its golden glow from eyes little used to weep, and sentiments were expressed by those humble folk most affecting in their purity and solemnity;—such is the influence of sacred sorrow on the spirits of all the children of the dust.

Hurried feet were heard descending the stair, and the sound died away at distance in the outer night. The old nurse ventured into the room, and lo! with one arm below the head of the corpse, and the other across its breast, lay the mother in a profound sleep! Both faces were alike pale, and the same angelical smile was on both,—but no one else was present, and it was plain that the father had sought, in his distraction, the less insufferable solitude of the woods or glens, now shone over by the midnight moon and stars.

On he went, blind and deaf to all outward things, yet unconsciously drawn, as if by the power of some invisible spirit, towards the solitary parish church that stood, among its multitude of burial heaps, under the gloom of an old pine-grove. Lonesome was the road he took, up a ravine darkened with trees, and filled with the constant [22] thunder of waterfalls. To his ear the place was silent as the grave. Unappalled he passed along the edges of precipices, and close to the brink of many an abyss, like one walking in his sleep, and to whom danger is not, because he has no fear. The confused sense of some unimaginable calamity drove him along; for his soul in its passion could no longer grapple with realities, and all it knew was that there had been most dismal death. Misery more than man could endure was quaking at his heart—but his reason was so shaken, that it lost hold of the cause why of all God's creatures on this wretched earth he should be the most wretched, and thus ordered out for ever and ever into the haunted wilderness.

There came a pause to his agony, and lifting up his eyes, once more he knew the heavens, and wept. Then the image of his child lay before him, with its face looking up to all those glorious luminaries, and he remembered that she was dead. His seat was a gravestone—the shadows of the church-tower lay across the moonlight burial-ground—and the far-off mysterious murmur of midnight was as a sound from another world.

Then arose, in the silence of that lonesome church-yard, the clamour of a grief that knew not how great it was till, far away from human voice and eye, it thus poured itself forth like a torrent, sounding along when all living things were asleep. All the blessings that Providence had bestowed,—so many, so pure, so high, and so undeserved,—were now all forgotten, or remembered in bitterness of [23] spirit, almost with an upbraiding ingratitude. "What means the goodness of God, since he has gathered all his gifts into one, and then destroyed them all by one dread decree? Better, oh better far, that she had never been born,—that smiles such as hers had never been, since they have all passed away,—that mine eyes had never seen her kneeling in prayer,—that——Oh, thou great, and thou dreadful God! is her voice indeed mute for ever?—Can it be that our Emmeline is dead,—and soon, soon to be buried among these hideous tombstones?" He dashed himself down on a cold stone slab, green with the mosses of many years, and writhing like a wounded worm, muttered curses on his existence, supplications for pardon, wailings for the dead, and prayers in behalf of her over whom, although he now knew it not, God had thrown the mantle of a profound sleep, out of which she was to awake in perfect resignation, even with her only child lying a corpse in her bosom!

A shadow moved over the church-yard, there was a sound as of steps, and the miserable man felt himself in the presence of some one whom he could not yet discern.—The feeling of that presence disarmed his grief,—something like shame for his weakness blended with the recollection of its rueful cause,—and starting to his feet, by a sudden effort of self-command he prepared himself to be seen and spoken to by one of his fellow christians. The figure of an old man stood close beside him, and he at once recognized the solemn countenance of him who had been [24] praying to his daughter on her death-bed. It seemed as if tears were in those aged eyes; pity overspread all his features, pity was in his locks white as the snow, pity trembled in his folded hands, and pity bent down that body more even than the weight of three-score-and-ten years. "My son, this is a sacred place, and God will to the prayers of a contrite heart send down peace from heaven—even the Holy Ghost, the Comforter. I bid thee to be of good cheer,—for where can mortal creatures like us so feel the vanity of sorrow as in the field of graves?" There was a long silence, during which the heavens became more serene, each large lustrous star seeming nearer to the earth, and the solitary church-yard to be received into the very bosom of the sky. The soul of the bereaved father felt its immortality; and the dreadful darkness rolled off from the decrees of Providence. The mystery of the dream of life grew more supportable; and he thought he heard the voice of an angel singing a hymn. Well known and dearly beloved was that voice! For many blessed years it had been heard amidst the shadow and sunshine of this earth: but now it wavered away far off into the blue celestial depths, murmuring a holy, almost a joyful, farewell.

The old man bent over his son and wept. "O father, for by that name from youth upwards have I loved to call thee, join with me in humblest supplication to heaven for pardon of my mad impiety!" They knelt down together,—he, that grey-headed man, [25] who had long been familiar with sorrow, and well acquainted with grief, and he that had never before bowed down at the bidding of a broken heart. The sighing and the sobbing were now all from the breast of him who had seemed unassailable to earthly troubles. Drenched were his wrinkled cheeks with tears, and he bowed his white hairs down even to the flowers that smiled in the moonlight on a grassy grave.

"O my son! pray thou also for thy poor old father! for know that only a few hours before I left my home to pray by little Emmeline's bed, my own daughter,—the sole daughter of my age,—was called away from me,—my Lucy lies like thy Emmeline—no more—no more than dust!"

O the great goodness, and the exceeding love of the human heart, that all life-long has been under the inspiration of a heaven-born faith! Utterly desolate was now the house of this aged minister of religion;—no one now to accompany him on his evening walk;—to read the chapter at morning and evening prayer;—to watch the daily change that steals over the face and the frame of him who had nearly reached the hill-foot of his pilgrimage; and to close his eyes at last when willingly they shall have become blind to this weary world!

The son now laid himself down at his father's feet, and in tenderest and most reverential embracement, bathed them in contrite tears. It was now his turn to be the comforter; and in that awful trance, his own [26] affliction changed into a sadness near akin to peace. He remembered that God chasteneth those he loves; the image of his wife, so beautiful in her resignation, and at that very hour cheered and strengthened by dreams sent from heaven, was brought suddenly before him; the promises contained in the Book of Life, holier and firmer far than any vows that can ever breathe from the lips of creatures of the clay, became embodied in those scriptural expressions so charged with love divine; and between the place where he and his father now stood, once more tranquil and without a groan, and the light of all those glorious stars and constellations, appeared for a moment the Shadow of a Cross.

The old man was the first to speak, and after that short fit of passion, his soul had subsided into the habitual and holy calm that broods over the declining years of the pious. Old age, too, by a gracious dispensation of Providence, becomes subdued in all its affections. Intense emotion it can contemplate with quiet sympathy in others; but when standing on the confines of another world, rightly considers all such emotion in its own case vanity of vanities. The past is as a painful or a pleasant dream; the future is felt to be the sole reality. He had parted with his daughter for a little while, and why should that little while be disturbed, blending as it was perceptibly with the dawning of an eternal day? "We shall meet, my son, on the sabbath-day, in the house of God. One funeral sermon will suffice for them both—your Emme- [27] line and my Lucy—few tears now have I to shed,—you may have many,—let them flow freely at morning and evening sacrifice."

Again and again they embraced one another with mutual benedictions; and then parted, each on the way to his own dwelling; the old man into the gloom of the upper glen, and his son away down the light that bathed the vale widening towards the plain and the sea.

Title

Galt, John. "The Witch." LS 1827. 97-102. [97]

THE WITCH.
BY JOHN GALT, ESQ.

They talk ignorantly of human nature who regard the abolished crime of witchcraft as having had its origin in the phantasma of superstition. Nothing is more common in the management of mankind than to see persons who, from having felt deference paid to their mental superiority, have assumed to themselves the prerogative of governing others by their dicta, rather than by the reasonable exercise of their understandings. In such assumption or arrogance consists the criminality of witchcraft—a crime as old as humanity, and as eternal as power and imbecility in the faculties of man. The following little anecdote is a demonstration of the moral theorem here propounded.

About the end of the reign of King James the First of Great Britain, a matronly woman of the name of Rebecca Swarth came to reside in the village of Stoke-Regis. Her appearance was rather, but in no remark [98] able degree, above her apparent condition. Some said she had surely been a gentlewoman; others were of opinion that her husband had been an apothecary; and the whole community of the village were somewhat surprised that she did not practise as a midwife. She lived, however, among them many years, avoiding the observation which she was evidently conscious of having attracted. During the whole period her manners were mild but reserved, and her conduct and deportment singularly unexceptionable.

This friendless and forlorn person at last became old; her means, from whatever source derived, whether from the industry with which she plied her own distaff, or from any undivulged source, gradually diminished, till she became almost a mendicant. She was not entirely so, because her wasted form, and the variety of wretchedness exhibited in her patched and unrenewed attire, attracted the charity she required without any solicitation on her part. She did not beg, she was only helped.

One day, it was in January, and after many stormy days of sleet and shower, she came to the door of Alice Thorwald, a neighbour, and requested the loan of a little meal or flour. Alice at the time was busy fondling her child, and answered the request—which was modestly enough made—harshly. Rebecca repeated it, and received a still more ungracious reply. Rebecca a third time begged the little loan of which she stood, as she said, really in great need; but the third answer was [99] still less kind than the former two, and she was told to apply elsewhere; "for," said Alice Thorwald, "I have something else to do with my dear child than to heed such applications."

Rebecca Swarth made no immediate reply, but drawing her cloak close around her, she looked sternly at Alice for a short space of time, and then replied—"Well as you love, or think you love, that darling, beware of the harm you are doomed to do to it!"

When the old woman had retired her words recoiled upon Alice, and when Eben Thorwald returned home in the evening Alice mentioned to him the occurrence and the malediction, for so she had felt it, of Rebecca Swarth.

Eben was of a gloomy frame of feeling, strong in resolution, and withal disposed to the worship of superiority, however constituted. He was naturally suspicious, and not untinctured with envy; hence, either from antipathy or from the effect of some experienced slight, he at once disliked Rebecca Swarth, and was awed by her sagacity.

He caused Alice, his wife, to repeat to him the malediction; he pondered on its intimation; he thought he could discern in it something of more than met the ear:—he stripped the child naked,—carefully examined all its body,—could find no mark of scathe upon its skin; and he finally concluded that if there were any power in the bodement, the evil thereof was to fall upon Alice.

Alice laughed at this conclusion, and for some time [101] afterwards no change was observable in her conduct; but in the end Eben saw, or thought he saw, that she did not treat the child with her wonted affection, and chided her for the neglect, reminding her at the same time of Rebecca Swarth's prophecy.

Alice, disturbed by his exhortations, affected to fondle and caress the baby ten times more than she would otherwise have done, till her anxiety grew to habitude, and all her neighbours spoke to her, and marvelled at the inordinate and foolish fondness for the child with which she embittered both her own life and that of her husband.—Eben himself became impatient at her exclusive endearments, and one day bethought, as a remedy to check the morbid affection of Alice, to apply to Rebecca Swarth for advice.

"Your wife," said Rebecca, "has had a dream or an omen, that has told her she is ordained to do mischief to the child."

From that moment Eben felt himself irresistibly drawn to watch the conduct of Alice. The hand of fate had indeed laid hold of him;—he felt it—he trembled;—but he could not shake it off.

One night, while he was observing Alice watching the baby as it lay asleep in its cradle, he saw, or fancied he saw, the fondness with which she was hanging over it suddenly change, and a ghastly and haggard expression supplant the wonted maternal benignity of her countenance.

"You so worship that child," said he, as if willing to be disenchanted from the impression which her agitation had produced,—"you so worship it, that one might think you make much of it in order to hide some intent to do it harm."

Alice burst into tears, and wept with impassioned grief over the child, who, awakened by her sobs, smiled at her sorrow.

    Eben was overawed at the effect of his remark, and endeavoured to soothe her with all his kindness; but his feelings received an irrecoverable shock when she informed him that she had one night dreamt a dream, in which she saw Rebecca Swarth come to her bedside with a knife in her hand, and heard her say—"cut the thread!" "From that hour," continued the comfortless Alice, "I have often seen a shadowy hand, holding a bloody knife, hovering over the cradle,—and the hand is like my own hand——"

    *   *   *   *   *   *

    These strange circumstances, after the execution of his infatuated wife, Eben Thorwald told to the rector, who caused Rebecca Swarth to be apprehended as a witch.—She was cast into prison, and several times examined; but no proof could be produced that she was in any way concerned in the murder of the child for which Alice had suffered;—Alice had confessed, when seized with the knife in her hand, that she had done the deed herself, from the instigations of a power whose dominion she knew not, [102] and whose influence she could not resist. But the poor old, forlorn, and wretched Rebecca's strength was soon exhausted. On her third examination she confessed herself a witch, and the worthy clergymen interrogated her as to the manner of her intercourse with the devil, and piously enquired what benefit she had derived for having sold to him her eternal jewel. "The end of my sufferings," was her only answer.

    The spot where she was burnt may yet be seen on the common: it is still bare and covered with ashes. Some say no bird ever alights on the ground there. The sheep nibble at a distance from it, so that it is as much distinguished by the rank growth of the herbage around as by the blackness of the ashes where she was consumed.

Title
R., E. [Roberts, Emma.] "The Bridal of St. Omer. A Tale." LS 1827. 145-163.
[145]

THE BRIDAL OF ST. OMER.
A TALE.

JACQUELINE folded up her embroidery, and sighed as she deposited the work in a drawer of an antique cabinet which stood in her chamber; for her hitherto obedient needle refused to trace those flowers which were wont to spring up beneath her creative fingers. She wandered into the garden, but its plants and blossoms no longer delighted her; the sickly tints of autumn had saddened the face of nature, and every surrounding object reminded her of her own faded hopes. Returning into the house, she sate down, and listened with anxious yet despairing ear for some stir or tumult, betokening the arrival of news; but no unusual sound disturbed the calm of the silent streets. The French soldiers basking in the sun in the front of their guard-room, now and then broke the stillness by snatches of old tunes, a fragment of some ancient romance chaunted to a national air, or the light laugh which occasionally followed a jest uttered in too low a tone to be heard beyond their own [146] circle. It was evident, from the careless gaiety of these men, that although the king of England was laying siege to Boulogne, they had no fear of being disturbed in the fortress so fraudulently wrested by Louis XI., the predecessor of the present monarch of France, from the house of Burgundy. Jacqueline's melancholy thoughts naturally turned upon the fallen fortunes of that luckless family. She herself retained a lively recollection of the beautiful orphan heiress, the Princess Mary, at the period of her deep distress, when, by the death of her gallant father, Charles the Bold Duke of Burgundy, she was left to the mercy of the factious citizens of Ghent, and exposed to the hostility of her most inveterate enemy, the cruel and crafty Louis. Jacqueline's heart burned with indignation as she reflected upon the disgraceful reverses which the Burgundians had sustained, from the period of their gallant sovereign's last fatal campaign in Germany; and she marvelled at the supineness displayed by Maximilian, in suffering the territories of his wife and her son (to whom, upon the decease of Mary, he had been constituted guardian) to remain in subjugation to the crown of France. The maiden gazed upon her delicate white hands as they hung listlessly over the arms of a high-backed chair on which she was reclining, and wished that they could be endowed with a giant's strength, to burst the fetters imposed by foreign power. She thought upon the heroic deeds achieved at Orleans by a frame as weak, and she almost fancied [147] that she could welcome the fate of Joan of Arc, to be, like her, the deliverer of her country. Suddenly the French guard sprang up from their recumbent attitudes, and the ponderous mail of the men at arms clashed as they rose in haste to salute their commanding officer, Count Bertrand de Montmorenci, the governor of St. Omer. For a moment Jacqueline hoped that he brought intelligence of the approach of the English or the Burgundians; that Boulogne had fallen, and that the town was threatened by a hostile force; but this expectation was soon dissipated: a few trifling orders, given with his usual affectation, sufficed to display the soldier's attention to his military duties. In another moment she heard the boisterous and hearty greetings offered by her father, and the interview was inevitable.

Ushered into the apartment by his friendly but unpolished host, Count Bertrand, attired in the extreme of the last Parisian fashion, advanced to pay his respects to the provincial rustic whose beauty and whose wealth had attracted him despite her country breeding. Jacqueline was an inattentive listener to her noble admirer's florid compliments, and little interested in the account of the hoods and wimples, the long training gowns, and flowing head-dresses, worn by the gay dames of the French capital, since she never desired to exchange her national costume for foreign vanities; and was only roused to animation when the conversation turned upon the politics of the day. [148]

"The English have forgotten the art of war," cried Montmorenci, "or love to fight only upon their own soil. A French herald is now in their camp, and when he can strike a bargain with these trading islanders our master will be free to pursue his conquests in Italy."

"And where then is Maximilian?" exclaimed Jacqueline; "will he look tamely on, and see the only chance of recovering his son's inheritance bartered away for a few paltry pieces of gold?"

"Know ye not," returned Montmorenci, "that the German beast is dull and slow of foot? Where was the recreant knight when Charles VIII. carried away his affianced bride, the heiress of Bretagne? Where is he now, when he should spur on his English allies to action? Engaged in some pitiful broil at home, he keeps aloof, giving Henry of Lancaster an excuse to follow his own sordid inclinations, and gather ducats instead of laurels in his wars."

Jacqueline, was grieved and angry at this disdainful mention of the king of the Romans, but felt that the reproach was but too just; she therefore remained silent, listening with wounded ear to the remarks of her father, who, devoted to France, rejoiced over the declining state of the Burgundian affairs.

Arnold von Rothfels, though descended from a noble family, had soiled his fingers by trade. His love of gain had in the first instance overcome his pride; but-a latent spark still existing in his breast, he was dazzled by the [149] prospect of uniting his daughter in marriage with the heir of the illustrious house of Montmorenci. The brilliant expectations which Count Bertrand's offer held out, effected an entire revolution in Arnold's sentiments. He forgot that he was by birth a Fleming; that he owed allegiance to the Duke of Burgundy; and that he had promised the hand of Jacqueline to one of Maximilian's most trusty knights, Maurice Waldenheim, the son of a deceased friend. The memory of the fair heiress of Von Rothfels was, however, more tenacious; she fondly recalled those happy days which she had spent at the court of Margaret, the dowager duchess of Burgundy, where Maurice Waldenheim had carried off the prizes at the tournaments, and laid them at her feet; and where she had embroidered a fair blue banner as the reward of his prowess, which the young soldier vowed, during a solemn banquet at which Maximilian carved the pheasant in person, should wave in proud victory over the French standard, now so exultingly floating above the towers of St. Omer. It was not in the power of the finical and haughty Montmorenci to banish these tender reminiscences. Jacqueline believed that her lover would religiously perform every iota of his promise; and there was little danger that her patriotic feelings would be subdued by the representations of Von Rothfels, of the superior advantages to be derived from living under the French dominion, while they were associated with the image of Maurice Waldenheim. [150]

    Count Bertrand, after he had sufficiently betrayed his contempt for both father and daughter, which, notwithstanding his pretended deference to the latter, was exceedingly obvious to Jacqueline's discriminating mind, at length took his leave; and, depressed in spirits by the assurance of a speedy peace between France and England, the object of this accomplished courtier's unwelcome homage threw a mantle around her, and ascending the ramparts, endeavoured, in the charms of the adjacent scenery, to dissipate those unpleasant sensations which clouded a mind until now a stranger to sorrow. The sun was still high in the heavens, and the whole landscape was bathed in its golden glories: it lit up the towers of Dunkirk and of Calais, as they rose to the right and left on the distant coast; threw an effulgent blaze of light upon the yellow sands between Dunkirk and Gravelines, and cast a strong illumination upon the dark walls of that gloomy fortress. The woods of Cassell were deeply embrowned with the hues of autumn, and a tempestuous night had stripped the trees which skirted the broad road across the flat country leading to the Netherlands so completely of their foliage, that every object proceeding from that quarter might be discerned at a considerable distance. It was the least interesting part of the landscape, yet thither Jacqueline continually directed her eyes: all was silent and solitary: vainly did she seek for the flash of the polished lance in the sun, and the waving of plumes and pennons: the naked [151] branches of the trees alone met her view, or showers of dead leaves, borne by the breeze, swept like small clouds through the empty space. Wearied with watching, she bent her steps to a home no longer sacred to felicity. A painful scene awaited the gentle girl. Unaccustomed to dispute a parent's will, she could only oppose tears and entreaties to the stern behest of Von Rothfels, when he commanded her to receive the Count de Montmorenci as her destined husband. She wept and prayed unavailingly, and her sole hope of escaping a union which she abhorred, rested in the speedy fulfilment of Waldenheim's oath. Jacqueline trusted that a token dispatched by a wandering minstrel to the Burgundian knight had made him acquainted with her perilous situation; and soothing her terrors with the fond idea that love would discover the means of preserving her from a fate she dreaded, she sought her couch, and obtained a transient oblivion from the cares which oppressed her burthened heart.

The next day, at the hour in which Montmorenci was engaged with the troops under his command, Jacqueline again repaired to the battlements, and again turned her expectant eyes towards the road leading to the Netherlands. An occasional traveller, a herd of cattle, or a peasant conveying the produce of his farm to market, were for some time the only objects that enlivened the scene. Still she continued to gaze; and just as the declining sun warned her of her long absence from home, her parting glance caught the gleam of spears in the dis- [152] tance. She paused,—looked again,—she was not deceived; and presently a body of archers and men at arms, accompanied by a squadron of *landznechts*, made their appearance, defiling in good order between the trees. Jacqueline's heart beat high. From the direction in which these soldiers marched, she had little doubt of their being Burgundians, led perchance by Waldenheim. In another instant she became convinced of the truth of her surmise; for, extended by a light breeze to its utmost length, the blue banner streamed along the martial line. Hope,—exultation,—joy,—sparkled in her eyes, and thrilled through her frame; but a chilling damp checked these delightful emotions, as with a feeling of bitter disappointment she contemplated the small number of warriors who followed Waldenheim's standard. Yet again was despondency banished from her sanguine breast, when she reflected that it was probably only the advanced guard who were now approaching the town; and if this brave band should dare attack, unsupported, a fortress rendered unusually strong both by nature and art, still fortune might and would befriend adventurous spirits, or all that she had read of desperate enterprises crowned with glorious success were false and deceitful legends, idle dreams, treacherously framed to betray the trusting heart to ruin.

The garrison of St. Omer soon caught the alarm; and Jacqueline, compelled to retire from the walls, heard only that a trumpet,—for Waldenheim's armament did not [153] boast a herald,—had arrived before the gate of St. Omer, formally demanding the surrender of the town in the name of Maximilian, a requisition which had been received with a laugh of deriding scorn.

The Burgundians pitched their tents at a convenient distance from the outworks, and made preparations for a regular siege. All was bustle and activity within the town; every street was filled with the din of arms; squires and lacqueys were seen burnishing the steel cuirass and the polished helm; the clink of the armourers' hammers resounded from all quarters; and soldiers hurrying to and fro hastened to relieve each other on the walls.

Suffering every alternation of bounding hope and the most chilling despair, Jacqueline, restless, anxious, impatient, now revolving some impracticable scheme of affording assistance to the besiegers, in the next moment sickening at the impossibility of becoming an active agent in their service, could only still the tumultuous sensations of her throbbing heart by prayer. She flew to the neighbouring cathedral, and poured forth her whole soul in supplication before the shrine of the virgin, listening, at the conclusion of every Ave, for the brazen roar of those dreadful engines which she concluded the enemy would bring to bear against the strong bulwarks of the fortress. But her vigil was not rewarded by the thunder of the deep-mouthed gun. Waldenheim then—and her heart panted with redoubled emotion at the thought—would venture to attack the walls armed only with the arrow, the battle-axe, and [154] the lance; a momentary thrill of terror shot across her mind, but it was instantly dissipated; she could not link the idea of defeat with the stout Burgundian soldier, and she rejoiced at a circumstance which would enhance the glory of his victory. Despite of these heroic feelings, Jacqueline could not contemplate the thought of the ghastly objects which she would, in all probability, encounter in her return home without horror; she feared to meet some mangled remnant of mortality borne, writhing in convulsive anguish, from the walls; to see blood flowing that she could not staunch, and to hear the deep groans wrung by torturing agony from a soul struggling in the pangs of death. Whilst absorbed in these painful anticipations, a burst of merriment greeted her astonished ear; the soldiers who had rushed in the morning to man the walls were returning leisurely to their quarters unhurt, not with the shout of triumph which would have followed a successful engagement, but humming, as usual, the lays of the Troubadours.

Annoyed and confounded by this unlooked for result of a day which she confidently expected would have been marked by some signal event, Jacqueline sought her own home. Montmorenci stood smiling at the portal, his dainty white plume unsoiled, and not a single fold disarranged in the silken mantle which flowed gracefully over his stainless and undinted armour.

"In faith, fair lady," he exclaimed, "these awkward Burgundians have played us a clumsy joke, doubtless the [155] braggart knaves think it a fine thing to have detained a cavalier of France for the space of six hours in harness under a hot sun, but, pardie, a warm bath and a little Hungary water will repair the damage."

"Did not Walden—, did not the enemy," returned Jacqueline, correcting her hasty speech, "make any attempt to scale the walls."

"No," cried Montmorenci, "nor did they adventure within a bow-shot of the garrison. By mine honour and St. Denis, if the Lombards give us not exercise for our good swords, they are like to grow rusty in these campaigns with the English and their timorous allies."

"So thought the Mareschal des Cordes," said Jacqueline, rather scornfully, "yet the fall of Dixmude taught him another lesson. This is but a feint of the besiegers to draw you out into the open field, for never yet did the Burgundian chivalry quail before the arms of France."

Hastening up to her chamber, Jacqueline relieved her full heart by a flood of tears. Though persuading herself that the craven conduct displayed by Waldenheim's soldiers was prompted by some deep-laid artifice, yet she could not avoid feeling very painful misgivings. The force which her lover had brought against St. Omer was certainly inadequate for the capture of so strong a town; Maurice would, perchance, imagine that he had redeemed his pledge by merely appearing before the frowning ramparts, and had probably no intention of endangering either life or limb in her service. Nothing disturbed the [156] tranquillity of the besieged during the following day; the anxious maiden saw Montmorenci armed at all points, preparing to make a sortie on the foe, and, from an upper window, she watched him as he returned in the same gallant array, not a feather broken from the plume that waved over his casque, his armour without spot or blemish, and his mantle still undisordered and stainless. Pleading a head-ache Jacqueline refused to join the count and her father, and thus was spared the disgraceful taunts which the haughty Frenchman cast upon a knight once ranked among the flower of Maximilian's chivalry.

Two more days elapsed, and, perceiving that de Montmorenci no longer led his soldiers in person to the ramparts, the now desponding Jacqueline emerged from her seclusion to learn the cause.

"The Burgundians have retreated?" said she, as she saw Count Bertrand lounging idly in her father's hall.

"Not so," replied Montmorenci, "they tilt with the air in yonder plain, taking especial care to keep beyond the reach of our cross-bows; come to the walls and you shall see the cooks and scullions of St. Omer, armed with their spits and basting ladles, drive these redoubtable assailants like a flock of geese before them to the entrenchments of their camp."

"I will not," cried Jacqueline, "do the soldiers of Maximilian so much wrong as to witness so base an indignity."

"Then," exclaimed Montmorenci, "I will condescend [157] to lead the attack again, trusting that the animating sight of beauty may inspire the degenerate Waldenheim with the spirit of a knight. To stir the lazy current of a dastard's veins, and to kindle a blaze of martial ardor in a clod of mere dull earth, will be an exploit worthy of the loveliest maid who ever smiled upon a warrior's suit." The count then calling for his armour, sallied out at the gate as Jacqueline ascended the rampart.

The plain below was enlivened with the careering steeds of Waldenheim's men at arms, as, with pennons flying and trumpets sounding, they advanced to the walls. The long blue banner floated majestically over the well-appointed troop; and its fair embroideress, as she contemplated the martial appearance of her lover's followers, again felt her hopes revive, and stood in strong expectation that they would on this day wipe off the deep stain which sullied their honour: but her wishes and her prayers were alike fruitless; the Burgundians awaited not the shock of de Montmorenci's battle-axe; he no sooner approached them, than, like affrighted deer, away ran the whole of the squadron, Waldenheim foremost in the disgraceful flight, and the blue banner trailing in the dust behind him. The heart of the knight's betrothed beat high with indignation. Had she beheld her lover fairly vanquished in open fight she would have felt respect and admiration for him in his defeat; but to see him act a coward's part, retreating thus dishonoured without daring to hazard a single blow, she could not endure the shame, [158]the ignominy of such a spectacle. Oh! rather, much rather, would she have gazed upon his bleeding corse borne from the field, secure, in a warrior's death, from the reproach which now must cling to his name for ever. Jacqueline's heroism, and her affection alike, failed her in this trial. Had Waldenheim acquitted himself like a soldier, or even like a man, the convent or a grave would have afforded her an asylum from the hated Montmorenci; but while she brooded over his fall from honour, her resolution was shaken; she could not wound, or, perchance, break a doting parent's heart, for the sake of one so worthless, so utterly undeserving love which should only be lavished on the brave: and, though she would have gladly buried herself and her sorrows in a monastery, duty forbade the indulgence of her wishes, and, with a dejected air, streaming eyes, and listless steps, she returned to her home, listened with mute indifference to the addresses of Count Bertrand, and allowed her father to promise that she would meet him at the altar at the expiration of six days, without offering a dissentient word.

  Nothing was heard of the Burgundians, and if a faint spark of hope was ever re-kindled in Jacqueline's breast, it was now entirely quenched. Vainly did returning love suggest an excuse for Waldenheim's conduct, or endeavour to point at the means by which he might retrieve a reputation now sunk below scorn; he had refused to meet Count Bertrand singly in the field, and even if at the head of a reinforcement he should, at some future [159] period, triumph over the arms of France, such a victory could not efface the indelible stain of cowardice, the disgrace branded upon him in that fatal retreat before the paltry force brought out by Montmorenci to oppose him. Jacqueline prepared for her approaching marriage,—for the sacrifice of every chance of happiness,—with a feeling of melancholy satisfaction. She knew that she was condemned to be the slave of a tyrannical and contemptuous husband; to misery which, under any other circumstances, would have been too bitter for endurance; but now, perfectly reckless of the destiny that awaited her, she experienced some consolation in the thought that the morbid feelings and blighted affections of a joyless heart would not destroy the happiness of one who, in seeking her reluctant hand, only strove to enrich himself. Could jewels and splendid apparel have reconciled Jacqueline to her fate, she must have been perfectly content. The taste and the magnificence of Count Bertrand were lavishly displayed in the bridal paraphernalia, and every citizen of St. Omer was employed under his immediate inspection in executing some new and brilliant device. The hour of midnight was appointed for the celebration of the nuptials, and the spirits of the bride sank as the time approached; a thousand tender recollections crowded upon her mind, and subdued the stern determination which had hitherto supported her. As noon advanced she stole away from her garden, and, under the friendly screen of a tall buttress, cast an anxious glance towards the Burgundian [160] camp. But nothing, save the long grass and the boughs of the naked trees, was stirring in that quarter; the rampart, on which she stood was deserted; a postern gate left negligently open, and the guard dispersed about the town, surveying the preparations for the evening festivities. Jacqueline felt strongly tempted to seize the favourable moment for escape, and to fly from a union which, despite of all her efforts, she regarded with horror. Where, however, could she go, and for whom should she forfeit the treasure of an unstained name? Alas! Waldenheim was unworthy of the sacrifice; he had abandoned her, or, if still lingering in the vicinity of St. Omer, was too indifferent even to reconnoitre the place, and to take advantage of the carelessness of the garrison to communicate with one so ready to listen to his justification, and to discredit the evidence of her senses against the warm and eloquent pleadings of the man she loved. Successfully combating her weakness, the afflicted Jacqueline quitted the dangerous spot and sought for protection from her own rebellious heart under the paternal roof. Evening came, and with it the bride-maids and tire-women; the rich and massy chain, the satin robe lined with costly furs, the broidery of goldsmith's work, and the sparkling circlet inlaid with pearl and precious stones, vainly courted admiration from their unhappy wearer's averted and tearful eyes; but, rallying her failing energies, she prepared to accompany the procession to the church, and, nerving her trembling limbs, advanced towards the altar with an unfaltering step; but [161] there Jacqueline's courage and fortitude melted away; she feared that she had been too precipitate in breaking those vows so solemnly pledged to Waldenheim, and she would have given worlds to have recalled the promise she had made to her father. The nave of the cathedral was brilliantly illuminated, but the vast edifice presented many distant aisles and extensive recesses involved in deep gloom, and, as her eyes wandered restlessly around, she almost fancied she could perceive the frowning countenance of the man she had forsaken in each dark and empty space. 'Twas only the vision of a distempered imagination. The light danced upon waving plumes, glittering tunics, and faces beaming with joy. Pleasure seemed to rule the hour, and Jacqueline alone, pale, sad, and motionless, offered a contrast to the gay throng who crowded round the steps of the altar. The ceremony was about to commence, the officiating priest had opened his missal, and the bridegroom, anticipating the moment in which he should place the ring on the finger of the bride, had stretched out his hand to clasp that of his trembling companion, when a whisper ran through the outer circle: a short pause ensued, but the alarm, if such it were, subsided; all was profoundly quiet, and the solemnity commenced. In another instant, a shout, a din of arms, groans, shrieks, and cries of terror, were distinctly heard; but ere the bridal party could look around them, all other sounds were stifled in one wild acclamation. The [162] doors of the church were burst open, and the whole of the interior filled with Burgundian soldiers: numbers of the wedding guests were stretched bleeding on the ground; de Montmorenci, torn from Jacqueline's side, would have fallen a sacrifice to the fury of four assailants, but for the opportune appearance of Waldenheim, who, springing from a monument over the heads of his *landznechts*, interposed his authority, and stayed the work of devastation.

"Now, Count Bertrand," he cried; "now shall my trusty sword vindicate the honour which you have dared to stigmatize; we meet on equal terms:" and throwing off his helmet, his coat of mail, and all other defensive armour (the bridegroom being arrayed in a vest and surcoat of velvet), the two knights drew their gleaming falchions, and encountered each other with deadly animosity;—fire flew from their clashing weapons, and every stroke seemed the herald of death. Jacqueline, speechless and clinging to her father's arm, gazed, with intense anxiety, on the sanguinary conflict. Both fought with untiring and desperate energy; at length the arm of the Burgundian appeared to relax, but, in the next moment, he charged again with redoubled fierceness, and Montmorenci, disarmed and beaten to the ground, received the boon of life from his generous antagonist. The terror-stricken bride saw not the termination of the combat; her senses fled ere Waldenheim had gained the vantage ground which he had so nearly lost, and she was only [163] restored to animation by the passionate exclamations of her lover, and the assurance that Bertrand still lived.

The strenuous exertions of Waldenheim preserved the town from pillage. On the following morning, after a solemn mass, he offered the blue banner at the altar of the cathedral, and received the hand of Jacqueline, who was now convinced that, with his slender force, it was only by lulling the garrison into security that he could have hoped to win the strong towers of St. Omer.

E.R.

Title

Croker, Thomas Crofton. "Clough Na Cuddy. A Killarney Legend." LS 1827. 233-243. [233]

CLOUGH NA CUDDY.
A Killarney Legend.
BY T. CROFTON CROKER, ESQ.

Above all the islands in the Lakes of Killarney, give ma Innisfallen—"sweet Innisfallen," as the melodious Moore calls it. It is in truth a fairy isle, although I have no fairy story to tell you about it; and if I had, these are such unbelieving times, and people of late have grown so sceptical, that they only smile at my stories and doubt them.

However, none will doubt that a monastery once stood upon Innisfallen island, for its ruins may still be seen; neither, that within its Walls dwelt certain pious and learned persons called monks. A very pleasant set of fellows they were, I make not the smallest doubt; and I am sure of this, that they had a very pleasant spot to enjoy themselves in after dinner:—the proper time, believe me, and I am no bad judge of such matters, for the enjoyment of a fine prospect.

Out of all the monks you could not pick a better fellow [234] nor a merrier soul than Father Cuddy;—he sang a good song, he told a good story, and had a jolly, comfortable looking paunch of his own that was a credit to any refectory table. He was distinguished above all the rest by the name of "the fat Father." Now there are many that will take huff at a name; but Father Cuddy had no nonsense of that kind about him; he laughed at it, and well able he was to laugh, for his mouth nearly reached from one ear to the other,—his might, in truth, be called an open countenance. As his paunch was no disgrace to his food, neither was his nose to his drink. Tis a question to me if there were not more carbuncles upon it than ever were seen at the bottom of the lake, which is said to be full of them. His eyes had a right merry twinkle in them, like moonshine dancing on the water, and his cheeks had the roundness and crimson glow of ripe arbutus berries.
He eat, and drank, and prayed, and slept,—what then?
He eat, and drank, and prayed, and slept again!

Such was the tenor of his simple life; but when he prayed a certain drowsiness would come upon him, which it must be confessed never occurred when a well-filled "black-jack" stood before him. Hence his prayers were short, and his draughts were long. The world loved him, and he saw no reason why he should not in return love its venison and its usquebaugh. But, as times went, he must have been a pious man, or else what befel him never would have happened. [235]

Spiritual affairs—for it was respecting the importation of a tun of wine into the island monastery demanded the presence of one of the brotherhood of Innisfallen at the abbey of Irelagh, now called Muckruss. The superintendance of this important matter was committed to Father Cuddy, who felt too deeply interested in the future welfare of any community of which he was a member to neglect or delay such mission. With the morning's light he was seen guiding his shallop across the crimson waters of the lake towards the peninsula of Muckruss, and having moored his little bark in safety beneath the shelter of a wave-worn rock, he advanced with becoming dignity towards the abbey.

The stillness of the bright and balmy hour was broken by the heavy footsteps of the zealous father:—at the sound the startled deer, shaking the dew from their sides, sprang up from their lair, and as they bounded off—"Hah," exclaimed Cuddy, "what a noble haunch goes there!—how delicious it would look smoking upon a goodly platter."

As he proceeded, the mountain bee hummed his tune of gladness around the holy man, save when buried in the fox-glove bell, or revelling upon a fragrant bunch of thyme,--and even then, the little voice murmured out happiness in low and broken tones of voluptuous delight. Father Cuddy derived no small comfort from the sound, for it presaged a good metheglin season; and metheglin he considered, if well manufactured, to be no bad liquor, [236] particularly when there was no stint of usquebaugh in the brewing.

Arrived within the abbey garth, he was received with due respect by the brethren of Irelagh, and arrangements for the embarkation of the wine were completed to his entire satisfaction.—"Welcome, Father Cuddy!" said the prior, "grace be on you."

"Grace before meat then," said Cuddy, "for a long walk always makes me hungry, and I am certain I have not walked less than half a mile this morning, to say nothing of crossing the water."

A pasty of choice flavour felt the truth of this assertion as regarded Father Cuddy's appetite. After such consoling repast, it would have been a reflection on monastic hospitality to have departed without partaking of the grace-cup:—moreover, Father Cuddy had a particular respect for the antiquity of that custom. He liked the taste of the grace-cup well;—he tried another,—it was no less excellent; and when he had swallowed the third he found his heart expand, and put forth its fibres, as willing to embrace all mankind!—Surely then there is christian love and charity in wine!

I said he sung a good song. Now though psalms are good songs, and in accordance with his vocation, I did not mean to imply that he was a mere psalm-singer. It was well known to the brethren, that wherever Father Cuddy was, mirth and melody were with him. Mirth in his eye, and melody on his tongue; and these, from [237] experience, are equally well known to be thirsty commodities; but he took good care never to let them run dry. To please the brotherhood, whose excellent wine pleased him, he sung, and as "*in vino veritas,*" his song will well become this veritable history.

"Quam pulchra sunt ova
Cum alba et nova
In stabulo scite leguntur;
Et a Margery bella
Quae festiva puella!
Lardi pinguis cum frustis coquuntur.

"Ut belles in prato
Aprico et lato
Sub sole tarn laete renident,
Ova tosta in mensa,
Mappa bene extensa
Nitidissima lance consident."

O 'tis eggs are a treat
When so white and so sweet
From under the manger they're taken;
And by fair Margery,
Och! 'tis she's full of glee,
They are fried with fat rashers of bacon.

Just like daisies all spread
O'er a broad sunny mead
In the sun-beams so beauteously shining,
Are fried eggs, well displayed
On a dish, when we've laid
The cloth, and are thinking of dining.
[238]

Such was his song. Father Cuddy smacked his lips at the recollection of Margery's delicious fried eggs, which always imparted a peculiar relish to his liquor. The very idea provoked Cuddy to raise the cup to his mouth, and, with one hearty pull thereat, he finished its contents.

This is, and ever was, a censorious world, often construing what is only a fair allowance into an excess;—but I scorn to reckon up any man's drink like an unrelenting host; therefore, I cannot tell how many brimming draughts of wine, bedecked with *the venerable Bead*, Father Cuddy emptied into his "soul-case,"—so he figuratively termed the body.

His respect for the goodly company of the monks of Irelagh detained him until their adjournment to vespers, when he set forward on his return to

Innisfallen. Whether his mind was occupied in philosophic contemplation or wrapped in pious musings, I cannot declare; but the honest Father wandered on in a different direction from that in which his shallop lay. Far be it from me to insinuate that the good liquor, which he had so commended, had caused him to forget his road, or that his track was irregular and unsteady. Oh no!—he carried his drink bravely, as became a decent man and a good christian; yet, somehow, he thought he could distinguish two moons. "Bless my eyes," said Father Cuddy, "everything is changing now a days!—the very stars are not in the same places they used to be;—I think *Camcéachta* (the plough) is driving on at a rate I never saw it before [239] to-night, but I suppose the driver is drunk, for there are blackguards everywhere."

Cuddy had scarcely uttered these words, when he saw, or fancied he saw, the form of a young woman; who, holding up a bottle, beckoned him towards her. The night was extremely beautiful, and the white dress of the girl floated gracefully in the moonlight, as with gay step she tripped on before the worthy rather, archly looking back upon him over her shoulder. "Ah, Margery,—merry Margery!"—cried Cuddy, "you tempting little rogue—*'Et a Margery bella—Quae festiva puella.'*—I see you—I see you and the bottle!—let me but catch you, Margery *bella*." And on he followed, panting and smiling, after this alluring apparition.

At length his feet grew weary, and his breath failed, which obliged him to give up the chace; yet such was his piety, that unwilling to rest in any attitude but that of prayer, down dropt Father Cuddy on his knees. Sleep as usual stole upon his devotions, and the morning was far advanced when he awoke from dreams, in which tables groaned beneath their load of viands, and wine poured itself free and sparkling as the mountain spring.

Rubbing his eyes, he looked about him, and the more he looked the more he wondered at the alterations which appeared in the face of the country. "Bless my soul and body," said the good Father, "I saw the stars changing last night, but here is a change!" Doubting his senses he looked again. The hills bore the same ma-[240]jestic outline as on the preceding day, and the lake spread itself beneath his view in the same tranquil beauty, and was studded with the same number of islands; but every smaller feature in the landscape was strangely altered;—what had been naked rocks, were now clothed with holly and arbutus. Whole woods had disappeared, and waste places had become cultivated fields; and, to complete the work of enchantment, the very season itself seemed changed. In the rosy dawn of a summer's morning he had left the monastery of Innisfallen, and he now felt in every sight and sound the dreariness of winter;—the hard ground was covered with withered leaves;—icicles depended from leafless branches;—lie heard the sweet low note of the robin who familiarly approached him, and he felt his fingers numbed by the nipping frost. Father Cuddy found it rather difficult to account for such sudden transformations, and to convince himself it was not the illusion of a dream, he was about to arise; when lo! he discovered that both his knees were buried at least six inches in the solid stone: for notwithstanding all these changes, he had never altered his devout position.

Cuddy was now wide awake, and felt, when he got up, his joints sadly cramped, which it was only natural they should be, considering the hard texture of the stone, and the depth his knees had sunk into it. The great difficulty was, to explain how, in one night, summer had become winter—whole woods had been cut down, and well-grown trees had sprouted up. The miracle, nothing else could [241] he conclude it to be, urged him to hasten his return to Innisfallen, where he might learn some explanation of these marvellous events.

Seeing a boat moored within reach of the shore, he delayed not, in the midst of such wonders, to seek his own bark, but, seizing the oars, pulled stoutly towards the island; and here new wonders awaited him.

Father Cuddy waddled, as fast as cramped limbs could carry his rotund corporation, to the gate of the monastery, where he loudly demanded admittance.

"Holloa! whence come you, master monk, and what's your business?" demanded a stranger who occupied the porter's place.

"Business—my business!" repeated the confounded Cuddy, "why do you not know me? Has the wine arrived safely?"

"Hence, fellow," said the porter's representative in a surly tone, "nor think to impose on me with your monkish tales."

"Fellow!" exclaimed the Father, "mercy upon us that I should be so spoken to at the gate of my own house!—Scoundrel!" cried Cuddy, raising his voice, "do you not see my garb—my holy garb?----"

"Ay, fellow," replied he of the keys, "the garb of laziness, and filthy debauchery, which has been expelled from out these walls. Know you not, idle knave, of the suppression of this nest of superstition, and that the abbey lands and possessions were granted in August last to [242] Master Robert Collan, by our Lady Elizabeth, sovereign queen of England, and paragon of all beauty, whom God preserve!"

"Queen of England," said Cuddy; "there never was a sovereign queen of England;—this is but a piece with the rest. I saw how it was going with the stars last night—the world's turned upside down. But surely this is Innisfallen Island, and I am the Father Cuddy who yesterday morning went over to the Abbey of Irelagh respecting the tun of wine. Do you know me now?"

"Know you! how should I know you?" said the keeper of the abbey—"yet true it is, that I have heard my grandmother, whose mother remembered the man, often speak of the fat Father Cuddy of Innisfallen, who made a profane and godless ballad in praise of fried eggs, of which he and his vile crew knew more than they did of the word of God, and who, being drunk, it was said, tumbled into the lake one night and was drowned; but that must have been a hundred—ay, more than a hundred years since."

"'Twas I who composed that song, in praise of Margery's fried eggs, which is no profane and godless ballad. No other Father Cuddy than myself ever belonged to Innisfallen," earnestly exclaimed the holy man. "A hundred years! What was your great grandmother's name?"

"She was a Mahony of Dunlow, Margaret ni Mahony; and my grandmother—.

"What, merry Margery of Dunlow your great grand- [243] mother!" shouted Cuddy; "St Brandon help me! the wicked wench, with that tempting bottle—why 'twas only last night—a hundred years—your great grandmother said you? Mercy on us, there has been a strange torpor over me. I must have slept all this time!"

That Father Cuddy had done so, I think is sufficiently proved, by the changes which occurred during his nap. A reformation, and a serious one it was for him, had taken place. Eggs fried by the pretty Margery were no longer to be had in Innisfallen, and, with heart as heavy as his footsteps, the worthy man directed his course towards Dingle, where he embarked in a vessel on the point of sailing for Malaga. The rich wine of that place had of old impressed him with a high respect for its monastic establishments, in one of which he quietly wore out the remnant of his days.

The stone impressed with the mark of Father Cuddy's knees may be seen to this day. Should any incredulous persons doubt my story, I request them to go to Killarney, where Clough na Cuddy—so is the stone called,—remains in Lord Kenmare's park, an indisputable evidence of the fact: and Spillane, the bugle man, will be able to point it out to them, as he did to me.

Title

Delta. [Moir, D.L.] "Auld Robin Gray. The Original Story." LS 1827. 301-322.

PLATE: Auld Robin Gray
Steel plate engraving; painted by R. Farrier;
engraved by J. Romney [301]

AULD ROBIN GRAY.
The Original Story.

> Jamie hadna been awa a twelvemonth and a day
> When my father brak his arm, and mir cow was stown away,
> My mither she fell sick, and my Jamie at the Ma,
> When Auld Robin Gray cam a courting me.
> My father condna work, and my mither condna spin;
> I toiled day and night, but their bread I coudna win:
> Auld Rob maintained them baith, and, wi' tears in his ee.
> Said, Jeanie, for their sakes, O marry me!
>
> *Ballad.*

JEANIE GRAHAME was ane of the blithest, bonniest lasses to be seen in the auncient kingdom of Fife, from the Leven Loch to the Bay of St. Andrews; at least she was (speaking of her as I first saw her) happy as a summer mavis, and bright as a June rose. What she afterwards saw and underwent was eneuch to have wasted and withered a' the beauty that was e'er bequeathed from heaven to woman.

The affairs of auld Walter Grahame had been lang back-going, and were now come to a poor pass. It would, indeed, be difficult preceesely to point out the cause; but the guids and gear, collected by the grandfather, Wattie o' the strong back (so called from his being famous [302] at putting the stane), had begun to dwindle in the days of his son, Alexander, who succeeded him in the farm of Rowan-brae; and so great was the confusion to which things had been allowed to run, that Walter, the second o' the name, and Jeanie's father, might be said to have fallen to a fruitless inheritance, and to have been left warstling in a sea of troubles.

Being the head of a family, and come to that time of life when moving about the warld has muckle mair of incumbrance than pleasure in't, Walter struggled hard to better his lot. He was up early, and lay down late,—drove his ain cart to the market,—toiled in the fields,—hedged and ditched,—and submitted to every drudgery along with the maist menial o' his warkmen. All, however, wadna do. It seemed as if the bow of Providence was bent against him,—that he was a doomed man,—and that naething was destined to thrive in his unfortunate hands.

His wife and he had foregathered in their better days, and if it may be said *he* bore up wi' a strong fortitude, it maun be confessed, that oh *she* tholed ill the deprivations to which their straitened means compelled them. When a high speerited, careless young lassie, she had married for love (as the saying is), against the will o' her relations, that were a' wealthy and well to do in the world; and, when she could afford to keep up her degree, and brush by them in a gown of French silk, to the full as guid as their ain, every thing was weil eneuch. It was otherwise [303] however, when, year by year, obleeged her to dispense with some wee bit article o' accustomed finery, and a back-going fortune estranged faces that had often smiled around her mair plentiful table. True it is, that with the changes o' life so we change; and that with the turns o' fortune we are oure apt to turn. Her temper began to sour; she took to liking an ill tale against her neighbour; and, as the family purse began to grow lighter, so in proportion did her wounded pride begin to show itself. Wad she petition her friends for help? Wad she condescend to bow down before them that had sae lang treated her as an outcast frae their family? Na—na—that wad have been as much as owning she had been in error, and they in the right. Sooner wad she perish of cauld and hunger; or be forced away into stranger districts, to beg, from door to door, a crust o' bread, and a drink o' water, from the hands of the charitable.

Oh, but Jeanie Grahame, the dochter, was a dear; sweet, bonny lassie! I was half in love wi' her mysell; and that is muckle for a douce married man to confess. Her behaviour to her parents, during all the time of their backgoing and misfortunes, was most pattern-like,—a sight to see as guid as a sermon to hear. She was the very heart and soul o' their howshold, and seemed to shed a glint of true pleasure oure the hame of honest poverty. Educated to the best o' the means that even their most prosperous days allowed them, she submitted to every accumulating little want without a murmur. Still she [304] was the same innocent, contented, cheerfu' lassie; still she was the light o' her father's ee, the pride o' her mother's heart. With them beside her, she seemed to fear nae evil, and to despise every hardship; her duty seemed aboon a'. She soothed all their misfortunes,—checked all their vain repinings,—cheered them with the smiles o' her sweet face,—and seemed ane that, to a stranger, had nae cause for tears in this world; but, for a' that, she sometimes grat to hersell in secret.

Auld Robin Gray, the Laird of Stanedykes, I mind him weil. He was a tall, lour-shouthered carle, a guid way up in his sixties at the time; wi' strong, hard-set features, and a brown, three-story wig. His face was remarkable for naething but his rough, bushy ee-bree, that, grizzled wi' years, lookit like snawy arches thrown oure a pair o' grey sparkling een. Mony and mony a time, when a callant, passing that road, have I seen him, standing at the bit parapet wa' before his house, with his hands in his pepper-and-salt coat pockets, his staff aneath his oxter, and his blue bonnet on his pow, looking at the folk passing on the road frae Wemyss to Dysart, or glinting his ee oure his braid fields, surrounded wi' fine auld trees, where the cows stood chewing the cud of fatness, and his whistling ploughlads turned up the mools wi' the glittering share; proud nae doubt a' the time to ken himself the laird o' sic a rich inheritance. Except for his keen hawk's ee, ane could scarcely have fand him out; however, there are surer ways of discovering a man's heart, than from [305] the cut of his coat, or his bodily looks; and where was the neibour that ever had occasion to lend him a guid word, or the beggar that e'er depairted frae his gate muttering a blessing?

The lang and the short of the story is, that auld Robin was a doure, hard-hearted, selfish man,—the king of misers; scraping and scraping frae a' corners from day to day, and from year to year; screwing what he could by all lawful shifts out o' ithers; and denying himself amaist the necessaries of life. In the early pairt of his youth, he had married a cousin of his ain, a dochter of the Laird of Lowth; who, after living wi' him six or seven miserable years, took farewell o' this world it is to be houpit for a better, the latter pairt o' her life having been waur than purgatory,—a dull, broken-hearted creature, that left him the father of an only son and heir.

In the course of years and nature, the son, Jamie, grew up a bonny, black-haired laddie, fu' of the milk of human kindness, funny and frolicksome; and seemingly determined to mak up, in the eyes o' the world, for the sourness of his father's disposition, by the sweetness of his ain. In all games and exercises he was the foremost; and no a lass in the parishes of Dysart or Kirkaldy wad have scrupled to have set her cap at him.

Mony a girn, and mony a bitter word did the laird gie; yet the outbreakings of youth were borne by the gruff auld carle better than could have been expectit. Whether, however, as he grew aulder, the father's temper grew mair [306] fractious, or his affection to his callant grew mair cauld, was hard to discover; but it becam visible to all, from: the usage he underwent, and the drudgeries to which he was made to yield, that the matter wad soon be past the endurance of a proud-hearted, free-speerited lad,—and so it happened; for, in a fit of resentment and sorrow, he betook himself to a vessel setting sail frae Leith to the West Indies; leaving to the doure, gruff, auld miser, and to his housekeeper, sand-blind Nancy, to mak a kirk and a mill of the pleasureless domicile and property of Stanedykes.

On the night before Jamie set off there was a grievous parting between him and Jeanie Grahame. They seemed made for ane anither; and if, as some suppose, Nature formed human creatures in pairs, these were the twa that it meant to meet. From the years in which the heart first opens to love, they had loved each ither like brother and sister; but with feelings still more warmly kindled, and more deeply rooted. Neither had ever been in love before—it was first love, full to the overflowing wi' passion and power,—to which a' the ither loves of life (if man can really and truly love twice) are but as sounding brass and a tinkling cymbal. Sair, sair, did Jeanie greet, and beg o' him no to gang away; lang did she hing upon his neck, while her burning tears drappit down on his hands; but na—his purpose was fixed,—fixed by an oath, as if he had been an auld Mede or Persian; so, after explaining to her the absurdity of his remaining at a hame where he [307] could never better himself; and of his submitting to a state of miserable and slavish dependence, he said he was only aboot trying to push his ain way in the world, and to get into a situation that would not render their coming together a thing, as it now was, altogether hopeless. "No—no," he said, "Jeanie," taking a farewell kiss from her lips, "you maunna cry,—it cannot be otherwise. It were cruel to you, as weel as mysell, to stay where I now am. I must—must leave you, Jeanie, and mind this,—if I get on in the world you will see me soon, if not, try to forget what has passed; and, my dear, dear, Jeanie, mind that I leave you a free creature,—as free in promise as God's daylight,—as free as before I saw ye:—and, when I am far away oure the sea, and forgotten, refuse not a guid offer for the sake of the foolish, silly, thoughtless memory o' what has passed betwixt us. So, may be, when I come hame—if ever it be my fortune to come hame,—a crazy, weather-beaten, broken-down, auld man, I may see ye surrounded wi' yere bonny bairns, and yere proud gudeman——No, hang me, I wad be sooner shot thro' the head, like a dog, than see the mon that daured, in my hearing, to ca' Jeanie Grahame his, Wife!!"

When the auld miser fand that his son had taen his will in his ain hands, and had decampit, he had a grievous contention wi' the bitterness and blackness of his ain speerit, and he vowed that, only son as he was of his, he wad cut him off wi' a shilling, come what liket of [308] the guids, gear, and chattels, he lamentit he could na carry to the grave with him. Naething wad mak him relax in his purpose, his determination was as fixed as the whunstane rock; and the friends that were sae forward as to presume offering a word o' advice, fand that they were only rivetting the nail of hatred more firmly in the laird's bosom.

Considering the ties o' nature, ane wad have thocht, that the course of time must have blunted his wrath, and reconceeled him to Jamie; but far otherwise. His speerit had got a bend that couldna be straightened; so, instead of relenting, every day appeared to mak him mair inveterately cruel. Twa simmers had passed oure, when the laird received a letter from his son, in which Jamie lamented the step he had taken, and the way they had pairted, hoping that, when he saw him again,—as he shortly expectit to do,—a' the past wad be forgotten.

The auld neerdoweel had scarcely patience to read the letter thro', ere he tore it into a thousand tatters, and strampit them below his feet. "Come hame when ye like, my man," cried the unnatural father, in the bitterness of his doure rage, "come hame when ye like, ye'se never mair be son of mine. Ye have brewed the cup o' wilful disobedience, and ye maun drink it to the dregs—deevil cares hoo bitter the dregs may be. Forgie ye! faith lad, ye little ken me. I'm no the willow whand to be bowed to your purpose. Do ye hear that?" added he, tapping sandblind Nancy, his housekeeper, on the [309] shouther, an auld, withered looking witchwife, that deserved a tar-barrel on the top o' Lomond hill, far better than mony that suffered there; "do ye hear that? Our bonnie son Jamie is thinking of paying us a veesit soon. Do you hear what I'm saying?"

"Nonsense, laird, nonsense. Jamie coming hame!" answered clootie's dochter, wi' a grin that showed her blackened stumps. "Ou, ay, he'll be coming to marry his bit bonny sweetheart, oure by, Wattie Grahame's dochter, ye understand, laird."

This was setting fire to tinder. The laird lookit first black and then blue; glowred in Nancy's withered face for a minute without speaking, like a man lost within himself, then gieing his head a shake, and screwing his mouth up to a whissle, like a man that has, after muckle trouble, seen his way thro' a puzzle, he clappit his bonnet on his pow, and away down the road to Rowan-brae.

At Walter's every thing was looking dowie and mair dowie, gloomier and gloomier. The cattle, ane after anither, had been selled to pay the landlord his rent. The barn yard was threshed out and empty. Sheriff-offishers frae Edinburgh were seen like wild cats in the gloaming, prowling aboot his bounds wi' docketted accounts in their side pockets, threatening poinding and horning; while, to crown a', Walter himself, by a tumble frae his cart shaft in the dark, had gotten his arm broken. It was a hame o' cauldrife poverty and wretchedness. Misfortune after misfortune showring down upon them, [310] had at length soured Walter's heart, and broken doun his speerit. His wife, wha could have tholed her puir fate better had she been among strangers, began to sink under a pride so mortally wounded, and she grew every day mair crabbit and ill-tempered, as she harpit oure the thocht o' their afflictions affording a cause of crowing to her neglectful relations. The warst of all, however, was, that they were neither o' them sae young as they once were; the snaws of auld age had begun to gather round their brows; and they hadna the warm hopes of youth, to see bright days amid years to come. Jeanie, puir thing, bore up wonderfully, and tho' doing every thing for the best, she took hard words, and crabbit looks, without a murmur; exerted hersell frae morning till night in managing the howshold concerns; and lookit like a stray sunbeam let into a dwelling of darkness.

Ane might naturally ask,—had she nae consolation which helpit her to oppose this brave speerit to the storm? had she nae secret help? nae kind letter? nae blithe tidings f Nane—nane; frae the night of the pairting she had heard not a syllable from or about him. She kent from his own lips that he was aff to the West Indies, and she had heard from ithers that the West Indies is the European's grave!

Auld Robin, the laird, saw the desolation of his neibour's dwelling, and he laid his schemes accordingly. He blew and braggit of his siller;—tell't Wattie that he understood a' his difficulties;—that he had nae objections [311] to lend him a helping hand;—and that, to crown all, he wad make Jeanie his wife, and the leddy of Stanedykes.

Walter's countenance brightened up. It was like torchlight suddenly let in on folk that have a lang time been sitting in darkness. But an hour afore he had thocht his case desperate, and now!——yet he could scarcely credit his ears. Sooner wad he have expectit a shower of gold frae the gloomy November clouds than help frae the hand of the laird of Stanedykes. But, tho' blinded like a man by a flash of lightning, even then, when he thocht o' his daughter, the young, the bonny, the dutiful,—of sacrificing her in this gate,—it was eneuch to stagger him, and make his flesh creep. It was, however, the only star he saw in his night of black darkness; and the laird stuck to him.

"Now, ye've gien me your hand," said Robin, rising to gang awa, "ye've gien me your hand, that ye'll do your utmost wi' my bonnie Jeanie. I've mair, Walter, than either you or her ken aboot, but the day she takes me she'll be mistress o't a'. She'll hae naething to do ava, but sit, and sew, and churm like a lintie, and tak her pleasure, wi' a ponie to ride on when she likes the open air; and as mony maidens to wait on her,—if she likes attendance,—as ony lord's leddy frae Earlsferry Abbey to Culzean Castle. When ye bring me oure word that she's consentit (she's your daughter, ye ken, Walter, my gude freen; and Scripture tells ye, ye can mak her do what ye like), bring oure a' yere bills and bunds to [312] me, and I'll pit my name on the back o' them. Then ye ken," he added, snapping his fingers, "they'll be worth twenty siller shillings to the pound; and as gude as the Bank o' Scotland. But mind ye, I canna wait; and, if I hear nae her consent the morn, I maun een look anither way."

It is hard to say, when he thocht of Jeanie in her teens, and the laird wi' ae foot in the grave, whether pleasure or grief was uppermost in Walter's heart; but at night, when they were sitting oure their cheerless ingle, he took an opportunity of breaking the subject to his daughter. "It's true, Jeanie, my dear," he said, giving her a kind clap on the shouther, "it's true we canna get every thing we like in this weary world. Ye're mither and me there married, like fools, for love, and lippenit to guid fortune for the plenishing. Ye see what we have been able to mak o't! No that I wad yet change her for ony ane, na—na, guidwife; hooever, I'm no speaking about that at present. Ye see, Jeanie, my dear, the state to which we are reduced;—every thing gaun back wi' us—empty barns, and horseless stables—naething but cauld poverty,—and me, wi' my broken arm, every day in the fear o' being thrown into the jail. I wush, my dear Jeanie, ye could help us."

"Me! how can I help ye," said Jeanie, dighting away the tears, that had started in her een, wi' the corner of her apron, as she stoppit her spinning-wheel. "Ay, faither, if it lay in my power, if it lay between me and [313] the end of the World, to help ye, I wadna weary o' the way."

"Deed, Jeanie, it is in your power—and ye maun tak him. Ye wad, nae doubt, like a younger man if he offered; but mak hay, my dear, when the sun shines; and when ance ye're the leddy of Stanedykes, ye may smirk in your sleeve at them a'."

"Stanedykes!—but, faither," askit Jeanie, innocently, "hoo can ye ca' Jamie Gray an auld man?—or, tho' I were to get him, hoo could either *I*, or ony ither body, be leddy o' Stanedykes when the auld laird is living?"

"Young Jamie I" quo' Walter, gieing a lauch, "na, na, lass, that were a kettle of fish to fry. Wha kens aboot that scapegrace? I'se warrant he's married abroad; or may be, wha kens, dead and buried long ago. It's the laird himsell I'm speaking aboot."

"The laird his faither!!" cried Jeanie, while her heart flaffed as if it wad have loupit thro' her stays. "Never speak in that way. Do ye think the laird wad marry me, that might be his grandchild?" and she gaed a wild lauch that sounded hardly canny.

"Tak ye, Jeanie!" said Walter, kindly patting her cheek, that had momently grown pale as the driven sna', "ay, and be glad to get ye.—Oh, Jeanie," he said, rising hurriedly frae his seat, and pacing aboot the floor in a distractit-like way, "think on the state we are in; look at me,—look at your puir mother,—we are beggared out [314] o' house and hal',—and, in a few days, may not have a mouthfu' to eat, or a roof to cover us."

"Jeanie, my dear bairn," said her mother, leaning her hand on her shouther, hear what your faither says, it is God's truth. Ye've aye done your duty; come what will, I'll aye say that o' ye. But what signifies a', what matters by ganes, if, when a word o' your mouth could lift us out o' this mire o' meesery and wretchedness, ye keep your teeth close, and determine to act the pairt o' an undutiful dochter?"

Jeanie's heart swelled to her mouth; and while she sat wi' her hands claspit before her, and the tears running like beads of boiling water down her cheeks, her voice died within her, and she couldna utter ae word. Her mind seemed to have fairly gien way; and when, in a while, her recollection began to come back, she started, as out of a fearfu' sleep, and in a broken, half-screaming way, cried out, "It wad ruin me here and hereafter—no—no—no—I daur not, cannot do it. —Oh, I wish—I wish I was dead and buried!!!" With this she drappit from her chair on the floor, and gaed away in a dwam, second only in soundness to the awfu' sleep of death.

Next morning, however, she was up betimes, and gaun aboot the wee affairs of the house (indeed there was now little or naething for her to look after); but her pale cheek, and sunken ee, told what she had suffered, and [315] was suffering. She seemed to shudder within hersell at the bare idea of the struggle which she kent must again be renewed, as the bleating goat is said to shudder whea driven into the den of the hungry wild beast.

So great, however, was the effect of the terrible conflict of yestreen, and such an impression had it made on the minds baith of father and mother, that, when they regarded the agoneezed countenance of Jeanie, they hesitated to put the thing to the test, though they kent that, in the course of a few hours, the battle must be either lost or won for ever. Breakfast passed without scarcely being tasted, while Jeanie glanced with a fearfu' ee on them baith, as dauting her, and hinging about her, they yet feared and kept aloof frae the momentous subject. The dark cloud, she perceived, had not yet passed over their heads. Hour after hour glided away. In the course o' the forenoon, Wattie hurriedly shut the auld family Bible, which he had sat down, as if to pore over; and, putting on his hat, dawndered away out like a tipsy man amang the fields, without kenning where his path lay.

Jeanie at last sat down to her spinning-wheel as usual, tho' she crooned not away at either of her favourite tunes, "Cowden Knowes," or, "The Flowers o' the Forest;" and her mother, putting on her spectacles, opened the book her father had shut. Neither seemed inclined to converse; and, save the humming of Jeanie's wheel, and now and then the mewing of the kitten, that wandered about among the empty dishes in search of its accustomed [316] milk, the haill house was silent. It didna, however, lang remain so. Walter came hurrying in with visible perplexity in his features; and, throwing his hat into a corner, sank down into a chair by the window. Jeanie turned and looked him i' the face, but, in the anxiety there painted, saw eneuch to prevent her looking a second time. The shadow of desolation cam' oure her speerit.

"Jeanie, my dear bairn," cried W alter, rising up behind her, and patting her tenderly on the back, "Oh! Jeanie, have mercy on us,—speak the word afore it be oure late. Could ye bear to see the father that brought ye up, and the mither that bore ye—could ye bear to see yere auld mither and me begging our bread frae door to door, or lying on the straw of a poor-house? We thochtna—thochtna to have come to that—and you have it in your power to put every thing right. Say but the word; every thing depends on you,—our comfort, nay, even our very existence. We'll lie down on our knees before ye on the floor,—the paurents that gied ye being will throw themsells at yere feet. Ye surely canna spurn them awa wi' disdain! Ye canna shut yere heart to our prayers! Ye canna think there is a hereafter—and yet see us starving here!"

This was past human tholing. "What maun I do—what maun I do?" said Jeanie, eagerly, "tell me what I maun do?"

"Ye maun just say, my dear lassie, that ye'll marry Laird Gray. That's a' Jeanie we want ye to say; and [317] that's na muckle."—And, as Walter spoke these words, his voice trembled with anxiety and earnestness. Where could Jeanie look for council? She lookit in her mither's face—and her mither's een seemed to say, "Oh! Jeanie, do it, or my heart will break." Jeanie's heart was all but broken!

"To be sure, to be sure," she said, putting her hand within her mother's, "I'll do whate'er ye want me. Ony thing, ony thing."

At this very moment Robin Gray, whose coming ours the fields Walter had seen before hurrying in, tapped at the door, carrying in his hand a pair o' fat ducks, his first present of courtship to a famishing family.

It wad be needless here, and a waste baith of time and paper, to gang thro' wi' all the circumstantialities that took place before the wadding, which caused a titter of astonishment and jeering laughter alang the haill shore of Fife. But married they were, to the no small consternation of sand-blind Nancy, the veteran housekeeper, wha heesitated about gieing up the keys; till, at last, forced to believe her ain een, she concluded that the laird had grown dormant, and lost his right senses. Scarcely less thunderstruck were Walter Grahame and his wife, when they fand what a few days had brought forth: but the accepted bills, the stockit pantry, and the calls of mony, that scarce a week agone passed their door, like the Levite, on the opposite side, assured them that all wasna a dream. [318]

Jeanie saw her faither and mother once more raised frae misery to comfort, and felt hersell the leddy o' Stanedykes. Of guids and gear she had eneuch, and to spare. Some, of course, wad tak it for granted she was happy; that, however, is another question.

It was in the thoughtfu' month of September, when the yellowing leaves, the heavy clouds, and the shortening days, remind man of the fate that sooner or later awaits him; and, it might be, some five or six weeks from the date of puir Jeanie's marriage, that, ae gloaming, as she was sitting at the far end o' the garden, behind the house, under the bourtree-bush, thinking, maybe, mournfully o' the days that were gone, a man dressed in a sailor's jacket burst suddenly thro' the hedge, and stood before her!

They gazed on each other for some time without speaking. His een were rivetted upon her, and pierced thro' Jeanie's soul; yet she couldna turn her head away. What, oh heaven and earth! maun she have felt, when she saw wha stood before her—when she saw her ain Jamie Gray looking into her heart—when she thocht of what had passed atween them, and when she thocht on what she now was—his father's wife!

He spoke not a word; but, with a smile of deevilish contempt, slowly raising up his finger opposite her face, he gave a long slow hiss of the bitterest scorn, turned onhbis heel, and depairted.

Jeanie was carried to bed in a raging fever; and the [319] laird, who had heard of his son's arrival, imputed it at ance, in the jaundice of his jealousy, to the right cause. With the wild fury of a madman, he taxed her with having broken thro' the vow she had sae lately sworn to afore the minister. All the wicked passions of his wicked heart were roused up, like serpents frae their dens. He stampit and swore about his son in the whirlwind -of his unnatural hatred: he shook his head oure the deeing Jeanie, telling her that she, like the rest, was but born to deceive him; and cursed the day that ever gave birth to such an unfortunate, miserable wretch as himself.

An awful night of tempestuous horror frowned over, and next morning Jeanie was out o' mind and delirious. She muttered and raved constantly about Jamie, asking why he had been sae lang, lang o' coming! What place of the West Indies they had buried him in!—and to take away the man in the sailor's claes that was aye standing afore her. Force was at last used to confine her to her bed; and auld sand-blind Nancy, standing wi' her hands in her sides in the middle of the floor, casting a leer first on the bed where lay the distracted and dying bride, and then on the laird, that was pacing up and down the room wi' his hands behind his back, mumbled, wi' hellish rejoicing, between her teeth, "What think ye now, maister, o' yere bonny bit wifie?"

Her strength at last totally exhausted, Jeanie fell asleep -late in the afternoon; and the laird, bidding a' body leave the room, darkened the windows, and sat doun to doze in [320] the leather elbow chair by the bedside, where the sick-nurse had been sitting. Scarcely had he closed his een "when he fand something desperately squeezing him. He started forrit, and lookit up. It was Jeanie's hand that held a grup of his coat sleeve, so forcibly that he felt her finger nails piercing the flesh o' his withered arm. Scarcely could the hand be drawn away, though the spark of life had fled for ever!

Jamie was never seen in Fife after. Some say that he was shot in a sea-fight off the Nore, and others that he was the stranger that throw himself oure the pier of Leith. The truth is, that naebody ever heard ony mair about him.

Auld Laird Gray spun out ten years after Jeanie's judgment-like departure; but he never could be said, from that time, to be properly in his right mind, losing his faculties, ane after anither, and growing, wi' the frailties of age, a kind of second bairn, or rather natural. However, let the truth aye be spoken, he had his beef-tea, or chicken-soup, regularly every day; and his swelled legs, carefully wrappit up in the finest Welch flannel, were laid on a stool wi' a silk cushion, by the dutifu' bands of sand-blind Nancy.

Jeanie's gravestane is in the southmost corner of the kirkyard of Dysart; but the reading is now scarcely legible, from the effects of the rain and sea-winds on a soft stane. On the tap o't there's the figure of a wee angel blawing a trumpet; but sae defaced as no to be [321] able to scare away the sea-gulls, that, coming up frae the shore, sail round and round about it, and at last light upon't wi' a scream, as if it was the grave of some auld sailor of their acquaintance they had come up on purpose to pay a visit to.

It may very readily be supposed that this is the story on which the very beautiful Scottish ballad of Auld Robin Gray is founded; though, with a fine discrimination, Lady Mary Lindsay, leaving out the unpleasant parts of the narrative, has felicitously converted it from a tale of guilt and suffering to one of unmingled tenderness and beauty.

The circumstances throughout, even as connected with the ballad, bear too evidently the impress of *truth* to be the mere mental imaginings of any sentimental poet or poetess; and though, like the ancient legend of Gil Morrice, on which Home founded his exquisite national tragedy, or the pathetic tale of Girolamo and Sylvestra, from which Barry Cornwall drew the finest of his dramatic scenes, "The Broken Heart,"—these circumstances now only appeal to our feelings in the lines to which the singing of Miss Stephens has added a more deserved celebrity; yet we see life, real life, and actual occurrence, in every stanza, most visibly and distinctly.

We believe there is no existing record of the time at which the ballad was composed; but from the authoress having died within the last year, though at a very ad- [322] vanced age, we may with certainty assign to it a date considerably posterior to the prose record, whose language in many places exhibits the idiomatic Scotch simplicity of the latter portion of the seventeenth century. In other parts, the hand of some impertinent transcriber, who has used the liberty of interlarding the narrative with his own less Doric, though more modern expressions, is but too perceptible to escape censure.

Literary Annual

The Literary Souvenir; or, Cabinet of Poetry and Romance. Ed. Alaric A. Watts. London: Longman, Rees, Orme, Brown, & Green, 1828. Printer: Bradbury & Co., Bolt Court, Fleet Street.[4]

Title

By Author of "Holland Tide." [Griffin, Gerald.] "The Dilemma of Phadrig. A Tale of the Shannon Side." LS 1828. 3-19. [3]

THE DILEMMA OF PHADRIG.
A Tale of the Shannon Side.
BY THE AUTHOR OF 'HOLLAND TIDE.'

"There's no use in talken about it, Phadrig. I know an I feel that all's over wit me. My pains are all gone, to be sure—but in place o' that, there's a weight like a quern stone down upon my heart, an I feel it blackenen within me. All I have to say is—think o' your own Mauria when she's gone, an be kind to poor Patcy."

"Ah, darlen, don't talk that way—there's hopes yet—what'll I do—what'll the child do witout you?—"

"Phadrig, there's noan. I'm goen fast, an ,if you have any regard for me, you wont say anythin that'll bring the thoughts o' you an him between me an the thoughts o' heaven, for that's what I must think of now. An if you marry again——"

"Oh, Mauria, honey, will you kill me entirely? Is it *I'll* marry again?"

——"If it be a thing you should marry again," Mauria resumed, without taking any notice of her hus- [4] band's interruption, "you'll bear in mind, that the best mother that ever walked the ground, will love her own above another's. It stands with raisin an natur. The gander abroad will pull a strange goslen out of his own flock; and you know yourself, we could never get the bracket hen to sit upon Nelly O'Leary's chickens, do what we could. Every thing loves its own. Then, Phadrig, if you see the flowery potaties—an the top o' the milk—an the warm seat be the hob—an the biggest bit o' meat on a Sunday goen away from Patcy—you'll think o' your poor Mauria, an do her part by him; just quietly, an softly, an without blamen the woman—for it is only what's nait'rel, an what many a stepmother does without thinking o' themselves. An above all things, Phadrig, take care to make him mind his books and his religion, to keep out o' bad company, an study his readin-made-aisy, and that's the way he'll be a blessing an a comfort to you in

---

4 Plain text for all short stories included here for the 1828 *Literary Souvenir* obtained from Google Books and then compared against the original volume. For full citation, see References.
< http://books.google.com/books?id=7WwEAAAAQAAJ&dq=1828%20The%20Literary%20Souvenir%3B%20or%2C%20Cabinet%20of%20Poetry%20and%20Romance&pg=PP13#v=onepage&q&f=false>

your old days, as I once thought he would be to me, in mine."

Here her husband renewed his promises, in a tone of deep affliction.

"An now for yourself, Phadrig. Remember the charge that's upon you, and don't be goen out venturen your life in a little canvas canoe, on the bad autumn days, at Ballybunion; nor wit foolish boys at the Glin and Tarbert fairs;—an don't be so wake-minded, as to be trusten to card-drawers, an fairy doctors, an the like; for its the last word the priest said to me was, that you [5] were too superstitious, and that's a great shame an a heavy sin. But tee you![5] Phadrig, dear, there's that rogue of a pig at the poaties over———"

Phadrig turned out the grunting intruder, bolted the hurdle-door, and returned to the bedside of his expiring helpmate. That tidy housekeeper, however, exhausted by the exertion which she had made to preserve, from the mastication of the swinish tusk, the fair produce of her husband's conacre of white-eyes, had fallen back on the pillow and breathed her last.

Great was the grief of the widowed Phadrig for her loss—great were the lamentations of her female friends at the evening wake—and great was the jug of whiskey-punch which the mourners imbibed at the mouth, in order to supply the loss of fluid which was expended from the eyes. According to the usual cottage etiquette, the mother of the deceased, who acted as mistress of the ceremonies, occupied a capacious hay-bottomed chair near the fire-place—from which she only rose, when courtesy called on her to join each of her female acquaintances as they arrived, in the death-wail which (as in politeness bound) they poured forth over the pale piece of earth that lay coffined in the centre of the room. This mark of attention, however, the old lady was observed to omit with regard to one of the fair guests—a round faced, middle-aged woman, called Milly Rue—or Red Milly, probably because her head might have [6] furnished a solution of the popular conundrum, "Why is a red-haired lady like a sentinel on his post?"

The fair Milly, however, did not appear to resent this slight, which was occasioned (so the whisper went among the guests) by the fact, that she had been an old and neglected love of the new widower. All the fiery ingredients in Milly's constitution appeared to be comprehended in her glowing ringlets—and those, report says, were as ardent in hue, as their owner was calm and regulated in her temper. It would be a cold morning indeed, that a sight of Milly's head would not warm you—and a hot fit of anger, which a few tones of her kind and wrath-disarming voice would not cool. She dropped, after she had concluded her 'cry,' a conciliating courtesy to the sullen old lady, took an unobtrusive seat at the foot of the bed, talked of the 'notable' qualities of the deceased, and was particularly attentive to the flaxen-headed little Patcy, whom she held in her lap during the whole night, cross-examining him in his reading and multiplication, and presenting him, at parting, in token of her satisfaction at his proficiency, with a copy of 'The Seven

---

5 To you! Beware!

Champions of Christendom,' with a fine marble cover and pictures. Milly acted in this instance, under the advice of a prudent mother, who exhorted her, "whenever she thought o' maken presents, that way, not to be layen her money out in cakes or gingerbread, or things that would be ett off at wanst, an no more about them or the giver—but [7] to give a strong toy, or a book, or somethen that would last, and bring her to mind now and then, so as that when a person 'ud ask where they got that, or who gev it, they'd say, 'from Milly Rue,' or ' Milly gev it, we're obleest to her,' an be talken an thinken of her when she'd be away."

To curb in my tale, which may otherwise become restive and unmanageable—Milly's deep affliction and generous sympathy, made a serious impression on the mind of the widower, who more than all, was touched by that singularly accidental attachment which she seemed to have conceived for little Patcy. Nothing could be farther from his own wishes, than any design of, a second time, changing his condition; but he felt that it would be doing a grievous wrong to the memory of his first wife, if he neglected this opportunity of providing her favourite Patcy with a protector, so well calculated to supply her place. He demurred a little on the score of true love, and the violence which he was about to do his own constant heart—but like the bluff King Henry, his conscience, 'aye—his conscience,'—touched him, and the issue was, that a roaring wedding shook the walls which had echoed to the wail of death within the few preceding months.

Milly Rue not only supplied the place of a mother to young Patcy, but presented him in the course of a few years-, with two merry playfellows, a brother and a sister. To do her handsome justice, too, poor Mauria's antici- [8] pations were completely disproved by her conduct, and it would have been impossible for a stranger to have detected the step son of the house from any shade of undue partiality in the mother. The harmony in which they dwelt, was unbroken by any accident for many years.

The first shock which burst in with a sudden violence upon their happiness, was one of a direful nature. Disease, that pale and hungry fiend, who haunts alike the abodes of wealth and of penury; who brushes away with his baleful wing the bloom from beauty's cheek, and the balm of slumber from the pillow of age; who troubles the hope of the young mother with dreams of ghastliness and gloom, and fears that come suddenly, she knows not why nor whence; who sheds his poisonous dews alike on the heart that is buoyant, and the heart that is broken; this stern and conquering demon scorned not to knock, one summer morning, at the door of Phadrig's cow-house, and to lay his iron fingers upon a fine milch-cow, a sheeted stripper, which constituted (to use his own emphatic phrase) the poor farmer's 'substance,' and to which he might have applied the well known lines which run nearly as follows:—

"She's straight in her back, and thin in her tail;
She's fine in her horn, and good at the pail;

She's calm in her eyes, and soft in her skin;
She's a grazier's without, and a butcher's within."

All the 'cures' in the pharmacopeia of the village [9] apothecary were expended on the poor animal, without any beneficial effect; and Phadrig, after many conscientious qualms about the dying words of his first wife, resolved to have recourse to that infallible refuge in such cases—a fairy doctor.

He said nothing to the afflicted Milly about his intention, but slipped out of the cottage in the afternoon, hurried to the Shannon side near Moneypoint, unmoored his light, canvas-built canoe, seated himself in the frail vessel, and fixing his paddles on the *towl-pin*, sped away over the calm face of the waters towards the isle of Scattery, where the renowned Crohoore-na-Oona, or Connor-of-the-Sheep, the Mohammed of the cottages, at this time took up his residence. This mysterious personage, whose prophecies are still commented on among the cottage circles with looks of deep awe and wonder, was much revered by his contemporaries, as a man 'who had seen a dale;' of what nature those sights or visions were, was intimated by a mysterious look, and a solemn nod of the head.

In a little time Phadrig ran his little canoe aground on the sandy beach of Scattery, and, drawing her above high-water mark, proceeded to the humble dwelling of the gifted Sheep-shearer, with feelings of profound fear and anxiety. He passed the lofty round tower—the ruined grave of St. Senanus, in the centre of the little isle—the mouldering church, on which the eye of the poring antiquary may still discern the sculptured image of the two- [10] headed monster, with which cottage tradition says the Saint sustained so fierce a conflict on landing in the islet—and which the translator of Odranus has vividly described as "a dragon, with his fore part covered with huge bristles, standing on end, like those of a boar; his mouth gaping wide open, with a double row of crooked, sharp tusks, and with such openings that his entrails might be seen; his back like a round island, full of scales and shells; his legs short and hairy, with such steely talons, that the pebble-stones, as he ran along them, sparkled—parching the way wherever he went, and making the sea boil about him where he dived—such was his excessive fiery heat." Phadrig's knees shook beneath him when he remembered this awful description—and thought of the legends of Lough Dhoola, on the summit of Mount Callon, to which the hideous animal was banished by the Saint, to fast on a trout and a half per diem to the end of time; and where, to this day, the neighbouring fishermen declare that, in dragging the lake with their nets, they find the half trout as regularly divided in the centre, as if it were done with a knife and scale.

While Phadrig remained, with mouth and eyes almost as wide open as those of the sculptured image of the monster which had fascinated him to the spot, a sudden crash among the stones and dock-weed, in an opposite corner of the ruin, made him start and yell as if the original were about to quit Lough Dhoola on parole of honour, and use him as a relish after the trout and a

[11] half. The noise was occasioned by a little rotund personage, who had sprung from the mouldering wall, and now stood gazing fixedly on the terrified Phadrig, who continued returning that steady glance with a half frightened, half crying face—one hand fast clenched upon his breast, and the other extended, with an action of avoidance and deprecation. The person of the stranger was stout and short, rendered still more so by a stoop, which might almost have been taken for a hump—his arms hung forward from his shoulders, like those of a long-armed ape—his hair was grey and bushy, like that of a wanderoo—and his sullen grey eye seemed to be inflamed with ill-humour—his feet were bare, and as broad as a camel's—and a leathern girdle buckling round his waist, secured a tattered grey frieze riding-coat, and held an enormous pair of shears, which might have dipt off a man's head as readily, perhaps, as a lock of wool. This last article of costume afforded a sufficient indication to Phadrig that he stood in the presence of the awful object of his search.

"Well! an who are *you?*" growled the Sheep-shearer, after surveying Phadrig attentively for some moments.

The first gruff sound of his voice made the latter renew his start and roar for fright; after which, composing his terrors as well as he might, he replied, in the words of Autolycus—"I am only a poor fellow, Sir."

"Well! an what's your business with me?"

"A cure, Sir, I wanted for her. A cow o' mine [12] that's very bad inwardly, an we can do nothen for her; an I thought may be you'd know what is it ail'ded her—an prevail on THEM" [this word was pronounced with an emphasis of deep meaning] "to leave her to uz."

"Huth!" the Sheep-shearer thundered out, in a tone that made poor Phadrig jump six feet backwards, with a fresh yell, "do you daare to spake of *them* before me. Go along! you villyan o' the airth, an wait for me outside the church, an I'll tell you all about it there; but, first—do you think I can get the *gentlemen* to do any thing for me *gratish*—without offeren 'em a trate or a haip'orth?"

"If their honours would'nt think two tinpennies and a fi'penny bit too little.—It's all I'm worth in the wide world."

"Well! we'll see what they'll say to it. Give it here to me. Go now—be off with yourself—if you don't want to have 'em all a-top o'you in a minnit."

This last hint made our hero scamper over the stones like a startled fawn; nor did he think himself safe, until he reached the spot where he had left his canoe, and where he expected the coming of the Sheep-shearer; conscience-struck by the breach of his promise to his dying Mauria, and in a state of agonising anxiety with respect to the lowing patient in the cow-house.

He was soon after rejoined by Connor of the Sheep.

"There is one way," said he, "of saving your cow—but you must lose one of your childer if you wish to save it." [13]

"0, heaven presarve uz, Sir, how is hat, if you plase?"

"You must go home," said the Sheep-shearer, "and say nothen to any body, but fix in your mind which o' your three childer you'll give for the cow; an when you do that, look in his eyes, an he'll sneeze, and den't you bless him, for the world. Then look in his eyes again, an he'll sneeze again, an still don't think o' blessen him, be any mains. The third time you'll look in his eyes, he'll sneeze a third time—an if you don't bless him the third time, he'll die—but your cow will live."

"An this is the only cure you have to gi' me?" exclaimed Phadrig, his indignation at the moment overcoming his natural timidity.

"The only cure.—It was by a dale to do, I could prevail on them to let you make the choice itself."

Phadrig declared stoutly against this decree, and even threw out some hints, that he would try whether or no Shaun Lauther, or Strong John, a young rival of the sheep-shearing fairy Doctor, might be able to make a better bargain for him with the "gentlemen."

"Shaun Lauther!" exclaimed Connor of the Sheep, in high anger—"Do you compare me to a man that never seen any more than yourself?—that never saw so much as the skirt of a dead man's shroud in the moonlight—or heard as much as the moanen of a sowlth[6] in an old grave-yard? Do you know me?—Ask them that [14] do—an they'll tell you how often I'm called up in the night, and kep posten over bog an mountain, till I'm ready to drop down with the sleep,—while feow voices are heard, I'll be bail, at Shaun Lauther's windey—an little knollidge given him in his drames. It is then that I get mine. Didn't I say before the King o' France was beheaded, that a blow would be struck wit an axe in that place, that the sound of it would be heard all over Europe?—An wasn't it true? Didn't I hear the shots that were fired at Gibaralthur, an tell it over in Dooly's forge, that the place was relieved that day?—an didn't the news come afterwards in a month's time, that I toult noten but the truth?"

Phadrig had nothing to say in answer to this overwhelming list of interrogatories—but to apologise for his want of credulity, and to express himself perfectly satisfied.

With a heavy heart he put forth in his canoe upon the water, and prepared to return. It was already twilight, and as he glided along the peaceful shores, he ruminated mournfully within his mind, on the course which he should pursue. The loss of the cow would be, he considered, almost equivalent to total ruin—and the loss of any one of his lovely children, was a probability which he could hardly bear to dwell on for a moment. Still, it behoved him to weigh the matter well. Which of them, now—supposing it possible that he could think of sacrificing any—which of them would he select for the [15] purpose? The choice was a hard

6 Bodiless spirit.

one. There was little Mauria, a fair-haired, blue-eyed little girl—but he could not, for an instant, think of losing her, as she happened to be named after his first wife; her brother, little Shamus, was the least useful of the three, but he was the youngest!—"the child of his old age—a little one!" his heart bled at the idea; he would lose the cow and the pig along with it, before he would harm a hair of the darling infant's head. He thought of Patcy—and he shuddered—and leaned heavier on his oars, as if to flee away from the horrible doubt which stole into his heart with that name. It must be one of the three, or the cow was lost for ever. The two first mentioned, be certainly would not lose—and Patcy—— Again he bade the fiend begone, and trembling in every limb, made the canoe speed rapidly over the tide in the direction of his home.

He drew the little vessel ashore, and proceeded towards his cabin. They had been waiting supper for him, and he learned with renewed anxiety, that the object of his solicitude, the milch cow, had rather fallen away than improved in her condition during his absence. He sat down in sorrowful silence with his wife and children, to their humble supper of potatoes and thick milk.

He gazed intently on the features of each of the young innocents, as they took their places on the suggan chairs that flanked the board. Little Mauria and her [16] brother Shamus, looked fresh, mirthful, and blooming, from their noisy play in the adjoining paddock, while their elder brother, who had spent the day at school, wore—or seemed, to the distempered mind of his father, to wear a look of sullenness and chagrin. He was thinner too than most boys of his age—a circumstance which Phadrig had never remarked before. It might be the first indications of his poor mother's disease, consumption, that were beginning to declare themselves in his constitution, and if so—his doom was already sealed—and whether the cow died or not, Patcy was certain to be lost. Still the father could not bring his mind to resolve on any settled course, and their meal proceeded in silence.

Suddenly, the latch of the door was lifted by some person outside, and a neighbour entered to inform Phadrig, that the agent to his landlord had arrived in the adjacent village, for the purpose of driving matters to extremity against all those tenants who remained in arrear. At the same moment, too, a low moan of anguish from the cow outside, announced the access of a fresh paroxysm of her distemper, which it was very evident the poor animal could never come through in safety.

In an agony of distress and horror, the distracted father laid his clenched fingers on the table, and looked fixedly in the eyes of the unsuspecting Patcy. The child sneezed, and Phadrig closed his lips hard, for fear [17] a blessing might escape them. The child, at the same time, he observed, looked paler than before.

Fearful lest the remorse which began to awake within his heart might oversway his resolution, and prevent the accomplishment of his unnatural design, he looked hurriedly, a second time, into the eyes of the little victim. Again, the latter sneezed—and again the father, using a violent effort, restrained the blessing which was struggling at his heart. The poor child drooped his head upon his bosom, and letting the untasted food fall from his hand, looked so pale and mournful, as to remind his murderer of the look which his mother wore in dying.

It was long—very long—before the heart-struck parent could prevail on himself to complete the sacrifice. The visitor departed; and the first beams of a full moon began to supplant the faint and lingering twilight which was fast fading in the west. The dead of the night drew on before the family rose from their silent and comfortless meal. The agonies of the devoted animal now drew rapidly to a close, and Phadrig still remained tortured by remorse on the one hand, and by selfish anxiety on the other.

A sudden sound of anguish from the cow-house made him start from his seat. A third time he fixed his eyes on those of his child—a third time the boy sneezed—but here the charm was broken.

Milly Rue, looking with surprise and tenderness on the fainting boy, said—" Why, then, heaven bless you, [18] child!—it must be a cold you caught, you're sneezen so often."

Immediately, the cow sent forth a bellow of deep agony, and expired; and, at the same moment, a low and plaintive voice outside the door was heard, exclaiming—"And heaven bless you, Milly! and the Almighty bless you, and spare you a long time over your children!"

Phadrig staggered back against the wall—his blood froze in his veins—his face grew white as death—his teeth chattered—his eyes stared—his hair moved upon his brow, and the chilling damp of terror exuded over all his frame. He recognised the voice of his first wife; and her pale, cold eye met his at that moment, as her shade flitted by the window in the thin moonlight, and darted on him a glance of mournful reproach. He covered his eyes with his hands, and sunk, senseless, into a chair;—while the affrighted Milly, and Patcy, who at once assumed his glowing health and vigour, hastened to his assistance. They had all heard the voice, but no one saw the shade, nor recognised the tone, excepting the conscience-smitten Phadrig.

Seeing that so great a man as Giraldus Cambrensis did not esteem it beneath him to enshrine in several pages of hard Latin, the popular superstitions of the people, to whose real character he is said to have done [19] so little justice, *we* cannot claim credit for much humility in devoting some good and bad English to the same purpose. They are foibles which the assaults of modern intelligence have ' dashed to air like dew-drops from the lion's mane,'—butwhile we rejoice in the progress of that information, which is clipping the wings of those light and fanciful follies, it can be of no injury to lay hold on a few of the most interesting legends to which they have given rise, and preserve them, as voyagers do their knotted cords of measurement, if only for the purpose of shewing what way that magnificent vessel, the human mind, has made in the mighty ocean of knowledge. What might not be made of the people, whose very weaknesses evince a depth of feeling, and a reach of imagination, which are denied to many a cultivated intellect?

Title
Maginn, William. "The City of the Demons." LS 1828. 73-84. [73]

THE CITY OF THE DEMONS.
BY WILLIAM MAGINN, ESQ.

In days of yore, there lived in the flourishing city of Cairo a Hebrew Rabbi, by name Jochonan, who was the most learned of his nation. His fame went over the East, and the most distant people sent their young men to imbibe wisdom from his lips. He was deeply skilled in the traditions of the fathers, and his word on a disputed point was decisive. He was pious, just, temperate and strict; but he had one vice,—a love of gold had seized upon his heart, and he opened not his hand to the poor. Yet he was wealthy above most, his wisdom being to him the source of riches. The Hebrews of the city were grieved at this blemish on the wisest of their people; but though the elders of the tribes continued to reverence him for his fame, the women and children of Cairo called him by no other name than that of Rabbi Jochonan the miser.

None knew, so well as he, the ceremonies necessary for initiation into the religion of Moses; and consequently, the exercise of those solemn offices was to him [74] another source of gain. One day, as he walked in the fields about Cairo, conversing with a youth on the interpretation of the law, it so happened that the angel of death smote the young man suddenly, and he fell dead before the feet of the Rabbi, even while he was yet speaking. When the Rabbi found that the youth was dead, he rent his garments, and glorified the Lord. But his heart was touched, and the thoughts of death troubled him in the visions of the night. He felt uneasy when he reflected on his hardness to the poor, and he said "Blessed be the name of the Lord! The first good thing that I am asked to do, in that holy name, will I perform,"—but he sighed, for he feared that some one might ask of him a portion of his gold.

While yet he thought upon these things, there came a loud cry at his gate.

"Awake, thou sleeper!" said the voice, "awake! A child is in danger of death, and the mother hath sent me for thee, that thou may'st do thine office."

"The night is dark and gloomy," said the Rabbi, coming to his casement, "and mine age is great; are there not younger men than I in Cairo?"

"For thee only, Rabbi Jochonan, whom some call the wise, but whom others call Rabbi Jochonan the miser, was I sent. Here is gold," said he, taking out a purse of sequins,—"I want not thy labour for nothing. I adjure thee to come, in the name of the living God."

So the Rabbi thought upon the vow he had just made, and he groaned in spirit, for the purse sounded heavy. [75]

"As thou hast adjured me by that name, I go with thee," said he to the man, "but I hope the distance is not far. Put up thy gold."

"The place is at hand," said the stranger, who was a gallant youth, in magnificent attire. "Be speedy, for time presses."

Jochonan arose, dressed himself, and accompanied the stranger, after having carefully locked up all the doors of his house, and deposited his keys in a secret place—at which the stranger smiled.

"I never remember," said the Rabbi, "so dark a night. Be thou to me as a guide, for I can hardly see the way."

"I know it well," replied the stranger with a sigh, "it is a way much frequented, and travelled hourly by many; lean upon mine arm, and fear not."

They journeyed on; and though the darkness was great, yet the Rabbi could see when it occasionally brightened that he was in a place strange to him. "I thought," said he, "I knew all the country for leagues about Cairo, yet I know not where I am. I hope, young man," said he to his companion, "that thou hast not missed the way;" and his heart misgave him.

"Fear not," returned the stranger. "Your journey is even now done," and, as he spoke, the feet of the Rabbi slipped from under him, and he rolled down a great height. When he recovered, he found that his companion had fallen also, and stood by his side.

"Nay, young man," said the Rabbi, "if thus thou [76] sportest with the grey hairs of age, thy days are numbered. Woe unto him who insults the hoary head!"

The stranger made an excuse, and they journeyed on some little further in silence. The darkness grew less, and the astonished Rabbi, lifting up his eyes, found that they had come to the gates of a city which he had never before seen. Yet he knew all the cities of the land of Egypt, and he had walked but half an hour from his dwelling in Cairo. So he knew not what to think, but followed the man with trembling.

They soon entered the gates of the city, which was lighted up as if there were a festival in every house. The streets were full of revellers, and nothing but a sound of joy could be heard. But when Jochonan looked upon their faces—they were the faces of men pained within; and he saw, by the marks they bore, that they were Mazikin[7]. He was terrified in his soul; and, by the light of the torches, he looked also upon the face of his companion, and, behold! he saw upon him too, the mark that shewed him to be a Demon. The Rabbi feared excessively—almost to fainting; but he thought it better to be silent, and sadly he followed his guide, who brought him to a splendid house, in the most magnificent quarter of the city.

"Enter here," said the Demon to Jochonan, "for this house is mine. The lady and the child are in the upper chamber;" and, accordingly, the sorrowful

---
7 Demons.

Rabbi ascended the stair to find them. [77] The lady, whose dazzling beauty was shrouded by melancholy beyond hope, lay in bed; the child, in rich raiment, slumbered on the lap of the nurse, by her side.

"I have brought to thee, light of my eyes!" said the Demon, "Rebecca, beloved of my soul! I have brought thee Rabbi Jochanan the wise, for whom thou didst desire. Let him, then, speedily begin his office; I shall fetch all things necessary, for he is in haste to depart." He smiled bitterly as he said these words, looking at the Rabbi; and left the room, followed by the nurse.

When Jochanan and the lady were alone, she turned in the bed towards him, and said:—

"Unhappy man that thou art! knowest thou where thou hast been brought?"

"I do," said he, with a heavy groan; "I know that I am in a city of the Mazikin."

"Know then, further," said she, and the tears gushed from eyes brighter than the diamond, "know then, further, that no one is ever brought here, unless he hath sinned before the Lord. What my sin hath been imports not to thee—and I seek not to know thine. But here thou remainest for ever—lost, even as I am lost." And she wept again.

The Rabbi dashed his turban on the ground, and tearing his hair, exclaimed, "Woe is me! Who art thou, woman, that speakest to me thus!"

"I am a Hebrew woman," said she, "the daughter of a [78] Doctor of the Laws, in the city of Bagdad; and being brought hither, it matters not how, I am married to a prince among the Mazikin, even him who was sent for thee. And that child, whom thou sawest, is our firstborn, and I could not bear the thought that the soul of our innocent babe should perish. I therefore besought my husband to try to bring hither a priest, that the law of Moses (blessed be his memory!) should be done; and thy fame, which has spread to Bagdad, and lands further towards the rising of the sun, made me think of thee. Now my husband, though great among the Mazikin, is more just than the other Demons; and he loves me, whom he hath ruined, with a love of despair. So he said, that the name of Jochanan the wise was familiar unto him, and that he knew thou wouldst not be able to refuse. What thou hast done, to give him power over thee, is known to thyself."

"I swear, before Heaven," said the Rabbi, "that I have ever diligently kept the law, and walked steadfastly according to the traditions of our fathers, from the day of my youth upward. I have wronged no man in word or deed, and I have daily worshipped the Lord; minutely performing all the ceremonies thereto needful."

"Nay," said the lady, "all this thou mightest have done, and more, and yet be in the power of the Demons. But time passes, for I hear the foot of my husband mounting the stair. There is one chance of thine escape." [79]

"What is that? O lady of beauty!" said the agonized Rabbi.

"Eat not, drink not, nor take fee or reward while here; and as long as thou canst do thus, the Mazikin have no power over thee, dead or alive. Have courage, and persevere."

As she ceased from speaking, her husband entered the room, followed by the nurse, who bore all things requisite for the ministration of the Rabbi. With a heavy heart he performed his duty, and the child was numbered among the faithful. But when, as usual, at the conclusion of the ceremony, the wine was handed round to be tasted by the child, the mother, and the Rabbi, he refused it, when it came to him, saying:—

"Spare me, my lord, for I have made a vow that I fast this day; and I will eat not, neither will I drink."

"Be it as thou pleasest," said the Demon, "I will not that thou shouldst break thy vow:" and he laughed aloud.

So the poor Rabbi was taken into a chamber, looking into a garden, where he passed the remainder of the night and the day, weeping, and praying to the Lord that he would deliver him from the city of Demons. But when the twelfth hour came, and the sun was set, the Prince of the Mazikin came again unto him, and said:—

"Eat now, I pray thee, for the day of thy vow is past;" and he set meat before him. [80]

"Pardon again thy servant, my lord," said Jochonan, "in this thing. I have another vow for this day also. I pray thee be not angry with thy servant."

"I am not angry," said the Demon, "be it as thou pleasest, I respect thy vow:" and he laughed louder than before.

So the Rabbi sat another day in his chamber by the garden, weeping and praying. And when the sun had gone behind the hills, the Prince of the Mazikin again stood before him, and said:—

"Eat now, for thou must be an hungered. It was a sore vow of thine;" and he offered him daintier meats.

And Jochonan felt a strong desire to eat, but he prayed inwardly to the Lord, and the temptation passed, and he answered:—

"Excuse thy servant yet a third time, my lord, that I eat not. I have renewed my vow."

"Be it so then," said the other; "arise, and follow me."

The Demon took a torch in his hand, and led the Rabbi through winding passages of his palace, to the door of a lofty chamber, which he opened with a key that he took from a niche in the wall. On entering the room, Jochonan saw that it was of solid silver, floor, ceiling, walls, even to the threshold and the door-posts. And the curiously carved roof and borders of the ceiling shone in the torch-light, as if they were the fanciful work of [81] frost. In the midst were heaps of silver money, piled up in immense urns of the same metal, even over the brim.

"Thou hast done me a serviceable act, Rabbi," said the Demon—"take of these what thou pleasest; aye, were it the whole."

"I cannot, my lord," said Jochonan. "I was adjured by thee to come hither in the name of God; and in that name I came, not for fee or for reward."

"Follow me," said the Prince of the Mazikin; and Jochonan did so, into an inner chamber.

It was of gold, as the other was of silver. Its golden roof was supported by pillars and pilasters of gold, resting upon a golden floor. The treasures of the kings of the earth would not purchase one of the four-and-twenty vessels of golden coins, which were disposed in six rows along the room. No wonder! for they were filled by the constant labours of the Demons of the mine. The heart of Jochonan was moved by avarice, when he saw them shining in yellow light, like the autumnal sun, as they reflected the beams of the torch. But God enabled him to persevere.

"These are thine," said the Demon; "one of the vessels which thou beholdest, would make thee richest of the sons of men—and I give thee them all."

But Jochonan refused again; and the Prince of the Mazikin opened the door of a third chamber, which was called the Hall of Diamonds. When the Rabbi [82] entered, he screamed aloud, and put his hands over his eyes, for the lustre of the jewels dazzled him, as if he had looked upon the noonday sun. In vases of agate were heaped diamonds beyond numeration, the smallest of which was larger than a pigeon's egg. On alabaster tables lay amethysts, topazes, rubies, beryls, and all other precious stones, wrought by the hands of skilful artists, beyond power of computation. The room was lighted by a carbuncle, which, from the end of the hall, poured its ever living light, brighter than the rays of noontide, but cooler than the gentle radiance of the dewy moon. This was a sore trial on the Rabbi; but he was strengthened from above, and he refused again.

"Thou knowest me then I perceive, O Jochonan, son of Ben-David," said the Prince of the Mazikin; "I am a Demon who would tempt thee to destruction. As thou hast withstood so far, I tempt thee no more. Thou hast done a service which, though I value it not, is acceptable in the sight of her whose love is dearer to me than the light of life. Sad has been that love to thee, my Rebecca! Why should I do that which would make thy cureless grief more grievous?—You have yet another chamber to see," said he to Jochonan, who had closed his eyes, and was praying fervently to the Lord, beating his breast.

Far different from the other chambers, the one into which the Rabbi was next introduced, was a mean and paltry apartment without furniture. On its filthy walls hung innumerable bunches of rusty keys of all sizes, [83] disposed without order. Among them, to the astonishment of Jochonan, hung the keys of his own house, those which he had put to hide when he came on this miserable journey, and he gazed upon them intently.

"What dost thou see," said the Demon, "that makes thee look so eagerly? Can he who has refused silver and gold, and diamonds, be moved by a paltry bunch of rusty iron?"

"They are mine own, my lord," said the Rabbi, "them will I take, if they be offered me."

"Take them, then," said the Demon, putting them into his hand;—"thou may'st depart. But Rabbi, open not thy house only, when thou returnest to Cairo, but thy heart also. That thou didst not open it before, was that which gave me power over thee. It was well that thou didst one act of charity in coming with me without reward, for it has been thy salvation. Be no more Rabbi Jochanan the miser."

The Rabbi bowed to the ground, and blessed the Lord for his escape. "But how," said he "am I to return, for I know not the way?"

"Close thine eyes," said the Demon. He did so, and, in the space of a moment, heard the voice of the Prince of the Mazikin ordering him to open them again. And behold, when he opened them, he stood in the centre of his own chamber, in his house at Cairo, with the keys in his hand.

When he recovered from his surprise, and had offered [84] thanksgivings to God, he opened his house, and his heart also. He gave alms to the poor, he cheered the heart of the widow, and lightened the destitution of the orphan. His hospitable board was open to the stranger, and his purse was at the service of all who needed to share it. His life was a perpetual act of benevolence, and the blessings showered upon him by all, were returned bountifully upon him by the hand of God.

But people wondered, and said; "Is not this the man who was called Rabbi Jochanan the miser? What hath made the change?"—And it became a saying in Cairo. When it came to the ears of the Rabbi, he called his friends together, and he avowed his former love of gold, and the danger to which it had exposed him, relating all which has been above told, in the hall of the new palace that he built by the side of the river, on the left hand, as thou goest down the course of the great stream. And wise men, who were scribes, wrote it down from his mouth, for the memory of mankind, that they might profit thereby. And a venerable man, with a beard of snow, who had read it in these books, and at whose feet I sat, that I might learn the wisdom of the old time, told it to me. And I write it in the tongue of England, the merry and the free, on the tenth day of the month Nisan, in the year according to the lesser supputation, five hundred, ninety and seven, that thou may'st learn good thereof. If not, the fault be upon thee.

Title

Delta. [Moir, D.L.] "The Pneumatologist." LS 1828. 325-334. [325]

THE PNEUMATOLOGIST.

> ———Unsphere
> The spirit of Plato, to' unfold
> What worlds, or whrt rast regions hold
> The immortal mind, that hath forsook
> Her mansion in this fleshly nook-
> *Il Penseroso.*

THE year was now on the wane, and the gorgeous tints of summer were mellowing into the less obtrusive hues of autumn. The foliage, so lately of a fresh, glossy emerald green, now partook of a tinge of the sallow; and the sky, which for a long period had remained of a pure, unstained Ausonian blue, became regularly clouded, as the sun neared his western declension; at which time also, a chill wind arose, attended with those marshy exhalations, so noted throughout the Campagna, as the pestilent source of the malaria. Nature was as yet, however, only half rifled of her sweets; for, in the delightful land of Italy, the natural spirit of life breathes with freedom and health. The vineyards groaned beneath their gushing and purpled clusters;—the fruitage hung in ripeness throughout orchard and garden;—and the flowers of the latter blossomed in all their rich and beautiful varieties. [326]

As if on purpose to disappoint the studious Pietro Giannone of his accustomed and favorite sunset walk, the dews descended almost in a shower; and every thing without doors looked so cheerless and uncomfortable, that he found himself compelled to occupy his twilight breathing time from research, by seating himself beside a window that overlooked one of the principal thoroughfares of the city of Pavia, and surveying the motley groups that were passing to and fro on the pavé. Here some noble Dama whirled along in her chariot to an evening coterie; and there a brawny porter bent under his Herculean load. In one corner stood a patient girl, waiting her turn for a pitcher of water from the public fountain; and, in another, a knot of noisy urchins had congregated for sportive pastime.

As twilight deepened, the crowd were thrown into greater obscurity; but the occasional lighting up of the warehouses of the different merchants cast a transient gleam over the faces and garments of such as chanced to cross the openings. One after another, in rapid succession, the street-lamps sparkled brilliantly, displaying in a long vista, down the squares and alleys, a far-off line of lights, gradually losing themselves in the distant haziness of night. The fruiterers had removed their linen-covered stalls; and, as the gathering stars began to glitter from on high, the bustle and the business of day gradually subsided into the quiet of evening.

As Pietro sat musing, his mind naturally reverted to the [327] theme of his philosophical researches; and they had that day lain among the intricacies of metaphysical speculation. He had turned from one philosopher to another. He had read, and re-read, only to find doubt and perplexity. All was a labyrinth of intricacy—a chaos of contradiction—a maze of obscurity—a sea without a shore!

One result, and one only, was obvious to him,—and that was the vigorous and unwearied aspiration of the soul after Truth,—the deep interest of the mind in the knowledge of its own hidden nature and destiny. At the same time, he felt chagrined at the miserably narrow and circumscribed view which our human faculties allow us to take of the subject.

Instead of a solution of those doubts, on account of which he had assiduously pored over the folios of a host of ethical sophists, he had ended in greater perplexity than he had set out; for, what at first seemed only difficult and tangled, now appeared 'a maze without a plan;' and his attention, fatigued with grasping at illusive theories, had sunk down into that state of dreamy listlessness which so uniformly follows over-excitement. He did not allow his acquiescence in the noble belief of Socrates, or the profound speculations of Plato, concerning the soul's perpetuity, to be disturbed by the cold, hesitating calculations of the Stagyrite, or the apathetic scepticism of Lucretius and Pliny. From the profane he had turned altogether to the Sacred writings,—from [328] the efforts of unassisted reason, to the illuminated pages of revelation; and he found that Scripture made that as clear as noonday, which had formerly been seen, ' but as through a glass darkly.'

One point of his restless research, however, yet remained unexplained; and he had vainly puzzled himself with the curious, but somewhat idle doctrines concerning the intermediate state of the soul.

Deeply aware of their unsatisfactory tendency, he had scarcely power to prevent his mind from indulging in those mystical trains of thought which had bewildered the Pneumatologists of the middle ages. However, though the reveries of Cardan, Psellus, Sprenger, and Iamblicus, were enough to dazzle and mislead the imaginations of romantic enthusiasts, they were insufficient to satisfy the judgment of one, so discriminating and logical as Pietro; and though the Gnostics of early Christian times, following Plato, had attempted to classify the different orders of angelic beings, and had thus, to their own satisfaction, formed a hierarchy of beatified spirits, according to their own whimsical superstitions, our inquirer after truth but too plainly saw, not only that their structure was raised on idle conjecture, but was in many respects repugnant to sound reason and common sense.

"Yet," thought he, "it is a curious fact, corroborated by the traditions of all nations, and by all historians, however discordant, that a belief in disembodied spirits [329] having power 'to revisit the glimpses of the moon,' and reveal themselves to earthly survivors, universally prevails. It is a matter of record, alike in the Talmud of the Jews—the Iliad of the Greeks—the Aeneid of the Romans—and the Edda of the Scandinavians. Can such a point of belief, seemingly co-extensive with the dispersion of the human race, be other than an inherent principle in our nature?"

Vividly did the recollection of that period awaken to memory, when some years before, he had pursued the same speculations, in conjunction with his friend Vasco Cellini; and many deep feelings, interwoven with that remembrance, now obtruded themselves. Both were convinced that the soul was an immortal and imperishable essence, embodied for a season in a human and perishable frame; yet, where goes it on its immediate separation from the body? Lies it dormant for ages in the cold grave? Does death absolve all its ties to earth? Is there an intermediate state between the confines of time and eternity? On some points of faith there existed a difference of belief between the two friends, and this, even in essentials. Truth is no Janus, it looks but one way; and mentally convinced as either was, how were they, between them, to elicit conviction?

Their lodgings having been in the same street, they had been accustomed to enjoy each other's company in unceremonious evening visits, at which they talked over the subjects of their daily researches together. Once, it [330] so chanced, that after much unavailing speculation on the subject alluded to, a colloquy to the following effect took place:

"This subject, my dear Vasco, is not to be unravelled; for, how can we draw sound conclusions from a topic, which is at best conjectural?"

"True," answered Vasco, "but it is not less on that account a subject of deep interest, and worthy of all the investigation, that our limited powers enable us to bestow upon it. I would sacrifice one half of my paternal inheritance, for a solution of my doubts."

Pietro, who was perambulating the apartment with measured steps, stopped short opposite one of the windows; and, having drawn aside the hangings, exclaimed—"How brightly yon myriads of stars sparkle in the dark blue firmament! The idea may be foolish, but it has often struck me, that the soul may be transferred from one of those bodies to another, in long succession; continually in its progressive course, becoming more and more purified from the stains of its terrestrial pilgrimage; throwing off its accquired infirmities; and approximating to the nature of a pure and blessed spirit."

"The idea," replied his companion, "is as novel, as it is orthodox: but proof—proof—proof, Pietro. We toss as before in a sea of idle conjecture. Where is our assurance of such things'! Hypothesis—suggestion—probability—are not certainty." [331]

"True, my friend, such things are but idle fashionings out of the inquiring and unsatisfied spirit,—whims of excursive fancy, supported neither by revelation, nor logical deduction. These things lie ' within the vail,' and are shut out from the explorations of human intellect. Imagination may hover around; but, like Noah's dove, it brings no token of assurance. Provided, however, it be not a warring against the fixed laws of nature, one of us may at least be made aware of the truth, even before leaving this sublunary stage. Do you attend to me?"

"I am all attention——Proceed."

"Well, then, my suggestion is this. Let which ever of us die first, return, in spirit, for the immediate information of the survivor."

"Agreed, with all my heart;" said Vasco, proffering his hand, which was cordially grasped by his friend:—"But how know we that such things are allowed?"

"At all events," returned Pietro, "one of us shall learn as much by the issue, in the accomplishment, or the non-fulfilment of this paction. If a disembodied soul may return to earth, and reveal the mystery, we are individually bound so to do."—

Pietro, sitting with his listless gaze fixed on the flickering fire, felt this conversation repass through his mind, with a vivid distinctness. Perhaps the same intensely renewed perception of the intangible nature of the [332] subject, which had occupied his mind on that memorable evening, by awakening trains of association, had now brought to recollection the ideas connected with such an unsatisfactory speculation more acutely.

As Pietro laid him down to rest, the clock struck eleven. The night was calm; the city silent; and starry darkness reigned over the wide, silent, serene hemisphere. Contrary to his wonted habit, his sleep was dreamy, disturbed, and unrefreshing. The dim pageantries of by-past years flitted before his mind's eye in feverish and gloomy succession, and mixing up with the heavy lethargic, leaden coinage of the brain, melted away in dim, shadowy indistinctness. In vain, turning from side to side, he courted the refreshing repose which eluded him. Still phantasmagorial crowds awaited the closing of his eyelids; and a mystical perplexity haunted his thoughts.

In this uncomfortable, dissatisfied state, he determined to shake off altogether the disposition to slumber; and, leaving his couch, he put on his morning robe,—lighted his taper,—and sat down, in the silence of the breathless night, to pursue his metaphysical speculations. Hour lapsed away after hour, till at length the grey dawn began to glimmer in at the casement.

The earliest morning was clouded, but silent; so that the twitter of the swallows, which harboured beneath the eaves, was distinctly audible. Opposite were some tall poplars whose summits stood motionless. From the thickness of [333] the air, it was evident that a heavy dew was falling:—the silence felt almost unearthly:—and sorely did Pietro miss his favorite blackbird, whose sweet, clear, thrilling song used to welcome in the dawn. The ticking of the old Venetian clock on the staircase, sounded to his painfully attentive ear like the audible pulse of time. Suddenly a violent knocking was heard at the street door, the portico over which almost shewed itself at his window sill. He started from his reverie, listening in anxious suspense;—what could it be, this untimely summons? He did not bestir himself; but waited a little, in the hope that some one of the servants would answer. In a few seconds it was repeated, and more violently, yet not a foot was stirring. Pietro lost his self-possession, a sudden awe fell shadow-like over his heart, and almost deprived him of the power of motion. The third peal sounded; just as, recovering himself, his foot touched the carpet.

He rushed forward to the window, the sash of which he was about to throw up—when, lo! what meets his view? He beholds his friend, Vasco Cellini, galloping down the centre of the street, on a horse white as the falling snows of January. Behind him streamed a long white mantle; and once he reverted his head, and waved his arm, as if in token of farewell. Could it be real? Was it not a dream? He glanced round the apartment, and then again after the figure; but the illusive pageant had vanished, like a shadow in the sunshine; and nought [334] was seen but the voiceless and deserted street under the sombre covering of a cloudy sky, and wet with the dews of morning.

The perturbed and agitated student could not help exclaiming aloud to himself. "And art thou, my friend, dead!—Hast thou left earth for ever?—Are we now separated by the gulf of eternity? Heaven hath shewed me by thee, that it is impious to pry too narrowly into its hidden mysteries. Light enough has been granted us, to lead our steps through the bewildering labyrinth of life. Plain are the ways of truth; and the road to heaven is not obstructed by complex speculations. There the unlettered hind may as surely go, as the most learned philosopher. I shall henceforth wait in faith: I have been fully and fearfully answered in this thing!"

Pietro mentioned the circumstance at breakfast; and the family tried to make him regard it as a mental hallucination, occasioned by over-exertion of thought; but, aware that Vasco had been travelling in Germany, he requested them to stay their mirth, till a sufficient lapse of time should counteract his impression. From that hour, Pietro Giannone was an altered man.

In four days a letter arrived, stating that the friend of Pietro had been drowned in the Danube, by the upsetting of a pleasure boat. On a fly-leaf of his Bible was found written, in a fine hand; 'This to be forwarded to Pisa, after my decease. It is a legacy from Vasco Cellini, to Pietro Giannone.'

Δ.

Literary Annual

The Literary Souvenir. Ed. Alaric A. Watts. London: Longman, Rees, Orme, Brown & Green, 1829. Printer: S. Manning & Co., London House Yard, St. Paul's.[8]

Title

Anonymous. "The Sisters." LS 1829. 1-33.

FRONTISPIECE TO *Literary Souvenir*;
PLATE: The Sisters
Steel plate engraving;
painted by Philip Francis Stephanoff;
engraving by John H. Robinson [1]

---

[8] Plain text for all short stories included here for the 1829 *Literary Souvenir* obtained from Google Books and then compared against the original volume. For full citation, see References:
< http://books.google.com/books?id=7mwEAAAAQAAJ&dq=1829%20The%20Literary%20Souvenir%3B%20or%2C%20Cabinet%20of%20Poetry%20and%20Romance&pg=PR3#v=onepage&q&f=false>

THE SISTERS.

THERE lies in the north of England a considerable tract of land, now known by the name of the Waste Lands, which once formed the richest property of two wealthy families by whom untoward circumstances had caused it to be deserted. For some time, it was looked after by stewards, too much bent upon profiting themselves to regard the interests of their employers. The tenantry, who, drained of their hard earnings, were obliged to vex the land till it became a bed of stones, dropped off one by one. The hedge-rows, being unremittingly assisted in the progress of decay by the paupers of the neighbourhood, were soon reduced to nothing but dock-weeds and brambles; which gradually uniting from the opposite ends of the fields, the property became a huge thicket, too encumbered ever to be worth clearing, and only valuable to poachers and gypsies, to whom it still affords abundant booty and a secure hiding place.

The two mansions have kept pace in ruin with the lands around them. The persons left in charge of them, [2] being subject to no supervision, put themselves but little out of their way to preserve that which was so lightly regarded by the owners. Too careless to repair the dilapidations of time and the weather, they were driven, by broken windows and rickety doors, from office to office, and from parlour to parlour, till ruin fairly pursued them into the grand saloon; where the Turkey carpets were tattered by hob-nails, and the dogs of the chase licked their paws upon sofas of silk and satin. In due time, the rain forced its way through the roofs, and the occupiers having no orders to stop it with a tile, the breach became wider and wider. Soon the fine papering began to shew discoloured patches, and display the lath and plaster which bulged through it; then the nails which supported the family portraits gave way with their burthens; and finally, the rafters began to yield, and the inhabitants wisely vacated the premises in time to avoid the last crash, rightly conjecturing that it was useless to leave the moveables behind to share in the common destruction, when there was so little likelihood of their ever being inquired after.

Thus ended the pride both of Heroncliff and Hazledell, which may still be seen, from each other, about a mile apart, shooting up a few parti-coloured walls from their untrimmed wildernesses, and seeming, like two desperate combatants, to stand to the last extremity; neither of them cheered by a sign of life, excepting the jackdaws which sit perched upon the dead tips of the old ash trees, [3] and the starlings that sweep around at sunset in circles, beyond which the country folks have rarely been hardy enough to intrude.

The last possessor who resided at Hazledell was an eccentric old bachelor, with a disposition so composed of kindness and petulance, that every body liked, and scarcely any one could live with him. His relations had been driven away from him, one after the other;—one because he presumed to plead the poverty of a tenant whom the old man had previously resolved upon forgiving his rent; another, because he mistook the choice bin of the cellar when wine was prescribed for the sickness of the poor; and a third, because he suffered himself to be convinced by him in politics, and thus deprived him of the opportunity of holding forth arguments which gave his company due time to discuss their good cheer. There was but one person who understood him, and this was his nephew; who continued to the last his only companion, and kept him alive solely by knowing how to manage him. He had the good taste never to remind him of his years by approaching him with that awe which is commonly demonstrated by young people towards the old; and the tact to observe exactly where his foibles would bear raillery, and where they required sympathy. He could lead him from one mood to another, so that the longest day in his company never seemed monotonous; or if he rambled away amongst the neighbourhood, he could return at night with a tale of adventures which sent him to bed without repining at the prospect of to-morrow. Unluckily the old man considered him too necessary to his comforts to part with him; and though merely the son of a younger brother, without fortune or expectations, he was not permitted to turn his mind to a profession, or to any thing beyond the present. The youth, however, was scarcely twenty-three; and at such an age, a well-supplied purse for the time being, leaves but little anxiety for the future. With a good education, picked up as he could, by snatches, a sprightly disposition, and a talent equal to any thing, young Vibert of Hazledell was as welcome abroad as he was at home; and it was augured that his handsome figure and countenance would stand him in the stead of the best profession going. The young ladies would turn from any beau at the county-ball to greet his arrival, and never think of engaging themselves to dance till they were quite sure that he was disposed of. One remarked upon the blackness of his hair, another upon the whiteness of his forehead; and the squires who were not jealous of him, would entertain them with his feats of horsemanship and adroitness at bringing down, right and left. Still Vibert was not spoiled, and the young ladies pulled up their kid gloves till they split, without making any visible impression upon him. His obstinacy was quite incomprehensible. Each ridiculed the disappointment of her friend, in the hope of concealing her own; and all turned for consolation, to the young master of Heroncliff. [5]

Marcus of Heroncliff was nearly of an age with Vibert, and was perhaps still more popular with the heads of families, if not with the younger branches; for lie had the advantage of an ample fortune. His person, also, was well formed, and his features were, for the most part, handsome, but the first had none of the grace of Vibert, and the last had a far different expression. His front, instead of being cast in that fine expansive mould, was contracted and low, and denoted more cunning than talent. His eye was too deeply sunk to indicate openness or generosity, and the *tout ensemble* gave an idea of sulkiness and double-dealing. It was held by many that this outward appearance was not a fair index of his disposition, which was said to be liberal and good natured. The only fault which they found with him was, that his conversation seemed over-much guarded for one of his age. He appeared unwilling to shew himself as he really was, and the greatest confidence which could be reposed in him produced no corresponding return. He walked in society like one who came to look on rather than to mix in it: and although his dependants lived in profusion, his table was rarely enlivened save by the dogs which had been the companions of his sport.

Vibert, whose character it was to judge always favourably, believed that his manner and mode of life proceeded from the consciousness of a faulty education, and a mistrust of his capacity to redeem lost time. He felt a friendliness for him, bordering upon compassion, and [6] their near neighbourhood affording him frequent opportunities of throwing himself in his way, a considerable degree of intimacy was, in course of time, established between them. Vibert was right, as far as he went, in his estimate of his friend's mind; but he never detected its grand feature. Marcus was sensible that he was below par amongst those of his rank, and a proud heart made him bitterly jealous of all who had the advantage of him. It was this that gave verity to the expression which we have before noticed in his features; made him a torment to himself; and rendered him incapable of sympathising with others. If a word were addressed to him, he believed that it was designed to afford an opportunity of ridiculing his reply; if contradiction was opposed to him, his visage blackened as though he felt that he had been insulted. Vibert, so open to examination, was the only person whom he did not suspect and dread. They hunted, shot, and went into society together; and it was observed that Marcus lost nothing by the contact. His confidence increased, his reserve in some degree disappeared, and Vibert secretly congratulated himself on having fashioned a battery to receive the flattering attentions from which he was anxious to escape. His ambition, indeed, was otherwise directed.

At a few miles distance from Hazledell was a pretty estate, called Silvermere, from a small lake, which reflected the front of the dwelling and the high grounds and rich limber behind it. It was inhabited by persons [7] of consideration in the county, who were too happy at home to mix much with their neighbours. In fact, of a numerous family, there was but one daughter old enough to be introduced; and she was of a beauty so rare, that there was little danger in keeping her upon hand until her sister was of an age to accompany her into society.

In this family, Vibert had been for some time a favourite, and had been fascinated on his first introduction to it. The beauty of whom we have made mention, and her sister, a year or two younger, were placed on either side of him; and it was hard to know whether most to admire the wild tongue and laughing loveliness of the younger—the fair-haired Edith; or the retiring, but smiling dignity of the black eyes and pale fine features of the elder—the graceful Marion. They were, perhaps, both pleased to see the hero of the county conversations; but the younger one was the foremost to display it: without being a flirt, she was frank, and had the rare, natural gift of saying and doing what she pleased without danger of misconstruction.

The daring but feminine gaiety of this young creature speedily dispelled from the mind of Vibert all idea of his recent acquaintance. On his making some mention of it, she assured him that, on her part, the acquaintance was by no means recent, for she had heard him discussed as often as any Knight of the Round Table.

"To place you upon an equality with us," she said, "I will tell you what sort of persons we are, and you [8] can judge whether at any future time, when your horse happens to knock up in our neighbourhood, and your dinner to be five miles off, you will condescend to take advantage of us. Papa and mamma, who you see have been a handsome couple, and would think themselves so still, if they had not such a well grown family, are by no means rigid, exacting, fault-finding and disagreeable, like papas and mammas in general. They have had the good taste to discover our precose talents, and profit by being our companions instead of our rulers, from the time we learned the art of spelling words of one syllable, and doing as we were not bidden. Instead of scolding us for our misdeeds, they used to reason with us as to their propriety, and generally got the worst of the argument; so, saving that in virtue of our old companionship we make them the confidants of most of our dilemmas, they have brought us up charmingly undutiful and self-willed.

"As for Marion, she is a young lady erroneously supposed to be the pride of the family, and who presumes to regard me with a patronising complacency which seems to intimate an idea that, one of these days, I shall really learn to talk. She is a sedate personage, who tries to reflect upon things; but as the same deep study has shaded her brow as long as I can recollect, I imagine that she does not often come to a conclusion. Yet the falsely-styled pride of Silvermere does not blanch her cheeks in the unwholesome atmosphere of learned tomes; [9] nor by spinning the globes, nor by hunting the stars. Her character is a little touched with romance, and her study is how to mend a bad world, which continues ailing in spite of her. She gives all her consolation, and half of her pin-money, to a tribe of old dames and young damsels, who, under such patronage, only pull our hedges in greater security, or add fresh colours to the costume which is to flaunt triumphant on the fair day. The urchins whom she teaches "to guess their lessons," and buys off from aiding in the toils of their parents, are the most mischievous in the neighbourhood; and, in short, things go on worse and worse, and poor Marion does not know what to make of it. From the humbler world, so different from the Arcadian affair of her imagination, she turns with despair to the sphere in which she is herself to move, and shudders at the prospect of disappointment there also. Where amongst such a community of young ladies battling for precedence, and young gentlemen vowing eternal constancy to a dozen at a time, can she look for the friend of her soul, or the more favoured being who is to console her for the want of one! Alas, the pride of Silvermere! with feelings so delicate that a gossamer might wound them, how can she accommodate herself to any world but that of the fairy tales which delighted our nursery, or expect tranquillity in any place but a cloister ."

Vibert's calls were repeated often, each one affording a pretext for another, and each visit growing longer than [10] the last. The father of his two attractions was required frequently by his affairs in London, where he spent weeks at a time, and their mother was generally confined by delicate health to her chamber. Thus Vibert's intimacy with them had but little ceremony to restrain its rapid advancement; and he soon felt, what has perhaps been felt by many, that the simple smile of the dignified and retiring, is more perilous than the brightest glance of wit and vivacity. Indeed, Edith was too gay to be suspected of any thought beyond that of amusement; but the actions of Marion were more measured, and her approbation was the more flattering. Vibert laughed when he encountered the first; but his pulse beat quicker at the sight of the last.

There seems in the affairs of the heart, to be an unaccountable intelligence, by which, without the use of external signs, the tremours of the one generally find their reverberation in the other. Often as Vibert entered to share in the morning amusements of the sisters, to give an account of the horse that he was breaking in for Marion, or the dog he was teaching antics for Edith, it was impossible for him to be insensible to an increasing flush of satisfaction at his appearance, and by degrees he gave up all other society, and had no pastime to which Marion was not a party. Both young, both interested in the other's happiness, it was not likely that they should reflect, how the brightest flowers may be the seat of poison, and the sweetest moments the parents of [11] misery. Their intimacy became more confidential; and Edith left them more and more to themselves, to seek amusement elsewhere. Still there was no question of love. Vibert knew that without fortune or expectations, he could have no pretension to Marion; and that the number of her young brothers and sisters must render it impossible for her father to remedy the deficiency. It was then that he felt the extent of the sacrifice he had made in devoting himself so entirely to his uncle. Had he adopted any profession, he might have obtained a home of his own, to say the least; and, however humble that home might have been, would Marion have shrunk from it? Would Marion have failed to make it the richest spot upon earth? He was yet only of an age when many commence their career; his mind was too active and too brilliant to suffer his habits to become so fixed but that he could apply them to any thing. He determined upon breaking the matter to his uncle: and, as Edith was now eighteen, and the sisters were just about to appear in public, there was no time to be lost. If Marion were not to go forth with a hand already engaged, what had he not to apprehend? Fortunes and honours would be at her feet—friends would reason—parents might command, and what had she to reply? She loved an idler who lived upon another's bounty, and whose future means were something worse than precarious. He seized upon what he thought a good opportunity, the same evening. His uncle was enjoying his arm-chair and slippers beside [12] an ample fire, to which the pattering of a November storm gave additional comfort.

"Vibert," said he, "what have been your adventures to day?"

"I have been to Silvermere."

"Folks tell me you have been there every day for the last twelvemonth,—and who have you seen there?"

"I have seen Marion."

"Well, nephew, she is good-looking, you say; and sensible, and all that. Why do not you marry her, and bring her home to make tea for us?"

"Alas! I would willingly do so, had I the means."

"We can get over that obstacle, I think, by doubling your allowance."

"My dear Sir, you do not understand its full extent. Marion's family would never consent, unless she were to be the mistress of an establishment of her own."

"We can remedy that, too, Vibert. Divide the house with me at the middle of the cellar, and brick up the communications. Divide the stables and the horses, have new wheels and new arms to the old family rumble-tumble, and make any farther arrangements you please. You have been a good boy, to bear with a crazy old man so long, and I should not like you to be a loser by it."

"My dear uncle, there was no need of this additional generosity to secure my gratitude and endeavours to prove it. I did not speak for the purpose of placing any farther tax upon you, but merely to consult you whether [13] it were not better that I thought of some profession, by which I might attain a position in life not liable to reverse."

"A profession!—what, one that would call you away from Hazledell?"

"I fear all professions would subject me to that affliction."

The uncle's colour rose, and his brow darkened.

"Vibert leave me in my old age, when I have become entirely dependent upon him! Vibert knock away the only crutch that props me up from the grave—bequeath me to the mercy of hired servants, with not a soul to exchange a word of comfort with me?—What fortune could you obtain which would compensate for reflections like these?

"Stay, nephew, and see me into my grave—the reverse which you apprehend,—I never thought that you could so coldly contemplate my extinction; but it is right and natural that you should do so. Only stay,—and I promise you that I will not keep you long,—I will curtail my expenses, banish my few old friends, dismiss my servants, and live upon bread and water, to save what I can for you from the estate. I cannot cause it to descend to you; but at all events, I can save for you as much as you would be likely to make by leaving me. Yet, if it be your wish to go, e'en go; I had rather you would leave me miserable, than stay to wish me dead."

The old man had worked himself into a fit of childish agitation, and Vibert saw that argument was useless.

"Uncle," he replied, with a look and voice of despair, "make yourself easy. Marion will find another husband, who will perhaps render her happier than I could, and I will remain with you as I have done hitherto."

From this time, Vibert spared no effort to overcome his ill-starred passion, as well for Marion's sake as for his own; seeking every possible pretext to render his visits less frequent, and to pay them in company. Marion perceived the change at the moment it took place, and, although she could not dispute its propriety, her sensibility was wounded to the quick. She commenced her first round of provincial gaiety with a fever at her heart, and an ominous presage of sorrow.

The appearance of the Silvermere party formed an epoch in the annals of the county,—and, as Vibert had foreseen, there was not a squire of the smallest pretensions who did not address himself sedulously to make the agreeable to them. They had little encouragement, however, in their attempts, excepting from Edith. Her heart was free, and her tongue was full of joy; but Marion was looking for the return of Vibert; and the reserved glance of her eye kept flattery at a distance, and hope in fetters. Still he returned not—she never met him in society, but she constantly heard of his having been at balls and merry-makings where she was not. It was in the vain pursuit of his peace of mind; and she was too generous [15] to attribute it to any thing else. On his occasional visits of ceremony, she received him as if nothing material had happened; but the flush was gone from her cheek, and the smile that remained, was cold and sickly.

Meantime, rumour was liberal in assigning to each of the sisters her share of intended husbands. Vibert listened to the catalogue with all the trepidation of a lover who had really entertained hopes. Alas! if that selfish principle of denying to another what we cannot enjoy ourselves be excusable in any case, it is so in love. The loved object which belongs to no other, still appears to be in some degree our own; and fancy conjures up in spite of us, an indefinable trust in the future, of which the total destruction falls like the blow of an assassin. It was thus with Vibert, when, after writhing long in secret anguish at the mention of any name connected with that of Marion, report from all quarters concurred in the same uncontradicted tale. Marion was receiving the addresses of Marcus of Heroncliff: of him, for whom he had himself, from motives of the purest kindness, secured the good thoughts of her family—him whom he had made the confidant of his love—him who had professed himself to be only waiting for encouragement to throw himself at the feet of her sister! That he should have met him daily, and never hinted at the change in his intentions!—Yet might it not have been that he feared to inflict pain? That he should have deserted Edith when his conduct had implied all that was devoted!—Yet, was it not for Marion? But [16] then, that Marion should have become the rival of her sister? Yet, oh! how soon she had overcome the remembrance of him, and how natural was it for the cold in love to become the faithless in friendship. Thus Vibert went on arguing for and against all the parties, and winding up with a forced ejaculation of, "it is nothing to me—it is no affair of mine;"—it was meant to confirm his pride, but only proved his wretchedness.

Upon this principle, and from a sense of his want of self-possession, the name of Marion never passed his lips in the presence of Marcus, who, on his part, was equally silent.

The report upon which this conduct was adopted was not so destitute of reason as those which had preceded it. Marcus, with the failing already noticed, was incapable of being a true friend; and though at his first introduction at Silvermere, the marked intelligence between Marion and Vibert reduced him to the necessity of devoting his attentions to Edith, yet the bare circumstance of her sister's preference for another was sufficient to kindle in his heart the most burning anxiety to obtain her for himself. Without considering Vibert's earlier acquaintance, he felt himself eclipsed, and his honour wounded. The moment, therefore, that his friend's visits were discontinued, his own were redoubled. They were naturally, from his previous behaviour, laid by the family to the account of Edith; and upon this conviction, Marion often used him as a protection against the advances [17] of her unwelcome host of admirers. If she was asked to dance, she was engaged to Marcus, and his arm was always ready to conduct her to her carriage. It was observed that she received much more of his attention than was bestowed upon her sister; and insensibly their manner in public became the practice in private, where there was no need for it. His hopes rose high, and he scrupled not to advance them by endeavouring to extirpate the last kind feeling, which he thought might yet linger, for poor Vibert. One while he affected chagrin, and invented excesses on the part of his friend as the cause of it: at another time he was incensed at injurious words, which he alleged to have been employed by Vibert towards herself. At last, when he thought himself quite secure, he disclosed his passion, and was rejected with astonishment.

The sting for one like him had a thousand barbs: he loved the beautiful Marion with all the energy of a soul which had never before loved a human being. Common report, and his confidence in her resentment against Vibert, had made him consider her as already his own. His triumph over all the competitors that he had feared, envied, and detested, was, as he deemed, on the eve of completion; and now he was to be the object of derision, and mock pity! The means which he had used to ingratiate himself would probably be divulged. The inmost core of his heart would be exposed and scorned; and Vibert, whom he felt to be the latent cause of his rejec- [18] tion, was perhaps finally to be reinstated, and to flaunt his triumph daily before his eyes! The very evils which bad minds have attempted to inflict upon others, become a provocation to themselves: they have been defeated, and therefore they have been injured! and the rejected suitor returned home pallid, and quivering with an ague fit of mortal hate.

The attentions of Marcus had never been discussed between the sisters until the occurrence of this catastrophe. He left them in a shaded alley of the pleasure-grounds, which were beginning to be strewed with the yellow leaves of autumn; and a clouded sunset cast a few long streaks across the sward, and made the deep recesses look still more sombre.

There are few who do not feel a melancholy peculiar to this period of the year. Marion had a double reason; for it was about the same time in the preceding autumn, and in the summer-house but a few steps before her, that she had passed the last happy hour with Vibert!

"Marion," said Edith, as they walked on, with their arms fondly resting upon each other's neck, "you are not well. It is long since you were well; but I had hoped that the attachment of Marcus would have dispelled a deep grief, of which you forbade me ever to speak. I trusted that your heart had been arrested in its progress of sorrow, and I was silent, lest you should think me jealous of my sweet rival."

"Heavens! that my apathy should have been so [19] great as to mistake his attentions. I only bore with him because I thought him yours."

"Marion, I love him not; and never should have wished him loved by you, had I not felt that your life depended on the diversion of your thoughts. I have been mistaken; you have been dying daily, and unless you would have me die with you, let me write to Vibert. Sweet Marion, let me write, as from myself, in my own wild way, merely to bid him come and dance on my birth-day."

"No, Edith, no. He would suspect the reason; it is too humiliating. I have still pride enough left to save me from contempt, if not to support me from—— Edith, let us talk of other things."

She leaned her head upon her sister's bosom, and both were weeping, when they were startled by the gallop of a horse, and a ring at the garden gate. Edith saw that it was the servant of Vibert, and she sprang like a fawn to inquire his commission. He brought a letter for Marion, and thus it ran:

"The relations who stood between me and the succession to the estates of Hazledell, are dead. I am now my uncle's heir; hut I fear too late. The sorrow of withdrawing myself to my proper distance when I was poor, is probably to be followed up by the anguish of being forbidden to return now that I am rich. I dare not appear before you till I hear the refutation of your reported engagements with Marcus—till you bid me [20] look forward to a termination of the misery which a feeling of honour obliged me to inflict upon myself."

Marion sank for support against the ivy-twined pillar of the summer-house. Edith kissed her pale cheek, and fondly whispered, "I told you so: what answer will you send?" After the first moments of tremulous agitation—after an interval of silence, to lull the tumults of her heart, Marion merely ejaculated, "Poor Vibert! I thought he had forgotten me!"

"Rather say, poor Edith," replied her sister, with a burst of that natural gaiety which had of late almost forsaken her; "poor Edith has now the willow-wreath all to herself. Alas! for some doughty champion to twine it round the neck of the false lord of Heroncliff!—'Tis time that I endow you with all my finery, and prepare for a nunnery."

With that she playfully took from her neck a simple hair-chain, the appendage to which had always been carefully hidden in her bosom, and cast it over the unadorned head of Marion. "Look!" she exclaimed, with increased archness, and gazing upon her averted eyes, to see if the smile had yet returned to them, "look what a jewel I bestow upon you; I have cherished it ever since we sat for our miniatures, and the artist amused himself between whiles with studying a head for Apollo. Why do you not look?"

Marion turned her eyes, and was surprised by her lover's likeness. [21]

"Then Marion *can* smile? Oh, the joy to see it! I begged this little jewel for your wedding-present; but, in truth, this seems no bad opportunity, as the cavalier may now speak for himself. See what a sad brow—what an imploring eye. Here—here is a pencil—the servant waits for a reply."

Marion tore the back from her letter, and wrote—"The reports are unfounded—the future is in your power."

"Edith!" she said, when the messenger was dismissed; "give me your arm back to the house, for I feel faint. In the midst of all this happiness, there is a sickness at my heart,—a strange boding, that I am only tantalized by chimeras, and meant for misfortune. Perhaps I deceive myself. Perhaps it is only the strange bewilderment occasioned by this revolution in all that interests me. I cannot help it."

The messenger, who had been dispatched by Vibert the moment he became aware of his happy fortune, did not return in time for him to profit ere the morrow by Marion's answer. It was a gusty and querulous night—the old trees by his window groaned as though they were in trouble, and the scud swept along the sky like a host of spectres. He felt low and oppressed, in spite of himself. His uncle had left him ominously distressed at the news which he had lately received. After having retired for the night, he had come back to shake hands with him again. The younger ones, he said, were dropping about him, and leaving him desolate, to lament the luckless [22] humour which had impeded him from adding to their comforts, as he might have done. Every joint of him trembled, lest he should live too long. "God bless you, Vibert," he added, "you have always been a good boy, and have borne kindly with my infirmities—God bless you!—God bless you! Vibert, you will go to-morrow to Silvermere? I have long prevented you from being happy, and you owe me no thanks that you are so at last. Go to bed,—you have grown thin from want of sleep; and it is all my fault."

He quitted him again with affectionate, and almost childish reluctance; and Vibert paced his room, in a fever of anticipation, till the rising of the sun, which had seemed as if it never meant to rise again. It was still too early to set out for Silvermere, but he knew that Marcus rose with the dawn for his field-sports, and his generous mind was unwilling to lose an instant in acknowledging and asking pardon for the suspicions which he had entertained of his friendship. He walked rapidly to Heroncliff, and found Marcus, as he had anticipated, up and dressed; in fact, he had passed the night in the same manner as he himself had done, and his face looked haggard and wild.

"Marcus," said Vibert, "I come to tell you a piece of strange news."

"I know it already," replied Marcus, with an attempt to look glad. "I met your servant going to Silvermere with it. Your uncles in India are dead." [23]

"I scarcely recollect them, and it would therefore he ridiculous to affect much grief for their loss; but the circumstance has been the means of shewing me an injustice committed against yourself, at which I am sincerely grieved. I believed that you entertained an intention of supplanting me in the love of Marion; and although my reason had nothing to object to it, my heart felt that it was not the part which I would have acted towards you. I have accused you bitterly; but see, Marion has herself exculpated you; and you must even forgive me as one who has been too unhappily bewildered to be master of himself."

Marcus took his offered hand and laughed, but with a fearful expression, which he strove to hide by casting his eyes on the ground.

"Then Marion," he observed, "looks forward to being the lady of Hazledell?"

"Ay, and to do the honours of it to her sister, the lady of Heroncliff. My son shall marry your daughter, and we will join the estates in one."

Marcus drew in his breath with a harrowing sound.

"Vibert," he said, "we had best remain unmarried; we are more independent to pursue our pastimes; we are not obliged to receive the society which is odious to us; and whilst we are free, we are the more welcomed abroad. Promise me you will think no more of it."

"You would not ask it, if you felt, like me, that you were beloved by Marion. What do I care for indepen- [24] dence and my reception abroad, when I have such a thraldom and such a paradise at home!"

"You are determined, then?"

"Can you doubt it? I am even now on my way to Silvermere. I should arrive too soon on horseback, and am therefore obliged to walk, for I cannot be easy until I find myself on my way thither. Come, take your gun and accompany me."

"I will accompany, in the hope of dissuading you, and bringing you back before you arrive there."

"And I will drag you into fetters whether you will or not. Come; it is time to start, if we would be there by breakfast time. What ails you?—You look pale and shivering this morning; and see,—for the first time in your life, you have forgotten your gun."

With that he kindly took it from where it stood, and presented it to him.

"I will not take it," said Marcus, vaguely; "I am nervous, and cannot shoot."

"Tut, man; take your gun, I say; a good shot will put you in spirits. There is an outlying deer from Hazledell in the Black Valley, and you must kill him for our wedding-feast."

Marcus bit his white lips, and did as he was bidden; and the companions set out upon their walk.

The weather was still gusty and uncertain. The faint gleam of the sun was rapidly traversed by the clouds, which seemed to overrun each other, in wild and [25] fearful confusion. Several large trees were blown across the pathways, and the crows skimmed aloft in unsettled course, as though they were afraid to perch.

"How I love this bracing air!" said Vibert. "I feel as if I could fly."

"You feel elastic from your errand. I have no such cause, and I would fain that the morning had been calmer. I think that long usage to blustering weather would have a strong effect upon men's passions, and render them too daring and reckless."

As they descended the brow of fern and scattered plantations, from his bleak residence, his persuasions that Vibert would return, became more and more urgent. He used in a wild, disjointed manner, all the vain arguments to which the selfish and the dissipated generally resort, to dissuade their friends from what they call a sacrifice of liberty. They were easily overruled, and his agitation grew the more violent. In this manner they arrived at the entrance of the Black Valley, a gorge of rock, and varied earth, choked up by trees and bushes, chance-sown by the birds and the winds. This valley was between two and three miles in length, its gloom was unbroken by a single habitation, and it had been the witness of many atrocities. It was a place usually avoided; but it was the shortest road to Silvermere, and Vibert never visited it by any other.

"I do not like this valley!" said Marcus, "we will take the upper road." [26]

"It is too far about,—come on—you are not yourself this morning, and the sooner Edith laughs at you the better."

They were making a short cut through the tangled thicket, from one path to another, and had reached a more gloomy and savage spot than they had hitherto encountered. Marcus sat down upon a piece of splintered timber, and motioned Vibert, with a gasping earnestness which was not to be disputed, to seat himself beside him.

"Marcus," said the latter, as he complied, "your conduct is inexplicable. Why are you so anxious that I should not go to Silvermere, nor renew my acquaintance with Marion? You must have some reason for all this; and, if so, why conceal it from me?"

"If nothing short of such an extremity will induce you to follow my counsel, I must even come to it. Marion is not what you have supposed her.—You imagine that her love for you has kept her single. Ask of whom you will, if such be the general opinion. Till yesterday, she gave herself to another, who cannot aspire to a thousandth part of your merit, but who happened to be more favoured by fortune. Last night, you became the richest, and she changed; but would Vibert be contented with a partner who preferred another?"

"Marcus!—this other! It is of yourself you speak?"

"Ask all the world, if she did not make herself notorious with me. She made me distrust all womankind. [27] Vibert, let us both leave her to the reflections of one who has deserved to be forsaken."

"May it not be that you, and not I, have mistaken her? She might have preferred your company because you were my friend, and you might have fancied that she loved you because you loved her. It is needless to contradict me; men do not tremble and turn pale because their friends are going to marry jilts. I do not blame you; for not to love Marion is beyond the power even of friendship. Let us only be fair rivals, and not attempt to discourage each other by doing her injustice. Let us go hand in hand, and each prefer his suit. For my part, I promise you, that, if you succeed, I will yield without enmity."

Marcus staggered as he arose; Vibert's countenance was grave, but not unfriendly.

"Go on, then," said the former, in a deep, broken voice, and with every feature convulsed; at the same time, he turned himself homeward; and Vibert, seeing that it was advisable to part company, pursued his course towards Silvermere. Marcus made but a few strides, and paused. He clenched his teeth, and cast a wild glance at the fine form that was retreating from him—made one or two hesitating steps, and then bounded after.

The restlessness which pervaded the other personages of our story during the night, was not spared to Marion or her sister. They talked of their future prospects, [28] until Edith was elevated to her highest flight of spirits. She arranged, that when Marion became the lady of Hazledell, she also was to call it her home; make herself the sole object of attraction and tournament to all the squires round about, and display her true dignity by remaining a scornful lady and a respectable maiden aunt! By degrees, her fancy ceased castle-building,—a few unconnected sparkles of gaiety grew fainter and fainter, and she dropped asleep. Marion had no wish or power to repose; her nervous sense of apprehension continued to increase;—she tried every effort to direct her thoughts to other subjects; but they invariably became entangled, and again pressed with a dead weight upon her heart. In this mood, she was startled by Edith laughing in her sleep, with a sound which terrified her.

"Edith!" she cried, shaking her till she partially awoke,—"Edith, you frighten me—why do you laugh in your sleep?".

"I laughed," replied Edith, drowsily, and scarce knowing what she said,—"I laughed at some one who preached to me of the vanity of human expectations." She again muttered a laugh, and a second time dropped asleep. She still remained so when Marion arose in the morning and hastily dressed herself to profit by the fresh air; and did not awaken until she had been left some hours alone. The servants told her that her sister had walked out upon the road to Hazledell, and thither Edith followed her. [29]

Marion was led on by the hope of meeting Vibert, who in former days had often arrived to breakfast, so far as the commencement of the Black Valley. At other times, she had shared in the general terror inspired by the spot; but her feelings were now concentrated upon another subject, and she mused along, heedless of the gloom which surrounded her. In this mood she was startled by a sound like the report of a gun; but the wind was too high to distinguish clearly, and it might have been only the cracking of some time-worn stem. Her heart beat quicker, and she hastened her step. It was Vibert, perhaps, on his way to meet her; and her lips unconsciously pronounced the words,—"Vibert, God bless you!" Presently she distinguished the figure of a man rapidly advancing towards her. He stopped a moment where two paths separated, as if hesitating which he should take; then hurried on, without perceiving her until he found himself by her side. It was the rejected Marcus. His face was distorted and convulsed, his clothes and flesh rent by the brambles, and his voice like that of one from the grave.

"Marion!" he exclaimed, standing stiff and motionless, as though he had been suddenly frozen; "what evil spirit has sent you to confront your victim? Go home, Marion, and leave the maniac to his den."

She regarded him a moment in extreme astonishment, and then burst into tears.

"Good God!" she cried, "is it possible that a person [30] so valueless as I am can have caused this dreadful change! How could I love you, when my heart had long been another's? I offered you my friendship—from my soul I offer it again. For my sake, for Vibert's, do not cloud our happiness by the thought that we have wounded the peace of another, much less of one who will be so dear to us. Return with me home; dear Edith has still a heart to give you."

He answered, with a smile of savage bitterness,—"I thank her,—I do not want it. Yours has cost me somewhat, and it is hard to labour in vain. Promise me, Marion, promise me, in case of Vibert's—death,"—

"Of Vibert's death!—what mean such horrible words. All things seem ominous of woe to me. In Heaven's name, speak again, and do not stand so motionless and ghastly. What is it that you see?"

Marcus slowly raised his arm, and pointed to a raven, which was battling its way against the wind. He spoke not a word, but kept his eye fixed upon the bird till it toiled over their heads, and, at a short distance, swooped into the thicket. It was followed by another, and another. He maintained the same aspect, and Marion, astonished by the strange scene, which accorded so well with her previous presentiments, could scarcely restrain a stifled scream.

Marcus was roused. "It is a strange instinct," said he. "Those heaven-instructed birds seem formed for the detection of—of the farmer's lost cattle, which have [31] strayed away and died! They scent blood afar off,—their note is harrowing!—Come away,—come away,—I will conduct you home!"

He grasped Marion by the wrist, and was leading her away, when two of the ravens rose up in clamorous combat for a disputed morsel. Unable to direct their course, the wind carried them back towards the spot where Marcus and Marion were standing; and a part of the contended booty, dropping from their beaks, was wafted to the feet of the latter. She eagerly snatched it up,—it was a curly lock of black hair! A momentary impulse endowed her with twice the strength of Marcus, and she wrenched her arm from his grasp.

"Yonder carcass," she exclaimed hysterically, "is neither stag nor steer;" and she sprang towards the scene with a supernatural swiftness. Marcus uttered a vain cry to restrain her, and disappeared, feeling his way more than seeing it, as though the world afforded no home and no purpose to direct his course.

Shortly after, Edith arrived at the place where they had parted, having traced the small foot of her sister in the damp soil. She was alarmed to find it turn in amongst the brambles, and called out, but received no answer! The wind blew her voice back, and the tortuous stems of ragged Scots fir, intermixed with every other species of hardy plant, permitted her eager glance to penetrate but a few yards. She forced her way into the maze, and, by the aid of the boughs, clambered [32] partly up the side of the valley, to where a large scale that had fallen from the rocks had separated into fragments upon a bank of yellow sand, overgrown with fern and furze. It was called the Badger's Bank, being filled with the earths of that animal, which shared it in common with the wild cat, and birds of prey that came thither to gorge upon victims! Amidst the ruin of this scene stood Marion,—her long black hair streaming in the blast, and her arms extended to scare away a multitude of the dismal birds which had directed her thither. At her feet lay the form of Vibert,—his face overspread with its last hue, and his temples shattered to pieces!

When search was made, the sisters were found still protecting the body, and both bereft of reason! Edith had loved Vibert no less fervently than Marion had done; but her devotion to her had rendered silence no sacrifice. To see her sister happy was to be blessed herself; and had it not been for this unlooked-for catastrophe, her secret would never have been known!

We will not swell our history with an account of the long interval that elapsed ere the sisters were restored, in a degree, to their right minds. Their first question, on their partial recovery, related to Vibert's uncle: his infirm frame had sunk beneath his affliction, and he lay in the family vault, beside his unfortunate nephew! There was yet another name, which neither of them dared to pronounce! But the question was divined; and Marcus, they were told, had never been heard of;—a body, too decayed to [33] be recognized, had been found in a distant forest, and might have been his; it was but a surmise, and, whether true or false, there has never been any other.

Years passed away; but the characters of Marion and Edith resumed no more their natural tone. The last was never seen to smile again, nor the first to drop a tear;—misfortune had stricken them into a strange apathy, and . their only pleasure was to wander, linked in each other's arms, upon the high grounds, from whence they could descry the church where Vibert lay. They were never seen elsewhere, nor in any society but that of each other, although all the world were their friends. Those who had loved them respected their sorrow too much to intrude upon it; and those who had been jealous of being outshone, had ceased to have any cause. The admirers who had pursued them turned sadly from their vague regard, and would as soon have thought of obtaining the stars themselves.

This lasted but a few years. The fatal remembrance, which slept neither night nor day, drank greedily of the springs of life! They faded almost to phantoms, and death seemed to think his prey scarcely worth the striking; for their departure was unmarked by a single pang. Edith, whose natural temperament had the least repose, was the first to drop;—she died clasping her sister's neck; and Marion followed, in time to be interred in the same grave![9]

---

9 The leading incidents of this little narrative are true; the names of the parties only having been altered.

Title

By Author of "Pelham." [Bulwer, Edward Lytton.] "A Manuscript found in a Madhouse." LS 1829. 56-66. [56]

A MANUSCRIPT FOUND IN A MADHOUSE.
BY THE AUTHOR OF 'PELHAM.'

I AM the eldest son of a numerous family,—noble in birth, and eminent for wealth. My brothers are a vigorous and comely race,—my sisters are more beautiful than dreams. By what fatality was it that I alone was thrust into this glorious world distorted, and dwarf-like, and hideous,—my limbs a mockery, my countenance a horror, myself a blackness on the surface of creation,—a discord in the harmony of nature, a living misery, an animated curse? I am shut out from the aims and objects of my race;—with the deepest sources of affection in my heart, I am doomed to find no living thing on which to pour them. Love!—out upon the word—I am its very loathing and abhorrence: friendship turns from me in disgust; pity beholds me, and withers to aversion. Wheresoever I wander, I am encompassed with hatred as with an atmosphere. Whatever I attempt, I am in [57] the impassable circle of a dreadful and accursed doom. Ambition—pleasure—philanthropy—fame—the common blessing of social intercourse—are all as *other* circles, which *mine* can touch hut in *one* point, and that point is torture. I have knowledge to which the wisdom of ordinary sages is as dust to gold;—I have energies to which relaxation is pain;—I have benevolence which sheds itself in charity and love over a worm! For what—merciful God!—for what are these blessings of nature or of learning?—The instant I employ them, I must enter among men: the moment I enter among men, my being blackens into an agony. Laughter grins upon me—terror dogs my steps;—I exist upon poisons, and my nourishment is scorn!

At my birth the nurse refused me suck; my mother saw me and became delirious; my father ordered that I should be stifled as a monster. The physicians saved my life—accursed be they for the act! One woman—she was old and childless—took compassion upon me; she reared and fed me. I grew up—I asked for something to love; I loved every thing; the common earth—the fresh grass—the living insect—the household brute;—from the dead stone I trod on, to the sublime countenance of man, made to behold the stars and to scorn me;—from the noblest thing to the prettiest—the fairest to the foulest—*I* loved them *all*! I knelt to my mother, and besought her to love me—she shuddered. I fled to my father,—and he spurned me! The lowest minion [58] of the human race that had its limbs shapen and its countenance formed, refused to consort with me;—the very dog (I only dared to seek out one that seemed more rugged and hideous than its fellows), the very dog dreaded me, and slunk away! I grew up lonely and wretched; I was like the reptile whose prison is the stone's heart,—immured in the eternal penthouse of a solitude to which the breath of fellowship never came;—girded with a wall of barrenness, and flint, and doomed to vegetate and batten on my own suffocating and poisoned meditations. But while this was my *heart's* dungeon, they could not take from the *external* senses the sweet face of the Universal Nature;—they could not bar me from commune with the voices of the mighty Dead. Earth opened to me her marvels, and the volumes of the wise their stores. I read—I mused—I examined—I descended into the deep wells of Truth—and mirrored in my soul the holiness of her divine beauty. The past lay before me like a scroll; the mysteries of this breathing world rose from the present like clouds;—even of the dark future, experience shadowed forth something of a token and a sign; and over the wonders of the world, I hung the intoxicating and mingled spells of poesy and of knowledge. But I could not without a struggle live in a world of love, and be the only thing doomed to hatred. "I will travel," said I, "to other quarters of the globe. All earth's tribes have not the proud stamp of angels and of gods, and amongst its infinite variety I may find a [59] being who will not sicken at myself." I took leave of the only one who had not loathed me—the woman who had given me food, and reared me up to life. She had now become imbecile, and doting, and blind;—so she did not disdain to lay her hand upon my distorted head, and to bless me. "But better," she said, even as she blessed me and in despite of her dotage,—"better that you had perished in the womb!" And I laughed with a loud laugh when I heard her, and rushed from the house.

One evening, in my wanderings, as I issued from a wood, I came abruptly upon the house of a village priest. Around it, from a thick and lofty fence of shrubs which the twilight of summer bathed in dew, the honeysuckle, and the sweetbrier, and the wild rose sent forth those gifts of fragrance and delight which were not denied even unto me. As I walked slowly behind the hedge, I heard voices on the opposite side; they were the voices of women, and I paused to listen. They spoke of love, and of the qualities which should create it.

"No," said one, and the words, couched in a tone of music, thrilled to my heart,—"no, it is not beauty which I require in a lover; it is the mind which can command others, and the passion which would bow that mind unto me. I ask for genius and affection. I ask for nothing else."

"But," said the other voice, "you could not love a monster in person, even if he were a miracle of intellect and of love!"

"I could," answered the first speaker, fervently; "if [60] I know my own heart, I could. You remember the fable of a girl whom a monster loved! I could have loved *that* monster."

And with these words they passed from my hearing; but I stole round, and through a small crevice in the fence, beheld the face and form of the speaker, whose words had opened, as it were, a glimpse of Heaven to my heart. Her eyes were soft, and deep,—her hair parting from her girlish, and smooth brow, was of the hue of gold,—her aspect was pensive and melancholy,—and over the delicate and transparent paleness of her cheek, hung the wanness, but also the eloquence of thought. To other eyes she might not have been beautiful,—to mine, her face was as an angel's.—Oh! lovelier far than the visions of the Carian, or the shapes that floated before the eyes of the daughters of Delos, is the countenance of one that bringeth to the dark breast the first glimmerings of Hope! From that hour my resolution was taken; I concealed myself in the wood that bordered her house; I made my home with the wild fox in the cavern, and the shade; the day-light passed in dreams, and passionate delirium,—and at evening I wandered forth, to watch afar off her footstep; or creep through the copse, unseen, to listen to her voice; or through the long and lone night to lie beneath the shadow of the house, and fix my soul, watchful as a star, upon the windows of the chamber where she slept. I strewed her walks with the leaves of poetry, and at [61] midnight I made the air audible with the breath of music. In my writings and my songs, whatever in the smooth accents of praise, or the burning language of passion, or the liquid melodies of verse, could awaken her fancy or excite her interest, I attempted. Curses on the attempt! May the hand wither!—may the brain burn! May the heart shrivel, and parch like a leaf that a flame devours—from which the cravings of my ghastly and unnatural love found a channel, or an aid! I told her in my verses, in my letters, that I had overheard her confession. I told her that I was more hideous than the demons which the imagination of a Northern savage had ever bodied forth;—I told her that I was a thing which the day-light loathed to look upon;—but I told her also, that I adored her: and I breathed both my story and my love in the numbers of song, and sung them to the silver chords of my lute, with a voice which belied my form, and was not out of harmony with nature. She answered me,—and her answer filled the air, that had hitherto been to me a breathing torture, with enchantment and rapture. She repeated, that beauty was as nothing in her estimation—that to her all loveliness was in the soul. She told me that one who wrote as I wrote—who felt as I felt—could not be loathsome in her eyes. She told me that she could love me, be my form even more monstrous than I had portrayed it. Fool!—miserable fool that I was, to believe her! So then, shrouded among the [62] trees, and wrapped from head to foot in a mantle, and safe in the oath by which I had bound her not to seek to penetrate my secret, or to behold my form before the hour I myself should appoint, arrived—I held commune with her in the deep nights of summer, and beneath the unconscious stars; and while I unrolled to her earnest spirit the marvels of the mystic world, and the glories of wisdom, I mingled with my instruction the pathos and the passion of love!

"Go," said she one night as we conferred together, and through the matted trees I saw—though she beheld me not—that her cheek blushed as she spoke; "Go,—and win from others the wonder that you have won from me. Go,—pour forth your knowledge to the crowd; go, gain the glory of fame—the glory which makes man immortal—and then come back, and claim me,—I will be yours!"

"Swear it!" cried I.

"I swear!" she said; and as she spoke the moonlight streamed upon her face, flushed as it was with the ardour of the moment and the strangeness of the scene; her eye burnt with a steady and deep fire—her lip was firm—and her figure, round which the light fell like the glory of a halo, seemed instinct and swelling, as it were, with the determinate energy of the soul. I gazed—and my heart leapt within me;—I answered not—but I stole silently away: for months she heard of me no more.

I fled to a lonely and far spot,—I surrounded myself [63] once more with books. I explored once more the arcana of science; I ransacked once more the starry regions of poetry; and then upon the mute page I poured the thoughts and the treasures which I had stored within me! I sent the product, without a name, upon the world: the world received it; approved it; and it became fame. Philosophers bowed in wonder before my discoveries; the pale student in cell and cloister, pored over the mines of learning which I had dragged into day; the maidens in their bowers blushed and sighed, as they drank in the burning pathos of my verse. The old and the young,—all sects and all countries, united in applause and enthusiasm for the unknown being who held, as they averred, the Genii of wisdom and the Spirits of verse in mighty and wizard spells, which few had ever won, and none had ever blended before.

I returned to her,—I sought a meeting under the same mystery and conditions as of old,—I proved myself that unknown whose fame filled all ears, and occupied all tongues. Her heart had foreboded it already! I claimed my reward! And in the depth and deadness of night, when not a star crept through the curtain of cloud and gloom—when not a gleam struggled against the blackness—not a breath stirred the heavy torpor around us—that reward was yielded. The dense woods and the eternal hills were the sole witness of our bridals;—and girt with darkness as with a robe, she leant upon my bosom, and shuddered not at the place of her repose! [64] Thus only we met;—but for months we did meet, and I was blessed. At last, the fruit of our ominous love could no longer be concealed. It became necessary, either that I should fly with her, or wed her with the rites and ceremonies of man—as I had done amidst the more sacred solemnities of nature. In either case, disclosure was imperious and unavoidable;—I took therefore that which gratitude ordained. Beguiled by her assurances—touched by her trust, and tenderness—maddened by her tears—duped by my own heart—I agreed to meet her, and for the first time openly reveal myself—at the foot of the altar!

The appointed day came. At our mutual wish, only two witnesses were present, beside the priest and the aged and broken-hearted father, who consented solely to our singular marriage because mystery was less terrible to him than disgrace. *She* had prepared them to see a distorted and fearful abortion,—but—ha! ha! ha!—she had not prepared them to see *me*! I entered:—all eyes, but *her's* were turned to me,—an unanimous cry was uttered—the priest involuntarily closed the book, and muttered the exorcism for a fiend—the father covered his face with his hands, and sunk upon the ground—the other witnesses—ha! ha! ha! (it was rare mirth)—rushed screaming from the chapel! It was twilight—the tapers burned dim and faint—I approached my bride—who, trembling and weeping beneath her long veil, had not dared to look at me. "Behold me!"—said [65] I—"my bride, my beloved!—behold thy husband!"—I raised her veil—she saw my countenance glare full upon her—uttered one shriek, and fell senseless on the floor. I raised her not—I stirred not—I spoke not.—I saw my doom was fixed, my curse complete; and my heart lay mute, and cold, and dead within me, like a stone! Others entered, they bore away the bride. By little and little, the crowd assembled, to gaze upon the monster in mingled derision and dread;—*then* I recollected myself and arose. I scattered them in terror before me,—and uttering a single and piercing cry, I rushed forth, and hid myself in the wood.

But at night, at the hour in which I had been accustomed to meet her, I stole forth again. I approached the house, I climbed the wall, I entered the window; I was in her chamber. All was still and solitary; I saw not a living thing there; but the lights burned bright and clear. I drew near to the bed; I beheld a figure stretched upon it—a taper at the feet, and a taper at the head,—so there was plenty of light for me to see my bride. She was a corpse! I did not speak—nor faint—nor groan;—but I laughed aloud. Verily it is a glorious mirth, to behold the only thing one loves stiff, and white, and shrunken, and food for the red, playful, creeping worm! I raised my eyes, and saw upon a table near the bed, something covered with a black cloth. I lifted the cloth, and beheld—ha! ha! ha!—by the foul fiend—a dead—but beautiful likeness of myself! A little [66] infant monster! The ghastly mouth, and the laidley features—and the delicate, green, corpse-like hue—and the black shaggy hair—and the horrible limbs, and the unnatural shape—there—ha! ha!—there they were—my wife and my child! I took them both in my arms—I hurried from the house—I carried them into the wood. I concealed them in a cavern—I watched over them—and lay beside them,—and played with the worms—that played with them—ha! ha! ha!—it was a jovial time that, in the old cavern!

And so when they were all gone but the bones, I buried them quietly and took my way to my home. My father was dead, and my brothers hoped that I was dead also. But I turned them out of the house, and took possession of the titles and the wealth. And then I went to see the doting old woman who had nursed me; and they shewed me where she slept—a little green mound in the church-yard—and I wept—Oh, so bitterly! I never shed a tear for my wife—or—ha! ha! ha!—for my beautiful child!

And so I lived *happily* enough for a short time; but at last they discovered that I was the unknown philosopher—the divine poet whom the world rung of. And the crowd came—and the mob beset me—and my rooms were filled with eyes—large, staring eyes, all surveying me from head to foot—and peals of laughter and shrieks wandered about the air, like disembodied and damned spirits and I was never alone again!

Title

By Author of "Holland Tide." [Griffin, Gerald.] "The Rock of the Candle. A Tale of an Irish Ruin." LS 1829. 73-110. [73]

THE ROCK OF THE CANDLE.
A Tale of an Irish Ruin.
BY THE AUTHOR OF 'ROLLAND-TIDE.'

> *Soldiers.*—Room, ho!—tell Antony, Brutus is ta'en.
> *Antony.*—This is not Brutus, friends; but I assure you,
>   A prize no less in worth. Keep this man safe,
>   Give him all kindness. I had rather have
>   Such men my friends than enemies.
>   JULIUS CAESAR.

REMEMBER ye not, my fair young friend, in one of those excursions which rendered the summer of the past year so sweet in the enjoyment, and so mournful in the recollection—remember ye not my having pointed out to your observation the ruined battlements of Carrigogunniel (the Rock of the Candle), which shoot upward from a craggy hillock on the Shannon side, within view of the ancient city of Limerick? I told you the legend from which the place originally derived its name—a legend, which I thought was distinguished (especially in the closing incident), by a tenderness and delicacy of imagination, [74] worthy of a Grecian origin. You, too, acknowledged the simple beauty of that incident; and your approval induces me to hope for that of the world.

On a misty evening in spring, when all the west is filled with a hazy sunshine, and the low clouds stoop and cling around the hill tops, there are few nobler spectacles to contemplate, than the ruins of Carrigogunniel Castle. This fine building, which was dismantled by one of William's generals, stands on the very brink of a broken hill, which, toward the water, looks bare and craggy, but on the landward side slopes gently down, under a close and verdant cover of elms and underwood. It is when seen from this side, standing high above the trees, and against the red and broken clouds that are gathered in the west, that the ruin assumes its most imposing aspect.

Such was the look it wore on the evening of an autumn day, when the village beauty, young Minny O'Donnell, put aside the woodbines from her window, and looked out upon the Rock. Her father's cottage was situated close to the foot of the hill, and the battlements seemed to frown downward upon it, with a royal and overtopping haughtiness.

"Hoo! murder, Minny honey, what is that you're doing l Looking out at the Rock at this hour, and the sun just going down behind the turret?"

"Why not, aunt?"

"Why not?—Do you remember nothing of the candle?" [75]

"Oh, I don't know what to think of it; I am inclined to doubt the story very much; I have been listening to that frightful tale of the Death Light since I was born, and I have never seen it yet."

"You may consider yourself fortunate in that, child, and I advise you not to be too anxious to prove the truth of the story. I .was standing by the side of poor young Dillon myself, on the very day of his marriage, when he looked out upon it through the wicket, and was blasted as if by a thunder-stroke. I never will forget the anguish of the dear young bride—it was heart breaking, to see her torn from his side when the life had left him. Poor creature! her shrieks are piercing my ears at this very moment."

"That story terrifies me, aunt. Speak of it no more, and I will leave the window. I wonder if Cormac knows this story of the Fatal Candle."

The good old woman smiled knowingly on her pretty niece, as, instead of answering her half query, she asked—"Do you not expect him here before sunset?"

Minny turned hastily round, and seated herself opposite a small mirror, adorned by one of those highly carved frames which were popular at the toilets of our grandmammas. She did so with the double view, of completing her evening toilet, and at the same time screening herself from the inquisitive glances of her sharp old relative, while she continued the conversation.

"He promised to be here before," she replied; "but it is a long way." [76]

"I hope he will not turn his eyes upon the Rock, if he should be detained after night-fall. I suspect, Minny, that his eyes will be wandering in another direction. I think he will be safe, after all."

"For shame, aunt Norry! You ought to be ashamed of yourself, an old woman of your kind, to speak in that way. Come now, and tell me something funny, while I am dressing my hair, to put the recollection of that frightful adventure of the Candle out of my head. Would not that be a good figure for a Banthee?" she added, shaking out her long bright hair with one hand, in the manner which is often attributed to the warning spirit, and casting at the same time, a not indifferent glance at the mirror above mentioned.

"Partly indeed,—but the Banthee (meaning no offence at the same time), is far from being so young or so blooming in the cheeks; and by all accounts, the eyes tell a different story from yours—a story of death, and not of marriage. Merry would the Banthee be, that would be going to get young Mr. Cormac for a husband tomorrow morning early."

"I'll go look at the Rock again, if you continue to talk such nonsense."

"Oh, bubboo!—rest easy, darling—and I'll say nothing.—Well, what story is it I'm to be telling you?"

"Something funny."

"O yeh, my heart is bothered with 'em for stories. I don't know what I'll tell you. Are you 'cute at all?"

PLATE: Minny O'Donnell's Toilet - 76/77
Steel plate engraving; painted by Robert Farrier;
engraved by Edward Portbury; printed by McQueen [77]

"I don't know. Only middling, I believe."

"Well—I'll tell you a story of a boy that flogged Europe for 'cuteness—so that if you have a mind to be ready with an answer for every cross question that 'ill be put to you, you can learn it after him;—a thing that may be useful to you one time or another, when the charge of the house is left in your hands."

"Well, let me hear it."

"I will, then, do that. Goon with your dress, and I'll have my story done

Literary Souvenir

before you are ready to receive Mr. Cormac."

So saying, she drew a stool near her niece, and leaning forward with her chin on her hand, commenced the following tale.

"There was a couple there, long ago, and they had a son that they didn't know rightly what was it they'd do with him, for they had not money to get him Latin enough for a priest, and there was only poor call for day labourers in the country. 'I'll tell you what I'll do,' says the father, says he; 'I'll make a thief of him,' says he; 'sorrow a better trade there is going than the roguery—or more money-making for a boy that would be industrious.' 'Its true for you,' says the wife, making answer to him; 'but where will you get a master for him, or who'll take him for an apprentice in such a business?' 'I'll tell you that,' says the husband to her again. 'I'll send him to Kerry. Sorrow better hand would you get at the business any where, [78] than there are about the mountains there—and I'll be bound he'll come home to us a good hand at his business,' says he. Well and good, they sent off the boy to Kerry, and bound him for seven years to a thief that was well known in these parts, and counted a very clever man in his line. They heard no more of him for the seven years, nor hardly knew that they were out, when he walked in to them one morning, with his 'Save all here!' and took his seat at the table along with them—a fine, handsome lad, and mighty well spoken. 'Well, Mun,' says the father, 'I hope you're master o' your business?' Pretty well for that, father,' says he; 'wait till we can have a trial of it.' 'With all my heart,' says the father; 'and I hope to see that you haven't been making a bad use o' your time while you were away!' Well, the news ran among the neighbours, what a fine able thief Mun had come home, and the landlord himself came to hear of it, amongst the rest. So when the father went to his work the next morning, he made up to him, and—'Well,' says he, 'this is a queer thing I'm told about you, that you had your son bound to a thief in Kerry, and that he's come home to you a great hand at the business.' 'Passable, indeed, he tells me, sir,' says the father, quite proud in himself. 'Well, I'll tell you what it is,' says the gentleman; 'I have a fine horse in my stable, and I'll put a guard upon him to-night—and if your son be that great hand that he's reported to be, let him come and steal him out from among the [79] people to-night—and if he does, he shall have my daughter in marriage, and my estate, when I die,' says he. 'A great offer, surely,' says the poor man. 'But if he fails,' says the gentleman, 'I'll prosecute him, and have him hanged, and you along with him, for serving his time to a thief; a thing that's clearly again all law,' says he. Well, 'tis unknown what a *whilliloo* the father set up when he heard this. 'O, murther, sir,' says he, 'and sure 'tis well, you know, that if a spirit itself was there he couldn't steal the horse that would be guarded that way—let alone my poor boy,' says he; 'and how will it he with us, or what did we ever do to you, sir, that you'd hang us that way?' 'I have my own reasons for it,' says the gentleman, 'and you'd better go home at once, and tell the boy about it, if you have a mind he should try his chance.' Well, the father went home, crying and bawling, as if all belonging to him were dead. 'E', what ails you, father,' says the son, 'or what is it makes you be bawling that way?' says he. So he up and told him the whole business, how they were to be hanged, the two of them, in the morning, if he wouldn't have the racer stolen. 'That beats Ireland,' says the son, 'to hang a man for *not* stealing a thing is droll, surely; but make your mind easy, father, my master would think no more of doing that than he would of eating a boiled potatoe.' Well, the old man was in great spirits when he heard the boy talk so stout, although he wasn't without having his doubts upon the business, for all that. The boy set to [80] work when the evening drew on, and dressed himself like an old *bucaughi*[10] with a tattered frieze coat about him, and stockings without any soles to 'em, with an old *caubean* of a straw hat upon the side of his head, and a tin can under his arm. 'Tis what he had in the tin can, I tell you, was a good sup of spirits, with a little poppy juice squeezed into it, to make them sleepy that would be after drinking it. Well and good, Minny, my child, he made towards the gentleman's house, and when he was passing the parlour window, he saw a beautiful young lady, as fair as a lily, and with a fine blush, entirely sitting and looking out about the country for herself. So he took off his hat, and turned out his toes, and made her a low bow, quite elegant. 'I declare to my heart,' says the young lady, speaking to her servant that stood behind her, 'I wouldn't desire to see a handsomer man than that.—If he had a better *shoot* of clothes upon him, he'd be equal to any gentleman, he's so slim and delicate.' And who was this but the gentleman's daughter all the while! Well, it's well became Mun, he went on to the stable door, and there he found the lads all watching the racer. I'll tell you the way they watched her. They had one upon her back, and another at her head, where she was tied to the manger, and a great number of them about the place, sitting down between her and the door. 'Save all here!' says Mun, putting in his head at the door; 'E', what are ye doing [81] here, boys?' says he. So they up and told him they were guarding the racer, from a great Kerry thief they expected to be stealing her that night. 'Why then, he'll be a smart fellow, if he gets her out of that,' says Mun, making as if he knew nothing. 'I'd be for ever obliged to ye, if ye'd let me light a pipe and sit down awhile with ye, and I'll do my part to make the company agreeable.' 'Why then,' says they, 'we have but poor treatment to offer you, for though there's plenty to eat here, we have nothing to drink—the master wouldn't allow us a ha'p'orth, in dread we'd get sleepy, and let the horse go.' 'Oh! the nourishment is all I want,' says Mun, 'I'm no way dry at all.' Well and good, in he came, and he sat among them telling stories until past midnight, eating and laughing; and every now and then, when he'd stop in the story, he'd turn about and make as if he was taking a good drink out of the can. 'You seem to be very fond of that tin can, whatever you have in it,' says one of the men that was sitting near him. 'Oh, its no signify,' says Mun, shutting it up as if not anxious to share it. Well, they got the smell of it about the

---

10 A lame man—idiomatically, beggar-man.

place, and 'tis little pleasure they took in the stories after, only every now and then throwing an eye at the can, and snuffing with their noses, like pointer swhen game is in the wind. "'Tis n't any spring water you'd have in that, I believe,i says one of them. 'You're welcome to try it,' says Mun, 'only I thought you might have some objection in regard of what you said when I came in.' [82] 'None in the world,' says they. So he filled a few little noggins for 'em, and for the man on the horse, and the man near the manger, and they all drank until they slept like troopers. When they were all fast, up got the youth, and he drew on a pair of worsted stockings over every one of the horse's legs, so they wouldn't make any noise, and he got a rope and fastened the man I tell you was upon the racer's back, by the shoulders, up to the rafters, when he drew the horse from under him, and left him hanging fast asleep. Well became him, he led the horse out of the stable, and had him home at his father's while a cat would be shaking his ears, and made up comfortably in a little out-house. 'Well,' says the old man, when he woke in the morning and saw the horse stolen—'if it was an angel was there,' says he, 'he couldn't do the business cleverer than that.' And the same thing he said to the landlord, when he met him in the field the same morning. 'It's true for you, indeed,' said the gentleman, 'nothing could be better done, and I'll take it as an honour if your son and yourself will give me your company at dinner to-day, and I'll have the pleasure of introducing him to my daughter.' 'E', is it me dine at your honour's table?' says the old man, looking down at his dress. "'Tis just,' says the gentleman again,—'and I'll take no apology whatever.' Well and good, they made themselves ready, the two of them, and young Mun came riding upon the racer, covered all over with the best of wearables, and looking like a real [83] gentleman. 'E,' what's that there, my child?' says the father, pointing to a gallows, that was planted right opposite the gentleman's hall door. 'I don't know—a gallows, I'm thinking,' says the son,—'sure 'tisn't to hang us he would be after asking us to his house, unless it be a thing he means to give us our dinner first and our dessert after, as the fashion goes,' says he. Well, in with them, and they found the company all waiting, a power of ladies and lords, and great people entirely. 'I'm sorry to keep you waiting,' says Mun, making up to them, quite free and easy, 'but the time stole upon us.' 'You couldn't blame the time for taking after yourself,' says the gentleman. 'It's true, indeed,' says Mun, 'I stole many is the thing in my time, but there's one thing I'd rather thieve than all the rest—the good will o' the ladies,' says he, smiling, and looking round at them. 'Why then, I wouldn't trust you very far with that either,' says the young lady of the house. Well and good, they sat down and they eat their dinner, and after the cloth was removed, there was a covered dish laid upon the table. 'Well,' says the gentleman, 'I have one trial more to make of your wit—and I'll tell you what it is:—let me know what is it I have in this covered dish; and if you don't, I'll hang you and your father upon that gallows over, for stealing my racer.' 'O, murther! d'ye hear this?' says the father—'and wasn't it your honour's bidding to steal her, or you'd hang us? Sure we're to be pitied with your honour,' says the poor old man. [84] 'Very well,' says the gentleman, 'I tell you a fact, and your only chance is to answer my question.' 'Well, sir,' says Mun, giving all up for lost, 'I have nothing to say to you—although far the fox may go, he'll be caught by the tail at last.' 'I declare you have it,' says the gentleman, uncovering the dish, and what should be in it only a fox's tail! Well, they gave it up to Mun, that he was the greatest rogue going, and the young lady married him upon the spot. They had the master's estate when he died; and if they didn't live happy, I wish that you and I may."

"Amen to that, aunt. Will you lay this mirror aside for a moment.—Ha! whose fault was that?"

"Oh, Minny, you have broken the mirror—O, my child! my child!"

"Why so! It is not so valuable." "Valuable! It is not the worth of the paltry glass, darling,—but don't you know it is not good! It is not lucky—and the night before your bridal, too!"

"I am very sorry for it," said the girl, bending a somewhat serious gaze on the shattered fragments of the antique looking-glass. Then, by a transition which it would require some knowledge of the maiden's history to account for, she said, "I wonder if Cormac was with the Knight, when he made the sally at the castle, yesterday."

The answer of the elderly lady was interrupted by the sound of several voices, in an outer apartment, [85] exclaiming, "Cormac! Cormac! Welcome, Cormac! It is Cormac!"

"And it is Cormac!" echoed Minny, starting from her seat, and glancing at the spot where the mirror ought to have been—"You were right, aunt," she added, in a disappointed tone, as she bounded out of the room, "it was unlucky to break the mirror."

"It might for them that would want it," replied the old lady, following at a less lively pace; "but for you, I hope, it will bring nothing worse than the loss of it for this night."

She found Minny seated, with one hand clasped in those of a young soldier, dressed in the uniform of the White Knight, smiling and blushing with all the artlessness in the world. The young man wore a close fitting *truis*, which displayed a handsome form to the best advantage, and contrasted well with the loose and flowing drapery of his mantle. The *birrede* of green cloth, which had confined his hair, was laid aside; and a leathern girdle appeared at his waist, which held a bright skene and pistol. The appearance of both figures—the expression of both countenances, secure of present, and confident of future happiness, formed a, picture—

Which some would smile, and more perhaps would sigh at;

A picture, which would bring back pleasing recollections enough to sweeten the temper of the sourest pair that [86] Hymen ever disunited, and to move the spleen of the best-natured old bachelor that ever dedicated his hearth to Dian and solitude.

The evening proceeded as the eve of a bridal might be supposed to do, with its proportion of mirth and mischief. The lovers had been acquainted from childhood; and every one who knew them felt an interest in their fortunes, and a share in the happiness which they enjoyed. The sun had been already long gone down, when Minny, in compliance with the wish of her old aunt, sang the following words, to an air, which was only remarkable for its simplicity and tenderness:—

I.

I love my love in the morning,
    For she, like morn, is fair—
Her blushing cheek, its crimson streak,
    Its clouds, her golden hair;
Her glance, its beam, so soft and kind;
    Her tears, its dewy showers;
And her voice, the tender whispering wind
    That stirs the early bowers.

II.

I love my love in the morning,
    I love my love at noon;
For she is bright, as the lord of light,
    Yet mild as autumn's moon:
Her beauty is my bosom's sun,
    Her faith my fostering shade;
And I will love my darling one,
    Till even that sun shall fade.

III.

I love my love in the morning,
    I love my love at even;
Her smile's soft play is like the ray
    That lights the western heaven:
I loved her when the sun was high,
    I loved her when he rose;
But, best of all, when evening's sigh
    Was murmuring at its close.

The song was scarcely ended, when Minny felt her arm grasped with an unusual force by the young soldier. Turning round, in some alarm, she beheld a sight which filled her with fear and anxiety. Her lover sat erect in his chair, gazing fixedly on the open casement, through which a strong and whitish light shone full upon his face and person. It was an interlunar night,—and Minny felt utterly at a loss to conjecture what the cause could be, of this extraordinary appearance.

"Minny," said her lover, "look yonder! I see a candle burning on the very summit of the rock above us! Although the wind is bending every tree upon the hillside, the flame does not flicker or change in the slightest degree. Look on it!"

"Do not look!" exclaimed the old aunt, with a shrill cry—"May heaven be about us! do not glance at the window. It is the death-light!"

Minny clasped her hands, and sank back into her chair.

"Let some one close the window," said the young [88] soldier, speaking in a faint tone, "I am growing ill—let some one close the window."

The old woman advanced cautiously toward the casement, and extending the handle of a broomstick, at the utmost stretch of her arm, was endeavouring to push the shutter to, when Minny, recovering from her astonishment, darted at her an indignant look, ran to the window, closed it, and left the room in darkness deeper than midnight.

"What was that strange light!" asked the young soldier, looking somewhat relieved.

With some hesitation, and a few prophetic groans and oscillations of the head, the old story-teller informed him that it was a light, whose appearance was commemorial with the rock itself, and that it usually foreboded considerable danger or misfortune, if not death, to any unhappy being on whom its beams might chance to fall. It appeared, indeed, but rarely,—yet there never was an instance known, in which the indication proved fallacious.

The soldier recovered heart enough to laugh away the anxiety which had begun to creep upon the company; and, in a little time, the mirthful tone of the assemblage was fully restored. Lights, of a more terrestrial description than that which figured on the haunted rock, were introduced; songs were sung; jests echoed from lip to lip, and merry feet pattered against the earthen floor, to the air of the national *rinceadh fadha*. The [89] merriment of the little party was at its highest point, when a galloping of horses, intermingled with a distant rolling of musketry, was heard outside the cottage.

"My fears were just!" exclaimed Cormac, stopping short in the dance, while he still retained the hand of his lovely partner; "the English have taken the castle, and the White Knight is flying for his life!"

His surmise was confirmed by the occurrence which instantly followed. The door was dashed back upon its hinges; and the White Knight, accompanied by two of his retainers, rushed into the house. The chieftain's face was pale and anxious, and his dress was bespattered with blood and mire. The three fugitives remained in a group near the door, as if listening for the sounds of pursuit; while the revellers hurried together like startled fawns, and gazed, with countenances indicative of strong interest or wild alarm, upon the baffled warriors.

"Cormac!" cried the Knight, perceiving the bridegroom among the company, "my good fellow, I missed you in an unlucky hour. These English dogs have worried us from our hold, and are still hot upon our scent. I have only time to bid my stout soldiers farewell, and go to meet them,—for I will not have this happy floor stained with blood to night."

"That shall not be, Knight," exclaimed the bridegroom; "we will meet them, or fly together. You were my father's foster child."

"It is in vain—look there!" He laid bare his left [90] arm, which was severely gashed on one side.—"They have had a taste of me already, and the bloodhounds will never tire till they have tracked me home. And yet, if I had but one day's space—Kavanagh and his followers are at Kilmallock, and the castle might be mine again before the moon rises to-morrow evening."

"Kavanagh at Kilmallock!" exclaimed Cormac. Oh, my chieftain! what do you here? Fly, while you have time, and leave us to deal with the foe."

"It were idle," repeated the Knight, "their horses are fresher than ours, and my dress would betray me."

"My mare will bear you safe," cried the young soldier, with a burst of enthusiasm; "and for your dress, take mine—and let me play the White Knight for once."

The chieftain's eyes brightened at the word, and a hope seemed to bloom out upon his cheek,—but a low sound of suppressed agony from the bride, checked it in the spring.

"No, Cormac," he said, "I will not be your murderer."

"There is no fear," said Cormac, warmly, "you will be back in time to prevent mischief; and if you remain, it will be only to see me share your fate. This is my only chance for life; for I will give the world leave to cry shame upon my head, if ever I outlive my master."

"What says the bride?" inquired the Knight, bending on her a look of mingled pity and admiration. [91]

"I will answer for her," said Cormac,—"she had rather be the widow of a true Irishman, than the wife of a false one."

"0, allilu! we'll all be murthered if ye don't hurry," said the aunt. "What do you say, Minny, my child?"

"Cormac speaks the truth," replied the trembling girl, hanging, in her weakness, on his shoulder; "if there be no other way, I am content it should be so."

She was rewarded for this effort of heroism, by a fervent pressure of the hand from her betrothed; and the exchange of accoutrements was presently effected. The Knight mounted Cormac's mare, and prepared to depart.

"My gallant fellow," he said, holding out his hand to the generous bridegroom, "you do not mock the part you act, for nobility is stamped upon your soul. If you suffer for this, I have a vow, that I will never more wear any other garb than yours; for you are the knightlier of the two. Let me clasp your hand—than which a nobler never closed on gauntlet."

They joined hands in silence, and the chieftain galloped away, with his retainers. When they were out of hearing, Cormac turned to his bride, and again pressing her hand, while he looked fixedly into her eyes, he said, "Now, Minny, you will shew that you are fit for a soldier's wife. Go, with your aunt Norry, into your room. No one here will be molested, but those who are in arms for the Knight—and I will contrive to postpone any violence, for a day, at least." [92]

"I will not leave you, Cormac," said Minny, speaking more firmly than she had done since the interruption of their festivity; "I am somewhat more to you, than you are to the White Knight."

Cormac smiled, and seemed to acquiesce, for some time, in her wishes. He took his seat at the hearth with the bespattered garb and sullied weapon of the Knight, and awaited in silence the approach of the pursuers, while Minny occupied a chair as near him as might be decorous, taking his new rank into consideration. They listened for a considerable time to the changeful rushing of the night wind among the trees that clothed the hill side—and the howling of the wolves, who were disturbed in their retreats by the sounds of combat. Those sounds, renewed after long intervals, and in an irregular manner, gradually approached more near; and they could plainly distinguish the trampling of horses' feet, over the beaten track that winded among the crags as far as the cottage door. Again, and with great earnestness, Cormac entreated his love to secure herself from the chances of their first encounter, by joining the family in the inner room: but she refused, in a resolute tone; and on his persisting, she assumed an impatience, and even a desperation of manner, which shewed that her purpose was not to be shaken.

"Ask me not to leave you," she said: "any other command, I am ready to obey. I will be silent—I will not shriek, nor murmur, even though——"she shud- [93] dered, and let her head droop upon his hand. "I will not leave you, Cormac. Whatever your fate shall be, I must remain to witness it. Do not doubt my firmness; only say that you will freely trust me, and I am ready for the worst that can happen. I feel that I can be calm, if you will only give me your confidence."

There are some spirits which, like the myrtle, require to be bruised and broken by affliction before their sweetness can be discovered. The young bride of Cormac might now have exhibited an instance of this moral truth. So perfectly did her manner indicate the degree of self-possession which she promised to maintain, that Cormac yielded, without further argument, to her entreaty, and resumed his place at the fire-side.

Scarcely had he performed this movement when a loud knocking was again heard at the door; and immediately after, as if this slight ceremony were only used in mockery, the frail barrier was once more dashed inward on its hinges. A crowd of soldiers rushed into the apartment, and stopped short on seeing the bridegroom habited in the accoutrements of the White Knight, and standing in a posture of defence between his foes and the young girl, who seemed to be restrained, rather by her deference to his wishes, than by any personal apprehension, from pressing forward to his side.

"Stand back!" said Cormac, levelling his blade at the foremost of the throng; "before you advance further, say what it is you seek. The inmates of this house (all [94] but one) are under the protection of the English law, and can only be molested at your great peril."

"If you be the White Knight, as your dress bespeaks you," returned an English officer, surrender your sword and person into our hands. It is only them we seek; and no one else shall be disturbed, further than to answer our claim of *bonaght bar*: rest and refreshment for our small troop until the morning breaks."

"I am not so thirsty of blood for the sake of shedding it merely," returned the pseudo knight, "that I would destroy a life of Heaven's bestowing in a vain encounter. Here is my sword; although I am well aware, that in yielding it without a struggle, I do not add a single one to my chances (if any I had) of safety in the hands of my Lord President."

"It would be dishonorable in me to deceive you," said the Englishman, "your ready, though late surrender, can avail you little. I have here the warrant, which commands that the execution of the rebel captain should not be deferred longer than six hours after his arrest. I am not disposed, however, to be more rigid than my instructions compel me to be, so that you may call the whole six hours your own, if you can find use for so much time in this world."

Cormac turned pale, and thought of Minny; but he dared not look at her. The poor girl endeavoured to support herself against the chair which her lover had left vacant, and retired a little, lest he should observe [95] and participate in the agitation which this fatal announcement had occasioned.

"I thought it probable," said Cormac, with some hesitation, "that I might have had a day, at all events, to prepare for my fate; but my Lord President is a pious man, and must be better aware than I, how much time a sinner under arms might require to collect his evidence for that last and fearful court marshal whose decision is irrevocable. A soldier's conscience, sir officer, is too often the only thing about him which he allows to gather rust. If I had been careful to preserve that as unsullied as my sword, I would not esteem your six hours so short a space as they now appear."

"The gift of grace, sir knight," said a solemn-looking sergeant, "is not like an earthly plant, which requires much time and toil to bring its blossom forth. Heard ye not of the graceless traveller, who, riding somewhat more than a Sabbath-day's journey on the seventh, was thrown from his horse and killed near a place of worship? The congregation thought his doom was sealed for both worlds, and yet—

>Between the stirrup and the ground,
>Merey he sought, and mercy found.

"Aye," said the captive—"there are some persons who look on this world as mere billeting quarters, and require no more time to prepare for the eternal route, than they might to brace up a haversac; but my memory [96] is not so light of carriage. I remember to have heard, at Mungharid, a Latin adage, which might shake the courage of any one who was inclined to rely venturously on his powers of spiritual dispatch—

>Unus erat—ne desperes:
>Unas tantum—ne presumas.

However, I shall be as far wide of the first peril, as I should wish to be of the last. Come, sirs, you forget your supper; leave me to my own thoughts, and pray respect this maiden, who will attend to your wants, while I rest."

"She seems as if she would more willingly omit that office," said the Englishman. "The maiden droops sorely for your misfortune, Knight."

"Poor girl!" Cormac exclaimed, venturing to look round upon her for the first time since his capture—"it is little wonder that she should wear a troubled brow. You have disturbed her bridal feast." Then taking her hand, and pressing it significantly while he spoke, he added—"Your husband was reckoned a true man; and I know him well enough to be convinced, that he would not place his heart in the keeping of an unworthy or a selfish love. I know, therefore, that you could not make him happier, than by acting on this occasion with that firmness which he expects from you. Tell him, I knew better the value of life than to lament my fate—at least, for my own sake; and remember likewise, Minny [97] (is not that your name?) if ever Cormac should, like me, be hurried off by an untimely stroke of fate—if ever"—he renewed the pressure of the hand, which he still held in his—"if ever you should see him led, as I must now be, to an early death, remember, my girl, that none but the craven-hearted are short-lived on earth. A brave roan, who has fulfilled all-his duties, can never die untimely; but a coward would, though every hair were grey upon his brow."

He strove to withdraw his hand; but Minny, who felt as if he were tearing her heart away from her, held it fast between both hers, and pressed it with the grasp of a drowning person. Cormac felt, by the trembling and moistness of her hand, that she was on the point of placing all in danger, by bursting into a passion of grief. He lowered his voice to a tone of grave reproof—and said—

"Remember, Minny—let him not find that he has been deceived in you. That would be a worse stroke than the headsman's."

The forlorn girl collected all her strength, and felt the tumult that was rising in her breast subside, like the uproar of the Northern tempest, at the voice of the Reimkennar. She let his hand go, and stood erect, while he passed on, followed by several of the party, into another room. Strange as sorrow had ever been to her bosom, she could not have anticipated, and was wholly incapable of supporting the dreadful desolation of spirit which [98] came upon her after she was left alone. She remained for some time motionless, in the attitude of one who listens intently, until she heard the door of a small inner apartment, into which he had been conducted, close upon her lover; and then, gathering her hands across her bosom, and walking slowly to the vacant chair, she sank down in a violent and hysterical excess of grief.

It is strange that the effusion of a few drops of a briny liquid at the eyes, should enable the soul to give more tranquil entertainment to a painful thought or feeling—but it is a fact, however, which Minny experienced, in common with all who have known what painful feelings are. She pictured to herself the probable nature of the fate which awaited her betrothed; and from the horror which she felt in the contemplation, proceeded to devise expedients for its prevention. This, however, appeared now to be a hopeless undertaking. The warrant of the Lord President must needs be executed within the time; and it was improbable that the White Knight could return before the expiration of the six hours. Would it be possible to contrive a scheme for his liberation? His guards were vigilant and numerous, and there was but one way by which he could return from the room—and that was occupied by sentinels. If Mun, or the Kerry thief, his master, were on the spot, of what a load might, they relieve her heart! She would have given worlds to be mistress, for one night, of the roguery of the adept in aunt Norry's tale. [99] We shall leave her for the present, involved, like a bungling dramatist, in a labyrinth of ravelled plots and contrivances, while we shift the scene to the unfortunate hero of the night, who lay in his room, expecting the catastrophe with no very enviable sensations.

The soldiers had left him, to make the necessary preparations for his approaching fate, in darkness and solitude. He was now on the point of achieving a character, not without precedent in the history of his country—namely, that of a martyr to his own heroic fidelity—and he was determined to bear his part like a warrior, to the last. Still, however, to a lover, conscious of being loved again—to a young man, with prospects so fair, and present happiness so nearly perfect—to a bridegroom, snatched from the altar to the scaffold, at the very moment when he was about to become doubly bound to life, by a tie so holy and so dear—to such an one, though brave as a fiery heart and youthful blood could make him, it was impossible that death should not wear a grim and most unwelcome aspect. Neither is the man to be envied, whose nature could undergo so direful a change without emotion. True bravery consists, not in ignorance of, or insensibility to danger, but in the resolution which can meet and defy it, when duty renders such collision necessary. Fear, in common with all the, other passions of our nature, has been given us for the purpose of exercising our reason, and acquiring a virtue by its subjugation; and the man (if any such ever lived) [100] who is ignorant of the feeling, is a monster, and not a hero. The truly courageous man, is he who has a heart to feel what danger is, and a soul to triumph over that feeling, when it would tempt him to the neglect of any moral or religious obligation. Such was the temper of Cormac. He believed that he was performing his duty, and did not even entertain a thought of any other line of conduct than that which he was pursuing—but this did not prevent his being deeply and bitterly conscious of the hardness of his fortunes, in this unlooked-for and untimely separation.

Exhausted by the intensity of his sensations, he had dropped for some time into a troubled and uneasy slumber, when the pressure of a soft hand upon his brow made him lift up his eyes, and raise himself upon his elbow. He beheld Minny stooping over him, with a dim rushlight burning in one hand, while with the other she motioned him to express no surprise, and to preserve silence.

"Hush, hush!" she said, in a low whisper, "Cormac, are you willing to make an effort for liberty?"

He stared strangely upon her, and stood on his feet.

"What is the meaning of this, Minny; how came you here?"

"The soldiers have been merrier than they intended, and I drugged their drink for them. Slip off your brogs, and steal out in your *truis* only. They are now sleeping in the next room, and I have left them in the dark. [101] Fear not their muskets; I have drenched the matchlocks for them. There are only two waking, who are on guard outside the door; and for these, we must even place our hopes in heaven, and take the chance of their bad marksmanship. Ah, Cormac!—but there is no time to lose; come with me."

"My glorious heroine!" cried the astonished soldier, "I could not have thought this possible."

"Hush! your raptures will betray us."

"But whither do you intend to fly?"

"To the cavern on the western side of the hill, where Fitzgerald lay on the night of the great massacre at Adare Castle. Keep close to me, and I think it likely we shall pass the sleepers."

She extinguished the light; and both crept, with noiseless footsteps, into the adjoining room, which was the chamber of the heroic maiden herself. As they endeavoured to steal between the soldiers, who lay locked in slumber on the ground, Minny set her foot on some brittle substance, which cracked beneath her weight, with a noise sufficient to awaken one of the soldiers.

"It is the mirror!" said Minny, to herself, "my aunt Norry's prophecy was but too correct, and my vanity has ruined every thing."

Still, however, her presence of mind did not forsake her. The soldier, turning suddenly round, laid hold of Cormac's *cotaigh*, or mantle, and arrested his progress.

"Ho! ho!" he exclaimed, "who have we here?"[102]

"Pr'y thee, let go my dress, master soldier," returned the young girl; "this freedom tallies not well with your sermon on Grace to the White Knight.—I doubt you for a solemn hypocrite."

"I knew you not, wench," replied the sergeant, letting Cormac's mantle fall; "or I would as soon have thought of clapping palms with Beelzebub, as of fingering any part of your Irish trumpery. Whither do ye travel, at this time of the night?"

"Even to kindle my rushlight, at our hearth-stone in the next room. Turn on your pallet, sergeant, and let me go, else you maybe troubled with unholy dreams."

They passed on, and reached the outer room in safety.

"Now, Minny," said Cormac, "it is my turn to make a suggestion. Do you pass out, and await me at the stream that runs by the edge of the wood. The sentinels will suffer you to proceed, and the risk of detection will be lessened. Nay, never stop to dispute the point—its advantages are unquestionable."

Minny would not even trust herself with a farewell, before she obeyed the wishes of her lover. A few passing jests were all she had to encounter from the sentinels, and Cormac had the satisfaction to see her hurry on, unmolested, in the direction of the stream. When he supposed a sufficient time had elapsed to enable her to reach the place of rendezvous, he threw aside his mantle, and prepared to take the sentinels by surprise. The door stood open, and he could plainly see the two guards pacing to and [103] fro in the moonlight. Pausing for a moment, he uplifted his clasped hands to heaven, and breathed a short and agitated prayer, of mingled hope and resignation. Then, summoning the resolution which never failed him in his need, he darted through the doorway, into the open air.

Astonishment and perplexity kept the sentinels motionless for some moments, and Cormac had fled a considerable distance, before they became sensible of the nature of the occurrence which had taken place. Both instantly discharged their pieces in the direction of the fugitive, and with loud shouts summoned their comrades to assist in the pursuit- The bullets tore up the earth on either side of Cormac, who could hear, as he hurried on, the execrations and uproar of the awakened troop, at finding their arms rendered incapable of service. He dashed onward toward the wood; and had the happiness, while the sounds of pursuit yet lingered far behind him, to discern the white dress of his betrothed fluttering in distinct relief, against the dark and shadowy foliage of the elm wood. Snatching her up in his arms, with as little difficulty as a mother feels in supporting her infant, he hurried across the stream, and was quickly hurried in the recesses of the wood.

The morning broke before they had reached the appointed place of concealment. It was one of those ancient receptacles for the noble dead, which were hollowed out of the earth in various parts of the country, [104] and were frequently used, during the persecutions of foreign invaders, as places of refuge and concealment for the persons and properties of the people. When they found themselves safely sheltered within the bosom of this close retreat, the customary effect of long restrained anxiety and sudden joy, was produced upon the lovers. They flung themselves, with broken exclamations of delight and affection, into each other's arms, and remained for a considerable time incapable of acting or speaking with any degree of self-possession. The necessity, however, of providing for their safety during the ensuing day, recalled them to a more distinct perception of the difficulties of their situation, and suggested expedients for their alleviation or removal.

They ventured not beyond the precincts of their Druidical sojourn until the approach of evening, and even then it was but to look upon the sunlight, and hurry back again to their lurking-place, in greater anxiety than before. The English had discovered, and were fast approaching the mouth of their retreat.

Cormac, signifying to his bride that she should remain silent in the interior of the cave, drew his sword and stood near the entrance, just as the light became obscured by the persons of the party who were about to enter. They paused for some time on hearing the voice of Cormac, who threatened to sacrifice the first person that should venture to place his foot inside the mouth of the recess. In a few moments after, the devoted pair were [105] perplexed to hear the sound of stones and earth thrown together, as if to erect some building near the cave. Unable to form any conjecture as to the nature and object of this proceeding, they clung together, in silence and increased anxiety, awaiting the issue.

On a sudden, a strong whitish light streamed into the cavern, casting the dark and lengthened shadows of the party who stood without, in sharp distinctness of outline, upon the broken rocks on the opposite side.

"Look there, Minny!" exclaimed the youth, "it is the moon-rise—and we may shortly look for the return of our chief."

"It cannot be, Cormac. The shadows would fall, in that case, to the westward, and not to the south. It is a more fatal signal, it is the death-light of the Rock!"

Cormac paused for some moments. "Fatal it may be," he replied,—"but do you observe, Minny, that no part of its ghastly lustre has fallen upon us? It is shining bright upon our enemies. There is a promise in that, if there be in reality any supernatural meaning in the appearance."

Minny sighed anxiously, while she hung upon his arm—but made no answer to this cheering suggestion. The party outside continued their labour, and in a little time the light was only discernible, as if penetrating through small crevices at the entrance.

"What can they intend?" said Minny, after a pause of some minutes, during which the party outside main- [106] tained profound silence. "All-merciful Heaven!" she continued, starting to her feet in renewed alarm,—"we are about to suffer the fate of Desmond's Kernes—they are going to suffocate us with fire!"

A dense volume of smoke, which rolled into the cavern through the crevices before-mentioned, confirmed this terrific conjecture. The practice, all barbarous as it was, had been frequently resorted to by the conquering party, in the subjugation of the inland districts of the island. Feeble as he had been rendered by fatigue, anxiety, and want of food, Cormac resolved to make a desperate effort to escape the horrible death which menaced them, and rushed, sword in hand, to the mouth of the cave. But he was met by a mass of heated vapour, which deprived him of the power of proceeding, or even calling aloud to their destroyers. He tottered back to where he had left his bride, and sinking down on the earth beside her, felt a horrid sense of despair weigh down his energies, like cowardice. Again he arose, and attempted to force his way through the entrance, and again he was compelled to relinquish the effort. He cried aloud to them—offered to surrender—and entreated that they would at least have mercy on his companion. But no answer was returned—and the dreadful conclusion remained to be deduced, that, contented with having made the work of death secure, they had retired to a distance from the place.

With a sickening heart, eyes swollen and painful, and [107] a reeling brain, Cormac once more resumed his place by the side of his betrothed. She had fallen into a kind of delirium, and extended her arms towards him with an expression of suffering, which made his heart ache more keenly than his own agonies.

"I want air, Cormac!—oh, Cormac, my love! take me home with you—take me into the green fields—for I am dying here.—Air, Cormac! air, for the love of heaven!"

"My own love, you shall have it—look up, and beat a good heart for two minutes, and we shall all be happy again."

"This place is horrible—it is like hell! It is hell! Are we living yet? I have been a sinner; and yet, I hoped, too, Cormac—I always hoped"—

"Hope yet, Minny, and you shall not hope in vain—keep your face near the earth, where the air is freest. Ha! listen to that. The White Knight is returned, and we are safe!"

A rolling of musketry, succeeded by yells, shouts, and cries of triumph and of anguish, was heard outside the cavern. Cormac and his bride stood erect once more; but poor Minny's strength failed her in the effort, and she sank lifeless into the arms of her lover. In a few moments the mouth of the cavern was cleared; and a flood of the cool sweet air rushed, like a welcome to life and happiness, into the bosoms of the sufferers. Recovering new vigour with the draught, Cormac staggered toward the entrance, and passed out into the open air, [108] with his fainting bride on his shoulder, and a drawn sword in his right hand—presenting to the troop of liberators, who were gathered outside, a picture not unlike that of Theseus, bearing the beauteous queen of Dis from the descent of Avernus. His pale cheeks looking paler in the moonlight: his wild staring eyes, scattered hair, and military attire, contributed to render the resemblance still more striking.

The White Knight received him with open arms; but Cormac would hold no more lengthened communication, until his bride was restored to health and consciousness.

In this no great difficulty was encountered; and tradition says, that the White Knight was one of the merriest dancers at the bridal feast, which was given at the cottage in a few days after these occurrences.

I learned from a person curious in old legends, an account of the manner in which the "Candle on the Rock" was exorcised,—for it has not been seen now for a long lapse of time. About two years after the marriage of Cormac and Minny, they were both seated, on a calm winter evening, in the room, which had been the scene of so much tumult and disaster on the occasion above-mentioned. Minny was occupied in instructing a little rosy child (whose property it was, my fair readers may perhaps conjecture), in the rudiments of locomotion; while Cormac—(young husbands will, play the fool sometimes)—held out his arms to receive the daring adventurer, after his hazardous journey of no less than two [109] yards, on foot, across the floor. The tyro-pedestrian had executed about half his undertaking without meeting with any accident worthy of commemoration, and lo! aunt Norry was bending over him, with a smile and a "*Ma gra hu!*" of overflowing affection, when an aged man presented himself at the open door, and solicited charity for the love of Heaven!

Minny placed a small cake of griddle bread in the arms of the infant, and bade him take it to the stranger. The child tottered across the floor with his burthen, and deposited it in the hat of the poor pilgrim, who laid his withered hand on the glossy ringlets of the little innocent, and blessed him with much fervency. At that moment, the fatal light of the Rock streamed through the doorway, and bathed in its lustre the persons of the wayfarer and his guileless entertainer. The poor mother shrieked aloud, and was about to rush towards the child, when the pilgrim assuming, on a sudden, a lofty and majestic attitude, bade her remain where she stood, and suffer him to protect the child.

"I know," said he, "the cause of your fear, and I hope to end it. The evil spirit who possesses that fatal signal, is as much under the control of the Almighty as the feeblest mortal amongst us; and if there be on earth a being who is exempt from the pernicious influence which the demon is permitted to exercise, surely the fiend may, with the chiefest security, be defied by innocence and charity." [110]

Having thus said, he knelt down, with the child between him and the Rock, and commenced a silent prayer, while his clasped hands rested on the head of the infant, his long grey hair hung down upon his shoulders, and his clear blue eye was fixed steadily upon the fatal Candle. As he prayed, the anxious parents observed the light grow fainter and fainter, and the shadows of the old man and child become less and less distinct, until at length the sallow hue of the pilgrim's countenance could scarcely be distinguished from the bloom that glowed upon the fresh cheeks of the infant. Before his prayer was ended, the light had disappeared altogether, and the child came running into the arms of its enraptured mother. When the first burst of joy had been indulged in, she looked up to thank the stranger; but he was nowhere to be seen!

The death-light has never since re-appeared upon the Rock, although it preserves the name which it received from that phantom. Cormac and Minny long continued to exercise the virtue of hospitality to which they owed so much in this instance; and, I am told, that the child became a bishop, in course of time. This, surely, is good fortune enough to enable one to wind up a long story with credit; and I have only to conclude, after aunt Norry's favourite form, by wishing—IF THEY DIDN'T LIVE HAPPY, THAT YOU AND I MAY.

Title
Maginn, William. "A Vision of Purgatory." LS 1829. 228-246. [228]

A VISION OF PURGATORY.
BY WILLIAM MAGINN, ESQ.

THE church-yard of Inistubber is as lonely a one as you would wish to see on a summer's day, or avoid on a winter's night. It is situated in a narrow valley, at the bottom of three low, barren, miserable hills, on which there is nothing green to meet the eye, tree or shrub, grass or weed. The country beyond these hills is pleasant and smiling;—rich fields of corn, fair clumps of oaks, sparkling streams of water, houses beautifully dotting the scenery, which gently undulates round and round, as far as the eye can reach: but once cross the north side of Inistubber-hill, and you look upon desolation. There is nothing to see but, down in the hollow, the solitary churchyard, with its broken wall, and the long, lank grass growing over the grave-stones, mocking with its melancholy verdure the barrenness of the rest of the landscape. It is a sad thing to reflect that the only green spot in the prospect springs from the grave! [229]

Under the east window is a mouldering vault of the De Lacys,—a branch of a family descended from one of the conquerors of Ireland; and there they are buried, when the allotted time calls them to the tomb. On these occasions a numerous cavalcade, poured from the adjoining districts in all the pomp and circumstance of woe, is wont to fill the deserted church-yard; and the slumbering echoes are awakened to the voice of prayer and wailing, and charged with the sigh that marks the heart bursting with grief, or the laugh escaping from the bosom mirth-making under the cloak of mourning. Which of these feelings was predominant, when Sir Theodore De Lacy died, is not written in history; nor is it necessary to inquire. He had lived a jolly, thoughtless life, rising early for the hunt, and retiring late from the bottle. A good-humoured bachelor who took no care about the management of his household, provided that the hounds were in order for his going out, and the table ready on his coming in. As for the rest,—an easy landlord, a quiet master, a lenient magistrate (except to poachers), and a very excellent foreman of a grand jury. He died one evening while laughing at a story which he had heard regularly thrice a week for the last fifteen years of his life, and his spirit mingled with the claret.

In former times when the De Lacys were buried, there was a grand breakfast, and all the party rode over to the church to see the last rites paid. The keeners lamented; the country people had a wake before the [230] funeral, and a dinner after it—and there was an end. But with the march of mind comes trouble and vexation. A man has now-a-days no certainty of quietness in his coffin—unless it be a patent one. He is laid down in the grave, and the next morning finds himself called upon to demonstrate an interesting fact! No one, I believe, admires this ceremony, and it is not to be wondered at that Sir Theodore De Lacy held it in especial horror. "I'd like," he said one evening, "to catch one of the thieves coming after me when I'm dead—By the God of War, I'd break every bone in his body;—but," he added with a sigh, "as I suppose I'll not be able to take my own part then, upon you I leave it, Larry Sweeny, to watch me three days and three nights after they plant me under the sod. There's Doctor Dickenson there, I see the fellow looking at me—fill your glass, Doctor—here's your health! and shoot him, Larry, do you hear, shoot the Doctor like a cock, if he ever comes stirring up my poor old bones from their roost of Inistubber."

"Why, then," Larry answered, accepting the glass which followed this command, "long life to both your honours; and it's I that would like to be putting a bullet into Dr. Dickenson—heaven between him and harm—for hauling your honour away, as if you was a horse's head, to a bonfire. There's nothing, I 'shure you, gintlemin, poor as I am, that would give me greater pleasure."

"We feel obliged, Larry," said Sir Theodore, "for your good wishes." [231]

"Is it I pull you out of the grave, indeed?" continued the whipper-in, for such he was,—"I'd let nobody pull your honour out of any place, saving 'twas purgatory; and out of that I'd pull you myself, if I saw you going there."

"I am of opinion, Larry," said Dr. Dickenson, "you would turn tail if you saw Sir Theodore on that road. You might go further, and fare worse, you know."

"Turn tail!" replied Larry, "it is I that wouldn't—I appale to St. Patrick himself over beyond"—pointing to a picture of the Prime Saint of Ireland, which hung in gilt daubery behind his master's chair, right opposite to him.

To Larry's horror and astonishment, the picture fixing its eyes upon him, winked with the most knowing air, as if acknowledging the appeal.

"What makes you turn so white then at the very thought," said the doctor, interpreting the visible consternation of our hero in his own way.

"Nothing particular," answered Larry; "but a wakeness has come strong over me, gintlemin, and if you'd have no objection, I'd like to go into the air for a bit."

Leave was of course granted, and Larry retired amid the laughter of the guests—but as he retreated, he could not avoid casting a glance on the awful picture—and again the Saint winked, with a most malicious smile. It was impossible to endure the repeated infliction, and Larry rushed down the stairs in an agony of fright and amazement. [232]

"Maybe," thought he, "it might he my own eyes that wasn't quite steady—or the flame of the candle. But no—he winked at me as plain as ever I winked at Judy Donaghue of a May morning. What he manes by it I can't say—but there's no use of thinking about it—no, nor of talking neither, for who'd believe me if I tould them of it?"

The next evening Sir Theodore died, as has been mentioned; and in due time thereafter was buried according to the custom of the family, by torch-light, in the churchyard of Inistubber. All was fitly performed; and although Dickenson had no design upon the jovial knight—and if he had not, there was nobody within fifteen miles that could be suspected of such an outrage,—yet Larry Sweeny was determined to make good his promise of watching his master. "I'd think little of telling a lie to him, by the way of no harm, when he was alive," said he, wiping his eyes, as soon as the last of the train had departed, leaving him with a single companion in the lonely cemetery; "but now that he's dead—God rest his soul!—I'd scorn it. So Jack Kinaley, as behoves my first cousin's son, stay you with me here this blessed night, for betune (between) you and I, it an't lucky to stay by one's self in this ruinated old rookery, where ghosts, God help us, is as thick as bottles in Sir Theodore's cellar!"

"Never you mind that, Larry," said Kinaley, a discharged soldier, who had been through all the campaigns of the Peninsula; "never mind, I say, such botherations. [233] Han't I lain in bivouack on the field at Salamanca, and Tallawara, and the Pyrumnees, and many another place beside, where there was dead corpses lying about in piles, and there was no more ghosts than kneebuckles in a ridgemint of Highlanders. Here, let me prime them pieces, and hand us over the bottle; we'll stay snug under this east window, for the wind's coming down the hill, and I defy"—

"None of that bould talk, Jack," said his cousin; "as for what ye saw in foreign parts, of dead men killed a-fighting, sure that's nothing to the dead—God rest 'em!—that's here. There you see, they had company one with the other, and being killed fresh-like that morning, had no heart to stir; but here, faith! 'tis a horse of another colour."

"Maybe it is," said Jack, "but the night's coming on; so I'll turn in. Wake me if you sees anything; and after I've got my two hours' rest, I'll relieve you."

With these words the soldier turned on his side, under shelter of a grave, and as his libations had been rather copious during the day, it was not long before he gave audible testimony that the dread of supernatural visitants had had no effect in disturbing the even current of his fancy.

Although Larry had not opposed the proposition of his kinsman, yet he felt by no means at ease. He put in practice all the usually recommended nostrums for keeping away unpleasant thoughts:—he whistled, but the echo [234] sounded so sad and dismal that he did not venture to repeat the experiment;—he sang, but when no more than five notes had passed his lips he found it impossible to get out a sixth, for the chorus reverberated from the ruinous walls was destruction to all earthly harmony;—he cleared his throat—he hemmed—he stamped—he endeavoured to walk—all would not do. He wished sincerely that Sir Theodore had gone to heaven—he dared not suggest even to himself, just then, the existence of any other region—without leaving on him the perilous task of guarding his mortal remains in so desperate a place. Flesh and blood could hardly resist it! even the preternatural snoring of Jack Kinaley added to the horrors of his position; and if his application to the spirituous soother of grief beside him was frequent, it is more to be deplored on the score of morality, than wondered at on the score of metaphysics. He who censures our hero too severely, has never watched the body of a dead baronet in the church-yard of Inistubber, at midnight.

"If it was a common, dacent, quite (quiet), well-behaved church-yard a'self," thought Larry, half-aloud—"but when 'tis a place like this forsaken ould berrin'-ground, which is noted for villany"—

"For what, Larry?" said a gentleman, stepping out of a niche which contained the only statue time had spared. It was the figure of Saint Colman, to whom the church was dedicated. Larry had been looking at the figure, as it shone forth in ebon and ivory in the light and shadow of the now high-careering moon. [235] "For what, Larry," said the gentleman,—"for what do you say the church-yard is noted?"

"For nothing at all, plase your honour," replied Larry, "except the height of gentility."

The stranger was about four feet high, dressed in what might be called flowing garments,—if, in spite of their form, their rigidity did not deprive them of all claim to such an appellation. He wore an antique mitre upon his head; his hands were folded upon his breast; and over his right shoulder rested a pastoral crook. There was a solemn expression in his countenance, and his eye might truly be called stony. His beard could not be well said to wave upon his bosom; but it lay upon it in ample profusion, stiffer than that of a Jew on a frosty morning after mist. In short, as Larry soon discovered to his horror, on looking up at the niche, it was no other than Saint Colman himself, who had stept forth, indignant (in all probability) at the stigma cast by the watcher of the dead on the church-yard of which his Saintship was patron.

He smiled with a grisly solemnity—just such a smile as you might imagine would play round the lips of a milestone (if it had any), at the recantation so quickly volunteered by Larry. "Well," said he, "Lawrence Sweeny"—

"How well the old rogue," thought Larry, "knows my name!"

"Since you profess yourself such an admirer of the merits of the church-yard of Inistubber, get up and [236] follow me, till I shew you the civilities of the place—for I am master here, and must do the honours."

"Willingly would I go with your worship," replied our friend; "but you see here I am engaged to Sir Theodore, who, though a good master, was a mighty passionate man when every thing was not done as he ordered it; and I am feared to stir."

"Sir Theodore," said the Saint, "will not blame you for following me. I assure you he will not."

"But then," said Larry—

"Follow me!" cried the Saint, in a hollow voice, and casting upon him his stony eye, drew poor Larry after him, as the bridal guest was drawn by the lapidary glance of the Ancient Mariner; or, as Larry himself afterwards expressed it, "as a jaw tooth is wrinched out of an ould woman with a pair of pinchers."

The Saint strode before him in silence, not in the least incommoded by the stones and rubbish, which at every step sadly contributed to the discomfiture of Larry's shins, who followed his marble conductor into a low vault, situated at the west end of the church. In accomplishing this, poor Larry contrived to bestow upon his head an additional organ, the utility of which he was not craniologist enough to discover.

The path lay through coffins piled up on each side of the way in various degrees of decomposition; and, excepting that the solid footsteps of the saintly guide, as they smote heavily on the floor of stone, broke the deadly [237] silence, all was still. Stumbling and staggering along, directed only by the casual glimpses of light afforded by the moon, where it broke through the dilapidated roof of the vault, and served to discover only sights of woe, Larry followed. He soon felt that he was descending, and could not help wondering at the length of the journey. He. began to entertain the most unpleasant suspicions as to the character of his conductor;—but what could he do? Flight was out of the question, and to think of resistance was absurd. "Needs must, they say," thought he to himself, "when the devil drives. I see it's much the same when a saint leads."

At last the dolorous march had an end; and not a little to Larry's amazement, he found that his guide had brought him to the gate of a lofty hall, before which a silver lamp, filled with naphtha, "yielded light, as from a sky."—From within loud sounds of merriment were ringing; and it was evident, from the jocular harmony and the tinkling of glasses, that some subterraneous catch-club were not idly employed over the bottle.

"Who's there?" said a porter, roughly responding to the knock of Saint Colman,

"Be so good," said the Saint, mildly, "my very good fellow, as to open the door without further questions, or I'll break your head. I'm bringing a gentleman here on a visit, whose business is pressing."

"May be so," thought Larry, "but what that business may be, is more than I can tell." [238] The porter sulkily complied with the order, after having apparently communicated the intelligence that a stranger was at hand; for a deep silence immediately followed the tipsy clamour; and Larry, sticking close to his guide, whom he now looked upon almost as a friend, when compared with these under-ground revellers to whom he was about to be introduced, followed him through a spacious vestibule, which gradually sloped into a low-arched room, where the company was assembled.

And a strange-looking company it was. Seated round a long table were three-and-twenty grave and venerable personages, bearded, mitred, stoled, and croriered,—all living statues of stone, like the Saint who had walked out of his niche. On the drapery before them were figured the images of the sun, moon, and stars—the inexplicable bear—the mystic temple, built by the hand of Hiram—and other symbols, of which the uninitiated know nothing. The square, the line, the trowel, were not wanting, and the hammer was lying in front of the chair. Labour, however, was over, and the time for refreshment having arrived, each of the stony brotherhood had a flagon before him; and when we mention that the Saints were Irish, and that St. Patrick in person was in the chair, it is not to be wondered at that the mitres, in some instances, hung rather loosely on the side of the heads of some of the canonized compotators. Among the company were found St. Senanus of Limerick, St. Declan of Ardmore, St. Canice of Kilkenny, St. Finbar of Cork, St. Michan of Dublin, [239] St. Brandon of Kerry, St. Fachnan of Ross, and others of that holy brotherhood; a vacant place, which completed the four-and-twentieth, was left for St. Colman, who, as everybody knows, is of Cloyne; and he, having taken his seat, addressed the President, to inform him that he had brought the man.

The man (viz. Larry himself) was awestruck with the company in which he so unexpectedly found himself; and trembled all over when, on the notice of his guide, the eight-and-forty eyes of stone were turned directly upon himself.

"You have just nicked the night to a shaving, Larry," said St. Patrick: "this is our chapter-night, and myself and brethren are here 'assembled on merry occasion.'—You know who I am?"

"God bless your Reverence," said Larry, "it's I that do well. Often did I see your picture hanging over the door of places where it is"—lowering his voice—"pleasanter to be than here, buried under an ould church."

"You may as well say it out, Larry," said St. Patrick; "and don't think I'm going to be angry with you about it; for I was once flesh and blood myself. But you remember, the other night, saying that you would think nothing of pulling your master out of purgatory, if you could get at him there, and appealing to me to stand by your words.

"Y-e-e-s," said Larry, most mournfully; for he recollected the significant look he had received from the picture. [240] "And," continued St. Patrick, "you remember also that I gave you a wink, which you know is as good, any day, as a nod—at least, to a blind horse."

"I'm sure your Reverence," said Larry, with a beating heart, "is too much of a gintleman to hold a poor man hard to every word he may say of an evening, and, therefore"—

"I was thinking so," said the Saint, "I guessed you'd prove a poltroon when put to the push. What do you think, my brethren, I should do to this fellow?"

A hollow sound burst from the bosoms of the unanimous assembly. The verdict was short, but decisive:—

"Knock out his brains!"

And in order to suit the action to the word, the whole four-and-twenty arose at once, and with their immoveable eyes fixed firmly on the face of our hero—who, horror-struck with the sight as he was, could not close his—they began to glide slowly but regularly towards him, bending their line into the form of a crescent, so as to environ him on all sides. In vain he fled to the door; its massive folds resisted mortal might. In vain he cast his eyes around in quest of a loophole of retreat—there was none. Closer and closer pressed on the slowly-moving phalanx, and the uplifted croziers threatened soon to put their sentence into execution. Supplication was all that remained—and Larry sunk upon his knees.

"Ah! then" said he, "gintlemin and ancient ould saints as you are, don't kill the father of a large small [241] family, who never did hurt to you or yours. Sure, if 'tis your will that I should go to—no matter who, for there's no use in naming his name—might I not as well make up my mind to go there, alive and well, stout and hearty, and able to face him,—as with my head knocked into bits, as if I had been after a fair or a patthren?"

"You say right," said St. Patrick, checking with a motion of his crozier the advancing assailants, who returned to their seats. "I am glad to see you coming to reason. Prepare for your journey."

"And how, please your Saintship, am I to go?" asked Larry.

"Why," said St. Patrick, "as Colman here has guided you so far, he may guide you further. But as the journey is into foreign parts, where you arn't likely to be known, you had better take this letter of introduction, which may be of use to you."

"And here, also, Lawrence," said a Dublin Saint—perhaps Michan—"take you this box also, and make use of it as he to whom you speak shall suggest."

"Take a hold, and a firm one," said St. Colman, "Lawrence, of my cassock, and we'll start."

"All right behind?" cried St. Patrick."

"All right!" was the reply.

In an instant! vault—table—saints—bell—church, faded into air; a rustling hiss of wings was all that was heard; and Larry felt his cheek swept by a current, as if a covey of birds of enormous size were passing him. (It [242] was, in all probability, the flight of the saints returning to heaven, but on that point nothing certain hag reached us up to the present time of writing). He had not a long time to wonder at the phenomenon, for he himself soon began to soar, dangling in mid sky to the skirt of the cassock of his sainted guide. Earth, and all that appertains thereto, speedily passed from his eyes, and they were alone in the midst of circumfused ether, glowing with a sunless light. Above, in immense distance, was fixed the firmament, fastened up with bright stars, fencing around the world with its azure wall. They fled far, before any distinguishable object met their eyes. At length, a long white streak, shining like silver in the moonbeam, was visible to their sight.

"That," said St. Colman, "is the Limbo which adjoins the earth, and is the highway for ghosts departing the world. It is called in Milton, a book which I suppose, Larry, you never have read"—

"And how could I, please your worship," said Larry, "seein' I don't know a B from a bull's foot!"

"Well, it is called in Milton the Paradise of Fools: and if it were indeed peopled by all of that tribe who leave the world, it would contain the best company that ever figured on the earth. To the north, you see a bright speck!"

"I do."

"That marks the upward path,—narrow and hard to find. To the south you may see a darksome road—broad, [243] smooth, and easy of descent; that is the lower way. It is thronged with the great ones of the world; you may see their figures in the gloom. Those who are soaring upwards are wrapt in the flood of light flowing perpetually from that single spot, and you cannot see them. The silver path on which we enter is the Limbo. Here I part with you. You are to give your letter to the first person you meet. Do your best;—be courageous, but observe particularly that you profane no holy name, or I will not answer for the consequences."

His guide had scarcely vanished, when Larry heard the tinkling of a bell in the distance, and turning his eyes in the quarter whence it proceeded, he saw a grave-looking man in black, with eyes of fire, driving before him a flock of ghosts with a switch, as you see turkeys driven on the western road, at the approach of Christmas. They were on the highway to Purgatory. The ghosts were shivering in the thin air, which pinched them severely, now that they had lost the covering of their bodies. Among the group, Larry recognized his old master, by the same means that Ulysses, Aeneas, and others, recognized the bodiless forms of *their* friends in the regions of Acheron.

"What brings a living person," said the man in black, "on this pathway? I shall make legal capture of you, Larry Sweeny, for trespassing. You have no business here."

"I have come," said Larry, plucking up courage, "to [244] bring your honour's glory a letter from a company of gintlemin with whom I had the pleasure of spending the evening, underneath the ould church of Inistubber."

"A letter," said the man in black, "where is if!"

"Here, my lord," said Larry.

"Ho!" cried the black gentleman, on opening it, "I know the hand-writing. It won't do, however, my lad,—I see they want to throw dust in my eyes."

"Whew!" thought Larry, "that's the very thing. Tis for that the ould Dublin boy gave me the box. I'd lay a tenpenny to a brass farthing that it's filled with Lundy-Foot."

Opening the box, therefore, he flung its contents right into the fiery eyes of the man in black, while he was still occupied with reading the letter,—and the experiment was successful.

"Curses,—tche-tche-tche,—Curses on it," exclaimed he, clapping his hand before his eyes, and sneezing most lustily.—

"Run, you villains, run," cried Larry, to the ghosts—"run, you villains, now that his eyes are off of you. O master, master! Sir Theodore, jewel! run to the right-hand side, make for the bright speck, and God give you luck."

He had forgotten his injunction. The moment the word was uttered he felt the silvery ground sliding from under him; and with the swiftness of thought he found himself on the flat of his back, under the very niche of [245] *the* old church wail whence he had started, dizzy and confused with the measureless tumble. The emancipated ghosts floated in all directions, emitting their shrill and stridulous cries in the gleaming expanse. Some were again gathered by their old conductor; some scudding about at random, took the right-hand path, others the left, into which of them Sir Theodore struck, is not recorded; but as he had heard the direction, let us hope that he made the proper choice.

Larry had not much time given him to recover from his fall, for almost in an instant he heard an angry snorting rapidly approaching, and, looking up, whom should he see but the gentleman in black, with eyes gleaming more furiously than ever, and his horns (for, in his haste he had let his hat fall) relieved in strong shadow against the moon. Up started Larry—away ran his pursuer after him. The safest refuge was, of course, the church,—thither ran our hero—
As darts the dolphin from the shark,
Or the deer before the hounds;
and after him—fiercer than the shark, swifter than the hounds—fled the black gentleman. The church is cleared; the chancel entered; and the hot breath of his pursuer glows upon the outstretched neck of Larry. Escape is impossible—the extended talons of the fiend have clutched him by the hair. [246]

"You are mine," cried the demon,—"if I have lost any of my flock, I have at last got you."

"Oh, St. Patrick!" exclaimed our hero, in horror,—"oh, St. Patrick have mercy upon me, and save me!"

"I tell you what, cousin Larry," said Kinaley, chucking him up from behind a gravestone, where he had fallen,—"all the St. Patricks that ever were born would not have saved you from ould Tom Picton, if he caught you sleeping on your post as I've caught you now. By the word of an ould soldier, he'd have had the provost-marshal upon you, and I'd not give two-pence for the loan of your life. And then, too, I see you have drank every drop in the bottle. What can you say for yourself!"

"Nothing at all," said Larry, scratching his head,—"but it was an unlucky dream, and I'm glad its over."

Title

By the Author of "The Mummy." [Loundon, J.C.] "The Grotto of Akteleg. A Hungarian Legend." LS 1829. 330-343 [330]

THE GROTTO OF AKTELEG.
BY THE AUTHOR OF 'THE MUMMY.'

NEAR the village of Azelas in Hungary, is an immense cavern, or rather, a vast succession of caverns, extending for many miles under ground, and known by the general name of the 'Grotto of Akteleg.' Nothing can be more romantic than its situation: fir and box trees cover the steep hills in its vicinity, and fields of Turkish maize fertilize the valleys; the bright yellow of the corn, as the tall stalks wave in the passing gale, and their heavy heads dash against each other, contrasting strikingly with the dark masses of the fir and the glossy verdure of the box.

This wild, solitary-looking spot, which is now almost inaccessible even to the foot of man, was once, according to tradition, a splendid city; indeed, traces are still pointed out, of the carriage wheels which once rolled through its streets; whilst the altar, pillars, and sculptures of its magnificent cathedral may also be discovered [331] through the mass of stalactites which now encrust them, and which reflect back the torch of the inquisitive visitor in a thousand varied tints. Dazzling, indeed, is the magical effect of this spacious cavern, when lights flash through its dark recesses. It resembles a crystal palace, whose walls, hung with diamonds and a thousand other precious stones, are so brilliant as to make the eye ache with beholding them;—vault after vault thus sparkles with ineffable brightness, till the spectator almost fancies himself in the paradise of the Chaldeans, and turns away at length bewildered by the blaze. One chamber is, however, an exception to this description; for in that, all is dark, save a single pillar of pale amber, emitting a mild, softened light; which, when compared with the intensity of the glare in the entrance to the cave, falls upon the eye like faint moon-beams feebly struggling through the deep shadows of a thick grove. Soothing is the effect produced upon the mind by this gentle lustre; but the pleasing sensations it excites are soon converted into astonishment—for when the pillar is struck with iron, it sends forth tones so plaintive and so sweet that few can hear them without emotion. The legend annexed to this singular phenomenon is far from being uninteresting.

In the reign of the apostate Julian, Akteleg was the metropolis of a flourishing kingdom; the monarch of which—a stern, avaricious man—eagerly followed the example of the emperor, and endeavoured to restore Paganism throughout his dominions. Although he was, [332] like all new converts, very zealous in the cause he had thus adopted, it was whispered that his persecuting fervour arose less from real enmity to the Christians, than from his earnest desire to seize upon the wealth they had accumulated; and this supposition was confirmed by his reconversion to Christianity on the fall of his master: a change which was, however, principally attributed to the influence of his beautiful daughter Monica, who was a pious follower of Jesus, and whom he had always permitted to practise freely the rites of her religion.

The fame of the court of Akteleg for its magnificence, and for the encouragement afforded by its monarch to the professors of the fine arts, drew to that city a number of learned men from all nations; and of these, none were so kindly received, or so warmly patronised, as those skilled in the occult sciences. It was the very era for superstition; as Paganism was labouring under all the weakness of dotage, and Christianity had scarcely risen into its full strength. The minds of men were unsettled,—and in the absence of some fixed faith upon which they could firmly build their hopes, they clung eagerly to the strong excitement produced by magic. In those days, when men were only imperfectly acquainted with the secrets of nature, knowledge was indeed power, and the happy few who possessed it were so superior to the rest, as to be readily supposed to hold communication with supernatural beings. It is a remarkable fact in the history of the human mind, that almost every person has some par- [333] ticular weakness, over which the judgment has no influence,—and which, even in sensible men, often degenerates into downright folly: whilst this feeling, although sedulously concealed from the world, is fondly cherished in private by its possessor; perhaps upon the principle that induces a mother to manifest more affection for her deformed children than for her more perfect offspring. This was the case with the king of Akteleg: no one possessed a stronger mind, more acute penetration, or a sounder judgment than he, as to the general affairs of his kingdom; and yet, no one was more credulous in all that related to astrology,—demonology,—astrobolism,—divination,—or, in fact, to any of those forbidden studies, whose very name of occult invested them with indescribable charms.

The most celebrated sage at the court of the Hungarian monarch, was an Egyptian of the name of Merops, who, it was affirmed, had existed in those far-distant days when Egypt, in science as well as power, shone mistress of the world, and even Greece was, as yet unknown. No one could tell by what mysterious arts his life had been protracted so far beyond the period usually assigned to that of man; yet, no one doubted the truth of the report; for no tale was so wild or so absurd as not at that time to find implicit belief. Merops was fully aware of the awe he inspired; and no one knew better than himself, how to maintain the station to which the credulity of his admirers had raised him. His abilities and knowledge, [334] however, were solely directed to one object—the gratification of his ambition; and for this, he denied himself all the pleasures and even comforts of life;—for this, he exhausted the powers of his mighty mind in abstruse studies;—and for this, he condescended to become the idol of the multitude. By these means, though of obscure origin, he had already risen into fame; he was followed, courted, nay, almost adored, till at length he reached the climax of his wishes, and was ordered to appear before the sovereign himself.

The king received Merops with breathless anxiety. Legends of the immense treasures buried in ancient times beneath the Hungarian mountains, had long haunted his imagination; and the hopes he had conceived, that this almost omniscient man might reveal their hidden depository, were so overpowering, that for a moment they nearly deprived him of speech; Merops marked the inward agitation of the king, and smiled in the proud consciousness of mental superiority. The conference was short; for the spirit of the king quailed before the haughty glance of the stranger: the power which after times have attributed to the eyes of the rattlesnake, seemed exercised upon him; and although he felt he could not turn from that steadfast gaze, his soul sickened under its influence.

In the meantime, the heart of Merops throbbed with joy, for he knew that he should now attain the summit of his wishes. The king had heedlessly put himself into the power of his subject; he had confided to the hands of [335] Merops, the master-key of his passions, and the wily philosopher did not hesitate to avail himself amply of the knowledge he had acquired. Though Merops despised wealth for its own sake, he was too well aware of the influence which gold exerts over the minds of men, not to wish to obtain it as a means of furthering his ambition. For this purpose he had searched the most hidden recesses of the mountains, to endeavour to discover the treasures said to be concealed in them; and had at length succeeded in discovering a valley of crystallizations, which, when they reflected the rays of the setting sun, assumed the appearance of precious stones. By torch-light, this effect was considerably increased; and the active mind of Merops easily divined an expedient, by which he might avail himself of this spectacle to inflame to its utmost the cupidity of the king, and at the same time to convince him that he possessed the power of gratifying it.

Having made the arrangements necessary to effect his purpose, Merops once more stood before his sovereign: the monarch greeted him eagerly; and with a trembling voice, asked if he had discovered the hidden treasures.

"In obedience to thy command, sire," replied the sage, "thy slave has summoned to his aid the demons of the earth, and they have shewn to him a treasure which has dazzled his eyes with its glory."

"Where! where is it?" cried the monarch.

"It is permitted to the humble slave of the mighty king of Akteleg, to shew this splendour to his sovereign: [336] but neither the king, nor his devoted attendant, may presume to touch the glittering jewels which they are destined to behold, without first propitiating the demons appointed to guard them from the world."

"And how are they to be propitiated?"

"There are rites," murmured the sage, in a deep, hollow tone, fixing his eyes, which seemed to glare with supernatural brightness, upon the king. "There are rites, which the unenlightened describe as impious; but which"—

"Oh, father! dearest father!" cried Monica, bursting into the room, and falling at the monarch's feet; "do not listen to him."

"Whence came you, my child; and why do you meddle with matters so far above your comprehension?"

"They are not above my comprehension;—alas! alas! I but too well understand their meaning. He would urge you to destruction, father; but resist the tempter—I inadvertently overheard your conversation, and I am come to save you."

Monica paused. All that fine devotedness of purpose, which had already distinguished so many of her sex and religion in those ages of persecution, glowed upon her cheek and brightened in her eye; whilst, like them, she also seemed prepared to die a martyr to her faith. The king was affected; he could not gaze upon the beautiful features of his daughter, ennobled as they were by the grandeur of her soul, without feeling ashamed of his own [337] vacillation, yet he could not conquer it; his mind was incapable of the high resolve which sat enthroned upon his daughter's brow; for avarice debases its possessor, and like the snail, pollutes with its foul slime every thing that it touches. The Egyptian saw his hesitation, and knew that he was successful; for such is the natural disposition of man to evil, that when he suffers his mind to waver, even for an instant, between vice and virtue, it is quite certain that the former will soon gain the ascendency.

"I do but wish to see the wonders that this man can exhibit;" said the king, after a short silence. "There can be no harm in beholding the treasures which he speaks of."

Monica shook her head. "Then let me accompany you," said she.

Merops was by no means pleased with this proposition, but the king caught at it with eagerness, and the Egyptian was too prudent to disgust his neophyte, by even offering an objection. The night fixed upon for their expedition was one of pitchy darkness, and the road lay entirely through dense forests of the black pine. The king, although he moved, himself, with trembling steps, was yet obliged to support the delicate form of his lovely daughter, who clung fondly to him; whilst the stern magician, arrayed in the flowing garb of his order, bore aloft the torch which alone served to light them on their way. No sound broke upon the silence of the night, save the wind, which howled mournfully through the pine trees; [338] the withered cones and dried leaves rattling with every gust. It is scarcely possible to imagine a scene more calculated to inspire horror; and the spirits of both Monica and her father, sank beneath its influence. No one spoke; and with noiseless steps they slowly wound round the side of a steep mountain, till they reached the top, when a scene burst upon them, which inspired even the tranquil Monica with a transport of delight.

In every fissure of the rocks that surrounded the valley of crystal, the magician had placed a torch of pine wood, and having previously illuminated them, the effulgence of light which burst upon the eyes of the! astonished king and his daughter, seemed almost more than mortals could endure. The cheeks of the lovely Monica, however, became pale as the sculptured marble of the tomb, when she had gazed a few seconds upon this splendid vision.

"Oh, father! dearest father! let us fly," exclaimed she, in trembling accents; "it is enchantment—a vile delusion, to destroy us—let us fly, whilst we have yet the power."

The king did not reply—his eyes were fixed upon the glittering valley.

"Father! dearest father!" cried Monica, hanging round his neck;—still she was unheeded—and the eyes of the king remained chained, as if by magic, to the spot. Monica was in despair: one only method presented itself, by which she hoped to drag her father from the influence of this fatal fascination; and although it was repugnant [339] to the natural timidity of her sex, she determined to brave every possible danger in such a cause. She looked again imploringly at the king; but his eye was glazed, and he seemed insensible of her presence.

"I go,—will you not accompany me, my father?" said she, clinging closer to him. He did not reply; all his faculties seemed absorbed in the contemplation of the deceitful treasures before him. "Nay, then, I go alone," said the maiden firmly,—and loosing her hold, she walked hastily away. Violent were the emotions which throbbed in her father's breast as she departed; but, after a struggle, parental love prevailed. He could not trust his Monica, his tender, gentle child, alone to tread that dark and dangerous way; he looked after her a moment, and til he saw her slight form vanishing amongst the trees, the lesser passion was absorbed; he felt how worthless would be his gold, should fate deprive him of his daughter; and he left the gorgeous scene he had been contemplating to pursue her footsteps, without heaving a single sigh.

The demon of avarice, however, although driven from the field, was by no means vanquished; for, as soon as the king's apprehensions for the safety of his daughter were removed, his thoughts reverted to the splendid valley. Monica marked her father's abstraction, and implored him to pray for Divine assistance to repel the tempter. The king did not reply; and, in fact, had no sooner conducted her to her own apartments, than he flew back in search [340] of the magnificent spectacle which had so lately enchanted him. It was vanished; the wary magician had taken advantage of his absence, to extinguish the torches and when the king again stood upon the brow of the hill, all around was gloom. Maddened with disappointment, fancy exaggerated what he had lost; and when he again encountered Merops, his mind was in a fit state to be wrought to desperation by that artful conspirator. It would be useless to detail by what means the king was induced to offer a sacrifice to propitiate the demons who guarded the treasures; yet, such was the fact, and the following night was fixed upon for the completion of the crime. The Egyptians were profound chemists; and though Merops did not, as rumours idly whispered, derive his existence from that nation, yet he had studied under a descendant from one of its sages, and from him had learned the secret of compounding a magic powder, which, when ignited, would explode with such force as to destroy every object in its vicinity. Having prepared a quantity of this destructive drug, he buried it under a pavilion in the garden belonging to the palace, and then persuaded the credulous monarch to offer there a burnt sacrifice to the evil spirits. Merops had contrived that he should not be present at this ceremony, which he confidently hoped would end in the destruction of his sovereign,—and he had prepared the ministers of state and chief officers of the court to regard such an event as a dispensation of Heaven; whilst he had laid another plan, [341] equally well arranged, through which he meant, by means of his chemical secrets, to terrify the people into appointing him as the king's successor.

Weak, however, are the designs of mortals, if Omnipotence frown upon their projects: the schemes of Merops were laid with almost supernatural sagacity;—every difficulty was foreseen, and every objection anticipated; yet it was all in vain; and the consummate skill shewn by the crafty plotter, only hastened his own destruction. Unconscious of the strength of the ingredients he had employed, he had buried so much of the fatal powder that one single spark was sufficient to involve the whole city in ruin. Of this he was not aware; and fancying that the pavilion in which the sacrifice was to be offered up would alone suffer, he calmly awaited the event in the adjoining palace. With fiend-like barbarity, however, he determined that the innocent Monica should not survive her father; and for this purpose he informed her of the king's intentions the very instant before they were to be put into execution. Monica was struck with horror at the intimation; and, as the crafty magician had anticipated, she resolved to interfere to prevent the consummation of so great a sin. She accordingly, at the very moment when the king was about to light the unhallowed pile, rushed into the pavilion, and threw herself at his feet. She could not speak,—but her panting breast and dishevelled hair bespoke her agitation, and her imploring eyes pierced her father's heart. [342]

"My Monica," said he, "this is no place for you. Return, my child,—I will join you soon."

"Never!" exclaimed Monica, firmly, "never will I leave this place, unless you accompany me."

"This is childish, Monica. I have but some rites to perform, in which I would not have you participate; when they are concluded, I will join you."

"And what rites must those be, which a parent refuses to participate with his child? At my entreaty you renounced the errors of Paganism—but this is worse. Oh, father!—dearest father! reflect, ere it be too late."

The king paused,—he looked fondly at his daughter.—"It is but for thy sake," said he, "that I wish to acquire riches."

"Then, wish no longer," cried Monica, her eyes sparkling with animation, "risk not thy precious soul for my sake. I want not gold. Hear me, as I swear—solemnly swear! to live henceforward as the anchorite of the desert. Never will I again touch gold—never again shall costly viands pollute my lips,—my food shall be simply the fruits of the earth, and my drink, water from the spring!"

"My child! my child! what have you said?"

"What I mean steadily to perform," returned Monica, a bright smile passing over her countenance as she spoke; "let me save my father from everlasting destruction, and the luxuries of life fade as nothing in the scale!"

The king looked at her with emotion; to his heated imagination it seemed no longer his daughter, but his [343] guardian angel that stood before him: his better feelings prevailed—he threw down the censer, and clasping her in his arms, whispered softly—"thou hast conquered!"

That instant a peal, like thunder broke upon their ears, a hollow rumbling noise succeeded, and the ground heaved like the billows of the sea. Fire had fallen from the censer when the king cast it from him; the fatal powder ignited, and as the mine exploded, the rocks were torn asunder with a convulsion which seemed the last throe of expiring nature. Palaces and towers tottered to their fall; the lofty dome of the cathedral rocked like a pine branch tossing in a storm; earth yawned for her prey, and the fair city sank into her bosom. Mountains closed over it, and the very name of Akteleg is now almost forgotten. No mortal being escaped alive the horrors of that fatal night; but the moonlight softness of the pale amber pillar, seems emblematic of the lovely Monica; and as its sweet though mournful notes melt upon the ear, to a fanciful mind the tender music seems still to sigh over the fallen fortunes of her country.

Literary Annual
The Literary Souvenir. Ed. Alaric A. Watts. London: Longman, Rees, Orme, Brown & Green, 1830. Printer: Samuel Manning and Co., London-House Yard, St. Paul's.[11]

Title
By the Author of "High-Ways and By-Ways." [Grattan, Thomas Colley.] "The Love-Draught. A Tale of the Barrow-Side." LS 1830. 1-19. [1]

THE LOVE-DRAUGHT.
A Tale of the Barrow-Side.
BY THE AUTHOR OF "HIGH-WAYS AND BY-WAYS."

WHOEVER has journeyed along the banks of the river Barrow, in that part of its course which separates the Queen's County from the county of Kildare, must have remarked the remains of Grange-Mellon, the former residence of the St. Ledger family. The long avenue, choked with grass and weeds,—the wooded grounds, stretching along the river's edge,—the dilapidated gateway and mansion-walls,—the loud cawing from the rookery,—all combined to mark the place as one which ought to furnish some legend of antiquity and romance. Such was surely to be had there for those who would seek it. But Grange - Mellon is only linked to my memory by an humble love-story of almost modern date, yet tragical enough, heaven knows, to have had its source in the very oldest days of magic and misery.

I can state nothing of the tender dames, or youths of gentle blood, who inhabited the castle before it tumbled [2] quite to decay. The only beings connected with the existence of the place (and that in the very last stage of its occupation) whom I would attempt to commemorate, were Lanty the whipper-in, and Biddy Keenahan the dairy-maid. Lanty was a kind, frank, honest-hearted lad as ever lived. He was a great favourite with the family and the servants, particularly the females. The whole pack of hounds loved him; and a cheering word from his voice could keep them together in the thickest cover, even if there were half-a-dozen hares a-foot; when Brian Oge, the veteran huntsman, might tantivy himself hoarse, and only frighten the whelps and vex the old dogs for his pains. Lanty was, indeed, in the words of the ballad,
Beloved much by man and baste.

But if he was welcome in the kitchen and the kennel, as surely he was, how many a thousand times more welcome. was he, when he came home from the

---

11 Plain text for all short stories included here for the 1830 *Literary Souvenir* obtained from Google Books and then compared against the original volume. For full citation, see References: <http://books.google.com/books?id=EG0EAAAAQAAJ&dq=1830%20The%20Literary%20Souvenir%3B%20or%2C%20Cabinet%20of%20Poetry%20and%20Romance&pg=PR3#v=onepage&q&f=false>

chase, cheering the tired harriers along, and stopping to say, "How is it wid you, Biddy?" or, "What a fine night it is, Biddy!" or some such passing phrase, at the dairy door; where Biddy was sure to be waiting, with a ready answer and a kind look. Ay, welcome indeed was the commonest word which came from Lanty's lips; and the more so, as not a syllable of a more direct tendency had he ever uttered; although it was plain to every one in the world, that he had been in love with Biddy for full a year and a half. [3]

"Ah, Brine!" said he to the old huntsman, one day when they were returning home after a couple of hard runs, followed by the limping pack, "Ah, Brine! it's no use talking! It's no use, you see; for I niver can bring myself to say the words to her, out and out. I love her little finger betther nor the whole 'varsal world: but, by this Cross-Pathrick!" (and he put his finger on his whip handle, making a very positive cross) "it's unpossible for me to tell her so."

Brian Oge, who was a regular male match-maker, and who thought that "the b'ys and girls ought to hunt in couples, any how," was resolved that it should not be his fault if Biddy Keenahan did not know the true state of the case; or if she did not take proper measures to bring matters to a speedy issue between herself and Lanty. He, therefore (as he himself expressed it), "up an' tould her what Lanty had said; an' advised her, as the only way of bringin' him to rason, to go straight to Peg Morrin the fortin-teller, at the fut of Magany Bridge, who 'd soon give her a charm that 'd make Lanty folly her an' spake to the point, as sartin as the rots (rats) folly'd Terry the rot-catcher; an' sure enough he could make thim spake too, if he thought it worth his while!"

This counsel was too palatable to be rejected by poor Biddy. Her spotted cotton handkerchief fluttered over her bosom while Brian Oge was giving his advice; and had it been of muslin, the deep glow of delight might [4] have been seen through it. Her face had no covering to conceal its blushes; and her eyes swam in tears.

"Och, then, *mushu*, Brine Oge!" said she, "it's myself that's behoulden to you for your good nath'r. Why, then, can it be true what you tell me? Little I thought than Lanty cared a *thraneen* for me, though, in troth, it's myself that loves the ground he walks on. Why, then, why wouldn't he tell me so at oncet? If it wasn't that it wouldn't be becomin' in a young girl to spake first, I'd soon tell him what's neither a shame nor a sin, any how. But I'll folly your word, Brine Oge; for you're an ould man, an' a kind one, an' one that knows what's fit for the b'ys an' the girls, an' that niver stands between thim but to bring thim closer to one another; an' here's a noggin of rale crame for you, Brine, jew'l, for it's tired you must be, afther the hunt.

"While Brian drank off the cream, to which he had added something from a leather-covered bottle that he had a habit of carrying in his side-pocket, Biddy went on to tell him that she would not lose any time, but would step down that very night as far as Maganyford, and cross over in Tom Pagan the miller's cot, which would land her at the very field in which Peg Morrin's cabin stood. Brian, after wiping his lips with the cuff of his faded green hunting frock, gave Biddy a very fatherly kiss; and, wishing that a blessing might be on her path, he left her to make her preparations. [5]

When night had fairly set in, so that there was little danger of her course being observed, Biddy, having arranged all the affairs of the dairy, put her grey cloak on her shoulders, and drew the hood well over her head. She tied her shoes fast on, as she had a rough path to follow for a couple of miles by the river's bank, and pulling her woollen mittens on her hands and arms, she finally slipped out of the back window, made the sign of the cross on her breast, and with a short prayer fervently put up, started on her expedition. She knew her way very well, even had it been pitch dark; but as there was moonlight, and as she stepped buoyantly forward, she reached Tom Fagan's cabin by the river side, without once stumbling or tripping over stone or bramble.

"God save all here!" said Biddy, as she raised the latch and entered the cabin, where the miller and his wife were eating their supper by the fire.

"God save you, kindly!" replied they; and the next words in both their mouths were expressions of surprise at this late visit from little Biddy.

"Why, thin, what's corned over you, Biddy, *avic*" said Molly Fagan. "Sure, thin, some misfortin it is that brings you to our cabin this time o' night. But it's welcome you are, *alanna*, any how; an' the greather your throuble the gladder we are to see you."

"Thank you, kindly, Molly, *asthore*; but it's no throuble at all; only I'd be after throublin' Tom jist to ferry me across the river in the cot, that's all." [6]

"Wid all the pleasure in life, and heartily welcome, Biddy, my darling," said Tom Pagan, a friendly young fellow, who was always ready to do a kind turn, particularly to a pretty girl. But his wife's curiosity was not so easily satisfied.

"Why, thin, the Lord save us, Biddy!" said she, "where is it you'd be goin' across the river, into the Queen's County, in the dark night. There's niver a wake nor a weddin' goin' on, nor a dance even, in the three parishes. Where in the world are you goin', Biddy?"

"In troth, it's only jist to see a friend, Molly; and Tom'll tell you who when he comes hack."

"Och! is that the way wid you, Biddy? I see how it is. It's ould Peg you're agoin' to; an' all along of Lanty. There's no use in denyin' it—an' more's the pity, Biddy, *agra*! It's twice you ought to think of what you're about to do; that's not oncet before an' oncet after,—but two times both together, Biddy; for it's a foolish thing, an' one you'll be sorry for, may be. Take my advice, an' have nawthin' to do with ould Peg and her grasy pack o'cards. It's bad fortin they'll bring you, Biddy, dear, when she's afther tellin' you all that's good. For your own sake an' poor

Lanty's, keep away from her; an' let thrue love take its coorse!"

This sensible warning had little effect on Biddy Keenahan. Youth and love were bad subjects to reason with. Backed by Brian Oge's advice, Biddy was resolved to pursue her adventure. She thought, that if [7] Molly Fagan had wanted a husband for herself, she would not have been so averse to a consultation with "the wise woman." But, to satisfy her friend, she put a salvo on her own conscience, and vowed that she "wouldn't let th' ould pack o' cards be cut or shuffled the night;" for that all she wanted was "a little bit of advice, which no one, barrin' Peg Morrin, could give her."

The moon was smothered in clouds, when Biddy stepped into a little flat-bottomed boat, called a cot, and placed herself at one of the pointed ends that might have been called the prow had not the other been quite similar, there being in fact no stern. At this other end, Tom Fagan stood; and, with a long pole, shoved his fragile canoe across the broad, and at that passage, somewhat rapid stream. The fortune-teller's cabin looked like a black patch on the face of the little field, in a corner of which it stood. And, as Biddy threw a furtive glance at the massive bridge of Magany, with its vaguely defined arches, and thought of the many stories which proclaimed it to be haunted, she involuntarily shuddered.

"Is it shiverin' you are, Biddy, dear?" said the compassionate miller; "wrap your cloak over you, for the night wind creeps up against the strame, an' stales into one's buzzum, without givin' a word's warnin'."

"It's not the wind, Tom, *agra*. It's something that's inside of the heart within me that's trimblin'! It's a dreary place you live in, Tom. Plase the Lord I 'm doin' the right thing, in goin' to ould Peg!" [8]

"Arrah, niver fear, Biddy! The divil a harm she'll do you. What if she does look on your palm, or cut the cards wid you? Sure, an' it's thrue enough, she tould me my fortin afore I married Molly, and every word comed to pass. Don't be turned agin her, by what Molly says. She's a very superstitious woman, Biddy; that's God's thruth, an' believes nawthin' but what Father Rice at the Friary tells her. So keep up your heart, like a good girl as you are. Here's the field—an' there's Peg Morrin's cabin—an' God speed you wid her. I 'll wait here till you 're ready, an' bring you back all the way home to the Grange. Now, jump over the flaggers—that's it! cliver an' clane—away wid you!"

And away tripped Biddy, with a beating heart, though greatly reassured by Tom Pagan's cheering words. She kept her eye on the cabin before her, and neither looked to the right nor the left; for she was in the very field where young William Barrington had been recently killed by Gillespie, in a duel rarely paralleled for ferocity; and there was not man nor woman, on either side of the river, that could walk fearlessly through that field of a dark night, much less live in it, except Peg Morrin. But it was well known that she carried a protection about her from all supernatural ills; and well might she walk or sleep, without fear of hurt or harm.

"The Lord save us!" exclaimed Biddy, with a suppressed scream, crossing herself, and clasping her hands together, as a rustling in the large alder bush close to the [9] cabin was followed by a loud whine; while a pair of fiery eyes seemed to fix themselves on the terrified girl. It was only old Peg's black cat, as Biddy was in a moment convinced. In another, she was close to, and tapping gently at, the door.

"Come in, Biddy Keenahan; rise the latch, an' niver mind blessin' or crossin' when you step over the thrashhold!" muttered the voice of the old hag inside. Biddy started back at hearing her own name thus pronounced; but she raised the latch and stepped in, being glad of any refuge from the darkness; and she took care not to say "God save you!" Just as she entered, she received a sharp blow, from some hard but feathery substance above the door. She was afraid to say "Lord bless us!" but she stooped low, and looked up sideways, and saw a large owl flapping his wing at her, from a nook over the entrance.

"Ah, then, how did you know it was me that tapped at the dure, Misthress Morrin?" asked Biddy, timidly, by way of beginning the conversation.

"Didn't you hear the black cat spaking, as you come up the field, Biddy Keenahan?" replied the hag.

"The blessed Cross be about us!" was on Biddy's lips, but she dared not let the words escape.

"Sit down on that stool, Biddy, an' I'll soon give you what you want," continued old Peg, who was herself seated on just such a three-legged implement as she pointed to, with a little table before her, traced with [10] many mystical lines, a lump of chalk being in one of her hands for that purpose; while the other held a pack of cards, which a cryptical incrustation of dirt and grease had brought to a perfect equality of appearance.

"There, Biddy, I'll put the cards away—for it isn't thim you want to dale with the night. Whin the fortin's cast, and the fate doomed, whether it's hangin' or drownin', or a weddin' or a berrin', there's no use in the cards, Biddy—an' it's yours an' Lanty's, that's settled long ago!"

With these words the crone screwed up her mouth and frowned, and thrust her dirty cards into a huge pocket; and then crossing her arms, she looked on Biddy with the half scowl and half smile of lawless power and vulgar patronage.

"Och, Misthress Morrin, *avic*, don't be after frightnin' me this blessed night! It's for your advice I 'm corned, an' sure it's yourself can sarve me, an' do me a good turn. It's ould Brine Oge, the huntsman, that put me upon comin' to you, or I wouldn't be bould enough to throuble you this-a-way."

"Brine Oge is a dacent man, an' one that nobody need be afeard to do wrong in follyin' his advice. Thin what do you want wid me, Biddy Keenahan? May be it's a love pouther for Lanty?"

"Och, then, Misthress Morrin, jew'l! what's the use of your axing me any questions at all at all, when you can answer thim before you ax thim? Then sure enough it's jist *that* I want from you." [11]

"There it is, Biddy Keenahan, ready for you; for I knew you were comin', an' what you'd be afther axin' for. Put out your lift hand, an' take hould of that paper on the shelf beside you, an' put it in your buzzum, for it's the heart that works on the heart! An' take it home wid you, an' mix the pouther wid whatever Lanty likes best—an' what 'd he like betther nor a bowl o' sillybub, the crathur!—An' stir it lift-handed, an' don't look at it, an' throw the paper over your lift shoulder, an' give it to your lovyer—for he's the b'y that loves you, Biddy, dear—wid your own hands, an' watch him while he drinks it, an' say somethin' to yourself all the while, ar a wish, ar what you most wish for in the world. An' from that minute out the charm 'll work, an' the philthur—for that's the name av it in the mysthery—'ll do the rest. An' good look be on you, Biddy Keenahan, wid Lanty your lovyer, who'll soon spake the right speech to you, an 'll only want the word av Father Rice at the Friary afther that, to be your own flish an' blood, Biddy, an' the father if your childer, which may good fortin presarve! Give me half-a-crown, Biddy, an' good night to you! for the miller's cot 'll be waitin', an' the wind's risin', an' it's a hard push Tom Fagan 'll have up the strame to the Grange."

Biddy, in a conflict of wonderment at this knowledge of her movements, and of delight at the wise woman's discourse, put the paper well under the folds of her handkerchief, and felt her heart working against it, sure [12] enough. And she handed the fee to Peg Morrin, and wished her good night, and gave her half-a-dozen blessings, whether the hag liked them or not; stooped low to avoid another slap from the owl's wing, and closing the door hastily, ran down the path without venturing to look at the alder bush, for fear of the black cat. In a minute or two she was at the water's edge, and safe over the side of the cot. In an hour afterwards she was landed on the "quay" of Grange-Mellon, as the little wharf for facilitating the loading and unloading of turf boats and others, was called. Tom Fagan had done all in his power to make the two miles voyage up the river beside the windings, as cheerful as he could to his passenger. She wished him a safe return home, and a good night's rest, and long life to him; and, in high spirits and hopes, with her hand upon the treasure she carried in her bosom, she soon gained her sleeping place and crept into bed, without ever being missed or inquired for.

The next morning, at sun-rise, Biddy was deeply employed in the business of her dairy. Never did she milk her cows, or set her pans, or prepare her churns, with such alacrity and pleasure. A minute's idleness would have been torture to her: she was afraid of having leisure to think; for in spite of every thing,—Brian Oge's and Tom Fagan's encouragement, Peg Morrin's assurances, and her own bright dreams during the night,—the warning of the miller's wife came across her sometimes, [13] like a black shadow on a path of sunshine. She kept the gloomy feeling down by the mere force of employment; and she sung as loudly, and apparently as gaily, during her morning's work, as if it was not to be followed by the most important action of her life.

The love-draught was at length prepared. A richly-frothing bowl of syllabub received the whole contents of Peg Morrin's paper. Biddy never ventured to look on the charm, curious as she felt, as she shook it carefully into the bowl, and conscientiously stirred the whole with her left hand for several minutes. But she had not thus completed her work when she heard the loud music of the hounds, as they left the kennel, and saw Brian Oge and Lanty come riding along, round the offices and orchard.

"God bless your work, Biddy!" said old Brian, reining up his horse at the dairy-door,—the common salutation to any one, however employed. Biddy felt her blood curdle at the words, for she did not think the mysterious and underhand work she was about was a holy one: but this was a moment's thought. She threw the empty paper over her left shoulder, and advanced to the door.

"The top o' the mornin' to you, Biddy!" said Lanty, with a sort of half-look of mingled kindness and timidity.

"God save ye kindly, both!" was Biddy's almost inaudible reply; for the faintness of anxiety, the mixture of hope and fear, almost overcame her. [14]

"An' what have you for us this mornin', Biddy, *machree*?" said Brian, looking significantly at the two bowls of syllabub which he saw on the slab of Kilkenny marble, on which the milk-pans were ranged.

Biddy handed him his bowl, at which he smacked his lips; and having carefully added somewhat from his private bottle, he drank off the whole, and said

"Why, thin, long life to you, Biddy Keenahan; for it's yourself that's the sowl of a dairy-maid! An' happy's the b'y that'll get you! Lanty, my lad, you can throt afther me an' the dogs, round by the bawn an' across the tin-acre field, an' meet us up at the rath: so don't hurry yourself. May be Biddy has somethin' to say to you. My blessin' on ye both!"

Brian had good reason for this speech, for he had called at Peg Morrin's cabin the previous evening, anxious to have his full share in the business, by warning the fortune-teller of the visit she was to expect, and putting her on the lookout for Biddy as she was to come ferried across the river by Tom Fagan. The sound of the huntsman's horse's feet were still echoing in Biddy's ears when she offered the love-draught to Lanty, with trembling hands and averted face. She would have given the world that Brian had waited, to sanction the deed by his presence. But she felt a sort of comfort in the very noise of the horse's feet, and hastened to present the bowl, ere she was quite alone with Lanty.

We know that a Roman empress gave to her tyrant [15] husband, a philter to soothe his rage; and that the odious Isabeau of France administered one to her spouse, Charles the Sixth, to attach him to her and her vile purposes. But how much more affecting than all the recorded instances of royal superstition, is the picture of this poor Irish girl, watching, in her simplicity, the effect of her charmed potion, as the thirsty youth drained every drop of the bowl, unconscious of the draught of mutual destruction, so fondly prepared and so unsuspectingly quaffed. Lanty had alighted from his horse ere he drank, intending to act on the old huntsman's hint, and to while away a quarter of an hour with his sweetheart, as was his wont on every possible occasion. He had thrown the bridle over a branch of one of the shrubs that kept the dairy in shade; and he stood at the door as he drank.

    Biddy could not resist her desire to mark the progress of her charm. She stole a sidelong glance at Lanty. His first look, as he gave back the bowl, was one of simple satisfaction at the highly-flavoured draught, which, however, the anxious girl did not fail to interpret into an expression of rising love. In a moment more, Lanty stretched forth his hand, placed it on Biddy's shoulder, and tottered towards her. Her heart bounded at these tokens of increasing passion: she looked up again. A wild convulsion passed over the poor lad's face. He stretched forward both his arms; and as Biddy shrunk back with a pang of horror, he fell extended on the floor, [16]

    Fixed to the spot, Biddy could not attempt to offer, nor had she the power to call for aid. A few moments of frightful silence ensued, broken only by the shrill voice of Brian leading the hounds, the yelp of some young dog, or the deep tone of an old one which had caught the scent. At these sounds, poor Lanty's horse neighed and pawed the ground. The unfortunate young man, whose senses had been entirely stunned by the first shock of the overcharged draught, but which were now revived by the fierce revulsion of every spring of sensation, bounded upwards from the floor, staggered round in the wild drunkenness of insanity, rushed to the door, passed the poor agent and victim of his ruin, leaped upon his saddle, and clapping spurs into his too ardent steed, set off at full gallop, in the direction of the pack, which had already found a hare, and was now in full cry.

    The course of the furious chase which Lanty rode that morning, is still marked out by many a trace. Those who witnessed it, declared that aught so terrible had never met their view. All who had joined the huntsman stopped, in surprise at first, and afterwards in affright, as Lanty drove his steed along, over ditch and wall, his hair flying in the wind, and spurs and whip perpetually urged into the flanks of the half-maddened animal. Brian Oge,. almost thunderstruck at what he saw, pulled up his horse, and with clasped hands gazed wildly on, while the unheeded dogs ran far and wide, in all the riot of the chase. At length the gallant hunter that had borne [17] the poor whipper-in for so many a hard day's run, fell utterly exhausted to the earth; and its unfortunate rider lay under it, in raging helplessness.

    Biddy had stood by the dairy door, transfixed in a trance of despair, and marking almost the whole appalling extent of her lover's progress, when she was aroused by the approach of an old woman, who came towards her, with hurried yet enfeebled steps; and as she approached she called out: "Biddy Keenahan, Biddy Keenahan, you *didn't* give him the philthur? say you didn't, girl;—don't daare to tell me that you did—ruination and misery is on us all if Lanty tasted the drug—spake, spake! why don't you?—Did he drink it—did he drink it?"—and with these words the trembling hag shook Biddy into sensation, and she answered, "He did, he did, Peg Morrin."

"Thin the doom is upon us all—or how could I ever let you take, or yourself come to take the wrong pouther—a pouther that would drive an elephant mad! Bow down your head, misfort'nate crathur—the curse is comin' over us

The poor girl, choking with emotions of terror that now reached their climax, fell into a fit of violent hysterics. Servants and others rushed in from various quarters, alarmed by sundry reports of evil. Lanty was brought back towards the house, raging mad. As his hapless sweetheart recovered her senses, they were shocked once more by the hoarse screaming of his voice, which, even [18] in those heart-rending tones she recognised as his. The persons about her had struggled out when she recovered from the fit, in newly-excited curiosity, to witness the maniac's approach:—seizing the moment when she could unobstructedly escape, poor Biddy, driven beyond endurance by her mental agony, and the fierce denunciation of the fortune-teller pursuing her like a blade of fire, rushed to the river's edge, and flinging herself from the little quay where she had landed the preceding night so full of hope and happiness, sought to quench in the river's depths, her burning misery and remorse. Tom Fagan the miller, coming up in his cot that morning, with some sacks of flour for the Grange, found its progress suddenly stopped on one of the shallows by a heavy substance looking white on the sand bank. On moving it with his pole, the body of poor Biddy Keenahan rose to the surface; and a number of people running along the river's edge, in too tardy search, explained to him the previous horrors of the morning.

Lanty, after undergoing for two or three days, excruciating tortures, in confirmed and outrageous madness, was led, as a faint chance of recovery, by some well-meaning theorist, to see the dead body of his sweetheart, laid out in her shroud, and ready for the grave. This, as was expected, produced a fierce shock and frightful crisis. Lanty recovered from insanity. But, with a hideous burst of laughter heralding the change, he instantly sunk into incurable idiocy, and so remained till [19] the day of his death. From what motive I have never been able to learn (perhaps in the hope that the sufferer might forget even his own identity with the transactions it involved) the country folk dropped the habit of calling Lanty by his own name; and changed it into that of John King, by which he was always afterwards known. He wandered about after a while, harmlessly and unobstructed, haunting the scenes of this terrible catastrophe, or straggling through the streets of the neighbouring town: a living lesson of the danger of forcing the development of even good passions; and proving the axiom of Molly Fagan the miller's wife, that "Thrue love should be let to run its coorse."

Title
Conway, Derwent. [Inglis, Henry.] "The City of the Desert." LS 1830. 64-71. [64]

THE CITY OF THE DESERT.
BY DERWENT CONWAY.

ELEVEN days had I trodden these trackless solitudes: eleven times had I seen the sun rise from the vast level that stretched around me. It was now evening, and as the oblique rays shot athwart the desert, I fancied I descried the appearance of columns rising on the far horizon. I strained my aching eye-balls, to pierce as it were, between the desert and the sky, that I might be assured no moving pillars of sand had been mistaken for the vestiges of human labour; but the appearances continued immovable. This, then, was the City of the Desert; here it was, that on the morning of the twelfth day, as my vision had revealed, I should obtain the promised gift—contentment! A thousand times had I bewailed the shortness of human life: "it is a worthless possession," I have exclaimed, "too brief for enjoyment: oh, that I might live for a thousand years!" "Go," said the vision; "go to the City of the Desert, and there learn contentment." [65]

As the morning of the twelfth day dawned, it revealed the object of my search. An irregular line of varied elevations, evidently the work of man, shewed, either the existence or the remains of his habitation. As I approached, the line grew into greater distinctness, and soon, the uprisen sun bathed in gold the pinnacles of a hundred temples. I knew not if the City were inhabited; this, my vision had not revealed; and I stopped to listen if any sound of life came over the desert. The profoundest stillness reigned,—the City was as silent as the wilderness that surrounded it; and, as I passed within the walls, I believed myself to be the only human being they inclosed. It was a solemn and imposing spectacle. I wandered through long and spacious streets all silent as the grave: palaces, temples, and private dwellings, stood, some as if they were yet the habitations of the living: some crumbling into ruins. Columns, upon which the art of man had been exhausted, lay prostrate, or stood yet erect, though mouldering away,—bright in the rays of the morning sun, that for centuries had risen and set upon their silent beauty. I was suddenly awakened from a deep reverie by the sound of a footstep. An aged man stood within a few paces of me; and, as I involuntarily stepped back, somewhat awed by the presence of one whose appearance bespoke a nature if not different, yet less evanescent than my own: "Fear nothing," said he, in a tongue that had long ceased to be the language of living lips, "fear [66] nothing; comest thou hither to learn, from one over whose head centuries have passed, the misery of length of years? Thou doest well: follow me, and thou shalt hear of the curse that has rested upon me for a thousand years." I obeyed my conductor, who led me into a garden, where, in the centre, shaded by date trees, stood a fountain, and on the ground, a marble basin, into which the water fell, drop by drop. "See," said he, "there is only one pebble in this basin," and an exulting smile passed over his shrivelled countenance; "once there were a thousand,—but nine hundred and ninety-nine are resting on the ground: I have taken one from the heap, each year of the nine hundred and ninety-nine that the curse has endured, that I might know my hour; to-night, when the moonbeam shall tip the date tree, I will throw this on the ground also: sit down upon these steps," continued the patriarch, "and listen to the story of my life." I sat down beside the man of a thousand years, as thus he spoke:—

"The City which now contains but thee and me, and which has been for a thousand years the dwelling-place of only one, was once the habitation of a million of living men and women. Tens of thousands in lusty manhood, once walked these silent streets; and the light glee of children who lived not to be men, mingled with the noise of the waters that once gushed from this fountain, and with the sounds of happy living creatures that filled the air, or gambolled on the earth. I see it all, but as yesterday. [67] But a curse came upon the City; and the curse has rested upon me. Famine came first; many died,—but they who had bread, gave to them who had none—all, save me, and my kindred; we ate abundantly, while famished men fought with the dogs for putrid offals. Then came disease; thousands died in a day, and thousands were each day newly smitten; but no man refused to tend the sick,—all were kind and compassionate, save me. When famine alone had visited us, I did not desert my kindred, because we had abundance; but now, I forsook all. My father was stricken, my mother—she who had so often watched over me,—my mother was stricken—sisters, brethren, all were stricken; but I visited them not, nor helped them. I garnered my own dwelling with provisions and costly wines, and secluded myself from all intercourse with the diseased; there I prayed a selfish prayer for life. I said, ' Let all die; but grant life to me.' Alas! my prayer—my guilty prayer—was heard.

"'Live,' said a voice, as my prayer expired on my lips; ' live, foolish Azib, be cursed with life; life for a thousand years!'

"I understood not then, how life could be a curse. I exulted in the anticipation of length of years. Death, that to others is always near, to me was afar off. Life, that to others was uncertain, was to me assured; life for a thousand years. The period at which I was resolved to return to the world, had not yet arrived: but the pro- [68] mise of life was sufficient security, even although disease should still be raging; and I came forth from my solitude. As I passed through this garden (for yonder, where that one column still stands, was my dwelling), I marvelled at the great stillness that filled the air; but I guessed not the curse that was upon me: that the City was half depeopled, I believed; that my friends, that my kindred had perished, might be; but not that all had perished! I entered the house of my kindred; I went into many chambers, but they were empty. I heard a noise in that which was my mother's; and as I approached the door, a hyaena came forth. Oh!

what a spectacle was reserved for me! I passed quickly into the streets,—they were silent and empty. I entered the houses,—in those that were shut, I found the dead; in those that were open, I found both the dead and the living; the dead of my own species, the living of another. Night came, and I again sought my dwelling. Now I prayed for death; but I heard the curse again pronounced, 'Live! be cursed with life,—life for a thousand years!' I again walked out into the streets, in search of death; but the hyaena and the wolf passed by, and avoided me. Now I knew that the curse was upon me, and that mine was a charmed life; and I returned to this garden, and sat down upon the marble steps where we now rest. I knew that life must endure for a thousand years, and I picked up a thousand pebbles, and placed them in that marble basin, where now but one remains. [69]

"Yet, hope had not entirely left me. I sought in the remotest and most obscure dwellings, if perchance I might find some human being—some child,—whom disease, or at least death had not reached; but I found none; and when assured I had no living associate, I felt a strange consolation in the companionship of the dead. In their faces and forms, there were recollections of living men; and I sat by them for hours and days, and disputed the possession of them with the wild beasts: but, one by one, they snatched them from me; and the traces of the living passed away, till nothing remained to remind me of my race. Next, the brute creation disappeared: during fifty years, birds and beasts sometimes visited the City; but at length they came no more. The last creature I have seen, was a Pelican, that more than nine hundred years ago, sat one morning, on the sun-dial before the great temple.

"Dreadful has been the curse of life, and more dreadful has it been every day. I would have made a companion of the hyaena; I would have associated with any thing that had life. While watching the winged race, called into existence by the sunbeams, I have felt less wretched; for, like me, they were endued with life: but many centuries have passed away since this small sympathy has been mine. A curse is upon earth and air, as well as upon me; even the insects that used to float in this basin, and with whose imperfect life I have felt some sympathy, have long been extinct. I would have [70] given,—but what had I to give? yet had I possessed one blessing, I would have resigned it, to have heard even the cry of a jackal, or the scream of a vulture!

"When life in animated beings could no longer be found, I sought life or motion in inanimate things. I have sat on these steps, and listened for centuries to the gushing of that fountain; but it has long ceased to afford this consolation, for see, the water comes drop by drop. I have watched the flowers that grew, watered by its spray, and the weeds that sprung up among the ruins, but they are all withered; and the country around is a desert: these date trees, that afford me sustenance, alone survive. All this, is the curse of selfishness, the punishment of longing after length of years. I might have given my sympathy, and died with my kindred;

but I refused it, and lo! I have received none for a thousand years. A thousand years have I wandered, the sole tenant of these silent streets: I have seen the tooth of time gnaw the records of perishing men; its triumphs are the sole disturbers of the silence that reigns around, as columns fall to the earth, or dwellings crumble into dust."

The aged man paused for a moment. "It is now only mid-day," continued he; "Go, walk through the City, meditate on what thou hast heard, and return hither at sunset."

I went into the City; I entered the habitations that had been tenantless a thousand years. I entered the dwelling of kings, and saw the vacant throne, and the enamelled [71] floor, once swept by the purple of past ages. I stood among the ruins of temples, and stumbled over the mutilated idols that were mingling with the dust of those who had worshipped them; and I gazed on the sun-dial, that time had spared, to be his chronicler.

At sunset, I returned to the garden: the aged man still sat on the marble steps, and seemed to be watching the far horizon: I sat down beside him, and both were silent. The light of day was fast waning; the rosy hues of sunset died away; fainter grew the scene; at length a pale light on the horizon appeared, and grew, till the moon rose slowly up into the wide sky: soon, the date tree, and the pinnacle of the fountain were tipped with silver: the aged man then arose, and taking the last pebble from the basin, threw it on the ground. One drop of water hung trembling from the fountain; it fell, but none other came; and when I raised my eyes to the countenance of the old man, I saw that his race was ended.

I quitted the garden to enter again upon my journey through the desert; and as I passed by the sun-dial, I saw that time had no longer a record in the City of the Desert: the pedestal which had supported it, had fallen!

Title
Galt, John. "The Confession." LS 1830. 202-207. [202]

THE CONFESSION.
BY JOHN GALT, ESQ.

My furlough had nearly expired; and, as I was to leave the village the next morning to join my regiment, then on the point of being shipped off at Portsmouth, for India, several of my old companions spent the evening with me, in the Marquis of Granby. They were joyous, hearty lads; but mirth bred thirst, and drinking begot contention.

I was myself the soberest of the squad, and did what I could to appease their quarrels. The liquor, however, had more power than my persuasion, and at last it so exasperated some foolish difference about a song, between Dick Winlaw and Jem Bradley, that they fell to fighting, and so the party broke up.

Bradley was a handsome, bold, fine fellow, and I had more than once urged him to enlist in our corps. Soon after quitting the house, he joined me in my way home, and I spoke to him again about enlisting, but his blood was still hot—he would abide no reason—he could only swear of the revenge he would inflict upon Winlaw. This led to some remonstrance on my part, for Bradley [203] was to blame in the dispute; till, from less to more, we both grew fierce, and he struck me such a blow in the face, that my bayonet leaped into his heart.

My passion was in the same moment quenched. I saw him dead at my feet—I heard footsteps approaching—I fled towards my father's house—the door was left unbolted for me—I crept softly, but in a flutter, to bed,—but I could not sleep. I was stunned;—a fearful consternation was upon me;—a hurry was in my brain—my mind was fire. I could not believe that I had killed Bradley. I thought it was the nightmare which had so poisoned my sleep. My tongue became as parched as charcoal: had I been choking with ashes, my throat could not have been filled with more horrible thirst. I breathed as if I were suffocating with the dry dust into which the dead are changed.

After a time, that fit of burning agony went off;—tears came into my eyes;—my nature was softened. I thought of Bradley when we were boys, and of the summer days we had spent together. I never owed him a grudge—his blow was occasioned by the liquor—a freer heart than his, mercy never opened; and I wept like a maiden.

The day at last began to dawn. I had thrown myself on the bed without undressing, and I started up involuntarily, and moved hastily—I should rather say instinctively—towards the door. My father heard the stir, and inquired wherefore I was departing so early. I begged [204] him not to be disturbed; my voice was troubled, and he spoke to me kindly and encouragingly, exhorting me to eschew riotous companions. I could make no reply—indeed I heard no more—there was a blank between his blessing and the time when I found myself crossing the Common, near the place of execution.

But through all that horror and frenzy, I felt not that I had committed a crime—the deed was the doing of a flash. I was conscious I could never in cold blood have harmed a hair of Bradley's head. I considered myself unfortunate, but not guilty; and this fond persuasion so pacified my alarms, that, by the time I reached Portsmouth, I almost thought as lightly of what I had done, as of the fate of the gallant French dragoon, whom I sabred at Salamanca.

But ever and anon, during the course of our long voyage to India, sadder afterthoughts often came upon me. In those trances, I saw, as it were, our pleasant village green, all sparkling again with schoolboys at their pastimes; then I fancied them gathering into groups, and telling the story of the murder; again, moving away in silence towards the church-yard, to look at the grave of poor Bradley. Still, however, I was loth to believe myself a criminal; and so, from day to day, the time passed on, without any outward change revealing what was passing within, to the observance or suspicions of my comrades. When the regiment was sent against the Burmese, the bravery of the war, and the hardships of [205] our adventures, so won me from reflection, that I began almost to forget the accident of that fatal night.

One day, however, while I was waiting in an outer room of the Colonel's quarters, I chanced to take up a London newspaper, and the first thing in it which caught my eye was, an account of the trial and execution of Dick Winlaw, for the murder of Bradley. The dreadful story scorched my eyes;—I read it as if every word had been fire,—it was a wild and wonderful account of all. The farewell party at the Granby was described by the witnesses. I was spoken of by them with kindness and commendation; the quarrel between Bradley and Winlaw was described, as in a picture; and my attempt to restrain them was pointed out by the judge, in his charge to the jury, as a beautiful example of loving old companionship. Winlaw had been found near the body, and the presumptions of guilt were so strong and manifold, that the jury, without retiring, found him guilty. He was executed on the Common, and his body hung in chains. Then it was, that I first felt I was indeed a murderer,—then it was that the molten sulphur of remorse was poured into my bosom, rushing, spreading, burning, and devouring; but it changed not the bronze with which hardship had masked my cheek, nor the steel to which danger had tempered my nerves.

I obeyed the Colonel's orders as unmoved as if nothing had happened. I did my duty with habitual precision,—my hand was steady, my limbs were firm; but my [206] tongue was incapable of uttering a word. My comrades as they came towards me, suddenly halted, and turned aside,—strangers looked at me, as if I bore the impress of some fearful thing. I was removed, as it were, out of myself—I was in another state of being—I was in hell.

Next morning we had a skirmish, in which I received this wound in the knee; and soon afterwards, with other invalids, I was ordered home. We were landed at Portsmouth, and I proceeded to my native village. But in this I had no will nor choice; a chain was around me, which I could not resist, drawing me on. Often did I pause and turn, wishing to change my route; but Fate held me fast, and I was enchanted by the spell of many an old and dear recollection, to revisit those things which had lost all their innocence and holiness to me.

The day had been sultry, the sun set with a drowsy eye, and the evening air was moist, warm, and oppressive. It weighed heavily alike on mind and body. I was crippled by my wound,—the journey was longer than my strength could sustain much further,—still I resolved to persevere, for I longed to be again in my father's house; and I fancied were I once there, that the burning in my bosom would abate.

During my absence in India, the new road across the Common had been opened. By the time I reached it, the night was closed in,—a dull, starless, breezeless, dumb, sluggish, and unwholesome night; and those things which still retained in their shapes some black-[207]ness, deeper than the darkness, seemed, as I slowly passed by, to be endowed with a mysterious intelligence, with which my spirit would have held communion but for dread.

While I was frozen with the influence of this dreadful phantasy, I saw a pale, glimmering, ineffectual light, rising before me. It was neither lamp, fire, nor candle; and though like, it was yet not flame. I took it at first for the lustre of a reflection from some unseen light, and I walked towards it, in the hope of finding a cottage or an alehouse, where I might obtain some refreshment and a little rest. I advanced,—its form enlarged, but its beam became no brighter; and the horror, which had for a moment left me when it was first discovered, returned with overwhelming power. I rushed forward, but soon halted,—for I saw that it hung in the air, and as I approached, that it began to take a ghastly and spectral form! I discerned the lineaments of a head, and the hideous outlines of a shapeless anatomy. I stood rivetted to the spot; for I thought that I saw behind it, a dark and vast thing, in whose hand it was held forth. In that moment, a voice said,—"It is Winlaw the murderer; his bones often, in the moist summer nights, shine out in this way; it is thought to be an acknowledgment of his guilt, for he died protesting his innocence."—The person who addressed me was your Honor's gamekeeper, and the story I have told, is the cause of my having desired him to bring me here.

ITHRAN THE DEMONIAC.
BY WILLIAM HOWITT, ESQ.

It was during the latter part of that remarkable period in the history of the world, when the Hebrews, passing from Egypt to Canaan, had encamped in the wilderness of Kadesh, that a young hunter went forth one morning from the borders of Mount Seir. He had pursued a herd of wild antelopes across one of the wide, sandy tracts of those regions till he beheld them take refuge among some rocky hills at a considerable distance before him. When he reached this craggy solitude, a variety of narrow valleys that opened between the cliffs, distracted his attention, and, pausing to consider which he should pursue, he observed for the first time— what his enthusiasm had hitherto prevented him from noticing—that the sun had nearly reached the mid-heaven, that the heat was intense, and that a burning thirst and a throbbing brow demanded the refreshments of shade and water. Added to this pressing necessity, he knew that to attempt to retrace those scorching sands till the heat of the day was past, was next to impossible; and beside, he hoped yet to surprise his game in some of the seclusions of these rocks. Selecting there [290] fore, in preference to the others, a glen, which, by the dampness of the sand in its bottom, gave indication of water higher up, he followed its windings for a long time with great perseverance, and, at length, found his patience rewarded by the sight of one of those little, paradisiacal valleys often hidden in the bosom of these stony Oases. There the stream, which at his entrance was absorbed by the hot and ever-thirsty sand, came murmuring along with all the transparency and liveliness of a mountain rivulet; and, while all the tops of the eminences around were bare and burning peaks, its banks were brightened with the most green and flowery verdure; the large white lily, the globe amaranth, and abundance of other plants of the most splendid hues, and of the richest aroma, bending over its margin; the aloe, here and there, spreading out its ample round of dark-green leaves, and lifting up its lofty blossomed stem; thickets of tamarind, rose-laurel, cotton, and a variety of aromatic shrubs scattered about between the water and the feet of the dark granite rocks, aloft in whose interstices, the lovely rose of Jericho waved its glowing blooms, and acacias, dates, and various species of palm, cast at once shade and beauty.

After quenching his thirst, and cooling his feet repeatedly in the stream, he slowly wandered farther up the valley, and soon beheld, to his mortification, that it was terminated by lofty cliffs, down which the brook came scattering loudly its waters. One nook attracted his steps by the luxuriant, dependant foliage of a vast wild [291] vine, and he was about to seat himself beneath it, when he started back on discovering that it concealed the entrance to a gloomy cavern. Instinctively he glanced upon the ground to discern, by footmarks, what might be the nature of its inhabitants, if any; and he beheld, not the print of the wild-beast's paw, nor the sandal of man, but that of a large naked human foot. He was about to retreat y but, on turning round, his eye fell upon the wildest figure it had ever yet encountered.

It was that of a tall and slightly-built man, whose only clothing was a long robe of goat and camel's hair, and whose locks and beard had grown to a wonderful extravagance. He reclined beneath a broad sycamore tree, on a large fragment of rock; and, observing him more closely, the youth was struck with signs of sickness and exhaustion. His heart, at the view, lost at once its fear; he saw only before him an object of distress;—he advanced, and spoke.

The stranger lifted up his eyes, with a vague wildness for a moment; then, closing them again, the tears gushed silently down his cheeks. He was silent; but it was evidently the silence of emotion. At length, lifting up his hands, he grasped that of the youth fervently, and made signs for him to sit down. He obeyed,—but the stranger still continuing silent, he asked if he could render him any service. He replied, with a melancholy emphasis, "Thou mayest! but start not when thou knowest for whom. Knowest thou for whom thou art interested? [292] knowest thou the "Demon of the Desert?" At that dreadful name the youth started to his feet with a shuddering groan; but he was rivetted to the spot,—and the stranger cried imploringly, "Nay!—fly not, fear not, my son! The time has been when thy visit hither would have been death; but that time is past—I am not what I was.—I am dying. At this moment, the presence of a human soul is precious to me. Thou canst hear me—thou canst bury me."

The eyes of the youth attested the truth of what his fearful companion declared; and with a strange mixture of awe, curiosity, and sympathy, he listened to the following narrative.

"I am not what thy countrymen have deemed me—I am not originally, and altogether, a demon; but Ithran, an outcast of Israel. It is not entirely unknown to the nations among whom that people has now so long sojourned, that, although their dreadful God has kept them wholly by his might, making nature bend its ancient laws to their use, and surrounding them with terror as with a wall, they have been but imperfectly sensible of the glory of their lot, and have often provoked the Lord to anger. But it has been, in these latter years, that this spirit of unbelief and ingratitude has grown to the most marvellous height. In vain were the overwhelming terrors of God displayed on the Mount;—in vain did blazing serpents spread death; and the burning bolts of Divine vengeance burst suddenly upon the heads [293] of the rebellious, in ruin; in vain was the beautiful and majestic Miriam, who went out dancing before the virgins of Israel, and singing that triumphant song of victory over Pharaoh, cast, a leprous object, out of the camp before their eyes;—since their abode in Kadesh the spirit of wickedness was become monstrous. God had refused to go up before them to the Promised Land; the Amalekites had discomfited them, and they were full of despondency. Add to this, famine was in the camp. Except the manna and the quails, food now universally loathed, there was nothing. The stock of cattle was exhausted; and the desert seemed to become, every day, more fierce and inhospitable.

"But the day of Annual Expiation was at hand; and hope awoke in all hearts. God had appointed, in his mercy, a way to free Israel from its sins. He had empowered the High Priest to lay all their crimes on the head of a goat, which should bear them away into the wilderness. The day arrived;—all Israel was assembled before the sanctuary;—a breathless anxiety prevailed;—the various offerings were made;—the devoted goat was brought forth; the mysterious words which charged it with the whole sin of Israel, were pronounced; and a weight, and a gloom, seemed to pass from the hearts of the people. It only remained to send the goat away, by the hand of a fit man. And now a fearful and eager curiosity ran through the multitude, to know who this man should be. It was an important trust. The two victim goats had [294] been procured with much difficulty,—such was our poverty; and they had been guarded with much care, for such was the wickedness of the time, that some sons of Belial had attempted to break in, and carry them off; and it was expected that they would lie in wait to kill the scape-goat in the wilderness. I was a prophet, and the son of a prophet; and young as I was, my zeal in the cause of God, and of Moses, had given me great favour in the eyes of the elders.—I was chosen as the *fit man*.

"It was deemed necessary that I should go two days' journey into the wilderness. A great number of the most illustrious of the Hebrew youth accompanied me till the sun began to decline; then, with many blessings, I went on alone. As I saw the friendly band retracing their steps, a sensation of pride, such as I never felt before, arose in my heart, that I should be deemed most worthy of this most momentous trust. I marched lightly on;—the sun went down;—all night I pursued my way, unceasingly; so strongly did that exaltation of spirit bear me on. I never thought of food or sleep, till the next day as the sun became hot, when I sought the shade of a rock for rest and refreshment. When I looked for my scrip, it was gone;—during this state of self-gratulating excitement, it had slipped off, unperceived. I was stung with a sudden and unreasonable anger; and rising up, I smote the goat, and went on. The craving of hunger the torture of thirst—the sense of my loss, the conscious-[295]ness that several days must elapse before I should regain the camp, angered and appalled me. My frame was already debilitated and rendered irritable, by the effects of the famine, and of the strict fast preparatory to the day of expiation: in vain I all day looked out for water, for a wild fig, a date, a melon;—there was nothing around me but burning sand. The goat, as well as myself, appeared exhausted. We went on and on;—the day seemed as though it would never end; and, to add to my anguish, the ground was now everywhere covered with a prickly plant, which lacerated my feet, and filled them with its spines. A suggestion arose in me, to return; but my pride instantly rejected it; and again I smote the goat, and we sped forward with increased exertion. The sun at length did set; and, to my joy, I saw some rocks before me:—but there was neither tree, nor herb, nor water. I tied the goat to a stone, and flung myself down in despair beneath the rocks. But if my body was spent, my mind was full of a bitter activity. A thousand troublous and depressing thoughts passed through me; the sense of my loss preyed on me; the vast distance I imagined myself from men, terrified me; the goat lay and slept quietly before me. At that sight my perturbation was aggravated tenfold. It could forget its pains; but I, who suffered on its account, might not. I cursed the foolish pride which led me to undertake the enterprise. At this moment a thought arose—kill and eat. The horrible idea struck me like a thunderclap;— [296] I started up, and waited hastily away to escape from it; but it pursued me, and to evade it by action, I loosed the goat, and endeavoured to drive it away. But it was too much fatigued: it sank again on the ground. I had now, however, fulfilled my mission—I might return; but the view of the dreary boundlessness of the desert depressed my heart:—I despaired of ever recrossing it, and, with a fond fatality, lingered near the goat. I endeavoured to fill my mind with a vivid sense of the enormity of the suggested crime; but, in spite of myself, my sense of the guilt grew less, and less, and my appetite became furious. 'What avails!' I exclaimed, 'at the price of my own existence, to spare a life which must soon be terminated!' and drawing the knife from my girdle, I rushed on the goat; and plunged it into its neck. The blood spouted freely; I thought not of Moses or his laws; to me it was the stream of life—and pressing my parched lips to the wound, I drank with ravenous avidity. I was instantly seized with a delirious joy. I waited not for the life to depart; but kneeling down, I feasted on the flesh. A spirit of triumphant intoxication, a whirl of extravagant transport possessed me;—my vigour seemed restored tenfold;—I sat and laughed over my victim. But the wickedness of thousands,—the inspiration and madness of all crime and outrage, had passed into me from the dedicated animal, and I rushed away in its strength.

"At length I fell, and slept—I know not how long; [297] but when I awoke the intoxication was past, and the darkness and despair of inexpiable guilt was upon me. The depth of my fall—its utterness—its hopelessness—my eternal separation from the house of Israel,—all rushed upon my soul, and my first impulse was that of self destruction. For this purpose I arose and sought for the place of my crime; for there were left the knife and the cord which had bound the goat. The spot I found; but they and the remains of the animal were gone. The demoniac spirit which possessed me, now boiled up in furious anger. *Now* it was evident man was near—he had robbed me of my prey; and my murderous passion turned from myself upon him.

A fierce and malignant desire of human destruction fastened upon me; I stalked along with the ravenous heart of a beast of prey; and it was not long before I descried, at the foot of a rocky range, a small Ishmaelitish encampment. Like the tiger, I lurked in the crevices of the crags till nightfall; and when I deemed sleep was upon the inhabitants, I rushed into the nearest tent. But the inmates were awake; at the sight of my wild visage, they fled shrieking; the alarm was communicated to the neighbouring tents, and I soon found myself in solitary possession of them all. At the sight of their soft couches, and various comforts, I was seized with envy and hatred intolerable. My first impulse was to set fire to the whole; but the wealth, the gold, the pearls, the rich robes,—treasures of these merchants, caught my [298] eye, and a grasping avarice instantly took hold of me. Thoughtless of danger—forgetting, for the time, my thirst after human life,—I immediately set about digging a pit at the foot of a rock to bury a kingly spoil, when the people recovering from their surprise, returned. At the sight of their numbers I fled—fled upwards to the rocks. They pursued me, accustomed as they were to follow the wild goat and the chamois;—but I too had, from my youth, scaled the cliffs of the desert; and now a spell was on me which gave me supernatural power and speed, that annihilated all fear:—they pursued me in vain. I leaped from point to point, I swung by the pliant tree from ledge to ledge, and was gone. From that hour the terrors of my name spread through the wilderness—a thousand marvellous acts were atrributed to me round the evening fires, and I became known as the "Demon of the Desert." For months I ranged from place to place, driven by the unquenchable spirit of the murderer, but unable to gratify my fiendish desires. My fame went before me, and I found myself for ever in solitude. "Exasperated with fruitless endeavours, my wrath turned from man to God: I became filled, at once, with a spirit of blasphemy and of idolatrous fear. I knelt to the sun at his rising, and kissed my hand to the moon and stars nightly;—to the Great Being who made them, I was full of hatred and defiance. In the vehemence of my impious rage, I traversed the deserts, and climbed by night to the lonely summits of Horeb and Sinai. There [299] no longer rested the dark and threatening clouds; no thunders shook the hills to their foundations; above, the clear sky, and the myriad stars shone silently,—around all was one waste sea of bare and splintered peaks. It is awful to think of the madness of impiety which there possessed me. I defied the Eternal on the very mountain of his power; and called on him, if he lived, to reveal himself once more in his thunders! I listened,—but a vast silence was around; the breeze only sighed carelessly on its way, as in mockery of my insignificance, I descended—my heart devoured with the most venomous feelings against God, and against Moses, whom I cursed as a juggling impostor.

"But if the sacred hills were quiet, not so was the earth beneath them. A sound of rushing wings swept by me; dark whispers were in my ears; shadowy shapes went to and fro, turning upon me their eyes gleaming with strange fires; and dusky forms arose out of the very ground before me. I had dared to challenge God; but I shrunk trembling from these dismal spirits! I fled to my cave for refuge; but where is the refuge for him who has surrendered the guardianship of the Author of Nature! Thunders shook the rocks over my head; crags fell crashing and echoing into the dell below; lightnings gleamed through the more than midnight darkness of my stronghold; and finally, a purple light issuing from the wall of solid granite, preceded the terrible Gods of the heathen, who passed slowly athwart the cavern. [300] They gazed silently upon me, but spoke not; as if their only purpose were to receive my homage. I beheld the colossal majesty of Baal; the imperial form, and lofty, yet smiling countenance of Ashtaroth, the queen of heaven—diademed with the horned moon, and a constellation of intensely beaming stars floating around her. Her steps were followed by the soft, voluptuous figure of Semel, the queen of love; and by Pibeseth, the blushing and shame-faced goddess, with her eyes on the ground. Then came the hideous Dagon rolling on his fishy rear; followed by the aged and stony-featured Chiun; the stern and savage gloom of Moloch, enveloped in the furnace-glow of his own flames; and lastly, Nehushtan, the haughty serpent, walking rather than gliding on his undulating volumes; lifting aloft his crowned head and human countenance; and clad in vivid scales, of scarlet, blue, and yellow, from beneath which streamed the radiance of internal fires. They passed; but I was not the morea lone. The bottom of the cave swarmed with the pygmy forms of the Gemedim; and from every nook and chink of wall and roof, gleamed down the green eyes and goatish visages of the Shoirim, grotesque but hideous.

"The idolatrous passion was extinguished. It was impossible to worship these fearful things;—it was terrible to be conscious of their presence. This vision rekindled my longing after human society, and human sympathies; but where were they to be found? Far around I was to the inhabitants what these beings were to me. I determined, [301] therefore, to abandon the deserts; and travelling on, from night to night, I, at length, found myself in a cultivated land, and at the gates of a city of stupendous walls and towers. It was Argob, the city of Og;—who has not heard of that last of the Anakims, and of his great bedstead of iron"! I was surrounded by a band of fierce, shaggy, and monstrous men who led me into his presence. He sate on a massy bench, beneath a sycamore, at the gate of his ponderous palace, and his sons, and his old warriors, a race of giants, stood around. I was overwhelmed, for a moment, by the sight of so huge and terrible a being; tall as I am, I reached not to his girdle. Hopeless of life—-careless of death, which to me could not be worse than life itself,—I avowed myself a prophet of Israel. A lying and cunning spirit was upon me. I declared that I fled from the despotism of Moses, and would rather receive death at the hands of the king, than live in those of the tyrant of my people. The spirit of delusion seized the giant-monarch. The nations of the Anakims had fallen around him beneath the arms of the Israelites; he awaited daily his own trial, and he grasped at the intelligence I might give as a saving branch in the moment of his fall. I was received with favour and honour. I encouraged him—feigned to reveal to him the secret of the Hebrew strength, and assured him of victory. Kindled by my words, he determined not to expect, but to pour forth on his enemies. At once the whole land was in motion like a swarm of hornets. The [302] din of arms, the tumult of processions and sacrifices, filled it from end to end. The giant sons of the king, like inflamed demons, flew from place to place;—the almost equally gigantic daughters, creatures of a fierce and superhuman beauty and stature, their proud necks loaded with strings of pearls, their hair flowing on their shoulders, glittering with gold and jewels, their arms and ancles bound with massy clasps of gold, and tinkling bells of silver, excited to madness the priests by their kindled charms, and their presents of embroidered hangings for the tabernacles of their polluted groves. Dreadful was the rage which boiled through the sanguinary multitudes—dreadful were the cries of human victims—thrilling the shrieks of tender infants cast into the flaming furnaces of Adrammelec.

"But in the midst of this tumultuous scene of guilt and terror, one beautiful and serene object shone like a solitary star upon a tempestuous ocean. It was the youngest daughter of the king, the daughter of a captive descendant of Esau. Of the ordinary stature of humanity, the richness of her beauty, and the gentleness of her spirit, presented only the image of her deceased mother. She was fair as the lily of the valley, but her eyes and flowing locks were dark as night. She had heard of the true God, and of his dealings with her ancestors, from her mother, in childhood; she looked on the savage natures of those with whom she dwelt, with horror and detestation; and my words roused in her soul the most intense [303] and anxious interest. While all others were absorbed in the preparations for war, from day to day, she besought me with questions. In her presence my former tone of mind, my former happiness, seemed to return; a spirit of sacred inspiration was even permitted to me; and I displayed, with glowing enthusiasm, the true history of man—the dispensations of God to Israel—the speedy and utter annihilation of this people. When I ceased, I beheld her kneeling upon the ground, her lovely face turned with a sublime and adoring expression towards heaven. She arose. 'I fear not to die,' she meekly said, "but I fain would not die in the midst of this idolatrous people. Oh! that I was but the lowest handmaid in the tents of my mother's kindred!'

"Already deeply affected by her beauty, I was now aroused by her devotion. 'Fly,' I exclaimed. 'I know the deserts, and vow to become thy faithful conductor.'

"With much entreaty I prevailed;—but when I counselled her to bear away the teraphim of the king, she paused; her pure soul shrank from any thing like theft; and those golden and jewelled teraphim, worth almost half his kingdom,—those household gods from which, morn and evening, he invoked prosperity,—it was too much. But my zeal—my character of a prophet—my solemn representations that it was a testimony against idolatry demanded by God, shook her spirit—she struggled long, but gave way. In a thicket, not far from [304] the city, I concealed two swift dromedaries. At night, I awaited her at the foot of a tower upon the wall, whence, with the teraphim, she descended in a basket. We had already reached the thicket, when her giant-brothers sprang forth with dreadful yells. I beheld her in their grasp—I heard her cries—I saw the sword red with her blood: resistance was vain—I fled! Darkness and my destiny favoured my flight; but the blood of that fair and gentle creature lay on my soul like fire. Remorse—pity—love—drove me on in desperation, I knew not whither. At length I was stopped by a range of rocks; I climbed to their top, and sate down in a state of dreamy torpor. . From that height I beheld the armies of Israel in march; I saw the host of the Anakims come down like a foaming sea; anon, they were scattered like mist, and the Israelites pursued, slaying to the bounds of the vast horizon. I followed, and in a few days beheld all that monstrous nation utterly destroyed, and walked amongst the smoking ashes of their groves and idol-temples.

"But I saw a thing there more hateful than even the Anakims. I saw the Israelites dwelling at peace in the cities and in the fertile fields—in a plenteous possession, from which I was cut off for ever. I retired from the intolerable spectacle once more to the desert. The tempestuous energy of those passions, which had successively visited me, seemed now exhausted. I was feeble and faint as a child; yet a burning envy consumed my [305] heart of the blessings of my brethren, and a malignant cruelty towards the weak and defenceless possessed me. I trod with vindictive malice on the beetle that crawled on the sand before me; and when the lizard ran up the sunny rock, and looked cheerfully in my face, I took up a stone and crushed it. Even this petty force of evil departed, and I was left a powerless prey to remorse—to a vain longing after reunion with my people—to overwhelming terrors—terrors of God, of death, and of the powers of darkness.

"Oh, praise! boundless praise to Him, who, at length, drew back the arm of his wrath, and forgave. I lay at the mouth of this cave—I know not whether awake or in sleep, but I saw before me two angelic beings; and, by a closer contemplation of them, I recognized my parents. I heard my mother, as if addressing my father, say,—'How long have we interceded for our unhappy son, that he might be made a partaker of the annual benefit of the scape-goat, and, at length, it is granted. His latter career of crime has been but the career of a maniac—his real crime was the breach of his sacred trust—he has suffered as no man ever yet did, and he is forgiven.' She scattered upon me drops, as of water, from a crystal vase, and a thrill of joy—a warm sensation of human love, and tenderness, and hope, gushed upon my soul—tears came into my eyes, and I lay as in a soothing trance. During the space of a moon I have continued tranquil, breathing an atmosphere of love, and full of [306] adoration. But I am now spent; and the last good gift of

God is this—that he has sent thee to learn this awful lesson of unfaithful pride, and to save the bones of his repentant servant from the desert beast."

Before the sun had risen on the morrow, the youth had buried the prophet in his cave, and returned to his tribe with a story destined to carry down fear and wonder to countless generations.

The Forgotten Gothic

Literary Annual
The Literary Souvenir. Ed. Alaric A. Watts. London: Longman, Rees, Orme, Brown & Green, 1831. Printer: S. Manning & Co., London House Yard, St. Paul's.[12]

Title
Anonymous. "Lady Olivia's Decamerone." LS 1831. 17-30.

PLATE: The Narrative
Steel plate engraving; painted by Thomas Stothard, R.A.;
engraved by W. Greatbatch; printed by McQueen [17]

---

[12] Plain text for all short stories included here for the 1831 *Literary Souvenir* obtained from Google Books and then compared against the original volume. For full citation, see References: <http://books.google.com/books?id=Ol8EAAAAQAAJ&dq=1831%20The%20Literary%20Souvenir%3B%20or%2C%20Cabinet%20of%20Poetry%20and%20Romance&pg=PR3#v=onepage&q&f=false>

850

Literary Souvenir

LADY OLIVIA'S DECAMERONE.

Story, God bless you!—I have none to tell, Sir.
Anti-Jacobin.

THE great contest for the county, between Sir Jacob Dunder, of Dunder-Park, and Colonel Parrot, of Bencoolen Hall, will not speedily be forgotten by those who witnessed, or shared its horrors. It was then that the awful pestilence of party-spirit began its ravages in our ancient town. Years have rolled away; and Time, the universal physician, has passed through our streets with healing on his wings: but there is not, among us, one family in which you may not trace the vestiges of the dismal visitation.

The first symptoms of the disorder were, absence of mind, neglect of business, forgetfulness of the dinner hour, and a disposition to haunt the market-place, or loiter on the Exchange. Soon, the voice of the sufferer became loud and hoarse, the step hurried and unsteady, [18] the eye fierce and glaring. He began to mutter indistinctly to himself, to whisper mysteriously to those he met, to rave incoherently to crowds of such as were similarly affected: and his talk was full of strange and unconnected words,—liberty and social order, retrenchment and revolution, the debt and the pope; dangers he had not anticipated, blessings he had not dreamed of, till now. Fire does not spread more rapidly from rafter to rafter, than did the fearful contagion from man to man. The huge letters of a placard, the discordant echo of a song, the touching of a ribbon, the tasting of a cup, were sufficient to communicate its fury. No age, no sex, escaped; the maiden sickened in her minuet, and the matron at her whist; in the frenzy of the fever, the octagenarian broke his crutches, and overturned his easy chair; and when you asked his grandson the subject of his morning's lesson,—"the cause" quoth the urchin, "for which Hampden bled on the field, and Sidney perished on the scaffold!"

On Saturday evening. Lady Olivia's *conversazione* was attended by only seven of its fair frequenters. The president herself, her three nieces, Marguerita, Medora, and Sybilla, and their three bosom friends, Leonora, Laura, and Ruth, looked disconsolately at the long saloon and its vacant sofas, and turned away in weariness from the stuffed kingfishers, and the cabinet of conchology, the portfolio of prints, and the drowsy poodle. "I had expected," said Lady Olivia, "Professor [19] Bellows, with a Lecture on the Steam-engine, and Dr. Macklin with an Exposition of the Kantian Philosophy: Mr. Merrywether was to have administered his Laughing Gas, and dear Lucerida had promised her charming Ode on the Success of the Missions in Newfoundland. But you see how we are deserted. Since, then, we are afflicted by a worse than Boccaccio's plague, let us adopt Boccaccio's remedy: let us retire to some sequestered spot, where we may wander among shady groves and purling streams, the bleating of sheep and the warbling of birds, pitying the calamities of those whom we leave to the drums and the dinners, the speeches and the cockades; and beguiling our long summer afternoons with pleasant stories, which, when this season shall have passed by, we will give to the world, in emulation of the fame of the Decamerone."

The proposal was received without a dissentient voice. Nevertheless, Medora hinted at the tea-table what Filomena suggested in the church,—that the company of two or three cavaliers, if any could be found, neither orange nor blue, in their neighbourhood, would help in no slight degree towards the cheating of time, and the banishing of *ennui*: and Fortune favoured the wish ere it was uttered; for General Shakerly was announced, and Sergeant Ambigu, and Frank Melvil, all ready to fly from the scene of action—the General, because he would support no party; and the Lawyer, because he had promised to support both; and the Johnian, because [20] he had no means of supporting either. Every necessary arrangement was presently planned. Chateau Shakerly was to be prepared for the reception of the beauteous recluses, and the various pavilions and arbours with which its grounds were decorated, were to be carefully stored with books and chess-boards, sweetmeats and guitars. A sovereign was to be elected daily, for the direction of the next day's pastimes; and all were to pay implicit obedience to the commands of their ruler. On Monday morning, while the sheriff was proceeding with his trumpets and his criers, to open the poll for the election of a knight of the shire, Lady Olivia, the queen for the first day, assembled her little court, under the canopy of a magnificent old beech; and, after the example of her Florentine predecessors, issued orders for the proceedings of the household, and gave audience to the seneschal and the tire-women.

The day passed pleasantly enough. They strolled, as their author suggested, and their queen allowed, through the exquisite scenes of as lovely a spot as ever opulence furnished for the dwelling of taste. They admired the stuffed hermit, and the wooden nymph, and the gothic ruin, and the Chinese pagoda. They praised the sculpture of the monument, which was erected to the memory of nobody; and studied the tablet, which invited them to
> Sleep and dream,
> Lulled by the music of the stream,

[21] while their host promised them that the fountain, though out of order to-day, would discourse most eloquent music to-morrow. Their dinner was served in the conservatory; and after they had banqueted, as a translator of their Italian model would have said, "with all the elegance imaginable," the queen called upon Frank to relate the first of those narratives which were in after time to drive the Decamerone from the Temple of Fame. Frank was a thin, sallow young man, who had won a gold medal at Cambridge, and filled all the albums in the county with sighs and songs. The listeners, therefore, were hushed into mute attention, when he set down his glass of claret, and began.

FIRST TALE.

It was late on a tempestuous evening, at that season of the year when winter treads closely on the footsteps of autumn. Thick clouds gathered over the face of heaven as the sun went down, and sudden blasts of wind whistling through the almost leafless trees, gave token of the approaching storm. The peasant sought shelter for his flock, and the rich merchant thought of his argosies and trembled.

Mine host of the Black Hound,—it was the only tolerable inn in the little village of Barbadillo—exulted at the pattering of the rain-drops and the distant growling of the thunder. "Trust me," he said to the guests, whose flagon he was sharing—Master Tomaso, the [22] notary; Dr. Bartolo, the physician; and a holy priest, of the order of St. Francis,—"trust me, my friends, a night like this, though it may be ill-regarded by delicate damsel or silk-clad cavalier, is a night of bounty and blessing to us of the spit and spigot. Little inquisition is made at such a time, whether the omelet be fresh or the capon tender, or the wine of the right growth. Give him but a floor under foot, and a roof over head, and a dry cloak, and an extra log upon the hearth, and Lucifer himself will scarcely turn aside from the platter, or look thrice at the seal of the flask."

While he yet spoke, the heavy sound of horses' feet, advancing, as it seemed, at a long and regular trot, roused him from his seat, and in a moment a vehement ringing at the bell announced the approach of some visitor, to whom it seemed those common comforts, of which the good man spoke, were indeed matters of interest. Mine host of the Black Hound found at his gate a cavalier, mounted on a powerful grey horse. "In good time thou art come, my master," he said, as he ushered his worshipful guest into the gayest apartment of his hostelrie; "there is such a storm toward, as there hath not been since that in which the holy abbot Olivarez—blessed be his memory!—was drowned in the Dauro. Doubtless my honoured guest will be for supper, and that presently. Capons have we, and dried kid, and eggs and milk, and such a draught of wine as a cardinal might give thanks for." [23]

The stranger shook his head mournfully. "Thy parlour," he replied, "and thy kitchen, might entice a saint from his road to Paradise; but for me, I am too weary for the one, and too sick for the other. A bed-chamber, good friend, and the aid of a leech, if there be one within any reasonable distance, would glad me more than aught else thy diligence can provide."

Honest Jerome started at the deep and sepulchral tone in which the words were uttered. He gazed upon his abstemious lodger with no very satisfied feelings. The stranger was a stout, well-proportioned man, of middle age, handsomely, even splendidly attired, and bearing in his ruddy cheek and bright eye no traces of indisposition. "If thou wouldst do by my counsel," he replied, after a pause, "thou wouldst find a spiced cup excellent medicine for all the ailing thou ailest: but thy pleasure shall be done. My niece, Margaretta, shall light thee to thy chamber; and, for a leech, marry—there is one now sipping with me the liquor thy frowardness scorns. A man more learned in the mysteries of his art, never weighed out his drachms and scruples by the bed of a dying Pope. Fare-thee-well, Sir: I will drink to thy better health, and thy livelier appetite."

The stranger took up from the table a small bag of crimson velvet, which, as he dismounted from his steed, he had carefully removed from a pocket in the saddle. With a firm step he followed little Margaretta to the chamber which was prepared for him. He might have [24] travelled all the way to Burgos without finding a merrier lip or a brighter pair of eyes.

Margaretta came down the narrow staircase much faster than she had gone up. "Sick, quotha!" said she, as she handed the lamp to the man of medicine, who was preparing for his visit;—"now the foul fiend cure his sickness, say I." And she was closeted for the next half hour with Jacinta the cook-maid; but Jacinta was the discreetest of confidantes, and nothing transpired.

The bald dispenser of drugs advanced silently and on tiptoe to the bedside of his patient. He felt the pulse, its beats were perfectly regular: he examined the tongue, it was of an admirably healthy hue: he passed his hand over the brow, it was dry and cool. "Did he suffer any pain?"

"None," said the stranger.

"Had he received any wound?"

"None," said the stranger.

"By Santiago," quoth the learned Doctor Bartolo, "I am wasting time which might be better bestowed, in listening to our host's jest and swallowing his elixir vitae. My patient is as well as I am!"

"He is dying;" said the stranger. "I pray of thy kindness, good Doctor Bartolo, that thou wilt send hither some sage professor of the law; to whom I may commit such testamentary disposition of my worldly affairs, as may prevent the arising of any disputes among my [25] kindred touching my sublunary wealth, when my spirit shall have left this, its fleshly tabernacle. Go to, man! Thou hast seen the bursting of a bubble on the surface of a calm lake. Couldst thou have observed, the moment ere it vanished, the slightest inequality on its surface? I tell thee, I am dying. Is not this the eve of the day hallowed by the suffering of the blessed martyr Crispin? Why, then, I tell thee I am dying. I would see a notary; and, when I shall have said my say to him, I would speak with a priest. It is already eleven of the clock; and at midnight"——

The stranger shewed no inclination to complete the sentence; so that the physician retired from his post in no small astonishment, and informed his friend Master Tomaso, that his services were required by an obstinate fellow, who might probably make bequests without property, since he was dying without disease.

"Good master notary," said the stranger, "write, I pray thee, that I, being of sane mind and sound body, but nevertheless, within but a short distance of the unrest which my misdeeds have earned for me, bequeath my whole worldly estates, my just debts being first paid, to the monks of the monastery of St. Francis, which stands a bowshot from this place; to be employed by them in the performance of charitable works, and in the celebration of masses for a sinner's soul. And for the collecting of this, my sole bequest, the pious men will have little trouble; for the wealth with which Fortune hath [26] blessed me is all in this crimson bag,"—and he drew it from his pillow as he spoke.—"I will be buried in the vestments I now wear; and for my horse, I will have nothing set down concerning him. He who can rein him, may ride him."

The notary completed his task in as brief a space as his employer had occupied in giving his directions. The stranger added his signature to the document; and the paper was duly attested and sealed up. " Now," said the invalid, "I have but one more duty to perform. I have a long journey to travel this night, and I would fain relieve my heart of some portion of the heavy burthen which for long, long years it has borne. Alas! at such an hour, the purest spirit may well need the strengthening presence of a spiritual guide; but for me, who have been"——

The notary listened anxiously; but what more the stranger might have purposed to say, was checked by a heavy sigh. Yet was there a smile upon his lips, or a contortion which resembled one. The notary escaped with precipitation: and the monk took his place beside the couch of the unaccountable sufferer.

In the parlour of the Black Hound, while the sick man was occupied in his devotions, stories were told and conjectures hazarded, which made the lips of the speakers quiver and the cheeks of the listeners turn pale. Mine host swore that the eyes of his guest glared with an expression which never dwelt in the eyes of mortal man. [27] Margaretta declared that he had come out of the rain with garments as dry as if he had been sitting in the oven; and the stable boy vowed that his grey horse was a more incurably vicious quadruped than ever was foaled by earthly mare. The notary observed, that it was certainly a suspicious circumstance that he had disposed of his worldly goods in favour of the church; and the doctor averred, that if he should die with so healthy a pulse, he could not be aught else but the devil. Then they began to relate how often, within their own and their father's memory, the author of evil had walked visibly upon earth; how he had lived for fifty years at the Court of Naples, in a hat and doublet, and how he had been seen by hundreds in the streets of Constantinople, in a robe and turban; how he had come with Martin Luther to the Diet at Worms, and had fought side by side with the constable Bourbon at the storming of Rome. Whilst they thus talked, the holy man returned. He trembled from head to foot as he entered the room, and big drops of perspiration trickled from his brow. "A mad penitent!" he said, "and a wild confession. And now he prays ye, my friends, that ye will all do him so much grace as to visit him in his pains; for something he hath yet to communicate, from which we may all, he deems, be benefited."

Fear is a soul-subduing spectre; but I have never yet seen a fair battle between him and curiosity, in which curiosity did not beat him out of the field. All the [28] inmates of the Black Hound hurried up stairs; and stood round the traveller's bed, peeping dubiously over one another's shoulders, and prepared for immediate flight if there should arise occasion for it.

The stranger called for a pipe. It was brought to him; and in half a minute he was hidden from their gaze in a veil of impenetrable smoke. Then they heard his solemn and sonorous voice, speaking thus from the darkness.

"I have marred your mirth, my friends, this evening; I will revive it by a song. An old stave it is, and there is a moral in its rhymes. If ye find it not, I beseech ye remember that there are mysteries in heaven, and earth, and the wide ocean, which move the sage to meditate, and the poet to dream, and the fool to laugh;—but they are inscrutable alike to all." And without further preface he began his strange song; renewing between every stanza the cloud in which he was enveloped.

SONG.

There is a traveller oil a steed,
Riding away with valiant speed
    From the city of his birth;
Spur on, spur on!—but the leaves of the limes
Shall come and go a thousand times;
And the sands shall gush with leaping tills,
And the vales be turned to lofty hills,
    Ere ever he loose a girth.
[29]
There is a mariner in a bark,
While the wave is rough, and the night is dark,
    Ploughing the billows hoar;
Sail on, sail on!—but the light of day
And the mist of night shall pass away,
And the sea be dry beneath his prow,
And the winds be dead that cheer him now,
    Ere ever he come to shore.

There is a race that was never won;
There is a tale that was often begun,
    But no man knows the ending;
There is a suit in a Court of Law,
The gravest the Chancellor ever saw,

It was entered for trial long ago,
When the world was made with its mirth and woe,
   And still that suit is pending.

What is the life of mortal man?
Just what it was when time began,
   A welcome and farewell;—
The dreariest road must have a turning;
The dullest task is got by learning:
The greenest leaf must soon be sear;
And the pipe, good friends, that was lighted here
   May be finished perhaps"——

The stranger's never was finished! The clock of the distant monastery struck twelve. He was silent,—motionless,—dead.

"For mercy's sake! Frank," said Lady Olivia, "do let me know something of your hero. What was his name? and what was there in his crimson bag? and what had he to confess? and whence did he come, and whither did he go?" [30]

"His name, Lady Olivia, was never ascertained; for the signature upon the will was perfectly illegible. His crimson bag was empty. And for his confession, of course it was between his conscience and his ghostly comforter. It was never divulged. I might have invented a confession on purpose for him, full of murders and treasons, ghosts and hobgoblins, sulphur and brimstone,—but I scorn such frauds. I will add nothing to the truth."

"Then you have nothing more to tell us?"

"Nothing. Unless you are interested in the fate of the dead man's horse. There never was such an untameable beast. It ran away with a minister of state, dislocated a bishop's collar-bone, and flung, successively, a whole regiment of Walloons. At last, it came into the possession of a functionary of the Holy Inquisition, and in his hands was as quiet as a lamb."

It was voted too late to begin another story that evening; and the following morning, upon hearing that Sir Jacob had resigned, the party broke up by common consent, and returned to Town. Lady Olivia has grieved ever since for the failure of her scheme; though she has consoled herself by hanging up a large piece of canvas in her drawing-room, in which she is framed and glazed, in the character of Pampinea.

Title

Howitt, William. "The Last of the Titans." LS 1831. 116-132. [116]

THE LAST OF THE TITANS.
BY WILLIAM HOWITT.

DALOOM, the Bedouin poet, gave the hospitality of the night to a Mameluke who was speeding on secret embassage of state. The Mameluke, in return for his kindness, perpetrated the greatest outrage that can be inflicted on the heart of man;—and, instead of thanks, departed before daybreak with laughter of a fiend. Daloom, whose soul possessed all the fire and irritability of his race and profession, was furious with indignation and revenge;—and not he alone,—but his whole tribe was on flame. They surrounded his house in a tumultuous crowd. The sheik placed at his door the fleetest dromedary of the East;—one chief put into his hand a deadly ataghan;—a second, with his own girdle, braced him for the swiftest flight;—another group, laying hold of him, placed him in the saddle; and all, with ten thousand burning curses on the Atheist Mameluke, bade him begone. [117]

  He shot through the desert like a meteor. Cairo was his object; and in a few days he was treading its streets. He saw his detested enemy;—he watched him with a lynx's eyes;—he dogged 'him with a tiger's foot,—but it was in vain. He beheld him surrounded by crowds of his fellows, as callous, as reckless, as godless as himself. They feasted, they laughed, they lived as if care had never been on earth, God in heaven, or vengeance in hell: but the infuriated poet might as well have attempted to pull down the eternal sky, as to approach him. Rank, which he had not suspected beneath the ordinary guise of a Mameluke, surrounded him as with a wall of adamant. Between him and Daloom's dagger were a thousand quick eyes, a thousand fearless hearts; and if the injured man sought redress by complaint to his superiors, a laughter which thrilled through him as an echo of the peal of the Mameluke, as he shot from his door, was his only answer. His heart was choked within him with the excess of his wrath,—his brain was maddened to desperation; and pouring out imprecations against heaven, earth, and mankind, he flew back to his native regions.

  Three days he had driven along in the vehemence of his transport. Lost in the turmoil of his distracted spirit, he had seen nothing of the tract through which he had passed; he trusted his route to the dromedary, which flew on like an arrow. He woke with a start, as from a tumultuous dream, as he suddenly found himself [118] involved in a whirlwind, which raised the sands of the desert into a mighty cloud, and wrapped him in darkness and suffocation. The next moment he beheld the black hurricane rushing forwards; and having for a few seconds followed, with his eyes, its career with terror and astonishment, he looked round,—and was not the less amazed to behold himself at the foot of an obelisk, whose slender shaft arose into the very heaven,—and in the vast square of a gigantic city. The shock of his wonder was like that of lightning. The sudden transition from the fierce and boiling torrent of his own passionate thoughts, was marvellous. The scenes around were of a magnitude which astounded him; the silence sank into his soul with all its vastness—deep, lifeless, and terrific. He looked on all sides for some trace of existence;—he saw none, but in himself and dromedary. He glanced up the obelisk beside him till his eye recoiled dizzily from its fearful altitude; he turned his gaze upon the towers, and his spirit sank crushed, as it were, beneath the overwhelming sense of their immensity. What hands could have piled those massy and stupendous towers? What might of men, in millions, could have reared those ponderous and gigantic columns, which, baffling the eye with the immensity of their bulk, shot up to the loftiest regions of air, and bore incumbent pediments and dependent scrolls, whose dimensions the imagination laboured in vain to grasp.

Daloom would gladly have persuaded himself that he [119] was in a dream, but his convictions were positive of waking existence, and he stood oppressed with the greatness of all without, and the vanity of all within him. "What are the griefs, the passions, the interests of a creature like me; a pigmy—an atom of the dust? The beings glorious, and to my imagination, almost omnipotent, who built and inhabited these mysterious dwellings, have probably passed away; and if *they* have gone down to impenetrable oblivion, what will be my departure from the earth?—The ceasing of a momentary breeze in the illimitable air! the extinction of a spark in the conflagration of a city!" As he thus moralised, his eye involuntarily fixed itself on the colossal portal of a most august palace, which stood open before him. A peristyle of those enormous pillars composed its front; and on each hand a row of gigantic sphinges guarded its entrance. It was not till a long contemplation of the greatness of all these objects had, in some degree, familiarised him to their strangeness, that his curiosity overcame his awe, and he determined to enter.

When, however, he began to move, the diminutiveness of his steps, the feebleness of his motions, contrasted with the vastness and the solidity of every thing around him, redoubled his amazement, and forced upon his senses the infinite distance between these works and himself; and when he reached a pillar, and, looking up, found that his stature was not a tenth part of that of its base, he again stood fixed to the ground in wonder. [120] When he endeavoured to arouse himself, it was only to encounter fresh objects, that fell upon his labouring senses with a mountainous weight. The hall that he entered was as vast in its dimensions as every thing without. Its floor, its walls, its lofty dome, presented but one plain surface of black marble, which, polished to the highest lustre, reflected, wherever he went, his own minute shape: and in the centre arose what he at first conceived to be a mount of stone, but which, as he continued to gaze upon it, gradually grew upon his perception a finished animal shape—a mighty sphinx! Every moment that he contemplated it, its character more vividly developed itself to his mind, till it at length filled it with ideas of terror that served to render him stony as itself. He beheld in its stupendous form indications of fleetness, and of energies immense as its bulk; and in its eye the immeasurable depths of a sagacity, dark, deadly, and malignant. With ineffable terror—with the labour and debility of a dream—he turned from this horrible image, and effected his retreat into the next apartment.

Here, if his terrors were less excited, his admiration and awe were equally called forth. It was a saloon of the same amplitude, constructed of the richest porphyry;—the same eternal silence pervaded it; and on the floor stood vases, chalices, and various banqueting vessels, of a splendour that seemed only befitting gods; and of a size which startled Daloom with the conviction, [121] that whoever used them must have been proportionably gigantic with their abode. Who—what might they have been? And when had their fearful presence filled this mysterious pile? He felt it must have been in some far-off time; yet were these superb utensils bright and pure as when they first issued from the hands of their unknown workmen. Not a stain, not an atom of dust rested upon them, or upon the mighty room in which they stood. He gazed upon them with an augmenting wonder and admiration. Their materials were such as sunk in value all the riches of the earth. Some were of gold, some brilliant crystal; and others one pure mass of cool, rich, translucent beryl, emerald, or chrysolite. Their shapes were such as he had never seen; but so moulded by the very spirit of grace and beauty, that for the moment, banishing all fear, all other sense, they filled his soul with the most delicious and heavenly sensations. Drawn by this absorbing influence, he advanced, and laying his hand on the stem of one, he attempted to move it;—it stood firm as an eternal rock; and at once all the consciousness of his situation rushed back upon him. He lifted up his eyes, and saw, on the opposite wall, wrought in bold relief, a series of the most marvellous scenes and figures. They were all of dimensions accordant with the place.

First, a child playing with a radiant girdle; a kingly figure, with eager eyes, and hands outstretched to take it: then the same god-like shape, girt with that splendid [122] cestus, in a chariot drawn by sphinges, driving forth on a career of victory. Here, embattled hosts of the same Titan forms, vainly opposing him and his; their countenances hideous with the expression of unutterable hate; writhing fiercely and furiously beneath the consciousness of overwhelming power: then, multitudes prostrate before his chariot;—processions offering submission at the gates of cities: and here, the same conqueror feasting with seven beings of equal stature and dignity in a banqueting-house, and in vessels which Daloom immediately recognised as the room in which he stood, and as the vessels before him. The last was the representation of a king and queen, young and beautiful above expression, in a triumphal chariot, riding amid the acclamations of the people.

These scenes filled Daloom with a restless curiosity. He looked round, but there were no others; and perceiving a lofty, open door at the distant end of the saloon, he approached it. What words can do justice to his increased amaze! A dome, seeming to emulate the amplitude and loftiness of that of heaven, formed its roof,—a dome expanded in the form of a huge concave flower of azure, in whose centre a glorious carbuncle flung down the richness of its perpetual glow upon an amethystine pavement. At the farther end stood a throne of lustrous jet; over which a bird, large as the fabled Simourg, spread its awful wings as a canopy. But what were these? It was upon two figures [123] which stood upon the steps of the throne, that Daloom's attention was riveted. The one was a female, whose character, as it grew upon his gaze, was that of a beauty pure and sublime as the depths of heaven itself. It was that lofty beauty resulting from a body and soul in unison, at once full of majesty and power, of grace and gentleness; but the expression of her magnificent face was that of woe,—a woe deep, deep and irremediable,—a remorse that wrung and devoured her spirit with all that terrible energy of which such a being could alone be capable. She stood—her hands clenched—her eyes upon the ground, and the feeling of that unutterable woe so imbuing her whole air and form, that Daloom became speedily wrapped up in a sympathy, even for a creature of so stupendous a nature, that grew and grew into an intensity unspeakable. He seemed to behold that image of overwhelming woe filling the silence of eternity with its influence; and he felt as if he could thus stand before it for ever, to accompany it with an eternal sympathy.

But what was the other figure? And what was its connexion with this absorbing form? He turned, and recognised instantly the bearing and countenance of the youthful monarch, who, in the last representation on the wall of the banqueting-room, rode in his chariot, accompanied by his queen. He had the lofty stature of a god;—light, vigorous, and graceful: a countenance sublime, eagle-glanced, but betraying a fiery pride—an [124] immeasurable ambition. He stood in a lofty attitude of firmness and command, yet mingled somewhat with a sense of surprise and pain;—his figure erect, yet slightly thrown backward; his arms downward, yet a little advanced; his hands separately clenched, and his features raised and prominent, as if his attention were fixed on some one before him. There was no one; but at his feet lay a splendid flagon.

How long Daloom had been entranced in the contemplation of these marvellous scenes, it were impossible to tell. The intensity of his feelings had annihilated all ideas of time; the impression of those two figures overpowered all others, and especially that breathing the immensity of woe, absorbed his whole spirit and transfused itself through his whole imagination. He turned from it, as from a figure of enchantment; and attempting to break with a powerful effort the spell of its fascination, he sped on. His progress was still through vast rooms, vast corridors, and courts exhibiting traces" of fountains which had ceased, and statuary enormous as the beings which he had seen; but the figures before the throne still glowed upon his spirit, and he beheld nothing beside distinctly, till he issued, with a feeling of joy, to the open air.

It was night! and the moon, in solitary splendour, was casting her beams upon those towering abodes, and tracing upon the ground their awful shadows. But what was his astonishment and terror as he beheld, seated on [125] a fallen column just before him, in a leaning and melancholy attitude, a figure gigantic as those within! And this, he felt, must be a living figure,—were it not merely a phantom of his heated and bewildered brain. The moon now shone partially upon it. He looked up, with an agonized hope to discover it, however fearful, yet inanimate and stony as they. One glance froze him to the spot!—He beheld the light of a living eye! it was fixed upon him, and, in the same instant, he recognised, in the whole form and face, a vivid resemblance to the statue of the young king before the throne. Another moment, and a voice, gentle and low for a being of such a stature, thus addressed him.

"Son of the earth, by whatever means thou hast entered this city, it must be by the agency of God. Hitherto, no eye of man has beheld it; no foot of man has trodden its streets. Know then, that thou art in the city of *earth's primaeval race*. Thou hast seen what to thee are marvels; thou hast seen what man shall never see again;—hear therefore, what may not be lost, even upon thee.

"These towers were the dwellings of my ancestors,—a race of beings such as thou seest me; such as the scenes within have represented them,—beings less, far less in number than thy diminutive species; but possessed of faculties, of energies, of an intensity of passion and perception impossible to your feebler fabric. They were mortal, it is true; but the term of their existence was not [126] years, but thousands of years. My forefathers ruled this city; but an incident, trivial in itself, gave them at once dominion over the greater part of their race. A child playing on the bank of a river, found a radiant girdle, and bringing it into the palace, was amusing himself with it, when the prince beheld, and springing forward in a transport of joy, seized upon it. It was the girdle of an angel of power;—one of those strong angels who roll the newly-created orbs into the infinitude of space, and fix them in their eternal stations; or who, on less occasions, shake them with earthquakes to their centres. Girt with this glorious girdle the king subdued the fierce, the fearful, the cunning, and hitherto indomitable sphinges,—a race of creatures who possessed, in the shape of a beast, the faculties of a spirit and the malignity of a fiend; and dwelt in the solitary places of the earth. Yoked to his chariot, and to those of his warriors, they bore him in triumph from land to land,—mountains or seas formed no impediment to their course; they trod with equal ease, and with the velocity of lightning, earth, air, or water. Lord of these, and girt with the girdle of power, every city, save one, became his; and this city the capital of the world. Seven kings,—all, save one, that the earth knew,—became his captives; in these towers they feasted at one table, and one tomb contains them.

"When the kingdom became mine, what was there left for me to desire?

The world was my patrimony—the most beautiful and gifted of earth's daughters was my [127] queen. Oh! lovely and gentle Thua, what charms and enchantments were thine! In loftiness of stature, in glory of countenance, there was none like her—for I had seen all. In the thrilling mysteries of music, who could emulate her! She had gathered the strains of the earth from the farthest of her many thousand ages; and had wrought them into songs which were sung from side to side of creation. When I trod secretly through my streets, I heard the happy children singing them, and my heart leaped at the sound; when I took the path of my camp, I heard the soldier chant the victories of his fathers in her words; when I visited the most distant and solitary regions of the world, I heard the lonely woman beneath her palm-tree soothing her heart with the pensive melodies of Thua! What did I need?—There was one little city which had resisted all the efforts of my ancestors,—not by its numbers, nor by its superior strength, or wisdom, but because there dwelt the ancient, the oracular Sphinx. This had resisted all my ancestors,—this was wanting to my glory. I bore down upon it with all my power, and I subdued it, and brought hither in triumph its prince, and the ancient Sphinx.

"Cursed be the day of that conquest! Cursed be the day that the Sphinx entered this city! The world was mine. In one achievement I had concentrated all its glory; in one female I had concentrated all its charms and its love. What could I need; Oh man! knowest thou not that an earlier, and a greater race than ours— [128] the sons of heaven, were wrenched from the heart of the universe, and hurled into the unutterable depths, by the fiend Ambition? Knowest thou not what myriads of thy trivial race, like insects in the summer sunlight, have been scorched by the sudden lightnings of its wrath, and have perished in every age, leaving vain warnings to their children: Our race was not the less subject to its influence;—it is a power wide as nature, and irresistible as death. Will the little brook, as it bounds, laughing and sparkling from its native hill, content itself with being a brook? Does not the brook swell on into a river, the river into a sea, and the sea, grasping the world in its embrace, lift up its stormy waves in the face of heaven? Yes, Ambition is a spirit that climbs the loftiest pinnacles of earth's mountains only to grasp at the stars, though the gulf of eternity yawns at its feet. What did I need? There was one thing wanting;—to achieve immortality,—to become, not only the king of the world, but—its God! I sought the counsels of the Sphinx; and by these counsels the multitude was taught to hail me as a deity, the vanquisher, even of the Godhead. Curse on that degenerate race!—it was only too compliant. They were become proud and self-willed: their ancient faith had died away; the spirits of heaven had long ceased to visit them; like me, they grasped at immortality, and eagerly anticipated it at my hands. One only dared to oppose my design;—and that was Affod, the father of my Thua. Firm in the ancient faith, he had filled his daughter's [129] soul with his own lofty knowledge, and loftier aspirings. When I brought home the Sphinx he alone rejoiced not, but with a sorrowful countenance warned me against its counsels, and urged me to expel it from the city. Instead of surrendering himself to the pleasures that occupied all beside, he wandered from town to town, and from land to land, though a prince, foretelling woe, and calling upon the apostate race to return to the God of their fathers. None listened—I least of all—the power of that Godhead upon this earth I trusted to destroy for ever!

"In the Sphinx was my confidence: he knew the secrets of the world from its creation; our fathers had died, but he had lived through all. I sought him in his hall—by night, alone; and with a heart that trembled for the response, I asked—'Shall not the power of the unseen God come to an end on the earth?' It replied. 'It may.' 'But when?' I eagerly rejoined—'but when?' 'When there ceases to be a believer.' 'Oh!' I exclaimed—'what do I hear?—When there ceases to be a believer!'—'There are two!' 'Yes'—said the terrible monster, 'and they are in thy power!'

"Let oblivion cover the days of my spirit's torment that succeeded! Let the sound of those horrible words—'they are two—they are in thy power,' which rung through my soul, and tossed it on the billows of perdition, some time cease, oh God! Let those struggles with the virtue, the sublime faith, the fathomless energies of a female mind, swayed and smitten by the deeper energies [130] of a female's love, be held in sacred silence;—thus much only be there now revealed:—

"In the secret of our pavilion, Thua reclined before me, gazing forth upon those fountains and groves which are now destroyed. Her resplendent mind was in full play, throwing into her countenance most marvellous beauty; expatiating on our youth,—our loves, our glory; on the charms of that scene where her eyes were now wandering—the scene of our youthful felicity; and, at times, turning back into the treasures of antiquity, for lays, and traditions, and sentences, that accorded with her feelings at the moment. The darkness which I had of late cast upon her spirit seemed totally to have vanished;—the misery with which my projects and persuasions had wrung it, seemed forgotten; but while I gazed with wonder and admiration on her charms, and gloried in the wealth of her intellect, pouring forth thoughts like a river—my heart throbbed with the desperate emotions of the consciousness of my destiny. Starting from the momentary reverie into which she had beguiled me, I exclaimed—'Thua! knowest thou that this night decides our fate for ever! Knowest thou that this night the earth is free, or its people are no more?' Like a palm-tree suddenly shrivelled by the burning blast, Thua sank at once, as struck with instant death; but as suddenly starting up, she grasped my arm with a fearful energy, and, with a look of awful meaning, said faintly—'Arzalan! *what sayest thou? Where learnedst thou this?*' [131]

"'From the Sphinx.'

"'Oh, that dreadful Sphinx! Would to God it had never been brought hither! Once, once more only—Oh, Arzalan! let me be heard!—abandon the counsels of the cruel Sphinx,—shun, distrust him!'

"'Thua! listen! Can the Sphinx err? Is not his wisdom well known? Has he not for ages protected his city against the whole world?'

"'Has he protected it *now*? Oh, Arzalan! Arzalan! Fear him—shun him!—And my father!—shall the Sphinx prevail against my father?'

"'Thua! thy father shall partake our felicity. He shall drink of the cup of peace which the Sphinx has taught me to mingle:—a momentary sleep, and he shall rise to immortality. Will not all power be ours?—to restore—to create—to re-create?'

"'Oh, Arzalan! Oh, my beloved! by all that the ancients taught, of pure, holy, and eternal—by all that we have loved and rejoiced in—by the certainty of ages of bliss here—by our hope of eternal peace, trust not the dark speeches of this cruel creature. Spare! oh, spare my father!'

"'Thua! what askest thou! my life? and our immortality? I have sworn the irrevocable oath! This night, the Sphinx has said, this night I am a god, or nothing. Even *thou* believest the Sphinx when he foretells evil; this night yield me thy consent, or I cease for ever!'

"'Perish, then! if I cannot save thee, I can perish with thee!' [132]

"At these words, Affod himself entered. His eyes sought Thua with a look of unspeakable anguish; he stood and gazed upon her for a space, in the silence of misery, and exclaimed, ' Alas! my child!'

"'Affod,' I said, 'why troublest thou my reign? Take the cup of peace, and let it unite us for ever!' He took it from my hand;—I saw it in his face, that he knew its nature; but he was calm as in his hour of meditations; he drank it up. A shriek from Thua—I turned, and beheld her in that attitude of woe which has continued through ten thousand years—she had ceased to be!

"In the agony of despair, I gazed upon her father; but instead of that change which I anticipated—the change of death—a sudden glory had wrapped him. His mortal frame appeared to have melted away; and his spirit, glowing like the liquid mirror of the sun, stood before me; and, lifting aloft his radiant arm,—'Arzalan!' he pronounced, in a tone that has found an everlasting echo— 'thou hast brought all life to an end!' At that word the shudder of an earthquake passed through the palace;—dreadful thunders broke above, and one wild wail of ineffable woe rang through the air. I looked, but Affod had disappeared. I felt the freezing pang which severed my spirit from the body, and I departed to my doom. As I passed through the palace, through the city, through the whole land, I beheld that all life had ceased. Not a creature, great or small, breathed; the [133] very frames of the primaeval race were annihilated; and nothing remained but the scattered statues of our ancient heroes.

"Once in a thousand years, an angel of Power passes before me through the. desert, and lays open this scene of my glory and my crime, that I may behold the ruin I have produced; that I may gaze on that form of inextinguishable woe; and revive in my spirit all the strength of hell. Depart! it is for no living eye, much less for a nature frail as thine, to behold the terrors of my trial."

Appendix A: Comparison of Gothic Content

Annual	Year	Gothic Stories	Gothic Stories Pages Total	Volume Pages Overall	% Pgs Gothic Stories	Gothic Engravings	Engravings Overall
FMN	1823	1	21	392	5.4%	0	12
FMN	1824	3	36	366	9.8%	0	13
FMN	1825	2	36	393	9.2%	0	12
FMN	1826	8	135	386	35.0%	3	13
FMN	1827	6	116	395	29.4%	0	13
FMN	1828	4	50	417	12.0%	0	13
FMN	1829	8	114	418	27.3%	2	14
FMN	1830	10	125	418	30.0%	1	14
FMN	1831	8	135	371	36.3%	1	14
Totals	9 vols.	50	768	3556	21.0%	7	
FO	1824	0	0	222	0.0%	0	6
FO	1825	1	14	305	4.6%	0	26
FO	1826	2	34	397	8.6%	1	13
FO	1827	1	26	354	7.3%	0	11
FO	1828	0	0	384	0.0%	0	13
FO	1829	1	13	418	3.1%	1	13
FO	1830	1	12	384	3.1%	0	13
FO	1831	2	31	408	7.6%	1	13
Totals	8 vols.	8	130	2872	4.5%	3	
LS	1825	5	66	394	16.8%	1	13
LS	1826	4	73	410	17.8%	0	12
LS	1827	5	67	402	16.7%	1	12
LS	1828	3	39	406	9.6%	0	14
LS	1829	5	115	362	31.8%	2	12
LS	1830	4	50	364	13.7%	0	12
LS	1831	2	31	346	9.0%	1	12
Totals	7 vols.	28	441	2684	16.4%	5	
KS	1828	2	31	312	9.6%	2	19
KS	1829	4	109	360	30.3%	4	19
KS	1830	3	54	352	15.3%	4	18
KS	1831	1	21	322	6.5%	1	18
Totals	4 vols.	10	215	1346	15.9%	11	
Total	28 vols	96	1554			26	
				265	avg words/pg		
			411810	Words total			
				867			

Appendix B: Alphabetical List of Authors

A Traveller, The Lady of the Tower, FMN 1826, 166-177
Ainsworth, William Harrison, The Fortress of Saguntum, LS 1825, 259-263
—, The Ghost Laid, KS 1828, 286-300
—, Rosicrucian. A Tale, FO 1827, 38-63
—, A Tradition of the Fortress of Saguntum, LS 1825, 264-282
Anonymous, The Magic Mirror. A Polish Tale, FMN 1823, 133-153
Anonymous, The Ring; A True Narrative. From the Russian, FMN 1824, 107-125
Anonymous, The Grey Palmer: A Legend of Yorkshire, FMN 1824, 232-237
Anonymous, Pernicious Effects of Fortune-Telling, FMN 1824, 319-329
Anonymous, Lanucci. A Tale of the Thirteenth Century, FO 1825, 247-260
Anonymous, The Golden Snuff-Box, LS 1825, 127-148
Anonymous, The Phantom Voice, FMN 1826, 317-337
Anonymous, The Laughing Horseman. A Tale, FO 1826, 109-134
Anonymous, Forgiveness. A Tale, FO 1826, 240-247
Anonymous, The Diamond Watch, LS 1826, 53-74
Anonymous, The Magician of Vicenza, FMN 1829, 273-283
Anonymous, The Sisters, LS 1829, 1-33
Anonymous, Lady Olivia's Decamerone, LS 1831, 17-30
Barker, Matthew Henry, Greenwich Hospital, FMN 1830, 241-255
Beevor, M.L., The Benshee of Shane. A Tradition of the North of Ireland, FMN 1831, 123-136
—, St. Feinah's Tree. A Legend of Loch Neagh, FMN 1830, 155-163
Bird, John, The Cornet's Widow, FMN 1829, 131-144
—, The Convent of St. Ursula, FMN 1830, 361-379
—, The Haunted Chamber, FMN 1831, 279-300
Bowdich, Sarah, Eliza Carthago, FMN 1829, 57-64
Bulwer, Edward Lytton, A Manuscript found in a Madhouse, LS 1829, 56-66
Chorley, H. F., The Elves of Caer-Gwyn, FMN 1831, 73-95
Croker, Thomas Crofton, Clough Na Cuddy. A Killarney Legend, LS 1827, 233-243
D., L., New Year's Eve. The Omens, LS 1825, 159-175
Dods, Mary Diana, The Bridal Ornaments. A Legend of Thuringia, FMN 1827, 393-416
—, The Three Damsels. A Tale of Halloween, FMN 1827, 79-86
Flora, Bolton Abbey, FMN 1826, 19-26
Galt, John, The Witch, LS 1827, 97-102
—, The Omen, FMN 1830, 99-105
—, The Confession, LS 1830, 202-207

Gillies, Robert Pearch, The Warning. A German Legend, FO 1829, 93-105
Grattan, Thomas Colley, The Love-Draught. A Tale of the Barrow-Side, LS 1830, 1-19
Griffin, Gerald, The Dilemma of Phadrig. A Tale of the Shannon Side, LS 1828, 3-19
—, The Rock of the Candle. A Tale of an Irish Ruin, LS 1829, 73-110
Harral, Thomas, Days of Old, FMN 1826, 107-115
—, The House of Castelli, FMN 1828, 339-356
Hesketh, S. K., The Smuggler, FMN 1831, 165-182
Hofland, Barbara, The Maid of the Beryl, FMN 1829, 253-267
—, The Regretted Ghost, FMN 1826, 79-101
Hogg, James, The Border Chronicler, LS 1826, 257-279
Howitt, William, Ithran the Demoniac, LS 1830, 289-306
—, The Last of the Titans, LS 1831, 116-132
Inglis, Henry, Kathed and Eurelia. A Bohemian Legend, FMN 1828, 237-243
—The Musician of Augsburg, FMN 1829, 235-244
—, Rodolph, the Fratricide, FO,1830, 200-211
—, The Unholy Promise. A Norwegian Legend, FO 1831, 115-125
—, The City of the Desert, LS 1830, 64-71
Jewsbury, Maria Jane [?], The Grave of the Suicide, FMN 1825, 219-230
Kennedy, William, The Castle of St. Michael. A Tale, FO 1831, 159-178
Loundon, J.C., The Grotto of Akteleg. A Hungarian Legend, LS 1829, 330-343
MacNish, Robert, The Red Man, FMN 1830, 49-65
Maginn, William, The City of the Demons, LS 1828, 73-84
—, A Vision of Purgatory, LS 1829, 228-246
Maturin, Charles, Leixlip Castle. An Irish Family Legend, LS 1825, 211-232
McNaghten, Captain Sir William Hay, The Sacrifice. An Indian Tale, FMN 1831, 193-213
Moir, D.L., The Old Manor-House, LS 1826, 181-200
—, Auld Robin Gray. The Original Story, LS 1827, 301-322
—, The Pneumatologist, LS 1828, 325-334
—, Kemp, The Bandit. A Legend of Castle Campbell, FMN,1830, 209-227
—, Bessy Bell and Mary Gray. A Scottish Legend of 1666, FMN 1831, 361-370
Neele, Henry, The Comet, FMN 1827, 239-267
—, The Magician's Visiter, FMN 1828, 91-98
—, The Houri. A Persian Tale, FMN 1829, 165-178
Richardson, David Lester, The Soldier's Dream, FMN 1830, 234-237
Roberts, Emma, Rosamunda. A Venetian Fragment, LS 1826, 305-312
—, Maximilian and his Daughter, FMN 1827, 219-226

—, The Halt on the Mountain, FMN 1828, 362-378
—, The Bridal of St. Omer. A Tale, LS 1827, 145-163
Roby, John, The Haunted Manor-House, FMN 1827, 133-159
Rosa, Giuseppe Guercino, FMN 1829, 193-208
Scott, Sir Walter, My Aunt Margaret's Mirror, KS 1829, 1-44
Scott, Sir Walter, The Tapestried Chamber, or The Lady in the Sacque, KS 1829, 123-142
Shelley, Mary, Convent of Chaillot: or, Valliere and Louis XIV, KS 1828, 267-283
—, The Euthanasia. A Story of Modern Greece, FMN 1829, 95-120
—, Ferdinando Eboli. A Tale, KS 1829, 195-218
—, The Sisters of Albano, KS 1829, 80-100
—, The False Rhyme, KS 1830, 265-268
—, The Mourner, KS 1830, 71-97
—, The Evil Eye, KS 1830, 150-175
—, Transformation, KS 1831, 18-39
— or Maria Jane Jewsbury [?], Lacy de Vere, FMN 1827, 275-294
Stafford, William Cooke, Woman's Love, FMN 1826, 62-77
Stone, William L., The Grave of the Indian King, FMN 1831, 101-118
T., A.D., The Fairies' Grot, FMN 1826, 119-135
Thompson, W. G., Fanny Lee, FMN 1830, 261-271
Thomson, Richard, The Antiquary and His Fetch. A Legend of the Strand, FMN 1830, 279-302
—, Saint Agnes' Fountain. The Romance of a Finsbury Archer, FMN 1826, 350-378
—, The Haunted Hogshead. A Yankee Legend, FMN 1831, 145-154
White, Joseph Blanco, The Alcazar of Seville and the Tale of the Green Taper, FMN 1825, 31-54
Wilson, John, The Two Fathers, LS 1827, 19-27

Appendix C:
Other Literary Annual Contributions by Select Authors of Gothic Short Stories

Note: The first number is the literary annual year; numbers following are page numbers.

Ainsworth, W. Harrison
> *Friendship's Offering.*
>> Stanzas for Music "When the morning awakens in the valley," 26, 387.
>> The Rosicrucian: a Tale, 27, 38;
>> Written in an Album, "Gazing on childhood's careless face," 42, 215.
>
> *Literary Souvenir.*
>> The Fortress of Saguntum, "Tradition of the Fortress of Saguntum," 25, 259.
>> An Imperfect Portrait, "There is an hour by favouring heaven," 25, 287;
>
> *Keepsake.*
>> To...., "What is the aim with which the poet glows," 28, Fronts; (published anonymously)
>> Pocket-books and Keepsakes, 28, 1; (published anonymously)
>> The Ghost Laid, 28, 286 (published anonymously)
>> The Cook and the Doctor, "Blest be the man who first invented eating," 28, 242 (published anonymously)
>> Opera Reminiscences for 1827, 28, 302 (published anonymously)
>> Beatrice di Tenda; 41, 1;
>> To a Young Italian Lady, "Young beauty of the South! and must thou go?" 42, 217.

Beevor, Miss M.L.
> *Forget Me Not*
>> St. Feinah's Tree: a Legend of Loch Neagh, 30, 155;
>> The Benshee of Shane: a Tradition of the North of Ireland, 31, 123;
>> The Waltz: a Tale founded on facts, 34, 337.

Bird, John
> *Forget Me Not*
>> Agatha Gheranzi, 28, 305;

> The Faithful Guardian, "Sweet Innocence! how calm thou sleepest," 29, 65;
> The Cornet's Widow, 29, 131;
> Eva, "Farewell, sweet Eva! o'er yon brow," 30, 145;
> The Convent of St. Ursula, 30, 361;
> Spring, "What's lovelier than the Spring?" 31, 214;
> The Haunted Chamber, 31, 279;
> The Gladiator, "sweep on, Sweep on! your savage sport is o'er," 32, 155;
> The Last of the Family, 34, 309;
> Song, "Give me the flowers that breathe," 37, 256;
> Hope, "Beautiful Dream," 37, 355.

Bulwer (Edward George Bulwer-Lytton)
> *Friendship's Offering*
>> The Poet's Dream, "It was the minstrel's merry month of June." 32, 73;
>
> *Literary Souvenir*
>> Too Handsome for anything, 29, 45;
>> A Manuscript found in a Madhouse, 29, 56.
>
> *Keepsake*
>> Ode, The Last Separation, "We shall not rest together, love," 41, 58;
>> Jealousy, "I have thy love–I know no fear," 42, 122;
>> The Lawyer who cost his Client nothing (from the "Thresor d'Histoires admirables et Memorables de nostre Temps: par Simon Goulart, Senlisien, MDCXX), 48, 1;
>> The First Violets, "Who that has loved knows not the tender tale," 48, 17;
>> The Confirmed Valetudinarian, 51, 153;
>> The Modern Wooer, "Since Woman is blind," 55, 116.

Chorley, H. F.
> *Forget Me Not*
>> The Elves of Caergwyn, 31, 73;
>> Song, "Go hang my lyre upon the wall," 31, 121;
>> Sir Percival's Return, "Sir Percival returning from the fight," 32, 254;
>> Uncle Anthony's Blunder, 33, 231;
>> The Mother's Picture, "From many years of wandering, and many days of care," 34, 95;

The Silent Man, 34, 95;
Song, "Friend, whose smile had ever power," 35, 68;
My Aunt Lucy's Lesson, 35, 93;
The Rest of the Heart, "O for the quiet of the heart profound," 36, 50;
Juliana, 36, 153;
Annabel's Bridal, 37, 193;
Puss and the Poetess, 37, 193;
Coralie: a Brother's Tale, 38, 159;
A Night's Song, "O sleep, come down to me," 38, 318;
Phoebe May's Dream, 41, 11;
The Portrait of Miranda: A Deal Extravaganza, 42, 133;
The Indian Necklace: a Legend, 43, 125;
Aurora's Fan, 45, 173.

Friendship's Offering
Adelaide; or, The Lady of Song, "There is no maid of Italy, with bright and fervent glance," 31, 31;
Columbines, "Homely old English flowers!–without pretence," 34, 252.

Literary Souvenir
The Sleeper's Shrift, 33, 253;
An Hour of Song, "'Twas music's hour: just when the summer day," 35, 123;

Keepsake
Helen: a Sketch, 37, 97;
The Sisters of the Silver Palace: a Tale from the Italian Chronicles, 41, 129;
Foulebel's Serenade (from an unpublished Drama), 42, 237;
On the Portrait of Mrs. Horace Marryat, "Mother and child! so long as earth is ours," 50, 1;
On the Portrait of the Princess Marie of Baden, Marchioness of Douglas, and the Earl of Angus, "Prisoned in towns, I look, as in a dream," 51, 1;
On the Portrait of Miss de Horsey, "Gentle lady! with that painted look," 54, 49;
The Glee-Maiden's Spell, "Lean your head upon my breast," 56, 73;
On the Portrait of Lady Molesworth, "Sweets to the sweet, renown to the renowned," 57, 1.

Dods, Mary Diana (pseudonym, David Lyndsey)
  Forget Me Not
    The Three Damsels: a Tale of Halloween, 27, 79
    The Bridal Ornaments: a Tale of Thuringia, 27, 393.

  Literary Souvenir
    Firouz-Abdel: a Tale of the Upas Tree, 25, 341.

  Pledge of Friendship
    The Beacon Light: A Tale, 28, 208

Galt, John
  Forget Me Not
    The Omen, 30, 99;
    Salvatore Niente, 32, 279;

  Friendship's Offering
    To Sir Walter Scott, "O sure–when stretched on verdant knoll," 26, 177;
    A Reverie, "The stars were out, and the moon was up," 27, 255;
    The New Atlantis: an American Legend, 31, 217;
    The First Settlers on the Ohio: an American Story, 32, 243.

  Literary Souvenir
    A Feeling Neighbour: a Fragment, 26, 163;
    The Witch, 27, 97;
    The Confession, 30, 202.

Gillies, Robert Pearce
  Friendship's Offering
    The Warning: a German Legend, 29, 93.

Hogg, James
  Forget Me Not
    The Skylark, 28, 27
    The Descent of Love, 28, 217
    St. Mary of the Lows, 29, 25
    Eastern Apologues, 29, 309
    Seeking the Houdy, 33, 399
    A Sea Story, 31, 19

Maggy o'Buccleugh, 32, 182
The Battle of the Boyne, 32, 299
Scottish Haymakers, 34, 327
The Lord of Ballach, 36, 352

Friendship's Offering
The Minstrel Boy, 29, 209
Auld Joe Nicholson's Bonny Nannie, 29, 263
Ballad, 29, 415
Verses to a Beloved Young Friend, 29, 417
A Scots Luve Sang, 30, 185
The Fords of Callum, 30, 187
A Bard's Address to his Youngest Daughter, 30, 312

Literary Souvenir
Invocation to the Queen of the Fairies, 25, 122
Love's Jubilee, 26, 121
The Border Chronicler, Charlie Dinmont, 26, 257
Stanzas for Music, 27, 247

Amulet
A Lay of the Martyrs, 30, 145
A Tale of Pentland, 30, 219
A Cameronian Ballad, 31, 173
A Hymn to the Redeemer, 35, 118
Morning Hymn, 36, 42
The Judgment of Idumea, 36, 79

Pledge of Friendship
A Night Piece (written in 1811), 27, 231

Bijou
An aged widow's own words, 28, 26
Ane Waefu' Scots Pastoral, 28, 108
Woman, 29, 92; Cameo, 146
Superstition and Grace, 29, 129

Anniversary
The Carle of Invertime, 29, 100
The Cameronian Preacher's Tale, 29, 170

The Forgotten Gothic
>
> *Gem*
>> A Highland Eclogue, 30, 194
>
> *Remembrance*
>> A Boy's Song, 31, 74
>> The Two Valleys, 31, 121
>> The Covenanter's Scaffold Song, 31, 256
>
> *Juvenile Forget Me Not*
>> A Child's Prayer, 30, 114
>> A Child's Hymn for the Close of the Week, 31, 78
>
> *Ackermann's Juvenile Forget Me Not*
>> A Child's Prayer, 30, 176
>> What is sin? 30, 223
>> The Poachers, 31, 99
>> Hymn for Sabbath Morning, 31, 172
>> The Shepherd Boy's Song, 32, 157

Hofland, Barbara
> *Forget Me Not*
>> The Regretted Ghost, 26, 79;
>> The Sketch, 28, 225;
>> The Maid and the Beryl, 29, 253;
>> The Orphan Family, 30, 135;
>> The Disappointment, 32, 305.
>
> *Friendship's Offering*
>> The Comforts of Conceitedness, 28, 108;
>> The Masquerade, 30, 289.

Inglis, Henry (pseudonym, Derwent Conway)
> *Forget Me Not*
>> Communings with Nature, "As the tempest lifted the Northern Sea," 28, 85;
>> Kathed and Eurelia: a Bohemian Legend, 28, 237;
>> The Musician of Augsberg, 29, 235;
>> The Painter of Pisa, 31, 219;
>> Sergeant Hawkins, 32, 255;
>> Mayence, 32, 275;
>> Nurenberg, 33, 121;

The Rich Goldsmith of Zurich, 33, 191;
The Church of St. Pierre at Caen, 34, 125;
The Wife: a Tale of the Tyrol, founded on Fact, 34, 277;
The Merchant of Cadiz, 35, 69;
Milan Cathedral, 34, 153;
The Knell of the Parting Year, "Hark! 'tis the midnight chime," 44, 166.

Friendship's Offering
Rudolph, the Fratricide, 30, 201;
Forest Changes, "Spring is thy youth and winter is thy age," 31, 36;
The Unholy Promise: a Norwegian Legend, 31, 115;
The Temptation of the Capuchins: a Legend of Murcia, 32, 131;
Carl Bluven and the Strange Mariner: a Norwegian Tale, 33, 114;
The Lady and the Moor: an Andalusian Legend, 34, 97;
The Client's Story, 35, 39;
My Hermitage, "Where two wizard streamlets meet," 35, 77;
Retrospection, "I am not old in years, but I have seen," 36, 256;

Literary Souvenir
Sonnet to a Mountain Rivulet, "O! What a pleasant prattle thou dost make," 28, 147;
La Fiancee: ou, Les Grandes Eaux, 28, 253;
Sonnet to the Swallow Tribe, "White-bosomed strangers, wandering tribe, that bring," 29, 269;
The City of the Desert, 30, 64;
To the Turtle-dove, "Deep in the wood, thy voice I list and love," 30, 324;
Stanzas, "Thine and thy people's once, stern King!" 32, 108;
Reminiscences of Andalusia, "Seville–gay Seville–with its serenades," 32, 286.

Kennedy, William
Friendship's Offering
On Leaving Scotland, "I love the land," 29, 59;
History, "Close we the book–enough–the first dark page," 29, 109;
A Voice from the Sea, "Poor worm of the land, to vain terrors a slave," 29, 149;
Lyra, "Meet emblem of the fairest dreams," 30, 1;
The Outline of Life, 30, 45;

Thirty Years, "Summers I've numbered three time ten," 30, 1;
The Dream of the Seventh Son, "three times thy red lips kissed the cup," 31, 14;
The Castle of St. Michael: a Tale, 31, 159;
I shall think of it ever, "I shall think of it ever," 31, 257;
I dreamt last night, "I dreamt last night that I was wandering lonely," 31, 287;
The Dirge of the last Conqueror, "The flag of battle on its staff hangs drooping," 31, 287;
Poesie, "Beauty that language fails, yet pants, to picture," 31, 373;
The Artist, "And is he gone? It seems as yesterday," 32, 176;
To....., "Behind me lies the changing wood," 39, 347;
To my Scottish Friends, "My heart is with you on the Highland mountains," 39, 383;

Literary Souvenir
Timour's Death-bed, "Ungird the saddle from his back," 33, 59.

Maturin, Charles
Friendship's Offering
Wellington, "Son of proud sires–whose patriot blood," 26, 148.

Literary Souvenir
Leixlip Castle, 25, 211
The Sybil's Prophecy: a Dramatic Fragment, 26, 128.

Moir (Delta) D. L.
Forget Me Not
The Household Spaniel, "Poor Oscar! how feebly thou crawl'st to the door," 27, 5;
A Dream of Youth, "Still was the air and all the scene," 27, 175;
Gildeluec ha Guilladun: an Amorican Legend, "The stately knight, young Eliduc," 27, 309;
The Snow, "The snow, the snow, 'tis a pleasant thing," 28, 3;
Song, "Up among the mountains," 28, 89;
Song, Mary Dhu, "Sweet, sweet is the rosebud," 28, 161;
The Dying Jew to his Daughter, "Life's ebbing sands are almost run," 28, 245;
The Sundial, 28, 11;
Lang Syne, "Lang Syne! how doth the word come back," 29, 23;

Appendices

On a Portrait, "As breaks the sunbeam through the storm," 29, 145;
Sir Baldred's Farewell, "I will thee bless–I will thee bless," 29, 231;
The Blind Piper, "I love to hear the bagpipe sound," 29, 365;
The Deserted Churchyard, "There lay an ancient churchyard," 30, 164;
The Fourth of June, "The Fourth of June! the Fourth of June," 30, 181;
Kemp the Bandit, 30, 209;
The Improvisatrice, "Beside her cottage door she sate and sang," 30, 273;
Bessy Bell and Mary Gray: a Scottish Legend of 1666, 31, 361;
The Harebell, "Simplest of blossoms to mine eye," 32, 110;
Christmas Musings, "Time flies apace, another year hath perished," 32, 270;
A Portrait, addressed to a Lady, "I knew a lady once, and she was fair," 35, 152;
The Forsaken, "Oh, mine be the shade, which no eye might discover," 35, 257;
Faded Flowers, "Farewell, ye withered flowers," 36, 49;
Light, "Light is the emblem of the star," 37, 207;
To the Bust of my son Charles, "Fair image of our sainted boy," 40, 324;
The Glen of Roslin, "Hark! 'twas the trumpet rung," 44, 41;
Original Letter of Lord Byron's to the Ettrick Shepherd," 44, 353;
Highland Melodies:
1. The Chieftain's Lullaby, "Hush thee, babe, the stag is belling," 45, 109;
2. Farewell, our Fathers' Land, "Farewell, our Fathers' Land," 45, 110;
3. Mourn for the Brave, "Oh, mourn for the brave," 45, 111;
4. MacGregor's Wail, "On grey Benledi stern," 45, 113;
5. Oh, were I a Swan, "Oh! were I a swan on the blue blossom'd lake," 45, 114;
6. Luyalla, Adieu, "The last red tinge of purple light," 45, 115.

Friendship's Offering

Castle Campbell, "Behind us tower the Ochills green," 29, 143;
To Ianthe, "Would I were with thee! Out the bright stars to shine," 29, 186;
School Recollections, 29, 335;
The Home of Peace, "'Twas in the depth of dazzling May," 29, 352;

Mine Own, "I need not token flowers to tell," 30, 181;
The Angler, "'Twas a blithe morning in the aureate month," 31, 211;
Siberian Scenery, "Meadow and moor were passed," 31, 277;
The Palace, "I looked, and to the light of evening shone," 32, 303;
Letters from Home, "'Tis sweet, unutterably sweet," 33, 77;
Polar Scenes, "Whither, swift Fancy? Lo! the freezing seas,' 33, 223;
Thorny Bank Farm, "How turns when early hopes are overcast," 35, 156;
My Ain Bonnie Lassie "My ain lassie's blooming in yon castle hall," 35, 319;
The Dirge of Isobel, "As is in sympathy, the low-toned wind," 36, 292.

Literary Souvenir
To a Robin Redbreast, "Hark! 'tis the robin's shrill yet mellow pipe," 25, 97;
Stanzas, "I stood upon the shore," 25, 180;
The Old Manor House, 26, 181;
The Knight's Revenge, "A steel-clad knight stood at the gate," 26, 286;
To a Dead Eagle, "It is a desolate eve," 27, 133;
The Contadina, "Most cheerful Contadina! thy lapsing years glide o'er," 27,
    224;
Auld Robin Gray, the Original Story, 27, 301;
The Sword of Wallace, "The Patriot's sword, a talisman thou art," 27, 396;
The Wallflower, "The wallflower, the wallflower," 28, 87;
Canzonet, "Come, beloved, the Evening Star," 28, 138;
On the Death of Inez, "'Tis midnight-deep, the full round moon," 28, 161;
The Pneumatologist, 28, 325
Sonnet at Midnight, "And art thou but a vision of the past," 28, 337;
Lines, "Pride of my country! I delight," 28, 338;
Zadie and Astarti, "He sought her east, he sought her west," 29, 250;
Flodden Field, "'Twas on a sultry summer noon," 30, 173;
A Canticle of the Covenanters, "Ho! watcher of the silent hill," 36, 119.

Neele, Henry
    Forget Me Not

Stanzas, "Oh! pale is that cheek," 24, 362;
Forget me not, "Forget not, oh! forget me not," 25, 4;
The Lover's Tomb, "I'll gather my dark raven locks o'er my brow," 25, 29;
Sacontala: a Tale, "It was a day of joy and revelry," 25, 196;
Canzonet, "And must we, must we part?" 25, 264;
Stanzas, "Suns will set and moons will wane," 26, 383;
The Comet, 27, 239;
Thoughts, "I, saw a glow-worm on a grave," 27, 273;
The Magician's Visiter, 28, 91;
The Houri: A Persian Tale, 29, 165;
Song, "Hope still will mount–no timorous fears," 30, 144.

Friendship's Offering
The Comet, "O'er the blue heavens–majestic and alone," 26, 85;
Stanzas, "Sing me a lay, not of knightly feats," 27, 88;
What is Life? "Tell me, what is life, I pray," 27, 95;
Time, "I saw a child, whose downy cheek," 28, 384;
Love and Sorrow, "Mourn not, sweet maid, nor fondly try," 29, 36.

Literary Souvenir
Goodrich Castle, "Thou sylvan We, since last my feet," 27, 397.

Roberts, Emma
Forget Me Not
The Guelph and the Ghibelline: a scene from an Unpublished Tragedy, 27, 163;
Maximilian and his Daughter, 27, 219
The Hop Girl, "Blithe March, with thee the infant Spring," 28, 335;
The Halt on the Mountains: a Tale of the Spanish War, 28, 362;
Ballad, "I have left my own home," 30, 179;
Song, "Upon the Ganges' regal stream," 30, 179;
The Ghaut, 30, 381;
Benares, 31, 243;
Memory, "Talk not to me of memory," 32, 183.

Friendship's Offering
The Dream, 26, 48;
The Two Hussars: a German Tale, 26, 193;
Constance: a Tale, 26, 287;

The Painter of Munich: a Tale, 27, 110;
The White Wolf: a Guard-room Tale of the "Black Brunswickers," 27, 225;
The Maid of Normandy: a Tale, 28, 171;
The Blacksmith of Liege, 38, 292.

Literary Souvenir
Constantine the Great: a Dramatic Sketch, 26, 207;
Rosamunda: a Venetian Fragment, 26, 305;
The Bridal of St. Omer, 27, 145.

Scott, Walter

Forget Me Not
"When the lone pilgrim views afar," 34, 197;

Friendship's Offering
Song of the Chieftain's Daughter (from "Waverley"), "There is a mist on the mountain, and a night in the vale," 34, 169.

Literary Souvenir
Epilogue, "The Sages–for authority pray look," 25, 373.

Keepsake
My Aunt Margaret's Mirror, 29, 1;
The Tapestried Chamber; or, The Lady in the Sacque, 29, 123;
Death of the Laird's Jock, 29, 186;
Description of the Engraving entitled "A Scene at Abbotsford," 29, 258;
The House of Aspen: a Tragedy, 30, 1;
A Highland Anecdote, 32, 283;
Lines to Lady Cochrane, "I knew thee, lady! by that glorious eye," 53, 96.

Shelley, Mary

Forget Me Not
Lacy de Vere, 27, 275 [see FN]
The Euthanasia, 29, 95 [published as E⬛⬛; see FN]
Count Egmonts Jewels, 33, 15

Keepsake
Convent of Chaillot, 28, 267 [published anonymously; see FN]

The Sisters of Albano, 29, 80;
Ferdinando Eboli, 29, 195;
The Mourner, 30, 71;
The Evil Eye, 30, 150;
The False Rhyme, 30, 265;
Transformation, 31, 18;
Absence, "Ah! he is gone and I alone," 31, 39;
A Dirge, "This morn thy gallant bark, love," 31, 85;
The Swiss Peasant, 31, 121;
The Dream, 32, 22;
The Brother and Sister: an Italian Story, 33, 105;
The Invisible Girl, 33, 210;
The Mortal Immortal, 34, 71;
The Trial of Love, 35, 70;
The Parvenue, 37, 209;
Euphrasia: a Tale of Greece, 39, 179;
Stanzas, "How like a star you rose upon my life," 39, 179;
Stanzas, "O, come to me in dreams, my love!" 39, 201.

Stone, William
Forget Me Not
The Grave of the Indian King, 31, 101;
The White Lynx of the Long Knives, 32, 17;
The Murdered Tinman, 33, 273;
The Skeleton Hand, 34, 129;
Uncle Zim, 35, 311;
Life in the Woods, 36, 55.

Sources:
Boyle, Andrew. *An Index to the Annuals*. Vol. I. 1820-1850. Worcester: Andrew Boyle Ltd, 1967.
Crook, Nora. "Sleuthing towards a Mary Shelley Canon," Women's Writing 6:3 (Oct 1999): 413-424.
Harris, Katherine D. *Forget Me Not: A Hypertextual Archive of Ackermann's 19th-Century Literary Annual, an edition from the Poetess Archive*. 29 Jan 2011
 <http://www.orgs.muohio.edu/anthologies/FMN/>.
Hootman, Harry. *Index of British Literary Annuals*. 29 Jan 2011
 <http://www.britannuals.com>.
The Poetess Archive. Gen. ed. Laura Mandell. 29 Jan 2011
 <http://unixgen.muohio.edu/~poetess/>

Appendix D:
Chronological Index
of British Literary Annual Titles

The *Forget Me Not* was published 1823-1847 (with a final singular issue produced for 1856). By 1847, British literary annuals had lost much of their popular appeal; however, the American production of literary annuals doubled the number of British publications during the period, 1846-1857. By 1857, the literary annual genre had begun to lose public interest on both continents.

To illustrate the early and rapid rise in popularity of the annual, the title of each annual is listed under the year published. Beyond 1835, the number of annuals published each year is listed (instead of the titles).

1823

    English. (1) Forget Me Not.

1824

    English. (3) Forget Me Not; Friendship's Offering; Graces.

1825

    English. (9) Blossoms at Christmas; First Flowers; Forget Me Not; Friendship's Offering; Hommage aux Dames; Literary Coronal; Literary Souvenir; Poetical Album; Remember Me.

1826

    American. (4) Atlantic Souvenir; Philadelphia Souvenir; Souvenir; Wreath, a Collection of Poems.

    English. (9) Amulet; Blossoms at Christmas; First Flowers; Forget Me Not; Friendship's Offering; Janus; Literary Souvenir; Pledge of Friendship; Poetical Album.

1827

    American. (2) Atlantic Souvenir; Memorial.

    English. (9) Amulet; First Flowers; Forget Me Not; Friendship's Offering; Literary Souvenir; Pledge of Friendship; Poetical Album; Poole's Royal Sovereign; Royal Sovereign.

1828

American. (10) Amaranth, Bost.; Atlantic Souvenir; Juvenile Sketchbook; Juvenile Souvenir; Legendary; Memorial; Moral and Religious Souvenir; Oasis; Talisman; Token.

English. (15) Amulet; Bijou; Carcanet; Christmas Box; First Flowers; Forget Me Not; Friendship's Offering; Juvenile Forget Me Not; Keepsake; Literary Souvenir; Pledge of Friendship; Poetical Album; Times Telescope; Troubadour; Winter's Wreath.

1829

American. (15) Atlantic Souvenir; Cabinet; Casket, Bost.; Gift, Bost.; Holiday Tales; Jackson Wreath; Offering; Pearl; Remember Me, a Religious and Literary Miscellany; Tales and Poetry from the English Souvenirs; Talisman; Token; Unique; Visitor; Western Souvenir.

English. (25) Affections Offering; Amulet; Anniversary; Bijou; Cabinet of Curiosities; Casket; Christian Forget Me Not; Christmas Box; First Flowers; Forget Me Not; Friendship's Offering; Gem; Juvenile Forget Me Not; Juvenile Keepsake; Keepsake; Literary Souvenir; Musical Gem; Nautilus; New Year's Gift; Offering; Poetical Album; Souvenir Litteraire de France; Times Telescope; Winter's Wreath; Young Ladies Book.

1830

American. (9) Atlantic Souvenir; Casket, or Youth's Pocket Library; Garland, N.Y.; Lily; Offering of Sympathy; Pearl; Talisman; Token; Youth's Keepsake.

English. (43) Ackermann's Juvenile Forget Me Not; Affections Gift; Affections Offering; Amulet; Anniversary; Apollo's Gift; Bengal Annual; Bijou; Cabinet Album; Carcanet; Christian Souvenir; Comic Annual; Emanuel; Excitement; Fisher's National Portrait Gallery; Forget Me Not; Friendship's Offering; Gem; Gem of Art; Iris; Johnson's Shooter's Annual; Juvenile Forget Me Not; Juvenile Keepsake; Juvenile Landscape Annual; Keepsake; Keepsake Francais; Literary Souvenir; Looking Glass; Lyre; Musical Bijou; Musical Forget Me Not; Musical Gem; Musical Souvenir; New Year's Gift; Olive Branch; Remember Me; Times Telescope; Winter's Wreath; Zoölogical Keepsake.

1831

American. (13) Amaranth; Newburyport; American Comic Annual; Amethyst, Balto.; Atlantic Souvenir, Child's Annual, Phila.; Hyacinth, NY; Keepsake Americaine; Lily; Pearl; Scrap Table; Spirit of the Annuals; Tablet; Token; Youth's Keepsake.

English. (62) Ackermann's Juvenile Forget Me Not; Affection's Gift; Affection's Offering; Amulet; Apollo's Gift; Bengal Annual; Cabinet Album; Cadeau; Cameo; Chameleon; Comic Annual; Comic Offering; Dramatic Annual; English Keepsake; Excitement; Father's Present to his Son; Fisher's National Portrait Gallery; Forget Me Not; Friendship's Offering; Gem; Humorist; Infant's Annual; Iris; Juvenile Forget Me Not; Keepsake; Keepsake Francais; Ladies' and Gentlemen's Polite Assistant and Useful Remembrancer; Ladies' Poetical Album; Landscape Annual; Literary Souvenir; Looking Glass; Lyre; Marshall's Christmas Box; Mirror of the Graces; Mr. Matthews' Comic Annual; Mother's Present to her Daughter; Musical Bijou; Musical Forget Me Not; Musical Gem; New Comic Annual; New Musical Annual; New Year's Gift; Olive Branch; Phrenological Bijou; Pledge of Friendship; Poetical Offering; Regent; Remember Me; Remembrance; Royal Repository and Picturesque Diary; Sacred Harp; Sacred Offering; Scrap Table; Simpson's Gentleman's Almanack; Souvenir, Le; Talisman; Times Telescope; Tit-Bits; Vocal Annual; Winter's Wreath; Youth's Keepsake.

1832

American. (12) Affection's Gift, NY; Annual; Atlantic Souvenir; Christian Offering; Compliment for the Season; Keepsake Americaine; Lady's Cabinet Album; Lily; Odd Volume; Pearl; Token; Young Lady's Own Book.

English. (63) Ackermann's Juvenile Forget Me Not; Affection's Gift; Affection's Offering; Amaranth; Amethyst; Amulet; Bengal Annual; Botanical Annual; Bouquet; Cabinet Album; Cabinet for Youth; Cabinet of Literary Gems; Cadeau; Chameleon; Comic Annual; Comic Offering; Continental Annual; Diadem; Easter Gift; Easter Offering; Evergreen; Excitement; Fisher's Drawing Room Scrap Book; Fisher's National Portrait Gallery; Forget Me Not; Friendship's Offering; Gem; Geographical Annual; Heath's Picturesque Annual; Hibernian Keepsake; Hive; Humorist; Infant's Annual; Juvenile Album; Juvenile Forget Me Not; Keepsake; Landscape Album; Landscape Annual; Literary Souvenir; Looking Glass; Love's Offering; Marshall's Christmas Box; Musical Bijou; Musical Gem; New Year's Gift; Nosegay; Poetical Offering; Portfolio; Recordanza; Regent; Remember Me; Rose of Four Seasons; Sacred Harp; Sacred Lyre; Sacred Offering; Shipp's Military Bijou; Sister's Gift; Spiritual Gleaner; Vocal Annual; Waverley Album; Winter's Wreath; Yorkshire Literary Annual; Youth's Cornucopia.

1833

American. (11) Annual; Child's Gem; Miscellanies; Odd Volume; Pearl; Premium; Religious Souvenir; Token; Young Lady's Sunday Book; Young Man's Guide.

English. (39) Affection's Amethyst; Amulet; Aurora Boealis; Bengal Annual; Biblical Annual; Bouquet; Cadeau; Chameleon; Christmas Tales; Comic Annual; Comic Offering; Dramatic Souvenir; Ellis's Missionary Annual; Elgin Annual; Excitement; Father's Present to His Son; Fisher's Drawing Room Scrap Book; Fisher's National Portrait Gallery; Forget Me Not; Friendship's Offering; Geographical Annual; Heath's Book of Beauty; Heath's Picturesque Annual; Infant's Annual; Juvenile Forget Me Not; Keepsake; Landscape Annual; Literary Souvenir; Looking Glass; Missionary Annual; Musical Gem; New Year's Gift; Offering; Regent; Sacred Musical Offering; Sacred Offering; Turner's Annual Tour; Wreath of Friendship.

1834

American. (17) American Juvenile Keepsake; Annual; Casket, or Youth's Pocket Library; Child's Annual, Bost.; Daughter's Own Book; Ladies and Gentlemen's Pocket Annual; Lady's Cabinet Album; Lily; Oasis; Offering; Pearl; Religious Souvenir; Rosary; Token; Unique; Youth's Keep-Sake; Youth's Sketch Book.

English. (40) Album Wreath; Amethyst; Amulet; Annual Souvenir; Bengal Annual; Biblical Annual; Bouquet; Bow in the Cloud; Comic Annual; Comic Offering; Coronal; English Annual; Excitement; Fisher's Drawing Room Scrap Book; Forget Me Not; Friend's Annual; Friendship's Offering; Gage d'Amitié; Gem of Art; Geographical Annual; Heath's Book of Beauty; Heath's Picturesque Annual; Juvenile Forget Me Not; Keepsake; Landscape Album; Landscape Annual; Literary Gift Book; Literary Souvenir; Looking Glass; Midsummer Keepsake; New Year's Gift; Offering; Oriental Annual; Regent; Sacred Annual; Sacred Offering; Souvenir; Turner's Annual Tour; Wreath of Friendship; Young Gentleman's Annual.

1835

American. (14) American Juvenile Keepsake; Annual; Beauties of the English Annuals; Bouquet, Phila.; Gift, Concord; Lady's Cabinet Album; Lily; Odd Volume; Parent's Present; Portfolio for Youth; Premium; Religious Souvenir; Rosary; Token; Youth's Keep-Sake.

English. (43) Amulet; Angler's Souvenir; Annual Token; Biblical Keepsake; Christian Keepsake; Comic Almanac; Comic Annual; Comic Offering; Continental Landscape Annual of European Scenery; Continental Tourist; English Annual; Excitement; Finden's Tableaux; Fisher's Drawing Room Scrap Book; Forget Me Not; Friendship's Offering; Gage d'Amitié; Gem of Art; Geographical Annual; Heath's Book of Beauty; Heath's Picturesque Annual; Juvenile Amulet; Juvenile Forget Me Not; Juvenile Keepsake; Keepsake; Lady's Keepsake and Maternal Monitor; Landscape Annual; Landscape Souvenir; Literary Souvenir; Looking Glass; Marshall's Christmas Box; Musical Gem; New Year's Gift; New Year's Token; Nursery Offering; Orient Pearl; Oriental Annual; Pledge of Affection; Present; Regent; Sacred Offering; Souvenir; Turner's Annual Tour; Youth's Cabinet.

* * *

1846

American. (56)
English. (16)

* * *

1857

American. (15)
English. (3)

Source

Harris, Katherine D. "Chronological Index of British Literary Annual Titles." *Forget Me Not:*
> *A Hypertextual Archive of Ackermann's 19th-Century Literary Annual, an edition from the Poetess Archive.* 29 Jan 2011 <http://www.orgs.muohio.edu/anthologies/FMN/Chron_Ind.htm

References & Works Cited

Literary Annuals[1]
Forget Me Not, A Christmas and New Year's Present for 1823. Ed. [Frederic Shoberl]. London: R. Ackermann, 1823. Printer: C.E Knight, Butcher Row, East Smithfield.

Forget Me Not; A Christmas and New Year's Present for 1824. Ed. Frederic Shoberl. London: R. Ackermann, 1824. Printer: Thomas Davison, Whitefriars.

Forget Me Not; A Christmas and New Year's Present for 1825. Ed. Frederic Shoberl. London: R. Ackermann, 1825. Printer: J. Moyes, Bouverie Street, Fleet Street.

Forget Me Not; A Christmas and New Year's Present for 1826. Ed. Frederic Shoberl. London: R. Ackermann, 1826. Printer: J. Moyes, Bouverie Street, Fleet Street.

Forget Me Not; A Christmas and New Year's Present for MDCCCXXVII. Ed. Frederic Shoberl. London: R. Ackermann, 1827. Printer: Thomas Davison, Whitefriars.

Forget Me Not; A Christmas and New Year's Present for MDCCCXXVIII. Ed. Frederic Shoberl. London: R. Ackermann, 1828. Printer: Thomas Davison, Whitefriars.

Forget Me Not; A Christmas and New Year's Present for MDCCCXXIX. Ed. Frederic Shoberl. London: R. Ackermann, 1829. Printer: Thomas Davison, Whitefriars.

Forget Me Not; A Christmas, New Year's, and Birth-Day Present for MDCCCXXX. Ed. Frederic Shoberl. London: R. Ackermann & Co., 1830. Printer: Thomas Davison, Whitefriars.

Forget Me Not; A Christmas, New Year's, and Birth-Day Present for MDCCCXXXI. Ed. Frederic Shoberl. London: R. Ackermann, 1831. Printer: Thomas Davison, Whitefriars.

---

1 With the exception of Friendship's Offering 1829, all literary annuals from the Katherine D. Harris private collection.

Friendship's Offering; or, The Annual Remembrancer: A Christmas Present, or New Year's Gift, for 1825. Ed. Thomas K. Hervey. London: Lupton Relfe, 1825. Printer: D.S. Maurice, Fenchurch-street.

Friendship's Offering. A Literary Album. Ed. Thomas K. Hervey. London: Lupton Relfe, 1826. Printer: D.S. Maurice, Fenchurch-street.

Friendship's Offering. A Literary Album. Ed. Thomas K. Hervey. London: Lupton Relfe, 1827. Printer: D.S. Maurice, Fenchurch-street.

Friendship's Offering: A Literary Album, and Christmas and New Year's Present for MDCCCXXIX. Ed. Thomas Pringle. London: Smith, Elder, and Co., 1829. Printer: Littlewood & Co., Old Bailey.

Friendship's Offering: A Literary Album, and Christmas and New Year's Present for MDCCCXXX. Ed. Thomas Pringle. London: Smith, Elder, and Co., 1830. Printer: Littlewood & Co., Old Bailey.

Friendship's Offering: A Literary Album, and Christmas and New Year's Present for MDCCCXXXI. Ed. Thomas Pringle. London: Smith, Elder, and Co., 1831. Printer: Littlewood & Co., Old Bailey.

The Comic Annual [The Anniversary of the Literary Fun]. 2nd ed. Ed. Thomas Hood. London: Charles Tilt, 1830.

The Keepsake for 1828. Ed. William Harrison Ainsworth. London: Hurst, Chance, and Co., 1828. Printer: Thomas Davison, Whitefriars.

The Keepsake for MDCCCXXIX. Ed. Frederic Mansel Reynolds. London: Hurst, Chance, and Co., and R. Jennings, 1829. Printer: Thomas Davison, Whitefriars.

The Keepsake for MDCCCXXX. Ed. Frederic Mansel Reynolds. London: Hurst, Chance, and Co., and R. Jennings, 1830. Printer: Thomas Davison, Whitefriars.

The Keepsake for MDCCCXXXI. Ed. Frederic Mansel Reynolds. London: Hurst, Chance, and Co., and Jennings and Chaplin, 1831. Printer: Thomas Davison, Whitefriars.

The Keepsake for MDCCCXLI. Ed. Countess of Blessington. London: Longman, Orme, Brown, Green, and Longmans; New York: Appleton and Co.; Paris: Fisher and Co., 1841. Printer: William Wilcockson, Rolls Buildings, Fetter Lane.

The Literary Souvenir; or, Cabinet of Poetry and Romance. Ed. Alaric A. Watts. London: Hurst, Robinson and Co. and A. Constable and Co. Edinburgh, 1825. Printer: B. Bensley, Bolt Court, Fleet Street.

The Literary Souvenir; or, Cabinet of Poetry and Romance. Ed. Alaric A. Watts. London: Hurst, Robinson and Co. and A. Constable and Co. Edinburgh, 1826. Printer: T. and J.B. Flindel, 67, St. Martin's-Lane.

The Literary Souvenir; or, Cabinet of Poetry and Romance. Ed. Alaric A. Watts. London: Longman, Rees, Orme, Brown, & Green; and John Andrews, 1827. Printer: T. and J.B. Flindel, 67, St. Martin's-Lane.

The Literary Souvenir; or, Cabinet of Poetry and Romance. Ed. Alaric A. Watts. London: Longman, Rees, Orme, Brown, & Green, 1828. Printer: Bradbury & Co., Bolt Court, Fleet Street.

The Literary Souvenir. Ed. Alaric A. Watts. London: Longman, Rees, Orme, Brown & Green, 1829. Printer: S. Manning & Co., London House Yard, St. Paul's.

The Literary Souvenir. Ed. Alaric A. Watts. London: Longman, Rees, Orme, Brown & Green, 1830. Printer: Samuel Manning and Co., London-House Yard, St. Paul's.

The Literary Souvenir. Ed. Alaric A. Watts. London: Longman, Rees, Orme, Brown & Green, 1831. Printer: S. Manning & Co., London House Yard, St. Paul's.

Plain Text Sources[2]

Anonymous. "The Diamond Watch." The Literary Souvenir; or, Cabinet of Poetry and Romance. Ed. Alaric A. Watts. London: Hurst, Robinson and Co. and A. Constable and Co. Edinburgh, 1826. Google Books. 31 Jan 2011 < http://books.google.com/books?id=OF8EAAAAQAAJ&pg=PA414&dq=18 26+The+Literary+Souvenir;+or,+Cabinet+of+Poetry+and+Romance&hl=en& ei=WbRHTd39PISBlAfJ94ykBA&sa=X&oi=book_result&ct=result&resnum

---

2 For some stories, plain text was obtained from an online source, compared against the original print text, and edited for accuracy. Those plain text sources are indicated here.

=3&ved=0CDMQ6AEwAg#v=onepage&q&f=false>

Anonymous. "Forgiveness. A Tale." *Friendship's Offering. A Literary Album*. Ed. Thomas K. Hervey. London: Lupton Relfe, 1826. 240-247. Google Books. 30 Jan 2011<http://books.google.com/books?id=8jofAAAAMAAJ&lpg=PR13&ots=KaxUOMikST&dq=friendship's%20offering%201826&pg=PR1#v=onepage&q&f=false>

Anonymous. "The Laughing Horseman. A Tale." *Friendship's Offering. A Literary Album*. Ed. Thomas K. Hervey. London: Lupton Relfe, 1826. 109-134. Google Books. 30 Jan 2011 <http://books.google.com/books?id=8jofAAAAMAAJ&lpg=PR13&ots=KaxUOMikST&dq=friendship's%20offering%201826&pg=PR1#v=onepage&q&f=false>

Conway, Derwent. [Inglis, Henry Rodolph.] "The Unholy Promise. A Norwegian Legend." *Friendship's Offering: A Literary Album, and Christmas and New Year's Present for MDCCCXXXI*. Ed. Thomas Pringle. London: Smith, Elder, and Co., 1831. 115-125. Google Books. 30 Jan 2011 <http://books.google.com/books?id=0PcdAAAAMAAJ&ots=vzYElBobmQ&dq=friendship's%20offering%201831&pg=PR7#v=onepage&q=friendship's%20offering%201831&f=false>

Hogg, James. "The Border Chronicler." *The Literary Souvenir; or, Cabinet of Poetry and Romance*. Ed. Alaric A. Watts. London: Hurst, Robinson and Co. and A. Constable and Co. Edinburgh, 1826. Google Books. 31 Jan 2011 <http://books.google.com/books?id=OF8EAAAAQAAJ&pg=PA414&dq=1826+The+Literary+Souvenir;+or,+Cabinet+of+Poetry+and+Romance&hl=en&ei=WbRHTd39PISBlAfJ94ykBA&sa=X&oi=book_result&ct=result&resnum=3&ved=0CDMQ6AEwAg#v=onepage&q&f=false>

Kennedy, William. "The Castle of St. Michael. A Tale." *Friendship's Offering: A Literary Album, and Christmas and New Year's Present for MDCCCXXXI*. Ed. Thomas Pringle. London: Smith, Elder, and Co., 1831. ." 159-178. Google Books. 30 Jan 2011 <http://books.google.com/books?id=0PcdAAAAMAAJ&ots=vzYElBobmQ&dq=friendship's%20offering%201831&pg=PR7#v=onepage&q=friendship's%20offering%201831&f=false>

Gillies, Robert Pearch. "The Warning. A German Legend." *Friendship's Offering: A Literary Album, and Christmas and New Year's Present for MDCCCXXIX*. Ed. Thomas Pringle. London: Smith, Elder, and Co., 1829. 93-105. Google Books 29 Jan 2011<http://books.google.com/

books?id=1vcdAAAAMAAJ&pg=PA92- IA2#v=onepage&q&f=false>

The Literary Souvenir; or, Cabinet of Poetry and Romance. Ed. Alaric A. Watts. London: Longman, Rees, Orme, Brown, & Green; and John Andrews, 1827. Google Books. 31 Jan 2011 <http://books.google.com/books?id=aFUJAAA AQAAJ&ots=BUhL22ZoX1&dq=The%20Literary%20Souvenir%3B%20 or%2C%20Cabinet%20of%20Poetry%20and%20Romance&pg=PR1#v=onep age&q&f=false>.

The Literary Souvenir; or, Cabinet of Poetry and Romance. Ed. Alaric A. Watts. London: Longman, Rees, Orme, Brown, & Green, 1828. Google Books. 31 Jan 2011 <http://books.google.com/ books?id=7WwEAAAAQAAJ&dq=1828%20The%20Liter ary%20 Souvenir%3B%20or%2C%20Cabinet%20of%20Poetry%20and%20Roman ce&pg=PP13#v=onepage&q&f=false>.

The Literary Souvenir. Ed. Alaric A. Watts. London: Longman, Rees, Orme, Brown & Green, 1829. Printer: S. Manning & Co., London House Yard, St. Paul's. Google Books. 31 Jan 2011 <http://books.google. com/books?id=7mwEAAAAQAAJ&dq=1829%20The%20Literary%20 Souvenir%3B%20or%2C%20Cabinet%20of%20Poetry%20and%20Roman ce&pg=PR3#v=onepage&q&f=false>

The Literary Souvenir. Ed. Alaric A. Watts. London: Longman, Rees, Orme, Brown & Green, 1830. Printer: Samuel Manning and Co., London-House Yard, St. Paul's. Google Books. 31 Jan 2011 <http://books.google. com/books?id=EG0EAAAAQAAJ&dq=1830%20The%20Literary%20 Souvenir%3B%20or%2C%20Cabinet%20of%20Poetry%20and%20Romanc e&pg=PR3#v=onepage&q&f=false>

The Literary Souvenir. Ed. Alaric A. Watts. London: Longman, Rees, Orme, Brown & Green, 1831. Printer: S. Manning & Co., London House Yard, St. Paul's. Google Books. 31 Jan 2011 <http://books.google. com/books?id=Ol8EAAAAQAAJ&dq=1831%20The%20Literary%20 Souvenir%3B%20or%2C%20Cabinet%20of%20Poetry%20and%20Romance &pg=PR3#v=onepage&q&f=false>

Scott, Sir Walter. "My Aunt Margaret's Mirror." The Keepsake for MDCCCXXIX. Ed. Frederic Mansel Reynolds. London: Hurst, Chance, and Co., and R. Jennings, 1829. 1-44. Project Gutenberg. 30 Jan 2011 <http://www.gutenberg.org/ebooks/1667>

Scott, Sir Walter. "The Tapestried Chamber, or The Lady in the Sacque." *The Keepsake for MDCCCXXIX.* Ed. Frederic Mansel Reynolds. London: Hurst, Chance, and Co., and R. Jennings, 1829. 123-142. from Literature Online. 30 Jan 2011 <http://www.online-literature.com/walter_scott/2568/>

Shelley, Mary. "The Evil Eye." Arthur's Classic Novels. 30 Jan 2011 <http://arthursclassicnovels.com/shelley/eviley10.html>

Shelley, Mary. "The False Rhyme." *Great Literature Online.* 1997-2011. 30 Jan 2011 <http://shelley.classicauthors.net/falserhyme/>

Shelley, Mary. "Ferdinando Eboli. A Tale." *The Last Man: A Romantic Circles Electronic Edition.* Ed. Steven E. Jones. 30 Jan 2011 <http://www.rc.umd.edu/editions/mws/lastman/eboli.htm>

Shelley, Mary. "The Mourner." *The Last Man: A Romantic Circles Electronic Edition.* Ed. Steven E. Jones. 30 Jan 2011 <http://www.rc.umd.edu/editions/mws/lastman/mournr.htm>

Shelley, Mary. "The Transformation." Columbia University, Course Web Spaces. 30 Jan 2011 <http://www.columbia.edu/itc/english/f1102-005x01/readings/transformation.htm>

Online Resources for British Literary Annuals

Eckert, Lindsey. Nineteenth Century British Literary Annuals: An Online Exhibition of Materials from the University of Toronto. 29 Jan 2011 <http://bookhistory.fis.utoronto.ca/annuals/index.html>.

Harris, Katherine D. *Forget Me Not: A Hypertextual Archive of Ackermann's 19th-Century Literary Annual,* an edition from the Poetess Archive. 29 Jan 2011 <http://www.orgs.muohio.edu/anthologies/FMN/>.

Hoagwood, Terence, Kathryn Ledbetter, and Martin M. Jacobsen. LEL's "Verses" and The Keepsake for 1829. 29 Jan 2011 <http://www.rc.umd.edu/editions/lel/keepsake.htm>.

Hootman, Harry. Index of British Literary Annuals. 29 Jan 2011 <http://www.britannuals.com>.

Oxford Dictionary of National Biography

The Poetess Archive. Gen. ed. Laura Mandell. 29 Jan 2011 <http://unixgen.

muohio.edu/~poetess/>

Works Cited in Introduction & General Resources

"Ackermann, Rudolph." *The Encyclopedia of Romantic Literature*. Eds. Frederick Burwick, Nancy M. Goslee and Diane Long Hoeveler. Blackwell Publishers.

Ackermann, Rudolf [or William Coombe]. "Preface." *Forget Me Not, A Christmas and New Year's Present for 1823*. London: R. Ackermann, 1823.

Advertisement. *Forget Me Not, A Christmas and New Year's Present for 1823*. Ed. Rudolf Ackermann [or William Combe]. London: R. Ackermann, 1823. At conclusion of volume.

Advertisement. *Forget Me Not; A Christmas and New Year's Present for 1824*. Ed. Frederick Shoberl. London: R. Ackermann, 1824. [in back of volume].

Alexander, Christine. "'That Kingdom of Gloom': Charlotte Brontë, the Annuals, and the Gothic." *Nineteenth-Century Literature* 47:4 (March 1993): 409-36.

Altick, Richard D. *The English Common Reader: A Social History of the Mass Reading Public 1800-1900*. Chicago: U of Chicago P, 1957.

Anonymous. "The Annuals of Former Days," The Bookseller 1 (29 November 1858): 494.

Anonymous. Review of 1825 *Literary Souvenir*. British Critic. (Quoted in 1826 *Literary Souvenir* advertisements).

Anonymous. Review of 1827 *Amulet and 1827 Forget Me Not*. *The Monthly Review* (Nov 1826): 274-293.

Anonymous. Review of 1828 *Literary Souvenir*. *The Monthly Review* (Dec 1827): 519-525.

Anonymous. "The Annuals for 1832." *The Monthly Review* (Dec 1831): 523-549.
Bennett, Betty T. "Feminism and Editing Mary Wollstonecraft Shelley." *Palimpsests:Editorial Theory in the Humanities*. Eds. George Bornstein and Ralph G. Williams. Ann Arbor: U Michigan P, 1996. 67-96.

—. Mary Diana Dods: *A Gentleman and a Scholar*. Baltimore: Johns Hopkins UP, 1994.

Booth, Bradford M. "Taste in the Annuals." *American Literature* 14:3 (Nov 1942): 299-305.

Bose, A. "The Verse of the English ⊠Annuals." *The Review of English Studies* 4:13 (Jan. 1953): 38-51.

Boyle, Andrew. *An Index to the Annuals. Vol. I. 1820-1850*. Worcester: Andrew Boyle Ltd, 1967.

Carter, John. *ABC for Book Collectors*. 7th ed. rev. New Castle: Oak Knoll Press, 1995.

Clauren, H. [Karl Heun]. "Mimili." Vergissmeinnicht ein Taschenbuch. Leipzig, 1818.

—. "Mimili." *Forget Me Not; A Christmas and New Year's Present for 1824*. Ed. Frederic Shoberl. London: R. Ackermann, 1824. 38-103.

[Coleridge, Samuel Taylor.] *Critical Review* 2nd ser. 19 (1797 Feb): 194-200 in *The Monk: A Romance by Matthew Lewis*. Eds. David MacDonald and Kathleen Scherf. Orchard Park: Broadview, 2004. 398-402.

Crook, Nora. "Sleuthing towards a Mary Shelley Canon," *Women's Writing* 6:3 (Oct 1999): 413-424.

Dickinson, Cindy. "Creating a World of Books, Friends, and Flowers: Gift Books and Inscriptions, 1825-60." Winterthur Portfolio: A Journal of American Material Culture. 31:1 (Spring 1996): 53-66.

Erickson, Lee. The Economy of Literary Form: English Literature and Industrialization of Publishing, 1800-1850. Baltimore: Johns Hopkins Univ. Press, 1996.

Faxon, Frederick W. Literary Annuals and Gift Books: A Bibliography, 1823-1903. 1912.   Surrey: The Gresham Press, 1973.
Feldman, Paula R. Introduction. *The Keepsake for 1829*. Broadview Press, 2006. 7-25.

—. "The Poet and the Profits: Felicia Hemans and the Literary Marketplace." *Women's Poetry, Late Romantic to Late Victorian: Gender and Genre, 1830-1900.* Eds.

Isobel Armstrong, *Virginia Blain and Cora Kaplan.* New York: Macmillan-St. Martin's, 1999. 71-101.

—. "Women, Literary Annuals and the Evidence of Inscriptions." *Keats-Shelley Journal* 55 (2006): 54-62.

Gaull, Marilyn. *English Romanticism: The Human Context.* 6th ed. New York: W.W. Norton, 1988.

Harris, Katherine D. "Borrowing, Altering and Perfecting the Literary Annual Form – or What It is Not: Emblems, Almanacs, Pocket-books, Albums, Scrapbooks and Gifts Books" *The Poetess Archive Journal* 1.1 (2007) <unixgen.muohio.edu/~poetess/PAJournal/index.html>

—. "Feminizing the Textual Body: Women and their Literary Annuals in Nineteenth-Century Britain." *Publications of the Bibliographical Society of America.* 99:4 (Dec.   2005): 573-622.

Hawkins, Ann. "'Delectable' Books for 'Delicate' Readers: The 1830s Giftbook Market, Ackermann and Co, and the Countess of Blessington." *Kentucky Philological Review* 16 (2002): 20-26.

—. "'Formed with Curious Skill': Blessington's Curious Negotiation of the 'Poetess' in Flowers of Loveliness." *Romanticism on the Net* 29-30 (2003 Feb-May): 48   paragraphs

—. "Marketing Gender and Nationalism: Blessington's Gems of Beauty/L'Ecrin and the Mid-Century Book Trade" *Women's Writing* 12:2 (2005): 225-40.

Jump, Harriet Devine. "'The False Prudery of Public Taste': Scandalous Women and the Annuals, 1820-1850." *Feminist Readings of Victorian Popular Culture: Divergent Femininities.* Eds. Emma Liggins and Daniel Duffy. Aldershot, England: Ashgate, 2001. 1-17.

Kontje, Todd. "Male Fantasies, Female Readers: Fictions of the Nation in the

Early Restoration." *The German Quarterly* 68:2 (Spring 1995): 131-146.

Kutcher, Matthew. *Flowers of Friendship: Gift Books and Polite Culture in EarlyNineteenth-Century Britain.* Dissertation Abstract, 59:10 (April 1999). 3830-31.

Le Keux, Henry. "Seventh Plague of Egypt."[Engraving] *Forget Me Not for 1828.* Ed. Frederic Shoberl. London: R. Ackermann, 1828.

Ledbetter, Kathryn. "BeGemmed and beAmuletted': Tennyson and Those Vapid' Gift Books." *Victorian Poetry* 34:2 (Summer 1996): 235-45.

—. "'The Copper and Steel Manufactory' of Charles Heath." *Victorian Review* 28:2 (2002): 21-30.

—. "'White Vellum and Gilt Edges': Imaging The Keepsake." *Studies in the Literary Imagination* 30:1 (Spring 1997): 35-47.

—. *A Woman's Book: 'The Keepsake' Literary Annual. Dissertation Abstract*, 56:6 (Dec 1995). 2249A.

— and Terence Hoagwood. "Introduction to The Keepsake." *L.E.L.'s Verses and "TheKeepsake" for 1829: A Hypertext Edition.* Eds. Terence Hoagwood and Kathryn Ledbetter. *Romantic Circles*, Electronic Editions April 28, 2002. <http://www.rc.umd.edu/editions/contemps/lel/keepsake.htm>.

Linley, Margaret. "A Centre that Would Not Hold: Annuals and Cultural Democracy." *Nineteenth-Century Media and the Construction of Identities.* Eds. Laurel Brake, Bill Bell and David Finkelstein. New York: Palgrave, 2000. 54-74.

—. "The Early Victorian Annual (1822-1857)." *Victorian Review* 35:1 (2009 Spring): 13-19.

Lodge, Sara. "Romantic Reliquaries: Memory and Irony in the Literary Annuals." *Romanticism: The Journal of Romantic Culture and Criticism.* 10:1 (2004): 23-40.

Maidment, Brian. "⊠Penny' Wise, ⊠Penny' Foolish?: Popular Periodicals and the ⊠March of Intellect' in the 1820s and 1830s." *Nineteenth-Century Media and the Construction of Identities.* Eds. Laurel Brake, Bill Bell and David Finkelstein. New York: Palgrave, 2000. 104-121.

Mandell, Laura. "Hemans and the Gift-Book Aesthetic." *Cardiff Corvey: Reading the Romantic Text* 6 (June 2001).

—. "Putting Contents on the Table: The Disciplinary Anthology and the Field of Literary History." *The Poetess Archive Journal* 1:1 (April 2007).

Martin, John. "Seventh Plague of Egypt." Collections Database, Museum of Fine Arts Boston. 8 Nov 2004 <http://www.mfa.org/artemis/fullrecord.asp?oid=33665>

Mayo, Robert. "Gothic Romance in the Magazines." *PMLA* 65:5 (1950 Sept): 762-789.

—. "The Gothic Short Story in the Magazines." *Modern Language Review* 37 (1942): 448- 454.

Potter, Franz. *The History of Gothic Publishing 1800-1835: Exhuming the Trade*. New York: Palgrave Macmillan, 2005.

Pulham, Patricia. "'Jewels-Delights-Perfect Loves': Victorian Women Poets and the Annuals." *Victorian Women Poets: Essays and Studies*. Woodbridge, England: Brewer, 2003. 9-31.

Raven, James. *The Business of Books: Booksellers and the English Book Trade 1450-1850*. New Haven, Yale UP, 2007.

Renier, Anne. *Friendship's Offering: An Essay on the Annuals and Gift Books of the 19th Century*. London: Private Libraries Association, 1964.

Robinson, Charles. *Mary Shelley: Collected Tales and Stories with Original Engravings*. Baltimore: Johns Hopkins UP, 1990.

Robson, Catherine. "Standing on the Burning Deck: Poetry, Performance, History." *PMLA* 120.1 (January 2005): 148-162.

Sha, Richard. *The Visual and Verbal Sketch in British Romanticism*. Philadelphia: University of Pennsylvania Press, 1998.

St. Clair, William. *The Reading Nations in the Romantic Period*. Cambridge:

Cambridge UP, 2004.

Tallent-Bateman, Chas. T. "The 'Forget-Me-Not.'" *Papers of the Manchester Literary Club* 28 (1902): 78-98.

Thompson, Judith. "From Forum to Repository: A Case Study in Romantic Cultural Geography." *European Romantic Review* 15:2 (June 2004): 177-191.

Vera, Eugenia Roldán. *The British Book Trade and Spanish American Independence: Education and Knowledge Transmission in Transcontinental Perspective.* Ashgate, 2003.

Warne, Vanessa K. "'Purport and Design': Print Culture and Gender Politics in Early Victorian Literary Annuals." *Dissertation Abstracts* 62:10 (2002 April). 3407.

Substantial Library Collections of British Literary Annuals
English Gift Books and Literary Annuals 1823-1857, Chadwyck-Healey Microfiche Collection
Library of Congress
The Pforzheimer Collection of Shelley and His Circle, Stephen A. Schwarzman Building, New York Public Library
Rare Books & General Collection, British Library
Rare Books & Special Collections, University of South Carolina
Special Collections, Miami University of Ohio, Oxford
Special Collections, E.J. Pratt Library, Victoria University
Thomas Fisher Rare Book Library, the McLean Collection in the Robertson Davies Library, Massey College

Lightning Source UK Ltd.
Milton Keynes UK
UKHW012125121121
393874UK00003B/999